WASHINGTON IRVING

WASHINGTON IRVING

BRACEBRIDGE HALL
TALES OF A TRAVELLER
THE ALHAMBRA

THE LIBRARY OF AMERICA

The paper used in this publication meets the
minimum requirements of the American National Standard for
Information Sciences—Permanence of Paper for Printed
Library Materials, ANSI z39.48—1984.

Distributed to the trade in the United States
and Canada by the Viking Press.

Library of Congress Catalog Number: 90–62267
For cataloging information, see end of Notes
ISBN 0–940450–59–3

First Printing
The Library of America—52

Manufactured in the United States of America

ANDREW B. MYERS
WROTE THE NOTES FOR THIS VOLUME

This volume prints the texts of Bracebridge Hall, Tales of a Traveller, and The Alhambra from The Complete Works of Washington Irving edited by Herbert F. Smith, William T. Lenehan, Andrew B. Myers, Judith Giblin Haig, Henry A. Pochmann, Herbert L. Kleinfield, Richard Dilworth Rust, and Edwin T. Bowden and published by Twayne Publishers.

Grateful acknowledgment is made to the National Endowment for the Humanities, the Ford Foundation, and the Andrew W. Mellon Foundation for their generous support of this series.

Contents

BRACEBRIDGE HALL

or

The Humourists

A MEDLEY
BY GEOFFERY CRAYON, GENT.

*Under this cloud I walk gentlemen; pardon my rude
assault. I am a traveller, who, having surveyed most
of the terrestrial angles of this globe, am hither
arrived to peruse this little spot.*

CHRISTMAS ORDINARY

Contents

Volume II

The Author

WORTHY READER!

On again taking pen in hand, I would fain make a few observations at the outset, by way of bespeaking a right understanding. The volumes which I have already published have met with a reception far beyond my most sanguine expectations. I would willingly attribute this to their intrinsic merits; but, in spite of the vanity of authorship, I cannot but be sensible that their success has, in a great measure, been owing to a less flattering cause. It has been a matter of marvel, that a man from the wilds of America should express himself in tolerable English. I was looked upon as something new and strange in literature; a kind of demi-savage, with a feather in his hand, instead of on his head; and there was a curiosity to hear what such a being had to say about civilized society.

This novelty is now at an end, and of course the feeling of indulgence which it produced. I must now expect to bear the scrutiny of sterner criticism, and to be measured by the same standard with contemporary writers; and the very favour which has been shown to my previous writings, will cause these to be treated with the greater rigour; as there is nothing for which the world is apt to punish a man more severely, than for having been over-praised. On this head, therefore, I wish to forestall the censoriousness of the reader; and I entreat he will not think the worse of me for the many injudicious things that may have been said in my commendation.

I am aware that I often travel over beaten ground, and treat of subjects that have already been discussed by abler pens. Indeed, various authors have been mentioned as my models, to whom I should feel flattered if I thought I bore the slightest resemblance; but in truth I write after no model that I am conscious of, and I write with no idea of imitation or competition. In venturing occasionally on topics that have already been almost exhausted by English authors, I do it, not with the presumption of challenging a comparison, but with the hope that some new interest may be given to such topics, when discussed by the pen of a stranger.

If, therefore, I should sometimes be found dwelling with fondness on subjects that are trite and common-placed with the reader, I beg the circumstances under which I write may be kept in recollection. Having been born and brought up in a new country, yet educated from infancy in the literature of an old one, my mind was early filled with historical and poetical associations, connected with places, and manners, and customs of Europe; but which could rarely be applied to those of my own country. To a mind thus peculiarly prepared, the most ordinary objects and scenes, on arriving in Europe, are full of strange matter and interesting novelty. England is as classic ground to an American as Italy is to an Englishman; and old London teems with as much historical association as mighty Rome.

Indeed, it is difficult to describe the whimsical medley of ideas that throng upon his mind on landing among English scenes. He for the first time sees a world about which he has been reading and thinking in every stage of his existence. The recollected ideas of infancy, youth, and manhood; of the nursery, the school, and the study, come swarming at once upon him; and his attention is distracted between great and little objects; each of which, perhaps, awakens an equally delightful train of remembrances.

But what more especially attracts his notice are those peculiarities which distinguish an old country and an old state of society from a new one. I have never yet grown familiar enough with the crumbling monuments of past ages, to blunt the intense interest with which I at first beheld them. Accustomed always to scenes where history was, in a manner, in anticipation; where every thing in art was new and progressive, and pointed to the future rather than to the past; where, in short, the works of man gave no ideas but those of young existence, and prospective improvement; there was something inexpressibly touching in the sight of enormous piles of architecture, gray with antiquity, and sinking to decay. I cannot describe the mute but deep-felt enthusiasm with which I have contemplated a vast monastic ruin, like Tintern Abbey, buried in the bosom of a quiet valley, and shut up from the world, as though it had existed merely for itself; or a warrior pile, like Conway Castle, standing in stern loneliness on its rocky height, a mere hollow yet threatening phantom of departed power. They spread a grand, and melancholy, and, to me, an unusual charm over the landscape; I for the first time beheld signs of national old age, and empire's decay, and proofs of the transient and perishing glories of art, amidst the ever-springing and reviving fertility of nature.

But, in fact, to me every thing was full of matter; the foot-steps of history were every where to be traced; and poetry had breathed over and sanctified the land. I experienced the delightful freshness of feeling of a child, to whom every thing is new. I pictured to myself a set of inhabitants and a mode of life for every habitation that I saw, from the aristocratical mansion, amidst the lordly repose of stately groves and soli-tary parks, to the straw-thatched cottage, with its scanty gar-den and its cherished woodbine. I thought I never could be sated with the sweetness and freshness of a country so com-pletely carpeted with verdure; where every air breathed of the balmy pasture, and the honeysuckled hedge. I was continually coming upon some little document of poetry in the blos-somed hawthorn, the daisy, the cowslip, the primrose, or some other simple object that has received a supernatural value from the muse. The first time that I heard the song of the nightingale, I was intoxicated more by the delicious crowd of remembered associations than by the melody of its notes; and I shall never forget the thrill of ecstasy with which I first saw the lark rise, almost from beneath my feet, and wing its musical flight up into the morning sky.

In this way I traversed England, a grown-up child, de-lighted by every object great and small; and betraying a won-dering ignorance, and simple enjoyment, that provoked many a stare and a smile from my wiser and more experienced fel-low-travellers. Such too was the odd confusion of associations that kept breaking upon me as I first approached London. One of my earliest wishes had been to see this great metrop-olis. I had read so much about it in the earliest books that had been put into my infant hands; and I had heard so much about it from those around me who had come from the "old countries," that I was familiar with the names of its streets and squares, and public places, before I knew those of my native city. It was, to me, the great centre of the world, round which every thing seemed to revolve. I recollect contemplating so wistfully when a boy, a paltry little print of the Thames, and London Bridge, and St. Paul's, that was in front of an old magazine; and a picture of Kensington Gardens, with gentlemen in three-cornered hats and broad skirts, and ladies in hoops and lappets, that hung up in my bedroom; even the venerable cut of St. John's Gate, that has stood, time out of mind, in front of the Gentleman's Magazine, was not without its charms to me; and I envied the odd looking little men that appeared to be loitering about its arches.

How then did my heart warm when the towers of Westminster Abbey were pointed out to me, rising above the rich groves of St. James's Park, with a thin blue haze about their gray pinnacles! I could not behold this great mausoleum of what is most illustrious in our paternal history, without feeling my enthusiasm in a glow. With what eagerness did I explore every part of the metropolis! I was not content with those matters which occupy the dignified research of the learned traveller; I delighted to call up all the feelings of childhood, and to seek after those objects which had been the wonders of my infancy. London Bridge, so famous in nursery song; the far-famed Monument; Gog and Magog, and the Lions in the Tower, all brought back many a recollection of infantine delight, and of good old beings, now no more, who had gossiped about them to my wondering ear. Nor was it without a recurrence of childish interest that I first peeped into Mr. Newberry's shop, in St. Paul's Church-yard, that fountain-head of literature. Mr. Newberry was the first that ever filled my infant mind with the idea of a great and good man. He published all the picture books of the day; and, out of his abundant love for children, he charged "nothing for either paper or print, and only a penny-halfpenny for the binding!"

I have mentioned these circumstances, worthy reader, to show you the whimsical crowd of associations that are apt to beset my mind on mingling among English scenes. I hope they may, in some measure, plead my apology, should I be found harping upon stale and trivial themes, or indulging an over-fondness for any thing antique and obsolete. I know it is the humour, not to say cant of the day, to run riot about old times, old books, old customs, and old buildings; with myself, however, as far as I have caught the contagion, the feeling is genuine. To a man from a young country all old things are in a manner new; and he may surely be excused in being a little curious about antiquities, whose native land, unfortunately, cannot boast of a single ruin.

Having been brought up, also, in the comparative simplicity of a republic, I am apt to be struck with even the ordinary circumstances incident to an aristocratical state of society. If, however, I should at any time amuse myself by pointing out some of the eccentricities, and some of the poetical characteristics of the latter, I would not be understood as pretending to decide upon its political merits. My only aim is to paint characters and manners. I am no politician. The more I have considered the study of politics, the more I have found it full of perplexity; and I have contented myself, as I have in my religion, with the faith in which I was brought up, regulating my own conduct by its precepts; but leaving to abler heads the task of making converts.

I shall continue on, therefore, in the course I have hitherto pursued; looking at things poetically, rather than politically; describing them as they are, rather than pretending to point out how they should be; and endeavouring to see the world in as pleasant a light as circumstances will permit.

I have always had an opinion that much good might be done by keeping mankind in good humour with one another. I may be wrong in my philosophy, but I shall continue to practise it until convinced of its fallacy. When I discover the world to be all that it has been represented by sneering cynics and whining poets, I will turn to and abuse it also; in the mean while, worthy reader, I hope you will not think lightly of me, because I cannot believe this to be so very bad a world as it is represented.

Thine truly,
GEOFFREY CRAYON

The Hall

The ancientest house, and the best for housekeeping in this county or the next; and though the master of it write but squire, I know no lord like him.

Merry Beggars

THE READER, if he has perused the volumes of the Sketch Book, will probably recollect something of the Bracebridge family, with which I once passed a Christmas. I am now on another visit at the Hall, having been invited to a wedding which is shortly to take place. The squire's second son, Guy, a fine, spirited young captain in the army, is about to be married to his father's ward, the fair Julia Templeton. A gathering of relations and friends has already commenced, to celebrate the joyful occasion; for the old gentleman is an enemy to quiet, private weddings. "There is nothing," he says, "like launching a young couple gaily, and cheering them from the shore; a good outset is half the voyage."

Before proceeding any further, I would beg that the squire might not be confounded with that class of hard-riding, fox-hunting gentlemen so often described, and, in fact, so nearly extinct in England. I use this rural title partly because it is his universal appellation throughout the neighbourhood, and partly because it saves me the frequent repetition of his name, which is one of those rough old English names at which Frenchmen exclaim in despair.

The squire is, in fact, a lingering specimen of the old English country gentleman; rusticated a little by living almost entirely on his estate, and something of a humourist, as Englishmen are apt to become when they have an opportunity of living in their own way. I like his hobby passing well, however, which is, a bigoted devotion to old English manners and customs; it jumps a little with my own humour, having as yet a lively and unsated curiosity about the ancient and genuine characteristics of my "father land."

There are some traits about the squire's family also, which appear to me to be national. It is one of those old aristocratical families, which, I believe, are peculiar to England, and

13

scarcely understood in other countries; that is to say, families of the ancient gentry, who, though destitute of titled rank, maintain a high ancestral pride: who look down upon all nobility of recent creation, and would consider it a sacrifice of dignity to merge the venerable name of their house in a modern title.

This feeling is very much fostered by the importance which they enjoy on their hereditary domains. The family mansion is an old manor-house, standing in a retired and beautiful part of Yorkshire. Its inhabitants have been always regarded through the surrounding country, as "the great ones of the earth;" and the little village near the Hall looks up to the squire with almost feudal homage. An old manor-house, and an old family of this kind, are rarely to be met with at the present day; and it is probably the peculiar humour of the squire that has retained this secluded specimen of English housekeeping in something like the genuine old style.

I am again quartered in the pannelled chamber, in the antique wing of the house. The prospect from my window, however, has quite a different aspect from that which it wore on my winter visit. Though early in the month of April, yet a few warm, sunshiny days have drawn forth the beauties of the spring, which, I think, are always most captivating on their first opening. The parterres of the old fashioned garden are gay with flowers; and the gardener has brought out his exotics, and placed them along the stone balustrades. The trees are clothed with green buds and tender leaves; when I throw open my jingling casement, I smell the odour of mignionette, and hear the hum of the bees from the flowers against the sunny wall, with the varied song of the throstle, and the cheerful notes of the tuneful little wren.

While sojourning in this strong hold of old fashions, it is my intention to make occasional sketches of the scenes and characters before me. I would have it understood, however, that I am not writing a novel, and have nothing of intricate plot, or marvellous adventure, to promise the reader. The Hall of which I treat, has, for aught I know, neither trap-door, nor sliding-pannel, nor donjon-keep; and indeed appears to have no mystery about it. The family is a worthy well-meaning family, that, in all probability, will eat and drink, and go to bed, and get up regularly, from one end of my work to the other; and the squire is so kind-hearted an old gentleman that I see no likelihood of his throwing any kind of distress in the way of the approaching nuptials. In a word, I cannot foresee a single extraordinary event that is likely to occur in the whole term of my sojourn at the Hall.

I tell this honestly to the reader, lest, when he finds me dallying along, through every-day English scenes, he may hurry ahead, in hopes of meeting with some marvellous adventure further on. I invite him, on the contrary, to ramble gently on with me, as he would saunter out into the fields, stopping occasionally to gather a flower, or listen to a bird, or admire a prospect, without any anxiety to arrive at the end of his career. Should I, however, in the course of my loiterings about this old mansion, see or hear any thing curious, that might serve to vary the monotony of this every-day life, I shall not fail to report it for the reader's entertainment:

> For freshest wits I know will soon be wearie,
> Of any book, how grave so e'er it be,
> Except it have odd matter, strange and merrie,
> Well sauc'd with lies and glared all with glee.*

*Mirror for Magistrates.

The Busy Man

A decayed gentleman, who lives most upon his own mirth and my master's means, and much good do him with it. He does hold my master up with his stories, and songs, and catches, and such tricks and jigs, you would admire—he is with him now.

Jovial Crew

B Y NO ONE has my return to the Hall been more heartily greeted than by Mr. Simon Bracebridge, or Master Simon, as the squire most commonly calls him. I encountered him just as I entered the park, where he was breaking a pointer, and he received me with all the hospitable cordiality with which a man welcomes a friend to another one's house. I have already introduced him to the reader as a brisk old bachelor-looking little man; the wit and superannuated beau of a large family connexion, and the squire's factotum. I found him, as usual, full of bustle; with a thousand petty things to do, and persons to attend to, and in chirping good-humour; for there are few happier beings than a busy idler; that is to say, a man who is eternally busy about nothing.

I visited him, the morning after my arrival, in his chamber, which is in a remote corner of the mansion, as he says he likes to be to himself, and out of the way. He has fitted it up in his own taste, so that it is a perfect epitome of an old bachelor's notions of convenience and arrangement. The furniture is made up of odd pieces from all parts of the house, chosen on account of their suiting his notions, or fitting some corner of his apartment; and he is very eloquent in praise of an ancient elbow chair, from which he takes occasion to digress into a censure on modern chairs, as having degenerated from the dignity and comfort of high-backed antiquity.

Adjoining to his room is a small cabinet, which he calls his study. Here are some hanging shelves, of his own construction, on which are several old works on hawking, hunting, and farriery, and a collection or two of poems and songs of the reign of Elizabeth, which he studies out of compliment to the squire; together with the Novelist's Magazine, the Sporting Magazine, the Racing Calendar, a volume or two of the Newgate Calendar, a book of peerage, and another of heraldry.

His sporting dresses hang on pegs in a small closet; and about the walls of his apartment are hooks to hold his fishing-tackle, whips, spurs, and a favourite fowling-piece, curiously wrought and inlaid, which he inherits from his grandfather. He has also a couple of old single-keyed flutes, and a fiddle, which he has repeatedly patched and mended himself, affirming it to be a veritable Cremona; though I have never heard him extract a single note from it that was not enough to make one's blood run cold.

From this little nest his fiddle will often be heard, in the stillness of midday, drowsily sawing some long-forgotten tune; for he prides himself on having a choice collection of good old English music, and will scarcely have any thing to do with modern composers. The time, however, at which his musical powers are of most use, is now and then of an evening, when he plays for the children to dance in the Hall, and he passes among them and the servants for a perfect Orpheus.

His chamber also bears evidence of his various avocations: there are half-copied sheets of music; designs for needlework; sketches of landscapes, very indifferently executed; a camera lucida; a magic lantern, for which he is endeavouring to paint glasses; in a word, it is the cabinet of a man of many accomplishments, who knows a little of every thing, and does nothing well.

After I had spent some time in his apartment, admiring the ingenuity of his small inventions, he took me about the establishment, to visit the stables, dog-kennel, and other dependencies, in which he appeared like a general visiting the different quarters of his camp; as the squire leaves the control of all these matters to him, when he is at the Hall. He inquired into the state of the horses; examined their feet; prescribed a drench for one, and bleeding for another; and then took me to look at his own horse, on the merits of which he dwelt with great prolixity, and which, I noticed, had the best stall in the stable.

After this I was taken to a new toy of his and the squire's, which he termed the falconry, where there were several unhappy birds in durance, completing their education. Among

the number was a fine falcon, which Master Simon had in
especial training, and he told me that he would show me, in
a few days, some rare sport of the good old-fashioned kind.
In the course of our round, I noticed that the grooms, gamekeeper, whippers-in, and other retainers, seemed all to be on
somewhat of a familiar footing with Master Simon, and fond
of having a joke with him, though it was evident they had
great deference for his opinion in matters relating to their
functions.

There was one exception, however, in a testy old huntsman, as hot as a pepper-corn; a meagre, wiry old fellow, in a
thread-bare velvet jockey-cap, and a pair of leather breeches,
that, from much wear, shone as though they had been japanned. He was very contradictory and pragmatical, and apt,
as I thought, to differ from Master Simon now and then, out
of mere captiousness. This was particularly the case with respect to the treatment of the hawk, which the old man
seemed to have under his peculiar care, and, according to
Master Simon, was in a fair way to ruin: the latter had a vast
deal to say about *casting*, and *imping*, and *gleaming*, and *enseaming*, and giving the hawk the *rangle*, which I saw was all
heathen Greek to old Christy; but he maintained his point
notwithstanding, and seemed to hold all this technical lore in
utter disrespect.

I was surprised at the good humour with which Master
Simon bore his contradictions till he explained the matter to
me afterwards. Old Christy is the most ancient servant in the
place, having lived among dogs and horses the greater part of
a century, and been in the service of Mr. Bracebridge's father.
He knows the pedigree of every horse on the place, and has
bestrode the great-great grandsires of most of them. He can
give a circumstantial detail of every fox-hunt for the last sixty
or seventy years, and has a history for every stag's head about
the house, and every hunting trophy nailed to the door of the
dog-kennel.

All the present race have grown up under his eye, and humour him in his old age. He once attended the squire to Oxford when he was a student there, and enlightened the whole
university with his hunting lore. All this is enough to make
the old man opinionated, since he finds on all these matters

of first-rate importance, he knows more than the rest of the world. Indeed, Master Simon had been his pupil, and acknowledges that he derived his first knowledge in hunting from the instructions of Christy; and I much question whether the old man does not still look upon him as rather a greenhorn.

On our return homewards, as we were crossing the lawn in front of the house, we heard the porter's bell ring at the lodge, and shortly afterwards, a kind of cavalcade advanced slowly up the avenue. At sight of it my companion paused, considered it for a moment, and then, making a sudden exclamation, hurried away to meet it. As it approached I discovered a fair fresh-looking elderly lady, dressed in an old-fashioned riding-habit, with a broad-brimmed white beaver hat, such as may be seen in Sir Joshua Reynolds' paintings. She rode a sleek white pony, and was followed by a footman in rich livery, mounted on an over-fed hunter. At a little distance in the rear came an ancient cumbrous chariot, drawn by two very corpulent horses, driven by as corpulent a coachman, beside whom sat a page dressed in a fanciful green livery. Inside of the chariot was a starched prim personage, with a look somewhat between a lady's companion and a lady's maid, and two pampered curs, that showed their ugly faces and barked out of each window.

There was a general turning out of the garrison to receive this new comer. The squire assisted her to alight, and saluted her affectionately; the fair Julia flew into her arms, and they embraced with the romantic fervour of boarding-school friends: she was escorted into the house by Julia's lover, towards whom she showed distinguished favour; and a line of the old servants, who had collected in the Hall, bowed most profoundly as she passed.

I observed that Master Simon was most assiduous and devout in his attentions upon this old lady. He walked by the side of her pony up the avenue; and, while she was receiving the salutations of the rest of the family, he took occasion to notice the fat coachman; to pat the sleek carriage horses, and, above all, to say a civil word to my lady's gentlewoman, the prim, sour-looking vestal in the chariot.

I had no more of his company for the rest of the morning.

He was swept off in the vortex that followed in the wake of this lady. Once indeed he paused for a moment, as he was hurrying on some errand of the good lady's, to let me know that this was Lady Lillycraft, a sister of the squire's, of large fortune, which the captain would inherit, and that her estate lay in one of the best sporting countries in all England.

Family Servants

Verily old servants are the vouchers of worthy housekeeping.
They are like rats in a mansion, or mites in a cheese, bespeaking
the antiquity and fatness of their abode.

IN MY CASUAL anecdotes of the Hall, I may often be tempted to dwell on circumstances of a trite and ordinary nature, from their appearing to me illustrative of genuine national character. It seems to be the study of the squire to adhere, as much as possible, to what he considers the old landmarks of English manners. His servants all understand his ways, and for the most part have been accustomed to them from infancy; so that, upon the whole, his household presents one of the few tolerable specimens that can now be met with, of the establishment of an English country gentleman of the old school.

By the bye, the servants are not the least characteristic part of the household: the housekeeper, for instance, has been born and brought up at the Hall, and has never been twenty miles from it; yet she has a stately air that would not disgrace a lady that had figured at the court of Queen Elizabeth.

I am half inclined to think that she has caught it from living so much among the old family pictures. It may, however, be owing to a consciousness of her importance in the sphere in which she has always moved; for she is greatly respected in the neighbouring village, and among the farmers' wives, and has high authority in the household, ruling over the servants with quiet, but undisputed sway.

She is a thin old lady, with blue eyes and pointed nose and chin. Her dress is always the same as to fashion. She wears a small, well-starched ruff, a laced stomacher, full petticoats, and a gown festooned and open in front, which, on particular occasions, is of ancient silk, the legacy of some former dame of the family, or an inheritance from her mother, who was housekeeper before her. I have a reverence for these old garments, as I make no doubt they have figured about these apartments in days long past, when they have set off the charms of some peerless family beauty; and I have sometimes

looked from the old housekeeper to the neighbouring portraits, to see whether I could not recognize her antiquated
brocade in the dress of some one of those long-waisted dames
that smile on me from the walls.

Her hair, which is quite white, is frizzed out in front, and
she wears over it a small cap, nicely plaited, and brought
down under the chin. Her manners are simple and primitive,
heightened a little by a proper dignity of station.

The Hall is her world, and the history of the family the
only history she knows, excepting that which she has read in
the Bible. She can give a biography of every portrait in the
picture gallery, and is a complete family chronicle.

She is treated with great consideration by the squire. Indeed, Master Simon tells me that there is a traditional anecdote current among the servants, of the squire's having been
seen kissing her in the picture gallery, when they were both
young. As, however, nothing further was ever noticed between them, the circumstance caused no great scandal; only
she was observed to take to reading Pamela shortly afterwards, and refused the hand of the village innkeeper, whom
she had previously smiled on.

The old butler, who was formerly footman, and a rejected
admirer of hers, used to tell the anecdote now and then, at
those little cabals that will occasionally take place among the
most orderly servants, arising from the common propensity
of the governed to talk against administration; but he has left
it off, of late years, since he has risen into place, and shakes
his head rebukingly when it is mentioned.

It is certain that the old lady will, to this day, dwell on the
looks of the squire when he was a young man at college; and
she maintains that none of his sons can compare with their
father when he was of their age, and was dressed out in his
full suit of scarlet, with his hair craped and powdered, and his
three-cornered hat.

She has an orphan niece, a pretty, soft-hearted baggage,
named Phœbe Wilkins, who has been transplanted to the Hall
within a year or two, and been nearly spoiled for any condition of life. She is a kind of attendant and companion of the
fair Julia's; and from loitering about the young lady's apartments, reading scraps of novels, and inheriting second-hand

finery, has become something between a waiting-maid and a slip-shod fine lady.

She is considered a kind of heiress among the servants, as she will inherit all her aunt's property; which, if report be true, must be a round sum of good golden guineas, the accumulated wealth of two housekeepers' savings; not to mention the hereditary wardrobe, and the many little valuables and knick-knacks treasured up in the housekeeper's room. Indeed the old housekeeper has the reputation among the servants and the villagers of being passing rich; and there is a japanned chest of drawers and a large iron-bound coffer in her room, which are supposed, by the housemaids, to hold treasures of wealth.

The old lady is a great friend of Master Simon, who, indeed, pays a little court to her, as to a person high in authority; and they have many discussions on points of family history, in which, notwithstanding his extensive information, and pride of knowledge, he commonly admits her superior accuracy. He seldom returns to the Hall, after one of his visits to the other branches of the family, without bringing Mrs. Wilkins some remembrance from the ladies of the house where he has been staying.

Indeed all the children of the house look up to the old lady with habitual respect and attachment, and she seems almost to consider them as her own, from their having grown up under her eye. The Oxonian, however, is her favourite, probably from being the youngest, though he is the most mischievous, and has been apt to play tricks upon her from boyhood.

I cannot help mentioning one little ceremony, which, I believe, is peculiar to the Hall. After the cloth is removed at dinner, the old housekeeper sails into the room and stands behind the squire's chair, when he fills her a glass of wine with his own hands, in which she drinks the health of the company in a truly respectful yet dignified manner, and then retires. The squire received the custom from his father, and has always continued it.

There is a peculiar character about the servants of old English families that reside principally in the country. They have a quiet, orderly, respectful mode of doing their duties. They are always neat in their persons, and appropriately, and, if I may use the phrase, technically dressed; they move about the house without hurry or noise; there is nothing of the bustle of employment, or the voice of command; nothing of that obtrusive housewifery that amounts to a torment. You are not persecuted by the process of making you comfortable; yet every thing is done, and is done well. The work of the house is performed as if by magic, but it is the magic of system. Nothing is done by fits and starts, nor at awkward seasons; the whole goes on like well-oiled clock-work, where there is no noise nor jarring in its operations.

English servants, in general, are not treated with great indulgence, nor rewarded by many commendations; for the English are laconic and reserved towards their domestics; but an approving nod and a kind word from master or mistress goes as far here, as an excess of praise or indulgence elsewhere. Neither do servants often exhibit any animated marks of affection to their employers; yet, though quiet, they are strong in their attachments; and the reciprocal regard of masters and servants, though not ardently expressed, is powerful and lasting in old English families.

The title of "an old family servant" carries with it a thousand kind associations in all parts of the world; and there is no claim upon the home-bred charities of the heart more irresistible than that of having been "born in the house." It is common to see gray-headed domestics of this kind attached to an English family of the "old school," who continue in it to the day of their death, in the enjoyment of steady unaffected kindness, and the performance of faithful, unofficious duty. I think such instances of attachment speak well for both master and servant, and the frequency of them speaks well for national character.

These observations, however, hold good only with families of the description I have mentioned; and with such as are somewhat retired, and pass the greater part of their time in the country. As to the powdered menials that throng the halls of fashionable town residences, they equally reflect the character of the establishments to which they belong; and I know no more complete epitomes of dissolute heartlessness, and pampered inutility.

But the good "old family servant!"—The one who has

always been linked, in idea, with the home of our heart; who has led us to school in the days of prattling childhood; who has been the confidant of our boyish cares, and schemes, and enterprises; who has hailed us as we came home at vacations, and been the promotor of all our holiday sports; who, when we, in wandering manhood, have left the paternal roof, and only return thither at intervals, will welcome us with a joy inferior only to that of our parents; who, now grown gray and infirm with age, still totters about the house of our fathers in fond and faithful servitude; who claims us, in a manner, as his own; and hastens with querulous eagerness to anticipate his fellow-domestics in waiting upon us at table; and who, when we retire at night to the chamber that still goes by our name, will linger about the room to have one more kind look, and one more pleasant word about times that are past—who does not experience towards such a being a feeling of almost filial affection?

I have met with several instances of epitaphs on the grave-stones of such valuable domestics, recorded with the simple truth of natural feeling. I have two before me at this moment; one copied from a tombstone of a churchyard in Warwick-shire:

"Here lieth the body of Joseph Batte, confidential servant to George Birch, Esq. of Hamstead Hall. His grateful friend and master caused this inscription to be written in memory of his discretion, fidelity, diligence, and continence. He died (a bachelor) aged 84, having lived 44 years in the same family."

The other was taken from a tombstone in Eltham church-yard:

"Here lie the remains of Mr. James Tappy, who departed this life on the 8th of September, 1818, aged 84, after a faithful service of 60 years in one family; by each individual of which he lived respected, and died lamented by the sole survivor."

Few monuments, even of the illustrious, have given me the glow about the heart that I felt while copying this honest epitaph in the churchyard of Eltham. I sympathised with this "sole survivor" of a family mourning over the grave of the faithful follower of his race, who had been, no doubt, a living memento of times and friends that had passed away; and in considering this record of long and devoted service, I called to mind the touching speech of Old Adam in "As You Like It," when tottering after the youthful son of his ancient master:

> "Master, go on, and I will follow thee
> To the last gasp, with truth and loyalty!"

NOTE—I cannot but mention a tablet which I have seen somewhere in the chapel of Windsor Castle, put up by the late king to the memory of a family servant, who had been a faithful attendant of his lamented daughter, the Princess Amelia. George III possessed much of the strong, domestic feeling of the old English country gentleman; and it is an incident curious in monumental history, and creditable to the human heart, a monarch erecting a monument in honour of the humble virtues of a menial.

The Widow

She was so charitable and pitious
She would weep if that she saw a mous
Caught in a trap, if it were dead or bled;
Of small hounds had she, that she fed
With rost flesh, milke, and wastel bread,
But sore wept she if any of them were dead,
Or if man smote them with a yard smart.

Chaucer

NOTWITHSTANDING the whimsical parade made by Lady Lillycraft on her arrival, she has none of the petty stateliness that I had imagined; but, on the contrary, she has a degree of naïveté, and simple-heartedness, if I may use the phrase, that mingles well with her old fashioned manners and harmless ostentation. She dresses in rich silks, with long waist; she rouges considerably, and her hair, which is nearly white, is frizzed out, and put up with pins. Her face is pitted with the small-pox, but the delicacy of her features shows that she may once have been beautiful; and she has a very fair and well-shaped hand and arm, of which, if I mistake not, the good lady is still a little vain.

I have had the curiosity to gather a few particulars concerning her. She was a great belle in town between thirty and forty years since, and reigned for two seasons with all the insolence of beauty, refusing several excellent offers; when, unfortunately, she was robbed of her charms and her lovers by an attack of the small-pox. She retired immediately into the country, where she sometime after inherited an estate, and married a baronet, a former admirer, whose passion had suddenly revived; "having," as he said, "always loved her mind rather than her person."

The baronet did not enjoy her mind and fortune above six months, and had scarcely grown very tired of her, when he broke his neck in a fox-chase, and left her free, rich, and disconsolate. She has remained on her estate in the country ever since, and has never shown any desire to return to town, and revisit the scene of her early triumphs and fatal malady. All her favourite recollections, however, revert to that short period of her youthful beauty. She has no idea of town but as it was at that time; and continually forgets that the place and people must have changed materially in the course of nearly half a century. She will often speak of the toasts of those days as if still reigning; and, until very recently, used to talk with delight of the royal family, and the beauty of the young princes and princesses. She cannot be brought to think of the present king otherwise than as an elegant young man, rather wild, but who danced a minuet divinely; and before he came to the crown, would often mention him as the "sweet young prince."

She talks also of the walks in Kensington Garden, where the gentlemen appeared in gold-laced coats and cocked hats, and the ladies in hoops, and swept so proudly along the grassy avenues; and she thinks the ladies let themselves sadly down in their dignity, when they gave up cushioned head-dresses, and high-heeled shoes. She has much to say too of the officers who were in the train of her admirers; and speaks familiarly of many wild young blades, that are now, perhaps, hobbling about watering-places with crutches and gouty shoes.

Whether the taste the good lady had of matrimony discouraged her or not, I cannot say; but, though her merits and her riches have attracted many suitors, she has never been tempted to venture again into the happy state. This is singular too, for she seems of a most soft and susceptible heart; is always talking of love and connubial felicity; and is a great stickler for old-fashioned gallantry, devoted attentions, and eternal constancy, on the part of the gentlemen. She lives, however, after her own taste. Her house, I am told, must have been built and furnished about the time of Sir Charles Grandison. Everything about it is somewhat formal and stately; but has been softened down into a degree of voluptuousness, characteristic of an old lady very tender-hearted and romantic, and that loves her ease. The cushions of the great arm-chairs and wide sofas almost bury you when you sit down on them. Flowers of the most rare and delicate kind are placed about the rooms and on little japanned stands; and sweet bags lie about the tables and mantel-pieces. The house is full of pet dogs, Angola cats, and singing birds, who are as carefully waited upon as she is herself.

She is dainty in her living, and a little of an epicure, living on white meats, and little ladylike dishes, though her servants have substantial old English fare, as their looks bear witness. Indeed, they are so indulged, that they are all spoiled; and when they lose their present place, they will be fit for no other. Her ladyship is one of those easy-tempered beings that are always doomed to be much liked, but ill served by their domestics, and cheated by all the world.

Much of her time is past in reading novels, of which she has a most extensive library, and has a constant supply from the publishers in town. Her erudition in this line of literature is immense; she has kept pace with the press for half a century. Her mind is stuffed with love-tales of all kinds, from the stately amours of the old books of chivalry, down to the last blue-covered romance, reeking from the press; though she evidently gives the preference to those that came out in the days of her youth, and when she was first in love. She maintains that there are no novels written now-a-days equal to Pamela and Sir Charles Grandison; and she places the Castle of Otranto at the head of all romances.

She does a vast deal of good in her neighbourhood, and is imposed upon by every beggar in the county. She is the benefactress of a village adjoining to her estate, and takes an especial interest in all its love-affairs. She knows of every courtship that is going on; every love-lorn damsel is sure to find a patient listener and a sage adviser in her ladyship. She takes great pains to reconcile all love-quarrels, and should any faithless swain persist in his inconstancy, he is sure to draw on himself the good lady's violent indignation.

I have learned these particulars partly from Frank Bracebridge, and partly from Master Simon. I am now able to account for the assiduous attention of the latter to her ladyship. Her house is one of his favourite resorts, where he is a very important personage. He makes her a visit of business once a year, when he looks into all her affairs; which, as she is no manager, are apt to get into confusion. He examines the books of the overseer, and shoots about the estate, which, he says, is well stocked with game, notwithstanding that it is poached by all the vagabonds in the neighbourhood.

It is thought, as I before hinted, that the captain will inherit the greater part of her property, having always been her chief favourite; for, in fact, she is partial to a red coat. She has now come to the Hall to be present at his nuptials, having a great disposition to interest herself in all matters of love and matrimony.

The Lovers

Rise up, my love, my fair one, and come away: for lo the winter is past, the rain is over and gone; the flowers appear on the earth, the time of the singing of birds is come, and the voice of the turtle is heard in the land.

Song of Solomon

To a man who is a little of a philosopher, and a bachelor to boot; and who, by dint of some experience in the follies of life, begins to look with a learned eye upon the ways of man, and eke of woman; to such a man, I say, there is something very entertaining in noticing the conduct of a pair of young lovers. It may not be as grave and scientific a study as the loves of the plants, but it is certainly as interesting.

I have therefore derived much pleasure, since my arrival at the Hall, from observing the fair Julia and her lover. She has all the delightful, blushing consciousness of an artless girl, inexperienced in coquetry, who has made her first conquest; while the captain regards her with that mixture of fondness and exultation, with which a youthful lover is apt to contemplate so beauteous a prize.

I observed them yesterday in the garden, advancing along one of the retired walks. The sun was shining with delicious warmth, making great masses of bright verdure, and deep blue shade. The cuckoo, that "harbinger of spring," was faintly heard from a distance; the thrush piped from the hawthorn, and the yellow butterflies sported, and toyed, and coquetted in the air.

The fair Julia was leaning on her lover's arm, listening to his conversation, with her eyes cast down, a soft blush on her cheek, and a quiet smile on her lips, while in the hand that hung negligently by her side was a bunch of flowers. In this way they were sauntering slowly along, and when I considered them, and the scene in which they were moving, I could not but think it a thousand pities that the season should ever change, or that young people should ever grow older, or that blossoms should give way to fruit, or that lovers should ever get married.

From what I have gathered of family anecdote, I understand that the fair Julia is the daughter of a favourite college friend of the squire; who after leaving Oxford, had entered the army, and served for many years in India, where he was mortally wounded in a skirmish with the natives. In his last moments he had, with a faltering pen, recommended his wife and daughter to the kindness of his early friend.

The widow and her child returned to England helpless, and almost hopeless. When Mr. Bracebridge received accounts of their situation, he hastened to their relief. He reached them just in time to soothe the last moments of the mother, who was dying of a consumption, and to make her happy in the assurance that her child should never want a protector.

The good squire returned with his prattling charge to his strong hold, where he has brought her up with a tenderness truly paternal. As he has taken some pains to superintend her education, and form her taste, she has grown up with many of his notions, and considers him the wisest, as well as the best of men. Much of her time, too, has been passed with Lady Lillycraft, who has instructed her in the manners of the old school, and enriched her mind with all kinds of novels and romances. Indeed, her ladyship has had a great hand in promoting the match between Julia and the captain, having had them together at her country seat, the moment she found there was an attachment growing up between them; the good lady being never so happy as when she has a pair of turtles cooing about her.

I have been pleased to see the fondness with which the fair Julia is regarded by the old servants at the Hall. She has been a pet with them from childhood, and every one seems to lay some claim to her education; so that it is no wonder that she should be extremely accomplished. The gardener taught her to rear flowers, of which she is extremely fond. Old Christy, the pragmatical huntsman, softens when she approaches; and as she sits lightly and gracefully in her saddle, claims the merit of having taught her to ride; while the housekeeper, who almost looks upon her as a daughter, intimates that she first gave her an insight into the mysteries of the toilet, having been dressing-maid in her young days to the late Mrs. Bracebridge. I am inclined to credit this last claim, as I have noticed that the dress of the young lady had an air of the old school, though managed with native taste, and that her hair was put up very much in the style of Sir Peter Lely's portraits in the picture-gallery.

Her very musical attainments partake of this old-fashioned character; and most of her songs are such as are not at the present day to be found on the piano of a modern performer. I have, however, seen so much of modern fashions, modern accomplishments, and modern fine ladies, that I relish this tinge of antiquated style in so young and lovely a girl; and I have had as much pleasure in hearing her warble one of the old songs of Herrick, or Carew, or Suckling, adapted to some simple old melody, as I have had from listening to a lady amateur sky-lark it up and down through the finest bravura of Rossini or Mozart.

We have very pretty music in the evenings, occasionally, between her and the captain, assisted sometimes by Master Simon, who scrapes, dubiously, on his violin; being very apt to get out, and to halt a note or two in the rear. Sometimes he even thrums a little on the piano, and takes a part in a trio, in which his voice can generally be distinguished by a certain quavering tone, and an occasional false note.

I was praising the fair Julia's performance to him after one of her songs, when I found he took to himself the whole credit of having formed her musical taste, assuring me that she was very apt; and, indeed, summing up her whole character in his knowing way, by adding, that "she was a very nice girl, and had no nonsense about her."

Family Reliques

My Infelice's face, her brow, her eye,
The dimple on her cheek: and such sweet skill
Hath from the cunning workman's pencil flown,
These lips look fresh and lively as her own.
False colours last after the true be dead.
Of all the roses grafted on her cheeks,
Of all the graces dancing in her eyes,
Of all the music set upon her tongue,
Of all that was past woman's excellence
In her white bosom; look, a painted board
Circumscribes all!

Dekker

AN OLD ENGLISH family mansion is a fertile subject for study. It abounds with illustrations of former times, and traces of the tastes, and humours, and manners, of successive generations. The alterations and additions, in different styles of architecture; the furniture, plate, pictures, hangings; the warlike and sporting implements of different ages and fancies; all furnish food for curious and amusing speculation. As the squire is very careful in collecting and preserving all family reliques, the Hall is full of remembrances of the kind. In looking about the establishment, I can picture to myself the character and habits that have prevailed at different eras of the family history. I have mentioned on a former occasion the armour of the crusader which hangs up in the Hall. There are also several jack-boots, with enormously thick soles and high heels, that belonged to a set of cavaliers, who filled the Hall with the din and stir of arms during the time of the Covenanters. A number of enormous drinking vessels of antique fashion, with huge Venice glasses, and green hock-glasses, with the apostles in relief on them, remain as monuments of a generation or two of hard-livers, that led a life of roaring revelry, and first introduced the gout into the family.

I shall pass over several more such indications of temporary tastes of the squire's predecessors; but I cannot forbear to notice a pair of antlers in the great hall, which is one of the trophies of a hard-riding squire of former times, who was the Nimrod of these parts. There are many traditions of his wonderful feats in hunting still existing, which are related by old Christy, the huntsman, who gets exceedingly nettled if they are in the least doubted. Indeed, there is a frightful chasm, a few miles from the Hall, which goes by the name of the Squire's Leap, from his having cleared it in the ardour of the chase; there can be no doubt of the fact, for old Christy shows the very dints of the horse's hoofs on the rocks on each side of the chasm.

Master Simon holds the memory of this squire in great veneration, and has a number of extraordinary stories to tell concerning him, which he repeats at all hunting dinners; and I am told that they wax more and more marvellous the older they grow. He has also a pair of Rippon spurs which belonged to this mighty hunter of yore, and which he only wears on particular occasions.

The place, however, which abounds most with mementos of past times, is the picture gallery; and there is something strangely pleasing, though melancholy, in considering the long rows of portraits which compose the greater part of the collection. They furnish a kind of narrative of the lives of the family worthies, which I am enabled to read with the assistance of the venerable housekeeper, who is the family chronicler, prompted occasionally by Master Simon. There is the progress of a fine lady, for instance, through a variety of portraits. One represents her as a little girl, with a long waist and hoop, holding a kitten in her arms, and ogling the spectator out of the corners of her eyes, as if she could not turn her head. In another we find her in the freshness of youthful beauty, when she was a celebrated belle, and so hard-hearted as to cause several unfortunate gentlemen to run desperate and write bad poetry. In another she is depicted as a stately dame, in the maturity of her charms; next to the portrait of her husband, a gallant colonel in full-bottomed wig and gold-laced hat, who was killed abroad; and, finally, her monument is in the church, the spire of which may be seen from the window, where her effigy is carved in marble, and represents her as a venerable dame of seventy-six.

In like manner I have followed some of the family great

men through a series of pictures, from early boyhood to the robe of dignity, or truncheon of command, so on by degrees, until they were garnered up in the common repository, the neighbouring church.

There is one group that particularly interested me. It consisted of four sisters of nearly the same age, who flourished about a century since, and, if I may judge from their portraits, were extremely beautiful. I can imagine what a scene of gaiety and romance this old mansion must have been, when they were in the hey-day of their charms; when they passed like beautiful visions through its halls, or stepped daintily to music in the revels and dances of the cedar gallery; or printed, with delicate feet, the velvet verdure of these lawns. How must they have been looked up to with mingled love, and pride, and reverence, by the old family servants; and followed with almost painful admiration by the aching eyes of rival admirers! How must melody, and song, and tender serenade, have breathed about these courts, and their echoes whispered to the loitering tread of lovers! How must these very turrets have made the hearts of the young galliards thrill, as they first discerned them from afar, rising from among the trees, and pictured to themselves the beauties casketed like gems within these walls! Indeed I have discovered about the place several faint records of this reign of love and romance, when the Hall was a kind of Court of Beauty. Several of the old romances in the library have marginal notes expressing sympathy and approbation, where there are long speeches extolling ladies' charms, or protesting eternal fidelity, or bewailing the cruelty of some tyrannical fair one. The interviews, and declarations, and parting scenes of tender lovers, also bear evidence of having been frequently read, and are scored, and marked with notes of admiration, and have initials written on the margins; most of which annotations have the day of the month and year annexed to them. Several of the windows, too, have scraps of poetry engraved on them with diamonds, taken from the writings of the fair Mrs. Philips, the once celebrated Orinda. Some of these seem to have been inscribed by lovers; and others, in a delicate and unsteady hand, and a little inaccurate in the spelling, have evidently been written by the young ladies themselves, or by female friends, who have been on visits to the Hall. Mrs. Philips seems to have been their favourite author, and they have distributed the names of her heroes and heroines among their circle of intimacy. Sometimes, in a male hand, the verse bewails the cruelty of beauty, and the sufferings of constant love; while in a female hand it prudishly confines itself to lamenting the parting of female friends. The bow-window of my bed-room, which has, doubtless, been inhabited by one of these beauties, has several of these inscriptions. I have one at this moment before my eyes, called "Camilla parting with Leonora:"

> "How perished is the joy that's past,
>   The present how unsteady!
> What comfort can be great and last,
>   When this is gone already?"

And close by it is another, written, perhaps, by some adventurous lover, who had stolen into the lady's chamber during her absence:

> "THEODOSIUS TO CAMILLA.
> I'd rather in your favour live,
>   Than in a lasting name;
> And much a greater rate would give
>   For happiness than fame.
>   THEODOSIUS. 1700."

When I look at these faint records of gallantry and tenderness; when I contemplate the fading portraits of these beautiful girls, and think too that they have long since bloomed, reigned, grown old, died, and passed away, and with them all their graces, their triumphs, their rivalries, their admirers; the whole empire of love and pleasure in which they ruled—"all dead, all buried, all forgotten," I find a cloud of melancholy stealing over the present gaieties around me. I was gazing, in a musing mood, this very morning, at the portrait of the lady, whose husband was killed abroad, when the fair Julia entered the gallery, leaning on the arm of the captain. The sun shone through the row of windows on her as she passed along, and she seemed to beam out each time into brightness, and relapse into shade, until the door at the bottom of the gallery closed after her. I felt a sadness of heart at the idea, that this was an emblem of her lot: a few more years of sunshine and shade, and all this life, and loveliness, and enjoyment, will have ceased, and nothing be left to commemorate this beautiful being but one more perishable portrait; to awaken, perhaps, the trite speculations of some future loiterer, like myself, when I and my scribblings shall have lived through our brief existence and been forgotten.

An Old Soldier

I've worn some leather out abroad; let out a heathen soul or
two; fed this good sword with the black blood of pagan Christians; converted a few infidels with it.—But let that pass.

The Ordinary

THE HALL was thrown into some little agitation, a few
days since, by the arrival of General Harbottle. He had
been expected for several days, and had been looked for,
rather impatiently, by several of the family. Master Simon assured me that I would like the general hugely, for he was a
blade of the old school, and an excellent table companion.
Lady Lillycraft, also, appeared to be somewhat fluttered, on
the morning of the general's arrival, for he had been one of
her early admirers; and she recollected him only as a dashing
young ensign, just come upon the town. She actually spent
an hour longer at her toilette, and made her appearance with
her hair uncommonly frizzed and powdered, and an additional quantity of rouge. She was evidently a little surprised
and shocked, therefore, at finding the lithe dashing ensign
transformed into a corpulent old general, with a double chin;
though it was a perfect picture to witness their salutations;
the graciousness of her profound curtsy, and the air of the
old school with which the general took off his hat, swayed it
gently in his hand, and bowed his powdered head.

All this bustle and anticipation has caused me to study the
general with a little more attention than, perhaps, I should
otherwise have done; and the few days that he has already
passed at the Hall have enabled me, I think, to furnish a tolerable likeness of him to the reader.

He is, as Master Simon observed, a soldier of the old
school, with powdered head, side locks, and pigtail. His face
is shaped like the stern of a Dutch man of war, narrow at top,
and wide at bottom, with full rosy cheeks and a double chin;
so that, to use the cant of the day, his organs of eating may
be said to be powerfully developed.

The general, though a veteran, has seen very little active
service, except the taking of Seringapatam, which forms an

era in his history. He wears a large emerald in his bosom, and a diamond on his finger, which he got on that occasion, and whoever is unlucky enough to notice either, is sure to involve himself in the whole history of the siege. To judge from the general's conversation, the taking of Seringapatam is the most important affair that has occurred for the last century.

On the approach of warlike times on the continent, he was rapidly promoted, to get him out of the way of younger officers of merit; until having been hoisted to the rank of general, he was quietly laid on the shelf. Since that time his campaigns have been principally confined to watering places; where he drinks the waters for a slight touch of the liver which he got in India; and plays whist with old dowagers, with whom he has flirted in his younger days. Indeed he talks of all the fine women of the last half century, and, according to hints which he now and then drops, has enjoyed the particular smiles of many of them.

He has seen considerable garrison duty, and can speak of almost every place famous for good quarters, and where the inhabitants give good dinners. He is a diner out of first-rate currency, when in town; being invited to one place, because he has been seen at another. In the same way he is invited about to country-seats, and can describe half the seats in the kingdom, from actual observation; nor is any one better versed in court gossip, and the pedigrees and intermarriages of the nobility.

As the general is an old bachelor, and an old beau, and there are several ladies at the Hall, especially his quondam flame Lady Lillycraft, he is put rather upon his gallantry. He commonly passes some time, therefore, at his toilette, and takes the field at a late hour every morning, with his hair dressed out and powdered, and a rose in his button-hole. After he has breakfasted, he walks up and down the terrace in the sunshine, humming an air, and hemming between every stave, carrying one hand behind his back, and with the other touching his cane to the ground, and then raising it up to his shoulder. Should he, in these morning promenades, meet any of the elder ladies of the family, as he frequently does Lady Lillycraft, his hat is immediately in his hand, and it is enough

to remind one of those courtly groups of ladies and gentlemen, in old prints of Windsor Terrace, or Kensington Garden.

He talks frequently about "the service," and is fond of
humming the old song,

> Why, soldiers, why,
> Should we be melancholy, boys?
> Why, soldiers, why,
> Whose business 'tis to die!

I cannot discover, however, that the general has ever run any
great risk of dying, excepting from an apoplexy, or an indiges-
tion. He criticises all the battles on the continent, and dis-
cusses the merits of the commanders, but never fails to bring
the conversation, ultimately, to Tippoo Saib and Seringapatam. I am told that the general was a perfect champion at
drawing-rooms, parades, and watering-places, during the late
war, and was looked to with hope and confidence by many an
old lady, when labouring under the terror of Bonaparte's
invasion.

He is thoroughly loyal, and attends punctually on levees
when in town. He has treasured up many remarkable sayings
of the late king, particularly one which the king made to him
on a field-day, complimenting him on the excellence of his
horse. He extols the whole royal family, but especially the
present king, whom he pronounces the most perfect gentleman and best whist-player in Europe. The general swears
rather more than is the fashion of the present day; but it was
the mode in the old school. He is, however, very strict in
religious matters, and a stanch churchman. He repeats the re-
sponses very loudly in church, and is emphatical in praying
for the king and royal family.

At table his loyalty waxes very fervent with his second
bottle, and the song of "God save the King" puts him into a
perfect ecstacy. He is amazingly well contented with the present state of things, and apt to get a little impatient at any talk
about national ruin and agricultural distress. He says he has
travelled about the country as much as any man, and has met
with nothing but prosperity; and to confess the truth, a great
part of his time is spent in visiting from one country seat to

another, and riding about the parks of his friends. "They talk of public distress," said the general this day to me, at dinner, as he smacked a glass of rich burgundy, and cast his eyes about the ample board; "they talk of public distress, but where do we find it, sir? I see none. I see no reason any one has to complain. Take my word for it, sir, this talk about public distress is all humbug!"

The Widow's Retinue

Little dogs and all!
Lear

IN GIVING an account of the arrival of Lady Lillycraft at the Hall, I ought to have mentioned the entertainment which I derived from witnessing the unpacking of her carriage, and the disposing of her retinue. There is something extremely amusing to me in the number of factitious wants, the loads of imaginary conveniences, but real incumbrances, with which the luxurious are apt to burthen themselves. I like to watch the whimsical stir and display about one of these petty progresses. The number of robustious footmen and retainers of all kinds bustling about, with looks of infinite gravity and importance, to do almost nothing. The number of heavy trunks, and parcels, and bandboxes belonging to my lady; and the solicitude exhibited about some humble, odd-looking box, by my lady's maid; the cushions piled in the carriage to make a soft seat still softer, and to prevent the dreaded possibility of a jolt; the smelling-bottles, the cordials, the baskets of biscuit and fruit; the new publications; all provided to guard against hunger, fatigue, or ennui; the led horses to vary the mode of travelling; and all this preparation and parade to move, perhaps, some very good-for-nothing personage about a little space of earth!

I do not mean to apply the latter part of these observations to Lady Lillycraft, for whose simple kindheartedness I have a very great respect, and who is really a most amiable and worthy being. I cannot refrain, however, from mentioning some of the motley retinue she has brought with her; and which, indeed, bespeak the overflowing kindness of her nature, which requires her to be surrounded with objects on which to lavish it.

In the first place, her ladyship has a pampered coachman, with a red face, and cheeks that hang down like dew-laps. He evidently domineers over her a little with respect to the fat horses; and only drives out when he thinks proper, and when he thinks it will be "good for the cattle."

43

She has a favourite page to attend upon her person: a handsome boy of about twelve years of age, but a mischievous varlet, very much spoiled, and in a fair way to be good for nothing. He is dressed in green, with a profusion of gold cord and gilt buttons about his clothes. She always has one or two attendants of the kind, who are replaced by others as soon as they grow to fourteen years of age. She has brought two dogs with her also, out of a number of pets which she maintains at home. One is a fat spaniel, called Zephyr— though heaven defend me from such a zephyr! He is fed out of all shape and comfort; his eyes are nearly strained out of his head; he wheezes with corpulency, and cannot walk without great difficulty. The other is a little, old, gray-muzzled curmudgeon, with an unhappy eye, that kindles like a coal if you only look at him; his nose turns up; his mouth is drawn into wrinkles, so as to show his teeth; in short, he has altogether the look of a dog far gone in misanthropy, and totally sick of the world. When he walks, he has his tail curled up so tight that it seems to lift his feet from the ground; and he seldom makes use of more than three legs at a time, keeping the other drawn up as a reserve. This last wretch is called Beauty.

These dogs are full of elegant ailments unknown to vulgar dogs; and are petted and nursed by Lady Lillycraft with the tenderest kindness. They are pampered and fed with delicacies by their fellow-minion, the page; but their stomachs are often weak and out of order, so that they cannot eat; though I have now and then seen the page give them a mischievous pinch, or thwack over the head, when his mistress was not by. They have cushions for their express use, on which they lie before the fire, and yet are apt to shiver and moan if there is the least draught of air. When any one enters the room, they make a most tyrannical barking that is absolutely deafening. They are insolent to all the other dogs of the establishment. There is a noble stag-hound, a great favourite of the squire's, who is a privileged visitor to the parlour; but the moment he makes his appearance, these intruders fly at him with furious rage; and I have admired the sovereign indifference and contempt with which he seems to look down upon his puny assailants. When her ladyship drives out, these dogs are generally carried

with her to take the air; when they look out of each window
of the carriage, and bark at all vulgar pedestrian dogs. These
dogs are a continual source of misery to the household; as
they are always in the way, they every now and then get their
toes trod on, and then there is a yelping on their part, and a
loud lamentation on the part of their mistress, that fill the
room with clamour and confusion.

Lastly, there is her ladyship's waiting-gentlewoman, Mrs.
Hannah, a prim, pragmatical old maid; one of the most intolerable and intolerant virgins that ever lived. She has kept
her virtue by her until it has turned sour, and now every word
and look smacks of verjuice. She is the very opposite to her
mistress, for one hates, and the other loves, all mankind. How
they first came together I cannot imagine; but they have lived
together for many years; and the abigail's temper being tart
and encroaching, and her ladyship's easy and yielding, the former has got the complete upper hand, and tyrannises over the
good lady in secret.

Lady Lillycraft now and then complains of it, in great confidence, to her friends, but hushes up the subject immediately,
if Mrs. Hannah makes her appearance. Indeed, she has been
so accustomed to be attended by her, that she thinks she
could not do without her; though one great study of her life
is to keep Mrs. Hannah in good humour, by little presents
and kindnesses.

Master Simon has a most devout abhorrence, mingled with
awe, for this ancient spinster. He told me the other day, in a
whisper, that she was a cursed brimstone—in fact, he added
another epithet, which I would not repeat for the world. I
have remarked, however, that he is always extremely civil to
her when they meet.

Ready Money Jack

My purse, it is my privy wyfe,
This song I dare both syng and say,
It keepeth men from grievous stryfe
When every man for hymself shall pay.
As I ryde in ryche array
For gold and sylver men wyll me floryshe;
By thys matter I dare well saye,
Ever gramercy myne owne purse.

Book of Hunting

ON THE SKIRTS of the neighbouring village there lives a kind of small potentate, who, for aught I know, is a representative of one of the most ancient legitimate lines of the present day; for the empire over which he reigns has belonged to his family time out of mind. His territories comprise a considerable number of good fat acres; and his seat of power is in an old farm-house, where he enjoys, unmolested, the stout oaken chair of his ancestors. The personage to whom I allude is a sturdy old yeoman of the name of John Tibbets, or rather Ready Money Jack Tibbets, as he is called throughout the neighbourhood.

The first place where he attracted my attention was in the churchyard on Sunday; where he sat on a tombstone after the service, with his hat a little on one side, holding forth to a small circle of auditors; and, as I presumed, expounding the law and the prophets; until, on drawing a little nearer, I found he was only expatiating on the merits of a brown horse. He presented so faithful a picture of a substantial English yeoman, such as he is often described in books, heightened, indeed, by some little finery, peculiar to himself, that I could not but take note of his whole appearance.

He was between fifty and sixty, of a strong, muscular frame, and at least six feet high, with a physiognomy as grave as a lion's, and set off with short, curling, iron-gray locks. His shirt-collar was turned down, and displayed a neck covered with the same short, curling, gray hair; and he wore a coloured silk neckcloth, tied very loosely, and tucked in at the bosom, with a green paste brooch on the knot. His coat was of dark green cloth, with silver buttons, on each of which was engraved a stag, with his own name, John Tibbets, underneath. He had an inner waistcoat of figured chintz, between which and his coat was another of scarlet cloth, unbuttoned. His breeches were also left unbuttoned at the knees, not from any slovenliness, but to show a broad pair of scarlet garters. His stockings were blue, with white clocks; he wore large silver shoe-buckles; a broad paste buckle in his hatband; his sleeve-buttons were gold seven shilling pieces; and he had two or three guineas hanging as ornaments to his watch-chain.

On making some inquiries about him, I gathered, that he was descended from a line of farmers that had always lived on the same spot, and owned the same property; and that half of the churchyard was taken up with the tombstones of his race. He has all his life been an important character in the place. When a youngster, he was one of the most roaring blades of the neighbourhood. No one could match him at wrestling, pitching the bar, cudgel play, and other athletic exercises. Like the renowned Pinner of Wakefield, he was the village champion, carried off the prize at all the fairs, and threw his gauntlet at the country round. Even to this day the old people talk of his prowess, and undervalue, in comparison, all heroes of the green that have succeeded him; nay, they say, that if Ready Money Jack were to take the field even now, there is no one could stand before him.

When Jack's father died, the neighbours shook their heads, and predicted that young hopeful would soon make way with the old homestead; but Jack falsified all their predictions. The moment he succeeded to the paternal farm he assumed a new character; took a wife; attended resolutely to his affairs, and became an industrious, thrifty farmer. With the family property he inherited a set of old family maxims, to which he steadily adhered. He saw to every thing himself; put his own hand to the plough; worked hard; ate heartily; slept soundly; paid for every thing in cash down; and never danced except he could do it to the music of his own money in both pockets. He has never been without a hundred or two pounds in gold by him, and never allows a debt to stand unpaid. This has gained him his current name, of which, by the bye, he is a little proud; and has caused him to be looked upon as a very wealthy man by all the village.

Notwithstanding his thrift, however, he has never denied himself the amusements of life, but has taken a share in every passing pleasure. It is his maxim, that "he that works hard can afford to play." He is, therefore, an attendant at all the country fairs and wakes, and has signalized himself by feats of strength and prowess on every village green in the shire. He often makes his appearance at horse races, and sports his half guinea, and even his guinea at a time; keeps a good horse for his own riding, and to this day is fond of following the hounds, and is generally in at the death. He keeps up the rustic revels, and hospitalities too, for which his paternal farm-house has always been noted; has plenty of good cheer and dancing at harvest-home, and, above all, keeps the "merry night,"* as it is termed, at Christmas.

With all his love of amusement, however, Jack is by no means a boisterous jovial companion. He is seldom known to laugh even in the midst of his gaiety; but maintains the same grave, lion-like demeanour. He is very slow at comprehending a joke; and is apt to sit puzzling at it, with a perplexed look, while the rest of the company is in a roar. This gravity has, perhaps, grown on him with the growing weight of his character; for he is gradually rising into patriarchal dignity in his native place. Though he no longer takes an active part in athletic sports, yet he always presides at them, and is appealed to on all occasions as umpire. He maintains the peace on the village-green at holiday games, and quells all brawls and quarrels by collaring the parties and shaking them heartily, if refractory. No one ever pretends to raise a hand against him, or to contend against his decisions; the young men having grown up in habitual awe of his prowess, and in implicit deference to him as the champion and lord of the green.

He is a regular frequenter of the village inn, the landlady having been a sweetheart of his in early life, and he having

---

*MERRY NIGHT. A rustic merry-making in a farm-house about Christmas, common in some parts of Yorkshire. There is abundance of homely fare, tea, cakes, fruit, and ale; various feats of agility, amusing games, romping, dancing, and kissing withal. They commonly break up at midnight.

always continued on kind terms with her. He seldom, however, drinks any thing but a draught of ale; smokes his pipe,
and pays his reckoning before leaving the tap-room. Here he
"gives his little senate laws;" decides bets, which are very generally referred to him; determines upon the characters and
qualities of horses; and indeed plays now and then the part
of a judge, in settling petty disputes between neighbours,
which otherwise might have been nursed by country attornies
into tolerable law-suits. Jack is very candid and impartial in
his decisions, but he has not a head to carry a long argument,
and is very apt to get perplexed and out of patience if there
is much pleading. He generally breaks through the argument
with a strong voice, and brings matters to a summary conclusion, by pronouncing what he calls the "upshot of the business," or, in other words, "the long and the short of the
matter."

Jack once made a journey to London a great many years
since, which has furnished him with topics of conversation
ever since. He saw the old king on the terrace at Windsor,
who stopped, and pointed him out to one of the princesses,
being probably struck with Jack's truly yeoman-like appearance. This is a favourite anecdote with him, and has no doubt
had a great effect in making him a most loyal subject ever
since, in spite of taxes and poors' rates. He was also at Bar-
tholomew-fair, where he had half the buttons cut off his coat;
and a gang of pickpockets, attracted by his external show of
gold and silver, made a regular attempt to hustle him as he
was gazing at a show; but for once they found that they had
caught a tartar; for Jack enacted as great wonders among the
gang as Samson did among the Philistines. One of his neighbours, who had accompanied him to town, and was with him
at the fair, brought back an account of his exploits, which
raised the pride of the whole village; who considered their
champion as having subdued all London, and eclipsed the
achievements of Friar Tuck, or even the renowned Robin
Hood himself.

Of late years the old fellow has begun to take the world
easily; he works less, and indulges in greater leisure, his son
having grown up, and succeeded to him both in the labours
of the farm, and the exploits of the green. Like all sons of

distinguished men, however, his father's renown is a disadvantage to him, for he can never come up to public expectation. Though a fine active fellow of three and twenty, and quite the "cock of the walk," yet the old people declare he is nothing like what Ready Money Jack was at his time of life. The youngster himself acknowledges his inferiority, and has a wonderful opinion of the old man, who indeed taught him all his athletic accomplishments, and holds such a sway over him, that I am told, even to this day, he would have no hesitation to take him in hands, if he rebelled against paternal government.

The squire holds Jack in very high esteem, and shows him to all his visitors as a specimen of old English "heart of oak." He frequently calls at his house, and tastes some of his home-brewed, which is excellent. He made Jack a present of old Tusser's "Hundred Points of good Husbandrie," which has furnished him with reading ever since, and is his text book and manual in all agricultural and domestic concerns. He has made dog's ears at the most favourite passages, and knows many of the poetical maxims by heart.

Tibbets, though not a man to be daunted or fluttered by high acquaintances, and though he cherishes a sturdy independence of mind and manner, yet is evidently gratified by the attentions of the squire, whom he has known from boyhood, and pronounces "a true gentleman every inch of him." He is also on excellent terms with Master Simon, who is a kind of privy counsellor to the family; but his great favourite is the Oxonian, whom he taught to wrestle and play at quarter-staff when a boy, and considers the most promising young gentleman in the whole county.

Bachelors

The Bachelor most joyfully
  In pleasant plight doth pass his daies,
Goodfellowship and companie
  He doth maintain and kepe alwaies.
Evans' Old Ballads

THERE IS no character in the comedy of human life that is more difficult to play well, than that of an old Bachelor. When a single gentleman, therefore, arrives at that critical period, when he begins to consider it an impertinent question to be asked his age, I would advise him to look well to his ways. This period, it is true, is much later with some men than with others; I have witnessed more than once the meeting of two wrinkled old lads of this kind, who had not seen each other for several years, and have been amused by the amicable exchange of compliments on each other's appearance that takes place on such occasions. There is always one invariable observation; "Why, bless my soul! you look younger than when last I saw you!" Whenever a man's friends begin to compliment him about looking young, he may be sure that they think he is growing old.

I am led to make these remarks by the conduct of Master Simon and the general, who have become great cronies. As the former is the youngest by many years, he is regarded as quite a youthful blade by the general, who moreover looks upon him as a man of great wit and prodigious acquirements. I have already hinted that Master Simon is a family beau, and considered rather a young fellow by all the elderly ladies of the connexion; for an old bachelor, in an old family connexion, is something like an actor in a regular dramatic corps, who seems "to flourish in immortal youth," and will continue to play the Romeos and Rangers for half a century together.

Master Simon, too, is a little of the camelion, and takes a different hue with every different companion. He is very attentive and officious, and somewhat sentimental, with Lady Lillycraft; copies out little namby-pamby ditties and love-songs for her, and draws quivers, and doves, and darts, and

Cupids to be worked on the corners of her pocket handker-
chiefs. He indulges, however, in very considerable latitude
with the other married ladies of the family; and has many sly
pleasantries to whisper to them, that provoke an equivocal
laugh and a tap of the fan. But when he gets among young
company, such as Frank Bracebridge, the Oxonian, and the
general, he is apt to put on the mad wag, and to talk in a
very bachelor-like strain about the sex.

In this he has been encouraged by the example of the general, whom he looks up to as a man that has seen the world.
The general, in fact, tells shocking stories after dinner, when
the ladies have retired, which he gives as some of the choice
things that are served up at the Mulligatawney club: a knot
of boon companions in London. He also repeats the fat jokes
of old Major Pendergast, the wit of the club, and which,
though the general can hardly repeat them for laughing,
always make Mr. Bracebridge look grave, he having a great
antipathy to an indecent jest. In a word, the general is a
complete instance of the declension in gay life, by which a
young man of pleasure is apt to cool down into an obscene
old gentleman.

I saw him and Master Simon, an evening or two since, conversing with a buxom milkmaid in a meadow; and from their
elbowing each other now and then, and the general's shaking
his shoulders, blowing up his cheeks, and breaking out into a
short fit of irrepressible laughter, I had no doubt they were
playing the mischief with the girl.

As I looked at them through a hedge, I could not but think
they would have made a tolerable group for a modern picture
of Susannah and the two elders. It is true, the girl seemed in
no wise alarmed at the force of the enemy; and I question,
had either of them been alone, whether she would not have
been more than they would have ventured to encounter. Such
veteran roysters are daring wags when together, and will put
any female to the blush with their jokes; but they are as quiet as
lambs when they fall singly into the clutches of a fine woman.

In spite of the general's years, he evidently is a little vain of
his person, and ambitious of conquests. I have observed him
on Sunday in church, eying the country girls most suspi-
ciously; and have seen him leer upon them with a downright

amorous look, even when he has been gallanting Lady Lilly-craft, with great ceremony, through the churchyard. The general, in fact, is a veteran in the service of Cupid rather than of Mars, having signalized himself in all the garrison towns and country quarters, and seen service in every ball-room of England. Not a celebrated beauty but he has laid siege to; and, if his word may be taken in a matter wherein no man is apt to be over veracious, it is incredible the success he has had with the fair. At present he is like a worn-out warrior, retired from service; but who still cocks his beaver with a military air, and talks stoutly of fighting whenever he comes within the smell of gunpowder.

I have heard him speak his mind very freely over his bottle, about the folly of the captain in taking a wife; as he thinks a young soldier should care for nothing but his "bottle and kind landlady." But, in fact, he says, the service on the continent has had a sad effect upon the young men; they have been ruined by light wines and French quadrilles. "They've nothing," he says, "of the spirit of the old service. There are none of your six-bottle men left, that were the souls of a mess-dinner, and used to play the very deuce among the women."

As to a bachelor, the general affirms that he is a free and easy man, with no baggage to take care of but his portmanteau; but a married man, with his wife hanging on his arm, always puts him in mind of a chamber candlestick, with its extinguisher hitched to it. I should not mind all this if it were merely confined to the general; but I fear he will be the ruin of my friend, Master Simon, who already begins to echo his heresies, and to talk in the style of a gentleman that has seen life, and lived upon the town. Indeed, the general seems to have taken Master Simon in hand, and talks of showing him the lions when he comes to town, and of introducing him to a knot of choice spirits at the Mulligatawney club; which, I understand, is composed of old nabobs, officers in the company's employ, and other "men of Ind," that have seen service in the East, and returned home burnt out with curry, and touched with the liver complaint. They have their regular club, where they eat Mulligatawney soup, smoke the hookah, talk about Tippoo Saib, Seringapatam, and tiger-hunting; and are tediously agreeable in each other's company.

Wives

Believe me, man, there is no greater blisse
Than is the quiet joy of loving wife;
Which whoso wants, half of himselfe doth misse;
Friend without change, play-fellow without strife,
Food without fulnesse, counsaile without pride,
Is this sweet doubling of our single life.

Sir P. Sidney

THERE IS so much talk about matrimony going on round me, in consequence of the approaching event for which we are assembled at the Hall, that I confess I find my thoughts singularly exercised on the subject. Indeed, all the bachelors of the establishment seem to be passing through a kind of fiery ordeal; for Lady Lillycraft is one of those tender, romance-read dames of the old school, whose mind is filled with flames and darts, and who breathe nothing but constancy and wedlock. She is for ever immersed in the concerns of the heart; and, to use a poetical phrase, is perfectly surrounded by "the purple light of love." The very general seems to feel the influence of this sentimental atmosphere; to melt as he approaches her ladyship, and, for the time, to forget all his heresies about matrimony and the sex.

The good lady is generally surrounded by little documents of her prevalent taste; novels of a tender nature; richly bound little books of poetry, that are filled with sonnets and love tales, and perfumed with rose-leaves; and she has always an album at hand, for which she claims the contributions of all her friends. On looking over this last repository the other day, I found a series of poetical extracts, in the squire's handwriting, which might have been intended as matrimonial hints to his ward. I was so much struck with several of them, that I took the liberty of copying them out. They are from the old play of Thomas Davenport, published in 1661, intitled "The City Night-cap;" in which is drawn out and exemplified, in the part of Abstemia, the character of a patient and faithful wife, which, I think, might vie with that of the renowned Griselda.

I have often thought it a pity that plays and novels should always end at the wedding, and should not give us another act, and another volume, to let us know how the hero and heroine conducted themselves when married. Their main object seems to be merely to instruct young ladies how to get husbands, but not how to keep them: now this last, I speak it with all due diffidence, appears to me to be a desideratum in modern married life. It is appalling to those who have not yet adventured into the holy state, to see how soon the flame of romantic love burns out, or rather is quenched in matrimony; and how deplorably the passionate, poetic lover declines into the phlegmatic, prosaic husband. I am inclined to attribute this very much to the defect just mentioned in the plays and novels, which form so important a branch of study of our young ladies; and which teach them how to be heroines, but leave them totally at a loss when they come to be wives. The play from which the quotations before me were made, however, is an exception to this remark; and I cannot refuse myself the pleasure of adducing some of them for the benefit of the reader, and for the honour of an old writer, who has bravely attempted to awaken dramatic interest in favour of a woman, even after she was married!

The following is a commendation of Abstemia to her husband Lorenzo:

> She's modest, but not sullen, and loves silence;
> Not that she wants apt words (for when she speaks,
> She inflames love with wonder), but because
> She calls wise silence the soul's harmony.
> She's truly chaste; yet such a foe to coyness,
> The poorest call her courteous; and, which is excellent,
> (Though fair and young) she shuns to expose herself
> To the opinion of strange eyes. She either seldom
> Or never walks abroad but in your company;
> And then with such sweet bashfulness, as if
> She were venturing on crack'd ice, and takes delight
> To step into the print your foot hath made,
> And will follow you whole fields; so she will drive
> Tediousness out of time with her sweet character.

Notwithstanding all this excellence, Abstemia has the

misfortune to incur the unmerited jealousy of her husband. Instead, however, of resenting his harsh treatment with clamorous upbraidings, and with the stormy violence of high, windy virtue, by which the sparks of anger are so often blown into a flame; she endures it with the meekness of conscious, but patient, virtue; and makes the following beautiful appeal to a friend who has witnessed her long suffering:

> —— Hast thou not seen me
> Bear all his injuries, as the ocean suffers
> The angry bark to plough thorough her bosom,
> And yet is presently so smooth, the eye
> Cannot perceive where the wide wound was made?

Lorenzo, being wrought on by false representations, at length repudiates her. To the last, however, she maintains her patient sweetness, and her love for him, in spite of his cruelty. She deplores his error, even more than his unkindness; and laments the delusion which has turned his very affection into a source of bitterness. There is a moving pathos in her parting address to Lorenzo after their divorce:

> —— Farewell, Lorenzo,
> Whom my soul doth love: if you e'er marry,
> May you meet a good wife; so good, that you
> May not suspect her, nor may she be worthy
> Of your suspicion: and if you hear hereafter
> That I am dead, inquire but my last words,
> And you shall know that to the last I lov'd you.
> And when you walk forth with your second choice,
> Into the pleasant fields, and by chance talk of me,
> Imagine that you see me, lean and pale,
> Strewing your path with flowers. —
> But may she never live to pay my debts: (*weeps*)
> If but in thought she wrong you, may she die
> In the conception of the injury.
> Pray make me wealthy with one kiss: farewell, sir:
> Let it not grieve you when you shall remember
> That I was innocent: nor this forget,
> Though innocence here suffer, sigh, and groan,
> She walks but thorow thorns to find a throne.

In a short time Lorenzo discovers his error, and the innocence of his injured wife. In the transports of his repentance,
he calls to mind all her feminine excellence; her gentle, un-
complaining, womanly fortitude under wrongs and sorrows:

> —— Oh, Abstemia!
> How lovely thou lookest now! now thou appearest
> Chaster than is the morning's modesty,
> That rises with a blush, over whose bosom
> The western wind creeps softly; now I remember
> How, when she sat at table, her obedient eye
> Would dwell on mine, as if it were not well,
> Unless it look'd where I look'd: oh how proud
> She was, when she could cross herself to please me!
> But where now is this fair soul? Like a silver cloud
> She hath wept herself, I fear, into the dread sea,
> And will be found no more.

It is but doing right by the reader, if interested in the fate
of Abstemia by the preceding extracts, to say, that she was
restored to the arms and affections of her husband, rendered
fonder than ever, by that disposition in every good heart, to
atone for past injustice, by an overflowing measure of returning kindness:

> Thou wealth worth more than kingdoms; I am now
> Confirmed past all suspicion; thou art far
> Sweeter in thy sincere truth than a sacrifice
> Deck'd up for death with garlands. The Indian winds
> That blow from off the coast, and cheer the sailor
> With the sweet savour of their spices, want
> The delight flows in thee.

I have been more affected and interested by this little dramatic picture than by many a popular love tale; though, as I
said before, I do not think it likely either Abstemia or patient
Grizzle stand much chance of being taken for a model. Still I
like to see poetry now and then extending its views beyond
the wedding-day, and teaching a lady how to make herself
attractive even after marriage. There is no great need of enforcing on an unmarried lady the necessity of being agreeable;
nor is there any great art requisite in a youthful beauty to

enable her to please. Nature has multiplied attractions round
her. Youth is in itself attractive. The freshness of budding
beauty needs no foreign aid to set it off; it pleases merely
because it is fresh, and budding, and beautiful. But it is for
the married state that a woman needs the most instruction,
and in which she should be most on her guard to maintain
her powers of pleasing. No woman can expect to be to her
husband all that he fancied her when he was a lover. Men are
always doomed to be duped, not so much by the arts of the
sex, as by their own imaginations. They are always wooing
goddesses, and marrying mere mortals. A woman should
therefore ascertain what was the charm that rendered her so
fascinating when a girl, and endeavour to keep it up when she
has become a wife. One great thing undoubtedly was, the
chariness of herself and her conduct, which an unmarried female always observes. She should maintain the same niceness
and reserve in her person and habits, and endeavour still to
preserve a freshness and virgin delicacy in the eye of her husband. She should remember that the province of woman is to
be wooed, not to woo; to be caressed, not to caress. Man is
an ungrateful being in love; bounty loses instead of winning
him. The secret of a woman's power does not consist so much
in giving, as in withholding. A woman may give up too much
even to her husband. It is to a thousand little delicacies of
conduct that she must trust to keep alive passion, and to protect herself from that dangerous familiarity, that thorough acquaintance with every weakness and imperfection incident to
matrimony. By these means she may still maintain her power,
though she has surrendered her person, and may continue the
romance of love even beyond the honey-moon.

"She that hath a wise husband," says Jeremy Taylor, "must
entice him to an eternal dearnesse by the veil of modesty, and
the grave robes of chastity, the ornament of meeknesse, and
the jewels of faith and charity. She must have no painting but
blushings; her brightness must be purity, and she must shine
round about with sweetnesses and friendship; and she shall be
pleasant while she lives, and desired when she dies."

I have wandered into a rambling series of remarks on a trite
subject, and a dangerous one for a bachelor to meddle with.
That I may not, however, appear to confine my observations

entirely to the wife, I will conclude with another quotation from Jeremy Taylor, in which the duties of both parties are mentioned; while I would recommend his sermon on the marriage ring to all those who, wiser than myself, are about entering the happy state of wedlock.

"There is scarce any matter of duty but it concerns them both alike, and is only distinguished by names, and hath its variety by circumstances and little accidents; and what in one is called love, in the other is called reverence; and what in the wife is obedience, the same in the man is duty. He provides, and she dispenses; he gives commandments, and she rules by them; he rules her by authority, and she rules him by love; she ought by all means to please him, and he must by no means displease her."

Story Telling

A FAVOURITE evening pastime at the Hall, and one which the worthy squire is fond of promoting, is story telling, "a good old-fashioned fire-side amusement," as he terms it. Indeed, I believe he promotes it chiefly because it was one of the choice recreations in those days of yore, when ladies and gentlemen were not much in the habit of reading. Be this as it may, he will often, at supper table, when conversation flags, call on some one or other of the company for a story, as it was formerly the custom to call for a song; and it is edifying to see the exemplary patience, and even satisfaction, with which the good old gentleman will sit and listen to some hackneyed tale that he has heard for at least a hundred times.

In this way one evening the current of anecdotes and stories ran upon mysterious personages that have figured at different times, and filled the world with doubt and conjecture; such as the Wandering Jew, the Man with the Iron Mask, who tormented the curiosity of all Europe; the Invisible Girl, and last, though not least, the Pigfaced Lady.

At length one of the company was called upon that had the most unpromising physiognomy for a story teller that ever I had seen. He was a thin, pale, weazen-faced man, extremely nervous, that had sat at one corner of the table, shrunk up, as it were, into himself, and almost swallowed up in the cape of his coat, as a turtle in its shell.

The very demand seemed to throw him into a nervous agitation, yet he did not refuse. He emerged his head out of his shell, made a few odd grimaces and gesticulations, before he could get his muscles into order, or his voice under command, and then offered to give some account of a mysterious personage that he had recently encountered in the course of his travels, and one whom he thought fully entitled of being classed with the Man with the Iron Mask.

I was so much struck with his extraordinary narrative, that I have written it out to the best of my recollection, for the amusement of the reader. I think it has in it all the elements of that mysterious and romantic narrative, so greedily sought after at the present day.

The Stout Gentleman

A Stage Coach Romance

"I'll cross it, though it blast me!"
Hamlet

IT WAS a rainy Sunday, in the gloomy month of November.
I had been detained, in the course of a journey, by a slight
indisposition, from which I was recovering; but I was still
feverish, and was obliged to keep within doors all day, in an
inn of the small town of Derby. A wet Sunday in a country
inn! whoever has had the luck to experience one can alone
judge of my situation. The rain pattered against the casements; the bells tolled for church with a melancholy sound. I
went to the windows in quest of something to amuse the eye;
but it seemed as if I had been placed completely out of the
reach of all amusement. The windows of my bed-room
looked out among tiled roofs and stacks of chimneys, while
those of my sitting-room commanded a full view of the
stable-yard. I know of nothing more calculated to make a man
sick of this world than a stable-yard on a rainy day. The place
was littered with wet straw that had been kicked about by
travellers and stable-boys. In one corner was a stagnant pool
of water, surrounding an island of muck; there were several
half-drowned fowls crowded together under a cart, among
which was a miserable, crest-fallen cock, drenched out of all
life and spirit; his drooping tail matted, as it were, into a
single feather, along which the water trickled from his back;
near the cart was a half-dozing cow, chewing the cud, and
standing patiently to be rained on, with wreaths of vapour
rising from her reeking hide; a wall-eyed horse, tired of the
loneliness of the stable, was poking his spectral head out of a
window, with the rain dripping on it from the eaves; an unhappy cur, chained to a doghouse hard by, uttered something
every now and then, between a bark and a yelp; a drab of a
kitchen wench tramped backwards and forwards through the
yard in pattens, looking as sulky as the weather itself; every
thing, in short, was comfortless and forlorn, excepting a crew of

61

hard-drinking ducks, assembled like boon companions round a puddle, and making a riotous noise over their liquor.

I was lonely and listless, and wanted amusement. My room soon became insupportable. I abandoned it, and sought what is technically called the travellers'-room. This is a public room set apart at most inns for the accommodation of a class of wayfarers, called travellers, or riders; a kind of commercial knights errant, who are incessantly scouring the kingdom in gigs, on horseback, or by coach. They are the only successors that I know of at the present day, to the knights errant of yore. They lead the same kind of roving adventurous life, only changing the lance for a driving-whip, the buckler for a pattern-card, and the coat of mail for an upper Benjamin. Instead of vindicating the charms of peerless beauty, they rove about, spreading the fame and standing of some substantial tradesman, or manufacturer, and are ready at any time to bargain in his name; it being the fashion now-a-days to trade, instead of fight, with one another. As the room of the hostel, in the good old fighting times, would be hung round at night with the armour of way-worn warriors, such as coats of mail, falchions, and yawning helmets; so the travellers'-room is garnished with the harnessing of their successors, with box coats, whips of all kinds, spurs, gaiters, and oil-cloth covered hats.

I was in hopes of finding some of these worthies to talk with, but was disappointed. There were, indeed, two or three in the room; but I could make nothing of them. One was just finishing his breakfast, quarrelling with his bread and butter, and huffing the waiter; another buttoned on a pair of gaiters, with many execrations at Boots for not having cleaned his shoes well; a third sat drumming on the table with his fingers and looking at the rain as it streamed down the window-glass; they all appeared infected by the weather, and disappeared, one after the other, without exchanging a word.

I sauntered to the window and stood gazing at the people, picking their way to church, with petticoats hoisted midleg high, and dripping umbrellas. The bell ceased to toll, and the streets became silent. I then amused myself with watching the daughters of a tradesman opposite; who, being confined to the house for fear of wetting their Sunday finery, played off their charms at the front windows, to fascinate the chance tenants of the inn. They at length were summoned away by a vigilant vinegar-faced mother, and I had nothing further from without to amuse me.

What was I to do to pass away the long-lived day? I was sadly nervous and lonely; and every thing about an inn seems calculated to make a dull day ten times duller. Old news-papers, smelling of beer and tobacco smoke, and which I had already read half a dozen times. Good for nothing books, that were worse than rainy weather. I bored myself to death with an old volume of the Lady's Magazine. I read all the common-placed names of ambitious travellers scrawled on the panes of glass; the eternal families of the Smiths and the Browns, and the Jacksons, and the Johnsons, and all the other sons; and I decyphered several scraps of fatiguing inn-window poetry which I have met with in all parts of the world.

The day continued lowering and gloomy; the slovenly, rag-ged, spongy clouds drifted heavily along; there was no variety even in the rain; it was one dull, continued, monotonous patter—patter—patter, excepting that now and then I was enlivened by the idea of a brisk shower, from the rattling of the drops upon a passing umbrella.

It was quite *refreshing* (if I may be allowed a hackneyed phrase of the day) when, in the course of the morning, a horn blew, and a stage coach whirled through the street, with out-side passengers stuck all over it, cowering under cotton um-brellas, and seethed together, and reeking with the steams of wet box-coats and upper Benjamins.

The sound brought out from their lurking-places a crew of vagabond boys, and vagabond dogs, and the carroty-headed hostler, and that non-descript animal ycleped Boots, and all the other vagabond race that infest the purlieus of an inn; but the bustle was transient; the coach again whirled on its way; and boy and dog, and hostler and Boots, all slunk back again to their holes; the street again became silent, and the rain continued to rain on. In fact, there was no hope of its clearing up; the barometer pointed to rainy weather; mine hostess's tortoise-shell cat sat by the fire washing her face, and rubbing her paws over her ears; and, on referring to the Almanack, I found a direful prediction stretching from the top of the page to the bottom through the whole month, "expect—much—rain—about—this—time!"

I was dreadfully hipped. The hours seemed as if they would never creep by. The very ticking of the clock became irksome. At length the stillness of the house was interrupted by the ringing of a bell. Shortly after I heard the voice of a waiter at the bar: "The stout gentleman in No. 13, wants his breakfast. Tea and bread and butter, with ham and eggs; the eggs not to be too much done."

In such a situation as mine every incident is of importance. Here was a subject of speculation presented to my mind, and ample exercise for my imagination. I am prone to paint pictures to myself, and on this occasion I had some materials to work upon. Had the guest up stairs been mentioned as Mr. Smith, or Mr. Brown, or Mr. Jackson, or Mr. Johnson, or merely as "the gentleman in No. 13," it would have been a perfect blank to me. I should have thought nothing of it; but "The Stout Gentleman!"—the very name had something in it of the picturesque. It at once gave the size; it embodied the personage to my mind's eye; and my fancy did the rest.

He was stout, or, as some term it, lusty; in all probability, therefore, he was advanced in life, some people expanding as they grow old. By his breakfasting rather late, and in his own room, he must be a man accustomed to live at his ease, and above the necessity of early rising; no doubt a round, rosy, lusty old gentleman.

There was another violent ringing. The stout gentleman was impatient for his breakfast. He was evidently a man of importance; "well to do in the world;" accustomed to be promptly waited upon; of a keen appetite, and a little cross when hungry; "perhaps," thought I, "he may be some London Alderman; or who knows but he may be a Member of Parliament?"

The breakfast was sent up, and there was a short interval of silence; he was, doubtless, making the tea. Presently there was a violent ringing; and before it could be answered, another ringing still more violent. "Bless me! what a choleric old gentleman!" The waiter came down in a huff. The butter was rancid, the eggs were over-done, the ham was too salt:—the stout gentleman was evidently nice in his eating; one of those who eat and growl, and keep the waiter on the trot, and live in a state militant with the household.

The hostess got into a fume. I should observe that she was a brisk, coquettish woman; a little of a shrew, and something of a slammerkin, but very pretty withal; with a nincompoop for a husband, as shrews are apt to have. She rated the servants roundly for their negligence in sending up so bad a breakfast, but said not a word against the stout gentleman; by which I clearly perceived that he must be a man of consequence, intitled to make a noise and to give trouble at a country inn. Other eggs, and ham, and bread and butter were sent up. They appeared to be more graciously received; at least there was no further complaint.

I had not made many turns about the travellers'-room, when there was another ringing. Shortly afterwards there was a stir and an inquest about the house. The stout gentleman wanted the Times or the Chronicle newspaper. I set him down, therefore, for a whig; or rather, from his being so absolute and lordly where he had a chance, I suspected him of being a radical. Hunt, I had heard, was a large man; "who knows," thought I, "but it is Hunt himself?"

My curiosity began to be awakened. I inquired of the waiter who was this stout gentleman that was making all this stir; but I could get no information. Nobody seemed to know his name. The landlords of bustling inns seldom trouble their heads about the names or occupations of their transient guests. The colour of a coat, the shape or size of the person, is enough to suggest a travelling name. It is either the tall gentleman, or the short gentleman, or the gentleman in black, or the gentleman in snuff-colour; or, as in the present instance, the stout gentleman. A designation of the kind once hit on answers every purpose, and saves all further inquiry.

Rain—rain—rain! pitiless, ceaseless rain! No such thing as putting a foot out of doors, and no occupation nor amusement within. By and by I heard some one walking over head. It was in the stout gentleman's room. He evidently was a large man by the heaviness of his tread; and an old man from his wearing such creaking soles. "He is doubtless," thought I, "some rich old square-toes of regular habits, and is now taking exercise after breakfast."

I now read all the advertisements of coaches and hotels that were stuck about the mantel-piece. The Lady's Magazine had become an abomination to me; it was as tedious as the day itself. I wandered out, not knowing what to do, and ascended again to my room. I had not been there long, when there was a squall from a neighbouring bed-room. A door opened and slammed violently; a chambermaid, that I had remarked for having a ruddy, good-humoured face, went down stairs in a violent flurry. The stout gentleman had been rude to her!

This sent a whole host of my deductions to the deuce in a moment. This unknown personage could not be an old gentleman; for old gentlemen are not apt to be so obstreperous to chambermaids. He could not be a young gentleman; for young gentlemen are not apt to inspire such indignation. He must be a middle-aged man, and confounded ugly into the bargain, or the girl would not have taken the matter in such terrible dudgeon. I confess I was sorely puzzled.

In a few minutes I heard the voice of my landlady. I caught a glance of her as she came tramping up stairs; her face glowing, her cap flaring, her tongue wagging the whole way. "She'd have no such doings in her house, she'd warrant! If gentlemen did spend money freely, it was no rule. She'd have no servant maids of hers treated in that way, when they were about their work, that's what she wouldn't!"

As I hate squabbles, particularly with women, and above all with pretty women, I slunk back into my room, and partly closed the door; but my curiosity was too much excited not to listen. The landlady marched intrepidly to the enemy's citadel, and entered it with a storm. The door closed after her. I heard her voice in high, windy clamour for a moment or two. Then it gradually subsided, like a gust of wind in a garret; then there was a laugh; then I heard nothing more.

After a little while my landlady came out with an odd smile on her face, adjusting her cap, which was a little on one side. As she went down stairs I heard the landlord ask her what was the matter; she said, "Nothing at all, only the girl's a fool."—I was more than ever perplexed what to make of this unaccountable personage, who could put a good-natured chambermaid in a passion, and send away a termagant land-

lady in smiles. He could not be so old, nor cross, nor ugly
either.

I had to go to work at his picture again, and to paint him
entirely different. I now set him down for one of those stout
gentlemen that are frequently met with swaggering about the
doors of country inns. Moist, merry fellows, in Belcher hand-
kerchiefs, whose bulk is a little assisted by malt-liquors. Men
who have seen the world, and been sworn at Highgate; who
are used to tavern life; up to all the tricks of tapsters, and
knowing in the ways of sinful publicans. Free-livers on a small
scale; who are prodigal within the compass of a guinea; who
call all the waiters by name, touzle the maids, gossip with the
landlady at the bar, and prose over a pint of port, or a glass
of negus, after dinner.

The morning wore away in forming of these and similar
surmises. As fast as I wove one system of belief, some movement of the unknown would completely overturn it, and
throw all my thoughts again into confusion. Such are the
solitary operations of a feverish mind. I was, as I have said,
extremely nervous; and the continual meditation on the concerns of this invisible personage began to have its effect:
—I was getting a fit of the fidgets.

Dinner-time came. I hoped the stout gentleman might dine
in the travellers'-room, and that I might at length get a view
of his person; but no—he had dinner served in his own
room. What could be the meaning of this solitude and mystery? He could not be a radical; there was something too aristocratical in thus keeping himself apart from the rest of the
world, and condemning himself to his own dull company
throughout a rainy day. And then, too, he lived too well for
a discontented politician. He seemed to expatiate on a variety
of dishes, and to sit over his wine like a jolly friend of good-
living. Indeed, my doubts on this head were soon at an end;
for he could not have finished his first bottle before I could
faintly hear him humming a tune; and on listening, I found
it to be "God save the King." 'Twas plain, then, he was no
radical, but a faithful subject; one that grew loyal over his
bottle, and was ready to stand by king and constitution, when
he could stand by nothing else. But who could he be! My
conjectures began to run wild. Was he not some personage of

distinction travelling incog.? "God knows!" said I, at my wit's end; "it may be one of the royal family, for aught I know, for they are all stout gentlemen!"

The weather continued rainy. The mysterious unknown kept his room, and, as far as I could judge, his chair, for I did not hear him move. In the mean time, as the day advanced, the travellers'-room began to be frequented. Some, who had just arrived, came in buttoned up in box-coats; others came home who had been dispersed about the town. Some took their dinners, and some their tea. Had I been in a different mood, I should have found entertainment in studying this peculiar class of men. There were two especially, who were regular wags of the road, and up to all the standing jokes of travellers. They had a thousand sly things to say to the waiting-maid, whom they called Louisa, and Ethelinda, and a dozen other fine names, changing the name every time, and chuckling amazingly at their own waggery. My mind, however, had become completely engrossed by the stout gentleman. He had kept my fancy in chase during a long day, and it was not now to be diverted from the scent.

The evening gradually wore away. The travellers read the papers two or three times over. Some drew round the fire and told long stories about their horses, about their adventures, their overturns, and breakings-down. They discussed the credits of different merchants and different inns; and the two wags told several choice anecdotes of pretty chambermaids, and kind landladies. All this passed as they were quietly taking what they called their night-caps, that is to say, strong glasses of brandy and water and sugar, or some other mixture of the kind; after which they one after another rang for "Boots" and the chambermaid, and walked off to bed in old shoes cut down into marvellously uncomfortable slippers.

There was only one man left; a short-legged, long-bodied, plethoric fellow, with a very large, sandy head. He sat by himself, with a glass of port wine negus, and a spoon; sipping and stirring, and meditating and sipping, until nothing was left but the spoon. He gradually fell asleep bolt upright in his chair, with the empty glass standing before him; and the candle seemed to fall asleep too, for the wick grew long, and black, and cabbaged at the end, and dimmed the little light that remained in the chamber. The gloom that now prevailed was contagious. Around hung the shapeless, and almost spectral, box-coats of departed travellers, long since buried in deep sleep. I only heard the ticking of the clock, with the deep-drawn breathings of the sleeping toper, and the drippings of the rain, drop—drop—drop, from the eaves of the house. The church bells chimed midnight. All at once the stout gentleman began to walk over head, pacing slowly backwards and forwards. There was something extremely awful in all this, especially to one in my state of nerves. These ghastly great coats, these guttural breathings, and the creaking footsteps of this mysterious being. His steps grew fainter and fainter, and at length died away. I could bear it no longer. I was wound up to the desperation of a hero of romance. "Be he who or what he may," said I to myself, "I'll have a sight of him!" I seized a chamber candle, and hurried up to number 13. The door stood ajar. I hesitated—I entered: the room was deserted. There stood a large, broad-bottomed elbow-chair at a table, on which was an empty tumbler, and a "Times" newspaper, and the room smelt powerfully of Stilton cheese.

The mysterious stranger had evidently but just retired. I turned off, sorely disappointed, to my room, which had been changed to the front of the house. As I went along the corridor, I saw a large pair of boots, with dirty, waxed tops, standing at the door of a bed-chamber. They doubtless belonged to the unknown; but it would not do to disturb so redoubtable a personage in his den; he might discharge a pistol, or something worse, at my head. I went to bed, therefore, and lay awake half the night in a terribly nervous state; and even when I fell asleep, I was still haunted in my dreams by the idea of the stout gentleman and his wax-topped boots.

I slept rather late the next morning, and was awakened by some stir and bustle in the house, which I could not at first comprehend; until getting more awake, I found there was a mail-coach starting from the door. Suddenly there was a cry from below, "The gentleman has forgot his umbrella! look for the gentleman's umbrella in No. 13!" I heard an immediate scampering of a chambermaid along the passage, and a shrill reply as she ran, "here it is! here's the gentleman's umbrella!"

The mysterious stranger then was on the point of setting

off. This was the only chance I should ever have of knowing him. I sprang out of bed, scrambled to the window, snatched aside the curtains, and just caught a glimpse of the rear of a person getting in at the coach-door. The skirts of a brown coat parted behind, and gave me a full view of the broad disk of a pair of drab breeches. The door closed—"all right!" was the word—the coach whirled off:—and that was all I ever saw of the stout gentleman!

Forest Trees

"A living gallery of aged trees."

ONE OF the favourite themes of boasting with the squire
is the noble trees on his estate, which, in truth, has some
of the finest that I have seen in England. There is something
august and solemn in the great avenues of stately oaks that
gather their branches together high in air, and seem to reduce
the pedestrians beneath them to mere pigmies. "An avenue of
oaks or elms," the squire observes, "is the true colonnade that
should lead to a gentleman's house. As to stone and marble,
any one can rear them at once, they are the work of the day;
but commend me to the colonnades that have grown old and
great with the family, and tell by their grandeur how long the
family has endured."

The squire has great reverence for certain venerable trees,
gray with moss, which he considers as the ancient nobility of
his domain. There is the ruin of an enormous oak, which has
been so much battered by time and tempest, that scarce any
thing is left; though he says Christy recollects when, in his
boyhood, it was healthy and flourishing, until it was struck by
lightning. It is now a mere trunk, with one twisted bough
stretching up into the air, bearing a green branch at the end
of it. This sturdy wreck is much valued by the squire; he calls
it his standard-bearer, and compares it to a veteran warrior
beaten down in battle, but bearing up his banner to the last.
He has actually had a fence built round it, to protect it as
much as possible from further injury.

It is with great difficulty that the squire can ever be
brought to have any tree cut down on his estate. To some he
looks with reverence, as having been planted by his ancestors;
to others with a kind of paternal affection, as having been
planted by himself; and he feels a degree of awe in bringing
down with a few strokes of the axe, what it has cost centuries
to build up. I confess I cannot but sympathize, in some degree, with the good squire on the subject. Though brought
up in a country overrun with forests, where trees are apt to be
considered mere incumbrances, and to be laid low without

hesitation or remorse, yet I could never see a fine tree hewn down without concern. The poets, who are naturally lovers of trees, as they are of every thing that is beautiful, have artfully awakened great interest in their favour, by representing them as the habitations of sylvan deities; insomuch that every great tree had its tutelar genius, or a nymph, whose existence was limited to its duration. Evelyn, in his Sylva, makes several pleasing and fanciful allusions to this superstition. "As the fall," says he, "of a very aged oak, giving a crack like thunder, has often been heard at many miles distance; constrained though I often am to fell them with reluctancy, I do not at any time remember to have heard the groans of those nymphs (grieving to be dispossessed of their ancient habitations) without some emotion and pity." And again, in alluding to a violent storm that had devastated the woodlands, he says; "Methinks I still hear, sure I am that I still feel, the dismal groans of our forests; the late dreadful hurricane having subverted so many thousands of goodly oaks, prostrating the trees, laying them in ghastly postures, like whole regiments fallen in battle by the sword of the conqueror, and crushing all that grew beneath them. The public accounts," he adds, "reckon no less than three thousand *brave oaks* in one part only of the forest of Dean blown down."

I have paused more than once in the wilderness of America, to contemplate the traces of some blast of wind, which seemed to have rushed down from the clouds, and ripped its way through the bosom of the woodlands; rooting up, shivering and splintering the stoutest trees, and leaving a long track of desolation. There was something awful in the vast havoc made among these gigantic plants; and in considering their magnificent remains, so rudely torn and mangled, and hurled down to perish prematurely on their native soil, I was conscious of a strong movement of the sympathy so feelingly expressed by Evelyn. I recollect, also, hearing a traveller, of poetical temperament, expressing the kind of horror which he felt on beholding, on the banks of the Missouri, an oak of prodigious size, which had been, in a manner, overpowered by an enormous wild grape-vine. The vine had clasped its huge folds round the trunk, and from thence had wound about every branch and twig, until the mighty tree had withered in its embrace. It seemed like Laocoon struggling ineffectually in the hideous coils of the monster Python. It was the lion of trees perishing in the embraces of a vegetable boa.

I am fond of listening to the conversation of English gentlemen on rural concerns, and of noticing with what taste and discrimination, and what strong, unaffected interest they will discuss topics, which in other countries are abandoned to mere woodmen, or rustic cultivators. I have heard a noble earl descant on park and forest scenery with the science and feeling of a painter. He dwelt on the shape and beauty of particular trees on his estate, with as much pride and technical precision as though he had been discussing the merits of statues in his collection. I found that he had even gone considerable distances to examine trees which were celebrated among rural amateurs; for it seems that trees, like horses, have their established points of excellence; and that there are some in England which enjoy very extensive celebrity among tree-fanciers from being perfect in their kind.

There is something nobly simple and pure in such a taste; it argues, I think, a sweet and generous nature, to have this strong relish for the beauties of vegetation, and this friendship for the hardy and glorious sons of the forest. There is a grandeur of thought connected with this part of rural economy. It is, if I may be allowed the figure, the heroic line of husbandry. It is worthy of liberal, and freeborn, and aspiring men. He who plants an oak looks forward to future ages, and plants for posterity. Nothing can be less selfish than this. He cannot expect to sit in its shade, nor enjoy its shelter; but he exults in the idea, that the acorn which he has buried in the earth shall grow up into a lofty pile, and shall keep on flourishing, and increasing, and benefiting mankind, long after he shall have ceased to tread his paternal fields. Indeed it is the nature of such occupations to lift the thoughts above mere worldliness. As the leaves of trees are said to absorb all noxious qualities of the air, and to breathe forth a purer atmosphere, so it seems to me as if they drew from us all sordid and angry passions, and breathed forth peace and philanthropy. There is a serene and settled majesty in woodland scenery, that enters into the soul, and dilates and elevates it, and fills it with noble inclinations. The ancient and hereditary groves, too, that embower this island, are most of them full of story. They are haunted by the recollections of great spirits of past ages, who have sought for relaxation among them from the tumult of arms, or the toils of state, or have wooed the muse beneath their shade. Who can walk, with soul un-moved, among the stately groves of Penshurst, where the gal-lant, the amiable, the elegant Sir Philip Sidney passed his boyhood; or can look without fondness upon the tree that is said to have been planted on his birthday; or can ramble among the classic bowers of Hagley; or can pause among the solitudes of Windsor Forest, and look at the oaks around, huge, gray, and time-worn, like the old castle towers, and not feel as if he were surrounded by so many monuments of long-enduring glory? It is, when viewed in this light, that planted groves, and stately avenues, and cultivated parks, have an ad-vantage over the more luxuriant beauties of unassisted nature. It is that they teem with moral associations, and keep up the ever-interesting story of human existence.

It is incumbent then, on the high and generous spirits of an ancient nation, to cherish these sacred groves that sur-round their ancestral mansions, and to perpetuate them to their descendants. Republican as I am by birth, and brought up as I have been in republican principles and habits, I can feel nothing of the servile reverence for titled rank, merely because it is titled; but I trust that I am neither churl nor bigot in my creed. I can both see and feel how hereditary distinction, when it falls to the lot of a generous mind, may elevate that mind into true nobility. It is one of the effects of hereditary rank, when it falls thus happily, that it multiplies the duties, and, as it were, extends the existence of the pos-sessor. He does not feel himself a mere individual link in cre-ation, responsible only for his own brief term of being. He carries back his existence in proud recollection, and he ex-tends it forward in honourable anticipation. He lives with his ancestry, and he lives with his posterity. To both does he con-sider himself involved in deep responsibilities. As he has re-ceived much from those that have gone before, so he feels bound to transmit much to those who are to come after him. His domestic undertakings seem to imply a longer existence than those of ordinary men; none are so apt to build and plant for future centuries, as noble-spirited men, who have received their heritages from foregone ages.

I cannot but applaud, therefore, the fondness and pride with which I have noticed English gentlemen, of generous temperaments, and high aristocratic feelings, contemplating those magnificent trees, which rise like towers and pyramids, from the midst of their paternal lands. There is an affinity between all nature, animate and inanimate; the oak, in the pride and lustihood of its growth, seems to me to take its range with the lion and the eagle, and to assimilate, in the grandeur of its attributes, to heroic and intellectual man. With its mighty pillar rising straight and direct towards heaven, bearing up its leafy honours from the impurities of earth, and supporting them aloft in free air and glorious sunshine, it is an emblem of what a true nobleman *should be*; a refuge for the weak, a shelter for the oppressed, a defence for the defenceless; warding off from them the peltings of the storm, or the scorching rays of arbitrary power. He who is *this*, is an ornament and a blessing to his native land. He who is *otherwise*, abuses his eminent advantages; abuses the grandeur and prosperity which he has drawn from the bosom of his country. Should tempests arise, and he be laid prostrate by the storm, who would mourn over his fall? Should he be borne down by the oppressive hand of power, who would murmur at his fate?—"why cumbereth he the ground?"

A Literary Antiquary

Printed bookes he contemnes, as a novelty of this latter age; but
a manuscript he pores on everlastingly; especially if the cover be
all moth-eaten, and the dust make a parenthesis betweene every
syllable.

Micro-Cosmographie, 1628

THE SQUIRE receives great sympathy and support, in his
antiquated humours, from the parson, of whom I made
some mention on my former visit to the Hall, and who acts
as a kind of family chaplain. He has been cherished by the
squire almost constantly since the time that they were fellow
students at Oxford; for it is one of the peculiar advantages of
these great universities, that they often link the poor scholar
to the rich patron, by early and heart-felt ties, that last
through life, without the usual humiliations of dependence
and patronage. Under the fostering protection of the squire,
therefore, the little parson has pursued his studies in peace.
Having lived almost entirely among books, and those, too,
old books, he is quite ignorant of the world, and his mind is
as antiquated as the garden at the Hall, where the flowers are
all arranged in formal beds, and the yew-trees clipped into
urns and peacocks.

His taste for literary antiquities was first imbibed in the
Bodleian Library at Oxford; where, when a student, he past
many an hour foraging among the old manuscripts. He has
since, at different times, visited most of the curious libraries
in England, and has ransacked many of the cathedrals. With
all his quaint and curious learning, he has nothing of arrogance or pedantry; but that unaffected earnestness and guileless simplicity which seem to belong to the literary antiquary.

He is a dark, mouldy little man, and rather dry in his manner; yet, on his favourite theme, he kindles up, and at times
is even eloquent. No fox-hunter, recounting his last day's
sport, could be more animated than I have seen the worthy
parson, when relating his search after a curious document,
which he had traced from library to library, until he fairly
unearthed it in the dusty chapter-house of a cathedral. When,
too, he describes some venerable manuscript, with its rich

illuminations, its thick creamy vellum, its glossy ink, and the odour of the cloisters that seems to exhale from it, he rivals the enthusiasm of a Parisian epicure, expatiating on the merits of a Perigord pie, or a *Paté de Strasbourg.*

His brain seems absolutely haunted with love-sick dreams about gorgeous old works in "silk linings, triple gold bands, and tinted leather, locked up in wire cases, and secured from the vulgar hands of the mere reader;" and, to continue the happy expressions of an ingenious writer, "dazzling one's eyes like eastern beauties, peering through their jealousies."*

He has a great desire, however, to read such works in the old libraries and chapter-houses to which they belong; for he thinks a black-letter volume reads best in one of those venerable chambers where the light struggles through dusty lancet windows and painted glass; and that it loses half its zest if taken away from the neighbourhood of the quaintly-carved oaken book-case and Gothic reading-desk. At his suggestion the squire has had the library furnished in this antique taste, and several of the windows glazed with painted glass, that they may throw a properly tempered light upon the pages of their favourite old authors.

The parson, I am told, has been for some time meditating a commentary on Strutt, Brand, and Douce, in which he means to detect them in sundry dangerous errors in respect to popular games and superstitions; a work to which the squire looks forward with great interest. He is, also, a casual contributor to that long-established repository of national customs and antiquities, the Gentleman's Magazine, and is one of those that every now and then make an inquiry concerning some obsolete custom or rare legend; nay, it is said that several of his communications have been at least six inches in length. He frequently receives parcels by coach from different parts of the kingdom, containing mouldy volumes and almost illegible manuscripts; for it is singular what an active correspondence is kept up among literary antiquaries, and how soon the fame of any rare volume, or unique copy, just discovered among the rubbish of a library, is circulated among them. The parson is more busy than common just

*D'Israeli. Curiosities of Literature.

now, being a little flurried by an advertisement of a work, said to be preparing for the press, on the mythology of the middle ages. The little man has long been gathering together all the hobgoblin tales he could collect, illustrative of the superstitions of former times; and he is in a complete fever, lest this formidable rival should take the field before him.

Shortly after my arrival at the Hall, I called at the parsonage, in company with Mr. Bracebridge and the general. The parson had not been seen for several days, which was a matter of some surprise, as he was an almost daily visitor at the Hall. We found him in his study; a small dusky chamber, lighted by a lattice window that looked into the church-yard, and was overshadowed by a yew-tree. His chair was surrounded by folios and quartos, piled upon the floor, and his table was covered with books and manuscripts. The cause of his seclusion was a work which he had recently received, and with which he had retired in rapture from the world, and shut himself up to enjoy a literary honeymoon undisturbed. Never did boarding-school girl devour the pages of a sentimental novel, or Don Quixote a chivalrous romance, with more intense delight than did the little man banquet on the pages of this delicious work. It was Dibdin's Bibliographical Tour; a work calculated to have as intoxicating an effect on the imaginations of literary antiquaries, as the adventures of the heroes of the round table, on all true knights; or the tales of the early American voyagers on the ardent spirits of the age, filling them with dreams of Mexican and Peruvian mines, and of the golden realm of El Dorado.

The good parson had looked forward to this Bibliographical expedition as of far greater importance than those to Africa, or the North Pole. With what eagerness he had seized upon the history of the enterprise! with what interest had he followed the redoubtable bibliographer and his graphical squire in their adventurous roamings among Norman castles and cathedrals, and French libraries, and German convents and universities; penetrating into the prison houses of vellum manuscripts, and exquisitely illuminated missals, and revealing their beauties to the world!

When the parson had finished a rapturous eulogy on this most curious and entertaining work, he drew forth from a

little drawer a manuscript, lately received from a correspondent, which had perplexed him sadly. It was written in
Norman French, in very ancient characters, and so faded and
mouldered away as to be almost illegible. It was apparently
an old Norman drinking song, that might have been brought
over by one of William the Conqueror's carousing followers.
The writing was just legible enough to keep a keen antiquity
hunter on a doubtful chase; here and there he would be completely thrown out, and then there would be a few words so
plainly written as to put him on the scent again. In this way
he had been led on for a whole day, until he had found himself completely at fault.

The squire endeavoured to assist him, but was equally baffled. The old general listened for some time to the discussion,
and then asked the parson, if he had read Captain Morris's,
or George Stevens', or Anacreon Moore's bacchanalian songs;
on the other replying in the negative, "Oh, then," said the
general, with a sagacious nod, "if you want a drinking song, I
can furnish you with the latest collection—I did not know
you had a turn for those kind of things; and I can lend you
the Encyclopedia of Wit into the bargain. I never travel without them; they're excellent reading at an inn."

It would not be easy to describe the odd look of surprise
and perplexity of the parson, at this proposal; or the difficulty
the squire had in making the general comprehend, that
though a jovial song of the present day was but a foolish
sound in the ears of wisdom, and beneath the notice of a
learned man, yet a trowl, written by a tosspot several hundred
years since, was a matter worthy of the gravest research, and
enough to set whole colleges by the ears.

I have since pondered much on this matter, and have figured to myself what may be the fate of our current literature,
when retrieved, piecemeal, by future antiquaries, from among
the rubbish of ages. What a Magnus Apollo, for instance, will
Moore become, among sober divines and dusty schoolmen!
Even his festive and amatory songs, which are now the mere
quickeners of our social moments, or the delights of our
drawing-rooms, will then become matters of laborious research and painful collation. How many a grave professor will
then waste his midnight oil, or worry his brain through a

long morning, endeavouring to restore the pure text, or illustrate the biographical hints of "Come, tell me, says Rosa, as kissing and kissed;" and how many an arid old book-worm, like the worthy little parson, will give up in despair, after vainly striving to fill up some fatal hiatus in "Fanny of Timmol!"

Nor is it merely such exquisite authors as Moore that are doomed to consume the oil of future antiquaries. Many a poor scribbler, who is now, apparently, sent to oblivion by pastry-cooks and cheesemongers, will then rise again in fragments, and flourish in learned immortality.

After all, thought I, time is not such an invariable destroyer as he is represented. If he pulls down, he likewise builds up; if he impoverishes one, he enriches another; his very dilapidations furnish matter for new works of controversy, and his rust is more precious than the most costly gilding. Under his plastic hand trifles rise into importance; the nonsense of one age becomes the wisdom of another; the levity of the wit gravitates into the learning of the pedant, and an ancient farthing moulders into infinitely more value than a modern guinea.

The Farm-House

—— "Love and hay
Are thick sown, but come up full of thistles."
Beaumont and Fletcher

I WAS so much pleased with the anecdotes which were told me of Ready Money Jack Tibbets, that I got Master Simon, a day or two since, to take me to his house. It was an old-fashioned farm-house, built of brick, with curiously twisted chimneys. It stood at a little distance from the road, with a southern exposure, looking upon a soft, green slope of meadow. There was a small garden in front, with a row of beehives humming among beds of sweet herbs and flowers. Well-scoured milking-tubs, with bright copper hoops, hung on the garden paling. Fruit-trees were trained up against the cottage, and pots of flowers stood in the windows. A fat, superannuated mastiff lay in the sunshine at the door; with a sleek cat sleeping peacefully across him.

Mr. Tibbets was from home at the time of our calling, but we were received with hearty and homely welcome by his wife; a notable, motherly woman, and a complete pattern for wives; since, according to Master Simon's account, she never contradicts honest Jack, and yet manages to have her own way, and to control him in every thing.

She received us in the main room of the house, a kind of parlour and hall, with great brown beams of timber across it, which Mr. Tibbets is apt to point out with some exultation, observing, that they don't put such timber in houses now-a-days. The furniture was old-fashioned, strong, and highly polished; the walls were hung with coloured prints of the story of the Prodigal Son, who was represented in a red coat and leather breeches. Over the fire-place was a blunderbuss, and a hard-favoured likeness of Ready Money Jack, taken, when he was a young man, by the same artist that painted the tavern sign; his mother having taken a notion that the Tibbetses had as much right to have a gallery of family portraits as the folks at the Hall.

The good dame pressed us very much to take some refreshment, and tempted us with a variety of household dainties, so that we were glad to compound by tasting some of her home-made wines. While we were there, the son and heir-apparent came home; a good-looking young fellow, and something of a rustic beau. He took us over the premises, and showed us the whole establishment. An air of homely but substantial plenty prevailed throughout; every thing was of the best materials, and in the best condition. Nothing was out of place, or ill-made; and you saw every where the signs of a man that took care to have the worth of his money, and that paid as he went.

The farm-yard was well stocked; under a shed was a taxed cart, in trim order, in which Ready Money Jack took his wife about the country. His well-fed horse neighed from the stable, and when led out into the yard, to use the words of young Jack, "he shone like a bottle;" for he said the old man made it a rule that every thing about him should fare as well as he did himself.

I was pleased to see the pride which the young fellow seemed to have of his father. He gave us several particulars concerning his habits, which were pretty much to the effect of those I have already mentioned. He had never suffered an account to stand in his life, always providing the money before he purchased any thing; and, if possible, paying in gold and silver. He had a great dislike to paper-money, and seldom went without a considerable sum in gold about him. On my observing that it was a wonder he had never been waylaid and robbed, the young fellow smiled at the idea of any one venturing upon such an exploit, for I believe he thinks the old man would be a match for Robin Hood and all his gang.

I have noticed that Master Simon seldom goes into any house without having a world of private talk with some one or other of the family, being a kind of universal counsellor and confidant. We had not been long at the farm, before the old dame got him into a corner of her parlour, where they had a long, whispering conference together; in which I saw by his shrugs that there were some dubious matters discussed, and by his nods that he agreed with every thing she said.

After we had come out, the young man accompanied us a little distance, and then, drawing Master Simon aside into a green lane, they walked and talked together for nearly half an hour. Master Simon, who has the usual propensity of confidants to blab every thing to the next friend they meet with, let me know that there was a love affair in question; the young fellow having been smitten with the charms of Phœbe Wilkins, the pretty niece of the housekeeper at the Hall. Like most other love concerns, it had brought its troubles and perplexities. Dame Tibbets had long been on intimate, gossiping terms with the housekeeper, who often visited the farm-house; but when the neighbours spoke to her of the likelihood of a match between her son and Phœbe Wilkins, "Marry come up!" she scouted the very idea. The girl had acted as lady's maid, and it was beneath the blood of the Tibbetses, who had lived on their own lands time out of mind, and owed reverence and thanks to nobody, to have the heir-apparent marry a servant!

These vapourings had faithfully been carried to the housekeeper's ear, by one of their mutual, go-between friends. The old housekeeper's blood, if not as ancient, was as quick as that of Dame Tibbets. She had been accustomed to carry a high head at the Hall, and among the villagers; and her faded brocade rustled with indignation at the slight cast upon her alliance by the wife of a petty farmer. She maintained that her niece had been a companion rather than a waiting-maid to the young ladies. "Thank heavens, she was not obliged to work for her living, and was as idle as any young lady in the land; and when somebody died, would receive something that would be worth the notice of some folks, with all their ready money."

A bitter feud had thus taken place between the two worthy dames, and the young people were forbidden to think of one another. As to young Jack, he was too much in love to reason upon the matter; and being a little heady, and not standing in much awe of his mother, was ready to sacrifice the whole dignity of the Tibbetses to his passion. He had lately, however, had a violent quarrel with his mistress, in consequence of some coquetry on her part, and at present stood aloof. The politic mother was exerting all her ingenuity to widen this accidental breach; but, as is most commonly the case, the more she meddled with this perverse inclination of her son, the stronger it grew. In the mean time Old Ready Money was kept completely in the dark; both parties were in awe and uncertainty as to what might be his way of taking the matter, and dreaded to awaken the sleeping lion. Between father and son, therefore, the worthy Mrs. Tibbets was full of business, and at her wits' end. It is true there was no great danger of honest Ready Money's finding the thing out, if left to himself; for he was of a most unsuspicious temper, and by no means quick of apprehension; but there was daily risk of his attention being aroused by those cobwebs which his indefatigable wife was continually spinning about his nose.

Such is the distracted state of politics in the domestic empire of Ready Money Jack; which only shows the intrigues and internal dangers to which the best regulated governments are liable. In this perplexed situation of their affairs, both mother and son have applied to Master Simon for counsel; and, with all his experience in meddling with other people's concerns, he finds it an exceedingly difficult part to play, to agree with both parties, seeing that their opinions and wishes are so diametrically opposite.

Horsemanship

A coach was a strange monster in those days, and the sight of
one put both horse and man into amazement. Some said it was
a great crabshell brought out of China, and some imagined it
to be one of the pagan temples, in which the canibals adored
the divell.

Taylor, the Water Poet

I HAVE MADE casual mention, more than once, of one of the
squire's antiquated retainers, old Christy the huntsman. I
find that his crabbed humour is a source of much entertainment among the young men of the family; the Oxonian, particularly, takes a mischievous pleasure now and then in slyly
rubbing the old man against the grain, and then smoothing
him down again; for the old fellow is as ready to bristle up
his back as a porcupine. He rides a venerable hunter called
Pepper, which is a counterpart of himself, a heady, cross-
grained animal, that frets the flesh off its bones; bites, kicks,
and plays all manner of villanous tricks. He is as tough, and
nearly as old as his rider, who has ridden him time out of
mind, and is, indeed, the only one that can do any thing with
him. Sometimes, however, they have a complete quarrel, and
a dispute for mastery, and then, I am told, it is as good as a
farce to see the heat they both get into, and the wrongheaded
contest that ensues; for they are quite knowing in each
other's ways, and in the art of teasing and fretting each
other. Notwithstanding these doughty brawls, however, there
is nothing that nettles old Christy sooner than to question
the merits of his horse; which he upholds as tenaciously as a
faithful husband will vindicate the virtues of the termagant
spouse, that gives him a curtain lecture every night of his life.

The young men call old Christy their "professor of equitation," and in accounting for the appellation, they let me into
some particulars of the squire's mode of bringing up his children. There is an odd mixture of eccentricity and good sense
in all the opinions of my worthy host. His mind is like modern Gothic, where plain brick-work is set off with pointed
arches and quaint tracery. Though the main groundwork of
his opinions is correct, yet he has a thousand little notions,

picked up from old books, which stand out whimsically on the surface of his mind.

Thus, in educating his boys, he chose Peachem, Markam, and such like old English writers, for his manuals. At an early age he took the lads out of their mother's hands, who was disposed, as mothers are apt to be, to make fine, orderly children of them, that should keep out of sun and rain, and never soil their hands, nor tear their clothes.

In place of this, the squire turned them loose to run free and wild about the park, without heeding wind or weather. He was also particularly attentive in making them bold and expert horsemen; and these were the days when old Christy, the huntsman, enjoyed great importance, as the lads were put under his care to practise them at the leaping-bars, and to keep an eye upon them in the chase.

The squire always objected to their riding in carriages of any kind, and is still a little tenacious on this point. He often rails against the universal use of carriages, and quotes the words of honest Nashe to that effect. "It was thought," says Nashe, in his Quaternio, "a kind of solecism, and to savour of effeminacy, for a young gentleman in the flourishing time of his age to creep into a coach, and to shrowd himself from wind and weather: our great delight was to out-brave the blustering Boreas upon a great horse; to arm and prepare ourselves to go with Mars and Bellona into the field was our sport and pastime; coaches and caroches we left unto them for whom they were first invented, for ladies and gentlemen, and decrepit age and impotent people."

The squire insists that the English gentlemen have lost much of their hardiness and manhood since the introduction of carriages. "Compare," he will say, "the fine gentleman of former times, ever on horseback, booted and spurred, and travel-stained, but open, frank, manly, and chivalrous, with the fine gentleman of the present day, full of affectation and effeminacy, rolling along a turnpike in his voluptuous vehicle. The young men of those days were rendered brave, and lofty, and generous in their notions, by almost living in their saddles, and having their foaming steeds 'like proud seas under them.' There is something," he adds, "in bestriding a fine horse that makes a man feel more than mortal. He seems to have doubled his nature, and to have added to his own courage and sagacity the power, the speed, and stateliness of the superb animal on which he is mounted."

"It is a great delight," says old Nashe, "to see a young gentleman with his skill and cunning, by his voice, rod and spur, better to manage and to command the great Bucephalus, than the strongest Milo, with all his strength; one while to see him make him tread, trot and gallop the ring; and one after to see him make him gather up roundly; to bear his head steadily; to run a full career swiftly; to stop a sudden lightly; anon after to see him make him advance, to yorke, to go back and side long, to turn on either hand; to gallop the gallop galliard; to do the capriole, the chambetta, and dance the curvetty."

In conformity to these ideas, the squire had them all on horseback at an early age, and made them ride, slap dash, about the country, without flinching at hedge, or ditch, or stone wall, to the imminent danger of their necks.

Even the fair Julia was partially included in this system; and, under the instructions of old Christy, has become one of the best horsewomen in the county. The squire says it is better than all the cosmetics and sweeteners of the breath that ever were invented. He extols the horsemanship of the ladies in former times, when Queen Elizabeth would scarcely suffer the rain to stop her accustomed ride. "And then think," he will say, "what nobler and sweeter beings it made them. What a difference must there be, both in mind and body, between a joyous high-spirited dame of those days, glowing with health and exercise, freshened by every breeze that blows, seated loftily and gracefully on her saddle, with plume on head, and hawk on hand, and her descendant of the present day, the pale victim of routs and ball-rooms, sunk languidly in one corner of an enervating carriage."

The squire's equestrian system has been attended with great success, for his sons, having passed through the whole course of instruction without breaking neck or limb, are now healthful, spirited, and active, and have the true Englishman's love for a horse. If their manliness and frankness are praised in their father's hearing, he quotes the old Persian maxim, and says, they have been taught "to ride, to shoot, and to speak the truth."

It is true the Oxonian has now and then practised the old gentleman's doctrines a little in the extreme. He is a gay youngster, rather fonder of his horse than his book, with a little dash of the dandy; though the ladies all declare that he is "the flower of the flock." The first year that he was sent to Oxford, he had a tutor appointed to overlook him, a dry chip of the university. When he returned home in the vacation, the squire made many inquiries about how he liked his college, his studies, and his tutor.

"Oh, as to my tutor, sir, I've parted with him some time since."

"You have; and, pray, why so?"

"Oh, sir, hunting was all the go at our college, and I was a little short of funds; so I discharged my tutor, and took a horse, you know."

"Ah, I was not aware of that, Tom," said the squire, mildly.

When Tom returned to college his allowance was doubled, that he might be enabled to keep both horse and tutor.

Love-Symptoms

I will now begin to sigh, read poets, look pale, go neatly, and be most apparently in love.

Marston

I SHOULD NOT be surprised if we should have another pair of turtles at the Hall, for Master Simon has informed me, in great confidence, that he suspects the general of some design upon the susceptible heart of Lady Lillycraft. I have, indeed, noticed a growing attention and courtesy in the veteran towards her ladyship; he softens very much in her company, sits by her at table, and entertains her with long stories about Seringapatam, and pleasant anecdotes of the Mulligatawney club. I have even seen him present her with a full blown rose from the hot-house, in a style of the most captivating gallantry, and it was accepted with great suavity and graciousness; for her ladyship delights in receiving the homage and attention of the sex.

Indeed, the general was one of the earliest admirers that dangled in her train during her short reign of beauty; and they flirted together for half a season in London, some thirty or forty years since. She reminded him lately, in the course of a conversation about former days, of the time when he used to ride a white horse, and to canter so gallantly by the side of her carriage in Hyde Park; whereupon I have remarked that the veteran has regularly escorted her since, when she rides out on horseback; and, I suspect, he almost persuades himself that he makes as captivating an appearance as in his youthful days.

It would be an interesting and memorable circumstance in the chronicles of Cupid, if this spark of the tender passion, after lying dormant for such a length of time, should again be fanned into a flame, from amidst the ashes of two burnt out hearts. It would be an instance of perdurable fidelity, worthy of being placed beside those recorded in one of the squire's favourite tomes, commemorating the constancy of the olden times; in which times, we are told, "Men and wymmen coulde love togyders seven yeres, and no licours lustes were

betwene them, and thenne was love, trouthe and feythfulnes;
and lo in lyke wyse was used love in Kyng Arthurs dayes."*

Still, however, this may be nothing but a little venerable
flirtation, the general being a veteran dangler, and the good
lady habituated to these kind of attentions. Master Simon, on
the other hand, thinks the general is looking about him with
the wary eye of an old campaigner; and now that he is on the
wane, is desirous of getting into warm winter quarters. Much
allowance, however, must be made for Master Simon's uneasiness on the subject, for he looks on Lady Lillycraft's house as
one of his strong holds, where he is lord of the ascendant;
and, with all his admiration of the general, I much doubt
whether he would like to see him lord of the lady and the
establishment.

There are certain other symptoms, notwithstanding, that
give an air of probability to Master Simon's intimations. Thus
for instance, I have observed that the general has been very
assiduous in his attentions to her ladyship's dogs, and has several times exposed his fingers to imminent jeopardy, in attempting to pat Beauty on the head. It is to be hoped his
advances to the mistress will be more favourably received, as
all his overtures towards a caress are greeted by the pestilent
little cur with a wary kindling of the eye, and a most venom-
ous growl.

He has, moreover, been very complaisant towards my
lady's gentlewoman, the immaculate Mrs. Hannah, whom he
used to speak of in a way that I do not choose to mention.
Whether she has the same suspicions with Master Simon or
not, I cannot say; but she receives his civilities with no better
grace than the implacable Beauty; unscrewing her mouth into
a most acid smile, and looking as though she could bite a
piece out of him. In short, the poor general seems to have as
formidable foes to contend with as a hero of ancient fairy tale;
who had to fight his way to his enchanted princess through
ferocious monsters of every kind, and to encounter the brimstone terrors of some fiery dragon.

There is still another circumstance which inclines me to
give very considerable credit to Master Simon's suspicions.

*Morte d'Arthur.

Lady Lillycraft is very fond of quoting poetry, and the conversation often turns upon it, on which occasions the general is thrown completely out. It happened the other day that Spenser's Fairy Queen was the theme for the great part of the morning, and the poor general sat perfectly silent. I found him not long after in the library, with spectacles on nose, a book in his hand, and fast asleep. On my approach he awoke, slipt the spectacles into his pocket, and began to read very attentively. After a little while he put a paper in the place, and laid the volume aside, which I perceived was the Fairy Queen. I have had the curiosity to watch how he got on in his poetical studies; but, though I have repeatedly seen him with the book in his hand, yet I find the paper has not advanced above three or four pages; the general being extremely apt to fall asleep when he reads.

Falconry

Ne is there hawk which mantleth on her perch,
  Whether high tow'ring or accousting low,
But I the measure of her flight doe search,
  And all her prey and all her diet know.

Spenser

THERE ARE several grand sources of lamentation furnished to the worthy squire, by the improvement of society, and the grievous advancement of knowledge; among which there is none, I believe, that causes him more frequent regret than the unfortunate invention of gunpowder. To this he continually traces the decay of some favourite custom, and, indeed, the general downfall of all chivalrous and romantic usages. "English soldiers," he says, "have never been the men they were in the days of the cross-bow and the long-bow; when they depended upon the strength of the arm, and the English archer could draw a clothyard shaft to the head. These were the times when at the battles of Cressy, Poictiers, and Agincourt, the French chivalry was completely destroyed by the bowmen of England. The yeomanry, too, have never been what they were, when, in times of peace, they were constantly exercised with the bow, and archery was a favourite holiday pastime."

Among the other evils which have followed in the train of this fatal invention of gunpowder, the squire classes the total decline of the noble art of falconry. "Shooting," he says, "is a skulking, treacherous, solitary sport in comparison; but hawking was a gallant, open, sunshiny recreation; it was the generous sport of hunting carried into the skies."

"It was, moreover," he says, "according to Braithwate, the stately amusement of 'high and mounting spirits;' for, as the old Welsh proverb affirms, in those times 'You might know a gentleman by his hawk, horse, and grayhound.' Indeed, a cavalier was seldom seen abroad without his hawk on his fist; and even a lady of rank did not think herself completely equipped, in riding forth, unless she had her tassel-gentel held by jesses on her delicate hand. It was thought in those

excellent days, according to an old writer, 'quite sufficient for noblemen to winde their horn, and to carry their hawke fair; and leave study and learning to the children of mean people.' "

Knowing the good squire's hobby, therefore, I have not been surprised at finding that, among the various recreations of former times which he has endeavoured to revive in the little world in which he rules, he has bestowed great attention on the noble art of falconry. In this he, of course, has been seconded by his indefatigable coadjutor, Master Simon; and even the parson has thrown considerable light on their labours, by various hints on the subject, which he has met with in old English works. As to the precious work of that famous dame Juliana Barnes; the Gentleman's Academie, by Markham; and the other well-known treatises that were the manuals of ancient sportsmen, they have them at their fingers' ends; but they have more especially studied some old tapestry in the house, whereon is represented a party of cavaliers and stately dames, with doublets, caps, and flaunting feathers, mounted on horse, with attendants on foot, all in animated pursuit of the game.

The squire has discountenanced the killing of any hawks in his neighbourhood, but gives a liberal bounty for all that are brought him alive; so that the Hall is well stocked with all kinds of birds of prey. On these he and Master Simon have exhausted their patience and ingenuity, endeavouring to "reclaim" them, as it is termed, and to train them up for the sport; but they have met with continual checks and disappointments. Their feathered school has turned out the most untractable and graceless scholars; nor is it the least of their trouble to drill the retainers who were to act as ushers under them, and to take immediate charge of these refractory birds. Old Christy and the gamekeeper both, for a time, set their faces against the whole plan of education; Christy having been nettled at hearing what he terms a wild-goose chase put on a par with a fox-hunt; and the gamekeeper having always been accustomed to look upon hawks as arrant poachers, which it was his duty to shoot down, and nail, in terrorem, against the out-houses.

Christy has at length taken the matter in hand, but has

done still more mischief by his intermeddling. He is as positive and wrong-headed about this, as he is about hunting. Master Simon has continual disputes with him as to feeding and training the hawks. He reads to him long passages from the old authors I have mentioned; but Christy, who cannot read, has a sovereign contempt for all book-knowledge, and persists in treating the hawks according to his own notions, which are drawn from his experience, in younger days, in the rearing of game-cocks.

The consequence is, that, between these jarring systems, the poor birds have had a most trying and unhappy time of it. Many have fallen victims to Christy's feeding and Master Simon's physicking; for the latter has gone to work *secundem artem*, and has given them all the vomitings and scourings laid down in the books; never were poor hawks so fed and physicked before. Others have been lost by being but half "reclaimed," or tamed: for on being taken into the field, they have "raked" after the game quite out of hearing of the call, and never returned to school.

All these disappointments had been petty, yet sore grievances to the squire, and had made him to despond about success. He has lately, however, been made happy by the receipt of a fine Welsh falcon, which Master Simon terms a stately highflyer. It is a present from the squire's friend, Sir Watkyn Williams Wynne; and is, no doubt, a descendant of some ancient line of Welsh princes of the air, that have long lorded it over their kingdom of clouds, from Wynnstay to the very summit of Snowden, or the brow of Penmanmawr.

Ever since the squire received this invaluable present, he has been as impatient to sally forth and make proof of it, as was Don Quixote to assay his suit of armour. There have been some demurs as to whether the bird was in proper health and training; but these have been overruled by the vehement desire to play with a new toy; and it has been determined, right or wrong, in season or out of season, to have a day's sport in hawking to-morrow.

The Hall, as usual, whenever the squire is about to make some new sally on his hobby, is all agog with the thing. Miss Templeton, who is brought up in reverence for all her guardian's humours, has proposed to be of the party, and Lady

Lillycraft has talked also of riding out to the scene of action and looking on. This has gratified the old gentleman extremely; he hails it as an auspicious omen of the revival of falconry, and does not despair but the time will come when it will be again the pride of a fine lady to carry about a noble falcon in preference to a parrot or a lap-dog.

I have amused myself with the bustling preparations of that busy spirit, Master Simon, and the continual thwartings he receives from that genuine son of a pepper-box, old Christy. They have had half a dozen consultations about how the hawk is to be prepared for the morning's sport. Old Nimrod, as usual, has always got in a pet, upon which Master Simon has invariably given up the point, observing, in a good-humoured tone, "Well, well, have it your own way, Christy; only don't put yourself in a passion;" a reply which always nettles the old man ten times more than ever.

Hawking

The soaring hawk, from fist that flies,
  Her falconer doth constrain
Sometimes to range the ground about
  To find her out again;
And if by sight, or sound of bell,
  His falcon he may see,
Wo ho! he cries, with cheerful voice—
  The gladdest man is he.

Handefull of Pleasant Delites

A T AN EARLY HOUR this morning the Hall was in a bustle,
preparing for the sport of the day. I heard Master Simon whistling and singing under my window at sunrise, as
he was preparing the jesses for the hawk's legs, and could
distinguish now and then a stanza of one of his favourite old
ditties:

"In peascod time, when hound to horn
  Gives note that buck be kill'd;
And little boy with pipe of corn
  Is tending sheep a-field," &c.

A hearty breakfast, well flanked by cold meats, was served
up in the great hall. The whole garrison of retainers and
hangers-on were in motion, reinforced by volunteer idlers
from the village. The horses were led up and down before the
door; every body had something to say, and something to do,
and hurried hither and thither; there was a direful yelping of
dogs; some that were to accompany us being eager to set off,
and others that were to stay at home being whipped back to
their kennels. In short, for once, the good squire's mansion
might have been taken as a good specimen of one of the
rantipole establishments of the good old feudal times.

Breakfast being finished, the chivalry of the Hall prepared
to take the field. The fair Julia was of the party, in a hunting
dress, with a light plume of feathers in her riding-hat. As she
mounted her favourite galloway, I remarked, with pleasure,
that old Christy forgot his usual crustiness, and hastened to

adjust her saddle and bridle. He touched his cap as she smiled on him and thanked him; and then, looking round at the other attendants, gave a knowing nod of his head, in which I read pride and exultation at the charming appearance of his pupil.

Lady Lillycraft had likewise determined to witness the sport. She was dressed in her broad white beaver, tied under the chin, and a riding-habit of the last century. She rode her sleek, ambling pony, whose motion was as easy as a rocking-chair; and was gallantly escorted by the general, who looked not unlike one of the doughty heroes in the old prints of the battle of Blenheim. The parson, likewise, accompanied her on the other side; for this was a learned amusement in which he took great interest; and, indeed, had given much council, from his knowledge of old customs.

At length every thing was arranged, and off we set from the Hall. The exercise on horseback puts one in fine spirits; and the scene was gay and animating. The young men of the family accompanied Miss Templeton. She sat lightly and gracefully in her saddle, her plumes dancing and waving in the air; and the group had a charming effect as they appeared and disappeared among the trees, cantering along with the bounding animation of youth. The squire and Master Simon rode together, accompanied by old Christy, mounted on Pepper. The latter bore the hawk on his fist, as he insisted the bird was most accustomed to him. There was a rabble rout on foot, composed of retainers from the Hall, and some idlers from the village, with two or three spaniels, for the purpose of starting the game.

A kind of corps de reserve came on quietly in the rear, composed of Lady Lillycraft, General Harbottle, the parson, and a fat footman. Her ladyship ambled gently along on her pony, while the general, mounted on a tall hunter, looked down upon her with an air of the most protecting gallantry.

For my part, being no sportsman, I kept with this last party, or rather lagged behind, that I might take in the whole picture; and the parson occasionally slackened his pace and jogged on in company with me.

The sport led us at some distance from the Hall, in a soft meadow, reeking with the moist verdure of spring. A little river ran through it, bordered by willows, which had put forth their tender early foliage. The sportsmen were in quest of herons which were said to keep about this stream.

There was some disputing, already, among the leaders of the sport. The squire, Master Simon, and old Christy, came every now and then to a pause, to consult together, like the field officers in an army; and I saw, by certain motions of the head, that Christy was as positive as any old wrong-headed German commander.

As we were prancing up this quiet meadow every sound we made was answered by a distinct echo, from the sunny wall of an old building that lay on the opposite margin of the stream; and I paused to listen to this "Spirit of a sound," which seems to love such quiet and beautiful places. The parson informed me that this was the ruin of an ancient grange, and was supposed, by the country people, to be haunted by a dobbie, a kind of rural sprite, something like Robin-good-fellow. They often fancied the echo to be the voice of the dobbie answering them, and were rather shy of disturbing it after dark. He added, that the squire was very careful of this ruin, on account of the superstition connected with it. As I considered this local habitation of an "airy nothing," I called to mind the fine description of an echo in Webster's Duchess of Malfy:

> —— " 'Yond side o' th' river lies a wall,
> Piece of a cloister, which in my opinion
> Gives the best echo that you ever heard;
> So plain in the distinction of our words,
> That many have supposed it a spirit
> That answers."

The parson went on to comment on a pleasing and fanciful appellation which the Jews of old gave to the echo, which they called Bath-kool, that is to say, "the daughter of the voice;" they considered it an oracle, supplying in the second temple the want of the urim and thummim, with which the first was honoured.* The little man was just entering very largely and learnedly upon the subject, when we were startled

*Bekker's Monde enchanté.

by a prodigious bawling, shouting, and yelping. A flight of crows, alarmed by the approach of our forces, had suddenly rose from a meadow; a cry was put up by the rabble rout on foot. "Now, Christy! now is your time, Christy!" The squire and Master Simon, who were beating up the river banks in quest of a heron, called out eagerly to Christy to keep quiet; the old man, vexed and bewildered by the confusion of voices, completely lost his head; in his flurry he slipped off the hood, cast off the falcon, and away flew the crows, and away soared the hawk.

I had paused on a rising ground, close to Lady Lillycraft and her escort, from whence I had a good view of the sport. I was pleased with the appearance of the party in the meadow, riding along in the direction that the bird flew; their bright beaming faces turned up to the bright skies as they watched the game; the attendants on foot scampering along, looking up, and calling out, and the dogs bounding and yelping with clamorous sympathy.

The hawk had singled out a quarry from among the carrion crew. It was curious to see the efforts of the two birds to get above each other; one to make the fatal swoop, the other to avoid it. Now they crossed athwart a bright feathery cloud, and now they were against the clear blue sky. I confess, being no sportsman, I was more interested for the poor bird that was striving for its life, than for the hawk that was playing the part of a mercenary soldier. At length the hawk got the upper hand, and made a rushing stoop at her quarry, but the latter made as sudden a surge downwards, and slanting up again evaded the blow, screaming and making the best of his way for a dry tree on the brow of a neighbouring hill; while the hawk, disappointed of her blow, soared up again into the air, and appeared to be "raking" off. It was in vain old Christy called, and whistled, and endeavoured to lure her down; she paid no regard to him: and, indeed, his calls were drowned in the shouts and yelps of the army of militia that had followed him into the field.

Just then an exclamation from Lady Lillycraft made me turn my head. I beheld a complete confusion among the sportsmen in the little vale below us. They were galloping and running towards the edge of a bank; and I was shocked to see Miss Templeton's horse galloping at large without his rider. I rode to the place to which the others were hurrying, and when I reached the bank, which almost overhung the stream, I saw at the foot of it, the fair Julia, pale, bleeding, and apparently lifeless, supported in the arms of her frantic lover.

In galloping heedlessly along, with her eyes turned upward, she had unwarily approached too near the bank; it had given way with her, and she and her horse had been precipitated to the pebbled margin of the river.

I never saw greater consternation. The captain was distracted; Lady Lillycraft fainting; the squire in dismay, and Master Simon at his wits' ends. The beautiful creature at length showed signs of returning life; she opened her eyes; looked around her upon the anxious group, and comprehending in a moment the nature of the scene, gave a sweet smile, and putting her hand in her lover's, exclaimed, feebly, "I am not much hurt, Guy!" I could have taken her to my heart for that single exclamation.

It was found, indeed, that she had escaped almost miraculously, with a contusion of the head, a sprained ankle, and some slight bruises. After her wound was stanched, she was taken to a neighbouring cottage, until a carriage could be summoned to convey her home; and when this had arrived, the cavalcade, which had issued forth so gaily on this enterprise, returned slowly and pensively to the Hall.

I had been charmed by the generous spirit shown by this young creature, who, amidst pain and danger, had been anxious only to relieve the distress of those around her. I was gratified, therefore, by the universal concern displayed by the domestics on our return. They came crowding down the avenue, each eager to render assistance. The butler stood ready with some curiously delicate cordial; the old housekeeper was provided with half a dozen nostrums, prepared by her own hands, according to the family receipt book; while her niece, the melting Phœbe, having no other way of assisting, stood wringing her hands, and weeping aloud.

The most material effect that is likely to follow this accident is a postponement of the nuptials, which were close at hand. Though I commiserate the impatience of the captain on that account, yet I shall not otherwise be sorry at the delay, as it will give me a better opportunity of studying the characters here assembled, with which I grow more and more entertained.

I cannot but perceive that the worthy squire is quite disconcerted at the unlucky result of his hawking experiment, and this unfortunate illustration of his eulogy on female equitation. Old Christy too is very waspish, having been sorely twitted by Master Simon for having let his hawk fly at carrion. As to the falcon, in the confusion occasioned by the fair Julia's disaster, the bird was totally forgotten. I make no doubt she has made the best of her way back to the hospitable Hall of Sir Watkyn Williams Wynne; and may very possibly, at this present writing, be pluming her wings among the breezy bowers of Wynnstay.

St. Mark's Eve

O 'tis a fearful thing to be no more.
Or if to be, to wander after death!
To walk as spirits do, in brakes all day,
And, when the darkness comes, to glide in paths
That lead to graves; and in the silent vault,
Where lies your own pale shroud, to hover o'er it,
Striving to enter your forbidden corpse.

Dryden

THE CONVERSATION this evening at supper-table took a curious turn on the subject of a superstition, formerly very prevalent in this part of the country, relative to the present night of the year, which is the Eve of St. Mark's. It was believed, the parson informed us, that if any one would watch in the church porch on this eve, for three successive years, from eleven to one o'clock at night, he would see, on the third year, the shades of those of the parish who were to die in the course of the year, pass by him into church, clad in their usual apparel.

Dismal as such a sight would be, he assured us that it was formerly a frequent thing for persons to make the necessary vigils. He had known more than one instance in his time. One old woman, who pretended to have seen this phantom procession, was an object of great awe for the whole year afterwards, and caused much uneasiness and mischief. If she shook her head mysteriously at a person, it was like a death warrant; and she had nearly caused the death of a sick person by looking ruefully in at the window.

There was also an old man, not many years since, of a sullen, melancholy temperament, who had kept two vigils, and began to excite some talk in the village, when, fortunately for the public comfort, he died shortly after his third watching; very probably from a cold that he had taken, as the night was tempestuous. It was reported about the village, however, that he had seen his own phantom pass by him into the church.

This led to the mention of another superstition of an equally strange and melancholy kind, which, however, is chiefly confined to Wales. It is respecting what are called corpse candles, little wandering fires, of a pale bluish light, that move about like tapers in the open air, and are supposed to designate the way some corpse is to go. One was seen at Lanylar, late at night, hovering up and down, along the bank of the Istwith, and was watched by the neighbours until they were tired, and went to bed. Not long afterwards there came a comely country lass, from Montgomeryshire, to see her friends, who dwelt on the opposite side of the river. She thought to ford the stream at the very place where the light had been first seen, but was dissuaded on account of the height of the flood. She walked to and fro along the bank, just where the candle had moved, waiting for the subsiding of the water. She at length endeavoured to cross, but the poor girl was drowned in the attempt.*

There was something mournful in this little anecdote of rural superstition, that seemed to affect all the listeners. Indeed, it is curious to remark how completely a conversation of the kind will absorb the attention of a circle, and sober down its gaiety, however boisterous. By degrees I noticed that every one was leaning forward over the table, with eyes earnestly fixed upon the parson, and at the mention of corpse candles which had been seen about the chamber of a young lady who died on the eve of her wedding-day, Lady Lillycraft turned pale.

I have witnessed the introduction of stories of the kind into various evening circles; they were often commenced in jest, and listened to with smiles; but I never knew the most gay or the most enlightened of audiences, that were not, if the conversation continued for any length of time, completely and solemnly interested in it. There is, I believe, a degree of superstition lurking in every mind; and I doubt if any one can thoroughly examine all his secret notions and impulses without detecting it, hidden, perhaps, even from himself. It seems, in fact, to be a part of our nature, like instinct in animals, acting independently of our reason. It is often found existing in lofty natures, especially those that are poetical and aspiring. A great and extraordinary poet of our day, whose life and

*Aubrey's Miscel.

writings evince a mind subject to powerful exaltation, is said to believe in omens and secret intimations. Cæsar, it is well known, was greatly under the influence of such belief; and Napoleon had his good and evil days, and his presiding star.

As to the worthy parson, I have no doubt that he is strongly inclined to superstition. He is naturally credulous, and passes so much of his time searching out popular traditions and supernatural tales, that his mind has probably become infected by them. He has lately been immersed in the Demonolatria of Nicholas Remigius, concerning supernatural occurrences in Lorraine, and the writings of Joachimus Camerarius, called by Vossius the Phœnix of Germany; and he entertains the ladies with stories from them, that make them almost afraid to go to bed at night. I have been charmed myself with some of the wild, little superstitions which he has adduced from Blefkénius, Scheffer, and others; such as those of the Laplanders about the domestic spirits which wake them at night, and summon them to go and fish; of Thor, the deity of thunder, who has power of life and death, health and sickness, and who, armed with the rainbow, shoots his arrows at those evil demons that live on the tops of rocks and mountains, and infest the lakes; of the Juhles or Juhlafolket, vagrant troops of spirits, which roam the air, and wander up and down by forests and mountains, and the moonlight sides of hills.

The parson never openly professes his belief in ghosts, but I have remarked that he has a suspicious way of pressing great names into the defence of supernatural doctrines, and making philosophers and saints fight for him. He expatiates at large on the opinions of the ancient philosophers about larves, or nocturnal phantoms, the spirits of the wicked, which wandered like exiles about the earth; and about those spiritual beings which abode in the air, but descended occasionally to earth, and mingled among mortals, acting as agents between them and the gods. He quotes also from Philo the rabbi, the contemporary of the apostles, and, according to some, the friend of St. Paul, who says that the air is full of spirits of different ranks; some destined to exist for a time in mortal bodies, from which, being emancipated, they pass and repass between heaven and earth, as agents or messengers in the service of the deity.

But the worthy little man assumes a bolder tone when he quotes from the fathers of the church; such as St. Jerome, who gives it as the opinion of all the doctors, that the air is filled with powers opposed to each other; and Lactantius, who says that corrupt and dangerous spirits wander over the earth, and seek to console themselves for their own fall by effecting the ruin of the human race; and Clemens Alexandrinus, who is of opinion that the souls of the blessed have knowledge of what passes among men, the same as angels have.

I am now alone in my chamber, but these themes have taken such hold of my imagination, that I cannot sleep. The room in which I sit is just fitted to foster such a state of mind. The walls are hung with tapestry, the figures of which are faded, and look like unsubstantial shapes melting away from sight. Over the fireplace is the portrait of a lady, who, according to the housekeeper's tradition, pined to death for the loss of her lover in the battle of Blenheim. She has a most pale and plaintive countenance, and seems to fix her eyes mournfully upon me. The family have long since retired. I have heard their steps die away, and the distant doors clap to after them. The murmur of voices, and the peal of remote laughter, no longer reach the ear. The clock from the church, in which so many of the former inhabitants of this house lie buried, has chimed the awful hour of midnight.

I have sat by the window and mused upon the dusky landscape, watching the lights disappearing, one by one, from the distant village; and the moon rising in her silent majesty, and leading up all the silver pomp of heaven. As I have gazed upon these quiet groves and shadowy lawns, silvered over, and imperfectly lighted by streaks of dewy moonshine, my mind has been crowded by "thick coming fancies" concerning those spiritual beings which

"—— walk the earth
Unseen, both when we wake and when we sleep."

Are there, indeed, such beings? Is this space between us and the deity filled up by innumerable orders of spiritual beings, forming the same gradations between the human soul and divine perfection, that we see prevailing from humanity

downwards to the meanest insect? It is a sublime and beautiful doctrine, inculcated by the early fathers, that there are
guardian angels appointed to watch over cities and nations;
to take care of the welfare of good men, and to guard and
guide the steps of helpless infancy. "Nothing," says St. Jerome, "gives us a greater idea of the dignity of our soul, than
that God has given each of us, at the moment of our birth,
an angel to have care of it."

Even the doctrine of departed spirits returning to visit the
scenes and beings which were dear to them during the body's
existence, though it has been debased by the absurd superstitions of the vulgar, in itself is awfully solemn and sublime.
However lightly it may be ridiculed, yet the attention involuntarily yielded to it whenever it is made the subject of
serious discussion; its prevalence in all ages and countries,
and even among newly discovered nations, that have had
no previous interchange of thought with other parts of
the world, prove it to be one of those mysterious, and almost
instinctive beliefs, to which, if left to ourselves, we should
naturally incline.

In spite of all the pride of reason and philosophy, a vague
doubt will still lurk in the mind, and perhaps will never be
perfectly eradicated; as it is concerning a matter that does not
admit of positive demonstration. Every thing connected with
our spiritual nature is full of doubt and difficulty. "We are
fearfully and wonderfully made;" we are surrounded by mysteries, and we are mysteries even to ourselves. Who yet has
been able to comprehend and describe the nature of the soul,
its connexion with the body, or in what part of the frame it is
situated? We know merely that it does exist; but whence it
came, and when it entered into us, and how it is retained, and
where it is seated, and how it operates, are all matters of mere
speculation, and contradictory theories. If, then, we are thus
ignorant of this spiritual essence, even while it forms a part
of ourselves, and is continually present to our consciousness,
how can we pretend to ascertain or to deny its powers and
operations when released from its fleshly prison-house? It is
more the manner, therefore, in which this superstition has
been degraded, than its intrinsic absurdity, that has brought
it into contempt. Raise it above the frivolous purposes to

which it has been applied, strip it of the gloom and horror with which it has been surrounded, and there is none of the whole circle of visionary creeds that could more delightfully elevate the imagination, or more tenderly affect the heart. It would become a sovereign comfort at the bed of death, soothing the bitter tear wrung from us by the agony of our mortal separation. What could be more consoling than the idea, that the souls of those whom we once loved were permitted to return and watch over our welfare? That affectionate and guardian spirits sat by our pillows when we slept, keeping a vigil over our most helpless hours? That beauty and innocence, which had languished into the tomb, yet smiled unseen around us, revealing themselves in those blest dreams wherein we live over again the hours of past endearment? A belief of this kind would, I should think, be a new incentive to virtue; rendering us circumspect even in our most secret moments, from the idea that those we once loved and honoured were invisible witnesses of all our actions.

It would take away, too, from that loneliness and destitution which we are apt to feel more and more as we get on in our pilgrimage through the wilderness of this world, and find that those who set forward with us, lovingly and cheerily, on the journey, have one by one dropped away from our side. Place the superstition in this light, and I confess I should like to be a believer in it. I see nothing in it that is incompatible with the tender and merciful nature of our religion, nor revolting to the wishes and affections of the heart.

There are departed beings that I have loved as I never again shall love in this world;—that have loved me as I never again shall be loved! If such beings do ever retain in their blessed spheres the attachments which they felt on earth; if they take an interest in the poor concerns of transient mortality, and are permitted to hold communion with those whom they have loved on earth, I feel as if now, at this deep hour of night, in this silence and solitude, I could receive their visitation with the most solemn, but unalloyed, delight.

In truth, such visitations would be too happy for this world; they would be incompatible with the nature of this imperfect state of being. We are here placed in a mere scene of spiritual thraldom and restraint. Our souls are shut in and limited by bounds and barriers; shackled by mortal infirmities, and subject to all the gross impediments of matter. In vain would they seek to act independently of the body, and to mingle together in spiritual intercourse. They can only act here through their fleshly organs. Their earthly loves are made up of transient embraces and long separations. The most intimate friendship, of what brief and scattered portions of time does it consist! We take each other by the hand, and we exchange a few words, and looks of kindness, and we rejoice together for a few short moments, and then days, months, years intervene, and we see and know nothing of each other. Or granting that we dwell together for the full season of this our mortal life, the grave soon closes its gates between us, and then our spirits are doomed to remain in separation and widowhood; until they meet again in that more perfect state of being, where soul will dwell with soul in blissful communion, and there will be neither death, nor absence, nor any thing else to interrupt our felicity.

――――――――

* * * In the foregoing paper I have alluded to the writings of some of the old Jewish rabbins. They abound with wild theories; but among them are many truly poetical flights; and their ideas are often very beautifully expressed. Their speculations on the nature of angels are curious and fanciful, though much resembling the doctrines of the ancient philosophers. In the writings of the Rabbi Eleazer is an account of the temptation of our first parents and the fall of the angels, which the parson pointed out to me as having probably furnished some of the ground-work for "Paradise Lost."

According to Eleazer, the ministering angels said to the Deity, "What is there in man that thou makest him of such importance? Is he any thing else than vanity? for he can scarcely reason a little on terrestrial things." To which God replied, "Do you imagine that I will be exalted and glorified only by you here above? I am the same below that I am here. Who is there among you that can call all the creatures by their names?" There was none found among them that could do so. At that moment Adam arose, and called all the creatures by their name. Seeing which, the ministering angels said among themselves, "Let us consult together how we may cause Adam to sin against the Creator, otherwise he will not fail to become our master."

Sammaël, who was a great prince in the heavens, was present at this council, with the saints of the first order, and the seraphim of six bands. Sammaël chose several out of the twelve orders to accompany him, and descended below, for the purpose of visiting all the creatures which God had created. He found none more cunning and more fit to do evil than the serpent.

The rabbi then treats of the seduction and the fall of man; of the consequent fall of the demon, and the punishment which God inflicted on Adam, Eve, and the serpent. "He made them all come before him; pronounced nine maledictions on Adam and Eve, and condemned them to suffer death; and he precipitated Sammaël and all his band from heaven. He cut off the feet of the serpent, which had before the figure of a camel (Sammaël having been mounted on him), and he cursed him among all beasts and animals."

Gentility

—— True Gentrie standeth in the trade
Of virtuous life, not in the fleshly line;
For bloud is knit, but Gentrie is divine.
Mirror for Magistrates

I HAVE MENTIONED some peculiarities of the squire in the education of his sons; but I would not have it thought that his instructions were directed chiefly to their personal accomplishments. He took great pains also to form their minds, and to inculcate what he calls good old English principles, such as are laid down in the writings of Peachem and his contemporaries. There is one author of whom he cannot speak without indignation, which is Chesterfield. He avers that he did much, for a time, to injure the true national character, and to introduce, instead of open manly sincerity, a hollow perfidious courtliness. "His maxims," he affirms, "were calculated to chill the delightful enthusiasm of youth, to make them ashamed of that romance which is the dawn of generous manhood, and to impart to them a cold polish and a premature worldliness.

"Many of Lord Chesterfield's maxims would make a young man a mere man of pleasure; but an English gentleman should not be a mere man of pleasure. He has no right to such selfish indulgence. His ease, his leisure, his opulence, are debts due to his country, which he must ever stand ready to discharge. He should be a man at all points; simple, frank, courteous, intelligent, accomplished, and informed; upright, intrepid, and disinterested; one that can mingle among freemen; that can cope with statesmen; that can champion his country and its rights either at home or abroad. In a country like England, where there is such free and unbounded scope for the exertion of intellect, and where opinion and example have such weight with the people, every gentleman of fortune and leisure should feel himself bound to employ himself in some way towards promoting the prosperity or glory of the nation. In a country where intellect and action are trammelled and restrained, men of rank and fortune may become idlers

and triflers with impunity; but an English coxcomb is inex-
cusable; and this, perhaps, is the reason why he is the most
offensive and insupportable coxcomb in the world."

The squire, as Frank Bracebridge informs me, would often
hold forth in this manner to his sons when they were about
leaving the paternal roof; one to travel abroad, one to go to
the army, and one to the university. He used to have them
with him in the library, which is hung with the portraits of
Sydney, Surrey, Raleigh, Wyat, and others. "Look at those
models of true English gentlemen, my sons," he would say
with enthusiasm; "those were men that wreathed the graces
of the most delicate and refined taste around the stern virtues
of the soldier; that mingled what was gentle and gracious,
with what was hardy and manly; that possessed the true chivalry of spirit, which is the exalted essence of manhood. They
are the lights by which the youth of the country should array
themselves. They were the patterns and the idols of their
country at home; they were the illustrators of its dignity
abroad. 'Surrey,' says Camden, 'was the first nobleman that
illustrated his high birth with the beauty of learning. He was
acknowledged to be the gallantest man, the politest lover, and
the completest gentleman of his time.' And as to Wyat, his
friend Surrey most amiably testifies of him, that his person
was majestic and beautiful, his visage 'stern and mild;' that he
sung, and played the lute with remarkable sweetness; spoke
foreign languages with grace and fluency, and possessed an
inexhaustible fund of wit. And see what a high commendation is passed upon these illustrious friends: 'They were the
two chieftains, who, having travelled into Italy, and there
tasted the sweet and stately measures and style of the Italian
poetry, greatly polished our rude and homely manner of vulgar poetry from what it had been before, and therefore may
be justly called the reformers of our English poetry and style.'
And Sir Philip Sydney, who has left us such monuments of
elegant thought, and generous sentiment, and who illustrated
his chivalrous spirit so gloriously in the field. And Sir Walter
Raleigh, the elegant courtier, the intrepid soldier, the enterprising discoverer, the enlightened philosopher, the magnanimous martyr. These are the men for English gentlemen to
study. Chesterfield, with his cold and courtly maxims, would

have chilled and impoverished such spirits. He would have blighted all the budding romance of their temperaments. Sydney would never have written his Arcadia, nor Surrey have challenged the world in vindication of the beauties of his Geraldine. These are the men, my sons," the squire will continue, "that show to what our national character may be exalted, when its strong and powerful qualities are duly wrought up and refined. The solidest bodies are capable of the highest polish; and there is no character that may be wrought to a more exquisite and unsullied brightness, than that of the true English gentleman."

When Guy was about to depart for the army, the squire again took him aside, and gave him a long exhortation. He warned him against that affectation of cool-blooded indifference, which he was told was cultivated by the young British officers, among whom it was a study to "sink the soldier" in the mere man of fashion. "A soldier," said he, "without pride and enthusiasm in his profession, is a mere sanguinary hireling. Nothing distinguishes him from the mercenary bravo but a spirit of patriotism, or a thirst for glory. It is the fashion, now-a-days, my son," said he, "to laugh at the spirit of chivalry; when that spirit is really extinct, the profession of the soldier becomes a mere trade of blood." He then set before him the conduct of Edward the Black Prince, who is his mirror of chivalry; valiant, generous, affable, humane; gallant in the field; but when he came to dwell on his courtesy towards his prisoner, the king of France; how he received him into his tent, rather as a conqueror than as a captive; attended on him at table like one of his retinue; rode uncovered beside him on his entry into London, mounted on a common palfrey, while his prisoner was mounted in state on a white steed of stately beauty; the tears of enthusiasm stood in the old gentleman's eyes.

Finally, on taking leave, the good squire put in his son's hands, as a manual, one of his favourite old volumes, the Life of the Chevalier Bayard, by Godefroy; on a blank page of which he had written an extract from the Morte d'Arthur, containing the eulogy of Sir Ector over the body of Sir Launcelot of the Lake, which the squire considers as comprising the excellencies of a true soldier. "Ah, Sir Lancelot! thou wert head of all Christian knights; now there thou liest: thou were never matched of none earthly knights-hands. And thou wert the curtiest knight that ever bare shield. And thou were the truest friend to thy lover that ever bestrood horse; and thou were the truest lover of a sinfull man that ever loved woman. And thou were the kindest man that ever strook with sword; and thou were the goodliest person that ever came among the presse of knights. And thou were the meekest man and the gentlest that ever eate in hall among ladies. And thou were the sternest knight to thy mortal foe that ever put speare in the rest."

Fortune Telling

Each city, each town, and every village,
Affords us either an alms or pillage.
And if the weather be cold and raw,
Then in a barn we tumble on straw.
If warm and fair, by yea-cock and nay-cock,
The fields will afford us a hedge or a hay-cock.

Merry Beggars

As I was walking one evening with the Oxonian, Master Simon, and the general, in a meadow not far from the village, we heard the sound of a fiddle, rudely played, and looking in the direction from whence it came, we saw a thread of smoke curling up from among the trees. The sound of music is always attractive; for, wherever there is music, there is good humour, or good-will. We passed along a footpath, and had a peep, through a break in the hedge, at the musician and his party, when the Oxonian gave us a wink, and told us that if we would follow him we should have some sport.

It proved to be a gipsy encampment, consisting of three or four little cabins, or tents, made of blankets and sail cloth, spread over hoops that were stuck in the ground. It was on one side of a green lane, close under a hawthorn hedge, with a broad beech-tree spreading above it. A small rill tinkled along close by, through the fresh sward, that looked like a carpet.

A tea-kettle was hanging by a crooked piece of iron, over a fire made from dry sticks and leaves, and two old gipsies, in red cloaks, sat crouched on the grass, gossiping over their evening cup of tea; for these creatures, though they live in the open air, have their ideas of fireside comforts. There were two or three children sleeping on the straw with which the tents were littered; a couple of donkeys were grazing in the lane, and a thievish-looking dog was lying before the fire. Some of the younger gipsies were dancing to the music of a fiddle, played by a tall slender stripling, in an old frock coat, with a peacock's feather stuck in his hatband.

As we approached, a gipsy girl, with a pair of fine roguish eyes, came up, and, as usual, offered to tell our fortunes. I could not but admire a certain degree of slattern elegance about the baggage. Her long black silken hair was curiously plaited in numerous small braids, and negligently put up in a picturesque style that a painter might have been proud to have devised. Her dress was of figured chintz, rather ragged, and not over clean, but of a variety of most harmonious and agreeable colours; for these beings have a singularly fine eye for colours. Her straw hat was in her hand, and a red cloak thrown over one arm.

The Oxonian offered at once to have his fortune told, and the girl began with the usual volubility of her race; but he drew her on one side, near the hedge, as he said he had no idea of having his secrets overheard. I saw he was talking to her instead of she to him, and by his glancing towards us now and then, that he was giving the baggage some private hints. When they returned to us, he assumed a very serious air. "Zounds!" said he, "it's very astonishing how these creatures come by their knowledge; this girl has told me some things that I thought no one knew but myself!"

The girl now assailed the general: "Come, your honour," said she, "I see by your face you're a lucky man; but you're not happy in your mind; you're not, indeed, sir: but have a good heart, and give me a good piece of silver, and I'll tell you a nice fortune."

The general had received all her approaches with a banter, and had suffered her to get hold of his hand; but at the mention of the piece of silver, he hemmed, looked grave, and turning to us, asked if we had not better continue our walk. "Come, my master," said the girl, archly, "you'd not be in such a hurry, if you knew all that I could tell you about a fair lady that has a notion for you. Come, sir, old love burns strong; there's many a one comes to see weddings that go away brides themselves!"—Here the girl whispered something in a low voice, at which the general coloured up, was a little fluttered, and suffered himself to be drawn aside under the hedge, where he appeared to listen to her with great earnestness, and at the end paid her half-a-crown with the air of a man that has got the worth of his money.

The girl next made her attack upon Master Simon, who, however, was too old a bird to be caught, knowing that it would end in an attack upon his purse, about which he is a little sensitive. As he has a great notion, however, of being considered a royster, he chucked her under the chin, played her off with rather broad jokes, and put on something of the rake-helly air, that we see now and then assumed on the stage, by the sad-boy gentlemen of the old school. "Ah, your honour," said the girl, with a malicious leer, "you were not in such a tantrum last year, when I told you about the widow you know who; but if you had taken a friend's advice, you'd never have come away from Doncaster races with a flea in your ear!"

There was a secret sting in this speech that seemed quite to disconcert Master Simon. He jerked away his hand in a pet, smacked his whip, whistled to his dogs, and intimated that it was high time to go home. The girl, however, was determined not to lose her harvest. She now turned upon me, and, as I have a weakness of spirit where there is a pretty face concerned, she soon wheedled me out of my money, and, in return, read me a fortune; which, if it prove true, and I am determined to believe it, will make me one of the luckiest men in the chronicles of Cupid.

I saw that the Oxonian was at the bottom of all this oracular mystery, and was disposed to amuse himself with the general, whose tender approaches to the widow have attracted the notice of the wag. I was a little curious, however, to know the meaning of the dark hints which had so suddenly disconcerted Master Simon; and took occasion to fall in the rear with the Oxonian on our way home, when he laughed heartily at my questions, and gave me ample information on the subject.

The truth of the matter is, that Master Simon has met with a sad rebuff since my Christmas visit to the Hall. He used at that time to be joked about a widow, a fine dashing woman, as he privately informed me. I had supposed the pleasure he betrayed on these occasions resulted from the usual fondness of old bachelors for being teased about getting married, and about flirting, and being fickle and false-hearted. I am assured, however, that Master Simon had really persuaded himself the widow had a kindness for him; in consequence of which he had been at some extraordinary expense in new clothes, and had actually got Frank Bracebridge to order him a coat from Stultz. He began to throw out hints about the importance of a man's settling himself in life before he grew old; he would look grave whenever the widow and matrimony were mentioned in the same sentence; and privately asked the opinion of the squire and parson about the prudence of marrying a widow with a rich jointure, but who had several children.

An important member of a great family connexion cannot harp much upon the theme of matrimony without its taking wind; and it soon got buzzed about that Mr. Simon Bracebridge was actually gone to Doncaster races, with a new horse; but that he meant to return in a curricle with a lady by his side. Master Simon did, indeed, go to the races, and that with a new horse; and the dashing widow did make her appearance in her curricle; but it was unfortunately driven by a strapping young Irish dragoon, with whom even Master Simon's self-complacency would not allow him to venture into competition, and to whom she was married shortly after.

It was a matter of sore chagrin to Master Simon for several months, having never before been fully committed. The dullest head in the family had a joke upon him; and there is no one that likes less to be bantered than an absolute joker. He took refuge for a time at Lady Lillycraft's, until the matter should blow over; and occupied himself by looking over her accounts, regulating the village choir, and inculcating loyalty into a pet bullfinch, by teaching him to whistle "God save the King."

He has now pretty nearly recovered from the mortification; holds up his head, and laughs as much as any one; again affects to pity married men, and is particularly facetious about widows, when Lady Lillycraft is not by. His only time of trial is when the general gets hold of him, who is infinitely heavy and persevering in his waggery, and will interweave a dull joke through the various topics of a whole dinner-time.

Master Simon often parries these attacks by a stanza from his old work of "Cupid's Solicitor for Love:"

> " 'Tis in vain to wooe a widow over long,
>   In once or twice her mind you may perceive;
> Widows are subtle, be they old or young,
>   And by their wiles young men they will deceive."

Love-Charms

—— Come, do not weep, my girl,
Forget him, pretty pensiveness; there will
Come others, every day, as good as he.
                                        Sir J. Suckling

THE APPROACH of a wedding in a family is always an event of great importance, but particularly so in a household like this, in a retired part of the country. Master Simon, who is a pervading spirit, and, through means of the butler and housekeeper, knows every thing that goes forward, tells me that the maid-servants are continually trying their fortunes, and that the servants'-hall has of late been quite a scene of incantation.

It is amusing to notice how the oddities of the head of a family flow down through all the branches. The squire, in the indulgence of his love of every thing that smacks of old times, has held so many grave conversations with the parson at table, about popular superstitions and traditional rites, that they have been carried from the parlour to the kitchen by the listening domestics, and, being apparently sanctioned by such high authority, the whole house has become infected by them.

The servants are all versed in the common modes of trying luck, and the charms to ensure constancy. They read their fortunes by drawing strokes in the ashes, or by repeating a form of words, and looking in a pail of water. St. Mark's eve, I am told, was a busy time with them; being an appointed night for certain mystic ceremonies. Several of them sowed hemp-seed to be reaped by their true lovers; and they even ventured upon the solemn and fearful preparation of the dumb-cake. This must be done fasting, and in silence. The ingredients are handed down in traditional form. "An egg-shell full of salt, an eggshell full of malt, and an eggshell full of barley-meal." When the cake is ready, it is put upon a pan over the fire, and the future husband will appear; turn the cake, and retire; but if a word is spoken, or a fast is broken, during this awful ceremony, there is no knowing what horrible consequences would ensue!

The experiments, in the present instance, came to no result; they that sowed the hemp-seed forgot the magic rhyme that they were to pronounce, so the true lover never appeared; and as to the dumb-cake, what between the awful stillness they had to keep, and the awfulness of the midnight hour, their hearts failed them when they had put the cake in the pan; so that, on the striking of the great house-clock in the servants'-hall, they were seized with a sudden panic, and ran out of the room, to which they did not return until morning, when they found the mystic cake burnt to a cinder.

The most persevering at these spells, however, is Phœbe Wilkins, the housekeeper's niece. As she is a kind of privileged personage, and rather idle, she has more time to occupy herself with these matters. She has always had her head full of love and matrimony. She knows the dream-book by heart, and is quite an oracle among the little girls of the family, who always come to her to interpret their dreams in the mornings.

During the present gaiety of the house, however, the poor girl has worn a face full of trouble; and, to use the housekeeper's words, "has fallen into a sad hystericky way lately." It seems that she was born and brought up in the village, where her father was parish clerk, and she was an early playmate and sweetheart of young Jack Tibbets. Since she has come to live at the Hall, however, her head has been a little turned. Being very pretty, and naturally genteel, she has been much noticed and indulged; and being the housekeeper's niece, she has held an equivocal station between a servant and a companion. She has learnt something of fashions and notions among the young ladies, which have effected quite a metamorphosis; insomuch that her finery at church on Sundays has given mortal offence to her former intimates in the village. This has occasioned the misrepresentations which have awakened the implacable family pride of Dame Tibbets. But what is worse, Phœbe, having a spice of coquetry in her disposition, showed it on one or two occasions to her lover, which produced a downright quarrel; and Jack, being very proud and fiery, has absolutely turned his back upon her for several successive Sundays.

The poor girl is full of sorrow and repentance, and would fain make up with her lover; but he feels his security, and stands aloof. In this he is doubtless encouraged by his mother, who is continually reminding him what he owes to his family; for this same family pride seems doomed to be the eternal bane of lovers.

As I hate to see a pretty face in trouble, I have felt quite concerned for the luckless Phœbe, ever since I heard her story. It is a sad thing to be thwarted in love at any time, but particularly so at this tender season of the year, when every living thing, even to the very butterfly, is sporting with its mate; and the green fields, and the budding groves, and the singing of the birds, and the sweet smell of the flowers, are enough to turn the head of a love-sick girl. I am told that the coolness of young Ready Money lies very heavy at poor Phœbe's heart. Instead of singing about the house as formerly, she goes about pale and sighing, and is apt to break into tears when her companions are full of merriment.

Mrs. Hannah, the vestal gentlewoman of my Lady Lillycraft, has had long talks and walks with Phœbe, up and down the avenue, of an evening; and has endeavoured to squeeze some of her own verjuice into the other's milky nature. She speaks with contempt and abhorrence of the whole sex, and advises Phœbe to despise all the men as heartily as she does. But Phœbe's loving temper is not to be curdled; she has no such thing as hatred or contempt for mankind in her whole composition. She has all the simple fondness of heart of poor, weak, loving woman; and her only thoughts at present are how to conciliate and reclaim her wayward swain.

The spells and love-charms, which are matters of sport to the other domestics, are serious concerns with this love-stricken damsel. She is continually trying her fortune in a variety of ways. I am told that she has absolutely fasted for six Wednesdays and three Fridays successively, having understood that it was a sovereign charm to ensure being married to one's liking within the year. She carries about, also, a lock of her sweetheart's hair, and a riband he once gave her, being a mode of producing constancy in a lover. She even went so far as to try her fortune by the moon, which has always had much to do with lovers' dreams and fancies. For this purpose she went out in the night of the full moon, knelt on a stone in the meadow, and repeated the old traditional rhyme:

"All hail to thee, moon, all hail to thee;
I pray thee, good moon, now show to me
The youth who my future husband shall be."

When she came back to the house, she was faint and pale, and went immediately to bed. The next morning she told the porter's wife that she had seen some one close by the hedge in the meadow, which she was sure was young Tibbets; at any rate, she had dreamt of him all night; both of which, the old dame assured her, were most happy signs. It has since turned out that the person in the meadow was old Christy, the huntsman, who was walking his nightly rounds with the great stag-hound; so that Phœbe's faith in the charm is completely shaken.

The Library

YESTERDAY the fair Julia made her first appearance down stairs since her accident; and the sight of her spread an universal cheerfulness through the household. She was extremely pale, however, and could not walk without pain and difficulty. She was assisted, therefore, to a sofa in the library, which is pleasant and retired, looking out among trees; and so quiet that the little birds come hopping upon the windows, and peering curiously into the apartment. Here several of the family gathered round, and devised means to amuse her, and make the day pass pleasantly. Lady Lillycraft lamented the want of some new novel to while away the time; and was almost in a pet, because the "Author of Waverley" had not produced a work for the last three months.

There was a motion made to call on the parson for some of his old legends or ghost stories; but to this Lady Lillycraft objected, as they were apt to give her the vapours. General Harbottle gave a minute account, for the sixth time, of the disaster of a friend in India, who had his leg bitten off by a tyger whilst he was hunting; and was proceeding to menace the company with a chapter or two about Tippoo Saib.

At length the captain bethought himself, and said, he believed he had a manuscript tale lying in one corner of his campaigning trunk, which, if he could find, and the company were desirous, he would read to them. The offer was eagerly accepted. He retired, and soon returned with a roll of blotted manuscript, in a very gentlemanlike, but nearly illegible, hand, and a great part written on cartridge paper.

"It is one of the scribblings," said he, "of my poor friend, Charles Lightly, of the dragoons. He was a curious, romantic, studious, fanciful fellow; the favourite, and often the unconscious butt of his fellow officers, who entertained themselves with his eccentricities. He was in some of the hardest service in the peninsula, and distinguished himself by his gallantry. When the intervals of duty permitted, he was fond of roving about the country, visiting noted places, and was extremely fond of Moorish ruins. When at his quarters, he was a great scribbler, and passed much of his leisure with his pen in his hand.

"As I was a much younger officer, and a very young man, he took me, in a manner, under his care, and we became close friends. He used often to read his writings to me, having a great confidence in my taste, for I always praised them. Poor fellow! he was shot down close by me at Waterloo. We lay wounded together for some time, during a hard contest that took place near at hand. As I was least hurt, I tried to relieve him, and to stanch the blood which flowed from a wound in his breast. He lay with his head in my lap, and looked up thankfully in my face, but shook his head faintly, and made a sign that it was all over with him; and, indeed, he died a few minutes afterwards, just as our men had repulsed the enemy, and came to our relief. I have his favourite dog and his pistols to this day, and several of his manuscripts, which he gave to me at different times. The one I am now going to read, is a tale which he said he wrote in Spain, during the time that he lay ill of a wound received at Salamanca."

We now arranged ourselves to hear the story. The captain seated himself on the sofa, beside the fair Julia, who I had noticed to be somewhat affected by the picture he had care-lessly drawn of wounds and dangers in a field of battle. She now leaned her arm fondly on his shoulder, and her eye glistened as it rested on the manuscript of the poor, literary dragoon. Lady Lillycraft buried herself in a deep, well-cushioned elbow-chair. Her dogs were nestled on soft mats at her feet; and the gallant general took his station, in an arm-chair, at her side, and toyed with her elegantly ornamented work-bag. The rest of the circle being all equally well accommodated, the captain began his story; a copy of which I have procured for the benefit of the reader.

The Student of Salamanca

What a life doe I lead with my master; nothing but blowing of
bellowes, beating of spirits, and scraping of croslets! It is a very
secret science, for none almost can understand the language
of it. Sublimation, almigation, calcination, rubification, albifica-
tion, and fermentation; with as many termes unpossible to be
uttered as the arte to be compassed.

Lilly's Gallathea

ONCE UPON A TIME, in the ancient city of Grenada, there
sojourned a young man of the name of Antonio de
Castros. He wore the garb of a student of Salamanca, and was
pursuing a course of reading in the library of the university;
and, at intervals of leisure, indulging his curiosity by examining those remains of Moorish magnificence for which Grenada is renowned.

Whilst occupied in his studies, he frequently noticed an old
man of a singular appearance, who was likewise a visitor to
the library. He was lean and withered, though apparently
more from study than from age. His eyes, though bright and
visionary, were sunk in his head, and thrown into shade by
overhanging eyebrows. His dress was always the same: a
black doublet, a short black cloak, very rusty and threadbare,
a small ruff, and a large overshadowing hat.

His appetite for knowledge seemed insatiable. He would
pass whole days in the library absorbed in study, consulting a
multiplicity of authors, as though he were pursuing some interesting subject through all its ramifications; so that, in general, when evening came, he was almost buried among books
and manuscripts.

The curiosity of Antonio was excited, and he inquired of
the attendants concerning the stranger. No one could give
him any information, excepting that he had been for some
time past a casual frequenter of the library; that his reading
lay chiefly among the works treating of the occult sciences,
and that he was particularly curious in his inquiries after Arabian manuscripts. They added, that he never held communication with any one, excepting to ask for particular works;
that, after a fit of studious application, he would disappear

for several days, and even weeks, and when he revisited the library, he would look more withered and haggard than ever. The student felt interested by this account; he was leading rather a desultory life, and had all that capricious curiosity which springs up in idleness. He determined to make himself acquainted with this book-worm, and find out who and what he was.

The next time that he saw the old man at the library he commenced his approaches, by requesting permission to look into one of the volumes with which the unknown appeared to have done. The latter merely bowed his head in token of assent. After pretending to look through the volume with great attention, he returned it with many acknowledgements. The stranger made no reply.

"May I ask, senor," said Antonio, with some hesitation, "may I ask what you are searching after in all these books?"

The old man raised his head, with an expression of surprise, at having his studies interrupted for the first time, and by so intrusive a question. He surveyed the student with a side glance from head to foot: "Wisdom, my son," said he, calmly; "and the search requires every moment of my attention." He then cast his eyes upon his book and resumed his studies.

"But, father," said Antonio, "cannot you spare a moment to point out the road to others? It is to experienced travellers, like you, that we strangers in the paths of knowledge must look for directions in our journey."

The stranger looked disturbed: "I have not time enough, my son, to learn," said he, "much less to teach. I am ignorant myself of the path of true knowledge; how then can I show it to others?"

"Well, but father———."

"Senor," said the old man, mildly, but earnestly, "you must see that I have but few steps more to the grave. In that short space have I to accomplish the whole business of my existence. I have no time for words; every word is as one grain of sand of my glass wasted. Suffer me to be alone."

There was no replying to so complete a closing of the door of intimacy. The student found himself calmly, but totally repulsed. Though curious and inquisitive, yet he was naturally modest, and on after-thoughts he blushed at his own intrusion. His mind soon became occupied by other objects. He passed several days wandering among the mouldering piles of Moorish architecture, those melancholy monuments of an elegant and voluptuous people. He paced the deserted halls of the Alhambra, the paradise of the Moorish kings. He visited the great court of the lions, famous for the perfidious massacre of the gallant Abencerrages. He gazed with admiration at its mosaic cupolas, gorgeously painted in gold and azure; its basins of marble, its alabaster vase, supported by lions, and storied with inscriptions.

His imagination kindled as he wandered among these scenes. They were calculated to awaken all the enthusiasm of a youthful mind. Most of the halls have anciently been beautified by fountains. The fine taste of the Arabs delighted in the sparkling purity and reviving freshness of water, and they erected, as it were, altars on every side, to that delicate element. Poetry mingles with architecture in the Alhambra. It breathes along the very walls. Wherever Antonio turned his eye, he beheld inscriptions in Arabic, wherein the perpetuity of Moorish power and splendour within these walls was confidently predicted. Alas! how has the prophecy been falsified! Many of the basins, where the fountains had once thrown up their sparkling showers, were dry and dusty. Some of the palaces were turned into gloomy convents, and the bare-foot monk paced through those courts, which had once glittered with the array, and echoed to the music of Moorish chivalry.

In the course of his rambles, the student more than once encountered the old man of the library. He was always alone, and so full of thought as not to notice any one about him. He appeared to be intent upon studying those half-buried inscriptions, which are found, here and there, among the Moorish ruins, and seem to murmur from the earth the tale of former greatness. The greater part of these have since been translated; but they were supposed by many, at the time, to contain symbolical revelations, and golden maxims of the Arabian sages and astrologers. As Antonio saw the stranger apparently deciphering these inscriptions, he felt an eager longing to make his acquaintance, and to participate in his curious researches; but the repulse he had met with at the library deterred him from making any further advances.

He had directed his steps one evening to the sacred mount, which overlooks the beautiful valley watered by the Darro, the fertile plain of the Vega, and all that rich diversity of vale and mountain, that surrounds Grenada with an earthly paradise. It was twilight when he found himself at the place, where, at the present day, are situated the chapels known by the name of the Sacred Furnaces. They are so called from grottoes, in which some of the primitive saints are said to have been burnt. At the time of Antonio's visit, the place was an object of much curiosity. In an excavation of these grottoes, several manuscripts had recently been discovered, engraved on plates of lead. They were written in the Arabian language, excepting one, which was in unknown characters. The pope had issued a bull, forbidding any one, under pain of excommunication, to speak of these manuscripts. The prohibition had only excited the greater curiosity; and many reports were whispered about, that these manuscripts contained treasures of dark and forbidden knowledge.

As Antonio was examining the place from whence these mysterious manuscripts had been drawn, he again observed the old man of the library, wandering among the ruins. His curiosity was now fully awakened; the time and place served to stimulate it. He resolved to watch this groper after secret and forgotten lore, and to trace him to his habitation. There was something like adventure in the thing, that charmed his romantic disposition. He followed the stranger, therefore, at a little distance; at first cautiously, but he soon observed him to be so wrapped in his own thoughts, as to take little heed of external objects.

They passed along the skirts of the mountain, and then by the shady banks of the Darro. They pursued their way, for some distance from Grenada, along a lonely road that led among the hills. The gloom of evening was gathering, and it was quite dark when the stranger stopped at the portal of a solitary mansion.

It appeared to be a mere wing, or ruined fragment, of what had once been a pile of some consequence. The walls were of great thickness; the windows narrow, and generally secured by iron bars. The door was of planks, studded with iron spikes, and had been of great strength, though at present it was much decayed. At one end of the mansion was a ruinous tower, in the Moorish style of architecture. The edifice had probably been a country retreat, or castle of pleasure, during the occupation of Grenada by the Moors, and rendered sufficiently strong to withstand any casual assault in those warlike times.

The old man knocked at the portal. A light appeared at a small window just above it, and a female head looked out. It might have served as a model for one of Raphael's saints. The hair was beautifully braided, and gathered in a silken net; and the complexion, as well as could be judged from the light, was that soft, rich brunette, so becoming in southern beauty.

"It is I, my child," said the old man. The face instantly disappeared, and soon after a wicket-door in the large portal opened. Antonio, who had ventured near to the building, caught a transient sight of a delicate female form. A pair of fine black eyes darted a look of surprise at seeing a stranger hovering near, and the door was precipitately closed.

There was something in this sudden gleam of beauty that wonderfully struck the imagination of the student. It was like a brilliant flashing from its dark casket. He sauntered about, regarding the gloomy pile with increasing interest. A few simple, wild notes, from among some rocks and trees at a little distance, attracted his attention. He found there a group of Gitanas, a vagabond gipsy race, which at that time abounded in Spain, and lived in hovels and caves of the hills about the neighbourhood of Grenada. Some were busy about a fire, and others were listening to the uncouth music which one of their companions, seated on a ledge of the rock, was making with a split reed.

Antonio endeavoured to obtain some information of them concerning the old building and its inhabitants. The one who appeared to be their spokesman was a gaunt fellow, with a subtle gait, a whispering voice, and a sinister roll of the eye. He shrugged his shoulders on the student's inquiries, and said that all was not right in that building. An old man inhabited it, whom nobody knew, and whose family appeared to be only a daughter and a female servant. He and his companions, he added, lived up among the neighbouring hills; and as they had been about at night, they had often seen strange lights, and heard strange sounds from the tower. Some of the country people, who worked in the vineyards among the hills, believed the old man to be one that dealt in the black art, and were not over fond of passing near the tower at night; "but for our parts," said the Gitano, "we are not a people that trouble ourselves much with fears of that kind."

The student endeavoured to gain more precise information, but they had none to furnish him. They began to be solicitous for a compensation for what they had already imparted; and recollecting the loneliness of the place, and the vagabond character of his companions, he was glad to give them a gratuity, and to hasten homewards.

He sat down to his studies, but his brain was too full of what he had seen and heard; his eye was upon the page, but his fancy still returned to the tower, and he was continually picturing the little window, with the beautiful head peeping out; or the door half open, and the nymph-like form within. He retired to bed, but the same objects haunted his dreams. He was young and susceptible; and the excited state of his feelings, from wandering among the abodes of departed grace and gallantry, had predisposed him for a sudden impression from female beauty.

The next morning he strolled again in the direction of the tower. It was still more forlorn by the broad glare of day than in the gloom of evening. The walls were crumbling, and weeds and moss were growing in every crevice. It had the look of a prison rather than a dwelling-house. In one angle, however, he remarked a window which seemed an exception to the surrounding squalidness. There was a curtain drawn within it, and flowers standing on the window-stone. Whilst he was looking at it the curtain was partially withdrawn, and a delicate white arm, of the most beautiful roundness, was put forth to water the flowers.

The student made a noise to attract the attention of the fair florist. He succeeded. The curtain was further drawn, and he had a glance of the same lovely face he had seen the evening before; it was but a mere glance; the curtain again fell, and the casement closed. All this was calculated to excite the feelings of a romantic youth. Had he seen the unknown under other circumstances, it is probable that he would not have been struck with her beauty; but this appearance of being shut up and kept apart gave her the value of a treasured gem. He passed and repassed before the house several times in the course of the day, but saw nothing more. He was there again in the evening. The whole aspect of the house was dreary. The narrow windows emitted no rays of cheerful light, to indicate that there was social life within. Antonio listened at the portal, but no sound of voices reached his ear. Just then he heard the clapping to a distant door, and fearing to be detected in the unworthy act of eaves-dropping, he precipitately drew off to the opposite side of the road, and stood in the shadow of a ruined archway.

He now remarked a light from a window in the tower. It was fitful and changeable; commonly feeble and yellowish, as if from a lamp; with an occasional glare of some vivid metallic colour, followed by a dusky glow. A column of dense smoke would now and then rise in the air, and hang like a canopy over the tower. There was altogether such a loneliness and seeming mystery about the building and its inhabitants, that Antonio was half inclined to indulge the country people's notions, and to fancy it the den of some powerful sorcerer, and the fair damsel he had seen to be some spell-bound beauty.

After some time had elapsed, a light appeared in the window where he had seen the beautiful arm. The curtain was down, but it was so thin that he could perceive the shadow of some one passing and repassing between it and the light. He fancied that he could distinguish that the form was delicate; and from the alacrity of its movements, it was evidently youthful. He had not a doubt but this was the bed-chamber of his beautiful unknown.

Presently he heard the sound of a guitar, and a female voice singing. He drew near cautiously, and listened. It was a plaintive Moorish ballad, and he recognised in it the lamentations of one of the Abencerrages on leaving the walls of lovely Grenada. It was full of passion and tenderness. It spoke of the delights of early life; the hours of love it had enjoyed on the banks of the Darro, and among the blissful abodes of the Alhambra. It bewailed the fallen honours of the Abencerrages, and imprecated vengeance on their oppressors. Antonio was affected by the music. It singularly coincided with the place.

It was like the voice of past times echoed in the present, and breathing among the monuments of its departed glories.

The voice ceased; after a time the light disappeared, and all was still. "She sleeps!" said Antonio, fondly. He lingered about the building with the devotion with which a lover lingers about the bower of sleeping beauty. The rising moon threw its silver beams on the gray walls, and glittered on the casement. The late gloomy landscape gradually became flooded with its radiance. Finding, therefore, that he could no longer move about in obscurity, and fearful that his loiterings might be observed, he reluctantly retired.

The curiosity which had at first drawn the young man to the tower was now seconded by feelings of a more romantic kind. His studies were almost entirely abandoned. He maintained a kind of blockade of the old mansion; he would take a book with him, and pass a great part of the day under the trees in its vicinity; keeping a vigilant eye upon it, and endeavouring to ascertain what were the walks of his mysterious charmer. He found, however, that she never went out except to mass, when she was accompanied by her father. He waited at the door of the church, and offered her the holy water, in the hopes of touching her hand; a little office of gallantry common in catholic countries. She, however, modestly declined, without raising her eyes to see who made the offer, and always took it herself from the font. She was attentive in her devotion; her eyes were never taken from the altar or the priest; and, on returning home, her countenance was almost entirely concealed by her mantilla.

Antonio had now carried on the pursuit for several days, and was hourly getting more and more interested in the chase, but never a step nearer to the game. His lurkings about the house had probably been noticed, for he no longer saw the fair face at the window, nor the white arm put forth to water the flowers. His only consolation was to repair nightly to his post of observation and listen to her warbling, and if by chance he could catch a sight of her shadow, passing and repassing before the window, he thought himself most fortunate.

As he was indulging in one of these evening vigils, which were complete revels of the imagination, the sound of approaching footsteps made him withdraw into the deep shadow of the ruined archway, opposite to the tower. A cavalier approached, wrapped in a large Spanish cloak. He paused under the window of the tower, and after a little while began a serenade, accompanied by his guitar, in the usual style of Spanish gallantry. His voice was rich and manly; he touched the instrument with skill, and sang with amorous and impassioned eloquence. The plume of his hat was buckled by jewels that sparkled in the moon-beams; and, as he played on the guitar, his cloak falling off from one shoulder, showed him to be richly dressed. It was evident that he was a person of rank.

The idea now flashed across Antonio's mind, that the affections of his unknown beauty might be engaged. She was young, and doubtless susceptible; and it was not in the nature of Spanish females to be deaf and insensible to music and admiration. The surmise brought with it a feeling of dreariness. There was a pleasant dream of several days suddenly dispelled. He had never before experienced any thing of the tender passion; and, as its morning dreams are always delightful, he would fain have continued in the delusion.

"But what have I to do with her attachments?" thought he, "I have no claim on her heart, nor even on her acquaintance. How do I know that she is worthy of affection? Or if she is, must not so gallant a lover as this, with his jewels, his rank, and his detestable music, have completely captivated her? What idle humour is this that I have fallen into? I must again to my books. Study, study will soon chase away all these idle fancies!"

The more he thought, however, the more he became entangled in the spell which his lively imagination had woven round him; and now that a rival had appeared, in addition to the other obstacles that environed this enchanted beauty, she appeared ten times more lovely and desirable. It was some slight consolation to him to perceive that the gallantry of the unknown met with no apparent return from the tower. The light at the window was extinguished. The curtain remained undrawn, and none of the customary signals were given to intimate that the serenade was accepted.

The cavalier lingered for some time about the place, and

sang several other tender airs with a taste and feeling that made Antonio's heart ache; at length he slowly retired. The student remained with folded arms, leaning against the ruined arch, endeavouring to summon up resolution enough to depart; but there was a romantic fascination that still enchained him to the place. "It is the last time," said he, willing to compromise between his feelings and his judgment, "it is the last time; then let me enjoy the dream a few moments longer."

As his eye ranged about the old building to take a farewell look, he observed the strange light in the tower, which he had noticed on a former occasion. It kept beaming up and declining as before. A pillar of smoke rose in the air, and hung in sable volumes. It was evident the old man was busied in some of those operations that had gained him the reputation of a sorcerer throughout the neighbourhood.

Suddenly an intense and brilliant glare shone through the casement, followed by a loud report, and then a fierce and ruddy glow. A figure appeared at the window, uttering cries of agony or alarm; but immediately disappeared, and a body of smoke and flame whirled out of the narrow aperture. Antonio rushed to the portal, and knocked at it with vehemence. He was only answered by loud shrieks, and found that the females were already in helpless consternation. With an exertion of desperate strength he forced the wicket from its hinges, and rushed into the house.

He found himself in a small vaulted hall, and by the light of the moon which entered at the door, he saw a staircase to the left. He hurried up it to a narrow corridor, through which was rolling a volume of smoke. He found here the two females in a frantic state of alarm; one of them clasped her hands, and implored him to save her father.

The corridor terminated in a spiral flight of steps, leading up to the tower. He sprang up it to a small door, through the chinks of which came a glow of light, and smoke was spuming out. He burst it open, and found himself in an antique vaulted chamber, furnished with furnace, and various chemical apparatus. A shattered retort lay on the stone floor; a quantity of combustibles, nearly consumed, with various half-burnt books and papers, were sending up an expiring flame, and filling the chamber with stifling smoke. Just within the threshold lay the reputed conjuror. He was bleeding, his clothes were scorched, and he appeared lifeless. Antonio caught him up, and bore him down the stairs to a chamber in which there was a light, and laid him on a bed. The female domestic was despatched for such appliances as the house afforded; but the daughter threw herself frantically beside her parent, and could not be reasoned out of her alarm. Her dress was all in disorder; her dishevelled hair hung in rich confusion about her neck and bosom, and never was there beheld a lovelier picture of terror and affliction.

The skilfull assiduities of the scholar soon produced signs of returning animation in his patient. The old man's wounds, though severe, were not dangerous. They had evidently been produced by the bursting of the retort; in his bewilderment he had been enveloped in the stifling metallic vapours, which had overpowered his feeble frame, and had not Antonio arrived to his assistance, it is possible he might never have recovered.

By slow degrees he came to his senses. He looked about with a bewildered air at the chamber, the agitated group around, and the student who was leaning over him.

"Where am I?" said he, wildly.

At the sound of his voice his daughter uttered a faint exclamation of delight. "My poor Inez!" said he, embracing her; then putting his hand to his head, and taking it away stained with blood, he seemed suddenly to recollect himself and to be overcome with emotion.

"Ay!" cried he, "all is over with me! all gone! all vanished! gone in a moment! the labour of a lifetime lost!"

His daughter attempted to soothe him, but he became slightly delirious, and raved incoherently about malignant demons, and about the habitation of the green lion being destroyed. His wounds being dressed, and such other remedies administered as his situation required, he sunk into a state of quiet. Antonio now turned his attention to the daughter, whose sufferings had been little inferior to those of her father. Having with great difficulty succeeded in tranquillizing her fears, he endeavoured to prevail upon her to retire, and seek the repose so necessary to her frame, proffering to remain by her father until morning. "I am a stranger," said he, "it is true, and my offer may appear intrusive; but I see you are lonely and helpless, and I cannot help venturing over the limits of mere ceremony. Should you feel any scruple or doubt, however, say but a word, and I will instantly retire."

There was a frankness, a kindness, and a modesty mingled in Antonio's deportment that inspired instant confidence; and his simple scholar's garb was a recommendation in the house of poverty. The females consented to resign the sufferer to his care, as they would be the better able to attend to him on the morrow. On retiring, the old domestic was profuse in her benedictions; the daughter only looked her thanks; but as they shone through the tears that filled her fine black eyes, the student thought them a thousand times the most eloquent.

Here, then, he was, by a singular turn of chance, completely housed within this mysterious mansion. When left to himself, and the bustle of the scene was over, his heart throbbed as he looked round the chamber in which he was sitting. It was the daughter's room, the promised land towards which he had cast so many a longing gaze. The furniture was old, and had probably belonged to the building in its prosperous days; but every thing was arranged with propriety. The flowers that he had seen her attend stood in the window; a guitar leaned against a table, on which stood a crucifix, and before it lay a missal and a rosary. There reigned an air of purity and serenity about this little nestling place of innocence; it was the emblem of a chaste and quiet mind. Some few articles of female dress lay on the chairs; and there was the very bed on which she had slept; the pillow on which her soft cheek had reclined! The poor scholar was treading enchanted ground; for what fairy land has more of magic in it than the bed-chamber of innocence and beauty?

From various expressions of the old man in his ravings, and from what he had noticed on a subsequent visit to the tower, to see that the fire was extinguished, Antonio had gathered that his patient was an alchymist. The philosopher's stone was an object eagerly sought after by visionaries in those days; but in consequence of the superstitious prejudices of the times, and the frequent persecutions of its votaries, they were apt to pursue their experiments in secret; in lonely houses, in caverns and ruins, or in the privacy of cloistered cells.

In the course of the night the old man had several fits of restlessness and delirium; he would call out upon Theophrastus, and Geber, and Albertus Magnus, and other sages of his art; and anon would murmur about fermentation and projection, until, towards daylight, he once more sunk into a salutary sleep. When the morning sun darted his rays into the casement, the fair Inez, attended by the female domestic, came blushing into the chamber. The student now took his leave, having himself need of repose, but obtained ready permission to return and inquire after the sufferer.

When he called again, he found the alchymist languid and in pain, but apparently suffering more in mind than in body. His delirium had left him, and he had been informed of the particulars of his deliverance, and of the subsequent attentions of the scholar. He could do little more than look his thanks, but Antonio did not require them; his own heart repaid him for all that he had done, and he almost rejoiced in the disaster that had gained him an entrance into this mysterious habitation. The alchymist was so helpless as to need much assistance; Antonio remained with him therefore the greater part of the day. He repeated his visit the next day, and the next. Every day his company seemed more pleasing to the invalid; and every day he felt his interest in the latter increasing. Perhaps the presence of the daughter might have been at the bottom of this solicitude.

He had frequent and long conversations with the alchymist. He found him, as men of his pursuits were apt to be, a mixture of enthusiasm and simplicity; of curious and extensive reading on points of little utility, with great inattention to the every-day occurrences of life, and profound ignorance of the world. He was deeply versed in singular and obscure branches of knowledge, and much given to visionary speculations. Antonio, whose mind was of a romantic cast, had himself given some attention to the occult sciences, and he entered upon those themes with an ardour that delighted the philosopher. Their conversations frequently turned upon astrology, divination, and the great secret. The old man would forget his aches and wounds, rise up like a spectre in his bed, and kindle into eloquence on his favourite topics. When gently admonished of his situation, it would but prompt him to another sally of thought.

"Alas, my son!" he would say, "is not this very decrepitude and suffering another proof of the importance of those secrets with which we are surrounded? Why are we trammelled by disease, withered by old age, and our spirits quenched, as it were, within us, but because we have lost those secrets of life and youth which were known to our parents before their fall? To regain these have philosophers been ever since aspiring; but just as they are on the point of securing the precious secrets for ever, the brief period of life is at an end; they die, and with them all their wisdom and experience. 'Nothing,' as De Nuysment observes, 'nothing is wanting for man's perfection but a longer life, less crossed with sorrows and maladies, to the attaining of the full and perfect knowledge of things.' "

At length Antonio so far gained on the heart of his patient, as to draw from him the outlines of his story.

Felix de Vasquez, the alchymist, was a native of Castile, and of an ancient and honourable line. Early in life he had married a beautiful female, a descendant from one of the Moorish families. The marriage displeased his father, who considered the pure Spanish blood contaminated by this foreign mixture. It is true, the lady traced her descent from one of the Abencerrages, the most gallant of Moorish cavaliers, who had embraced the christian faith on being exiled from the walls of Grenada. The injured pride of the father, however, was not to be appeased. He never saw his son afterwards; and on dying left him but a scanty portion of his estate; bequeathing the residue, in the piety and bitterness of his heart, to the erection of convents, and the performance of masses for souls in purgatory. Don Felix resided for a long time in the neighbourhood of Valladolid in a state of embarrassment and obscurity. He devoted himself to intense study, having, while at the university of Salamanca, imbibed a taste for the secret sciences. He was enthusiastic and speculative; he went on from one branch of knowledge to another, until he became zealous in the search after the grand Arcanum.

He had at first engaged in the pursuit with the hopes of raising himself from his present obscurity, and resuming the rank and dignity to which his birth entitled him; but, as usual, it ended in absorbing every thought, and becoming the business of his existence. He was at length aroused from this mental abstraction by the calamities of his household. A malignant fever swept off his wife and all his children, excepting an infant daughter. These losses for a time overwhelmed and stupefied him. His home had in a manner died away from around him, and he felt lonely and forlorn. When his spirit revived within him, he determined to abandon the scene of his humiliation and disaster; to bear away the child that was still left him, beyond the scene of contagion, and never to return to Castile until he should be enabled to reclaim the honours of his line.

He had ever since been wandering and unsettled in his abode. Sometimes the resident of populous cities, at other times of absolute solitudes. He had searched libraries, meditated on inscriptions, visited adepts of different countries, and sought to gather and concentrate the rays which had been thrown by various minds upon the secrets of alchymy. He had at one time travelled quite to Padua to search for the manuscripts of Pietro d'Abano, and to inspect an urn which had been dug up near Este, supposed to have been buried by Maximus Olybius, and to have contained the grand elixir.*

While at Padua he had met with an adept versed in Arabian lore, who talked of the invaluable manuscripts that must remain in the Spanish libraries, preserved from the spoils of the Moorish academies and universities; of the probability of meeting with precious unpublished writings of Geber, and Alfarabius, and Avicenna, the great physicians of the Arabian schools, who, it was well known, had treated much of alchymy; but above all, he spoke of the Arabian tablets of lead,

*This urn was found in 1533. It contained a lesser one, in which was a burning lamp betwixt two small vials, the one of gold, the other of silver, both of them full of a very clear liquor. On the largest was an inscription, stating that Maximus Olybius shut up in this small vessel elements which he had prepared with great toil. There were many disquisitions among the learned on the subject. It was the most received opinion, that this Maximus Olybius was an inhabitant of Padua, that he had discovered the great secret, and that these vessels contained liquor, one to transmute metals to gold, the other to silver. The peasants who found the urns, imagining this precious liquor to be common water, spilt every drop, so that the art of transmuting metals remains as much a secret as ever.

which had recently been dug up in the neighbourhood of Grenada, and which, it was confidently believed among adepts, contained the lost secrets of the art.

The indefatigable alchymist once more bent his steps for Spain, full of renovated hope. He had made his way to Grenada: he had wearied himself in the study of Arabic, in decyphering inscriptions, in rummaging libraries, and exploring every possible trace left by the Arabian sages.

In all his wanderings he had been accompanied by Inez; through the rough and the smooth, the pleasant and the adverse; never complaining, but rather seeking to soothe his cares by her innocent and playful caresses. Her instruction had been the employment and the delight of his hours of relaxation. She had grown up while they were wandering, and had scarcely ever known any home but by his side. He was family, friends, home, every thing to her. He had carried her in his arms when they first began their wayfaring; had nestled her, as an eagle does its young, among the rocky heights of the Sierra Morena; she had sported about him in childhood in the solitudes of the Bateucas; had followed him, as a lamb does the shepherd, over the rugged Pyrenees, and into the fair plains of Languedoc; and now she was grown up to support his feeble steps among the ruined abodes of her maternal ancestors.

His property had gradually wasted away in the course of his travels and his experiments. Still hope, the constant attendant of the alchymist, had led him on; ever on the point of reaping the reward of his labours, and ever disappointed. With the credulity that often attended his art, he attributed many of his disappointments to the machinations of the malignant spirits that beset the path of the alchymist, and torment him in his solitary labours. "It is their constant endeavour," he observed, "to close up every avenue to those sublime truths, which would enable man to rise above the abject state into which he has fallen, and to return to his original perfection." To the evil offices of these demons he attributed his late disaster. He had been on the very verge of the glorious discovery; never were the indications more completely auspicious; all was going on prosperously, when, at the critical moment which should have crowned his labours with success, and have placed him at the very summit of human power and felicity, the bursting of a retort had reduced his laboratory and himself to ruins.

"I must now," said he, "give up at the very threshold of success. My books and papers are burnt; my apparatus is broken. I am too old to bear up against these evils. The ardour that once inspired me is gone; my poor frame is exhausted by study and watchfulness, and this last misfortune has hurried me towards the grave." He concluded in a tone of deep dejection. Antonio endeavoured to comfort and reassure him; but the poor alchymist had for once awakened to a consciousness of the worldly ills that were gathering around him, and had sunk into despondency. After a pause, and some thoughtfulness and perplexity of brow, Antonio ventured to make a proposal.

"I have long," said he, "been filled with a love for the secret sciences, but have felt too ignorant and diffident to give myself up to them. You have acquired experience; you have amassed the knowledge of a lifetime; it were a pity it should be thrown away. You say you are too old to renew the toils of the laboratory; suffer me to undertake them. Add your knowledge to my youth and activity, and what shall we not accomplish? As a probationary fee, and a fund on which to proceed, I will bring into the common stock a sum of gold, the residue of a legacy, which has enabled me to complete my education. A poor scholar cannot boast much; but I trust we shall soon put ourselves beyond the reach of want; and if we should fail, why, I must depend, like other scholars, upon my brains to carry me through the world."

The philosopher's spirits, however, were more depressed than the student had imagined. This last shock, following in the rear of so many disappointments, had almost destroyed the reaction of his mind. The fire of an enthusiast, however, is never so low, but that it may be blown again into a flame. By degrees the old man was cheered and reanimated by the buoyancy and ardour of his sanguine companion. He at length agreed to accept of the services of the student, and once more to renew his experiments. He objected, however, to using the student's gold, notwithstanding that his own was nearly exhausted; but this objection was soon overcome; the student insisted on making it a common stock and common cause;—and then how absurd was any delicacy about such a trifle, with men who looked forward to discovering the philosopher's stone!

While, therefore, the alchymist was slowly recovering, the student busied himself in getting the laboratory once more in order. It was strewed with the wrecks of retorts and alembics, with old crucibles, boxes and phials of powders and tinctures, and half-burnt books and manuscripts.

As soon as the old man was sufficiently recovered, the studies and experiments were renewed. The student became a privileged and frequent visitor, and was indefatigable in his toils in the laboratory. The philosopher daily derived new zeal and spirits from the animation of his disciple. He was now enabled to prosecute the enterprise with continued exertion, having so active a coadjutor to divide the toil. While he was poring over the writings of Sandivogius, and Philalethes, and Dominus de Nuysment, and endeavouring to comprehend the symbolical language in which they have locked up their mysteries, Antonio would occupy himself among the retorts and crucibles, and keep the furnace in a perpetual glow.

With all his zeal, however, for the discovery of the golden art, the feelings of the student had not cooled as to the object that first drew him to this ruinous mansion. During the old man's illness, he had frequent opportunities of being near the daughter; and every day made him more sensible to her charms. There was a pure simplicity, and an almost passive gentleness in her manners; yet with all this was mingled something, whether mere maiden shyness, or a consciousness of high descent, or a dash of Castilian pride, or perhaps all united, that prevented undue familiarity, and made her difficult of approach. The danger of her father, and the measures to be taken for his relief, had at first overcome this coyness and reserve; but as he recovered and her alarm subsided, she seemed to shrink from the familiarity she had indulged with the youthful stranger, and to become every day more shy and silent.

Antonio had read many books, but this was the first volume of womankind that he had ever studied. He had been captivated with the very title-page; but the further he read the more he was delighted. She seemed formed to love; her soft black eye rolled languidly under its long silken lashes, and wherever it turned, it would linger and repose; there was tenderness in every beam. To him alone she was reserved and distant. Now that the common cares of the sick room were at an end, he saw little more of her than before his admission to the house. Sometimes he met her on his way to and from the laboratory, and at such times there was ever a smile and a blush; but, after a simple salutation, she glided on and disappeared.

" 'Tis plain," thought Antonio, "my presence is indifferent, if not irksome to her. She has noticed my admiration, and is determined to discourage it; nothing but a feeling of gratitude prevents her treating me with marked distaste—and then has she not another lover, rich, gallant, splendid, musical? how can I suppose she would turn her eyes from so brilliant a cavalier, to a poor obscure student, raking among the cinders of her father's laboratory?"

Indeed, the idea of the amorous serenader continually haunted his mind. He felt convinced that he was a favoured lover; yet, if so, why did he not frequent the tower? Why did he not make his approaches by noon-day? There was mystery in this eaves-dropping and musical courtship. Surely Inez could not be encouraging a secret intrigue! Oh, no! she was too artless, too pure, too ingenuous! But then the Spanish females were so prone to love and intrigue; and music and moonlight were so seductive, and Inez had such a tender soul languishing in every look.—"Oh!" would the poor scholar exclaim, clasping his hands, "Oh that I could but once behold those loving eyes beaming on me with affection!"

It is incredible to those who have not experienced it, on what scanty aliment human life and human love may be supported. A dry crust, thrown now and then to a starving man, will give him a new lease of existence; and a faint smile, or a kind look, bestowed at casual intervals, will keep a lover loving on, when a man in his sober senses would despair.

When Antonio found himself alone in the laboratory his mind would be haunted by one of these looks, or smiles, which he had received in passing. He would set it in every possible light, and argue on it with all the self-pleasing, self-teasing logic of a lover.

The country around him was enough to awaken that voluptuousness of feeling so favourable to the growth of passion. The window of the tower rose above the trees of the romantic valley of the Darro, and looked down upon some of the loveliest scenery of the Vega, where groves of citron and orange were refreshed by cool springs and brooks of the purest water. The Xenel and the Darro wound their shining streams along the plain, and gleamed from among its bowers. The surrounding hills were covered with vineyards, and the mountains crowned with snow seemed to melt into the blue sky. The delicate airs that played about the tower were perfumed by the fragrance of myrtle and orange blossoms, and the ear was charmed with the fond warbling of the nightingale, which, in these happy regions, sings the whole day long. Sometimes, too, there was the idle song of the muleteer, sauntering along the solitary road; or the notes of the guitar from some group of peasants dancing in the shade. All these were enough to fill the head of a young lover with poetic fancies; and Antonio would picture to himself how he could loiter among those happy groves, and wander by those gentle rivers, and love away his life with Inez.

He felt at times impatient at his own weakness, and would endeavour to brush away these cobwebs of the mind. He would turn his thought, with sudden effort, to his occult studies, or occupy himself in some perplexing process; but often, when he had partially succeeded in fixing his attention, the sound of Inez' lute, or the soft notes of her voice, would come stealing upon the stillness of the chamber, and, as it were, floating round the tower. There was no great art in her performance; but Antonio thought he had never heard music comparable to this. It was perfect witchcraft to hear her warble forth some of her national melodies; those little Spanish romances and Moorish ballads that transport the hearer, in idea, to the banks of the Guadalquiver, or the walls of the Alhambra, and make him dream of beauties, and balconies, and moonlight serenades.

Never was poor student more sadly beset than Antonio. Love is a troublesome companion in a study at the best of times; but in the laboratory of an alchymist his intrusion is terribly disastrous. Instead of attending to the retorts and crucibles, and watching the process of some experiment intrusted to his charge, the student would get entranced in one of these love-dreams, from which he would often be aroused by some fatal catastrophe. The philosopher, on returning from his researches in the libraries, would find every thing gone wrong, and Antonio in despair over the ruins of the whole day's work. The old man, however, took all quietly, for his had been a life of experiment and failure.

"We must have patience, my son," would he say, "as all the great masters that have gone before us have had. Errors, and accidents, and delays, are what we have to contend with. Did not Pontanus err two hundred times before he could obtain even the matter on which to found his experiments? The great Flamel, too, did he not labour four and twenty years, before he ascertained the first agent? What difficulties and hardships did not Cartilaceus encounter, at the very threshold of his discoveries? And Bernard de Treves, even after he had attained a knowledge of all the requisites, was he not delayed full three years? What you consider accidents, my son, are the machinations of our invisible enemies. The treasures and golden secrets of nature are surrounded by spirits hostile to man. The air about us teems with them. They lurk in the fire of the furnace, in the bottom of the crucible and the alembic, and are ever on the alert to take advantage of those moments when our minds are wandering from intense meditation on the great truth that we are seeking. We must only strive the more to purify ourselves from those gross and earthly feelings which becloud the soul, and prevent her from piercing into nature's arcana."

"Alas!" thought Antonio, "if to be purified from all earthly feeling requires that I should cease to love Inez, I fear I shall never discover the philosopher's stone!"

In this way matters went on for some time at the alchymist's. Day after day was sending the student's gold in vapour up the chimney; every blast of the furnace made him a ducat the poorer, without apparently helping him a jot nearer to the golden secret. Still the young man stood by, and saw piece after piece disappearing without a murmur; he had daily an opportunity of seeing Inez, and felt as if her favour would be better than silver or gold, and that every smile was worth a ducat.

Sometimes, in the cool of the evening, when the toils of the laboratory happened to be suspended, he would walk with the alchymist in what had once been a garden belonging to the mansion. There were still the remains of terraces and balustrades, and here and there a marble urn, or mutilated statue overturned, and buried among weeds and flowers run wild. It was the favourite resort of the alchymist in his hours of relaxation, where he would give full scope to his visionary flights. His mind was tinctured with the Rosycrucian doctrines. He believed in elementary beings; some favourable, others adverse to his pursuits; and in the exaltation of his fancy, had often imagined that he held communion with them in his solitary walks about the whispering groves and echoing walls of this old garden.

When accompanied by Antonio, he would prolong these evening recreations. Indeed, he sometimes did it out of consideration for his disciple, for he feared lest his too close application, and his incessant seclusion in the tower, should be injurious to his health. He was delighted and surprised by this extraordinary zeal and perseverance in so young a tyro, and looked upon him as destined to be one of the great luminaries of the art. Lest the student should repine at the time lost in these relaxations, the good alchymist would fill them up with wholesome knowledge, in matters connected with their pursuits; and would walk up and down the alleys with his disciple, imparting oral instruction, like an ancient philosopher. In all his visionary schemes there breathed a spirit of lofty, though chimerical, philanthropy, that won the admiration of the scholar. Nothing sordid, nor sensual; nothing petty nor selfish seemed to enter into his views, in respect to the grand discoveries he was anticipating. On the contrary his imagination kindled with conceptions of widely dispensated happiness. He looked forward to the time when he should be able to go about the earth relieving the indigent, comforting the distressed; and, by his unlimited means, devising and executing plans for the complete extirpation of poverty, and all its attendant sufferings and crimes. Never were grander schemes for general good, for the distribution of boundless wealth and universal competence, devised, than by this poor, indigent alchymist in his ruined tower.

Antonio would attend these peripatetic lectures with all the ardour of a devotee; but there was another circumstance which may have given a secret charm to them. The garden was the resort also of Inez, where she took her walks of recreation; the only exercise that her secluded life permitted. As Antonio was duteously pacing by the side of his instructor, he would often catch a glimpse of the daughter, walking pensively about the alleys in the soft twilight. Sometimes they would meet her unexpectedly, and the heart of the student would throb with agitation. A blush too would crimson the cheek of Inez, but still she passed on, and never joined them.

He had remained one evening, until rather a late hour, with the alchymist in this favourite resort. It was a delightful night after a sultry day, and the balmy air of the garden was peculiarly reviving. The old man was seated on a fragment of a pedestal, looking like a part of the ruin on which he sat. He was edifying his pupil by long lessons of wisdom from the stars, as they shone out with brilliant lustre in the dark blue vault of a southern sky; for he was deeply versed in Behmen, and other of the Rosicrucians, and talked much of the signature of earthly things, and passing events, which may be discerned in the heavens; of the power of the stars over corporeal beings, and their influence on the fortunes of the sons of men.

By degrees the moon rose, and shed her gleaming light among the groves. Antonio apparently listened with fixed attention to the sage, but his ear was drinking in the melody of Inez' voice, who was singing to her lute in one of the moonlight glades of the garden. The old man having exhausted his theme, sat gazing in silent reverie at the heavens. Antonio could not resist an inclination to steal a look at this coy beauty, who was thus playing the part of the nightingale, so sequestered and musical. Leaving the alchymist in his celestial reverie, he stole gently along one of the alleys. The music had ceased, and he thought he heard the sound of voices. He came to an angle of a copse that had screened a kind of green recess, ornamented by a marble fountain. The moon shone full upon the place, and by its light, he beheld his unknown serenading rival at the feet of Inez. He was detaining her by the hand, which he covered with kisses; but at sight of Antonio he started up and half drew his sword, while Inez, disengaged, fled back to the house.

All the jealous doubts and fears of Antonio were now confirmed. He did not remain to encounter the resentment of his happy rival at being thus interrupted, but turned from the place in sudden wretchedness of heart. That Inez should love another would have been misery enough; but that she should be capable of a dishonourable amour, shocked him to the soul. The idea of deception in so young and apparently artless a being, brought with it that sudden distrust in human nature, so sickening to a youthful and ingenuous mind; but when he thought of the kind, simple parent she was deceiving, whose affections all centered in her, he felt for a moment a sentiment of indignation, and almost of aversion.

He found the alchymist still seated in his visionary contemplation of the moon. "Come hither, my son," said he, with his usual enthusiasm; "come, read with me in this vast volume of wisdom, thus nightly unfolded for our perusal. Wisely did the Chaldean sages affirm, that the heaven is as a mystic page, uttering speech to those who can rightly understand; warning them of good and evil, and instructing them in the secret decrees of fate."

The student's heart ached for his venerable master; and, for a moment he felt the futility of all his occult wisdom. "Alas! poor old man!" thought he, "of what avails all thy study? Little dost thou dream, while busied in airy speculations among the stars, what a treason against thy happiness is going on under thine eyes; as it were, in thy very bosom!— Oh Inez! Inez! where shall we look for truth and innocence; where shall we repose confidence in woman, if even you can deceive?"

It was a trite apostrophe, such as every lover makes when he finds his mistress not quite such a goddess as he had painted her. With the student, however, it sprung from honest anguish of heart. He returned to his lodgings in pitiable confusion of mind. He now deplored the infatuation that had led him on until his feelings were so thoroughly engaged. He resolved to abandon his pursuits at the tower, and trust to absence to dispel the fascination by which he had been spellbound. He no longer thirsted after the discovery of the grand elixir: the dream of alchymy was over; for without Inez, what was the value of the philosopher's stone?

He rose, after a sleepless night, with the determination of taking his leave of the alchymist, and tearing himself from Grenada. For several days did he rise with the same resolution, and every night saw him come back to his pillow to repine at his want of resolution, and to make fresh determinations for the morrow. In the meanwhile he saw less of Inez than ever. She no longer walked in the garden, but remained almost entirely in her apartment. When she met him, she blushed more than usual; and once hesitated, as if she would have spoken; but after a temporary embarrassment, and still deeper blushes, she made some casual observation, and retired. Antonio read in this confusion, a consciousness of fault, and of that fault's being discovered. "What could she have wished to communicate? Perhaps to account for the scene in the garden;—but how can she account for it, or why should she account for it to me? What am I to her?—or rather, what is she to me?" exclaimed he, impatiently; with a new resolution to break through these entanglements of the heart, and fly from this enchanted spot for ever.

He was returning that very night to his lodgings, full of this excellent determination, when, in a shadowy part of the road, he passed a person, whom he recognized, by his height and form, for his rival. He was going in the direction of the tower. If any lingering doubts remained, here was an opportunity of settling them completely. He determined to follow this unknown cavalier, and, under favour of the darkness, observe his movements. If he obtained access to the tower, or in any way a favourable reception, Antonio felt as if it would be a relief to his mind, and would enable him to fix his wavering resolution.

The unknown, as he came near the tower, was more cautious and stealthy in his approaches. He was joined under a clump of trees by another person, and they had much whispering together. A light was burning in the chamber of Inez, the curtain was down, but the casement was left open, as the

night was warm. After some time, the light was extinguished.
A considerable interval elapsed. The cavalier and his companion remained under covert of the trees, as if keeping watch.
At length they approached the tower with silent and cautious
steps. The cavalier received a dark lantern from his companion, and threw off his cloak. The other then softly brought
something from the clump of trees, which Antonio perceived
to be a light ladder. He placed it against the wall, and the
serenader gently ascended. A sickening sensation came over
Antonio. Here was indeed a confirmation of every fear. He
was about to leave the place, never to return, when he heard
a stifled shriek from Inez' chamber.

In an instant the fellow that stood at the foot of the ladder
lay prostrate on the ground. Antonio wrested a stiletto from
his nerveless hand, and hurried up the ladder. He sprang in
at the window, and found Inez struggling in the grasp of his
fancied rival: the latter, disturbed from his prey, caught up
his lantern, turned its light full upon Antonio, and drawing
his sword, made a furious assault; luckily the student saw the
light gleam along the blade, and parried the thrust with the
stiletto. A fierce but unequal combat ensued. Antonio fought
exposed to the full glare of the light, while his antagonist was
in shadow. His stiletto, too, was but a poor defence against a
rapier. He saw that nothing would save him but closing with
his adversary and getting within his weapon; he rushed
furiously upon him, and gave him a severe blow with the
stiletto; but received a wound in return from the shortened
sword. At the same moment a blow was inflicted from behind, by the confederate, who had ascended the ladder; it
felled him to the floor, and his antagonists made their escape.

By this time the cries of Inez had brought her father and
the domestic to the room. Antonio was found weltering in
his blood, and senseless. He was conveyed to the chamber of
the alchymist, who now repaid in kind the attentions which
the student had once bestowed upon him. Among his varied
knowledge he possessed some skill in surgery, which at this
moment was of more value than even his chymical lore. He
stanched and dressed the wounds of his disciple, which on
examination proved less desperate than he had at first apprehended. For a few days, however, his case was anxious, and

attended with danger. The old man watched over him with the affection of a parent. He felt a double debt of gratitude towards him on account of his daughter and himself; he loved him too as a faithful and zealous disciple; and he dreaded lest the world should be deprived of the promising talents of so aspiring an alchymist.

An excellent constitution soon medicined his wounds; and there was a balsam in the looks and words of Inez, that had a healing effect on still severer wounds which he carried in his heart. She displayed the strongest interest in his safety; she called him her deliverer, her preserver. It seemed as if her grateful disposition sought, in the warmth of its acknowledgments, to repay him for past coldness. But what most contributed to Antonio's recovery, was her explanation concerning his supposed rival. It was some time since he had first beheld her at church, and he had ever since persecuted her with his attentions. He had beset her in her walks, until she had been obliged to confine herself to the house, except when accompanied by her father. He had besieged her with letters, serenades, and every art by which he could urge a vehement, but clandestine and dishonourable suit. The scene in the garden was as much of a surprise to her as to Antonio. Her persecutor had been attracted by her voice, and had found his way over a ruined part of the wall. He had come upon her unawares; was detaining her by force, and pleading his insulting passion, when the appearance of the student interrupted him, and enabled her to make her escape. She had forborne to mention to her father the persecution which she suffered; she wished to spare him unavailing anxiety and distress, and had determined to confine herself more rigorously to the house; though it appeared that even here she had not been safe from his daring enterprise.

Antonio inquired whether she knew the name of this impetuous admirer? She replied, that he had made his advances under a fictitious name; but that she had heard him once called by the name of Don Ambrosio de Loxa.

Antonio knew him, by report, for one of the most determined and dangerous libertines in all Grenada. Artful, accomplished, and, if he chose to be so, insinuating; but daring and headlong in the pursuit of his pleasures; violent and implacable in his resentments. He rejoiced to find that Inez had been proof against his seductions, and had been inspired with aversion by his splendid profligacy; but he trembled to think of the dangers she had run, and he felt solicitude about the dangers that must yet environ her.

At present, however, it was probable the enemy had a temporary quietus. The traces of blood had been found for some distance from the ladder, until they were lost among thickets; and as nothing had been heard or seen of him since, it was concluded that he had been seriously wounded.

As the student recovered from his wounds, he was enabled to join Inez and her father in their domestic intercourse. The chamber in which they usually met had probably been a saloon of state in former times. The floor was of marble; the walls partially covered with remains of tapestry; the chairs, richly carved and gilt, were crazed with age, and covered with tarnished and tattered brocade. Against the wall hung a long, rusty rapier, the only relique that the old man retained of the chivalry of his ancestors. There might have been something to provoke a smile in the contrast between the mansion and its inhabitants; between present poverty and the traces of departed grandeur; but the fancy of the student had thrown so much romance about the edifice and its inmates, that every thing was clothed with charms. The philosopher, with his broken-down pride, and his strange pursuits, seemed to comport with the melancholy ruin he inhabited; and there was a native elegance of spirit about the daughter, that showed she would have graced the mansion in its happier days.

What delicious moments were these to the student! Inez was no longer coy and reserved. She was naturally artless and confiding; though the kind of persecution she had experienced from one admirer had rendered her, for a time, suspicious and circumspect towards the other. She now felt an entire confidence in the sincerity and worth of Antonio, mingled with an overflowing gratitude. When her eyes met his, they beamed with sympathy and kindness; and Antonio, no longer haunted by the idea of a favoured rival, once more aspired to success.

At these domestic meetings, however, he had little opportunity of paying his court, except by looks. The alchymist

supposing him, like himself, absorbed in the study of alchymy, endeavoured to cheer the tediousness of his recovery
by long conversations on the art. He even brought several of
his half-burnt volumes, which the student had once rescued
from the flames, and rewarded him for their preservation, by
reading copious passages. He would entertain him with the
great and good acts of Flamel, which he effected through
means of the philosopher's stone, relieving widows and or-
phans, founding hospitals, building churches, and what not;
or with the interrogatories of King Kalid, and the answers of
Morienus, the Roman hermit of Hierusalem; or the profound
questions which Elardus, a necromancer of the province of
Catalonia, put to the Devil, touching the secrets of alchymy,
and the Devil's replies.

All these were couched in occult language, almost unintelligible to the unpractised ear of the disciple. Indeed, the old
man delighted in the mystic phrases and symbolical jargon in
which the writers that have treated of alchymy have wrapped
their communications; rendering them incomprehensible except to the initiated. With what rapture would he elevate his
voice at a triumphant passage, announcing the grand discovery! "Thou shalt see," would he exclaim in the words of
Henry Kuhnrade,* "the stone of the philosophers (our king)
go forth of the bedchamber of his glassy sepulchre into the
theatre of this world; that is to say, regenerated and made
perfect, a shining carbuncle, a most temperate splendour,
whose most subtle and depurated parts are inseparable, united
into one with a concordial mixture, exceeding equal, transparent as chrystal, shining red like a ruby, permanently colouring
or ringing, fixt in all temptations or tryals; yea, in the examination of the burning sulphur itself, and the devouring waters, and in the most vehement persecution of the fire, always
incombustible and permanent as a salamander!"

The student had a high veneration for the fathers of alchymy, and a profound respect for his instructor; but what
was Henry Kuhnrade, Geber, Lully, or even Albertus Magnus
himself, compared to the countenance of Inez, which presented such a page of beauty to his perusal? While, therefore,

*Amphitheatre of the Eternal Wisdom.

the good alchymist was doling out knowledge by the hour, his disciple would forget books, alchymy, every thing but the lovely object before him. Inez, too, unpractised in the science of the heart, was gradually becoming fascinated by the silent attentions of her lover. Day by day she seemed more and more perplexed by the kindling and strangely pleasing emotions of her bosom. Her eye was often cast down in thought. Blushes stole to her cheek without any apparent cause, and light, half-suppressed sighs, would follow these short fits of musing. Her little ballads, though the same that she had always sung, yet breathed a more tender spirit. Either the tones of her voice were more soft and touching, or some passages were delivered with a feeling which she had never before given them. Antonio, besides his love for the abstruse sciences, had a pretty turn for music; and never did philosopher touch the guitar more tastefully. As, by degrees, he conquered the mutual embarrassment that kept them asunder, he ventured to accompany Inez in some of her songs. He had a voice full of fire and tenderness; as he sang, one would have thought, from the kindling blushes of his companion, that he had been pleading his own passion in her ear. Let those who would keep two youthful hearts asunder beware of music. Oh! this leaning over chairs, and conning the same music book, and entwining of voices, and melting away in harmonies!—the German waltz is nothing to it.

The worthy alchymist saw nothing of all this. His mind could admit of no idea that was not connected with the discovery of the grand arcanum, and he supposed his youthful coadjutor equally devoted. He was a mere child as to human nature; and, as to the passion of love, whatever he might once have felt of it, he had long since forgotten that there was such an idle passion in existence. But, while he dreamed, the silent amour went on. The very quiet and seclusion of the place were favourable to the growth of romantic passion. The opening bud of love was able to put forth leaf by leaf, without an adverse wind to check its growth. There was neither officious friendship to chill by its advice, nor insidious envy to wither by its sneers, nor an observing world to look on and stare it out of countenance. There was neither declaration, nor vow, nor any other form of Cupid's canting school. Their hearts mingled together, and understood each other without the aid of language. They lapsed into the full current of affection, unconscious of its depth, and thoughtless of the rocks that might lurk beneath its surface. Happy lovers! who wanted nothing to make their felicity complete, but the discovery of the philosopher's stone!

At length Antonio's health was sufficiently restored to enable him to return to his lodgings in Grenada. He felt uneasy, however, at leaving the tower, while lurking danger might surround its almost defenceless inmates. He dreaded lest Don Ambrosio, recovered from his wounds, might plot some new attempt, by secret art, or open violence. From all that he had heard, he knew him to be too implacable to suffer his defeat to pass unavenged, and too rash and fearless, when his arts were unavailing, to stop at any daring deed in the accomplishment of his purposes. He urged his apprehensions to the alchymist and his daughter, and proposed that they should abandon the dangerous vicinity of Grenada.

"I have relations," said he, "in Valentia, poor indeed, but worthy and affectionate. Among them you will find friendship and quiet, and we may there pursue our labours unmolested." He went on to paint the beauties and delights of Valentia with all the fondness of a native, and all the eloquence with which a lover paints the fields and groves which he is picturing as the future scenes of his happiness. His eloquence, backed by the apprehensions of Inez, was successful with the alchymist, who, indeed, had led too unsettled a life to be particular about the place of his residence; and it was determined, that, as soon as Antonio's health was perfectly restored, they should abandon the tower, and seek the delicious neighbourhood of Valentia.*

*Here are the strongest silks, the sweetest wines, the excellent'st almonds, the best oyls and beautifull'st females of all Spain. The very bruit animals make themselves beds of rosemary, and other fragrant flowers hereabouts; and when one is at sea, if the winde blow from the shore, he may smell this soyl before he come in sight of it many leagues off, by the strong oderiferous scent it casts. As it is the most pleasant, so it is also the temperat'st clime of all Spain, and they commonly call it the second Italy, which made the Moors, whereof many thousands were disterr'd, and banish'd hence to Barbary, to think that Paradise was in that part of the heavens which hung over this citie.
HOWELL'S LETTERS.

To recruit his strength, the student suspended his toils in the laboratory, and spent the few remaining days, before departure, in taking a farewell look at the enchanting environs of Grenada. He felt returning health and vigour as he inhaled the pure temperate breezes that play about its hills; and the happy state of his mind contributed to his rapid recovery. Inez was often the companion of his walks. Her descent, by the mother's side, from one of the ancient Moorish families, gave her an interest in this once favourite seat of Arabian power. She gazed with enthusiasm upon its magnificent monuments, and her memory was filled with the traditional tales and ballads of Moorish chivalry. Indeed the solitary life she had led, and the visionary turn of her father's mind, had produced an effect upon her character, and given it a tinge of what, in modern days, would be termed romance. All this was called into full force by this new passion; for, when a woman first begins to love, life is all romance to her.

In one of their evening strolls, they had ascended to the mountain of the Sun, where is situated the Generaliffe, the palace of pleasure, in the days of Moorish dominion, but now a gloomy convent of capuchins. They had wandered about its garden, among groves of orange, citron, and cypress, where the waters, leaping in torrents, or gushing in fountains, or tossed aloft in sparkling jets, fill the air with music and freshness. There is a melancholy mingled with all the beauties of this garden, that gradually stole over the feelings of the lovers. The place is full of the sad story of past times. It was the favourite abode of the lovely queen of Grenada, where she was surrounded by the delights of a gay and voluptuous court. It was here, too, amidst her own bowers of roses, that her slanderers laid the base story of her dishonour, and struck a fatal blow to the line of the gallant Abencerrages.

The whole garden has a look of ruin and neglect. Many of the fountains are dry and broken; the streams have wandered from their marble channels, and are choked by weeds and yellow leaves. The reed whistles to the wind where it had once sported among roses, and shaken perfume from the orange blossom. The convent bell flings its sullen sound, or the drowsy vesper hymn floats along these solitudes, which once resounded with the song, and the dance, and the lover's serenade. Well may the Moors lament over the loss of this earthly paradise; well may they remember it in their prayers, and beseech heaven to restore it to the faithful; well may their ambassadors smite their breasts when they behold these monuments of their race, and sit down and weep among the fading glories of Grenada!

It is impossible to wander about these scenes of departed love and gaiety, and not feel the tenderness of the heart awakened. It was then that Antonio first ventured to breathe his passion, and to express by words what his eyes had long since so eloquently revealed. He made his avowal with fervour, but with frankness. He had no gay prospects to hold out: he was a poor scholar, dependent on his "good spirits to feed and clothe him." But a woman in love is no interested calculator. Inez listened to him with downcast eyes, but in them was a humid gleam that showed her heart was with him. She had no prudery in her nature; and she had not been sufficiently in society to acquire it. She loved him with all the absence of worldliness of a genuine woman; and, amidst timid smiles and blushes, he drew from her a modest acknowledgment of her affection.

They wandered about the garden with that sweet intoxication of the soul which none but happy lovers know. The world about them was all fairy land; and, indeed, it spread forth one of its fairest scenes before their eyes, as if to fulfil their dream of earthly happiness. They looked out from between groves of orange upon the towers of Grenada below them; the magnificent plain of the Vega beyond, streaked with evening sunshine, and the distant hills tinted with rosy and purple hues; it seemed an emblem of the happy future that love and hope were decking out for them.

As if to make the scene complete, a group of Andalusians struck up a dance, in one of the vistas of the garden, to the guitars of two wandering musicians. The Spanish music is wild and plaintive, yet the people dance to it with spirit and enthusiasm. The picturesque figures of the dancers; the girls with their hair in silken nets that hung in knots and tassels down their backs, their mantillas floating round their graceful forms, their slender feet peeping from under their basquinas, their arms tossed up in the air to play the castanets, had a beautiful effect on this airy height, with the rich evening landscape spreading out below them.

When the dance was ended, two of the parties approached Antonio and Inez; one of them began a soft and tender Moorish ballad, accompanied by the other on the lute. It alluded to the story of the garden, the wrongs of the fair queen of Grenada, and the misfortunes of the Abencerrages. It was one of those old ballads that abound in this part of Spain, and live, like echoes, about the ruins of Moorish greatness. The heart of Inez was at that moment open to every tender impression; the tears rose into her eyes as she listened to the tale. The singer approached nearer to her; she was striking in her appearance; young, beautiful, with a mixture of wildness and melancholy in her fine black eyes. She fixed them mournfully and expressively on Inez, and suddenly varying her manner, sang another ballad, which treated of impending danger and treachery. All this might have passed for a mere accidental caprice of the singer, had there not been something in her look, manner, and gesticulation, that made it pointed and startling.

Inez was about to ask the meaning of this evidently personal application of the song, when she was interrupted by Antonio, who gently drew her from the place. Whilst she had been lost in attention to the music, he had remarked a group of men, in the shadows of the trees, whispering together. They were enveloped in the broad hats and great cloaks, so much worn by the Spanish, and while they were regarding himself and Inez attentively, seemed anxious to avoid observation. Not knowing what might be their character or intention, he hastened to quit a place where the gathering shadows of evening might expose them to intrusion and insult. On their way down the hill, as they passed through the woods of elms, mingled with poplars and oleanders, that skirts the road leading from the Alhambra, he again saw these men, apparently following at a distance; and he afterwards caught sight of them among the trees on the banks of the Darro. He said nothing on the subject to Inez, nor her father, for he would not awaken unnecessary alarm; but he felt at a loss how to ascertain or to avert any machinations that might be devising against the helpless inhabitants of the tower.

He took his leave of them late at night, full of this perplexity. As he left the dreary old pile, he saw some one lurking in the shadow of the wall, apparently watching his movements. He hastened after the figure, but it glided away, and disappeared among some ruins. Shortly after he heard a low whistle, which was answered from a little distance. He had no longer a doubt but that some mischief was on foot, and turned to hasten back to the tower, and put its inmates on their guard. He had scarcely turned, however, before he found himself suddenly seized from behind by some one of Herculean strength. His struggles were in vain; he was surrounded by armed men. One threw a mantle over him that stifled his cries, and enveloped him in its folds; and he was hurried off with irresistible rapidity.

The next day passed without the appearance of Antonio at the alchymist's. Another, and another day succeeded, and yet he did not come; nor had any thing been heard of him at his lodgings. His absence caused, at first, surprise and conjecture, and at length alarm. Inez recollected the singular intimations of the ballad-singer upon the mountain, which seemed to warn her of impending danger, and her mind was full of vague forebodings. She sat listening to every sound at the gate, or footstep on the stairs. She would take up her guitar and strike a few notes, but it would not do; her heart was sickening with suspense and anxiety. She had never before felt what it was to be really lonely. She now was conscious of the force of that attachment which had taken possession of her breast; for never do we know how much we love, never do we know how necessary the object of our love is to our happiness, until we experience the weary void of separation.

The philosopher, too, felt the absence of his disciple almost as sensibly as did his daughter. The animating buoyancy of the youth had inspired him with new ardour, and had given to his labours the charm of full companionship. However, he had resources and consolations of which his daughter was destitute. His pursuits were of a nature to occupy every thought, and keep the spirits in a state of continual excitement. Certain indications, too, had lately manifested themselves, of the most favourable nature. Forty days and forty nights had the process gone on successfully; the old man's hopes were constantly rising, and he now considered the glorious moment once more at hand, when he should obtain not merely the major lunaria, but likewise the tinctura solaris, the means of multiplying gold, and of prolonging existence. He remained, therefore, continually shut up in his laboratory, watching his furnace; for a moment's inadvertency might once more defeat all his expectations.

He was sitting one evening at one of his solitary vigils, wrapped up in meditation; the hour was late, and his neighbour, the owl, was hooting from the battlement of the tower, when he heard the door open behind him. Supposing it to be his daughter coming to take her leave of him for the night, as was her frequent practice, he called her by name, but a harsh voice met his ear in reply. He was grasped by the arms, and looking up, perceived three strange men in the chamber. He attempted to shake them off, but in vain. He called for help, but they scoffed at his cries.

"Peace, dotard!" cried one, "think'st thou the servants of the most holy inquisition are to be daunted by thy clamours? Comrades, away with him!"

Without heeding his remonstrances and entreaties, they seized upon his books and papers, took some note of the apartment and the utensils, and then bore him off a prisoner.

Inez, left to herself, had passed a sad and lonely evening; seated by a casement which looked into the garden, she had pensively watched star after star sparkle out of the blue depths of the sky, and was indulging a crowd of anxious thoughts about her lover, until the rising tears began to flow. She was suddenly alarmed by the sound of voices that seemed to come from a distant part of the mansion. There was not long after a noise of several persons descending the stairs. Surprised at these unusual sounds in their lonely habitation, she remained for a few moments in a state of trembling, yet indistinct apprehension, when the servant rushed into the room, with terror in her countenance, and informed her that her father was carried off by armed men.

Inez did not stop to hear further, but flew down stairs to overtake them. She had scarcely passed the threshold, when she found herself in the grasp of strangers.—"Away!—

away!" cried she, wildly; "do not stop me—let me follow my father."

"We come to conduct you to him, senora," said one of the men, respectfully.

"Where is he, then?"

"He is gone to Grenada," replied the man: "an unexpected circumstance requires his presence there immediately; but he is among friends."

"We have no friends in Grenada," said Inez, drawing back; but then the idea of Antonio rushed into her mind; something relating to him might have called her father thither. "Is senor Antonio de Castros with him?" demanded she with agitation.

"I know not, senora," replied the man. "It is very possible. I only know that your father is among friends, and is anxious for you to follow him."

"Let us go, then," cried she, eagerly. The men led her a little distance to where a mule was waiting, and, assisting her to mount, they conducted her slowly towards the city.

Grenada was on that evening a scene of fanciful revel. It was one of the festivals of the Maestranza, an association of the nobility to keep up some of the gallant customs of ancient chivalry. There had been a representation of a tournament in one of the squares; the streets would still occasionally resound with the beat of a solitary drum, or the bray of a trumpet, from some straggling party of revellers. Sometimes they were met by cavaliers, richly dressed in ancient costumes, attended by their squires, and at one time they passed in sight of a palace brilliantly illuminated, from whence came the mingled sounds of music and the dance. Shortly after they came to the square, where the mock tournament had been held. It was thronged by the populace, recreating themselves among booths and stalls where refreshments were sold, and the glare of torches showed the temporary galleries, and gay-coloured awnings, and armorial trophies, and other paraphernalia of the show. The conductors of Inez endeavoured to keep out of observation, and to traverse a gloomy part of the square; but they were detained at one place by the pressure of a crowd surrounding a party of wandering musicians, singing one of those ballads of which the Spanish populace are so passionately fond. The torches which were held by some of the crowd, threw a strong mass of light upon Inez, and the sight of so beautiful a being, without mantilla or veil, looking so bewildered, and conducted by men, who seemed to take no gratification in the surrounding gaiety, occasioned expressions of curiosity. One of the ballad-singers approached, and striking her guitar with peculiar earnestness, began to sing a doleful air, full of sinister forebodings. Inez started with surprise. It was the same ballad-singer that had addressed her in the garden of Generaliffe. It was the same air that she had then sung. It spoke of impending dangers; they seemed, indeed, to be thickening around her. She was anxious to speak with the girl, and to ascertain whether she really had a knowledge of any definite evil that was threatening her; but as she attempted to address her, the mule, on which she rode, was suddenly seized, and led forcibly through the throng by one of her conductors, while she saw another addressing menacing words to the ballad-singer. The latter raised her hand with a warning gesture as Inez lost sight of her.

While she was yet lost in perplexity, caused by this singular occurrence, they stopped at the gate of a large mansion. One of her attendants knocked, the door was opened, and they entered a paved court. "Where are we?" demanded Inez, with anxiety. "At the house of a friend, senora," replied the man. "Ascend this staircase with me, and in a moment you will meet your father."

They ascended a staircase that led to a suite of splendid apartments. They passed through several until they came to an inner chamber. The door opened, some one approached; but what was her terror at perceiving, not her father, but Don Ambrosio!

The men who had seized upon the alchymist had, at least, been more honest in their professions. They were, indeed, familiars of the inquisition. He was conducted in silence to the gloomy prison of that horrible tribunal. It was a mansion whose very aspect withered joy, and almost shut out hope. It was one of those hideous abodes which the bad passions of men conjure up in this fair world, to rival the fancied dens of demons and the accursed.

Day after day went heavily by without any thing to mark

the lapse of time, but the decline and re-appearance of the light that feebly glimmered through the narrow window of the dungeon, in which the unfortunate alchymist was buried, rather than confined. His mind was harassed with uncertainties and fears about his daughter, so helpless and inexperienced. He endeavoured to gather tidings of her from the man who brought his daily portion of food. The fellow stared, as if astonished, at being asked a question in that mansion of silence and mystery, but departed without saying a word. Every succeeding attempt was equally fruitless.

The poor alchymist was oppressed by many griefs; and it was not the least that he had been again interrupted in his labours on the very point of success. Never was alchymist so near attaining the golden secret—a little longer, and all his hopes would have been realized. The thoughts of these disappointments afflicted him more even than the fear of all that he might suffer from the merciless inquisition. His waking thoughts would follow him into his dreams. He would be transported in fancy to his laboratory, busied again among retorts and alembics, and surrounded by Lully, by D'Abano, by Olybius, and the other masters of the sublime art. The moment of projection would arrive; a seraphic form would rise out of the furnace, holding forth a vessel, containing the precious elixir; but, before he could grasp the prize, he would awake, and find himself in a dungeon.

All the devices of inquisitorial ingenuity were employed to ensnare the old man, and to draw from him evidence that might be brought against himself, and might corroborate certain secret information that had been given against him. He had been accused of practising necromancy and judicial astrology, and a cloud of evidence had been secretly brought forward to substantiate the charge. It would be tedious to enumerate all the circumstances, apparently corroborative, which had been industriously cited by the secret accuser. The silence which prevailed about the tower, its desolateness, the very quiet of its inhabitants, had been adduced as proofs that something sinister was perpetrated within. The alchymist's conversations and soliloquies in the garden had been overheard and misrepresented. The lights and strange appearances at night, in the tower, were given with violent exaggerations.

Shrieks and yells were said to have been heard from thence at midnight, when, it was confidently asserted, the old man raised familiar spirits by his incantations, and even compelled the dead to rise from their graves, and answer to his questionings.

The alchymist, according to the custom of the inquisition, was kept in complete ignorance of his accuser; of the witnesses produced against him; even of the crimes of which he was accused. He was examined generally, whether he knew why he was arrested, and was conscious of any guilt that might deserve the notice of the holy office? He was examined as to his country, his life, his habits, his pursuits, his actions, and opinions. The old man was frank and simple in his replies; he was conscious of no guilt, capable of no art, practised in no dissimulation. After receiving a general admonition to bethink himself whether he had not committed any act deserving of punishment, and to prepare, by confession, to secure the well-known mercy of the tribunal, he was remanded to his cell.

He was now visited in his dungeon by crafty familiars of the inquisition; who, under pretence of sympathy and kindness, came to beguile the tediousness of his imprisonment with friendly conversation. They casually introduced the subject of alchymy, on which they touched with great caution and pretended indifference. There was no need of such craftiness. The honest enthusiast had no suspicion in his nature: the moment they touched upon his favourite theme, he forgot his misfortunes and imprisonment, and broke forth into rhapsodies about the divine science.

The conversation was artfully turned to the discussion of elementary beings. The alchymist readily avowed his belief in them; and that there had been instances of their attending upon philosophers, and administering to their wishes. He related many miracles said to have been performed by Apollonius Thyaneus through the aid of spirits or demons; insomuch that he was set up by the heathens in opposition to the Messiah; and was even regarded with reverence by many Christians. The familiars eagerly demanded whether he believed Apollonius to be a true and worthy philosopher. The unaffected piety of the alchymist protected him even in the midst of his simplicity, for he condemned Apollonius as a sorcerer and an impostor. No art could draw from him an admission that he had ever employed or invoked spiritual agencies in the prosecution of his pursuits, though he believed himself to have been frequently impeded by their invisible interference.

The inquisitors were sorely vexed at not being able to en-veigle him into a confession of a criminal nature; they attrib-uted their failure to craft, to obstinacy, to every cause but the right one, namely, that the harmless visionary had nothing guilty to confess. They had abundant proof of a secret nature against him; but it was the practice of the inquisition to en-deavour to procure confession from the prisoners. An auto da fé was at hand; the worthy fathers were eager for his con-viction, for they were always anxious to have a good number of culprits condemned to the stake, to grace these solemn triumphs. He was at length brought to a final examination.

The chamber of trial was spacious and gloomy. At one end was a huge crucifix, the standard of the inquisition. A long table extended through the centre of the room, at which sat the inquisitors and their secretary; at the other end a stool was placed for the prisoner.

He was brought in, according to custom, bare-headed and bare-legged. He was enfeebled by confinement and affliction; by constantly brooding over the unknown fate of his child, and the disastrous interruption of his experiments. He sat bowed down and listless; his head sunk upon his breast; his whole appearance that of one "past hope, abandoned, and by himself given over."

The accusation alleged against him was now brought for-ward in a specific form; he was called upon by name, Felix de Vasquez, formerly of Castile, to answer to the charges of nec-romancy and demonology. He was told that the charges were amply substantiated; and was asked whether he was ready, by full confession, to throw himself upon the well-known mercy of the holy inquisition.

The philosopher testified some slight surprise at the nature of the accusation, but simply replied, "I am innocent."

"What proof have you to give of your innocence?"

"It rather remains for you to prove your charges," said the old man. "I am a stranger and a sojourner in the land, and know no one out of the doors of my dwelling. I can give nothing in my vindication but the word of a nobleman and a Castilian."

The inquisitor shook his head, and went on to repeat the various inquiries that had before been made as to his mode of life and pursuit. The poor alchymist was too feeble and too weary at heart to make any but brief replies. He requested that some man of science might examine his laboratory, and all his books and papers, by which it would be made abundantly evident that he was merely engaged in the study of alchymy.

To this the inquisitor observed, that alchymy had become a mere covert for secret and deadly sins. That the practisers of it were apt to scruple at no means to satisfy their inordinate greediness of gold. Some had been known to use spells and impious ceremonies; to conjure the aid of evil spirits; nay, even to sell their souls to the enemy of mankind, so that they might riot in boundless wealth while living.

The poor alchymist had heard all patiently, or, at least, passively. He had disdained to vindicate his name otherwise than by his word; he had smiled at the accusations of sorcery, when applied merely to himself; but when the sublime art, which had been the study and passion of his life, was assailed, he could no longer listen in silence. His head gradually rose from his bosom; a hectic colour came in faint streaks to his cheek; played about there, disappeared, returned, and at length kindled into a burning glow. The clammy dampness dried from his forehead; his eyes, which had been nearly extinguished, lighted up again, and burned with their wonted and visionary fires. He entered into a vindication of his favourite art. His voice at first was feeble and broken; but it gathered strength as he proceeded, until it rolled in a deep and sonorous volume. He gradually rose from his seat as he rose with his subject; he threw back the scanty black mantle which had hitherto wrapped his limbs; the very uncouthness of his form and looks gave an impressive effect to what he uttered; it was as though a corpse had become suddenly animated.

He repelled with scorn the aspersions cast upon alchymy by the ignorant and vulgar. He affirmed it to be the mother

of all art and science, citing the opinions of Paracelsus, Sandivogius, Raymond Lully, and others, in support of his assertions. He maintained that it was pure and innocent, and
honourable both in its purposes and means. What were its
objects? The perpetuation of life and youth, and the production of gold. "The elixir vitæ," said he, "is no charmed po-
tion, but merely a concentration of those elements of vitality
which nature has scattered through her works. The philosopher's stone, or tincture, or powder, as it is variously called,
is no necromantic talisman, but consists simply of those particles which gold contains within itself for its reproduction;
for gold, like other things, has its seed within itself, though
bound up with inconceivable firmness, from the vigour of innate fixed salts and sulphurs. In seeking to discover the elixir
of life, then," continued he, "we seek only to apply some of
nature's own specifics against the disease and decay to which
our bodies are subjected; and what else does the physician,
when he tasks his art, and uses subtle compounds and cunning distillations to revive our languishing powers, and avert
the stroke of death for a season?

"In seeking to multiply the precious metals, also, we seek
but to germinate and multiply, by natural means, a particular
species of nature's productions; and what else does the hus-
bandman, who consults times and seasons, and, by what
might be deemed a natural magic, from the mere scattering
of his hand, covers a whole plain with golden vegetation? The
mysteries of our art, it is true, are deeply and darkly hidden;
but it requires so much the more innocence and purity of
thought to penetrate unto them. No, father! the true alchymist must be pure in mind and body; he must be temperate,
patient, chaste, watchful, meek, humble, devout. 'My son,'
says Hermes Trismegestes, the great master of our art, 'My
son, I recommend you above all things to fear God'. And
indeed it is only by devout castigation of the senses and
purification of the soul, that the alchymist is enabled to enter
into the sacred chambers of truth. 'Labour, pray, and read,' is
the motto of our science. As De Nuysement well observes,
'these high and singular favours are granted unto none, save
only unto the sons of God (that is to say, the virtuous and
devout), who, under his paternal benediction, have obtained

the opening of the same, by the helping hand of the queen of arts, divine Philosophy.' Indeed, so sacred has the nature of this knowledge been considered, that we are told it has four times been expressly communicated by God to man, having made a part of that cabalistical wisdom which was revealed to Adam to console him for the loss of Paradise; and to Moses in the bush, and to Solomon in a dream, and to Esdras by the angel.

"So far from demons and malign spirits being the friends and abettors of the alchymist, they are the continual foes with which he has to contend. It is their constant endeavour to shut up the avenues to those truths which would enable him to rise above the abject state into which he has fallen, and return to that excellence which was his original birthright. For what would be the effect of this length of days, and this abundant wealth, but to enable the possessor to go on from art to art, from science to science, with energies unimpaired by sickness, uninterrupted by death? For this have sages and philosophers shut themselves up in cells and solitudes; buried themselves in caves and dens of the earth; turning from the joys of life, and the pleasance of the world; enduring scorn, poverty, persecution. For this was Raymond Lully stoned to death in Mauritania. For this did the immortal Pietro D'Abano suffer persecution at Padua, and when he escaped from his oppressors by death, was despitefully burnt in effigy. For this have illustrious men of all nations intrepidly suffered martyrdom. For this, if unmolested, have they assiduously employed the latest hour of life, the expiring throb of existence; hoping to the last that they might yet seize upon the prize for which they had struggled, and pluck themselves back even from the very jaws of the grave!

"For, when once the alchymist shall have attained the object of his toils; when the sublime secret shall be revealed to his gaze, how glorious will be the change in his condition! How will he emerge from his solitary retreat, like the sun breaking forth from the darksome chamber of the night, and darting his beams throughout the earth! Gifted with perpetual youth and boundless riches, to what heights of wisdom may he attain! How may he carry on, uninterrupted, the thread of knowledge, which has hitherto been snapped at the death of each philosopher! And, as the increase of wisdom is the increase of virtue, how may he become the benefactor of his fellow-men; dispensing with liberal, but cautious and discriminating hand, that inexhaustible wealth which is at his disposal; banishing poverty, which is the cause of so much sorrow and wickedness; encouraging the arts; promoting discoveries, and enlarging all the means of virtuous enjoyment! His life will be the connecting band of generations. History will live in his recollection; distant ages will speak with his tongue. The nations of the earth will look to him as their preceptor, and kings will sit at his feet and learn wisdom. Oh glorious! Oh celestial alchymy!"—

Here he was interrupted by the inquisitor, who had suffered him to go on thus far, in hopes of gathering something from his unguarded enthusiasm. "Senor," said he, "this is all rambling, visionary talk. You are charged with sorcery, and in defence you give us a rhapsody about alchymy. Have you nothing better than this to offer in your defence?"

The old man slowly resumed his seat, but did not deign a reply. The fire that had beamed in his eye gradually expired. His cheek resumed its wonted paleness; but he did not relapse into inanity. He sat with a steady, serene, patient look, like one prepared not to contend but to suffer.

His trial continued for a long time, with cruel mockery of justice, for no witnesses were ever, in this court, confronted with the accused, and the latter had continually to defend himself in the dark. Some unknown and powerful enemy had alleged charges against the unfortunate alchymist, but who he could not imagine. Stranger and sojourner as he was in the land; solitary and harmless in his pursuits, how could he have provoked such hostility? The tide of secret testimony, however, was too strong against him; he was convicted of the crime of magic, and condemned to expiate his sins at the stake, at the approaching auto da fé.

While the unhappy alchymist was undergoing his trial at the inquisition, his daughter was exposed to trials no less severe. Don Ambrosio, into whose hands she had fallen, was, as has before been intimated, one of the most daring and lawless profligates in all Grenada. He was a man of hot blood and fiery passions, who stopped at nothing in the gratification of his desires; yet with all this he possessed manners, address, and accomplishments, that had made him eminently successful among the sex. From the palace to the cottage he had extended his amorous enterprises; his serenades harassed the slumbers of half the husbands of Grenada; no balcony was too high for his adventurous attempts; nor any cottage too lowly for his perfidious seductions. Yet he was as fickle as he was ardent; success had made him vain and capricious; he had no sentiment to attach him to the victim of his arts, and many a pale cheek and fading eye, languishing amidst the sparkling of jewels; and many a breaking heart, throbbing under the rustic boddice, bore testimony to his triumphs and his faithlessness.

He was sated, however, by easy conquests, and wearied of a life of continual and prompt gratification. There had been a degree of difficulty and enterprise in the pursuit of Inez, that he had never before experienced. It had aroused him from the monotony of mere sensual life, and stimulated him with the charm of adventure. He had become an epicure in pleasure; and now that he had this coy beauty in his power, he was determined to protract his enjoyment, by the gradual conquest of her scruples, and downfall of her virtue. He was vain of his person and address, which he thought no woman could long withstand; and it was a kind of trial of skill, to endeavour to gain by art and fascination, what he was secure of obtaining at any time by violence.

When Inez, therefore, was brought into his presence by his emissaries, he affected not to notice her terror and surprise; but received her with formal and stately courtesy. He was too wary a fowler to flutter the bird when just entangled in the net. To her eager and wild inquiries about her father, he begged her not to be alarmed; that he was safe, and had been there, but was engaged elsewhere in an affair of moment, from which he would soon return; in the mean time he had left word, that she should await his return in patience. After some stately expressions of general civility, Don Ambrosio made a ceremonious bow and retired.

The mind of Inez was full of trouble and perplexity. The stately formality of Don Ambrosio was so unexpected as to check the accusations and reproaches that were springing to her lips. Had he had evil designs, would he have treated her with such frigid ceremony when he had her in his power? But why, then, was she brought to his house? Was not the mysterious disappearance of Antonio connected with this? A thought suddenly darted into her mind. Antonio had again met with Don Ambrosio—they had fought—Antonio was wounded—perhaps dying!—It was him to whom her father had gone.—It was at his request that Don Ambrosio had sent for them to soothe his dying moments! These, and a thousand such horrible suggestions harassed her mind; but she tried in vain to get information from the domestics; they knew nothing but that her father had been there, had gone, and would soon return.

Thus passed a night of tumultuous thought and vague yet cruel apprehensions. She knew not what to do, or what to believe: whether she ought to fly, or to remain; but if to fly, how was she to extricate herself? and where was she to seek her father? As the day dawned without any intelligence of him, her alarm increased; at length a message was brought from him, saying that circumstances prevented his return to her, but begging her to hasten to him without delay.

With an eager and throbbing heart did she set forth with the men that were to conduct her. She little thought, however, that she was merely changing her prison-house. Don Ambrosio had feared lest she should be traced to his residence in Grenada; or that he might be interrupted there before he could accomplish his plan of seduction. He had her now conveyed, therefore, to a mansion which he possessed in one of the mountain solitudes in the neighbourhood of Grenada; a lonely, but beautiful retreat. In vain, on her arrival, did she look around for her father, or Antonio; none but strange faces met her eye; menials profoundly respectful, but who knew nor saw any thing but what their master pleased.

She had scarcely arrived before Don Ambrosio made his appearance, less stately in his manner, but still treating her with the utmost delicacy and deference. Inez was too much agitated and alarmed to be baffled by his courtesy, and became vehement in her demand to be conducted to her father.

Don Ambrosio now put on an appearance of the greatest embarrassment and emotion. After some delay, and much pretended confusion, he at length confessed that the seizure of her father was all a stratagem; a mere false alarm to procure him the present opportunity of having access to her, and endeavouring to mitigate that obduracy, and conquer that repugnance, which he declared had almost driven him to distraction.

He assured her that her father was again at home in safety, and occupied in his usual pursuits; having been fully satisfied that his daughter was in honourable hands, and would soon be restored to him. It was in vain that she threw herself at his feet, and implored to be set at liberty; he only replied, by gentle entreaties, that she would pardon the seeming violence he had to use; and that she would trust a little while to his honour. "You are here," said he, "absolute mistress of every thing; nothing shall be said or done to offend you; I will not even intrude upon your ear the unhappy passion that is devouring my heart. Should you require it, I will even absent myself from your presence; but to part with you entirely at present, with your mind full of doubts and resentments, would be worse than death to me. No, beautiful Inez, you must first know me a little better, and know by my conduct, that my passion for you is as delicate and respectful as it is vehement."

The assurance of her father's safety had relieved Inez from one cause of torturing anxiety, only to render her fears the more violent on her own account. Don Ambrosio, however, continued to treat her with artful deference, that insensibly lulled her apprehensions. It is true she found herself a captive, but no advantage appeared to be taken of her helplessness. She soothed herself with the idea that a little while would suffice to convince Don Ambrosio of the fallacy of his hopes, and that he would be induced to restore her to her home. Her transports of terror and affliction, therefore, subsided, in a few days, into a passive, yet anxious melancholy, with which she awaited the hoped-for event.

In the mean while all those artifices were employed that are calculated to charm the senses, ensnare the feelings, and dissolve the heart into tenderness. Don Ambrosio was a master of the subtil arts of seduction. His very mansion breathed an enervating atmosphere of languor and delight. It was here, amidst twilight saloons and dreamy chambers, buried among groves of orange and myrtle, that he shut himself up at times from the prying world, and gave free scope to the gratification of his pleasures.

The apartments were furnished in the most sumptuous and voluptuous manner; the silken couches swelled to the touch, and sunk in downy softness beneath the slightest pressure. The paintings and statues all told some classic tale of love, managed, however, with an insidious delicacy; which, while it banished the grossness that might disgust, was the more calculated to excite the imagination. There the blooming Adonis was seen, not breaking away to pursue the boisterous chase, but crowned with flowers, and languishing in the embraces of celestial beauty. There Acis wooed his Galatea in the shade, with the Sicilian sea spreading in halcyon serenity before them. There were depicted groups of fauns and dryads, fondly reclining in summer bowers, and listening to the liquid piping of the reed; or the wanton satyrs surprising some wood-nymph during her noontide slumber. There, too, on the storied tapestry, might be seen the chaste Diana, stealing, in the mystery of moonlight, to kiss the sleeping Endymion; while Cupid and Psyche, entwined in immortal marble, breathed on each other's lips the early kiss of love.

The ardent rays of the sun were excluded from these balmy halls; soft and tender music from unseen musicians floated around, seeming to mingle with the perfumes that were exhaled from a thousand flowers. At night, when the moon shed a fairy light over the scene, the tender serenade would rise from among the bowers of the garden, in which the fine voice of Don Ambrosio might often be distinguished; or the amorous flute would be heard along the mountain, breathing in its pensive cadences the very soul of a lover's melancholy.

Various entertainments were also devised to dispel her loneliness, and to charm away the idea of confinement. Groups of Andalusian dancers performed, in the splendid saloons, the various picturesque dances of their country; or represented little amorous ballets, which turned upon some pleasing scene of pastoral coquetry and courtship. Sometimes there were bands of singers, who, to the romantic guitar, warbled forth ditties full of passion and tenderness.

Thus all about her enticed to pleasure and voluptuousness; but the heart of Inez turned with distaste from this idle mockery. The tears would rush into her eyes as her thoughts reverted from this scene of profligate splendour, to the humble but virtuous home from whence she had been betrayed; or if the witching power of music ever soothed her into a tender reverie, it was to dwell with fondness on the image of Antonio. But if Don Ambrosio, deceived by this transient calm, should attempt at such time to whisper his passion, she would start as from a dream, and recoil from him with involuntary shuddering.

She had passed one long day of more than ordinary sadness, and in the evening a band of these hired performers were exerting all the animating powers of song and dance to amuse her. But while the lofty saloon resounded with their warblings, and the light sound of feet upon its marble pavement kept time to the cadence of the song, poor Inez, with her face buried in the silken couch on which she reclined, was only rendered more wretched by the sound of gaiety.

At length her attention was caught by the voice of one of the singers, that brought with it some indefinite recollections. She raised her head, and cast an anxious look at the performers, who, as usual, were at the lower end of the saloon. One of them advanced a little before the others. It was a female, dressed in a fanciful, pastoral garb, suited to the character she was sustaining; but her countenance was not to be mistaken. It was the same ballad-singer that had twice crossed her path, and given her mysterious intimations of the lurking mischief that surrounded her. When the rest of the performances were concluded, she seized a tambourine, and tossing it aloft, danced alone to the melody of her own voice. In the course of her dancing she approached to where Inez reclined; and as she struck the tambourine, contrived, dexterously, to throw a folded paper on the couch. Inez seized it with avidity, and concealed it in her bosom. The singing and dancing were at an end; the motley crew retired; and Inez, left alone, hastened with anxiety to unfold the paper thus mysteriously conveyed. It was written in an agitated, and almost illegible, handwriting; "Be on your guard! you are surrounded by treachery. Trust not to the forbearance of Don Ambrosio; you are marked out for his prey. An humble victim to his perfidy gives you this warning; she is encompassed by too many dangers to be more explicit.—Your father is in the dungeons of the inquisition!"

The brain of Inez reeled as she read this dreadful scroll. She was less filled with alarm at her own danger, than horror at her father's situation. The moment Don Ambrosio appeared, she rushed and threw herself at his feet, imploring him to save her father. Don Ambrosio started with astonishment; but immediately regaining his self-possession, endeavoured to soothe her by his blandishments, and by assurances that her father was in safety. She was not to be pacified; her fears were too much aroused to be trifled with. She declared her knowledge of her father's being a prisoner of the inquisition, and reiterated her frantic supplications that he would save him.

Don Ambrosio paused for a moment in perplexity, but was too adroit to be easily confounded. "That your father is a prisoner," replied he, "I have long known. I have concealed it from you, to save you from fruitless anxiety. You now know the real reason of the restraint I have put upon your liberty; I have been protecting instead of detaining you. Every exertion has been made in your father's favour; but I regret to say, the proofs of the offences of which he stands charged have been too strong to be controverted. Still," added he, "I have it in my power to save him; I have influence, I have means at my beck; it may involve me, it is true, in difficulties, perhaps in disgrace; but what would I not do in the hopes of being rewarded by your favour? Speak, beautiful Inez," said he, his eyes kindling with sudden eagerness, "it is with you to say the word that seals your father's fate. One kind word, say but you will be mine, and you will behold me at your feet, your father at liberty and in affluence, and we shall all be happy!"

Inez drew back from him with scorn and disbelief. "My father," exclaimed she, "is too innocent and blameless to be convicted of crime; this is some base, some cruel artifice!" Don Ambrosio repeated his asseverations, and with them also his dishonourable proposals; but his eagerness overshot its mark; her indignation and her incredulity were alike awakened by his base suggestions; and he retired from her presence checked and awed by the sudden pride and dignity of her demeanour.

The unfortunate Inez now became a prey to the most harrowing anxieties. Don Ambrosio saw that the mask had fallen from his face, and that the nature of his machinations was revealed. He had gone too far to retrace his steps, and assume the affectation of tenderness and respect; indeed he was mortified and incensed at her insensibility to his attractions, and now only sought to subdue her through her fears. He daily represented to her the dangers that threatened her father, and that it was in his power alone to avert them. Inez was still incredulous. She was too ignorant of the nature of the inquisition to know that even innocence was not always a protection from its cruelties; and she confided too surely in the virtue of her father to believe that any accusation could prevail against him.

At length, Don Ambrosio, to give an effectual blow to her confidence, brought her the proclamation of the approaching auto da fé, in which the prisoners were enumerated. She glanced her eye over it, and beheld her father's name, condemned to the stake for sorcery.

For a moment she stood transfixed with horror. Don Ambrosio seized upon the transient calm. "Think, now, beautiful Inez," said he, with a tone of affected tenderness, "his life is still in your hands; one word from you, one kind word, and I can yet save him."

"Monster! wretch!" cried she, coming to herself, and recoiling from him with insuperable abhorrence: " 'tis you that are the cause of this—'tis you that are his murderer!" Then, wringing her hands, she broke forth into exclamations of the most frantic agony.

The perfidious Ambrosio saw the torture of her soul, and anticipated from it a triumph. He saw that she was in no mood, during her present paroxysm, to listen to his words; but he trusted that the horrors of lonely rumination would break down her spirit, and subdue her to his will. In this, however, he was disappointed. Many were the vicissitudes of mind of the wretched Inez; one time she would embrace his knees with piercing supplications; at another she would shrink with nervous horror at his very approach; but any intimation of his passion only excited the same emotion of loathing and detestation.

At length the fatal day drew nigh. "To-morrow," said Don Ambrosio, as he left her one evening, "To-morrow is the auto da fé. To-morrow you will hear the sound of the bell that tolls your father to his death. You will almost see the smoke that rises from his funeral pile. I leave you to yourself. It is yet in my power to save him. Think whether you can stand to-morrow's horrors without shrinking. Think whether you can endure the after-reflection, that you were the cause of his death, and that merely through a perversity in refusing proffered happiness."

What a night was it to Inez! Her heart, already harassed and almost broken by repeated and protracted anxieties; her strength wasted and enfeebled. On every side horrors awaited her; her father's death, her own dishonour; there seemed no escape from misery or perdition. "Is there no relief from man—no pity in heaven?" exclaimed she. "What—what have we done that we should be thus wretched?"

As the dawn approached, the fever of her mind arose to agony; a thousand times did she try the doors and windows of her apartment, in the desperate hope of escaping. Alas! with all the splendour of her prison, it was too faithfully secured for her weak hands to work deliverance. Like a poor bird, that beats its wings against its gilded cage, until it sinks panting in despair, so she threw herself on the floor in hopeless anguish. Her blood grew hot in her veins, her tongue was parched, her temples throbbed with violence, she gasped rather than breathed; it seemed as if her brain was on fire. "Blessed Virgin!" exclaimed she, clasping her hands and turning up her strained eyes, "look down with pity, and support me in this dreadful hour!"

Just as the day began to dawn, she heard a key turn softly in the door of her apartment. She dreaded lest it should be Don Ambrosio; and the very thought of him gave her a sickening pang. It was a female, clad in a rustic dress, with her face concealed by her mantilla. She stepped silently into the room, looked cautiously round, and then, uncovering her face, revealed the well-known features of the ballad-singer. Inez uttered an exclamation of surprise, almost of joy. The unknown started back, pressed her finger on her lips enjoining silence, and beckoned her to follow. She hastily wrapped herself in her veil and obeyed. They passed with quick but noiseless steps through an antechamber, across a spacious hall, and along a corridor; all was silent; the household was yet locked in sleep. They came to a door, to which the unknown applied a key. Inez' heart misgave her; she knew not but some new treachery was menacing her; she laid her cold hand on the stranger's arm: "Whither are you leading me?" said she. "To liberty," replied the other, in a whisper.

"Do you know the passages about this mansion?"

"But too well!" replied the girl, with a melancholy shake of the head. There was an expression of sad veracity in her countenance that was not to be distrusted. The door opened on a small terrace, which was overlooked by several windows of the mansion.

"We must move across this quickly," said the girl, "or we may be observed."

They glided over it as if scarce touching the ground. A flight of steps led down into the garden; a wicket at the bottom was readily unbolted: they passed with breathless velocity along one of the alleys, still in sight of the mansion, in which, however, no person appeared to be stirring. At length they came to a low private door in the wall, partly hidden by a fig-tree. It was secured by rusty bolts, that refused to yield to their feeble efforts.

"Holy Virgin!" exclaimed the stranger, "what is to be done? one moment more, and we may be discovered."

She seized a stone that lay near by: a few blows, and the bolts flew back; the door grated harshly as they opened it, and the next moment they found themselves in a narrow road.

"Now," said the stranger, "for Grenada as quickly as possible! The nearer we approach it, the safer we shall be; for the road will be more frequented."

The imminent risk they ran of being pursued and taken gave supernatural strength to their limbs; they flew rather than ran. The day had dawned; the crimson streaks on the edge of the horizon gave tokens of the approaching sunrise; already the light clouds that floated in the western sky were tinged with gold and purple; though the broad plain of the Vega, which now began to open upon their view, was covered with the dark haze of morning. As yet they only passed a few straggling peasants on the road, who could have yielded them no assistance in case of their being overtaken. They continued to hurry forward, and had gained a considerable distance, when the strength of Inez, which had only been sustained by the fever of her mind, began to yield to fatigue. She slackened her pace, and faltered.

"Alas!" said she, "my limbs fail me! I can go no further!" "Bear up, bear up," replied her companion cheeringly; "a little further and we shall be safe: look! yonder is Grenada, just showing itself in the valley below us. A little further, and we shall come to the main road, and then we shall find plenty of passengers to protect us."

Inez, encouraged, made fresh efforts to get forward, but her weary limbs were unequal to the eagerness of her mind; her mouth and throat were parched by agony and terror; she gasped for breath, and leaned for support against a rock. "It is all in vain!" exclaimed she; "I feel as though I should faint."

"Lean on me," said the other; "let us get into the shelter of yon thicket, that will conceal us from the view; I hear the sound of water, which will refresh you."

With much difficulty they reached the thicket, which overhung a small mountain stream, just where its sparkling waters leaped over the rock and fell into a natural basin. Here Inez sank upon the ground exhausted. Her companion brought water in the palms of her hands, and bathed her pallid temples. The cooling drops revived her; she was enabled to get to the margin of the stream, and drink of its crystal current; then, reclining her head on the bosom of her deliverer, she was first enabled to murmur forth her heartfelt gratitude.

"Alas!" said the other, "I deserve no thanks; I deserve not the good opinion you express. In me you behold a victim of Don Ambrosio's arts. In early years he seduced me from the cottage of my parents; look! at the foot of yonder blue mountain in the distance lies my native village; but it is no longer a home for me. From thence he lured me when I was too young for reflection; he educated me, taught me various accomplishments, made me sensible to love, to splendour, to refinement; then, having grown weary of me, he neglected me, and cast me upon the world. Happily the accomplishments he taught me have kept me from utter want; and the love with which he inspired me has kept me from further degradation. Yes! I confess my weakness; all his perfidy and wrongs cannot efface him from my heart. I have been brought up to love him; I have no other idol; I know him to be base, yet I cannot help adoring him. I am content to mingle among the hireling throng that administer to his amusements, that I may still hover about him, and linger in those halls where I once reigned mistress. What merit, then, have I in assisting your escape? I scarce know whether I am acting from sympathy, and a desire to rescue another victim from his power; or jealousy, and an eagerness to remove too powerful a rival!"

While she was yet speaking, the sun rose in all its splendour; first lighting up the mountain summits, then stealing down height by height, until its rays gilded the domes and towers of Grenada, which they could partially see from between the trees, below them. Just then the heavy tones of a bell came sounding from a distance, echoing, in sullen clang, along the mountain. Inez turned pale at the sound. She knew it to be the great bell of the cathedral, rung at sunrise on the day of the auto da fé, to give note of funeral preparation. Every stroke beat upon her heart, and inflicted an absolute, corporeal pang. She started up wildly. "Let us be gone!" cried she; "there is not a moment for delay!"

"Stop!" exclaimed the other, "yonder are horsemen coming over the brow of that distant height; if I mistake not, Don Ambrosio is at their head.—Alas! 'tis he; we are lost. Hold!" continued she, "give me your scarf and veil; wrap yourself in this mantilla. I will fly up yon footpath that leads to the heights. I will let the veil flutter as I ascend; perhaps they may mistake me for you, and they must dismount to follow me. Do you hasten forward—you will soon reach the main road. You have jewels on your fingers; bribe the first muleteer you meet to assist you on your way."

All this was said with hurried and breathless rapidity. The exchange of garments was made in an instant. The girl darted up the mountain-path, her white veil fluttering among the dark shrubbery; while Inez, inspired with new strength, or rather new terror, flew to the road, and trusted to Providence to guide her tottering steps to Grenada.

All Grenada was in agitation on the morning of this dismal day. The heavy bell of the cathedral continued to utter its clanging tones, that pervaded every part of the city, summoning all persons to the tremendous spectacle that was about to be exhibited. The streets through which the procession was to pass were crowded with the populace. The windows, the roofs, every place that could admit a face or a foothold, was alive with spectators. In the great square a spacious scaffolding, like an amphitheatre, was erected, where the sentences of the prisoners were to be read, and the sermon of faith to be preached; and close by were the stakes prepared, where the condemned were to be burnt to death. Seats were arranged for the great, the gay, the beautiful; for such is the horrible curiosity of human nature, that this cruel sacrifice was attended with more eagerness than a theatre, or even a bull feast.

As the day advanced, the scaffolds and balconies were filled with expecting multitudes; the sun shone brightly upon fair faces and gallant dresses; one would have thought it some scene of elegant festivity, instead of an exhibition of human agony and death. But what a different spectacle and ceremony was this from those which Grenada exhibited in the days of her Moorish splendour. "Her galas, her tournaments, her sports of the ring, her fêtes of St. John, her music, her Zambras, and admirable tilts of canes! Her serenades, her concerts, her songs in Generaliffe! The costly liveries of the Abencerrages, their exquisite inventions, the skill and valour of the Alabaces, the superb dresses of the Zegries, Mazas, and Gomeles!"*—All these were at an end. The days of chivalry were over. Instead of the prancing cavalcade, with neighing steed and lively trumpet; with burnished lance, and helm, and buckler; with rich confusion of plume, and scarf, and banner, where purple, and scarlet, and green, and orange, and every gay colour were mingled with cloth of gold and fair embroidery; instead of this crept on the gloomy pageant of super-

*Rodd's Civil Wars of Grenada

stition, in cowl and sackcloth; with cross and coffin, and frightful symbols of human suffering. In place of the frank, hardy knight, open and brave, with his lady's favour in his casque, and amorous motto on his shield, looking, by gallant deeds, to win the smile of beauty, came the shaven, unmanly monk, with downcast eyes, and head and heart bleached in the cold cloister, secretly exulting in this bigot triumph.

The sound of the bells gave notice that the dismal procession was advancing. It passed slowly through the principal streets of the city, bearing in advance the awful banner of the holy office. The prisoners walked singly, attended by confessors, and guarded by familiars of the inquisition. They were clad in different garments, according to the nature of their punishments; those who were to suffer death wore the hideous Samarra, painted with flames and demons. The procession was swelled by choirs of boys, by different religious orders and public dignitaries, and, above all, by the fathers of the faith, moving "with slow pace, and profound gravity, truly triumphing, as becomes the principal generals of that great victory."*

As the sacred banner of the inquisition advanced, the countless throng sunk on their knees before it; they bowed their faces to the very earth as it passed, and then slowly rose again, like a great undulating billow. A murmur of tongues prevailed as the prisoners approached, and eager eyes were strained, and fingers pointed, to distinguish the different orders of penitents, whose habits denoted the degree of punishment they were to undergo. But as those drew near whose frightful garb marked them as destined to the flames, the noise of the rabble subsided; they seemed almost to hold in their breaths; filled with that strange and dismal interest with which we contemplate a human being on the verge of suffering and death.

It is an awful thing—a voiceless, noiseless multitude! The hushed and gazing stillness of the surrounding thousands, heaped on walls, and gates, and roofs, and hanging, as it were, in clusters, heightened the effect of the pageant that moved drearily on. The low murmuring of the priests could

*Gonsalvius, p. 135.

His creatures advanced to seize her. "Oh no! oh no!" cried she, with new terrors, and clinging to the familiars, "I have fled from no friends. He is not my protector! He is the murderer of my father!"

The familiars were perplexed; the crowd pressed on with eager curiosity. "Stand off!" cried the fiery Ambrosio, dashing the throng from around him. Then turning to the familiars, with sudden moderation, "My friends," said he, "deliver this poor girl to me. Her distress has turned her brain; she has escaped from her friends and protectors this morning; but a little quiet and kind treatment will restore her to tranquillity."

"I am not mad! I am not mad!" cried she vehemently. "Oh, save me!—save me from these men! I have no protector on earth but my father, and him they are murdering!"

The familiars shook their heads; her wildness corroborated the assertions of Don Ambrosio, and his apparent rank commanded respect and belief. They relinquished their charge to him, and he was consigning the struggling Inez to his creatures.—

"Let go your hold, villain!" cried a voice from among the crowd, and Antonio was seen eagerly tearing his way through the press of people.

"Seize him! seize him!" cried Don Ambrosio to the familiars: " 'tis an accomplice of the sorcerer's."

"Liar!" retorted Antonio, as he thrust the mob to the right and left, and forced himself to the spot.

The sword of Don Ambrosio flashed in an instant from the scabbard; the student was armed, and equally alert. There was a fierce clash of weapons; the crowd made way for them as they fought, and closed again, so as to hide them from the view of Inez. All was tumult and confusion for a moment; when there was a kind of shout from the spectators, and the mob again opening, she beheld, as she thought, Antonio weltering in his blood.

This new shock was too great for her already overstrained intellects. A giddiness seized upon her; every thing seemed to whirl before her eyes; she gasped some incoherent words, and sunk senseless upon the ground.

Days—weeks elapsed before Inez returned to consciousness. At length she opened her eyes, as if out of a troubled sleep. She was lying upon a magnificent bed, in a chamber richly furnished with pier glasses and massive tables inlaid with silver, of exquisite workmanship. The walls were covered with tapestry; the cornices richly gilded: through the door, which stood open, she perceived a superb saloon, with statues and crystal lustres, and a magnificent suite of apartments beyond. The casements of the room were open to admit the soft breath of summer, which stole in, laden with perfumes from a neighbouring garden; from whence, also, the refreshing sound of fountains and the sweet notes of birds came in mingled music to her ear.

Female attendants were moving, with noiseless step, about the chamber; but she feared to address them. She doubted whether this were not all delusion, or whether she was not still in the palace of Don Ambrosio, and that her escape, and all its circumstances, had not been but a feverish dream. She closed her eyes again, endeavouring to recall the past, and to separate the real from the imaginary. The last scenes of consciousness, however, rushed too forcibly, with all their horrors, to her mind to be doubted, and she turned shuddering from the recollection, to gaze once more on the quiet and serene magnificence around her. As she again opened her eyes, they rested on an object that at once dispelled every alarm. At the head of her bed sat a venerable form watching over her with a look of fond anxiety—it was her father!

I will not attempt to describe the scene that ensued; nor the moments of rapture which more than repaid all the sufferings that her affectionate heart had undergone. As soon as their feelings had become more calm, the alchymist stepped out of the room to introduce a stranger, to whom he was indebted for his life and liberty. He returned, leading in Antonio, no longer in his poor scholar's garb, but in the rich dress of a nobleman.

The feelings of Inez were almost overpowered by these sudden reverses, and it was some time before she was sufficiently composed to comprehend the explanation of this seeming romance.

It appeared that the lover, who had sought her affections

in the lowly guise of a student, was only son and heir of a powerful grandee of Valentia. He had been placed at the university of Salamanca; but a lively curiosity and an eagerness for adventure had induced him to abandon the university, without his father's consent, and to visit various parts of Spain. His rambling inclination satisfied, he had remained incognito for a time at Grenada, until, by further study and self-regulation, he could prepare himself to return home with credit, and atone for his transgressions against paternal authority.

How hard he had studied does not remain on record. All that we know is his romantic adventure of the tower. It was at first a mere youthful caprice, excited by a glimpse of a beautiful face. In becoming a disciple of the alchymist, he probably thought of nothing more than pursuing a light love-affair. Further acquaintance, however, had completely fixed his affections; and he had determined to conduct Inez and her father to Valentia, and to trust to her merits to secure his father's consent to their union.

In the mean time he had been traced to his concealment. His father had received intelligence of his being entangled in the snares of a mysterious adventurer and his daughter, and likely to become the dupe of the fascinations of the latter. Trusty emissaries had been despatched to seize upon him by main force, and convey him without delay to the paternal home.

What eloquence he had used with his father to convince him of the innocence, the honour, and the high descent of the alchymist, and of the exalted worth of his daughter, does not appear. All that we know is, that the father, though a very passionate, was a very reasonable man, as appears by his consenting that his son should return to Grenada, and conduct Inez, as his affianced bride, to Valentia.

Away, then, Don Antonio hurried back, full of joyous anticipations. He still forbore to throw off his disguise, fondly picturing to himself what would be the surprise of Inez, when, having won her heart and hand as a poor wandering scholar, he should raise her and her father at once to opulence and splendour.

On his arrival he had been shocked at finding the tower

deserted by its inhabitants. In vain he sought for intelligence concerning them; a mystery hung over their disappearance which he could not penetrate, until he was thunderstruck, on accidentally reading a list of the prisoners at the impending auto da fé, to find the name of his venerable master among the condemned.

It was the very morning of the execution. The procession was already on its way to the grand square. Not a moment was to be lost. The grand inquisitor was a relation of Don Antonio, though they had never met. His first impulse was to make himself known; to exert all his family influence, the weight of his name, and the power of his eloquence, in vindication of the alchymist. But the grand inquisitor was already proceeding, in all his pomp, to the place where the fatal ceremony was to be performed. How was he to be approached? Antonio threw himself into the crowd, in a fever of anxiety, and was forcing his way to the scene of horror, when he arrived just in time to rescue Inez, as has been mentioned.

It was Don Ambrosio that fell in their contest. Being desperately wounded, and thinking his end approaching, he had confessed, to an attending father of the inquisition, that he was the sole cause of the alchymist's condemnation, and that the evidence on which it was grounded was altogether false. The testimony of Don Antonio came in corroboration of this avowal; and his relationship to the grand inquisitor had, in all probability, its proper weight. Thus was the poor alchymist snatched, in a manner, from the very flames; and so great had been the sympathy awakened in his case, that for once a populace rejoiced at being disappointed of an execution.

The residue of the story may readily be imagined by every one versed in this valuable kind of history. Don Antonio espoused the lovely Inez, and took her and her father with him to Valentia. As she had been a loving and dutiful daughter, so she proved a true and tender wife. It was not long before Don Antonio succeeded to his father's titles and estates, and he and his fair spouse were renowned for being the handsomest and happiest couple in all Valentia.

As to Don Ambrosio, he partially recovered to the enjoyment of a broken constitution and a blasted name, and hid his remorse and disgraces in a convent; while the poor victim of his arts, who had assisted Inez in her escape, unable to conquer the early passion that he had awakened in her bosom, though convinced of the baseness of the object, retired from the world, and became a humble sister in a nunnery.

The worthy alchymist took up his abode with his children. A pavilion, in the garden of their palace, was assigned to him as a laboratory, where he resumed his researches, with renovated ardour, after the grand secret. He was now and then assisted by his son-in-law; but the latter slackened grievously in his zeal and diligence, after marriage. Still he would listen with profound gravity and attention to the old man's rhapsodies, and his quotations from Paracelsus, Sandivogius, and Pietro D'Abano, which daily grew longer and longer. In this way the good alchymist lived on quietly and comfortably, to what is called a good old age, that is to say, an age that is good for nothing, and, unfortunately for mankind, was hurried out of life in his ninetieth year, just as he was on the point of discovering the philosopher's stone.

Such was the story of the captain's friend, with which we whiled away the morning. The captain was, every now and then, interrupted by questions and remarks, which I have not mentioned, lest I should break the continuity of the tale. He was a little disturbed, also, once or twice, by the general, who fell asleep, and breathed rather hard, to the great horror and annoyance of Lady Lillycraft. In a long and tender love-scene, also, which was particularly to her ladyship's taste, the unlucky general, having his head a little sunk upon his breast, kept making a sound at regular intervals, very much like the word *pish*, long drawn out. At length he made an odd abrupt guttural sound, that suddenly awoke him; he hemmed, looked about with a slight degree of consternation, and then began to play with her ladyship's work-bag, which, however, she rather pettishly withdrew. The steady sound of the captain's voice was still too potent a soporific for the poor general; he kept gleaming up and sinking in the socket, until the cessation of the tale again roused him, when he started awake, put his foot down upon Lady Lillycraft's cur, the sleeping

Beauty, which yelped, and seized him by the leg, and, in a moment, the whole library resounded with yelpings and exclamations. Never did a man more completely mar his fortunes while he was asleep. Silence being at length restored, the company expressed their thanks to the captain, and gave various opinions of the story. The parson's mind, I found, had been continually running upon the leaden manuscripts, mentioned in the beginning, as dug up at Grenada, and he put several eager questions to the captain on the subject. The general could not well make out the drift of the story, but thought it a little confused. "I am glad, however," said he, "that they burnt the old chap of the tower; I have no doubt he was a notorious imposter."

END OF VOL. I

English Country Gentlemen

His certain life, that never can deceive him,
  Is full of thousand sweets, and rich content;
The smooth-leav'd beeches in the field receive him
  With coolest shade, till noontide's heat be spent.
His life is neither tost in boist'rous seas,
Or the vexatious world; or lost in slothful ease.
Pleased and full blest he lives, when he his God can please.
Phineas Fletcher

I TAKE GREAT PLEASURE in accompanying the squire in his perambulations about his estate, in which he is often attended by a kind of cabinet council. His prime minister, the steward, is a very worthy and honest old man, that assumes a right of way; that is to say, a right to have his own way, from having lived time out of mind on the place. He loves the estate even better than he does the squire; and thwarts the latter sadly in many of his projects of improvement, being a little prone to disapprove of every plan that does not originate with himself.

In the course of one of these perambulations, I have known the squire to point out some important alteration which he was contemplating, in the disposition or cultivation of the grounds; this of course would be opposed by the steward, and a long argument would ensue over a stile, or on a rising piece of ground, until the squire, who has a high opinion of the other's ability and integrity, would be fain to give up the point. This concession, I observed, would immediately mollify the old man, and, after walking over a field or two in silence, with his hands behind his back, chewing the cud of reflection, he would suddenly turn to the squire and observe, that "he had been turning the matter over in his mind, and, upon the whole, he believed he would take his honour's advice."

Christy, the huntsman, is another of the squire's occasional attendants, to whom he continually refers in all matters of local history, as to a chronicle of the estate, having, in a manner, been acquainted with many of the trees from the very time that they were acorns. Old Nimrod, as has been shown, is rather pragmatical in those points of knowledge on which he values himself; but the squire rarely contradicts him, and is, in fact, one of the most indulgent potentates that ever was hen-pecked by his ministry.

He often laughs about it himself, and evidently yields to these old men more from the bent of his own humour, than from any want of proper authority. He likes this honest independence of old age, and is well aware that these trusty followers love and honour him in their hearts. He is perfectly at ease about his own dignity and the respect of those around him; nothing disgusts him sooner than any appearance of fawning or sycophancy.

I really have seen no display of royal state that could compare with one of the squire's progresses about his paternal fields and through his hereditary woodlands, with several of these faithful adherents about him, and followed by a body-guard of dogs. He encourages a frankness and manliness of deportment among his dependents, and is the personal friend of his tenants; inquiring into their concerns, and assisting them in times of difficulty and hardship. This has rendered him one of the most popular, and of course one of the happiest of landlords.

Indeed, I do not know a more enviable condition of life, than that of an English gentleman, of sound judgment and good feelings, who passes the greater part of his time on an hereditary estate in the country. From the excellence of the roads and the rapidity and exactness of the public conveyances, he is enabled to command all the comforts and conveniences, all the intelligence and novelties of the capital, while he is removed from its hurry and distraction. He has ample means of occupation and amusement within his own domains; he may diversify his time by rural occupations, by rural sports, by study, and by the delights of friendly society collected within his own hospitable halls.

Or if his views and feelings are of a more extensive and liberal nature, he has it greatly in his power to do good, and to have that good immediately reflected back upon himself. He can render essential service to his country, by assisting in the disinterested administration of the laws; by watching over the opinions and principles of the lower orders around him; by diffusing among them those lights which may be important to their welfare; by mingling frankly among them, gaining their confidence, becoming the immediate auditor of their complaints, informing himself of their wants, making himself a channel through which their grievances may be quietly communicated to the proper sources of mitigation and relief; or by becoming, if need be, the intrepid and incorruptible guardian of their liberties—the enlightened champion of their rights.

All this, it appears to me, can be done without any sacrifice of personal dignity, without any degrading arts of popularity, without any truckling to vulgar prejudices, or concurrence in vulgar clamour; but by the steady influence of sincere and friendly counsel, of fair, upright, and generous deportment. Whatever may be said of English mobs and English demagogues, I have never met with a people more open to reason, more considerate in their tempers, more tractable by argument in the roughest times, than the English. They are remarkably quick at discerning and appreciating whatever is manly and honourable. They are by nature and habit methodical and orderly: and they feel the value of all that is regular and respectable. They may occasionally be deceived by sophistry, and excited into turbulence by public distresses and the misrepresentations of designing men; but open their eyes, and they will eventually rally round the land-marks of steady truth and deliberate good sense. They are fond of established customs, they are fond of long established names, and that love of order and quiet which characterizes the nation, gives a vast influence to the descendants of the old families, whose forefathers have been lords of the soil from time immemorial.

It is when the rich and well-educated and highly privileged classes neglect their duties, when they neglect to study the interests, and conciliate the affections, and instruct the opinions and champion the rights of the people, that the latter become discontented and turbulent, and fall into the hands of demagogues: the demagogue always steps in where the patriot is wanting. There is a common high-handed cant among the high-feeding, and, as they fancy themselves, high-minded men, about putting down the mob; but all true physicians know that it is better to sweeten the blood than attack the tumour, to apply the emollient rather than the cautery. It is absurd in a country like England, where there is so much freedom, and such a jealousy of right, for any man to assume an aristocratical tone, and to talk superciliously of the common people. There is no rank that makes him independent of the opinions and affections of his fellow-men, there is no rank nor distinction that severs him from his fellow-subject; and if, by any gradual neglect or assumption on the one side, and discontent and jealousy on the other, the orders of society should really separate, let those who stand on the eminence beware that the chasm is not mining at their feet. The orders of society in all well constituted governments are mutually bound together, and important to each other; there can be no such thing in a free government as a vacuum; and whenever one is likely to take place, by the drawing off of the rich and intelligent from the poor, the bad passions of society will rush in to fill up the space, and rend the whole asunder.

Though born and brought up in a republic, and more and more confirmed in republican principles by every year's observation and experience, yet I am not insensible to the excellence that may exist in other forms of government, nor to the fact that they may be more suitable to the situation and circumstances of the countries in which they exist: I have endeavoured rather to look at them as they are, and to observe how they are calculated to effect the end which they propose. Considering, therefore, the mixed nature of the government of this country, and its representative form, I have looked with admiration at the manner in which the wealth and influence and intelligence were spread over its whole surface; not as in some monarchies, drained from the country, and collected in towns and cities. I have considered the great rural establishments of the nobility, and the lesser establishments of the gentry, as so many reservoirs of wealth and intelligence distributed about the kingdom, apart from the towns, to irrigate, freshen, and fertilize the surrounding country. I have looked upon them too, as the august retreats of patriots and statesmen, where, in the enjoyment of honourable independence and elegant leisure, they might train up their minds to appear in those legislative assemblies, whose debates and decisions form the study and precedents of other nations, and involve the interests of the world.

I have been both surprised and disappointed, therefore, at finding, that on this subject I was often indulging in an Utopian dream, rather than a well-founded opinion. I have been concerned at finding that these fine estates were too often involved, and mortgaged, or placed in the hands of creditors, and the owners exiled from their paternal lands. There is an extravagance, I am told, that runs parallel with wealth; a lavish expenditure among the great; a senseless competition among the aspiring; a heedless, joyless dissipation, among all the upper ranks, that often beggars even these splendid establishments, breaks down the pride and principles of their possessors, and makes too many of them mere place-hunters, or shifting absentees. It is thus that so many are thrown into the hands of government; and a court, which ought to be the most pure and honourable in Europe, is so often degraded by noble, but importunate time-servers. It is thus, too, that so many become exiles from their native land, crowding the hotels of foreign countries, and expending upon thankless strangers the wealth so hardly drained from their laborious peasantry. I have looked upon these latter with a mixture of censure and concern. Knowing the almost bigoted fondness of an Englishman for his native home, I can conceive what must be their compunction and regret, when, amidst the sunburnt plains of France, they call to mind the green fields of England; the hereditary groves which they have abandoned, and the hospitable roof of their fathers, which they have left desolate, or to be inhabited by strangers. But retrenchment is no plea for an abandonment of country. They have risen with the prosperity of the land; let them abide its fluctuations, and conform to its fortunes. It is not for the rich to fly because the country is suffering: let them share, in their relative proportion, the common lot; they owe it to the land that has elevated them to honour and affluence. When the poor have to diminish their scanty morsel of bread; when they have to compound with the cravings of nature, and study with how little they can do, and not be starved; it is not then for the rich to fly, and diminish still further the resources of the poor, that they themselves may live in splendour in a cheaper country. Let them rather retire to their estates, and there practise retrenchment. Let them return to that noble simplicity, that practical good sense, that honest pride, which form the foundation of true English character, and from them they may again rear the edifice of fair and honourable prosperity.

On the rural habits of the English nobility and gentry; on the manner in which they discharge their duties on their patrimonial possessions, depend greatly the virtue and welfare of the nation. So long as they pass the greater part of their time in the quiet and purity of the country; surrounded by the monuments of their illustrious ancestors; surrounded by every thing that can inspire generous pride, noble emulation, and amiable magnanimous sentiment; so long they are safe, and in them the nation may repose its interests and its honour. But the moment that they become the servile throngers of court avenues, and give themselves up to the political intrigues and heartless dissipations of the metropolis, that moment they lose the real nobility of their natures, and become the mere leeches of the country.

That the great majority of nobility and gentry in England are endowed with high notions of honour and independence, I thoroughly believe. They have evidenced it lately on very important questions, and have given an example of adherence to principle, in preference to party and power, that must have astonished many of the venal and obsequious courts of Europe. Such are the glorious effects of freedom, when infused into a constitution. But it seems to me that they are apt to forget the positive nature of their duties, and to fancy that their eminent privileges are only so many means of self-indulgence. They should recollect, that in a constitution like that of England, the titled orders are intended to be as useful as they are ornamental, and it is their virtues alone that can render them both. Their duties are divided between the sovereign and the subject; surrounding and giving lustre and dignity to the throne, and at the same time tempering and mitigating its rays, until they are transmitted in mild and genial radiance to the people. Born to leisure and opulence, they owe the exercise of their talents, and the expenditure of their wealth, to their native country. They may be compared to the clouds; which, being drawn up by the sun, and elevated in the heavens, reflect and magnify his splendour; while they repay the earth, from which they derive their sustenance, by returning their treasures to its bosom in fertilizing showers.

A Bachelor's Confessions

"I'll live a private, pensive, single life."
The Collier of Croydon

I WAS SITTING in my room a morning or two since, reading, when some one tapped at the door, and Master Simon entered. He had an unusually fresh appearance; he had put on a bright green riding-coat, with a bunch of violets in the button-hole, and had the air of an old bachelor trying to rejuvenate himself. He had not, however, his usual briskness and vivacity; but loitered about the room with somewhat of absence of manner, humming the old song, — "Go, lovely rose, tell her that wastes her time and me;" and then, leaning against the window, and looking upon the landscape, he uttered a very audible sigh. As I had not been accustomed to see Master Simon in a pensive mood, I thought there might be some vexation preying on his mind, and I endeavoured to introduce a cheerful strain of conversation; but he was not in the vein to follow it up, and proposed that we should take a walk.

It was a beautiful morning of that soft vernal temperature, that seems to thaw all the frost out of one's blood, and to set all nature in a ferment. The very fishes felt its influence; the cautious trout ventured out of his dark hole to seek his mate, the roach and the dace rose up to the surface of the brook to bask in the sunshine, and the amorous frog piped from among the rushes. If ever an oyster can really fall in love, as has been said or sung, it must be on such a morning.

The weather certainly had its effect even upon Master Simon, for he seemed obstinately bent upon the pensive mood. Instead of stepping briskly along, smacking his dog-whip, whistling quaint ditties, or telling sporting anecdotes, he leaned on my arm, and talked about the approaching nuptials; from whence he made several digressions upon the character of womankind, touched a little upon the tender passion, and made sundry very excellent, though rather trite, observations upon disappointments in love. It was evident that he had something on his mind which he wished to impart, but felt awkward in approaching it. I was curious to see to what this strain would lead; but I was determined not to assist him. Indeed, I mischievously pretended to turn the conversation, and talked of his usual topics, dogs, horses, and hunting; but he was very brief in his replies, and invariably got back, by hook or by crook, into the sentimental vein.

At length we came to a clump of trees that overhung a whispering brook, with a rustic bench at their feet. The trees were grievously scored with letters and devices, which had grown out of all shape and size by the growth of the bark; and it appeared that this grove had served as a kind of register of the family loves from time immemorial. Here Master Simon made a pause, pulled up a tuft of flowers, threw them one by one into the water, and at length, turning somewhat abruptly upon me, asked me if I had ever been in love. I confess the question startled me a little, as I am not over fond of making confessions of my amorous follies; and above all should never dream of choosing my friend Master Simon for a confidant. He did not wait, however, for a reply; the inquiry was merely a prelude to a confession on his own part, and after several circumlocutions and whimsical preambles, he fairly disburthened himself of a very tolerable story of his having been crossed in love.

The reader will, very probably, suppose that it related to the gay widow who jilted him not long since at Doncaster races;—no such thing. It was about a sentimental passion that he once had for a most beautiful young lady, who wrote poetry and played on the harp. He used to serenade her; and indeed he described several tender and gallant scenes, in which he was evidently picturing himself in his mind's eye as some elegant hero of romance, though, unfortunately for the tale, I only saw him as he stood before me, a dapper little old bachelor, with a face like an apple that has dried with the bloom on it.

What were the particulars of this tender tale I have already forgotten; indeed I listened to it with a heart like a very pebble stone, having hard work to repress a smile while Master Simon was putting on the amorous swain, uttering every now and then a sigh, and endeavouring to look sentimental and melancholy.

All that I recollect is, that the lady, according to his account, was certainly a little touched; for she used to accept all the music that he copied for her harp, and all the patterns that he drew for her dresses; and he began to flatter himself, after a long course of delicate attentions, that he was gradually fanning up a gentle flame in her heart, when she suddenly accepted the hand of a rich, boisterous, fox-hunting baronet, without either music or sentiment, who carried her by storm, after a fortnight's courtship.

Master Simon could not help concluding by some observation about "modest merit," and the power of gold over the sex. As a remembrance of his passion, he pointed out a heart carved on the bark of one of the trees; but which, in the process of time, had grown out into a large excrescence: and he showed me a lock of her hair, which he wore in a true lover's knot, in a large gold brooch.

I have seldom met with an old bachelor that had not, at some time or other, his nonsensical moment, when he would become tender and sentimental, talk about the concerns of the heart, and have some confession of a delicate nature to make. Almost every man has some little trait of romance in his life, which he looks back to with fondness, and about which he is apt to grow garrulous occasionally. He recollects himself as he was at the time, young and gamesome; and forgets that his hearers have no other idea of the hero of the tale, but such as he may appear at the time of telling it; peradventure, a withered, whimsical, spindle-shanked old gentleman. With married men, it is true, this is not so frequently the case; their amorous romance is apt to decline after marriage; why, I cannot for the life of me imagine; but with a bachelor, though it may slumber, it never dies. It is always liable to break out again in transient flashes, and never so much as on a spring morning in the country; or on a winter evening, when seated in his solitary chamber, stirring up the fire and talking of matrimony.

The moment that Master Simon had gone through his confession, and, to use the common phrase, "had made a clean breast of it," he became quite himself again. He had settled the point which had been worrying his mind, and doubtless considered himself established as a man of sentiment in my opinion. Before we had finished our morning's stroll, he was singing as blithe as a grasshopper, whistling to his dogs, and telling droll stories; and I recollect that he was particularly facetious that day at dinner, on the subject of matrimony, and uttered several excellent jokes, not to be found in Joe Miller, that made the bride elect blush and look down; but set all the old gentlemen at the table in a roar, and absolutely brought tears into the general's eyes.

English Gravity

"Merrie England!"
Ancient Phrase

THERE IS NOTHING so rare as for a man to ride his hobby without molestation. I find the squire has not so undisturbed an indulgence in his humours as I had imagined; but has been repeatedly thwarted of late, and has suffered a kind of well-meaning persecution from a Mr. Faddy, an old gentleman of some weight, at least of purse, who has recently moved into the neighbourhood. He is a worthy and substantial manufacturer, who, having accumulated a large fortune by dint of steam-engines and spinning jennies, has retired from business, and set up for a country gentleman. He has taken an old country seat and refitted it, and painted and plastered it, until it looks not unlike his own manufactory. He has been particularly careful in mending the walls and hedges, and putting up notices of spring-guns and man-traps in every part of his premises. Indeed he shows great jealousy about his territorial rights, having stopped up a foot-path that led across his fields; and given warning, in staring letters, that whoever was found trespassing on those grounds would be prosecuted with the utmost rigour of the law. He has brought into the country with him all the practical maxims of town, and the bustling habits of business; and is one of those sensible, useful, prosing, troublesome, intolerable old gentlemen that go about wearying and worrying society with excellent plans for public utility.

He is very much disposed to be on intimate terms with the squire, and calls on him every now and then, with some project for the good of the neighbourhood, which happens to run diametrically opposite to some one or other of the squire's peculiar notions; but which is "too sensible a measure" to be openly opposed. He has annoyed him excessively by enforcing the vagrant laws; persecuting the gipsies, and endeavouring to suppress country wakes and holiday games; which he considers great nuisances, and reprobates as causes of the deadly sin of idleness.

There is evidently in all this a little of the ostentation of newly acquired consequence; the tradesman is gradually swelling into the aristocrat; and he begins to grow excessively intolerant of every thing that is not genteel. He has a great deal to say about "the common people;" talks much of his park, his preserves, and the necessity of enforcing the game laws more strictly; and makes frequent use of the phrase, "the gentry of the neighbourhood."

He came to the hall lately, with a face full of business, that he and the squire, to use his own words, "might lay their heads together," to hit upon some mode of putting a stop to the frolicking at the village on the approaching May-day. It drew, he said, idle people together from all parts of the neighbourhood, who spent the day fiddling, dancing, and carousing, instead of staying at home to work for their families.

Now, as the squire, unluckily, is at the bottom of these May-day revels, it may be supposed that the suggestions of the sagacious Mr. Faddy were not received with the best grace in the world. It is true, the old gentleman is too courteous to show any temper to a guest in his own house, but no sooner was he gone than the indignation of the squire found vent, at having his poetical cobwebs invaded by this buzzing, blue-bottle fly of traffic. In his warmth he inveighed against the whole race of manufacturers, who, I found, were sore disturbers of his comfort. "Sir," said he, with emotion, "it makes my heart bleed to see all our fine streams dammed up and bestrode by cotton mills; our valleys smoking with steam-engines, and the din of the hammer and the loom scaring away all our rural delights. What's to become of merry old England, when its manor houses are all turned into manufactories, and its sturdy peasantry into pin-makers and stocking-weavers? I have looked in vain for merry Sherwood, and all the greenwood haunts of Robin Hood; the whole country is covered with manufacturing towns. I have stood on the ruins of Dudley Castle, and looked round, with an aching heart, on what were once its feudal domains of verdant and beautiful country. Sir, I beheld a mere campus phlegræ; a region of fire; reeking with coal-pits, and furnaces, and smelting-houses, vomiting forth flames and smoke. The pale and ghastly people, toiling among vile exhalations, looked more

like demons than human beings; the clanking wheels and
engines, seen through the murky atmosphere, looked like instruments of torture in this pandemonium. What is to become of the country with these evils rankling in its very core?
Sir, these manufacturers will be the ruin of our rural manners;
they will destroy the national character; they will not leave
materials for a single line of poetry!"

The squire is apt to wax eloquent on such themes; and I
could hardly help smiling at this whimsical lamentation over
national industry and public improvement. I am told, however, that he really grieves at the growing spirit of trade, as
destroying the charm of life. He considers every new short-
hand mode of doing things, as an inroad of snug sordid
method; and thinks that this will soon become a mere matter
of fact world, where life will be reduced to a mathematical
calculation of conveniences, and every thing will be done by
steam.

He maintains also, that the nation has declined in its free
and joyous spirit in proportion as it has turned its attention to
commerce and manufactures; and that in old times, when England was an idler, it was also a merrier little island. In support of this opinion he adduces the frequency and splendour
of ancient festivals and merry-makings, and the hearty spirit
with which they were kept up by all classes of people. His
memory is stored with the accounts given by Stow, in his
Survey of London, of the holiday revels at the inns of court,
the Christmas mummeries, and the masquings and bonfires
about the streets. London, he says, in those days, resembled
the continental cities in its picturesque manners and amusements. The court used to dance after dinner on public occasions. After the coronation dinner of Richard II, for example,
the king, the prelates, the nobles, the knights, and the rest of
the company danced in Westminster Hall to the music of the
minstrels. The example of the court was followed by the mid-
dling classes, and so down to the lowest, and the whole
nation was a dancing, jovial nation. He quotes a lively city
picture of the times, given by Stow, which resembles the
lively scenes one may often see in the gay city of Paris; for he
tells us that on holidays, after evening prayers, the maidens in
London used to assemble before the door, in sight of their

masters and dames, and while one played on a timbrel, the others danced for garlands, hanged athwart the street.

"Where will we meet with such merry groups now-a-days?" the squire will exclaim, shaking his head mournfully;—"and then as to the gaiety that prevailed in dress throughout all ranks of society; and made the very streets so fine and picturesque. 'I have myself,' says Gervaise Markham, 'met an ordinary tapster in his silk stockings, garters deep fringed with gold lace, the rest of his apparel suitable, with cloak lined with velvet!' Nashe, too, who wrote in 1593, exclaims at the finery of the nation. 'England, the players stage of gorgeous attire, the ape of all nations superfluities, the continual masquer in outlandish habiliments.' "

Such are a few of the authorities quoted by the squire by way of contrasting what he supposes to have been the former vivacity of the nation with its present monotonous character. "John Bull," he will say, "was then a gay cavalier, with a sword by his side and a feather in his cap; but he is now a plodding citizen, in snuff-coloured coat and gaiters."

By the bye, there really appears to have been some change in the national character since the days of which the squire is so fond of talking; those days when this little island acquired its favourite old title of "merry England." This may be attributed in part to the growing hardships of the times, and the necessity of turning the whole attention to the means of subsistence; but England's gayest customs prevailed at times when her common people enjoyed comparatively few of the comforts and conveniences that they do at present. It may be still more attributed to the universal spirit of gain, and the calculating habits that commerce has introduced; but I am inclined to attribute it chiefly to the gradual increase of the liberty of the subject, and the growing freedom and activity of opinion.

A free people are apt to be grave and thoughtful. They have high and important matters to occupy their minds. They feel that it is their right, their interest, and their duty to mingle in public concerns, and to watch over the general welfare. The continual exercise of the mind on political topics gives intenser habits of thinking, and a more serious and earnest demeanour. A nation becomes less gay, but more intellectually active and vigorous. It evinces less play of the fancy, but more power of the imagination; less taste and elegance, but more grandeur of mind; less animated vivacity, but deeper enthusiasm.

It is when men are shut out of the regions of manly thought by a despotic government; when every grave and lofty theme is rendered perilous to discussion and almost to reflection; it is then that they turn to the safer occupations of taste and amusement; trifles rise to importance, and occupy the craving activity of intellect. No being is more void of care and reflection than the slave; none dances more gaily in his intervals of labour; but make him free, give him rights and interests to guard, and he becomes thoughtful and laborious.

The French are a gayer people than the English. Why? Partly from temperament, perhaps; but greatly because they have been accustomed to governments which surrounded the free exercise of thought with danger, and where he only was safe who shut his eyes and ears to public events, and enjoyed the passing pleasure of the day. Within late years they have had more opportunity of exercising their minds; and within late years the national character has essentially changed. Never did the French enjoy such a degree of freedom as they do at this moment: and at this moment the French are comparatively a grave people.

Gipsies

What's that to absolute freedom; such as the very beggars have;
to feast and revel here today, and yonder tomorrow; next day
where they please, and so on still, the whole country or kingdom over? There's liberty! the birds of the air can take no more.

Jovial Crew

SINCE THE MEETING with the gipsies, which I have related
in a former paper, I have observed several of them haunting the purlieus of the Hall, in spite of a positive interdiction
of the squire. They are part of a gang that has long kept about
this neighbourhood, to the great annoyance of the farmers,
whose poultry-yards often suffer from their nocturnal invasions. They are, however, in some measure, patronised by
the squire, who considers the race as belonging to the good
old times which, to confess the private truth, seem to have
abounded with good-for-nothing characters.

This roving crew is called "Star-light Tom's Gang," from
the name of its chieftain, a notorious poacher. I have heard
repeatedly of the misdeeds of this "minion of the moon;" for
every midnight depredation that takes place in park, or fold,
or farm-yard, is laid to his charge. Star-light Tom, in fact,
answers to his name; he seems to walk in darkness, and, like
a fox, to be traced in the morning by the mischief he has
done. He reminds me of that fearful personage in the nursery
rhyme:

> Who goes round the house at night?
>   None but bloody Tom!
> Who steals all the sheep at night?
>   None but one by one!

In short, Star-light Tom is the scape-goat of the neighbourhood; but so cunning and adroit, that there is no detecting him. Old Christy and the game-keeper have watched
many a night in hopes of entrapping him; and Christy
often patrols the park with his dogs, for the purpose, but
all in vain. It is said that the squire winks hard at his mis-

deeds, having an indulgent feeling towards the vagabond, because of his being very expert at all kinds of games, a great shot with the cross-bow, and the best morrice dancer in the country.

The squire also suffers the gang to lurk unmolested about the skirts of his estate, on condition that they do not come about the house. The approaching wedding, however, has made a kind of Saturnalia at the Hall, and has caused a suspension of all sober rule. It has produced a great sensation throughout the female part of the household; not a housemaid but dreams of wedding favours, and has a husband running in her head. Such a time is a harvest for the gipsies; there is a public foot-path leading across one part of the park, by which they have free ingress, and they are continually hovering about the grounds, telling the servant girls' fortunes, or getting smuggled in to the young ladies.

I believe the Oxonian amuses himself very much by furnishing them with hints in private, and bewildering all the weak brains in the house with their wonderful revelations. The general certainly was very much astonished by the communications made to him the other evening by the gipsy girl: he kept a wary silence towards us on the subject, and affected to treat it lightly; but I have noticed that he has since redoubled his attentions to Lady Lillycraft and her dogs.

I have seen also Phœbe Wilkins, the housekeeper's pretty and lovesick niece, holding a long conference with one of these old sibyls behind a large tree in the avenue, and often looking round to see that she was not observed. I make no doubt that she was endeavouring to get some favourable augury about the result of her love-quarrel with young Ready Money, as oracles have always been more consulted on love-affairs than upon any thing else. I fear, however, that in this instance the response was not so favourable as usual, for I perceived poor Phœbe returning pensively towards the house; her head hanging down, her hat in her hand, and the riband trailing along the ground.

At another time, as I turned a corner of a terrace, at the bottom of the garden, just by a clump of trees, and a large stone urn, I came upon a bevy of the young girls of the family, attended by this same Phœbe Wilkins. I was at a loss to comprehend the meaning of their blushing and giggling, and their apparent agitation, until I saw the red cloak of a gipsy vanishing among the shrubbery. A few moments after I caught sight of Master Simon and the Oxonian stealing along one of the walks of the garden, chuckling and laughing at their successful waggery; having evidently put the gipsy up to the thing, and instructed her what to say.

After all, there is something strangely pleasing in these tamperings with the future, even where we are convinced of the fallacy of the prediction. It is singular how willingly the mind will half deceive itself, and with what a degree of awe we will listen even to these babblers about futurity. For my part, I cannot feel angry with these poor vagabonds, that seek to deceive us into bright hopes and expectations. I have always been something of a castle-builder, and have found my liveliest pleasures to arise from the illusions which fancy has cast over common-place realities. As I get on in life, I find it more difficult to deceive myself in this delightful manner; and I should be thankful to any prophet, however false, that would conjure the clouds which hang over futurity into palaces, and all its doubtful regions into fairy-land.

The squire, who, as I have observed, has a private good will towards gipsies, has suffered considerable annoyance on their account. Not that they requite his indulgence with ingratitude, for they do not depredate very flagrantly on his estate; but because their pilferings and misdeeds occasion loud murmurs in the village. I can readily understand the old gentleman's humour on this point; I have a great toleration for all kinds of vagrant sunshiny existence, and must confess I take a pleasure in observing the ways of gipsies. The English, who are accustomed to them from childhood, and often suffer from their petty depredations, consider them as mere nuisances; but I have been very much struck with their peculiarities. I like to behold their clear olive complexions, their romantic black eyes, their raven locks, their lithe slender figures, and to hear them, in low silver tones, dealing forth magnificent promises of honours, and estates, of world's wealth, and ladies' love.

Their mode of life, too, has something in it very fanciful and picturesque. They are the free denizens of nature, and maintain a primitive independence, in spite of law and gospel; of county gaols and country magistrates. It is curious to see this obstinate adherence to the wild unsettled habits of savage life transmitted from generation to generation, and preserved in the midst of one of the most cultivated, populous, and systematic countries in the world. They are totally distinct from the busy, thrifty people about them. They seem to be, like the Indians of America, either above or below the ordinary cares and anxieties of mankind. Heedless of power, of honours, of wealth; and indifferent to the fluctuations of the times; the rise or fall of grain, or stock, or empires, they seem to laugh at the toiling, fretting world around them, and to live according to the philosophy of the old song:

> "Who would ambition shun,
>   And loves to lie i' the sun,
>   Seeking the food he eats,
>   And pleased with what he gets,
>   Come hither, come hither, come hither;
>   Here shall he see
>   No enemy,
>   But winter and rough weather."

In this way they wander from county to county; keeping about the purlieus of villages, or in plenteous neighbourhoods, where there are fat farms and rich country-seats. Their encampments are generally made in some beautiful spot; either a green shady nook of a road; or on the border of a common, under a sheltering hedge; or on the skirts of a fine spreading wood. They are always to be found lurking about fairs and races, and rustic gatherings, wherever there is pleasure, and throng, and idleness. They are the oracles of milk maids and simple serving girls; and sometimes have even the honour of perusing the white hands of gentlemen's daughters, when rambling about their fathers' grounds. They are the bane of good housewives and thrifty farmers, and odious in the eyes of country justices; but, like all other vagabond beings, they have something to commend them to the fancy. They are among the last traces, in these matter-of-fact days, of the motley population of former times; and are whimsically associated in my mind with fairies and witches, Robin Good Fellow, Robin Hood, and the other fantastical personages of poetry.

May-Day Customs

Happy the age, and harmlesse were the dayes,
  (For then true love and amity was found)
When every village did a May-pole raise,
  And Whitson-ales and May-games did abound:
And all the lusty yonkers in a rout,
With merry lasses daunc'd the rod about,
Then friendship to their banquets bid the guests,
And poore men far'd the better for their feasts.

Pasquil's Palinodia

T HE MONTH of April has nearly passed away, and we are
fast approaching that poetical day which was considered,
in old times, as the boundary that parted the frontiers of
winter and summer. With all its caprices, however, I like the
month of April. I like these laughing and crying days, when
sun and shade seem to run in billows over the landscape. I
like to see the sudden shower coursing over the meadow, and
giving all nature a greener smile; and the bright sunbeams
chasing the flying cloud, and turning all its drops into
diamonds.

I was enjoying a morning of the kind in company with the
squire in one of the finest parts of the park. We were skirting
a beautiful grove, and he was giving me a kind of biographical account of several of his favourite forest trees, when we
heard the strokes of an axe from the midst of a thick copse.
The squire paused and listened, with manifest signs of uneasiness. He turned his steps in the direction of the sound. The
strokes grew louder and louder as we advanced; there was
evidently a vigorous arm wielding the axe. The squire quick-
ened his pace, but in vain; a loud crack and a succeeding crash
told that the mischief had been done, and some child of the
forest laid low. When we came to the place, we found Master
Simon and several others standing about a tall and beautifully
straight young tree, which had just been felled.

The squire, though a man of most harmonious disposi-
tions, was completely put out of tune by this circumstance.
He felt like a monarch witnessing the murder of one of his

liege subjects, and demanded, with some asperity, the meaning of the outrage. It turned out to be an affair of Master Simon's, who had selected the tree, from its height and straightness, for a May-pole, the old one which stood on the village green being unfit for further service. If any thing could have soothed the ire of my worthy host, it would have been the reflection that his tree had fallen in so good a cause; and I saw that there was a great struggle between his fondness for his groves, and his devotion to May-day. He could not contemplate the prostrate tree, however, without indulging in lamentation, and making a kind of funeral eulogy, like Mark Anthony over the body of Cæsar; and he forbade that any tree should thenceforward be cut down on his estate without a warrant from himself; being determined, he said, to hold the sovereign power of life and death in his own hands.

This mention of the May-pole struck my attention, and I inquired whether the old customs connected with it were really kept up in this part of the country. The squire shook his head mournfully; and I found I had touched on one of his tender points, for he grew quite melancholy in bewailing the total decline of old May-day. Though it is regularly celebrated in the neighbouring village, yet it has been merely resuscitated by the worthy squire, and is kept up in a forced state of existence at his expense. He meets with continual discouragements; and finds great difficulty in getting the country bumpkins to play their parts tolerably. He manages to have every year a "Queen of the May;" but as to Robin Hood, Friar Tuck, the Dragon, the Hobby Horse, and all the other motley crew that used to enliven the day with their mummery, he has not ventured to introduce them.

Still I look forward with some interest to the promised shadow of old May-day, even though it be but a shadow; and I feel more and more pleased with the whimsical, yet harmless hobby of my host, which is surrounding him with agreeable associations, and making a little world of poetry about him. Brought up, as I have been, in a new country, I may appreciate too highly the faint vestiges of ancient customs which I now and then meet with, and the interest I express in them may provoke a smile from those who are negligently suffering them to pass away. But with whatever indifference they may be regarded by those "to the manner born," yet in my mind the lingering flavour of them imparts a charm to rustic life, which nothing else could readily supply.

I shall never forget the delight I felt on first seeing a May-pole. It was on the banks of the Dee, close by the picturesque old bridge that stretches across the river from the quaint little city of Chester. I had already been carried back into former days by the antiquities of that venerable place; the examination of which is equal to turning over the pages of a black letter volume, or gazing on the pictures in Froissart. The May-pole on the margin of that poetic stream completed the illusion. My fancy adorned it with wreaths of flowers, and peopled the green bank with all the dancing revelry of May-day. The mere sight of this May-pole gave a glow to my feelings, and spread a charm over the country for the rest of the day; and as I traversed a part of the fair plain of Cheshire, and the beautiful borders of Wales, and looked from among swelling hills down a long green valley, through which "the Deva wound its wizard stream," my imagination turned all into a perfect Arcadia.

Whether it be owing to such poetical associations early instilled into my mind, or whether there is, as it were, a sympathetic revival and budding forth of the feelings at this season, certain it is, that I always experience, wherever I may be placed, a delightful expansion of the heart at the return of May. It is said that birds about this time will become restless in their cages, as if instinct with the season, conscious of the revelry that is going on in the groves, and impatient to break from their bondage, and join in the jubilee of the year. In like manner I have felt myself excited, even in the midst of the metropolis, when the windows, which had been churlishly closed all winter, were again thrown open to receive the balmy breath of May; when the sweets of the country were breathed into the town, and flowers were cried about the streets. I have considered the treasures of flowers thus poured in, as so many missives from nature inviting us forth to enjoy the virgin beauty of the year, before its freshness is exhaled by the heats of sunny summer.

One can readily imagine what a gay scene it must have been in jolly old London, when the doors were decorated with flowering branches, when every hat was decked with haw-thorn, and Robin Hood, Friar Tuck, Maid Marian, the mor-rice dancers, and all the other fantastic masks and revellers, were performing their antics about the May-pole in every part of the city.

I am not a bigoted admirer of old times and old customs merely because of their antiquity. But while I rejoice in the decline of many of the rude usages and coarse amusements of former days, I cannot but regret that this innocent and fanci-ful festival has fallen into disuse. It seemed appropriate to this verdant and pastoral country, and calculated to light up the too pervading gravity of the nation. I value every custom that tends to infuse poetical feeling into the common people, and to sweeten and soften the rudeness of rustic manners, without destroying their simplicity. Indeed, it is to the decline of this happy simplicity that the decline of this custom may be traced; and the rural dance on the green and the homely May-day pageant have gradually disappeared, in proportion as the peasantry have become expensive and artificial in their plea-sures, and too knowing for simple enjoyment.

Some attempts, the squire informs me, have been made of late years, by men of both taste and learning, to rally back the popular feeling to these standards of primitive simplicity; but the time has gone by, the feeling has become chilled by habits of gain and traffic, the country apes the manners and amuse-ments of the town, and little is heard of May-day at present, except from the lamentations of authors, who sigh after it from among the brick walls of the city:

"For O, for O, the Hobby Horse is forgot."

Village Worthies

Nay, I tell you, I am so well beloved in our town, that not the worst dog in the street will hurt my little finger.

Collier of Croydon

As the neighbouring village is one of those out-of-the-way, but gossiping little places, where a small matter makes a great stir, it is not to be supposed that the approach of a festival like that of May-day can be regarded with indifference, especially since it is made a matter of such moment by the great folks at the Hall. Master Simon, who is the faithful factotum of the worthy squire, and jumps with his humour in every thing, is frequent just now in his visits to the village, to give directions for the impending fête; and as I have taken the liberty occasionally of accompanying him, I have been enabled to get some insight into the characters and internal politics of this very sagacious little community.

Master Simon is in fact the Cæsar of the village. It is true the squire is the protecting power, but his factotum is the active and busy agent. He intermeddles in all its concerns, is acquainted with all the inhabitants and their domestic history, gives counsel to the old folks in their business matters, and the young folks in their love affairs, and enjoys the proud satisfaction of being a great man in a little world.

He is the dispenser too of the squire's charity, which is bounteous; and, to do Master Simon justice, he performs this part of his functions with great alacrity. Indeed I have been entertained with the mixture of bustle, importance, and kind-heartedness which he displays. He is of too vivacious a temperament to comfort the afflicted by sitting down moping and whining and blowing noses in concert; but goes whisking about like a sparrow, chirping consolation into every hole and corner of the village. I have seen an old woman, in a red cloak, hold him for half an hour together with some long phthisical tale of distress, which Master Simon listened to with many a bob of the head, smack of his dog-whip, and other symptoms of impatience, though he afterwards made a most faithful and circumstantial report of the case to the squire. I have watched him too, during one of his pop visits into the cottage of a superannuated villager, who is a pensioner of the squire, where he fidgeted about the room without sitting down, made many excellent off-hand reflections with the old invalid, who was propped up in his chair, about the shortness of life, the certainty of death, and the necessity of preparing for "that awful change;" quoted several texts of scripture very incorrectly, but much to the edification of the cottager's wife; and on coming out pinched the daughter's rosy cheek, and wondered what was in the young men, that such a pretty face did not get a husband.

He has also his cabinet councillors in the village, with whom he is very busy just now, preparing for the May-day ceremonies. Among these is the village tailor, a pale-faced fellow, that plays the clarinet in the church choir; and, being a great musical genius, has frequent meetings of the band at his house, where they "make night hideous" by their concerts. He is, in consequence, high in favour with Master Simon; and, through his influence, has the making, or rather marring, of all the liveries of the Hall; which generally look as though they had been cut out by one of those scientific tailors of the Flying Island of Laputa, who took measure of their customers with a quadrant. The tailor, in fact, might rise to be one of the monied men of the village, was he not rather too prone to gossip, and keep holidays, and give concerts, and blow all his substance, real and personal, through his clarinet; which literally keeps him poor both in body and estate. He has for the present thrown by all his regular work, and suffered the breeches of the village to go unmade and unmended, while he is occupied in making garlands of party-coloured rags, in imitation of flowers, for the decoration of the May-pole.

Another of Master Simon's councillors is the apothecary, a short and rather fat man, with a pair of prominent eyes that diverge like those of a lobster. He is the village wise man; very sententious, and full of profound remarks on shallow subjects. Master Simon often quotes his sayings, and mentions him as rather an extraordinary man; and even consults him occasionally in desperate cases of the dogs and horses. Indeed he seems to have been overwhelmed by the apothecary's philosophy, which is exactly one observation deep, consisting of indisputable maxims, such as may be gathered from the mottos of tobacco-boxes. I had a specimen of his philosophy in my very first conversation with him; in the course of which he observed, with great solemnity and emphasis, that "man is a compound of wisdom and folly;" upon which Master Simon, who had hold of my arm, pressed very hard upon it, and whispered in my ear, "that's a devilish shrewd remark!"

The Schoolmaster

There will no mosse stick to the stone of Sisiphus, no grasse
hang on the heeles of Mercury, no butter cleave on the bread of
a traveller. For as the eagle at every flight loseth a feather, which
maketh her bauld in her age, so the traveller in every country
loseth some fleece, which maketh him a beggar in his youth, by
buying that for a pound which he cannot sell again for a
penny—repentance.

Lilly's Euphues

A MONG THE WORTHIES of the village that enjoy the peculiar confidence of Master Simon is one who has struck
my fancy so much, that I have thought him worthy of a separate notice. It is Slingsby, the schoolmaster, a thin elderly
man, rather threadbare and slovenly, somewhat indolent in
manner, and with an easy, good-humoured look, not often
met with in his craft. I have been interested in his favour by a
few anecdotes which I have picked up concerning him.

He is a native of the village, and was a contemporary and
playmate of Ready Money Jack in the days of their boyhood.
Indeed, they carried on a kind of league of mutual good offices. Slingsby was rather puny, and withal somewhat of a
coward, but very apt at his learning: Jack, on the contrary,
was bully-boy out of doors, but a sad laggard at his books.
Slingsby helped Jack, therefore, to all his lessons; Jack fought
all Slingsby's battles; and they were inseparable friends. This
mutual kindness continued even after they left the school,
notwithstanding the dissimilarity of their characters. Jack
took to ploughing and reaping, and prepared himself to till
his paternal acres; while the other loitered negligently on in
the path of learning, until he penetrated even into the confines of Latin and mathematics.

In an unlucky hour, however, he took to reading voyages and
travels, and was smitten with a desire to see the world. This
desire increased upon him as he grew up; so, early one bright
sunny morning he put all his effects in a knapsack, slung it on
his back, took staff in hand, and called in his way to take leave
of his early schoolmate. Jack was just going out with the
plough; the friends shook hands over the farm-house gate;

Jack drove his team afield, and Slingsby whistled "over the hills and far away," and sallied forth gaily to "seek his fortune."

Years and years passed by, and young Tom Slingsby was forgotten; when, one mellow Sunday afternoon in autumn, a thin man, somewhat advanced in life, with a coat out at elbows, a pair of old nankeen gaiters, and a few things tied in a handkerchief, and slung on the end of a stick, was seen loitering through the village. He appeared to regard several houses attentively, to peer into the windows that were open, to eye the villagers wistfully as they returned from church, and then to pass some time in the church-yard, reading the tomb-stones.

At length he found his way to the farm-house of Ready Money Jack, but paused ere he attempted the wicket; contemplating the picture of substantial independence before him. In the porch of the house sat Ready Money Jack, in his Sunday dress; with his hat upon his head, his pipe in his mouth, and his tankard before him, the monarch of all he surveyed. Beside him lay his fat house-dog. The varied sounds of poultry were heard from the well-stocked farm-yard; the bees hummed from their hives in the garden; the cattle lowed in the rich meadow; while the crammed barns and ample stacks bore proof of an abundant harvest.

The stranger opened the gate and advanced dubiously towards the house. The mastiff growled at the sight of the suspicious-looking intruder; but was immediately silenced by his master; who, taking his pipe from his mouth, awaited with inquiring aspect the address of this equivocal personage. The stranger eyed old Jack for a moment, so portly in his dimensions, and decked out in gorgeous apparel; then cast a glance upon his own threadbare and starveling condition, and the scanty bundle which he held in his hand; then giving his shrunk waistcoat a twitch to make it meet his receding waistband; and casting another look, half sad, half humorous, at the sturdy yeoman, "I suppose," said he, "Mr. Tibbets, you have forgot old times and old playmates."

The latter gazed at him with scrutinizing look, but acknowledged that he had no recollection of him.

"Like enough, like enough," said the stranger; "every body seems to have forgotten poor Slingsby!"

"Why, no sure! it can't be Tom Slingsby!"

"Yes, but it is, though!" replied the stranger, shaking his head.

Ready Money Jack was on his feet in a twinkling; thrust out his hand, gave his ancient crony the gripe of a giant, and slapping the other hand on a bench, "Sit down there," cried he, "Tom Slingsby!"

A long conversation ensued about old times, while Slingsby was regaled with the best cheer that the farm-house afforded; for he was hungry as well as wayworn, and had the keen appetite of a poor pedestrian. The early playmates then talked over their subsequent lives and adventures. Jack had but little to relate, and was never good at a long story. A prosperous life, passed at home, has little incident for narrative; it is only poor devils, that are tossed about the world, that are the true heroes of story. Jack had stuck by the paternal farm, followed the same plough that his forefathers had driven, and had waxed richer the richer as he grew older. As to Tom Slingsby, he was an exemplification of the old proverb, "a rolling stone gathers no moss." He had sought his fortune about the world, without ever finding it, being a thing oftener found at home than abroad. He had been in all kinds of situations, and had learnt a dozen different modes of making a living; but had found his way back to his native village rather poorer than when he left it, his knapsack having dwindled down to a scanty bundle.

As luck would have it, the squire was passing by the farm-house that very evening, and called there, as is often his custom. He found the two school-mates still gossiping in the porch, and according to the good old Scottish song, "taking a cup of kindness yet, for auld lang syne." The squire was struck by the contrast in appearance and fortunes of these early playmates. Ready Money Jack, seated in lordly state, surrounded by the good things of this life, with golden guineas hanging to his very watch-chain, and the poor pilgrim Slingsby, thin as a weasel, with all his worldly effects, his bundle, hat, and walking-staff, lying on the ground beside him.

The good squire's heart warmed towards the luckless cosmopolite, for he is a little prone to like such half-vagrant characters. He cast about in his mind how he should contrive once more to anchor Slingsby in his native village. Honest Jack had already offered him a present shelter under his roof, in spite of the hints, and winks, and half remonstrances of the shrewd Dame Tibbets; but how to provide for his permanent maintenance was the question. Luckily the squire bethought himself that the village school was without a teacher. A little further conversation convinced him that Slingsby was as fit for that as for any thing else, and in a day or two he was seen swaying the rod of empire in the very school-house where he had often been horsed in the days of his boyhood.

Here he has remained for several years, and being honoured by the countenance of the squire and the fast friendship of Mr. Tibbets, he has grown into much importance and consideration in the village. I am told, however, that he still shows, now and then, a degree of restlessness, and a disposition to rove abroad again, and see a little more of the world; and inclination which seems particularly to haunt him about spring-time. There is nothing so difficult to conquer as the vagrant humour, when once it has been fully indulged.

Since I have heard these anecdotes of poor Slingsby, I have more than once mused upon the picture presented by him and his schoolmate Ready Money Jack, on their coming together again after so long a separation. It is difficult to determine between lots in life, where each is attended with its peculiar discontents. He who never leaves his home repines at his monotonous existence, and envies the traveller, whose life is a constant tissue of wonder and adventure; while he, who is tossed about the world, looks back with many a sigh to the safe and quiet shore which he has abandoned. I cannot help thinking, however, that the man that stays at home, and cultivates the comforts and pleasures daily springing up around him, stands the best chance for happiness. There is nothing so fascinating to a young mind as the idea of travelling; and there is very witchcraft in the old phrase found in every nursery tale, of "going to seek one's fortune." A continual change of place and change of object promises a continual succession of adventure and gratification of curiosity. But there is a limit to all our enjoyments, and every desire bears its death in its very gratification. Curiosity languishes under repeated stimulants, novelties cease to excite surprise, until at length we cannot wonder even at a miracle. He who has sallied forth into the world like poor Slingsby, full of sunny anticipations, finds too soon how different the distant scene becomes when visited. The smooth place roughens as he approaches; the wild place becomes tame and barren; the fairy tints that beguiled him on still fly to the distant hill, or gather upon the land he has left behind, and every part of the landscape seems greener than the spot he stands on.

The School

> But to come down from great men and higher matters to my
> little children and poor school house again; I will, God willing,
> go forward orderly, as I purposed, to instruct children and
> young men both for learning and manners.
>
> *Roger Ascham*

HAVING GIVEN the reader a slight sketch of the village
schoolmaster, he may be curious to learn something
concerning his school. As the squire takes much interest in
the education of the neighbouring children, he put into the
hands of the teacher, on first installing him in office, a copy
of Roger Ascham's Schoolmaster, and advised him, moreover, to con over that portion of old Peachem which treats of
the duty of masters, and which condemns the favourite
method of making boys wise by flagellation.

He exhorted Slingsby not to break down or depress the
free spirit of the boys, by harshness and slavish fear, but to
lead them freely and joyously on in the path of knowledge,
making it pleasant and desirable in their eyes. He wished to
see the youth trained up in the manners and habitudes of the
peasantry of the good old times, and thus to lay a foundation
for the accomplishment of his favourite object, the revival of
old English customs and character. He recommended that all
the ancient holidays should be observed, and that the sports
of the boys, in their hours of play, should be regulated according to the standard authorities laid down in Strutt, a
copy of whose invaluable work, decorated with plates, was
deposited in the school-house. Above all, he exhorted the
pedagogue to abstain from the use of birch, an instrument of
instruction which the good squire regards with abhorrence,
as fit only for the coercion of brute natures, that cannot be
reasoned with.

Mr. Slingsby has followed the squire's instructions to the
best of his disposition and abilities. He never flogs the boys, because he is too easy, good-humoured a creature to inflict pain
on a worm. He is bountiful in holidays, because he loves holiday himself, and has a sympathy with the urchins' impatience
of confinement, from having divers times experienced its irk-

someness during the time that he was seeing the world. As to sports and pastimes, the boys are faithfully exercised in all that are on record, quoits, races, prison-bars, tipcat, trap-ball, bandy-ball, wrestling, leaping, and what not. The only misfortune is, that having banished the birch, honest Slingsby has not studied Roger Ascham sufficiently to find out a substitute, or rather he has not the management in his nature to apply one; his school, therefore, though one of the happiest, is one of the most unruly in the country; and never was a pedagogue more liked or less heeded by his disciples than Slingsby.

He has lately taken a coadjutor worthy of himself, being another stray sheep that has returned to the village fold. This is no other than the son of the musical tailor, who had bestowed some cost upon his education, hoping to see him one day arrive at the dignity of an exciseman, or at least of a parish clerk. The lad grew up, however, as idle and musical as his father; and, being captivated by the drum and fife of a recruiting party, he followed them off to the army. He returned not long since, out of money, and out at the elbows, the prodigal son of the village. He remained for some time lounging about the place in half-tattered soldier's dress, with a foraging cap on one side of his head, jerking stones across the brook, or loitering about the tavern door, a burthen to his father, and regarded with great coldness by all warm householders.

Something, however, drew honest Slingsby towards the youth. It might be the kindness he bore to his father, who is one of the schoolmaster's great cronies; it might be that secret sympathy, which draws men of vagrant propensities towards each other, for there is something truly magnetic in the vagabond feeling; or it might be that he remembered the time, when he himself had come back like this youngster, a wreck to his native place. At any rate, whatever the motive, Slingsby drew towards the youth. They had many conversations in the village tap-room about foreign parts, and the various scenes and places they had witnessed during their wayfaring about the world. The more Slingsby talked with him the more he found him to his taste: and finding him almost as learned as himself, he forthwith engaged him as an assistant, or usher, in the school.

Under such admirable tuition the school, as may be supposed, flourishes apace; and if the scholars do not become versed in all the holiday accomplishments of the good old times, to the squire's heart's content, it will not be the fault of their teachers. The prodigal son has become almost as popular among the boys as the pedagogue himself. His instructions are not limited to school-hours; and having inherited the musical taste and talents of his father, he has bitten the whole school with the mania. He is a great hand at beating a drum, which is often heard rumbling from the rear of the school-house. He is teaching half the boys of the village, also, to play the fife, and the pandean pipes; and they weary the whole neighbourhood with their vague pipings, as they sit perched on stiles, or loitering about the barn-doors in the evenings. Among the other exercises of the school, also, he has introduced the ancient art of archery, one of the squire's favourite themes, with such success, that the whipsters roam in truant bands about the neighbourhood, practising with their bows and arrows upon the birds of the air, and the beasts of the field; and not unfrequently making a foray into the squire's domains, to the great indignation of the game-keepers. In a word, so completely are the ancient English customs and habits cultivated at this school, that I should not be surprised if the squire should live to see one of his poetic visions realised, and a brood reared up, worthy successors to Robin Hood, and his merry gang of outlaws.

A Village Politician

I am a rogue if I do not think I was designed for the helm of
state; I am so full of nimble stratagems, that I should have ordered affairs and carried it against the stream of a faction with
as much ease as a skipper would laver against the wind.

The Goblins

IN ONE of my visits to the village with Master Simon, he
proposed that we should stop at the inn, which he wished
to show me, as a specimen of a real country inn, the head-
quarters of village gossip. I had remarked it before, in my
perambulations about the place. It has a deep old-fashioned
porch, leading into a large hall, which serves for tap-room
and travellers'-room; having a wide fire-place, with high
backed settles on each side, where the wise men of the village
gossip over their ale, and hold their sessions during the long
winter evenings. The landlord is an easy, indolent fellow,
shaped a little like one of his own beer barrels, and is apt to
stand gossiping at his door, with his wig on one side, and his
hands in his pockets, whilst his wife and daughter attend to
customers. His wife, however, is fully competent to manage
the establishment; and, indeed, from long habitude, rules
over all the frequenters of the tap-room as completely as if
they were her dependents instead of her patrons. Not a veteran ale-bibber but pays homage to her, having, no doubt,
been often in her arrears. I have already hinted that she is on
very good terms with Ready Money Jack. He was a sweetheart of hers in early life, and has always countenanced the
tavern on her account. Indeed, he is quite the "cock of the
walk" at the tap-room.

As we approached the inn, we heard some one talking
with great volubility, and distinguished the ominous words
"taxes," "poor's rates," and "agricultural distress." It proved
to be a thin, loquacious fellow, who had penned the landlord
up in one corner of the porch, with his hands in his pockets
as usual, listening with an air of the most vacant acquiescence.

The sight seemed to have a curious effect on Master Simon,
as he squeezed my arm, and altering his course, sheered wide
of the porch, as though he had not had any idea of entering.

This evident evasion induced me to notice the orator more particularly. He was meagre, but active in his make, with a long, pale, bilious face; a black beard, so ill-shaven as to bloody his shirt-collar, a feverish eye, and a hat sharpened up at the sides into a most pragmatical shape. He had a news-paper in his hand, and seemed to be commenting on its con-tents, to the thorough conviction of mine host.

At sight of Master Simon the landlord was evidently a little flurried, and began to rub his hands, edge away from his corner, and make several profound publican bows; while the orator took no other notice of my companion than to talk rather louder than before, and with, as I thought, something of an air of defiance. Master Simon, however, as I have before said, sheered off from the porch and passed on, pressing my arm within his, and whispering as we got by, in a tone of awe and horror, "That's a radical! he reads Cobbett!"

I endeavoured to get a more particular account of him from my companion, but he seemed unwilling even to talk about him, answering only in general terms, that he was "a cursed busy fellow, that had a confounded trick of talking, and was apt to bother one about the national debt, and such non-sense;" from which I suspected that Master Simon had been rendered wary of him by some accidental encounter on the field of argument; for these radicals are continually roving about in quest of wordy warfare, and never so happy as when they can tilt a gentleman logician out of his saddle.

On subsequent inquiry my suspicions have been confirmed. I find the radical has but recently found his way into the vil-lage, where he threatens to commit fearful devastations with his doctrines. He has already made two or three complete converts, or new lights; has shaken the faith of several others; and has grievously puzzled the brains of many of the oldest villagers, who had never thought about politics, or scarce any thing else, during their whole lives.

He is lean and meagre from the constant restlessness of mind and body; worrying about with newspapers and pam-phlets in his pockets, which he is ready to pull out on all occasions. He has shocked several of the stanchest villagers by talking lightly of the squire and his family; and hinting that it would be better the park should be cut up into small farms and kitchen-gardens, or feed good mutton instead of worthless deer.

He is a great thorn in the side of the squire, who is sadly afraid that he will introduce politics into the village, and turn it into an unhappy, thinking community. He is a still greater grievance to Master Simon, who has hitherto been able to sway the political opinions of the place, without much cost of learning or logic; but has been very much puzzled of late to weed out the doubts and heresies already sown by this champion of reform. Indeed, the latter has taken complete command at the tap-room of the tavern, not so much because he has convinced, as because he has out-talked all the old established oracles. The apothecary, with all his philosophy, was as naught before him. He has convinced and converted the landlord at least a dozen times; who, however, is liable to be convinced and converted the other way by the next person with whom he talks. It is true the radical has a violent antagonist in the landlady, who is vehemently loyal, and thoroughly devoted to the king, Master Simon, and the squire. She now and then comes out upon the reformer with all the fierceness of a cat-o'-mountain, and does not spare her own soft-headed husband, for listening to what she terms such "low-lived politics." What makes the good woman the more violent, is the perfect coolness with which the radical listens to her attacks, drawing his face up into a provoking, supercilious smile; and when she has talked herself out of breath, quietly asking her for a taste of her home-brewed.

The only person that is in any way a match for this redoubtable politician is Ready Money Jack Tibbets; who maintains his stand in the tap-room, in defiance of the radical and all his works. Jack is one of the most loyal men in the country, without being able to reason about the matter. He has that admirable quality for a tough arguer, also, that he never knows when he is beat. He has half a dozen old maxims, which he advances on all occasions, and though his antagonist may overturn them never so often, yet he always brings them anew to the field. He is like the robber in Ariosto, who, though his head might be cut off half a hundred times, yet whipped it on his shoulders again in a twinkling, and returned as sound a man as ever to the charge.

Whatever does not square with Jack's simple and obvious creed he sets down for "French politics;" for, notwithstanding the peace, he cannot be persuaded that the French are not still laying plots to ruin the nation, and to get hold of the Bank of England. The radical attempted to overwhelm him one day by a long passage from a newspaper; but Jack neither reads nor believes in newspapers. In reply he gave him one of the stanzas which he has by heart from his favourite, and indeed only author, old Tusser, and which he calls his Golden Rules:

> Leave princes' affairs undescanted on,
> And tend to such doings as stand thee upon;
> Fear God, and offend not the king nor his laws,
> And keep thyself out of the magistrate's claws.

When Tibbets had pronounced this with great emphasis, he pulled out a well-filled leathern purse, took out a handful of gold and silver, paid his score at the bar with great punctuality, returned his money, piece by piece, into his purse, his purse into his pocket, which he buttoned up; and then, giving his cudgel a stout thump upon the floor, and bidding the radical "good morning, sir!" with the tone of a man who conceives he has completely done for his antagonist, he walked with lion-like gravity out of the house. Two or three of Jack's admirers who were present, and had been afraid to take the field themselves, looked upon this as a perfect triumph, and winked at each other when the radical's back was turned. "Ay, ay!" said mine host, as soon as the radical was out of hearing, "let old Jack alone; I'll warrant he'll give him his own!"

The Rookery

But cawing rooks, and kites that swim sublime
In still repeated circles, screaming loud,
The jay, the pie, and e'en the boding owl,
That hails the rising moon, have charms for me.
Cowper

IN A GROVE of tall oaks and beeches that crowns a terrace-walk, just on the skirts of the garden, is an ancient rookery; which is one of the most important provinces in the squire's rural domains. The old gentleman sets great store by his rooks, and will not suffer one of them to be killed; in consequence of which they have increased amazingly; the tree-tops are loaded with their nests; they have encroached upon the great avenue, and have even established, in times long past, a colony among the elms and pines of the churchyard, which, like other distant colonies, has already thrown off allegiance to the mother-country.

The rooks are looked upon by the squire as a very ancient and honourable line of gentry, highly aristocratical in their notions, fond of place, and attached to church and state; as their building so loftily, keeping about churches and cathedrals, and in the venerable groves of old castles and manor-houses, sufficiently manifests. The good opinion thus expressed by the squire put me upon observing more narrowly these very respectable birds; for I confess, to my shame, I had been apt to confound them with their cousins-german the crows, to whom, at the first glance, they bear so great a family resemblance. Nothing, it seems, could be more unjust or injurious than such a mistake. The rooks and crows are, among the feathered tribes, what the Spaniards and Portuguese are among nations, the least loving, in consequence of their neighbourhood and similarity. The rooks are old-established housekeepers, high-minded gentlefolk, that have had their hereditary abodes time out of mind; but as to the poor crows, they are a kind of vagabond, predatory, gipsy race, roving about the country without any settled home; "their hands are against every body, and every body's against them," and they are gibbeted in every corn-field. Master Simon assures me that a female rook, that should so far forget herself as to consort with a crow, would inevitably be disinherited, and indeed would be totally discarded by all her genteel acquaintance.

The squire is very watchful over the interests and concerns of his sable neighbours. As to Master Simon, he even pretends to know many of them by sight, and to have given names to them; he points out several, which he says are old heads of families, and compares them to worthy old citizens, beforehand in the world, that wear cocked-hats, and silver buckles in their shoes. Notwithstanding the protecting benevolence of the squire, and their being residents in his empire, they seem to acknowledge no allegiance, and to hold no intercourse or intimacy. Their airy tenements are built almost out of the reach of gun-shot; and, notwithstanding their vicinity to the Hall, they maintain a most reserved and distrustful shyness of mankind.

There is one season of the year, however, which brings all birds in a manner to a level, and tames the pride of the loftiest highflyer; which is the season of building their nests. This takes place early in the spring, when the forest-trees first begin to show their buds; the long, withy ends of the branches to turn green; when the wild strawberry, and other herbage of the sheltered woodlands, put forth their tender and tinted leaves; and the daisy and the primrose peep from under the hedges. At this time there is a general bustle among the feathered tribes; an incessant fluttering about, and a cheerful chirping; indicative, like the germination of the vegetable world, of the reviving life and fecundity of the year.

It is then that the rooks forget their usual stateliness, and their shy and lofty habits. Instead of keeping up in the high regions of the air, swinging on the breezy tree-tops, and looking down with sovereign contempt upon the humble crawlers upon earth, they are fain to throw off for a time the dignity of the gentleman, to come down to the ground, and put on the pains-taking and industrious character of a labourer. They now lose their natural shyness, become fearless and familiar, and may be seen plying about in all directions, with an air of great assiduity, in search of building materials. Every now and then your path will be crossed by one of these busy old gentlemen, worrying about with awkward gait, as if troubled with the gout, or with corns on his toes, casting about many a prying look, turning down first one eye, then the other, in earnest consideration, upon every straw he meets with, until, espying some mighty twig, large enough to make a rafter for his air-castle, he will seize upon it with avidity, and hurry away with it to the tree-top; fearing, apparently, lest you should dispute with him the invaluable prize.

Like other castle-builders, these airy architects seem rather fanciful in the materials with which they build, and to like those most which come from a distance. Thus, though there are abundance of dry twigs on the surrounding trees, yet they never think of making use of them, but go foraging in distant lands, and come sailing home, one by one, from the ends of the earth, each bearing in his bill some precious piece of timber.

Nor must I avoid mentioning, what, I grieve to say, rather derogates from the grave and honourable character of these ancient gentlefolk, that, during the architectural season, they are subject to great dissensions among themselves; that they make no scruple to defraud and plunder each other; and that sometimes the rookery is a scene of hideous brawl and commotion, in consequence of some delinquency of the kind. One of the partners generally remains on the nest to guard it from depredation; and I have seen severe contests, when some sly neighbour has endeavoured to filch away a tempting rafter that had captivated his eye. As I am not willing to admit any suspicion hastily that should throw a stigma on the general character of so worshipful a people, I am inclined to think that these larcenies are very much discountenanced by the higher classes, and even rigorously punished by those in authority; for I have now and then seen a whole gang of rooks fall upon the nest of some individual, pull it all to pieces, carry off the spoils, and even buffet the luckless proprietor. I have concluded this to be some signal punishment inflicted upon him, by the officers of the police, for some pilfering misdemeanor; or, perhaps, that it was a crew of bailiffs carrying an execution into his house.

I have been amused with another of their movements

during the building season. The steward has suffered a considerable number of sheep to graze on a lawn near the house, somewhat to the annoyance of the squire, who thinks this an innovation on the dignity of a park, which ought to be devoted to deer only. Be this as it may, there is a green knoll, not far from the drawing-room window, where the ewes and lambs are accustomed to assemble towards evening, for the benefit of the setting sun. No sooner were they gathered here, at the time when these politic birds were building, than a stately old rook, who Master Simon assured me was the chief magistrate of this community, would settle down upon the head of one of the ewes, who, seeming conscious of this condescension, would desist from grazing, and stand fixed in motionless reverence of her august burthen; the rest of the rookery would then come wheeling down, in imitation of their leader, until every ewe had two or three of them cawing, and fluttering, and battling upon her back. Whether they requited the submission of the sheep, by levying a contribution upon their fleece for the benefit of the rookery, I am not certain; though I presume they followed the usual custom of protecting powers.

The latter part of May is the time of great tribulation among the rookeries, when the young are just able to leave the nests, and balance themselves on the neighbouring branches. Now comes on the season of "rook shooting;" a terrible slaughter of the innocents. The squire, of course, prohibits all invasion of the kind on his territories; but I am told that a lamentable havoc takes place in the colony about the old church. Upon this devoted commonwealth the village charges "with all its chivalry." Every idle wight that is lucky enough to possess an old gun or blunderbuss, together with all the archery of Slingsby's school, takes the field on the occasion. In vain does the little parson interfere, or remonstrate, in angry tones, from his study window that looks into the churchyard; there is a continual popping from morning till night. Being no great marksmen, their shots are not often effective; but every now and then a great shout from the besieging army of bumpkins makes known the downfall of some unlucky, squab rook, which comes to the ground with the emphasis of a squashed apple-dumpling.

Nor is the rookery entirely free from other troubles and disasters. In so aristocratical and lofty-minded a community, which boasts so much ancient blood and hereditary pride, it is natural to suppose that questions of etiquette will sometimes arise, and affairs of honour ensue. In fact, this is very often the case; bitter quarrels break out between individuals, which produce sad scufflings on the tree-tops, and I have more than once seen a regular duel take place between two doughty heroes of the rookery. Their field of battle is generally the air; and their contest is managed in the most scientific and elegant manner; wheeling round and round each other, and towering higher and higher to get the 'vantage ground, until they sometimes disappear in the clouds before the combat is determined.

They have also fierce combats now and then with an invading hawk, and will drive him off from their territories by a *posse comitatis*. They are also extremely tenacious of their domains, and will suffer no other bird to inhabit the grove or its vicinity. There was a very ancient and respectable old bachelor owl that had long had his lodgings in a corner of the grove, but has been fairly ejected by the rooks; and has retired, disgusted with the world, to a neighbouring wood, where he leads the life of a hermit, and makes nightly complaints of his ill treatment.

The hootings of this unhappy gentleman may generally be heard in the still evenings, when the rooks are all at rest; and I have often listened to them of a moonlight night, with a kind of mysterious gratification. This gray-bearded misanthrope of course is highly respected by the squire; but the servants have superstitious notions about him; and it would be difficult to get the dairy-maid to venture after dark near to the wood which he inhabits.

Besides the private quarrels of the rooks, there are other misfortunes to which they are liable, and which often bring distress into the most respectable families of the rookery. Having the true baronial spirit of the good old feudal times, they are apt now and then to issue forth from their castles on a foray, and to lay the plebeian fields of the neighbouring country under contribution; in the course of which chivalrous expeditions they now and then get a shot from the rusty

artillery of some refractory farmer. Occasionally, too, while
they are quietly taking the air beyond the park boundaries,
they have the incaution to come within the reach of the truant
bowmen of Slingsby's school, and receive a flight shot from
some unlucky urchin's arrow. In such case the wounded adventurer will sometimes have just strength enough to bring
himself home, and, giving up the ghost at the rookery, will
hang dangling "all abroad" on a bough, like a thief on a gibbet; an awful warning to his friends and an object of great
commiseration to the squire.

But, maugre all these untoward incidents, the rooks have,
upon the whole, a happy holiday life of it. When their young
are reared, and fairly launched upon their native element the
air, the cares of the old folks seem over, and they resume all
their aristocratical dignity and idleness. I have envied them
the enjoyment which they appear to have in their ethereal
heights, sporting with clamorous exultation about their lofty
bowers; sometimes hovering over them, sometimes partially
alighting upon the topmost branches, and there balancing
with outstretched wings, and swinging in the breeze. Sometimes they seem to take a fashionable drive to the church, and
amuse themselves by circling in airy rings about its spire; at
other times a mere garrison is left at home to mount guard in
their strong hold at the grove, while the rest roam abroad to
enjoy the fine weather. About sunset the garrison gives notice
of their return; their faint cawing will be heard from a great
distance, and they will be seen far off like a sable cloud, and
then, nearer and nearer, until they all come soaring home.
Then they perform several grand circuits in the air, over
the Hall and garden, wheeling closer and closer, until they
gradually settle down upon the grove when a prodigious
cawing takes place, as though they were relating their day's
adventures.

I like at such times to walk about these dusky groves, and
hear the various sounds of these airy people roosted so high
above me. As the gloom increases, their conversation sub-
sides, and they seem to be gradually dropping asleep; but
every now and then there is a querulous note, as if some one
was quarrelling for a pillow, or a little more of the blanket. It

is late in the evening before they completely sink to repose, and then their old anchorite neighbour, the owl, begins his lonely hootings from his bachelor's-hall, in the wood.

May-Day

It is the choice time of the year,
For the violets now appear;
Now the rose receives its birth,
And pretty primrose decks the earth.
　　Then to the May-pole come away,
　　For it is now a holiday.
Actæon and Diana

A s I was lying in bed this morning, enjoying one of those half-dreams, half reveries, which are so pleasant in the country, when the birds are singing about the window, and the sunbeams peeping through the curtains, I was roused by the sound of music. On going down stairs, I found a number of villagers dressed in their holiday clothes, bearing a pole, ornamented with garlands and ribands, and accompanied by the village band of music, under the direction of the tailor, the pale fellow who plays on the claironet. They had all sprigs of hawthorn, or, as it is called, "the May," in their hats, and had brought green branches and flowers to decorate the Hall door and windows. They had come to give notice that the May-pole was reared on the green, and to invite the household to witness the sports. The Hall, according to custom, became a scene of hurry and delighted confusion. The servants were all agog with May and music; and there was no keeping either the tongues or the feet of the maids quiet, who were anticipating the sports of the green, and the evening dance.

I repaired to the village at an early hour to enjoy the merry-making. The morning was pure and sunny, such as a May morning is always described. The fields were white with daisies, the hawthorn was covered with its fragrant blossoms, the bee hummed about every bank, and the swallow played high in the air about the village steeple. It was one of those genial days when we seem to draw in pleasure with the very air we breathe, and to feel happy we know not why. Whoever has felt the worth of worthy man, or has doted on lovely woman, will, on such a day, call them tenderly to mind, and feel his heart all alive with long-buried recollections. "For thenne," says the excellent romance of king Arthur, "lovers call ageyne to their mynde old gentilnes and old servyse, and many kind dedes that were forgotten by neglygence."

Before reaching the village, I saw the May-pole towering above the cottages, with its gay garlands and streamers, and heard the sound of music. I found that there had been booths set up near it, for the reception of company; and a bower of green branches and flowers for the Queen of May, a fresh, rosy-cheeked girl of the village.

A band of morrice dancers were capering on the green in their fantastic dresses, jingling with hawks' bells, with a boy dressed up as Maid Marian, and the attendant fool rattling his box to collect contributions from the bystanders. The gipsy-women too were already plying their mystery in by-corners of the village, reading the hands of the simple country girls, and no doubt promising them all good husbands and tribes of children.

The squire made his appearance in the course of the morning, attended by the parson, and was received with loud acclamations. He mingled among the country people throughout the day, giving and receiving pleasure wherever he went. The amusements of the day were under the management of Slingsby, the schoolmaster, who is not merely lord of misrule in his school, but master of the revels to the village. He was bustling about with the perplexed and anxious air of a man who has the oppressive burthen of promoting other people's merriment upon his mind. He had involved himself in a dozen scrapes in consequence of a politic intrigue, which, by the bye, Master Simon and the Oxonian were at the bottom of, which had for object the election of the Queen of May. He had met with violent opposition from a faction of ale-drinkers, who were in favour of a bouncing bar-maid, the daughter of the innkeeper; but he had been too strongly backed not to carry his point, though it shows that these rural crowns, like all others, are objects of great ambition and heart-burning. I am told that Master Simon takes great interest, though in an underhand way, in the election of these May-day Queens, and that the chaplet is generally secured for some rustic beauty that has found favour in his eyes.

In the course of the day there were various games of strength and agility on the green, at which a knot of village veterans presided, as judges of the lists. Among these I perceived that Ready Money Jack took the lead, looking with a learned and critical eye on the merits of the different candidates; and though he was very laconic, and sometimes merely expressed himself by a nod, yet it was evident that his opinions far outweighed those of the most loquacious.

Young Jack Tibbets was the hero of the day, and carried off most of the prizes, though in some of the feats of agility, he was rivalled by the "prodigal son," who appeared much in his element on this occasion; but his most formidable competitor was the notorious gipsy, the redoubtable "Star-light Tom." I was rejoiced at having an opportunity of seeing this "minion of the moon" in broad daylight. I found him a tall, swarthy, good-looking fellow, with a lofty air, something like what I have seen in an Indian chieftain; and with a certain lounging, easy, and almost graceful carriage, which I have often remarked in beings of the lazaroni order, that lead an idle, loitering life, and have a gentlemanlike contempt of labour.

Master Simon and the old general reconnoitered the ground together, and indulged a vast deal of harmless raking among the buxom country girls. Master Simon would give some of them a kiss on meeting with them, and would ask after their sisters, for he is acquainted with most of the farmers' families. Sometimes he would whisper, and affect to talk mischievously with them, and, if bantered on the subject, would turn it off with a laugh, though it was evident he liked to be suspected of being a gay Lothario amongst them.

He had much to say to the farmers about their farms; and seemed to know all their horses by name. There was an old fellow, with a round ruddy face, and a night-cap under his hat, the village wit, who took several occasions to crack a joke with him in the hearing of his companions, to whom he would turn and wink hard when Master Simon had passed.

The harmony of the day, however, had nearly, at one time, been interrupted, by the appearance of the radical on the ground, with two or three of his disciples. He soon got engaged in argument in the very thick of the throng, above which I could hear his voice, and now and then see his meagre hand, half a mile out of the sleeve, elevated in the air in violent gesticulation, and flourishing a pamphlet by way of truncheon. He was decrying these idle nonsensical amusements in times of public distress, when it was every one's business to think of other matters, and to be miserable. The honest village logicians could make no stand against him, especially as he was seconded by his proselytes; when, to their great joy, Master Simon and the general came drifting down into the field of action. I saw that Master Simon was for making off, as soon as he found himself in the neighbourhood of this fireship; but the general was too loyal to suffer such talk in his hearing, and thought, no doubt, that a look and a word from a gentleman would be sufficient to shut up so shabby an orator. The latter, however, was no respecter of persons, but rather seemed to exult in having such important antagonists. He talked with greater volubility than ever, and soon drowned them in declamation on the subject of taxes, poor's rates, and the national debt. Master Simon endeavoured to brush along in his usual excursive manner, which had always answered amazingly well with the villagers; but the radical was one of those pestilent fellows that pin a man down to facts, and, indeed, he had two or three pamphlets in his pocket, to support every thing he advanced by printed documents. The general, too, found himself betrayed into a more serious action than his dignity could brook; and looked like a mighty Dutch Indiaman grievously peppered by a petty privateer. It was in vain that he swelled and looked big; and talked large, and endeavoured to make up by pomp of manner for poverty of matter; every home-thrust of the radical made him wheeze like a bellows, and seemed to let a volume of wind out of him. In a word, the two worthies from the Hall were completely dumb-founded, and this too in the presence of several of Master Simon's stanch admirers, who had always looked up to him as infallible. I do not know how he and the general would have managed to draw their forces decently from the field, had there not been a match at grinning through a horse-collar announced, whereupon the radical retired with great expression of contempt, and, as soon as his back was turned, the argument was carried against him all hollow.

"Did you ever hear such a pack of stuff, general?" said Master Simon; "there's no talking with one of these chaps when he once gets that confounded Cobbett in his head."

"S'blood, sir!" said the general, wiping his forehead, "such fellows ought all to be transported!"

In the latter part of the day the ladies from the Hall paid a visit to the green. The fair Julia made her appearance, leaning on her lover's arm, and looking extremely pale and interesting. As she is a great favourite in the village, where she has been known from childhood; and as her late accident had been much talked about, the sight of her caused very manifest delight, and some of the old women of the village blessed her sweet face as she passed.

While they were walking about, I noticed the schoolmaster in earnest conversation with the young girl that represented the Queen of May, evidently endeavouring to spirit her up to some formidable undertaking. At length, as the party from the Hall approached her bower, she came forth, faltering at every step, until she reached the spot where the fair Julia stood between her lover and Lady Lillycraft. The little Queen then took the chaplet of flowers from her head, and attempted to put it on that of the bride elect; but the confusion of both was so great, that the wreath would have fallen to the ground, had not the officer caught it, and, laughing, placed it upon the blushing brows of his mistress. There was something charming in the very embarrassment of these two young creatures, both so beautiful, yet so different in their kinds of beauty. Master Simon told me, afterwards, that the Queen of May was to have spoken a few verses which the schoolmaster had written for her; but that she had neither wit to understand, nor memory to recollect them. "Besides," added he, "between you and I, she murders the king's English abominably; so she has acted the part of a wise woman in holding her tongue, and trusting to her pretty face."

Among the other characters from the Hall was Mrs. Hannah, my Lady Lillycraft's gentlewoman: to my surprise she

was escorted by old Christy the huntsman, and followed by
his ghost of a greyhound; but I find they are very old acquaintances; being drawn together by some sympathy of disposition. Mrs. Hannah moved about with starched dignity
among the rustics, who drew back from her with more awe
than they did from her mistress. Her mouth seemed shut as
with a clasp; excepting that I now and then heard the word
"fellows!" escape from between her lips, as she got accidentally jostled in the crowd.

But there was one other heart present that did not enter
into the merriment of the scene, which was that of the simple
Phœbe Wilkins, the housekeeper's niece. The poor girl has
continued to pine and whine for some time past, in consequence of the obstinate coldness of her lover; never was a
little flirtation more severely punished. She appeared this day
on the green, gallanted by a smart servant out of livery, and
had evidently resolved to try the hazardous experiment of
awakening the jealousy of her lover. She was dressed in her
very best; affected an air of great gaiety; talked loud and girl-
ishly, and laughed when there was nothing to laugh at. There
was, however, an aching, heavy heart, in the poor baggage's
bosom, in spite of all her levity. Her eye turned every now
and then in quest of her reckless lover, and her cheek grew
pale, and her fictitious gaiety vanished, on seeing him paying
his rustic homage to the little May-day Queen.

My attention was now diverted by a fresh stir and bustle.
Music was heard from a distance; a banner was seen advancing up the road, preceded by a rustic band playing something
like a march, and followed by a sturdy throng of country lads,
the chivalry of a neighbouring and rival village.

No sooner had they reached the green than they challenged
the heroes of the day to new trials of strength and activity.
Several gymnastic contests ensued for the honour of the
respective villages. In the course of these exercises, young
Tibbets and the champion of the adverse party had an obstinate match at wrestling. They tugged, and strained, and panted,
without either getting the mastery, until both came to the
ground, and rolled upon the green. Just then the disconsolate
Phœbe came by. She saw her recreant lover in fierce contest,
as she thought, and in danger. In a moment pride, pique, and

coquetry were forgotten: she rushed into the ring, seized upon the rival champion by the hair, and was on the point of wreaking on him her puny vengeance, when a buxom, strapping country lass, the sweetheart of the prostrate swain, pounced upon her like a hawk, and would have stripped her of her fine plumage in a twinkling, had she also not been seized in her turn.

A complete tumult ensued. The chivalry of the two villages became embroiled. Blows began to be dealt, and sticks to be flourished. Phœbe was carried off from the field in hysterics. In vain did the sages of the village interfere. The sententious apothecary endeavoured to pour the soothing oil of his philosophy upon this tempestuous sea of passion, but was tumbled into the dust. Slingsby the pedagogue, who is a great lover of peace, went into the midst of the throng, as marshal of the day, to put an end to the commotion; but was rent in twain, and came out with his garment hanging in two strips from his shoulders: upon which the prodigal son dashed in with fury to revenge the insult which his patron had sustained. The tumult thickened; I caught glimpses of the jockey-cap of old Christy, like the helmet of a chieftain, bobbing about in the midst of the scuffle; while Mistress Hannah, separated from her doughty protector, was squalling and striking at right and left with a faded parasol; being tossed and tousled about by the crowd in such wise as never happened to maiden gentlewoman before.

At length I beheld old Ready Money Jack making his way into the very thickest of the throng; tearing it, as it were, apart, and enforcing peace *vi et armis*. It was surprising to see the sudden quiet that ensued. The storm settled down at once into tranquillity. The parties, having no real grounds of hostility, were readily pacified, and in fact were a little at a loss to know why and how they had got by the ears. Slingsby was speedily stitched together again by his friend the tailor, and resumed his usual good humour. Mrs. Hannah drew on one side to plume her rumpled feathers; and old Christy having repaired his damages, took her under his arm, and they swept back again to the Hall, ten times more bitter against mankind than ever.

The Tibbets family alone seemed slow in recovering from

the agitation of the scene. Young Jack was evidently very much moved by the heroism of the unlucky Phœbe. His mother, who had been summoned to the field of action by news of the affray, was in a sad panic, and had need of all her management to keep him from following his mistress, and coming to a perfect reconciliation.

What heightened the alarm and perplexity of the good managing dame was, that the matter had aroused the slow apprehension of old Ready Money himself; who was very much struck by the intrepid interference of so pretty and delicate a girl, and was sadly puzzled to understand the meaning of the violent agitation in his family.

When all this came to the ears of the squire, he was grievously scandalized that his May-day fête should have been disgraced by such a brawl. He ordered Phœbe to appear before him, but the girl was so frightened and distressed, that she came sobbing and trembling, and, at the first question he asked, fell again into hysterics. Lady Lillycraft, who had understood that there was an affair of the heart at the bottom of this distress, immediately took the girl into great favour and protection, and made her peace with the squire. This was the only thing that disturbed the harmony of the day, if we except the discomfiture of Master Simon and the general by the radical. Upon the whole, therefore, the squire had very fair reason to be satisfied that he had rode his hobby throughout the day without any other molestation.

The reader, learned in these matters, will perceive that all this was but a faint shadow of the once gay and fanciful rites of May. The peasantry have lost the proper feeling for these rites, and have grown almost as strange to them as the boors of La Mancha were to the customs of chivalry in the days of the valorous Don Quixote. Indeed, I considered it a proof of the discretion with which the squire rides his hobby, that he had not pushed the thing any further, nor attempted to revive many obsolete usages of the day, which, in the present matter-of-fact times, would appear affected and absurd. I must say, though I do it under the rose, the general brawl in which this festival had nearly terminated, has made me doubt whether these rural customs of the good old times were always so very loving and innocent as we are apt to fancy them;

and whether the peasantry in those times were really so Arcadian as they have been fondly represented. I begin to fear—

> —— "Those days were never; airy dreams
> Sat for the picture, and the poet's hand,
> Imparting substance to an empty shade,
> Impos'd a gay delirium for a truth.
> Grant it; I still must envy them an age
> That favoured such a dream."

The Manuscript

YESTERDAY was a day of quiet and repose after the bustle of May-day. During the morning I joined the ladies in a small sitting-room, the windows of which came down to the floor, and opened upon a terrace of the garden, which was set out with delicate shrubs and flowers. The soft sunshine that fell into the room through the branches of trees that over-hung the windows, the sweet smell of the flowers, and the singing of the birds, seemed to produce a pleasing, yet calming effect on the whole party, for some time elapsed without any one speaking. Lady Lillycraft and Miss Templeton were sitting by an elegant work-table, near one of the windows, occupied with some pretty lady-like work. The captain was on a stool at his mistress' feet, looking over some music, and poor Phœbe Wilkins, who has always been a kind of pet among the ladies, but who has risen vastly in favour with Lady Lillycraft, in consequence of some tender confessions, sat in one corner of the room, with swoln eyes, working pensively at some of the fair Julia's wedding ornaments.

The silence was interrupted by her ladyship, who suddenly proposed a task to the captain. "I am in your debt," said she, "for that tale you read to us the other day; I will now furnish one in return, if you'll read it: and it is just suited to this sweet May morning, for it is all about love!"

The proposition seemed to delight every one present. The captain smiled assent. Her ladyship rung for her page, and despatched him to her room for the manuscript. "As the captain," said she, "gave us an account of the author of his story, it is but right I should give one of mine. It was written by the parson of the parish where I reside. He is a thin, elderly man, of a delicate constitution, but positively one of the most charming men that ever lived. He lost his wife a few years since; one of the sweetest women you ever saw. He has two sons, whom he educates himself; both of whom already write delightful poetry. His parsonage is a lovely place, close by the church, all overrun with ivy and honeysuckles; with the sweetest flower-garden about it; for, you know, our country clergymen are almost always fond of flowers, and make their parsonages perfect pictures.

"His living is a very good one, and he is very much beloved, and does a great deal of good in the neighbourhood, and among the poor. And then such sermons as he preaches! Oh, if you could only hear one taken from a text in Solomon's Song, all about love and matrimony, one of the sweetest things you ever heard! He preaches it at least once a year, in spring time, for he knows I am fond of it. He always dines with me on Sundays, and often brings me some of the sweetest pieces of poetry, all about the pleasures of melancholy, and such subjects, that make me cry so, you can't think. I wish he would publish. I think he has some things as sweet as any thing in Moore or Lord Byron.

"He fell into very ill health some time ago, and was advised to go to the continent; and I gave him no peace until he went, and promised to take care of his two boys until he returned.

"He was gone for above a year, and was quite restored. When he came back, he sent me the tale I'm going to show you.—Oh, here it is!" said she, as the page put in her hands a beautiful box of satin-wood. She unlocked it, and from among several parcels of notes on embossed paper, cards of charades, and copies of verses, she drew out a crimson velvet case, that smelt very much of perfumes. From this she took a manuscript, daintily written on gilt-edged vellum paper, and stitched with a light blue riband. This she handed to the captain, who read the following tale, which I have procured for the entertainment of the reader.

Annette Delarbre

The soldier frae the war returns,
And the merchant from the main,
But I hae parted wi' my love,
And ne'er to meet again,
      My dear,
And ne'er to meet again.

When day is gone, and night is come,
And a' are boun to sleep,
I think on them that's far awa
The lee-lang night and weep,
      My dear,
The lee-lang night and weep.
Old Scotch Ballad

IN THE COURSE of a tour that I once made in Lower Normandy I remained for a day or two at the old town of Honfleur, which stands near the mouth of the Seine. It was the time of a fête, and all the world was thronging in the evening to dance at the fair, held before the chapel of Our Lady of Grace. As I like all kinds of innocent merry-making, I joined the throng.

The chapel is situated at the top of a high hill, or promontory, from whence its bell may be heard at a distance by the mariner at night. It is said to have given the name to the port of Havre de Grace, which lies directly opposite, on the other side of the Seine. The road up to the chapel went in a zig-zag course, along the brow of the steep coast; it was shaded by trees, from between which I had beautiful peeps at the ancient towers of Honfleur below, the varied scenery of the opposite shore, the white buildings of Havre in the distance, and the wide sea beyond. The road was enlivened by groups of peasant girls, in their bright crimson dresses, and tall caps; and I found all the flower of the neighbourhood assembled on the green that crowns the summit of the hill.

The chapel of Notre Dame de Grace is a favourite resort of the inhabitants of Honfleur and its vicinity, both for pleasure and devotion. At this little chapel prayers are put up by the mariners of the port previous to their voyages, and by their friends during their absence; and votive offerings are hung about its walls, in fulfilment of vows made during times of shipwreck and disaster. The chapel is surrounded by trees. Over the portal is an image of the Virgin and Child, with an inscription which struck me as being quite poetical:

> "Etoile de la mer, priez pour nous!"
> (Star of the sea, pray for us.)

On a level spot near the chapel, under a grove of noble trees, the populace dance on fine summer evenings; and here are held frequent fairs and fêtes, which assemble all the rustic beauty of the loveliest parts of Lower Normandy. The present was an occasion of the kind. Booths and tents were erected among the trees; there were the usual displays of finery to tempt the rural coquette, and of wonderful shows to entice the curious; mountebanks were exerting their eloquence; jugglers and fortune-tellers astonishing the credulous; while whole rows of grotesque saints, in wood and wax-work, were offered for the purchase of the pious.

The fête had assembled in one view all the picturesque costumes of the Pays d'Auge, and the Coté de Caux. I beheld tall, stately caps, and trim boddices, according to fashions which have been handed down from mother to daughter for centuries, the exact counterparts of those worn in the time of the Conqueror; and which surprised me by their faithful resemblance to those which I had seen in the old pictures of Froissart's Chronicles, and in the paintings of illuminated manuscripts. Any one, also, that has been in Lower Normandy, must have remarked the beauty of the peasantry, and that air of native elegance which prevails among them. It is to this country, undoubtedly, that the English owe their good looks. It was from hence that the bright carnation, the fine blue eye, the light auburn hair, passed over to England in the train of the Conqueror, and filled the land with beauty.

The scene before me was perfectly enchanting; the assemblage of so many fresh and blooming faces; the gay groups in fanciful dresses; some dancing on the green, others strolling about, or seated on the grass; the fine clumps of trees in the foreground, bordering the brow of this airy height, and the broad green sea, sleeping in summer tranquillity, in the distance.

Whilst I was regarding this animated picture, I was struck with the appearance of a beautiful girl, who passed through the crowd without seeming to take any interest in their amusements. She was slender and delicate in her form; she had not the bloom upon her cheek that is usual among the peasantry of Normandy, and her blue eyes had a singular and melancholy expression. She was accompanied by a venerable looking man, whom I presumed to be her father. There was a whisper among the bystanders, and a wistful look after her as she passed; the young men touched their hats, and some of the children followed her at a little distance, watching her movements. She approached the edge of the hill, where there is a little platform, from whence the people of Honfleur look out for the approach of vessels. Here she stood for some time waving her handkerchief, though there was nothing to be seen but two or three fishing-boats, like mere specks on the bosom of the distant ocean.

These circumstances excited my curiosity, and I made some inquiries about her, which were answered with readiness and intelligence by a priest of the neighbouring chapel. Our conversation drew together several of the bystanders, each of whom had something to communicate, and from them all I gathered the following particulars.

Annette Delarbre was the only daughter of one of the higher order of farmers, or small proprietors, as they are called, who lived at Pont l'Eveque, a pleasant village not far from Honfleur, in that rich pastoral part of Lower Normandy called the Pays d'Auge. Annette was the pride and delight of her parents, and was brought up with the fondest indulgence. She was gay, tender, petulant, and susceptible. All her feelings were quick and ardent; and having never experienced contradiction or restraint, she was little practised in self-control: nothing but the native goodness of her heart kept her from running continually into error.

Even while a child, her susceptibility was evinced in an attachment which she formed to a playmate, Eugene La Forgue, the only son of a widow who lived in the neighbourhood. Their childish love was an epitome of maturer passion; it had its caprices, and jealousies, and quarrels, and reconciliations. It was assuming something of a graver character as Annette entered her fifteenth, and Eugene his nineteenth year, when he was suddenly carried off to the army by the conscription.

It was a heavy blow to his widowed mother, for he was her only pride and comfort; but it was one of those sudden bereavements which mothers were perpetually doomed to feel in France, during the time that continual and bloody wars were incessantly draining her youth. It was a temporary affliction also to Annette, to lose her lover. With tender embraces, half childish, half womanish, she parted from him. The tears streamed from her blue eyes, as she bound a braid of her fair hair round his wrist; but the smiles still broke through; for she was yet too young to feel how serious a thing is separation, and how many chances there are, when parting in this wide world, against our ever meeting again.

Weeks, months, years flew by. Annette increased in beauty as she increased in years, and was the reigning belle of the neighbourhood. Her time passed innocently and happily. Her father was a man of some consequence in the rural community, and his house was the resort of the gayest of the village. Annette held a kind of rural court; she was always surrounded by companions of her own age, among whom she shone unrivalled. Much of their time was past in making lace, the prevalent manufacture of the neighbourhood. As they sat at this delicate and feminine labour, the merry tale and sprightly song went round: none laughed with a lighter heart than Annette; and if she sang, her voice was perfect melody. Their evenings were enlivened by the dance, or by those pleasant social games so prevalent among the French; and when she appeared at the village ball on Sunday evenings, she was the theme of universal admiration.

As she was a rural heiress, she did not want for suitors. Many advantageous offers were made her, but she refused them all. She laughed at the pretended pangs of her admirers, and triumphed over them with the caprice of buoyant youth and conscious beauty. With all her apparent levity, however, could any one have read the story of her heart, they might

have traced in it some fond remembrance of her early playmate, not so deeply graven as to be painful, but too deep to
be easily obliterated; and they might have noticed, amidst all
her gaiety, the tenderness that marked her manner towards
the mother of Eugene. She would often steal away from her
youthful companions and their amusements, to pass whole
days with the good widow; listening to her fond talk about
her boy, and blushing with secret pleasure when his letters
were read, at finding herself a constant theme of recollection
and inquiry.

At length the sudden return of peace, which sent many a
warrior to his native cottage, brought back Eugene, a young
sun-burnt soldier, to the village. I need not say how rap-
turously his return was greeted by his mother, who saw in
him the pride and staff of her old age. He had risen in the
service by his merit; but brought away little from the wars,
excepting a soldier-like air, a gallant name, and a scar across
the forehead. He brought back, however, a nature unspoiled
by the camp. He was frank, open, generous, and ardent. His
heart was quick and kind in its impulses, and was perhaps
a little softer from having suffered: it was full of tenderness
for Annette. He had received frequent accounts of her from
his mother; and the mention of her kindness to his lonely
parent had rendered her doubly dear to him. He had been
wounded; he had been a prisoner; he had been in various
troubles, but he had always preserved the braid of her hair,
which she had bound round his arm. It had been a kind of
talisman to him; he had many a time looked upon it as he lay
on the hard ground, and the thought that he might one day
see Annette again, and the fair fields about his native village,
had cheered his heart, and enabled him to bear up against
every hardship.

He had left Annette almost a child; he found her a blooming woman. If he had loved her before, he now adored her.
Annette was equally struck with the improvement which time
had made in her lover. She noticed, with secret admiration,
his superiority to the other young men of the village; the
frank, lofty, military air, that distinguished him from all
the rest at their rural gatherings. The more she saw him, the
more her light, playful fondness of former years deepened into

ardent and powerful affection. But Annette was a rural belle. She had tasted the sweets of dominion, and had been rendered wilful and capricious by constant indulgence at home, and admiration abroad. She was conscious of her power over Eugene, and delighted in exercising it. She sometimes treated him with petulant caprice, enjoying the pain which she inflicted by her frowns, from the idea how soon she would chase it away again by her smiles. She took a pleasure in alarming his fears, by affecting a temporary preference for some one or other of his rivals; and then would delight in allaying them by an ample measure of returning kindness. Perhaps there was some degree of vanity gratified by all this; it might be a matter of triumph to show her absolute power over the young soldier, who was the universal object of female admiration. Eugene, however, was of too serious and ardent a nature to be trifled with. He loved too fervently not to be filled with doubt. He saw Annette surrounded by admirers, and full of animation; the gayest among the gay at all their rural festivities, and apparently most gay when he was most dejected. Every one saw through this caprice but himself; every one saw that in reality she doted on him; but Eugene alone suspected the sincerity of her affection. For some time he bore this coquetry with secret impatience and distrust; but his feelings grew sore and irritable, and overcame his self-command. A slight misunderstanding took place; a quarrel ensued. Annette, unaccustomed to be thwarted and contradicted, and full of the insolence of youthful beauty, assumed an air of disdain. She refused all explanations to her lover, and they parted in anger. That very evening Eugene saw her, full of gaiety, dancing with one of his rivals; and as her eye caught his, fixed on her with unfeigned distress, it sparkled with more than usual vivacity. It was a finishing blow to his hopes, already so much impaired by secret distrust. Pride and resentment both struggled in his breast, and seemed to rouse his spirit to all its wonted energy. He retired from her presence with the hasty determination never to see her again.

A woman is more considerate in affairs of love than a man; because love is more the study and business of her life. Annette soon repented of her indiscretion; she felt that she had

used her lover unkindly; she felt that she had trifled with his
sincere and generous nature—and then he looked so handsome when he parted after their quarrel—his fine features
lighted up by indignation. She had intended making up with
him at the evening dance; but his sudden departure prevented
her. She now promised herself that when next they met she
would amply repay him by the sweets of a perfect reconciliation, and that, thenceforward, she would never—never tease
him more! That promise was not to be fulfilled. Day after day
passed; but Eugene did not make his appearance. Sunday
evening came, the usual time when all the gaiety of the village
assembled; but Eugene was not there. She inquired after him;
he had left the village. She now became alarmed, and, forgetting all coyness and affected indifference, called on Eugene's
mother for an explanation. She found her full of affliction,
and learnt with surprise and consternation that Eugene had
gone to sea.

While his feelings were yet smarting with her affected disdain, and his heart a prey to alternate indignation and despair,
he had suddenly embraced an invitation which had repeatedly
been made him by a relation, who was fitting out a ship from
the port of Honfleur, and who wished him to be the companion of his voyage. Absence appeared to him the only cure for
his unlucky passion; and in the temporary transports of his
feelings, there was something gratifying in the idea of having
half the world intervene between them. The hurry necessary
for his departure left no time for cool reflection; it rendered
him deaf to the remonstrances of his afflicted mother. He hastened to Honfleur just in time to make the needful preparations for the voyage; and the first news that Annette received
of this sudden determination was a letter delivered by his
mother, returning her pledges of affection, particularly the
long-treasured braid of her hair, and bidding her a last farewell, in terms more full of sorrow and tenderness than upbraiding.

This was the first stroke of real anguish that Annette had
ever received, and it overcame her. The vivacity of her spirits
were apt to hurry her to extremes; she for a time gave way to
ungovernable transports of affliction and remorse, and manifested, in the violence of her grief, the real ardour of her

affection. The thought occurred to her that the ship might not yet have sailed; she seized on the hope with eagerness, and hastened with her father to Honfleur. The ship had sailed that very morning. From the heights above the town she saw it lessening to a speck on the broad bosom of the ocean, and before evening the white sail had faded from her sight. She turned full of anguish to the neighbouring chapel of Our Lady of Grace, and throwing herself on the pavement, poured out prayers and tears for the safe return of her lover.

When she returned home the cheerfulness of her spirits was at an end. She looked back with remorse and self-upbraiding at her past caprices; she turned with distaste from the adulation of her admirers, and had no longer any relish for the amusements of the village. With humiliation and diffidence she sought the widowed mother of Eugene; but was received by her with an overflowing heart; for she only beheld in Annette one who could sympathise in her doting fondness for her son. It seemed some alleviation of her remorse to sit by the mother all day, to study her wants, to beguile her heavy hours, to hang about her with the caressing endearments of a daughter, and to seek by every means, if possible, to supply the place of the son, whom she reproached herself with having driven away.

In the mean time the ship made a prosperous voyage to her destined port. Eugene's mother received a letter from him, in which he lamented the precipitancy of his departure. The voyage had given him time for sober reflection. If Annette had been unkind to him, he ought not to have forgotten what was due to his mother, who was now advanced in years. He accused himself of selfishness in only listening to the suggestions of his own inconsiderate passions. He promised to return with the ship, to make his mind up to his disappointment, and to think of nothing but making his mother happy—— "And when he does return," said Annette, clasping her hands with transport, "it shall not be my fault if he ever leaves us again."

The time approached for the ship's return. She was daily expected, when the weather became dreadfully tempestuous. Day after day brought news of vessels foundered, or driven on shore, and the sea coast was strewed with wrecks. Intelligence was received of the looked-for ship having been seen dismasted in a violent storm, and the greatest fears were entertained for her safety.

Annette never left the side of Eugene's mother. She watched every change of her countenance with painful solicitude, and endeavoured to cheer her with hopes, while her own mind was racked by anxiety. She tasked her efforts to be gay; but it was a forced and unnatural gaiety: a sigh from the mother would completely check it; and when she could no longer restrain the rising tears, she would hurry away and pour out her agony in secret. Every anxious look, every anxious inquiry of the mother, whenever a door opened, or a strange face appeared, was an arrow to her soul. She considered every disappointment as a pang of her own infliction, and her heart sickened under the care-worn expression of the maternal eye. At length this suspense became insupportable. She left the village and hastened to Honfleur, hoping every hour, every moment, to receive some tidings of her lover. She paced the pier, and wearied the seamen of the port with her inquiries. She made a daily pilgrimage to the chapel of Our Lady of Grace; hung votive garlands on the wall, and passed hours either kneeling before the altar, or looking out from the brow of the hill upon the angry sea.

At length word was brought that the long-wished-for vessel was in sight. She was seen standing into the mouth of the Seine, shattered and crippled, bearing marks of having been sadly tempest-tossed. There was a general joy diffused by her return; and there was not a brighter eye, nor a lighter heart, than Annette's in the little port of Honfleur. The ship came to anchor in the river; and shortly after a boat put off for the shore. The populace crowded down to the pier-head to welcome it. Annette stood blushing, and smiling, and trembling, and weeping; for a thousand painfully pleasing emotions agitated her breast at the thoughts of the meeting and reconciliation about to take place. Her heart throbbed to pour itself out, and atone to her gallant lover for all its errors. At one moment she would place herself in a conspicuous situation, where she might catch his view at once, and surprise him by her welcome; but the next moment a doubt would come across her mind, and she would shrink among the throng, trembling and faint, and gasping with her emotions. Her agitation increased as the boat drew near, until it became distressing; and it was almost a relief to her when she perceived that her lover was not there. She presumed that some accident had detained him on board of the ship; and she felt that the delay would enable her to gather more self-possession for the meeting. As the boat neared the shore, many inquiries were made, and laconic answers returned. At length Annette heard some inquiries after her lover. Her heart palpitated; there was a moment's pause: the reply was brief, but awful. He had been washed from the deck, with two of the crew, in the midst of a stormy night, when it was impossible to render any assistance. A piercing shriek broke from among the crowd; and Annette had nearly fallen into the waves.

The sudden revulsion of feelings after such a transient gleam of happiness, was too much for her harassed frame. She was carried home senseless. Her life was for some time despaired of, and it was months before she recovered her health; but she never had perfectly recovered her mind: it still remained unsettled with respect to her lover's fate.

"The subject," continued my informer, "is never mentioned in her hearing; but she sometimes speaks of it herself, and it seems as though there were some vague train of impressions in her mind, in which hope and fear are strangely mingled; some imperfect idea of her lover's shipwreck, and yet some expectation of his return.

"Her parents have tried every means to cheer her, and to banish these gloomy images from her thoughts. They assemble round her the young companions in whose society she used to delight; and they will work, and chat, and sing, and laugh, as formerly; but she will sit silently among them, and will sometimes weep in the midst of their gaiety; and, if spoken to, will make no reply, but look up with streaming eyes, and sing a dismal little song, which she has learned somewhere, about a shipwreck. It makes every one's heart ache to see her in this way, for she used to be the happiest creature in the village.

"She passes the greater part of the time with Eugene's mother; whose only consolation is her society, and who dotes on her with a mother's tenderness. She is the only one that has perfect influence over Annette in every mood. The poor girl seems, as formerly, to make an effort to be cheerful in her company; but will sometimes gaze upon her with the most piteous look, and then kiss her gray hairs, and fall on her neck and weep.

"She is not always melancholy, however; she has occasional intervals when she will be bright and animated for days together; but there is a degree of wildness attending these fits of gaiety, that prevents their yielding any satisfaction to her friends. At such times she will arrange her room, which is all covered with pictures of ships and legends of saints; and will wreath a white chaplet, as if for a wedding, and prepare wedding ornaments. She will listen anxiously at the door, and look frequently out at the window, as if expecting some one's arrival. It is supposed that at such times she is looking for her lover's return; but, as no one touches upon the theme, or mentions his name in her presence, the current of her thoughts is mere matter of conjecture. Now and then she will make a pilgrimage to the chapel of Notre Dame de Grace; where she will pray for hours at the altar, and decorate the images with wreaths that she has woven; or will wave her handkerchief from the terrace, as you have seen, if there is any vessel in the distance."

Upwards of a year, he informed me, had now elapsed without effacing from her mind this singular taint of insanity; still her friends hoped it might gradually wear away. They had at one time removed her to a distant part of the country, in hopes that absence from the scenes connected with her story might have a salutary effect; but, when her periodical melancholy returned, she became more restless and wretched than usual, and, secretly escaping from her friends, set out on foot, without knowing the road, on one of her pilgrimages to the chapel.

This little story entirely drew my attention from the gay scene of the fête, and fixed it upon the beautiful Annette. While she was yet standing on the terrace the vesper-bell was rung from the neighbouring chapel. She listened for a moment, and then, drawing a small rosary from her bosom, walked in that direction. Several of the peasantry followed her in silence; and I felt too much interested not to do the same.

The chapel, as I said before, is in the midst of a grove, on the high promontory. The inside is hung round with little models of ships, and rude paintings of wrecks and perils at sea, and providential deliverances; the votive offerings of captains and crews that have been saved. On entering, Annette paused for a moment before a picture of the Virgin, which, I observed, had recently been decorated with a wreath of artificial flowers. When she reached the middle of the chapel she knelt down, and those who followed her involuntarily did the same at a little distance. The evening sun shone softly through the chequered grove into one window of the chapel. A perfect stillness reigned within; and this stillness was the more impressive, contrasted with the distant sound of music and merriment from the fair. I could not take my eyes off from the poor suppliant; her lips moved as she told her beads, but her prayers were breathed in silence. It might have been mere fancy excited by the scene, that, as she raised her eyes to heaven, I thought they had an expression truly seraphic. But I am easily affected by female beauty, and there was something in this mixture of love, devotion, and partial insanity, that was inexpressibly touching.

As the poor girl left the chapel, there was a sweet serenity in her looks; and I was told that she would return home, and in all probability be calm and cheerful for days, and even weeks; in which time it was supposed that hope predominated in her mental malady; and that when the dark side of her mind, as her friends call it, was about to turn up, it would be known by her neglecting her distaff or her lace, singing plaintive songs, and weeping in silence.

She passed on from the chapel without noticing the fête, but smiling and speaking to many as she passed. I followed her with my eye as she descended the winding road towards Honfleur, leaning on her father's arm. "Heaven," thought I, "has ever its store of balms for the hurt mind and wounded spirit, and may in time rear up this broken flower to be once more the pride and joy of the valley. The very delusion in which the poor girl walks may be one of those mists kindly diffused by Providence over the regions of thought, when they become too fruitful of misery. The veil may gradually be raised which obscures the horizon of her mind, as she is enabled steadily and calmly to contemplate the sorrows at present hidden in mercy from her view."

On my return from Paris, about a year afterwards, I turned off from the beaten route at Rouen, to revisit some of the most striking scenes of Lower Normandy. Having passed through the lovely country of the Pays d'Auge, I reached Honfleur on a fine afternoon, intending to cross to Havre the next morning, and embark for England. As I had no better way of passing the evening, I strolled up the hill to enjoy the fine prospect from the chapel of Notre Dame de Grace; and while there, I thought of inquiring after the fate of poor Annette Delarbre. The priest who had told me her story was officiating at vespers, after which I accosted him, and learnt from him the remaining circumstances. He told me that from the time I had seen her at the chapel, her disorder took a sudden turn for the worse, and her health rapidly declined. Her cheerful intervals became shorter and less frequent, and attended with more incoherency. She grew languid, silent, and moody in her melancholy; her form was wasted, her looks pale and disconsolate, and it was feared she would never recover. She became impatient of all sounds of gaiety, and was never so contented as when Eugene's mother was near her. The good woman watched over her with patient, yearning solicitude; and in seeking to beguile her sorrows, would half forget her own. Sometimes, as she sat looking upon her pallid face, the tears would fill her eyes, which, when Annette perceived, she would anxiously wipe them away, and tell her not to grieve, for that Eugene would soon return; and then she would affect a forced gaiety, as in former times, and sing a lively air; but a sudden recollection would come over her, and she would burst into tears, hang on the poor mother's neck, and entreat her not to curse her for having destroyed her son.

Just at this time, to the astonishment of every one, news was received of Eugene; who, it appeared, was still living. When almost drowned, he had fortunately seized upon a spar which had been washed from the ship's deck. Finding himself nearly exhausted, he had fastened himself to it, and floated for a day and night, until all sense had left him. On recovering, he had found himself on board a vessel bound to India, but so ill as not to move without assistance. His health had continued precarious throughout the voyage; on arriving in India he had experienced many vicissitudes, and had been transferred from ship to ship, and hospital to hospital. His constitution had enabled him to struggle through every hardship; and he was now in a distant port, waiting only for the sailing of a ship to return home.

Great caution was necessary in imparting these tidings to the mother, and even then she was nearly overcome by the transports of her joy. But how to impart them to Annette was a matter of still greater perplexity. Her state of mind had been so morbid; she had been subject to such violent changes, and the cause of her derangement had been of such an inconsolable and hopeless kind, that her friends had always forborne to tamper with her feelings. They had never even hinted at the subject of her griefs, nor encouraged the theme when she adverted to it, but had passed it over in silence, hoping that time would gradually wear the traces of it from her recollection, or, at least, would render them less painful. They now felt at a loss how to undeceive her even in her misery, lest the sudden recurrence of happiness might confirm the estrangement of her reason, or might overpower her enfeebled frame. They ventured, however, to probe those wounds which they formerly did not dare to touch, for they now had the balm to pour into them. They led the conversation to those topics which they had hitherto shunned, and endeavoured to ascertain the current of her thoughts in those varying moods that had formerly perplexed them. They found, however, that her mind was even more affected than they had imagined. All her ideas were confused and wandering. Her bright and cheerful moods, which now grew seldomer than ever, were all the effects of mental delusion. At such times she had no recollection of her lover's having been in danger, but was only anticipating his arrival. "When the winter has passed away," said she, "and the trees put on their blossoms, and the swallow comes back over the sea, he will return." When she was drooping and desponding, it was in vain to remind her of what she had said in her gayer moments, and to assure her that Eugene would indeed return shortly. She wept on in silence, and appeared insensible to their words. But at times

her agitation became violent, when she would upbraid herself
with having driven Eugene from his mother, and brought
sorrow on her gray hairs. Her mind admitted but one leading
idea at a time, which nothing could divert or efface; or if they
ever succeeded in interrupting the current of her fancy, it only
became the more incoherent, and increased the feverishness
that preyed upon both mind and body. Her friends felt more
alarm for her than ever, for they feared that her senses were
irrecoverably gone, and her constitution completely undermined.

In the mean time Eugene returned to the village. He was
violently affected when the story of Annette was told him.
With bitterness of heart he upbraided his own rashness and
infatuation that had hurried him away from her, and accused
himself as the author of all her woes. His mother would describe to him all the anguish and remorse of poor Annette;
the tenderness with which she clung to her, and endeavoured,
even in the midst of her insanity, to console her for the loss
of her son, and the touching expressions of affection that
were mingled with her most incoherent wanderings of
thought, until his feelings would be wound up to agony, and
he would entreat her to desist from the recital. They did not
dare as yet to bring him into Annette's sight; but he was permitted to see her when she was sleeping. The tears streamed
down his sunburnt cheeks as he contemplated the ravages
which grief and malady had made; and his heart swelled almost to breaking as he beheld round her neck the very braid
of hair which she once gave him in token of girlish affection,
and which he had returned to her in anger.

At length the physician that attended her determined to
adventure upon an experiment; to take advantage of one of
those cheerful moods when her mind was visited by hope,
and to endeavour to ingraft, as it were, the reality upon the
delusions of her fancy. These moods had now become very
rare, for nature was sinking under the continual pressure of
her mental malady, and the principle of reaction was daily
growing weaker. Every effort was tried to bring on a cheerful
interval of the kind. Several of her most favourite companions
were kept continually about her; they chatted gaily, they
laughed, and sang, and danced; but Annette reclined with

languid frame and hollow eye, and took no part in their
gaiety. At length the winter was gone; the trees put forth
their leaves; the swallows began to build in the eaves of the
house, and the robin and wren piped all day beneath the window. Annette's spirits gradually revived. She began to deck
her person with unusual care; and bringing forth a basket of
artificial flowers, she went to work to wreathe a bridal chaplet
of white roses. Her companions asked her why she prepared
the chaplet. "What!" said she with a smile, "have you not
noticed the trees putting on their wedding dresses of blossoms? Has not the swallow flown back over the sea? Do you
not know that the time is come for Eugene to return? that he
will be home to-morrow, and that on Sunday we are to be
married?"

Her words were repeated to the physician, and he seized
on them at once. He directed that her idea should be encouraged and acted upon. Her words were echoed through the
house. Every one talked of the return of Eugene as a matter
of course; they congratulated her upon her approaching happiness, and assisted her in her preparations. The next morning
the same theme was resumed. She was dressed out to receive
her lover. Every bosom fluttered with anxiety. A cabriolet
drove into the village. "Eugene is coming!" was the cry. She
saw him alight at the door, and rushed with a shriek into his
arms.

Her friends trembled for the result of this critical experiment; but she did not sink under it, for her fancy had prepared her for his return. She was as one in a dream, to whom
a tide of unlooked-for prosperity, that would have overwhelmed his waking reason, seems but the natural current of
circumstances. Her conversation, however, showed that her
senses were wandering. There was an absolute forgetfulness
of all past sorrow; a wild and feverish gaiety that at times was
incoherent.

The next morning she awoke languid and exhausted. All
the occurrences of the preceding day had passed away from
her mind as though they had been the mere illusions of her
fancy. She rose melancholy and abstracted, and as she dressed
herself, was heard to sing one of her plaintive ballads. When
she entered the parlour her eyes were swoln with weeping.

She heard Eugene's voice without and started. She passed her hand across her forehead, and stood musing, like one endeavouring to recall a dream. Eugene entered the room, and advanced towards her; she looked at him with an eager, searching look, murmured some indistinct words, and, before he could reach her, sank upon the floor.

She relapsed into a wild and unsettled state of mind; but now that the first shock was over, the physician ordered that Eugene should keep continually in her sight. Sometimes she did not know him; at other times she would talk to him as if he were going to sea, and would implore him not to part from her in anger; and when he was not present, she would speak of him as if buried in the ocean, and would sit, with clasped hands, looking upon the ground, the picture of despair.

As the agitation of her feelings subsided, and her frame recovered from the shock which it had received, she became more placid and coherent. Eugene kept almost continually near her. He formed the real object round which her scattered ideas once more gathered, and which linked them once more with the realities of life. But her changeful disorder now appeared to take a new turn. She became languid and inert, and would sit for hours silent, and almost in a state of lethargy. If roused from this stupor, it seemed as if her mind would make some attempts to follow up a train of thought, but would soon become confused. She would regard every one that approached her with an anxious and inquiring eye, that seemed continually to disappoint itself. Sometimes, as her lover sat holding her hand, she would look pensively in his face without saying a word, until his heart was overcome; and after these transient fits of intellectual exertion, she would sink again into lethargy.

By degrees this stupor increased; her mind appeared to have subsided into a stagnant and almost deathlike calm. For the greater part of the time her eyes were closed; her face almost as fixed and passionless as that of a corpse. She no longer took any notice of surrounding objects. There was an awfulness in this tranquillity that filled her friends with apprehension. The physician ordered that she should be kept perfectly quiet; or that, if she evinced any agitation, she should be gently lulled, like a child, by some favourite tune.

She remained in this state for hours, hardly seeming to breathe, and apparently sinking into the sleep of death. Her chamber was profoundly still. The attendants moved about it with noiseless tread; every thing was communicated by signs and whispers. Her lover sat by her side watching her with painful anxiety, and fearing that every breath which stole from her pale lips would be the last.

At length she heaved a deep sigh; and from some convulsive motions, appeared to be troubled in her sleep. Her agitation increased, accompanied by an indistinct moaning. One of her companions, remembering the physician's instructions, endeavoured to lull her by singing, in a low voice, a tender little air, which was a particular favourite of Annette's. Probably it had some connexion in her mind with her own story; for every fond girl has some ditty of the kind, linked in her thoughts with sweet and sad remembrances.

As she sang, the agitation of Annette subsided. A streak of faint colour came into her cheeks; her eyelids became swoln with rising tears, which trembled there for a moment, and then, stealing forth, coursed down her pallid cheek. When the song was ended, she opened her eyes and looked about her, as one awaking in a strange place.

"Oh, Eugene! Eugene!" said she, "it seems as if I have had a long and dismal dream: what has happened, and what has been the matter with me?"

The questions were embarrassing; and before they could be answered, the physician, who was in the next room, entered. She took him by the hand, looked up in his face, and made the same inquiry. He endeavoured to put her off with some evasive answer;—"No, no!" cried she, "I know I've been ill, and I have been dreaming strangely. I thought Eugene had left us—and that he had gone to sea—and that he was drowned!—But he *has* been to sea!" added she earnestly, as recollection kept flashing upon her, "and he has been wrecked—and we were all so wretched—and he came home again one bright morning—and—Oh!" said she, pressing her hand against her forehead with a sickly smile, "I see how it is; all has not been right here, I begin to recollect—but it is all past now—Eugene is here! and his mother is happy—and we shall never—never part again—shall we, Eugene?"

She sunk back in her chair exhausted; the tears streamed down her cheeks. Her companions hovered round her, not knowing what to make of this sudden dawn of reason. Her lover sobbed aloud. She opened her eyes again, and looked upon them with an air of the sweetest acknowledgment. "You are all so good to me!" said she, faintly.

The physician drew the father aside. "Your daughter's mind is restored," said he; "she is sensible that she has been deranged; she is growing conscious of the past, and conscious of the present. All that now remains is to keep her calm and quiet until her health is re-established, and then let her be married, in God's name!"

"The wedding took place," continued the good priest, "but a short time since; they were here at the last fête during their honey-moon, and a handsomer and happier couple was not to be seen as they danced under yonder trees. The young man, his wife, and mother, now live on a fine farm at Pont L'Eveque; and that model of a ship which you see yonder, with white flowers wreathed round it, is Annette's offering of thanks to our Lady of Grace, for having listened to her prayers and protected her lover in the hour of peril."*

The captain having finished, there was a momentary silence. The tender-hearted Lady Lillycraft, who knew the story by heart, had led the way in weeping, and indeed had often begun to shed tears before they had come to the right place.

The fair Julia was a little flurried at the passage where wedding preparations were mentioned; but the auditor most affected was the simple Phœbe Wilkins. She had gradually dropt her work in her lap, and sat sobbing through the latter part of the story, until towards the end, when the happy

*Whoever has seen the pathetic ballet of Nina, may be reminded of it by some of the passages in the latter part of the above tale. The story, it is true, was sketched before seeing that ballet; but in re-writing it, the author's memory was haunted by the inimitable performance of Bigottini, in Nina, and the vivid recollection of it may have produced an occasional similarity. He is in some measure prompted to make this acknowledgment, for the purpose of expressing his admiration of the wonderful powers of that actress; who has given a dignity and pathos to the ballet, of which he had not supposed it capable.

reverse had nearly produced another scene of hystericks. "Go, take this case to my room again, child," said Lady Lillycraft kindly, "and don't cry so much."

"I won't, an't please your ladyship, if I can help it;—but I'm glad they made all up again, and were married!"

By the way, the case of this love-lorn damsel begins to make some talk in the household, especially among certain little ladies, not far in their teens, of whom she has made confidants. She is a great favourite with them all, but particularly so since she has confided to them her love secrets. They enter into her concerns with all the violent zeal and overwhelming sympathy with which little boarding-school ladies engage in the politics of a love affair.

I have noticed them frequently clustering about her in private conferences, or walking up and down the garden terrace under my window, listening to some long and dolorous story of her afflictions; of which I could now and then distinguish the ever-recurring phrases "says he," and "says she."

I accidentally interrupted one of these little councils of war, when they were all huddled together under a tree, and seemed to be earnestly considering some interesting document. The flutter at my approach showed that there were some secrets under discussion; and I observed the disconsolate Phœbe crumbling into her bosom either a love-letter or an old valentine, and brushing away the tears from her cheeks.

The girl is a good girl, of a soft melting nature, and shows her concern at the cruelty of her lover only in tears and drooping looks; but with the little ladies who have espoused her cause, it sparkles up into fiery indignation: and I have noticed on Sunday many a glance darted at the pew of the Tibbetses, enough even to melt down the silver buttons on old Ready Money's jacket.

Travelling

A citizen, for recreation sake,
To see the country would a journey take
Some dozen mile, or very little more;
Taking his leave with friends two months before,
With drinking healths, and shaking by the hand,
As he had travail'd to some new-found land.

Doctor Merrie-Man, 1609

THE SQUIRE has lately received another shock in the saddle, and been almost unseated by his marplot neighbour
the indefatigable Mr. Faddy, who rides his jog-trot hobby
with equal zeal; and is so bent upon improving and reform-
ing the neighbourhood, that the squire thinks, in a little
while, it will be scarce worth living in. The enormity that
has just discomposed my worthy host, is an attempt of the
manufacturer to have a line of coaches established, that shall
diverge from the old route, and pass through the neighbouring village.

I believe I have mentioned that the Hall is situated in a
retired part of the country, at a distance from any great coach
road; insomuch that the arrival of a traveller is apt to make
every one look out of the window, and to cause some talk
among the ale-drinkers at the little inn. I was at a loss, therefore, to account for the squire's indignation at a measure
apparently fraught with convenience and advantage, until I
found that the conveniences of travelling were among his
greatest grievances.

In fact, he rails against stage-coaches, post-chaises, and
turnpike-roads, as serious causes of the corruption of English
rural manners. They have given facilities, he says, to every
hum-drum citizen to trundle his family about the kingdom,
and have sent the follies and fashions of town whirling, in
coach-loads, to the remotest parts of the island. The whole
country, he says, is traversed by these flying cargoes; every
by-road is explored by enterprising tourists from Cheapside
and the Poultry, and every gentleman's park and lawns in-

vaded by cockney sketchers of both sexes, with portable chairs
and portfolios for drawing.

He laments over this as destroying the charm of privacy,
and interrupting the quiet of country life; but more especially
as affecting the simplicity of the peasantry, and filling their
heads with half-city notions. A great coach inn, he says, is
enough to ruin the manners of a whole village. It creates a
horde of sots and idlers; makes gapers and gazers and news-
mongers of the common people, and knowing jockeys of the
country bumpkins.

The squire has something of the old feudal feeling. He
looks back with regret to the "good old times," when journeys were only made on horseback, and the extraordinary
difficulties of travelling, owing to bad roads, bad accommodations, and highway robbers, seemed to separate
each village and hamlet from the rest of the world. The lord
of the manor was then a kind of monarch in the little realm
around him. He held his court in his paternal hall, and was
looked up to with almost as much loyalty and deference as
the king himself. Every neighbourhood was a little world
within itself, having its local manners and customs, its local
history, and local opinions. The inhabitants were fonder of
their homes, and thought less of wandering. It was looked
upon as an expedition to travel out of sight of the parish steeple; and a man that had been to London was a village oracle
for the rest of his life.

What a difference between the mode of travelling in those
days and at present! At that time, when a gentleman went on
a distant visit, he sallied forth like a knight-errant on an
enterprise, and every family excursion was a pageant. How
splendid and fanciful must one of those domestic cavalcades
have been, when the beautiful dames were mounted on pal-
fries magnificently caparisoned, with embroidered harness, all
tinkling with silver bells; attended by cavaliers richly attired
on prancing steeds, and followed by pages and serving-men,
as we see them represented in old tapestry. The gentry, as
they travelled about in those days, were like moving pictures.
They delighted the eyes and awakened the admiration of the
common people, and passed before them like superior beings;
and indeed they were so; there was a hardy and healthful

exercise connected with this equestrian style, that made them generous and noble.

In his fondness for the old style of travelling, the squire makes most of his journeys on horseback, though he laments the modern deficiency of incident on the road, from the want of fellow-wayfarers, and the rapidity with which every one else is whirled along in coaches and post-chaises. In the "good old times," on the contrary, a cavalier jogged on through bog and mire, from town to town, and hamlet to hamlet, conversing with friars and franklens, and all other chance companions of the road; beguiling the way with travellers' tales, which then were truly wonderful, for every thing beyond one's neighbourhood was full of marvel and romance; stopping at night at some "hostel," where the bush over the door proclaimed good wine, or a pretty hostess made bad wine palatable; meeting at supper with travellers like himself; discussing their day's adventures, or listening to the song or merry story of the host, who was generally a boon companion, and presided at his own board; for, according to old Tusser's "Innholder's Posie,"

> "At meales my friend who vitleth here
>   And sitteth with his host,
>   Shall both be sure of better cheere,
>   And 'scape with lesser cost."

The squire is fond, too, of stopping at those inns which may be met with, here and there, in ancient houses of wood and plaster, or calimanco houses, as they are called by antiquaries, with deep porches, diamond-paned bow-windows, panneled rooms, and great fire-places. He will prefer them to more spacious and modern inns, and will cheerfully put up with bad cheer and bad accommodations in the gratification of his humour. They give him, he says, the feeling of old times, insomuch that he almost expects, in the dusk of the evening, to see some party of weary travellers ride up to the door, with plumes and mantles, trunk-hose, wide boots, and long rapiers.

The good squire's remarks brought to mind a visit that I once paid to the Tabard Inn, famous for being the place of assemblage from whence Chaucer's pilgrims set forth for

Canterbury. It is in the borough of Southwark, not far from London Bridge, and bears, at present, the name of "the Talbot." It has sadly declined in dignity since the days of Chaucer, being a mere rendezvous and packing place of the great waggons that travel into Kent. The court-yard, which was anciently the mustering-place of the pilgrims previous to their departure, was now lumbered with huge waggons. Crates, boxes, hampers, and baskets, containing the good things of town and country, were piled about them; while, among the straw and litter, the motherly hens scratched and clucked, with their hungry broods at their heels. Instead of Chaucer's motley and splendid throng, I only saw a group of waggoners, and stable-boys enjoying a circulating pot of ale; while a long-bodied dog sat by, with head on one side, ear cocked up, and wistful gaze, as if waiting for his turn at the tankard.

Notwithstanding this grievous declension, however, I was gratified at perceiving that the present occupants were not unconscious of the poetical renown of their mansion. An inscription over the gateway proclaimed it to be the inn where Chaucer's pilgrims slept on the night previous to their departure, and at the bottom of the yard was a magnificent sign, representing them in the act of sallying forth. I was pleased, too, at noticing, that though the present inn was comparatively modern, yet the form of the old inn was preserved. There were galleries round the yard, as in old times, on which opened the chambers of the guests. To these ancient inns have antiquaries ascribed the present forms of our theatres. Plays were originally acted in inn-yards. The guests lolled over the galleries which answered to our modern dress-circle; the critical mob clustered in the yard instead of the pit; and the groups gazing from the garret windows, were no bad representatives of the gods of the shilling gallery. When, therefore, the drama grew important enough to have a house of its own, the architects took a hint for its construction from the yard of the ancient "hostel."

I was so well pleased at finding these remembrances of Chaucer and his poem, that I ordered my dinner in the little parlour of the Talbot. Whilst it was preparing, I sat at the window, musing and gazing into the court-yard, and conjuring up recollections of the scenes depicted in such lively

colours by the poet, until, by degrees, bales, boxes and hampers, boys, waggoners, and dogs, faded from sight, and my
fancy peopled the place with the motley throng of Canterbury
pilgrims. The galleries once more swarmed with idle gazers in
the rich dresses of Chaucer's time, and the whole cavalcade
seemed to pass before me. There was the stately knight on
sober steed, who had ridden in Christendom and heathenesse,
and had "foughten for our faith at Tramissene;"—and his
son, the young squire, a lover, and a lusty bachelor, with
curled locks and gay embroidery; a bold rider, a dancer, and
a writer of verses, singing and fluting all day long, and "fresh
as the month of May;"—and his "knot-headed" yeoman; a
bold forester, in green, with horn, and baudrick, and dagger,
a mighty bow in hand, and a sheaf of peacock arrows shining
beneath his belt;—and the coy, smiling, simple nun, with her
gray eyes, her small red mouth and fair forehead, her dainty
person clad in featly cloak and " 'ypinched wimple," her coral
beads about her arm, her golden brooch with a love motto,
and her pretty oath "by Saint Eloy;"—and the merchant, solemn in speech and high on horse, with forked beard and
"Flaundrish bever hat;"—and the lusty monk, "full fat and in
good point," with berry brown palfrey, his hood fastened
with gold pin, wrought with a love-knot, his bald head shining like glass, and his face glistening as though it had been
anointed;—and the lean, logical, sententious clerke of Oxen-
forde, upon his half-starved, scholar-like horse;—and the
bowsing sompnour, with fiery-cherub face, all knobbed with
pimples, an eater of garlick and onions, and drinker of
"strong wine, red as blood," that carried a cake for a buckler,
and babbled Latin in his cups; of whose brimstone visage
"children were sore aferd;"—and the buxom wife of Bath,
the widow of five husbands, upon her ambling nag, with her
hat broad as a buckler, her red stockings and sharp spurs;—
and the slender, choleric reeve of Norfolk, bestriding his good
gray stot; with close-shaven beard, his hair cropped round his
ears, long, lean, calfless legs, and a rusty blade by his side,—
and the jolly Limitour, with lisping tongue and twinkling
eye, well beloved of franklens and housewives, a great promoter of marriages among young women, known at the taverns in every town, and by every "hosteler and gay tapstere."

In short, before I was roused from my reverie by the less poetical, but more substantial apparition of a smoking beef-steak, I had seen the whole cavalcade issue forth from the hostel-gate, with the brawny, double-jointed, red-haired miller, playing the bagpipes before them, and the ancient host of the Tabard giving them his farewell God-send to Canter-bury.

When I told the squire of the existence of this legitimate descendant of the ancient Tabard Inn, his eyes absolutely glis-tened with delight. He determined to hunt it up the very first time he visited London, and to eat a dinner there, and drink a cup of mine host's best wine, in memory of old Chaucer. The general, who happened to be present, immediately begged to be of the party, for he liked to encourage these long-established houses, as they are apt to have choice old wines.

Popular Superstitions

Farewell rewards and fairies
  Good housewives now may say;
For now fowle sluts in dairies
  Do fare as well as they:
And though they sweepe their hearths no lesse
  Than maids were wont to doe,
Yet who of late for cleanlinesse
  Finds sixpence in her shooe?
Bishop Corbet

I HAVE MENTIONED the squire's fondness for the marvellous, and his predilection for legends and romances. His library contains a curious collection of old works of this kind, which bear evident marks of having been much read. In his great love for all that is antiquated, he cherishes popular superstitions, and listens, with very grave attention, to every tale, however strange; so that, through his countenance, the household, and, indeed, the whole neighbourhood, is well stocked with wonderful stories; and if ever a doubt is expressed of any one of them, the narrator will generally observe, that "the squire thinks there's something in it."

The Hall of course comes in for its share, the common people having always a propensity to furnish a great superannuated building of the kind with supernatural inhabitants. The gloomy galleries of such old family mansions; the stately chambers, adorned with grotesque carvings and faded paintings; the sounds that vaguely echo about them; the moaning of the wind; the cries of rooks and ravens from the trees and chimney-tops; all produce a state of mind favourable to superstitious fancies.

In one chamber of the Hall, just opposite a door which opens upon a dusky passage, there is a full length portrait of a warrior in armour; when, on suddenly turning into the passage, I have caught a sight of the portrait, thrown into strong relief by the dark pannelling against which it hangs, I have more than once been startled, as though it were a figure advancing towards me.

To superstitious minds, therefore, predisposed by the strange and melancholy stories that are connected with family paintings, it needs but little stretch of fancy, on a moonlight night, or by the flickering light of a candle, to set the old pictures on the walls in motion, sweeping in their robes and trains about the galleries.

To tell the truth, the squire confesses that he used to take a pleasure in his younger days in setting marvellous stories afloat, and connecting them with the lonely and peculiar places of the neighbourhood. Whenever he read any legend of a striking nature, he endeavoured to transplant it, and give it a local habitation among the scenes of his boyhood. Many of these stories took root, and he says he is often amused with the odd shapes in which they will come back to him in some old woman's narrative, after they have been circulating for years among the peasantry, and undergoing rustic additions and amendments. Among these may doubtless be numbered that of the crusader's ghost, which I have mentioned in the account of my Christmas visit; and another about the hard-riding squire of yore, the family Nimrod, who is sometimes heard on stormy winter nights, galloping, with hound and horn, over a wild moor a few miles distant from the Hall. This I apprehend to have had its origin in the famous story of the wild huntsman, the favourite goblin in German tales; though, by-the-bye, as I was talking on the subject with Master Simon the other evening in the dark avenue, he hinted, that he had himself once or twice heard odd sounds at night, very like a pack of hounds in cry; and that once, as he was returning rather late from a hunting-dinner, he had seen a strange figure galloping along this same moor; but as he was riding rather fast at the time, and in a hurry to get home, he did not stop to ascertain what it was.

Popular superstitions are fast fading away in England, owing to the general diffusion of knowledge, and the bustling intercourse kept up throughout the country: still they have their strong holds and lingering places, and a retired neighbourhood like this is apt to be one of them. The parson tells me that he meets with many traditional beliefs and notions among the common people, which he has been able to draw from them in the course of familiar conversation, though they are rather shy of avowing them to strangers, and particularly to "the gentry," who are apt to laugh at them. He says there are several of his old parishioners who remember when the village had its bar-guest, or bar-ghost; a spirit supposed to belong to a town or village, and to predict any impending misfortune by midnight shrieks and wailings. The last time it was heard was just before the death of Mr. Bracebridge's father, who was much beloved throughout the neighbourhood; though there are not wanting some obstinate unbelievers, who insisted that it was nothing but the howling of a watch-dog. I have been greatly delighted, however, at meeting with some traces of my old favourite, Robin Good-fellow, though under a different appellation from any of those by which I have heretofore heard him called. The parson assures me that many of the peasantry believe in household goblins, called Dobbies, which live about particular farms and houses, in the same way that Robin Good-fellow did of old. Sometimes they haunt the barns and outhouses, and now and then will assist the farmer wonderfully, by getting in all his hay or corn in a single night. In general, however, they prefer to live within doors, and are fond of keeping about the great hearths, and basking at night, after the family have gone to bed, by the glowing embers. When put in particular good humour by the warmth of their lodgings, and the tidiness of the housemaids, they will overcome their natural laziness, and do a vast deal of household work before morning; churning the cream, brewing the beer, or spinning all the good dame's flax. All this is precisely the conduct of Robin Good-fellow, described so charmingly by Milton:

> "Tells how the drudging goblin sweat
> To earn his cream-bowl duly set,
> When in one night, ere glimpse of morn,
> His shadowy flail had thresh'd the corn
> That ten day labourers could not end;
> Then lays him down the lubber-fiend,
> And stretch'd out all the chimney's length
> Basks at the fire his hairy strength,
> And crop-full, out of door he flings
> Ere the first cock his matin rings."

But beside these household Dobbies, there are others of a more gloomy and unsocial nature, that keep about lonely barns at a distance from any dwelling-house, or about ruins and old bridges. These are full of mischievous, and often malignant tricks, and are fond of playing pranks upon benighted travellers. There is a story, among the old people, of one that haunted a ruined mill, just by a bridge that crosses a small stream; how that late one night, as a traveller was passing on horseback, the Dobbie jumped up behind him, and grasped him so close round the body that he had no power to help himself, but expected to be squeezed to death: luckily his heels were loose, with which he plied the sides of his steed, and was carried, with the wonderful instinct of a traveller's horse, straight to the village inn. Had the inn been at any greater distance, there is no doubt but he would have been strangled to death; as it was, the good people were a long time in bringing him to his senses, and it was remarked that the first sign he showed of returning consciousness was to call for a bottom of brandy.

These mischievous Dobbies bear much resemblance in their natures and habits to those sprites which Heywood in his Hierarchie calls pugs or hobgoblins:

> "—— Their dwellings be
> In corners of old houses least frequented,
> Or beneath stacks of wood, and these convented,
> Make fearfull noise in butteries and in dairies;
> Robin Goodfellow some, some call them faries.
> In solitarie rooms these uprores keep,
> And beate at doores, to wake men from their slepe,
> Seeming to force lockes, be they nere so strong,
> And keeping Christmasse gambols all night long.
> Pots, glasses, trenchers, dishes, pannes and kettles
> They will make dance about the shelves and settles,
> As if about the kitchen tost and cast,
> Yet in the morning, nothing found misplac't.
> Others such houses to their use have fitted
> In which base murthers have been once committed.
> Some have their fearful habitations taken
> In desolat houses, ruin'd and forsaken."

In the account of our unfortunate hawking expedition, I mentioned an instance of one of these sprites supposed to haunt the ruined grange that stands in a lonely meadow, and has a remarkable echo. The parson informs me also, that the belief was once very prevalent, that a household Dobbie kept about the old farm-house of the Tibbetses. It has long been traditional, he says, that one of these good-natured goblins is attached to the Tibbets' family, and came with them when they moved into this part of the country; for it is one of the peculiarities of these household sprites, that they attach themselves to the fortunes of certain families, and follow them in all their removals.

There is a large old-fashioned fire-place in the farm-house, which affords fine quarters for a chimney-corner sprite that likes to lie warm; especially as Ready Money Jack keeps up rousing fires in the winter time. The old people of the village recollect many stories about this goblin that were current in their young days. It was thought to have brought good luck to the house, and to be the reason why the Tibbetses were always beforehand in the world, and why their farm was always in better order, their hay got in sooner, and their corn better stacked than that of their neighbours. The present Mrs. Tibbets, at the time of her courtship, had a number of these stories told her by the country gossips; and when married, was a little fearful about living in a house where such a hobgoblin was said to haunt: Jack, however, who has always treated this story with great contempt, assured her that there was no spirit kept about his house that he could not at any time lay in the Red sea with one flourish of his cudgel. Still his wife has never got completely over her notions on the subject, but has a horse-shoe nailed on the threshold, and keeps a branch of rauntry, or mountain-ash, with its red berries suspended from one of the great beams in the parlour, —a sure protection from all evil spirits.

These stories, however, as I before observed, are fast fading away, and in another generation or two will probably be completely forgotten. There is something, however, about these rural superstitions that is extremely pleasing to the imagination; particularly those which relate to the good-humoured race of household demons, and indeed to the whole

fairy mythology. The English have given an inexpressible
charm to these superstitions, by the manner in which they
have associated them with whatever is most home-felt and
delightful in rustic life, or refreshing and beautiful in nature.
I do not know a more fascinating race of beings than these
little fabled people that haunted the southern sides of hills
and mountains, lurked in flowers and about fountain heads,
glided through key-holes into ancient halls, watched over
farm-houses and dairies, danced on the green by summer
moonlight, and on the kitchen hearth in winter. They seem
to me to accord with the nature of English housekeeping and
English scenery. I always have them in mind when I see a fine
old English mansion, with its wide hall and spacious kitchen;
or a venerable farm-house, in which there is so much fire-side
comfort and good housewifery. There was something of national character in their love of order and cleanliness; in the
vigilance with which they watched over the economy of the
kitchen, and the functions of the servants; munificently re-
warding, with silver sixpence in shoe, the tidy housemaid, but
venting their direful wrath, in midnight bobs and pinches,
upon the sluttish dairymaid. I think I can trace the good effects of this ancient fairy sway over household concerns, in
the care that prevails to the present day among English housemaids, to put their kitchens in order before they go to bed.

I have said, too, that these fairy superstitions seemed to me
to accord with the nature of English scenery. They suit these
small landscapes, which are divided by honeysuckled hedges
into sheltered fields and meadows, where the grass is mingled
with daisies, buttercups, and hare-bells. When I first found
myself among English scenery, I was continually reminded of
the sweet pastoral images which distinguish their fairy mythology; and when for the first time a circle in the grass was
pointed out to me as one of the rings where they were formerly supposed to have held their moonlight revels, it seemed
for a moment as if fairy land were no longer a fable. Brown,
in his Britannia's Pastorals, gives a picture of the kind of
scenery to which I allude:

> "—— A pleasant mead
> Where fairies often did their measures tread;

> Which in the meadows makes such circles green
> As if with garlands it had crowned been.
> Within one of these rounds was to be seen
> A hillock rise, where oft the fairy queen
> At twilight sat."

And there is another picture of the same, in a poem ascribed to Ben Jonson.

> "By wells and rills in the meadowes green,
>   We nightly dance our hey-day guise,
> And to our fairy king and queen
>   We chant our moonlight minstrelsies."

Indeed it seems to me, that the older British poets, with that true feeling for nature which distinguishes them, have closely adhered to the simple and familiar imagery which they found in these popular superstitions, and have thus given to their fairy mythology those continual allusions to the farm-house and the dairy, the green meadow and the fountain-head, that fill our minds with the delightful associations of rural life. It is curious to observe how the most beautiful fictions have their origin among the rude and ignorant. There is an indescribable charm about the illusions with which chimerical ignorance once clothed every subject. These twilight views of nature are often more captivating than any which are revealed by the rays of enlightened philosophy. The most accomplished and poetical minds, therefore, have been fain to search back into these accidental conceptions of what are termed barbarous ages, and to draw from them their finest imagery and machinery. If we look through our most admired poets, we shall find that their minds have been impregnated by these popular fancies, and that those have succeeded best who have adhered closest to the simplicity of their rustic originals. Such is the case with Shakspeare in his Midsummer-Night's Dream, which so minutely describes the employments and amusements of fairies, and embodies all the notions concerning them which were current among the vulgar. It is thus that poetry in England has echoed back every rustic note, softened into perfect melody; it is thus that it has spread its charms over every-day life, displacing nothing, taking things as it found them, but tinting them up with its own magical hues, until every green hill and fountain head, every fresh meadow, nay, every humble flower, is full of song and story.

I am dwelling too long, perhaps, upon a threadbare subject; yet it brings up with it a thousand delicious recollections of those happy days of childhood, when the imperfect knowledge I have since obtained had not yet dawned upon my mind, and when a fairy tale was true history to me. I have often been so transported by the pleasure of these recollections, as almost to wish that I had been born in the days when the fictions of poetry were believed. Even now I cannot look upon those fanciful creations of ignorance and credulity, without a lurking regret that they have all passed away. The experience of my early days tells me, that they were sources of exquisite delight; and I sometimes question whether the naturalist who can dissect the flowers of the field, receives half the pleasure from contemplating them, that he did who considered them the abode of elves and fairies. I feel convinced that the true interests and solid happiness of man are promoted by the advancement of truth; yet I cannot but mourn over the pleasant errors which it has trampled down in its progress. The fauns and sylphs, the household sprite, the moonlight revel, Oberon, Queen Mab, and the delicious realms of fairy land, all vanish before the light of true philosophy; but who does not sometimes turn with distaste from the cold realities of morning, and seek to recall the sweet visions of the night?

The Culprit

From fire, from water, and all things amiss,
Deliver the house of an honest justice.
The Widow

THE SERENITY of the Hall has been suddenly interrupted by a very important occurrence. In the course of this morning a posse of villagers was seen trooping up the avenue, with boys shouting in advance. As it drew near, we perceived Ready Money Jack Tibbets striding along, wielding his cudgel in one hand, and with the other grasping the collar of a tall fellow, whom, on still nearer approach, we recognised for the redoubtable gipsy hero, Starlight Tom. He was now, however, completely cowed and crest-fallen, and his courage seemed to have quailed in the iron gripe of the lion-hearted Jack.

The whole gang of gipsy-women and children came draggling in the rear; some in tears, others making a violent clamour about the ears of old Ready Money, who, however, trudged on in silence with his prey, heeding their abuse as little a hawk that has pounced upon a barn-door hero regards the outcries and cacklings of his whole feathered seraglio.

He had passed through the village on his way to the Hall, and of course had made a great sensation in that most excitable place, where every event is a matter of gaze and gossip. The report flew like wildfire, that Starlight Tom was in custody. The ale-drinkers forthwith abandoned the tap-room; Slingsby's school broke loose, and master and boys swelled the tide that came rolling at the heels of old Ready Money and his captive.

The uproar increased as they approached the Hall; it aroused the whole garrison of dogs, and the crew of hangers-on. The great mastiff barked from the dog-house; the stag-hound and the greyhound, and the spaniel issued barking from the hall-door, and my Lady Lillycraft's little dogs ramped and barked from the parlour window. I remarked, however, that the gipsy dogs made no reply to all these menaces and insults, but crept close to the gang, looking round with a guilty, poaching air, and now and then glancing up a dubious eye to their owners; which shows that the moral dignity, even of dogs, may be ruined by bad company!

When the throng reached the front of the house, they were brought to a halt by a kind of advanced guard, composed of old Christy, the gamekeeper, and two or three servants of the house, who had been brought out by the noise. The common herd of the village fell back with respect; the boys were driven back by Christy and his compeers; while Ready Money Jack maintained his ground and his hold of the prisoner, and was surrounded by the tailor, the schoolmaster, and several other dignitaries of the village, and by the clamorous brood of gipsies, who were neither to be silenced nor intimidated.

By this time the whole household were brought to the doors and windows, and the squire to the portal. An audience was demanded by Ready Money Jack, who had detected the prisoner in the very act of sheep-stealing on his domains, and had borne him off to be examined before the squire, who is in the commission of the peace.

A kind of tribunal was immediately held in the servants' hall, a large chamber, with a stone floor and a long table in the centre, at one end of which, just under an enormous clock, was placed the squire's chair of justice, while Master Simon took his place at the table as clerk of the court. An attempt had been made by old Christy to keep out the gipsy gang, but in vain; and they, with the village worthies, and the household, half filled the hall. The old housekeeper and the butler were in a panic at this dangerous irruption. They hurried away all the valuable things and portable articles that were at hand, and even kept a dragon watch on the gipsies, lest they should carry off the house clock, or the deal table.

Old Christy, and his faithful coadjutor the gamekeeper, acted as constables to guard the prisoner, triumphing in having at last got this terrible offender in their clutches. Indeed I am inclined to think the old man bore some peevish recollection of having been handled rather roughly by the gipsy in the chance-medley affair of May-day.

Silence was now commanded by Master Simon; but it was difficult to be enforced in such a motley assemblage. There was a continual snarling and yelping of dogs, and, as fast as it was quelled in one corner, it broke out in another. The poor gipsy curs, who, like errant thieves, could not hold up their heads in an honest house, were worried and insulted by the gentlemen dogs of the establishment, without offering to make resistance; the very curs of my Lady Lillycraft bullied them with impunity.

The examination was conducted with great mildness and indulgence by the squire, partly from the kindness of his nature, and partly, I suspect, because his heart yearned towards the culprit, who had found great favour in his eyes, as I have already observed, from the skill he had at various times displayed in archery, morrice dancing, and other obsolete accomplishments. Proofs, however, were too strong. Ready Money Jack told his story in a straight-forward independent way, nothing daunted by the presence in which he found himself. He had suffered from various depredations on his sheepfold and poultry-yard, and had at length kept watch, and caught the delinquent in the very act of making off with a sheep on his shoulders.

Tibbets was repeatedly interrupted, in the course of his testimony, by the culprit's mother, a furious old beldame, with an insufferable tongue, and who, in fact, was several times kept, with some difficulty, from flying at him tooth and nail. The wife, too, of the prisoner, whom I am told he does not beat above half a dozen times a week, completely interested Lady Lillycraft in her husband's behalf, by her tears and supplications; and several of the other gipsy women were awakening strong sympathy among the young girls and maidservants in the back-ground. The pretty black-eyed gipsy-girl, whom I have mentioned on a former occasion as the sibyl that read the fortunes of the general, endeavoured to wheedle that doughty warrior into their interests, and even made some approaches to her old acquaintance, Master Simon; but was repelled by the latter with all the dignity of office, having assumed a look of gravity and importance suitable to the occasion.

I was a little surprised at first, to find honest Slingsby, the schoolmaster, rather opposed to his old crony Tibbets, and coming forward as a kind of advocate for the accused. It seems that he had taken compassion on the forlorn fortunes of Starlight Tom, and had been trying his eloquence in his favour the whole way from the village, but without effect. During the examination of Ready Money Jack, Slingsby had stood like "dejected pity at his side," seeking every now and then, by a soft word, to soothe any exacerbation of his ire or to qualify any harsh expression. He now ventured to make a few observations to the squire in palliation of the delinquent's offence; but poor Slingsby spoke more from the heart than the head, and was evidently actuated merely by a general sympathy for every poor devil in trouble, and a liberal toleration for all kinds of vagabond existence.

The ladies, too, large and small, with the kind-heartedness of the sex, were zealous on the side of mercy, and interceded strenuously with the squire; insomuch that the prisoner, finding himself unexpectedly surrounded by active friends, once more reared his crest, and seemed disposed for a time to put on the air of injured innocence. The squire, however, with all his benevolence of heart, and his lurking weakness towards the prisoner, was too conscientious to swerve from the strict path of justice. There was abundant concurring testimony that made the proof of guilt incontrovertible, and Starlight Tom's mittimus was made out accordingly.

The sympathy of the ladies was now greater than ever; they even made some attempts to mollify the ire of Ready Money Jack; but that sturdy potentate had been too much incensed by the repeated incursions that had been made into his territories by the predatory band of Starlight Tom, and he was resolved, he said, to drive the "varment reptiles" out of the neighbourhood. To avoid all further importunities, as soon as the mittimus was made out, he girded up his loins, and strode back to his seat of empire, accompanied by his interceding friend, Slingsby, and followed by a detachment of the gipsy gang, who hung on his rear, assailing him with mingled prayers and execrations.

The question now was, how to dispose of the prisoner; a matter of great moment in this peaceful establishment, where so formidable a character as Starlight Tom was like a hawk entrapped in a dove-cote. As the hubbub and examination had occupied a considerable time, it was too late in the day to send him to the county prison, and that of the village was sadly out of repair from long want of occupation. Old Christy, who took great interest in the affair, proposed that the culprit should be committed for the night to an upper loft of a kind of tower in one of the out-houses, where he and the gamekeeper would mount guard. After much deliberation this measure was adopted; the premises in question were examined and made secure, and Christy and his trusty ally, the one armed with a fowling-piece, the other with an ancient blunderbuss, turned out as sentries to keep watch over this donjon-keep.

Such is the momentous affair that has just taken place, and it is an event of too great moment in this quiet little world, not to turn it completely topsy-turvy. Labour is at a stand. The house has been a scene of confusion the whole evening. It has been beleagured by gipsy women, with their children on their backs, wailing and lamenting; while the old virago of a mother has cruised up and down the lawn in front, shaking her head and muttering to herself, or now and then breaking into a paroxysm of rage, brandishing her fist at the Hall, and denouncing ill luck upon Ready Money Jack, and even upon the squire himself.

Lady Lillycraft has given repeated audiences to the culprit's weeping wife, at the Hall door; and the servant maids have stolen out to confer with the gipsy women under the trees. As to the little ladies of the family, they are all outrageous at Ready Money Jack, whom they look upon in the light of a tyrannical giant of fairy tale. Phœbe Wilkins, contrary to her usual nature, is the only one that is pitiless in the affair. She thinks Mr. Tibbets quite in the right; and thinks the gipsies deserve to be punished severely for meddling with the sheep of the Tibbetses.

In the mean time the females of the family have evinced all the provident kindness of the sex, ever ready to soothe and succour the distressed, right or wrong. Lady Lillycraft has had a mattress taken to the outhouse, and comforts and delicacies of all kinds have been taken to the prisoner; even the little girls have sent their cakes and sweetmeats; so that, I'll warrant, the vagabond has never fared so well in his life before. Old Christy, it is true, looks upon every thing with a wary eye; struts about with his blunderbuss with the air of a veteran campaigner, and will hardly allow himself to be spoken to. The gipsy women dare not come within gunshot, and every tatterdemallion of a boy has been frightened from the park. The old fellow is determined to lodge Starlight Tom in prison with his own hands; and hopes, he says, to see one of the poaching crew made an example of.

I doubt, after all, whether the worthy squire is not the greatest sufferer in the whole affair. His honourable sense of duty obliges him to be rigid, but the overflowing kindness of his nature makes this a grievous trial to him.

He is not accustomed to have such demands upon his justice in his truly patriarchal domain; and it wounds his benevolent spirit, that while prosperity and happiness are flowing in thus bounteously upon him, he should have to inflict misery upon a fellow-being.

He has been troubled and cast down the whole evening; took leave of the family, on going to bed, with a sigh, instead of his usual hearty and affectionate tone; and will, in all probability, have a far more sleepless night than his prisoner. Indeed this unlucky affair has cast a damp upon the whole household, as there appears to be an universal opinion that the unlucky culprit will come to the gallows.

Morning.—The clouds of last evening are all blown over. A load has been taken from the squire's heart, and every face is once more in smiles. The gamekeeper made his appearance at an early hour, completely shame-faced and crest-fallen. Starlight Tom had made his escape in the night; how he had got out of the loft no one could tell: the Devil they think must have assisted him. Old Christy was so mortified that he would not show his face, but had shut himself up in his strong-hold at the dog-kennel, and would not be spoken with. What has particularly relieved the squire is, that there is very little likelihood of the culprit's being retaken, having gone off on one of the old gentleman's best hunters.

Family Misfortunes

"The night has been unruly; where we lay,
The chimneys were blown down."
Macbeth

WE HAVE for a day or two past had a flaw of unruly
weather, which has intruded itself into this fair and
flowery month, and for a time has quite marred the beauty of
the landscape. Last night the storm attained its crisis; the rain
beat in torrents against the casements, and the wind piped
and blustered about the old Hall with quite a wintry vehemence. The morning, however, dawned clear and serene; the
face of the heavens seemed as if newly washed, and the sun
shone with a brightness that was undimmed by a single vapour. Nothing over-head gave traces of the recent storm; but
on looking from my window I beheld sad ravage among the
shrubs and flowers; the garden walks had formed the channels
for little torrents; trees were lopped of their branches, and a
small silver stream that wound through the park, and ran at
the bottom of the lawn, had swelled into a turbid, yellow
sheet of water.

In an establishment like this, where the mansion is vast,
ancient, and somewhat afflicted with the infirmities of age,
and where there are numerous and extensive dependencies, a
storm is an event of a very grave nature, and brings in its train
a multiplicity of cares and disasters.

While the squire was taking his breakfast in the great hall,
he was continually interrupted by some bearer of ill tidings
from some part or other of his domains; he appeared to me
like the commander of a besieged city, after some grand assault, receiving at his head-quarters reports of damages sustained in the various quarters of the place. At one time the
housekeeper brought him intelligence of a chimney blown
down, and a desperate leak sprung in the roof over the picture-gallery, which threatened to obliterate a whole generation of his ancestors. Then the steward came in with a doleful
story of the mischief done in the woodlands; while the gamekeeper bemoaned the loss of one of his finest bucks, whose

bloated carcass was seen floating along the swoln current of the river.

When the squire issued forth, he was accosted, before the door, by the old, paralytic gardener, with a face full of trouble, reporting, as I supposed, the devastation of his flower-beds, and the destruction of his wall-fruit. I remarked, however, that his intelligence caused a peculiar expression of concern not only with the squire and Master Simon, but with the fair Julia and Lady Lillycraft, who happened to be present. From a few words which reached my ear, I found there was some tale of domestic calamity in the case, and that some unfortunate family had been rendered houseless by the storm. Many ejaculations of pity broke from the ladies; I heard the expressions of "poor helpless beings," and "unfortunate little creatures," several times repeated; to which the old gardener replied by very melancholy shakes of the head.

I felt so interested, that I could not help calling to the gardener, as he was retiring, and asking what unfortunate family it was that had suffered so severely? The old man touched his hat, and gazed at me for an instant, as if hardly comprehending my question. "Family!" replied he: "there be no family in the case, your honour; but here have been sad mischief done in the rookery!"

I had noticed the day before that the high and gusty winds which prevailed had occasioned great disquiet among these airy householders; their nests being all filled with young, who were in danger of being tilted out of their tree-rocked cradles. Indeed, the old birds themselves seemed to have hard work to maintain a foothold; some kept hovering and cawing in the air; or if they ventured to alight, they had to hold fast, flap their wings, and spread their tails, and thus remain seesawing on the topmost twigs.

In the course of the night, however, an awful calamity had taken place in this most sage and politic community. There was a great tree, the tallest in the grove, which seemed to have been the kind of court-end of the metropolis, and crowded with the residences of those whom Master Simon considers the nobility and gentry. A decayed limb of this tree had given way with the violence of the storm, and had come down with all its air-castles.

One should be well aware of the humours of the good squire and his household, to understand the general concern expressed at this disaster. It was quite a public calamity in this rural empire, and all seemed to feel for the poor rooks as for fellow-citizens in distress.

The ground had been strewed with the callow young, which were now cherished in the aprons and bosoms of the maid servants, and the little ladies of the family. I was pleased with this touch of nature: this feminine sympathy in the sufferings of the offspring, and the maternal anxiety of the parent birds.

It was interesting, too, to witness the general agitation and distress that seemed to prevail throughout the feathered community. The common cause that was made of it; and the incessant hovering, and fluttering, and lamenting, that took place in the whole rookery. There is a chord of sympathy that runs through the whole feathered race as to any misfortunes of the young; and the cries of a wounded bird in the breeding season will throw a whole grove in a flutter and an alarm. Indeed, why should I confine it to the feathered tribe? Nature seems to me to have implanted an exquisite sympathy on this subject, which extends through all her works. It is an invariable attribute of the female heart, to melt at the cry of early helplessness, and to take an instinctive interest in the distresses of the parent and its young. On the present occasion the ladies of the family were full of pity and commiseration; and I shall never forget the look that Lady Lillycraft gave the general, on his observing that the young birds would make an excellent curry, or an especial good rook-pie.

Lovers' Troubles

"The poor soul sat singing by a sycamore tree,
    Sing all a green willow;
Her hand on her bosom, her head on her knee,
    Sing willow, willow, willow;
Sing all a green willow must be my garland."

Old Song

THE FAIR JULIA having nearly recovered from the effects of her hawking disaster, it begins to be thought high time to appoint a day for the wedding. As every domestic event in a venerable and aristocratic family connexion like this is a matter of moment, the fixing upon this important day has, of course, given rise to much conference and debate.

Some slight difficulties and demurs have lately sprung up, originating in the peculiar humours that are prevalent at the Hall. Thus, I have overheard a very solemn consultation between Lady Lillycraft, the parson, and Master Simon, as to whether the marriage ought not to be postponed until the coming month.

With all the charms of the flowery month of May, there is, I find, an ancient prejudice against it as a marrying month. An old proverb says, "To wed in May is to wed poverty." Now, as Lady Lillycraft is very much given to believe in lucky and unlucky times and seasons, and indeed is very superstitious on all points relating to the tender passion, this old proverb seems to have taken great hold upon her mind. She recollects two or three instances in her own knowledge of matches that took place in this month, and proved very unfortunate. Indeed, an own cousin of hers, who married on a May-day, lost her husband by a fall from his horse, after they had lived happily together for twenty years.

The parson appeared to give great weight to her ladyship's objections, and acknowledged the existence of a prejudice of the kind, not merely confined to modern times, but prevalent likewise among the ancients. In confirmation of this, he quoted a passage from Ovid, which had a great effect on Lady Lillycraft, being given in a language which she did not understand. Even Master Simon was staggered by it; for he listened with a puzzled air; and then, shaking his head, sagaciously observed that Ovid was certainly a very wise man.

From this sage conference I likewise gathered several other important pieces of information relative to weddings; such as that, if two were celebrated in the same church, on the same day, the first would be happy, the second unfortunate. If, on going to church, the bridal party should meet the funeral of a female, it was an omen that the bride would die first; if of a male, the bridegroom. If the newly married couple were to dance together on their wedding-day, the wife would thenceforth rule the roast; with many other curious and unquestionable facts of the same nature, all which made me ponder more than ever upon the perils which surround this happy state, and the thoughtless ignorance of mortals as to the awful risks they run in venturing upon it. I abstain, however, from enlarging upon this topic, having no inclination to promote the increase of bachelors.

Notwithstanding the due weight which the squire gives to traditional saws and ancient opinions, yet I am happy to find that he makes a firm stand for the credit of this loving month, and brings to his aid a whole legion of poetical authorities; all which, I presume, have been conclusive with the young couple, as I understand they are perfectly willing to marry in May, and abide the consequences. In a few days, therefore, the wedding is to take place, and the Hall is in a buzz of anticipation. The housekeeper is bustling about from morning till night, with a look full of business and importance, having a thousand arrangements to make, the squire intending to keep open house on the occasion; and as to the housemaids, you cannot look one of them in the face, but the rogue begins to colour up and simper.

While, however, this leading love affair is going on with a tranquillity quite inconsistent with the rules of romance, I cannot say that the under-plots are equally propitious. The "opening bud of love" between the general and Lady Lillycraft seems to have experienced some blight in the course of this genial season. I do not think the general has ever been able to retrieve the ground he lost, when he fell asleep during the captain's story. Indeed, Master Simon thinks his case is completely desperate, her ladyship having determined that he is quite destitute of sentiment.

The season has been equally unpropitious to the love-lorn Phœbe Wilkins. I fear the reader will be impatient at having this humble amour so often alluded to; but I confess I am apt to take a great interest in the love troubles of simple girls of this class. Few people have an idea of the world of care and perplexity that these poor damsels have in managing the affairs of the heart.

We talk and write about the tender passion; we give it all the colourings of sentiment and romance, and lay the scene of its influence in high life; but, after all, I doubt whether its sway is not more absolute among females of a humbler sphere. How often, could we but look into the heart, should we find the sentiment throbbing in all its violence, in the bosom of the poor lady's-maid, rather than in that of the brilliant beauty she is decking out for conquest; whose brain is probably bewildered with beaux, ball-rooms, and wax-light chandeliers.

With these humble beings love is an honest, engrossing concern. They have no ideas of settlements, establishments, equipages, and pin-money. The heart—the heart is all-in-all with them, poor things! There is seldom one of them but has her love cares, and love secrets; her doubts, and hopes, and fears, equal to those of any heroine of romance, and ten times as sincere. And then, too, there is her secret hoard of love documents;—the broken sixpence, the gilded brooch, the lock of hair, the unintelligible love-scrawl, all treasured up in her box of Sunday finery, for private contemplation.

How many crosses and trials is she exposed to from some lynx-eyed dame, or staid old vestal of a mistress, who keeps a dragon watch over her virtue, and scouts the lover from the door. But then, how sweet are the little love scenes, snatched at distant intervals of holiday, and fondly dwelt on through many a long day of household labour and confinement. If in the country—it is the dance at the fair or wake, the interview in the churchyard after service, or the evening stroll in the green lane. If in town, it is perhaps merely a stolen moment of delicious talk between the bars of the area, fearful every instant of being seen;—and then, how lightly will the simple creature carol all day afterwards at her labour!

Poor baggage! after all her crosses and difficulties, when she marries, what is it but to exchange a life of comparative ease and comfort, for one of toil and uncertainty? Perhaps, too, the lover for whom in the fondness of her nature she has committed herself to fortune's freaks, turns out a worthless churl, the dissolute, hard-hearted husband of low life; who, taking to the ale-house, leaves her to a cheerless home, to labour, penury, and child-bearing.

When I see poor Phœbe going about with dropping eye, and her head hanging "all o' one side," I cannot help calling to mind the pathetic little picture drawn by Desdemona:—

> "My mother had a maid, called Barbara;
> She was in love; and he she loved proved mad,
> And did forsake her: she had a song of willow,
> An old thing 'twas; but it express'd her fortune,
> And she died singing it."

I hope, however, that a better lot is in reserve for Phœbe Wilkins, and that she may yet "rule the roast," in the ancient empire of the Tibbetses! She is not fit to battle with hard hearts or hard times. She was, I am told, the pet of her poor mother, who was proud of the beauty of her child, and brought her up more tenderly than a village girl ought to be; and, ever since she has been left an orphan, the good ladies at the Hall have completed the softening and spoiling of her.

I have recently observed her holding long conferences in the churchyard, and up and down one of the lanes near the village, with Slingsby the schoolmaster. I at first thought the pedagogue might be touched with the tender malady so prevalent in these parts of late; but I did him injustice. Honest Slingsby, it seems, was a friend and crony of her late father, the parish clerk; and is on intimate terms with the Tibbets family: prompted, therefore, by his good-will towards all parties, and secretly instigated, perhaps, by the managing dame Tibbets, he has undertaken to talk with Phœbe upon the subject. He gives her, however, but little encouragement. Slingsby has a formidable opinion of the aristocratical feeling of old Ready Money, and thinks, if Phœbe were even to make the matter up with the son, she would find the father totally hostile to the match. The poor damsel, therefore, is reduced almost to despair; and Slingsby, who is too good-natured not to sympathise in her distress, has advised her to give up all thoughts of young Jack, and has proposed as a substitute his learned coadjutor, the prodigal son. He has even, in the fulness of his heart, offered to give up the school-house to them; though it would leave him once more adrift in the wide world.

The Historian

> *Hermione.*   Pray you sit by us,
> And tell's a tale.
> *Mamilius.*   Merry, or sad shall't be?
> *Hermione.*   As merry as you will.
> *Mamilius.*   A sad tale's best for winter.
> I have one of sprites and goblins.
> *Hermione.*   Let's have that, sir.
> *Winter's Tale*

A s this is a story-telling age, I have been tempted occasionally to give the reader one of the many tales that are served up with supper at the Hall. I might, indeed, have furnished a series almost equal in number to the Arabian Nights; but some were rather hackneyed and tedious; others I did not feel warranted in betraying into print; and many more were of the old general's relating, and turned principally upon tiger-hunting, elephant-riding, and Seringapatam, enlivened by the wonderful deeds of Tippoo Saib, and the excellent jokes of Major Pendergast.

I had all along maintained a quiet post at a corner of the table, where I had been able to indulge my humour undisturbed; listening attentively when the story was very good, and dozing a little when it was rather dull, which I consider the perfection of auditorship.

I was roused the other evening from a slight trance into which I had fallen during one of the general's histories, by a sudden call from the squire to furnish some entertainment of the kind in my turn. Having been so profound a listener to others, I could not in conscience refuse; but neither my memory nor invention being ready to answer so unexpected a demand, I begged leave to read a manuscript tale from the pen of my fellow-countryman, the late Mr. Diedrich Knickerbocker, the historian of New York. As this ancient chronicler may not be better known to my readers than he was to the company at the Hall, a word or two concerning him may not be amiss, before proceeding to his manuscript.

Diedrich Knickerbocker was a native of New York, a de-

scendant from one of the ancient Dutch families which originally settled that province, and remained there after it was
taken possession of by the English in 1664. The descendants
of these Dutch families still remain in villages and neighbourhoods in various parts of the country, retaining, with singular
obstinacy, the dresses, manners, and even language of their
ancestors, and forming a very distinct and curious feature in
the motley population of the state. In a hamlet whose spire
may be seen from New York, rising from above the brow of
a hill on the opposite side of the Hudson, many of the old
folks, even at the present day, speak English with an accent,
and the Dominie preaches in Dutch; and so completely is the
hereditary love of quiet and silence maintained, that in one of
these drowsy little villages, in the middle of a warm summer's
day, the buzzing of a stout blue-bottle fly will resound from
one end of the place to the other.

With the laudable hereditary feeling thus kept up among
these worthy people, did Mr. Knickerbocker undertake to
write a history of his native city, comprising the reign of its
three Dutch governors during the time that it was yet under
the domination of the Hogen-mogens of Holland. In the execution of this design the little Dutchman has displayed great
historical research, and a wonderful consciousness of the
dignity of his subject. His work, however, has been so little
understood, as to be pronounced a mere work of humour,
satirising the follies of the times, both in politics and morals,
and giving whimsical views of human nature.

Be this as it may: — among the papers left behind him were
several tales of a lighter nature, apparently thrown together
from materials which he had gathered during his profound
researches for his history, and which he seems to have cast by
with neglect, as unworthy of publication. Some of these have
fallen into my hands by an accident which it is needless at
present to mention; and one of these very stories, with its
prelude in the words of Mr. Knickerbocker, I undertook to
read, by way of acquitting myself of the debt which I owed
to the other story-tellers at the Hall. I subjoin it for such of
my readers as are fond of stories.*

*I find that the tale of Rip Van Winkle, given in the Sketch Book, has been
discovered by divers writers in magazines, to have been founded on a

little German tradition, and the matter has been revealed to the world as if it were a foul instance of plagiarism marvellously brought to light. In a note which follows that tale I had alluded to the superstition on which it was founded, and I thought a mere allusion was sufficient, as the tradition was so notorious as to be inserted in almost every collection of German legends. I had seen it myself in three. I could hardly have hoped, therefore, in the present age, when every source of ghost and goblin story is ransacked, that the origin of the tale would escape discovery. In fact, I had considered popular traditions of the kind as fair foundations for authors of fiction to build upon, and had made use of the one in question accordingly. I am not disposed to contest the matter, however, and indeed consider myself so completely overpaid by the public for my trivial performances, that I am content to submit to any deduction which, in their after-thoughts, they may think proper to make.

The Haunted House

From the Mss. of the Late
Diedrich Knickerbocker

Formerly almost every place had a house of this kind. If a house
was seated on some melancholy place, or built in some old romantic manner, or if any particular accident had happened in it,
such as murder, sudden death, or the like, to be sure that house
had a mark set on it, and was afterwards esteemed the habitation of a ghost.

Bourne's Antiquities

IN THE NEIGHBOURHOOD of the ancient city of the Manhattoes there stood, not very many years since, an old
mansion, which, when I was a boy, went by the name of the
Haunted House. It was one of the very few remains of the
architecture of the early Dutch settlers, and must have been a
house of some consequence at the time when it was built. It
consisted of a centre and two wings, the gable ends of which
were shaped like stairs. It was built partly of wood, and partly
of small Dutch bricks, such as the worthy colonists brought
with them from Holland, before they discovered that bricks
could be manufactured elsewhere. The house stood remote
from the road, in the centre of a large field, with an avenue of
old locust* trees leading up to it, several of which had been
shivered by lightning, and two or three blown down. A few
apple trees grew straggling about the field; there were traces
also of what had been a kitchen-garden; but the fences were
broken down, the vegetables had disappeared, or had grown
wild and turned to little better than weeds, with here and
there a ragged rose-bush, or a tall sunflower shooting up
from among brambles, and hanging its head sorrowfully, as if
contemplating the surrounding desolation. Part of the roof of
the old house had fallen in, the windows were shattered, the
pannels of the doors broken, and mended with rough boards,
and there were two rusty weathercocks at the ends of the
house which made a great jingling and whistling as they
whirled about, but always pointed wrong. The appearance of

*Acacias.

the whole place was forlorn and desolate at the best of times; but, in unruly weather, the howling of the wind about the crazy old mansion, the screeching of the weathercocks, the slamming and banging of a few loose window-shutters, had altogether so wild and dreary an effect, that the neighbourhood stood perfectly in awe of the place, and pronounced it the rendezvous of hobgoblins. I recollect the old building well; for I remember how many times, when an idle, unlucky urchin, I have prowled round its precincts, with some of my graceless companions, on holiday afternoons, when out on a freebooting cruise among the orchards. There was a tree standing near the house that bore the most beautiful and tempting fruit; but then it was on enchanted ground, for the place was so charmed by frightful stories that we dreaded to approach it. Sometimes we would venture in a body, and get near the Hesperian tree, keeping an eye upon the old mansion, and darting fearful glances into its shattered windows; when, just as we were about to seize upon our prize, an exclamation from one of the gang, or an accidental noise, would throw us all into a panic, and we would scamper headlong from the place, nor stop until we had got quite into the road. Then there were sure to be a host of fearful anecdotes told of strange cries and groans, or of some hideous face suddenly seen staring out of one of the windows. By degrees we ceased to venture into these lonely grounds, but would stand at a distance and throw stones at the building; and there was something fearfully pleasing in the sound as they rattled along the roof, or sometimes struck some jingling fragments of glass out of the windows.

The origin of this house was lost in the obscurity that covers the early period of the province, while under the government of their high mightinesses the states-general. Some reported it to have been a country residence of Wilhelmus Kieft, commonly called the Testy, one of the Dutch governors of New Amsterdam; others said that it had been built by a naval commander who served under Van Tromp, and who, on being disappointed of preferment, retired from the service in disgust, became a philosopher through sheer spite, and brought over all his wealth to the province, that he might live according to his humour, and despise the world. The reason of its having fallen to decay was likewise a matter of dispute; some said that it was in chancery, and had already cost more than its worth in legal expenses; but the most current, and, of course, the most probable account, was that it was haunted, and that nobody could live quietly in it. There can, in fact, be very little doubt that this last was the case, there were so many corroborating stories to prove it,—not an old woman in the neighbourhood but could furnish at least a score. There was a gray-headed curmudgeon of a negro that lived hard by, who had a whole budget of them to tell, many of which had happened to himself. I recollect many a time stopping with my schoolmates, and getting him to relate some. The old crone lived in a hovel, in the midst of a small patch of potatoes, and Indian corn, which his master had given him on setting him free. He would come to us, with his hoe in his hand, and as we sat perched, like a row of swallows, on the rail of the fence, in the mellow twilight of a summer evening, he would tell us such fearful stories, accompanied by such awful rollings of his white eyes, that we were almost afraid of our own footsteps as we returned home afterwards in the dark.

Poor old Pompey! many years are past since he died, and went to keep company with the ghosts he was so fond of talking about. He was buried in a corner of his own little potatoe patch; the plough soon passed over his grave, and levelled it with the rest of the field, and nobody thought any more of the gray-headed negro. By singular chance I was strolling in that neighbourhood several years afterwards, when I had grown up to be a young man, and I found a knot of gossips speculating on a skull which had just been turned up by a ploughshare. They of course determined it to be the remains of some one that had been murdered, and they had raked up with it some of the traditionary tales of the haunted house. I knew it at once to be the relic of poor Pompey, but I held my tongue; for I am too considerate of other people's enjoyment ever to mar a story of a ghost or a murder. I took care, however, to see the bones of my old friend once more buried in a place where they were not likely to be disturbed. As I sat on the turf and watched the interment, I fell into a long conversation with an old gentleman of the neighbourhood, John Josse Vandermoere, a pleasant gossiping man, whose whole life was spent in hearing and telling the news of the province. He recollected old Pompey, and his stories about the Haunted House; but he assured me he could give me one still more strange than any that Pompey had related; and on my expressing a great curiosity to hear it, he sat down beside me on the turf, and told the following tale. I have endeavoured to give it as nearly as possible in his words; but it is now many years since, and I am grown old, and my memory is not over good. I cannot therefore vouch for the language, but I am always scrupulous as to facts.

D. K.

Dolph Heyliger

"I take the town to concord, where I dwell,
All Kilborn be my witness, if I were not
Begot in bashfulness, brought up in shamefacedness:
Let 'un bring a dog but to my vace that can
Zay I have beat 'un, and without a vault;
Or but a cat will swear upon a book,
I have as much as zet a vire her tail,
And I'll give him or her a crown for 'mends."

Tale of a Tub

IN THE EARLY TIME of the province of New York, while it groaned under the tyranny of the English governor, Lord Cornbury, who carried his cruelties towards the Dutch inhabitants so far as to allow no Dominie, or schoolmaster, to officiate in their language, without his special licence; about this time, there lived in the jolly, little old city of the Manhattoes a kind motherly dame, known by the name of Dame Heyliger. She was the widow of a Dutch sea captain, who died suddenly of a fever, in consequence of working too hard, and eating too heartily, at the time when all the inhabitants turned out in a panic, to fortify the place against the invasion of a small French privateer.* He left her with very little money, and one infant son, the only survivor of several children. The good woman had need of much management to make both ends meet, and keep up a decent appearance. However, as her husband had fallen a victim to his zeal for the public safety, it was universally agreed that "something ought to be done for the widow;" and on the hopes of this "something" she lived tolerably for some years; in the meantime every body pitied and spoke well of her, and that helped along.

She lived in a small house, in a small street, called Garden-street, very probably from a garden which may have flourished there some time or other. As her necessities every year grew greater, and the talk of the public about doing "something for her" grew less, she had to cast about for some mode of doing something for herself, by way of helping out her

*1705.

304

slender means, and maintaining her independence, of which she was somewhat tenacious.

Living in a mercantile town, she had caught something of the spirit, and determined to venture a little in the great lottery of commerce. On a sudden, therefore, to the great surprise of the street, there appeared at her window a grand array of gingerbread kings and queens, with their arms stuck a-kimbo, after the invariable royal manner. There were also several broken tumblers, some filled with sugar-plums, some with marbles; there were, moreover, cakes of various kinds, and barley-sugar, and Holland dolls, and wooden horses, with here and there gilt-covered picture-books, and now and then a skein of thread, or a dangling pound of candles. At the door of the house sat the good old dame's cat, a decent de-mure-looking personage, that seemed to scan every body that passed, to criticise their dress, and now and then to stretch her neck, and look out with sudden curiosity, to see what was going on at the other end of the street; but if by chance any idle vagabond dog came by, and offered to be uncivil—hoity-toity!—how she would bristle up, and growl, and spit, and strike out her paws! she was as indignant as ever was an ancient and ugly spinster on the approach of some graceless profligate.

But though the good woman had to come down to those humble means of subsistence, yet she still kept up a feeling of family pride, having descended from the Vanderspiegels, of Amsterdam; and she had the family arms painted and framed, and hung over her mantel-piece. She was, in truth, much re-spected by all the poorer people of the place; her house was quite a resort of the old wives of the neighbourhood; they would drop in there of a winter's afternoon, as she sat knit-ting on one side of her fire-place, her cat purring on the other, and the tea-kettle singing before it; and they would gossip with her until late in the evening. There was always an arm chair for Peter de Groodt, sometimes called Long Peter, and sometimes Peter Longlegs, the clerk and sexton of the little Lutheran church, who was her great crony, and indeed the oracle of her fire-side. Nay, the Dominie himself did not disdain, now and then, to step in, converse about the state of her mind, and take a glass of her special good cherry-brandy.

Indeed, he never failed to call on new year's day, and wish her a happy new year; and the good dame, who was a little vain on some points, always piqued herself on giving him as large a cake as any one in town.

I have said that she had one son. He was the child of her old age; but could hardly be called the comfort, for, of all unlucky urchins, Dolph Heyliger was the most mischievous. Not that the whipster was really vicious; he was only full of fun and frolic, and had that daring, gamesome spirit, which is extolled in a rich man's child, but execrated in a poor man's. He was continually getting into scrapes; his mother was incessantly harassed with complaints of some waggish pranks which he had played off; bills were sent in for windows that he had broken; in a word, he had not reached his fourteenth year before he was pronounced, by all the neighbourhood, to be a "wicked dog, the wickedest dog in the street!" Nay, one old gentleman, in a claret-coloured coat, with a thin red face, and ferret eyes, went so far as to assure dame Heyliger, that her son would, one day or other, come to the gallows!

Yet, notwithstanding all this, the poor old soul loved her boy. It seemed as though she loved him the better the worse he behaved; and that he grew more in her favour, the more he grew out of favour with the world. Mothers are foolish, fond-hearted beings; there's no reasoning them out of their dotage; and, indeed, this poor woman's child was all that was left to love her in this world;—so we must not think it hard that she turned a deaf ear to her good friends, who sought to prove to her that Dolph would come to a halter.

To do the varlet justice, too, he was strongly attached to his parent. He would not willingly have given her pain on any account; and when he had been doing wrong, it was but for him to catch his poor mother's eye fixed wistfully and sorrowfully upon him, to fill his heart with bitterness and contrition. But he was a heedless youngster, and could not, for the life of him, resist any new temptation to fun and mischief. Though quick at his learning, whenever he could be brought to apply himself, yet he was always prone to be led away by idle company, and would play truant to hunt after birds' nests, to rob orchards, or to swim in the Hudson.

In this way he grew up, a tall, lubberly boy; and his mother began to be greatly perplexed what to do with him, or how to put him in a way to do for himself; for he had acquired such an unlucky reputation, that no one seemed willing to employ him.

Many were the consultations that she held with Peter de Groodt, the clerk and sexton, who was her prime councillor. Peter was as much perplexed as herself, for he had no great opinion of the boy, and thought he would never come to good. He at one time advised her to send him to sea; a piece of advice only given in the most desperate cases; but Dame Heyliger would not listen to such an idea; she could not think of letting Dolph go out of her sight. She was sitting one day knitting by her fire-side, in great perplexity, when the sexton entered with an air of unusual vivacity and briskness. He had just come from a funeral. It had been that of a boy of Dolph's years, who had been apprentice to a famous German doctor, and had died of a consumption. It is true, there had been a whisper that the deceased had been brought to his end by being made the subject of the doctor's experiments, on which he was apt to try the effects of a new compound, or a quieting draught. This, however, it is likely was a mere scandal; at any rate, Peter de Groodt did not think it worth mentioning; though, had we time to philosophise, it would be a curious matter for speculation, why a doctor's family is apt to be so lean and cadaverous, and a butcher's so jolly and rubicund.

Peter de Groodt, as I said before, entered the house of Dame Heyliger with unusual alacrity. He was full of a bright idea that had popped into his head at the funeral, and over which he had chuckled as he shovelled the earth into the grave of the doctor's disciple. It had occurred to him, that, as the situation of the deceased was vacant at the doctor's, it would be the very place for Dolph. The boy had parts, and could pound a pestle, and run an errand with any boy in the town, and what more was wanted in a student?

The suggestion of the sage Peter was a vision of glory to the mother. She already saw Dolph, in her mind's eye, with a cane at his nose, a knocker at his door, and an M.D. at the end of his name—one of the established dignitaries of the town.

The matter, once undertaken, was soon effected: the sexton

had some influence with the doctor, they having had much dealing together in the way of their separate professions; and the very next morning he called and conducted the urchin, clad in his Sunday clothes, to undergo the inspection of Dr. Karl Lodovick Knipperhausen.

They found the doctor seated in an elbow chair, in one corner of his study, or laboratory, with a large volume, in German print, before him. He was a short fat man, with a dark square face, rendered more dark by a black velvet cap. He had a little nobbed nose, not unlike the ace of spades, with a pair of spectacles gleaming on each side of his dusky countenance, like a couple of bow windows.

Dolph felt struck with awe on entering into the presence of this learned man; and gazed about him with boyish wonder at the furniture of this chamber of knowledge; which appeared to him almost as the den of a magician. In the centre stood a claw-footed table, with pestle and mortar, phials and gallipots, and a pair of small burnished scales. At one end was a heavy clothes-press, turned into a receptacle for drugs and compounds; against which hung the doctor's hat and cloak, and gold-headed cane, and on the top grinned a human skull. Along the mantel-piece were glass vessels, in which were snakes and lizards, and a human fœtus preserved in spirits. A closet, the doors of which were taken off, contained three whole shelves of books, and some too of mighty folio dimensions; a collection, the like of which Dolph had never before beheld. As, however, the library did not take up the whole of the closet, the doctor's thrifty housekeeper had occupied the rest with pots of pickles and preserves; and had hung about the room, among awful implements of the healing art, strings of red pepper and corpulent cucumbers, carefully preserved for seed.

Peter de Groodt, and his protegé, were received with great gravity and stateliness by the doctor, who was a very wise, dignified little man, and never smiled. He surveyed Dolph from head to foot, above, and under, and through his spectacles, and the poor lad's heart quailed as these great glasses glared on him like two full moons. The doctor heard all that Peter de Groodt had to say in favour of the youthful candidate; and then, wetting his thumb with the end of his tongue, he began deliberately to turn over page after page of the great black volume before him. At length, after many hums and haws, and strokings of the chin, and all that hesitation and deliberation with which a wise man proceeds to do what he intended to do from the very first, the doctor agreed to take the lad as a disciple; to give him bed, board, and clothing, and to instruct him in the healing art; in return for which he was to have his services until his twenty-first year.

Behold, then, our hero, all at once transformed from an unlucky urchin, running wild about the streets, to a student of medicine, diligently pounding a pestle, under the auspices of the learned Doctor Karl Lodovick Knipperhausen. It was a happy transition for his fond old mother. She was delighted with the idea of her boy's being brought up worthy of his ancestors; and anticipated the day when he would be able to hold up his head with the lawyer, that lived in the large house opposite; or, peradventure, with the Dominie himself.

Doctor Knipperhausen was a native of the Palatinate in Germany; from whence, in company with many of his countrymen, he had taken refuge in England, on account of religious persecution. He was one of nearly three thousand Palatines, who came over from England in 1710, under the protection of Governor Hunter. Where the doctor had studied, how he had acquired his medical knowledge, and where he had received his diploma, it is hard at present to say, for nobody knew at the time; yet it is certain that his profound skill and abstruse knowledge were the talk and wonder of the common people, far and near.

His practice was totally different from that of any other physician; consisting in mysterious compounds, known only to himself, in the preparing and administering of which, it was said, he always consulted the stars. So high an opinion was entertained of his skill, particularly by the German and Dutch inhabitants, that they always resorted to him in desperate cases. He was one of those infallible doctors, that are always effecting sudden and surprising cures, when the patient has been given up by all the regular physicians; unless, as is shrewdly observed, the case has been left too long before it was put into their hands. The doctor's library was the talk and marvel of the neighbourhood, I might almost say of the entire burgh. The good people looked with reverence at a man that had read three whole shelves full of books, and some of them too as large as a family Bible. There were many disputes among the members of the little Lutheran church, as to which was the wisest man, the doctor or the Dominie. Some of his admirers even went so far as to say, that he knew more than the governor himself—in a word, it was thought that there was no end to his knowledge!

No sooner was Dolph received into the doctor's family, than he was put in possession of the lodging of his predecessor. It was a garret-room of a steep-roofed Dutch house, where the rain pattered on the shingles, and the lightning gleamed, and the wind piped through the crannies in stormy weather; and where whole troops of hungry rats, like Don Cossacks, galloped about, in defiance of traps and ratsbane.

He was soon up to his ears in medical studies, being employed, morning, noon, and night, in rolling pills, filtering tinctures, or pounding the pestle and mortar in one corner of the laboratory; while the doctor would take his seat in another corner, when he had nothing else to do, or expected visitors, and, arrayed in his morning gown and velvet cap, would pore over the contents of some folio volume. It is true, that the regular thumping of Dolph's pestle, or, perhaps, the drowsy buzzing of the summer flies, would now and then lull the little man into a slumber; but then his spectacles were always wide awake, and studiously regarding the book.

There was another personage in the house, however, to whom Dolph was obliged to pay allegiance. Though a bachelor, and a man of such great dignity and importance, yet the doctor was, like many other wise men, subject to petticoat government. He was completely under the sway of his housekeeper; a spare, busy, fretting housewife, in a little, round, quilted German cap, with a huge bunch of keys jingling at the girdle of an exceedingly long waist. Frau Ilsé (or Frow Ilsy as it was pronounced) had accompanied him in his various migrations from Germany to England, and from England to the province; managing his establishment and himself too: ruling him, it is true, with a gentle hand, but carrying a high hand with all the world beside. How she had acquired such ascendancy I do not pretend to say. People, it is true, did talk—but have not people been prone to talk ever since the world began? Who can tell how women generally contrive to get the upper hand? A husband, it is true, may now and then be master in his own house; but who ever knew a bachelor that was not managed by his housekeeper?

Indeed, Frau Ilsy's power was not confined to the doctor's household. She was one of those prying gossips that knew every one's business better than they do themselves; and whose all-seeing eyes, and all-telling tongues, are terrors throughout a neighbourhood.

Nothing of any moment transpired in the world of scandal of this little burgh, but it was known to Frau Ilsy. She had her crew of cronies, that were perpetually hurrying to her little parlour with some precious bit of news; nay, she would sometimes discuss a whole volume of secret history, as she held the street-door ajar, and gossiped with one of these garrulous crones in the very teeth of a December blast.

Between the doctor and the housekeeper it may easily be supposed that Dolph had a busy life of it. As Frau Ilsy kept the keys, and literally ruled the roast, it was starvation to offend her, though he found the study of her temper more perplexing even than that of medicine. When not busy in the laboratory, she kept him running hither and thither on her errands; and on Sundays he was obliged to accompany her to and from church, and carry her Bible. Many a time has the poor varlet stood shivering and blowing his fingers, or holding his frost-bitten nose, in the church-yard, while Ilsy and her cronies were huddled together, wagging their heads, and tearing some unlucky character to pieces.

With all his advantages, however, Dolph made very slow progress in his art. This was no fault of the doctor's, certainly, for he took unwearied pains with the lad, keeping him close to the pestle and mortar, or on the trot about town with phials and pill-boxes; and if he ever flagged in his industry, which he was rather apt to do, the doctor would fly into a passion, and ask him if he ever expected to learn his profession, unless he applied himself closer to the study. The fact is, he still retained the fondness for sport and mischief that had marked his childhood; the habit, indeed, had strengthened with his years, and gained force from being thwarted and constrained. He daily grew more and more untractable, and lost favour in the eyes both of the doctor and the house-keeper.

In the mean time the doctor went on, waxing wealthy and renowned. He was famous for his skill in managing cases not laid down in the books. He had cured several old women and young girls of witchcraft; a terrible complaint, nearly as prev-alent in the province in those days as hydrophobia is at present. He had even restored one strapping country girl to perfect health, who had gone so far as to vomit crooked pins and needles; which is considered a desperate stage of the malady. It was whispered, also, that he was possessed of the art of preparing love-powders; and many applications had he in consequence from love-sick patients of both sexes. But all these cases formed the mysterious part of his practice, in which, according to the cant phrase, "secrecy and honour might be depended on." Dolph, therefore, was obliged to turn out of the study whenever such consultations occurred, though it is said he learnt more of the secrets of the art at the key-hole, than by all the rest of his studies put together.

As the doctor increased in wealth, he began to extend his possessions, and to look forward, like other great men, to the time when he should retire to the repose of a country seat. For this purpose he had purchased a farm, or as the Dutch settlers called it, a *bowerie*, a few miles from town. It had been the residence of a wealthy family, that had returned some time since to Holland. A large mansion-house stood in the centre of it, very much out of repair, and which, in conse-quence of certain reports, had received the appellation of the Haunted House. Either from these reports, or from its actual dreariness, the doctor had found it impossible to get a tenant; and, that the place might not fall to ruin before he could reside in it himself, he had placed a country boor, with his family, in one wing, with the privilege of cultivating the farm on shares.

The doctor now felt all the dignity of a landholder rising within him. He had a little of the German pride of territory in his composition, and almost looked upon himself as owner of a principality. He began to complain of the fatigue of busi-ness; and was fond of riding out "to look at his estate." His little expeditions to his lands were attended with a bustle and parade that created a sensation throughout the neighbourhood. His wall-eyed horse stood stamping, and whisking off the flies, for a full hour before the house. Then the doctor's saddle-bags would be brought out and adjusted; then, after a little while, his cloak would be rolled up and strapped to the saddle; then his umbrella would be buckled to the cloak; while, in the mean time, a group of ragged boys, that observant class of beings, would gather before the door. At length the doctor would issue forth, in a pair of jack-boots that reached above his knees, and a cocked hat flapped down in front. As he was a short, fat man, he took some time to mount into the saddle; and when there, he took some time to have the saddle and stirrups properly adjusted, enjoying the wonder and admiration of the urchin crowd. Even after he had set off, he would pause in the middle of the street, or trot back two or three times to give some parting orders, which were answered by the housekeeper from the door, or Dolph from the study, or the black cook from the cellar, or the chambermaid from the garret window; and there were generally some last words bawled after him, just as he was turning the corner.

The whole neighbourhood would be aroused by this pomp and circumstance. The cobbler would leave his last; the barber would thrust out his frizzed head, with a comb sticking in it; a knot would collect at the grocer's door, and the word would be buzzed from one end of the street to the other, "The doctor's riding out to his country seat!"

These were golden moments for Dolph. No sooner was the doctor out of sight, than pestle and mortar were abandoned; the laboratory was left to take care of itself, and the student was off on some mad-cap frolic.

Indeed, it must be confessed, the youngster, as he grew up, seemed in a fair way to fulfil the prediction of the old, claret-coloured gentleman. He was the ringleader of all holiday sports, and midnight gambols; ready for all kinds of mischievous pranks, and hare-brained adventures.

There is nothing so troublesome as a hero on a small scale, or rather, a hero in a small town. Dolph soon became the abhorrence of all drowsy, housekeeping, old citizens, who hated noise, and had no relish for waggery. The good dames, too, considered him as little better than a reprobate, gathered their daughters under their wings whenever he approached, and pointed him out as a warning to their sons. No one seemed to hold him in much regard, excepting the wild striplings of the place, who were captivated by his open-hearted, daring manners, and the negroes, who always look upon every idle, do-nothing youngster, as a kind of gentleman. Even the good Peter de Groodt, who had considered himself a kind of patron of the lad, began to despair of him; and would shake his head dubiously, as he listened to a long complaint from the housekeeper, and sipped a glass of her raspberry brandy.

Still his mother was not to be wearied out of her affection by all the waywardness of her boy; nor disheartened by the stories of his misdeeds, with which her good friends were continually regaling her. She had, it is true, very little of the pleasure which rich people enjoy, in always hearing their children praised; but she considered all this ill-will as a kind of persecution which he suffered, and she liked him the better on that account. She saw him growing up a fine, tall, good-looking youngster, and she looked at him with the secret pride of a mother's heart. It was her great desire that Dolph should appear like a gentleman, and all the money she could save went towards helping out his pocket and his wardrobe. She would look out of the window after him, as he sallied forth in his best array, and her heart would yearn with delight; and once, when Peter de Groodt, struck with the youngster's gallant appearance on a bright Sunday morning, observed, "Well, after all, Dolph does grow a comely fellow!" the tear of pride started into the mother's eye: "Ah, neighbour! neighbour!" exclaimed she, "they may say what they please; poor Dolph will yet hold up his head with the best of them!"

Dolph Heyliger had now nearly attained his one-and-twentieth year, and the term of his medical studies was just expiring; yet it must be confessed that he knew little more of the profession than when he first entered the doctor's doors. This, however, could not be from any want of quickness of parts, for he showed amazing aptness in mastering other branches of knowledge, which he could only have studied at intervals. He was, for instance, a sure marksman, and won all the geese and turkeys at Christmas-holidays. He was a bold rider; he was famous for leaping and wrestling; he played tolerably on the fiddle; could swim like a fish; and was the best hand in the whole place at fives or ninepins.

All these accomplishments, however, procured him no favour in the eyes of the doctor, who grew more and more crabbed and intolerant the nearer the term of apprenticeship approached. Frau Ilsy, too, was for ever finding some occasion to raise a windy tempest about his ears; and seldom encountered him about the house, without a clatter of the tongue; so that at length the jingling of her keys, as she approached, was to Dolph like the ringing of the prompter's bell, that gives notice of a theatrical thunder-storm. Nothing but the infinite good humour of the heedless youngster enabled him to bear all this domestic tyranny without open rebellion. It was evident that the doctor and his housekeeper were preparing to beat the poor youth out of the nest, the moment his term should have expired; a short hand mode which the doctor had of providing for useless disciples.

Indeed the little man had been rendered more than usually irritable lately, in consequence of various cares and vexations which his country estate had brought upon him. The doctor had been repeatedly annoyed by the rumours and tales which prevailed concerning the old mansion; and found it difficult to prevail even upon the countryman and his family to remain there rent free. Every time he rode out to the farm he was teased by some fresh complaint of strange noises and fearful sights, with which the tenants were disturbed at night; and the doctor would come home fretting and fuming, and vent his spleen upon the whole household. It was indeed a sore grievance, that affected him both in pride and purse. He was threatened with an absolute loss of the profits of his property; and then, what a blow to his territorial consequence, to be the landlord of a haunted house!

It was observed, however, that with all his vexation, the doctor never proposed to sleep in the house himself; nay, he could never be prevailed upon to remain on the premises after dark, but made the best of his way for town as soon as the bats began to flit about in the twilight. The fact was, the doctor had a secret belief in ghosts, having passed the early part of his life in a country where they particularly abound; and indeed the story went, that, when a boy, he had once seen the devil upon the Hartz mountains in Germany.

At length the doctor's vexations on this head were brought to a crisis. One morning, as he sat dozing over a volume in his study, he was suddenly startled from his slumbers by the bustling in of the housekeeper.

"Here's a fine to do!" cried she, as she entered the room. "Here's Claus Hopper come in, bag and baggage, from the farm, and swears he'll have nothing more to do with it. The whole family have been frightened out of their wits; for there's such racketing and rummaging about the old house, that they can't sleep quiet in their beds!"

"Donner und Blitzen!" cried the doctor, impatiently; "will they never have done chattering about that house? What a pack of fools, to let a few rats and mice frighten them out of good quarters!"

"Nay, nay," said the housekeeper, wagging her head knowingly, and piqued at having a good ghost-story doubted, "there's more in it than rats and mice. All the neighbourhood talks about the house; and then such sights have been seen in it! Peter de Groodt tells me, that the family that sold you the house, and went to Holland, dropped several strange hints about it, and said, 'they wished you joy of your bargain;' and you know yourself there's no getting any family to live in it."

"Peter de Groodt's a ninny—an old woman," said the doctor, peevishly; "I'll warrant he's been filling these people's heads full of stories. It's just like his nonsense about the ghost that haunted the church belfry, as an excuse for not ringing the bell that cold night when Hermanus Brinkherhoff's house was on fire. Send Claus to me."

Claus Hopper now made his appearance: a simple country lout, full of awe at finding himself in the very study of Dr. Knipperhausen, and too much embarrassed to enter in much detail of the matters that had caused his alarm. He stood twirling his hat in one hand, resting sometimes on one leg, sometimes on the other, looking occasionally at the doctor, and now and then stealing a fearful glance at the death's head that seemed ogling him from the top of the clothes-press.

The doctor tried every means to persuade him to return to the farm, but all in vain; he maintained a dogged determination on the subject; and at the close of every argument or solicitation would make the same brief, inflexible reply, "Ich kan nicht, mynheer." The doctor was a "little pot, and soon hot;" his patience was exhausted by these continual vexations about his estate. The stubborn refusal of Claus Hopper seemed to him like flat rebellion; his temper suddenly boiled over, and Claus was glad to make a rapid retreat to escape scalding.

When the bumpkin got to the housekeeper's room, he found Peter de Groodt, and several other true believers, ready to receive him. Here he indemnified himself for the restraint he had suffered in the study, and opened a budget of stories about the haunted house that astonished all his hearers. The housekeeper believed them all, if it was only to spite the doctor for having received her intelligence so uncourteously. Peter de Groodt matched them with many a wonderful legend of the times of the Dutch dynasty, and of the Devil's Stepping-stones; and of the pirate that was hanged at Gibbet Island, and continued to swing there at night long after the gallows was taken down; and of the ghost of the unfortunate Governor Leisler, who was hanged for treason, which haunted the old fort and the government-house. The gossiping knot dispersed, each charged with direful intelligence. The sexton disburdened himself at a vestry meeting that was held that very day, and the black cook forsook her kitchen, and spent half of the day at the street-pump, that gossiping place of servants, dealing forth the news to all that came for water. In a little time the whole town was in a buzz with tales about the haunted house. Some said that Claus Hopper had seen the devil, while others hinted that the house was haunted by the ghosts of some of the patients whom the doctor had physicked out of the world, and that was the reason why he did not venture to live in it himself.

All this put the little doctor in a terrible fume. He threatened vengeance on any one who should affect the value of his property by exciting popular prejudices. He complained loudly of thus being in a manner dispossessed of his territories by mere bugbears; but he secretly determined to have the house exorcised by the Dominie. Great was his relief, therefore, when, in the midst of his perplexities, Dolph stepped forward and undertook to garrison the haunted house. The youngster had been listening to all the stories of Claus Hopper and Peter de Groodt; he was fond of adventure, he loved the marvellous, and his imagination had become quite excited by these tales of wonder. Besides, he had led such an uncomfortable life at the doctor's, being subjected to the intolerable thraldom of early hours, that he was delighted at the prospect of having a house to himself, even though it should be a haunted one. His offer was eagerly accepted, and it was determined that he should mount guard that very night. His only stipulation was, that the enterprise should be kept secret from his mother; for he knew the poor soul would not sleep a wink if she knew that her son was waging war with the powers of darkness.

When night came on he set out on this perilous expedition. The old black cook, his only friend in the household, had provided him with a little mess for supper, and a rush-light; and she tied round his neck an amulet, given her by an African conjurer, as a charm against evil spirits. Dolph was escorted on his way by the doctor and Peter de Groodt, who had agreed to accompany him to the house, and to see him safe lodged. The night was overcast, and it was very dark when they arrived at the grounds which surrounded the mansion. The sexton led the way with a lantern. As they walked along the avenue of acacias, the fitful light, catching from bush to bush, and tree to tree, often startled the doughty Peter, and made him fall back upon his followers; and the doctor grappled still closer hold of Dolph's arm, observing that the ground was very slippery and uneven. At one time they were nearly put to total rout by a bat, which came flitting about the lantern; and the notes of the insects from the trees, and the frogs from a neighbouring pond, formed a most drowsy and doleful concert.

The front door of the mansion opened with a grating sound, that made the doctor turn pale. They entered a tolerably large hall, such as is common in American country-houses, and which serves for a sitting room in warm weather. From hence they went up a wide staircase, that groaned and creaked as they trod, every step making its particular note, like the key of a harpsichord. This led to another hall on the second story, from whence they entered the room where Dolph was to sleep. It was large, and scantily furnished; the shutters were closed; but as they were much broken, there was no want of a circulation of air. It appeared to have been that sacred chamber, known among Dutch housewives by the name of "the best bed-room;" which is the best furnished room in the house, but in which scarce any body is ever permitted to sleep. Its splendour, however, was all at an end. There were a few broken articles of furniture about the room, and in the centre stood a heavy deal table and a large arm-chair, both of which had the look of being coeval with the mansion. The fire-place was wide, and had been faced with Dutch tiles, representing scripture stories; but some of them had fallen out of their places, and lay shattered about the hearth. The sexton had lit the rushlight; and the doctor, looking fearfully about the room, was just exhorting Dolph to be of good cheer, and to pluck up a stout heart, when a noise in the chimney, like voices and struggling, struck a sudden panic into the sexton. He took to his heels with the lantern; the doctor followed hard after him; the stairs groaned and creaked as they hurried down, increasing their agitation and speed by its noises. The front door slammed after them; and Dolph heard them scrambling down the avenue, till the sound of their feet was lost in the distance. That he did not join in this precipitate retreat might have been owing to his possessing a little more courage than his companions, or perhaps that he had caught a glimpse of the cause of their dismay, in a nest of chimney swallows, that came tumbling down into the fire-place.

Being now left to himself, he secured the front door by a strong bolt and bar; and having seen that the other entrances were fastened, he returned to his desolate chamber. Having made his supper from the basket which the good old cook had provided, he locked the chamber door, and retired to rest on a mattress in one corner. The night was calm and still; and nothing broke upon the profound quiet, but the lonely chirping of a cricket from the chimney of a distant chamber. The rushlight, which stood in the centre of the deal table, shed a feeble yellow ray, dimly illumining the chamber, and making uncouth shapes and shadows on the walls, from the clothes which Dolph had thrown over a chair.

With all his boldness of heart there was something subduing in this desolate scene; and he felt his spirits flag within him, as he lay on his hard bed and gazed about the room. He was turning over in his mind his idle habits, his doubtful prospects, and now and then heaving a heavy sigh, as he thought on his poor old mother; for there is nothing like the silence and loneliness of night to bring dark shadows over the brightest mind. By-and-by he thought he heard a sound as if some one was walking below stairs. He listened, and distinctly heard a step on the great staircase. It approached solemnly and slowly, tramp—tramp—tramp! It was evidently the tread of some heavy personage; and yet how could he have got into the house without making a noise? He had examined all the fastenings, and was certain that every entrance was secure. Still the steps advanced, tramp—tramp—tramp! It was evident that the person approaching could not be a robber, the step was too loud and deliberate; a robber would either be stealthy or precipitate. And now the footsteps had ascended the staircase; they were slowly advancing along the passage, resounding through the silent and empty apartments. The very cricket had ceased its melancholy note, and nothing interrupted their awful distinctness. The door, which had been locked on the inside, slowly swung open, as if self-moved. The footsteps entered the room; but no one was to be seen. They passed slowly and audibly across it, tramp—tramp—tramp! but whatever made the sound was invisible. Dolph rubbed his eyes, and stared about him; he could see to every part of the dimly-lighted chamber; all was vacant; yet still he heard those mysterious footsteps, solemnly walking about the chamber. They ceased, and all was dead silence. There was something more appalling in this invisible visitation, than there would have been in any thing that addressed itself to the eyesight. It was awfully vague and indefinite. He felt his heart beat against his ribs; a cold sweat broke out upon his forehead; he lay for some time in a state of violent agitation; nothing, however, occurred to increase his alarm. His light gradually burnt down into the socket, and he fell asleep. When he awoke it was broad daylight; the sun was peering through the cracks of the window-shutters, and the birds were merrily singing about the house. The bright cheery day soon put to flight all the terrors of the preceding night. Dolph laughed, or rather tried to laugh, at all that had passed, and endeavoured to persuade himself that it was a mere freak of the imagination, conjured up by the stories he had heard; but he was a little puzzled to find the door of his room locked on the inside, notwithstanding that he had positively seen it swing open as the footsteps had entered. He returned to town in a state of considerable perplexity; but he determined to say nothing on the subject, until his doubts were either confirmed or removed by another night's watching. His silence was a grievous disappointment to the gossips who had gathered at the doctor's mansion. They had prepared their minds to hear direful tales; and they were almost in a rage at being assured that he had nothing to relate.

The next night, then, Dolph repeated his vigil. He now entered the house with some trepidation. He was particular in examining the fastenings of all the doors, and securing them well. He locked the door of his chamber, and placed a chair against it; then having despatched his supper, he threw himself on his mattress and endeavoured to sleep. It was all in vain; a thousand crowding fancies kept him waking. The time slowly dragged on, as if minutes were spinning themselves out into hours. As the night advanced, he grew more and more nervous; and he almost started from his couch when he heard the mysterious footstep again on the staircase. Up it came, as before, solemnly and slowly, tramp—tramp—tramp! It approached along the passage; the door again swung open, as if there had been neither lock nor impediment, and a strange looking figure stalked into the room. It was an elderly man, large and robust, clothed in the old Flemish fashion. He had on a kind of short cloak, with a garment under it, belted round the waist; trunk hose, with great bunches or bows at the knees; and a pair of russet boots, very large at top, and standing widely from his legs. His hat was broad and slouched, with a feather trailing over one side. His iron-gray hair hung in thick masses on his neck; and he had a short grizzled beard. He walked slowly round the room, as if examining that all was safe; then, hanging his hat on a peg beside the door, he sat down in the elbow-chair, and, leaning his elbow on the table, he fixed his eyes on Dolph with an unmoving and deadening stare.

Dolph was not naturally a coward; but he had been brought up in an implicit belief in ghosts and goblins. A thousand stories came swarming to his mind that he had heard about this building; and as he looked at this strange personage, with his uncouth garb, his pale visage, his grizzly beard, and his fixed, staring, fish-like eye, his teeth began to chatter, his hair to rise on his head, and a cold sweat to break out all over his body. How long he remained in this situation he could not tell, for he was like one fascinated. He could not take his gaze off from the spectre; but lay staring at him, with his whole intellect absorbed in the contemplation. The old man remained seated behind the table, without stirring, or turning an eye, always keeping a dead steady glare upon Dolph. At length the household cock, from a neighbouring farm, clapped his wings, and gave a loud cheerful crow that rung over the fields. At the sound the old man slowly rose, and took down his hat from the peg; the door opened, and closed after him; he was heard to go slowly down the stair-case, tramp—tramp—tramp!—and when he had got to the bottom, all was again silent. Dolph lay and listened earnestly; counted every footfall; listened, and listened if the steps should return, until, exhausted with watching and agitation, he fell into a troubled sleep.

Daylight again brought fresh courage and assurance. He would fain have considered all that had passed as a mere dream; yet there stood the chair in which the unknown had seated himself; there was the table on which he had leaned; there was the peg on which he had hung his hat; and there was the door, locked precisely as he himself had locked it, with the chair placed against it. He hastened down stairs, and examined the doors and windows; all were exactly in the same state in which he had left them, and there was no apparent way by which any being could have entered and left the house, without leaving some trace behind. "Pooh!" said

Dolph to himself, "it was all a dream:"—but it would not do; the more he endeavoured to shake the scene off from his mind, the more it haunted him.

Though he persisted in a strict silence as to all that he had seen and heard, yet his looks betrayed the uncomfortable night that he had passed. It was evident that there was something wonderful hidden under this mysterious reserve. The doctor took him into the study, locked the door, and sought to have a full and confidential communication; but he could get nothing out of him. Frau Ilsy took him aside into the pantry, but to as little purpose; and Peter de Groodt held him by the button for a full hour, in the churchyard, the very place to get at the bottom of a ghost story, but came off not a whit wiser than the rest. It is always the case, however, that one truth concealed makes a dozen current lies. It is like a guinea locked up in a bank, that has a dozen paper representatives. Before the day was over, the neighbourhood was full of reports. Some said that Dolph Heyliger watched in the haunted house, with pistols loaded with silver bullets; others, that he had a long talk with a spectre without a head; others, that Doctor Knipperhausen and the sexton had been hunted down the Bowery-lane, and quite into town, by a legion of ghosts of their customers. Some shook their heads; and thought it a shame that the doctor should put Dolph to pass the night alone in that dismal house, where he might be spirited away, no one knew whither; while others observed, with a shrug, that if the devil did carry off the youngster, it would but be taking his own.

These rumours at length reached the ears of the good Dame Heyliger, and, as may be supposed, threw her into a terrible alarm. For her son to have exposed himself to danger from living foes, would have been nothing so dreadful in her eyes, as to dare alone the terrors of the Haunted House. She hastened to the doctor's, and passed a great part of the day in attempting to dissuade Dolph from repeating his vigil; she told him a score of tales, which her gossiping friends had just related to her, of persons who had been carried off, when watching alone, in old ruinous houses. It was all to no effect. Dolph's pride, as well as curiosity, was piqued. He endeavoured to calm the apprehensions of his mother, and to

assure her that there was no truth in all the rumours she had
heard. She looked at him dubiously, and shook her head; but
finding his determination was not to be shaken, she brought
him a little thick Dutch Bible, with brass clasps, to take with
him, as a sword wherewith to fight the powers of darkness;
and, lest that might not be sufficient, the housekeeper gave
him the Heidelburgh catechism by way of dagger.

The next night, therefore, Dolph took up his quarters for
the third time in the old mansion. Whether dream or not, the
same thing was repeated. Towards midnight, when every
thing was still, the same sound echoed through the empty
halls—tramp—tramp—tramp! The stairs were again ascended; the door again swung open; the old man entered;
walked round the room; hung up his hat, and seated himself
by the table. The same fear and trembling came over poor
Dolph, though not in so violent a degree. He lay in the same
way, motionless and fascinated, staring at the figure, which
regarded him as before with a dead, fixed, chilling gaze. In
this way they remained for a long time, till, by degrees,
Dolph's courage began gradually to revive. Whether alive or
dead, this being had certainly some object in his visitation;
and he recollected to have heard it said, that spirits have no
power to speak until they are spoken to. Summoning up resolution, therefore, and making two or three attempts, before
he could get his parched tongue in motion, he addressed the
unknown in the most solemn form of adjuration that he
could recollect, and demanded to know what was the motive
of his visit.

No sooner had he finished, than the old man rose, took
down his hat, the door opened, and he went out, looking
back upon Dolph just as he crossed the threshold, as if expecting him to follow. The youngster did not hesitate an instant. He took the candle in his hand, and the Bible under his
arm, and obeyed the tacit invitation. The candle emitted a
feeble, uncertain ray; but still he could see the figure before
him, slowly descending the stairs. He followed, trembling.
When it had reached the bottom of the stairs, it turned
through the hall towards the back-door of the mansion.
Dolph held the light over the balustrades; but, in his eagerness to catch a sight of the unknown, he flared his feeble taper

so suddenly, that it went out. Still there was sufficient light from the pale moonbeams, that fell through a narrow window, to give him an indistinct view of the figure, near the door. He followed, therefore, down stairs, and turned towards the place; but when he had got there, the unknown had disappeared. The door remained fast barred and bolted; there was no other mode of exit; yet the being, whatever he might be, was gone. He unfastened the door, and looked out into the fields. It was a hazy, moonlight night, so that the eye could distinguish objects at some distance. He thought he saw the unknown in a footpath that led from the door. He was not mistaken; but how had he got out of the house? He did not pause to think, but followed on. The old man proceeded at a measured pace, without looking about him, his footsteps sounding on the hard ground. He passed through the orchard of apple-trees that stood near the house, always keeping the footpath. It led to a well, situated in a little hollow, which had supplied the farm with water. Just at this well Dolph lost sight of him. He rubbed his eyes and looked again; but nothing was to be seen of the unknown. He reached the well, but nobody was there. All the surrounding ground was open and clear; there was no bush nor hiding-place. He looked down the well and saw, at a great depth, the reflection of the sky in the still water. After remaining here for some time, without seeing or hearing any thing more of his mysterious conductor, he returned to the house, full of awe and wonder. He bolted the door, groped his way back to bed, and it was long before he could compose himself to sleep.

His dreams were strange and troubled. He thought he was following the old man along the side of a great river, until they came to a vessel that was on the point of sailing; and that his conductor led him on board and vanished. He remembered the commander of the vessel, a short swarthy man, with crisped black hair, blind of one eye, and lame of one leg; but the rest of his dream was very confused. Sometimes he was sailing; sometimes on shore; now amidst storms and tempests, and now wandering quietly in unknown streets. The figure of the old man was strangely mingled up with the incidents of the dream; and the whole distinctly wound up by his finding himself on board of the vessel again, returning home, with a great bag of money!

When he woke, the gray, cool light of dawn was streaking the horizon, and the cocks passing the *réveil* from farm to farm throughout the country. He rose more harassed and perplexed than ever. He was singularly confounded by all that he had seen and dreamt, and began to doubt whether his mind was not affected, and whether all that was passing in his thoughts might not be mere feverish fantasy. In his present state of mind, he did not feel disposed to return immediately to the doctor's, and undergo the cross-questioning of the household. He made a scanty breakfast, therefore, on the remains of last night's provisions, and then wandered out into the fields to meditate on all that had befallen him. Lost in thought, he rambled about, gradually approaching the town, until the morning was far advanced, when he was roused by a hurry and bustle around him. He found himself near the water's edge, in a throng of people, hurrying to a pier, where there was a vessel ready to make sail. He was unconsciously carried along by the impulse of the crowd, and found that it was a sloop, on the point of sailing up the Hudson to Albany. There was much leave-taking, and kissing of old women and children, and great activity in carrying on board baskets of bread and cakes, and provisions of all kinds, notwithstanding the mighty joints of meat that dangled over the stern; for a voyage to Albany was an expedition of great moment in those days. The commander of the sloop was hurrying about, and giving a world of orders, which were not very strictly attended to; one man being busy in lighting his pipe, and another in sharpening his snicker-snee.

The appearance of the commander suddenly caught Dolph's attention. He was short and swarthy, with crisped black hair; blind of one eye, and lame of one leg—the very commander he had seen in his dream! Surprised and aroused, he considered the scene more attentively, and recalled still further traces of his dream: the appearance of the vessel, of the river, and of a variety of other objects, accorded with the imperfect images vaguely rising to recollection.

As he stood musing on these circumstances, the captain suddenly called to him in Dutch, "Step on board, young man, or you'll be left behind!" He was startled by the summons; he saw that the sloop was cast loose, and was actually moving from the pier; it seemed as if he was actuated by some irresistible impulse; he sprang upon the deck, and the next moment the sloop was hurried off by the wind and tide. Dolph's thoughts and feelings were all in tumult and confusion. He had been strongly worked upon by the events that had recently befallen him, and could not but think that there was some connexion between his present situation and his last night's dream. He felt as if he was under supernatural influence; and he tried to assure himself with an old and favourite maxim of his, that "one way or other, all would turn out for the best." For a moment, the indignation of the doctor at his departure, without leave, passed across his mind, but that was matter of little moment; then he thought of the distress of his mother at his strange disappearance, and the idea gave him a sudden pang. He would have entreated to be put on shore; but he knew with such wind and tide the entreaty would have been in vain. Then the inspiring love of novelty and adventure came rushing in full tide through his bosom; he felt himself launched strangely and suddenly on the world, and under full way to explore the regions of wonder that lay up this mighty river, and beyond those blue mountains that had bounded his horizon since childhood. While he was lost in this whirl of thought, the sails strained to the breeze; the shores seemed to hurry away behind him; and, before he perfectly recovered his self-possession, the sloop was ploughing her way past Spiking-devil and Yonkers, and the tallest chimney of the Manhattoes had faded from his sight.

I have said that a voyage up the Hudson in those days was an undertaking of some moment; indeed, it was as much thought of as a voyage to Europe is at present. The sloops were often many days on the way; the cautious navigators taking in sail when it blew fresh, and coming to anchor at night; and stopping to send the boat ashore for milk for tea; without which it was impossible for the worthy old lady passengers to subsist. And then there were the much-talked-of perils of the Tappaan-zee, and the highlands. In short, a prudent Dutch burgher would talk of such a voyage for months, and even years, beforehand; and never undertook it without putting his affairs in order, making his will, and having prayers said for him in the Low Dutch churches.

In the course of such a voyage, therefore, Dolph was satisfied he would have time enough to reflect, and to make up his mind as to what he should do when he arrived at Albany. The captain, with his blind eye, and lame leg, would, it is true, bring his strange dream to mind, and perplex him sadly for a few moments; but of late his life had been made up so much of dreams and realities, his nights and days had been so jumbled together, that he seemed to be moving continually in a delusion. There is always, however, a kind of vagabond consolation in a man's having nothing in this world to lose; with this Dolph comforted his heart, and determined to make the most of the present enjoyment.

In the second day of the voyage they came to the highlands. It was the latter part of a calm, sultry day that they floated gently with the tide between these stern mountains. There was that perfect quiet which prevails over nature in the languor of summer heat; the turning of a plank, or the accidental falling of an oar on deck, was echoed from the mountain-side, and reverberated along the shores; and if by chance the captain gave a shout of command, there were airy tongues that mocked it from every cliff.

Dolph gazed about him in mute delight and wonder at these scenes of nature's magnificence. To the left the Dunderberg reared its woody precipices, height over height, forest over forest, away into the deep summer sky. To the right strutted forth the bold promontory of Anthony's Nose, with a solitary eagle wheeling about it; while beyond, mountain succeeded mountain, until they seemed to lock their arms together, and confine this mighty river in their embraces. There was a feeling of quiet luxury in gazing at the broad, green bosoms here and there scooped out among the precipices; or at woodlands high in air, nodding over the edge of some beetling bluff, and their foliage all transparent in the yellow sunshine.

In the midst of his admiration, Dolph remarked a pile of bright, snowy clouds peering above the western heights. It was succeeded by another and another, each seemingly pushing onwards its predecessor, and towering, with dazzling

brilliancy, in the deep blue atmosphere: and now muttering
peals of thunder were faintly heard rolling behind the mountains. The river, hitherto still and glassy, reflecting pictures of
the sky and land, now showed a dark ripple at a distance, as
the breeze came creeping up it. The fish-hawks wheeled and
screamed, and sought their nests on the high dry trees; the
crows flew clamorously to the crevices of the rocks, and all
nature seemed conscious of the approaching thunder-gust.

The clouds now rolled in volumes over the mountain tops;
their summits still bright and snowy, but the lower parts of
an inky blackness. The rain began to patter down in broad
and scattered drops; the wind freshened, and curled up the
waves; at length it seemed as if the bellying clouds were torn
open by the mountain tops, and complete torrents of rain
came rattling down. The lightning leaped from cloud to
cloud, and streamed quivering against the rocks, splitting and
rending the stoutest forest trees. The thunder burst in tremendous explosions; the peals were echoed from mountain
to mountain; they crashed upon Dunderberg, and rolled up
the long defile of the highlands, each headland making a new
echo, until old Bull-hill seemed to bellow back the storm.

For a time the scudding rack and mist, and the sheeted
rain, almost hid the landscape from the sight. There was a
fearful gloom, illumined still more fearfully by the streams of
lightning which glittered among the rain-drops. Never had
Dolph beheld such an absolute warring of the elements; it
seemed as if the storm was tearing and rending its way
through this mountain defile, and had brought all the artillery
of heaven into action.

The vessel was hurried on by the increasing wind, until she
came to where the river makes a sudden bend, the only one in
the whole course of its majestic career.* Just as they turned
the point, a violent flaw of wind came sweeping down a
mountain-gully, bending the forest before it, and, in a moment, lashing up the river into white froth and foam. The
captain saw the danger, and cried out to lower the sail. Before
the order could be obeyed, the flaw struck the sloop, and
threw her on her beam-ends. Every thing now was fright and

*This must have been the bend at West point.

confusion: the flapping of the sails, the whistling and rushing of the wind, the bawling of the captain and crew, the shrieking of the passengers, all mingled with the rolling and bellowing of the thunder. In the midst of the uproar the sloop righted; at the same time the mainsail shifted, the boom came sweeping the quarter-deck, and Dolph, who was gazing unguardedly at the clouds, found himself, in a moment, floundering in the river.

For once in his life one of his idle accomplishments was of use to him. The many truant hours which he had devoted to sporting in the Hudson had made him an expert swimmer; yet with all his strength and skill, he found great difficulty in reaching the shore. His disappearance from the deck had not been noticed by the crew, who were all occupied by their own danger. The sloop was driven along with inconceivable rapidity. She had hard work to weather a long promontory on the eastern shore, round which the river turned, and which completely shut her from Dolph's view.

It was on a point of the western shore that he landed, and, scrambling up the rocks, he threw himself, faint and exhausted, at the foot of a tree. By degrees the thunder-gust passed over. The clouds rolled away to the east, where they lay piled in feathery masses, tinted with the last rosy rays of the sun. The distant play of the lightning might be still seen about their dark bases, and now and then might be heard the faint muttering of the thunder. Dolph rose, and sought about to see if any path led from the shore, but all was savage and trackless. The rocks were piled upon each other; great trunks of trees lay shattered about, as they had been blown down by the strong winds which draw through these mountains, or had fallen through age. The rocks too, were overhung with wild vines and briars, which completely matted themselves together, and opposed a barrier to all ingress; every movement that he made shook down a shower from the dripping foliage. He attempted to scale one of these almost perpendicular heights; but, though strong and agile, he found it an Herculean undertaking. Often he was supported merely by crumbling projections of the rock, and sometimes he clung to roots and branches of trees, and hung almost suspended in the air. The wood-pigeon came cleaving his whistling flight by him, and the eagle screamed from the brow of the impending cliff. As he was thus clambering, he was on the point of seizing hold of a shrub to aid his ascent, when something rustled among the leaves, and he saw a snake quivering along like lightning, almost from under his hand. It coiled itself up immediately, in an attitude of defiance, with flattened head, distended jaws, and quickly vibrating tongue, that played like a little flame about its mouth. Dolph's heart turned faint within him, and he had well nigh let go his hold, and tumbled down the precipice. The serpent stood on the defensive but for an instant; it was an instinctive movement of defence; and, finding there was no attack, it glided away into a cleft of the rock. Dolph's eye followed it with fearful intensity; and he saw at a glance that he was in the vicinity of a nest of adders, that lay knotted, and writhing, and hissing in the chasm. He hastened with all speed to escape from so frightful a neighbourhood. His imagination was full of this new horror; he saw an adder in every curling vine, and heard the tail of a rattle-snake in every dry leaf that rustled.

At length he succeeded in scrambling to the summit of a precipice; but it was covered by a dense forest. Wherever he could gain a look out between the trees, he saw that the coast rose in heights and cliffs, one rising beyond another, until huge mountains overtopped the whole. There were no signs of cultivation; nor any smoke curling amongst the trees to indicate a human residence. Every thing was wild and solitary. As he was standing on the edge of a precipice that overlooked a deep ravine fringed with trees, his feet detached a great fragment of rock; it fell, crashing its way through the tree tops, down into the chasm. A loud whoop, or rather yell, issued from the bottom of the glen; the moment after there was the report of a gun; and a ball came whistling over his head, cutting the twigs and leaves, and burying itself deep in the bark of a chestnut-tree.

Dolph did not wait for a second shot, but made a precipitate retreat; fearing every moment to hear the enemy in pursuit. He succeeded, however, in returning unmolested to the shore, and determined to penetrate no further into a country so beset with savage perils.

He sat himself down, dripping disconsolately, on a wet

stone. What was to be done? where was he to shelter himself? The hour of repose was approaching; the birds were seeking their nests, the bat began to flit about in the twilight, and the night-hawk, soaring high in heaven, seemed to be calling out the stars. Night gradually closed in, and wrapped every thing in gloom; and though it was the latter part of summer, yet the breeze stealing along the river, and among these dripping forests, was chilly and penetrating, especially to a half-drowned man.

As he sat drooping and despondent in this comfortless condition, he perceived a light gleaming through the trees near the shore, where the winding of the river made a deep bay. It cheered him with the hopes that there might be some human habitation where he might get something to appease the clamourous cravings of his stomach, and, what was equally necessary in his shipwrecked condition, a comfortable shelter for the night. It was with extreme difficulty that he made his way towards the light, along ledges of rocks, down which he was in danger of sliding into the river, and over great trunks of fallen trees; some of which had been blown down in the late storm, and lay so thickly together, that he had to struggle through their branches. At length he came to the brow of a rock that overhung a small dell, from whence the light proceeded. It was from a fire at the foot of a great tree that stood in the midst of a grassy interval or plat among the rocks. The fire cast up a red glare among the gray crags, and impending trees; leaving chasms of deep gloom, that resembled entrances to caverns. A small brook rippled close by, betrayed by the quivering reflection of the flame. There were two figures moving about the fire, and others squatted before it. As they were between him and the light, they were in complete shadow; but one of them happening to move round to the opposite side, Dolph was startled at perceiving, by the full glare falling on painted features, and glittering on silver ornaments, that he was an Indian. He now looked more narrowly, and saw guns leaning against a tree, and a dead body lying on the ground.

Dolph began to doubt whether he was not in a worse condition than before; here was the very foe that had fired at him from the glen. He endeavoured to retreat quietly, not caring to entrust himself to these half-human beings in so savage and lonely a place. It was too late; the Indian, with that eagle quickness of eye so remarkable in his race, perceived something stirring among the bushes on the rock; he seized one of the guns that leaned against the tree; one moment more, and Dolph might have had his passion for adventure cured by a bullet. He hallooed loudly, with the Indian salutation of friendship. The whole party sprang upon their feet; the salutation was returned, and the straggler was invited to join them at the fire.

On approaching he found to his consolation, that the party was composed of white men, as well as Indians. One, who was evidently the principal personage, or commander, was seated on a trunk of a tree before the fire. He was a large stout man, somewhat advanced in life, but hale and hearty. His face was bronzed almost to the colour of an Indian's; he had strong but rather jovial features, an aquiline nose, and a mouth shaped like a mastiff's. His face was half thrown in shade by a broad hat, with a buck's tail in it. His gray hair hung short in his neck. He wore a hunting frock, with Indian leggings, and mockasins, and a tomahawk in the broad wampum belt round his waist. As Dolph caught a distinct view of his person and features, he was struck with something that reminded him of the old man of the Haunted House. The man before him, however, was different in his dress and age; he was more cheery too in his aspect, and it was hard to define where the vague resemblance lay; but a resemblance there certainly was. Dolph felt some degree of awe in approaching him; but was assured by the frank, hearty welcome with which he was received. As he cast his eyes about, too, he was still further encouraged, by perceiving that the dead body, which had caused him some alarm, was that of a deer; and his satisfaction was complete in discerning, by the savoury steams which issued from a kettle, suspended by a hooked stick over the fire, that there was a part cooking for the evening's repast.

He now found that he had fallen in with a rambling hunting party; such as often took place in those days among the settlers along the river. The hunter is always hospitable; and nothing makes men more social and unceremonious than meeting in the wilderness. The commander of the party poured him out a dram of cheering liquor, which he gave him with a merry leer, to warm his heart; and ordered one of his followers to fetch some garments from a pinnace, which was moored in a cove close by; while those in which our hero was dripping might be dried before the fire.

Dolph found, as he had suspected, that the shot from the glen, which had come so near giving him his quietus when on the precipice, was from the party before him. He had nearly crushed one of them by the fragment of rock which he had detached; and the jovial old hunter, in the broad hat and buck tail, had fired at the place where he saw the bushes move, supposing it to be some wild animal. He laughed heartily at the blunder; it being what is considered an exceeding good joke among hunters; "but, faith, my lad," said he, "if I had but caught a glimpse of you to take sight at, you would have followed the rock. Antony Vander Heyden is seldom known to miss his aim." These last words were at once a clue to Dolph's curiosity; and a few questions let him completely into the character of the man before him, and of his band of woodland rangers. The commander in the broad hat and hunting frock was no less a personage than the Heer Antony Vander Heyden, of Albany, of whom Dolph had many a time heard. He was, in fact, the hero of many a story; being a man of singular humours and whimsical habits, that were matters of wonder to his quiet Dutch neighbours. As he was a man of property, having had a father before him, from whom he inherited large tracts of wild land, and whole barrels full of wampum, he could indulge his humours without control. Instead of staying quietly at home; eating and drinking at regular meal-times; amusing himself by smoking his pipe on the bench before the door; and then turning into a comfortable bed at night; he delighted in all kinds of rough, wild expeditions. He was never so happy as when on a hunting party in the wilderness, sleeping under trees or bark sheds, or cruising down the river, or on some woodland lake, fishing and fowling, and living the Lord knows how.

He was a great friend to Indians, and to an Indian mode of life, which he considered true natural liberty and manly enjoyment. When at home he had always several Indian hangers-on, who loitered about his house, sleeping like hounds in the sunshine, or preparing hunting and fishing-tackle for some new expedition, or shooting at marks with bows and arrows.

Over these vagrant beings Heer Antony had as perfect command as a huntsman over his pack; though they were great nuisances to the regular people of his neighbourhood. As he was a rich man, no one ventured to thwart his humours; indeed, he had a hearty, joyous manner about him, that made him universally popular. He would troll a Dutch song as he tramped along the street; hail every one a mile off; and when he entered a house, he would slap the good man familiarly on the back, shake him by the hand till he roared, and kiss his wife and daughters before his face—in short, there was no pride nor ill humour about Heer Antony.

Besides his Indian hangers on, he had three or four humble friends among the white men, who looked up to him as a patron, and had the run of his kitchen, and the favour of being taken with him occasionally on his expeditions. It was with a medley of such retainers that he was at present on a cruise along the shores of the Hudson, in a pinnace which he kept for his own recreation. There were two white men with him, dressed partly in the Indian style, with mocassins and hunting shirts; the rest of his crew consisted of four favourite Indians. They had been prowling about the river, without any definite object, until they found themselves in the highlands; where they had passed two or three days, hunting the deer which still lingered among these mountains.

"It is a lucky circumstance, young man," said Antony Vander Heyden, "that you happened to be knocked overboard to-day; as tomorrow morning we start early on our return homewards; and you might then have looked in vain for a meal among these mountains—but come, lads, stir about! stir about! Let's see what prog we have for supper; the kettle has boiled long enough; my stomach cries cupboard; and I'll warrant our guest is in no mood to dally with his trencher."

There was a bustle now in the little encampment; one took off the kettle and turned a part of the contents into a huge wooden bowl. Another prepared a flat rock for a table; while a third brought various utensils from the pinnace; and Heer

Antony himself brought a flask or two of precious liquor from his own private locker; knowing his boon companions too well to trust any of them with the key.

A rude but hearty repast was soon spread; consisting of venison smoking from the kettle, with cold bacon, boiled Indian corn, and mighty loaves of good brown household bread. Never had Dolph made a more delicious repast; and when he had washed it down by two or three draughts from the Heer Antony's flask, and felt the jolly liquor sending its warmth through his veins, and glowing round his very heart, he would not have changed his situation, no, not with the governor of the province.

The Heer Antony, too, grew chirping and joyous; told half a dozen fat stories, at which his white followers laughed immoderately, though the Indians, as usual, maintained an invincible gravity.

"This is your true life, my boy!" said he, slapping Dolph on the shoulder; "a man is never a man till he can defy wind and weather, range woods and wilds, sleep under a tree, and live on bass-wood leaves!"

And then would he sing a stave or two of a Dutch drinking song, swaying a short, squab Dutch bottle in his hand, while his myrmidons would join in chorus, until the woods echoed again;—as the good old song has it:

> "They all with a shout made the elements ring,
>   So soon as the office was o'er;
> To feasting they went, with true merriment,
>   And tippled strong liquor gillore."

In the midst of his joviality, however, Heer Antony did not lose sight of discretion. Though he pushed the bottle without reserve to Dolph, yet he always took care to help his followers himself, knowing the beings he had to deal with; and he was particular in granting but a moderate allowance to the Indians. The repast being ended, the Indians having drunk their liquor, and smoked their pipes, now wrapped themselves in their blankets, stretched themselves on the ground, with their feet to the fire, and soon fell asleep, like so many tired hounds. The rest of the party remained chatting before the fire, which the gloom of the forest, and the dampness of the air from the late storm, rendered extremely grateful and comforting. The conversation gradually moderated from the hilarity of supper-time, and turned upon hunting adventures, and exploits and perils in the wilderness; many of which were so strange and improbable, that I will not venture to repeat them, lest the veracity of Antony Vander Heyden and his comrades should be brought into question. There were many legendary tales told, also, about the river, and the settlements on its borders; in which valuable kind of lore the Heer Antony seemed deeply versed. As the sturdy bush-beater sat in a twisted root of a tree, that served him for a kind of arm-chair, dealing forth these wild stories, with the fire gleaming on his strongly marked visage, Dolph was again repeatedly perplexed by something that reminded him of the phantom of the Haunted House; some vague resemblance that could not be fixed upon any precise feature or lineament, but which pervaded the general air of his countenance and figure.

The circumstance of Dolph's falling overboard being again discussed, led to the relation of divers disasters and singular mishaps that had befallen voyagers on this great river, particularly in the earlier periods of colonial history; most of which the Heer deliberately attributed to supernatural causes. Dolph stared at this suggestion; but the old gentleman assured him that it was very currently believed by the settlers along the river, that these highlands were under the dominion of supernatural and mischievous beings, which seemed to have taken some pique against the Dutch colonists in the early time of the settlement. In consequence of this, they have ever since taken particular delight in venting their spleen, and indulging their humours, upon the Dutch skippers; bothering them with flaws, head-winds, counter-currents, and all kinds of impediments; insomuch, that a Dutch navigator was always obliged to be exceedingly wary and deliberate in his proceedings; to come to anchor at dusk; to drop his peak, or take in sail, whenever he saw a swag-bellied cloud rolling over the mountains; in short, to take so many precautions, that he was often apt to be an incredible time in toiling up the river.

Some, he said, believed these mischievous powers of the air to be evil spirits conjured up by the Indian wizards, in the early times of the province, to revenge themselves on the strangers who had dispossessed them of their country. They even attributed to their incantations the misadventure which befell the renowned Hendrick Hudson, when he sailed so gallantly up this river in quest of a northwest passage, and, as he thought, run his ship aground; which they affirm was nothing more nor less than a spell of these same wizards, to prevent his getting to China in this direction.

The greater part, however, Heer Antony observed, accounted for all the extraordinary circumstances attending this river, and the perplexities of the skippers which navigated it, by the old legend of the Storm-ship which haunted Point-no-point. On finding Dolph to be utterly ignorant of this tradition, the Heer stared at him for a moment with surprise, and wondered where he had passed his life, to be uninformed on so important a point of history. To pass away the remainder of the evening, therefore, he undertook the tale, as far as his memory would serve, in the very words in which it had been written out by Mynheer Selyne, an early poet of the New Nederlandts. Giving then, a stir to the fire, that sent up its sparks among the trees like a little volcano, he adjusted himself comfortably in his root of a tree; and throwing back his head, and closing his eyes for a few moments, to summon up his recollection, he related the following legend.

The Storm-Ship

IN THE GOLDEN AGE of the province of the New Netherlands, when it was under the sway of Wouter Van Twiller,
otherwise called the Doubter, the people of the Manhattoes
were alarmed one sultry afternoon, just about the time of the
summer solstice, by a tremendous storm of thunder and lightning. The rain descended in such torrents as absolutely to
spatter up and smoke along the ground. It seemed as if the
thunder rattled and rolled over the very roofs of the houses;
the lightning was seen to play about the church of St. Nicholas, and to strive three times, in vain, to strike its weathercock.
Garret Van Horne's new chimney was split almost from top
to bottom; and Doffue Mildeberger was struck speechless
from his bald-faced mare, just as he was riding into town. In
a word, it was one of those unparalleled storms, that only
happen once within the memory of that venerable personage, known in all towns by the appellation of "the oldest inhabitant."

Great was the terror of the good old women of the Manhattoes. They gathered their children together, and took refuge in the cellars; after having hung a shoe on the iron point
of every bed-post, lest it should attract the lightning. At
length the storm abated; the thunder sunk into a growl, and
the setting sun, breaking from under the fringed borders of
the clouds, made the broad bosom of the bay to gleam like a
sea of molten gold.

The word was given from the fort that a ship was standing
up the bay. It passed from mouth to mouth, and street to
street, and soon put the little capital in a bustle. The arrival
of a ship, in those early times of the settlement, was an event
of vast importance to the inhabitants. It brought them news
from the old world, from the land of their birth, from which
they were so completely severed. To the yearly ship, too, they
looked for their supply of luxuries, of finery, of comforts, and
almost of necessaries. The good vrouw could not have her
new cap nor new gown until the arrival of the ship; the artist
waited for it for his tools, the burgomaster for his pipe
and his supply of Hollands, the schoolboy for his top and

marbles, and the lordly landholder for the bricks with which
he was to build his new mansion. Thus every one, rich and
poor, great and small, looked out for the arrival of the ship. It
was the great yearly event of the town of New Amsterdam;
and from one end of the year to the other, the ship—the
ship—the ship—was the continual topic of conversation.

The news from the fort, therefore, brought all the populace
down to the battery, to behold the wished-for sight. It was
not exactly the time when she had been expected to arrive,
and the circumstance was a matter of some speculation. Many
were the groups collected about the battery. Here and there
might be seen a burgomaster, of slow and pompous gravity,
giving his opinion with great confidence to a crowd of old
women and idle boys. At another place was a knot of old
weather-beaten fellows, who had been seamen or fishermen
in their times, and were great authorities on such occasions;
these gave different opinions, and caused great disputes
among their several adherents: but the man most looked up
to, and followed and watched by the crowd, was Hans Van
Pelt, an old Dutch sea captain retired from service, the nau-
tical oracle of the place. He reconnoitred the ship through an
ancient telescope, covered with tarry canvas, hummed a
Dutch tune to himself, and said nothing. A hum, however,
from Hans Van Pelt had always more weight with the public
than a speech from another man.

In the mean time the ship became more distinct to the naked eye: she was a stout, round, Dutch-built vessel, with high
bow and poop, and bearing Dutch colours. The evening sun
gilded her bellying canvas, as she came riding over the long
waving billows. The centinel who had given notice of her approach, declared, that he first got sight of her when she was
in the centre of the bay; and that she broke suddenly on his
sight, just as if she had come out of the bosom of the black
thunder-cloud. The bystanders looked at Hans Van Pelt, to
see what he would say to this report: Hans Van Pelt screwed
his mouth closer together, and said nothing; upon which
some shook their heads, and others shrugged their shoulders.

The ship was now repeatedly hailed, but made no reply,
and passing by the fort, stood on up the Hudson. A gun was
brought to bear on her, and, with some difficulty, loaded and

fired by Hans Van Pelt, the garrison not being expert in artillery. The shot seemed absolutely to pass through the ship, and to skip along the water on the other side, but no notice was taken of it! What was strange, she had all her sails set, and sailed right against wind and tide, which were both down the river. Upon this Hans Van Pelt, who was likewise harbour-master, ordered his boat, and set off to board her; but after rowing two or three hours, he returned without success. Sometimes he would get within one or two hundred yards of her, and then, in a twinkling, she would be half a mile off. Some said it was because his oars-men, who were rather pursy and short-winded, stopped every now and then to take breath, and spit on their hands; but this it is probable was a mere scandal. He got near enough, however, to see the crew; who were all dressed in the Dutch style, the officers in doublets and high hats and feathers. Not a word was spoken by any one on board; they stood as motionless as so many statues, and the ship seemed as if left to her own government. Thus she kept on, away up the river, lessening and lessening in the evening sunshine, until she faded from sight, like a little white cloud melting away in the summer sky.

The appearance of this ship threw the governor into one of the deepest doubts that ever beset him in the whole course of his administration. Fears were entertained for the security of the infant settlements on the river, lest this might be an enemy's ship in disguise, sent to take possession. The governor called together his council repeatedly, to assist him with their conjectures. He sat in his chair of state, built of timber from the sacred forest of the Hague, and smoked his long jasmin pipe, and listened to all that his counsellors had to say on a subject about which they knew nothing; but in spite of all the conjecturing of the sagest and oldest heads, the governor still continued to doubt.

Messengers were despatched to different places on the river; but they returned without any tidings—the ship had made no port. Day after day, and week after week, elapsed, but she never returned down the Hudson. As, however, the council seemed solicitous for intelligence, they had it in abundance. The captains of the sloops seldom arrived without bringing some report of having seen the strange ship at different parts of the river; sometimes near the Pallisadoes, sometimes off Croton Point, and sometimes in the highlands; but she never was reported as having been seen above the highlands. The crews of the sloops, it is true, generally differed among themselves in their accounts of these apparitions; but that may have arisen from the uncertain situations in which they saw her. Sometimes it was by the flashes of the thunder-storm lighting up a pitchy night, and giving glimpses of her careering across Tappaan Zee, or the wide waste of Haverstraw Bay. At one moment she would appear close upon them, as if likely to run them down, and would throw them into great bustle and alarm; but the next flash would show her far off, always sailing against the wind. Sometimes, in quiet moonlight nights, she would be seen under some high bluff of the highlands, all in deep shadow, excepting her top-sails glittering in the moonbeams; by the time, however, that the voyagers would reach the place, there would be no ship to be seen; and when they had past on for some distance, and looked back, behold! there she was again, with her top-sails in the moonshine! Her appearance was always just after, or just before, or just in the midst of unruly weather; and she was known by all the skippers and voyagers of the Hudson by the name of "the storm-ship."

These reports perplexed the governor and his council more than ever; and it would be endless to repeat the conjectures and opinions that were uttered on the subject. Some quoted cases in point, of ships seen off the coast of New England, navigated by witches and goblins. Old Hans Van Pelt, who had been more than once to the Dutch colony at the Cape of Good Hope, insisted that this must be the flying Dutchman which had so long haunted Table Bay; but being unable to make port, had now sought another harbour. Others suggested, that, if it really was a supernatural apparition, as there was every natural reason to believe, it might be Hendrick Hudson, and his crew of the Half-moon; who, it was well known, had once run aground in the upper part of the river, in seeking a north-west passage to China. This opinion had very little weight with the governor, but it passed current out of doors; for indeed it had already been reported, that Hendrick Hudson and his crew haunted the Kaatskill Mountain;

and it appeared very reasonable to suppose, that his ship might infest the river where the enterprise was baffled, or that it might bear the shadowy crew to their periodical revels in the mountain.

Other events occurred to occupy the thoughts and doubts of the sage Wouter and his council, and the storm-ship ceased to be a subject of deliberation at the board. It continued, however, to be a matter of popular belief and marvellous anecdote through the whole time of the Dutch government, and particularly just before the capture of New Amsterdam, and the subjugation of the province by the English squadron. About that time the storm-ship was repeatedly seen in the Tappaan-Zee, and about Weehawk, and even down as far as Hoboken; and her appearance was supposed to be ominous of the approaching squall in public affairs, and the downfall of Dutch domination.

Since that time we have no authentic accounts of her; though it is said she still haunts the highlands, and cruises about Point-no-point. People who live along the river, insist that they sometimes see her in summer moonlight; and that in a deep still midnight they have heard the chant of her crew, as if heaving the lead; but sights and sounds are so deceptive along the mountainous shores, and about the wide bays and long reaches of this great river, that I confess I have very strong doubts upon the subject.

It is certain, nevertheless, that strange things have been seen in these highlands in storms, which are considered as connected with the old story of the ship. The captains of the river craft talk of a little bulbous-bottomed Dutch goblin, in trunk hose and sugar-loafed hat, with a speaking-trumpet in his hand, which they say keeps about the Dunderberg.* They declare that they have heard him, in stormy weather, in the midst of the turmoil, giving orders in low Dutch for the piping up of a fresh gust of wind, or the rattling off of another thunder-clap. That sometimes he has been seen surrounded by a crew of little imps in broad breeches and short doublets; tumbling head over heels in the rack and mist, and playing a thousand gambols in the air; or buzzing like a swarm of flies

---

*i.e. the "Thunder-Mountain," so called from its echoes.

about Anthony's Nose; and that, at such times, the hurry-scurry of the storm was always greatest. One time a sloop, in passing by the Dunderberg, was overtaken by a thunder-gust, that came scouring round the mountain, and seemed to burst just over the vessel. Though tight and well ballasted, yet she laboured dreadfully, until the water came over the gunwale. All the crew were amazed, when it was discovered that there was a little white sugarloaf-hat on the mast head, which was known at once to be the hat of the Heer of the Dunderberg. Nobody, however, dared to climb to the mast-head, and get rid of this terrible hat. The sloop continued labouring and rocking, as if she would have rolled her mast overboard. She seemed in continual danger either of upsetting or of running on shore. In this way she drove quite through the highlands, until she had passed Pollopol's Island, where, it is said, the jurisdiction of the Dunderberg potentate ceases. No sooner had she passed this bourne, than the little hat, all at once, spun up into the air like a top; whirled up all the clouds into a vortex, and hurried them back to the summit of the Dunderberg; while the sloop righted herself, and sailed on as quietly as if in a mill-pond. Nothing saved her from utter wreck but the fortunate circumstance of having a horse-shoe nailed against the mast; a wise precaution against evil spirits, which has since been adopted by all the Dutch captains that navigate this haunted river.

There is another story told of this foul-weather urchin, by Skipper Daniel Ouslesticker, of Fishkill, who was never known to tell a lie. He declared, that, in a severe squall, he saw him seated astride of his bowsprit, riding the sloop ashore, full butt against Anthony's Nose, and that he was ex-orcised by Dominie Van Gieson, of Esopus, who happened to be on board, and who sung the hymn of St. Nicholas; whereupon the goblin threw himself up in the air like a ball, and went off in a whirlwind, carrying away with him the night-cap of the Dominie's wife; which was discovered the next Sunday morning hanging on the weather-cock of Eso-pus' church steeple, at least forty miles off! After several events of this kind had taken place, the regular skippers of the river, for a long time, did not venture to pass the Dunder-berg, without lowering their peaks, out of homage to the

Heer of the mountain; and it was observed that all such as paid this tribute of respect were suffered to pass unmolested.*

"Such," said Antony Vander Heyden, "are a few of the stories written down by Selyne the poet, concerning this storm-ship; which he affirms to have brought this colony of mischievous imps into the province, from some old ghost-ridden country of Europe. I could give you a host more, if necessary; for all the accidents that so often befall the river craft in the highlands are said to be tricks played off by these imps of the Dunderberg; but I see that you are nodding, so let us turn in for the night."—

The moon had just raised her silver horns above the round back of Old Bull Hill, and lit up the gray rocks and shagged forests, and glittered on the waving bosom of the river. The night dew was falling, and the late gloomy mountains began to soften and put on a gray aerial tint in the dewy light. The hunters stirred the fire, and threw on fresh fuel to qualify the damp of the night air. They then prepared a bed of branches and dry leaves under a ledge of rocks for Dolph; while Antony Vander Heyden, wrapping himself up in a huge coat made of skins, stretched himself before the fire. It was some

*Among the superstitions which prevailed in the colonies, during the early times of the settlements, there seems to have been a singular one about phantom ships. The superstitious fancies of men are always apt to turn upon those objects which concern their daily occupations. The solitary ship, which, from year to year, came like a raven in the wilderness, bringing to the inhabitants of a settlement the comforts of life from the world from which they were cut off, was apt to be present to their dreams, whether sleeping or waking. The accidental sight from shore of a sail gliding along the horizon in those, as yet, lonely seas, was apt to be a matter of much talk and speculation. There is mention made in one of the early New England writers, of a ship navigated by witches, with a great horse that stood by the mainmast. I have met with another story, somewhere, of a ship that drove on shore, in fair, sunny, tranquil weather, with sails all set and a table spread in the cabin, as if to regale a number of guests, yet not a living being on board. These phantom ships always sailed in the eye of the wind; or ploughed their way with great velocity, making the smooth sea foam before their bows, when not a breath of air was stirring.

Moore has finely wrought up one of these legends of the sea into a little tale, which, within a small compass, contains the very essence of this species of supernatural fiction. I allude to his Spectre-Ship bound to Deadman's Isle.

time, however, before Dolph could close his eyes. He lay contemplating the strange scene before him: the wild woods and rocks around; the fire throwing fitful gleams on the faces of the sleeping savages; and the Heer Antony, too, who so singularly, yet vaguely, reminded him of the nightly visitant to the Haunted House. Now and then he heard the cry of some animal from the forest; or the hooting of the owl; or the notes of the whip-poor-will, which seemed to abound among these solitudes; or the splash of a sturgeon, leaping out of the river, and falling back full length on its placid surface. He contrasted all this with his accustomed nest in the garret room of the doctor's mansion; where the only sounds he heard at night were the church clock telling the hour; the drowsy voice of the watchman, drawling out all was well; the deep snoring of the doctor's clubbed nose from below stairs; or the cautious labours of some carpenter rat gnawing in the wainscot. His thoughts then wandered to his poor old mother: what would she think of his mysterious disappearance—what anxiety and distress would she not suffer? This was the thought that would continually intrude itself to mar his present enjoyment. It brought with it a feeling of pain and compunction, and he fell asleep with the tears yet standing in his eyes.

Were this a mere tale of fancy, here would be a fine opportunity for weaving in strange adventures among these wild mountains, and roving hunters; and, after involving my hero in a variety of perils and difficulties, rescuing him from them all by some miraculous contrivance; but as this is absolutely a true story, I must content myself with simple facts, and keep to probabilities.

At an early hour of the next day, therefore, after a hearty morning's meal, the encampment broke up, and our adventurers embarked in the pinnace of Antony Vander Heyden. There being no wind for the sails, the Indians rowed her gently along, keeping time to a kind of chant of one of the white men. The day was serene and beautiful; the river without a wave; and as the vessel cleft the glassy water, it left a long, undulating track behind. The crows, who had scented the hunters' banquet, were already gathering and hovering in the air, just where a column of thin, blue smoke, rising from among the trees, showed the place of their last night's quarters. As they coasted along the bases of the mountains, the Heer Antony pointed out to Dolph a bald eagle, the sovereign of these regions, who sat perched on a dry tree that projected over the river; and, with eye turned upwards, seemed to be drinking in the splendour of the morning sun. Their approach disturbed the monarch's meditations. He first spread one wing, and then the other; balanced himself for a moment; and then, quitting his perch with dignified composure, wheeled slowly over their heads. Dolph snatched up a gun, and sent a whistling ball after him that cut some of the feathers from his wing; the report of the gun leaped sharply from rock to rock, and awakened a thousand echoes; but the monarch of the air sailed calmly on, ascending higher and higher, and wheeling widely as he ascended, soaring up the green bosom of the woody mountain, until he disappeared over the brow of a beetling precipice. Dolph felt in a manner rebuked by this proud tranquillity, and almost reproached himself for having so wantonly insulted this majestic bird. Heer Antony told him, laughing, to remember that he was not yet out of the territories of the lord of the Dunderberg; and an old Indian shook his head, and observed, that there was bad luck in killing an eagle; the hunter, on the contrary, should always leave him a portion of his spoils.

Nothing, however, occurred to molest them on their voyage. They passed pleasantly through magnificent and lonely scenes, until they came to where Pollopol's Island lay, like a floating bower, at the extremity of the highlands. Here they landed, until the heat of the day should abate, or a breeze spring up, that might supersede the labour of the oar. Some prepared the mid-day meal, while others reposed under the shade of the trees in luxurious summer indolence, looking drowsily forth upon the beauty of the scene. On the one side were the highlands, vast and cragged, feathered to the top with forests, and throwing their shadows on the glassy water that dimpled at their feet. On the other side was a wide expanse of the river, like a broad lake, with long sunny reaches, and green headlands; and the distant line of Shawungunk mountains waving along a clear horizon, or chequered by a fleecy cloud.

But I forbear to dwell on the particulars of their cruise along the river. This vagrant amphibious life, careering across silver sheets of water; coasting wild woodland shores; banqueting on shady promontories, with the spreading tree over head, the river curling its light foam to one's feet, and distant mountain, and rock, and tree, and snowy cloud, and deep blue sky, all mingling in summer beauty before one; all this, though never cloying in the enjoyment, would be but tedious in narration.

When encamped by the water-side, some of the party would go into the woods and hunt; others would fish; sometimes they would amuse themselves by shooting at a mark, by leaping, by running, by wrestling; and Dolph gained great favour in the eyes of Antony Vander Heyden, by his skill and adroitness in all these exercises, which the Heer considered as the highest of manly accomplishments.

Thus did they coast jollily on, choosing only the pleasant hours for voyaging; sometimes in the cool morning dawn, sometimes in the sober evening twilight, and sometimes when the moonshine spangled the crisp curling waves that whispered along the sides of their little bark. Never had Dolph felt so completely in his element; never had he met with any thing so completely to his taste as this wild, hap-hazard life. He was the very man to second Antony Vander Heyden in his rambling humours, and gained continually on his affections. The heart of the old bush-whacker yearned towards the young man, who seemed thus growing up in his own likeness; and as they approached the end of their voyage, he could not help inquiring a little into his history. Dolph frankly told him his course of life, his severe medical studies, his little proficiency, and his very dubious prospects. The Heer was shocked to find that such amazing talents and accomplishments were to be cramped and buried under a doctor's wig. He had a sovereign contempt for the healing art, having never had any other physician than the butcher. He bore a mortal grudge to all kinds of study also, ever since he had been flogged about an unintelligible book when he was a boy. But to think that a young fellow like Dolph, of such wonderful abilities, who could shoot, fish, run, jump, ride, and wrestle, should be obliged to roll pills, and administer juleps for a living—'twas monstrous!

He told Dolph never to despair, but to "throw physic to the dogs;" for a young fellow of his prodigious talents could never fail to make his way. "As you seem to have no acquaintance in Albany," said Heer Antony, "you shall go home with me, and remain under my roof until you can look about you; and in the meantime we can take an occasional bout at shooting and fishing, for it is a pity such talents should lie idle."

Dolph, who was at the mercy of chance, was not hard to be persuaded. Indeed, on turning over matters in his mind, which he did very sagely and deliberately, he could not but think that Antony Vander Heyden was, "some how or other," connected with the story of the Haunted House; that the misadventure in the highlands, which had thrown them so strangely together, was, "some how or other," to work out something good: in short, there is nothing so convenient as this "some how or other" way of accommodating one's self to circumstances; it is the main stay of a heedless actor, and tardy reasoner, like Dolph Heyliger; and he who can, in this loose, easy way, link foregone evil to anticipated good, possesses a secret of happiness almost equal to the philosopher's stone.

On their arrival at Albany, the sight of Dolph's companion seemed to cause universal satisfaction. Many were the greetings at the river-side, and the salutations in the streets; the dogs bounded before him; the boys whooped as he passed; every body seemed to know Antony Vander Heyden. Dolph followed on in silence, admiring the neatness of this worthy burgh; for in those days Albany was in all its glory, and inhabited almost exclusively by the descendants of the original Dutch settlers, for it has not as yet been discovered and colonized by the restless people of New England. Every thing was quiet and orderly; every thing was conducted calmly and leisurely; no hurry, no bustle, no struggling and scrambling for existence. The grass grew about the unpaved streets, and relieved the eye by its refreshing verdure. Tall sycamores or pendent willows shaded the houses, with caterpillars swinging, in long silken strings, from their branches, or moths, fluttering about like coxcombs, in joy at their gay transformation. The houses were built in the old Dutch style, with the gable ends towards the street. The thrifty housewife was seated on

a bench before her door, in close crimped cap, bright flow-
ered gown, and white apron, busily employed in knitting.
The husband smoked his pipe on the opposite bench, and the
little pet negro girl, seated on the step at her mistress' feet,
was industriously plying her needle. The swallows sported
about the eaves, or skimmed along the streets, and brought
back some rich booty for their clamorous young; and the
little housekeeping wren flew in and out of a Lilliputian
house, or an old hat nailed against the wall. The cows were
coming home, lowing through the streets, to be milked at their
owner's door; and if, perchance, there were any loiterers,
some negro urchin, with a long goad, was gently urging them
homewards.

As Dolph's companion passed on, he received a tranquil
nod from the burghers, and a friendly word from their wives;
all calling him familiarly by the name of Antony; for it was
the custom in this strong hold of the patriarchs, where they
had all grown up together from childhood, to call every one
by the christian name. The Heer did not pause to have his
usual jokes with them, for he was impatient to reach his
home. At length they arrived at his mansion. It was of some
magnitude, in the Dutch style, with large iron figures on the
gables, that gave the date of its erection, and showed that it
had been built in the earliest times of the settlement.

The news of Heer Antony's arrival had preceded him, and
the whole household was on the look out. A crew of negroes,
large and small, had collected in front of the house to receive
him. The old, white-headed ones, who had grown gray in his
service, grinned for joy, and made many awkward bows and
grimaces, and the little ones capered about his knees. But the
most happy being in the household was a little, plump,
blooming lass, his only child, and the darling of his heart. She
came bounding out of the house; but the sight of a strange
young man with her father called up, for a moment, all the
bashfulness of a home-bred damsel. Dolph gazed at her with
wonder and delight; never had he seen, as he thought, any
thing so comely in the shape of woman. She was dressed in
the good old Dutch taste, with long stays, and full, short petticoats, so admirably adapted to show and set off the female
form. Her hair, turned up under a small round cap, displayed

the fairness of her forehead; she had fine blue, laughing eyes; a trim, slender waist, and soft swel——but, in a word, she was a little Dutch divinity; and Dolph, who never stopt half-way in a new impulse, fell desperately in love with her.

Dolph was now ushered into the house with a hearty welcome. In the interior was a mingled display of Heer Antony's taste and habits, and of the opulence of his predecessors. The chambers were furnished with good old mahogany; the beaufets and cupboards glittered with embossed silver, and painted china. Over the parlour fire-place was, as usual, the family coat of arms, painted and framed; above which was a long, duck fowling-piece, flanked by an Indian pouch, and a powder-horn. The room was decorated with many Indian articles, such as pipes of peace, tomahawks, scalping knives, hunting pouches, and belts of wampum; and there were various kinds of fishing tackle, and two or three fowling-pieces in the corners. The household affairs seemed to be conducted, in some measure, after the master's humours; corrected, perhaps, by a little quiet management of the daughter's. There was a great degree of patriarchal simplicity, and good-humored indulgence. The negroes came into the room without being called, merely to look at their master, and hear of his adventures; they would stand listening at the door until he had finished a story, and then go off on a broad grin, to repeat it in the kitchen. A couple of pet negro children were playing about the floor with the dogs, and sharing with them their bread and butter. All the domestics looked hearty and happy; and when the table was set for the evening repast, the variety and abundance of good household luxuries bore testimony to the open-handed liberality of the Heer, and the notable housewifery of his daughter.

In the evening there dropped in several of the worthies of the place, the Van Rennsellaers, and the Gansevoorts, and the Rosebooms, and others of Antony Vander Heyden's intimates, to hear an account of his expedition; for he was the Sindbad of Albany, and his exploits and adventures were favourite topics of conversation among the inhabitants. While these sat gossiping together about the door of the hall, and telling long twilight stories, Dolph was cozily seated, entertaining the daughter on a window-bench. He had already got

on intimate terms; for those were not times of false reserve
and idle ceremony: and, besides, there is something wonderfully propitious to a lover's suit, in the delightful dusk of a
long summer evening; it gives courage to the most timid
tongue, and hides the blushes of the bashful. The stars alone
twinkled brightly; and now and then a fire-fly streamed his
transient light before the window, or, wandering into the
room, flew gleaming about the ceiling.

What Dolph whispered in her ear that long summer evening it is impossible to say. His words were so low and indistinct, that they never reached the ear of the historian. It is
probable, however, that they were to the purpose; for he had
a natural talent at pleasing the sex, and was never long in the
company with a petticoat without paying proper court to it.
In the mean time the visitors, one by one, departed; Antony
Vander Heyden, who had fairly talked himself silent, sat nodding alone in his chair by the door, when he was suddenly
aroused by a hearty salute with which Dolph Heyliger had
unguardedly rounded off one of his periods, and which
echoed through the still chamber like the report of a pistol.
The Heer started up, rubbed his eyes, called for lights, and
observed, that it was high time to go to bed; though, on
parting for the night, he squeezed Dolph heartily by the
hand, looked kindly in his face, and shook his head knowingly; for the Heer well remembered what he himself had
been at the youngster's age.

The chamber in which our hero was lodged was spacious,
and pannelled with oak. It was furnished with clothes presses,
and mighty chests of drawers, well waxed, and glittering with
brass ornaments. These contained ample stock of family linen;
for the Dutch housewives had always a laudable pride in
showing off their household treasures to strangers.

Dolph's mind, however, was too full to take particular note
of the objects around him; yet he could not help continually
comparing the free, open-hearted cheeriness of this establishment, with the starveling, sordid, joyless housekeeping, at
Doctor Knipperhausen's. Still there was something that
marred the enjoyment; the idea that he must take leave of his
hearty host, and pretty hostess and cast himself once more
adrift upon the world. To linger here would be folly; he

should only get deeper in love: and for a poor varlet, like himself, to aspire to the daughter of the great Heer Vander Heyden—it was madness to think of such a thing! The very kindness that the girl had shown towards him prompted him, on reflection, to hasten his departure; it would be a poor return for the frank hospitality of his host, to entangle his daughter's heart in an injudicious attachment. In a word, Dolph was, like many other young reasoners, of exceeding good hearts, and giddy heads; who think after they act, and act differently from what they think; who make excellent determinations over night, and forget to keep them the next morning.

"This is a fine conclusion, truly, of my voyage," said he, as he almost buried himself in a sumptuous feather-bed, and drew the fresh white sheets up to his chin. "Here am I, instead of finding a bag of money to carry home, launched in a strange place, with scarcely a stiver in my pocket; and, what is worse, have jumped ashore up to my very ears in love into the bargain. However," added he, after some pause, stretching himself, and turning himself in bed, "I'm in good quarters for the present, at least; so I'll e'en enjoy the present moment, and let the next take care of itself. I dare say all will work out, 'some how or other,' for the best."

As he said these words, he reached out his hand to extinguish the candle, when he was suddenly struck with astonishment and dismay, for he thought he beheld the phantom of the Haunted House, staring on him from a dusky part of the chamber. A second look reassured him, as he perceived that what he had taken for the spectre was, in fact, nothing but a Flemish portrait, that hung in a shadowy corner, just behind a clothes press. It was, however, the precise representation of his nightly visitor. The same cloak and belted jerkin, the same grizzled beard and fixed eye, the same broad slouched hat, with a feather hanging over one side. Dolph now called to mind the resemblance he had frequently remarked between his host and the old man of the Haunted House; and was fully convinced that they were in some way connected, and that some especial destiny had governed his voyage. He lay gazing on the portrait with almost as much awe as he had gazed on the ghostly original, until the shrill house clock warned him of the lateness of the hour. He put out the light; but remained for a long time turning over these curious circumstances and coincidences in his mind, until he fell asleep. His dreams partook of the nature of his waking thoughts. He fancied that he still lay gazing on the picture, until, by degrees, it became animated; that the figure descended from the wall, and walked out of the room; that he followed it, and found himself by the well, to which the old man pointed, smiled on him, and disappeared.

In the morning, when Dolph waked, he found his host standing by his bed-side, who gave him a hearty morning's salutation, and asked him how he had slept. Dolph answered cheerily; but took occasion to inquire about the portrait that hung against the wall. "Ah," said Heer Antony, "that's a portrait of old Killian Vander Spiegel, once a burgomaster of Amsterdam, who, on some popular troubles, abandoned Holland, and came over to the province during the government of Peter Stuyvesant. He was my ancestor by the mother's side, and an old miserly curmudgeon he was. When the English took possession of New Amsterdam, in 1664, he retired into the country. He fell into a melancholy, apprehending that his wealth would be taken from him, and that he would come to beggary. He turned all his property into cash, and used to hide it away. He was for a year or two concealed in various places, fancying himself sought after by the English, to strip him of his wealth; and finally was found dead in his bed one morning, without any one being able to discover where he had concealed the greater part of his money."

When his host had left the room, Dolph remained for some time lost in thought. His whole mind was occupied by what he had heard. Vander Spiegel was his mother's family name; and he recollected to have heard her speak of this very Killian Vander Spiegel as one of her ancestors. He had heard her say, too, that her father was Killian's rightful heir, only that the old man died without leaving any thing to be inherited. It now appeared that Heer Antony was likewise a descendant, and perhaps an heir also, of this poor rich man; and that thus the Heyligers and the Vander Heydens were remotely connected. "What," thought he, "if, after all, this is the interpretation of my dream, that this is the way I am to make my

fortune by this voyage to Albany, and that I am to find the
old man's hidden wealth in the bottom of that well? But what
an odd round-about mode of communicating the matter!
Why the plague could not the old goblin have told me about
the well at once, without sending me all the way to Albany,
to hear a story that was to send me all the way back again?"

These thoughts passed through his mind while he was
dressing. He descended the stairs, full of perplexity, when the
bright face of Marie Vander Heyden suddenly beamed in
smiles upon him, and seemed to give him a clue to the whole
mystery. "After all," thought he, "the old goblin is in the
right. If I am to get his wealth, he means that I shall marry
his pretty descendant; thus both branches of the family
will be again united, and the property go on in the proper
channel."

No sooner did this idea enter his head, than it carried conviction with it. He was now all impatience to hurry back and
secure the treasure, which, he did not doubt, lay at the bottom of the well, and which he feared every moment might be
discovered by some other person. "Who knows," thought he,
"but this night-walking old fellow of the Haunted House may
be in the habit of haunting every visitor, and may give a hint
to some shrewder fellow than myself, who will take a shorter
cut to the well than by the way of Albany?" He wished a
thousand times that the babbling old ghost was laid in the
Red Sea, and his rambling portrait with him. He was in a
perfect fever to depart. Two or three days elapsed before any
opportunity presented for returning down the river. They
were ages to Dolph, notwithstanding that he was basking in
the smiles of the pretty Marie, and daily getting more and
more enamoured.

At length the very sloop from which he had been knocked
overboard prepared to make sail. Dolph made an awkward
apology to his host for his sudden departure. Antony Vander
Heyden was sorely astonished. He had concerted half a dozen
excursions into the wilderness; and his Indians were actually
preparing for a grand expedition to one of the lakes. He took
Dolph aside, and exerted his eloquence to get him to abandon
all thoughts of business and to remain with him, but in vain;
and he at length gave up the attempt, observing, "that it was

a thousand pities so fine a young man should throw himself away." Heer Antony, however, gave him a hearty shake by the hand at parting, with a favourite fowling-piece, and an invitation to come to his house whenever he revisited Albany. The pretty little Marie said nothing; but as he gave her a farewell kiss, her dimpled cheek turned pale, and a tear stood in her eye.

Dolph sprang lightly on board of the vessel. They hoisted sail; the wind was fair; they soon lost sight of Albany, and its green hills, and embowered islands. They were wafted gaily past the Kaatskill mountains, whose fairy heights were bright and cloudless. They passed prosperously through the high-lands, without any molestation from the Dunderberg goblin and his crew; they swept on across Haverstraw Bay, and by Croton Point, and through the Tappaan Zee, and under the Pallisadoes, until, in the afternoon of the third day, they saw the promontory of Hoboken, hanging like a cloud in the air; and, shortly after, the roofs of the Manhattoes rising out of the water.

Dolph's first care was to repair to his mother's house; for he was continually goaded by the idea of the uneasiness she must experience on his account. He was puzzling his brains, as he went along, to think how he should account for his absence, without betraying the secrets of the Haunted House. In the midst of these cogitations, he entered the street in which his mother's house was situated, when he was thunder-struck at beholding it a heap of ruins.

There had evidently been a great fire, which had destroyed several large houses, and the humble dwelling of poor dame Heyliger had been involved in the conflagration. The walls were not so completely destroyed, but that Dolph could distinguish some traces of the scene of his childhood. The fire-place, about which he had often played, still remained, orna-mented with Dutch tiles, illustrating passages in Bible history, on which he had many a time gazed with admiration. Among the rubbish lay the wreck of the good dame's elbow-chair, from which she had given him so many a wholesome precept; and hard by it was the family Bible, with brass clasps; now, alas! reduced almost to a cinder.

For a moment Dolph was overcome by this dismal sight,

for he was seized with the fear that his mother had perished in the flames. He was relieved, however, from this horrible apprehension, by one of the neighbours who happened to come by, and who informed him that his mother was yet alive.

The good woman had, indeed, lost every thing by this unlooked-for calamity; for the populace had been so intent upon saving the fine furniture of her rich neighbours, that the little tenement and the little all of poor dame Heyliger had been suffered to consume without interruption; nay, had it not been for the gallant assistance of her old crony, Peter de Groodt, the worthy dame and her cat might have shared the fate of their habitation.

As it was, she had been overcome with fright and affliction, and lay ill in body, and sick at heart. The public, however, had showed her its wonted kindness. The furniture of her rich neighbours being, as far as possible, rescued from the flames; themselves duly and ceremoniously visited and condoled with on the injury of their property, and their ladies commiserated on the agitation of their nerves; the public, at length, began to recollect something about poor dame Heyliger. She forthwith became again a subject of universal sympathy; every body pitied her more than ever; and if pity could but have been coined into cash—good Lord! how rich she would have been!

It was now determined, in good earnest, that something ought to be done for her without delay. The Dominie, therefore, put up prayers for her on Sunday, in which all the congregation joined most heartily. Even Cobus Groesbeek, the alderman, and Mynheer Milledollar, the great Dutch merchant, stood up in their pews, and did not spare their voices on the occasion; and it was thought the prayers of such great men could not but have their due weight. Doctor Knipperhausen, too, visited her professionally, and gave her abundance of advice gratis, and was universally lauded for his charity. As to her old friend, Peter de Groodt, he was a poor man, whose pity, and prayers, and advice, could be of but little avail, so he gave her all that was in his power—he gave her shelter.

To the humble dwelling of Peter de Groodt, then, did

Dolph turn his steps. On his way thither, he recalled all the tenderness and kindness of his simple-hearted parent, her indulgence of his errors, her blindness to his faults; and then he bethought himself of his own idle, harum-scarum life. "I've been a sad scapegrace," said Dolph, shaking his head sorrowfully. "I've been a complete sink-pocket, that's the truth of it!—But," added he briskly, and clasping his hands, "only let her live—only let her live—and I'll show myself indeed a son!"

As Dolph approached the house he met Peter de Groodt coming out of it. The old man started back aghast, doubting whether it was not a ghost that stood before him. It being bright daylight, however, Peter soon plucked up heart, satisfied that no ghost dare show his face in such clear sunshine. Dolph now learned from the worthy sexton the consternation and rumour to which his mysterious disappearance had given rise. It had been universally believed that he had been spirited away by those hobgoblin gentry that infested the Haunted House; and old Abraham Vandozer, who lived by the great Button-wood trees, at the three mile stone, affirmed, that he had heard a terrible noise in the air, as he was going home late at night, which seemed just as if a flight of wild-geese were over-head, passing towards the northward. The Haunted House was, in consequence, looked upon with ten times more awe than ever; nobody would venture to pass a night in it for the world, and even the doctor had ceased to make his expeditions to it in the daytime.

It required some preparation before Dolph's return could be made known to his mother, the poor soul having bewailed him as lost; and her spirits having been sorely broken down by a number of comforters, who daily cheered her with stories of ghosts, and of people carried away by the devil. He found her confined to her bed, with the other member of the Heyliger family, the good dame's cat, purring beside her, but sadly singed, and utterly despoiled of those whiskers which were the glory of her physiognomy. The poor woman threw her arms about Dolph's neck: "My boy! my boy! art thou still alive?" For a time she seemed to have forgotten all her losses and troubles in her joy at his return. Even the sage grimalkin showed indubitable signs of joy at the return of the youngster. She saw, perhaps, that they were a forlorn and undone family, and felt a touch of that kindliness which fellow-sufferers only know. But, in truth, cats are a slandered people; they have more affection in them than the world commonly gives them credit for.

The good dame's eyes glistened as she saw one being, at least, beside herself, rejoiced at her son's return. "Tib knows thee! poor dumb beast!" said she, smoothing down the mottled coat of her favourite; then recollecting herself, with a melancholy shake of the head, "Ah, my poor Dolph!" exclaimed she, "thy mother can help thee no longer! She can no longer help herself! What will become of thee, my poor boy!"

"Mother," said Dolph, "don't talk in that strain; I've been too long a charge upon you; it's now my part to take care of you in your old days. Come! be of good heart! You, and I, and Tib, will all see better days. I'm here, you see, young, and sound, and hearty; then don't let us despair; I dare say things will all, some how or other, turn out for the best."

While this scene was going on with the Heyliger family, the news was carried to Doctor Knipperhausen, of the safe return of his disciple. The little doctor scarcely knew whether to rejoice or be sorry at the tidings. He was happy at having the foul reports which had prevailed concerning his country mansion thus disproved; but he grieved at having his disciple, of whom he had supposed himself fairly disencumbered, thus drifting back, a heavy charge upon his hands. While he was balancing between these two feelings, he was determined by the counsels of Frau Ilsy, who advised him to take advantage of the truant absence of the youngster, and shut the door upon him for ever.

At the hour of bed-time, therefore, when it was supposed the recreant disciple would seek his old quarters, every thing was prepared for his reception. Dolph, having talked his mother into a state of tranquillity, sought the mansion of his quondam master, and raised the knocker with a faltering hand. Scarcely, however, had it given a dubious rap, when the doctor's head, in a red night-cap, popped out of one window, and the housekeeper's, in a white night-cap, out of another. He was now greeted with a tremendous volley of hard names and hard language, mingled with invaluable pieces of advice, such as are seldom ventured to be given excepting to a friend in distress, or a culprit at the bar. In a few moments, not a window in the street but had its particular night-cap, listening to the shrill treble of Frau Ilsy, and the guttural croaking of Dr. Knipperhausen; and the word went from window to window, "Ah! here's Dolph Heyliger come back, and at his old pranks again." In short, poor Dolph found he was likely to get nothing from the doctor but good advice; a commodity so abundant as even to be thrown out of the window; so he was fain to beat a retreat, and take up his quarters for the night under the lowly roof of honest Peter de Groodt.

The next morning, bright and early, Dolph was out at the Haunted House. Every thing looked just as he had left it. The fields were grass-grown and matted, and it appeared as if nobody had traversed them since his departure. With palpitating heart he hastened to the well. He looked down into it, and saw that it was of great depth, with water at the bottom. He had provided himself with a strong line, such as the fishermen use on the banks of Newfoundland. At the end was a heavy plummet and a large fish-hook. With this he began to sound the bottom of the well, and to angle about in the water. He found that the water was of some depth; there appeared also to be much rubbish, stones from the top having fallen in. Several times his hook got entangled, and he came near breaking his line. Now and then, too, he hauled up mere trash, such as the skull of a horse, an iron hoop, and a shattered iron-bound bucket. He had now been several hours employed without finding any thing to repay his trouble, or to encourage him to proceed. He began to think himself a great fool, to be thus decoyed into a wild-goose-chase by mere dreams, and was on the point of throwing line and all into the well, and giving up all further angling.

"One more cast of the line," said he, "and that shall be the last." As he sounded, he felt the plummet slip, as it were, through the interstices of loose stones; and as he drew back the line, he felt that the hook had taken hold of something heavy. He had to manage his line with great caution, lest it should be broken by the strain upon it. By degrees the rubbish that lay upon the article which he had hooked gave way; he drew it to the surface of the water, and what was his rap-

ture at seeing something like silver glittering at the end of his
line! Almost breathless with anxiety, he drew it up to the
mouth of the well, surprised at its great weight, and fearing
every instant that his hook would slip from its hold, and his
prize tumble again to the bottom. At length he landed it safe
beside the well. It was a great silver porringer, of an ancient
form, richly embossed, and with armorial bearings, similar to
those over his mother's mantel-piece, engraved on its side.
The lid was fastened down by several twists of wire; Dolph
loosened them with a trembling hand, and, on lifting the lid,
behold! the vessel was filled with broad golden pieces, of a
coinage which he had never seen before! It was evident he
had lit on the place where old Killian Vander Spiegel had
concealed his treasure.

Fearful of being seen by some straggler, he cautiously retired, and buried his pot of money in a secret place. He now
spread terrible stories about the Haunted House, and deterred every one from approaching it, while he made frequent
visits to it in stormy days, when no one was stirring in the
neighbouring fields; though, to tell the truth, he did not care
to venture there in the dark. For once in his life he was diligent and industrious, and followed up his new trade of angling with such perseverance and success, that in a little while
he had hooked up wealth enough to make him, in those moderate days, a rich burgher for life.

It would be tedious to detail minutely the rest of his story.
To tell how he gradually managed to bring his property into
use without exciting surprise and inquiry—how he satisfied
all scruples with regard to retaining the property, and at the
same time gratified his own feelings by marrying the pretty
Marie Vander Heyden—and how he and Heer Antony had
many a merry and roving expedition together.

I must not omit to say, however, that Dolph took his
mother home to live with him, and cherished her in her old
days. The good dame, too, had the satisfaction of no longer
hearing her son made the theme of censure; on the contrary,
he grew daily in public esteem; every body spoke well of him
and his wines; and the lordliest burgomaster was never
known to decline his invitation to dinner. Dolph often related, at his own table, the wicked pranks which had once

been the abhorrence of the town; but they were now considered excellent jokes, and the gravest dignitary was fain to hold his sides when listening to them. No one was more struck with Dolph's increasing merit than his old master the doctor; and so forgiving was Dolph, that he absolutely employed the doctor as his family physician, only taking care that his prescriptions should be always thrown out of the window. His mother had often her junto of old cronies to take a snug cup of tea with her in her comfortable little parlour; and Peter de Groodt, as he sat by the fireside, with one of her grandchildren on his knee, would many a time congratulate her upon her son turning out so great a man; upon which the good old soul would wag her head with exultation, and exclaim, "Ah, neighbour, neighbour! did I not say that Dolph would one day or other hold up his head with the best of them?"

Thus did Dolph Heyliger go on, cheerily and prosperously, growing merrier as he grew older and wiser, and completely falsifying the old proverb about money got over the devil's back; for he made good use of his wealth, and became a distinguished citizen, and a valuable member of the community. He was a great promoter of public institutions, such as beef-steak societies and catch-clubs. He presided at all public dinners, and was the first that introduced turtle from the West Indies. He improved the breed of race-horses and game-cocks, and was so great a patron of modest merit, that any-one, who could sing a good song, or tell a good story, was sure to find a place at his table.

He was a member, too, of the corporation, made several laws for the protection of game and oysters, and bequeathed to the board a large silver punch-bowl, made out of the identical porringer before-mentioned, and which is in the possession of the corporation to this very day.

Finally, he died, in a florid old age, of an apoplexy at a corporation feast, and was buried with great honours in the yard of the little Dutch church in Garden-street, where his tombstone may still be seen, with a modest epitaph in Dutch, by his friend Mynheer Justus Benson, an ancient and excellent poet of the province.

The foregoing tale rests on better authority than most tales of the kind, as I have it at second hand from the lips of Dolph

Heyliger himself. He never related it till towards the latter part of his life, and then in great confidence, (for he was very discreet) to a few of his particular cronies at his own table, over a supernumerary bowl of punch; and, strange as the hobgoblin parts of the story may seem, there never was a single doubt expressed on the subject by any of his guests. It may not be amiss, before concluding, to observe that, in addition to his other accomplishments, Dolph Heyliger was noted for being the ablest drawer of the long-bow in the whole province.

The Wedding

No more, no more, much honor aye betide
The lofty bridegroom, and the lovely bride;
That all of their succeeding days may say,
Each day appears like to a wedding-day.

Braithwaite

NOTWITHSTANDING the doubts and demurs of Lady Lillycraft, and all the grave objections that were conjured up against the month of May, yet the wedding has at length happily taken place. It was celebrated at the village church, in presence of a numerous company of relatives and friends, and many of the tenantry. The squire must needs have something of the old ceremonies observed on the occasion; so at the gate of the church-yard, several little girls of the village, dressed in white, were in readiness with baskets of flowers, which they strewed before the bride; and the butler bore before her the bride cup, a great silver embossed bowl, one of the family reliques from the days of the hard drinkers. This was filled with rich wine, and decorated with a branch of rosemary, tied with gay ribands, according to ancient custom.

"Happy is the bride that the sun shines on," says the old proverb; and it was as sunny and auspicious a morning as heart could wish. The bride looked uncommonly beautiful; but, in fact, what woman does not look interesting on her wedding-day? I know no sight more charming and touching than that of a young and timid bride, in her robes of virgin white, led up trembling to the altar. When I thus behold a lovely girl, in the tenderness of her years, forsaking the house of her fathers, and the home of her childhood; and, with the implicit confiding, and the sweet self-abandonment, which belong to woman, giving up all the world for the man of her choice; when I hear her, in the good old language of the ritual, yielding herself to him, "for better for worse, for richer for poorer, in sickness and in health, to love, honour, and obey, till death us do part," it brings to my mind the beautiful and affecting self-devotion of Ruth: "Whither thou goest I

will go, and where thou lodgest I will lodge; thy people shall
be my people, and thy God my God."

The fair Julia was supported on the trying occasion by
Lady Lillycraft, whose heart was overflowing with its wonted
sympathy in all matters of love and matrimony. As the bride
approached the altar, her face would be one moment covered
with blushes, and the next deadly pale; and she seemed almost
ready to shrink from sight among her female companions.

I do not know what it is that makes every one serious, and,
as it were, awe-struck at a marriage ceremony; which is generally considered as an occasion of festivity and rejoicing. As
the ceremony was performing, I observed many a rosy face
among the country girls turn pale, and I did not see a smile
throughout the church. The young ladies from the Hall were
almost as much frightened as if it had been their own case,
and stole many a look of sympathy at their trembling
companion. A tear stood in the eye of the sensitive Lady
Lillycraft; and as to Phœbe Wilkins, who was present, she
absolutely wept and sobbed aloud; but it is hard to tell, half
the time, what these fond foolish creatures are crying about.

The captain, too, though naturally gay and unconcerned,
was much agitated on the occasion; and, in attempting to put
the ring upon the bride's finger, dropped it on the floor;
which Lady Lillycraft has since assured me is a very lucky
omen. Even Master Simon had lost his usual vivacity, and had
assumed a most whimsically solemn face, which he is apt to
do on all occasions of ceremony. He had much whispering
with the parson and parish-clerk, for he is always a busy personage in the scene; and he echoed the clerk's amen with a
solemnity and devotion that edified the whole assemblage.

The moment, however, that the ceremony was over, the
transition was magical. The bride cup was passed round, according to ancient usage, for the company to drink to a happy
union; every one's feelings seemed to break forth from restraint; Master Simon had a world of bachelor pleasantries to
utter, and as to the gallant general, he bowed and cooed
about the dulcet Lady Lillycraft, like a mighty cock pigeon
about his dame.

The villagers gathered in the church-yard, to cheer the
happy couple as they left the church; and the musical tailor

had marshalled his band, and set up a hideous discord, as the blushing and smiling bride passed through a lane of honest peasantry to her carriage. The children shouted and threw up their hats; the bells rung a merry peal that set all the crows and rooks flying and cawing about the air, and threatened to bring down the battlements of the old tower; and there was a continual popping off of rusty firelocks from every part of the neighbourhood.

The prodigal son distinguished himself on the occasion, having hoisted a flag on the top of the school-house, and kept the village in a hubbub from sun-rise, with the sound of drum and fife and pandean pipe; in which species of music several of his scholars are making wonderful proficiency. In his great zeal, however, he had nearly done mischief; for on returning from church, the horses of the bride's carriage took fright from the discharge of a row of old gun-barrels, which he had mounted as a park of artillery in front of the school-house, to give the captain a military salute as he passed.

The day passed off with great rustic rejoicings. Tables were spread under the trees in the park, where all the peasantry of the neighbourhood were regaled with roast beef and plum-pudding, and oceans of ale. Ready Money Jack presided at one of the tables, and became so full of good cheer, as to unbend from his usual gravity, to sing a song out of all tune, and give two or three shouts of laughter, that almost electrified his neighbours, like so many peals of thunder. The schoolmaster and the apothecary vied with each other in making speeches over their liquor; and there were occasional glees and musical performances by the village band, that must have frightened every faun and dryad from the park. Even old Christy, who had got on a new dress, from top to toe, and shone in all the splendor of bright leather breeches, and an enormous wedding favour in his cap, forgot his usual crustiness, became inspired by wine and wassel, and absolutely danced a hornpipe on one of the tables, with all the grace and agility of a mannikin hung upon wires.

Equal gaiety reigned within doors, where a large party of friends were entertained. Every one laughed at his own pleasantry, without attending to that of his neighbours. Loads of bride-cake were distributed. The young ladies were all busy in passing morsels of it through the wedding ring to dream on, and I myself assisted a fine little boarding-school girl in putting up a quantity for her companions, which I have no doubt will set all the little heads in the school gadding, for a week at least.

After dinner all the company, great and small, gentle and simple, abandoned themselves to the dance: not the modern quadrille, with its graceful gravity, but the merry, social, old country dance; the true dance, as the squire says, for a wedding occasion; as it sets all the world jigging in couples, hand in hand, and makes every eye and every heart dance merrily to the music. According to frank old usage, the gentlefolks of the Hall mingled for a time in the dance of the peasantry, who had a great tent erected for a ball-room; and I think I never saw Master Simon more in his element than when figuring about among his rustic admirers, as master of the ceremonies; and, with a mingled air of protection and gallantry, leading out the quondam Queen of May; all blushing at the signal honour conferred upon her.

In the evening the whole village was illuminated, excepting the house of the radical, who has not shown his face during the rejoicings. There was a display of fireworks at the school-house, got up by the prodigal son, which had well nigh set fire to the building. The squire is so much pleased with the extraordinary services of this last-mentioned worthy, that he talks of enrolling him in his list of valuable retainers, and promoting him to some important post on the estate; peradventure to be falconer, if the hawks can ever be brought into proper training.

There is a well-known old proverb, that says, "one wedding makes many,"—or something to the same purpose; and I should not be surprised if it holds good in the present instance. I have seen several flirtations among the young people, that have been brought together on this occasion; and a great deal of strolling about in pairs, among the retired walks and blossoming shrubberies of the old garden; and if groves were really given to whispering, as poets would fain make us believe, Heaven knows what love-tales the grave-looking old trees about this venerable country seat might blab to the world.

The general, too, has waxed very zealous in his devotions within the last few days, as the time of her ladyship's departure approaches. I observed him casting many a tender look at her during the wedding-dinner, while the courses were changing; though he was always liable to be interrupted in his adoration by the appearance of any new delicacy. The general, in fact, has arrived at that time of life, when the heart and the stomach maintain a kind of balance of power; and when a man is apt to be perplexed in his affections between a fine woman and a truffled turkey. Her ladyship was certainly rivalled through the whole of the first course by a dish of stewed carp; and there was one glance, which was evidently intended to be a point-blank shot at her heart, and could scarcely have failed to effect a practicable breach, had it not unluckily been diverted away to a tempting breast of lamb, in which it immediately produced a formidable incision.

Thus did this faithless general go on, coquetting during the whole dinner, and committing an infidelity with every new dish; until, in the end, he was so overpowered by the attentions he had paid to fish, flesh, and fowl; to pastry, jelly, cream, and blanc-mange, that he seemed to sink within himself; his eyes swam beneath their lids, and their fire was so much slackened, that he could no longer discharge a single glance that would reach across the table. Upon the whole, I fear the general ate himself into as much disgrace, at this memorable dinner, as I have seen him sleep himself into on a former occasion.

I am told, moreover, that young Jack Tibbets was so touched by the wedding ceremony, at which he was present, and so captivated by the sensibility of poor Phœbe Wilkins, who certainly looked all the better for her tears, that he had a reconciliation with her that very day, after dinner, in one of the groves of the park, and danced with her in the evening; to the complete confusion of all Dame Tibbets' domestic politics. I met them walking together in the park, shortly after the reconciliation must have taken place. Young Jack carried himself gaily and manfully; but Phœbe hung her head, blushing, as I approached. However, just as she passed me, and dropped a curtesy, I caught a shy gleam of her eye from under her bonnet; but it was immediately cast down again. I saw enough in that single gleam, and in the involuntary smile that dimpled about her rosy lips, to feel satisfied that the little gipsy's heart was happy again.

What is more, Lady Lillycraft, with her usual benevolence and zeal in all matters of this tender nature, on hearing of the reconciliation of the lovers, undertook the critical task of breaking the matter to Ready Money Jack. She thought there was no time like the present, and attacked the sturdy old yeoman that very evening in the park, while his heart was yet lifted up with the squire's good cheer. Jack was a little surprised at being drawn aside by her ladyship, but was not to be flurried by such an honour: he was still more surprised by the nature of her communication, and by this first intelligence of an affair that had been passing under his eye. He listened, however, with his usual gravity, as her ladyship represented the advantages of the match, the good qualities of the girl, and the distress which she had lately suffered; at length his eye began to kindle, and his hand to play with the head of his cudgel. Lady Lillycraft saw that something in the narrative had gone wrong, and hastened to mollify his rising ire by reiterating the soft-hearted Phœbe's merit and fidelity, and her great unhappiness; when old Ready Money suddenly interrupted her by exclaiming, that if Jack did not marry the wench, he'd break every bone in his body! The match, therefore, is considered a settled thing; Dame Tibbets and the housekeeper have made friends, and drunk tea together; and Phœbe has again recovered her good looks and good spirits, and is carolling from morning till night like a lark.

But the most whimsical caprice of Cupid is one that I should be almost afraid to mention, did I not know that I was writing for readers well experienced in the waywardness of this most mischievous deity. The morning after the wedding, therefore, while Lady Lillycraft was making preparations for her departure, an audience was requested by her immaculate handmaid, Mrs. Hannah, who, with much primming of the mouth, and many maidenly hesitations, requested leave to stay behind, and that Lady Lillycraft would supply her place with some other servant. Her ladyship was astonished: "What! Hannah going to quit her, that had lived with her so long!"

"Why, one could not help it; one must settle in life some time or other."

The good lady was still lost in amazement; at length the secret was gasped from the dry lips of the maiden gentle-woman: "she had been some time thinking of changing her condition, and at length had given her word, last evening, to Mr. Christy, the huntsman."

How, or when, or where this singular courtship had been carried on, I have not been able to learn; nor how she has been able, with the vinegar of her disposition, to soften the stony heart of old Nimrod. So, however, it is, and it has as-tonished every one. With all her ladyship's love of match-making, this last fume of Hymen's torch has been too much for her. She has endeavoured to reason with Mrs. Hannah, but all in vain; her mind was made up, and she grew tart on the least contradiction. Lady Lillycraft applied to the squire for his interference. "She did not know what she should do without Mrs. Hannah, she had been used to have her about her so long a time."

The squire, on the contrary, rejoiced in the match, as relieving the good lady from a kind of toilet-tyrant, under whose sway she had suffered for years. Instead of thwarting the affair, therefore, he has given it his full countenance; and declares that he will set up the young couple in one of the best cottages on his estate. The approbation of the squire has been followed by that of the whole household; they all de-clare, that if ever matches are really made in heaven, this must have been; for that old Christy and Mrs. Hannah were as evidently formed to be linked together as ever were pepper-box and vinegar-cruet.

As soon as this matter was arranged, Lady Lillycraft took her leave of the family at the Hall; taking with her the captain and his blushing bride, who are to pass the honeymoon with her. Master Simon accompanied them on horseback, and indeed means to ride on ahead to make preparations. The general, who was fishing in vain for an invitation to her seat, handed her ladyship into her carriage with a heavy sigh; upon which his bosom friend, Master Simon, who was just mount-ing his horse, gave me a knowing wink, made an abominably wry face, and leaning from his saddle, whispered loudly in my

ear, "it won't do!" Then putting spurs to his horse, away he
cantered off. The general stood for some time waving his hat
after the carriage as it rolled down the avenue, until he was
seized with a fit of sneezing, from exposing his head to the
cool breeze. I observed that he returned rather thoughtfully
to the house; whistling softly to himself, with his hands behind his back, and an exceedingly dubious air.

The company have now almost all taken their departure. I
have determined to do the same to-morrow morning; and I
hope my reader may not think that I have already lingered
too long at the Hall. I have been tempted to do so, however,
because I thought I had lit upon one of the retired places
where there are yet some traces to be met with of old English
character. A little while hence, and all these will probably
have passed away. Ready Money Jack will sleep with his fathers. The good squire, and all his peculiarities, will be buried
in the neighbouring church. The old Hall will be modernised
into a fashionable country-seat, or peradventure a manufactory. The park will be cut up into petty farms and kitchen-
gardens. A daily coach will run through the village; it will
become, like all other common-place villages, thronged with
coachmen, post-boys, tipplers, and politicians; and Christmas,
May-day, and all the other hearty merry-makings of the
"good old times" will be forgotten.

The Author's Farewell

And so, without more circumstance at all,
I hold it fit that we shake hands, and part.
Hamlet

HAVING TAKEN leave of the Hall and its inmates, and brought the history of my visit to something like a close, there seems to remain nothing further than to make my bow and exit. It is my foible, however, to get on such companionable terms with my reader in the course of a work, that it really costs me some pain to part with him, and I am apt to keep him by the hand, and have a few farewell words at the end of my last volume.

When I cast an eye back upon the work I am just concluding, I cannot but be sensible how full it must be of errors and imperfections; indeed, how should it be otherwise, writing as I do, about subjects and scenes with which, as a stranger, I am but partially acquainted? Many will, doubtless, find cause to smile at very obvious blunders which I may have made; and many may, perhaps, be offended at what they may conceive prejudiced representations. Some will think I might have said much more on such subjects as may suit their peculiar tastes; whilst others will think I had done wiser to have left those subjects entirely alone.

It will, probably, be said, too, by some, that I view England with a partial eye. Perhaps I do; for I can never forget that it is my "father land." And yet the circumstances under which I have viewed it have by no means been such as were calculated to produce favourable impressions. For the greater part of the time that I have resided in it, I have lived almost unknowing and unknown; seeking no favours, and receiving none; "a stranger and a sojourner in the land," and subject to all the chills and neglects that are the common lot of the stranger.

When I consider these circumstances, and recollect how often I have taken up my pen, with a mind ill at ease, and spirits much dejected and cast down; I cannot but think I was not likely to err on the favourable side of the picture. The

opinions I have given of English character have been the result of much quiet, dispassionate, and varied observation. It is
a character not to be hastily studied, for it always puts on a
repulsive and ungracious aspect to a stranger. Let those, then,
who condemn my representations as too favourable, observe
this people as closely and deliberately as I have done, and they
will, probably, change their opinion. Of one thing, at any
rate, I am certain, that I have spoken honestly and sincerely,
from the convictions of my mind, and the dictates of my
heart. When I first published my former writings, it was with
no hope of gaining favour in English eyes, for I little thought
they were to become current out of my own country; and had
I merely sought popularity among my own countrymen, I
should have taken a more direct and obvious way, by gratifying rather than rebuking the angry feelings that were then
prevalent against England.

And here let me acknowledge my warm, my thankful feelings, at the effect produced by one of my trivial lucubrations.
I allude to the essay in the Sketch-Book, on the subject of the
literary feuds between England and America. I cannot express
the heartfelt delight I have experienced, at the unexpected
sympathy and approbation with which those remarks have
been received on both sides of the Atlantic. I speak this not
from any paltry feelings of gratified vanity; for I attribute the
effect to no merit of my pen. The paper in question was brief
and casual, and the ideas it conveyed were simple and obvious. "It was the cause; it was the cause" alone. There was a
predisposition on the part of my readers to be favourably affected. My countrymen responded in heart to the filial feelings I had avowed in their name towards the parent country;
and there was a generous sympathy in every English bosom
towards a solitary individual, lifting up his voice in a strange
land, to vindicate the injured character of his nation. There
are some causes so sacred as to carry with them an irresistible
appeal to every virtuous bosom; and he needs but little power
of eloquence, who defends the honour of his wife, his
mother, or his country.

I hail, therefore, the success of that brief paper, as showing
how much good may be done by a kind word, however feeble, when spoken in season—as showing how much dormant

good feeling actually exists in each country, towards the other, which only wants the slightest spark to kindle it into a genial flame—as showing, in fact, what I have all along believed and asserted, that the two nations would grow together in esteem and amity, if meddling and malignant spirits would but throw by their mischievous pens, and leave kindred hearts to the kindly impulses of nature.

I once more assert, and I assert it with increased conviction of its truth, that there exists, among the great majority of my countrymen, a favourable feeling towards England. I repeat this assertion, because I think it a truth that cannot too often be reiterated, and because it has met with some contradiction. Among all the liberal and enlightened minds of my countrymen, among all those which eventually give a tone to national opinion, there exists a cordial desire to be on terms of courtesy and friendship. But, at the same time, there exists in those very minds a distrust of reciprocal good will on the part of England. They have been rendered morbidly sensitive by the attacks made upon their country by the English press; and their occasional irritability on this subject has been misinterpreted into a settled and unnatural hostility.

For my part, I consider this jealous sensibility as belonging to generous natures. I should look upon my countrymen as fallen indeed from that independence of spirit which is their birth-gift; as fallen indeed from that pride of character which they inherit from the proud nation from which they sprung, could they tamely sit down under the infliction of contumely and insult. Indeed the very impatience which they show as to the misrepresentations of the press, proves their respect for English opinion, and their desire for English amity; for there is never jealousy where there is not strong regard.

It is easy to say that these attacks are all the effusions of worthless scribblers, and treated with silent contempt by the nation; but alas! the slanders of the scribbler travel abroad, and the silent contempt of the nation is only known at home. With England, then, it remains, as I have formerly asserted, to promote a mutual spirit of conciliation; she has but to hold the language of friendship and respect, and she is secure of the good will of every American bosom.

In expressing these sentiments I would utter nothing that

should commit the proper spirit of my countrymen. We seek no boon at England's hands. We ask nothing as a favour. Her friendship is not necessary, nor would her hostility be dangerous to our well-being. We ask nothing from abroad that we cannot reciprocate. But with respect to England, we have a warm feeling of the heart, the glow of consanguinity that still lingers in our blood. Interest apart—past differences forgotten—we extend the hand of old relationship. We merely ask, do not estrange us from you; do not destroy the ancient tie of blood; do not let scoffers and slanderers drive a kindred nation from your side: we would fain be friends; do not compel us to be enemies.

There needs no better rallying ground for international amity, than that furnished by an eminent English writer: "There is," says he, "a sacred bond between us of blood and of language, which no circumstances can break. Our literature must always be theirs; and though their laws are no longer the same as ours, we have the same Bible, and we address our common Father in the same prayer. Nations are too ready to admit that they have natural enemies; why should they be less willing to believe that they have natural friends?"*

To the magnanimous spirits of both countries must we trust to carry such a natural alliance of affection into full effect. To pens more powerful than mine I leave the noble task of promoting the cause of national amity. To the intelligent and enlightened of my own country, I address my parting voice, entreating them to show themselves superior to the petty attacks of the ignorant and the worthless, and still to look with dispassionate and philosophic eye to the moral character of England, as the intellectual source of our rising greatness; while I appeal to every generous-minded Englishman from the slanders which disgrace the press, insult the understanding, and belie the magnanimity of his country: and I invite him to look to America, as to a kindred nation, worthy of its origin; giving, in the healthy vigour of its growth, the best of comments on its parent stock; and reflecting, in

*From an article (said to be by Robert Southey, Esq.), published in the Quarterly Review. It is to be lamented that that publication should so often forget the generous text here given!

the dawning brightness of its fame, the moral effulgence of British glory.

I am sure that such appeal will not be made in vain. Indeed I have noticed, for some time past, an essential change in English sentiment with regard to America. In parliament, that fountain-head of public opinion, there seems to be an emulation, on both sides of the house, in holding the language of courtesy and friendship. The same spirit is daily becoming more and more prevalent in good society. There is a growing curiosity concerning my country; a craving desire for correct information, that cannot fail to lead to a favourable understanding. The scoffer, I trust, has had his day; the time of the slanderer is gone by. The ribald jokes, the stale commonplaces, which have so long passed current when America was the theme, are now banished to the ignorant and the vulgar, or only perpetuated by the hireling scribblers and traditional jesters of the press. The intelligent and high-minded now pride themselves upon making America a study.

But however my feelings may be understood or reciprocated on either side of the Atlantic, I utter them without reserve, for I have ever found that to speak frankly is to speak safely. I am not so sanguine as to believe that the two nations are ever to be bound together by any romantic ties of feeling; but I believe that much may be done towards keeping alive cordial sentiments, were every well disposed mind occasionally to throw in a simple word of kindness. If I have, indeed, produced any such effect by my writings, it will be a soothing reflection to me, that for once, in the course of a rather negligent life, I have been useful; that for once, by the casual exercise of a pen which has been in general but too unprofitably employed, I have awakened a chord of sympathy between the land of my fathers and the dear land that gave me birth.

In the spirit of these sentiments I now take my farewell of the paternal soil. With anxious eye do I behold the clouds of doubt and difficulty that are lowering over it, and earnestly do I hope that they may all clear up into serene and settled sunshine. In bidding this last adieu, my heart is filled with fond, yet melancholy emotions; and still I linger, and still, like a child, leaving the venerable abodes of his forefathers, I turn to breathe forth a filial benediction: "Peace be within thy walls, oh England! and plenteousness within thy palaces; for my brethren and my companions' sake I will now say, Peace be within thee!"

THE END

TALES OF A TRAVELLER
BY
GEOFFREY CRAYON, GENT.

I am neither your minotaure, nor your centaure, nor your satyr, nor your hyæna, nor your babion, but your meer traveller, believe me.

BEN JONSON

Contents

To the Reader

WORTHY AND DEAR READER!
Hast thou ever been waylaid in the midst of a pleasant tour by some treacherous malady; thy heels tripped up, and thou left to count the tedious minutes as they passed, in the solitude of an inn chamber? If thou hast, thou wilt be able to pity me. Behold me, interrupted in the course of my journeying up the fair banks of the Rhine, and laid up by indisposition in this old frontier town of Mentz. I have worn out every source of amusement. I know the sound of every clock that strikes, and bell that rings, in the place. I know to a second when to listen for the first tap of the Prussian drum, as it summons the garrison to parade; or at what hour to expect the distant sound of the Austrian military band. All these have grown wearisome to me, and even the well known step of my doctor, as he slowly paces the corridor, with healing in the creak of his shoes, no longer affords an agreeable interruption to the monotony of my apartment.

For a time I attempted to beguile the weary hours by studying German under the tuition of mine host's pretty little daughter, Katrine; but I soon found even German had not power to charm a languid ear, and that the conjugating of *ich liebe* might be powerless, however rosy the lips which uttered it.

I tried to read, but my mind would not fix itself; I turned over volume after volume, but threw them by with distaste: "Well, then," said I at length in despair, "if I cannot read a book, I will write one." Never was there a more lucky idea; it at once gave me occupation and amusement.

The writing of a book was considered, in old times, as an enterprise of toil and difficulty, insomuch that the most trifling lucubration was denominated a "work," and the world talked with awe and reverence of "the labours of the learned." These matters are better understood now adays. Thanks to the improvements in all kind of manufactures, the art of book making has been made familiar to the meanest capacity. Every body is an author. The scribbling of a quarto is the mere pastime of the idle; the young gentleman throws off his brace of duodecimos in the intervals of the sporting season, and the young lady produces her set of volumes with the same facility that her great grandmother worked a set of chair bottoms.

The idea having struck me, therefore, to write a book, the reader will easily perceive that the execution of it was no difficult matter. I rummaged my portfolio, and cast about, in my recollection, for those floating materials which a man naturally collects in travelling; and here I have arranged them in this little work.

As I know this to be a story telling and a story reading age, and that the world is fond of being taught by apologue, I have digested the instruction I would convey into a number of tales. They may not possess the power of amusement which the tales told by many of my contemporaries possess; but then I value myself on the sound moral which each of them contains. This may not be apparent at first, but the reader will be sure to find it out in the end. I am for curing the world by gentle alteratives, not by violent doses; indeed the patient should never be conscious that he is taking a dose. I have learnt this much from my experience under the hands of the worthy Hippocrates of Mentz.

I am not, therefore, for those barefaced tales which carry their moral on the surface, staring one in the face; they are enough to deter the squeamish reader. On the contrary, I have often hid my moral from sight, and disguised it as much as possible by sweets and spices, so that while the simple reader is listening with open mouth to a ghost or a love story, he may have a bolus of sound morality popped down his throat, and be never the wiser for the fraud.

As the public is apt to be curious about the sources whence an author draws his stories, doubtless that it may know how far to put faith in them, I would observe, that the Adventure of the German Student, or rather the latter part of it, is founded on an anecdote related to me as existing somewhere in French; and, indeed, I have been told, since writing it, that an ingenious tale has been founded on it by an English writer; but I have never met with either the former or the latter in print. Some of the circumstances in the Adventure of the Mysterious Picture, and in the Story of the Young Italian, are vague recollections of anecdotes related to me some years since; but from what source derived I do not know. The Adventure of the Young Painter among the banditti is taken almost entirely from an authentic narrative in manuscript.

As to the other tales contained in this work, and, indeed, to my tales generally, I can make but one observation. I am an old traveller. I have read somewhat, heard and seen more, and dreamt more than all. My brain is filled, therefore, with all kinds of odds and ends. In travelling, these heterogeneous matters have become shaken up in my mind, as the articles are apt to be in an ill packed travelling trunk; so that when I attempt to draw forth a fact, I cannot determine whether I have read, heard, or dreamt it; and I am always at a loss to know how much to believe of my own stories.

These matters being premised, fall to, worthy reader, with good appetite, and, above all, with good humour, to what is here set before thee. If the tales I have furnished should prove to be bad, they will at least be found short; so that no one will be wearied long on the same theme. "Variety is charming," as some poet observes. There is a certain relief in change, even though it be from bad to worse; as I have found in travelling in a stage coach, that it is often a comfort to shift one's position and be bruised in a new place.

Ever thine,
GEOFFREY CRAYON

Dated from the HOTEL DE DARMSTADT,
ci-devant HOTEL DE PARIS,
MENTZ, *otherwise called* MAYENCE.

PART I

STRANGE STORIES

BY A NERVOUS GENTLEMAN

I'll tell you more; there was a fish taken,
A monstrous fish, with a sword by's side, a long sword,
A pike in's neck, and a gun in's nose, a huge gun.
And letters of mart in's mouth, from the Duke of Florence.
   Cleanthes. This is a monstrous lie.
   Tony. I do confess it.
Do you think I'd tell you truths?
FLETCHER'S WIFE FOR A MONTH

The Great Unknown

The following adventures were related to me by the same nervous gentleman who told me the romantic tale of THE STOUT GENTLEMAN, published in Bracebridge Hall.

It is very singular, that although I expressly stated that story to have been told to me, and described the very person who told it, still it has been received as an adventure that happened to myself. Now, I protest I never met with any adventure of the kind. I should not have grieved at this, had it not been intimated by the author of Waverley, in an introduction to his novel of Peveril of the Peak, that he was himself the Stout Gentleman alluded to. I have ever since been importuned by questions and letters from gentlemen, and particularly from ladies without number, touching what I had seen of the great unknown.

Now, all this is extremely tantalizing. It is like being congratulated on the high prize when one has drawn a blank; for I have just as great a desire as any one of the public to penetrate the mystery of that very singular personage, whose voice fills every corner of the world, without any one being able to tell whence it comes.

My friend, the nervous gentleman, also, who is a man of very shy retired habits, complains that he has been excessively annoyed in consequence of its getting about in his neighbourhood that he is the fortunate personage. Insomuch, that he has become a character of considerable notoriety in two or three country towns; and has been repeatedly teased to exhibit himself at blue stocking parties, for no other reason than that of being "the gentleman who has had a glimpse of the author of Waverley."

Indeed, the poor man has grown ten times as nervous as ever, since he has discovered, on such good authority, who the stout gentleman was; and will never forgive himself for not having made a more resolute effort to get a full sight of him. He has anxiously endeavoured to call up a recollection of what he saw of that portly personage; and has ever since kept a curious eye on all gentlemen of more than ordinary dimensions, whom he has seen getting into stage coaches. All in vain! The features he had caught a glimpse of seem common to the whole race of stout gentlemen; and the great unknown remains as great an unknown as ever.

————

Having premised these circumstances, I will now let the nervous gentleman proceed with his stories.

The Hunting Dinner

I was once at a hunting dinner, given by a worthy fox-hunting old Baronet, who kept Bachelor's Hall in jovial style, in an ancient rook-haunted family mansion, in one of the middle counties. He had been a devoted admirer of the fair sex in his young days; but having travelled much, studied the sex in various countries with distinguished success, and returned home profoundly instructed, as he supposed, in the ways of woman, and a perfect master of the art of pleasing, he had the mortification of being jilted by a little boarding school girl, who was scarcely versed in the accidence of love.

The Baronet was completely overcome by such an incredible defeat; retired from the world in disgust, put himself under the government of his housekeeper, and took to fox hunting like a perfect Nimrod. Whatever poets may say to the contrary, a man will grow out of love as he grows old; and a pack of fox hounds may chase out of his heart even the memory of a boarding school goddess. The Baronet was when I saw him as merry and mellow an old bachelor as ever followed a hound; and the love he had once felt for one woman had spread itself over the whole sex; so that there was not a pretty face in the whole country round, but came in for a share.

The dinner was prolonged till a late hour; for our host having no ladies in his household to summon us to the drawing room, the bottle maintained its true bachelor sway, unrivalled by its potent enemy the tea kettle. The old hall in which we dined echoed to bursts of robustious fox hunting merriment, that made the ancient antlers shake on the walls. By degrees, however, the wine and wassail of mine host began to operate

upon bodies already a little jaded by the chase. The choice
spirits which flashed up at the beginning of the dinner, sparkled for a time, then gradually went out one after another, or
only emitted now and then a faint gleam from the socket.
Some of the briskest talkers, who had given tongue so bravely
at the first burst, fell fast asleep; and none kept on their way
but certain of those long winded prosers, who, like short
legged hounds, worry on unnoticed at the bottom of conversation, but are sure to be in at the death. Even these at length
subsided into silence; and scarcely any thing was heard but
the nasal communications of two or three veteran masticators,
who, having been silent while awake, were indemnifying the
company in their sleep.

At length the announcement of tea and coffee in the cedar
parlour roused all hands from this temporary torpor. Every
one awoke marvellously renovated, and while sipping the
refreshing beverage out of the Baronet's old fashioned hereditary china, began to think of departing for their several
homes. But here a sudden difficulty arose. While we had been
prolonging our repast, a heavy winter storm had set in, with
snow, rain, and sleet, driven by such bitter blasts of wind,
that they threatened to penetrate to the very bone.

"It's all in vain," said our hospitable host, "to think of putting one's head out of doors in such weather. So, gentlemen,
I hold you my guests for this night at least, and will have your
quarters prepared accordingly."

The unruly weather, which became more and more tempestuous, rendered the hospitable suggestion unanswerable. The
only question was, whether such an unexpected accession of
company, to an already crowded house, would not put the
housekeeper to her trumps to accommodate them.

"Pshaw," cried mine host, "did you ever know of a Bachelor's Hall that was not elastic, and able to accommodate twice
as many as it could hold?" So out of a good humoured pique
the housekeeper was summoned to consultation before us all.
The old lady appeared, in her gala suit of faded brocade,
which rustled with flurry and agitation, for in spite of our
host's bravado, she was a little perplexed. But in a bachelor's
house, and with bachelor guests, these matters are readily managed. There is no lady of the house to stand upon squeamish

points about lodging gentlemen in odd holes and corners, and exposing the shabby parts of the establishment. A bachelor's housekeeper is used to shifts and emergencies; so, after much worrying to and fro; and divers consultations about the red room, and the blue room, and the chintz room, and the damask room, and the little room with the bow window, the matter was finally arranged.

When all this was done, we were once more summoned to the standing rural amusement of eating. The time that had been consumed in dozing after dinner, and in the refreshment and consultation of the cedar parlour, was sufficient, in the opinion of the rosy faced butler, to engender a reasonable appetite for supper. A slight repast had therefore been tricked up from the residue of dinner, consisting of a cold sirloin of beef; hashed venison; a devilled leg of a turkey or so, and a few other of those light articles taken by country gentlemen to ensure sound sleep and heavy snoring.

The nap after dinner had brightened up every one's wit; and a great deal of excellent humour was expended upon the perplexities of mine host and his housekeeper, by certain married gentlemen of the company, who considered themselves privileged in joking with a bachelor's establishment. From this the banter turned as to what quarters each would find, on being thus suddenly billeted in so antiquated a mansion.

"By my soul," said an Irish captain of dragoons, one of the most merry and boisterous of the party—"by my soul, but I should not be surprised if some of those good looking gentlefolks that hang along the walls, should walk about the rooms of this stormy night; or if I should find the ghost of one of these long waisted ladies turning into my bed in mistake for her grave in the church yard."

"Do you believe in ghosts, then?" said a thin hatchet-faced gentleman, with projecting eyes like a lobster.

I had remarked this last personage during dinner time for one of those incessant questioners, who have a craving, unhealthy, appetite in conversation. He never seemed satisfied with the whole of a story; never laughed when others laughed; but always put the joke to the question. He could never enjoy the kernel of the nut, but pestered himself to get more out of the shell.

"Do you believe in ghosts, then?" said the inquisitive gentleman.

"Faith, but I do," replied the jovial Irishman; "I was brought up in the fear and belief of them: we had a Benshee in our own family, honey."

"A Benshee—and what's that?" cried the questioner.

"Why an old lady ghost that tends upon your real Milesian families, and wails at their window to let them know when some of them are to die."

"A mighty pleasant piece of information," cried an elderly gentleman, with a knowing look and a flexible nose, to which he could give a whimsical twist when he wished to be waggish.

"By my soul, but I'd have you to know it's a piece of distinction to be waited on by a Benshee. It's a proof that one has pure blood in one's veins. But i'faith, now we are talking of ghosts, there never was a house or a night better fitted than the present for a ghost adventure. Pray, Sir John, haven't you such a thing as a haunted chamber to put a guest in?"

"Perhaps," said the Baronet smiling, "I might accommodate you even on that point."

"Oh, I should like it of all things, my jewel. Some dark oaken room, with ugly wobegone portraits that stare dismally at one, and about which the housekeeper has a power of delightful stories of love and murder. And then a dim lamp, a table with a rusty sword across it, and a spectre all in white to draw aside one's curtains at midnight"——

"In truth," said an old gentleman at one end of the table, "you put me in mind of an anecdote"——

"Oh, a ghost story! a ghost story!" was vociferated round the board, every one edging his chair a little nearer.

The attention of the whole company was now turned upon the speaker. He was an old gentleman, one side of whose face was no match for the other. The eyelid drooped and hung down like an unhinged window shutter. Indeed, the whole side of his head was dilapidated, and seemed like the wing of a house shut up and haunted. I'll warrant that side was well stuffed with ghost stories.

There was a universal demand for the tale.

"Nay," said the old gentleman, "it's a mere anecdote—and a very commonplace one; but such as it is you shall have it. It is a story that I once heard my uncle tell as having happened to himself. He was a man very apt to meet with strange adventures. I have heard him tell of others much more singular."

"What kind of man was your uncle?" said the questioning gentleman.

"Why, he was rather a dry, shrewd kind of body; a great traveller, and fond of telling his adventures."

"Pray, how old might he have been when this happened?"

"When what happened?" cried the gentleman with the flexible nose, impatiently—"Egad, you have not given any thing a chance to happen—come, never mind our uncle's age; let us have his adventures."

The inquisitive gentleman being for the moment silenced, the old gentleman with the haunted head proceeded.

The Adventure of My Uncle

Many years since, some time before the French revolution, my uncle passed several months at Paris. The English and French were on better terms, in those days, than at present, and mingled cordially in society. The English went abroad to spend money then, and the French were always ready to help them: they go abroad to save money at present, and that they can do without French assistance. Perhaps the travelling English were fewer and choicer than at present, when the whole nation has broke loose, and inundated the continent. At any rate, they circulated more readily and currently in foreign society, and my uncle, during his residence at Paris, made many very intimate acquaintances among the French noblesse.

Some time afterwards, he was making a journey in the winter time, in that part of Normandy called the Pays de Caux, when, as evening was closing in, he perceived the turrets of an ancient chateau rising out of the trees of its walled park, each turret with its high conical roof of grey slate, like a candle with an extinguisher on it.

"To whom does that chateau belong, friend?" cried my uncle to a meagre but fiery postillion, who, with tremendous jack boots and cocked hat, was floundering on before him.

"To Monseigneur the Marquis de ——," said the postillion, touching his hat, partly out of respect to my uncle, and partly out of reverence to the noble name pronounced. My uncle recollected the Marquis for a particular friend in Paris, who had often expressed a wish to see him at his paternal chateau. My uncle was an old traveller, one who knew how to turn things to account. He revolved for a few moments in his mind how agreeable it would be to his friend the Marquis to be surprised in this sociable way by a pop visit; and how much more agreeable to himself to get into snug quarters in a chateau, and have a relish of the Marquis's well known kitchen, and a smack of his superior champagne and burgundy; rather than put up with the miserable lodgement, and miserable fare of a provincial inn. In a few minutes, therefore, the meagre postillion was cracking his whip like a very devil, or like a true Frenchman, up the long straight avenue that led to the chateau.

You have no doubt all seen French chateaus, as every body travels in France now adays. This was one of the oldest; standing naked and alone, in the midst of a desert of gravel walks and cold stone terraces; with a cold looking formal garden, cut into angles and rhomboids; and a cold leafless park, divided geometrically by straight alleys; and two or three cold looking noseless statues; and fountains spouting cold water enough to make one's teeth chatter. At least, such was the feeling they imparted on the wintry day of my uncle's visit; though, in hot summer weather, I'll warrant there was glare enough to scorch one's eyes out.

The smacking of the postillion's whip, which grew more and more intense the nearer they approached, frightened a flight of pigeons out of the dove cote, and rooks out of the roofs; and finally a crew of servants out of the chateau, with the Marquis at their head. He was enchanted to see my uncle; for his chateau, like the house of our worthy host, had not many more guests at the time than it could accommodate. So he kissed my uncle on each cheek, after the French fashion, and ushered him into the castle.

The Marquis did the honours of the house with the urbanity of his country. In fact, he was proud of his old family chateau; for part of it was extremely old. There was a tower

and chapel which had been built almost before the memory of
man; but the rest was more modern; the castle having been
nearly demolished during the wars of the League. The Marquis dwelt upon this event with great satisfaction, and seemed
really to entertain a grateful feeling towards Henry the
Fourth, for having thought his paternal mansion worth bat-
tering down. He had many stories to tell of the prowess of his
ancestors, and several skull caps, helmets and cross bows, and
divers huge boots and buff jerkins, to show, which had been
worn by the Leaguers. Above all, there was a two handled
sword, which he could hardly wield; but which he displayed
as a proof that there had been giants in his family.

In truth, he was but a small descendant from such great
warriors. When you looked at their bluff visages and brawny
limbs, as depicted in their portraits, and then at the little Marquis, with his spindle shanks, and his sallow lanthern visage,
flanked with a pair of powdered ear locks, or *ailes de pigeon*,
that seemed ready to fly away with it; you could hardly believe him to be of the same race. But when you looked at the
eyes that sparkled out like a beetle's from each side of his
hooked nose, you saw at once that he inherited all the fiery
spirit of his forefathers. In fact, a Frenchman's spirit never
exhales, however his body may dwindle. It rather rarifies, and
grows more inflammable, as the earthy particles diminish; and
I have seen valour enough in a little fiery hearted French
dwarf, to have furnished out a tolerable giant.

When once the Marquis, as he was wont, put on one of the
old helmets stuck up in his hall; though his head no more
filled it than a dry pea its pease cod; yet his eyes flashed from
the bottom of the iron cavern with the brilliancy of car-
buncles; and when he poised the ponderous two handled
sword of his ancestors, you would have thought you saw
the doughty little David wielding the sword of Goliah, which
was unto him like a weaver's beam.

However, gentlemen, I am dwelling too long on this description of the Marquis and his chateau; but you must excuse
me; he was an old friend of my uncle's, and whenever my
uncle told the story, he was always fond of talking a great deal
about his host.—Poor little Marquis! He was one of that
handful of gallant courtiers, who made such a devoted, but

hopeless stand in the cause of their sovereign, in the chateau of the Tuilleries, against the irruption of the mob, on the sad tenth of August. He displayed the valour of a preux French chevalier to the last; flourished feebly his little court sword with a sa-sa! in face of a whole legion of *sans culottes*; but was pinned to the wall like a butterfly, by the pike of a poissarde, and his heroic soul was borne up to heaven on his *ailes de pigeon*.

But all this has nothing to do with my story: to the point then:—When the hour arrived for retiring for the night, my uncle was shown to his room, in a venerable old tower. It was the oldest part of the chateau, and had in ancient times been the Donjon or strong hold; of course the chamber was none of the best. The Marquis had put him there, however, because he knew him to be a traveller of taste, and fond of antiquities; and also because the better apartments were already occupied. Indeed, he perfectly reconciled my uncle to his quarters by mentioning the great personages who had once inhabited them, all of whom were in some way or other connected with the family. If you would take his word for it, John Baliol, or as he called him Jean de Bailleul had died of chagrin in this very chamber on hearing of the success of his rival, Robert the Bruce, at the battle of Bannockburn; and when he added that the Duke de Guise had slept in it, my uncle was fain to felicitate himself upon being honoured with such distinguished quarters.

The night was shrewd and windy, and the chamber none of the warmest. An old long faced, long bodied servant in quaint livery, who attended upon my uncle, threw down an armful of wood beside the fire place, gave a queer look about the room, and then wished him *bon repos*, with a grimace and a shrug that would have been suspicious from any other than an old French servant. The chamber had indeed a wild crazy look, enough to strike any one who had read romances with apprehension and foreboding. The windows were high and narrow, and had once been loop holes, but had been rudely enlarged, as well as the extreme thickness of the walls would permit; and the ill fitted casements rattled to every breeze. You would have thought, on a windy night, some of the old Leaguers were tramping and clanking about the apartment in their huge boots and rattling spurs. A door which stood ajar, and like a true French door would stand ajar, in spite of every reason and effort to the contrary, opened upon a long dark corridor, that led the Lord knows whither, and seemed just made for ghosts to air themselves in, when they turned out of their graves at midnight. The wind would spring up into a hoarse murmur through this passage, and creak the door to and fro, as if some dubious ghost were balancing in its mind whether to come in or not. In a word, it was precisely the kind of comfortless apartment that a ghost, if ghost there were in the chateau, would single out for its favourite lounge.

My uncle, however, though a man accustomed to meet with strange adventures, apprehended none at the time. He made several attempts to shut the door, but in vain. Not that he apprehended any thing, for he was too old a traveller to be daunted by a wild looking apartment; but the night, as I have said, was cold and gusty, and the wind howled about the old turret, pretty much as it does round this old mansion at this moment; and the breeze from the long dark corridor came in as damp and chilly as if from a dungeon. My uncle, therefore, since he could not close the door threw a quantity of wood on the fire, which soon sent up a flame in the great wide mouthed chimney that illumined the whole chamber, and made the shadow of the tongs, on the opposite wall, look like a long legged giant. My uncle now clambered on top of the half score of mattresses which form a French bed, and which stood in a deep recess; then tucking himself snugly in, and burying himself up to the chin in the bed clothes, he lay looking at the fire, and listening to the wind, and thinking how knowingly he had come over his friend the Marquis for a night's lodging: and so he fell asleep.

He had not taken above half of his first nap, when he was awakened by the clock of the chateau, in the turret over his chamber, which struck midnight. It was just such an old clock as ghosts are fond of. It had a deep, dismal tone, and struck so slowly and tediously that my uncle thought it would never have done. He counted and counted till he was confident he counted thirteen, and then it stopped.

The fire had burnt low, and the blaze of the last faggot was almost expiring, burning in small blue flames, which now and then lengthened up into little white gleams. My uncle lay with his eyes half closed, and his nightcap drawn almost down to his nose. His fancy was already wandering, and began to mingle up the present scene with the crater of Vesuvius, the French opera, the Coliseum at Rome, Dolly's chop house in London, and all the farrago of noted places with which the brain of a traveller is crammed—in a word, he was just falling asleep.

Suddenly he was roused by the sound of footsteps slowly pacing along the corridor. My uncle, as I have often heard him say himself, was a man not easily frightened; so he lay quiet, supposing this some other guest, or some servant on his way to bed. The footsteps, however, approached the door; the door gently opened; whether of its own accord, or whether pushed open, my uncle could not distinguish:—a figure all in white glided in. It was a female, tall and stately, and of a commanding air. Her dress was of an ancient fashion, ample in volume and sweeping the floor. She walked up to the fire place without regarding my uncle; who raised his nightcap with one hand, and stared earnestly at her. She remained for some time standing by the fire, which flashing up at intervals cast blue and white gleams of light that enabled my uncle to remark her appearance minutely.

Her face was ghastly pale, and perhaps rendered still more so by the blueish light of the fire. It possessed beauty, but its beauty was saddened by care and anxiety. There was the look of one accustomed to trouble, but of one whom trouble could not cast down nor subdue; for there was still the predominating air of proud, unconquerable resolution. Such at least was the opinion formed by my uncle, and he considered himself a great physiognomist.

The figure remained, as I said, for some time by the fire, putting out first one hand, then the other, then each foot alternately, as if warming itself; for your ghosts, if ghost it really was, are apt to be cold. My uncle furthermore remarked that it wore high heeled shoes, after an ancient fashion, with paste or diamond buckles, that sparkled as though they were alive. At length the figure turned gently round, casting a glassy look about the apartment, which, as it passed over my uncle, made his blood run cold, and chilled the very marrow in his bones. It then stretched its arms towards heaven, clasped its hands, and wringing them in a supplicating manner, glided slowly out of the room.

My uncle lay for some time meditating on this visitation, for (as he remarked when he told me the story) though a man of firmness, he was also a man of reflection, and did not reject a thing because it was out of the regular course of events. However, being as I have before said, a great traveller, and accustomed to strange adventures, he drew his nightcap resolutely over his eyes, turned his back to the door, hoisted the bed clothes high over his shoulders, and gradually fell asleep.

How long he slept he could not say, when he was awakened by the voice of some one at his bed side. He turned round and beheld the old French servant, with his ear locks in tight buckles on each side of a long, lanthorn face, on which habit had deeply wrinkled an everlasting smile. He made a thousand grimaces and asked a thousand pardons for disturbing Monsieur, but the morning was considerably advanced. While my uncle was dressing, he called vaguely to mind the visitor of the preceding night. He asked the ancient domestic what lady was in the habit of rambling about this part of the chateau at night. The old valet shrugged his shoulders as high as his head, laid one hand on his bosom, threw open the other with every finger extended; made a most whimsical grimace, which he meant to be complimentary, and replied, that it was not for him to know any thing of *les bonnes fortunes* of Monsieur.

My uncle saw there was nothing satisfactory to be learnt in this quarter.—After breakfast he was walking with the Marquis through the modern apartments of the chateau; sliding over the well waxed floors of silken saloons, amidst furniture rich in gilding and brocade; until they came to a long picture gallery, containing many portraits, some in oil and some in chalks.

Here was an ample field for the eloquence of his host, who had all the family pride of a nobleman of the *ancien regime*. There was not a grand name in Normandy, and hardly one in France, which was not, in some way or other, connected with his house. My uncle stood listening with inward impatience, resting sometimes on one leg, sometimes on the other, as the little Marquis descanted, with his usual fire and vivacity, on the achievements of his ancestors, whose portraits hung along the wall; from the martial deeds of the stern warriors in steel, to the gallantries and intrigues of the blue eyed gentlemen, with fair smiling faces, powdered ear locks, laced ruffles, and pink and blue silk coats and breeches; not forgetting the conquests of the lovely shepherdesses, with hoop petticoats and waists no thicker than an hour glass, who appeared ruling over their sheep and their swains with dainty crooks decorated with fluttering ribbands.

In the midst of his friend's discourse my uncle was startled on beholding a full length portrait, the very counterpart of his visitor of the preceding night.

"Methinks," said he, pointing to it, "I have seen the original of this portrait."

"*Pardonnez moi,*" replied the Marquis politely, "that can hardly be, as the lady has been dead more than a hundred years. That was the beautiful Duchess de Longueville, who figured during the minority of Louis the Fourteenth."

"And was there any thing remarkable in her history?"

Never was question more unlucky. The little Marquis immediately threw himself into the attitude of a man about to tell a long story. In fact, my uncle had pulled upon himself the whole history of the civil war of the Fronde, in which the beautiful Duchess had played so distinguished a part. Turenne, Coligni, Mazarin, were called up from their graves to grace his narration; nor were the affairs of the Barricadoes, nor the chivalry of the Port Cocheres forgotten. My uncle began to wish himself a thousand leagues off from the Marquis and his merciless memory, when suddenly the little man's recollections took a more interesting turn. He was relating the imprisonment of the Duke de Longueville, with the Princes Condé and Conti, in the chateau of Vincennes, and the ineffectual efforts of the Duchess to rouse the sturdy Normans to their rescue. He had come to that part where she was invested by the royal forces in the Castle of Dieppe.

"The spirit of the Duchess," proceeded the Marquis, "rose with her trials. It was astonishing to see so delicate and beautiful a being buffet so resolutely with hardships. She determined on a desperate means of escape. You may have seen the chateau in which she was mewed up; an old ragged wart of an edifice, standing on the knuckle of a hill, just above the rusty little town of Dieppe. One dark unruly night, she issued secretly out of a small postern gate of the castle, which the enemy had neglected to guard. The postern gate is there to this very day; opening upon a narrow bridge over a deep fosse between the castle and the brow of the hill. She was followed by her female attendants, a few domestics, and some gallant cavaliers who still remained faithful to her fortunes. Her object was to gain a small port about two leagues distant, where she had privately provided a vessel for her escape in case of emergency.

"The little band of fugitives were obliged to perform the distance on foot. When they arrived at the port the wind was high and stormy, the tide contrary, the vessel anchored far off in the road, and no means of getting on board, but by a fishing shallop which lay tossing like a cockle shell on the edge of the surf. The Duchess determined to risk the attempt. The seamen endeavoured to dissuade her, but the imminence of her danger on shore, and the magnanimity of her spirit urged her on. She had to be borne to the shallop in the arms of a mariner. Such was the violence of the wind and waves, that he faltered, lost his foothold, and let his precious burthen fall into the sea.

"The Duchess was nearly drowned; but partly through her own struggles, partly by the exertions of the seamen, she got to land. As soon as she had a little recovered strength, she insisted on renewing the attempt. The storm, however, had by this time become so violent as to set all efforts at defiance. To delay, was to be discovered and taken prisoner. As the only resource left, she procured horses; mounted with her female attendants *en croupe* behind the gallant gentlemen who accompanied her; and scoured the country to seek some temporary asylum.

"While the Duchess," continued the Marquis, laying his forefinger on my uncle's breast to arouse his flagging attention, "while the Duchess, poor lady, was wandering amid the tempest in this disconsolate manner, she arrived at this chateau. Her approach caused some uneasiness; for the clattering of a troop of horse, at dead of night, up the avenue of a lonely chateau, in those unsettled times, and in a troubled part of the country, was enough to occasion alarm.

"A tall, broad shouldered chasseur, armed to the teeth, gallopped ahead, and announced the name of the visitor. All uneasiness was dispelled. The household turned out with flambeaux to receive her, and never did torches gleam on a more weather beaten, travel stained band than came tramping into the court. Such pale, careworn faces, such bedraggled dresses, as the poor Duchess and her females presented, each seated behind her cavalier; while half drenched, half drowsy pages and attendants, seemed ready to fall from their horses with sleep and fatigue.

"The Duchess was received with a hearty welcome by my ancestor. She was ushered into the Hall of the chateau, and the fires soon crackled and blazed to cheer herself and her train; and every spit and stewpan was put in requisition to prepare ample refreshments for the wayfarers.

"She had a right to our hospitalities," continued the little Marquis, drawing himself up with a slight degree of stateliness, "for she was related to our family. I'll tell you how it was: Her father, Henry de Bourbon, Prince of Condé"——

"But did the Duchess pass the night in the chateau?" said my uncle rather abruptly, terrified at the idea of getting involved in one of the Marquis's genealogical discussions.

"Oh, as to the Duchess, she was put into the very apartment you occupied last night; which, at that time, was a kind of state apartment. Her followers were quartered in the chambers opening upon the neighbouring corridor, and her favourite page slept in an adjoining closet. Up and down the corridor walked the great chasseur, who had announced her arrival, and who acted as a kind of sentinel or guard. He was a dark, stern, powerful looking fellow, and as the light of a lamp in the corridor fell upon his deeply marked face and sinewy form, he seemed capable of defending the castle with his single arm.

"It was a rough, rude night; about this time of the year.—*Apropos*—now I think of it, last night was the anniversary of her visit. I may well remember the precise date, for it was a night not to be forgotten by our house. There is a singular tradition concerning it in our family." Here the Marquis hesitated, and a cloud seemed to gather about his bushy eyebrows. "There is a tradition—that a strange occurrence took place that night—a strange, mysterious, inexplicable occurrence."

Here he checked himself and paused.

"Did it relate to that Lady?" inquired my uncle, eagerly.

"It was past the hour of midnight," resumed the Marquis— "when the whole chateau——"

Here he paused again—my uncle made a movement of anxious curiosity.

"Excuse me," said the Marquis—a slight blush streaking his sallow visage. "There are some circumstances connected with our family history which I do not like to relate. That was a rude period. A time of great crimes among great men: for you know high blood, when it runs wrong, will not run tamely like blood of the *canaille*—poor lady!—But I have a little family pride, that—excuse me—we will change the subject if you please."—

My uncle's curiosity was piqued. The pompous and magnificent introduction had led him to expect something wonderful in the story to which it served as a kind of avenue. He had no idea of being cheated out of it by a sudden fit of unreasonable squeamishness. Besides, being a traveller, in quest of information, he considered it his duty to inquire into every thing.

The Marquis, however, evaded every question.

"Well," said my uncle, a little petulantly, "whatever you may think of it, I saw that lady last night."

The Marquis stepped back and gazed at him with surprise.

"She paid me a visit in my bed chamber."

The Marquis pulled out his snuff box with a shrug and a smile; taking this no doubt for an awkward piece of English pleasantry, which politeness required him to be charmed with. My uncle went on gravely, however, and related the whole circumstance. The Marquis heard him through with profound attention, holding his snuff box unopened in his hand. When the story was finished he tapped on the lid of his box deliberately; took a long sonorous pinch of snuff—

"Bah!" said the Marquis, and walked towards the other end of the gallery.——

———

Here the narrator paused. The company waited for some time for him to resume his narration; but he continued silent.

"Well," said the inquisitive gentleman, "and what did your uncle say then?"

"Nothing," replied the other.

"And what did the Marquis say further?"

"Nothing."

"And is that all?"

"That is all," said the narrator filling a glass of wine.

"I surmise," said the shrewd old gentleman with the waggish nose—"I surmise the ghost must have been the old housekeeper walking her rounds to see that all was right."

"Bah!" said the narrator, "my uncle was too much accustomed to strange sights not to know a ghost from a housekeeper!"

There was a murmur round the table half of merriment half of disappointment. I was inclined to think the old gentleman had really an afterpart of his story in reserve; but he sipped his wine and said nothing more; and there was an odd expression about his dilapidated countenance which left me in doubt whether he were in drollery or earnest.

"Egad," said the knowing gentleman with the flexible nose, "this story of your uncle puts me in mind of one that used to be told of an aunt of mine, by the mother's side; though I don't know that it will bear a comparison; as the good lady was not so prone to meet with strange adventures. But at any rate, you shall have it."

The Adventure of My Aunt

My aunt was a lady of large frame, strong mind, and great resolution; she was what might be termed a very manly woman. My uncle was a thin, puny little man, very meek and acquiescent, and no match for my aunt. It was observed that he dwindled and dwindled gradually away, from the day of his marriage. His wife's powerful mind was too much for him; it wore him out. My aunt, however, took all possible care of him, had half the doctors in town to prescribe for him, made him take all their prescriptions, and dosed him with physic enough to cure a whole hospital. All was in vain. My uncle grew worse and worse the more dosing and nursing he underwent, until in the end he added another to the long list of matrimonial victims, who have been killed with kindness.

"And was it his ghost that appeared to her?" asked the inquisitive gentleman, who had questioned the former story teller.

"You shall hear," replied the narrator:—My aunt took on mightily for the death of her poor dear husband! Perhaps she felt some compunction at having given him so much physic, and nursed him into his grave. At any rate, she did all that a widow could do to honour his memory. She spared no expense in either the quantity or quality of her mourning weeds; wore a miniature of him about her neck, as large as a little sun dial; and had a full length portrait of him always hanging in her bed chamber. All the world extolled her conduct to the skies; and it was determined, that a woman who behaved so well to the memory of one husband, deserved soon to get another.

It was not long after this that she went to take up her residence in an old country seat in Derbyshire, which had long been in the care of merely a steward and housekeeper. She took most of her servants with her, intending to make it her principal abode. The house stood in a lonely, wild part of the country, among the grey Derbyshire hills; with a murderer hanging in chains on a bleak height in full view.

The servants from town were half frightened out of their wits, at the idea of living in such a dismal, pagan looking place; especially when they got together in the servants' hall in the evening, and compared notes on all the hobgoblin stories picked up in the course of the day. They were afraid to venture alone about the gloomy, black looking chambers. My lady's maid, who was troubled with nerves, declared she could never sleep alone in such a "gashly, rummaging old building;" and the footman, who was a kind hearted young fellow, did all in his power to cheer her up.

My aunt was struck with the lonely appearance of the house. Before going to bed, therefore, she examined well the fastenings of the doors and windows, locked up the plate with her own hands, and carried the keys, together with a little box of money and jewels, to her own room; for she was a notable woman, and always saw to all things herself. Having put the keys under her pillow, and dismissed her maid, she sat by her toilet arranging her hair; for, being, in spite of her grief for my uncle, rather a buxom widow, she was somewhat particular about her person. She sat for a little while looking at her face in the glass, first on one side, then on the other, as ladies are apt to do, when they would ascertain whether they have been in good looks; for a roystering country squire of the neighbourhood, with whom she had flirted when a girl, had called that day to welcome her to the country.

All of a sudden she thought she heard something move behind her. She looked hastily round, but there was nothing to be seen. Nothing but the grimly painted portrait of her poor dear man, hanging against the wall. She gave a heavy sigh to his memory, as she was accustomed to do, whenever she spoke of him in company; and then went on adjusting her night dress, and thinking of the squire. Her sigh was re-echoed; or answered by a long drawn breath. She looked round again, but no one was to be seen. She ascribed these sounds to the wind, oozing through the rat holes of the old mansion; and proceeded leisurely to put her hair in papers, when, all at once, she thought she perceived one of the eyes of the portrait move.

"The back of her head being towards it!" said the story teller with the ruined head, "good!"

"Yes sir!" replied drily the narrator, "her back being towards the portrait, but her eye fixed on its reflection in the glass."

Well, as I was saying, she perceived one of the eyes of the portrait move. So strange a circumstance, as you may well suppose, gave her a sudden shock. To assure herself of the fact, she put one hand to her forehead, as if rubbing it; peeped through her fingers, and moved the candle with the other hand. The light of the taper gleamed on the eye, and was reflected from it. She was sure it moved. Nay, more, it seemed to give her a wink, as she had sometimes known her husband to do when living! It struck a momentary chill to her heart; for she was a lone woman, and felt herself fearfully situated.

The chill was but transient. My aunt, who was almost as resolute a personage as your uncle, sir, (turning to the old story teller,) became instantly calm and collected. She went on adjusting her dress. She even hummed an air, and did not make a single false note. She casually overturned a dressing box; took a candle and picked up the articles, one by one, from the floor; pursued a rolling pin cushion that was making the best of its way under the bed; then opened the door; looked for an instant into the corridor, as if in doubt whether to go; and then walked quietly out.

She hastened down stairs, ordered the servants to arm themselves with the weapons first at hand, placed herself at their head, and returned almost immediately.

Her hastily levied army presented a formidable force. The steward had a rusty blunderbuss; the coachman a loaded whip; the footman a pair of horse pistols; the cook a huge chopping knife, and the butler a bottle in each hand. My aunt led the van with a red hot poker; and, in my opinion, she was the most formidable of the party. The waiting maid, who dreaded to stay alone in the servants' hall, brought up the rear, smelling to a broken bottle of volatile salts, and expressing her terror of the ghosteses.

"Ghosts!" said my aunt resolutely, "I'll singe their whiskers for them!"

They entered the chamber. All was still and undisturbed as when she left it. They approached the portrait of my uncle.

"Pull me down that picture!" cried my aunt.

A heavy groan, and a sound like the chattering of teeth, issued from the portrait. The servants shrunk back. The maid uttered a faint shriek, and clung to the footman for support.

"Instantly!" added my aunt, with a stamp of the foot.

The picture was pulled down, and from a recess behind it, in which had formerly stood a clock, they hauled forth a round shouldered, black bearded varlet, with a knife as long as my arm, but trembling all over like an aspen leaf.

"Well, and who was he? No ghost, I suppose!" said the inquisitive gentleman.

"A Knight of the Post," replied the narrator, "who had been smitten with the worth of the wealthy widow; or rather a marauding Tarquin, who had stolen into her chamber to violate her purse and rifle her strong box when all the house should be asleep. In plain terms," continued he, "the vagabond was a loose idle fellow of the neighbourhood, who had once been a servant in the house, and had been employed to assist in arranging it for the reception of its mistress. He confessed that he had contrived this hiding place for his nefarious purposes, and had borrowed an eye from the portrait by way of a reconnoitering hole."

"And what did they do with him—did they hang him?" resumed the questioner.

"Hang him?—how could they?" exclaimed a beetle browed barrister, with a hawk's nose—"the offence was not capital—no robbery, nor assault had been committed—no forcible entry or breaking into the premises"——

"My aunt," said the narrator, "was a woman of spirit, and apt to take the law into her own hands. She had her own notions of cleanliness also. She ordered the fellow to be drawn through the horsepond to cleanse away all offences, and then to be well rubbed down with an oaken towel."

"And what became of him afterwards?" said the inquisitive gentleman.

"I do not exactly know—I believe he was sent on a voyage of improvement to Botany Bay."

"And your aunt"—said the inquisitive gentleman—"I'll warrant she took care to make her maid sleep in the room with her after that."

"No, sir, she did better—she gave her hand shortly after to the roystering squire; for she used to observe it was a dismal thing for a woman to sleep alone in the country."

"She was right," observed the inquisitive gentleman, nodding sagaciously—"but I am sorry they did not hang that fellow."

It was agreed on all hands that the last narrator had brought his tale to the most satisfactory conclusion; though a country clergyman present regretted that the uncle and aunt, who figured in the different stories, had not been married together. They certainly would have been well matched.

"But I don't see, after all," said the inquisitive gentleman, "that there was any ghost in this last story."

"Oh, if it's ghosts you want, honey," cried the Irish captain of dragoons, "if it's ghosts you want, you shall have a whole regiment of them. And since these gentlemen have given the adventures of their uncles and aunts, faith and I'll e'en give you a chapter out of my own family history."

The Bold Dragoon, or the Adventure of My Grandfather

My grandfather was a bold dragoon, for it's a profession, d'ye see, that has run in the family. All my forefathers have been dragoons and died upon the field of honour except myself, and I hope my posterity may be able to say the same; however, I don't mean to be vainglorious. Well, my grandfather, as I said, was a bold dragoon, and had served in the Low Countries. In fact, he was one of that very army, which, according to my uncle Toby, "swore so terribly in Flanders." He could swear a good stick himself; and, moreover, was the very man that introduced the doctrine Corporal Trim mentions, of radical heat and radical moisture; or in other words, the mode of keeping out the damps of ditch water by burnt brandy. Be that as it may, it's nothing to the purport of my story. I only tell it to show you that my grandfather was a man not easily to be humbugged. He had seen service; or, according to his own phrase, "he had seen the divil"—and that's saying every thing.

Well, gentlemen, my grandfather was on his way to England, for which he intended to embark at Ostend;—bad luck to the place for one where I was kept by storms and head winds for three long days, and the divil of a jolly companion or pretty face to comfort me. Well, as I was saying, my grandfather was on his way to England, or rather to Ostend—no matter which, it's all the same. So one evening, towards nightfall, he rode jollily into Bruges. Very like you all know Bruges, gentlemen, a queer, old fashioned Flemish town, once they say a great place for trade and money making, in old times, when the Mynheers were in their glory; but almost as large and as empty as an Irishman's pocket at the present day. Well, gentlemen, it was the time of the annual fair. All Bruges was crowded; and the canals swarmed with Dutch boats, and the streets swarmed with Dutch merchants; and there was hardly any getting along for goods, wares, and merchandises, and peasants in big breeches, and women in half a score of petticoats.

My grandfather rode jollily along, in his easy slashing way, for he was a saucy, sunshiny fellow—staring about him at the motley crowd, and the old houses with gabel ends to the street and storks' nests on the chimneys; winking at the ya vrouws who showed their faces at the windows, and joking the women right and left in the street; all of whom laughed and took it in amazing good part; for though he did not know a word of their language, yet he had always a knack of making himself understood among the women.

Well, gentlemen, it being the time of the annual fair, all the town was crowded; every inn and tavern full, and my grandfather applied in vain from one to the other for admittance. At length he rode up to an old rackety inn that looked ready to fall to pieces, and which all the rats would have run away from, if they could have found room in any other house to put their heads. It was just such a queer building as you see in Dutch pictures, with a tall roof that reached up into the clouds; and as many garrets, one over the other, as the seven heavens of Mahomet.—Nothing had saved it from tumbling down but a stork's nest on the chimney, which always brings good luck to a house in the Low Countries; and at the very time of my grandfather's arrival, there were two of these long legged birds of grace, standing like ghosts on the chimney top. Faith, but they've kept the house on its legs to this very day; for you may see it any time you pass through Bruges, as it stands there yet; only it is turned into a brewery—a brewery of strong Flemish beer; at least it was so when I came that way after the battle of Waterloo.

My grandfather eyed the house curiously as he approached.

It might not altogether have struck his fancy, had he not seen in large letters over the door,

HEER VERKOOPT MAN GOEDEN DRANK.

My grandfather had learnt enough of the language to know that the sign promised good liquor. "This is the house for me," said he, stopping short before the door.

The sudden appearance of a dashing dragoon was an event in an old inn, frequented only by the peaceful sons of traffick. A rich burgher of Antwerp, a stately ample man, in a broad Flemish hat, and who was the great man and great patron of the establishment, sat smoking a clean long pipe on one side of the door; a fat little distiller of Geneva from Schiedam, sat smoking on the other, and the bottle nosed host stood in the door, and the comely hostess, in crimped cap, beside him; and the hostess' daughter, a plump Flanders lass, with long gold pendants in her ears, was at a side window.

"Humph!" said the rich burgher of Antwerp, with a sulky glance at the stranger.

"Die duyvel!" said the fat little distiller of Schiedam.

The landlord saw with the quick glance of a publican that the new guest was not at all to the taste of the old ones; and to tell the truth, he did not like my grandfather's saucy eye. He shook his head—"Not a garret in the house but was full."

"Not a garret!" echoed the landlady.

"Not a garret!" echoed the daughter.

The burgher of Antwerp and the little distiller of Schiedam continued to smoke their pipes sullenly, eyed the enemy askance from under their broad hats, but said nothing.

My grandfather was not a man to be browbeaten. He threw the reins on his horse's neck, cocked his hat on one side, stuck one arm akimbo—

"Faith and troth!" said he, "but I'll sleep in this house this very night!"

As he said this he gave a slap on his thigh, by way of emphasis—the slap went to the landlady's heart.

He followed up the vow by jumping off his horse, and making his way past the staring Mynheers into the public room.—May be you've been in the bar room of an old Flemish inn—faith, but a handsome chamber it was as you'd wish to see; with a brick floor, and a great fire place, with the whole bible history in glazed tiles; and then the mantle piece, pitching itself head foremost out of the wall, with a whole regiment of cracked tea pots and earthen jugs paraded on it; not to mention half a dozen great Delft platters hung about the room by way of pictures; and the little bar in one corner, and the bouncing bar maid inside of it with a red calico cap and yellow ear drops.

My grandfather snapped his fingers over his head, as he cast an eye round the room: "Faith, this is the very house I've been looking after," said he.

There was some further show of resistance on the part of the garrison, but my grandfather was an old soldier, and an Irishman to boot, and not easily repulsed, especially after he had got into the fortress. So he blarney'd the landlord, kissed the landlord's wife, tickled the landlord's daughter, chucked the bar maid under the chin; and it was agreed on all hands that it would be a thousand pities, and a burning shame into the bargain, to turn such a bold dragoon into the streets. So they laid their heads together, that is to say, my grandfather and the landlady, and it was at length agreed to accommodate him with an old chamber that had for some time been shut up.

"Some say it's haunted!" whispered the landlord's daughter, "but you're a bold dragoon, and I dare say don't fear ghosts."

"The divil a bit!" said my grandfather, pinching her plump cheek; "but if I should be troubled by ghosts, I've been to the Red Sea in my time, and have a pleasant way of laying them, my darling!"

And then he whispered something to the girl which made her laugh, and give him a good humoured box on the ear. In short, there was nobody knew better how to make his way among the petticoats than my grandfather.

In a little while, as was his usual way, he took complete possession of the house; swaggering all over it:—into the stable to look after his horse; into the kitchen to look after his supper. He had something to say or do with every one; smoked with the Dutchmen; drank with the Germans; slapped the landlord on the shoulder, romped with his daughter and the bar maid:—never since the days of Ally Croaker had such a rattling blade been seen. The landlord stared at him with astonishment; the landlord's daughter hung her head and giggled whenever he came near; and as he swaggered along the corridor, with his sword trailing by his side, the maids looked after him, and whispered to one another—"What a proper man!"

At supper my grandfather took command of the table d'hôte as though he had been at home; helped every body, not forgetting himself; talked with every one, whether he understood their language or not; and made his way into the intimacy of the rich burgher of Antwerp, who had never been known to be sociable with any one during his life. In fact, he revolutionized the whole establishment, and gave it such a rouse, that the very house reeled with it. He outsat every one at table excepting the little fat distiller of Schiedam, who sat soaking a long time before he broke forth; but when he did, he was a very devil incarnate. He took a violent affection for my grandfather; so they sat drinking, and smoking, and telling stories, and singing Dutch and Irish songs, without understanding a word each other said, until the little Hollander was fairly swampt with his own gin and water, and carried off to bed, whooping and hiccuping, and trolling the burthen of a Low Dutch love song.

Well, gentlemen, my grandfather was shown to his quarters, up a large staircase composed of loads of hewn timber; and through long rigmarole passages, hung with blackened paintings of fruit, and fish, and game, and country frolicks, and huge kitchens, and portly burgomasters, such as you see about old fashioned Flemish inns, till at length he arrived at his room.

An old times chamber it was, sure enough, and crowded with all kinds of trumpery. It looked like an infirmary for decayed and superannuated furniture; where every thing diseased and disabled was sent to nurse, or to be forgotten. Or rather, it might have been taken for a general congress of old legitimate moveables, where every kind and country had a representative. No two chairs were alike: such high backs and low backs, and leather bottoms and worsted bottoms, and straw bottoms, and no bottoms; and cracked marble tables

with curiously carved legs, holding balls in their claws, as
though they were going to play at ninepins.

My grandfather made a bow to the motley assemblage as he
entered, and having undressed himself, placed his light in the
fire place, asking pardon of the tongs, which seemed to be
making love to the shovel in the chimney corner, and whispering soft nonsense in its ear.

The rest of the guests were by this time sound asleep; for
your Mynheers are huge sleepers. The house maids, one by
one, crept up yawning to their atticks, and not a female head
in the inn was laid on a pillow that night without dreaming of
the Bold Dragoon.

My grandfather, for his part, got into bed, and drew over
him one of those great bags of down, under which they
smother a man in the Low Countries; and there he lay, melting between two feather beds, like an anchovy sandwich
between two slices of toast and butter. He was a warm
complexioned man, and this smothering played the very
deuce with him. So, sure enough, in a little time it seemed as
if a legion of imps were twitching at him, and all the blood in
his veins was in fever heat.

He lay still, however, until all the house was quiet, excepting the snoring of the Mynheers from the different chambers;
who answered one another in all kinds of tones and cadences,
like so many bull frogs in a swamp. The quieter the house
became, the more unquiet became my grandfather. He waxed
warmer and warmer, until at length the bed became too hot
to hold him.

"May be the maid had warmed it too much?" said the curious gentleman inquiringly.

"I rather think the contrary," replied the Irishman. "But be
that as it may, it grew too hot for my grandfather."

"Faith there's no standing this any longer," says he; so he
jumped out of bed and went strolling about the house.

"What for?" said the inquisitive gentleman.

"Why, to cool himself to be sure—or perhaps to find a
more comfortable bed—or perhaps——but no matter what
he went for—he never mentioned; and there's no use in
taking up our time in conjecturing."

Well, my grandfather had been for some time absent from

his room, and was returning, perfectly cool, when just as he reached the door he heard a strange noise within. He paused and listened. It seemed as if some one were trying to hum a tune in defiance of the asthma. He recollected the report of the room's being haunted; but he was no believer in ghosts. So he pushed the door gently open, and peeped in.

Egad, gentlemen, there was a gambol carrying on within enough to have astonished St. Anthony himself.

By the light of the fire he saw a pale weazen-faced fellow in a long flannel gown and a tall white nightcap with a tassel to it, who sat by the fire, with a bellows under his arm by way of bagpipe, from which he forced the asthmatical music that had bothered my grandfather. As he played, too, he kept twitching about with a thousand queer contortions; nodding his head and bobbing about his tasselled nightcap.

My grandfather thought this very odd, and mighty presumptuous, and was about to demand what business he had to play his wind instrument in another gentleman's quarters, when a new cause of astonishment met his eye. From the opposite side of the room a long backed, bandy legged chair, covered with leather, and studded all over in a coxcomical fashion with little brass nails, got suddenly into motion; thrust out first a claw foot, then a crooked arm, and at length, making a leg, slided gracefully up to an easy chair, of tarnished brocade, with a hole in its bottom, and led it gallantly out in a ghostly minuet about the floor.

The musician now played fiercer and fiercer, and bobbed his head and his nightcap about like mad. By degrees the dancing mania seemed to seize upon all the other pieces of furniture. The antique, long bodied chairs paired off in couples and led down a country dance; a three legged stool danced a hornpipe, though horribly puzzled by its supernumerary limb; while the amorous tongs seized the shovel round the waist, and whirled it about the room in a German waltz. In short, all the moveables got in motion; pirouetting, hands across, right and left, like so many devils, all except a great clothes press, which kept curtseying and curtseying in one corner, like a dowager, in exquisite time to the music; — being either too corpulent to dance, or perhaps at a loss for a partner.

My grandfather concluded the latter to be the reason; so, being, like a true Irishman, devoted to the sex, and at all times ready for a frolick, he bounced into the room, calling to the musician to strike up "Paddy O'Rafferty," capered up to the clothes press and seized upon two handles to lead her out:— When, whirr!—the whole revel was at an end. The chairs, tables, tongs, and shovel slunk in an instant as quietly into their places as if nothing had happened; and the musician vanished up the chimney, leaving the bellows behind him in his hurry. My grandfather found himself seated in the middle of the floor, with the clothes press sprawling before him, and the two handles jerked off and in his hands.

"Then after all, this was a mere dream!" said the inquisitive gentleman.

"The divil a bit of a dream!" replied the Irishman: "there never was a truer fact in this world. Faith, I should have liked to see any man tell my grandfather it was a dream."

Well, gentlemen, as the clothes press was a mighty heavy body, and my grandfather likewise, particularly in rear, you may easily suppose two such heavy bodies coming to the ground would make a bit of a noise. Faith, the old mansion shook as though it had mistaken it for an earthquake. The whole garrison was alarmed. The landlord, who slept below, hurried up with a candle to inquire the cause, but with all his haste his daughter had arrived at the scene of uproar before him. The landlord was followed by the landlady, who was followed by the bouncing bar maid, who was followed by the simpering chambermaids all holding together, as well as they could, such garments as they had first laid hands on; but all in a terrible hurry to see what the deuce was to pay in the chamber of the bold dragoon.

My grandfather related the marvellous scene he had witnessed, and the broken handles of the prostrate clothes press bore testimony to the fact. There was no contesting such evidence; particularly with a lad of my grandfather's complexion, who seemed able to make good every word either with sword or shillelah. So the landlord scratched his head and looked silly, as he was apt to do when puzzled. The landlady scratched—no, she did not scratch her head,—but she knit her brow, and did not seem half pleased with the explanation.

But the landlady's daughter corroborated it, by recollecting that the last person who had dwelt in that chamber was a famous juggler who had died of St. Vitus's dance, and no doubt had infected all the furniture.

This set all things to rights, particularly when the chambermaids declared that they had all witnessed strange carryings on in that room;—and as they declared this "upon their honours," there could not remain a doubt upon the subject.

"And did your grandfather go to bed again in that room?" said the inquisitive gentleman.

"That's more than I can tell. Where he passed the rest of the night was a secret he never disclosed. In fact, though he had seen much service, he was but indifferently acquainted with geography, and apt to make blunders in his travels about inns at night, which it would have puzzled him sadly to account for in the morning."

"Was he ever apt to walk in his sleep?" said the knowing old gentleman.

"Never that I heard of."

There was a little pause after this rigmarole Irish romance, when the old gentleman with the haunted head observed, that the stories hitherto related had rather a burlesque tendency. "I recollect an adventure, however," added he, "which I heard of during a residence at Paris, for the truth of which I can undertake to vouch, and which is of a very grave and singular nature."

The Adventure of the German Student

On a stormy night, in the tempestuous times of the French revolution, a young German was returning to his lodgings, at a late hour, across the old part of Paris. The lightning gleamed, and the loud claps of thunder rattled through the lofty, narrow streets—but I should first tell you something about this young German.

Gottfried Wolfgang was a young man of good family. He had studied for some time at Göttingen, but being of a visionary and enthusiastic character, he had wandered into those wild and speculative doctrines which have so often bewildered German students. His secluded life, his intense application, and the singular nature of his studies, had an effect on both mind and body. His health was impaired; his imagination diseased. He had been indulging in fanciful speculations on spiritual essences until, like Swedenborg, he had an ideal world of his own around him. He took up a notion, I do not know from what cause, that there was an evil influence hanging over him; an evil genius or spirit seeking to ensnare him and ensure his perdition. Such an idea working on his melancholy temperament produced the most gloomy effects. He became haggard and desponding. His friends discovered the mental malady preying upon him, and determined that the best cure was a change of scene; he was sent, therefore, to finish his studies amidst the splendours and gaieties of Paris.

Wolfgang arrived at Paris at the breaking out of the revolution. The popular delirium at first caught his enthusiastic mind, and he was captivated by the political and philosophical theories of the day: but the scenes of blood which followed shocked his sensitive nature; disgusted him with society and the world, and made him more than ever a recluse. He shut himself up in a solitary apartment in the *Pays Latin*, the quarter of students. There in a gloomy street not far from the monastic walls of the Sorbonne, he pursued his favourite speculations. Sometimes he spent hours together in the great libraries of Paris, those catacombs of departed authors, rummaging among their hoards of dusty and obsolete works in quest of food for his unhealthy appetite. He was, in a manner, a literary goul, feeding in the charnel house of decayed literature.

Wolfgang, though solitary and recluse, was of an ardent temperament, but for a time it operated merely upon his imagination. He was too shy and ignorant of the world to make any advances to the fair, but he was a passionate admirer of female beauty, and in his lonely chamber would often lose himself in reveries on forms and faces which he had seen, and his fancy would deck out images of loveliness far surpassing the reality.

While his mind was in this excited and sublimated state, a dream produced an extraordinary effect upon him. It was of a female face of transcendent beauty. So strong was the impression made, that he dreamt of it again and again. It haunted his thoughts by day, his slumbers by night; in fine, he became passionately enamoured of this shadow of a dream. This lasted so long, that it became one of those fixed ideas which haunt the minds of melancholy men, and are at times mistaken for madness.

Such was Gottfried Wolfgang, and such his situation at the time I mentioned. He was returning home late one stormy night, through some of the old and gloomy streets of the *Marais*, the ancient part of Paris. The loud claps of thunder rattled among the high houses of the narrow streets. He came to the Place de Grève, the square where public executions are performed. The lightning quivered about the pinnacles of the ancient Hôtel de Ville, and shed flickering gleams over the open space in front. As Wolfgang was crossing the square, he shrank back with horror at finding himself close by the guillotine. It was the height of the reign of terror, when this dreadful instrument of death stood ever ready, and its scaffold was continually running with the blood of the virtuous and the brave. It had that very day been actively employed in the work of carnage, and there it stood in grim array amidst a silent and sleeping city, waiting for fresh victims.

Wolfgang's heart sickened within him, and he was turning shuddering from the horrible engine, when he beheld a shadowy form cowering as it were at the foot of the steps which led up to the scaffold. A succession of vivid flashes of lightning revealed it more distinctly. It was a female figure, dressed in black. She was seated on one of the lower steps of the scaffold, leaning forward, her face hid in her lap, and her long dishevelled tresses hanging to the ground, streaming with the rain which fell in torrents. Wolfgang paused. There was something awful in this solitary monument of wo. The female had the appearance of being above the common order. He knew the times to be full of vicissitude, and that many a fair head, which had once been pillowed on down, now wandered houseless. Perhaps this was some poor mourner whom the dreadful axe had rendered desolate, and who sat here heartbroken on the strand of existence, from which all that was dear to her had been launched into eternity.

He approached, and addressed her in the accents of sympathy. She raised her head and gazed wildly at him. What was his astonishment at beholding, by the bright glare of the lightning, the very face which had haunted him in his dreams. It was pale and disconsolate, but ravishingly beautiful.

Trembling with violent and conflicting emotions, Wolfgang again accosted her. He spoke something of her being exposed at such an hour of the night, and to the fury of such a storm, and offered to conduct her to her friends. She pointed to the guillotine with a gesture of dreadful signification.

"I have no friend on earth!" said she.

"But you have a home," said Wolfgang.

"Yes—in the grave!"

The heart of the student melted at the words.

"If a stranger dare make an offer," said he, "without danger of being misunderstood, I would offer my humble dwelling as a shelter; myself as a devoted friend. I am friendless myself in Paris, and a stranger in the land; but if my life could be of service, it is at your disposal, and should be sacrificed before harm or indignity should come to you."

There was an honest earnestness in the young man's manner that had its effect. His foreign accent, too, was in his favour; it showed him not to be a hackneyed inhabitant of Paris. Indeed there is an eloquence in true enthusiasm that is not to be doubted. The homeless stranger confided herself implicitly to the protection of the student.

He supported her faltering steps across the Pont Neuf, and by the place where the statue of Henry the Fourth had been overthrown by the populace. The storm had abated, and the thunder rumbled at a distance. All Paris was quiet; that great volcano of human passion slumbered for a while, to gather fresh strength for the next day's eruption. The student conducted his charge through the ancient streets of the *Pays Latin*, and by the dusky walls of the Sorbonne to the great, dingy hotel which he inhabited. The old portress who admitted them stared with surprise at the unusual sight of the melancholy Wolfgang with a female companion.

On entering his apartment, the student, for the first time, blushed at the scantiness and indifference of his dwelling. He had but one chamber—an old fashioned saloon—heavily carved and fantastically furnished with the remains of former magnificence, for it was one of those hotels in the quarter of the Luxembourg palace which had once belonged to nobility. It was lumbered with books and papers, and all the usual apparatus of a student, and his bed stood in a recess at one end.

When lights were brought, and Wolfgang had a better opportunity of contemplating the stranger, he was more than ever intoxicated by her beauty. Her face was pale, but of a dazzling fairness, set off by a profusion of raven hair that hung clustering about it. Her eyes were large and brilliant, with a singular expression approaching almost to wildness. As far as her black dress permitted her shape to be seen, it was of perfect symmetry. Her whole appearance was highly striking, though she was dressed in the simplest style. The only thing approaching to an ornament which she wore was a broad, black band round her neck, clasped by diamonds.

The perplexity now commenced with the student how to dispose of the helpless being thus thrown upon his protection. He thought of abandoning his chamber to her, and seeking shelter for himself elsewhere. Still he was so fascinated by her charms, there seemed to be such a spell upon his thoughts and senses, that he could not tear himself from her presence. Her manner, too, was singular and unaccountable. She spoke no more of the guillotine. Her grief had abated. The attentions of the student had first won her confidence, and then, apparently, her heart. She was evidently an enthusiast like himself, and enthusiasts soon understand each other.

In the infatuation of the moment Wolfgang avowed his passion for her. He told her the story of his mysterious dream, and how she had possessed his heart before he had even seen her. She was strangely affected by his recital, and acknowledged to have felt an impulse towards him equally unaccountable. It was the time for wild theory and wild actions. Old prejudices and superstitions were done away; every thing was under the sway of the "Goddess of Reason." Among other rubbish of the old times, the forms and ceremonies of marriage began to be considered superfluous bonds for honourable minds. Social compacts were the vogue. Wolfgang was too much of a theorist not to be tainted by the liberal doctrines of the day.

"Why should we separate?" said he: "our hearts are united; in the eye of reason and honour we are as one. What need is there of sordid forms to bind high souls together?"

The stranger listened with emotion: she had evidently received illumination at the same school.

"You have no home nor family," continued he; "let me be every thing to you, or rather let us be every thing to one another. If form is necessary, form shall be observed—there is my hand. I pledge myself to you for ever."

"For ever?" said the stranger, solemnly.

"For ever!" repeated Wolfgang.

The stranger clasped the hand extended to her: "Then I am yours," murmured she, and sank upon his bosom.

The next morning the student left his bride sleeping, and sallied forth at an early hour to seek more spacious apartments, suitable to the change in his situation. When he returned, he found the stranger lying with her head hanging over the bed, and one arm thrown over it. He spoke to her, but received no reply. He advanced to awaken her from her uneasy posture. On taking her hand, it was cold—there was no pulsation—her face was pallid and ghastly.—In a word—she was a corpse.

Horrified and frantic, he alarmed the house. A scene of confusion ensued. The police was summoned. As the officer of police entered the room, he started back on beholding the corpse.

"Great heaven!" cried he, "how did this woman come here?"

"Do you know any thing about her?" said Wolfgang, eagerly.

"Do I?" exclaimed the police officer: "she was guillotined yesterday!"

He stepped forward; undid the black collar round the neck of the corpse, and the head rolled on the floor!

The student burst into a frenzy. "The fiend! the fiend has gained possession of me!" shrieked he: "I am lost for ever!"

They tried to soothe him, but in vain. He was possessed

with the frightful belief that an evil spirit had reanimated the dead body to ensnare him. He went distracted, and died in a madhouse.

———

Here the old gentleman with the haunted head finished his narrative.

"And is this really a fact?" said the inquisitive gentleman.

"A fact not to be doubted," replied the other. "I had it from the best authority. The student told it me himself. I saw him in a madhouse at Paris."

The Adventure of the Mysterious Picture

As one story of the kind produces another, and as all the company seemed fully engrossed by the subject, and disposed to bring their relatives and ancestors upon the scene, there is no knowing how many more strange adventures we might have heard, had not a corpulent old fox hunter, who had slept soundly through the whole, now suddenly awakened, with a loud and long drawn yawn. The sound broke the charm; the ghosts took to flight as though it had been cock-crowing, and there was a universal move for bed.

"And now for the haunted chamber," said the Irish captain, taking his candle.

"Aye, who's to be the hero of the night?" said the gentleman with the ruined head.

"That we shall see in the morning," said the old gentleman with the nose: "whoever looks pale and grizzly will have seen the ghost."

"Well, gentlemen," said the Baronet, "there's many a true thing said in jest. In fact, one of you will sleep in a room tonight"——

"What—a haunted room? a haunted room? I claim the adventure—and I—and I—and I," cried a dozen guests, talking and laughing at the same time.

"No—no," said mine host, "there is a secret about one of my rooms on which I feel disposed to try an experiment. So, gentlemen, none of you shall know who has the haunted chamber, until circumstances reveal it. I will not even know it myself, but will leave it to chance and the allotment of the housekeeper. At the same time, if it will be any satisfaction to you, I will observe, for the honour of my paternal mansion, that there's scarcely a chamber in it but is well worthy of being haunted."

We now separated for the night, and each went to his allotted room. Mine was in one wing of the building, and I could not but smile at its resemblance in style to those eventful apartments described in the tales of the supper table. It was spacious and gloomy, decorated with lamp black portraits, a bed of ancient damask, with a tester sufficiently lofty to grace a couch of state, and a number of massive pieces of old fashioned furniture. I drew a great claw-footed arm chair before the wide fire place; stirred up the fire; sat looking into it, and musing upon the odd stories I had heard; until, partly overcome by the fatigue of the day's hunting, and partly by the wine and wassail of mine host, I fell asleep in my chair.

The uneasiness of my position made my slumber troubled, and laid me at the mercy of all kinds of wild and fearful dreams; now it was that my perfidious dinner and supper rose in rebellion against my peace. I was hag-ridden by a fat saddle of mutton; a plum pudding weighed like lead upon my conscience; the merry thought of a capon filled me with horrible suggestions; and a devilled leg of a turkey stalked in all kinds of diabolical shapes through my imagination. In short, I had a violent fit of the nightmare. Some strange indefinite evil seemed hanging over me which I could not avert; something terrible and loathsome oppressed me which I could not shake off. I was conscious of being asleep, and strove to rouse myself, but every effort redoubled the evil; until gasping, struggling, almost strangling, I suddenly sprang bolt upright in my chair, and awoke.

The light on the mantle piece had burnt low, and the wick was divided; there was a great winding sheet made by the dripping wax, on the side towards me. The disordered taper emitted a broad flaring flame, and threw a strong light on a painting over the fire place, which I had not hitherto observed.

It consisted merely of a head, or rather a face, staring full upon me, with an expression that was startling. It was without a frame, and at the first glance I could hardly persuade myself that it was not a real face, thrusting itself out of the dark oaken pannel. I sat in my chair gazing at it, and the more I gazed the more it disquieted me. I had never before been affected in the same way by any painting. The emotions it caused were strange and indefinite. They were something like what I have heard ascribed to the eyes of the basilisk; or like that mysterious influence in reptiles termed fascination. I passed my hand over my eyes several times, as if seeking instinctively to brush away the illusion—in vain—they instantly reverted to the picture, and its chilling, creeping influence over my flesh and blood was redoubled.

I looked round the room on other pictures, either to divert my attention, or to see whether the same effect would be produced by them. Some of them were grim enough to produce the effect, if the mere grimness of the painting produced it—no such thing. My eye passed over them all with perfect indifference, but the moment it reverted to this visage over the fire place, it was as if an electric shock darted through me. The other pictures were dim and faded; but this one protruded from a plain black ground in the strongest relief, and with wonderful truth of colouring. The expression was that of agony—the agony of intense bodily pain; but a menace scowled upon the brow, and a few sprinklings of blood added to its ghastliness. Yet it was not all these characteristics—it was some horror of the mind, some inscrutable antipathy awakened by this picture, which harrowed up my feelings.

I tried to persuade myself that this was chimerical; that my brain was confused by the fumes of mine host's good cheer, and, in some measure, by the odd stories about paintings which had been told at supper. I determined to shake off these vapours of the mind; rose from my chair, and walked about the room; snapped my fingers; rallied myself; laughed aloud. It was a forced laugh, and the echo of it in the old chamber jarred upon my ear. I walked to the window; tried to discern the landscape through the glass. It was pitch darkness, and howling storm without; and as I heard the wind moan among the trees, I caught a reflection of this accursed visage in the pane of glass, as though it were staring through the window at me. Even the reflection of it was thrilling.

How was this vile nervous fit, for such I now persuaded myself it was, to be conquered? I determined to force myself not to look at the painting, but to undress quickly and get into bed. I began to undress, but in spite of every effort I could not keep myself from stealing a glance every now and then at the picture; and a glance was now sufficient to distress me. Even when my back was turned to it, the idea of this strange face behind me, peering over my shoulder, was insufferable. I threw off my clothes and hurried into bed; but still this visage gazed upon me. I had a full view of it in my bed, and for some time could not take my eyes from it. I had grown nervous to a dismal degree.

I put out the light, and tried to force myself to sleep;—all in vain! The fire gleaming up a little, threw an uncertain light about the room, leaving, however, the region of the picture in deep shadow. What, thought I, if this be the chamber about which mine host spoke as having a mystery reigning over it?—I had taken his words merely as spoken in jest; might they have a real import? I looked around. The faintly lighted apartment had all the qualifications requisite for a haunted chamber. It began in my infected imagination to assume strange appearances. The old portraits turned paler and paler, and blacker and blacker; the streaks of light and shadow thrown among the quaint articles of furniture, gave them more singular shapes and characters. There was a huge dark clothes press of antique form, gorgeous in brass and lustrous with wax, that began to grow oppressive to me.

Am I then, thought I, indeed, the hero of the haunted room? Is there really a spell laid upon me, or is this all some contrivance of mine host, to raise a laugh at my expense? The idea of being hag-ridden by my own fancy all night, and then bantered on my haggard looks the next day was intolerable; but the very idea was sufficient to produce the effect, and to render me still more nervous. Pish, said I, it can be no such thing. How could my worthy host imagine that I, or any man would be so worried by a mere picture? It is my own diseased imagination that torments me. I turned in bed, and shifted from side to side, to try to fall asleep; but all in vain. When one cannot get asleep by lying quiet, it is seldom that tossing about will effect the purpose. The fire gradually went out and left the room in darkness. Still I had the idea of that inexplicable countenance gazing and keeping watch upon me through the gloom. Nay, what was worse, the very darkness seemed to magnify its terrors. It was like having an unseen enemy hanging about one in the night. Instead of having one picture now to worry me, I had a hundred. I fancied it in every direction. There it is, thought I,—and there, and there, —with its horrible and mysterious expression, still gazing and gazing on me. No—if I must suffer this strange and dismal influence, it were better face a single foe, than thus be haunted by a thousand images of it.

Whoever has been in a state of nervous agitation, must know that the longer it continues, the more uncontroulable it grows; the very air of the chamber seemed at length infected by the baleful presence of this picture. I fancied it hovering over me. I almost felt the fearful visage from the wall approaching my face,—it seemed breathing upon me. This is not to be borne, said I, at length, springing out of bed. I can stand this no longer. I shall only tumble and toss about here all night; make a very spectre of myself, and become the hero of the haunted chamber in good earnest. Whatever be the ill consequence, I'll quit this cursed room, and seek a night's rest elsewhere. They can but laugh at me at all events, and they'll be sure to have the laugh upon me if I pass a sleepless night and show them a haggard and wobegone visage in the morning.

All this was half muttered to myself, as I hastily slipped on my clothes; which having done, I groped my way out of the room, and down stairs to the drawing room. Here, after tumbling over two or three pieces of furniture, I made out to reach a sopha, and stretching myself upon it determined to bivouack there for the night.

The moment I found myself out of the neighbourhood of that strange picture, it seemed as if the charm were broken. All its influence was at an end. I felt assured that it was confined to its own dreary chamber, for I had, with a sort of instinctive caution, turned the key when I closed the door. I soon calmed down, therefore, into a state of tranquillity; from that into a drowsiness, and finally into a deep sleep; out of which I did not awake, until the housemaid, with her besom and her matin song, came to put the room in order. She stared at finding me stretched upon the sofa; but I presume circumstances of the kind were not uncommon after hunting dinners, in her master's bachelor establishment; for she went on with her song and her work, and took no further heed of me.

I had an unconquerable repugnance to return to my chamber; so I found my way to the butler's quarters, made my toilette in the best way circumstances would permit, and was among the first to appear at the breakfast table. Our breakfast was a substantial fox-hunter's repast, and the company were generally assembled at it. When ample justice had been done to the tea, coffee, cold meats, and humming ale, for all these were furnished in abundance, according to the tastes of the different guests, the conversation began to break out, with all the liveliness and freshness of morning mirth.

"But who is the hero of the haunted chamber?—Who has seen the ghost last night?" said the inquisitive gentleman, rolling his lobster eyes about the table.

The question set every tongue in motion; a vast deal of bantering; criticizing of countenances; of mutual accusation and retort took place. Some had drunk deep, and some were unshaven, so that there were suspicious faces enough in the assembly. I alone could not enter with ease and vivacity into the joke. I felt tongue-tied—embarrassed. A recollection of what I had seen and felt the preceding night still haunted my mind. It seemed as if the mysterious picture still held a thrall upon me. I thought also that our host's eye was turned on me with an air of curiosity. In short, I was conscious that I was the hero of the night, and felt as if every one might read it in my looks.

The joke, however, passed over, and no suspicion seemed to attach to me. I was just congratulating myself on my escape, when a servant came in, saying, that the gentleman who had slept on the sofa in the drawing room, had left his watch under one of the pillows. My repeater was in his hand.

"What!" said the inquisitive gentleman, "did any gentleman sleep on the sofa?"

"Soho! soho! a hare—a hare!" cried the old gentleman with the flexible nose.

I could not avoid acknowledging the watch, and was rising in great confusion, when a boisterous old squire who sat beside me, exclaimed, slapping me on the shoulder, " 'Sblood, lad! thou'rt the man as has seen the ghost!"

The attention of the company was immediately turned to me; if my face had been pale the moment before, it now glowed almost to burning. I tried to laugh, but could only make a grimace; and found the muscles of my face twitching at sixes and sevens, and totally out of all controul.

It takes but little to raise a laugh among a set of fox hunters. There was a world of merriment and joking on the subject; and as I never relished a joke overmuch when it was at my own expense, I began to feel a little nettled. I tried to look cool and calm and to restrain my pique; but the coolness and calmness of a man in a passion are confounded treacherous.

Gentlemen, said I, with a slight cocking of the chin, and a bad attempt at a smile, this is all very pleasant—ha! ha!— very pleasant—but I'd have you know I am as little superstitious as any of you—ha! ha!—and as to any thing like timidity—you may smile, gentlemen—but I trust there's no one here means to insinuate that.——As to a room's being haunted, I repeat, gentlemen—(growing a little warm at seeing a cursed grin breaking out round me)—as to a room's being haunted, I have as little faith in such silly stories as any one. But, since you put the matter home to me, I will say that I have met with something in my room strange and inexplicable to me—(a shout of laughter.) Gentlemen, I am serious— I know well what I am saying—I am calm, gentlemen, (striking my fist upon the table)—by heaven I am calm. I am neither trifling, nor do I wish to be trifled with—(the laughter of the company suppressed with ludicrous attempts at gravity.) There is a picture in the room in which I was put last night, that has had an effect upon me the most singular and incomprehensible.

"A picture!" said the old gentleman with the haunted head. "A picture!" cried the narrator with the nose. "A picture! a picture!" echoed several voices. Here there was an ungovernable peal of laughter.

I could not contain myself. I started up from my seat—looked round on the company with fiery indignation—thrust both my hands into my pockets, and strode up to one of the windows, as though I would have walked through it. I stopped short; looked out upon the landscape without distinguishing a feature of it; and felt my gorge rising almost to suffocation.

Mine host saw it was time to interfere. He had maintained an air of gravity through the whole of the scene, and now stepped forth as if to shelter me from the overwhelming merriment of my companions.

"Gentlemen," said he, "I dislike to spoil sport, but you have had your laugh, and the joke of the haunted chamber has been enjoyed. I must now take the part of my guest. I must not only vindicate him from your pleasantries, but I must reconcile him to himself, for I suspect he is a little out of humour with his own feelings; and above all, I must crave his pardon for having made him the subject of a kind of experiment.

"Yes, gentlemen, there is something strange and peculiar in the chamber to which our friend was shown last night. There is a picture in my house which possesses a singular and mysterious influence; and with which there is connected a very curious story. It is a picture to which I attach a value from a variety of circumstances; and though I have often been tempted to destroy it, from the odd and uncomfortable sensations it produces in every one that beholds it; yet I have never been able to prevail upon myself to make the sacrifice. It is a picture I never like to look upon myself; and which is held in awe by all my servants. I have therefore banished it to a room but rarely used; and should have had it covered last night, had not the nature of our conversation, and the whimsical talk about a haunted chamber tempted me to let it remain, by way of experiment, to see whether a stranger, totally unacquainted with its story, would be affected by it."

The words of the Baronet had turned every thought into a different channel; all were anxious to hear the story of the mysterious picture; and for myself, so strongly were my feelings interested, that I forgot to feel piqued at the experiment which my host had made upon my nerves, and joined eagerly in the general entreaty.

As the morning was stormy, and denied all egress, my host was glad of any means of entertaining his company; so drawing his arm chair towards the fire, he began—

The Adventure of the Mysterious Stranger

Many years since, when I was a young man, and had just left Oxford, I was sent on the grand tour to finish my education. I believe my parents had tried in vain to inoculate me with wisdom; so they sent me to mingle with society, in hopes I might take it the natural way. Such, at least, appears the reason for which nine tenths of our youngsters are sent abroad.

In the course of my tour I remained some time at Venice. The romantic character of the place delighted me; I was very much amused by the air of adventure and intrigue prevalent in this region of masks and gondolas; and I was exceedingly smitten by a pair of languishing black eyes, that played upon my heart from under an Italian mantle. So I persuaded myself that I was lingering at Venice to study men and manners. At least I persuaded my friends so, and that answered all my purpose. Indeed, I was a little prone to be struck by peculiarities in character and conduct, and my imagination was so full of romantic associations with Italy, that I was always on the look out for adventure.

Every thing chimed in with such a humour in this old mermaid of a city. My suite of apartments were in a proud, melancholy palace on the grand canal, formerly the residence of a Magnifico, and sumptuous with the traces of decayed grandeur. My gondolier was one of the shrewdest of his class, active, merry, intelligent, and, like his brethren, secret as the grave; that is to say, secret to all the world except his master. I had not had him a week before he put me behind all the curtains in Venice. I liked the silence and mystery of the place, and when I sometimes saw from my window a black gondola gliding mysteriously along in the dusk of the evening, with nothing visible but its little glimmering lantern, I would jump into my own zendaletto, and give a signal for pursuit. But I am running away from my subject with the recollection of youthful follies, said the Baronet, checking himself, "let us come to the point."

Among my familiar resorts was a Cassino under the Arcades on one side of the grand square of St. Mark. Here I used frequently to lounge and take my ice on those warm summer nights when in Italy every body lives abroad until morning. I was seated here one evening, when a groupe of Italians took seats at a table on the opposite side of the saloon. Their conversation was gay and animated, and carried on with Italian vivacity and gesticulation.

I remarked among them one young man, however, who appeared to take no share, and find no enjoyment in the conversation; though he seemed to force himself to attend to it. He was tall and slender, and of extremely prepossessing appearance. His features were fine, though emaciated. He had a profusion of black glossy hair that curled lightly about his head, and contrasted with the extreme paleness of his countenance. His brow was haggard; deep furrows seemed to have been ploughed into his visage by care, not by age, for he was evidently in the prime of youth. His eye was full of expression and fire, but wild and unsteady. He seemed to be tormented by some strange fancy or apprehension. In spite of every effort to fix his attention on the conversation of his companions, I noticed that every now and then he would turn his head slowly round, give a glance over his shoulder, and then withdraw it with a sudden jerk, as if something painful met his eye. This was repeated at intervals of about a minute; and he appeared hardly to have recovered from one shock, before I saw him slowly preparing to encounter another.

After sitting some time in the Cassino, the party paid for the refreshments they had taken, and departed. The young man was the last to leave the saloon, and I remarked him glancing behind him in the same way, just as he passed out of the door. I could not resist the impulse to rise and follow him; for I was at an age when a romantic feeling of curiosity is easily awakened. The party walked slowly down the Arcades, talking and laughing as they went. They crossed the Piazzetta, but paused in the middle of it to enjoy the scene. It was one of those moonlight nights so brilliant and clear in the pure atmosphere of Italy. The moon beams streamed on the

tall tower of St. Mark, and lighted up the magnificent front
and swelling domes of the Cathedral. The party expressed
their delight in animated terms. I kept my eye upon the
young man. He alone seemed abstracted and self occupied. I
noticed the same singular, and as it were, furtive glance over
the shoulder which had attracted my attention in the Cassino.
The party moved on, and I followed; they passed along the
walk called the Broglio; turned the corner of the Ducal palace, and getting into a gondola, glided swiftly away.

The countenance and conduct of this young man dwelt
upon my mind, and interested me exceedingly. I met him a
day or two afterwards in a gallery of paintings. He was
evidently a connoisseur, for he always singled out the most
masterly productions, and the few remarks drawn from him
by his companions showed an intimate acquaintance with the
art. His own taste, however, ran on singular extremes. On
Salvator Rosa in his most savage and solitary scenes; on
Raphael, Titian and Correggio in their softest delineations of
female beauty. On these he would occasionally gaze with
transient enthusiasm. But this seemed only a momentary forgetfulness. Still would recur that cautious glance behind, and
always quickly withdrawn, as though something terrible met
his view.

I encountered him frequently afterwards. At the theatre, at
balls, at concerts; at the promenades in the gardens of San
Georgio; at the grotesque exhibitions in the square of St.
Mark; among the throng of merchants on the Exchange by
the Rialto. He seemed, in fact, to seek crowds; to hunt after
bustle and amusement; yet never to take any interest in either
the business or gaiety of the scene. Ever an air of painful
thought, of wretched abstraction; and ever that strange and
recurring movement, of glancing fearfully over the shoulder. I
did not know at first but this might be caused by apprehension of arrest; or perhaps from dread of assassination. But, if
so, why should he go thus continually abroad; why expose
himself at all times and in all places?

I became anxious to know this stranger. I was drawn to
him by that romantic sympathy which sometimes draws
young men towards each other. His melancholy threw a
charm about him, no doubt heightened by the touching ex-

pression of his countenance, and the manly graces of his person; for manly beauty has its effect even upon men. I had an Englishman's habitual diffidence and awkwardness to contend with; but from frequently meeting him in the Cassino, I gradually edged myself into his acquaintance. I had no reserve on his part to contend with. He seemed on the contrary to court society; and in fact to seek any thing rather than be alone.

When he found I really took an interest in him he threw himself entirely upon my friendship. He clung to me like a drowning man. He would walk with me for hours up and down the place of St. Mark—or would sit until night was far advanced in my apartments; he took rooms under the same roof with me; and his constant request was, that I would permit him, when it did not incommode me, to sit by me in my saloon. It was not that he seemed to take a particular delight in my conversation; but rather that he craved the vicinity of a human being; and above all, of a being that sympathized with him. "I have often heard," said he, "of the sincerity of Englishmen—thank God I have one at length for a friend!"

Yet he never seemed disposed to avail himself of my sympathy other than by mere companionship. He never sought to unbosom himself to me; there appeared to be a settled corroding anguish in his bosom that neither could be soothed "by silence nor by speaking." A devouring melancholy preyed upon his heart, and seemed to be drying up the very blood in his veins. It was not a soft melancholy—the disease of the affections; but a parching withering agony. I could see at times that his mouth was dry and feverish; he panted rather than breathed; his eyes were bloodshot; his cheeks pale and livid; with now and then faint streaks of red athwart them— baleful gleams of the fire that was consuming his heart. As my arm was within his, I felt him press it at times with a convulsive motion to his side; his hands would clinch themselves involuntarily, and a kind of shudder would run through his frame. I reasoned with him about his melancholy, and sought to draw from him the cause—he shrunk from all confiding. "Do not seek to know it," said he, "you could not relieve it if you knew it; you would not even seek to relieve it—on the contrary, I should lose your sympathy; and that," said he, pressing my hand convulsively, "that I feel has become too dear to me to risk."

I endeavoured to awaken hope within him. He was young; life had a thousand pleasures in store for him; there is a healthy reaction in the youthful heart; it medicines all its own wounds—"Come, come," said I, "there is no grief so great that youth cannot outgrow it."—"No! no!" said he, clinching his teeth, and striking repeatedly, with the energy of despair, upon his bosom—"It is here—here—deep rooted; draining my heart's blood. It grows and grows, while my heart withers and withers! I have a dreadful monitor that gives me no re-pose—that follows me step by step; and will follow me step by step, until it pushes me into my grave!"

As he said this he gave involuntarily one of those fearful glances over his shoulder, and shrunk back with more than usual horror. I could not resist the temptation, to allude to this movement, which I supposed to be some mere malady of the nerves. The moment I mentioned it his face became crim-soned and convulsed—he grasped me by both hands: "For God's sake," exclaimed he, with a piercing voice—"never al-lude to that again—let us avoid this subject, my friend: you cannot relieve me, indeed you cannot relieve me; but you may add to the torments I suffer;—at some future day you shall know all."

I never resumed the subject; for however much my curios-ity might be roused, I felt too true a compassion for his suf-ferings to increase them by my intrusion. I sought various ways to divert his mind, and to arouse him from the constant meditations in which he was plunged. He saw my efforts, and seconded them as far as in his power, for there was nothing moody or wayward in his nature; on the contrary, there was something frank, generous, unassuming, in his whole deport-ment. All the sentiments he uttered were noble and lofty. He claimed no indulgence, asked no toleration, but seemed con-tent to carry his load of misery in silence, and only sought to carry it by my side. There was a mute beseeching manner about him, as if he craved companionship as a charitable boon; and a tacit thankfulness in his looks, as if he felt grate-ful to me for not repulsing him.

I felt this melancholy to be infectious. It stole over my

spirits; interfered with all my gay pursuits, and gradually saddened my life; yet I could not prevail upon myself to shake
off a being who seemed to hang upon me for support. In
truth, the generous traits of character which beamed through
all this gloom penetrated to my heart. His bounty was lavish
and open handed. His charity melting and spontaneous. Not
confined to mere donations, which humiliate as much as they
relieve. The tone of his voice, the beam of his eye, enhanced
every gift, and surprised the poor suppliant with that rarest
and sweetest of charities, the charity not merely of the hand
but of the heart. Indeed, his liberality seemed to have something in it of self abasement and expiation. He, in a manner,
humbled himself before the mendicant. "What right have I to
ease and affluence," would he murmur to himself, "when innocence wanders in misery and rags?"

The Carnival time arrived. I hoped the gay scenes then presented might have some cheering effect. I mingled with him
in the motley throng that crowded the place of St. Mark. We
frequented operas, masquerades, balls. All in vain. The evil
kept growing on him; he became more and more haggard
and agitated. Often, after we had returned from one of these
scenes of revelry, I have entered his room, and found him
lying on his face on the sofa: his hands clinched in his fine
hair, and his whole countenance bearing traces of the convulsions of his mind.

The Carnival passed away; the time of Lent succeeded; Passion week arrived. We attended one evening a solemn service
in one of the churches; in the course of which, a grand piece
of vocal and instrumental music was performed relating to the
death of our Saviour.

I had remarked that he was always powerfully affected by
music; on this occasion he was so in an extraordinary degree.
As the pealing notes swelled through the lofty aisles, he
seemed to kindle with fervour. His eyes rolled upwards, until
nothing but the whites were visible; his hands were clasped
together, until the fingers were deeply imprinted in the flesh.
When the music expressed the dying agony, his face gradually
sank upon his knees; and at the touching words resounding
through the church *"Jesu mori,"* sobs burst from him uncon-
trouled. I had never seen him weep before; his had always

been agony rather than sorrow. I augured well from the circumstance, and let him weep on uninterrupted. When the service was ended, we left the church. He hung on my arm as we walked homewards, with something of a softer and more subdued manner; instead of that nervous agitation I had been accustomed to witness. He alluded to the service we had heard. "Music," said he, "is indeed the voice of heaven; never before have I felt more impressed by the story of the atonement of our Saviour. Yes, my friend," said he, clasping his hands with a kind of transport, "I know that my Redeemer liveth."

We parted for the night. His room was not far from mine, and I heard him for some time busied in it. I fell asleep, but was awakened before daylight. The young man stood by my bed side, dressed for travelling. He held a sealed pacquet and a large parcel in his hand, which he laid on the table. "Farewell, my friend," said he, "I am about to set forth on a long journey; but, before I go, I leave with you these remembrances. In this pacquet you will find the particulars of my story. When you read them, I shall be far away; do not remember me with aversion. You have been, indeed, a friend to me. You have poured oil into a broken heart,—but you could not heal it.—Farewell—let me kiss your hand—I am unworthy to embrace you." He sank on his knees, seized my hand in despite of my efforts to the contrary, and covered it with kisses. I was so surprised by all this scene that I had not been able to say a word.

"But we shall meet again," said I, hastily, as I saw him hurrying towards the door.

"Never—never in this world!" said he solemnly. He sprang once more to my bed side—seized my hand, pressed it to his heart and to his lips, and rushed out of the room.

Here the Baronet paused. He seemed lost in thought, and sat looking upon the floor and drumming with his fingers on the arm of his chair.

"And did this mysterious personage return?" said the inquisitive gentleman. "Never!" replied the Baronet, with a pensive shake of the head: "I never saw him again." "And pray what has all this to do with the picture?" inquired the old gentleman with the nose—"True!" said the questioner—

"Is it the portrait of that crack brained Italian?" "No!" said the Baronet, drily, not half liking the appellation given to his hero; "but this picture was inclosed in the parcel he left with me. The sealed pacquet contained its explanation. There was a request on the outside that I would not open it until six months had elapsed. I kept my promise, in spite of my curiosity. I have a translation of it by me, and had meant to read it, by way of accounting for the mystery of the chamber, but I fear I have already detained the company too long."

Here there was a general wish expressed to have the manuscript read; particularly on the part of the inquisitive gentleman. So the worthy Baronet drew out a fairly written manuscript, and wiping his spectacles, read aloud the following story: —

The Story of the Young Italian

I was born at Naples. My parents, though of noble rank, were limited in fortune, or rather my father was ostentatious beyond his means, and expended so much on his palace, his equipage, and his retinue, that he was continually straightened in his pecuniary circumstances. I was a younger son, and looked upon with indifference by my father, who, from a principle of family pride, wished to leave all his property to my elder brother.

I showed, when quite a child, an extreme sensibility. Every thing affected me violently. While yet an infant in my mother's arms, and before I had learnt to talk, I could be wrought upon to a wonderful degree of anguish or delight by the power of music. As I grew older my feelings remained equally acute, and I was easily transported into paroxysms of pleasure or rage. It was the amusement of my relatives and of the domestics to play upon this irritable temperament. I was moved to tears, tickled to laughter, provoked to fury, for the entertainment of company, who were amused by such a tempest of mighty passion in a pigmy frame. They little thought, or perhaps little heeded the dangerous sensibilities they were fostering. I thus became a little creature of passion, before reason was developed. In a short time I grew too old to be a play-thing, and then I became a torment. The tricks and passions I had been teased into became irksome, and I was disliked by my teachers for the very lessons they had taught me.

My mother died; and my power as a spoiled child was at an end. There was no longer any necessity to humour or tolerate me, for there was nothing to be gained by it, as I was no favourite of my father. I therefore experienced the fate of a spoiled child in such a situation, and was neglected, or noticed only to be crossed and contradicted. Such was the early treatment of a heart, which, if I can judge of it at all, was naturally disposed to the extremes of tenderness and affection.

My father, as I have already said, never liked me—in fact he never understood me; he looked upon me as wilful and wayward, as deficient in natural affection:—it was the stateliness of his own manner; the loftiness and grandeur of his own look which had repelled me from his arms. I always pictured him to myself as I had seen him clad in his senatorial robes, rustling with pomp and pride. The magnificence of his person daunted my young imagination. I could never approach him with the confiding affection of a child.

My father's feelings were wrapped up in my elder brother. He was to be the inheritor of the family title and the family dignity, and every thing was sacrificed to him—I, as well as every thing else. It was determined to devote me to the church, that so my humours and myself might be removed out of the way, either of tasking my father's time and trouble, or interfering with the interests of my brother. At an early age, therefore, before my mind had dawned upon the world and its delights, or known any thing of it beyond the precincts of my father's palace, I was sent to a convent, the superior of which was my uncle, and was confided entirely to his care.

My uncle was a man totally estranged from the world; he had never relished, for he had never tasted its pleasures; and he regarded rigid self denial as the great basis of Christian virtue. He considered every one's temperament like his own; or at least he made them conform to it. His character and habits had an influence over the fraternity of which he was superior. A more gloomy saturnine set of beings were never

sembled together. The convent, too, was calculated to
waken sad and solitary thoughts. It was situated in a gloomy
rge of those mountains away south of Vesuvius. All distant
ws were shut out by sterile volcanic heights. A mountain
eam raved beneath its walls, and eagles screamed about its
rets.

had been sent to this place at so tender an age as soon to
all distinct recollection of the scenes I had left behind. As
mind expanded, therefore, it formed its idea of the world
n the convent and its vicinity, and a dreary world it ap-
ed to me. An early tinge of melancholy was thus infused
my character; and the dismal stories of the monks, about
ils and evil spirits, with which they affrighted my young
gination, gave me a tendency to superstition, which I
ld never effectually shake off. They took the same delight
work upon my ardent feelings that had been so mischie-
usly executed by my father's household.

I can recollect the horrors with which they fed my heated
fancy during an eruption of Vesuvius. We were distant from
that volcano, with mountains between us; but its convulsive
throes shook the solid foundations of nature. Earthquakes
threatened to topple down our convent towers. A lurid, baleful light hung in the heavens at night, and showers of ashes,
borne by the wind, fell in our narrow valley. The monks
talked of the earth being honey-combed beneath us; of
streams of molten lava raging through its veins; of caverns of
sulphurous flames roaring in the centre, the abodes of demons and the damned; of fiery gulfs ready to yawn beneath
our feet. All these tales were told to the doleful accompaniment of the mountain's thunders, whose low bellowing made
the walls of our convent vibrate.

One of the monks had been a painter, but had retired from
the world, and embraced this dismal life in expiation of some
crime. He was a melancholy man, who pursued his art in the
solitude of his cell, but made it a source of penance to him.
His employment was to portray, either on canvass or in
waxen models, the human face and human form, in the agonies of death, and in all the stages of dissolution and decay.
The fearful mysteries of the charnel house were unfolded in
his labours—the loathsome banquet of the beetle and the

worm.——I turn with shuddering even from the recollection of his works. Yet, at the time, my strong but ill directed imagination seized with ardour upon his instructions in his art. Any thing was a variety from the dry studies and monotonous duties of the cloister. In a little while I became expert with my pencil, and my gloomy productions were thought worthy of decorating some of the altars of the chapel.

In this dismal way was a creature of feeling and fancy brought up. Every thing genial and amiable in my nature was repressed, and nothing brought out but what was unprofitable and ungracious. I was ardent in my temperament; quick, mercurial, impetuous, formed to be a creature all love and adoration; but a leaden hand was laid on all my finer qualities. I was taught nothing but fear and hatred. I hated my uncle, I hated the monks, I hated the convent in which I was immured. I hated the world, and I almost hated myself, for being, as I supposed, so hating and hateful an animal.

When I had nearly attained the age of sixteen, I was suffered, on one occasion, to accompany one of the brethren on a mission to a distant part of the country. We soon left behind us the gloomy valley in which I had been pent up for so many years, and after a short journey among the mountains, emerged upon the voluptuous landscape that spreads itself about the Bay of Naples. Heavens! how transported was I, when I stretched my gaze over a vast reach of delicious sunny country, gay with groves and vineyards; with Vesuvius rearing its forked summit to my right; the blue Mediterranean to my left, with its enchanting coast, studded with shining towns and sumptuous villas; and Naples, my native Naples, gleaming far, far in the distance.

Good God! was this the lovely world from which I had been excluded! I had reached that age when the sensibilities are in all their bloom and freshness. Mine had been checked and chilled. They now burst forth with the suddenness of a retarded spring time. My heart, hitherto unnaturally shrunk up, expanded into a riot of vague but delicious emotions. The beauty of nature intoxicated, bewildered me. The song of the peasants; their cheerful looks; their happy avocations; the picturesque gaiety of their dresses; their rustic music; their dances; all broke upon me like witchcraft. My soul responded to the music; my heart danced in my bosom. All the men appeared amiable, all the women lovely.

I returned to the convent, that is to say, my body returned, but my heart and soul never entered there again. I could not forget this glimpse of a beautiful and a happy world; a world so suited to my natural character. I had felt so happy while in it; so different a being from what I felt myself when in the convent—that tomb of the living. I contrasted the countenances of the beings I had seen, full of fire and freshness and enjoyment, with the pallid, leaden, lack lustre visages of the monks; the music of the dance, with the droning chant of the chapel. I had before found the exercises of the cloister wearisome; they now became intolerable. The dull round of duties wore away my spirit; my nerves became irritated by the fretful tinkling of the convent bell; evermore dinging among the mountain echoes; evermore calling me from my repose at night, my pencil by day, to attend to some tedious and mechanical ceremony of devotion.

I was not of a nature to meditate long, without putting my thoughts into action. My spirit had been suddenly aroused, and was now all awake within me. I watched an opportunity, fled from the convent, and made my way on foot to Naples. As I entered its gay and crowded streets, and beheld the variety and stir of life around me, the luxury of palaces, the splendour of equipages, and the pantomimic animation of the motley populace, I seemed as if awakened to a world of enchantment, and solemnly vowed that nothing should force me back to the monotony of the cloister.

I had to inquire my way to my father's palace, for I had been so young on leaving it, that I knew not its situation. I found some difficulty in getting admitted to my father's presence, for the domestics scarcely knew that there was such a being as myself in existence, and my monastic dress did ⸻ in my favour. Even ⸻ recollection of my person. I told him my name, threw myself at his feet, implored his forgiveness, and entreated that I might not be sent back to the convent.

He received me with the condescension of a patron rather than the fondness of a parent: listened patiently, but coldly to my tale of monastic grievances and disgusts, and promised to

think what else could be done for me. This coldness blighted
and drove back all the frank affection of my nature that was
ready to spring forth at the least warmth of parental kindness.
All my early feelings towards my father revived; I again
looked up to him as the stately magnificent being that had
daunted my childish imagination, and felt as if I had no pretensions to his sympathies. My brother engrossed all his care
and love; he inherited his nature, and carried himself towards
me with a protecting rather than a fraternal air. It wounded
my pride, which was great. I could brook condescension from
my father, for I looked up to him with awe as a superior
being; but I could not brook patronage from a brother, who,
I felt, was intellectually my inferior. The servants perceived
that I was an unwelcome intruder in the paternal mansion,
and, menial-like, they treated me with neglect. Thus baffled at
every point; my affections outraged wherever they would attach themselves, I became sullen, silent and desponding. My
feelings driven back upon myself, entered and preyed upon
my own heart. I remained for some days an unwelcome guest
rather than a restored son in my father's house. I was doomed
never to be properly known there. I was made, by wrong
treatment, strange even to myself; and they judged of me
from my strangeness.

I was startled one day at the sight of one of the monks of
my convent, gliding out of my father's room. He saw me, but
pretended not to notice me; and this very hypocrisy made me
suspect something. I had become sore and susceptible in my
feelings; every thing inflicted a wound on them. In this state
of mind I was treated with marked disrespect by a pampered
minion, the favourite servant of my father. All the pride and
passion of my nature rose in an instant, and I struck him to
the earth.

My father was passing by; he stopped not to inquire the
reason, nor indeed could he read the long course of mental
sufferings which were the real cause. He rebuked me with
anger and scorn; summoning all the haughtiness of his nature, and grandeur of his look, to give weight to the contumely with which he treated me. I felt I had not deserved
it—I felt that I was not appreciated—I felt that I had that
within me which merited better treatment; my heart swelled

against a father's injustice. I broke through my habitual awe of him. I replied to him with impatience; my hot spirit flushed in my cheek and kindled in my eye, but my sensitive heart swelled as quickly, and before I had half vented my passion I felt it suffocated and quenched in my tears. My father was astonished and incensed at this turning of the worm, and ordered me to my chamber. I retired in silence, choking with contending emotions.

I had not been long there when I overheard voices in an adjoining apartment. It was a consultation between my father and the monk, about the means of getting me back quietly to the convent. My resolution was taken. I had no longer a home nor a father. That very night I left the paternal roof. I got on board a vessel about making sail from the harbour, and abandoned myself to the wide world. No matter to what port she steered; any part of so beautiful a world was better than my convent. No matter where I was cast by fortune; any place would be more a home to me than the home I had left behind. The vessel was bound to Genoa. We arrived there after a voyage of a few days.

As I entered the harbour, between the moles which embrace it, and beheld the amphitheatre of palaces and churches and splendid gardens, rising one above another, I felt at once its title to the appellation of Genoa the Superb. I landed on the mole an utter stranger, without knowing what to do, or whither to direct my steps. No matter; I was released from the thraldom of the convent and the humiliations of home! When I traversed the Strada Balbi and the Strada Nuova, those streets of palaces, and gazed at the wonders of architecture around me; when I wandered at close of day, amid a gay throng of the brilliant and the beautiful, through the green alleys of the Aqua Verde, or among the colonnades and terraces of the magnificent Doria Gardens; I thought it impossible to be ever otherwise than happy in Genoa.

A few days sufficed to show me my mistake. My scanty purse was exhausted, and for the first time in my life I experienced the sordid distress of penury. I had never known the want of money, and had never adverted to the possibility of such an evil. I was ignorant of the world and all its ways; and when first the idea of destitution came over my mind its effect was withering. I was wandering pensively through the streets which no longer delighted my eyes, when chance led my steps into the magnificent church of the Annunciata.

A celebrated painter of the day was at that moment superintending the placing of one of his pictures over an altar. The proficiency which I had acquired in his art during my residence in the convent had made me an enthusiastic amateur. I was struck, at the first glance, with the painting. It was the face of a Madonna. So innocent, so lovely, such a divine expression of maternal tenderness! I lost for the moment all recollection of myself in the enthusiasm of my art. I clasped my hands together, and uttered an ejaculation of delight. The painter perceived my emotion. He was flattered and gratified by it. My air and manner pleased him, and he accosted me. I felt too much the want of friendship to repel the advances of a stranger, and there was something in this one so benevolent and winning that in a moment he gained my confidence.

I told him my story and my situation, concealing only my name and rank. He appeared strongly interested by my recital; invited me to his house, and from that time I became his favourite pupil. He thought he perceived in me extraordinary talents for the art, and his encomiums awakened all my ardour. What a blissful period of my existence was it that I passed beneath his roof. Another being seemed created within me, or rather, all that was amiable and excellent was drawn out. I was as recluse as ever I had been at the convent, but how different was my seclusion. My time was spent in storing my mind with lofty and poetical ideas; in meditating on all that was striking and noble in history and fiction; in studying and tracing all that was sublime and beautiful in nature. I was always a visionary imaginative being, but now my reveries and imaginings all elevated me to rapture.

I looked up to my master as to a benevolent genius that had opened to me a region of enchantment. He was not a native of Genoa, but had been drawn thither by the solicitations of several of the nobility, and had resided there but a few years, for the completion of certain works. His health was delicate, and he had to confide much of the filling up of his designs to the pencils of his scholars. He considered me as particularly happy in delineating the human countenance; in seizing upon characteristic, though fleeting expressions, and fixing them powerfully upon my canvas. I was employed continually, therefore, in sketching faces, and often when some particular grace or beauty of expression was wanted in a countenance, it was entrusted to my pencil. My benefactor was fond of bringing me forward; and partly, perhaps, through my actual skill, and partly through his partial praises, I began to be noted for the expressions of my countenances.

Among the various works which he had undertaken, was an historical piece for one of the palaces of Genoa, in which were to be introduced the likenesses of several of the family. Among these was one entrusted to my pencil. It was that of a young girl, as yet in a convent for her education. She came out for the purpose of sitting for the picture. I first saw her in an apartment of one of the sumptuous palaces of Genoa. She stood before a casement that looked out upon the bay: a stream of vernal sunshine fell upon her, and shed a kind of glory round her as it lit up the rich crimson chamber. She was but sixteen years of age—and oh how lovely! The scene broke upon me like a mere vision of spring, and youth, and beauty. I could have fallen down and worshipped her. She was like one of those fictions of poets and painters, when they would express the *beau ideal* that haunts their minds with shapes of indescribable perfection.

I was permitted to sketch her countenance in various positions, and I fondly protracted the study that was undoing me. The more I gazed on her the more I became enamoured; there was something almost painful in my intense admiration. I was but nineteen years of age; shy, diffident, and inexperienced. I was treated with attention by her mother; for my youth and my enthusiasm in my art had won favour for me; and I am inclined to think something in my air and manner inspired interest and respect. Still the kindness with which I was treated could not dispel the embarrassment into which my own imagination threw me when in presence of this lovely being. It elevated her into something almost more than mortal. She seemed too exquisite for earthly use; too delicate and exalted for human attainment. As I sat tracing her charms on my canvas, with my eyes occasionally riveted on her features, I drank in delicious poison that made me giddy. My heart alternately gushed with tenderness, and ached with despair. Now I became more than ever sensible of the violent fires that had lain dormant at the bottom of my soul. You who are born in a more temperate climate and under a cooler sky, have little idea of the violence of passion in our southern bosoms.

A few days finished my task; Bianca returned to her convent, but her image remained indelibly impressed upon my heart. It dwelt in my imagination; it became my pervading idea of beauty. It had an effect even upon my pencil; I became noted for my felicity in depicting female loveliness; it was but because I multiplied the image of Bianca. I soothed, and yet fed my fancy, by introducing her in all the productions of my master. I have stood with delight in one of the chapels of the Annunciata, and heard the crowd extol the seraphic beauty of a saint which I had painted; I have seen them bow down in adoration before the painting: they were bowing before the loveliness of Bianca.

I existed in this kind of dream, I might almost say delirium, for upwards of a year. Such is the tenacity of my imagination that the image which was formed in it continued in all its power and freshness. I was a solitary, meditative being, much given to reverie, and apt to foster ideas which had once taken strong possession of me. I was roused from this fond, melancholy, delicious dream by the death of my worthy benefactor. I cannot describe the pangs his death occasioned me. It left me alone and almost broken hearted. He bequeathed to me his little property; which, from the liberality of his disposition and his expensive style of living, was indeed but small; and he most particularly recommended me, in dying, to the protection of a nobleman who had been his patron.

The latter was a man who passed for munificent. He was a lover and an encourager of the arts, and evidently wished to be thought so. He fancied he saw in me indications of future excellence; my pencil had already attracted attention; he took me at once under his protection; seeing that I was overwhelmed with grief, and incapable of exerting myself in the mansion of my late benefactor, he invited me to sojourn for a time at a villa which he possessed on the border of the sea, in the picturesque neighbourhood of Sestri di Ponente.

I found at the villa the Count's only son Filippo: he was nearly of my age, prepossessing in his appearance, and fascinating in his manners; he attached himself to me, and seemed to court my good opinion. I thought there was something of profession in his kindness, and of caprice in his disposition; but I had nothing else near me to attach myself to, and my heart felt the need of something to repose upon. His education had been neglected; he looked upon me as his superior in mental powers and acquirements, and tacitly acknowledged my superiority. I felt that I was his equal in birth, and that gave an independence to my manner, which had its effect. The caprice and tyranny I saw sometimes exercised on others, over whom he had power, were never manifested towards me. We became intimate friends, and frequent companions. Still I loved to be alone, and to indulge in the reveries of my own imagination, among the scenery by which I was surrounded.

The villa commanded a wide view of the Mediterranean, and the picturesque Ligurian coast. It stood alone in the midst of ornamented grounds, finely decorated with statues and fountains, and laid out into groves and alleys, and shady lawns. Every thing was assembled here that could gratify the taste or agreeably occupy the mind. Soothed by the tranquillity of this elegant retreat, the turbulence of my feelings gradually subsided, and, blending with the romantic spell which still reigned over my imagination, produced a soft voluptuous melancholy.

I had not been long under the roof of the Count, when our solitude was enlivened by another inhabitant. It was the daughter of a relative of the Count, who had lately died in reduced circumstances, bequeathing this only child to his protection. I had heard much of her beauty from Filippo, but my fancy had become so engrossed by one idea of beauty as not to admit of any other. We were in the central saloon of the villa when she arrived. She was still in mourning, and approached, leaning on the Count's arm. As they ascended the marble portico, I was struck by the elegance of her figure and movement, by the grace with which the *mezzaro*, the bewitching veil of Genoa, was folded about her slender form. They entered. Heavens! what was my surprise when I beheld Bianca before me. It was herself; pale with grief; but still more matured in loveliness than when I had last beheld her. The time that had elapsed had developed the graces of her person; and the sorrow she had undergone had diffused over her countenance an irresistible tenderness.

She blushed and trembled at seeing me, and tears rushed into her eyes, for she remembered in whose company she had been accustomed to behold me. For my part, I cannot express what were my emotions. By degrees I overcame the extreme shyness that had formerly paralyzed me in her presence. We were drawn together by sympathy of situation. We had each lost our best friend in the world; we were each, in some measure, thrown upon the kindness of others. When I came to know her intellectually, all my ideal picturings of her were confirmed. Her newness to the world, her delightful susceptibility to every thing beautiful and agreeable in nature, reminded me of my own emotions when first I escaped from the convent. Her rectitude of thinking delighted my judgment; the sweetness of her nature wrapped itself round my heart; and then her young and tender and budding loveliness, sent a delicious madness to my brain.

I gazed upon her with a kind of idolatry, as something more than mortal; and I felt humiliated at the idea of my comparative unworthiness. Yet she was mortal; and one of mortality's most susceptible and loving compounds; for she loved me!

How first I discovered the transporting truth I cannot recollect; I believe it stole upon me by degrees, as a wonder past hope or belief. We were both at such a tender and loving age; in constant intercourse with each other; mingling in the same elegant pursuits; for music, poetry and painting were our mutual delights, and we were almost separated from society, among lovely and romantic scenery! Is it strange that two young hearts thus brought together should readily twine round each other?

Oh gods! what a dream—a transient dream! of unalloyed delight then passed over my soul! Then it was that the world around me was indeed a paradise, for I had woman—lovely, delicious woman, to share it with me. How often have I rambled along the picturesque shores of Sestri, or climbed its wild mountains, with the coast gemmed with villas, and the blue sea far below me, and the slender Pharo of Genoa on its romantic promontory in the distance; and as I sustained the faltering steps of Bianca, have thought there could no unhappiness enter into so beautiful a world. How often have we listened together to the nightingale, as it poured forth its rich notes among the moonlight bowers of the garden, and have wondered that poets could ever have fancied any thing melancholy in its song! Why, oh why is this budding season of life and tenderness so transient—why is this rosy cloud of love that sheds such a glow over the morning of our days so prone to brew up into the whirlwind and the storm!

I was the first to awaken from this blissful delirium of the affections. I had gained Bianca's heart; what was I to do with it? I had no wealth nor prospects to entitle me to her hand. Was I to take advantage of her ignorance of the world, of her confiding affection, and draw her down to my own poverty? Was this requiting the hospitality of the Count?—was this requiting the love of Bianca?

Now first I began to feel that even successful love may have its bitterness. A corroding care gathered about my heart. I moved about the palace like a guilty being. I felt as if I had abused its hospitality—as if I were a thief within its walls. I could no longer look with unembarrassed mien in the countenance of the Count. I accused myself of perfidy to him, and I thought he read it in my looks, and began to distrust and despise me. His manner had always been ostentatious and condescending, it now appeared cold and haughty. Filippo, too, became reserved and distant; or at least I suspected him to be so. Heavens!—was this mere coinage of my brain: was I to become suspicious of all the world?—a poor surmising wretch; watching looks and gestures; and torturing myself with misconstructions. Or if true—was I to remain beneath a roof where I was merely tolerated, and linger there on sufferance? "This is not to be endured!" exclaimed I, "I will tear myself from this state of self abasement; I will break through this fascination and fly——Fly?—whither?—from the world?—for where is the world when I leave Bianca behind me!"

My spirit was naturally proud, and swelled within me at the idea of being looked upon with contumely. Many times I was on the point of declaring my family and rank, and asserting my equality, in the presence of Bianca, when I thought her relatives assumed an air of superiority. But the feeling was transient. I considered myself discarded and contemned by my family; and had solemnly vowed never to own relationship to them, until they themselves should claim it.

The struggle of my mind preyed upon my happiness and my health. It seemed as if the uncertainty of being loved would be less intolerable than thus to be assured of it, and yet not dare to enjoy the conviction. I was no longer the enraptured admirer of Bianca; I no longer hung in ecstacy on the tones of her voice, nor drank in with insatiate gaze the beauty of her countenance. Her very smiles ceased to delight me, for I felt culpable in having won them.

She could not but be sensible of the change in me, and inquired the cause with her usual frankness and simplicity. I could not evade the inquiry, for my heart was full to aching. I told her all the conflict of my soul; my devouring passion, my bitter self upbraiding. "Yes!" said I, "I am unworthy of you. I am an offcast from my family—a wanderer—a nameless, homeless wanderer, with nothing but poverty for my portion, and yet I have dared to love you—have dared to aspire to your love!"

My agitation moved her to tears; but she saw nothing in my situation so hopeless as I had depicted it. Brought up in a convent, she knew nothing of the world, its wants, its cares;—and indeed, what woman is a worldly casuist in matters of the heart!—Nay, more—she kindled into a sweet enthusiasm when she spoke of my fortunes and myself. We had dwelt together on the works of the famous masters. I had related to her their histories; the high reputation, the influence, the magnificence to which they had attained;—the companions of princes, the favourites of kings, the pride and boast of nations. All this she applied to me. Her love saw nothing in all their great productions that I was not able to achieve; and when I beheld the lovely creature glow with fervour, and her whole countenance radiant with visions of my glory, I was snatched up for the moment into the heaven of her own imagination.

I am dwelling too long upon this part of my story; yet I

cannot help lingering over a period of my life, on which, with all its cares and conflicts, I look back with fondness; for as yet my soul was unstained by a crime. I do not know what might have been the result of this struggle between pride, delicacy, and passion, had I not read in a Neapolitan gazette an account of the sudden death of my brother. It was accompanied by an earnest inquiry for intelligence concerning me, and a prayer, should this notice meet my eye, that I would hasten to Naples, to comfort an infirm and afflicted father.

I was naturally of an affectionate disposition; but my brother had never been as a brother to me; I had long considered myself as disconnected from him, and his death caused me but little emotion. The thoughts of my father, infirm and suffering, touched me, however, to the quick; and when I thought of him, that lofty magnificent being, now bowed down and desolate, and suing to me for comfort, all my resentment for past neglect was subdued, and a glow of filial affection was awakened within me.

The predominant feeling, however, that overpowered all others was transport at the sudden change in my whole fortunes. A home—a name—rank—wealth awaited me; and love painted a still more rapturous prospect in the distance. I hastened to Bianca, and threw myself at her feet. "Oh, Bianca," exclaimed I, "at length I can claim you for my own. I am no longer a nameless adventurer, a neglected, rejected outcast. Look—read, behold the tidings that restore me to my name and to myself!"

I will not dwell on the scene that ensued. Bianca rejoiced in the reverse of my situation, because she saw it lightened my heart of a load of care; for her own part she had loved me for myself, and had never doubted that my own merits would command both fame and fortune.

I now felt all my native pride buoyant within me. I no longer walked with my eyes bent to the dust; hope elevated them to the skies; my soul was lit up with fresh fires, and beamed from my countenance.

I wished to impart the change in my circumstances to the Count; to let him know who and what I was, and to make formal proposals for the hand of Bianca; but he was absent on a distant estate. I opened my whole soul to Filippo. Now first

I told him of my passion; of the doubts and fears that had distracted me, and of the tidings that had suddenly dispelled them. He overwhelmed me with congratulations and with the warmest expressions of sympathy. I embraced him in the fullness of my heart. I felt compunctious for having suspected him of coldness, and asked him forgiveness for having ever doubted his friendship.

Nothing is so warm and enthusiastic as a sudden expansion of the heart between young men. Filippo entered into our concerns with the most eager interest. He was our confidant and counsellor. It was determined that I should hasten at once to Naples to re-establish myself in my father's affections and my paternal home, and the moment the reconciliation was effected and my father's consent insured, I should return and demand Bianca of the Count. Filippo engaged to secure his father's acquiescence; indeed, he undertook to watch over our interests, and was to be the channel through which we might correspond.

My parting with Bianca was tender—delicious—agonizing. It was in a little pavilion of the garden which had been one of our favourite resorts. How often and often did I return to have one more adieu—to have her look once more on me in speechless emotion—to enjoy once more the rapturous sight of those tears streaming down her lovely cheeks—to seize once more on that delicate hand, the frankly accorded pledge of love, and cover it with tears and kisses! Heavens! There is a delight even in the parting agony of two lovers worth a thousand tame pleasures of the world. I have her at this moment before my eyes—at the window of the pavilion, putting aside the vines which clustered about the casement— her light form beaming forth in virgin white—her countenance all tears and smiles—sending a thousand and a thousand adieus after me, as, hesitating, in a delirium of fondness and agitation, I faltered my way down the avenue.

As the bark bore me out of the harbour of Genoa, how eagerly my eye stretched along the coast of Sestri, till it discovered the villa gleaming from among trees at the foot of the mountain. As long as day lasted, I gazed and gazed upon it, till it lessened and lessened to a mere white speck in the distance; and still my intense and fixed gaze discerned it, when all other objects of the coast had blended into indistinct confusion, or were lost in the evening gloom.

On arriving at Naples, I hastened to my paternal home. My heart yearned for the long withheld blessing of a father's love. As I entered the proud portal of the ancestral palace, my emotions were so great that I could not speak. No one knew me. The servants gazed at me with curiosity and surprise. A few years of intellectual elevation and development had made a prodigious change in the poor fugitive stripling from the convent. Still that no one should know me in my rightful home was overpowering. I felt like the prodigal son returned. I was a stranger in the house of my father. I burst into tears, and wept aloud. When I made myself known, however, all was changed. I, who had once been almost repulsed from its walls, and forced to fly as an exile, was welcomed back with acclamation, with servility. One of the servants hastened to prepare my father for my reception; my eagerness to receive the paternal embrace was so great that I could not await his return; but hurried after him.

What a spectacle met my eyes as I entered the chamber. My father, whom I had left in the pride of vigourous age, whose noble and majestic bearing had so awed my young imagination, was bowed down and withered into decrepitude. A paralysis had ravaged his stately form, and left it a shaking ruin. He sat propped up in his chair, with pale relaxed visage and glassy wandering eye. His intellects had evidently shared in the ravage of his frame. The servant was endeavouring to make him comprehend the visitor that was at hand. I tottered up to him and sank at his feet. All his past coldness and neglect were forgotten in his present sufferings. I remembered only that he was my parent, and that I had deserted him. I clasped his knees; my voice was almost stifled with convulsive sobs. "Pardon—pardon—oh my father!" was all that I could utter. His apprehension seemed slowly to return to him. He gazed at me for some moments with a vague, inquiring look; a convulsive tremor quivered about his lips; he feebly extended a shaking hand, laid it upon my head, and burst into an infantine flow of tears.

From that moment he would scarcely spare me from his sight. I appeared the only object that his heart responded to in the world: all else was as a blank to him. He had almost lost the powers of speech, and the reasoning faculty seemed at an end. He was mute and passive; excepting that fits of child-like weeping would sometimes come over him without any immediate cause. If I left the room at any time, his eye was incessantly fixed on the door till my return, and on my entrance there was another gush of tears.

To talk with him of my concerns, in this ruined state of mind, would have been worse than useless: to have left him, for ever so short a time, would have been cruel, unnatural. Here then was a new trial for my affections. I wrote to Bianca an account of my return and of my actual situation; painting in colours vivid, for they were true, the torments I suffered at our being thus separated; for to the youthful lover every day of absence is an age of love lost. I enclosed the letter in one to Filippo who was the channel of our correspondence. I received a reply from him full of friendship and sympathy; from Bianca full of assurances of affection and constancy.

Week after week; month after month elapsed, without making any change in my circumstances. The vital flame, which had seemed nearly extinct when first I met my father, kept fluttering on without any apparent diminution. I watched him constantly, faithfully—I had almost said patiently. I knew that his death alone would set me free; yet I never at any moment wished it. I felt too glad to be able to make any atonement for past disobedience; and, denied as I had been all endearments of relationship in my early days, my heart yearned towards a father, who, in his age and helplessness, had thrown himself entirely on me for comfort. My passion for Bianca gained daily more force from absence; by constant meditation it wore itself a deeper and deeper channel. I made no new friends nor acquaintances; sought none of the pleasures of Naples which my rank and fortune threw open to me. Mine was a heart that confined itself to few objects, but dwelt upon them with the intenser passion. To sit by my father, administer to his wants, and to meditate on Bianca in the silence of his chamber, was my constant habit. Sometimes I amused myself with my pencil in portraying the image ever present to my imagination. I transferred to canvas every look and smile of hers that dwelt in my heart. I showed them to my father in hopes of awakening an interest in his bosom for the mere shadow of my love; but he was too far sunk in intellect to take any notice of them.

When I received a letter from Bianca it was a new source of solitary luxury. Her letters, it is true, were less and less frequent, but they were always full of assurances of unabated affection. They breathed not the frank and innocent warmth, with which she expressed herself in conversation, but I accounted for it from the embarrassment which inexperienced minds have often to express themselves upon paper. Filippo assured me of her unaltered constancy. They both lamented in the strongest terms our continued separation, though they did justice to the filial piety that kept me by my father's side.

Nearly two years elapsed in this protracted exile. To me they were so many ages. Ardent and impetuous by nature, I scarcely know how I should have supported so long an absence, had I not felt assured that the faith of Bianca was equal to my own. At length my father died. Life went from him almost imperceptibly. I hung over him in mute affliction, and watched the expiring spasms of nature. His last faltering accents whispered repeatedly a blessing on me—alas! how has it been fulfilled!

When I had paid due honours to his remains, and laid them in the tomb of our ancestors, I arranged briefly my affairs; put them in a posture to be easily at my command from a distance, and embarked once more, with a bounding heart for Genoa.

Our voyage was propitious, and oh! what was my rapture when first, in the dawn of morning, I saw the shadowy summits of the Apennines rising almost like clouds above the horizon. The sweet breath of summer just moved us over the long wavering billows that were rolling us on towards Genoa. By degrees the coast of Sestri rose like a creation of enchantment from the silver bosom of the deep. I beheld the line of villages and palaces studding its borders. My eye reverted to a well known point, and at length, from the confusion of distant objects, it singled out the villa which contained Bianca. It was a mere speck in the landscape, but glimmering from afar, the polar star of my heart.

Again I gazed at it for a livelong summer's day; but oh

how different the emotions between departure and return. It now kept growing and growing, instead of lessening and lessening on my sight. My heart seemed to dilate with it. I looked at it through a telescope. I gradually defined one feature after another. The balconies of the central saloon where first I met Bianca beneath its roof; the terrace where we so often had passed the delightful summer evenings; the awning which shaded her chamber window—I almost fancied I saw her form beneath it. Could she but know her lover was in the bark whose white sail now gleamed on the sunny bosom of the sea! My fond impatience increased as we neared the coast. The ship seemed to lag lazily over the billows; I could almost have sprung into the sea and swam to the desired shore.

The shadows of evening gradually shrouded the scene, but the moon arose in all her fullness and beauty, and shed the tender light so dear to lovers, over the romantic coast of Sestri. My soul was bathed in unutterable tenderness. I anticipated the heavenly evenings I should pass in once more wandering with Bianca by the light of that blessed moon.

It was late at night before we entered the harbour. As early next morning as I could get released from the formalities of landing I threw myself on horseback and hastened to the villa. As I gallopped round the rocky promontory on which stands the Faro, and saw the coast of Sestri opening upon me, a thousand anxieties and doubts suddenly sprang up in my bosom. There is something fearful in returning to those we love, while yet uncertain what ills or changes absence may have effected. The turbulence of my agitation shook my very frame. I spurred my horse to redoubled speed; he was covered with foam when we both arrived panting at the gateway that opened to the grounds around the villa. I left my horse at a cottage and walked through the grounds that I might regain tranquillity for the approaching interview. I chid myself for having suffered mere doubts and surmises thus suddenly to overcome me; but I was always prone to be carried away by gusts of the feelings.

On entering the garden every thing bore the same look as when I had left it; and this unchanged aspect of things reassured me. There were the alleys in which I had so often

walked with Bianca as we listened to the song of the nightingale; the same shades under which we had so often sat during
the noontide heat. There were the same flowers of which she
was fond; and which appeared still to be under the ministry
of her hand. Every thing looked and breathed of Bianca; hope
and joy flushed in my bosom at every step. I passed a little
arbour in which we had often sat and read together. A book
and a glove lay on the bench. It was Bianca's glove; it was a
volume of the Metastasio I had given her. The glove lay in my
favourite passage. I clasped them to my heart with rapture.
"All is safe!" exclaimed I, "she loves me! she is still my own!"

I bounded lightly along the avenue down which I had faltered so slowly at my departure. I beheld her favourite pavilion which had witnessed our parting scene. The window was
open, with the same vine clambering about it, precisely as
when she waved and wept me an adieu. Oh! how transporting was the contrast in my situation. As I passed near the
pavilion, I heard the tones of a female voice. They thrilled
through me with an appeal to my heart not to be mistaken.
Before I could think, I *felt* they were Bianca's. For an instant I
paused, overpowered with agitation. I feared to break in so
suddenly upon her. I softly ascended the steps of the pavilion.
The door was open. I saw Bianca seated at a table; her back
was towards me; she was warbling a soft melancholy air, and
was occupied in drawing. A glance sufficed to show me that
she was copying one of my own paintings. I gazed on her for
a moment in a delicious tumult of emotions. She paused in
her singing; a heavy sigh, almost a sob followed. I could no
longer contain myself. "Bianca!" exclaimed I, in a half smothered voice. She started at the sound; brushed back the ringlets
that hung clustering about her face; darted a glance at me;
uttered a piercing shriek, and would have fallen to the earth,
had I not caught her in my arms.

"Bianca! my own Bianca!" exclaimed I, folding her to my
bosom; my voice stifled in sobs of convulsive joy. She lay in
my arms without sense or motion. Alarmed at the effects of
my precipitation, I scarce knew what to do. I tried by a thousand endearing words to call her back to consciousness. She
slowly recovered, and half opening her eyes—"where am I?"
murmured she faintly. "Here," exclaimed I, pressing her to

my bosom, "Here! close to the heart that adores you; in the arms of your faithful Ottavio!"

"Oh no! no! no!" shrieked she, starting into sudden life and terror—"away! away! leave me! leave me!"

She tore herself from my arms; rushed to a corner of the saloon, and covered her face with her hands, as if the very sight of me were baleful. I was thunderstruck—I could not believe my senses. I followed her, trembling, confounded. I endeavoured to take her hand, but she shrunk from my very touch with horror.

"Good heavens, Bianca," exclaimed I, "what is the meaning of this? Is this my reception after so long an absence? Is this the love you professed for me?"

At the mention of love, a shuddering ran through her. She turned to me a face wild with anguish. "No more of that! no more of that!" gasped she—"talk not to me of love—I—I—am married!"

I reeled as if I had received a mortal blow. A sickness struck to my very heart. I caught at a window frame for support. For a moment or two, every thing was chaos around me. When I recovered, I beheld Bianca lying on a sofa; her face buried in the pillow, and sobbing convulsively. Indignation at her fickleness for a moment overpowered every other feeling.

"Faithless—perjured—" cried I, striding across the room. But another glance at that beautiful being in distress, checked all my wrath. Anger could not dwell together with her idea in my soul.

"Oh Bianca," exclaimed I, in anguish, "could I have dreamt of this; could I have suspected you would have been false to me?"

She raised her face all streaming with tears, all disordered with emotion, and gave me one appealing look—"False to you!——they told me you were dead!"

"What," said I, "in spite of our constant correspondence?"

She gazed wildly at me—"correspondence!—what correspondence?"

"Have you not repeatedly received and replied to my letters?"

She clasped her hands with solemnity and fervour—"As I hope for mercy, never!"

A horrible surmise shot through my brain—"Who told you I was dead?"

"It was reported that the ship in which you embarked for Naples perished at sea."

"But who told you the report?"

She paused for an instant, and trembled—

"Filippo!"

"May the God of heaven curse him!" cried I, extending my clinched fists aloft.

"Oh do not curse him—do not curse him!" exclaimed she—"He is—he is—my husband!"

This was all that was wanting to unfold the perfidy that had been practised upon me. My blood boiled like liquid fire in my veins. I gasped with rage too great for utterance. I remained for a time bewildered by the whirl of horrible thoughts that rushed through my mind. The poor victim of deception before me thought it was with her I was incensed. She faintly murmured forth her exculpation. I will not dwell upon it. I saw in it more than she meant to reveal. I saw with a glance how both of us had been betrayed. "'Tis well!" muttered I to myself in smothered accents of concentrated fury. "He shall render an account of all this!"

Bianca overheard me. New terror flashed in her countenance. "For mercy's sake do not meet him—say nothing of what has passed—for my sake say nothing to him—I only shall be the sufferer!"

A new suspicion darted across my mind—"what!" exclaimed I—"do you then *fear* him—is he *unkind* to you—tell me," reiterated I, grasping her hand and looking her eagerly in the face—"tell me—*dares* he to use you harshly!"

"No! no! no!" cried she faltering and embarrassed; but the glance at her face had told me volumes. I saw in her pallid and wasted features; in the prompt terror and subdued agony of her eye a whole history of a mind broken down by tyranny. Great God! and was this beauteous flower snatched from me to be thus trampled upon. The idea roused me to madness. I clinched my teeth and my hands; I foamed at the mouth; every passion seemed to have resolved itself into the fury that like a lava boiled within my heart. Bianca shrunk from me in speechless affright. As I strode by the window my eye darted

down the alley. Fatal moment! I beheld Filippo at a distance!
My brain was in delirium—I sprang from the pavilion, and
was before him with the quickness of lightning. He saw me as
I came rushing upon him—he turned pale, looked wildly to
right and left, as if he would have fled, and trembling drew
his sword:—

"Wretch!" cried I, "well may you draw your weapon!"

I spoke not another word—I snatched forth a stiletto, put
by the sword which trembled in his hand, and buried my
poniard in his bosom. He fell with the blow, but my rage was
unsated. I sprang upon him with the blood thirsty feeling of
a tiger; redoubled my blows; mangled him in my frenzy,
grasped him by the throat, until with reiterated wounds and
strangling convulsions he expired in my grasp. I remained
glaring on the countenance, horrible in death, that seemed to
stare back with its protruded eyes upon me. Piercing shrieks
roused me from my delirium. I looked round and beheld
Bianca flying distractedly towards us. My brain whirled. I
waited not to meet her, but fled from the scene of horror. I
fled forth from the garden like another Cain, a hell within my
bosom, and a curse upon my head. I fled without knowing
whither—almost without knowing why—my only idea was
to get farther and farther from the horrors I had left behind;
as if I could throw space between myself and my conscience. I
fled to the Apennines, and wandered for days and days
among their savage heights. How I existed I cannot tell—
what rocks and precipices I braved, and how I braved them, I
know not. I kept on and on—trying to outtravel the curse
that clung to me. Alas, the shrieks of Bianca rung for ever in
my ears. The horrible countenance of my victim was for ever
before my eyes. "The blood of Filippo cried to me from the
ground." Rocks, trees, and torrents all resounded with my
crime.

Then it was I felt how much more insupportable is the anguish of remorse than every other mental pang. Oh! could I
but have cast off this crime that festered in my heart; could I
but have regained the innocence that reigned in my breast as
I entered the garden at Sestri; could I but have restored my
victim to life, I felt as if I could look on with transport even
though Bianca were in his arms.

By degrees this frenzied fever of remorse settled into a permanent malady of the mind. Into one of the most horrible
that ever poor wretch was cursed with. Wherever I went the
countenance of him I had slain appeared to follow me. Whenever I turned my head I beheld it behind me, hideous with
the contortions of the dying moment. I have tried in every
way to escape from this horrible phantom; but in vain. I
know not whether it be an illusion of the mind, the consequence of my dismal education at the convent, or whether a
phantom really sent by heaven to punish me; but there it ever
is—at all times—in all places—nor has time nor habit had
any effect in familiarizing me with its terrors. I have travelled
from place to place, plunged into amusements—tried dissipation and distraction of every kind—all—all in vain.

I once had recourse to my pencil as a desperate experiment.
I painted an exact resemblance of this phantom face. I placed
it before me in hopes that by constantly contemplating the
copy I might diminish the effect of the original. But I only
doubled instead of diminishing the misery.

Such is the curse that has clung to my footsteps—that has
made my life a burthen—but the thought of death, terrible.
God knows what I have suffered. What days and days, and
nights and nights, of sleepless torment. What a never dying
worm has preyed upon my heart; what an unquenchable fire
has burned within my brain. He knows the wrongs that
wrought upon my poor weak nature; that converted the tenderest of affections into the deadliest of fury. He knows best
whether a frail erring creature has expiated by long enduring
torture and measureless remorse, the crime of a moment of
madness. Often, often have I prostrated myself in the dust,
and implored that he would give me a sign of his forgiveness,
and let me die.——

Thus far had I written some time since. I had meant to
leave this record of misery and crime with you, to be read
when I should be no more. My prayer to heaven has at length
been heard. You were witness to my emotions last evening at
the church, when the vaulted temple resounded with the
words of atonement and redemption. I heard a voice speaking
to me from the midst of the music; I heard it rising above the
pealing of the organ and the voices of the choir: it spoke to

me in tones of celestial melody; it promised mercy and for-giveness, but demanded from me full expiation. I go to make it. Tomorrow I shall be on my way to Genoa to surrender myself to justice. You who have pitied my sufferings; who have poured the balm of sympathy into my wounds, do not shrink from my memory with abhorrence now that you know my story. Recollect, when you read of my crime I shall have atoned for it with my blood!

———

When the Baronet had finished, there was a universal desire expressed to see the painting of this frightful visage. After much entreaty the Baronet consented, on condition that they should only visit it one by one. He called his housekeeper and gave her charge to conduct the gentlemen singly to the cham-ber. They all returned varying in their stories: some affected in one way, some in another; some more, some less; but all agreeing that there was a certain something about the paint-ing that had a very odd effect upon the feelings.

I stood in a deep bow window with the Baronet, and could not help expressing my wonder. "After all," said I, "there are certain mysteries in our nature, certain inscrutable impulses and influences, which warrant one in being superstitious. Who can account for so many persons of different characters being thus strangely affected by a mere painting?"

"And especially when not one of them has seen it!" said the Baronet with a smile.

"How?" exclaimed I, "not seen it?"

"Not one of them!" replied he, laying his finger on his lips in sign of secrecy. "I saw that some of them were in a banter-ing vein, and I did not choose that the memento of the poor Italian should be made a jest of. So I gave the housekeeper a hint to show them all to a different chamber!"

———

Thus end the Stories of the Nervous Gentleman.

PART II

BUCKTHORNE AND HIS FRIENDS

This world is the best that we live in,
To lend, or to spend, or to give in;
But to beg, or to borrow, or get a man's own,
'Tis the very worst world, sir, that ever was known.
                    LINES FROM AN INN WINDOW

Literary Life

Among other subjects of a traveller's curiosity, I had at one time a great craving after anecdotes of literary life; and being at London, one of the most noted places for the production of books, I was excessively anxious to know something of the animals which produced them. Chance fortunately threw me in the way of a literary man by the name of Buckthorne, an eccentric personage, who had lived much in the metropolis, and could give me the natural history of every odd animal to be met with in that wilderness of men. He readily imparted to me some useful hints upon the subject of my inquiry.

"The literary world," said he, "is made up of little confederacies, each looking upon its own members as the lights of the universe; and considering all others as mere transient meteors, doomed soon to fall and be forgotten, while its own luminaries are to shine steadily on to immortality."

"And pray," said I, "how is a man to get a peep into those confederacies you speak of? I presume an intercourse with authors is a kind of intellectual exchange, where one must bring his commodities to barter, and always give a quid pro quo."

"Pooh, pooh—how you mistake," said Buckthorne, smiling: "you must never think to become popular among wits by shining. They go into society to shine themselves, not to admire the brilliancy of others. I once thought as you do, and never went into literary society without studying my part before hand. The consequence was, I soon got the name of an intolerable proser, and should in a little while have been completely excommunicated had I not changed my plan of operations. No, sir, no character succeeds so well among wits as that of a good listener, or if ever you are eloquent, let it be when tête-à-tête with an author, and then in praise of his own works, or what is nearly as acceptable, in disparagement of the works of his contemporaries. If ever he speaks favourably of the productions of a particular friend, dissent boldly from him; pronounce his friend to be a blockhead; never fear his being vexed; much as people speak of the irritability of authors, I never found one to take offense at such contradictions. No-no sir, authors are particularly candid in admitting the faults of their friends.

"Indeed I would advise you to be extremely sparing of remarks on all modern works, excepting to make sarcastic observations on the most distinguished writers of the day."

"Faith," said I, "I'll praise none that have not been dead for at least half a century."

"Even then," observed Mr. Buckthorne, "I would advise you to be rather cautious; for you must know that many old writers have been enlisted under the banners of different sects, and their merits have become as complete topics of party discussion as the merits of living statesmen and politicians. Nay, there have been whole periods of literature absolutely *taboo'd*, to use a South Sea phrase. It is, for example, as much as a man's critical reputation is worth, in some circles, to say a word in praise of any writers of the reign of Charles the Second, or even of Queen Anne; they being all declared Frenchmen in disguise."

"And pray then," said I, "when am I to know that I am on safe grounds; being totally unacquainted with the literary landmarks and the boundary lines of fashionable taste?"

"Oh," replied he, "there is fortunately one tract of literature which forms a kind of neutral ground, on which all the literary meet amicably, and run riot in the excess of their good humour. And this is, the reigns of Elizabeth and James. Here you may praise away at random; here it is 'cut and come again,' and the more obscure the author, and the more quaint and crabbed his style; the more your admiration will smack of the real relish of the Connoisseur; whose taste, like that of an Epicure, is always for game that has an antiquated flavour.

"But," continued he, "as you seem anxious to know something of literary society I will take an opportunity to introduce you to some coterie, where the talents of the day are assembled. I cannot promise you, however, that they will all be of the first order. Some how or other, our great geniuses are not gregarious, they do not go in flocks; but fly singly in general society. They prefer mingling, like common men, with the multitude; and are apt to carry nothing of the author about them but the reputation. It is only the inferior orders that herd together, acquire strength and importance by their confederacies, and bear all the distinctive characteristics of their species."

A Literary Dinner

A few days after this conversation with Mr. Buckthorne, he called upon me, and took me with him to a regular literary dinner. It was given by a great Bookseller, or rather a company of Booksellers, whose firm surpassed in length even that of Shadrach, Meshach and Abed-nego.

I was surprised to find between twenty and thirty guests assembled, most of whom I had never seen before. Buckthorne explained this to me, by informing me that this was a "business dinner," or kind of field day which the house gave about twice a year to its authors. It is true they did occasionally give snug dinners to three or four literary men at a time; but then these were generally select authors; favourites of the public; such as had arrived at their sixth or seventh editions. "There are," said he, "certain geographical boundaries in the land of literature, and you may judge tolerably well of an author's popularity, by the wine his bookseller gives him. An author crosses the port line about the third edition and gets into claret, but when he has reached the sixth and seventh, he may revel in champagne and burgundy."

"And pray," said I, "how far may these gentlemen have reached that I see around me; are any of these claret drinkers?"

"Not exactly, not exactly. You find at these great dinners the common steady run of authors, one, two-edition men; or if any others are invited they are aware that it is a kind of republican meeting.—You understand me—a meeting of the republic of letters, and that they must expect nothing but plain substantial fare."

These hints enabled me to comprehend more fully the arrangement of the table. The two ends were occupied by two partners of the House—and the host seemed to have adopted Addison's idea as to the literary precedence of his guests. A popular poet had the post of honour, opposite to whom was a hotpressed traveller in Quarto with plates. A grave looking antiquarian, who had produced several solid works, which were much quoted and little read, was treated with great respect, and seated next to a neat dressy gentleman in black, who had written a thin, genteel, hotpressed octavo on political economy that was getting into fashion. Several three volume duodecimo men of fair currency were placed about the centre of the table; while the lower end was taken up with small poets, translators and authors who had not as yet risen into much notoriety.

The conversation during dinner was by fits and starts; breaking out here and there in various parts of the table in small flashes, and ending in smoke. The poet who had the confidence of a man on good terms with the world and independent of his bookseller, was very gay and brilliant, and said many clever things, which set the partner next him in a roar, and delighted all the company. The other partner, however, maintained his sedateness and kept carving on, with the air of a thorough man of business, intent upon the occupation of the moment. His gravity was explained to me by my friend Buckthorne. He informed me that the concerns of the house were admirably distributed among the partners. "Thus, for instance," said he. "The grave gentleman is the carving partner who attends to the joints, and the other is the laughing partner who attends to the jokes."

The general conversation was chiefly carried on at the upper end of the table; as the authors there seemed to possess the greatest courage of the tongue. As to the crew at the lower end, if they did not make much figure in talking they did in eating. Never was there a more determined, inveterate, thoroughly sustained attack on the trencher, than by this phalanx of masticators. When the cloth was removed, and the wine began to circulate, they grew very merry and jocose among themselves. Their jokes, however, if by chance any of them reached the upper end of the table, seldom produced much effect. Even the laughing partner did not think it necessary to honour them with a smile; which my neighbour Buckthorne accounted for, by informing me that there was a certain degree of popularity to be obtained, before a bookseller could afford to laugh at an author's jokes.

Among this crew of questionable gentlemen thus seated below the salt, my eye singled out one in particular. He was rather shabbily dressed; though he had evidently made the most of a rusty black coat, and wore his shirt frill plaited and puffed out voluminously at the bosom. His face was dusky, but florid, perhaps a little too florid, particularly about the nose; though the rosy hue gave the greater lustre to a twinkling black eye. He had a little the look of a boon companion, with that dash of the poor devil in it which gives an inexpressibly mellow tone to a man's humour. I had seldom seen a face of richer promise; but never was promise so ill kept. He said nothing; ate and drank with the keen appetite of a Garretteer, and scarcely stopped to laugh even at the good jokes from the upper end of the table. I inquired who he was. Buckthorne looked at him attentively; "Gad," said he, "I have seen that face before but where I cannot recollect. He cannot be an author of any note. I suppose some writer of sermons or grinder of foreign travels."

After dinner we retired to another room to take tea and coffee, where we were reinforced by a cloud of inferior guests. Authors of small volumes in boards, and pamphlets stitched in blue paper. These had not as yet arrived to the importance of a dinner invitation, but were invited occasionally to pass the evening "in a friendly way." They were very respectful to the partners, and indeed seemed to stand a little in awe of them; but they paid devoted court to the Lady of the house, and were extravagantly fond of the children. Some few, who did not feel confidence enough to make such advances, stood shyly off in corners, talking to one another; or turned over the portfolios of prints, which they had not seen above five thousand times, or moused over the music on the forte-piano.

The poet and the thin octavo gentleman were the persons most current and at their ease in the drawing room; being men evidently of circulation in the west end. They got on each side of the lady of the house, and paid her a thousand compliments and civilities, at some of which I thought she would have expired with delight. Every thing they said and did had the odour of fashionable life. I looked round in vain for the poor devil author in the rusty black coat; he had disappeared immediately after leaving the table; having a dread, no doubt, of the glaring light of a drawing room. Finding nothing further to interest my attention, I took my departure soon after coffee had been served, leaving the poet and the thin, genteel, hotpressed, octavo gentleman, masters of the field.

The Club of Queer Fellows

I think it was but the very next evening that in coming out of Covent Garden theatre with my excentric friend Buckthorne, he proposed to give me another peep at life and character. Finding me willing for any research of the kind, he took me through a variety of the narrow courts and lanes about Covent Garden until we stopped before a tavern from which we heard the bursts of merriment of a jovial party. There would be a loud peal of laughter, then an interval, then another peal, as if a prime wag were telling a story. After a little while there was a song, and at the close of each stanza a hearty roar and a vehement thumping on the table.

"This is the place," whispered Buckthorne. "It is the 'club of queer fellows,' a great resort of the small wits, third rate actors, and newspaper critics of the theatres. Any one can go in, on paying a sixpence at the bar for the use of the club."

We entered, therefore, without ceremony and took our seats at a lone table in a dusky corner of the room. The club was assembled round a table, on which stood beverages of various kinds, according to the taste of the individual. The members were a set of queer fellows indeed; but what was my surprize on recognizing in the prime wit of the meeting the poor devil author, whom I had remarked at the Booksellers' dinner for his promising face and his complete taciturnity. Matters, however, were entirely changed with him. There he was a mere cypher: here he was lord of the ascendant; the choice spirit, the dominant genius. He sat at the head of the table with his hat on, and an eye beaming even more luminously than his nose. He had a quip and a fillip for every one, and a good thing on every occasion. Nothing could be said or done without eliciting a spark from him; and I solemnly declare I have heard much worse wit even from noblemen. His jokes it must be confessed, were rather wet, but they suited the circle in which he presided. The company were in that maudlin mood when a little wit goes a great way. Every time he opened his lips there was sure to be a roar, and even sometimes before he had time to speak.

We were fortunate enough to enter in time for a glee composed by him expressly for the club, and which he sang with two boon companions who would have been worthy subjects for Hogarth's pencil. As they were each provided with a written copy; I was enabled to procure the reading of it.

> Merrily, merrily push round the glass,
> And merrily troll the glee,
> For he who won't drink till he wink is an ass,
> So neighbour I drink to thee.
>
> Merrily, merrily fuddle thy nose,
> Until it right rosy shall be;
> For a jolly red nose, I speak under the rose,
> Is a sign of good company.

We waited until the party broke up, and no one but the wit remained. He sat at the table with his legs stretched under it, and wide apart; his hands in his breeches pockets; his head drooped upon his breast; and gazing with lack lustre countenance on an empty tankard. His gaiety was gone, his fire completely quenched.

My companion approached and startled him from his fit of brown study, introducing himself on the strength of their having dined together at the Booksellers'.

"By the way," said he, "it seems to me I have seen you before; your face is surely that of an old acquaintance, though for the life of me I cannot tell where I have known you."

"Very likely," replied he with a smile; "many of my old friends have forgotten me. Though, to tell the truth my memory in this instance is as bad as your own. If however it will assist your recollection in any way, my name is Thomas Dribble, at your service."

"What. Tom Dribble, who was at old Birchell's school in Warwickshire—"

"The same," said the other, coolly. "Why then we are old schoolmates, though it's no wonder you don't recollect me. I was your junior by several years; don't you recollect little Jack Buckthorne?"

Here then ensued a scene of school fellow recognition—and a world of talk about old school times and school pranks. Mr. Dribble ended by observing with a heavy sigh "that times were sadly changed since those days."

"Faith, Mr. Dribble," said I, "you seem quite a different man here from what you were at dinner. I had no idea that you had so much stuff in you. There you were all silence; but here you absolutely keep the table in a roar."

"Ah my dear sir," replied he, with a shake of the head and a shrug of the shoulder, "I'm a mere glow worm. I never shine by daylight. Besides, it's a hard thing for a poor devil of an author to shine at the table of a rich bookseller. Who, do you think, would laugh at any thing I could say, when I had some of the current wits of the day about me? But, here, though a poor devil, I am among still poorer devils than myself: men who look up to me as a man of letters and a bel esprit, and all my jokes pass as sterling gold from the mint."

"You surely do yourself injustice, sir," said I. "I have certainly heard more good things from you this evening, than from any of those beaux esprits by whom you appear to have been so daunted."

"Ah, sir! but they have luck on their side; they are in the fashion—there's nothing like being in fashion. A man that has once got his character up for a wit, is always sure of a laugh, say what he may. He may utter as much nonsense as he pleases, and all will pass current. No one stops to question the coin of a rich man; but a poor devil cannot pass off either a joke or a guinea, without its being examined on both sides. Wit and coin are always doubted with a threadbare coat.

"For my part," continued he, giving his hat a twitch a little more on one side, "for my part, I hate your fine dinners; there's nothing, sir, like the freedom of a chop house. I'd rather, any time, have my steak and tankard among my own set, than drink claret and eat venison with your cursed civil, elegant company who never laugh at a good joke from a poor devil for fear of its being vulgar. A good joke grows in a wet soil; it flourishes in low places, but withers on your d——d high, dry grounds. I once kept high company, sir, until I nearly ruined myself, I grew so dull, and vapid and genteel. Nothing saved me but being arrested by my Landlady and thrown into prison; where a course of catch clubs, eightpenny ale and poor devil company, manured my mind and brought it back to itself again."

As it was now growing late we parted for the evening; though I felt anxious to know more of this practical philosopher. I was glad therefore when Buckthorne proposed to have another meeting to talk over old school times, and inquired his schoolmate's address. The latter seemed at first a little shy of naming his lodgings; but suddenly assuming an air of hardihood—"Green Arbour Court Sir," exclaimed he— "number —— in Green Arbour Court. You must know the place. Classic ground, sir! classic ground! It was there Goldsmith wrote his Vicar of Wakefield—I always like to live in literary haunts—"

I was amused with this whimsical apology for shabby quarters. On our way homewards Buckthorne assured me that this Dribble had been the prime wit and great wag of the school in their boyish days and one of those unlucky urchins denominated bright geniuses. As he perceived me curious respecting his old schoolmate he promised to take me with him in his proposed visit to Green Arbour Court.

A few mornings afterwards he called upon me and we set forth on our Expedition. He led me through a variety of singular alleys, and courts, and blind passages; for he appeared to be profoundly versed in all the intricate geography of the metropolis. At length we came out upon Fleet Market and traversing it turned up a narrow street to the bottom of a long steep flight of stone steps called Break neck Stairs. These he told me led up to Green Arbour Court, and that, down them poor Goldsmith might many a time have risked his neck. When we entered the court, I could not but smile to think in what out of the way corners genius produces her bantlings! And the muses, those capricious dames, who forsooth, so often refuse to visit palaces, and deny a single smile to votaries in splendid studies and gilded drawing rooms,—what holes and burrows will they frequent to lavish their favours on some ragged disciple!

This Green Arbour Court I found to be a small square surrounded by tall miserable houses, the very intestines of which seemed turned inside out, to judge from the old garments and frippery fluttering from every window. It appeared to be a region of washerwomen, and lines were stretched about the little square, on which clothes were dangling to dry. Just as we entered the square, a scuffle took place between two viragos about a disputed right to a washtub, and immediately the whole community was in a hubbub. Heads in mob caps popped out of every window, and such a clamour of tongues ensued that I was fain to stop my ears. Every Amazon took part with one or other of the disputants, and brandished her arms dripping with soapsuds, and fired away from her window as from the embrazure of a fortress; while the swarms of children nestled and cradled in every procreant chamber of this hive, waking with the noise, set up their shrill pipes to swell the general concert.

Poor Goldsmith! what a time must he have had of it, with his quiet disposition and nervous habits, penned up in this den of noise and vulgarity. How strange that while every sight and sound was sufficient to embitter the heart and fill it with misanthropy, his pen should be dropping the honey of Hybla. Yet it is more than probable that he drew many of his inimitable pictures of low life from the scenes which surrounded him in this abode. The circumstance of Mrs. Tibbs being obliged to wash her husband's two shirts in a neighbour's house, who refused to lend her washtub, may have been no sport of fancy, but a fact passing under his own eye. His landlady may have sat for the picture, and Beau Tibbs' scanty wardrobe have been a fac simile of his own.

It was with some difficulty that we found our way to Dribble's lodgings. They were up two pair of stairs, in a room that looked upon the Court, and when we entered he was seated on the edge of his bed, writing at a broken table. He received us, however, with a free, open, poor devil air, that was irresistible. It is true he did at first appear slightly confused; buttoned up his waistcoat a little higher and tucked in a stray frill of linen. But he recollected himself in an instant; gave a half swagger, half leer as he stepped forth to receive us; drew a three legged stool for Mr. Buckthorne; pointed me to a lumbering old Damask chair that looked like a dethroned monarch in exile, and bade us welcome to his garret.

We soon got engaged in conversation. Buckthorne and he had much to say about early school scenes, and as nothing opens a man's heart more than recollections of the kind we soon drew from him a brief outline of his literary career.

The Poor Devil Author

I began life unluckily by being the wag and bright fellow at school; and I had the further misfortune of becoming the great genius of my native village. My father was a country attorney, and intended I should succeed him in business; but I had too much genius to study, and he was too fond of my genius to force it into the traces. So I fell into bad company and took to bad habits. Do not mistake me. I mean that I fell into the company of village literati and village blues, and took to writing village poetry.

It was quite the fashion in the village to be literary. There was a little knot of choice spirits of us who assembled frequently together, formed ourselves into a Literary, Scientific and Philosophical Society, and fancied ourselves the most learned philos in existence. Every one had a great character assigned him, suggested by some casual habit or affectation. One heavy fellow drank an enormous quantity of tea; rolled in his arm chair, talked sententiously, pronounced dogmatically, and was considered a second Dr. Johnson; another who happened to be a curate uttered coarse jokes, wrote doggerel rhymes, and was the Swift of our association. Thus we had also our Popes, and Goldsmiths and Addisons, and a blue stocking lady whose drawing room we frequented, who corresponded about nothing, with all the world, and wrote letters with the stiffness and formality of a printed book, was

cried up as another Mrs. Montagu. I was, by common consent, the juvenile prodigy, the poetical youth, the great genius, the pride and hope of the village, through whom it was
to become one day as celebrated as Stratford on Avon.

My father died and left me his blessing and his business.
His blessing brought no money into my pocket; and as to his
business it soon deserted me: for I was busy writing poetry,
and could not attend to law; and my clients, though they
had great respect for my talents, had no faith in a poetical
attorney.

I lost my business, therefore, spent my money and finished
my poem. It was the Pleasures of Melancholy, and was cried
up to the skies by the whole circle. The Pleasures of Imagination, the Pleasures of Hope and the Pleasures of Memory
though each had placed its author in the first rank of poets,
were blank prose in comparison. Our Mrs. Montagu would
cry over it from beginning to end. It was pronounced by all
the members of the Literary, Scientific and Philosophical Society, the greatest poem of the age, and all anticipated the
noise it would make in the great world. There was not a
doubt but the London booksellers would be mad after it, and
the only fear of my friends was, that I would make a sacrifice
by selling it too cheap. Every time they talked the matter over
they encreased the price. They reckoned up the great sums
given for the poems of certain popular writers, and determined that mine was worth more than all put together, and
ought to be paid for accordingly. For my part, I was modest
in my expectations, and determined that I would be satisfied
with a thousand guineas. So I put my poem in my pocket and
set off for London.

My journey was joyous. My heart was light as my purse,
and my head full of anticipations of fame and fortune. With
what swelling pride did I cast my eyes upon old London from
the heights of Highgate. I was like a general looking down
upon a place he expects to conquer. The great metropolis lay
stretched before me, buried under a home made cloud of
murky smoke, that wrapped it from the brightness of a sunny
day, and formed for it a kind of artificial bad weather. At the
outskirts of the city, away to the west, the smoke gradually

decreased until all was clear and sunny, and the view stretched uninterrupted to the blue line of the Kentish Hills.

My eye turned fondly to where the mighty cupola of St. Paul's swelled dimly through this misty chaos, and I pictured to myself the solemn realm of learning that lies about its base. How soon should the Pleasures of Melancholy throw this world of Booksellers and printers into a bustle of business and delight! How soon should I hear my name repeated by printers' devils throughout Paternoster Row, and Angel Court, and Ave Maria Lane, until Amen Corner should echo back the sound!

Arrived in town, I repaired at once to the most fashionable publisher. Every new author patronizes him of course. In fact, it had been determined in the village circle that he should be the fortunate man. I cannot tell you how vaingloriously I walked the streets; my head was in the clouds. I felt the airs of heaven playing about it, and fancied it already encircled by a halo of literary glory. As I passed by the windows of bookshops, I anticipated the time when my work would be shining among the hotpressed wonders of the day; and my face, scratched on copper, or cut in wood, figuring in fellowship with those of Scott and Byron and Moore.

When I applied at the publisher's house there was something in the loftiness of my air, and the dinginess of my dress, that struck the clerks with reverence. They doubtless took me for some person of consequence, probably a digger of Greek roots or a penetrater of pyramids. A proud man in a dirty shirt is always an imposing character in the world of letters; one must feel intellectually secure before he can venture to dress shabbily; none but a great scholar or a great genius dares to be dirty; so I was ushered at once, to the sanctum sanctorum of this high priest of Minerva.

The publishing of books is a very different affair now adays, from what it was in the time of Bernard Lintot. I found the publisher a fashionably dressed man, in an elegant drawing room, furnished with sophas; and portraits of celebrated authors, and cases of splendidly bound books. He was writing letters at an elegant table. This was transacting business in style. The place seemed suited to the magnificent

publications that issued from it. I rejoiced at the choice I had
made of a publisher, for I always liked to encourage men of
taste and spirit.

I stepped up to the table with the lofty poetical port I had
been accustomed to maintain in our village circle; though I
threw in it something of a patronizing air, such as one feels
when about to make a man's fortune. The publisher paused
with his pen in hand, and seemed waiting in mute suspense to
know what was to be announced by so singular an apparition.

I put him at his ease in a moment, for I felt that I had but
to come, see and conquer. I made known my name, and the
name of my poem; produced my precious roll of blotted
manuscript, laid it on the table with an emphasis, and told
him at once, to save time and come directly to the point, the
price was one thousand guineas.

I had given him no time to speak, nor did he seem so
inclined. He continued looking at me for a moment with an
air of whimsical perplexity; scanned me from head to foot;
looked down at the manuscript; then up again at me, then
pointed to a chair; and whistling softly to himself, went on
writing his letter.

I sat for some time waiting his reply; supposing he was
making up his mind; but he only paused occasionally to take a
fresh dip of ink; to stroke his chin or the tip of his nose and
then resumed his writing. It was evident his mind was in-
tently occupied upon some other subject; but I had no idea
that any other subject should be attended to and my poem lie
unnoticed on the table. I had supposed that every thing
would make way for the Pleasures of Melancholy.

My gorge at length rose within me. I took up my manuscript; thrust it into my pocket, and walked out of the room;
making some noise as I went, to let my departure be heard.
The publisher, however, was too much buried in minor concerns to notice it. I was suffered to walk down stairs without
being called back. I sallied forth into the street, but no clerk
was sent after me; nor did the publisher call after me from the
drawing room window. I have been told since, that he considered me either a madman or a fool. I leave you to judge
how much he was in the wrong in his opinion.

When I turned the corner my crest fell. I cooled down in

my pride and my expectations, and reduced my terms with the next bookseller to whom I applied. I had no better success: nor with a third; nor with a fourth. I then desired the booksellers to make an offer themselves; but the deuce an offer would they make. They told me poetry was a mere drug; every body wrote poetry; the market was overstocked with it. And then, they said, the title of my poem was not taking: that pleasures of all kinds were worn threadbare, nothing but horrors did now adays, and even those were almost worn out. Tales of Pirates, Robbers and bloody Turks might answer tolerably well; but then they must come from some established well known name, or the public would not look at them.

At last I offered to leave my poem with a bookseller to read it and judge for himself. "Why really, my dear Mr.——a—a—I forget your name," said he, cutting an eye at my rusty coat and shabby gaiters, "really, sir, we are so pressed with business just now, and have so many manuscripts on hand to read, that we have not time to look at any new production, but if you can call again in a week or two, or say the middle of next month, we may be able to look over your writings and give you an answer. Don't forget, the month after next——good morning, sir—happy to see you any time you are passing this way—"; so saying he bowed me out in the civilest way imaginable.—In short, sir, instead of an eager competition to secure my poem, I could not even get it read! In the meantime I was harrassed by letters from my friends, wanting to know when the work was to appear; who was to be my publisher; but above all things warning me not to let it go too cheap.

There was but one alternative left. I determined to publish the poem myself; and to have my triumph over the booksellers, when it should become the fashion of the day. I accordingly published the Pleasures of Melancholy and ruined myself. Excepting the copies sent to the reviews, and to my friends in the country, not one I believe ever left the bookseller's ware house. The printer's bill drained my purse, and the only notice that was taken of my work was contained in the advertisements paid for by myself.

I could have borne all this, and have attributed it as usual to the mismanagement of the publisher; or the want of taste in the public; and could have made the usual appeal to posterity; but my village friends would not let me rest in quiet. They were picturing me to themselves feasting with the great, communing with the literary, and in the high career of fortune and renown. Every little while, some one would call on me with a letter of introduction from the village circle, recommending him to my attentions, and requesting that I would make him known in society: with a hint that an introduction to a celebrated literary nobleman would be extremely agreeable.

I determined, therefore, to change my lodgings, drop my correspondence, and disappear altogether from the view of my village admirers. Besides, I was anxious to make one more poetic attempt. I was by no means disheartened by the failure of my first. My poem was evidently too didactic. The public was wise enough. It no longer read for instruction. "They want horrors, do they?" said I, "I'faith then they shall have enough of them." So I looked out for some quiet retired place, where I might be out of reach of my friends, and have leisure to cook up some delectable dish of poetical "hell-broth."

I had some difficulty in finding a place to my mind, when chance threw me in the way of Canonbury Castle. It is an ancient brick tower, hard by "merry Islington;" the remains of a hunting seat of Queen Elizabeth, where she took the pleasures of the country, when the neighbourhood was all woodland. What gave it particular interest in my eyes was the circumstance that it had been the residence of a Poet. It was here Goldsmith resided when he wrote his Deserted Village. I was shown the very apartment. It was a relique of the original style of the castle, with pannelled wainscots and Gothic windows. I was pleased with its air of antiquity, and with its having been the residence of poor Goldy. "Goldsmith was a pretty poet," said I to myself, "a very pretty poet; though rather of the old school. He did not think and feel so strongly as is the fashion now adays; but had he lived in these times of hot hearts and hot heads, he would no doubt have written quite differently."

In a few days I was quietly established in my new quarters; my books all arranged, my writing desk placed by a window

looking out into the fields; and I felt as snug as Robinson
Crusoe, when he had finished his bower. For several days I
enjoyed all the novelty of change and the charms which grace
new lodgings before one has found out their defects. I rambled about the fields where I fancied Goldsmith had rambled.
I explored merry Islington; ate my solitary dinner at the Black
Bull, which according to tradition was a country seat of Sir
Walter Raleigh, and would sit and sip my wine and muse on
old times in a quaint old room, where many a council had
been held.

All this did very well for a few days; I was stimulated by
novelty; inspired by the associations awakened in my mind by
these curious haunts; and began to think I felt the spirit of
composition stirring within me; but Sunday came, and with it
the whole city world, swarming about Canonbury Castle. I
could not open my window but I was stunned with shouts
and noises from the cricket ground. The late quiet road beneath my window, was alive with the tread of feet and clack
of tongues, and to complete my misery, I found that my quiet
retreat was absolutely a "show house!" the tower and its contents being shewn to strangers at sixpence a head.

There was a perpetual tramping up stairs of citizens and
their families, to look about the country from the top of the
tower, and to take a peep at the city through the telescope, to
try if they could discern their own chimnies. And then, in the
midst of a vein of thought, or a moment of inspiration, I was
interrupted and all my ideas put to flight, by my intolerable
landlady's tapping at the door, and asking me, if I would "jist
please to let a lady and gentleman come in to take a look at
Mr. Goldsmith's room."

If you know any thing what an author's study is, and what
an author is himself, you must know that there was no standing this. I put a positive interdict on my room's being exhibited; but then it was shewn when I was absent and my papers
put in confusion; and on returning home one day, I absolutely found a cursed tradesman and his daughters gaping
over my manuscripts; and my landlady in a panic at my appearance. I tried to make out a little longer by taking the key
in my pocket, but it would not do. I overheard mine hostess
one day telling some of her customers on the stairs that the

room was occupied by an author, who was always in a tantrum if interrupted; and I immediately perceived, by a slight noise at the door, that they were peeping at me through the keyhole. By the head of Apollo, but this was quite too much! With all my eagerness for fame, and my ambition of the stare of the million, I had no idea of being exhibited by retail at sixpence a head, and that through a Key hole. So I bade adieu to Canonbury Castle, Merry Islington, and the haunts of poor Goldsmith, without having advanced a single line in my labours.

My next quarters were at a small white washed cottage, which stands not far from Hampstead, just on the brow of a hill; looking over Chalk Farm, and Camden Town, remarkable for the rival houses of Mother Red Cap and Mother Black Cap; and so across Crackscull Common to the distant city.

The cottage was in no wise remarkable in itself; but I regarded it with reverence, for it had been the asylum of a persecuted author. Hither poor Steele had retreated and lain perdu, when persecuted by creditors and bailiffs; those immemorial plagues of authors and free spirited gentlemen; and here he had written many numbers of the Spectator. It was hence, too, that he had dispatched those little notes to his lady, so full of affection and whimsicality; in which the fond husband, the careless gentleman, and the shifting spendthrift, were so oddly blended. I thought, as I first eyed the window of his apartment, that I could sit within it, and write volumes.

No such thing! It was Haymaking season, and, as ill luck would have it, immediately opposite the cottage was a little ale house with the sign of the Load of Hay. Whether it was there in Steele's time I cannot say; but it set all attempts at conception or inspiration at defiance. It was the resort of all the Irish Haymakers who mow the broad fields in the neighbourhood; and of drovers and teamsters who travel that road. Here would they gather in the endless summer twilight, or by the light of the harvest moon, and sit round a table at the door; and tipple, and laugh, and quarrel, and fight, and sing drowsy songs, and dawdle away the hours until the deep solemn notes of St. Paul's clock would warn the varlets home.

In the day time I was still less able to write. It was broad summer. The haymakers were at work in the fields, and the perfume of the new mown hay brought with it the recollection of my native fields. So instead of remaining in my room to write, I went wandering about Primrose Hill and Hampstead Heights and Shepherd's Fields; and all those Arcadian scenes so celebrated by London Bards. I cannot tell you how many delicious hours I have passed lying on the cocks of new mown hay, on the pleasant slopes of some of those hills, inhaling the fragrance of the fields; while the summer fly buzzed about me, or the grasshopper leaped into my bosom; and how I have gazed with half shut eye upon the smoky mass of London, and listened to the distant sound of its population; and pitied the poor sons of earth, toiling in its bowels, like Gnomes in the "dark gold mine."

People may say what they please about Cockney pastorals; but after all, there is a vast deal of rural beauty about the western vicinity of London; and any one that has looked down upon the valley of West End, with its soft bosom of green pasturage, lying open to the south and dotted with cattle; the steeple of Hampstead rising among rich groves on the brow of the hill; and the learned height of Harrow in the distance; will confess that never has he seen a more absolutely rural landscape in the vicinity of a great metropolis.

Still, however, I found myself not a whit the better off for my frequent change of lodgings; and I began to discover that in literature, as in trade, the old proverb holds good, "a rolling stone gathers no moss."

The tranquil beauty of the country played the very vengeance with me. I could not mount my fancy into the termagant vein. I could not conceive, amidst the smiling landscape, a scene of blood and murder; and the smug citizens in breeches and gaiters, put all ideas of heroes and Bandits out of my brain. I could think of nothing but dulcet subjects— "the pleasures of spring"—"the pleasures of solitude"—"the pleasures of tranquility"—"the pleasures of sentiment"— nothing but pleasures; and I had the painful experience of "the pleasures of melancholy" too strongly in my recollection to be beguiled by them.

Chance at length befriended me. I had frequently in my ramblings loitered about Hampstead Hill; which is a kind of

Parnassus of the metropolis. At such times I occasionally took
my dinner at Jack Straw's Castle. It is a country Inn so
named. The very spot where that notorious rebel and his followers held their council of war. It is a favourite resort of
citizens when rurally inclined, as it commands fine fresh air
and a good view of the city.

I sat one day in the public room of this Inn, ruminating
over a beefsteak and a pint of port, when my imagination
kindled up with ancient and heroic images. I had long wanted
a theme and a hero; both suddenly broke upon my mind; I
determined to write a poem on the history of Jack Straw. I
was so full of my subject that I was fearful of being anticipated; I wondered that none of the poets of the day, in their
search after ruffian heroes, had ever thought of Jack Straw. I
went to work pell mell, blotted several sheets of paper with
choice floating thoughts, and battles and descriptions, to be
ready at a moment's warning. In a few days' time I sketched
out the skeleton of my poem, and nothing was wanting but
to give it flesh and blood. I used to take my manuscript and
stroll about Caen Wood, and read aloud; and would dine at
the castle, by way of keeping up the vein of thought.

I was there one day, at rather a late hour, in the public
room. There was no other company but one man, who sat
enjoying his pint of port at a window, and noticing the passers by. He was dressed in a green shooting coat. His countenance was strongly marked. He had a hooked nose, a
romantic eye, excepting that it had something of a squint, and
altogether, as I thought, a poetical style of head. I was quite
taken with the man, for you must know I am a little of a
physiognomist; I set him down at once for either a poet or a
philosopher.

As I like to make new acquaintances, considering every
man a volume of human nature, I soon fell into conversation
with the stranger, who, I was pleased to find, was by no
means difficult of access. After I had dined, I joined him at
the window, and we became so sociable that I proposed a
bottle of wine together, to which he most cheerfully assented.

I was too full of my poem to keep long quiet on the subject, and began to talk about the origin of the tavern and the
history of Jack Straw. I found my new acquaintance to be

perfectly at home on the topic, and to jump exactly with my humour in every respect. I became elevated by the wine and the conversation. In the fullness of an author's feelings, I told him of my projected poem, and repeated some passages, and he was in raptures. He was evidently of a strong poetical turn.

"Sir," said he, filling my glass at the same time, "our poets don't look at home. I don't see why we need go out of old England for robbers and rebels to write about. I like your Jack Straw, sir. He's a home made hero. I like him, sir. I like him exceedingly. He's English to the back bone—damme—Give me honest old England after all; them's my sentiments, sir!"

"I honour your sentiment," cried I zealously, "it is exactly my own. An English ruffian is as good a ruffian for poetry as any in Italy, or Germany, or the Archipelago; but it is hard to make our poets think so."

"More shame for them!" replied the man in green. "What a plague would they have? What have we to do with their Archipelagos of Italy and Germany? Haven't we heaths and commons and high ways on our own little island?—Aye and stout fellows to pad the hoof over them too? Stick to home, I say—them's my sentiments.—Come sir, my service to you— I agree with you perfectly."

"Poets in old times had right notions on this subject," continued I; "witness the fine old ballads about Robin Hood, Allan a'Dale and other staunch blades of yore." "Right, sir, right," interrupted he. "Robin Hood! He was the lad to cry stand! to a man, and never flinch."

"Ah sir!" said I, "they had famous bands of robbers in the good old times. Those were glorious poetical days. The merry crew of Sherwood Forest, who led such a roving picturesque life, 'under the greenwood tree.' I have often wished to visit their haunts, and tread the scenes of the exploits of Friar Tuck, and Clym of the Clough, and Sir William of Cloudeslie."

"Nay sir," said the gentleman in green, "we have had several very pretty gangs since their day. Those gallant dogs that kept about the great heaths in the neighbourhood of London; about Bagshot, and Hounslow, and Blackheath, for instance. Come sir, my service to you. You don't drink."

"I suppose," said I, emptying my glass, "I suppose you have

heard of the famous Turpin who was born in this very village of Hampstead, and who used to lurk with his gang in Epping Forest, about a hundred years since."

"Have I?" cried he. "To be sure I have! A hearty old blade that, sound as pitch. Old Turpentine!—as we used to call him. A famous fine fellow, sir."

"Well sir," continued I, "I have visited Waltham Abbey, and Chingford Church merely from the stories I heard when a boy of his exploits there, and I have searched Epping Forest for the cavern where he used to conceal himself. You must know," added I, "that I am a sort of amateur of Highwaymen. They were dashing, daring fellows; the last apologies that we had for the Knights errants of yore. Ah sir! the country has been sinking gradually into tameness and common place. We are losing the old English spirit. The bold Knights of the Post have all dwindled down into lurking footpads and sneaking pickpockets. There's no such thing as a dashing gentlemanlike robbery committed now adays on the King's high way. A man may roll from one end of England to the other, in a drowsy coach or jingling postchaise without any other adventure than that of being occasionally overturned, sleeping in damp sheets, or having an ill cooked dinner.

"We hear no more of public coaches being stopped and robbed by a well mounted gang of resolute fellows with pistols in their hands and crapes over their faces. What a pretty poetical incident was it for example, in domestic life, for a family carriage, on its way to a country seat, to be attacked about dusk, the old gentleman eased of his purse and watch, the ladies of their necklaces and ear rings, by a politely spoken Highwayman on a blood mare, who afterwards leaped the hedge and galloped across the country, to the admiration of Miss Carolina the daughter, who would write a long and romantic account of the adventure to her friend Miss Juliana in town. Ah sir! we meet with nothing of such incidents now adays!"

"That, sir,—" said my companion, taking advantage of a pause, when I stopped to recover breath and to take a glass of wine, which he had just poured out—"that, sir, craving your pardon, is not owing to any want of old English pluck. It is the effect of this cursed system of banking. People do not travel with bags of gold, as they did formerly. They have post notes and drafts on Bankers. To rob a coach is like catching a crow; where you have nothing but carrion flesh and feathers for your pains. But a coach in old times, sir, was as rich as a Spanish Galloon. It turned out the yellow boys bravely. And a private carriage was a cool hundred or two at least."

I cannot express how much I was delighted with the sallies of my new acquaintance. He told me that he often frequented the castle, and would be glad to know more of me; and I promised myself many a pleasant afternoon with him, when I should read him my poem, as it proceeded, and benefit by his remarks; for it was evident he had the true poetical feeling.

"Come, sir!" said he, pushing the bottle, "Damme I like you!—You're a man after my own heart; I'm cursed slow in making new acquaintances. One must be on the reserve, you know. But when I meet with a man of your kidney, damme my heart jumps at once to him—Them's my sentiments, sir—Come, sir, here's Jack Straw's health! I presume one can drink it now adays without treason!"

"With all my heart," said I gaily, "and Dick Turpin's into the bargain!"

"Ah, sir!" said the man in green, "those are the kind of men for poetry. The Newgate Kalender, sir! the Newgate Kalender is your only reading! There's the place to look for bold deeds and dashing fellows."

We were so much pleased with each other that we sat until a late hour. I insisted on paying the bill, for both my purse and my heart were full, and I agreed that he should pay the score at our next meeting. As the coaches had all gone that run between Hampstead and London he had to return on foot. He was so delighted with the idea of my poem that he could talk of nothing else. He made me repeat such passages as I could remember, and though I did it in a very mangled manner, having a wretched memory, yet he was in raptures.

Every now and then he would break out with some scrap which he would misquote most terribly, but would rub his hands and exclaim, "By Jupiter that's fine! that's noble! Damme, sir, if I can conceive how you hit upon such ideas!"

I must confess I did not always relish his misquotations, which sometimes made absolute nonsense of the passages; but what author stands upon trifles when he is praised?

Never had I spent a more delightful evening. I did not perceive how the time flew. I could not bear to separate but continued walking on, arm in arm, with him, past my lodgings, through Camden Town, and across Crackscull Common talking the whole way about my poem.

When we were half way across the common he interrupted me in the midst of a quotation by telling me that this had been a famous place for footpads, and was still occasionally infested by them; and that a man had recently been shot there in attempting to defend himself.

"The more fool he!" cried I. "A man is an ideot to risk life, or even limb, to save a paltry purse of money. It's quite a different case from that of a duel, where one's honour is concerned. For my part," added I, "I should never think of making resistance against one of those desperadoes."

"Say you so?" cried my friend in green, turning suddenly upon me, and putting a pistol to my breast, "Why then have at you my lad!—come—disburse! empty! unsack!"

In a word, I found that the muse had played me another of her tricks, and had betrayed me into the hands of a footpad. There was no time to parley; he made me turn my pockets inside out; and hearing the sound of distant footsteps, he made one fell swoop upon purse, watch and all, gave me a thwack over my unlucky pate that laid me sprawling on the ground; and scampered away with his booty.

I saw no more of my friend in green until a year or two afterwards; when I caught a sight of his poetical countenance among a crew of scapegraces, heavily ironed, who were on the way for transportation. He recognized me at once, tipped me an impudent wink, and asked me how I came on with the history of Jack Straw's Castle.

The catastrophe at Crackscull Common put an end to my summer's campaign. I was cured of my poetical enthusiasm for rebels, robbers and highwaymen. I was put out of conceit of my subject, and what was worse I was lightened of my purse, in which was almost every farthing I had in the world. So I abandoned Sir Richard Steele's cottage in despair, and crept into less celebrated, though no less poetical and airy lodgings in a garret in town.

I now determined to cultivate the society of the literary, and to enrol myself in the fraternity of authorship. It is by the constant collision of mind, thought I, that authors strike out the sparks of genius, and kindle up with glorious conceptions. Poetry is evidently a contagious complaint: I will keep company with poets; who knows but I may catch it as others have done?

I found no difficulty in making a circle of literary acquaintances, not having the sin of success lying at my door; indeed, the failure of my poem was a kind of recommendation to their favour. It is true my new friends were not of the most brilliant names in literature; but then, if you would take their words for it, they were like the prophets of old, men of whom the world was not worthy; and who were to live in future ages, when the ephemeral favourites of the day should be forgotten.

I soon discovered, however, that the more I mingled in literary society, the less I felt capacitated to write; that poetry was not so catching as I imagined; and that in familiar life there was often nothing less poetical than a poet. Besides, I wanted the *esprit du corps* to turn these literary fellowships to any account. I could not bring myself to enlist in any particular sect: I saw something to like in them all, but found that would never do, for that the tacit condition on which a man enters into one of these sects is, that he abuses all the rest.

I perceived that there were little knots of authors who lived with, and for, and by one another. They considered themselves the salt of the earth. They fostered and kept up a conventional vein of thinking and talking, and joking on all subjects; and they cried each other up to the skies. Each sect had its particular creed; and set up certain authors as divinities, and fell down and worshipped them; and considered every one who did not worship them, or who worshipped any other, as a heretic and an infidel.

In quoting the writers of the day, I generally found them extolling names of which I had scarcely heard, and talking slightingly of others who were the favourites of the public. If I mentioned any recent work from the pen of a first rate

author, they had not read it; they had not time to read all that
was spawned from the press; he wrote too much to write
well;—and then they would break out into raptures about
some Mr. Timson, or Tomson, or Jackson, whose works were
neglected at the present day, but who was to be the wonder
and delight of posterity. Alas! what heavy debts is this ne-
glectful world daily accumulating on the shoulders of poor
posterity!

But above all, it was edifying to hear with what contempt
they would talk of the great. Ye gods! how immeasurably the
great are despised by the small fry of literature! It is true, an
exception was now and then made of some nobleman, with
whom, perhaps, they had casually shaken hands at an election,
or hob or nobbed at a public dinner, and who was pronounced a "devilish good fellow," and "no humbug;" but, in
general, it was enough for a man to have a title to be the
object of their sovereign disdain: you have no idea how poetically and philosophically they would talk of nobility.

For my part, this affected me but little; for though I had no
bitterness against the great, and did not think the worse of a
man for having innocently been born to a title, yet I did not
feel myself at present called upon to resent the indignities
poured upon them by the little. But the hostility to the great
writers of the day went sorely against the grain with me. I
could not enter into such feuds, nor participate in such ani-
mosities. I had not become author sufficiently to hate other
authors. I could still find pleasure in the novelties of the press,
and could find it in my heart to praise a contemporary, even
though he were successful. Indeed, I was miscellaneous in
my taste, and could not confine it to any age or growth of
writers. I could turn with delight from the glowing pages of
Byron to the cool and polished raillery of Pope; and, after
wandering among the sacred groves of Paradise Lost, I could
give myself up to voluptuous abandonment in the enchanted
bowers of Lalla Rookh.

"I would have my authors," said I, "as various as my wines,
and, in relishing the strong and the racy, would never decry
the sparkling and exhilarating. Port and sherry are excellent
stand-by's, and so is Madeira; but claret and Burgundy may
be drunk now and then without disparagement to one's

palate; and Champagne is a beverage by no means to be despised."

Such was the tirade I uttered one day, when a little flushed with ale, at a literary club. I uttered it, too, with something of a flourish, for I thought my simile a clever one. Unluckily, my auditors were men who drank beer and hated Pope; so my figure about wines went for nothing, and my critical toleration was looked upon as downright heterodoxy. In a word, I soon became like a freethinker in religion, an outlaw from every sect, and fair game for all. Such are the melancholy consequences of not hating in literature.

I see you are growing weary, so I will be brief with the residue of my literary career. I will not detain you with a detail of my various attempts to get astride of Pegasus; of the poems I have written which were never printed, the plays I have presented which were never performed, and the tracts I have published which were never purchased.—It seemed as if booksellers, managers, and the very public, had entered into a conspiracy to starve me. Still I could not prevail upon myself to give up the trial nor abandon those dreams of renown in which I had indulged. How should I ever be able to look the literary circle of my native village in the face, if I were so completely to falsify their predictions. For some time longer therefore I continued to write for fame, and of course was the most miserable dog in existence, besides being in continual risk of starvation. I accumulated loads of literary treasure on my shelves—loads which were to be treasures to posterity; but, alas! they put not a penny into my purse. What was all this wealth to my present necessities? I could not patch my elbows with an ode; nor satisfy my hunger with blank verse. "Shall a man fill his belly with the east wind?" says the proverb. He may as well do so as with poetry.

I have many a time strolled sorrowfully along, with a sad heart and an empty stomach, about five o'clock, and looked wistfully down the areas in the west end of the town; and seen through the kitchen windows the fires gleaming, and the joints of meat turning on the spits and dripping with gravy; and the cook maids beating up puddings, or trussing turkeys, and felt for the moment that if I could but have the run of one of those kitchens, Apollo and the muses might have the

hungry heights of Parnassus for me. Oh sir! talk of meditations among the tombs—they are nothing so melancholy as
the meditations of a poor devil without penny in pouch,
along a line of kitchen windows towards dinner time.

At length, when almost reduced to famine and despair, the
idea all at once entered my head, that perhaps I was not so
clever a fellow as the village and myself had supposed. It was
the salvation of me. The moment the idea popped into my
brain it brought conviction and comfort with it. I awoke as
from a dream. I gave up immortal fame to those who could
live on air; took to writing for mere bread; and have ever
since led a very tolerable life of it. There is no man of letters
so much at his ease, sir, as he who has no character to gain or
lose. I had to train myself to it a little, and to clip my wings
short at first, or they would have carried me up into poetry in
spite of myself. So I determined to begin by the opposite
extreme, and abandoning the higher regions of the craft I
came plump down to the lowest, and turned Creeper.

"Creeper! and pray what is that?" said I. "Oh sir! I see you
are ignorant of the language of the craft; a creeper is one who
furnishes the newspapers with paragraphs at so much a line:
one who goes about in quest of misfortunes; attends the Bow
Street Office; the courts of justice and every other den of mischief and iniquity. We are paid at the rate of a penny a line,
and as we can sell the same paragraph to almost every paper,
we sometimes pick up a very decent day's work. Now and
then the muse is unkind, or the day uncommonly quiet, and
then we rather starve; and sometimes the unconscionable editors will clip our paragraphs when they are a little too rhetorical, and snip off twopence or threepence at a go. I have many
a time had my pot of porter snipped off of my dinner in this
way; and have had to dine with dry lips. However I cannot
complain. I rose gradually in the lower ranks of the craft, and
am now I think in the most comfortable region of literature."

"And pray," said I, "what may you be at present?"

"At present," said he, "I am a regular job writer and turn
my hand to any thing. I work up the writings of others at so
much a sheet; turn off translations; write second rate articles
to fill up reviews and magazines; compile travels and voyages,
and furnish theatrical criticisms for the newspapers. All this

authorship, you perceive, is anonymous; it gives no reputation, except among the trade, where I am considered an
author of all work, and am always sure of employ. That's
the only reputation I want. I sleep soundly, without dread
of duns or critics, and leave immortal fame to those that
choose to fret and fight about it. Take my word for it, the only
happy author in this world is he who is below the care of
reputation."

Notoriety

When we had emerged from the literary nest of honest Dribble, and had passed safely through the dangers of Break neck
Stairs, and the labyrinths of Fleet Market, Buckthorne indulged in many comments upon the peep into literary life
which he had furnished me.

I expressed my surprise at finding it so different a world
from what I had imagined. "It is always so," said he, "with
strangers. The land of literature is a fairy land to those who
view it from a distance, but like all other landscapes, the
charm fades on a nearer approach, and the thorns and briars
become visible. The republic of letters is the most factious
and discordant of all republics, ancient or modern."

"Yet," said I, smiling, "you would not have me take honest
Dribble's experience as a view of the land. He is but a mousing owl; a mere groundling. We should have quite a different
strain from one of those fortunate authors whom we see
sporting about the empyreal heights of fashion, like swallows
in the blue sky of a summer's day."

"Perhaps we might," replied he, "but I doubt it. I doubt
whether if any one, even of the most successful, were to tell
his actual feelings, you would not find the truth of friend
Dribble's philosophy with respect to reputation. One you
would find carrying a gay face to the world, while some vulture critic was preying upon his very liver. Another, who was
simple enough to mistake fashion for fame, you would find
watching countenances, and cultivating invitations, more ambitious to figure in the *beau monde* than the world of letters,

and apt to be rendered wretched by the neglect of an illiterate peer, or a dissipated duchess. Those who were rising to fame, you would find tormented with anxiety to get higher; and those who had gained the summit, in constant apprehension of a decline.

"Even those who are indifferent to the buzz of notoriety, and the farce of fashion, are not much better off, being incessantly harassed by intrusions on their leisure, and interruptions of their pursuits; for, whatever may be his feelings, when once an author is launched into notoriety, he must go the rounds until the idle curiosity of the day is satisfied, and he is thrown aside to make way for some new caprice. Upon the whole, I do not know but he is most fortunate who engages in the whirl through ambition, however tormenting; as it is doubly irksome to be obliged to join in the game without being interested in the stake.

"There is a constant demand in the fashionable world for novelty; every nine days must have its wonder, no matter of what kind. At one time it is an author; at another a fire eater; at another a composer, an Indian juggler, or an Indian chief; a man from the North Pole or the Pyramids: each figures through his brief term of notoriety, and then makes way for the succeeding wonder. You must know that we have oddity fanciers among our ladies of rank, who collect about them all kinds of remarkable beings: fiddlers, statesmen, singers, warriors, artists, philosophers, actors, and poets; every kind of personage, in short, who is noted for something peculiar: so that their routs are like fancy balls, where every one comes 'in character.'

"I have had infinite amusement at these parties in noticing how industriously every one was playing a part, and acting out of his natural line. There is not a more complete game at cross purposes than the intercourse of the literary and the great. The fine gentleman is always anxious to be thought a wit, and the wit a fine gentleman.

"I have noticed a lord endeavouring to look wise and to talk learnedly with a man of letters, who was aiming at a fashionable air, and the tone of a man who had lived about town. The peer quoted a score or two of learned authors, with whom he would fain be thought intimate, while the author talked of Sir John this, and Sir Harry that, and extolled the Burgundy he had drank at Lord Such-a-one's.—Each seemed to forget that he could only be interesting to the other in his proper character. Had the peer been merely a man of erudition, the author would never have listened to his prosing; and had the author known all the nobility in the Court Calendar, it would have given him no interest in the eyes of the peer.

"In the same way I have seen a fine lady, remarkable for beauty, weary a philosopher with flimsy metaphysics, while the philosopher put on an awkward air of gallantry, played with her fan, and prattled about the Opera. I have heard a sentimental poet talk very stupidly with a statesman about the national debt; and on joining a knot of scientific old gentlemen conversing in a corner, expecting to hear the discussion of some valuable discovery, I found they were only amusing themselves with a fat story."

A Practical Philosopher

The anecdotes I had heard of Buckthorne's early schoolmate, together with a variety of peculiarities which I had remarked in himself, gave me a strong curiosity to know something of his own history. I am a traveller of the good old school, and am fond of the custom laid down in books, according to which, whenever travellers met, they sat down forthwith, and gave a history of themselves and their adventures. This Buckthorne, too, was a man much to my taste; he had seen the world, and mingled with society, yet retained the strong eccentricities of a man who had lived much alone. There was a careless dash of good humour about him which pleased me exceedingly, and at times an odd tinge of melancholy mingled with his humour and gave it an additional zest. He was apt to run into long speculations upon society and manners, and to indulge in whimsical views of human nature; yet there was nothing ill tempered in his satire. It ran more upon the follies than the vices of mankind; and even the follies of his fellow man were treated with the leniency of one who felt himself to be but frail. He had evidently been a little chilled and buffetted by fortune, without being soured thereby; as some fruits become mellower and more generous in their flavour from having been bruised and frostbitten.

I have always had a great relish for the conversation of practical philosophers of this stamp, who have profited by the "sweet uses" of adversity without imbibing its bitterness; who have learnt to estimate the world rightly, yet good humouredly; and who, while they perceive the truth of the saying, that "all is vanity," are yet able to do so without vexation of spirit.

Such a man was Buckthorne. In general a laughing philosopher; and if at any time a shade of sadness stole across his brow, it was but transient; like a summer cloud, which soon goes by, and freshens and revives the fields over which it passes.

I was walking with him one day in Kensington Gardens—for he was a knowing epicure in all the cheap pleasures and rural haunts within reach of the metropolis. It was a delightful warm morning in spring; and he was in the happy mood of a pastoral citizen, when just turned loose into grass and sunshine. He had been watching a lark which, rising from a bed of daisies and yellow cups, had sung his way up to a bright snowy cloud floating in the deep blue sky.

"Of all birds," said he, "I should like to be a lark. He revels in the brightest time of the day, in the happiest season of the year, among fresh meadows and opening flowers; and when he has sated himself with the sweetness of earth, he wings his flight up to Heaven as if he would drink in the melody of the morning stars. Hark to that note! How it comes trilling down upon the ear! What a stream of music, note falling over note in delicious cadence! Who would trouble his head about operas and concerts when he could walk in the fields and hear such music for nothing? These are the enjoyments which set riches at scorn, and make even a poor man independent:

> I care not, Fortune, what you do deny:—
>   You cannot rob me of free nature's grace;
> You cannot shut the windows of the sky,
>   Through which Aurora shows her bright'ning face;

You cannot bar my constant feet to trace
The woods and lawns by living streams at eve——

"Sir, there are homilies in nature's works worth all the wisdom of the schools, if we could but read them rightly; and one of the pleasantest lessons I ever received in a time of trouble, was from hearing the notes of a lark."

I profited by this communicative vein to intimate to Buckthorne a wish to know something of the events of his life, which I fancied must have been an eventful one.

He smiled when I expressed my desire. "I have no great story," said he, "to relate. A mere tissue of errors and follies. But, such as it is, you shall have one epoch of it, by which you may judge of the rest." And so, without any further prelude, he gave me the following anecdotes of his early adventures.

Buckthorne, or the Young Man of Great Expectations

I was born to very little property, but to great expectations; which is perhaps one of the most unlucky fortunes a man can be born to. My father was a country gentleman, the last of a very ancient and honourable but decayed family, and resided in an old hunting lodge in Warwickshire. He was a keen sportsman and lived to the extent of his moderate income, so that I had little to expect from that quarter; but then I had a rich uncle by the mother's side, a penurious, accumulating curmudgeon, who it was confidently expected would make me his heir; because he was an old Bachelor; because I was named after him, and because he hated all the world except myself.

He was, in fact, an inveterate hater; a miser even in misanthropy, and hoarded up a grudge as he did a guinea. Thus, though my mother was an only sister, he had never forgiven her marriage with my father, against whom he had a cold, still, immoveable pique, which had lain at the bottom of his heart, like a stone in a well, ever since they had been school boys together. My mother, however, considered me as the intermediate being that was to bring every thing again into harmony, for she looked upon me as a prodigy—God bless her! My heart overflows whenever I recall her tenderness. She was the most excellent, the most indulgent of mothers. I was her only child; it was a pity she had no more, for she had fondness of heart enough to have spoiled a dozen!

I was sent at an early age to a public school sorely against my mother's wishes; but my father insisted that it was the only way to make boys hardy. The school was kept by a conscientious prig of the ancient system who did his duty by the boys entrusted to his care; that is to say we were flogged soundly when we did not get our lessons. We were put into classes and thus flogged on in droves along the highways of knowledge, in much the same manner as cattle are driven to market, where those that are heavy in gait or short in leg have to suffer for the superior alertness or longer limbs of their companions.

For my part, I confess it with shame, I was an incorrigible laggard. I have always had the poetical feeling, that is to say I have always been an idle fellow and prone to play the vagabond. I used to get away from my books and school whenever I could and ramble about the fields. I was surrounded by seductions for such a temperament. The school house was an old fashioned whitewashed mansion of wood and plaister, standing on the skirts of a beautiful village. Close by it was the venerable church with a tall Gothic spire. Before it spread a lovely green valley, with a little stream glistening along through willow groves; while a line of blue hills bounding the landscape gave rise to many a summer day dream as to the fairy land that lay beyond.

In spite of all the scourgings I suffered at that school to make me love my book I cannot but look back upon the place with fondness. Indeed I considered this frequent flagellation as the common lot of humanity and the regular mode in which scholars were made. My kind mother used to lament over my details of the sore trials I underwent in the cause of learning; but my father turned a deaf ear to her expostulations. He had been flogged through school himself and swore there was no other way of making a man of parts; though, let

me speak it with all due reverence, my father was but an indifferent illustration of his theory, for he was considered a
grievous blockhead.

My poetical temperament evinced itself at a very early period. The village church was attended every Sunday by a
neighbouring squire; the lord of the manor, whose park
stretched quite to the village and whose spacious country seat
seemed to take the church under its protection. Indeed you
would have thought the church had been consecrated to him
instead of to the Deity. The parish clerk bowed low before
him and the vergers humbled themselves unto the dust in his
presence. He always entered a little late and with some stir,
striking his cane emphatically on the ground; swaying his hat
in his hand, and looking loftily to the right and left as he
walked slowly up the aisle, and the parson, who always ate his
Sunday dinner with him, never commenced service until he
appeared. He sat with his family in a large pew gorgeously
lined, humbling himself devoutly on velvet cushions and reading lessons of meekness and lowliness of spirit out of splendid
gold and morocco prayer books. Whenever the parson spoke
of the difficulty of a rich man's entering the kingdom of
heaven, the eyes of the congregation would turn towards the
"grand pew," and I thought the squire seemed pleased with
the application.

The pomp of this pew and the aristocratical air of the family struck my imagination wonderfully and I fell desperately in
love with a little daughter of the squire's, about twelve years
of age. This freak of fancy made me more truant from my
studies than ever. I used to stroll about the squire's park, and
lurk near the house: to catch glimpses of this little damsel at
the windows, or playing about the lawns; or walking out with
her governess.

I had not enterprize, nor impudence enough to venture
from my concealment; indeed I felt like an arrant poacher,
until I read one or two of Ovid's Metamorphoses, when I
pictured myself as some sylvan deity and she a coy wood
nymph of whom I was in pursuit. There is something extremely delicious in these early awakenings of the tender
passion. I can feel, even at this moment, the thrilling of my
boyish bosom, whenever by chance I caught a glimpse of her

white frock fluttering among the shrubbery. I carried about in my bosom a volume of Waller, which I had purloined from my mother's library; and I applied to my little fair one all the compliments lavished upon Sacharissa.

At length I danced with her at a school ball. I was so awkward a booby that I dared scarcely speak to her; I was filled with awe and embarrassment in her presence; but I was so inspired that my poetical temperament for the first time broke out in verse and I fabricated some glowing lines, in which I berhymed the little lady under the favourite name of Sacharissa. I slipped the verses, trembling and blushing, into her hand the next Sunday as she came out of church. The little prude handed them to her mamma; the mamma handed them to the squire; the squire, who had no soul for poetry, sent them in dudgeon to the schoolmaster; and the schoolmaster, with a barbarity worthy of the dark ages, gave me a sound and peculiarly humiliating flogging for thus trespassing upon Parnassus.

This was a sad outset for a votary of the muse. It ought to have cured me of my passion for poetry; but it only confirmed it, for I felt the spirit of a martyr rising within me. What was as well, perhaps, it cured me of my passion for the young lady, for I felt so indignant at the ignominious horsing I had incurred in celebrating her charms, that I could not hold up my head in church.

Fortunately for my wounded sensibility the midsummer holydays came on, and I returned home. My mother, as usual, enquired into all my school concerns, my little pleasures, and cares, and sorrows; for boyhood has its share of the one as well as of the others. I told her all, and she was indignant at the treatment I had experienced. She fired up at the arrogance of the squire, and the prudery of the daughter; and as to the schoolmaster, she wondered where was the use of having schoolmasters, and why boys could not remain at home and be educated by tutors, under the eye of their mothers. She asked to see the verses I had written, and she was delighted with them, for to confess the truth, she had a pretty taste in poetry. She even shewed them to the parson's wife, who protested they were charming, and the parson's three daughters insisted on each having a copy of them.

All this was exceedingly balsamic, and I was still more consoled and encouraged when the young ladies, who were the
blue stockings of the neighbourhood, and had read Dr.
Johnson's Lives quite through, assured my mother that great
geniuses never studied, but were always idle; upon which I
began to surmise that I was myself something out of the common run. My father, however, was of a very different opinion, for when my mother, in the pride of her heart, shewed
him my copy of verses, he threw them out of the window,
asking her "if she meant to make a ballad monger of the boy."
But he was a careless, common thinking man, and I cannot
say that I ever loved him much; my mother absorbed all my
filial affection.

I used occasionally during holydays to be sent on short visits to the uncle, who was to make me his heir; they thought it
would keep me in his mind and render him fond of me. He
was a withered, anxious looking old fellow, and lived in a
desolate old country seat, which he suffered to go to ruin
from absolute niggardliness. He kept but one man servant
who had lived, or rather starved with him for years. No
woman was allowed to sleep in the house. A daughter of the
old servant lived by the gate in what had been a porter's
lodge, and was permitted to come into the house about an
hour each day, to make the beds, and cook a morsel of provisions.

The park that surrounded the house was all run wild; the
trees grown out of shape; the fish ponds stagnant; the urns
and statues fallen from their pedestals and buried among the
rank grass. The hares and pheasants were so little molested,
except by poachers, that they bred in great abundance, and
sported about the rough lawns and weedy avenues. To guard
the premises and frighten off robbers, of whom he was somewhat apprehensive, and visitors, whom he held in almost
equal awe, my uncle kept two or three blood hounds, who
were always prowling round the house, and were the dread
of the neighbouring peasantry. They were gaunt and half
starved, seemed ready to devour one from mere hunger, and
were an effectual check on any stranger's approach to this
wizard castle.

Such was my uncle's house, which I used to visit now and

then during the holydays. I was, as I before said, the old
man's favourite; that is to say he did not hate me so much as
he did the rest of the world. I had been apprised of his character and cautioned to cultivate his good will; but I was too
young and careless to be a courtier; and indeed have never
been sufficiently studious of my interests, to let them govern
my feelings. However, we jogged on very well together, and
as my visits cost him almost nothing, they did not seem to be
very unwelcome. I brought with me my fishing rod and half
supplied the table from the fish ponds.

Our meals were solitary and unsocial. My uncle rarely
spoke; he pointed for whatever he wanted and the servant
perfectly understood him. Indeed his man John, or Iron John
as he was called in the neighbourhood, was a counterpart of
his master. He was a tall bony old fellow, with a dry wig that
seemed made of cow's tail and a face as tough as though it
had been made of bull's hide. He was generally clad in a long,
patched livery coat, taken out of the wardrobe of the house;
and which bagged loosely about him, having evidently belonged to some corpulent predecessor, in the more plenteous
days of the mansion. From long habits of taciturnity the
hinges of his jaws seemed to have grown absolutely rusty; and
it cost him as much effort to set them ajar, and to let out a
tolerable sentence, as it would have done to set open the iron
gates of the park and let out the old family carriage that was
dropping to pieces in the coach house.

I cannot say, however, but that I was for some time amused
with my uncle's peculiarities. Even the very desolateness of
the establishment had something in it that hit my fancy.
When the weather was fine I used to amuse myself, in a solitary way, by rambling about the park, and coursing like a colt
across its lawns. The hares and pheasants seemed to stare with
surprize to see a human being walking these forbidden
grounds by day light. Sometimes I amused myself by jerking
stones, or shooting at birds with a bow and arrows; for to
have used a gun would have been treason. Now and then my
path was crossed by a little red-headed ragged-tailed urchin,
the son of the woman at the lodge, who ran wild about the
premises. I tried to draw him into familiarity and to make a
companion of him; but he seemed to have imbibed the

strange, unsocial character of every thing around him; and always kept aloof; so I considered him as another Orson, and amused myself with shooting at him with my bow and arrows, and he would hold up his breeches with one hand and scamper away like a deer.

There was something in all this loneliness and wildness strangely pleasing to me. The great stables, empty and weather broken, with the names of favourite horses over the vacant stalls; the windows bricked and boarded up; the broken roofs, garrisoned by Rooks and Jackdaws; all had a singularly forlorn appearance: One would have concluded the house to be totally uninhabited, were it not for a little thread of blue smoke, which now and then curled up like a cork-screw, from the center of one of the wide chimnies, when my uncle's starveling meal was cooking.

My uncle's room was in a remote corner of the building, strongly secured and generally locked; I was never admitted into this strong hold; where the old man would remain for the greater part of the time, drawn up like a veteran spider, in the citadel of his web. The rest of the mansion, however, was open to me, and I wandered about it, unconstrained. The damp and rain which beat in through the broken windows, crumbled the paper from the walls; mouldered the pictures and gradually destroyed the furniture. I loved to rove about the wide waste chambers in bad weather, and listen to the howling of the wind, and the banging about of the doors and window shutters. I pleased myself with the idea how completely, when I came to the estate, I would renovate all things, and make the old building ring with merriment, till it was astonished at its own jocundity.

The chamber which I occupied on these visits had been my mother's, when a girl. There was still the toilet table of her own adorning; the landscapes of her own drawing. She had never seen it since her marriage, but would often ask me if every thing was still the same. All was just the same, for I loved that chamber on her account, and had taken pains to put every thing in order, and to mend all the flaws in the windows with my own hands. I anticipated the time when I should once more welcome her to the house of her fathers, and restore her to this little nestling place of her childhood.

At length my evil genius, or, what perhaps is the same thing, the muse, inspired me with the notion of rhyming again. My uncle, who never went to church, used on Sundays to read chapters out of the bible, and Iron John, the woman from the lodge and myself were his congregation. It seemed to be all one to him what he read, so long as it was something from the bible; sometimes therefore it would be the Song of Solomon, and this withered anatomy would read about being "stayed with flaggons and comforted with apples, for he was sick of love." Sometimes he would hobble with spectacles on nose, through whole chapters of hard Hebrew names in Deuteronomy; at which the poor woman would sigh and groan as if wonderfully moved. His favourite book however was "The Pilgrim's Progress," and when he came to that part which treats of Doubting Castle and Giant Despair, I thought invariably of him and his desolate old country seat. So much did the idea amuse me, that I took to scribbling about it under the trees in the park; and in a few days had made some progress in a poem, in which I had given a description of the place, under the name of Doubting Castle, and personified my uncle as Giant Despair.

I lost my poem somewhere about the house, and I soon suspected that my uncle had found it; as he harshly intimated to me that I could return home, and that I need not come and see him again until he should send for me.

Just about this time my mother died.—I cannot dwell upon the circumstance; my heart, careless and wayworn as it is, gushes with the recollection. Her death was an event that perhaps gave a turn to all my after fortunes. With her died all that made home attractive. I had no longer any body whom I was ambitious to please, or fearful to offend. My father was a good kind of man in his way, but he had bad maxims in education, and we differed on material points. It makes a vast difference in opinion about the utility of the rod, which end happens to fall to one's share. I never could be brought into my father's way of thinking on the subject.

I now, therefore, began to grow very impatient of remaining at school to be flogged for things that I did not like. I longed for variety, especially now that I had not my uncle's to resort to, by way of diversifying the dullness of school with the dreariness of his country seat. I was now almost seventeen, tall for my age and full of idle fancies. I had a roving, inextinguishable desire to see different kinds of life, and different orders of society; and this vagrant humour had been fostered in me by Tom Dribble, the prime wag and great genius of the school, who had all the rambling propensities of a poet.

I used to sit at my desk in the school, on a fine summer's day, and instead of studying the book which lay open before me, my eye was gazing through the window on the green fields and blue hills. How I envied the happy groups seated on the tops of stage coaches chatting, and joking, and laughing, as they were whirled by the school house, on their way to the metropolis. Even the Waggoners trudging along beside their ponderous teams, and traversing the Kingdom, from one end to the other, were objects of envy to me. I fancied to myself what adventures they must experience, and what odd scenes of life they must witness. All this was, doubtless, the poetical temperament working within me and tempting me forth into a world of its own creation, which I mistook for the world of real life.

While my mother lived this strong propensity to rove was counteracted by the stronger attractions of home and by the powerful ties of affection which drew me to her side; but now that she was gone, the attractions had ceased; the ties were severed. I had no longer an anchorage ground for my heart; but was at the mercy of every vagrant impulse. Nothing but the narrow allowance on which my father kept me, and the consequent penury of my purse, prevented me from mounting the top of a stage coach and launching myself adrift on the great ocean of life.

Just about this time the village was agitated for a day or two, by the passing through of several caravans, containing wild beasts, and other spectacles for a great fair annually held at a neighbouring town.

I had never seen a fair of any consequence, and my curiosity was powerfully awakened by this bustle of preparation. I gazed with respect and wonder at the vagrant personages who accompanied these caravans. I loitered about the village inn, listening with curiosity and delight to the slang talk and cant jokes of the showmen and their followers; and I felt an eager desire to witness this fair, which my fancy decked out as something wonderfully fine.

A holyday afternoon presented, when I could be absent from noon until evening. A waggon was going from the village to the fair. I could not resist the temptation, nor the eloquence of Tom Dribble, who was a truant to the very heart's core. We hired seats, and set off full of boyish expectation. I promised myself that I would but take a peep at the land of promise, and hasten back again before my absence should be noticed.

Heavens! how happy I was on arriving at the fair! How I was enchanted with the world of fun and pageantry around me! The humours of Punch, the feats of the Equestrians, the magical tricks of the Conjurors! But what principally caught my attention was—an itinerant theatre; where a tragedy, pantomime and farce were all acted in the course of half an hour, and more of the Dramatis personæ murdered, than at either Drury Lane or Covent Garden in the course of a whole evening. I have since seen many a play performed by the best actors in the world, but never have I derived half the delight from any, that I did from this first representation.

There was a ferocious tyrant in a skull cap, like an inverted porringer, and a dress of red baize, magnificently embroidered with gilt leather; with his face so be-whiskered and his eyebrows so knit and expanded with burnt cork, that he made my heart quake within me as he stamped about the little stage. I was enraptured too with the surpassing beauty of a distressed damsel, in faded pink silk, and dirty white muslin, whom he held in cruel captivity by way of gaining her affections; and who wept and wrung her hands and flourished a ragged white handkerchief from the top of an impregnable tower, of the size of a band box.

Even after I had come out from the play, I could not tear myself from the vicinity of the theatre; but lingered, gazing and wondering, and laughing at the dramatis personæ, as they performed their antics, or danced upon a stage in front of the booth, to decoy a new set of spectators.

I was so bewildered by the scene, and so lost in the crowd of sensations that kept swarming upon me, that I was like one entranced. I lost my companion Tom Dribble in a tumult and scuffle that took place near one of the shows, but I was too much occupied in mind to think long about him. I strolled about until dark, when the fair was lighted up, and a new scene of magic opened upon me. The illumination of the tents and booths; the brilliant effect of the stages decorated with lamps, with dramatic groups flaunting about them in gaudy dresses, contrasted splendidly with the surrounding darkness; while the uproar of drums, trumpets, fiddles, hautboys and cymbals, mingled with the harangues of the showmen, the squeaking of Punch, and the shouts and laughter of the crowd, all united to complete my giddy distraction.

Time flew without my perceiving it. When I came to myself and thought of the school, I hastened to return. I enquired for the waggon in which I had come: it had been gone for hours. I asked the time. It was almost midnight! A sudden quaking seized me. How was I to get back to school? I was too weary to make the journey on foot, and I knew not where to apply for a conveyance. Even if I should find one, could I venture to disturb the school house long after midnight?—to arouse that sleeping lion the usher, in the very midst of his night's rest? The idea was too dreadful for a delinquent schoolboy. All the horrors of return rushed upon me—my absence must long before this have been remarked—and absent for a whole night!—a deed of darkness not easily to be expiated. The rod of the pedagogue budded forth into tenfold terrors before my affrighted fancy. I pictured to myself punishment and humiliation in every variety of form; and my heart sickened at the picture. Alas! how often are the petty ills of boyhood as painful to our tender natures, as are the sterner evils of manhood to our robuster minds.

I wandered about among the booths, and I might have derived a lesson from my actual feelings, how much the charms of this world depend upon ourselves; for I no longer saw any thing gay or delightful in the revelry around me. At length I lay down, wearied and perplexed, behind one of the large tents, and, covering myself with the margin of the tent cloth, to keep off the night chill, I soon fell asleep.

I had not slept long when I was awakened by the noise of merriment within an adjoining booth. It was the itinerant theatre, rudely constructed of boards and canvass. I peeped through an aperture and saw the whole dramatis personæ, tragedy, comedy and pantomime all refreshing themselves after the final dismissal of their auditors. They were merry and gamesome and made the flimsy theatre ring with their laughter. I was astonished to see the Tragedy tyrant in red baize and fierce whiskers who had made my heart quake as he strutted about the boards; now transformed into a fat, good humoured fellow; the beaming porringer laid aside from his brow, and his jolly face washed from all the terrors of burnt cork. I was delighted, too, to see the distressed damsel, in faded silk and dirty muslin, who had trembled under his tyranny, and afflicted me so much by her sorrows; now seated familiarly on his knee, and quaffing from the same tankard. Harlequin lay asleep on one of the benches; and monks, satyrs and vestal virgins were grouped together, laughing outrageously at a broad story, told by an unhappy count who had been barbarously murdered in the tragedy.

This was, indeed, novelty to me. It was a peep into another planet. I gazed and listened with intense curiosity and enjoyment. They had a thousand odd stories and jokes about the events of the day; and burlesque descriptions and mimickings of the spectators, who had been admiring them. Their conversation was full of allusions to their adventures at different places where they had exhibited; the characters they had met with in different villages; and the ludicrous difficulties in which they had occasionally been involved. All past cares and troubles were now turned by these thoughtless beings into matter of merriment; and made to contribute to the gaiety of the moment. They had been moving from fair to fair about the kingdom, and were the next morning, to set out on their way to London.

My resolution was taken. I stole from my nest; and crept through a hedge into a neighbouring field, where I went to work to make a tatterdemalion of myself. I tore my clothes; soiled them with dirt; begrimed my face and hands; and, crawling near one of the booths, purloined an old hat, and left my new one in its place. It was an honest theft, and I hope may not hereafter rise up in judgment against me.

I now ventured to the scene of merrymaking, and, presenting myself before the Dramatic corps, offered myself as a volunteer. I felt terribly agitated and abashed, for—"never before stood I in such a presence." I had addressed myself to the manager of the company. He was a fat man dressed in dirty white; with a red sash fringed with tinsel, swathed round his body. His face was smeared with paint, and a majestic plume towered from an old spangled black bonnet. He was the Jupiter Tonans of this Olympus, and was surrounded by the inferior gods and goddesses of his court. He sat on the end of a bench, by a table, with one arm akimbo and the other extended to the handle of a tankard, which he had slowly set down from his lips, as he surveyed me from head to foot. It was a moment of awful scrutiny, and I fancied the groupes around, all watching us in silent suspense, and waiting for the imperial nod.

He questioned me as to who I was; what were my qualifications; and what terms I expected. I passed myself off for a discharged servant from a gentleman's family; and as, happily, one does not require a special recommendation to get admitted into bad company, the questions on that head were easily satisfied. As to my accomplishments, I could spout a little poetry, and knew several scenes of plays, which I had learnt at school exhibitions. I could dance——that was enough; no further questions were asked me as to accomplishments; it was the very thing they wanted; and, as I asked no wages, but merely meat and drink, and safe conduct about the world, a bargain was struck in a moment.

Behold me, therefore, transformed of a sudden, from a gentleman student, to a dancing buffoon; for such, in fact, was the character in which I made my debut. I was one of those who formed the groupes in the dramas, and were principally employed on the stage in front of the booth, to attract company. I was equipped as a Satyr, in a dress of drab frize that fitted to my shape; with a great laughing mask, ornamented with huge ears and short horns. I was pleased with the disguise, because it kept me from the danger of being discovered, whilst we were in that part of the country; and, as I had merely to dance and make antics, the character was favourable to a debutant; being almost on a par with Simon Snug's part of the Lion, which required nothing but roaring.

I cannot tell you how happy I was at this sudden change in my situation. I felt no degradation, for I had seen too little of society to be thoughtful about the differences of rank; and a boy of sixteen is seldom aristocratical. I had given up no friend; for there seemed to be no one in the world that cared for me, now my poor mother was dead. I had given up no pleasure; for my pleasure was to ramble about and indulge the flow of a poetical imagination; and I now enjoyed it in perfection. There is no life so truly poetical as that of a dancing buffoon.

It may be said that all this argued grovelling inclinations. I do not think so. Not that I mean to vindicate myself in any great degree; I know too well what a whimsical compound I am. But in this instance I was seduced by no love of low company, nor disposition to indulge in low vices. I have always despised the brutally vulgar, and had a disgust at vice, whether in high or low life. I was governed merely by a sudden and thoughtless impulse. I had no idea of resorting to this profession as a mode of life; or of attaching myself to these people, as my future class of society. I thought merely of a temporary gratification of my curiosity, and an indulgence of my humours. I had already a strong relish for the peculiarities of character and the varieties of situation, and I have always been fond of the comedy of life and desirous of seeing it through all its shifting scenes.

In mingling, therefore, among mountebanks and buffoons I was protected by the very vivacity of imagination which had led me among them. I moved about envelloped, as it were, in a protecting delusion, which my fancy spread around me. I assimilated to these people only as they struck me poetically; their whimsical ways and a certain picturesqueness in their mode of life entertained me; but I was neither amused nor corrupted by their vices. In short, I mingled among them, as Prince Hal did among his graceless associates, merely to gratify my humour.

I did not investigate my motives in this manner, at the time, for I was too careless and thoughtless to reason about the matter; but I do so now, when I look back with trembling to think of the ordeal to which I unthinkingly exposed myself and the manner in which I passed through it. Nothing, I am convinced, but the poetical temperament, that hurried me into the scrape, brought me out of it without my becoming an arrant vagabond.

Full of the enjoyment of the moment, giddy with the wildness of animal spirits, so rapturous in a boy; I capered, I danced, I played a thousand fantastic tricks about the stage, in the villages in which we exhibited; and I was universally pronounced the most agreeable monster that had ever been seen in those parts. My disappearance from school had awakened my father's anxiety; for I one day heard a description of myself cried before the very booth in which I was exhibiting; with the offer of a reward for any intelligence of me. I had no great scruple about letting my father suffer a little uneasiness on my account; it would punish him for past indifference, and would make him value me the more when he found me again. I have wondered that some of my comrades did not recognize in me the stray sheep that was cried; but they were all, no doubt, occupied by their own concerns. They were all labouring seriously in their antic vocation; for folly was a mere trade with most of them, and they often grinned and capered with heavy hearts. With me, on the contrary, it was all real. I acted *con amore*, and rattled and laughed from the irrepressible gaiety of my spirits. It is true that, now and then, I started and looked grave on receiving a sudden thwack from the wooden sword of Harlequin, in the course of my gambols; as it brought to mind the birch of my schoolmaster. But I soon got accustomed to it; and bore all the cuffing, and kicking, and tumbling about, which form the practical wit of your itinerant pantomime, with a good humour that made me a prodigious favourite.

The country campaign of the troop was soon at an end, and we set off for the metropolis, to perform at the fairs which are held in its vicinity. The greater part of our theatrical property was sent on direct, to be in a state of preparation for the opening of the fairs; while a detachment of the company travelled slowly on, foraging among the villages. I was amused with the desultory, hap hazard kind of life we led; here today and gone tomorrow. Sometimes revelling in ale houses, sometimes feasting under hedges in the green fields. When audiences were crowded and business profitable we

fared well, and when otherwise, we fared scantily, and consoled ourselves with anticipations of the next day's success.

At length the increasing frequency of coaches hurrying past
us, covered with passengers; the increasing number of
carriages, carts, waggons, gigs, droves of cattle and flocks of
sheep, all thronging the road; the snug country boxes with
trim flower gardens twelve feet square, and their trees twelve
feet high, all powdered with dust; and the innumerable semi-
naries for young ladies and gentlemen, situated along the road
for the benefit of country air and rural retirement; all these
insignia announced that the mighty London was at hand. The
hurry, and the crowd and the bustle and the noise, and the
dust, increased as we proceeded, until I saw the great cloud of
smoke hanging in the air, like a canopy of state, over this
queen of cities.

In this way, then, did I enter the metropolis; a strolling
vagabond; on the top of a caravan with a crew of vagabonds
about me; but I was as happy as a prince, for, like Prince Hal,
I felt myself superior to my situation, and knew that I could
at any time cast it off and emerge into my proper sphere.

How my eyes sparkled as we passed Hyde Park Corner, and
I saw splendid equipages rolling by, with powdered footmen
behind, in rich liveries; and fine nosegays and gold headed
canes; and with lovely women within, so sumptuously dressed
and so surpassingly fair. I was always extremely sensible to
female beauty; and here I saw it in all its fascination, for,
whatever may be said of "beauty unadorned," there is something almost awful in female loveliness decked out in jewelled
state. The swanlike neck encircled with diamonds; the raven
locks, clustered with pearls; the ruby glowing on the snowy
bosom are objects which I could never contemplate without
emotion; and a dazzling white arm clasped with bracelets, and
taper transparent fingers laden with sparkling rings are to me
irresistible. My very eyes ached as I gazed at the high and
courtly beauty before me. It surpassed all that my imagination
had conceived of the sex. I shrank, for a moment, into shame
at the company in which I was placed, and repined at the vast
distance that seemed to intervene between me and these magnificent beings.

I forbear to give a detail of the happy life I led about the skirts of the metropolis, playing at the various fairs held there during the latter part of spring and the beginning of summer. This continual change from place to place, and scene to scene, fed my imagination with novelties, and kept my spirits in a perpetual state of excitement.

As I was tall of my age I aspired, at one time, to play heroes in tragedy; but after two or three trials, I was pronounced, by the manager, totally unfit for the line; and our first tragic actress, who was a large woman, and held a small hero in abhorrence, confirmed his decision.

The fact is I had attempted to give point to language which had no point, and nature to scenes which had no nature. They said I did not fill out my characters; and they were right. The characters had all been prepared for a different sort of man. Our Tragedy hero was a round robustious fellow, with an amazing voice; who stamped, and slapped his breast until his wig shook again; and who roared and bellowed out his bombast, until every phraze swelled upon the ear like the sound of a Kettle drum. I might as well have attempted to fill out his clothes as his characters. When we had a dialogue together I was nothing before him, with my slender voice and discriminating manner. I might as well have attempted to parry a cudgel with a small sword. If he found me in any way gaining ground upon him, he would take refuge in his mighty voice and throw his tones like peals of thunder at me, until they were drowned in the still louder thunders of applause from the audience.

To tell the truth, I suspect that I was not shewn fair play, and that there was management at the bottom; for without vanity, I think I was a better actor than he. As I had not embarked in the vagabond line through ambition I did not repine at lack of preferment; but I was grieved to find that a vagrant life was not without its cares and anxieties, and that jealousies, intrigues and mad ambition were to be found even among vagabonds.

Indeed, as I became more familiar with my situation, and the delusions of fancy gradually faded away, I began to find that my associates were not the happy careless creatures I had at first imagined them. They were jealous of each other's talents; they quarrelled about parts, the same as the actors on

the grand theatres; they quarrelled about dresses; and there
was one robe of yellow silk, trimmed with red, and a head-
dress of three rumpled ostrich feathers, which were continually setting the ladies of the Company by the ears. Even those
who had attained the highest honours, were not more happy
than the rest; for Mr. Flimsey himself, our first tragedian, and
apparently a jovial good humoured fellow, confessed to me
one day, in the fullness of his heart, that he was a miserable
man. He had a brother in law—a relative by marriage,
though not by blood; who was manager of a theatre in a
small country town. And this same Brother ("a little more
than kin but less than kind") looked down upon him, and
treated him with contumely, because forsooth he was but a
strolling player. I tried to console him with the thoughts of
the vast applause he daily received, but it was all in vain. He
declared that it gave him no delight, and that he should never
be a happy man until the name of Flimsey rivalled the name
of Crimp.

How little do those before the scenes know of what passes
behind; how little can they judge, from the countenances of
actors, of what is passing in their hearts. I have known two
lovers quarrel like cats behind the scenes, who were, the moment after, to fly into each other's embraces. And I have
dreaded, when our Belvidera was to take her farewell kiss of
her Jaffier, lest she should bite a piece out of his cheek. Our
tragedian was a rough joker off the stage; our prime clown
the most peevish mortal living. The latter used to go about
snapping and snarling, with a broad laugh painted on his
countenance; and I can assure you that, whatever may be said
of the gravity of a monkey; or the melancholy of a gibed cat;
there is no more melancholy creature in existence than a
mountebank off duty.

The only thing in which all parties agreed, was to back bite
the manager, and cabal against his regulations. This, however,
I have since discovered to be a common trait of human nature, and to take place in all communities. It would seem to
be the main business of man to repine at government. In all
situations of life into which I have looked, I have found mankind divided into two grand parties; those who ride, and
those who are ridden. The great struggle of life seems to be

which shall keep in the saddle. This it appears to me is the fundamental principle of politics, whether in great or little life.—However, I do not mean to moralize; but one cannot always sink the philosopher.

Well then, to return to myself. It was determined, as I said, that I was not fit for tragedy; and, unluckily, as my study was bad, having a very poor memory, I was pronounced unfit for comedy also; besides, the line of young gentlemen was already engrossed by an actor with whom I could not pretend to enter into competition, he having filled it for almost half a century. I came down again therefore to pantomime. In consequence, however, of the good offices of the manager's lady, who had taken a liking to me, I was promoted from the part of the satyr to that of the Lover; and with my face patched and painted; a huge cravat of paper; a steeple crowned hat, and dangling long skirted, sky blue coat, was metamorphosed into the lover of Columbine. My part did not call for much of the tender and sentimental. I had merely to pursue the fugitive fair one; to have a door now and then slammed in my face; to run my head occasionally against a post; to tumble and roll about with Pantaloon and the Clown; and to endure the hearty thwacks of Harlequin's wooden sword.

As ill luck would have it, my poetical temperament began to ferment within me, and to work out new troubles. The inflammatory air of a great metropolis; added to the rural scenes in which the fairs were held; such as Greenwich Park; Epping Forest; and the lovely valley of West End, had a powerful effect upon me. While in Greenwich Park I was witness to the old holyday games of running down hill; and kissing in the ring; and then the firmament of blooming faces and blue eyes that would be turned towards me, as I was playing antics on the stage; all these set my young blood, and my poetical vein, in full flow. In short, I played my character to the life and became desperately enamoured of Columbine. She was a trim, well made, tempting girl; with a roguish dimpling face, and fine chesnut hair clustering all about it. The moment I got fairly smitten, there was an end to all playing. I was such a creature of fancy and feeling, that I could not put on a pretended, when I was powerfully affected by a real emotion. I could not sport with a fiction that came so near to the fact. I became too natural in my acting to succeed. And then; what a situation for a lover! I was a mere stripling, and she played with my passion; for girls soon grow more adroit and knowing in these matters than your awkward youngsters. What agonies had I to suffer. Every time that she danced in front of the booth, and made such liberal displays of her charms, I was in torment. To complete my misery, I had a real rival in Harlequin; an active, vigorous, knowing varlet of six and twenty. What had a raw inexperienced youngster like me to hope from such a competition.

I had still, however, some advantages in my favour. In spite of my change of life, I retained that indescribable something which always distinguishes the gentleman; that something which dwells in a man's air and deportment, and not in his clothes; and which is as difficult for a gentleman to put off, as for a vulgar fellow to put on. The company generally felt it, and used to call me little gentleman Jack. The girl felt it too; and in spite of her predilection for my powerful rival; she liked to flirt with me. This only aggravated my troubles, by encreasing my passion, and awakening the jealousy of her particoloured Lover.

Alas! think what I suffered, at being obliged to keep up an ineffectual chase after my Columbine through whole pantomimes; to see her carried off in the vigorous arms of the happy Harlequin; and to be obliged instead of snatching her from him to tumble sprawling with Pantaloon and the clown; and bear the infernal and degrading thwacks of my rival's weapon of lath; which, may heaven confound him! (excuse my passion) the villain laid on with a malicious good will; nay I could absolutely hear him chuckle and laugh beneath his accursed mask.—I beg pardon for growing a little warm in my narration. I wish to be cool, but these recollections will sometimes agitate me. I have heard and read of many desperate and deplorable situations of lovers; but none I think in which true love was ever exposed to so severe and peculiar a trial.

This could not last long! Flesh and blood, at least such flesh and blood as mine, could not bear it. I had repeated heart-burnings and quarrels with my rival, in which he treated me with the mortifying forbearance of a man towards a child.

Had he quarrelled outright with me I could have stomached it; at least I should have known what part to take; but to be humoured and treated as a child in the presence of my mistress; when I felt all the bantam spirit of a little man swelling within me—gods, it was insufferable!

At length we were exhibiting one day at West End fair, which was at that time a very fashionable resort, and often beleaguered by gay equipages from town. Among the spectators that filled the front row of our little canvas theatre one afternoon, when I had to figure in a pantomime, was a party of young ladies from a boarding school, with their governess. Guess my confusion, when, in the midst of my antics, I beheld among the number my quondam flame; her whom I had berhymed at school; her for whose charms I had smarted so severely; the cruel Sacharissa! What was worse, I fancied she recollected me; and was repeating the story of my humiliating flagellation, for I saw her whispering her companions and her governess. I lost all consciousness of the part I was acting, and of the place where I was. I felt shrunk to nothing, and could have crept into a rat hole—unluckily, none was open to receive me. Before I could recover from my confusion I was tumbled over by Pantaloon and the clown; and I felt the sword of Harlequin making vigorous assaults in a manner most degrading to my dignity.

Heaven and earth! was I again to suffer martyrdom in this ignominious manner, in the knowledge, and even before the very eyes, of this most beautiful, but most disdainful of fair ones? All my long smothered wrath broke out at once; the dormant feelings of the gentleman arose within me; stung to the quick by intolerable mortification. I sprang on my feet in an instant; leaped upon Harlequin like a young tiger; tore off his mask; buffetted him in the face, and soon shed more blood on the stage, than had been spilt upon it during a whole tragic campaign of battles and murders.

As soon as Harlequin recovered from his surprize he returned my assault with interest. I was nothing in his hands. I was game to be sure, for I was a gentleman; but he had the clownish advantages of bone and muscle. I felt as if I could have fought even unto the death; and I was likely to do so; for he was, according to the boxing phraze, "putting my head into Chancery," when the gentle Columbine flew to my assistance. God bless the women! they are always on the side of the weak and the oppressed!

The battle now became general; the dramatis personæ ranged on either side. The manager interposed in vain. In vain were his spangled black bonnet and towering white feathers seen whisking about, and nodding, and bobbing, in the thickest of the fight. Warriors, Ladies, Priests, Satyrs, Kings, Queens, gods and goddesses all joined pell mell in the fray. Never, since the conflict under the walls of Troy, had there been such a chance medley warfare of combatants, human and divine. The audience applauded; the ladies shrieked and fled from the theatre, and a scene of discord ensued that baffles all description.

Nothing but the interference of the peace officers restored some degree of order. The havoc, however, among dresses and decorations put an end to all further acting for that day. The battle over, the next thing was to enquire why it was begun; a common question among politicians, after a bloody and unprofitable war; and one not always easy to be answered. It was soon traced to me, and my unaccountable transport of passion, which they could only attribute to my having *run a muck*. The manager was judge, and jury, and plaintiff into the bargain, and in such cases justice is always speedily administered. He came out of the fight as sublime a wreck as the Santissima Trinidada. His gallant plumes which once towered aloft, were drooping about his ears. His robe of state hung in ribbands from his back, and but ill concealed the ravages he had suffered in the rear. He had received kicks and cuffs from all sides, during the tumult; for every one took the opportunity of slyly gratifying some lurking grudge on his fat carcass. He was a discreet man and did not choose to declare war with all his company; so he swore all those kicks and cuffs had been given by me, and I let him enjoy the opinion. Some wounds he bore, however, which were the incontestable traces of a woman's warfare. His sleek rosy cheek was scored by trickling furrows which were ascribed to the nails of my intrepid and devoted Columbine. The ire of the monarch was not to be appeased. He had suffered in his person, and he had suffered in his purse; his dignity too had been insulted,

and that went for something; for dignity is always more iras-
cible, the more petty the potentate. He wreaked his wrath
upon the beginners of the affray, and Columbine and myself
were discharged, at once, from the Company.

Figure me, then, to yourself, a stripling of little more than
sixteen; a gentleman by birth; a vagabond by trade; turned
adrift upon the world; making the best of my way through
the crowd of West End fair; my mountebank dress fluttering
in rags about me; the weeping Columbine hanging upon my
arm, in splendid, but tattered finery; the tears coursing one by
one down her face; carrying off the red paint in torrents, and
literally "preying upon her damask cheek."

The crowd made way for us as we passed and hooted in
our rear. I felt the ridicule of my situation, but had too much
gallantry to desert this fair one, who had sacrificed every thing
for me. Having wandered through the fair, we emerged, like
another Adam and Eve, into unknown regions, and "had the
world before us, where to choose." Never was a more disconsolate pair seen in the soft valley of West End. The luckless
Columbine cast back many a lingering look at the fair, which
seemed to put on a more than usual splendour; its tents, and
booths, and party coloured groups, all brightening in the sunshine, and gleaming among the trees; and its gay flags and
streamers playing and fluttering in the light summer airs.
With a heavy sigh she would lean on my arm and proceed. I
had no hope nor consolation to give her; but she had linked
herself to my fortunes; and she was too much of a woman to
desert me.

Pensive and silent, then, we traversed the beautiful fields
which lie behind Hampstead, and wandered on, until the fiddle, and the hautboy, and the shout, and the laugh, were
swallowed up in the deep sound of the big bass drum, and
even that died away into a distant rumble. We passed along
the pleasant sequestered walk of Nightingale Lane. For a pair
of lovers what scene could be more propitious?—But such a
pair of lovers! Not a nightingale sang to soothe us; the very
gipsies who were encamped there during the fair made no
offer to tell the fortunes of such an ill omened couple, whose
fortunes, I suppose, they thought too legibly written to need
an interpreter; and the gipsey children crawled into their

cabins and peeped out fearfully at us as we went by. For a moment I paused, and was almost tempted to turn gipsey, but the poetical feeling for the present was fully satisfied, and I passed on. Thus we travelled, and travelled, like a prince and princess in Nursery Tale, until we had traversed a part of Hampstead Heath and arrived in the vicinity of Jack Straw's Castle.

Here, wearied and dispirited we seated ourselves on the margin of the hill, hard by the very mile stone where Whittington of yore heard the Bow bells ring out the presage of his future greatness. Alas! no Bell rung an invitation to us, as we looked disconsolately upon the distant city. Old London seemed to wrap itself unsociably in its mantle of brown smoke; and to offer no encouragement to such a couple of tatterdemalions.

For once at least the usual course of the pantomime was reversed. Harlequin was jilted and the lover had carried off Columbine in good earnest. But what was I to do with her? I could not take her in my hand, return to my father, throw myself on my knees, and crave his forgiveness and his blessing according to dramatic usage. The very dogs would have chased such a draggletailed beauty from the grounds.

In the midst of my doleful dumps, some one tapped me on the shoulder, and looking up I saw a couple of rough sturdy fellows standing behind me. Not knowing what to expect I jumped on my legs and was preparing again to make battle; but I was tripped up and secured in a twinkling.

"Come, come, young master," said one of the fellows in a gruff, but good humoured tone, "don't let's have any of your tantrums. One would have thought you had had swing enough for this bout. Come, it's high time to leave off harlequinading, and go home to your father."

In fact I had fallen into the hands of remorseless men. The cruel Sacharissa had proclaimed who I was, and that a reward had been offered throughout the country for any tidings of me; and they had seen a description of me which had been inserted in the public papers. Those harpies, therefore, for the mere sake of filthy lucre, were resolved to deliver me over into the hands of my father and the clutches of my Pedagogue.

In vain I swore I would not leave my faithful and afflicted

Columbine. In vain I tore myself from their grasp, and flew to
her; and vowed to protect her; and wiped the tears from her
cheek, and with them a whole blush that might have vied
with the Carnation for brilliancy. My persecutors were inflexible: they even seemed to exult in our distress; and to enjoy
this theatrical display of dirt, and finery, and tribulation. I was
carried off in despair, leaving my Columbine destitute in the
wide world; but many a look of agony did I cast back at her,
as she stood gazing piteously after me from the brink of
Hampstead Hill; so forlorn, so fine, so ragged, so bedraggled,
yet so beautiful.

   Thus ended my first peep into the world. I returned home,
rich in good-for-nothing experience, and dreading the reward
I was to receive for my improvement. My reception, however,
was quite different from what I had expected. My father had a
spice of the devil in him, and did not seem to like me the
worse for my freak, which he termed "sewing my wild oats."
He happened to have several of his sporting friends to dine
the very day of my return; they made me tell some of my
adventures; and laughed heartily at them. One old fellow with
an outrageously red nose took to me hugely. I heard him
whisper to my father that I was a lad of mettle and might
make something clever, to which my father replied that "I had
good points, but was an ill broken whelp and required a great
deal of the whip." Perhaps this very conversation raised me a
little in his esteem, for I found the red nosed old gentleman
was a veteran fox hunter of the neighbourhood, for whose
opinion my father had vast deference. Indeed I believe he
would have pardoned any thing in me more readily than poetry; which he called a cursed sneaking, puling, housekeeping
employment, the bane of all true manhood. He swore it was
unworthy of a youngster of my expectations, who was one
day to have so great an estate, and would be able to keep
horses and hounds and hire poets to write songs for him into
the bargain.

   I had now satisfied, for a time, my roving propensity. I had
exhausted the poetical feeling. I had been heartily buffetted
out of my love for theatrical display. I felt humiliated by my
exposure and willing to hide my head any where for a season;
so that I might be out of the way of the ridicule of the world;

for I found folks not altogether so indulgent abroad, as they were at my father's table. I could not stay at home; the house was intolerably doleful now that my mother was no longer there to cherish me. Every thing around spoke mournfully of her. The little flower garden in which she delighted, was all in disorder and overrun with weeds. I attempted, for a day or two, to arrange it, but my heart grew heavier and heavier as I laboured. Every little broken down flower, that I had seen her rear so tenderly, seemed to plead in mute eloquence to my feelings. There was a favourite honeysuckle which I had seen her often training with assiduity and had heard her say it should be the pride of her garden. I found it grovelling along the ground, tangled and wild, and twining round every worthless weed, and it struck me as an emblem of myself, a mere scatterling, running to waste and uselessness. I could work no longer in the garden.

My father sent me to pay a visit to my uncle, by way of keeping the old gentleman in mind of me. I was received, as usual, without any expression of discontent; which we always considered equivalent to a hearty welcome. Whether he had ever heard of my strolling freak or not I could not discover; he and his man were both so taciturn. I spent a day or two roaming about the dreary mansion and neglected park; and felt at one time, I believe, a touch of poetry, for I was tempted to drown myself in a fish pond; I rebuked the evil spirit, however, and it left me. I found the same redheaded boy running wild about the park, but I felt in no humour to hunt him at present. On the contrary I tried to coax him to me, and to make friends with him, but the young savage was untameable.

When I returned from my uncle's I remained at home for some time, for my father was disposed, he said, to make a man of me. He took me out hunting with him, and I became a great favourite of the red nosed squire, because I rode at every thing, never refused the boldest leap, and was always sure to be in at the death. I used often however to offend my father at hunting dinners, by taking the wrong side in politics. My father was amazingly ignorant, so ignorant in fact as not to know, that he knew nothing. He was staunch, however, to church and King, and full of old fashioned prejudices. Now I had picked up a little knowledge in politics and religion, during my rambles with the strollers, and found myself capable of setting him right as to many of his antiquated notions. I felt it my duty to do so; we were apt therefore to differ occasionally in the political discussions which sometimes arose at these hunting dinners.

I was at that age when a man knows least and is most vain of his knowledge; and when he is extremely tenacious in defending his opinion upon subjects about which he knows nothing. My father was a hard man for any one to argue with, for he never knew when he was refuted. I sometimes posed him a little, but then he had one argument that always settled the question; he would threaten to knock me down. I believe he at last grew tired of me, because I both outtalked and outrode him. The red nosed squire too got out of conceit of me, because in the heat of the chace, I rode over him one day as he and his horse lay sprawling in the dirt. My father, therefore, thought it high time to send me to college — and accordingly to Trinity College at Oxford was I sent.

I had lost my habits of study while at home; and I was not likely to find them again at college. I found that study was not the fashion at college, and that a lad of spirit only ate his terms; and grew wise by dint of knife and fork. I was always prone to follow the fashions of the company into which I fell; so I threw by my books, and became a man of spirit. As my father made me a tolerable allowance, notwithstanding the narrowness of his income, having an eye always to my great expectations, I was enabled to appear to advantage among my fellow students. I cultivated all kinds of sports and exercises. I was one of the most expert oarsmen that rowed on the Isis. I boxed, fenced, angled, shot, and hunted, and my rooms in college were always decorated with whips of all kinds, spurs, fowling pieces, fishing rods, foils and boxing gloves. A pair of leather breeches would seem to be throwing one leg out of the half open drawers, and empty bottles lumbered the bottom of every closet.

I soon grew tired of this; and relapsed into my vein of mere poetical indulgence. I was charmed with Oxford for it was full of poetry to me. I thought I should never grow tired of wandering about its courts and cloisters; and visiting the different college halls. I used to love to get in places surrounded by the colleges, where all modern buildings were screened from the sight; and to walk about them in twilight, and see the professors and students sweeping along in the dusk in their caps and gowns. There was complete delusion in the scene. It seemed to transport me among the edifices and the people of old times. It was a great luxury, too, for me to attend the evening service, in the New College Chapel; and to hear the fine organ and the choir swelling an anthem in that solemn building; where painting and music and architecture seem to combine their grandest effects.

I became a loiterer, also, about the Bodleian library, and a great dipper into books; but too idle to follow any course of study or vein of research. One of my favourite haunts was the beautiful walk, bordered by lofty elms, along the Isis, under the old grey walls of Magdalen College, which goes by the name of Addison's Walk; and was his resort when a student at the college. I used to take a volume of poetry in my hand and stroll up and down this walk for hours.

My father came to see me at college. He asked me how I came on with my studies; and what kind of hunting there was in the neighbourhood. He examined my sporting apparatus; wanted to know if any of the professors were fox hunters; and whether they were generally good shots; for he suspected this reading so much was rather hurtful to the sight. Such was the only person to whom I was responsible for my improvement: is it matter of wonder therefore that I became a confirmed idler?

I do not know how it is, but I cannot be idle long without getting in love. I became deeply enamoured of a shopkeeper's daughter in the High Street; who in fact was the admiration of many of the students. I wrote several sonnets in praise of her, and spent half of my pocket money at the shop, in buying articles which I did not want, that I might have an opportunity of speaking to her. Her father, a severe looking old gentleman, with bright silver buckles and a crisp curled wig, kept a strict guard on her; as the fathers generally do upon their daughters in Oxford; and well they may. I tried to get into his good graces, and to be sociable with him, but all in vain. I said several good things in his shop, but he never laughed; he had no relish for wit and humour. He was one of those dry old gentlemen who keep youngsters at bay. He had already brought up two or three daughters, and was experienced in the ways of students. He was as knowing and wary as a grey old badger that has often been hunted. To see him on Sunday, so stiff and starched in his demeanour; so precise in his dress; with his daughter under his arm, was enough to deter all graceless youngsters from approaching.

I managed, however, in spite of his vigilance, to have several conversations with the daughter, as I cheapened articles in the shop. I made terrible long bargains, and examined the articles over and over, before I purchased. In the mean time, I would convey a sonnet or an acrostic under cover of a piece of cambric, or slipped into a pair of stockings; I would whisper soft nonsense into her ear as I haggled about the price; and would squeeze her hand tenderly as I received my halfpence of change, in a bit of whity-brown paper. Let this serve as a hint to all haberdashers, who have pretty daughters for shop girls, and young students for customers. I do not know whether my words and looks were very eloquent; but my poetry was irresistible; for, to tell the truth, the girl had some literary taste, and was seldom without a book from the circulating library.

By the divine power of poetry, therefore, which is so potent with the lovely sex, did I subdue the heart of this fair little Haberdasher. We carried on a sentimental correspondence for a time across the counter, and I supplied her with rhyme by the stocking full. At length I prevailed on her to grant an assignation. But how was this to be effected? Her father kept her always under his eye; she never walked out alone; and the house was locked up the moment that the shop was shut. All these difficulties served but to give zest to the adventure. I proposed that the assignation should be in her own chamber, into which I would climb at night. The plan was irresistible. A cruel father, a secret lover, and a clandestine meeting! All the little girl's studies from the circulating library seemed about to be realized.

But what had I in view in making this assignation? Indeed I know not. I had no evil intentions; nor can I say that I had any good ones. I liked the girl, and wanted to have an opportunity of seeing more of her; and the assignation was made, as I have done many things else, heedlessly and without fore thought. I asked myself a few questions of the kind, after all my arrangements were made; but the answers were very unsatisfactory. "Am I to ruin this poor thoughtless girl?" said I to myself. "No!" was the prompt and indignant answer. "Am I to run away with her?"—"Whither—and to what purpose?"—"Well then, am I to marry her?"—"Pah! a man of my expectations marry a shopkeeper's daughter!"—"What then am I to do with her?"—"Hum—Why—Let me get into her chamber first, and then consider,"—and so the self examination ended.

Well sir, "come what come might," I stole under cover of the darkness to the dwelling of my dulcinea. All was quiet. At the concerted signal her window was gently opened. It was just above the projecting bow window of her father's shop, which assisted me in mounting. The house was low, and I was enabled to scale the fortress with tolerable ease. I clambered with a beating heart; I reached the casement; I hoisted my body half into the chamber and was welcomed, not by the embraces of my expecting fair one, but by the grasp of the crabbed looking old father in the crisp curled wig.

I extricated myself from his clutches and endeavoured to make my retreat; but I was confounded by his cries of thieves! and robbers! I was bothered too by his Sunday cane; which was amazingly busy about my head as I descended; and against which my hat was but a poor protection. Never before had I an idea of the activity of an old man's arm, and hardness of the knob of an Ivory headed cane. In my hurry and confusion I missed my footing, and fell sprawling on the pavement. I was immediately surrounded by myrmidons, who I doubt not were on the watch for me. Indeed I was in no situation to escape, for I had sprained my ancle in the fall, and could not stand. I was seized as a housebreaker; and to exonerate myself from a greater crime I had to accuse myself of a less—I made known who I was, and why I came there. Alas! the varlets knew it already, and were only amusing themselves at my expense. My perfidious muse had been playing me one of her slippery tricks. The old curmudgeon of a father had found my sonnets and acrostics hid away in holes and corners of his shop; he had no taste for poetry like his daughter, and had instituted a rigorous though silent observation. He had moused upon our letters; detected our plans, and prepared every thing for my reception. Thus was I ever doomed to be led into scrapes by the muse. Let no man henceforth carry on a secret amour in poetry!

The old man's ire was in some measure appeased by the pummelling of my head, and the anguish of my sprain; so he did not put me to death on the spot. He was even humane enough to furnish a shutter, on which I was carried back to college like a wounded warrior. The porter was roused to admit me; the college gate was thrown open for my entry; the affair was blazed abroad the next morning, and became the joke of the college from the Buttry to the Hall.

I had leisure to repent during several weeks' confinement by my sprain, which I passed in translating Boethius' Consolations of Philosophy. I received a most tender and ill spelled letter from my mistress, who had been sent to a relation in Coventry. She protested her innocence of my misfortunes and vowed to be true to me "till deth." I took no notice of the letter, for I was cured, for the present, both of love and poetry. Women, however, are more constant in their attachments than men, whatever philosophers may say to the contrary. I am assured that she actually remained faithful to her vow for several months; but she had to deal with a cruel father whose heart was as hard as the knob of his cane. He was not to be touched by tears or poetry; but absolutely compelled her to marry a reputable young tradesman; who made her a happy woman in spite of herself, and of all the rules of romance; and what is more, the mother of several children. They are at this very day a thriving couple, and keep a snug corner shop, just opposite the figure of Peeping Tom at Coventry.

I will not fatigue you by any more details of my studies at Oxford, though they were not always as severe as these; nor did I always pay as dear for my lessons. People may say what they please, a studious life has its charms and there are many places more gloomy than the cloisters of a university.

To be brief then, I lived on in my usual miscellaneous manner, gradually getting a knowledge of good and evil until I had attained my twenty first year. I had scarcely come of age when I heard of the sudden death of my father. The shock was severe, for though he had never treated me with much kindness, still he was my father, and at his death I felt alone in the world.

I returned home, and found myself the solitary master of the paternal mansion. A crowd of gloomy feelings came thronging upon me. It was a place that always sobered me, and brought me to reflection. Now especially, it looked so deserted and melancholy. I entered the little breakfasting room. There were my father's whip and spurs hanging by the fire place; the Stud Book, Sporting Magazine, and Racing Calendar, his only reading. His favourite spaniel lay on the hearth rug. The poor animal, who had never before noticed me, now came fondling about me, licked my hand, then looked round the room, whined, wagged his tail slightly, and gazed wistfully in my face. I felt the full force of the appeal. "Poor Dash!" said I, "we are both alone in the world, with no body to care for us, and we'll take care of one another."— The dog never quitted me afterwards.

I could not go into my mother's room: my heart swelled when I passed within sight of the door. Her portrait hung in the parlour just over the place where she used to sit. As I cast my eyes on it I thought it looked at me with tenderness, and I burst into tears. My heart had long been seared by living in public schools, and buffetting about among strangers who cared nothing for me; but the recollection of a mother's tenderness was overcoming.

I was not of an age or a temperament to be long depressed. There was a reaction in my system that always brought me up again after every pressure; and indeed my spirits were most buoyant after a temporary prostration. I settled the concerns of the estate as soon as possible; realized my property, which was not very considerable; but which appeared a vast deal to me, having a poetical eye that magnified every thing; and finding myself at the end of a few months, free of all further business or restraint, I determined to go to London and enjoy myself. Why should not I?—I was young, animated, joyous; had plenty of funds for present pleasures, and my uncle's estate in the perspective. Let those mope at college and pore

over books, thought I, who have their way to make in the
world; it would be ridiculous drudgery in a youth of my expectations.

Away to London, therefore, I rattled in a tandem, determined to take the town gaily. I passed through several of the
villages where I had played the jack pudding a few years before; and I visited the scenes of many of my adventures and
follies, merely from that feeling of melancholy pleasure which
we have in stepping again in the footprints of foregone existence, even when they have passed among weeds and briars. I
made a circuit in the latter part of my journey, so as to take in
West End and Hampstead, the scenes of my last dramatic exploit, and of the battle royal of the Booth. As I drove along
the ridge of Hampstead Hill, by Jack Straw's Castle, I paused
at the spot where Columbine and I had sat down so disconsolately in our ragged finery, and had looked dubiously upon
London. I almost expected to see her again, standing on the
hill's brink, "like Niobe all tears;"—mournful as Babylon in
ruins!

"Poor Columbine!" said I, with a heavy sigh, "thou wert a
gallant, generous girl—a true woman; faithful to the distressed, and ready to sacrifice thyself in the cause of worthless
man!"

I tried to whistle off the recollection of her, for there was
always something of self reproach with it. I drove gaily along
the road, enjoying the stare of Hostlers and stable boys as I
managed my horses knowingly down the steep street of
Hampstead; when, just at the skirts of the village, one of the
traces of my leader came loose. I pulled up, and, as the animal
was restive, and my servant a bungler, I called for assistance
to the robustious master of a snug ale house, who stood at his
door with a tankard in his hand. He came readily to assist me,
followed by his wife with her bosom half open, a child in her
arms, and two more at her heels. I stared for a moment as if
doubting my eyes. I could not be mistaken: in the fat beer-
blown landlord of the ale house I recollected my old rival
Harlequin, and in his slattern spouse, the once trim and dimpling Columbine.

The change of my looks, from youth to manhood, and the
change of my circumstances, prevented them from recog-

nizing me. They could not suspect, in the dashing young buck, fashionably dressed, and driving his own equipage, the painted beau, with old peaked hat and long, flimsy, sky blue coat. My heart yearned with kindness towards Columbine, and I was glad to see her establishment a thriving one. As soon as the harness was adjusted I tossed a small purse of gold into her ample bosom; and then, pretending to give my horses a hearty cut of the whip, I made the lash curl with a whistling about the sleek sides of ancient Harlequin. The horses dashed off like lightning, and I was whirled out of sight, before either of the parties could get over their surprize at my liberal donations. I have always considered this as one of the greatest proofs of my poetical genius. It was distributing poetical justice in perfection.

I now entered London *en cavalier*, and became a blood upon town. I took fashionable lodgings in the west end; employed the first Taylor; frequented the regular lounges; gambled a little; lost my money good humouredly, and gained a number of fashionable, good for nothing acquaintances. I gained some reputation, also, for a man of science, having become an expert boxer in the course of my studies at Oxford. I was distinguished, therefore, among the gentlemen of the fancy; became hand and glove with certain boxing noblemen, and was the admiration of the Fives Court. A gentleman's science, however, is apt to get him into sad scrapes: he is too prone to play the knight errant, and to pick up quarrels which less scientific gentlemen would quietly avoid. I undertook one day to punish the insolence of a porter; he was a Hercules of a fellow, but then I was so secure in my science! I gained the victory of course. The porter pocketed his humiliation, bound up his broken head, and went about his business as unconcernedly as though nothing had happened; while I went to bed with my victory, and did not dare to show my battered face for a fortnight, by which I discovered that a gentleman may have the worst of the battle even when victorious.

I am naturally a philosopher, and no one can moralize better after a misfortune has taken place: so I lay on my bed and moralized on this sorry ambition, which levels the gentleman with the clown. I know it is the opinion of many sages, who have thought deeply on these matters, that the noble science of boxing keeps up the bull dog courage of the nation; and far be it from me to decry the advantage of becoming a nation of bull dogs; but I now saw clearly that it was calculated to keep up the breed of English ruffians. "What is the Fives Court," said I to myself, as I turned uncomfortably in bed, "but a college of scoundrelism, where every bully ruffian in the land may gain a fellowship? What is the slang language of 'The Fancy' but a jargon by which fools and knaves commune and understand each other, and enjoy a kind of superiority over the uninitiated? What is a boxing match but an arena, where the noble and the illustrious are jostled into familiarity with the infamous and the vulgar? What, in fact, is The Fancy itself, but a chain of easy communication, extending from the peer down to the pickpocket, through the medium of which, a man of rank may find, he has shaken hands, at three removes, with the murderer on the gibbet? —

"Enough!" ejaculated I, thoroughly convinced through the force of my philosophy, and the pain of my bruises — "I'll have nothing more to do with The Fancy." So when I had recovered from my victory, I turned my attention to softer themes, and became a devoted admirer of the ladies. Had I had more industry and ambition in my nature, I might have worked my way to the very height of fashion; as I saw many laborious gentlemen doing around me. But it is a toilsome, an anxious, and an unhappy life; there are few beings so sleepless and miserable as your cultivators of fashionable smiles.

I was quite content with that kind of society which forms the frontiers of fashion, and may be easily taken possession of. I found it a light, easy, productive soil. I had but to go about and sow visiting cards, and I reaped a whole harvest of invitations. Indeed my figure and address were by no means against me. It was whispered, too, among the young ladies, that I was prodigiously clever, and wrote poetry; and the old ladies had ascertained that I was a young gentleman of good family, handsome fortune, and "great expectations."

I now was carried away by the hurry of gay life; so intoxicating to a young man; and which a man of poetical temperament enjoys so highly on his first tasting of it. That rapid variety of sensations; that whirl of brilliant objects; that succession of pungent pleasures! I had no time for thought, I only felt. I never attempted to write poetry; my poetry seemed all to go off by transpiration. I lived poetry; it was all a poetical dream to me. A mere sensualist knows nothing of the delights of a splendid metropolis. He lives in a round of animal gratifications and heartless habits. But to a young man of poetical feelings it is an ideal world; a scene of enchantment and delusion; his imagination is in perpetual excitement, and gives a spiritual zest to every pleasure.

A season of town life, however, somewhat sobered me of my intoxication; or rather I was rendered more serious by one of my old complaints—I fell in love. It was with a very pretty, though a very haughty fair one; who had come to London under the care of an old maiden aunt, to enjoy the pleasures of a winter in town, and to get married. There was not a doubt of her commanding a choice of lovers; for she had long been the belle of a little cathedral town; and one of the prebendaries had absolutely celebrated her beauty in a copy of Latin verses. The most extravagant anticipations were formed by her friends of the sensation she would produce. It was feared by some that she might be precipitate in her choice, and take up with some inferior title. The aunt was determined nothing should gain her under a lord.

Alas! with all her charms, the young lady lacked the one thing needful—she had no money. So she waited in vain for duke, marquis, or earl, to throw himself at her feet. As the season waned, so did the lady's expectations; when, just towards the close, I made my advances.

I was most favourably received by both the young lady and her aunt. It is true, I had no title; but then such great expectations! A marked preference was immediately shewn me, over two rivals, the younger son of a needy Baronet, and a captain of Dragoons on half pay. I did not absolutely take the field in form, for I was determined not to be precipitate; but I drove my equipage frequently through the street in which she lived, and was always sure to see her at the window, generally with a book in her hand. I resumed my knack at rhyming, and sent her a long copy of verses; anonymously to be sure; but she knew my hand writing. Both aunt and niece, however, displayed the most delightful ignorance on the subject. The young lady shewed them to me; wondered who they could be written by; and declared there was nothing in this world she loved so much as poetry: while the maiden aunt would put her pinching spectacles on her nose, and read them, with blunders in sense and sound, excruciating to an author's ears; protesting there was nothing equal to them in the whole Elegant Extracts.

The fashionable season closed without my adventuring to make a declaration, though I certainly had encouragement. I was not perfectly sure that I had effected a lodgement in the young lady's heart; and, to tell the truth the aunt overdid her part, and was a little too extravagant in her liking of me. I knew that maiden aunts were not apt to be captivated by the mere personal merits of their nieces' admirers, and I wanted to ascertain how much of all this favour I owed to driving an equipage and having great expectations.

I had received many hints how charming their native town was during the summer months; what pleasant society they had; and what beautiful drives about the neighbourhood. They had not, therefore, returned home long before I made my appearance in dashing style, driving down the principal street. It is an easy thing to put a little quiet cathedral town in a buzz. The very next morning, I was seen at prayers, seated in the pew of the reigning belle. All the congregation was in a flutter. The prebends eyed me from their stalls; questions were whispered about the aisles after service, "who is he?" and "what is he?" and the replies were as usual—"a young gentleman of good family and fortune, and great expectations."

I was pleased with the peculiarities of a cathedral town, where I found I was a personage of some consequence. I was quite a brilliant acquisition to the young ladies of the cathedral circle, who were glad to have a beau that was not in a black coat and clerical wig. You must know that there was a vast distinction between the classes of society of the town. As it was a place of some trade, there were many wealthy inhabitants among the commercial and manufacturing classes, who lived in style and gave many entertainments. Nothing of trade, however, was admitted into the cathedral circle— faugh! the thing could not be thought of. The cathedral circle, therefore, was apt to be very select, very dignified, and very dull. They had evening parties, at which the old ladies played cards with the Prebends and the young ladies sat and looked on, and shifted from one chair to another about the room, until it was time to go home.

It was difficult to get up a ball from the want of partners, the cathedral circle being very deficient in dancers; and on those occasions, there was an occasional drafting among the dancing men of the other circle, who, however, were generally regarded with great reserve and condescension by the gentlemen in powdered wigs. Several of the young ladies, assured me, in confidence, that they had often looked with a wistful eye at the gaiety of the other circle, where there was such plenty of young beaux, and where they all seemed to enjoy themselves so merrily; but that it would be degradation to think of descending from their sphere.

I admired the degree of old fashioned ceremony, and superannuated courtesy that prevailed in this little place. The bowings and curtseyings that would take place about the cathedral porch after morning service; where knots of old gentlemen and ladies would collect together to ask after each other's health, and settle the card party for the evening. The little presents of fruit and delicacies, and the thousand petty messages that would pass from house to house; for in a tranquil community like this, living entirely at ease and having little to do, little duties and little civilities and little amusements, fill up the day. I have smiled, as I looked from my window on a quiet street near the cathedral, in the middle of a warm summer day, to see a corpulent powdered footman in rich livery, carrying a small tart on a large silver salver. A dainty tit bit, sent, no doubt, by some worthy old dowager, to top off the dinner of her favourite Prebend.

Nothing could be more delectable, also, than the breaking up of one of their evening card parties. Such shakings of hands; such mobbing up in cloaks and tippets! There were two or three old sedan chairs that did the duty of the whole place; though the greater part made their exit in clogs or pattens, with a footman or waiting maid carrying a lanthorn in advance; and at a certain hour of the night the clank of pattens and the gleam of these jack lanthorns, here and there, about the quiet little town, gave notice, that the cathedral card party had dissolved, and the luminaries were severally seeking their homes.

To such a community therefore, or at least to the female part of it, the accession of a gay dashing young beau was a matter of some importance. The old ladies eyed me with complacency through their spectacles, and the young ladies pronounced me divine. Every body received me favourably, excepting the gentleman who had written the Latin verses on the Belle.—Not that he was jealous of my success with the Lady, for he had no pretensions to her; but he heard my verses praised wherever he went, and he could not endure a rival with the muse.

I was thus carrying every thing before me, I was the Adonis of the cathedral circle; when one evening there was a public ball which was attended likewise by the gentry of the neighbourhood. I took great pains with my toilet on the occasion and I had never looked better. I had determined that night to make my grand assault on the heart of the young lady, to batter it with all my forces, and the next morning to demand a surrender in due form.

I entered the ball room amidst a buzz and flutter, which generally took place among the young ladies on my appearance. I was in fine spirits, for to tell the truth I had exhilarated myself by a cheerful glass of wine on the occasion. I talked, and rattled, and said a thousand silly things, slap dash, with all the confidence of a man sure of his auditors; and every thing had its effect.

In the midst of my triumph I observed a little knot gathering together in the upper part of the room. By degrees it encreased. A tittering broke out there; and glances were cast round at me, and then there would be fresh tittering. Some of the young ladies would hurry away to distant parts of the room, and whisper to their friends; wherever they went there was still this tittering and glancing at me. I did not know what to make of all this: I looked at myself from head to foot; and peeped at my back in a glass, to see if any thing was odd about my person; any awkward exposure; any whimsical tag hanging out—no—every thing was right. I was a perfect picture. I determined that it must be some choice saying of mine, that was bandied about in this knot of merry beauties, and I determined to enjoy one of my good things in the rebound.

I stepped gently, therefore, up the room, smiling at every one as I passed, who I must say all smiled and tittered in return. I approached the group, smirking and perking my chin, like a man who is full of pleasant feeling, and sure of being well received. The cluster of little belles opened as I advanced.

Heavens and earth! whom should I perceive in the midst of them, but my early and tormenting flame, the everlasting Sacharissa! She was grown, it is true, into the full beauty of Womanhood, but shewed by the provoking merriment of her countenance, that she perfectly recollected me, and the ridiculous flagellations of which she had twice been the cause.

I saw at once the exterminating cloud of ridicule bursting over me. My crest fell. The flame of love went suddenly out, or was extinguished by overwhelming shame. How I got down the room I know not; I fancied every one tittering at me. Just as I reached the door I caught a glance of my mistress and her aunt listening to the whispers of my poetic rival; the old lady raising her hands and eyes, and the face of the young one lighted up with scorn ineffable. I paused to see no more; but made two steps from the top of the stairs to the bottom. The next morning, before sunrise, I beat a retreat; and did not feel the blushes cool from my tingling cheeks, until I had lost sight of the old towers of the Cathedral.

I now returned to town thoughtful and crestfallen. My money was nearly spent, for I had lived freely and without calculation. The dream of love was over, and the reign of pleasure at an end. I determined to retrench while I had yet a trifle left; so, selling my equipage and horses for half their value, I quietly put the money in my pocket, and turned pedestrian. I had not a doubt that, with my great expectations, I could at any time raise funds, either on usury or by borrowing; but I was principled against both, and resolved, by strict economy, to make my slender purse hold out, until my uncle should give up the ghost; or rather, the estate.

I staid at home, therefore, and read, and would have written; but I had already suffered too much from my poetical productions, which had generally involved me in some ridiculous scrape. I gradually acquired a rusty look, and had a straightened, money borrowing air, upon which the world began to shy me. I have never felt disposed to quarrel with the world for its conduct. It has always used me well. When I have been flush, and gay, and disposed for society, it has caressed me, and when I have been pinched, and reduced, and wished to be alone, why, it has left me alone; and what more could a man desire?—Take my word for it, this world is a more obliging world than people generally represent it.

Well sir—In the midst of my retrenchment, my retirement, and my studiousness, I received news that my uncle was dangerously ill. I hastened on the wings of an heir's affections to receive his dying breath and his last testament. I found him attended by his faithful valet old Iron John; by the woman who occasionally worked about the house; and by the foxy headed boy young Orson, whom I had occasionally hunted about the park. Iron John gasped a kind of asthmatical salutation as I entered the room, and received me with something almost like a smile of welcome. The woman sat blubbering at the foot of the bed; and the foxy headed Orson, who had now grown up to be a lubberly lout, stood gazing in stupid vacancy at a distance.

My uncle lay stretched upon his back. The chamber was without fire, or any of the comforts of a sick room. The cobwebs flaunted from the ceiling. The tester was covered with dust and the curtains were tattered. From underneath the bed peeped out one end of his strong box. Against the wainscot were suspended rusty blunderbusses; horse pistols and a cut and thrust sword, with which he had fortified his room to defend his life and treasure. He had employed no physician during his illness, and from the scanty relics lying on the table, seemed almost to have denied himself the assistance of a cook.

When I entered the room he was lying motionless; his eyes fixed and his mouth open; at the first look I thought him a corpse. The noise of my entrance made him turn his head. At the sight of me a ghastly smile came over his face, and his glazing eye gleamed with satisfaction. It was the only smile he had ever given me, and it went to my heart. "Poor old man!"

thought I, "why would you force me to leave you thus desolate; when I see that my presence has the power to cheer you?"

"Nephew," said he, after several efforts and in a low gasping voice—"I am glad you are come. I shall now die with satisfaction. Look—" said he, raising his withered hand and pointing—"look—in that box on the table you will find that I have not forgotten you."

I pressed his hand to my heart, and the tears stood in my eyes. I sat down by his bed side, and watched him, but he never spoke again. My presence, however, gave him evident satisfaction—for every now and then as he looked at me a vague smile would come over his visage, and he would feebly point to the sealed box on the table. As the day wore away his life appeared to wear away with it. Towards sun set, his hand sank on the bed and lay motionless; his eyes grew glazed; his mouth remained open and thus he gradually died.

I could not but feel shocked at this absolute extinction of my kindred. I dropped a tear of real sorrow over this strange old man, who had thus reserved his smile of kindness, to his death bed; like an evening sun after a gloomy day, just shining out to set in darkness. Leaving the corpse in charge of the domestics I retired for the night.

It was a rough night. The winds seemed as if singing my uncle's requiem about the mansion; and the bloodhounds howled without as if they knew of the death of their old master. Iron John almost grudged me the tallow candle to burn in my apartment and light up its dreariness; so accustomed had he been to starveling economy. I could not sleep. The recollection of my uncle's dying scene and the dreary sounds about the house, affected my mind. These however were succeeded by plans for the future, and I lay awake the greater part of the night indulging the poetical anticipation, how soon I should make these old walls ring with cheerful life, and restore the hospitality of my mother's ancestors.

My uncle's funeral was decent but private. I knew that no body respected his memory; and I was determined none should be summoned to sneer over his funeral, and make merry at his grave. He was buried in the church of the neighbouring village, though it was not the burying place of his race; but he had expressly injoined that he should not be buried with his family; he had quarrelled with most of them when living, and he carried his resentments even into the grave.

I defrayed the expenses of the funeral out of my own purse, that I might have done with the undertakers at once, and clear the ill omened birds from the premises. I invited the parson of the parish, and the lawyer from the village to attend at the house the next morning and hear the reading of the will. I treated them to an excellent breakfast, a profusion that had not been seen at the house for many a year. As soon as the breakfast things were removed, I summoned Iron John, the woman and the boy, for I was particular in having every one present and proceeding regularly. The box was placed on the table. All was silence. I broke the seal; raised the lid; and beheld—not the will; but my accursed poem of Doubting Castle and Giant Despair!

Could any mortal have conceived that this old withered man; so taciturn, and apparently lost to feeling, could have treasured up for years the thoughtless pleasantry of a boy, to punish him with such cruel ingenuity? I now could account for his dying smile, the only one he had ever given me. He had been a grave man all his life; it was strange that he should die in the enjoyment of a joke; and it was hard that that joke should be at my expense.

The Lawyer and the Parson seemed at a loss to comprehend the matter. "Here must be some mistake," said the Lawyer, "there is no will here."

"Oh," said Iron John, creaking forth his rusty jaws, "if it is a will you are looking for, I believe I can find one."

He retired with the same singular smile with which he had greeted me on my arrival and which I now apprehended, boded me no good. In a little while he returned with a will, perfect at all points, properly signed and sealed and witnessed and worded with horrible correctness, in which he left large legacies to Iron John and his daughter, and the residue of his fortune to the foxy headed boy; who, to my utter astonishment, was his son by this very woman; he having married her privately, and, as I verily believe, for no other purpose than to have an heir and so baulk my father and his issue of the inheritance. There was one little proviso, in which he mentioned that having discovered his nephew to have a pretty turn for poetry, he presumed he had no occasion for wealth: he recommended him, however, to the patronage of his heir; and requested that he might have a garret, rent free, in Doubting Castle.

Grave Reflections of a Disappointed Man

Mr. Buckthorne had paused at the death of his uncle, and the downfall of his great expectations, which formed, as he said, an epoch in his history; and it was not until some little time afterwards, and in a very sober mood, that he resumed his particoloured narrative.

After leaving the domains of my defunct uncle, said he, when the gate closed between me and what was once to have been mine, I felt thrust out naked into the world, and completely abandoned to fortune. What was to become of me? I had been brought up to nothing but expectations, and they had all been disappointed. I had no relations to look to for counsel or assistance. The world seemed all to have died away from me. Wave after wave of relationship had ebbed off, and I was left a mere hulk upon the strand. I am not apt to be greatly cast down, but at this time I felt sadly disheartened. I could not realize my situation, nor form a conjecture how I was to get forward.

I was now to endeavour to make money. The idea was new and strange to me. It was like being asked to discover the philosophers' stone. I had never thought about money, other than to put my hand into my pocket and find it, or if there were none there, to wait until a new supply came from home. I had considered life as a mere space of time to be filled up with enjoyments; but to have it portioned out into long hours and days of toil, merely that I might gain bread to give me strength to toil on; to labour but for the purpose of perpetuating a life of labour was new and appalling to me. This may appear a very simple matter to some, but it will be understood by every unlucky wight in my predicament, who has had the misfortune of being born to great expectations.

I passed several days in rambling about the scenes of my boyhood; partly because I absolutely did not know what to do with myself, and partly because I did not know that I should ever see them again. I clung to them as one clings to a wreck, though he knows he must eventually cast himself loose and swim for his life. I sat down on a little hill within sight of my paternal home, but I did not venture to approach it, for I felt compunction at the thoughtlessness with which I had dissipated my patrimony. But was I to blame, when I had the rich possessions of my curmudgeon of an uncle in expectation?

The new possessor of the place was making great alterations. The house was almost rebuilt. The trees which stood about it were cut down; my mother's flower garden was thrown into a lawn; all was undergoing a change. I turned my back upon it with a sigh, and rambled to another part of the country.

How thoughtful a little adversity makes one. As I came within sight of the school house where I had so often been flogged in the cause of wisdom, you would hardly have recognized the truant boy who but a few years since had eloped so heedlessly from its walls. I leaned over the paling of the play ground and watched the scholars at their games and looked to see if there might not be some urchin among them, like I was once, full of gay dreams about life and the world. The play ground seemed smaller than when I used to sport about it. The house and park too of the neighbouring squire, the father of the cruel Sacharissa, had shrunk in size and diminished in magnificence. The distant hills no longer appeared so far off, and, alas! no longer awakened ideas of a fairy land beyond.

As I was rambling pensively through a neighbouring meadow, in which I had many a time gathered primroses, I met the very pedagogue who had been the tyrant and dread of my boyhood. I had sometimes vowed to myself, when suffering under his rod, that I would have my revenge if ever I met him when I had grown to be a man. The time had come; but I had no disposition to keep my vow. The few years which had matured me into a vigorous man had shrunk him into decrepitude. He appeared to have had a paralytic stroke. I looked at him, and wondered that this poor helpless mortal could have been an object of terror to me! That I should have watched with anxiety the glance of that failing eye, or dreaded the power of that trembling hand! He tottered feebly along the path and had some difficulty getting over a style. I ran and assisted him. He looked at me with surprize but did not recognize me and made a low bow of humility and thanks. I had no disposition to make myself known for I felt that I had nothing to boast of. The pains he had taken and the pains he had inflicted had been equally useless. His repeated predictions were fully verified, and I felt that little Jack Buckthorne the idle boy had grown up to be a very good for nothing man.

This is all very comfortless detail, but as I have told you of my follies, it is meet that I shew you how for once I was schooled for them. The most thoughtless of mortals will some time or other have this day of gloom when he will be compelled to reflect. I felt on this occasion as if I had a kind of penance to perform, and I made a pilgrimage in expiation of my past levity.

Having passed a night at Leamington, I set off by a private path which leads up a hill, through a grove, and across quiet fields, until I came to the small village, or rather hamlet of Lenington. I sought the village church. It is an old low edifice of grey stone on the brow of a small hill, looking over fertile fields towards where the proud towers of Warwick Castle lift themselves against the distant horizon. A part of the church yard is shaded by large trees. Under one of these my mother lay buried. You have no doubt thought me a light, heartless being. I thought myself so; but there are moments of adversity which let us into some feelings of our nature, to which we might otherwise remain perpetual strangers.

I sought my mother's grave. The weeds were already matted over it, and the tombstone was half hid among nettles. I cleared them away and they stung my hands; but I was heedless of the pain, for my heart ached too severely. I sat down on the grave, and read over and over again the epitaph on the stone.

It was simple, but it was true. I had written it myself. I had tried to write a poetical epitaph but in vain; my feelings refused to utter themselves in rhyme. My heart had gradually been filling during my lonely wanderings; it was now charged to the brim and overflowed. I sank upon the grave and buried my face in the tall grass and wept like a child. Yes, I wept in manhood upon the grave, as I had in infancy upon the bosom of my mother. Alas! how little do we appreciate a mother's tenderness while living! How heedless are we, in youth, of all her anxieties and kindness. But when she is dead and gone, when the cares and coldness of the world come withering to our hearts; when we find how hard it is to meet with true sympathy; how few love us for ourselves; how few will befriend us in our misfortunes; then it is we think of the mother we have lost. It is true I had always loved my mother, even in my most heedless days; but I felt how inconsiderate and ineffectual had been my love. My heart melted as I retraced the days of infancy, when I was led by a mother's hand, and rocked to sleep in a mother's arms, and was without care or sorrow. "Oh my mother!" exclaimed I, burying my face again in the grass of the grave. "Oh that I were once more by your side; sleeping never to wake again on the cares and troubles of this world!"

I am not naturally of a morbid temperament, and the violence of my emotion gradually exhausted itself. It was a hearty, honest, natural discharge of griefs which had been slowly accumulating, and gave me wonderful relief. I rose from the grave as if I had been offering up a sacrifice, and I felt as if that sacrifice had been accepted.

I sat down again on the grass and plucked, one by one, the weeds from her grave; the tears trickled more slowly down my cheeks, and ceased to be bitter. It was a comfort to think that she had died before sorrow and poverty came upon her child, and that all his great expectations were blasted.

I leaned my cheek upon my hand and looked upon the landscape. Its quiet beauty soothed me. The whistle of a peasant from an adjoining field came cheerily to my ear. I seemed to respire hope and comfort with the free air that whispered through the leaves and played lightly with my hair, and dried the tears upon my cheek. A lark, rising from the field before

me, and leaving, as it were, a stream of song behind him as he
rose, lifted my fancy with him. He hovered in the air just
above the place where the towers of Warwick Castle marked
the horizon; and seemed as if fluttering with delight at his
own melody. "Surely," thought I, "if there were such a thing
as transmigration of souls, this might be taken for some poet,
let loose from earth, but still revelling in song, and carrolling
about fair fields and lordly towers."

At this moment the long forgotten feeling of poetry rose
within me. A thought sprang at once into my mind. "I will
become an author!" said I. "I have hitherto indulged in
poetry as a pleasure and it has brought me nothing but pain.
Let me try what it will do, when I cultivate it with devotion
as a pursuit."

The resolution, thus suddenly aroused within me, heaved a
load from off my heart. I felt a confidence in it from the very
place where it was formed. It seemed as though my mother's
spirit whispered it to me from her grave. "I will henceforth,"
said I, "endeavour to be all that she fondly imagined me. I
will endeavour to act as if she were witness of my actions. I
will endeavour to acquit myself in such manner, that when
I revisit her grave there may, at least, be no compunctious
bitterness in my tears."

I bowed down and kissed the turf in solemn attestation of
my vow. I plucked some primroses that were growing there
and laid them next my heart. I left the church yard with my
spirits once more lifted up, and set out a third time for London, in the character of an author.

Here my companion made a pause, and I waited in anxious
suspence; hoping to have a whole volume of literary life unfolded to me. He seemed however to have sunk into a fit of
pensive musing; and when after some time I gently roused
him by a question or two as to his literary career—

"No," said he smiling, "over that part of my story I
wish to leave a cloud. Let the mysteries of the craft rest sacred
for me. Let those who have never adventured into the republic of letters still look upon it as a fairy land. Let them suppose the author the very being they picture him from his
works. I am not the man to mar their illusion. I am not
the man to hint, while one is admiring the silken web of

Persia, that it has been spun from the entrails of a miserable worm."

"Well," said I, "if you will tell me nothing of your literary history, let me know at least if you have had any further intelligence from Doubting Castle."

"Willingly," replied he, "though I have but little to communicate."

The Booby Squire

A long time elapsed, said Buckthorne, without my receiving any accounts of my cousin and his estate. Indeed I felt so much soreness on the subject, that I wished, if possible, to shut it from my thoughts. At length chance took me into that part of the country, and I could not refrain from making some enquiries.

I learnt that my cousin had grown up ignorant, self willed, and clownish. His ignorance and clownishness had prevented his mingling with the neighbouring gentry. In spite of his great fortune he had been unsuccessful in an attempt to gain the hand of the daughter of the Parson, and had at length shrunk into the limits of such society, as a mere man of wealth can gather in a country neighbourhood.

He kept horses and hounds and a roaring table, at which were collected the loose livers of the country round, and the shabby gentlemen of a village in the vicinity. When he could get no other company he would smoke and drink with his own servants, who in their turns fleeced and despised him. Still, with all this apparent prodigality, he had a leaven of the old man in him, which shewed that he was his true born son. He lived far within his income, was vulgar in his expenses, and penurious on many points on which a gentleman would be extravagant. His house servants were obliged occasionally to work on the estate, and part of the pleasure grounds were ploughed up and devoted to husbandry.

His table though plentiful was coarse; his liquors strong and bad; and more ale and whiskey were expended in his establishment than generous wine. He was loud and arrogant at his own table, and exacted a rich man's homage from his vulgar and obsequious guests.

As to Iron John, his old grandfather, he had grown impatient of the tight hand his own grandson kept over him and quarrelled with him soon after he came to the estate. The old man had retired to a neighbouring village where he lived on the legacy of his late master, in a small cottage, and was as seldom seen out of it as a rat out of his hole in day light.

The Cub, like Caliban, seemed to have an instinctive attachment to his mother. She resided with him; but from long habit she acted more as servant than as mistress of the mansion; for she toiled in all the domestic drudgery and was oftener in the kitchen than the parlour. Such was the information which I collected of my rival cousin who had so unexpectedly elbowed me out of all my expectations.

I now felt an irresistible hankering to pay a visit to this scene of my boyhood; and to get a peep at the odd kind of life that was passing within the mansion of my maternal ancestors. I determined to do so in disguise. My booby cousin had never seen enough of me to be very familiar with my countenance, and a few years make great difference between youth and manhood. I understood he was a breeder of cattle and proud of his stock. I dressed myself therefore as a substantial farmer, and with the assistance of a red scratch that came low down on my forehead, made a complete change in my physiognomy.

It was past three o'clock when I arrived at the gate of the park, and was admitted by an old woman, who was washing in a dilapidated building which had once been a porter's lodge. I advanced up the remains of a noble avenue, many of the trees of which had been cut down and sold for timber. The grounds were in scarcely better keeping than during my uncle's life time. The grass was overgrown with weeds, and the trees wanted pruning and clearing of dead branches. Cattle were grazing about the lawns and ducks and geese swimming in the fishponds.

The road to the house bore very few traces of carriage wheels as my Cousin received few visitors but such as came on foot or horseback, and never used a carriage himself. Once indeed, as I was told, he had had the old family carriage drawn out from among the dust and cobwebs of the coach house and furbished up, and had driven, with his mother, to the village church, to take formal possession of the family pew; but there was such hooting and laughing after them as they passed through the village, and such giggling and bantering about the church door, that the pageant had never made a reappearance.

As I approached the house a legion of whelps sallied out barking at me, accompanied by the low howling rather than barking of two old worn out bloodhounds, which I recognized for the ancient life guards of my uncle. The house had still a neglected, random appearance, though much altered for the better since my last visit. Several of the windows were broken and patched up with boards; and others had been bricked up, to save taxes. I observed smoke, however, rising from the chimneys; a phenomenon rarely witnessed in the ancient establishment. On passing that part of the house where the dining room was situated I heard the sound of boisterous merriment; where three or four voices were talking at once, and oaths and laughter were horribly mingled.

The uproar of the dogs had brought a servant to the door, a tall hardfisted country clown, with a livery coat put over the undergarments of a plowman. I requested to see the master of the house, but was told he was at dinner with some "gemmen" of the neighbourhood. I made known my business and sent in to know if I might talk with the master about his cattle; for I felt a great desire to have a peep at him at his orgies. Word was returned that he was engaged with company and could not attend to business, but that if I would "step in and take a drink of something, I was heartily welcome." I accordingly entered the hall, where whips and hats of all kinds and shapes were lying on an oaken table; two or three clownish servants were lounging about; every thing had a look of confusion and carelessness.

The apartments through which I passed had the same air of departed gentility and sluttish housekeeping. The once rich curtains were faded and dusty, the furniture greased and tarnished. On entering the dining room I found a number of odd vulgar looking rustic gentlemen seated round a table on which were bottles, decanters, tankards, pipes and tobacco.

Several dogs were lying about the room, or sitting and watching their masters, and one was gnawing a bone under a side table.

The master of the feast sat at the head of the board. He was greatly altered. He had grown thick set and rather gummy, with a fiery foxy head of hair. There was a singular mixture of foolishness, arrogance and conceit in his countenance. He was dressed in a vulgarly fine style, with leather breeches, a red waistcoat and green coat, and was evidently, like his guests, a little flushed with drinking. The whole company stared at me with a whimsical muzzy look; like men whose senses were a little obfuscated by beer rather than wine.

My Cousin, (God forgive me! the appellation sticks in my throat) my cousin invited me with awkward civility, or, as he intended it, condescension, to sit to the table and drink. We talked as usual, about the weather, the crops, politics, and hard times. My Cousin was a loud politician, and evidently accustomed to talk without contradiction at his own table. He was amazingly loyal, and talked of standing by the throne to the last guinea, "as every gentleman of fortune should do." The village Exciseman, who was half asleep, could just ejaculate "very true" to every thing he said.

The conversation turned upon cattle; he boasted of his breed, his mode of crossing it, and of the general management of his estate. This unluckily drew on a history of the place and of the family. He spoke of my late uncle with the greatest irreverence, which I could easily forgive. He mentioned my name, and my blood began to boil. He described my frequent visits to my uncle when I was a lad, and I found the varlet, even at that time, imp as he was, had known that he was to inherit the estate.

He described the scene of my uncle's death and the opening of the will, with a degree of coarse humour that I had not expected from him; and, vexed as I was, I could not help joining in the laugh; for I have always relished a joke, even though made at my own expense. He went on to speak of my various pursuits; my strolling freak, and that somewhat nettled me; at length he talked of my parents. He ridiculed my father; I stomached even that, though with great difficulty.

He mentioned my mother with a sneer—and in an instant he lay sprawling at my feet.

Here a tumult succeeded. The table was nearly overturned. Bottles, glasses and tankards rolled crashing and clattering about the floor. The company seized hold of both of us to keep us from doing any further mischief. I struggled to get loose, for I was boiling with fury. My cousin defied me to strip and fight him on the lawn. I agreed, for I felt the strength of a giant in me, and I longed to pummel him soundly.

Away then we were borne. A ring was formed. I had a second assigned me in true boxing style. My cousin, as he advanced to fight, said something about his generosity in shewing me such fair play, when I had made such an unprovoked attack upon him at his own table—

"Stop there!" cried I, in a rage.—"Unprovoked!—know that I am John Buckthorne, and you have insulted the memory of my mother."

The lout was suddenly struck by what I said. He drew back and thought for a moment.

"Nay, damn it," said he, "that's too much—that's clean another thing—I've a mother myself, and no one shall speak ill of her, bad as she is."—

He paused again: nature seemed to have a rough struggle in his rude bosom.

"Damn it cousin," cried he, "I'm sorry for what I said. Thou'st served me right in knocking me down, and I like thee the better for it. Here's my hand. Come and live with me, and damme but the best room in the house, and the best horse in the stable, shall be at thy service."

I declare to you I was strongly moved at this instance of nature, breaking her way through such a lump of flesh. I forgave the fellow in a moment his two heinous crimes of having been born in wedlock and inheriting my estate. I shook the hand he offered me, to convince him that I bore him no ill-will; and then making my way through the gaping crowd of toad eaters, bade adieu to my uncle's domains forever. This is the last I have seen or heard of my cousin or of the domestic concerns of Doubting Castle.

The Strolling Manager

As I was walking one morning with Buckthorne, near one of the principal theatres, he directed my attention to a groupe of those equivocal beings that may often be seen hovering about the stage doors of theatres. They were marvellously ill favoured in their attire, their coats buttoned up to their chins; yet they wore their hats smartly on one side, and had a certain knowing, dirty-gentlemanlike air, which is common to the subalterns of the drama. Buckthorne knew them well by early experience.

"These," said he, "are the ghosts of departed Kings and heroes; fellows who sway sceptres and truncheons; command kingdoms and armies; and after giving away realms and treasures over night, have scarce a shilling to pay for a breakfast in the morning. Yet they have the true vagabond abhorrence of all useful and industrious employment; and they have their pleasures too: one of which is to lounge in this way in the sunshine, at the stage door, during rehearsals, and make hackneyed theatrical jokes on all passers by.

"Nothing is more traditional and legitimate than the stage. Old scenery, old clothes, old sentiments, old ranting, and old jokes, are handed down from generation to generation; and will probably continue to be so until time shall be no more. Every hanger on of a theatre becomes a wag by inheritance, and flourishes about at tap rooms and sixpenny clubs with the property jokes of the green room."

While amusing ourselves with reconnoitering this groupe, we noticed one in particular who appeared to be the oracle. He was a weather beaten veteran, a little bronzed by time and beer, who had no doubt grown grey in the parts of robbers, cardinals, Roman senators, and walking noblemen.

"There's something in the set of that hat, and the turn of that physiognomy, extremely familiar to me," said Buckthorne. He looked a little closer. "I cannot be mistaken, that must be my old brother of the truncheon, Flimsey, the tragic hero of the Strolling Company."

It was he in fact. The poor fellow shewed evident signs that times went hard with him: he was so finely and shabbily dressed. His coat was some what threadbare, and of the Lord

Townly cut; single breasted, and scarcely capable of meeting in front of his body; which, from long intimacy, had acquired the symmetry and robustness of a beer barrel. He wore a pair of dingy white stockinet pantaloons, which had much ado to reach his waistcoat; a great quantity of dirty cravat; and a pair of old russet coloured tragedy boots.

When his companions had dispersed, Buckthorne drew him aside and made himself known to him. The tragic veteran could scarcely recognize him, or believe that he was really his quondam associate "little gentleman Jack." Buckthorne invited him to a neighbouring coffee house to talk over old times; and in the course of a little while we were put in possession of his history in brief.

He had continued to act the heroes in the Strolling Company for some time after Buckthorne had left it, or rather had been driven from it, so abruptly. At length the manager died and the troop was thrown into confusion. Every one aspired to the crown, every one was for taking the lead; and the manager's widow, although a tragedy queen, and a brimstone to boot, pronounced it utterly impossible for a woman to keep any controul over such a set of tempestuous rascallions.

"Upon this hint, I spake"—said Flimsey. I stepped forward, and offered my services in the most effectual way. They were accepted. In a week's time I married the widow and succeeded to the throne. "The funeral baked meats did coldly furnish forth the marriage table," as Hamlet says. But the ghost of my predecessor never haunted me; and I inherited crowns, sceptres, bowls, daggers, and all the stage trappings and trumpery, not omitting the widow, without the least molestation.

I now led a flourishing life of it; for our company was pretty strong and attractive, and as my wife and I took the heavy parts of tragedy, it was a great saving to the treasury. We carried off the palm from all the rival shows at country fairs; and I assure you we have even drawn full houses, and been applauded by the critics at Bartlemy Fair itself, though we had Astley's Troop, the Irish giant and "the death of Nelson" in wax work to contend against.

I soon began to experience, however, the cares of command. I discovered that there were cabals breaking out in the company, headed by the clown, who you may recollect was a terribly peevish, fractious fellow, and always in ill humour. I had a great mind to turn him off at once, but I could not do without him, for there was not a droller scoundrel on the stage. His very shape was comic, for he had but to turn his back upon the audience and all the ladies were ready to die with laughing. He felt his importance, and took advantage of it. He would keep the audience in a continual roar, and then come behind the scenes and fret and fume and play the very devil. I excused a great deal in him, however, knowing that comic actors are a little prone to this infirmity of temper.

I had another trouble of a nearer and dearer nature to struggle with; which was, the affection of my wife. As ill luck would have it she took it into her head to be very fond of me, and became intolerably jealous. I could not keep a pretty girl in the company, and hardly dared embrace an ugly one, even when my part required it. I have known her reduce a fine lady to tatters, "to very rags" as Hamlet says, in an instant, and destroy one of the very best dresses in the wardrobe; merely because she saw me kiss her at the side scenes;—though I give you my honour it was done merely by way of rehearsal.

This was doubly annoying, because I have a natural liking to pretty faces and wish to have them about me; and because they are indispensible to the success of a company at a fair, where one has to vie with so many rival theatres. But when once a jealous wife gets a freak in her head, there's no use in talking of interest or any thing else. Egad, sirs, I have more than once trembled when during a fit of her tantrums, she was playing high tragedy and flourishing her tin dagger on the stage, lest she should give way to her humour and stab some fancied rival in good earnest.

I went on better, however, than could be expected, considering the weakness of my flesh and the violence of my rib. I had not a much worse time of it than old Jupiter, whose spouse was continually ferretting out some new intrigue, and making the heavens almost too hot to hold him.

At length, as luck would have it, we were performing at a country fair, when I understood the theatre of a neighbouring town to be vacant. I had always been desirous to be enrolled in a settled company, and the height of my desire was to get on a par with a brother in law, who was manager of a regular theatre, and who had looked down upon me. Here was an opportunity not to be neglected. I concluded an agreement with the proprietors, and in a few days opened the theatre with great eclat.

Behold me now at the summit of my ambition, "the high top gallant of my joy," as Romeo says. No longer a chieftain of a wandering tribe, but the monarch of a legitimate throne; and entitled to call even the great potentates of Covent Garden and Drury Lane cousin. You no doubt think my happiness complete. Alas, sir! I was one of the most uncomfortable dogs living. No one knows, who has not tried, the miseries of a manager; but above all, of a country manager.—No one can conceive the contentions and quarrels within doors, the oppressions and vexations from without.

I was pestered with the bloods and loungers of a country town, who infested my green room, and played the mischief among my actresses. But there was no shaking them off. It would have been ruin to affront them; for, though troublesome friends, they would have been dangerous enemies. Then there were the village critics and village amateurs, who were continually tormenting me with advice, and getting into a passion if I would not take it:—especially the village doctor and the village attorney; who had both been to London occasionally, and knew what acting should be.

I had also to manage as arrant a crew of scape graces as were ever collected together within the walls of a theatre. I had been obliged to combine my original troop, with some of the former troop of the theatre, who were favourites with the public. Here was a mixture that produced perpetual ferment. They were all the time either fighting or frolicking with each other, and I scarcely know which mood was least troublesome. If they quarrelled every thing went wrong; and if they were friends they were continually playing off some confounded prank upon each other, or upon me; for I had unhappily acquired among them the character of an easy good natured fellow, the worst character that a manager can possess.

Their waggery at times drove me almost crazy; for there is nothing so vexatious as the hackneyed tricks and hoaxes and pleasantries of a veteran band of theatrical vagabonds. I relished them well enough, it is true, while I was merely one of the company, but as manager I found them detestable. They were incessantly bringing some disgrace upon the theatre by their tavern frolicks, and their pranks about the country town. All my lectures upon the importance of keeping up the dignity of the profession, and the respectability of the company, were in vain. The villains could not sympathize with the delicate feelings of a man in station. They even trifled with the seriousness of stage business. I have had the whole piece interrupted and a crowded audience of at least twenty five pounds kept waiting, because the actors had hid away the breeches of Rosalind; and have known Hamlet stalk solemnly on to deliver his soliloquy, with a dish clout pinned to his skirts. Such are the baleful consequences of a manager's getting a character for good nature.

I was intolerably annoyed, too, by the great actors who came down *Starring*, as it is called, from London. Of all baneful influences, keep me from that of a London Star. A first rate actress, going the rounds of the country theatres, is as bad as a blazing comet, whisking about the heavens, and shaking fire, and plagues, and discords from its tail.

The moment one of these "heavenly bodies" appeared on my horizon, I was sure to be in hot water. My theatre was overrun by provincial dandies, copper-washed counterfeits of Bond Street loungers; who are always proud to be in the train of an actress from town, and anxious to be thought on exceeding good terms with her. It was really a relief to me when some random young nobleman would come in pursuit of the bait, and awe all this small fry to a distance. I have always felt myself more at ease with a nobleman, than with the dandy of a country town.

And then the injuries I suffered in my personal dignity and my managerial authority from the visits of these great London actors. 'Sblood, sir, I was no longer master of myself or my throne. I was hectored and lectured in my own green room, and made an absolute nincompoop on my own stage. There is no tyrant so absolute and capricious as a London Star at a country theatre.

I dreaded the sight of all of them; and yet if I did not

engage them, I was sure of having the public clamourous against me. They drew full houses and appeared to be making my fortune, but they swallowed up all the profits by their insatiable demands. They were absolute tape worms to my little theatre; the more it took in, the poorer it grew. They were sure to leave me with an exhausted public, empty benches, and a score or two of affronts to settle among the town's folk, in consequence of misunderstandings about the taking of places.

But the worst thing I had to undergo in my managerial career was patronage. Oh sir, of all things deliver me from the patronage of the great people of a country town. It was my ruin. You must know that this town, though small, was filled with feuds, and parties, and great folks; being a busy little trading and manufacturing town. The mischief was that their greatness was of a kind not to be settled by reference to the court calender, or college of heraldry. It was therefore the most quarrelsome kind of greatness in existence. You smile sir, but let me tell you there are no feuds more furious than the frontier feuds, which take place on these "debateable lands" of gentility. The most violent dispute that I ever knew in high life, was one which occurred at a country town, on a question of precedence between the ladies of a manufacturer of pins, and a manufacturer of needles.

At the town where I was situated there were perpetual altercations of the kind. The head manufacturer's lady, for instance, was at daggers drawings with the head shopkeeper's, and both were too rich, and had too many friends to be treated lightly. The Doctor's and Lawyer's ladies held their heads still higher; but they in their turn were kept in check by the wife of a country banker, who kept her own carriage; while a masculine widow of cracked character, and second hand fashion, who lived in a large house, and claimed to be, in some way, related to nobility, looked down upon them all. To be sure her manners were not over elegant, nor her fortune over large, but then, sir, her blood—oh her blood carried it all hollow; there was no withstanding a woman with such blood in her veins.

After all, her claims to high connexion were questioned, and she had frequent battles for precedence at balls and

assemblies; with some of the sturdy dames of the neighbourhood, who stood upon their wealth and their virtue; but then
she had two dashing daughters, who dressed as fine as dragons, had as high blood as their mother, and seconded her in
every thing. So they carried their point with high heads, and
every body hated, abused, and stood in awe of the Fantadlins.

Such was the state of the fashionable world in this self important little town. Unluckily I was not as well acquainted
with its politics as I should have been. I had found myself a
stranger and in great perplexities during my first season; I
determined, therefore, to put myself under the patronage of
some powerful name, and thus to take the field with the prejudices of the public in my favour. I cast round my thoughts
for the purpose, and, in an evil hour they fell upon Mrs. Fantadlin. No one seemed to me to have a more absolute sway in
the world of fashion. I had always noticed that her party
slammed the box door the loudest at the theatre; had most
beaux attending on them; and talked and laughed loudest
during the performance; and then the Miss Fantadlins wore
always more feathers and flowers than any other ladies; and
used quizzing glasses incessantly. The first evening of my theatre's re-opening, therefore, was announced, in flaring capitals
on the play bills, "under the patronage of The Honourable
Mrs. Fantadlin."

Sir, the whole community flew to arms! The Banker's wife
felt her dignity grievously insulted, at not having the preference; her husband being high bailiff, and the richest man in
the place. She immediately issued invitations for a large party
for the night of the performance, and asked many a lady to it
whom she never had noticed before. Presume to patronize the
theatre! Insufferable! And then for me to dare to term her
"The Honourable!" What claim had she to the title, forsooth!
The fashionable world had long groaned under the tyranny of
the Fantadlins, and were glad to make a common cause
against this new instance of assumption. Those, too, who had
never before been noticed by the banker's lady, were ready to
enlist in any quarrel, for the honour of her acquaintance. All
minor feuds were forgotten. The Doctor's lady and the Lawyer's lady met together; and the Manufacturer's lady and the
Shopkeeper's lady kissed each other; and all, headed by the

Banker's lady, voted the theatre a *bore*, and determined to encourage nothing but the Indian Jugglers, and Mr. Walker's Eidouranion.

Alas for poor Pillgarlick! I little knew the mischief that was brewing against me. My box book remained blank. The evening arrived; but no audience. The musick struck up to a tolerable pit and gallery, but no fashionables! I peeped anxiously from behind the curtain, but the time passed away; the play was retarded until pit and gallery became furious; and I had to raise the curtain, and play my greatest part in tragedy to "a beggarly account of empty boxes."

It is true the Fantadlins came late, as was their custom, and entered like a tempest, with a flutter of feathers and red shawls; but they were evidently disconcerted at finding they had no one to admire and envy them; and were enraged at this glaring defection of their fashionable followers. All the beau monde were engaged at the Banker's lady's rout. They remained for some time in solitary and uncomfortable state, and though they had the theatre almost to themselves, yet, for the first time they talked in whispers. They left the house at the end of the first piece, and I never saw them afterwards.

Such was the rock on which I split. I never got over the patronage of the Fantadlin family. My house was deserted; my actors grew discontented because they were ill paid; my door became a hammering place for every bailiff in the county; and my wife became more and more shrewish and tormenting, the more I wanted comfort.

I tried for a time the usual consolation of a harassed and henpecked man: I took to the bottle, and tried to tipple away my cares, but in vain. I don't mean to decry the bottle; it is no doubt an excellent remedy in many cases, but it did not answer in mine. It cracked my voice, coppered my nose, but neither improved my wife nor my affairs.

My establishment became a scene of confusion and peculation. I was considered a ruined man, and of course fair game for every one to pluck at, as every one plunders a sinking ship. Day after day some of the troop deserted, and like deserting soldiers, carried off their arms and accoutrements with them. In this manner my wardrobe took legs and walked away; my finery strolled all over the country; my swords and daggers glittered in every barn; until at last my taylor made "one fell swoop," and carried off three dress coats, half a dozen doublets, and nineteen pair of flesh coloured pantaloons.

This was the "be all and the end all" of my fortune. I no longer hesitated what to do. Egad, thought I, since stealing is the order of the day I'll steal too. So I secretly gathered together the jewels of my wardrobe; packed up a hero's dress in a handkerchief, slung it on the end of a tragedy sword, and quietly stole off at dead of night, — "the bell then beating one," — leaving my queen and Kingdom to the mercy of my rebellious subjects, and my merciless foes the bumbailiffs.

Such, sir, was the "end of all my greatness." I was heartily cured of all passion for governing, and returned once more into the ranks. I had for some time the usual run of an actor's life. I played in various country theatres, at fairs and in barns; sometimes hard pushed, sometimes flush, until on one occasion I came within an ace of making my fortune, and becoming one of the wonders of the age.

I was playing the part of Richard the Third in a country barn and in my best style, for, to tell the truth, I was a little in liquor, and the critics of the company always observed that I played with most effect when I had a glass too much. There was a thunder of applause when I came to that part where Richard cries for "a horse! a horse!" My cracked voice had always a wonderful effect here; it was like two voices run into one; you would have thought two men had been calling for a horse, or that Richard had called for two horses. And when I flung the taunt at Richmond, "Richard is *hoarse* with calling thee to arms," I thought the barn would have come down about my ears with the raptures of the audience.

The very next morning a person waited upon me at my lodgings; I saw at once he was a gentleman by his dress, for he had a large brooch in his bosom, thick rings on his fingers, and used a quizzing glass. And a gentleman he proved to be, for I soon ascertained that he was a kept author, or kind of literary tailor to one of the great London theatres; one who worked under the manager's directions, and cut up and cut down plays, and patched and pieced, and new faced, and turned them inside out; in short, he was one of the readiest and greatest writers of the day.

He was now on a foraging excursion in quest of something that might be got up as a prodigy. The theatre it seems was in desperate condition—nothing but a miracle could save it. He had seen me act Richard the night before and had pitched upon me for that miracle. I had a remarkable bluster in my style and swagger in my gait; I certainly differed from all other heroes of the barn; so the thought struck the agent to bring me out as a theatrical wonder; as the restorer of natural and legitimate acting; as the only one who could understand and act Shakespeare rightly. When he opened his plan I shrunk from it with becoming modesty, for, well as I thought of myself, I doubted my competency to such an undertaking.

I hinted at my imperfect knowledge of Shakespeare, having played his characters only after mutilated copies, interlarded with a great deal of my own talk by way of helping memory or heightening the effect.

"So much the better," cried the gentleman with rings on his fingers; "so much the better. New readings, sir!—new readings! Don't study a line—let us have Shakespeare after your own fashion."

"But then my voice was cracked; it could not fill a London theatre."

"So much the better! so much the better! The public is tired of intonation—the *ore rotundo* has had its day. No, sir, your cracked voice is the very thing—spit and splutter, and snap and snarl, and 'play the very dog' about the stage, and you'll be the making of us."

"But then,"—I could not help blushing to the end of my very nose as I said it, but I was determined to be candid;— "but then," added I, "there is one awkward circumstance; I have an unlucky habit—my misfortunes, and the exposures to which one is subjected in country barns, have obliged me now and then to—to—take a drop of something comfortable—and so—and so——"

"What! you drink?" cried the agent eagerly.

I bowed my head in blushing acknowledgment.

"So much the better! so much the better! The irregularities of genius! A sober fellow is common place. The public like an actor that drinks.—Give me your hand, sir. You're the very man to make a dash with."

I still hung back with lingering diffidence, declaring myself unworthy of such praise.

" 'Sblood man!" cried he, "no praise at all. You don't imagine *I* think you a wonder. I only want the public to think so. Nothing so easy as gulling the public if you only set up a prodigy. Common talent any body can measure by common rule; but a prodigy sets all rule and measurement at defiance."

These words opened my eyes in an instant: we now came to a proper understanding; less flattering, it is true, to my vanity, but much more satisfactory to my judgment.

It was agreed that I should make my appearance before a London audience, as a dramatic sun just bursting from behind the clouds: one that was to banish all the lesser lights and false fires of the stage. Every precaution was to be taken to possess the public mind at every avenue. The pit was to be packed with sturdy clappers; the newspapers secured by vehement puffers; every theatrical resort to be haunted by hireling talkers. In a word, every engine of theatrical humbug was to be put in action. Wherever I differed from former actors, it was to be maintained that I was right and they were wrong. If I ranted, it was to be pure passion; if I were vulgar, it was to be pronounced a familiar touch of nature; if I made any queer blunder, it was to be a new reading. If my voice cracked, or I got out in my part, I was only to bounce, and grin, and snarl at the audience, and make any horrible grimace that came into my head, and my admirers were to call it "a great point," and to fall back and shout and yell with rapture.

"In short," said the gentleman with the quizzing glass, "strike out boldly and bravely: no matter how or what you do, so that it be but odd and strange. If you do but escape pelting the first night, your fortune and the fortune of the theatre is made."

I set off for London, therefore, in company with the kept author, full of new plans and new hopes. I was to be restorer of Shakespeare and nature, and the legitimate drama; my very swagger was to be heroic, and my cracked voice the standard of elocution. Alas sir! my usual luck attended me. Before I arrived at the metropolis a rival wonder had appeared. A woman who could dance the slack rope, and run up a cord from the stage to the gallery with fire works all round her.

She was seized on by the manager with avidity; she was the saving of the great national theatre for the season. Nothing was talked of but Madame Saqui's fire works and flame coloured pantaloons; and nature, Shakespeare, the legitimate drama and poor Pillgarlic were completely left in the lurch.

When Madame Saqui's performance grew stale, other wonders succeeded; horses, and harlequinades, and mummery of all kinds; until another dramatic prodigy was brought forward to play the very game for which I had been intended. I called upon the kept author for an explanation, but he was deeply engaged in writing a melo-drame or a pantomime, and was extremely testy on being interrupted in his studies.

However, as the theatre was in some measure pledged to provide for me, the manager acted, according to the usual phrase, "like a man of honour," and I received an appointment in the corps. It had been a turn up of a die whether I should be Alexander the Great or Alexander the Coppersmith: the latter carried it. I could not be put at the head of the drama so I was put at the tail. In other words I was enrolled among the number of what are called *useful men*; those who enact soldiers, senators, and Banquo's shadowy line. I was perfectly satisfied with my lot; for I have always been a bit of a philosopher. If my situation was not splendid, it at least was secure; and in fact I have seen half a dozen prodigies appear, dazzle, burst like bubbles and pass away, and yet here I am, snug, unenvied and unmolested at the foot of the profession.

You may smile; but let me tell you, we "useful men" are the only comfortable actors on the stage. We are safe from hisses and below the hope of applause. We fear not the success of rivals, nor dread the critic's pen. So long as we get the words of our parts, and they are not often many, it is all we care for. We have our own merriment, our own friends, and our own admirers; for every actor has his friends and admirers, from the highest to the lowest. The first rate actor dines with the noble amateur, and entertains a fashionable table with scraps and songs and theatrical slip-slop. The second rate actors have their second rate friends and admirers, with whom they likewise spout tragedy and talk slip-slop; and so down even to us; who have our friends and admirers among spruce clerks and aspiring apprentices, who treat us to a dinner now and then, and enjoy at tenth hand the same scraps, and songs, and slip-slop, that have been served up by our more fortunate breth-ren at the tables of the great.

I now for the first time in my theatrical life experience what true pleasure is. I have known enough of notoriety to pity the poor devils who are called favourites of the public. I would rather be a Kitten in the arms of a spoiled child to be one moment petted and pampered, and the next moment thumped over the head with the spoon. I smile to see our leading actors, fretting themselves with envy and jealousy about a trumpery renown, questionable in its quality and un-certain in its duration. I laugh too, though of course in my sleeve, at the bustle and importance and trouble and perplex-ities of our manager, who is harrassing himself to death in the hopeless effort to please every body.

I have found among my fellow subalterns two or three quondam managers, who like myself, have wielded the scep-tres of country theatres; and we have many a sly joke together at the expense of the manager and the public. Sometimes too we meet like deposed and exiled Kings, talk over the events of our respective reigns, moralize over a tankard of ale, and laugh at the humbug of the great and little world; which, I take it, is the essence of practical philosophy.

———

Thus end the anecdotes of Buckthorne and his friends. It grieves me much that I could not procure from him further particulars of his history, and especially of that part of it which passed in town. He had evidently seen much of literary life; and, as he had never risen to eminence in letters, and yet was free from the gall of disappointment, I had hoped to gain some candid intelligence concerning his contemporaries. The testimony of such an honest chronicler would have been par-ticularly valuable at the present time; when, owing to the ex-treme fecundity of the press, and the thousand anecdotes, criticisms, and biographical sketches that are daily poured forth concerning public characters, it is extremely difficult to get at any truth concerning them.

He was always, however, excessively reserved and fastidious

on this point, at which I very much wondered, authors in general appearing to think each other fair game, and being ready to serve each other up for the amusement of the public.

A few mornings after hearing the history of the ex manager, I was surprised by a visit from Buckthorne before I was out of bed. He was dressed for travelling.

"Give me joy! give me joy!" said he, rubbing his hands with the utmost glee; "my great expectations are realized!"

I gazed at him with a look of wonder and inquiry.

"My booby cousin is dead!" cried he, "may he rest in peace! He nearly broke his neck in a fall from his horse in a fox chace. By good luck he lived long enough to make his will. He has made me his heir, partly out of an odd feeling of retributive justice, and partly because, as he says, none of his own family or friends know how to enjoy such an estate. I'm off to the country to take possession. I've done with authorship.—That for the critics!" said he, snapping his fingers. "Come down to Doubting Castle when I get settled, and egad I'll give you a rouse." So saying he shook me heartily by the hand and bounded off in high spirits.

A long time elapsed before I heard from him again. Indeed it was but lately that I received a letter written in the happiest of moods. He was getting the estate into fine order; every thing went to his wishes, and what was more, he was married to Sacharissa; who it seems had always entertained an ardent though secret attachment for him, which he fortunately discovered just after coming to his estate.

"I find," said he, "you are a little given to the sin of authorship, which I renounce. If the anecdotes I have given you of my story are of any interest, you may make use of them; but come down to Doubting Castle and see how we live, and I'll give you my whole London life over a social glass; and a rattling history it shall be about authors and reviewers."

If ever I visit Doubting Castle, and get the history he promises, the public shall be sure to hear of it.

PART III

THE ITALIAN BANDITTI

The Inn at Terracina

Crack! crack! crack! crack! crack!

"Here comes the estafette from Naples," said mine host of the inn at Terracina, "bring out the relay."

The estafette came galloping up the road according to custom, brandishing over his head a short handled whip, with a long knotted lash; every smack of which made a report like a pistol. He was a tight square-set young fellow, in the usual uniform—a smart blue coat, ornamented with facings and gold lace, but so short behind as to reach scarcely below his waistband, and cocked up not unlike the tail of a wren. A cocked hat, edged with gold lace; a pair of stiff riding boots; but instead of the usual leathern breeches he had a fragment of a pair of drawers that scarcely furnished an apology for modesty to hide behind.

The estafette galloped up to the door and jumped from his horse.

"A glass of rosolio, a fresh horse, and a pair of breeches," said he, "and quickly—*per l'amor di Dio*, I am behind my time, and must be off."

"San Gennaro!" replied the host, "why, where hast thou left thy garment?"

"Among the robbers between this and Fondi."

"What! rob an estafette! I never heard of such folly. What could they hope to get from thee?"

"My leather breeches!" replied the estafette. "They were bran new, and shone like gold, and hit the fancy of the captain."

"Well, these fellows grow worse and worse. To meddle with an estafette! And that merely for the sake of a pair of leather breeches!"

The robbing of a government messenger seemed to strike the host with more astonishment than any other enormity that had taken place on the road; and indeed it was the first time so wanton an outrage had been committed; the robbers generally taking care not to meddle with any thing belonging to government.

The estafette was by this time equipped; for he had not lost an instant in making his preparations while talking. The relay was ready: the rosolio tossed off. He grasped the reins and the stirrup.

"Were there many robbers in the band?" said a handsome, dark young man, stepping forward from the door of the inn.

"As formidable a band as ever I saw," said the estafette, springing into the saddle.

"Are they cruel to travellers?" said a beautiful young Venetian lady, who had been hanging on the gentleman's arm.

"Cruel, signora!" echoed the estafette, giving a glance at the lady as he put spurs to his horse. "*Corpo di Bacco!* they stiletto all the men, and as to the women——"

Crack! crack! crack! crack! crack!—the last words were drowned in the smacking of the whip, and away galloped the estafette along the road to the Pontine marshes.

"Holy Virgin!" ejaculated the fair Venetian, "what will become of us!"

The inn of which we are speaking stands just outside of the walls of Terracina, under a vast precipitous height of rocks, crowned with the ruins of the castle of Theodoric the Goth. The situation of Terracina is remarkable. It is a little, ancient, lazy Italian town, on the frontiers of the Roman territory. There seems to be an idle pause in every thing about the place. The Mediterranean spreads before it—that sea without flux or reflux. The port is without a sail, excepting that once in a while a solitary felucca may be seen, disgorging its holy cargo of baccala, or codfish, the meagre provision for the Quaresima or Lent. The inhabitants are apparently a listless, heedless race, as people of soft, sunny climates are apt to be; but under this passive, indolent exterior are said to lurk dangerous qualities. They are supposed by many to be little better than the banditti of the neighbouring mountains, and indeed to hold a secret correspondence with them. The solitary watch towers, erected here and there along the coast, speak of pirates and corsairs which hover about these shores: while the low huts, as stations for soldiers, which dot the distant road, as it winds up through an olive grove, intimate that in the ascent there is danger for the traveller and facility for the bandit.

Indeed, it is between this town and Fondi, that the road to

Naples is most infested by banditti. It has several winding and solitary places, where the robbers are enabled to see the traveller from a distance, from the brows of hills or impending precipices, and to lie in wait for him, at lonely and difficult passes.

The Italian robbers are a desperate class of men that have almost formed themselves into an order of society. They wear a kind of uniform, or rather costume, which openly designates their profession. This is probably done to diminish its sculking, lawless character, and to give it something of a military air in the eyes of the common people; or, perhaps, to catch by outward show and finery the fancies of the young men of the villages, and thus to gain recruits. Their dresses are often very rich and picturesque. They wear jackets and breeches of bright colours, sometimes gaily embroidered; their breasts are covered with medals and relics; their hats are broad brimmed, with conical crowns, decorated with feathers, or variously coloured ribbands; their hair is sometimes gathered in silk nets; they wear a kind of sandal of cloth or leather, bound round the legs with thongs, and extremely flexible, to enable them to scramble with ease and celerity among the mountain precipices; a broad belt of cloth, or a sash of silk net, is stuck full of pistols and stilettos; a carbine is slung at the back, while about them is generally thrown, in a negligent manner, a great dingy mantle, which serves as a protection in storms, or a bed in their bivouacs among the mountains.

They range over a great extent of wild country, along the chain of Apennines bordering on different states; they know all the difficult passes, the short cuts for retreat, and the impracticable forests of the mountain summits, where no force dare follow them. They are secure of the good will of the inhabitants of those regions, a poor and semi-barbarous race, whom they never disturb and often enrich. Indeed, they are considered as a sort of illegitimate heroes among the mountain villages, and in certain frontier towns, where they dispose of their plunder. Thus countenanced, and sheltered and secure in the fastnesses of their mountains, the robbers have set the weak police of the Italian states at defiance. It is in vain that their names and descriptions are posted on the doors of country churches, and rewards offered for them alive or dead;

the villagers are either too much awed by the terrible instances of vengeance inflicted by the Brigands, or have too good an understanding with them to be their betrayers. It is true they are now and then hunted and shot down like beasts of prey by the *gens d'armes*, their heads put in iron cages and stuck upon posts by the road side, or their limbs hung up to blacken in the trees near the places where they have committed their atrocities; but these ghastly spectacles only serve to make some dreary pass of the road still more dreary, and to dismay the traveller without deterring the bandit.

At the time that the estafette made this sudden appearance, almost *in cuerpo*, as has been mentioned, the audacity of the robbers had risen to an unparalleled height. They had laid villas under contribution, they had sent messages into country towns, to tradesmen and rich burghers, demanding supplies of money, of clothing, or even of luxuries, with menaces of vengeance in case of refusal; they had their spies and emissaries in every town, village and inn, along the principal roads, to give them notice of the quality and movements of travellers. They had plundered carriages; carried people of rank and fortune into the mountains and obliged them to write for heavy ransoms; and had committed outrages on females who had fallen into their hands.

Such was briefly the state of the robbers, or rather such was the amount of the rumours prevalent concerning them, when the scene took place at the inn of Terracina. The dark, handsome, young man, and the Venetian lady, incidentally mentioned, had arrived early that afternoon in a private carriage, drawn by mules and attended by a single servant. They had been recently married, were spending the honey moon in travelling through these delicious countries, and were on their way to visit a rich aunt of the bride's at Naples.

The lady was young, and tender and timid. The stories she had heard along the road had filled her with apprehension, not more for herself than for her husband; for though she had been married almost a month, she still loved him almost to idolatry. When she reached Terracina the rumours of the road had increased to an alarming magnitude; and the sight of two robbers' skulls grinning in iron cages on each side of the old gateway of the town brought her to a pause. Her husband had tried in vain to reassure her. They had lingered all the afternoon at the inn, until it was too late to think of starting that evening, and the parting words of the estafette completed her affright.

"Let us return to Rome," said she, putting her arm within her husband's, and drawing towards him as if for protection—"let us return to Rome and give up this visit to Naples."

"And give up the visit to your aunt, too," said the husband.

"Nay—what is my aunt in comparison with your safety," said she, looking up tenderly in his face.

There was something in her tone and manner that showed she really was thinking more of her husband's safety at that moment than of her own; and being so recently married, and a match of pure affection, too, it is very possible that she was. At least her husband thought so. Indeed, any one who has heard the sweet, musical tone of a Venetian voice, and the melting tenderness of a Venetian phrase, and felt the soft witchery of a Venetian eye, would not wonder at the husband's believing whatever they professed.

He clasped the white hand that had been laid within his, put his arm round her slender waist, and drawing her fondly to his bosom—"This night at least," said he, "we will pass at Terracina."

Crack! crack! crack! crack! crack!

Another apparition of the road attracted the attention of mine host and his guests. From the direction of the Pontine marshes, a carriage drawn by half a dozen horses, came driving at a furious rate—the postillions smacking their whips like mad, as is the case when conscious of the greatness or the munificence of their fare. It was a landaulet, with a servant mounted on the dickey. The compact, highly finished, yet proudly simple construction of the carriage; the quantity of neat, well arranged trunks and conveniencies; the loads of box coats and upper benjamins on the dickey—and the fresh, burly, gruff looking face at the window, proclaimed at once that it was the equipage of an Englishman.

"Horses to Fondi," said the Englishman, as the landlord came bowing to the carriage door.

"Would not his Eccellenza alight and take some refreshment?"

"No—he did not mean to eat until he got to Fondi!"

"But the horses will be some time in getting ready—"

"Ah—that's always the case—nothing but delay in this cursed country."

"If his Eccellenza would only walk into the house——"

"No, no, no!—I tell you no!—I want nothing but horses, and as quick as possible. John! see that the horses are got ready, and don't let us be kept here an hour or two. Tell him if we're delayed over the time, I'll lodge a complaint with the postmaster."

John touched his hat, and set off to obey his master's orders, with the taciturn obedience of an English servant. He was a ruddy, round faced fellow, with hair cropped close; a short coat, drab breeches, and long gaiters; and appeared to have almost as much contempt as his master for every thing around him.

In the mean time the Englishman got out of the carriage and walked up and down before the inn, with his hands in his pockets: taking no notice of the crowd of idlers who were gazing at him and his equipage. He was tall, stout, and well made; dressed with neatness and precision, wore a travelling cap of the colour of gingerbread, and had rather an unhappy expression about the corners of his mouth; partly from not having yet made his dinner, and partly from not having been able to get on at a greater rate than seven miles an hour. Not that he had any other cause for haste than an Englishman's usual hurry to get to the end of a journey; or, to use the regular phrase, "to get on."

After some time the servant returned from the stable with as sour a look as his master.

"Are the horses ready, John?"

"No, sir—I never saw such a place. There's no getting any thing done. I think your honour had better step into the house and get something to eat; it will be a long while before we get to Fundy."

"D—n the house—it's a mere trick—I'll not eat any thing, just to spite them," said the Englishman, still more crusty at the prospect of being so long without his dinner.

"They say your honour's very wrong," said John, "to set off at this late hour. The road's full of highwaymen."

"Mere tales to get custom."

"The estafette which passed us was stopped by a whole gang," said John, increasing his emphasis with each additional piece of information.

"I don't believe a word of it."

"They robbed him of his breeches," said John, giving at the same time a hitch to his own waistband.

"All humbug!"

Here the dark, handsome young man stepped forward and addressing the Englishman very politely in broken English, invited him to partake of a repast he was about to make. "Thank'ee," said the Englishman, thrusting his hands deeper into his pockets, and casting a slight side glance of suspicion at the young man, as if he thought from his civility he must have a design upon his purse.

"We shall be most happy if you will do us that favour," said the lady, in her soft Venetian dialect. There was a sweetness in her accents that was most persuasive. The Englishman cast a look upon her countenance; her beauty was still more eloquent. His features instantly relaxed. He made an attempt at a civil bow. "With great pleasure, signora," said he.

In short, the eagerness to "get on" was suddenly slackened; the determination to famish himself as far as Fondi by way of punishing the landlord was abandoned; John chose the best apartment in the inn for his master's reception, and preparations were made to remain there until morning.

The carriage was unpacked of such of its contents as were indispensable for the night. There was the usual parade of trunks, and writing desks, and portfolios, and dressing boxes, and those other oppressive conveniencies which burthen a comfortable man. The observant loiterers about the inn door, wrapped up in great dirt coloured cloaks, with only a hawk's eye uncovered, made many remarks to each other on this quantity of luggage that seemed enough for an army. And the domestics of the inn talked with wonder of the splendid dressing case, with its gold and silver furniture that was spread out on the toilette table, and the bag of gold that chinked as it was taken out of the trunk. The strange

"Milor's" wealth, and the treasures he carried about him, were the talk, that evening, over all Terracina.

The Englishman took some time to make his ablutions and arrange his dress for table, and after considerable labour and effort in putting himself at his ease, made his appearance, with stiff white cravat, his clothes free from the least speck of dust, and adjusted with precision. He made a formal bow on entering, which no doubt he meant to be cordial, but which any one else would have considered cool, and took his seat.

The supper, as it was termed by the Italian, or dinner, as the Englishman called it, was now served. Heaven and earth, and the waters under the earth, had been moved to furnish it, for there were birds of the air and beasts of the field and fish of the sea. The Englishman's servant, too, had turned the kitchen topsy turvy in his zeal to cook his master a beefsteak; and made his appearance loaded with ketchup, and soy, and Cayenne pepper, and Harvey sauce, and a bottle of port wine, from that warehouse, the carriage, in which his master seemed desirous of carrying England about the world with him. Every thing, however, according to the Englishman, was execrable. The tureen of soup was a black sea, with livers and limbs and fragments of all kinds of birds and beasts, floating like wrecks about it. A meagre winged animal, which my host called a delicate chicken, was too delicate for his stomach, for it had evidently died of a consumption. The macaroni was smoked. The beefsteak was tough buffalo's flesh, and the countenance of mine host confirmed the assertion. Nothing seemed to hit his palate but a dish of stewed eels, of which he ate with great relish, but had nearly refunded them when told that they were vipers, caught among the rocks of Terracina, and esteemed a great delicacy.

In short, the Englishman ate and growled, and ate and growled, like a cat eating in company, pronouncing himself poisoned by every dish, yet eating on in defiance of death and the doctor. The Venetian lady, not accustomed to English travellers, almost repented having persuaded him to the meal; for though very gracious to her, he was so crusty to all the world beside, that she stood in awe of him. Nothing, how-ever, conquers John Bull's crustiness sooner than eating, whatever may be the cookery; and nothing brings him into good humour with his company sooner than eating together; the Englishman, therefore, had not half finished his repast and his bottle, before he began to think the Venetian a very tolerable fellow for a foreigner, and his wife almost handsome enough to be an Englishwoman.

In the course of the repast the usual topics of travellers were discussed, and among others, the reports of robbers which harassed the mind of the fair Venetian. The landlord and the waiter dipped into the conversation with that familiarity permitted on the continent, and served up so many bloody tales as they served up the dishes, that they almost frightened away the poor lady's appetite. The Englishman, who had a national antipathy to every thing technically called "humbug," listened to them all with a certain screw of the mouth, expressive of incredulity. There was the well known story of the school of Terracina, captured by the robbers; and one of the scholars coolly massacred, in order to bring the parents to terms for the ransom of the rest. And another, of a gentleman of Rome, who received his son's ear in a letter, with information, that his son would be remitted to him in this way, by instalments, until he paid the required ransom.

The fair Venetian shuddered as she heard these tales. The landlord, like a true narrator of the terrible, doubled the dose when he saw how it operated. He was just proceeding to relate the misfortunes of a great English lord and his family, when the Englishman, tired of his volubility, testily interrupted him, and pronounced these accounts mere travellers' tales, or the exaggerations of ignorant peasants and designing innkeepers. The landlord was indignant at the doubt levelled at his stories, and the inuendo levelled at his cloth; he cited, in corroboration, half a dozen tales still more terrible.

"I don't believe a word of them," said the Englishman.

"But the robbers have been tried and executed."

"All a farce!"

"But their heads are stuck up along the road."

"Old skulls accumulated during a century."

The landlord muttered to himself as he went out at the door, "San Gennaro, quanto sono singolari questi Inglesi."

A fresh hubbub outside of the inn announced the arrival of more travellers; and from the variety of voices, or rather clamours, the clattering of hoofs, the rattling of wheels, and the general uproar both within and without, the arrival seemed to be numerous. It was in fact the procaccio, and its convoy—a kind of caravan which sets out on certain days for the transportation of merchandise, with an escort of soldiery to protect it from the robbers. Travellers avail themselves of its protection, and a long file of carriages generally accompany it. A considerable time elapsed before either landlord or waiter returned, being hurried hither and thither by that tempest of noise and bustle which takes place in an Italian inn on the arrival of any considerable accession of custom. When mine host reappeared, there was a smile of triumph on his countenance.—"Perhaps," said he, as he cleared the table, "perhaps the signor has not heard of what has happened."

"What?" said the Englishman, drily.

"Why, the procaccio has brought accounts of fresh exploits of the robbers, signor."

"Pish!"

"There's more news of the English Milor and his family," said the host, exultingly.

"An English lord—What English lord?"

"Milor Popkin."

"Lord Popkins? I never heard of such a title!"

"*O Sicuro*—a great nobleman who passed through here lately with his mi ladi and her daughters—a magnifico—one of the grand councillors of London—un almanno."

"Almanno—almanno?—tut! he means alderman."

"Sicuro, aldermanno Popkin, and the principessa Popkin, and the signorine Popkin!" said mine host, triumphantly. He now put himself into an attitude, and would have launched into a full detail, had he not been thwarted by the Englishman, who seemed determined neither to credit nor indulge him in his stories, but drily motioned for him to clear away the table. An Italian tongue, however, is not easily checked: that of mine host continued to wag with increasing volubility as he conveyed the reliques of the repast out of the room, and the last that could be distinguished of his voice, as it died away along the corridor, was the iteration of the favourite word Popkin—Popkin—Popkin—pop—pop—pop.

The arrival of the procaccio had indeed filled the house

with stories as it had with guests. The Englishman and his companions walked after supper up and down the large hall, or common room of the inn, which ran through the centre of the building. It was spacious, and somewhat dirty, with tables placed in various parts, at which groups of travellers were seated; while others strolled about, waiting in famished impatience for their evening's meal.

It was a heterogeneous assemblage of people of all ranks and countries, who had arrived in all kinds of vehicles. Though distinct knots of travellers, yet the travelling together under one common escort had jumbled them into a certain degree of companionship on the road: besides, on the continent travellers are always familiar, and nothing is more motley than the groups which gather casually together in sociable conversation in the public rooms of inns. Their formidable number and the formidable guard of the procaccio had prevented any molestation from banditti; but every party of travellers had its tale of wonder, and one carriage vied with another in its budget of assertions and surmises. Fierce, whiskered faces had been seen peering over the rocks; carbines and stilettos gleaming from among the bushes; suspicious looking fellows, with flapped hats, and scowling eyes, had occasionally reconnoitred a straggling carriage, but had disappeared on seeing the guard.

The fair Venetian listened to all these stories with that avidity with which we always pamper any feeling of alarm. Even the Englishman began to feel interested in the common topic, and desirous of gaining more correct information than mere flying reports. He mingled in one of the groups which appeared to be the most respectable, and which was assembled round a tall thin Italian, with long aquiline nose, a high forehead, and lively prominent eye, beaming from under a green velvet travelling cap, with gold tassel. He was of Rome; a surgeon by profession, a poet by choice, and something of an improvvisatore.

In the present instance, however, he was talking in plain prose, but holding forth with the fluency of one who talks well and likes to exert his talent. A question or two from the Englishman drew copious replies; for an Englishman sociable among strangers is regarded as a phenomenon on the continent, and always treated with attention for the rarity's sake. The improvvisatore gave much the same account of the banditti that I have already furnished.

"But why does not the police exert itself and root them out?" demanded the Englishman.

"Because the police is too weak and the banditti are too strong," replied the other. "To root them out would be a more difficult task than you imagine. They are connected and almost identified with the mountain peasantry and the people of the villages. The numerous bands have an understanding with each other, and with the country round. A *gens d'armes* cannot stir without their being aware of it. They have their scouts every where, who lurk about towns, villages, and inns,—mingle in every crowd, and pervade every place of resort. I should not be surprised if some one should be supervising us at this moment."

The fair Venetian looked round fearfully and turned pale.

Here the improvvisatore was interrupted by a lively Neapolitan lawyer. "By the way," said he, "I recollect a little adventure of a learned doctor, a friend of mine, which happened in this very neighbourhood; not far from the ruins of Theodoric's Castle, which are on the top of those great, rocky heights above the town."

A wish was of course expressed to hear the adventure of the doctor by all excepting the improvvisatore, who being fond of talking and of hearing himself talk, and accustomed moreover to harangue without interruption, looked rather annoyed at being checked when in full career.

The Neapolitan, however, took no notice of his chagrin, but related the following anecdote.

The Adventure of the Little Antiquary

My friend the doctor was a thorough antiquary: a little rusty, musty old fellow, always groping among ruins. He relished a building as you Englishmen relish a cheese,—the more mouldy and crumbling it was, the more it suited his taste. A shell of an old nameless temple, or the cracked walls of a broken down amphitheatre, would throw him into raptures; and he took more delight in these crusts and cheese parings of antiquity than in the best conditioned modern palaces.

He was a curious collector of coins also, and had just gained an accession of wealth that almost turned his brain. He had picked up, for instance, several Roman Consulars, half a Roman As, two Punics, which had doubtless belonged to the soldiers of Hannibal, having been found on the very spot where they had encamped among the Apennines. He had, moreover, one Samnite, struck after the Social War, and a Philistis, a queen that never existed; but above all, he valued himself upon a coin, indescribable to any but the initiated in these matters, bearing a cross on one side, and a pegasus on the other, and which, by some antiquarian logic, the little man adduced as an historical document, illustrating the progress of christianity.

All these precious coins he carried about him in a leathern purse, buried deep in a pocket of his little black breeches.

The last maggot he had taken into his brain was to hunt after the ancient cities of the Pelasgi which are said to exist to this day among the mountains of the Abruzzi; but about which a singular degree of obscurity prevails.* He had made many discoveries concerning them, and had recorded a great many valuable notes and memorandums on the subject, in a voluminous book, which he always carried about with him, either for the purpose of frequent reference, or through fear lest the precious document should fall into the hands of brother antiquaries. He had therefore a large pocket in the

---

*Among the many fond speculations of antiquaries is that of the existence of traces of the ancient Pelasgian cities in the Apennines; and many a wistful eye is cast by the traveller, versed in antiquarian lore, at the richly wooded mountains of the Abruzzi, as a forbidden fairy land of research. These spots, so beautiful yet so inaccessible, from the rudeness of their inhabitants and the hordes of banditti which infest them, are a region of fable to the learned. Sometimes a wealthy virtuoso, whose purse and whose consequence could command a military escort, has penetrated to some individual point among the mountains; and sometimes a wandering artist or student, under protection of poverty or insignificance, has brought away some vague account, only calculated to give a keener edge to curiosity and conjecture.

By those who maintain the existence of the Pelasgian cities, it is affirmed, that the formation of the different kingdoms in the Peloponnesus gradually

skirt of his coat, where he bore about this inestimable tome, banging against his rear as he walked.

Thus heavily laden with the spoils of antiquity, the good little man, during a sojourn at Terracina, mounted one day the rocky cliffs which overhang the town, to visit the castle of Theodoric. He was groping about these ruins, towards the hour of sunset, buried in his reflections,—his wits no doubt wool gathering among the Goths and Romans, when he heard footsteps behind him.

He turned and beheld five or six young fellows, of rough, saucy demeanour, clad in a singular manner, half peasant, half huntsman, with carbines in their hands. Their whole appearance and carriage left him no doubt into what company he had fallen.

The doctor was a feeble little man, poor in look and poorer in purse. He had but little gold or silver to be robbed of; but then he had his curious ancient coin in his breeches pocket. He had, moreover, certain other valuables, such as an old silver watch, thick as a turnip, with figures on it large enough for a clock, and a set of seals at the end of a steel chain, dangling half way down to his knees. All these were of precious esteem, being family reliques. He had also a seal ring, a veritable antique intaglio, that covered half his knuckles. It was a Venus, which the old man almost worshipped with the zeal of

---

caused the expulsion thence of the Pelasgi; but that their great migration may be dated from the finishing the wall round Acropolis, and that at this period they came into Italy. To these, in the spirit of theory, they would ascribe the introduction of the elegant arts into the country. It is evident, however, that, as barbarians flying before the first dawn of civilization, they could bring little with them superior to the inventions of the aborigines, and nothing that would have survived to the antiquarian through such a lapse of ages. It would appear more probable, that these cities, improperly termed Pelasgian, were coeval with many that have been discovered. The romantic Aricia, built by Hippolytus before the siege of Troy, and the poetic Tibur, Æsculate and Proenes, built by Telegonus after the dispersion of the Greeks. These, lying contiguous to inhabited and cultivated spots, have been discovered. There are others, too, on the ruins of which the later and more civilized Grecian colonists have engrafted themselves, and which have become known by their merits or their medals. But that there are many still undiscovered, imbedded in the Abruzzi, it is the delight of the antiquarians to fancy. Strange that such a virgin soil for research, such an unknown realm of knowledge, should at this day remain in the very centre of hackneyed Italy!

a voluptuary. But what he most valued was, his inestimable collection of hints relative to the Pelasgian cities, which he would gladly have given all the money in his pocket to have had safe at the bottom of his trunk in Terracina.

However, he plucked up a stout heart; at least as stout a heart as he could, seeing that he was but a puny little man at the best of times. So, he wished the hunters a "buon giorno." They returned his salutation, giving the old gentleman a sociable slap on the back that made his heart leap into his throat.

They fell into conversation, and walked for some time together among the heights, the doctor wishing them all the while at the bottom of the crater of Vesuvius. At length they came to a small osteria on the mountain, where they proposed to enter and have a cup of wine together. The doctor consented; though he would as soon have been invited to drink hemlock.

One of the gang remained sentinel at the door; the others swaggered into the house; stood their guns in a corner of the room; and each drawing a pistol or stiletto out of his belt, laid it upon the table. They now drew benches round the board, called lustily for wine, and hailing the doctor as though he had been a boon companion of long standing, insisted upon his sitting down and making merry. The worthy man complied with forced grimace, but with fear and trembling; sitting uneasily on the edge of his chair; eyeing ruefully the black muzzled pistols, and cold, naked stilettos; and supping down heartburn with every drop of liquor. His new comrades, however, pushed the bottle bravely, and plied him vigorously; they sang, they laughed, told excellent stories of their robberies and combats, mingled with many ruffian jokes; and the little doctor was fain to laugh at all their cutthroat pleasantries, though his heart was dying away at the very bottom of his bosom.

By their own account they were young men from the villages, who had recently taken up this line of life out of the wild caprice of youth. They talked of their murderous exploits as a sportsman talks of his amusements. To shoot down a traveller seemed of little more consequence to them than to shoot a hare. They spoke with rapture of the glorious roving life they led; free as birds; here today, gone tomorrow; ranging the forests, climbing the rocks, scouring the valleys; the world their own wherever they could lay hold of it; full purses, merry companions; pretty women.——The little antiquary got fuddled with their talk and their wine, for they did not spare bumpers. He half forgot his fears, his seal ring and his family watch; even the treatise on the Pelasgian cities which was warming under him, for a time faded from his memory, in the glowing picture which they drew. He declares that he no longer wonders at the prevalence of this robber mania among the mountains; for he felt at the time, that had he been a young man and a strong man, and had there been no danger of the galleys in the back ground, he should have been half tempted himself to turn bandit.

At length the hour of separating arrived. The doctor was suddenly called to himself and his fears, by seeing the robbers resume their weapons. He now quaked for his valuables, and above all for his antiquarian treatise. He endeavoured, however, to look cool and unconcerned; and drew from out of his deep pocket a long, lank, leathern purse, far gone in consumption, at the bottom of which a few coin chinked with the trembling of his hand.

The chief of the party observed this movement; and laying his hand upon the antiquary's shoulder—"Harkee! Signor Dottore!" said he, "we have drunk together as friends and comrades, let us part as such. We understand you; we know who and what you are; for we know who every body is that sleeps at Terracina, or that puts foot upon the road. You are a rich man, but you carry all your wealth in your head. We cannot get at it, and we should not know what to do with it, if we could. I see you are uneasy about your ring; but don't worry yourself; it is not worth taking; you think it an antique, but it's a counterfeit—a mere sham."

Here the ire of the antiquary arose: the doctor forgot himself in his zeal for the character of his ring. Heaven and earth! his Venus a sham! Had they pronounced the wife of his bosom "no better than she should be," he could not have been more indignant. He fired up in vindication of his intaglio.

"Nay, nay," continued the robber, "we have no time to dispute about it. Value it as you please. Come, you're a brave little old signor—one more cup of wine and we'll pay the reckoning. No compliments—You shall not pay a grain— You are our guest—I insist upon it. So—now make the best of your way back to Terracina; it's growing late—buono viaggio!—and hark'ee, take care how you wander among these mountains,—you may not always fall into such good company."

They shouldered their guns, sprang gaily up the rocks, and the little doctor hobbled back to Terracina, rejoicing that the robbers had left his watch, his coins, and his treatise unmolested, but still indignant that they should have pronounced his Venus an imposter.

———

The improvvisatore had shown many symptoms of impatience during this recital. He saw his theme in danger of being taken out of his hands, which to an able talker is always a grievance; but to an improvvisatore is an absolute calamity: and then for it to be taken away by a Neapolitan was still more vexatious; the inhabitants of the different Italian states having an implacable jealousy of each other in all things, great and small. He took advantage of the first pause of the Neapolitan to catch hold again of the thread of the conversation.

"As I observed before," said he, "the prowlings of the banditti are so extensive; they are so much in league with one another, and so interwoven with various ranks of society"——

"For that matter," said the Neapolitan, "I have heard that your government has had some understanding with these gentry, or at least has winked at their misdeeds."

"My government?" said the Roman, impatiently.

"Aye—they say that Cardinal Gonsalvi"——

"Hush!" said the Roman, holding up his finger, and rolling his large eyes about the room.

"Nay—I only repeat what I heard commonly rumoured in Rome," replied the Neapolitan, sturdily. "It was openly said that the Cardinal had been up to the mountains, and had an interview with some of the chiefs. And I have been told, moreover, that while honest people have been kicking their heels in the Cardinal's anti-chamber, waiting by the hour for admittance, one of these stiletto looking fellows has elbowed his way through the crowd, and entered without ceremony into the Cardinal's presence."

"I know," observed the improvvisatore, "that there have been such reports; and it is not impossible that government may have made use of these men at particular periods, such as at the time of your late abortive revolution, when your carbonari were so busy with their machinations all over the country. The information which such men could collect, who were familiar, not merely with the recesses and secret places of the mountains, but also with the dark and dangerous recesses of society, who knew every suspicious character, and all his movements and all his lurkings; in a word, who knew all that was plotting in the world of mischief; the utility of such men as instruments in the hands of government was too obvious to be overlooked, and Cardinal Gonsalvi as a politic statesman may perhaps have made use of them. Besides, he knew that with all their atrocities the robbers were always respectful towards the church, and devout in their religion."

"Religion!—religion?" echoed the Englishman.

"Yes—religion!" repeated the Roman. "They have each their patron saint. They will cross themselves and say their prayers, whenever, in their mountain haunts, they hear the matin or the *ave maria* bells sounding from the valleys; and will often descend from their retreats, and run imminent risks to visit some favourite shrine. I recollect an instance in point: I was one evening in the village of Frascati, which stands on the beautiful brow of hills rising from the Campagna, just below the Abruzzi mountains. The people, as is usual in fine evenings in our Italian towns and villages, were recreating themselves in the open air, and chatting in groups in the public square. While I was conversing with a knot of friends, I noticed a tall fellow, wrapped in a great mantle, passing across the square, but skulking along in the dusk, as if anxious to avoid observation. The people drew back as he passed. It was whispered to me that he was a notorious bandit."

"But why was he not immediately seized?" said the Englishman.

"Because it was nobody's business; because nobody wished to incur the vengeance of his comrades; because there were not sufficient *gens d'armes* near to insure security against the numbers of desperadoes he might have at hand; because the *gens d'armes* might not have received particular instructions with respect to him, and might not feel disposed to engage in a hazardous conflict without compulsion. In short, I might give you a thousand reasons, rising out of the state of our government and manners, not one of which after all might appear satisfactory."

The Englishman shrugged his shoulders, with an air of contempt.

"I have been told," added the Roman, rather quickly, "that even in your metropolis of London, notorious thieves, well known to the police as such, walk the streets at noon day, in search of their prey, and are not molested unless caught in the very act of robbery."

The Englishman gave another shrug, but with a different expression.

"Well, sir, I fixed my eye on this daring wolf thus prowling through the fold, and saw him enter a church. I was curious to witness his devotions. You know our spacious, magnificent churches. The one in which he entered was vast and shrowded in the dusk of evening. At the extremity of the long aisles a couple of tapers feebly glimmered on the grand altar. In one of the side chapels was a votive candle placed before the image of a saint. Before this image the robber had prostrated himself. His mantle partly falling off from his shoulders as he knelt, revealed a form of Herculean strength; a stiletto and pistol glittered in his belt, and the light falling on his countenance showed features not unhandsome, but strongly and fiercely charactered. As he prayed he became vehemently agitated; his lips quivered; sighs and murmurs, almost groans burst from him; he beat his breast with violence, then clasped his hands and wrung them convulsively as he extended them towards the image. Never had I seen such a terrific picture of remorse. I felt fearful of being discovered watching him, and withdrew. Shortly afterwards I saw him issue from the church, wrapped in his mantle; he recrossed the square, and no doubt returned to his mountain with disburthened conscience, ready to incur a fresh arrear of crime."

Here the Neapolitan was about to get hold of the conversation, and had just preluded with the ominous remark, "That puts me in mind of a circumstance," when the improv-visatore, too adroit to suffer himself to be again superseded, went on, pretending not to hear the interruption.

"Among the many circumstances connected with the ban-ditti which serve to render the traveller uneasy and insecure, is the understanding which they sometimes have with innkeep-ers. Many an isolated inn among the lonely parts of the Ro-man territories, and especially about the mountains, are of a dangerous and perfidious character. They are places where the banditti gather information, and where the unwary traveller, remote from hearing or assistance, is betrayed to the midnight dagger. The robberies committed at such inns are often ac-companied by the most atrocious murders; for it is only by the complete extermination of their victims that the assassins can escape detection. I recollect an adventure," added he, "which occurred at one of these solitary mountain inns, which, as you all seem in a mood for robber anecdotes, may not be uninteresting."

Having secured the attention and awakened the curiosity of the bystanders, he paused for a moment, rolled up his large eyes as improvvisatori are apt to do when they would rec-ollect an impromptu, and then related with great dramatic effect the following story, which had, doubtless, been well prepared and digested beforehand.

The Belated Travellers

It was late one evening that a carriage, drawn by mules, slowly toiled its way up one of the passes of the Apennines. It was through one of the wildest defiles, where a hamlet oc-curred only at distant intervals, perched on the summit of some rocky height, or the white towers of a convent peeped out from among the thick mountain foliage. The carriage was of ancient and ponderous construction. Its faded embellish-ments spoke of former splendor, but its crazy springs and axletrees creaked out the tale of present decline. Within was seated a tall, thin old gentleman, in a kind of military travelling dress, and a foraging cap trimmed with fur, though the grey locks which stole from under it hinted that his fighting days were over. Beside him was a pale, beautiful girl of eighteen, dressed in something of a northern or Polish costume. One servant was seated in front, a rusty, crusty looking fellow, with a scar across his face; an orange-tawny *schnur-bart*, or pair of mustachios, bristling from under his nose, and altogether the air of an old soldier.

It was, in fact, the equipage of a Polish nobleman; a wreck of one of those princely families once of almost oriental magnificence, but broken down and impoverished by the disasters of Poland. The Count, like many other generous spirits, had been found guilty of the crime of patriotism, and was, in a manner, an exile from his country. He had resided for some time in the first cities of Italy for the education of his daughter, in whom all his cares and pleasures were now centred. He had taken her into society, where her beauty and her accomplishments gained her many admirers; and had she not been the daughter of a poor broken down Polish nobleman, it is more than probable many would have contended for her hand. Suddenly, however, her health became delicate and drooping; her gaiety fled with the roses of her cheek, and she sank into silence and debility. The old Count saw the change with the solicitude of a parent. "We must try a change of air and scene," said he; and in a few days the old family carriage was rumbling among the Apennines.

Their only attendant was the veteran Caspar, who had been born in the family, and grown rusty in its service. He had followed his master in all his fortunes; had fought by his side; had stood over him when fallen in battle; and had received, in his defence, the sabre cut which added such grimness to his countenance. He was now his valet, his steward, his butler, his factotum. The only being that rivalled his master in his affections was his youthful mistress; she had grown up under his eye. He had led her by the hand when she was a child, and he now looked upon her with the fondness of a parent; nay, he even took the freedom of a parent in giving his blunt opinion on all matters which he thought were for her good; and felt a parent's vanity in seeing her gazed at and admired.

The evening was thickening: they had been for some time

passing through narrow gorges of the mountains, along the edge of a tumbling stream. The scenery was lonely and savage. The rocks often beetled over the road, with flocks of white goats browsing on their brinks, and gazing down upon the travellers. They had between two and three leagues yet to go before they could reach any village; yet the muleteer, Pietro, a tippling old fellow, who had refreshed himself at the last halting place with a more than ordinary quantity of wine, sat singing and talking alternately to his mules, and suffering them to lag on at a snail's pace, in spite of the frequent entreaties of the Count and maledictions of Caspar.

The clouds began to roll in heavy masses among the mountains, shrouding their summits from view. The air was damp and chilly. The Count's solicitude on his daughter's account overcame his usual patience. He leaned from the carriage, and called to old Pietro in an angry tone.

"Forward!" said he. "It will be midnight before we arrive at our inn."

"Yonder it is, Signor," said the muleteer.

"Where?" demanded the Count.

"Yonder," said Pietro, pointing to a desolate pile about a quarter of a league distant.

"That the place?—why, it looks more like a ruin than an inn. I thought we were to put up for the night at a comfortable village."

Here Pietro uttered a string of piteous exclamations and ejaculations, such as are ever at the tip of the tongue of a delinquent muleteer. "Such roads! and such mountains! and then his poor animals were wayworn, and leg weary; they would fall lame; they would never be able to reach the village. And then what could his Eccellenza wish for better than the inn; a perfect castello—a palazza—and such people!—and such a larder!—and such beds!—His Eccellenza might fare as sumptuously and sleep as soundly there as a prince!"

The Count was easily persuaded, for he was anxious to get his daughter out of the night air; so in a little while the old carriage rattled and jingled into the great gateway of the inn.

The building did certainly in some measure answer to the muleteer's description. It was large enough for either castle or palazza; built in a strong, but simple and almost rude style;

with a great quantity of waste room. It had, in fact, been, in former times, a hunting seat for one of the Italian princes. There was space enough within its walls and outbuildings to have accommodated a little army.

A scanty household seemed now to people this dreary mansion. The faces that presented themselves on the arrival of the travellers were begrimed with dirt, and scowling in their expression. They all knew old Pietro, however, and gave him a welcome as he entered, singing and talking, and almost whooping, into the gateway.

The hostess of the inn waited herself on the Count and his daughter, to show them the apartments. They were conducted through a long gloomy corridor, and then through a suite of chambers opening into each other, with lofty ceilings, and great beams extending across them. Every thing, however, had a wretched, squalid look. The walls were damp and bare, excepting that here and there hung some great painting, large enough for a chapel, and blackened out of all distinctness.

They chose two bedrooms, one within another; the inner one for the daughter. The bedsteads were massive and misshapen; but on examining the beds, so vaunted by old Pietro, they found them stuffed with fibres of hemp, knotted in great lumps. The Count shrugged his shoulders, but there was no choice left.

The chilliness of the apartments crept to their bones; and they were glad to return to a common chamber, or kind of hall, where there was a fire burning in a huge cavern, miscalled a chimney. A quantity of green wood, just thrown on, puffed out volumes of smoke. The room corresponded to the rest of the mansion. The floor was paved and dirty. A great oaken table stood in the centre, immoveable from its size and weight.

The only thing that contradicted this prevalent air of indigence was the dress of the hostess. She was a slattern of course; yet her garments, though dirty and negligent, were of costly materials. She wore several rings of great value on her fingers, and jewels in her ears, and round her neck was a string of large pearls, to which was attached a sparkling crucifix. She had the remains of beauty; yet there was something in the expression of her countenance that inspired the young lady with singular aversion. She was officious and obsequious in her attentions, and both the Count and his daughter were relieved when she consigned them to the care of a dark, sullen looking servant maid, and went off to superintend the supper.

Caspar was indignant at the muleteer for having, either through negligence or design, subjected his master and mistress to such quarters; and vowed by his mustachios to have revenge on the old varlet the moment they were safe out from among the mountains. He kept up a continual quarrel with the sulky servant maid, which only served to increase the sinister expression with which she regarded the travellers, from under her strong dark eyebrows.

As to the Count, he was a good humoured, passive traveller. Perhaps real misfortunes had subdued his spirit, and rendered him tolerant of many of those petty evils which make prosperous men miserable. He drew a large, broken arm chair to the fireside for his daughter, and another for himself, and seizing an enormous pair of tongs, endeavoured to rearrange the wood so as to produce a blaze. His efforts, however, were only repaid by thicker puffs of smoke, which almost overcame the good gentleman's patience. He would draw back, cast a look upon his delicate daughter, then upon the cheerless, squalid apartment, and shrugging his shoulders, would give a fresh stir to the fire.

Of all the miseries of a comfortless inn, however, there is none greater than sulky attendance: the good Count for some time bore the smoke in silence, rather than address himself to the scowling servant maid. At length he was compelled to beg for drier firewood. The woman retired muttering. On re-entering the room hastily, with an armful of faggots, her foot slipped; she fell, and striking her head against the corner of a chair, cut her temple severely. The blow stunned her for a time, and the wound bled profusely. When she recovered, she found the Count's daughter administering to her wound, and binding it up with her own handkerchief. It was such an attention as any woman of ordinary feeling would have yielded; but perhaps there was something in the appearance of the lovely being who bent over her, or in the tones of her voice, that touched the heart of the woman, unused to be ministered to by such hands. Certain it is, she was strongly affected. She caught the delicate hand of the Polonaise, and pressed it fervently to her lips:

"May San Francesco watch over you, Signora!" exclaimed she.

A new arrival broke the stillness of the inn. It was a Spanish princess with a numerous retinue. The court yard was in an uproar; the house in a bustle; the landlady hurried to attend such distinguished guests; and the poor Count and his daughter, and their supper, were for the moment forgotten. The veteran Caspar muttered Polish maledictions enough to agonize an Italian ear; but it was impossible to convince the hostess of the superiority of his old master and young mistress to the whole nobility of Spain.

The noise of the arrival had attracted the daughter to the window just as the new comers had alighted. A young cavalier sprang out of the carriage, and handed out the princess. The latter was a little shrivelled old lady, with a face of parchment, and a sparkling black eye; she was richly and gaily dressed, and walked with the assistance of a gold headed cane as high as herself. The young man was tall and elegantly formed. The Count's daughter shrunk back at sight of him, though the deep frame of the window screened her from observation. She gave a heavy sigh as she closed the casement. What that sigh meant I cannot say. Perhaps it was at the contrast between the splendid equipage of the princess, and the crazy, rheumatic looking old vehicle of her father, which stood hard by. Whatever might be the reason, the young lady closed the casement with a sigh. She returned to her chair;— a slight shivering passed over her delicate frame; she leaned her elbow on the arm of the chair; rested her pale cheek in the palm of her hand, and looked mournfully into the fire.

The Count thought she appeared paler than usual.—

"Does any thing ail thee, my child?" said he.

"Nothing, dear father!" replied she, laying her hand within his, and looking up smiling in his face; but as she said so, a treacherous tear rose suddenly to her eye, and she turned away her head.

"The air of the window has chilled thee," said the Count, fondly, "but a good night's rest will make all well again."

The supper table was at length laid, and the supper about to be served, when the hostess appeared, with her usual obsequiousness, apologizing for showing in the new comers; but the night air was cold, and there was no other chamber in the inn with a fire in it.—She had scarcely made the apology when the Princess entered, leaning on the arm of the elegant young man.

The Count immediately recognized her for a lady whom he had met frequently in society both at Rome and Naples; and at whose conversaziones, in fact, he had constantly been invited. The cavalier, too, was her nephew and heir, who had been greatly admired in the gay circles both for his merits and prospects, and who had once been on a visit at the same time with his daughter and himself at the villa of a nobleman near Naples. Report had recently affianced him to a rich Spanish heiress.

The meeting was agreeable to both the Count and the Princess. The former was a gentleman of the old school, courteous in the extreme; the Princess had been a belle in her youth, and a woman of fashion all her life, and liked to be attended to.

The young man approached the daughter, and began something of a complimentary observation; but his manner was embarrassed, and his compliment ended in an indistinct murmur, while the daughter bowed without looking up, moved her lips without articulating a word, and sank again into her chair, where she sat gazing into the fire, with a thousand varying expressions passing over her countenance.

This singular greeting of the young people was not perceived by the old ones, who were occupied at the time with their own courteous salutations. It was arranged that they should sup together; and as the Princess travelled with her own cook, a very tolerable supper soon smoked upon the board; this, too, was assisted by choice wines, and liqueurs, and delicate confitures brought from one of her carriages; for she was a veteran epicure, and curious in her relish for the good things of this world. She was, in fact, a vivacious little old lady, who mingled the woman of dissipation with the devotee. She was actually on her way to Loretto to expiate a long life of gallantries and peccadilloes by a rich offering at the holy shrine. She was, to be sure, rather a luxurious penitent, and a contrast to the primitive pilgrims, with scrip, and staff, and cockleshell; but then it would be unreasonable to expect such self denial from people of fashion; and there was not a doubt of the ample efficacy of the rich crucifixes, and golden vessels, and jewelled ornaments, which she was bearing to the treasury of the blessed Virgin.

The Princess and the Count chatted much during supper about the scenes and society in which they had mingled, and did not notice that they had all the conversation to themselves: the young people were silent and constrained. The daughter ate nothing, in spite of the politeness of the Princess, who continually pressed her to taste one or other of the delicacies. The Count shook his head:

"She is not well this evening," said he. "I thought she would have fainted just now as she was looking out of the window at your carriage on its arrival."

A crimson glow flushed to the very temples of the daughter; but she leaned over her plate, and her tresses cast a shade over her countenance.

When supper was over, they drew their chairs about the great fireplace. The flame and smoke had subsided, and a heap of glowing embers diffused a grateful warmth. A guitar, which had been brought from the Count's carriage, leaned against the wall; the Princess perceived it: "Can we not have a little music before parting for the night?" demanded she.

The Count was proud of his daughter's accomplishment, and joined in the request. The young man made an effort of politeness, and taking up the guitar presented it, though in an embarrassed manner, to the fair musician. She would have declined it, but was too much confused to do so; indeed, she was so nervous and agitated, that she dared not trust her voice to make an excuse. She touched the instrument with a faltering hand, and, after preluding a little, accompanied herself in several Polish airs. Her father's eyes glistened as he sat gazing on her. Even the crusty Caspar lingered in the room, partly through a fondness for the music of his native country, but chiefly through his pride in the musician. Indeed, the melody of the voice, and the delicacy of the touch, were enough to have charmed more fastidious ears. The little Princess nodded her head and tapped her hand to the music, though exceedingly out of time; while the nephew sat buried in profound contemplation of a black picture on the opposite wall.

"And now," said the Count, patting her cheek fondly, "one more favour. Let the princess hear that little Spanish air you were so fond of. You can't think," added he, "what a proficiency she made in your language; though she has been a sad girl and neglected it of late."

The colour flushed the pale cheek of the daughter; she hesitated, murmured something; but with sudden effort collected herself, struck the guitar boldly, and began. It was a Spanish romance, with something of love and melancholy in it. She gave the first stanza with great expression, for the tremulous, melting tones of her voice went to the heart; but her articulation failed, her lip quivered, the song died away, and she burst into tears.

The Count folded her tenderly in his arms. "Thou art not well, my child," said he, "and I am tasking thee cruelly. Retire to thy chamber, and God bless thee!" She bowed to the company without raising her eyes, and glided out of the room.

The Count shook his head as the door closed. "Something is the matter with that child," said he, "which I cannot divine. She has lost all health and spirits lately. She was always a tender flower, and I had much pains to rear her. Excuse a father's foolishness," continued he, "but I have seen much trouble in my family; and this poor girl is all that is now left to me; and she used to be so lively—"

"May be she's in love!" said the little Princess, with a shrewd nod of the head.

"Impossible!" replied the good Count artlessly. "She has never mentioned a word of such a thing to me."

How little did the worthy gentleman dream of the thousand cares, and griefs, and mighty love concerns which agitate a virgin heart, and which a timid girl scarce breathes unto herself.

The nephew of the Princess rose abruptly and walked about the room.

When she found herself alone in her chamber, the feelings of the young lady, so long restrained, broke forth with violence. She opened the casement, that the cool air might blow upon her throbbing temples. Perhaps there was some little pride or pique mingled with her emotions; though her gentle nature did not seem calculated to harbour any such angry inmate.

"He saw me weep!" said she, with a sudden mantling of the cheek, and a swelling of the throat,—"but no matter!—no matter!"

And so saying, she threw her white arms across the window frame, buried her face in them, and abandoned herself to an agony of tears. She remained lost in a reverie, until the sound of her father's and Caspar's voices in the adjoining room gave token that the party had retired for the night. The lights gleaming from window to window, showed that they were conducting the Princess to her apartments, which were in the opposite wing of the inn; and she distinctly saw the figure of the nephew as he passed one of the casements.

She heaved a deep heart-drawn sigh, and was about to close the lattice, when her attention was caught by words spoken below her window by two persons who had just turned an angle of the building.

"But what will become of the poor young lady?" said a voice, which she recognized for that of the servant woman.

"Pooh! she must take her chance," was the reply from old Pietro.

"But cannot she be spared?" asked the other entreatingly; "she's so kind hearted!"

"Cospetto! what has got into thee?" replied the other petulantly: "would you mar the whole business for the sake of a silly girl?" By this time they had got so far from the window that the Polonaise could hear nothing further.

There was something in this fragment of conversation calculated to alarm. Did it relate to herself?—and if so, what was this impending danger from which it was entreated that she might be spared? She was several times on the point of tapping at her father's door, to tell him what she had heard; but she might have been mistaken; she might have heard indistinctly; the conversation might have alluded to some one else; at any rate it was too indefinite to lead to any conclusion. While in this state of irresolution, she was startled by a low knocking against the wainscot in a remote part of her gloomy chamber. On holding up the light, she beheld a small door there, which she had not before remarked. It was bolted on the inside. She advanced, and demanded who knocked, and was answered in the voice of the female domestic. On opening the door, the woman stood before it pale and agitated. She entered softly, laying her finger on her lips in sign of caution and secrecy.

"Fly!" said she: "leave this house instantly, or you are lost!"

The young lady, trembling with alarm, demanded an explanation.

"I have no time," replied the woman, "I dare not—I shall be missed if I linger here—but fly instantly, or you are lost."

"And leave my father?"

"Where is he?"

"In the adjoining chamber."

"Call him, then, but lose no time."

The young lady knocked at her father's door. He was not yet retired to bed. She hurried into his room, and told him of the fearful warning she had received. The Count returned with her into her chamber, followed by Caspar. His questions soon drew the truth out of the embarrassed answers of the woman. The inn was beset by robbers. They were to be introduced after midnight, when the attendants of the Princess and the rest of the travellers were sleeping, and would be an easy prey.

"But we can barricado the inn, we can defend ourselves," said the Count.

"What! when the people of the inn were in league with the banditti?"

"How then are we to escape? Can we not order out the carriage and depart?"

"San Francesco! for what? To give the alarm that the plot is discovered? That would make the robbers desperate, and bring them on you at once. They have had notice of the rich booty in the inn, and will not easily let it escape them."

"But how else are we to get off?"

"There is a horse behind the inn," said the woman, "from which the man has just dismounted who has been to summon the aid of a part of the band at a distance."

"One horse! and there are three of us!" said the Count.

"And the Spanish Princess!" cried the daughter anxiously—
"How can she be extricated from the danger?"

"Diavolo! what is she to me?" said the woman in sudden
passion. "It is *you* I come to save, and you will betray me, and
we shall all be lost! Hark!" continued she, "I am called—I
shall be discovered—one word more. This door leads by a
staircase to the court yard. Under the shed, in the rear of the
yard, is a small door leading out to the fields. You will find a
horse there; mount it; make a circuit under the shadow of a
ridge of rocks that you will see; proceed cautiously and quietly until you cross a brook, and find yourself on the road just
where there are three white crosses nailed against a tree; then
put your horse to his speed, and make the best of your way to
the village—but recollect, my life is in your hands—say
nothing of what you have heard or seen, whatever may happen at this inn."

The woman hurried away. A short and agitated consultation took place between the Count, his daughter, and the
veteran Caspar. The young lady seemed to have lost all
apprehension for herself in her solicitude for the safety of the
Princess. "To fly in selfish silence, and leave her to be massacred!"—A shuddering seized her at the very thought. The
gallantry of the Count, too, revolted at the idea. He could not
consent to turn his back upon a party of helpless travellers,
and leave them in ignorance of the danger which hung over
them.

"But what is to become of the young lady," said Caspar, "if
the alarm is given, and the inn thrown in a tumult? What may
happen to her in a chance medley affray?"

Here the feelings of the father were roused: he looked
upon his lovely, helpless child, and trembled at the chance of
her falling into the hands of ruffians.

The daughter, however, thought nothing of herself. "The
Princess! the Princess!—only let the Princess know her danger."—She was willing to share it with her.

At length Caspar interfered with the zeal of a faithful old
servant. No time was to be lost—the first thing was to get
the young lady out of danger. "Mount the horse," said he to
the Count, "take her behind you, and fly! Make for the
village, rouse the inhabitants, and send assistance. Leave me

here to give the alarm to the Princess and her people. I am an old soldier, and I think we shall be able to stand siege until you send us aid."

The daughter would again have insisted on staying with the Princess—

"For what?" said old Caspar, bluntly, "You could do no good—You would be in the way—We should have to take care of you instead of ourselves."

There was no answering these objections: the Count seized his pistols, and taking his daughter under his arm, moved towards the staircase. The young lady paused, stepped back, and said, faltering with agitation—"There is a young cavalier with the Princess—her nephew—perhaps he may—"

"I understand you, Mademoiselle," replied old Caspar with a significant nod; "not a hair of his head shall suffer harm if I can help it!"

The young lady blushed deeper than ever: she had not anticipated being so thoroughly understood by the blunt old servant.

"That is not what I mean," said she, hesitating. She would have added something, or made some explanation, but the moments were precious, and her father hurried her away.

They found their way through the court yard to the small postern gate, where the horse stood, fastened to a ring in the wall. The Count mounted, took his daughter behind him, and they proceeded as quietly as possible in the direction which the woman had pointed out. Many a fearful and an anxious look did the daughter cast back upon the gloomy pile: the lights which had feebly twinkled through the dusty casements were one by one disappearing, a sign that the inmates were gradually sinking to repose; and she trembled with impatience, lest succour should not arrive until that repose had been fatally interrupted.

They passed silently and safely along the skirts of the rocks, protected from observation by their overhanging shadows. They crossed the brook, and reached the place where three white crosses nailed against a tree told of some murder that had been committed there. Just as they had reached this ill omened spot they beheld several men in the gloom coming down a craggy defile among the rocks.

"Who goes there?" exclaimed a voice. The Count put spurs to his horse, but one of the men sprang forward and seized the bridle. The horse started back, and reared, and had not the young lady clung to her father, she would have been thrown off. The Count leaned forward, put a pistol to the very head of the ruffian, and fired. The latter fell dead. The horse sprang forward. Two or three shots were fired which whistled by the fugitives, but only served to augment their speed. They reached the village in safety.

The whole place was soon roused: but such was the awe in which the banditti were held, that the inhabitants shrunk at the idea of encountering them. A desperate band had for some time infested that pass through the mountains, and the inn had long been suspected of being one of those horrible places where the unsuspicious wayfarer is entrapped and silently disposed of. The rich ornaments worn by the slattern hostess of the inn had excited heavy suspicions. Several instances had occurred of small parties of travellers disappearing mysteriously on that road, who it was supposed, at first, had been carried off by the robbers for the purpose of ransom, but who had never been heard of more. Such were the tales buzzed in the ears of the Count by the villagers as he endeavoured to rouse them to the rescue of the princess and her train from their perilous situation. The daughter seconded the exertions of her father with all the eloquence of prayers, and tears, and beauty. Every moment that elapsed increased her anxiety until it became agonizing. Fortunately, there was a body of gens d'armes resting at the village. A number of the young villagers volunteered to accompany them, and the little army was put in motion. The Count having deposited his daughter in a place of safety, was too much of the old soldier not to hasten to the scene of danger. It would be difficult to paint the anxious agitation of the young lady while awaiting the result.

The party arrived at the inn just in time. The robbers, finding their plans discovered, and the travellers prepared for their reception, had become open and furious in their attack.

The Princess's party had barricadoed themselves in one suite of apartments, and repulsed the robbers from the doors and windows. Caspar had shown the generalship of a veteran, and the nephew of the Princess the dashing valour of a young soldier. Their ammunition, however, was nearly exhausted, and they would have found it difficult to hold out much longer, when a discharge from the musketry of the gens d'armes gave them the joyful tidings of succour.

A fierce fight ensued, for part of the robbers were surprised in the inn, and had to stand siege in their turn; while their comrades made desperate attempts to relieve them from under cover of the neighbouring rocks and thickets.

I cannot pretend to give a minute account of the fight, as I have heard it related in a variety of ways. Suffice it to say, the robbers were defeated; several of them killed, and several taken prisoners; which last, together with the people of the inn, were either executed or sent to the galleys.

I picked up these particulars in the course of a journey which I made some time after the event had taken place. I passed by the very inn. It was then dismantled, excepting one wing, in which a body of gens d'armes was stationed. They pointed out to me the shot holes in the window frames, the walls, and the pannels of the doors. There were a number of withered limbs dangling from the branches of a neighbouring tree, and blackening in the air, which I was told were the limbs of the robbers who had been slain, and the culprits who had been executed. The whole place had a dismal, wild, forlorn look.

"Were any of the Princess's party killed?" inquired the Englishman.

"As far as I can recollect, there were two or three."

"Not the nephew, I trust?" said the fair Venetian.

"Oh no: he hastened with the Count to relieve the anxiety of the daughter by the assurances of victory. The young lady had been sustained throughout the interval of suspense by the very intensity of her feelings. The moment she saw her father returning in safety, accompanied by the nephew of the Princess, she uttered a cry of rapture and fainted. Happily, however, she soon recovered, and what is more, was married shortly afterwards to the young cavalier, and the whole party accompanied the old Princess in her pilgrimage to Loretto, where her votive offerings may still be seen in the treasury of the Santa Casa."

————

It would be tedious to follow the devious course of the conversation as it wound through a maze of stories of the kind, until it was taken up by two other travellers who had come under convoy of the Procaccio: Mr. Hobbs and Mr. Dobbs, a linen draper and a green grocer, just returning from a hasty tour in Greece and the Holy Land. They were full of the story of Alderman Popkins. They were astonished that the robbers should dare to molest a man of his importance on 'Change, he being an eminent dry salter of Throgmorton Street, and a magistrate to boot.

In fact, the story of the Popkins family was but too true. It was attested by too many present to be for a moment doubted; and from the contradictory and concordant testimony of half a score, all eager to relate it, and all talking at the same time, the Englishman was enabled to gather the following particulars.

The Adventure of the Popkins Family

It was but a few days before that the carriage of Alderman Popkins had driven up to the inn of Terracina. Those who have seen an English family carriage on the continent, must have remarked the sensation it produces. It is an epitome of England; a little morsel of the old island rolling about the world—every thing about it compact, snug, finished and fitting. The wheels turning on patent axles without rattling; the body hanging so well on its springs, yielding to every motion, yet protecting from every shock. The ruddy faces gaping from the windows; sometimes, of a portly old citizen, sometimes of a voluminous dowager, and sometimes of a fine fresh hoyden, just from boarding school. And then the dickeys loaded with well dressed servants, beef fed and bluff; looking down from their heights with contempt on all the world around; profoundly ignorant of the country and the people, and devoutly certain that every thing not English must be wrong.

Such was the carriage of Alderman Popkins, as it made its appearance at Terracina. The courier who had preceded it, to order horses, and who was a Neapolitan, had given a magnificent account of the riches and greatness of his master, blundering with an Italian's splendour of imagination about the alderman's titles and dignities; the host had added his usual share of exaggeration, so that by the time the alderman drove up to the door, he was a Milor—Magnifico—Principe—— the Lord knows what!

The alderman was advised to take an escort to Fondi and Itri, but he refused. It was as much as a man's life was worth, he said, to stop him on the king's highway; he would complain of it to the ambassador at Naples; he would make a national affair of it. The principessa Popkins, a fresh, motherly dame, seemed perfectly secure in the protection of her husband, so omnipotent a man in the city. The signorine Popkins, two fine bouncing girls looked to their brother Tom, who had taken lessons in boxing; and as to the dandy himself, he swore no scaramouch of an Italian robber would dare to meddle with an Englishman. The landlord shrugged his shoulders and turned out the palms of his hands with a true Italian grimace, and the carriage of Milor Popkins rolled on.

They passed through several very suspicious places without any molestation. The Misses Popkins, who were very romantic, and had learnt to draw in water colours, were enchanted with the savage scenery around; it was so like what they had read in Mrs. Radcliffe's romances, they should like of all things to make sketches. At length, the carriage arrived at a place where the road wound up a long hill. Mrs. Popkins had sunk into a sleep; the young ladies were lost in the "Loves of the Angels;" and the dandy was hectoring the postilions from the coach box. The alderman got out, as he said, to stretch his legs up the hill. It was a long winding ascent, and obliged him every now and then to stop and blow and wipe his forehead with many a pish! and phew! being rather pursy and short of wind. As the carriage, however, was far behind him, and moved slowly under the weight of so many well stuffed trunks and well stuffed travellers, he had plenty of time to walk at leisure.

On a jutting point of rock that overhung the road nearly at the summit of the hill, just where the route began again to descend, he saw a solitary man seated, who appeared to be tending goats. Alderman Popkins was one of your shrewd travellers who always like to be picking up small information along the road, so he thought he'd just scramble up to the honest man, and have a little talk with him by way of learning the news and getting a lesson in Italian. As he drew near to the peasant he did not half like his looks. He was partly reclining on the rocks wrapped in the usual long mantle, which, with his slouched hat, only left a part of a swarthy visage, with a keen black eye, a beetle brow and a fierce moustache to be seen. He had whistled several times to his dog which was roving about the side of the hill. As the alderman approached he rose and greeted him. When standing erect he seemed almost gigantic, at least in the eyes of Alderman Popkins; who, however, being a short man, might be deceived.

The latter would gladly now have been back in the carriage, or even on 'change in London, for he was by no means well pleased with his company. However, he determined to put the best face on matters, and was beginning a conversation about the state of the weather, the baddishness of the crops and the price of goats in that part of the country, when he heard a violent screaming. He ran to the edge of the rock, and, looking over, beheld his carriage surrounded by robbers. One held down the fat footman, another had the dandy by his starched cravat, with a pistol to his head; one was rummaging a portmanteau, another rummaging the principessa's pockets, while the two Misses Popkins were screaming from each window of the carriage, and their waiting maid squalling from the dickey.

Alderman Popkins felt all the ire of the parent and the magistrate roused within him. He grasped his cane and was on the point of scrambling down the rocks, either to assault the robbers or to read the riot act, when he was suddenly seized by the arm. It was by his friend the goatherd, whose cloak, falling open, discovered a belt stuck full of pistols and stilettos. In short, he found himself in the clutches of the captain of the band, who had stationed himself on the rock to look out for travellers and to give notice to his men.

A sad ransacking took place. Trunks were turned inside out, and all the finery and frippery of the Popkins family scattered about the road. Such a chaos of Venice beads and Roman mosaics; and Paris bonnets of the young ladies, mingled with the alderman's night caps and lamb's wool stockings, and the dandy's hair brushes, stays, and starched cravats.

The gentlemen were eased of their purses and their watches; the ladies of their jewels, and the whole party were on the point of being carried up into the mountain, when fortunately the appearance of soldiery at a distance obliged the robbers to make off with the spoils they had secured, and leave the Popkins family to gather together the remnants of their effects, and make the best of their way to Fondi.

When safe arrived, the alderman made a terrible blustering at the inn; threatened to complain to the ambassador at Naples, and was ready to shake his cane at the whole country. The dandy had many stories to tell of his scuffles with the brigands, who overpowered him merely by numbers. As to the Misses Popkins, they were quite delighted with the adventure, and were occupied the whole evening in writing it in their journals. They declared the captain of the band to be a most romantic looking man; they dared to say some unfortunate lover, or exiled nobleman: and several of the band to be very handsome young men—"quite picturesque!"

"In verity," said mine host of Terracina, "they say the captain of the band is *un galant uomo*."

"A gallant man!" said the Englishman indignantly. "I'd have your gallant man hang'd like a dog!"

"To dare to meddle with Englishmen!" said Mr. Hobbs.

"And such a family as the Popkinses!" said Mr. Dobbs.

"They ought to come upon the county for damages!" said Mr. Hobbs.

"Our ambassador should make a complaint to the government of Naples," said Mr. Dobbs.

"They should be obliged to drive these rascals out of the country," said Hobbs.

"And if they did not, we should declare war against them!" said Dobbs.

"Pish!—humbug!" muttered the Englishman to himself, and walked away.

The Englishman had been a little wearied by this story, and by the ultra zeal of his countrymen, and was glad when a summons to their supper relieved him from the crowd of travellers. He walked out with his Venetian friends and a young Frenchman of an interesting demeanour, who had become sociable with them in the course of the conversation. They directed their steps toward the sea, which was lit up by the rising moon. The Venetian, out of politeness, left his beautiful wife to be escorted by the Englishman. The latter, however, either from shyness or reserve, did not avail himself of the civility, but walked on without offering his arm. The fair Venetian, with all her devotion to her husband, was a little nettled at a want of gallantry to which her charms had rendered her unaccustomed, and took the proffered arm of the Frenchman with a pretty air of pique, which, however, was entirely lost upon the phlegmatic delinquent.

As they strolled along the beach they came to where a body of soldiers were stationed in a circle. They were guarding a number of galley slaves, who were permitted to refresh themselves in the evening breeze, and sport and roll upon the sand.

The Frenchman paused, and pointed to the group of wretches at their sports. "It is difficult," said he, "to conceive a more frightful mass of crime than is here collected. Many of these have probably been robbers, such as you have heard described. Such is, too often, the career of crime in this country. The parricide, the fratricide, the infanticide, the miscreant of every kind first flies from justice and turns mountain bandit, and then, when wearied of a life of danger, becomes traitor to his brother desperadoes, betrays them to punishment, and thus buys a commutation of his own sentence from death to the galleys: happy in the privilege of wallowing on the shore an hour a day, in this mere state of animal enjoyment."

The fair Venetian shuddered as she cast a look at the horde of wretches at their evening amusement. "They seemed," she said, "like so many serpents writhing together." And yet the idea that some of them had been robbers, those formidable beings that haunted her imagination, made her still cast another fearful glance, as we contemplate some terrible beast of prey, with a degree of awe and horror, even though caged and chained.

The conversation reverted to the tales of banditti which they had heard at the inn. The Englishman condemned some of them as fabrications, others as exaggerations. As to the story of the improvvisatore, he pronounced it a mere piece of romance, originating in the heated brain of the narrator.

"And yet," said the Frenchman, "there is so much romance about the real life of those beings, and about the singular country they infest, that it is hard to tell what to reject on the ground of improbability. I have had an adventure happen to myself which gave me an opportunity of getting some insight into their manners and habits, which I found altogether out of the common run of existence."

There was an air of mingled frankness and modesty about the Frenchman which had gained the good will of the whole party, not even excepting the Englishman. They all eagerly inquired after the particulars of the circumstance he alluded to, and as they strolled slowly up and down the sea shore, he related the following adventure.

The Painter's Adventure

I am an historical painter by profession, and resided for some time in the family of a foreign prince, at his villa, about fifteen miles from Rome, among some of the most interesting scenery of Italy. It is situated on the heights of ancient Tusculum. In its neighbourhood are the ruins of the villas of Cicero, Sylla, Lucullus, Rufinus, and other illustrious Romans, who sought refuge here occasionally, from their toils, in the bosom of a soft and luxurious repose. From the midst of delightful bowers, refreshed by the pure mountain breeze, the eye looks over a romantic landscape full of poetical and historical associations. The Albanian mountains, Tivoli, once the favourite residence of Horace and Mæcenas; the vast, deserted, melancholy Campagna with the Tiber winding through it, and St. Peter's dome swelling in the midst, the monument—as it were, over the grave of ancient Rome.

I assisted the prince in researches which he was making among the classic ruins of his vicinity. His exertions were highly successful. Many wrecks of admirable statues and fragments of exquisite sculpture were dug up; monuments of the taste and magnificence that reigned in the ancient Tusculan abodes. He had studded his villa and its grounds with statues, relievos, vases and sarcophagi, thus retrieved from the bosom of the earth.

The mode of life pursued at the villa was delightfully serene, diversified by interesting occupations and elegant leisure. Every one passed the day according to his pleasure or pursuits; and we all assembled in a cheerful dinner party at sunset. It was on the fourth of November, a beautiful serene day, that we had assembled in the saloon at the sound of the first dinner bell. The family were surprised at the absence of the prince's confessor. They waited for him in vain, and at length placed themselves at table. They first attributed his absence to his having prolonged his customary walk; and the early part of the dinner passed without any uneasiness. When the desart was served, however, without his making his appearance, they began to feel anxious. They feared he might have been taken ill in some alley of the woods; or, might have fallen into the hands of robbers. Not far from the villa, with the interval of a small valley, rose the mountains of the Abruzzi, the strong hold of banditti. Indeed, the neighbourhood had, for some time past, been infested by them; and Barbone, a notorious bandit chief, had often been met prowling about the solitudes of Tusculum. The daring enterprises of these ruffians were well known; the objects of their cupidity or vengeance were insecure even in palaces. As yet they had respected the possessions of the prince; but the idea of such dangerous spirits hovering about the neighbourhood was sufficient to occasion alarm.

The fears of the company increased as evening closed in. The prince ordered out forest guards, and domestics with flambeaux to search for the confessor. They had not departed long, when a slight noise was heard in the corridor of the ground floor. The family were dining on the first floor, and the remaining domestics were occupied in attendance. There was no one on the ground floor at this moment but the housekeeper, the laundress, and three field labourers, who were resting themselves, and conversing with the women.

I heard the noise from below, and presuming it to be occasioned by the return of the absentee, I left the table, and hastened down stairs, eager to gain intelligence that might relieve the anxiety of the prince and princess. I had scarcely reached the last step, when I beheld before me a man dressed as a bandit; a carbine in his hand, and a stiletto and pistols in his belt. His countenance had a mingled expression of ferocity and trepidation. He sprang upon me, and exclaimed exultingly, "Ecco il principe!"

I saw at once into what hands I had fallen, but endeavoured to summon up coolness and presence of mind. A glance towards the lower end of the corridor, showed me several ruffians, clothed and armed in the same manner with the one who had seized me. They were guarding the two females and the field labourers. The robber, who held me firmly by the collar, demanded repeatedly whether or not I were the prince. His object evidently was to carry off the prince, and extort an immense ransom. He was enraged at receiving none but vague replies; for I felt the importance of misleading him.

A sudden thought struck me how I might extricate myself from his clutches. I was unarmed, it is true, but I was vigorous. His companions were at a distance. By a sudden exertion I might wrest myself from him, and spring up the staircase, whither he would not dare to follow me singly. The idea was put in practice as soon as conceived. The ruffian's throat was bare: with my right hand I seized him by it, with my left hand I grasped the arm which held the carbine. The suddenness of my attack took him completely unawares; and the strangling nature of my grasp paralized him. He choked and faltered. I felt his hand relaxing its hold, and was on the point of jerking myself away, and darting up the staircase before he could recover himself, when I was suddenly seized by some one from behind.

I had to let go my grasp. The bandit, once more released, fell upon me with fury, and gave me several blows with the butt end of his carbine, one of which wounded me severely in the forehead, and covered me with blood. He took advantage of my being stunned, to rifle me of my watch, and whatever valuables I had about my person.

When I recovered from the effects of the blow, I heard the voice of the chief of the banditti, who exclaimed, "Quello e il principe, siamo contente, andiamo!" (It is the prince, enough, let us be off.) The band immediately closed round me, and dragged me out of the palace, bearing off the three labourers likewise.

I had no hat on, and the blood flowed from my wound; I managed to staunch it, however, with my pocket handkerchief, which I bound round my forehead. The captain of the band conducted me in triumph, supposing me to be the prince. We had gone some distance, before he learnt his mistake from one of the labourers. His rage was terrible. It was too late to return to the villa, and endeavour to retrieve his error, for by this time the alarm must have been given, and every one in arms. He darted at me a ferocious look; swore I had deceived him, and caused him to miss his fortune; and told me to prepare for death. The rest of the robbers were equally furious. I saw their hands upon their poniards; and I knew that death was seldom an empty threat with these ruffians.

The labourers saw the peril into which their information had betrayed me, and eagerly assured the captain that I was a man for whom the prince would pay a great ransom. This produced a pause. For my part, I cannot say that I had been much dismayed by their menaces. I mean not to make any boast of courage; but I have been so schooled to hardship during the late revolutions, and have beheld death around me in so many perilous and disastrous scenes, that I have become, in some measure, callous to its terrors. The frequent hazard of life makes a man at length as reckless of it, as a gambler of his money. To their threat of death I replied, "that the sooner it was executed the better." This reply seemed to astonish the captain, and the prospect of ransom held out by the labourers had, no doubt, a still greater effect on him. He considered for a moment; assumed a calmer manner, and made a sign to his companions, who had remained waiting for my death warrant. *"Forward,"* said he, "we will see about this matter by and bye."

We descended rapidly towards the road of La Molara, which leads to Rocca Priori. In the midst of this road is a solitary inn. The captain ordered the troop to halt at the distance of a pistol shot from it; and enjoined profound silence. He approached the threshold alone, with noiseless steps. He examined the outside of the door very narrowly, and then returning precipitately, made a sign for the troop to continue its march in silence. It has since been ascertained, that this was one of those infamous inns which are the secret resorts of banditti. The innkeeper had an understanding with the captain, as he most probably had with the chiefs of the different bands. When any of the patroles and gens d'armes were quartered at his house, the brigands were warned of it by a preconcerted signal on the door; when there was no such signal, they might enter with safety, and be sure of welcome.

After pursuing our road a little further, we struck off towards the woody mountains, which envelope Rocca Priori. Our march was long and painful, with many circuits and windings; at length we clambered a steep ascent, covered with a thick forest, and when we had reached the centre, I was told to seat myself on the ground. No sooner had I done so, than at a sign from their chief, the robbers surrounded me, and spreading their great cloaks from one to the other, formed a kind of pavilion of mantles, to which their bodies might be said to serve as columns. The captain then struck a light, and a flambeau was lit immediately. The mantles were extended to prevent the light of the flambeau from being seen through the forest. Anxious as was my situation, I could not look round upon this screen of dusky drapery, relieved by the bright colours of the robbers' garments, the gleaming of their weapons, and the variety of strong marked countenances, lit up by the flambeau, without admiring the picturesque effect of the scene. It was quite theatrical.

The captain now held an inkhorn, and giving me pen and paper, ordered me to write what he should dictate. I obeyed.—It was a demand, couched in the style of robber eloquence, "that the prince should send three thousand dollars for my ransom, or that my death should be the consequence of a refusal."

I knew enough of the desperate character of these beings to

feel assured this was not an idle menace. Their only mode of insuring attention to their demands, is to make the infliction of the penalty inevitable. I saw at once, however, that the demand was preposterous, and made in improper language.

I told the captain so, and assured him, that so extravagant a sum would never be granted; "that I was neither a friend nor relative of the prince, but a mere artist, employed to execute certain paintings. That I had nothing to offer as a ransom but the price of my labours; if this were not sufficient, my life was at their disposal: it was a thing on which I set but little value."

I was the more hardy in my reply, because I saw that coolness and hardihood had an effect upon the robbers. It is true, as I finished speaking the captain laid his hand upon his stiletto, but he restrained himself, and snatching the letter, folded it, and ordered me, in a peremptory tone, to address it to the prince. He then despatched one of the labourers with it to Tusculum, who promised to return with all possible speed.

The robbers now prepared themselves for sleep, and I was told that I might do the same. They spread their great cloaks on the ground, and lay down around me. One was stationed at a little distance to keep watch, and was relieved every two hours. The strangeness and wildness of this mountain bivouac, among lawless beings whose hands seemed ever ready to grasp the stiletto, and with whom life was so trivial and insecure, was enough to banish repose. The coldness of the earth and of the dew, however, had a still greater effect than mental causes in disturbing my rest. The airs wafted to these mountains from the distant Mediterranean diffused a great chilliness as the night advanced. An expedient suggested itself. I called one of my fellow prisoners, the labourers, and made him lie down beside me. Whenever one of my limbs became chilled I approached it to the robust limb of my neighbour, and borrowed some of his warmth. In this way I was able to obtain a little sleep.

Day at length dawned, and I was roused from my slumber by the voice of the chieftain. He desired me to rise and follow him. I obeyed. On considering his physiognomy attentively, it appeared a little softened. He even assisted me in scrambling up the steep forest among rocks and brambles. Habit had made him a vigorous mountaineer; but I found it excessively toilsome to climb those rugged heights. We arrived at length at the summit of the mountain.

Here it was that I felt all the enthusiasm of my art suddenly awakened; and I forgot, in an instant, all my perils and fatigues at this magnificent view of the sunrise in the midst of the mountains of the Abruzzi. It was on these heights that Hannibal first pitched his camp, and pointed out Rome to his followers. The eye embraces a vast extent of country. The minor height of Tusculum, with its villas, and its sacred ruins, lie below; the Sabine hills and the Albanian mountains stretch on either hand, and beyond Tusculum and Frascati spreads out the immense Campagna, with its lines of tombs, and here and there a broken aqueduct stretching across it, and the towers and domes of the eternal city in the midst.

Fancy this scene lit up by the glories of a rising sun, and bursting upon my sight, as I looked forth from among the majestic forests of the Abruzzi. Fancy, too, the savage foreground, made still more savage by groups of banditti, armed and dressed in their wild picturesque manner, and you will not wonder that the enthusiasm of a painter for a moment overpowered all his other feelings.

The banditti were astonished at my admiration of a scene which familiarity had made so common in their eyes. I took advantage of their halting at this spot, drew forth a quire of drawing paper, and began to sketch the features of the landscape. The height, on which I was seated, was wild and solitary, separated from the ridge of Tusculum by a valley nearly three miles wide; though the distance appeared less from the purity of the atmosphere. This height was one of the favourite retreats of the banditti, commanding a look out over the country; while, at the same time, it was covered with forests, and distant from the populous haunts of men.

While I was sketching, my attention was called off for a moment by the cries of birds and the bleatings of sheep. I looked around, but could see nothing of the animals which uttered them. They were repeated, and appeared to come from the summits of the trees. On looking more narrowly, I perceived six of the robbers perched in the tops of oaks, which grew on the breezy crest of the mountain, and com-

manded an uninterrupted prospect. They were keeping a look
out, like so many vultures; casting their eyes into the depths
of the valley below us; communicating with each other by
signs, or holding discourse in sounds, which might be mistaken by the wayfarer, for the cries of hawks and crows, or
the bleating of the mountain flocks. After they had reconnoitred the neighbourhood, and finished their singular discourse,
they descended from their airy perch, and returned to their
prisoners. The captain posted three of them at three naked
sides of the mountain, while he remained to guard us with
what appeared his most trusty companion.

I had my book of sketches in my hand; he requested to see
it, and after having run his eye over it, expressed himself convinced of the truth of my assertion, that I was a painter. I
thought I saw a gleam of good feeling dawning in him, and
determined to avail myself of it. I knew that the worst of men
have their good points and their accessible sides, if one would
but study them carefully. Indeed, there is a singular mixture
in the character of the Italian robber. With reckless ferocity,
he often mingles traits of kindness and good humour. He is
not always radically bad, but driven to his course of life by
some unpremeditated crime, the effect of those sudden bursts
of passion to which the Italian temperament is prone. This
has compelled him to take to the mountains, or, as it is technically termed among them, "andare in Campagna." He has
become a robber by profession; but like a soldier, when not
in action, he can lay aside his weapon and his fierceness, and
become like other men.

I took occasion from the observations of the captain on my
sketchings, to fall into conversation with him and found him
sociable and communicative. By degrees I became completely
at my ease with him. I had fancied I perceived about him a
degree of self love, which I determined to make use of. I assumed an air of careless frankness, and told him that, as an
artist, I pretended to the power of judging of the physiognomy; that I thought I perceived something in his features
and demeanour, which announced him worthy of higher fortunes. That he was not formed to exercise the profession to
which he had abandoned himself; that he had talents and
qualities fitted for a nobler sphere of action; that he had but

to change his course of life, and in a legitimate career, the same courage and endowments which now made him an object of terror, would ensure him the applause and admiration of society.

I had not mistaken my man. My discourse both touched and excited him. He seized my hand, pressed it, and replied with strong emotion, "You have guessed the truth; you have judged of me rightly." He remained for a moment silent; then with a kind of effort he resumed. "I will tell you some particulars of my life, and you will perceive that it was the oppression of others, rather than my own crimes, which drove me to the mountains. I sought to serve my fellow men, and they have persecuted me from among them." We seated ourselves on the grass, and the robber gave me the following anecdotes of his history.

The Story of the Bandit Chieftain

I am a native of the village of Prossedi. My father was easy enough in circumstances, and we lived peaceably and independently, cultivating our fields. All went on well with us until a new chief of the Sbirri was sent to our village to take command of the police. He was an arbitrary fellow, prying into every thing, and practising all sorts of vexations and oppressions in the discharge of his office.

I was at that time eighteen years of age, and had a natural love of justice and good neighbourhood. I had also a little education, and knew something of history, so as to be able to judge a little of men and their actions. All this inspired me with hatred for this paltry despot. My own family, also, became the object of his suspicion or dislike, and felt more than once the arbitrary abuse of his power. These things worked together on my mind, and I gasped after vengeance. My character was always ardent and energetic; and acted upon by my love of justice, determined me by one blow to rid the country of the tyrant.

Full of my project I rose one morning before peep of day, and concealing a stiletto under my waistcoat—here you see it!—(and he drew forth a long keen poniard)—I lay in wait for him in the outskirts of the village. I knew all his haunts, and his habit of making his rounds and prowling about like a wolf, in the grey of the morning; at length I met him and attacked him with fury. He was armed, but I took him un-awares, and was full of youth and vigour. I gave him repeated blows to make sure work, and laid him lifeless at my feet.

When I was satisfied that I had done for him, I returned with all haste to the village, but had the ill luck to meet two of the Sbirri as I entered it. They accosted me and asked if I had seen their chief. I assumed an air of tranquillity, and told them I had not. They continued on their way, and, within a few hours, brought back the dead body to Prossedi. Their suspicions of me being already awakened, I was arrested and thrown into prison. Here I lay several weeks, when the prince who was Seigneur of Prossedi directed judicial proceedings against me. I was brought to trial, and a witness was pro-duced who pretended to have seen me flying with precipita-tion not far from the bleeding body, and so I was condemned to the galleys for thirty years.

"Curse on such laws," vociferated the bandit, foaming with rage; "curse on such a government, and ten thousand curses on the prince who caused me to be adjudged so rigorously, while so many other Roman princes harbour and protect as-sassins a thousand times more culpable. What had I done but what was inspired by a love of justice and my country? Why was my act more culpable than that of Brutus, when he sacri-ficed Cæsar to the cause of liberty and justice!"

There was something at once both lofty and ludicrous in the rhapsody of this robber chief, thus associating himself with one of the great names of antiquity. It showed, however, that he had at least the merit of knowing the remarkable facts in the history of his country. He became more calm, and re-sumed his narrative.

I was conducted to Civita Vecchia in fetters. My heart was burning with rage. I had been married scarce six months to a woman whom I passionately loved, and who was pregnant. My family was in despair. For a long time I made unsuccess-ful efforts to break my chain. At length I found a morsel of iron which I hid carefully, and endeavoured with a pointed flint to fashion it into a kind of file. I occupied myself in this work during the night time, and when it was finished, I made out, after a long time, to sever one of the rings of my chain. My flight was successful.

I wandered for several weeks in the mountains which surround Prossedi, and found means to inform my wife of the place where I was concealed. She came often to see me. I had determined to put myself at the head of an armed band. She endeavoured for a long time to dissuade me; but finding my resolution fixed, she at length united in my project of vengeance, and brought me, herself, my poniard.

By her means I communicated with several brave fellows of the neighbouring villages, who I knew to be ready to take to the mountains, and only panting for an opportunity to exercise their daring spirits. We soon formed a combination, procured arms, and we have had ample opportunities of revenging ourselves for the wrongs and injuries which most of us have suffered. Every thing has succeeded with us until now, and had it not been for our blunder in mistaking you for the prince, our fortunes would have been made.

———

Here the robber concluded his story. He had talked himself into complete companionship, and assured me he no longer bore me any grudge for the error of which I had been the innocent cause. He even professed a kindness for me, and wished me to remain some time with them. He promised to give me a sight of certain grottos which they occupied beyond Villetri, and whither they resorted during the intervals of their expeditions. He assured me that they led a jovial life there; had plenty of good cheer; slept on beds of moss, and were waited upon by young and beautiful females, whom I might take for models.

I confess I felt my curiosity roused by his descriptions of these grottos and their inhabitants: they realized those scenes in robber story which I had always looked upon as mere creations of the fancy. I should gladly have accepted his invitation, and paid a visit to those caverns, could I have felt more secure in my company.

I began to find my situation less painful. I had evidently

propitiated the good will of the chieftain, and hoped that he might release me for a moderate ransom. A new alarm, however, awaited me. While the captain was looking out with impatience for the return of the messenger who had been sent to the prince, the sentinel posted on the side of the mountain facing the plain of La Molara, came running towards us. "We are betrayed!" exclaimed he. "The police of Frascati are after us. A party of carabiniers have just stopped at the inn below the mountain." Then laying his hand on his stiletto, he swore, with a terrible oath, that if they made the least movement towards the mountain, my life and the lives of my fellow prisoners should answer for it.

The chieftain resumed all his ferocity of demeanour, and approved of what his companion said; but when the latter had returned to his post, he turned to me with a softened air: "I must act as chief," said he, "and humour my dangerous subalterns. It is a law with us to kill our prisoners rather than suffer them to be rescued; but do not be alarmed. In case we are surprised keep by me; fly with us, and I will consider myself responsible for your life."

There was nothing very consolatory in this arrangement, which would have placed me between two dangers; I scarcely knew in case of flight, which I should have most to apprehend from, the carbines of the pursuers, or the stilettos of the pursued. I remained silent, however, and endeavoured to maintain a look of tranquillity.

For an hour was I kept in this state of peril and anxiety. The robbers, crouching among their leafy coverts, kept an eagle watch upon the carabiniers below, as they loitered about the inn; sometimes lolling about the portal; sometimes disappearing for several minutes, then sallying out, examining their weapons, pointing in different directions and apparently asking questions about the neighbourhood; not a movement or gesture was lost upon the keen eyes of the brigands. At length we were relieved from our apprehensions. The carabiniers having finished their refreshment, seized their arms, continued along the valley towards the great road, and gradually left the mountain behind them. "I felt almost certain," said the chief, "that they could not be sent after us. They know too well how prisoners have fared in our hands on similar

occasions. Our laws in this respect are inflexible, and are necessary for our safety. If we once flinched from them, there
would no longer be such thing as a ransom to be procured."

There were no signs yet of the messenger's return. I was
preparing to resume my sketching, when the captain drew a
quire of paper from his knapsack—"Come," said he, laughing, "you are a painter; take my likeness. The leaves of your
portfolio are small; draw it on this." I gladly consented, for it
was a study that seldom presents itself to a painter. I recollected that Salvator Rosa in his youth had voluntarily sojourned for a time among the banditti of Calabria, and had
filled his mind with the savage scenery and savage associates
by which he was surrounded. I seized my pencil with enthusiasm at the thought. I found the captain the most docile of
subjects, and after various shiftings of position, I placed him
in an attitude to my mind.

Picture to yourself a stern muscular figure, in fanciful
bandit costume, with pistols and poniards in belt, his brawny
neck bare, a handkerchief loosely thrown round it, and the
two ends in front strung with rings of all kinds, the spoils of
travellers; reliques and medals hung on his breast; his hat decorated with various coloured ribbands; his vest and short
breeches of bright colours and finely embroidered; his legs in
buskins or leggins. Fancy him on a mountain height, among
wild rocks and rugged oaks, leaning on his carbine as if meditating some exploit, while far below are beheld villages and
villas, the scenes of his maraudings, with the wide Campagna
dimly extending in the distance.

The robber was pleased with the sketch, and seemed to
admire himself upon paper. I had scarcely finished, when the
labourer arrived who had been sent for my ransom. He had
reached Tusculum two hours after midnight. He brought me
a letter from the prince, who was in bed at the time of his
arrival. As I had predicted, he treated the demand as extravagant, but offered five hundred dollars for my ransom. Having
no money by him at the moment, he had sent a note for the
amount, payable to whomever should conduct me safe and
sound to Rome. I presented the note of hand to the chieftain,
he received it with a shrug. "Of what use are notes of hand to
us?" said he, "who can we send with you to Rome to receive

it? We are all marked men, known and described at every gate and military post, and village church door. No, we must have gold and silver; let the sum be paid in cash and you shall be restored to liberty."

The captain again placed a sheet of paper before me to communicate his determination to the prince. When I had finished the letter and took the sheet from the quire, I found on the opposite side of it the portrait which I had just been tracing. I was about to tear it off and give it to the chief.

"Hold," said he, "let it go to Rome; let them see what kind of looking fellow I am. Perhaps the prince and his friends may form as good an opinion of me from my face as you have done."

This was said sportively, yet it was evident there was vanity lurking at the bottom. Even this wary, distrustful chief of banditti forgot for a moment his usual foresight and precaution in the common wish to be admired. He never reflected what use might be made of this portrait in his pursuit and conviction.

The letter was folded and directed, and the messenger departed again for Tusculum. It was now eleven o'clock in the morning, and as yet we had eaten nothing. In spite of all my anxiety, I began to feel a craving appetite. I was glad therefore to hear the captain talk something of eating. He observed that for three days and nights they had been lurking about among rocks and woods, meditating their expedition to Tusculum, during which time all their provisions had been exhausted. He should now take measures to procure a supply. Leaving me therefore in the charge of his comrade, in whom he appeared to have implicit confidence, he departed, assuring me that in less than two hours we should make a good dinner. Where it was to come from was an enigma to me, though it was evident these beings had their secret friends and agents throughout the country.

Indeed, the inhabitants of these mountains and of the valleys which they embosom are a rude, half civilized set. The towns and villages among the forests of the Abruzzi, shut up from the rest of the world, are almost like savage dens. It is wonderful that such rude abodes, so little known and visited, should be embosomed in the midst of one of the most travelled and civilized countries of Europe. Among these regions the robber prowls unmolested, not a mountaineer hesitates to give him secret harbour and assistance. The shepherds, however, who tend their flocks among the mountains, are the favourite emissaries of the robbers, when they would send messages down to the valleys either for ransom or supplies. The shepherds of the Abruzzi are as wild as the scenes they frequent. They are clad in a rude garb of black or brown sheep skin, they have high conical hats, and coarse sandals of cloth bound round their legs with thongs, similar to those worn by the robbers. They carry long staffs, on which as they lean they form picturesque objects in the lonely landscape, and they are followed by their ever constant companion the dog. They are a curious questioning set, glad at any time to relieve the monotony of their solitude by the conversation of the passer by, and the dog will lend an attentive ear, and put on as sagacious and inquisitive a look as his master.

But I am wandering from my story. I was now left alone with one of the robbers, the confidential companion of the chief. He was the youngest and most vigorous of the band, and though his countenance had something of that dissolute fierceness which seems natural to this desperate, lawless mode of life, yet there were traits of manly beauty about it. As an artist I could not but admire it. I had remarked in him an air of abstraction and reverie, and at times a movement of inward suffering and impatience. He now sat on the ground; his elbows on his knees, his head resting between his clenched fists, and his eyes fixed on the earth with an expression of sad and bitter rumination. I had grown familiar with him from repeated conversations, and had found him superior in mind to the rest of the band. I was anxious to seize every opportunity of sounding the feelings of these singular beings. I fancied I read in the countenance of this one traces of self condemnation and remorse; and the ease with which I had drawn forth the confidence of the chieftain, encouraged me to hope the same with his follower.

After a little preliminary conversation I ventured to ask him if he did not feel regret at having abandoned his family, and taken to this dangerous profession. "I feel," replied he, "but one regret, and that will end only with my life." As he said this he pressed his clenched fists upon his bosom, drew his breath through his set teeth, and added with deep emotion, "I have something within here that stifles me; it is like a burning iron consuming my very heart. I could tell you a miserable story, but not now—another time."—He relapsed into his former position, and sat with his head between his hands, muttering to himself in broken ejaculations, and what appeared at times to be curses and maledictions. I saw he was not in a mood to be disturbed, so I left him to himself. In a little while the exhaustion of his feelings, and probably the fatigues he had undergone in this expedition, began to produce drowsiness. He struggled with it for a time, but the warmth and stillness of midday made it irresistible, and he at length stretched himself upon the herbage and fell asleep.

I now beheld a chance of escape within my reach. My guard lay before me at my mercy. His vigorous limbs relaxed by sleep; his bosom open for the blow; his carbine slipped from his nerveless grasp, and lying by his side; his stiletto half out of the pocket in which it was usually carried. But two of his comrades were in sight, and those at a considerable distance, on the edge of the mountain; their backs turned to us, and their attention occupied in keeping a look out upon the plain. Through a strip of intervening forest, and at the foot of a steep descent, I beheld the village of Rocca Priori. To have secured the carbine of the sleeping brigand, to have seized upon his poniard and have plunged it in his heart, would have been the work of an instant. Should he die without noise, I might dart through the forest and down to Rocca Priori before my flight might be discovered. In case of alarm, I should still have a fair start of the robbers, and a chance of getting beyond the reach of their shot.

Here then was an opportunity for both escape and vengeance; perilous, indeed, but powerfully tempting. Had my situation been more critical I could not have resisted it. I reflected, however, for a moment. The attempt, if successful, would be followed by the sacrifice of my two fellow prisoners, who were sleeping profoundly, and could not be awakened in time to escape. The labourer who had gone after the ransom might also fall a victim to the rage of the robbers, without the money which he brought being saved. Besides, the conduct of the chief towards me made me feel certain of speedy deliverance. These reflections overcame the first powerful impulse, and I calmed the turbulent agitation which it had awakened.

I again took out my materials for drawing, and amused myself with sketching the magnificent prospect. It was now about noon, and every thing had sunk into repose, like the sleeping bandit before me. The noontide stillness that reigned over these mountains, the vast landscape below, gleaming with distant towns and dotted with various habitations and signs of life, yet all so silent, had a powerful effect upon my mind. The intermediate valleys, too, which lie among the mountains have a peculiar air of solitude. Few sounds are heard at midday to break the quiet of the scene. Sometimes the whistle of a solitary muleteer, lagging with his lazy animal along the road which winds through the centre of the valley; sometimes the faint piping of a shepherd's reed from the side of the mountain, or sometimes the bell of an ass slowly pacing along, followed by a monk with bare feet and bare shining head; and carrying provisions to the convent.

I had continued to sketch for some time among my sleeping companions, when at length I saw the captain of the band approaching, followed by a peasant leading a mule, on which was a well filled sack. I at first apprehended that this was some new prey fallen into the hands of the robbers, but the contented look of the peasant soon relieved me, and I was rejoiced to hear that it was our promised repast. The brigands now came running from the three sides of the mountain, having the quick scent of vultures. Every one busied himself in unloading the mule and relieving the sack of its contents.

The first thing that made its appearance was an enormous ham of a colour and plumpness that would have inspired the pencil of Teniers. It was followed by a large cheese, a bag of boiled chesnuts, a little barrel of wine, and a quantity of good household bread. Every thing was arranged on the grass with a degree of symmetry, and the captain presenting me his knife, requested me to help myself. We all seated ourselves round the viands, and nothing was heard for a time but the sound of vigorous mastication, or the gurgling of the barrel of wine as it revolved briskly about the circle. My long fasting and the mountain air and exercise had given me a keen appetite, and never did repast appear to me more excellent or picturesque.

From time to time one of the band was despatched to keep a look out upon the plain: no enemy was at hand, and the dinner was undisturbed.

The peasant received nearly three times the value of his provisions, and set off down the mountain highly satisfied with his bargain. I felt invigorated by the hearty meal I had made, and notwithstanding that the wound I had received the evening before was painful, yet I could not but feel extremely interested and gratified by the singular scenes continually presented to me. Every thing was picturesque about these wild beings and their haunts. Their bivouacs, their groups on guard, their indolent noontide repose on the mountain brow, their rude repast on the herbage among rocks and trees, every thing presented a study for a painter. But it was towards the approach of evening that I felt the highest enthusiasm awakened.

The setting sun, declining beyond the vast Campagna, shed its rich yellow beams on the woody summits of the Abruzzi. Several mountains crowned with snow shone brilliantly in the distance, contrasting their brightness with others, which thrown into shade, assumed deep tints of purple and violet. As the evening advanced, the landscape darkened into a sterner character. The immense solitude around; the wild mountains broken into rocks and precipices, intermingled with vast oaks, corks and chesnuts; and the groups of banditti in the foreground, reminded me of the savage scenes of Salvator Rosa.

To beguile the time the captain proposed to his comrades to spread before me their jewels and cameos, as I must doubtless be a judge of such articles, and able to form an estimate of their value. He set the example, the others followed it, and in a few moments I saw the grass before me sparkling with jewels and gems that would have delighted the eyes of an antiquary or a fine lady. Among them were several precious jewels and antique intaglios and cameos of great value, the spoils doubtless of travellers of distinction. I found that they were in the habit of selling their booty in the frontier towns: but as these in general were thinly and poorly peopled, and little frequented by travellers, they could offer no market for such valuable articles of taste and luxury. I suggested to them the certainty of their readily obtaining great prices for these gems among the rich strangers with which Rome was thronged.

The impression made upon their greedy minds was immediately apparent. One of the band, a young man, and the least known, requested permission of the captain to depart the following day in disguise for Rome, for the purpose of traffick; promising on the faith of a bandit (a sacred pledge amongst them) to return in two days to any place he might appoint. The captain consented, and a curious scene took place. The robbers crowded round him eagerly, confiding to him such of their jewels as they wished to dispose of, and giving him instructions what to demand. There was much bargaining and exchanging and selling of trinkets among them, and I beheld my watch which had a chain and valuable seals, purchased by the young robber merchant of the ruffian who had plundered me, for sixty dollars. I now conceived a faint hope that if it went to Rome, I might somehow or other regain possession of it.*

In the mean time day declined, and no messenger returned from Tusculum.

The idea of passing another night in the woods was extremely disheartening; for I began to be satisfied with what I had seen of robber life. The chieftain now ordered his men to follow him that he might station them at their posts, adding, that if the messenger did not return before night they must shift their quarters to some other place.

I was again left alone with the young bandit who had before guarded me: he had the same gloomy air and haggard eye, with now and then a bitter sardonic smile. I was determined to probe this ulcerated heart, and reminded him of a kind of promise he had given me to tell me the cause of his suffering.

It seemed to me as if these troubled spirits were glad of an

*The hopes of the artist were not disappointed—the robber was stopped at one of the gates of Rome. Something in his looks or deportment had excited suspicion. He was searched, and the valuable trinkets found on him sufficiently evinced his character. On applying to the police, the artist's watch was returned to him.

opportunity to disburthen themselves; and of having some fresh undiseased mind with which they could communicate. I had hardly made the request but he seated himself by my side, and gave me his story in, as nearly as I can recollect, the following words.

The Story of the Young Robber

I was born at the little town of Frosinone, which lies at the skirts of the Abruzzi. My father had made a little property in trade, and gave me some education, as he intended me for the church, but I had kept gay company too much to relish the cowl, so I grew up a loiterer about the place. I was a heedless fellow, a little quarrelsome on occasions, but good humoured in the main, so I made my way very well for a time, until I fell in love. There lived in our town a surveyor, or land bailiff, of the prince's, who had a young daughter, a beautiful girl of sixteen. She was looked upon as something better than the common run of our townsfolk, and was kept almost entirely at home. I saw her occasionally, and became madly in love with her, she looked so fresh and tender, and so different from the sunburnt females to whom I had been accustomed.

As my father kept me in money, I always dressed well, and took all opportunities of showing myself off to advantage in the eyes of the little beauty. I used to see her at church; and as I could play a little upon the guitar, I gave a tune sometimes under her window of an evening; and I tried to have interviews with her in her father's vineyard, not far from the town, where she sometimes walked. She was evidently pleased with me, but she was young and shy, and her father kept a strict eye upon her, and took alarm at my attentions, for he had a bad opinion of me, and looked for a better match for his daughter. I became furious at the difficulties thrown in my way, having been accustomed always to easy success among the women, being considered one of the smartest young fellows of the place.

Her father brought home a suitor for her; a rich farmer from a neighbouring town. The wedding day was appointed, and preparations were making. I got sight of her at her window, and I thought she looked sadly at me. I determined the match should not take place, cost what it might. I met her intended bridegroom in the market place, and could not restrain the expression of my rage. A few hot words passed between us, when I drew my stiletto, and stabbed him to the heart. I fled to a neighbouring church for refuge; and with a little money I obtained absolution; but I did not dare to venture from my asylum.

At that time our captain was forming his troop. He had known me from boyhood, and hearing of my situation, came to me in secret, and made such offers, that I agreed to enrol myself among his followers. Indeed, I had more than once thought of taking to this mode of life, having known several brave fellows of the mountains, who used to spend their money freely among us youngsters of the town. I accordingly left my asylum late one night, repaired to the appointed place of meeting; took the oaths prescribed, and became one of the troop. We were for some time in a distant part of the mountains, and our wild adventurous kind of life hit my fancy wonderfully, and diverted my thoughts. At length they returned with all their violence to the recollection of Rosetta. The solitude in which I often found myself, gave me time to brood over her image, and as I have kept watch at night over our sleeping camp in the mountains, my feelings have been roused almost to a fever.

At length we shifted our ground, and determined to make a descent upon the road between Terracina and Naples. In the course of our expedition, we passed a day or two in the woody mountains which rise above Frosinone. I cannot tell you how I felt when I looked down upon the place, and distinguished the residence of Rosetta. I determined to have an interview with her; but to what purpose? I could not expect that she would quit her home, and accompany me in my hazardous life among the mountains. She had been brought up too tenderly for that; and when I looked upon the women who were associated with some of our troop, I could not have borne the thoughts of her being their companion. All return to my former life was likewise hopeless; for a price was set upon my head. Still I determined to see her; the very hazard and fruitlessness of the thing made me furious to accomplish it.

It is about three weeks since I persuaded our captain to draw down to the vicinity of Frosinone, in hopes of entrapping some of its principal inhabitants, and compelling them to a ransom. We were lying in ambush towards evening, not far from the vineyard of Rosetta's father. I stole quietly from my companions, and drew near to reconnoitre the place of her frequent walks.

How my heart beat when among the vines, I beheld the gleaming of a white dress! I knew it must be Rosetta's; it being rare for any female of the place to dress in white. I advanced secretly and without noise, until putting aside the vines, I stood suddenly before her. She uttered a piercing shriek, but I seized her in my arms, put my hand upon her mouth and conjured her to be silent. I poured out all the frenzy of my passion; offered to renounce my mode of life, to put my fate in her hands, to fly with her where we might live in safety together. All that I could say, or do, would not pacify her. Instead of love, horror and affright seemed to have taken possession of her breast.—She struggled partly from my grasp, and filled the air with her cries. In an instant the captain and the rest of my companions were around us. I would have given any thing at that moment had she been safe out of our hands, and in her father's house. It was too late. The captain pronounced her a prize, and ordered that she should be borne to the mountains. I represented to him that she was my prize, that I had a previous claim to her; and I mentioned my former attachment. He sneered bitterly in reply; observed that brigands had no business with village intrigues, and that, according to the laws of the troop, all spoils of the kind were determined by lot. Love and jealousy were raging in my heart, but I had to choose between obedience and death. I surrendered her to the captain, and we made for the mountains.

She was overcome by affright, and her steps were so feeble and faltering, that it was necessary to support her. I could not endure the idea that my comrades should touch her, and assuming a forced tranquillity, begged she might be confided to me, as one to whom she was more accustomed. The captain regarded me for a moment with a searching look, but I bore it without flinching, and he consented. I took her in my arms: she was almost senseless. Her head rested on my shoulder; I felt her breath on my face, and it seemed to fan the flame which devoured me. Oh God! to have this glowing treasure in my arms, and yet to think it was not mine!

We arrived at the foot of the mountain. I ascended it with difficulty, particularly where the woods were thick; but I would not relinquish my delicious burthen. I reflected with rage, however, that I must soon do so. The thoughts that so delicate a creature must be abandoned to my rude companions, maddened me. I felt tempted, the stiletto in my hand, to cut my way through them all, and bear her off in triumph. I scarcely conceived the idea, before I saw its rashness; but my brain was fevered with the thought that any but myself should enjoy her charms. I endeavoured to outstrip my companions by the quickness of my movements; and to get a little distance a head, in case any favourable opportunity of escape should present. Vain effort! The voice of the captain suddenly ordered a halt. I trembled, but had to obey. The poor girl partly opened a languid eye, but was without strength or motion. I laid her upon the grass. The captain darted on me a terrible look of suspicion, and ordered me to scour the woods with my companions, in search of some shepherd who might be sent to her father's to demand a ransom.

I saw at once the peril. To resist with violence was certain death; but to leave her alone, in the power of the captain!—I spoke out then with a fervour, inspired by my passion and my despair. I reminded the captain that I was the first to seize her; that she was my prize, and that my previous attachment for her ought to make her sacred among my companions. I insisted, therefore, that he should pledge me his word to respect her; otherwise I should refuse obedience to his orders. His only reply was, to cock his carbine; and at the signal my comrades did the same. They laughed with cruelty at my impotent rage. What could I do? I felt the madness of resistance. I was menaced on all hands, and my companions obliged me to follow them. She remained alone with the chief—yes, alone—and almost lifeless!——

Here the robber paused in his recital, overpowered by his

emotions. Great drops of sweat stood on his forehead; he panted rather than breathed; his brawny bosom rose and fell like the waves of a troubled sea. When he had become a little calm, he continued his recital.

I was not long in finding a shepherd, said he. I ran with the rapidity of a deer, eager, if possible, to get back before what I dreaded might take place. I had left my companions far behind, and I rejoined them before they had reached one half the distance I had made. I hurried them back to the place where we had left the captain. As we approached, I beheld him seated by the side of Rosetta. His triumphant look, and the desolate condition of the unfortunate girl, left me no doubt of her fate. I know not how I restrained my fury.

It was with extreme difficulty, and by guiding her hand, that she was made to trace a few characters, requesting her father to send three hundred dollars as her ransom. The letter was despatched by the shepherd. When he was gone, the chief turned sternly to me: "You have set an example," said he, "of mutiny and self will, which if indulged would be ruinous to the troop. Had I treated you as our laws require, this bullet would have been driven through your brain. But you are an old friend: I have borne patiently with your fury and your folly; I have even protected you from a foolish passion that would have unmanned you. As to this girl, the laws of our association must have their course." So saying, he gave his commands, lots were drawn, and the helpless girl was abandoned to the troop.

Here the robber paused again, panting with fury, and it was some moments before he could resume his story.

Hell, said he, was raging in my heart. I beheld the impossibility of avenging myself, and I felt that, according to the articles in which we stood bound to one another, the captain was in the right. I rushed with frenzy from the place. I threw myself upon the earth; tore up the grass with my hands, and beat my head, and gnashed my teeth in agony and rage. When at length I returned, I beheld the wretched victim, pale, dishevelled; her dress torn and disordered. An emotion of pity for a moment subdued my fiercer feelings. I bore her to the foot of a tree, and leaned her gently against it. I took my gourd, which was filled with wine, and applying it to her lips, endeavoured to make her swallow a little. To what a condition was she reduced! She, whom I had once seen the pride of Frosinone, who but a short time before I had beheld sporting in her father's vineyard, so fresh and beautiful and happy! Her teeth were clenched; her eyes fixed on the ground; her form without motion, and in a state of absolute insensibility. I hung over her in an agony of recollection of all that she had been, and of anguish at what I now beheld her. I darted round a look of horror at my companions, who seemed like so many fiends exulting in the downfall of an angel, and I felt a horror at myself for being their accomplice.

The captain, always suspicious, saw with his usual penetration what was passing within me, and ordered me to go upon the ridge of the woods to keep a look out over the neighbourhood and await the return of the shepherd. I obeyed, of course, stifling the fury that raged within me, though I felt for the moment that he was my most deadly foe.

On my way, however, a ray of reflection came across my mind. I perceived that the captain was but following with strictness the terrible laws to which we had sworn fidelity. That the passion by which I had been blinded might with justice have been fatal to me but for his forbearance; that he had penetrated my soul, and had taken precautions, by sending me out of the way, to prevent my committing any excess in my anger. From that instant I felt that I was capable of pardoning him.

Occupied with these thoughts, I arrived at the foot of the mountain. The country was solitary and secure; and in a short time I beheld the shepherd at a distance crossing the plain. I hastened to meet him. He had obtained nothing. He had found the father plunged in the deepest distress. He had read the letter with violent emotion, and then calming himself with a sudden exertion, he had replied coldly, "My daughter has been dishonoured by those wretches; let her be returned without ransom, or let her die!"

I shuddered at this reply. I knew, according to the laws of our troop, her death was inevitable. Our oaths required it. I felt, nevertheless, that, not having been able to have her to myself, I could be her executioner!

The robber again paused with agitation. I sat musing upon his last frightful words, which proved to what excess the passions may be carried when escaped from all moral restraint. There was a horrible verity in this story that reminded me of some of the tragic fictions of Dante.

We now come to a fatal moment, resumed the bandit. After the report of the shepherd, I returned with him, and the chieftain received from his lips the refusal of the father. At a signal, which we all understood, we followed him some distance from the victim. He there pronounced her sentence of death. Every one stood ready to execute his order; but I interfered. I observed that there was something due to pity, as well as to justice. That I was as ready as any one to approve the implacable law which was to serve as a warning to all those who hesitated to pay the ransoms demanded for our prisoners, but that, though the sacrifice was proper, it ought to be made without cruelty. The night is approaching, continued I; she will soon be wrapped in sleep: let her then be despatched. All I now claim on the score of former kindness is, let me strike the blow. I will do it as surely, though more tenderly than another.

Several raised their voices against my proposition, but the captain imposed silence on them. He told me I might conduct her into a thicket at some distance, and he relied upon my promise.

I hastened to seize my prey. There was a forlorn kind of triumph at having at length become her exclusive possessor. I bore her off into the thickness of the forest. She remained in the same state of insensibility or stupor. I was thankful that she did not recollect me; for had she once murmured my name, I should have been overcome. She slept at length in the arms of him who was to poniard her. Many were the conflicts I underwent before I could bring myself to strike the blow. But my heart had become sore by the recent conflicts it had undergone, and I dreaded lest, by procrastination, some other should become her executioner. When her repose had continued for some time, I separated myself gently from her, that I might not disturb her sleep, and seizing suddenly my poniard, plunged it into her bosom. A painful and concentrated murmur, but without any convulsive movement, accompanied her last sigh. So perished this unfortunate.

———

He ceased to speak. I sat horror struck, covering my face with my hands, seeking, as it were, to hide from myself the frightful images he had presented to my mind. I was roused from this silence, by the voice of the captain. "You sleep," said he, "and it is time to be off. Come, we must abandon this height, as night is setting in, and the messenger is not returned. I will post some one on the mountain edge, to conduct him to the place where we shall pass the night."

This was no agreeable news to me. I was sick at heart with the dismal story I had heard. I was harassed and fatigued, and the sight of the banditti began to grow insupportable to me.

The captain assembled his comrades. We rapidly descended the forest which we had mounted with so much difficulty in the morning, and soon arrived in what appeared to be a frequented road. The robbers proceeded with great caution, carrying their guns cocked, and looking on every side with wary and suspicious eyes. They were apprehensive of encountering the civic patrole. We left Rocca Priori behind us. There was a fountain near by, and as I was excessively thirsty, I begged permission to stop and drink. The captain himself went, and brought me water in his hat. We pursued our route, when, at the extremity of an alley which crossed the road, I perceived a female on horseback, dressed in white. She was alone. I recollected the fate of the poor girl in the story, and trembled for her safety.

One of the brigands saw her at the same instant, and plunging into the bushes, he ran precipitately in the direction towards her. Stopping on the border of the alley, he put one knee to the ground, presented his carbine ready to menace her, or to shoot her horse if she attempted to fly, and in this way awaited her approach. I kept my eyes fixed on her with intense anxiety. I felt tempted to shout, and warn her of her danger, though my own destruction would have been the consequence. It was awful to see this tiger crouching ready for a bound, and the poor innocent victim wandering unconsciously near him. Nothing but a mere chance could save her.

To my joy, the chance turned in her favour. She seemed almost accidentally to take an opposite path, which led outside of the wood, where the robber dared not venture. To this casual deviation, she owed her safety.

I could not imagine why the captain of the band had ventured to such a distance from the height, on which he had placed the sentinel to watch the return of the messenger. He seemed himself anxious at the risk to which he exposed himself. His movements were rapid and uneasy; I could scarce keep pace with him. At length, after three hours of what might be termed a forced march, we mounted the extremity of the same woods, the summit of which we had occupied during the day; and I learnt, with satisfaction, that we had reached our quarters for the night. "You must be fatigued," said the chieftain; "but it was necessary to survey the environs, so as not to be surprised during the night. Had we met with the famous civic guard of Rocca Priori you would have seen fine sport." Such was the indefatigable precaution and forethought of this robber chief, who really gave continual evidences of military talent.

The night was magnificent. The moon rising above the horizon in a cloudless sky, faintly lit up the grand features of the mountains, while lights twinkling here and there, like terrestrial stars, in the wide, dusky expanse of the landscape, betrayed the lonely cabins of the shepherds. Exhausted by fatigue, and by the many agitations I had experienced, I prepared to sleep, soothed by the hope of approaching deliverance. The captain ordered his companions to collect some dry moss; he arranged with his own hands a kind of mattress and pillow of it, and gave me his ample mantle as a covering. I could not but feel both surprised and gratified by such unexpected attentions on the part of this benevolent cut-throat: for there is nothing more striking than to find the ordinary charities, which are matters of course in common life, flourishing by the side of such stern and sterile crime. It is like finding the tender flowers and fresh herbage of the valley growing among the rocks and cinders of the volcano.

Before I fell asleep, I had some further discourse with the captain, who seemed to feel great confidence in me. He referred to our previous conversation of the morning, told me he was weary of his hazardous profession; that he had acquired sufficient property, and was anxious to return to the world and lead a peaceful life in the bosom of his family. He wished to know whether it was not in my power to procure him a passport for the United States of America. I applauded his good intentions, and promised to do every thing in my power to promote its success. We then parted for the night. I stretched myself upon my couch of moss, which, after my fatigues, felt like a bed of down, and sheltered by the robber's mantle from all humidity, I slept soundly without waking, until the signal to arise.

It was nearly six o'clock, and the day was just dawning. As the place where we had passed the night was too much exposed, we moved up into the thickness of the woods. A fire was kindled. While there was any flame, the mantles were again extended round it; but when nothing remained but glowing cinders, they were lowered, and the robbers seated themselves in a circle.

The scene before me reminded me of some of those described by Homer. There wanted only the victim on the coals, and the sacred knife, to cut off the succulent parts, and distribute them around. My companions might have rivaled the grim warriors of Greece. In place of the noble repasts, however, of Achilles and Agamemnon, I beheld displayed on the grass the remains of the ham which had sustained so vigorous an attack on the preceding evening, accompanied by the reliques of the bread, cheese and wine.

We had scarcely commenced our frugal breakfast, when I heard again an imitation of the bleating of sheep, similar to what I had heard the day before. The captain answered it in the same tone. Two men were soon after seen descending from the woody height, where we had passed the preceding evening. On nearer approach, they proved to be the sentinel and the messenger. The captain rose and went to meet them. He made a signal for his comrades to join him. They had a short conference, and then returning to me with great eagerness, "Your ransom is paid," said he; "you are free!"

Though I had anticipated deliverance, I cannot tell you what a rush of delight these tidings gave me. I cared not to finish my repast, but prepared to depart. The captain took me by the hand; requested permission to write to me, and begged me not to forget the passport. I replied, that I hoped to be of effectual service to him, and that I relied on his honour to return the prince's note for five hundred dollars, now that the cash was paid. He regarded me for a moment with surprise; then, seeming to recollect himself, "E giusto," said he, "eccolo—adio!"* He delivered me the note, pressed my hand once more, and we separated. The labourers were permitted to follow me, and we resumed with joy our road towards Tusculum.

———

The Frenchman ceased to speak; the party continued for a few moments to pace the shore in silence. The story had made a deep impression, particularly on the Venetian lady. At that part which related to the young girl of Frosinone, she was violently affected; sobs broke from her; she clung closer to her husband, and as she looked up to him as if for protection, the moon beams shining on her beautifully fair countenance showed it paler than usual, while tears glittered in her fine dark eyes.

"Corragio, mia vita!" said he, as he gently and fondly tapped the white hand that lay upon her arm.

The Englishman alone preserved his usual phlegm, and the fair Venetian was piqued at it.

She had pardoned him a want of gallantry towards herself, though a sin of omission seldom met with in the gallant climate of Italy, but the quiet coolness which he maintained in matters which so much affected her; and the slow credence which he had given to the stories which had filled her with alarm, were quite vexatious.

"Santa Maria!" said she to her husband as they retired for the night, "what insensible beings these English are!"

*It is just—there it is—adieu!

The Adventure of the Englishman

In the morning all was bustle in the inn at Terracina.

The procaccio had departed at day break, on its route towards Rome, but the Englishman was yet to start, and the departure of an English equipage is always enough to keep an inn in a bustle. On this occasion there was more than usual stir; for the Englishman having much property about him, and having been convinced of the real danger of the road, had applied to the police and obtained, by dint of liberal pay, an escort of eight dragoons and twelve foot soldiers, as far as Fondi.

Perhaps, too, there might have been a little ostentation at bottom, from which, with great delicacy be it spoken, English travellers are not always exempt; though to say the truth, he had nothing of it in his manner. He moved about taciturn and reserved as usual, among the gaping crowd, in his gingerbread coloured travelling cap, with his hands in his pockets. He gave laconic orders to John as he packed away the thousand and one indispensable conveniencies of the night, double loaded his pistols with great *sang froid*, and deposited them in the pockets of the carriage, taking no notice of a pair of keen eyes gazing on him from among the herd of loitering idlers. The fair Venetian now came up with a request made in her dulcet tones, that he would permit their carriage to proceed under protection of his escort. The Englishman, who was busy loading another pair of pistols for his servant, and held the ramrod between his teeth, nodded assent as a matter of course, but without lifting up his eyes. The fair Venetian was not accustomed to such indifference. "O Dio!" ejaculated she softly as she retired, "Quanto sono insensibili questi Inglesi." At length off they set in gallant style, the eight dragoons prancing in front, the twelve foot soldiers marching in rear, and the carriages moving slowly in the centre to enable the infantry to keep pace with them. They had proceeded but a few hundred yards when it was discovered that some indispensable article had been left behind.

In fact the Englishman's purse was missing, and John was despatched to the inn to search for it.

This occasioned a little delay, and the carriage of the Venetians drove slowly on. John came back out of breath and out of humour, the purse was not to be found, his master was irritated, he recollected the very place where it lay: the cursed Italian servant had pocketed it. John was again sent back. He returned once more, without the purse, but with the landlord and the whole household at his heels. A thousand ejaculations and protestations, accompanied by all sorts of grimaces and contortions. "No purse had been seen—his eccellenza must be mistaken."

No—his eccellenza was not mistaken; the purse lay on the marble table, under the mirror, a green purse, half full of gold and silver. Again a thousand grimaces and contortions, and vows by San Gennaro, that no purse of the kind had been seen.

The Englishman became furious. "The waiter had pocketed it. The landlord was a knave. The inn a den of thieves—it was a d——d country—he had been cheated and plundered from one end of it to the other—but he'd have satisfaction—he'd drive right off to the police."

He was on the point of ordering the postillions to turn back, when, on rising, he displaced the cushion of the carriage, and the purse of money fell chinking to the floor.

All the blood in his body seemed to rush into his face. "D—n the purse," said he, as he snatched it up. He dashed a handfull of money on the ground before the pale cringing waiter. "There—be off," cried he: "John, order the postillions to drive on."

Above half an hour had been exhausted in this altercation. The Venetian carriage had loitered along; its passengers looking out from time to time, and expecting the escort every moment to follow. They had gradually turned an angle of the road that shut them out of sight. The little army was again in motion, and made a very picturesque appearance as it wound along at the bottom of the rocks; the morning sunshine beaming upon the weapons of the soldiery.

The Englishman lolled back in his carriage, vexed with himself at what had passed, and consequently out of humour with all the world. As this, however, is no uncommon case with gentlemen who travel for their pleasure, it is hardly worthy of remark.

They had wound up from the coast among the hills, and

came to a part of the road that admitted of some prospect ahead.

"I see nothing of the lady's carriage, sir," said John, leaning down from the coach box.

"Hang the lady's carriage!" said the Englishman, crustily; "don't plague me about the lady's carriage; must I be continually pestered with strangers?"

John said not another word, for he understood his master's mood. The road grew more wild and lonely; they were slowly proceeding in a foot pace up a hill; the dragoons were some distance ahead, and had just reached the summit of the hill, when they uttered an exclamation, or rather shout, and galloped forward. The Englishman was roused from his sulky reverie. He stretched his head from the carriage which had attained the brow of the hill. Before him extended a long hollow defile, commanded on one side by rugged precipitous heights, covered with bushes and scanty forest. At some distance, he beheld the carriage of the Venetians overturned; a numerous gang of desperadoes were rifling it; the young man and his servant were overpowered and partly stripped, and the lady was in the hands of two of the ruffians. The Englishman seized his pistols, sprang from the carriage, and called upon John to follow him. In the mean time as the dragoons came forward, the robbers who were busy with the carriage quitted their spoil, formed themselves in the middle of the road, and taking deliberate aim, fired. One of the dragoons fell, another was wounded, and the whole were for a moment checked and thrown in confusion. The robbers loaded again in an instant. The dragoons discharged their carbines, but without apparent effect; they received another volley, which, though none fell, threw them again into confusion. The robbers were loading a second time, when they saw the foot soldiers at hand.— "Scampa via!" was the word. They abandoned their prey, and retreated up the rocks; the soldiers after them. They fought from cliff to cliff and bush to bush, the robbers turning every now and then to fire upon their pursuers; the soldiers scrambling after them, and discharging their muskets whenever they could get a chance. Sometimes a soldier or a robber was shot down, and came tumbling among the cliffs. The dragoons kept firing from below, whenever a robber came in sight.

The Englishman had hastened to the scene of action, and the balls discharged at the dragoons had whistled past him as he advanced. One object, however, engrossed his attention. It was the beautiful Venetian lady in the hands of two of the robbers, who during the confusion of the fight, carried her shrieking up the mountain. He saw her dress gleaming among the bushes, and he sprang up the rocks to intercept the robbers as they bore off their prey. The ruggedness of the steep and the entanglements of the bushes, delayed and impeded him. He lost sight of the lady, but was still guided by her cries, which grew fainter and fainter. They were off to the left, while the reports of muskets showed that the battle was raging to the right.

At length he came upon what appeared to be a rugged footpath, faintly worn in a gully of the rocks, and beheld the ruffians at some distance hurrying the lady up the defile. One of them hearing his approach let go his prey, advanced towards him, and levelling the carbine which had been slung on his back, fired. The ball whizzed through the Englishman's hat, and carried with it some of his hair. He returned the fire with one of his pistols; and the robber fell. The other brigand now dropped the lady, and drawing a long pistol from his belt, fired on his adversary with deliberate aim; the ball passed between his left arm and his side, slightly wounding the arm. The Englishman advanced and discharged his remaining pistol, which wounded the robber, but not severely. The brigand drew a stiletto, and rushed upon his adversary, who eluded the blow, receiving merely a slight wound, and defended himself with his pistol, which had a spring bayonet. They closed with one another, and a desperate struggle ensued. The robber was a square built, thick set man, powerful, muscular and active. The Englishman though of larger frame and greater strength, was less active and less accustomed to athletic exercises and feats of hardihood, but he showed himself practised and skilled in the art of defence. They were on a craggy height, and the Englishman perceived that his antagonist was striving to press him to the edge.

A side glance showed him also the robber whom he had first wounded, scrambling up to the assistance of his comrade, stiletto in hand. He had, in fact, attained the summit of the cliff, he was within a few steps, and the Englishman felt that his case was desperate, when he heard suddenly the report of a pistol and the ruffian fell. The shot came from John, who had arrived just in time to save his master.

The remaining robber, exhausted by loss of blood and the violence of the contest, showed signs of faltering. The Englishman pursued his advantage; pressed on him, and as his strength relaxed, dashed him headlong from the precipice. He looked after him and saw him lying motionless among the rocks below.

The Englishman now sought the fair Venetian. He found her senseless on the ground. With his servant's assistance he bore her down to the road, where her husband was raving like one distracted. He had sought her in vain, and had given her over for lost; and when he beheld her thus brought back in safety, his joy was equally wild and ungovernable. He would have caught her insensible form to his bosom had not the Englishman restrained him. The latter, now really aroused, displayed a true tenderness and manly gallantry which one would not have expected from his habitual phlegm. His kindness, however, was practical, not wasted in words. He despatched John to the carriage for restoratives of all kinds, and, totally thoughtless of himself, was anxious only about his lovely charge.

The occasional discharge of fire arms along the height showed that a retreating fight was still kept up by the robbers. The lady gave signs of reviving animation. The Englishman, eager to get her from this place of danger, conveyed her to his own carriage, and, committing her to the care of her husband, ordered the dragoons to escort them to Fondi. The Venetian would have insisted on the Englishman's getting into the carriage; but the latter refused. He poured forth a torrent of thanks and benedictions; but the Englishman beckoned to the postillions to drive on.

John now dressed his master's wounds, which were found not to be serious, though he was faint with loss of blood. The Venetian carriage had been righted, and the baggage replaced;

and, getting into it, they set out on their way towards Fondi, leaving the foot soldiers still engaged in ferreting out the banditti.

Before arriving at Fondi the fair Venetian had completely recovered from her swoon. She made the usual question —

"Where was she?"

"In the Englishman's carriage."

"How had she escaped from the robbers?"

"The Englishman had rescued her."

Her transports were unbounded; and mingled with them were enthusiastic ejaculations of gratitude to her deliverer. A thousand times did she reproach herself for having accused him of coldness and insensibility. The moment she saw him she rushed into his arms with the vivacity of her nation, and hung about his neck in a speechless transport of gratitude.

Never was man more embarrassed by the embraces of a fine woman.

"Tut! tut!" said the Englishman.

"You are wounded!" shrieked the fair Venetian, as she saw blood upon his clothes.

"Pooh—nothing at all!"

"My deliverer!—my angel!" exclaimed she, clasping him again round the neck and sobbing on his bosom.

"Pooh!" said the Englishman, looking somewhat foolish, "this is all nonsense."

PART IV

THE MONEY DIGGERS

FOUND AMONG THE PAPERS OF THE LATE DIEDRICH KNICKERBOCKER

> Now I remember those old women's words
> Who in my youth would tell me winter's tales;
> And speak of spirits and ghosts that glide by night
> About the place where treasure hath been hid.
> MARLOW'S JEW OF MALTA

Hell Gate

About six miles from the renowned city of the Manhattoes, in that Sound, or arm of the sea, which passes between the main land and Nassau or Long Island, there is a narrow strait, where the current is violently compressed between shouldering promontories, and horribly perplexed by rocks and shoals. Being at the best of times a very violent, impetuous current, it takes these impediments in mighty dudgeon; boiling in whirlpools; brawling and fretting in ripples; raging and roaring in rapids and breakers; and, in short, indulging in all kinds of wrong headed paroxysms. At such times, wo to any unlucky vessel that ventures within its clutches.

This termagant humour, however, prevails only at certain times of tide. At low water, for instance, it is as pacific a stream as you would wish to see; but as the tide rises, it begins to fret; at half tide it roars with might and main, like a bully bellowing for more drink; but when the tide is full it relapses into quiet, and for a time sleeps as soundly as an alderman after dinner. In fact, it may be compared to a quarrelsome toper, who is a peaceable fellow enough when he has no liquor at all, or when he has a skin full, but who, when half seas over, plays the very devil.

This mighty blustering, bullying, hard drinking little strait was a place of great danger and perplexity to the Dutch navigators of ancient days; hectoring their tub built barks in a most unruly style; whirling them about, in a manner to make any but a Dutchman giddy, and not unfrequently stranding them upon rocks and reefs, as it did the famous squadron of Oloffe the Dreamer, when seeking a place to found the city of the Manhattoes. Whereupon out of sheer spleen they denominated it Hellegat and solemnly gave it over to the devil. This appellation has since been aptly rendered into English by the name of Hell Gate; and into nonsense by the name of Hurl Gate, according to certain foreign intruders who neither understood Dutch nor English.—May St. Nicholas confound them!

This strait of Hell Gate was a place of great awe and perilous enterprise to me in my boyhood; having been much of a

navigator on those small seas, and having more than once run
the risk of shipwreck and drowning in the course of certain
holyday voyages, to which in common with other Dutch urchins I was rather prone. Indeed, partly from the name, and
partly from various strange circumstances connected with it,
this place had far more terrors in the eyes of my truant companions and myself than had Scylla and Charybdis for the
navigators of yore.

In the midst of this strait, and hard by a group of rocks
called "the Hen and Chickens," there lay the wreck of a vessel
which had been entangled in the whirlpools and stranded
during a storm. There was a wild story told to us of this being
the wreck of a pirate, and some tale of bloody murder which I
cannot now recollect, but which made us regard it with great
awe, and keep far from it in our cruisings. Indeed, the desolate look of this forlorn hulk, and the fearful place where it lay
rotting, were enough to awaken strange notions. A row of
timber heads, blackened by time, just peered above the surface at high water; but at low tide a considerable part of the
hull was bare, and its great ribs or timbers, partly stripped of
their planks and dripping with sea weeds, looked like the
huge skeleton of some sea monster. There was also the stump
of a mast, with a few ropes and blocks swinging about
and whistling in the wind, while the sea gull wheeled and
screamed around the melancholy carcass. I have a faint recollection of some hobgoblin tale of sailors' ghosts being seen
about this wreck at night, with bare sculls, and blue lights
in their sockets instead of eyes, but I have forgotten all the
particulars.

In fact, the whole of this neighbourhood was, like the
straits of Pylorus of yore, a region of fable and romance to
me. From the strait to the Manhattoes the borders of the
Sound are greatly diversified, being broken and indented by
rocky nooks overhung with trees, which give them a wild and
romantic look. In the time of my boyhood they abounded
with traditions about pirates, ghosts, smugglers, and buried
money; which had a wonderful effect upon the young minds
of my companions and myself.

As I grew to more mature years I made diligent research
after the truth of these strange traditions; for I have always

been a curious investigator of the valuable but obscure branches of the history of my native province. I found infinite difficulty, however, in arriving at any precise information. In seeking to dig up one fact it is incredible the number of fables which I unearthed. I will say nothing of the Devil's Stepping Stones, by which that arch fiend made his retreat from Connecticut to Long Island, across the Sound; seeing the subject is likely to be learnedly treated by a worthy friend and contemporary historian whom I have furnished with particulars thereof.* Neither will I say any thing of the black man in a three cornered hat, seated in the stern of a jolly boat who used to be seen about Hell Gate in stormy weather; and who went by the name of the Pirate's Spuke (i.e. Pirate's Ghost), and whom, it is said, old Governor Stuyvesant once shot with a silver bullet; because I never could meet with any person of stanch credibility who professed to have seen this spectrum; unless it were the widow of Manus Conklin the blacksmith of Frogs Neck; but then, poor woman, she was a little purblind, and might have been mistaken; though they say she saw farther than other folks in the dark.

All this, however, was but little satisfactory in regard to the tales of pirates and their buried money about which I was most curious; and the following is all that I could for a long time collect that had any thing like an air of authenticity.

Kidd the Pirate

In old times, just after the territory of the New Netherlands had been wrested from the hands of their High Mightinesses the Lords States General of Holland, by King Charles the Second, and while it was as yet in an unquiet state, the province was a great resort of random adventurers, loose livers, and all that class of haphazard fellows who live by their wits, and dislike the old fashioned restraint of law and gospel.

*For a very interesting and authentic account of the Devil and his Stepping Stones, see the valuable memoir read before the New-York Historical Society since the death of Mr. Knickerbocker, by his friend, an eminent jurist of the place.

Among these, the foremost were the Buccaneers. These were rovers of the deep, who, perhaps, in time of war had been educated in those schools of piracy, the privateers; but having once tasted the sweets of plunder, had ever retained a hankering after it. There is but a slight step from the privateersman to the pirate; both fight for the love of plunder; only that the latter is the bravest, as he dares both the enemy and the gallows.

But in whatever school they had been taught, the Buccaneers who kept about the English colonies were daring fellows, and made sad work in times of peace among the Spanish settlements and Spanish merchantmen. The easy access to the harbour of the Manhattoes, the number of hiding places about its waters, and the laxity of its scarcely organized government, made it a great rendezvous of the pirates, where they might dispose of their booty, and concert new depredations. As they brought home with them wealthy lading of all kinds, the luxuries of the tropics, and the sumptuous spoils of the Spanish provinces, and disposed of them with the proverbial carelessness of freebooters, they were welcome visitors to the thrifty traders of the Manhattoes. Crews of these desperadoes, therefore, the runagates of every country and every clime, might be seen swaggering, in open day, about the streets of the little burgh; elbowing its quiet Mynheers; trafficking away their rich outlandish plunder, at half or quarter price, to the wary merchant, and then squandering their prize money in taverns; drinking, gambling, singing, swearing, shouting, and astounding the neighbourhood with midnight brawl and ruffian revelry.

At length these excesses rose to such a height as to become a scandal to the provinces, and to call loudly for the interposition of government. Measures were accordingly taken to put a stop to the widely extended evil, and to ferret this vermin brood out of the colonies.

Among the agents employed to execute this purpose was the notorious Captain Kidd. He had long been an equivocal character; one of those nondescript animals of the ocean that are neither fish, flesh, nor fowl. He was somewhat of a trader, something more of a smuggler, with a considerable dash of the pickaroon. He had traded for many years among the pirates, in a little rakish, musquito built vessel, that could run into all kinds of waters. He knew all their haunts and lurking places; was always hooking about on mysterious voyages; and as busy as a Mother Cary's chicken in a storm.

This nondescript personage was pitched upon by government as the very man to hunt the pirates by sea, upon the good old maxim of "setting a rogue to catch a rogue;" or as otters are sometimes used to catch their cousins german, the fish. Kidd accordingly sailed for New York, in 1695, in a gallant vessel called the Adventure Galley, well armed and duly commissioned. On arriving at his old haunts, however, he shipped his crew on new terms; enlisted a number of his old comrades, lads of the knife and the pistol, and then set sail for the East. Instead of cruising against pirates he turned pirate himself: steered to the Madeiras, to Bonavista, and Madagascar, and cruised about the entrance of the Red Sea. Here, among other maritime robberies, he captured a rich Quedah merchantman, manned by Moors, though commanded by an Englishman. Kidd would fain have passed this off for a worthy exploit, as being a kind of crusade against the infidels; but government had long since lost all relish for such Christian triumphs.

After roaming the seas, trafficking his prizes, and changing from ship to ship, Kidd had the hardihood to return to Boston, laden with booty, with a crew of swaggering companions at his heels.

Times, however, had changed. The buccaneers could no longer show a whisker in the colonies with impunity. The new governor, Lord Bellamont, had signalized himself by his zeal in extirpating these offenders; and was doubly exasperated against Kidd, having been instrumental in appointing him to the trust which he had betrayed. No sooner, therefore, did he show himself in Boston, than the alarm was given of his reappearance, and measures were taken to arrest this cutpurse of the ocean. The daring character which Kidd had acquired, however, and the desperate fellows who followed like bull dogs at his heels, caused a little delay in his arrest. He took advantage of this, it is said, to bury the greater part of his treasures, and then carried a high head about the streets of Boston. He even attempted to defend himself when arrested;

but was secured and thrown into prison, with his followers. Such was the formidable character of this pirate and his crew, that it was thought advisable to despatch a frigate to bring them to England. Great exertions were made to screen him from justice, but in vain; he and his comrades were tried, condemned, and hanged at Execution Dock in London. Kidd died hard, for the rope with which he was first tied up broke with his weight, and he tumbled to the ground; he was tied up a second time, and more effectually; hence came, doubtless, the story of Kidd's having a charmed life, and that he had to be twice hanged.

Such is the main outline of Kidd's history; but it has given birth to an innumerable progeny of traditions. The report of his having buried great treasures of gold and jewels before his arrest set the brains of all the good people along the coast in a ferment. There were rumours on rumours of great sums of money found here and there; sometimes in one part of the country, sometimes in another; of coins with Moorish inscriptions, doubtless the spoils of his eastern prizes, but which the common people looked upon with superstitious awe, regarding the Moorish letters as diabolical or magical characters.

Some reported the treasure to have been buried in solitary unsettled places, about Plymouth and Cape Cod; but by degrees various other parts, not only on the eastern coast, but along the shores of the Sound, and even of Manhattan and Long Island, were gilded by these rumours. In fact, the rigorous measures of Lord Bellamont spread sudden consternation among the buccaneers in every part of the provinces: they secreted their money and jewels in lonely out of the way places, about the wild shores of the rivers and sea coast, and dispersed themselves over the face of the country. The hand of justice prevented many of them from ever returning to regain their buried treasures, which remained, and remain probably to this day, objects of enterprise for the money digger.

This is the cause of those frequent reports of trees and rocks bearing mysterious marks, supposed to indicate the spots where treasure lay hidden; and many have been the ransackings after the pirates' booty.

In all the stories which once abounded of these enterprizes

the devil played a conspicuous part. Either he was conciliated by ceremonies and invocations, or some solemn compact was made with him. Still he was ever prone to play the money diggers some slippery trick. Some would dig so far as to come to an iron chest, when some baffling circumstance was sure to take place. Either the earth would fall in and fill up the pit, or some direful noise or apparition would frighten the party from the place; and sometimes the devil himself would appear and bear off the prize when within their very grasp; and if they revisited the place the next day not a trace would be found of their labours of the preceding night.

All these rumours, however, were extremely vague, and for a long time tantalized without gratifying my curiosity. There is nothing in this world so hard to get at as truth, and there is nothing in this world but truth that I care for. I sought among all my favourite sources of authentic information, the oldest inhabitants, and particularly the old Dutch wives of the province; but though I flatter myself I am better versed than most men in the curious history of my native province, yet for a long time my inquiries were unattended with any substantial result.

At length it happened that, one calm day in the latter part of summer, I was relaxing myself from the toils of severe study by a day's amusement in fishing in those waters which had been the favourite resort of my boyhood. I was in company with several worthy burghers of my native city, among whom were more than one illustrious member of the corporation, whose names, did I dare to mention them, would do honour to my humble page. Our sport was indifferent; the fish did not bite freely; and we frequently changed our fishing ground, without bettering our luck. We were at length anchored close under a ledge of rocky coast, on the eastern side of the island of Mannahata. It was a still, warm day. The stream whirled and dimpled by us without a wave or even a ripple, and every thing was so calm and quiet, that it was almost startling when the kingfisher would pitch himself from the branch of some dry tree, and after suspending himself for a moment in the air to take his aim, would souse into the smooth water after his prey. While we were lolling in our boat, half drowsy with the warm stillness of the day and the dullness of our sport, one of our party, a worthy alderman, was overtaken by a slumber, and as he dozed suffered the sinker of his drop line to lie upon the bottom of the river. On waking he found he had caught something of importance, from the weight; on drawing it to the surface, we were much surprised to find a long pistol of very curious and outlandish fashion, which from its rusted condition, and its stock being worm eaten, and covered with barnacles, appeared to have lain a long time under water. The unexpected appearance of this document of warfare occasioned much speculation among my pacific companions. One supposed it to have fallen there during the revolutionary war. Another, from the peculiarity of its fashion, attributed it to the voyagers in the earliest days of the settlement; perchance to the renowned Adrian Block who explored the Sound and discovered Block Island, since so noted for its cheese. But a third, after regarding it for some time, pronounced it to be of veritable Spanish workmanship.

"I'll warrant," said he, "if this pistol could talk it would tell strange stories of hard fights among the Spanish Dons. I've no doubt but it is a relique of the buccaneers of old times—who knows but it belonged to Kidd himself?"

"Ah, that Kidd was a resolute fellow," cried an iron faced Cape Cod whaler. "There's a fine old song about him, all to the tune of

> 'My name is Robert Kidd,
> As I sailed, as I sailed.'

And then it tells all about how he gained the devil's good graces by burying the bible;

> 'I had the bible in my hand,
> As I sailed, as I sailed,
> And I buried it in the sand,
> As I sailed.'

Odsfish, if I thought this pistol had belonged to Kidd I should set great store by it for curiosity's sake. By the way, I recollect a story about a fellow who once dug up Kidd's buried money, which was written by a neighbour of mine, and which I learnt by heart. As the fish don't bite just now, I'll tell it to you, by way of passing away the time."—And so saying, he gave us the following narration.

The Devil and Tom Walker

A few miles from Boston, in Massachusetts, there is a deep inlet winding several miles into the interior of the country from Charles Bay, and terminating in a thickly wooded swamp, or morass. On one side of this inlet is a beautiful dark grove; on the opposite side the land rises abruptly from the water's edge, into a high ridge on which grow a few scattered oaks of great age and immense size. Under one of these gigantic trees, according to old stories, there was a great amount of treasure buried by Kidd the pirate. The inlet allowed a facility to bring the money in a boat secretly and at night to the very foot of the hill. The elevation of the place permitted a good look out to be kept that no one was at hand, while the remarkable trees formed good landmarks by which the place might easily be found again. The old stories add, moreover, that the devil presided at the hiding of the money, and took it under his guardianship; but this, it is well known, he always does with buried treasure, particularly when it has been ill gotten. Be that as it may, Kidd never returned to recover his wealth; being shortly after seized at Boston, sent out to England, and there hanged for a pirate.

About the year 1727, just at the time when earthquakes were prevalent in New England, and shook many tall sinners down upon their knees, there lived near this place a meagre miserly fellow of the name of Tom Walker. He had a wife as miserly as himself; they were so miserly that they even conspired to cheat each other. Whatever the woman could lay hands on she hid away: a hen could not cackle but she was on the alert to secure the new laid egg. Her husband was continually prying about to detect her secret hoards, and many and fierce were the conflicts that took place about what ought to have been common property. They lived in a forlorn looking house, that stood alone and had an air of starvation. A few straggling savin trees, emblems of sterility, grew near it; no smoke ever curled from its chimney; no traveller stopped at its door. A miserable horse, whose ribs were as articulate as the bars of a gridiron, stalked about a field where a thin carpet of moss, scarcely covering the ragged beds of pudding stone, tantalized and balked his hunger; and sometimes he would lean his head over the fence, look piteously at the passer by, and seem to petition deliverance from this land of famine. The house and its inmates had altogether a bad name. Tom's wife was a tall termagant, fierce of temper, loud of tongue, and strong of arm. Her voice was often heard in wordy warfare with her husband; and his face sometimes showed signs that their conflicts were not confined to words. No one ventured, however, to interfere between them; the lonely wayfarer shrank within himself at the horrid clamour and clapper clawing; eyed the den of discord askance, and hurried on his way, rejoicing, if a bachelor, in his celibacy.

One day that Tom Walker had been to a distant part of the neighbourhood, he took what he considered a short cut homewards through the swamp. Like most short cuts, it was an ill chosen route. The swamp was thickly grown with great gloomy pines and hemlocks, some of them ninety feet high; which made it dark at noonday, and a retreat for all the owls of the neighbourhood. It was full of pits and quagmires, partly covered with weeds and mosses; where the green surface often betrayed the traveller into a gulf of black smothering mud; there were also dark and stagnant pools, the abodes of the tadpole, the bull frog, and the water snake, where the trunks of pines and hemlocks lay half drowned, half rotting, looking like alligators, sleeping in the mire.

Tom had long been picking his way cautiously through this treacherous forest; stepping from tuft to tuft of rushes and roots which afforded precarious footholds among deep sloughs; or pacing carefully, like a cat, along the prostrate trunks of trees; startled now and then by the sudden screaming of the bittern, or the quacking of a wild duck, rising on the wing from some solitary pool. At length he arrived at a piece of firm ground, which ran out like a peninsula into the deep bosom of the swamp. It had been one of the strong holds of the Indians during their wars with the first colonists. Here they had thrown up a kind of fort which they had looked upon as almost impregnable, and had used as a place of refuge for their squaws and children. Nothing remained of the old Indian fort but a few embankments gradually sinking to the level of the surrounding earth, and already overgrown in part by oaks and other forest trees, the foliage of which formed a contrast to the dark pines and hemlocks of the swamp.

It was late in the dusk of evening when Tom Walker reached the old fort, and he paused there for a while to rest himself. Any one but he would have felt unwilling to linger in this lonely melancholy place, for the common people had a bad opinion of it from the stories handed down from the time of the Indian wars; when it was asserted that the savages held incantations here and made sacrifices to the evil spirit. Tom Walker, however, was not a man to be troubled with any fears of the kind.

He reposed himself for some time on the trunk of a fallen hemlock, listening to the boding cry of the tree toad, and delving with his walking staff into a mound of black mould at his feet. As he turned up the soil unconsciously, his staff struck against something hard. He raked it out of the vegetable mould, and lo! a cloven skull with an Indian tomahawk buried deep in it, lay before him. The rust on the weapon showed the time that had elapsed since this death blow had been given. It was a dreary memento of the fierce struggle that had taken place in this last foothold of the Indian warriors.

"Humph!" said Tom Walker, as he gave the skull a kick to shake the dirt from it.

"Let that skull alone!" said a gruff voice.

Tom lifted up his eyes and beheld a great black man, seated directly opposite him on the stump of a tree. He was exceedingly surprised, having neither seen nor heard any one approach, and he was still more perplexed on observing, as well as the gathering gloom would permit, that the stranger was neither negro nor Indian. It is true, he was dressed in a rude, half Indian garb, and had a red belt or sash swathed round his body, but his face was neither black nor copper colour, but swarthy and dingy and begrimed with soot, as if he had been accustomed to toil among fires and forges. He had a shock of coarse black hair, that stood out from his head in all directions; and bore an axe on his shoulder.

He scowled for a moment at Tom with a pair of great red eyes.

"What are you doing on my grounds?" said the black man, with a hoarse growling voice.

"Your grounds?" said Tom, with a sneer; "no more your grounds than mine: they belong to Deacon Peabody."

"Deacon Peabody be d——d," said the stranger, "as I flatter myself he will be, if he does not look more to his own sins and less to those of his neighbours. Look yonder, and see how Deacon Peabody is faring."

Tom looked in the direction that the stranger pointed, and beheld one of the great trees, fair and flourishing without, but rotten at the core, and saw that it had been nearly hewn through, so that the first high wind was likely to blow it down. On the bark of the tree was scored the name of Deacon Peabody, an eminent man, who had waxed wealthy by driving shrewd bargains with the Indians. He now looked round and found most of the tall trees marked with the name of some great man of the colony, and all more or less scored by the axe. The one on which he had been seated, and which had evidently just been hewn down, bore the name of Crowninshield; and he recollected a mighty rich man of that name, who made a vulgar display of wealth, which it was whispered he had acquired by buccaneering.

"He's just ready for burning!" said the black man, with a growl of triumph. "You see I am likely to have a good stock of firewood for winter."

"But what right have you," said Tom, "to cut down Deacon Peabody's timber?"

"The right of prior claim," said the other. "This woodland belonged to me long before one of your white faced race put foot upon the soil."

"And pray, who are you, if I may be so bold?" said Tom.

"Oh, I go by various names. I am the Wild Huntsman in some countries; the Black Miner in others. In this neighbourhood I am known by the name of the Black Woodsman. I am he to whom the red men consecrated this spot, and in honour of whom they now and then roasted a white man by way of

sweet smelling sacrifice. Since the red men have been extermi-
nated by you white savages, I amuse myself by presiding at
the persecutions of quakers and anabaptists; I am the great
patron and prompter of slave dealers, and the grand master of
the Salem witches."

"The upshot of all which is, that, if I mistake not," said
Tom, sturdily, "you are he commonly called Old Scratch."

"The same at your service!" replied the black man, with a
half civil nod.

Such was the opening of this interview, according to the
old story, though it has almost too familiar an air to be cred-
ited. One would think that to meet with such a singular
personage in this wild lonely place, would have shaken any
man's nerves: but Tom was a hard minded fellow, not easily
daunted, and he had lived so long with a termagant wife, that
he did not even fear the devil.

It is said that after this commencement, they had a long
and earnest conversation together, as Tom returned homewards. The black man told him of great sums of money buried by Kidd the pirate, under the oak trees on the high ridge
not far from the morass. All these were under his command
and protected by his power, so that none could find them but
such as propitiated his favour. These he offered to place
within Tom Walker's reach, having conceived an especial
kindness for him: but they were to be had only on certain
conditions. What these conditions were, may easily be surmised, though Tom never disclosed them publicly. They must
have been very hard, for he required time to think of them,
and he was not a man to stick at trifles where money was in
view. When they had reached the edge of the swamp the
stranger paused.

"What proof have I that all you have been telling me is
true?" said Tom.

"There is my signature," said the black man, pressing his
finger on Tom's forehead. So saying, he turned off among
the thickets of the swamp, and seemed, as Tom said, to go
down, down, down, into the earth, until nothing but his head
and shoulders could be seen, and so on until he totally disappeared.

When Tom reached home he found the black print of a

finger burnt, as it were, into his forehead, which nothing could obliterate.

The first news his wife had to tell him was the sudden death of Absalom Crowninshield the rich buccaneer. It was announced in the papers with the usual flourish, that "a great man had fallen in Israel."

Tom recollected the tree which his black friend had just hewn down, and which was ready for burning. "Let the free-booter roast," said Tom, "who cares!" He now felt convinced that all he had heard and seen was no illusion.

He was not prone to let his wife into his confidence; but as this was an uneasy secret, he willingly shared it with her. All her avarice was awakened at the mention of hidden gold, and she urged her husband to comply with the black man's terms and secure what would make them wealthy for life. However Tom might have felt disposed to sell himself to the devil, he was determined not to do so to oblige his wife; so he flatly refused out of the mere spirit of contradiction. Many and bitter were the quarrels they had on the subject, but the more she talked the more resolute was Tom not to be damned to please her. At length she determined to drive the bargain on her own account, and if she succeeded, to keep all the gain to herself.

Being of the same fearless temper as her husband, she set off for the old Indian fort towards the close of a summer's day. She was many hours absent. When she came back she was reserved and sullen in her replies. She spoke something of a black man whom she had met about twilight, hewing at the root of a tall tree. He was sulky, however, and would not come to terms; she was to go again with a propitiatory offering, but what it was she forbore to say.

The next evening she set off again for the swamp, with her apron heavily laden. Tom waited and waited for her, but in vain: midnight came, but she did not make her appearance; morning, noon, night returned, but still she did not come. Tom now grew uneasy for her safety; especially as he found she had carried off in her apron the silver teapot and spoons and every portable article of value. Another night elapsed, another morning came; but no wife. In a word, she was never heard of more.

What was her real fate nobody knows, in consequence of so many pretending to know. It is one of those facts which have become confounded by a variety of historians. Some asserted that she lost her way among the tangled mazes of the swamp and sank into some pit or slough; others, more uncharitable, hinted that she had eloped with the household booty, and made off to some other province; while others assert that the tempter had decoyed her into a dismal quagmire on top of which her hat was found lying. In confirmation of this, it was said a great black man with an axe on his shoulder was seen late that very evening coming out of the swamp, carrying a bundle tied in a check apron, with an air of surly triumph.

The most current and probable story, however, observes that Tom Walker grew so anxious about the fate of his wife and his property that he set out at length to seek them both at the Indian fort. During a long summer's afternoon he searched about the gloomy place, but no wife was to be seen. He called her name repeatedly, but she was no where to be heard. The bittern alone responded to his voice, as he flew screaming by; or the bull frog croaked dolefully from a neighbouring pool. At length, it is said, just in the brown hour of twilight, when the owls began to hoot and the bats to flit about, his attention was attracted by the clamour of carrion crows hovering about a cypress tree. He looked up and beheld a bundle tied in a check apron and hanging in the branches of the tree; with a great vulture perched hard by, as if keeping watch upon it. He leaped with joy, for he recognized his wife's apron, and supposed it to contain the household valuables.

"Let us get hold of the property," said he, consolingly to himself, "and we will endeavour to do without the woman."

As he scrambled up the tree the vulture spread its wide wings, and sailed off screaming into the deep shadows of the forest. Tom seized the check apron, but, woful sight! found nothing but a heart and liver tied up in it.

Such, according to the most authentic old story, was all that was to be found of Tom's wife. She had probably attempted to deal with the black man as she had been accustomed to deal with her husband; but though a female scold is generally considered a match for the devil, yet in this instance she appears to have had the worst of it. She must have died game however; for it is said Tom noticed many prints of cloven feet deeply stamped about the tree, and found handsful of hair, that looked as if they had been plucked from the coarse black shock of the woodsman. Tom knew his wife's prowess by experience. He shrugged his shoulders as he looked at the signs of a fierce clapper clawing. "Egad," said he to himself, "Old Scratch must have had a tough time of it!"

Tom consoled himself for the loss of his property with the loss of his wife; for he was a man of fortitude. He even felt something like gratitude towards the black woodsman, who he considered had done him a kindness. He sought, therefore, to cultivate a further acquaintance with him, but for some time without success; the old black legs played shy, for whatever people may think, he is not always to be had for calling for; he knows how to play his cards when pretty sure of his game.

At length, it is said, when delay had whetted Tom's eagerness to the quick, and prepared him to agree to any thing rather than not gain the promised treasure, he met the black man one evening in his usual woodman dress, with his axe on his shoulder, sauntering along the edge of the swamp, and humming a tune. He affected to receive Tom's advances with great indifference, made brief replies, and went on humming his tune.

By degrees, however, Tom brought him to business, and they began to haggle about the terms on which the former was to have the pirate's treasure. There was one condition which need not be mentioned, being generally understood in all cases where the devil grants favours; but there were others about which, though of less importance, he was inflexibly obstinate. He insisted that the money found through his means should be employed in his service. He proposed, therefore, that Tom should employ it in the black traffick; that is to say, that he should fit out a slave ship. This, however, Tom resolutely refused; he was bad enough in all conscience; but the devil himself could not tempt him to turn slave dealer.

Finding Tom so squeamish on this point, he did not insist upon it, but proposed instead that he should turn usurer; the devil being extremely anxious for the increase of usurers, looking upon them as his peculiar people.

To this no objections were made, for it was just to Tom's taste.

"You shall open a broker's shop in Boston next month," said the black man.

"I'll do it tomorrow, if you wish," said Tom Walker.

"You shall lend money at two per cent. a month."

"Egad, I'll charge four!" replied Tom Walker.

"You shall extort bonds, foreclose mortgages, drive the merchant to bankruptcy——"

"I'll drive him to the d——l," cried Tom Walker, eagerly.

"You are the usurer for my money!" said the black legs, with delight. "When will you want the rhino?"

"This very night."

"Done!" said the devil.

"Done!" said Tom Walker.—So they shook hands, and struck a bargain.

A few days' time saw Tom Walker seated behind his desk in a counting house in Boston. His reputation for a ready moneyed man, who would lend money out for a good consideration, soon spread abroad. Every body remembers the days of Governor Belcher, when money was particularly scarce. It was a time of paper credit. The country had been deluged with government bills; the famous Land Bank had been established; there had been a rage for speculating; the people had run mad with schemes for new settlements; for building cities in the wilderness; land jobbers went about with maps of grants, and townships, and Eldorados, lying nobody knew where, but which every body was ready to purchase. In a word, the great speculating fever which breaks out every now and then in the country, had raged to an alarming degree, and every body was dreaming of making sudden fortunes from nothing. As usual the fever had subsided; the dream had gone off, and the imaginary fortunes with it; the patients were left in doleful plight, and the whole country resounded with the consequent cry of "hard times."

At this propitious time of public distress did Tom Walker set up as a usurer in Boston. His door was soon thronged by customers. The needy and the adventurous; the gambling

speculator; the dreaming land jobber; the thriftless tradesman; the merchant with cracked credit; in short, every one
driven to raise money by desperate means and desperate sacrifices, hurried to Tom Walker.

Thus Tom was the universal friend of the needy, and he
acted like a "friend in need;" that is to say, he always exacted
good pay and good security. In proportion to the distress of
the applicant was the hardness of his terms. He accumulated
bonds and mortgages; gradually squeezed his customers
closer and closer; and sent them at length, dry as a sponge
from his door.

In this way he made money hand over hand; became a rich
and mighty man, and exalted his cocked hat upon change. He
built himself, as usual, a vast house, out of ostentation; but
left the greater part of it unfinished and unfurnished out of
parsimony. He even set up a carriage in the fullness of his
vain glory, though he nearly starved the horses which drew it;
and as the ungreased wheels groaned and screeched on the
axle trees, you would have thought you heard the souls of the
poor debtors he was squeezing.

As Tom waxed old, however, he grew thoughtful. Having
secured the good things of this world, he began to feel anxious about those of the next. He thought with regret on the
bargain he had made with his black friend, and set his wits to
work to cheat him out of the conditions. He became, therefore, all of a sudden, a violent church goer. He prayed loudly
and strenuously as if heaven were to be taken by force of
lungs. Indeed, one might always tell when he had sinned
most during the week, by the clamour of his Sunday devotion. The quiet christians who had been modestly and stead-
fastly travelling Zionward, were struck with self reproach at
seeing themselves so suddenly outstripped in their career by
this new made convert. Tom was as rigid in religious, as in
money matters; he was a stern supervisor and censurer of
his neighbours, and seemed to think every sin entered up to
their account became a credit on his own side of the page. He
even talked of the expediency of reviving the persecution of
quakers and anabaptists. In a word, Tom's zeal became as
notorious as his riches.

Still, in spite of all this strenuous attention to forms, Tom had a lurking dread that the devil, after all, would have his due. That he might not be taken unawares, therefore, it is said he always carried a small bible in his coat pocket. He had also a great folio bible on his counting house desk, and would frequently be found reading it when people called on business; on such occasions he would lay his green spectacles in the book, to mark the place, while he turned round to drive some usurious bargain.

Some say that Tom grew a little crack brained in his old days, and that fancying his end approaching, he had his horse new shod, saddled and bridled, and buried with his feet uppermost; because he supposed that at the last day the world would be turned upside down; in which case he should find his horse standing ready for mounting, and he was determined at the worst to give his old friend a run for it. This, however, is probably a mere old wives' fable. If he really did take such a precaution it was totally superfluous; at least so says the authentic old legend which closes his story in the following manner.

One hot afternoon in the dog days, just as a terrible black thundergust was coming up, Tom sat in his counting house in his white linen cap and India silk morning gown. He was on the point of foreclosing a mortgage, by which he would complete the ruin of an unlucky land speculator for whom he had professed the greatest friendship. The poor land jobber begged him to grant a few months' indulgence. Tom had grown testy and irritated and refused another day.

"My family will be ruined and brought upon the parish," said the land jobber. "Charity begins at home," replied Tom, "I must take care of myself in these hard times."

"You have made so much money out of me," said the speculator.

Tom lost his patience and his piety—"The devil take me," said he, "if I have made a farthing!"

Just then there were three loud knocks at the street door. He stepped out to see who was there. A black man was holding a black horse which neighed and stamped with impatience.

"Tom, you're come for!" said the black fellow, gruffly. Tom shrunk back, but too late. He had left his little bible at the bottom of his coat pocket, and his big bible on the desk buried under the mortgage he was about to foreclose: never was sinner taken more unawares. The black man whisked him like a child into the saddle, gave the horse a lash, and away he galloped, with Tom on his back, in the midst of a thunder storm. The clerks stuck their pens behind their ears and stared after him from the windows. Away went Tom Walker, dashing down the streets; his white cap bobbing up and down; his morning gown fluttering in the wind, and his steed striking fire out of the pavement at every bound. When the clerks turned to look for the black man he had disappeared.

Tom Walker never returned to foreclose the mortgage. A countryman who lived on the border of the swamp, reported that in the height of the thunder gust he had heard a great clattering of hoofs and a howling along the road, and running to the window caught sight of a figure, such as I have described, on a horse that galloped like mad across the fields, over the hills and down into the black hemlock swamp towards the old Indian fort; and that shortly after a thunderbolt falling in that direction seemed to set the whole forest in a blaze.

The good people of Boston shook their heads and shrugged their shoulders, but had been so much accustomed to witches and goblins and tricks of the devil in all kinds of shapes from the first settlement of the colony, that they were not so much horror struck as might have been expected. Trustees were appointed to take charge of Tom's effects. There was nothing, however, to administer upon. On searching his coffers all his bonds and mortgages were found reduced to cinders. In place of gold and silver his iron chest was filled with chips and shavings; two skeletons lay in his stable instead of his half starved horses, and the very next day his great house took fire and was burnt to the ground.

Such was the end of Tom Walker and his ill gotten wealth. Let all griping money brokers lay this story to heart. The truth of it is not to be doubted. The very hole under the oak trees, whence he dug Kidd's money is to be seen to this day; and the neighbouring swamp and old Indian fort are often haunted in stormy nights by a figure on horseback, in a morning gown and white cap, which is doubtless the troubled spirit of the usurer. In fact, the story has resolved itself into a proverb, and is the origin of that popular saying, prevalent throughout New England, of "The Devil and Tom Walker."

———

Such, as nearly as I can recollect, was the purport of the tale told by the Cape Cod whaler. There were divers trivial particulars which I have omitted, and which whiled away the morning very pleasantly, until the time of tide favourable for fishing being passed, it was proposed to land, and refresh ourselves under the trees, until the noontide heat should have abated.

We accordingly landed on a delectable part of the island of Mannahatta, in that shady and embowered tract formerly under dominion of the ancient family of the Hardenbrooks. It was a spot well known to me in the course of the aquatic expeditions of my boyhood. Not far from where we landed, was an old Dutch family vault, constructed in the side of a bank, which had been an object of great awe and fable among my school boy associates. We had peeped into it during one of our coasting voyages, and been startled by the sight of mouldering coffins and musty bones within; but what had given it the most fearful interest in our eyes, was its being in some way connected with the pirate wreck which lay rotting among the rocks of Hell Gate. There were also stories of smuggling connected with it, particularly relating to a time when this retired spot was owned by a noted burgher called Ready Money Prevost; a man of whom it was whispered that he had many and mysterious dealings with parts beyond seas. All these things, however, had been jumbled together in our minds in that vague way in which such themes are mingled up in the tales of boyhood.

While I was pondering upon these matters my companions had spread a repast, from the contents of our well stored pannier, under a broad chesnut, on the green sward which swept down to the water's edge. Here we solaced ourselves on the cool grassy carpet during the warm sunny hours of midday. While lolling on the grass, indulging in that kind of musing reverie of which I am fond, I summoned up the dusky recollections of my boyhood respecting this place, and repeated them like the imperfectly remembered traces of a dream, for the amusement of my companions. When I had finished a worthy old burgher, John Josse Vandermoere, the same who once related to me the adventures of Dolph Heyliger, broke silence and observed, that he recollected a story of money digging which occurred in this very neighbourhood, and might account for some of the traditions which I had heard in my boyhood. As we knew him to be one of the most authentic narrators in the province we begged him to let us have the particulars, and accordingly, while we solaced ourselves with a clean long pipe of Blase Moore's best tobacco, the authentic John Josse Vandermoere related the following tale.

Wolfert Webber, or Golden Dreams

In the year of grace one thousand seven hundred and—blank—for I do not remember the precise date; however, it was somewhere in the early part of the last century, there lived in the ancient city of the Manhattoes a worthy burgher, Wolfert Webber by name. He was descended from old Cobus Webber of the Brille in Holland, one of the original settlers, famous for introducing the cultivation of cabbages, and who came over to the province during the protectorship of Oloffe Van Kortlandt, otherwise called the Dreamer.

The field in which Cobus Webber first planted himself and his cabbages had remained ever since in the family, who continued in the same line of husbandry, with that praiseworthy perseverance for which our Dutch burghers are noted. The whole family genius, during several generations, was devoted to the study and development of this one noble vegetable; and to this concentration of intellect may doubtless be ascribed the prodigious size and renown to which the Webber cabbages attained.

The Webber dynasty continued in uninterrupted succession; and never did a line give more unquestionable proofs of legitimacy. The eldest son succeeded to the looks, as well as the territory of his sire; and had the portraits of this line of tranquil potentates been taken, they would have presented a row of heads marvellously resembling in shape and magnitude the vegetables over which they reigned.

The seat of government continued unchanged in the family mansion: — a Dutch built house, with a front, or rather gabel end of yellow brick, tapering to a point, with the customary iron weathercock at the top. Every thing about the building bore the air of long settled ease and security. Flights of martins peopled the little coops nailed against its walls, and swallows built their nests under the eaves; and every one knows that these house loving birds bring good luck to the dwelling where they take up their abode. In a bright sunny morning in early summer, it was delectable to hear their cheerful notes, as they sported about in the pure sweet air, chirping forth, as it were, the greatness and prosperity of the Webbers.

Thus quietly and comfortably did this excellent family vegetate under the shade of a mighty buttonwood tree, which by little and little grew so great as entirely to overshadow their palace. The city gradually spread its suburbs round their domain. Houses sprang up to interrupt their prospects. The rural lanes in the vicinity began to grow into the bustle and populousness of streets; in short, with all the habits of rustic life they began to find themselves the inhabitants of a city. Still, however, they maintained their hereditary character, and hereditary possessions, with all the tenacity of petty German princes in the midst of the Empire. Wolfert was the last of the line, and succeeded to the patriarchal bench at the door, under the family tree, and swayed the sceptre of his fathers, a kind of rural potentate in the midst of a metropolis.

To share the cares and sweets of sovereignty, he had taken unto himself a help mate, one of that excellent kind, called stirring women; that is to say, she was one of those notable little housewives who are always busy when there is nothing to do. Her activity, however, took one particular direction; her whole life seemed devoted to intense knitting; whether at home or abroad; walking, or sitting, her needles were continually in motion, and it is even affirmed that by her unwearied industry she very nearly supplied her household with stockings throughout the year. This worthy couple were blessed with one daughter, who was brought up with great tenderness and care; uncommon pains had been taken with her education, so that she could stitch in every variety of way; make all kinds of pickles and preserves, and mark her own name on a sampler. The influence of her taste was seen also in the family garden, where the ornamental began to mingle with the useful; whole rows of fiery marigolds and splendid hollyhocks bordered the cabbage beds; and gigantic sun flowers lolled their broad jolly faces over the fences, seeming to ogle most affectionately the passers by.

Thus reigned and vegetated Wolfert Webber over his paternal acres, peaceably and contentedly. Not but that, like all other sovereigns, he had his occasional cares and vexations. The growth of his native city sometimes caused him annoyance. His little territory gradually became hemmed in by streets and houses, which intercepted air and sunshine. He was now and then subjected to the irruptions of the border population, that infest the skirts of a metropolis, who would make midnight forays into his dominions, and carry off captive whole platoons of his noblest subjects. Vagrant swine would make a descent, too, now and then, when the gate was left open, and lay all waste before them; and mischievous urchins would decapitate the illustrious sunflowers, the glory of the garden, as they lolled their heads so fondly over the walls. Still all these were petty grievances, which might now and then ruffle the surface of his mind, as a summer breeze will ruffle the surface of a mill pond; but they could not disturb the deep seated quiet of his soul. He would but seize a trusty staff, that stood behind the door, issue suddenly out, and anoint the back of the aggressor, whether pig, or urchin, and then return within doors, marvellously refreshed and tranquillized.

The chief cause of anxiety to honest Wolfert, however, was the growing prosperity of the city. The expenses of living doubled and trebled; but he could not double and treble the magnitude of his cabbages; and the number of competitors prevented the increase of price; thus, therefore, while every one around him grew richer, Wolfert grew poorer, and he could not, for the life of him, perceive how the evil was to be remedied.

This growing care, which increased from day to day, had its gradual effect upon our worthy burgher; insomuch, that it at length implanted two or three wrinkles on his brow; things unknown before in the family of the Webbers; and it seemed to pinch up the corners of his cocked hat into an expression of anxiety, totally opposite to the tranquil, broad brimmed, low crowned beavers of his illustrious progenitors.

Perhaps even this would not have materially disturbed the serenity of his mind had he had only himself and his wife to care for; but there was his daughter gradually growing to maturity; and all the world knows when daughters begin to ripen no fruit or flower requires so much looking after. I have no talent at describing female charms, else fain would I depict the progress of this little Dutch beauty. How her blue eyes grew deeper and deeper, and her cherry lips redder and redder; and how she ripened and ripened, and rounded and rounded in the opening breath of sixteen summers, until, in her seventeenth spring, she seemed ready to burst out of her boddice, like a half blown rosebud.

Ah, well-a-day! could I but show her as she was then, tricked out on a Sunday morning, in the hereditary finery of the old Dutch clothes press, of which her mother had confided to her the key. The wedding dress of her grandmother, modernized for use, with sundry ornaments, handed down as heir looms in the family. Her pale brown hair smoothed with buttermilk in flat waving lines on each side of her fair forehead. The chain of yellow virgin gold, that encircled her neck; the little cross, that just rested at the entrance of a soft valley of happiness, as if it would sanctify the place. The—but pooh!—it is not for an old man like me to be prosing about female beauty: suffice it to say, Amy had attained her seventeenth year. Long since had her sampler exhibited hearts in couples desperately transfixed with arrows, and true lovers' knots worked in deep blue silk; and it was evident she began to languish for some more interesting occupation than the rearing of sunflowers or pickling of cucumbers.

At this critical period of female existence, when the heart within a damsel's bosom, like its emblem, the miniature which hangs without, is apt to be engrossed by a single image, a new visitor began to make his appearance under the roof of Wolfert Webber. This was Dirk Waldron, the only son of a poor widow, but who could boast of more fathers than

any lad in the province; for his mother had had four husbands, and this only child, so that though born in her last
wedlock, he might fairly claim to be the tardy fruit of a long
course of cultivation. This son of four fathers united the merits and the vigour of his sires. If he had not had a great family
before him, he seemed likely to have a great one after him; for
you had only to look at the fresh bucksome youth, to see that
he was formed to be the founder of a mighty race.

This youngster gradually became an intimate visitor of the
family. He talked little, but he sat long. He filled the father's
pipe when it was empty, gathered up the mother's knitting
needle, or ball of worsted when it fell to the ground; stroked
the sleek coat of the tortoise shell cat, and replenished the tea
pot for the daughter from the bright copper kettle that sang
before the fire. All these quiet little offices may seem of
trifling import, but when true love is translated into Low
Dutch, it is in this way that it eloquently expresses itself. They
were not lost upon the Webber family. The winning youngster found marvellous favour in the eyes of the mother; the
tortoise shell cat, albeit the most staid and demure of her
kind, gave indubitable signs of approbation of his visits, the
tea kettle seemed to sing out a cheery note of welcome at his
approach, and if the sly glances of the daughter might be
rightly read, as she sat bridling and dimpling, and sewing by
her mother's side, she was not a whit behind Dame Webber,
or grimalkin, or the tea kettle in good will.

Wolfert alone saw nothing of what was going on. Profoundly wrapt up in meditation on the growth of the city and
his cabbages, he sat looking in the fire, and puffing his pipe in
silence. One night, however, as the gentle Amy, according to
custom lighted her lover to the outer door, and he, according
to custom, took his parting salute, the smack resounded so
vigorously through the long, silent entry, as to startle even
the dull ear of Wolfert. He was slowly roused to a new source
of anxiety. It had never entered into his head, that this mere
child who, as it seemed but the other day, had been climbing
about his knees, and playing with dolls and baby houses,
could all at once be thinking of lovers and matrimony. He
rubbed his eyes, examined into the fact, and really found that
while he had been dreaming of other matters, she had actually

grown to be a woman, and what was worse, had fallen in love. Here arose new cares for poor Wolfert. He was a kind father, but he was a prudent man. The young man was a lively, stirring lad; but then he had neither money nor land. Wolfert's ideas all ran in one channel, and he saw no alternative in case of a marriage, but to portion off the young couple with a corner of his cabbage garden, the whole of which was barely sufficient for the support of his family.

Like a prudent father, therefore, he determined to nip this passion in the bud, and forbad the youngster the house, though sorely did it go against his fatherly heart, and many a silent tear did it cause in the bright eye of his daughter. She showed herself, however, a pattern of filial piety and obedience. She never pouted and sulked, she never flew in the face of parental authority; she never flew into a passion, nor fell into hysterics, as many romantic novel-read young ladies would do. Not she, indeed! She was none such heroical rebellious trumpery, I'll warrant ye. On the contrary, she acquiesced like an obedient daughter; shut the street door in her lover's face, and if ever she did grant him an interview, it was either out of the kitchen window, or over the garden fence.

Wolfert was deeply cogitating these matters in his mind, and his brow wrinkled with unusual care, as he wended his way one Saturday afternoon to a rural inn, about two miles from the city. It was a favourite resort of the Dutch part of the community from being always held by a Dutch line of landlords, and retaining an air and relish of the good old times. It was a Dutch built house, that had probably been a country seat of some opulent burgher in the early time of the settlement. It stood near a point of land, called Corlear's Hook, which stretches out into the Sound, and against which the tide, at its flux and reflux, sets with extraordinary rapidity. The venerable and somewhat crazy mansion was distinguished from afar, by a grove of elms and sycamores that seemed to wave a hospitable invitation, while a few weeping willows with their dank, drooping foliage, resembling falling waters, gave an idea of coolness, that rendered it an attractive spot during the heats of summer.

Here, therefore, as I said, resorted many of the old inhabitants of the Manhattoes, where, while some played at the

shuffle board and quoits and ninepins, others smoked a deliberate pipe, and talked over public affairs.

It was on a blustering autumnal afternoon that Wolfert
made his visit to the inn. The grove of elms and willows was
stripped of its leaves, which whirled in rustling eddies about
the fields. The ninepin alley was deserted, for the premature
chilliness of the day had driven the company within doors. As
it was Saturday afternoon, the habitual club was in session,
composed principally of regular Dutch burghers, though mingled occasionally with persons of various character and country, as is natural in a place of such motley population.

Beside the fire place, in a huge leather bottomed arm
chair, sat the dictator of this little world, the venerable Rem,
or, as it was pronounced, Ramm Rapelye. He was a man
of Walloon race, and illustrious for the antiquity of his
line, his great grandmother having been the first white
child born in the province. But he was still more illustrious
for his wealth and dignity: he had long filled the noble
office of alderman, and was a man to whom the governor
himself took off his hat. He had maintained possession of
the leathern bottomed chair from time immemorial; and
had gradually waxed in bulk as he sat in this seat of government, until in the course of years he filled its whole
magnitude. His word was decisive with his subjects; for he
was so rich a man, that he was never expected to support
any opinion by argument. The landlord waited on him with
peculiar officiousness; not that he paid better than his neighbours, but then the coin of a rich man seems always to be so
much more acceptable. The landlord had ever a pleasant word
and a joke, to insinuate in the ear of the august Ramm. It is
true, Ramm never laughed, and indeed, maintained a mastiff-
like gravity, and even surliness of aspect, yet he now and then
rewarded mine host with a token of approbation; which,
though nothing more nor less than a kind of grunt, yet delighted the landlord more than a broad laugh from a poorer
man.

"This will be a rough night for the money diggers," said
mine host, as a gust of wind howled round the house, and
rattled at the windows.

"What, are they at their works again?" said an English half-pay captain, with one eye, who was a frequent attendant at the inn.

"Aye, are they," said the landlord, "and well may they be. They've had luck of late. They say a great pot of money has been dug up in the field, just behind Stuyvesant's orchard. Folks think it must have been buried there in old times, by Peter Stuyvesant, the Dutch Governor."

"Fudge!" said the one eyed man of war, as he added a small portion of water to a bottom of brandy.

"Well, you may believe, or not, as you please," said mine host, somewhat nettled; "but every body knows that the old governor buried a great deal of his money at the time of the Dutch troubles, when the English red coats seized on the province. They say, too, the old gentleman walks; aye, and in the very same dress that he wears in the picture which hangs up in the family house."

"Fudge!" said the half-pay officer.

"Fudge, if you please!—But didn't Corney Van Zandt see him at midnight, stalking about in the meadow with his wooden leg, and a drawn sword in his hand, that flashed like fire? And what can he be walking for, but because people have been troubling the place where he buried his money in old times?"

Here the landlord was interrupted by several guttural sounds from Ramm Rapelye, betokening that he was labouring with the unusual production of an idea. As he was too great a man to be slighted by a prudent publican, mine host respectfully paused until he should deliver himself. The corpulent frame of this mighty burgher now gave all the symptoms of a volcanic mountain on the point of an eruption. First, there was a certain heaving of the abdomen, not unlike an earthquake; then was emitted a cloud of tobacco smoke from that crater, his mouth; then there was a kind of rattle in the throat, as if the idea were working its way up through a region of phlegm; then there were several disjointed members of a sentence thrown out, ending in a cough; at length his voice forced its way in the slow, but absolute tone of a man who feels the weight of his purse, if not of his ideas; every portion of his speech being marked by a testy puff of tobacco smoke.

"Who talks of old Peter Stuyvesant's walking?—puff—
Have people no respect for persons?—puff—puff—Peter
Stuyvesant knew better what to do with his money than to
bury it—puff—I know the Stuyvesant family—puff—every
one of them—puff—not a more respectable family in the
province—puff—old standers—puff—warm householders
—puff—none of your upstarts—puff—puff—puff.—Don't
talk to me of Peter Stuyvesant's walking—puff—puff—
puff—puff."

Here the redoubtable Ramm contracted his brow, clasped
up his mouth, till it wrinkled at each corner, and redoubled
his smoking with such vehemence, that the cloudy volumes
soon wreathed round his head, as the smoke envellops the
awful summit of Mount Etna.

A general silence followed the sudden rebuke of this very
rich man. The subject, however, was too interesting to be
readily abandoned. The conversation soon broke forth again
from the lips of Peechy Prauw Van Hook, the chronicler of
the club, one of those prosy, narrative old men who seem to
be troubled with an incontinence of words, as they grow old.

Peechy could at any time tell as many stories in an evening
as his hearers could digest in a month. He now resumed the
conversation, by affirming that, to his knowledge, money had
at different times been digged up in various parts of the island. The lucky persons who had discovered them had always
dreamt of them three times before hand, and what was worthy of remark, these treasures had never been found but by
some descendant of the good old Dutch families, which
clearly proved that they had been buried by Dutchmen in the
olden time.

"Fiddle stick with your Dutchmen!" cried the half-pay officer. "The Dutch had nothing to do with them. They were
all buried by Kidd, the pirate, and his crew."

Here a key note was touched which roused the whole company. The name of Captain Kidd was like a talisman in those
times, and was associated with a thousand marvellous stories.

The half-pay officer took the lead, and in his narrations fa-
thered upon Kidd all the plunderings and exploits of Morgan,
Blackbeard, and the whole list of bloody buccaneers.

The officer was a man of great weight among the peaceable

members of the club, by reason of his warlike character and gunpowder tales. All his golden stories of Kidd, however, and of the booty he had buried, were obstinately rivalled by the tales of Peechy Prauw, who, rather than suffer his Dutch progenitors to be eclipsed by a foreign freebooter, enriched every field and shore in the neighbourhood with the hidden wealth of Peter Stuyvesant and his contemporaries.

Not a word of this conversation was lost upon Wolfert Webber. He returned pensively home, full of magnificent ideas. The soil of his native island seemed to be turned into gold dust; and every field to teem with treasure. His head almost reeled at the thought how often he must have heedlessly rambled over places where countless sums lay, scarcely covered by the turf beneath his feet. His mind was in an uproar with this whirl of new ideas. As he came in sight of the venerable mansion of his forefathers, and the little realm where the Webbers had so long, and so contentedly flourished, his gorge rose at the narrowness of his destiny.

"Unlucky Wolfert!" exclaimed he; "others can go to bed and dream themselves into whole mines of wealth; they have but to seize a spade in the morning, and turn up doubloons like potatoes; but thou must dream of hardship, and rise to poverty—must dig thy field from year's end to year's end, and—and yet raise nothing but cabbages!"

Wolfert Webber went to bed with a heavy heart; and it was long before the golden visions that disturbed his brain, permitted him to sink into repose. The same visions, however, extended into his sleeping thoughts, and assumed a more definite form. He dreamt that he had discovered an immense treasure in the centre of his garden. At every stroke of the spade he laid bare a golden ingot; diamond crosses sparkled out of the dust; bags of money turned up their bellies, corpulent with pieces of eight, or venerable doubloons; and chests, wedged close with moidores, ducats, and pistareens, yawned before his ravished eyes, and vomited forth their glittering contents.

Wolfert awoke a poorer man than ever. He had no heart to go about his daily concerns, which appeared so paltry and profitless; but sat all day long in the chimney corner, picturing to himself ingots and heaps of gold in the fire. The next night his dream was repeated. He was again in his garden, digging, and laying open stores of hidden wealth. There was something very singular in this repetition. He passed another day of reverie, and though it was cleaning day, and the house, as usual in Dutch households, completely topsy turvy, yet he sat unmoved amidst the general uproar.

The third night he went to bed with a palpitating heart. He put on his red nightcap, wrong side outwards for good luck. It was deep midnight before his anxious mind could settle itself into sleep. Again the golden dream was repeated, and again he saw his garden teeming with ingots and money bags.

Wolfert rose the next morning in complete bewilderment. A dream three times repeated was never known to lie; and if so, his fortune was made.

In his agitation he put on his waistcoat with the hind part before, and this was a corroboration of good luck. He no longer doubted that a huge store of money lay buried somewhere in his cabbage field, coyly waiting to be sought for, and he repined at having so long been scratching about the surface of the soil, instead of digging to the centre.

He took his seat at the breakfast table full of these speculations; asked his daughter to put a lump of gold into his tea, and on handing his wife a plate of slap jacks, begged her to help herself to a doubloon.

His grand care now was how to secure this immense treasure without its being known. Instead of working regularly in his grounds in the day time, he now stole from his bed at night, and with spade and pickaxe, went to work to rip up and dig about his paternal acres, from one end to the other. In a little time the whole garden, which had presented such a goodly and regular appearance, with its phalanx of cabbages, like a vegetable army in battle array, was reduced to a scene of devastation, while the relentless Wolfert, with nightcap on head, and lantern and spade in hand, stalked through the slaughtered ranks, the destroying angel of his own vegetable world.

Every morning bore testimony to the ravages of the preceding night in cabbages of all ages and conditions, from the tender sprout to the full grown head, piteously rooted from their quiet beds like worthless weeds, and left to wither in the

sunshine. In vain Wolfert's wife remonstrated; in vain his darling daughter wept over the destruction of some favourite
marygold. "Thou shalt have gold of another guess sort," he
would cry, chucking her under the chin; "thou shalt have a
string of crooked ducats for thy wedding necklace, my child."
His family began really to fear that the poor man's wits were
diseased. He muttered in his sleep at night about mines of
wealth, about pearls and diamonds and bars of gold. In the
day time he was moody and abstracted, and walked about as
if in a trance. Dame Webber held frequent councils with all
the old women of the neighbourhood. Scarce an hour in the
day but a knot of them might be seen wagging their white
caps together round her door, while the poor woman made
some piteous recital. The daughter too was fain to seek for
more frequent consolation from the stolen interviews of her
favoured swain Dirk Waldron. The delectable little Dutch
songs with which she used to dulcify the house grew less and
less frequent, and she would forget her sewing and look wistfully in her father's face as he sat pondering by the fire side.
Wolfert caught her eye one day fixed on him thus anxiously,
and for a moment was roused from his golden reveries.—
"Cheer up my girl," said he, exultingly, "why dost thou
droop—thou shalt hold up thy head one day with the
Brinkerhoffs and the Schermerhorns, the Van Hornes, and the
Van Dams—By St. Nicholas, but the patroon himself shall be
glad to get thee for his son!"

Amy shook her head at this vain glorious boast, and was
more than ever in doubt of the soundness of the good man's
intellect.

In the mean time Wolfert went on digging and digging, but
the field was extensive, and as his dream had indicated no
precise spot, he had to dig at random. The winter set in before one tenth of the scene of promise had been explored. The
ground became frozen hard, and the nights too cold for the
labours of the spade. No sooner, however, did the returning
warmth of spring loosen the soil, and the small frogs begin to
pipe in the meadows, but Wolfert resumed his labours with
renovated zeal. Still, however, the hours of industry were
reversed. Instead of working cheerily all day, planting and
setting out his vegetables, he remained thoughtfully idle, until

the shades of night summoned him to his secret labours. In this way he continued to dig from night to night, and week to week, and month to month, but not a stiver did he find. On the contrary, the more he digged, the poorer he grew. The rich soil of his garden was digged away, and the sand and gravel from beneath were thrown to the surface, until the whole field presented an aspect of sandy barrenness.

In the mean time the seasons gradually rolled on. The little frogs which had piped in the meadows in early spring, croaked as bull frogs during the summer heats, and then sank into silence. The peach tree budded, blossomed, and bore its fruit. The swallows and martins came, twittered about the roof, built their nests, reared their young, held their congress along the eaves, and then winged their flight in search of another spring. The caterpillar spun its winding sheet, dangled in it from the great buttonwood tree before the house; turned into a moth, fluttered with the last sunshine of summer, and disappeared; and finally the leaves of the buttonwood tree turned yellow, then brown, then rustled one by one to the ground, and whirling about in little eddies of wind and dust, whispered that winter was at hand.

Wolfert gradually woke from his dream of wealth as the year declined. He had reared no crop for the supply of his household during the sterility of winter. The season was long and severe, and for the first time the family was really straightened in its comforts. By degrees a revulsion of thought took place in Wolfert's mind, common to those whose golden dreams have been disturbed by pinching realities. The idea gradually stole upon him that he should come to want. He already considered himself one of the most unfortunate men in the province, having lost such an incalculable amount of undiscovered treasure, and now, when thousands of pounds had eluded his search, to be perplexed for shillings and pence was cruel in the extreme.

Haggard care gathered about his brow; he went about with a money seeking air, his eyes bent downwards into the dust, and carrying his hands in his pockets, as men are apt to do when they have nothing else to put into them. He could not even pass the city almshouse without giving it a rueful glance, as if destined to be his future abode.

The strangeness of his conduct and of his looks occasioned much speculation and remark. For a long time he was suspected of being crazy, and then every body pitied him; at length it began to be suspected that he was poor, and then every body avoided him.

The rich old burghers of his acquaintance met him outside of the door when he called, entertained him hospitably on the threshold, pressed him warmly by the hand on parting, shook their heads as he walked away, with the kind hearted expression of "poor Wolfert," and turned a corner nimbly, if by chance they saw him approaching as they walked the streets. Even the barber and cobbler of the neighbourhood, and a tattered tailor in an alley hard by, three of the poorest and merriest rogues in the world, eyed him with that abundant sympathy which usually attends a lack of means; and there is not a doubt but their pockets would have been at his command, only that they happened to be empty.

Thus every body deserted the Webber mansion, as if poverty were contagious, like the plague; every body but honest Dirk Waldron, who still kept up his stolen visits to the daughter, and indeed seemed to wax more affectionate as the fortunes of his mistress were in the wane.

Many months had elapsed since Wolfert had frequented his old resort, the rural inn. He was taking a long lonely walk one Saturday afternoon, musing over his wants and disappointments, when his feet took instinctively their wonted direction, and on awaking out of a reverie, he found himself before the door of the inn. For some moments he hesitated whether to enter, but his heart yearned for companionship; and where can a ruined man find better companionship than at a tavern, where there is neither sober example nor sober advice to put him out of countenance?

Wolfert found several of the old frequenters of the tavern at their usual posts, and seated in their usual places; but one was missing, the great Ramm Rapelye, who for many years had filled the leather bottomed chair of state. His place was supplied by a stranger, who seemed, however, completely at home in the chair and the tavern. He was rather under size, but deep chested, square and muscular. His broad shoulders, double joints, and bow knees, gave tokens of prodigious strength. His face was dark and weather beaten; a deep scar, as if from the slash of a cutlass had almost divided his nose, and made a gash in his upper lip, through which his teeth shone like a bull dog's. A mop of iron grey hair gave a grizzly finish to his hard favoured visage. His dress was of an amphibious character. He wore an old hat edged with tarnished lace, and cocked in martial style, on one side of his head; a rusty blue military coat with brass buttons, and a wide pair of short petticoat trowsers, or rather breeches, for they were gathered up at the knees. He ordered every body about him, with an authoritative air; talked in a brattling voice, that sounded like the crackling of thorns under a pot; damned the landlord and servants with perfect impunity, and was waited upon with greater obsequiousness than had ever been shown to the mighty Ramm himself.

Wolfert's curiosity was awakened to know who and what was this stranger who had thus usurped absolute sway in this ancient domain. Peechy Prauw took him aside, into a remote corner of the hall, and there in an under voice, and with great caution, imparted to him all that he knew on the subject. The inn had been aroused several months before, on a dark stormy night, by repeated long shouts, that seemed like the howlings of a wolf. They came from the water side; and at length were distinguished to be hailing the house in the seafaring manner. "House-a-hoy!" The landlord turned out with his head waiter, tapster, hostler and errand boy—that is to say, with his old negro Cuff. On approaching the place whence the voice proceeded, they found this amphibious looking personage at the water's edge, quite alone, and seated on a great oaken sea chest. How he came there, whether he had been set on shore from some boat, or had floated to land on his chest, nobody could tell, for he did not seem disposed to answer questions, and there was something in his looks and manners that put a stop to all questioning. Suffice it to say, he took possession of a corner room of the inn, to which his chest was removed with great difficulty. Here he had remained ever since, keeping about the inn and its vicinity. Sometimes, it is true, he disappeared for one, two, or three days at a time, going and returning without giving any notice or account of his movements. He always appeared to have plenty of money, though often of very strange outlandish coinage; and he regularly paid his bill every evening before turning in.

He had fitted up his room to his own fancy, having slung a hammock from the ceiling instead of a bed, and decorated the walls with rusty pistols and cutlasses of foreign workmanship. A great part of his time was passed in this room, seated by the window, which commanded a wide view of the Sound, a short old fashioned pipe in his mouth, a glass of rum toddy at his elbow, and a pocket telescope in his hand, with which he reconnoitred every boat that moved upon the water. Large square rigged vessels seemed to excite but little attention; but the moment he descried any thing with a shoulder of mutton sail, or that a barge, or yawl, or jolly boat hove in sight, up went the telescope, and he examined it with the most scrupulous attention.

All this might have passed without much notice, for in those times the province was so much the resort of adventurers of all characters and climes that any oddity in dress or behaviour attracted but small attention. In a little while, however, this strange sea monster, thus strangely cast up on dry land, began to encroach upon the long established customs and customers of the place, and to interfere in a dictatorial manner in the affairs of the ninepin alley and the bar room, until in the end he usurped an absolute command over the whole inn. It was all in vain to attempt to withstand his authority. He was not exactly quarrelsome, but boisterous and peremptory, like one accustomed to tyrannize on a quarter deck; and there was a dare devil air about every thing he said and did, that inspired a wariness in all bystanders. Even the half-pay officer, so long the hero of the club, was soon silenced by him; and the quiet burghers stared with wonder at seeing their inflammable man of war so readily and quietly extinguished.

And then the tales that he would tell were enough to make a peaceable man's hair stand on end. There was not a sea fight, or marauding, or freebooting adventure that had happened within the last twenty years but he seemed perfectly versed in it. He delighted to talk of the exploits of the buccaneers in the West Indies and on the Spanish Main. How his eyes would glisten as he described the waylaying of treasure

ships, the desperate fights, yard arm and yard arm—broadside and broadside—the boarding and capturing of huge
Spanish galleons! with what chuckling relish would he describe the descent upon some rich Spanish colony; the rifling
of a church; the sacking of a convent! You would have
thought you heard some gormandizer dilating upon the roasting of a savory goose at Michaelmas as he described the roasting of some Spanish Don to make him discover his treasure—
a detail given with a minuteness that made every rich old
burgher present turn uncomfortably in his chair. All this
would be told with infinite glee, as if he considered it an excellent joke; and then he would give such a tyrannical leer in
the face of his next neighbour, that the poor man would be
fain to laugh out of sheer faint heartedness. If any one, however, pretended to contradict him in any of his stories he was
on fire in an instant. His very cocked hat assumed a momentary fierceness, and seemed to resent the contradiction.—
"How the devil should you know as well as I! I tell you it was
as I say!" and he would at the same time let slip a broadside
of thundering oaths and tremendous sea phrases, such as had
never been heard before within those peaceful walls.

Indeed, the worthy burghers began to surmise that he
knew more of these stories than mere hearsay. Day after day
their conjectures concerning him grew more and more wild
and fearful. The strangeness of his arrival, the strangeness of
his manners, the mystery that surrounded him, all made him
something incomprehensible in their eyes. He was a kind of
monster of the deep to them—he was a merman—he was
behemoth—he was leviathan—in short they knew not what
he was.

The domineering spirit of this boisterous sea urchin at
length grew quite intolerable. He was no respecter of persons; he contradicted the richest burghers without hesitation;
he took possession of the sacred elbow chair, which time out
of mind had been the seat of sovereignty of the illustrious
Ramm Rapelye. Nay, he even went so far in one of his rough
jocular moods, as to slap that mighty burgher on the back,
drink his toddy and wink in his face, a thing scarcely to be
believed. From this time Ramm Rapelye appeared no more at
the inn; his example was followed by several of the most em-

inent customers, who were too rich to tolerate being bullied out of their opinions, or being obliged to laugh at another man's jokes. The landlord was almost in despair, but he knew not how to get rid of this sea monster and his sea chest, which seemed both to have grown like fixtures, or excrescences on his establishment.

Such was the account whispered cautiously in Wolfert's ear, by the narrator, Peechy Prauw, as he held him by the button in a corner of the hall, casting a wary glance now and then towards the door of the bar room, lest he should be overheard by the terrible hero of his tale.

Wolfert took his seat in a remote part of the room in silence; impressed with profound awe of this unknown, so versed in freebooting history. It was to him a wonderful instance of the revolutions of mighty empires, to find the venerable Ramm Rapelye thus ousted from the throne, and a rugged tarpaulin dictating from his elbow chair, hectoring the patriarchs, and filling this tranquil little realm with brawl and bravado.

The stranger was on this evening in a more than usually communicative mood, and was narrating a number of astounding stories of plunderings and burnings upon the high seas. He dwelt upon them with peculiar relish, heightening the frightful particulars in proportion to their effect on his peaceful auditors. He gave a swaggering detail of the capture of a Spanish merchantman. She was lying becalmed during a long summer's day, just off from an island which was one of the lurking places of the pirates. They had reconnoitred her with their spy glasses from the shore, and ascertained her character and force. At night a picked crew of daring fellows set off for her in a whale boat. They approached with muffled oars, as she lay rocking idly with the undulations of the sea and her sails flapping against the masts. They were close under her stern before the guard on deck was aware of their approach. The alarm was given; the pirates threw hand grenades on deck and sprang up the main chains sword in hand.

The crew flew to arms, but in great confusion; some were shot down, others took refuge in the tops; others were driven overboard and drowned, while others fought hand to hand from the main deck to the quarter deck, disputing gallantly every inch of ground. There were three Spanish gentlemen on board with their ladies, who made the most desperate resistance. They defended the companion way, cut down several of their assailants, and fought like very devils, for they were maddened by the shrieks of the ladies from the cabin. One of the Dons was old and soon despatched. The other two kept their ground vigourously, even though the captain of the pirates was among their assailants. Just then there was a shout of victory from the main deck. "The ship is ours!" cried the pirates.

One of the Dons immediately dropped his sword and surrendered; the other, who was a hot headed youngster, and just married, gave the captain a slash in the face that laid all open. The captain just made out to articulate the words "no quarter."

"And what did they do with their prisoners?" said Peechy Prauw, eagerly.

"Threw them all overboard!" was the answer.

A dead pause followed this reply. Peechy Prauw shrunk quietly back like a man who had unwarily stolen upon the lair of a sleeping lion. The honest burghers cast fearful glances at the deep scar slashed across the visage of the stranger, and moved their chairs a little farther off. The seaman, however, smoked on without moving a muscle, as though he either did not perceive or did not regard the unfavourable effect he had produced upon his hearers.

The half-pay officer was the first to break the silence; for he was continually tempted to make ineffectual head against this tyrant of the seas, and to regain his lost consequence in the eyes of his ancient companions. He now tried to match the gunpowder tales of the stranger by others equally tremendous. Kidd, as usual, was his hero, concerning whom he seemed to have picked up many of the floating traditions of the province. The seaman had always evinced a settled pique against the one eyed warrior. On this occasion he listened with peculiar impatience. He sat with one arm akimbo, the other elbow on a table, the hand holding on to the small pipe he was pettishly puffing; his legs crossed, drumming with one foot on the ground and casting every now and then the side glance of a basilisk at the prosing captain. At length the latter spoke of Kidd's having ascended the Hudson with some of his crew, to land his plunder in secresy.

"Kidd up the Hudson!" burst forth the seaman, with a tremendous oath; "Kidd never was up the Hudson!"

"I tell you he was," said the other. "Aye, and they say he buried a quantity of treasure on the little flat that runs out into the river, called the Devil's Dans Kammer."

"The Devil's Dans Kammer in your teeth!" cried the seaman. "I tell you, Kidd never was up the Hudson—what a plague do you know of Kidd and his haunts?"

"What do I know?" echoed the half-pay officer; "why, I was in London at the time of his trial, aye, and I had the pleasure of seeing him hanged at Execution Dock."

"Then, sir, let me tell you that you saw as pretty a fellow hanged as ever trod shoe leather. Aye!" putting his face nearer to that of the officer, "and there was many a land lubber looked on, that might much better have swung in his stead."

The half-pay officer was silenced; but the indignation thus pent up in his bosom glowed with intense vehemence in his single eye, which kindled like a coal.

Peechy Prauw, who never could remain silent, observed that the gentleman certainly was in the right. Kidd never did bury money up the Hudson, nor indeed in any of those parts, though many affirmed such to be the fact. It was Bradish and others of the buccaneers who had buried money, some said in Turtle Bay, others on Long Island, others in the neighbourhood of Hell Gate. Indeed, added he, I recollect an adventure of Sam, the negro fisherman, many years ago, which some think had something to do with the buccaneers. As we are all friends here, and as it will go no farther, I'll tell it to you.

"Upon a dark night many years ago, as Black Sam was returning from fishing in Hell Gate——"

Here the story was nipped in the bud by a sudden movement from the unknown, who laying his iron fist on the table, knuckles downward, with a quiet force that indented the very boards, and looking grimly over his shoulder, with the grin of an angry bear. "Heark'ee, neighbour," said he, with significant nodding of the head, "you'd better let the buccaneers and their money alone—they're not for old men and old women to meddle with. They fought hard for their money, they gave body and soul for it, and wherever it lies buried, depend upon it he must have a tug with the devil who gets it."

This sudden explosion was succeeded by a blank silence throughout the room. Peechy Prauw shrunk within himself, and even the one eyed officer turned pale. Wolfert, who from a dark corner of the room, had listened with intense eagerness to all this talk about buried treasure, looked with mingled awe and reverence on this bold buccaneer, for such he really suspected him to be. There was a chinking of gold and a sparkling of jewels in all his stories about the Spanish Main that gave a value to every period, and Wolfert would have given any thing for the rummaging of the ponderous sea chest, which his imagination crammed full of golden chalices and crucifixes and jolly round bags of doubloons.

The dead stillness that had fallen upon the company was at length interrupted by the stranger, who pulled out a prodigious watch of curious and ancient workmanship, and which in Wolfert's eyes had a decidedly Spanish look. On touching a spring it struck ten o'clock; upon which the sailor called for his reckoning, and having paid it out of a handful of outlandish coin, he drank off the remainder of his beverage, and without taking leave of any one, rolled out of the room, muttering to himself, as he stumped up stairs to his chamber.

It was some time before the company could recover from the silence into which they had been thrown. The very footsteps of the stranger which were heard now and then as he traversed his chamber, inspired awe.

Still the conversation in which they had been engaged was too interesting not to be resumed. A heavy thunder gust had gathered up unnoticed while they were lost in talk, and the torrents of rain that fell forbade all thoughts of setting off for home until the storm should subside. They drew nearer together, therefore, and entreated the worthy Peechy Prauw to continue the tale which had been so discourteously interrupted. He readily complied, whispering, however, in a tone scarcely above his breath, and drowned occasionally by the rolling of the thunder; and he would pause every now and then, and listen with evident awe, as he heard the heavy foot-steps of the stranger pacing over head.

The following is the purport of his story.

The Adventure of the Black Fisherman

Every body knows Black Sam, the old negro fisherman, or, as he is commonly called, Mud Sam, who has fished about the Sound for the last half century. It is now many, many years since Sam, who was then as active a young negro as any in the province, and worked on the farm of Killian Suydam on Long Island, having finished his day's work at an early hour, was fishing, one still summer evening, just about the neigh-bourhood of Hell Gate. He was in a light skiff, and being well acquainted with the currents and eddies, had shifted his station according to the shifting of the tide, from the Hen and Chickens to the Hog's Back, from the Hog's Back to the Pot, and from the Pot to the Frying Pan; but in the eagerness of his sport he did not see that the tide was rapidly ebbing; until the roaring of the whirlpools and eddies warned him of his danger, and he had some difficulty in shooting his skiff from among the rocks and breakers, and getting to the point of Blackwell's Island. Here he cast anchor for some time, waiting the turn of the tide to enable him to return home-wards. As the night set in it grew blustering and gusty. Dark clouds came bundling up in the west; and now and then a growl of thunder or a flash of lightning told that a summer storm was at hand. Sam pulled over, therefore, under the lee of Manhattan Island, and coasting along came to a snug nook, just under a steep beetling rock, where he fastened his skiff to the root of a tree that shot out from a cleft and spread its broad branches like a canopy over the water. The gust came scouring along; the wind threw up the river in white surges; the rain rattled among the leaves, the thunder bel-lowed worse than that which is now bellowing, the lightning seemed to lick up the surges of the stream; but Sam, snugly sheltered under rock and tree, lay crouching in his skiff, rock-ing upon the billows until he fell asleep. When he woke all was quiet. The gust had passed away, and only now and then a faint gleam of lightning in the east showed which way it had gone. The night was dark and moonless; and from the state of the tide Sam concluded it was near midnight. He was on the point of making loose his skiff to return homewards, when he saw a light gleaming along the water from a distance, which seemed rapidly approaching. As it drew near he perceived it came from a lanthorn in the bow of a boat gliding along under shadow of the land. It pulled up in a small cove, close to where he was. A man jumped on shore, and searching about with the lanthorn exclaimed, "This is the place—here's the Iron ring." The boat was then made fast, and the man returning on board, assisted his comrades in conveying something heavy on shore. As the light gleamed among them, Sam saw that they were five stout desperate looking fellows, in red woollen caps, with a leader in a three cornered hat, and that some of them were armed with dirks, or long knives and pistols. They talked low to one another, and occasionally in some outlandish tongue which he could not understand.

On landing they made their way among the bushes, taking turns to relieve each other in lugging their burthen up the rocky bank. Sam's curiosity was now fully aroused, so leaving his skiff he clambered silently up a ridge that overlooked their path. They had stopped to rest for a moment, and the leader was looking about among the bushes with his lanthorn. "Have you brought the spades?" said one. "They are here," replied another, who had them on his shoulder. "We must dig deep, where there will be no risk of discovery," said a third.

A cold chill ran through Sam's veins. He fancied he saw before him a gang of murderers, about to bury their victim. His knees smote together. In his agitation he shook the branch of a tree with which he was supporting himself as he looked over the edge of the cliff.

"What's that?" cried one of the gang. "Some one stirs among the bushes!"

The lanthorn was held up in the direction of the noise. One of the red caps cocked a pistol, and pointed it towards the very place where Sam was standing. He stood motionless— breathless; expecting the next moment to be his last. Fortunately his dingy complexion was in his favour, and made no glare among the leaves.

"'Tis no one," said the man with the lanthorn. "What a plague! you would not fire off your pistol and alarm the country."

The pistol was uncocked; the burthen was resumed, and the party slowly toiled along the bank. Sam watched them as they went; the light sending back fitful gleams through the dripping bushes, and it was not till they were fairly out of sight that he ventured to draw breath freely. He now thought of getting back to his boat, and making his escape out of the reach of such dangerous neighbours; but curiosity was all powerful. He hesitated and lingered and listened. By and bye he heard the strokes of spades.

"They are digging the grave!" said he to himself; and the cold sweat started upon his forehead. Every stroke of a spade, as it sounded through the silent groves, went to his heart; it was evident there was as little noise made as possible; every thing had an air of terrible mystery and secresy. Sam had a great relish for the horrible,—a tale of murder was a treat for him; and he was a constant attendant at executions. He could not resist an impulse, in spite of every danger, to steal nearer to the scene of mystery, and overlook the midnight fellows at their work. He crawled along cautiously, therefore, inch by inch; stepping with the utmost care among the dry leaves, lest their rustling should betray him. He came at length to where a steep rock intervened between him and the gang; for he saw the light of their lanthorn shining up against the branches of the trees on the other side. Sam slowly and silently clambered up the surface of the rock, and raising his head above its naked edge, beheld the villains immediately below him, and so near that though he dreaded discovery he dared not withdraw lest the least movement should be heard. In this way he remained, with his round black face peering above the edge of the rock, like the sun just emerging above the edge of the horizon, or the round cheeked moon on the dial of a clock.

The red caps had nearly finished their work; the grave was filled up, and they were carefully replacing the turf. This done, they scattered dry leaves over the place. "And now," said the leader, "I defy the devil himself to find it out."

"The murderers!" exclaimed Sam, involuntarily.

The whole gang started, and looking up beheld the round black head of Sam just above them. His white eyes strained half out of their orbits; his white teeth chattering, and his whole visage shining with cold perspiration.

"We're discovered!" cried one.

"Down with him!" cried another.

Sam heard the cocking of a pistol, but did not pause for the report. He scrambled over rock and stone, through bush and briar; rolled down banks like a hedge hog; scrambled up others like a catamount. In every direction he heard some one or other of the gang hemming him in. At length he reached the rocky ridge along the river; one of the red caps was hard behind him. A steep rock like a wall rose directly in his way; it seemed to cut off all retreat, when fortunately he espied the strong cord-like branch of a grape vine, reaching half way down it. He sprang at it with the force of a desperate man, seized it with both hands, and being young and agile, succeeded in swinging himself to the summit of the cliff. Here he stood in full relief against the sky, when the red cap cocked his pistol and fired. The ball whistled by Sam's head. With the lucky thought of a man in an emergency, he uttered a yell, fell to the ground, and detached at the same time a fragment of the rock, which tumbled with a loud splash into the river.

"I've done his business," said the red cap, to one or two of his comrades as they arrived panting. "He'll tell no tales, except to the fishes in the river."

His pursuers now turned off to meet their companions. Sam sliding silently down the surface of the rock, let himself quietly into his skiff, cast loose the fastening, and abandoned himself to the rapid current, which in that place runs like a mill stream and soon swept him off from the neighbourhood. It was not, however, until he had drifted a great distance that he ventured to ply his oars; when he made his skiff dart like an arrow through the strait of Hell Gate, never heeding the danger of Pot, Frying Pan, or Hog's Back itself; nor did he feel himself thoroughly secure until safely nestled in bed in the cockloft of the ancient farm house of the Suydams.

Here the worthy Peechy Prauw paused to take breath and to take a sip of the gossip tankard that stood at his elbow. His auditors remained with open mouths and outstretched necks, gaping like a nest of swallows for an additional mouthful.

"And is that all?" exclaimed the half-pay officer.

"That's all that belongs to the story," said Peechy Prauw.

"And did Sam never find out what was buried by the red caps?" said Wolfert, eagerly; whose mind was haunted by nothing but ingots and doubloons.

"Not that I know of," said Peechy; "he had no time to spare from his work, and to tell the truth he did not like to run the risk of another race among the rocks. Besides, how should he recollect the spot where the grave had been digged? every thing would look so different by daylight. And then, where was the use of looking for a dead body, when there was no chance of hanging the murderers?"

"Aye, but are you sure it was a dead body they buried?" said Wolfert.

"To be sure," cried Peechy Prauw, exultingly. "Does it not haunt in the neighbourhood to this very day?"

"Haunts!" exclaimed several of the party, opening their eyes still wider and edging their chairs still closer.

"Aye, haunts," repeated Peechy, "has none of you heard of father red cap that haunts the old burnt farm house in the woods, on the border of the Sound, near Hell Gate?"

"Oh, to be sure, I've heard tell of something of the kind, but then I took it for some old wives' fable."

"Old wives' fable or not," said Peechy Prauw, "that farm house stands hard by the very spot. It's been unoccupied time out of mind, and stands in a lonely part of the coast; but those who fish in the neighbourhood have often heard strange noises there; and lights have been seen about the wood at night; and an old fellow in a red cap has been seen at the windows more than once, which people take to be the ghost of the body buried there. Once upon a time three soldiers took shelter in the building for the night, and rummaged it from top to bottom, when they found old father red cap astride of a cider barrel in the cellar, with a jug in one hand and a goblet in the other. He offered them a drink out of his goblet, but just as one of the soldiers was putting it to his mouth—Whew! a flash of fire blazed through the cellar, blinded every mother's son of them for several minutes, and when they recovered their eye sight, jug, goblet, and red cap had vanished, and nothing but the empty cider barrel remained."

Here the half-pay officer, who was growing very muzzy and sleepy, and nodding over his liquor, with half extinguished eye, suddenly gleamed up like an expiring rushlight.

"That's all fudge!" said he, as Peechy finished his last story.

"Well, I don't vouch for the truth of it myself," said Peechy Prauw, "though all the world knows that there's something strange about that house and grounds; but as to the story of Mud Sam, I believe it just as well as if it had happened to myself."

The deep interest taken in this conversation by the company, had made them unconscious of the uproar abroad among the elements, when suddenly they were electrified by a tremendous clap of thunder. A lumbering crash followed instantaneously shaking the building to its very foundation. All started from their seats, imagining it the shock of an earthquake, or that old father red cap was coming among them in all his terrors. They listened for a moment but only heard the rain pelting against the windows, and the wind howling among the trees. The explosion was soon explained by the apparition of an old negro's bald head thrust in at the door, his white goggle eyes contrasting with his jetty poll, which was wet with rain and shone like a bottle. In a jargon but half intelligible he announced that the kitchen chimney had been struck with lightning.

A sullen pause of the storm, which now rose and sunk in gusts, produced a momentary stillness. In this interval the report of a musket was heard, and a long shout, almost like a yell, resounded from the shore. Every one crowded to the window; another musket shot was heard, and another long shout, mingled wildly with a rising blast of wind. It seemed as if the cry came up from the bosom of the waters; for though incessant flashes of lightning spread a light about the shore, no one was to be seen.

Suddenly the window of the room overhead was opened, and a loud halloo uttered by the mysterious stranger. Several hailings passed from one party to the other, but in a language which none of the company in the bar room could understand; and presently they heard the window closed, and a great noise over head as if all the furniture were pulled and hauled about the room. The negro servant was summoned, and shortly afterwards was seen assisting the veteran to lug the ponderous sea chest down stairs.

The landlord was in amazement. "What, you are not going on the water in such a storm?"

"Storm!" said the other, scornfully, "do you call such a sputter of weather a storm?"

"You'll get drenched to the skin—You'll catch your death!" said Peechy Prauw, affectionately.

"Thunder and lightning!" exclaimed the merman, "don't preach about weather to a man that has cruised in whirlwinds and tornadoes."

The obsequious Peechy was again struck dumb. The voice from the water was heard once more in a tone of impatience; the bystanders stared with redoubled awe at this man of storms, who seemed to have come up out of the deep and to be summoned back to it again. As, with the assistance of the negro, he slowly bore his ponderous sea chest towards the shore, they eyed it with a superstitious feeling; half doubting whether he were not really about to embark upon it and launch forth upon the wild waves. They followed him at a distance with a lanthorn.

"Dowse the light!" roared the hoarse voice from the water. "No one wants lights here!"

"Thunder and lightning!" exclaimed the veteran, turning short upon them; "back to the house with you!"

Wolfert and his companions shrunk back in dismay. Still their curiosity would not allow them entirely to withdraw. A long sheet of lightning now flickered across the waves, and discovered a boat, filled with men, just under a rocky point, rising and sinking with the heaving surges, and swashing the water at every heave. It was with difficulty held to the rocks by a boat hook, for the current rushed furiously round the point. The veteran hoisted one end of the lumbering sea chest on the gunwale of the boat, and seized the handle at the other end to lift it in, when the motion propelled the boat from the shore; the chest slipped off from the gunwale, and, sinking into the waves, pulled the veteran headlong after it. A loud shriek was uttered by all on shore, and a volley of execrations by those on board; but boat and man were hurried away by the rushing swiftness of the tide. A pitchy darkness succeeded; Wolfert Webber indeed fancied that he distinguished a cry for help, and that he beheld the drowning man beckoning for assistance; but when the lightning again gleamed along the water all was void. Neither man nor boat was to be seen; nothing but the dashing and weltering of the waves as they hurried past.

The company returned to the tavern to await the subsiding of the storm. They resumed their seats and gazed on each other with dismay. The whole transaction had not occupied five minutes, and not a dozen words had been spoken. When they looked at the oaken chair they could scarcely realize the fact that the strange being who had so lately tenanted it, full of life and Herculean vigour, should already be a corpse. There was the very glass he had just drunk from; there lay the ashes from the pipe which he had smoked as it were with his last breath. As the worthy burghers pondered on these things, they felt a terrible conviction of the uncertainty of existence, and each felt as if the ground on which he stood was rendered less stable by this awful example.

As, however, the most of the company were possessed of that valuable philosophy which enables a man to bear up with fortitude against the misfortunes of his neighbours, they soon managed to console themselves for the tragic end of the veteran. The landlord was particularly happy that the poor dear man had paid his reckoning before he went; and made a kind of farewell speech on the occasion.

"He came," said he, "in a storm, and he went in a storm; he came in the night, and he went in the night; he came nobody knows whence, and he has gone nobody knows where. For aught I know he has gone to sea once more on his chest and may land to bother some people on the other side of the world! Though it's a thousand pities," added he, "if he has gone to Davy Jones' locker, that he had not left his own locker behind him."

"His locker! St. Nicholas preserve us!" cried Peechy Prauw. "I'd not have had that sea chest in the house for any money; I'll warrant he'd come racketing after it at nights, and making a haunted house of the inn. And as to his going to sea on his chest I recollect what happened to Skipper Onderdonk's ship on his voyage from Amsterdam.

"The boatswain died during a storm, so they wrapped him up in a sheet, and put him in his own sea chest, and threw him overboard; but they neglected in their hurry skurry to say prayers over him—and the storm raged and roared louder than ever, and they saw the dead man seated in his chest, with his shroud for a sail, coming hard after the ship; and the sea breaking before him in great sprays like fire, and there they kept scudding day after day and night after night, expecting every moment to go to wreck; and every night they saw the dead boatswain in his sea chest trying to get up with them, and they heard his whistle above the blasts of wind, and he seemed to send great seas mountain high after them, that would have swamped the ship if they had not put up the dead lights. And so it went on till they lost sight of him in the fogs of Newfoundland, and supposed he had veered ship and stood for Dead Man's Isle. So much for burying a man at sea without saying prayers over him."

The thundergust which had hitherto detained the company was now at an end. The cuckoo clock in the hall told midnight; every one pressed to depart, for seldom was such a late hour of the night trespassed on by these quiet burghers. As they sallied forth they found the heavens once more serene. The storm which had lately obscured them had rolled away, and lay piled up in fleecy masses on the horizon, lighted up by the bright crescent of the moon, which looked like a little silver lamp hung up in a palace of clouds.

The dismal occurrence of the night, and the dismal narrations they had made, had left a superstitious feeling in every mind. They cast a fearful glance at the spot where the buccaneer had disappeared, almost expecting to see him sailing on his chest in the cool moonshine. The trembling rays glittered along the waters, but all was placid; and the current dimpled over the spot where he had gone down. The party huddled together in a little crowd as they repaired homewards; particularly when they passed a lonely field where a man had been murdered; and even the sexton, who had to complete his journey alone, though accustomed, one would think, to ghosts and goblins, yet went a long way round, rather than pass by his own churchyard.

Wolfert Webber had now carried home a fresh stock of stories and notions to ruminate upon. These accounts of pots of money and Spanish treasures, buried here and there and every where, about the rocks and bays of these wild shores made him almost dizzy.

"Blessed St. Nicholas!" ejaculated he half aloud, "is it not possible to come upon one of these golden hoards, and so make one's self rich in a twinkling. How hard that I must go on, delving and delving, day in and day out, merely to make a morsel of bread, when one lucky stroke of a spade might enable me to ride in my carriage for the rest of my life!"

As he turned over in his thoughts all that had been told of the singular adventure of the negro fisherman, his imagination gave a totally different complexion to the tale. He saw in the gang of red caps nothing but a crew of pirates burying their spoils, and his cupidity was once more awakened by the possibility of at length getting on the traces of some of this lurking wealth. Indeed, his infected fancy tinged every thing with gold. He felt like the greedy inhabitant of Bagdad, when his eye had been greased with the magic ointment of the dervise, that gave him to see all the treasures of the earth. Caskets of buried jewels, chests of ingots, and barrels of outlandish coins, seemed to court him from their concealments, and supplicate him to relieve them from their untimely graves.

On making private inquiries about the grounds said to be haunted by Father red cap, he was more and more confirmed in his surmise. He learned that the place had several times been visited by experienced money diggers, who had heard Black Sam's story, though none of them had met with success. On the contrary, they had always been dogged with ill luck of some kind or other, in consequence, as Wolfert concluded, of not going to work at the proper time, and with the proper ceremonials. The last attempt had been made by Cobus Quackenbos, who dug for a whole night and met with incredible difficulty, for as fast as he threw one shovel full of earth out of the hole, two were thrown in by invisible hands. He succeeded so far, however, as to uncover an iron chest, when there was a terrible roaring, and ramping, and raging, of uncouth figures about the hole, and at length a shower of blows, dealt by invisible cudgels, fairly belaboured him off of the forbidden ground. This Cobus Quackenbos had declared on his death bed, so that there could not be any doubt of it. He was a man that had devoted many years of his life to money digging, and it was thought would have ultimately succeeded, had he not died recently of a brain fever in the alms house.

Wolfert Webber was now in a worry of trepidation and impatience; fearful lest some rival adventurer should get a scent of the buried gold. He determined privately to seek out the black fisherman and get him to serve as guide to the place where he had witnessed the mysterious scene of interment. Sam was easily found; for he was one of those old habitual beings that live about a neighbourhood until they wear themselves a place in the public mind, and become, in a manner, public characters. There was not an unlucky urchin about town that did not know Sam the fisherman, and think that he had a right to play his tricks upon the old negro. Sam had led an amphibious life for more than half a century, about the shores of the bay, and the fishing grounds of the Sound. He passed the greater part of his time on and in the water, particularly about Hell Gate; and might have been taken, in bad weather, for one of the hobgoblins that used to haunt that strait. There would he be seen, at all times, and in all weathers; sometimes in his skiff, anchored among the eddies, or prowling, like a shark about some wreck, where the fish are supposed to be most abundant. Sometimes seated on a rock from hour to hour, looking, in the mist and drizzle, like a solitary heron watching for its prey. He was well acquainted with every hole and corner of the Sound; from the Wallabout to Hell Gate, and from Hell Gate even unto the Devil's Stepping Stones; and it was even affirmed that he knew all the fish in the river by their christian names.

Wolfert found him at his cabin, which was not much larger than a tolerable dog house. It was rudely constructed of fragments of wrecks and drift wood, and built on the rocky shore, at the foot of the old fort, just about what at present forms the point of the Battery. A "most ancient and fish-like smell" pervaded the place. Oars, paddles, and fishing rods were leaning against the wall of the fort; a net was spread on the sands to dry; a skiff was drawn up on the beach, and at the door of his cabin was Mud Sam himself, indulging in the true negro luxury of sleeping in the sunshine.

Many years had passed away since the time of Sam's youthful adventure, and the snows of many a winter had grizzled the knotty wool upon his head. He perfectly recollected the circumstances, however, for he had often been called upon to relate them, though in his version of the story he differed in many points from Peechy Prauw; as is not unfrequently the case with authentic historians. As to the subsequent researches of money diggers, Sam knew nothing about them; they were matters quite out of his line; neither did the cautious Wolfert care to disturb his thoughts on that point. His only wish was to secure the old fisherman as a pilot to the spot, and this was readily effected. The long time that had intervened since his nocturnal adventure had effaced all Sam's awe of the place, and the promise of a trifling reward roused him at once from his sleep and his sunshine.

The tide was adverse to making the expedition by water, and Wolfert was too impatient to get to the land of promise, to wait for its turning; they set off, therefore, by land. A walk of four or five miles brought them to the edge of a wood, which at that time covered the greater part of the eastern side of the island. It was just beyond the pleasant region of Bloomen-dael. Here they struck into a long lane, straggling among trees and bushes, very much overgrown with weeds and mullein stalks as if but seldom used, and so completely overshadowed as to enjoy but a kind of twilight. Wild vines entangled the trees and flaunted in their faces; brambles and briars caught their clothes as they passed; the garter snake glided across their path; the spotted toad hopped and waddled before them, and the restless cat-bird mewed at them from every thicket. Had Wolfert Webber been deeply read in romantic legend he might have fancied himself entering upon forbidden enchanted ground; or that these were some of the guardians set to keep a watch upon buried treasure. As it was, the loneliness of the place, and the wild stories connected with it, had their effect upon his mind.

On reaching the lower end of the lane they found themselves near the shore of the Sound in a kind of amphitheatre, surrounded by forest trees. The area had once been a grass plot, but was now shagged with briars and rank weeds. At one end, and just on the river bank, was a ruined building, little better than a heap of rubbish, with a stack of chimneys rising like a solitary tower out of the centre. The current of the Sound rushed along just below it; with wildly grown trees drooping their branches into its waves.

Wolfert had not a doubt that this was the haunted house of Father red cap, and called to mind the story of Peechy Prauw. The evening was approaching and the light falling dubiously among these woody places, gave a melancholy tone to the scene, well calculated to foster any lurking feeling of awe or superstition. The night hawk, wheeling about in the highest regions of the air, emitted his peevish, boding cry. The woodpecker gave a lonely tap now and then on some hollow tree, and the fire bird* streamed by them with his deep red plumage.

They now came to an enclosure that had once been a garden. It extended along the foot of a rocky ridge, but was little better than a wilderness of weeds, with here and there a matted rose bush, or a peach or plum tree grown wild and ragged, and covered with moss. At the lower end of the garden they passed a kind of vault in the side of a bank, facing the water. It had the look of a root house. The door, though decayed, was still strong, and appeared to have been recently patched up. Wolfert pushed it open. It gave a harsh grating upon its hinges, and striking against something like a box, a rattling sound ensued, and a skull rolled on the floor. Wolfert drew back shuddering, but was reassured on being informed by the negro that this was a family vault belonging to one of the old Dutch families that owned this estate; an assertion corroborated by the sight of coffins of various sizes piled within. Sam had been familiar with all these scenes when a boy, and now knew that he could not be far from the place of which they were in quest.

They now made their way to the water's edge, scrambling along ledges of rocks that overhung the waves, and obliged

*Orchard Oreole.

often to hold by shrubs and grape vines to avoid slipping into the deep and hurried stream. At length they came to a small cove, or rather indent of the shore. It was protected by steep rocks and overshadowed by a thick copse of oaks and chesnuts, so as to be sheltered and almost concealed. The beach shelved gradually within the cove, but the current swept deep and black and rapid along its jutting points. The negro paused; raised his remnant of a hat, and scratching his grizzled poll for a moment, as he regarded this nook: then suddenly clapping his hands, he stepped exultingly forward and pointed to a large iron ring, stapled firmly in the rock, just where a broad shelve of stone furnished a commodious landing place. It was the very spot where the red caps had landed. Years had changed the more perishable features of the scene; but rock and iron yield slowly to the influence of time. On looking more closely, Wolfert remarked three crosses cut in the rock just above the ring, which had no doubt some mysterious signification. Old Sam now readily recognized the overhanging rock under which his skiff had been sheltered during the thundergust. To follow up the course which the midnight gang had taken, however, was a harder task. His mind had been so much taken up on that eventful occasion by the persons of the drama, as to pay but little attention to the scenes; and these places look so different by night and day. After wandering about for some time, however, they came to an opening among the trees which Sam thought resembled the place. There was a ledge of rock of moderate height like a wall on one side, which he thought might be the very ridge whence he had overlooked the diggers. Wolfert examined it narrowly, and at length discovered three crosses similar to those above the iron ring, cut deeply into the face of the rock, but nearly obliterated by the moss that had grown over them. His heart leaped with joy, for he doubted not they were the private marks of the buccaneers. All now that remained was to ascertain the precise spot where the treasure lay buried, for otherwise he might dig at random in the neighbourhood of the crosses without coming upon the spoils, and he had already had enough of such profitless labour. Here, however, the old negro was perfectly at a loss, and indeed perplexed him by a variety of opinions; for his recollections were all confused. Sometimes he declared it must have been at the foot of a mulberry tree hard by; then beside a great white stone; then under a small green knoll, a short distance from the ledge of rock; until at length Wolfert became as bewildered as himself.

The shadows of evening were now spreading themselves over the woods, and rock and tree began to mingle together. It was evidently too late to attempt any thing farther at present; and, indeed, Wolfert had come unprovided with implements to prosecute his researches. Satisfied, therefore, with having ascertained the place, he took note of all its landmarks, that he might recognize it again, and set out on his return homewards, resolved to prosecute this golden enterprise without delay.

The leading anxiety which had hitherto absorbed every feeling being now in some measure appeased, fancy began to wander, and to conjure up a thousand shapes and chimeras as he returned through this haunted region. Pirates hanging in chains seemed to swing from every tree, and he almost expected to see some Spanish Don, with his throat cut from ear to ear, rising slowly out of the ground, and shaking the ghost of a money bag.

Their way back lay through the desolate garden, and Wolfert's nerves had arrived at so sensitive a state that the flitting of a bird, the rustling of a leaf, or the falling of a nut was enough to startle him. As they entered the confines of the garden, they caught sight of a figure at a distance advancing slowly up one of the walks and bending under the weight of a burthen. They paused and regarded him attentively. He wore what appeared to be a woollen cap, and still more alarming, of a most sanguinary red. The figure moved slowly on, ascended the bank, and stopped at the very door of the sepulchral vault. Just before entering it he looked around. What was the affright of Wolfert when he recognized the grisly visage of the drowned buccaneer. He uttered an ejaculation of horror. The figure slowly raised his iron fist and shook it with a terrible menace. Wolfert did not pause to see any more, but hurried off as fast as his legs could carry him, nor was Sam slow in following at his heels, having all his ancient terrors revived. Away, then, did they scramble, through bush and brake, horribly frightened at every bramble that tugged at their skirts, nor did they pause to breathe, until they had blundered their way through this perilous wood and fairly reached the high road to the city.

Several days elapsed before Wolfert could summon courage enough to prosecute the enterprise, so much had he been dismayed by the apparition, whether living or dead, of the grisly buccaneer. In the mean time, what a conflict of mind did he suffer! He neglected all his concerns, was moody and restless all day, lost his appetite; wandered in his thoughts and words, and committed a thousand blunders. His rest was broken; and when he fell asleep the nightmare in shape of a huge money bag sat squatted upon his breast. He babbled about incalculable sums; fancied himself engaged in money digging; threw the bed clothes right and left, in the idea that he was shovelling away the dirt, groped under the bed in quest of the treasure, and lugged forth, as he supposed, an inestimable pot of gold.

Dame Webber and her daughter were in despair at what they conceived a returning touch of insanity. There are two family oracles, one or other of which Dutch house wives consult in all cases of great doubt and perplexity: the dominie and the doctor. In the present instance they repaired to the doctor. There was at that time a little dark mouldy man of medicine famous among the old wives of the Manhattoes for his skill not only in the healing art, but in all matters of strange and mysterious nature. His name was Dr. Knipperhausen, but he was more commonly known by the appellation of the High German doctor.* To him did the poor women repair for council and assistance touching the mental vagaries of Wolfert Webber.

They found the doctor seated in his little study, clad in his dark camblet robe of knowledge, with his black velvet cap, after the manner of Boerhaave, Van Helmont and other medical sages: a pair of green spectacles set in black horn upon his clubbed nose, and poring over a German folio that reflected back the darkness of his physiognomy. The doctor listened to

---

*The same, no doubt, of whom mention is made in the history of Dolph Heyliger.

their statement of the symptoms of Wolfert's malady with profound attention; but when they came to mention his raving about buried money, the little man pricked up his ears. Alas, poor women! they little knew the aid they had called in.

Dr. Knipperhausen had been half his life engaged in seeking the short cuts to fortune, in quest of which so many a long life time is wasted. He had passed some years of his youth among the Harz mountains of Germany, and had derived much valuable instruction from the miners, touching the mode of seeking treasure buried in the earth. He had prosecuted his studies also under a travelling sage who united the mysteries of medicine with magic and legerdemain. His mind therefore had become stored with all kinds of mystic lore: he had dabbled a little in astrology, alchemy, and divination; knew how to detect stolen money, and to tell where springs of water lay hidden; in a word, by the dark nature of his knowledge he had acquired the name of the High German doctor, which is pretty nearly equivalent to that of necromancer. The doctor had often heard rumours of treasure being buried in various parts of the island, and had long been anxious to get on the traces of it. No sooner were Wolfert's waking and sleeping vagaries confided to him, than he beheld in them the confirmed symptoms of a case of money digging, and lost no time in probing it to the bottom. Wolfert had long been sorely oppressed in mind by the golden secret, and as a family physician is a kind of father confessor, he was glad of an opportunity of unburthening himself. So far from curing, the doctor caught the malady from his patient. The circumstances unfolded to him awakened all his cupidity; he had not a doubt of money being buried somewhere in the neighbourhood of the mysterious crosses, and offered to join Wolfert in the search. He informed him that much secresy and caution must be observed in enterprises of the kind; that money is only to be digged for at night; with certain forms and ceremonies; the burning of drugs; the repeating of mystic words, and above all, that the seekers must first be provided with a divining rod, which had the wonderful property of pointing to the very spot on the surface of the earth under which treasure lay hidden. As the doctor had given much of his mind to these matters, he charged himself with all the necessary preparations, and, as the quarter of the moon was propitious, he undertook to have the divining rod ready by a certain night.*

Wolfert's heart leaped with joy at having met with so learned and able a coadjutor. Every thing went on secretly, but swimmingly. The doctor had many consultations with his patient, and the good women of the household lauded the comforting effect of his visits. In the mean time the wonderful divining rod, that great key to nature's secrets, was duly prepared. The doctor had thumbed over all his books of knowledge for the occasion; and the black fisherman was engaged to take them in his skiff to the scene of enterprise; to work with spade and pickaxe in unearthing the treasure; and

---

*The following note was found appended to this passage in the hand writing of Mr. Knickerbocker. "There has been much written against the divining rod by those light minds who are ever ready to scoff at the mysteries of nature, but I fully join with Dr. Knipperhausen in giving it my faith. I shall not insist upon its efficacy in discovering the concealment of stolen goods, the boundary stones of fields, the traces of robbers and murderers, or even the existence of subterraneous springs and streams of water: albeit, I think these properties not to be readily discredited; but of its potency in discovering veins of precious metal, and hidden sums of money and jewels I have not the least doubt. Some said that the rod turned only in the hands of persons who had been born in particular months of the year; hence astrologers had recourse to planetary influence when they would procure a talisman. Others declared that the properties of the rod were either an effect of chance, or the fraud of the holder, or the work of the devil. Thus sayeth the reverend father Gaspard Schott in his Treatise on Magic. 'Propter hæc et similia argumenta audacter ego pronuncio vim conversivam virgulæ bifurcatæ nequaquam naturalem esse, sed vel casu vel fraude virgulam tractantis vel ope diaboli,' &c.

"Georgius Agricola also was of opinion that it was a mere delusion of the devil to inveigle the avaricious and unwary into his clutches, and in his treatise 'de re Metallica,' lays particular stress on the mysterious words pronounced by those persons who employed the divining rod during his time. But I make not a doubt that the divining rod is one of those secrets of natural magic, the mystery of which is to be explained by the sympathies existing between physical things operated upon by the planets, and rendered efficacious by the strong faith of the individual. Let the divining rod be properly gathered at the proper time of the moon, cut into the proper form, used with the necessary ceremonies, and with a perfect faith in its efficacy, and I can confidently recommend it to my fellow citizens as an infallible means of discovering the various places on the Island of the Manhattoes where treasure hath been buried in the olden time.

D.K."

to freight his bark with the weighty spoils they were certain of finding.

At length the appointed night arrived for this perilous undertaking. Before Wolfert left his home he counselled his wife and daughter to go to bed, and feel no alarm if he should not return during the night. Like reasonable women, on being told not to feel alarm they fell immediately into a panic. They saw at once by his manner that something unusual was in agitation; all their fears about the unsettled state of his mind were revived with tenfold force: they hung about him entreating him not to expose himself to the night air, but all in vain. When once Wolfert was mounted on his hobby, it was no easy matter to get him out of the saddle. It was a clear starlight night, when he issued out of the portal of the Webber palace. He wore a large flapped hat tied under the chin with a handkerchief of his daughter's, to secure him from the night damp, while Dame Webber threw her long red cloak about his shoulders, and fastened it round his neck.

The doctor had been no less carefully armed and accoutred by his housekeeper, the vigilant Frau Ilsy; and sallied forth in his camblet robe by way of surtout; his black velvet cap under his cocked hat, a thick clasped book under his arm, a basket of drugs and dried herbs in one hand, and in the other the miraculous rod of divination.

The great church clock struck ten as Wolfert and the doctor passed by the church yard, and the watchman bawled in hoarse voice a long and doleful "all's well!" A deep sleep had already fallen upon this primitive little burgh: nothing disturbed this awful silence, excepting now and then the bark of some profligate night walking dog, or the serenade of some romantic cat. It is true, Wolfert fancied more than once that he heard the sound of a stealthy footfall at a distance behind them; but it might have been merely the echo of their own steps along the quiet streets. He thought also at one time that he saw a tall figure skulking after them—stopping when they stopped, and moving on as they proceeded; but the dim and uncertain lamp light threw such vague gleams and shadows, that this might all have been mere fancy.

They found the old fisherman waiting for them, smoking his pipe in the stern of his skiff, which was moored just in front of his little cabin. A pickaxe and spade were lying in the bottom of the boat, with a dark lanthorn, and a stone bottle of good Dutch courage in which honest Sam no doubt put even more faith than Dr. Knipperhausen in his drugs.

Thus then did these three worthies embark in their cockle shell of a skiff upon this nocturnal expedition, with a wisdom and valour equalled only by the three wise men of Gotham, who adventured to sea in a bowl. The tide was rising and running rapidly up the Sound. The current bore them along, almost without the aid of an oar. The profile of the town lay all in shadow. Here and there a light feebly glimmered from some sick chamber, or from the cabin window of some vessel at anchor in the stream. Not a cloud obscured the deep starry firmament, the lights of which wavered on the surface of the placid river; and a shooting meteor, streaking its pale course in the very direction they were taking, was interpreted by the doctor into a most propitious omen.

In a little while they glided by the point of Corlear's Hook with the rural inn which had been the scene of such night adventures. The family had retired to rest, and the house was dark and still. Wolfert felt a chill pass over him as they passed the point where the buccaneer had disappeared. He pointed it out to Dr. Knipperhausen. While regarding it they thought they saw a boat actually lurking at the very place; but the shore cast such a shadow over the border of the water that they could discern nothing distinctly. They had not proceeded far when they heard the low sounds of distant oars, as if cautiously pulled. Sam plied his oars with redoubled vigour, and knowing all the eddies and currents of the stream soon left their followers, if such they were, far astern. In a little while they stretched across Turtle Bay and Kip's Bay, then shrouded themselves in the deep shadows of the Manhattan shore, and glided swiftly along, secure from observation. At length the negro shot his skiff into a little cove, darkly embowered by trees, and made it fast to the well known iron ring. They now landed, and lighting the lanthorn, gathered their various implements and proceeded slowly through the bushes. Every sound startled them, even that of their own footsteps among the dry leaves; and the hooting of a screech owl, from the shattered chimney of the neighbouring ruin, made their blood run cold.

In spite of all Wolfert's caution in taking note of the landmarks, it was some time before they could find the open place among the trees, where the treasure was supposed to be buried. At length they came to the ledge of rock; and on examining its surface by the aid of the lanthorn, Wolfert recognized the three mystic crosses. Their hearts beat quick, for the momentous trial was at hand that was to determine their hopes.

The lanthorn was now held by Wolfert Webber, while the doctor produced the divining rod. It was a forked twig, one end of which was grasped firmly in each hand, while the centre, forming the stem, pointed perpendicularly upwards. The doctor moved this wand about, within a certain distance of the earth, from place to place, but for some time without any effect, while Wolfert kept the light of the lanthorn turned full upon it, and watched it with the most breathless interest. At length the rod began slowly to turn. The doctor grasped it with greater earnestness, his hands trembling with the agitation of his mind. The wand continued to turn gradually, until at length the stem had reversed its position, and pointed perpendicularly downward; and remained pointing to one spot as fixedly as the needle to the pole.

"This is the spot!" said the doctor in an almost inaudible tone.

Wolfert's heart was in his throat.

"Shall I dig?" said the negro, grasping the spade.

"*Pots tausends*, no!" replied the little doctor, hastily. He now ordered his companions to keep close by him and to maintain the most inflexible silence. That certain precautions must be taken and ceremonies used to prevent the evil spirits which keep about buried treasure from doing them any harm. He then drew a circle round the place, enough to include the whole party. He next gathered dry twigs and leaves, and made a fire, upon which he threw certain drugs and dried herbs which he had brought in his basket. A thick smoke rose, diffusing a potent odour, savouring marvellously of brimstone and assafœtida, which, however grateful it might be to the olfactory nerves of spirits, nearly strangled poor

Wolfert, and produced a fit of coughing and wheezing that made the whole grove resound. Doctor Knipperhausen then unclasped the volume which he had brought under his arm, which was printed in red and black characters in German text. While Wolfert held the lanthorn, the doctor, by the aid of his spectacles, read off several forms of conjuration in Latin and German. He then ordered Sam to seize the pickaxe and proceed to work. The close bound soil gave obstinate signs of not having been disturbed for many a year. After having picked his way through the surface, Sam came to a bed of sand and gravel which he threw briskly to right and left with the spade.

"Hark!" said Wolfert, who fancied he heard a trampling among the dry leaves, and a rustling through the bushes. Sam paused for a moment, and they listened.—No footstep was near. The bat flitted by them in silence; a bird roused from its roost by the light which glared up among the trees, flew circling about the flame. In the profound stillness of the woodland, they could distinguish the current rippling along the rocky shore, and the distant murmuring and roaring of Hell Gate.

The negro continued his labours, and had already digged a considerable hole. The doctor stood on the edge, reading formulæ every now and then from his black letter volume, or throwing more drugs and herbs upon the fire; while Wolfert bent anxiously over the pit, watching every stroke of the spade. Any one witnessing the scene thus lighted up by fire, lanthorn, and the reflection of Wolfert's red mantle, might have mistaken the little doctor for some foul magician, busied in his incantations, and the grizzly headed negro for some swart goblin, obedient to his commands.

At length the spade of the old fisherman struck upon something that sounded hollow. The sound vibrated to Wolfert's heart. He struck his spade again.

"'Tis a chest," said Sam.

"Full of gold, I'll warrant it!" cried Wolfert, clasping his hands with rapture.

Scarcely had he uttered the words when a sound from above caught his ear. He cast up his eyes, and lo! by the expiring light of the fire he beheld, just over the disk of the rock, what appeared to be the grim visage of the drowned buccaneer, grinning hideously down upon him.

Wolfert gave a loud cry, and let fall the lanthorn. His panic communicated itself to his companions. The negro leaped out of the hole, the doctor dropped his book and basket and began to pray in German. All was horror and confusion. The fire was scattered about, the lanthorn extinguished. In their hurry skurry they ran against and confounded one another. They fancied a legion of hobgoblins let loose upon them, and that they saw by the fitful gleams of the scattered embers, strange figures in red caps gibbering and ramping around them. The doctor ran one way, the negro another, and Wolfert made for the water side. As he plunged struggling onwards through bush and brake, he heard the tread of some one in pursuit. He scrambled frantically forward. The footsteps gained upon him. He felt himself grasped by his cloak, when suddenly his pursuer was attacked in turn: a fierce fight and struggle ensued—a pistol was discharged that lit up rock and bush for a second, and showed two figures grappling together—all was then darker than ever. The contest continued—the combatants clenched each other, and panted and groaned, and rolled among the rocks. There was snarling and growling as of a cur, mingled with curses in which Wolfert fancied he could recognize the voice of the buccaneer. He would fain have fled, but he was on the brink of a precipice and could go no farther.

Again the parties were on their feet; again there was a tugging and struggling, as if strength alone could decide the combat, until one was precipitated from the brow of the cliff and sent headlong into the deep stream that whirled below. Wolfert heard the plunge, and a kind of strangling bubbling murmur, but the darkness of the night hid every thing from him, and the swiftness of the current swept every thing instantly out of hearing. One of the combatants was disposed of, but whether friend or foe Wolfert could not tell, nor whether they might not both be foes. He heard the survivor approach, and his terror revived. He saw, where the profile of the rocks rose against the horizon, a human form advancing. He could not be mistaken: it must be the buccaneer. Whither should he fly! a precipice was on one side; a murderer on the other. The enemy approached: he was close at hand. Wolfert attempted to let himself down the face of the cliff. His cloak caught in a thorn that grew on the edge. He was jerked from off his feet, and held dangling in the air, half choaked by the string with which his careful wife had fastened the garment round his neck. Wolfert thought his last moment was arrived; already had he committed his soul to St. Nicholas, when the string broke, and he tumbled down the bank, bumping from rock to rock and bush to bush, and leaving the red cloak fluttering like a bloody banner in the air.

It was a long while before Wolfert came to himself. When he opened his eyes, the ruddy streaks of morning were already shooting up the sky. He found himself grievously battered, and lying in the bottom of a boat. He attempted to sit up, but was too sore and stiff to move. A voice requested him in friendly accents to lie still. He turned his eyes towards the speaker: it was Dirk Waldron. He had dogged the party, at the earnest request of Dame Webber and her daughter, who with the laudable curiosity of their sex had pried into the secret consultations of Wolfert and the doctor. Dirk had been completely distanced in following the light skiff of the fisherman, and had just come in time to rescue the poor money digger from his pursuer.

Thus ended this perilous enterprise. The doctor and Black Sam severally found their way back to the Manhattoes, each having some dreadful tale of peril to relate. As to poor Wolfert, instead of returning in triumph laden with bags of gold, he was borne home on a shutter, followed by a rabble rout of curious urchins. His wife and daughter saw the dismal pageant from a distance, and alarmed the neighbourhood with their cries: they thought the poor man had suddenly settled the great debt of nature in one of his wayward moods. Finding him, however, still living, they had him speedily to bed, and a jury of old matrons of the neighbourhood assembled to determine how he should be doctored. The whole town was in a buzz with the story of the money diggers. Many repaired to the scene of the previous night's adventures: but though they found the very place of the digging, they discovered nothing that compensated them for their trouble. Some say they found the fragments of an oaken chest, and an iron pot lid which savoured strongly of hidden money; and that in the old family vault there were traces of bales and boxes, but this is all very dubious.

In fact, the secret of all this story has never to this day been discovered: whether any treasure was ever actually buried at that place; whether, if so, it was carried off at night by those who had buried it; or whether it still remains there under the guardianship of gnomes and spirits until it shall be properly sought for, is all matter of conjecture. For my part I incline to the latter opinion; and make no doubt that great sums lie buried, both there and in many other parts of this island and its neighbourhood, ever since the times of the buccaneers and the Dutch colonists; and I would earnestly recommend the search after them to such of my fellow citizens as are not engaged in any other speculations.

There were many conjectures formed, also, as to who and what was the strange man of the seas who had domineered over the little fraternity at Corlear's Hook for a time; disappeared so strangely, and reappeared so fearfully. Some supposed him a smuggler stationed at that place to assist his comrades in landing their goods among the rocky coves of the island. Others that he was one of the ancient comrades of Kidd or Bradish, returned to convey away treasures formerly hidden in the vicinity. The only circumstance that throws any thing like a vague light over this mysterious matter is a report which prevailed of a strange foreign built shallop, with much the look of a piccaroon, having been seen hovering about the Sound for several days without landing or reporting herself, though boats were seen going to and from her at night: and that she was seen standing out of the mouth of the harbour, in the grey of the dawn after the catastrophe of the money diggers.

I must not omit to mention another report, also, which I confess is rather apocryphal, of the buccaneer, who was supposed to have been drowned, being seen before daybreak, with a lanthorn in his hand, seated astride his great sea chest and sailing through Hell Gate, which just then began to roar and bellow with redoubled fury.

While all the gossip world was thus filled with talk and rumour, poor Wolfert lay sick and sorrowful in his bed,

bruised in body and sorely beaten down in mind. His wife
and daughter did all they could to bind up his wounds both
corporal and spiritual. The good old dame never stirred from
his bed side, where she sat knitting from morning till night;
while his daughter busied herself about him with the fondest
care. Nor did they lack assistance from abroad. Whatever may
be said of the desertions of friends in distress, they had no
complaint of the kind to make. Not an old wife of the neighbourhood but abandoned her work to crowd to the mansion
of Wolfert Webber, inquire after his health and the particulars
of his story. Not one came moreover without her little pipkin
of pennyroyal, sage, balm, or other herb tea, delighted at an
opportunity of signalizing her kindness and her doctorship.
What drenchings did not the poor Wolfert undergo, and all in
vain. It was a moving sight to behold him wasting away day
by day; growing thinner and thinner and ghastlier and ghastlier, and staring with rueful visage from under an old patch-
work counterpane upon the jury of matrons kindly assembled
to sigh and groan and look unhappy around him.

Dirk Waldron was the only being that seemed to shed a ray
of sunshine into this house of mourning. He came in with
cheery look and manly spirit, and tried to reanimate the expiring heart of the poor money digger, but it was all in vain.
Wolfert was completely done over.—If any thing was wanting to complete his despair, it was a notice served upon him
in the midst of his distress, that the corporation were about to
run a new street through the very centre of his cabbage garden. He now saw nothing before him but poverty and ruin;
his last reliance, the garden of his forefathers, was to be laid
waste, and what then was to become of his poor wife and
child.

His eyes filled with tears as they followed the dutiful Amy
out of the room one morning. Dirk Waldron was seated beside him; Wolfert grasped his hand, pointed after his daughter, and for the first time since his illness broke the silence he
had maintained.

"I am going!" said he, shaking his head feebly, "and when I
am gone—my poor daughter——"

"Leave her to me, father!" said Dirk, manfully—"I'll take
care of her!"

Wolfert looked up in the face of the cheery strapping youngster, and saw there was none better able to take care of a woman.

"Enough," said he—"she is yours!—and now fetch me a lawyer—let me make my will and die."

The lawyer was brought—a dapper, bustling, round headed little man, Roorback (or Rollebuck as it was pronounced) by name. At the sight of him the women broke into loud lamentations, for they looked upon the signing of a will as the signing of a death warrant. Wolfert made a feeble motion for them to be silent. Poor Amy buried her face and her grief in the bed curtain. Dame Webber resumed her knitting to hide her distress, which betrayed itself, however, in a pellucid tear, which trickled silently down and hung at the end of her peaked nose; while the cat, the only unconcerned member of the family, played with the good dame's ball of worsted, as it rolled about the floor.

Wolfert lay on his back, his nightcap drawn over his forehead; his eyes closed; his whole visage the picture of death. He begged the lawyer to be brief, for he felt his end approaching, and that he had no time to lose. The lawyer nibbed his pen, spread out his paper, and prepared to write.

"I give and bequeath," said Wolfert, faintly, "my small farm——"

"What—all!" exclaimed the lawyer.

Wolfert half opened his eyes and looked upon the lawyer.

"Yes—all," said he.

"What! all that great patch of land with cabbages and sunflowers, which the corporation is just going to run a main street through?"

"The same," said Wolfert, with a heavy sigh, and sinking back upon his pillow.

"I wish him joy that inherits it!" said the little lawyer, chuckling and rubbing his hands involuntarily.

"What do you mean?" said Wolfert, again opening his eyes.

"That he'll be one of the richest men in the place!" cried little Rollebuck.

The expiring Wolfert seemed to step back from the threshold of existence: his eyes again lighted up; he raised himself in his bed, shoved back his red worsted nightcap, and stared broadly at the lawyer.

"You don't say so!" exclaimed he.

"Faith, but I do!" rejoined the other. "Why, when that great field and that huge meadow come to be laid out in streets, and cut up into snug building lots—why, whoever owns them need not pull off his hat to the patroon!"

"Say you so?" cried Wolfert, half thrusting one leg out of bed, "why, then I think I'll not make out my will yet!"

To the surprise of every body the dying man actually recovered. The vital spark which had glimmered faintly in the socket, received fresh fuel from the oil of gladness, which the little lawyer poured into his soul. It once more burnt up into a flame.

Give the physic to the heart, ye who would revive the body of a spirit broken man! In a few days Wolfert left his room; in a few days more his table was covered with deeds, plans of streets and building lots. Little Rollebuck was constantly with him, his right hand man and adviser, and instead of making his will, assisted in the more agreeable task of making his fortune. In fact, Wolfert Webber was one of those many worthy Dutch burghers of the Manhattoes whose fortunes have been made, in a manner, in spite of themselves. Who have tenaciously held on to their hereditary acres, raising turnips and cabbages about the skirts of the city, hardly able to make both ends meet, until the corporation has cruelly driven streets through their abodes, and they have suddenly awakened out of a lethargy, and, to their astonishment, found themselves rich men.

Before many months had elapsed a great bustling street passed through the very centre of the Webber garden, just where Wolfert had dreamed of finding a treasure. His golden dream was accomplished; he did indeed find an unlooked for source of wealth; for, when his paternal lands were distributed into building lots, and rented out to safe tenants, instead of producing a paltry crop of cabbages, they returned him an abundant crop of rents; insomuch that on quarter day, it was a goodly sight to see his tenants knocking at his door, from morning to night, each with a little round bellied bag of money, the golden produce of the soil.

The ancient mansion of his forefathers was still kept up, but instead of being a little yellow fronted Dutch house in a garden, it now stood boldly in the midst of a street, the grand house of the neighbourhood; for Wolfert enlarged it with a wing on each side, and a cupola or tea room on top, where he might climb up and smoke his pipe in hot weather; and in the course of time the whole mansion was overrun by the chubby progeny of Amy Webber and Dirk Waldron.

As Wolfert waxed old and rich and corpulent, he also set up a great gingerbread coloured carriage drawn by a pair of black Flanders mares with tails that swept the ground; and to commemorate the origin of his greatness he had for his crest a full blown cabbage painted on the pannels, with the pithy motto 𝔄𝔩𝔩𝔢𝔰 𝔎𝔬𝔭𝔣: that is to say, ALL HEAD; meaning thereby that he had risen by sheer head work.

To fill the measure of his greatness, in the fullness of time the renowned Ramm Rapelye slept with his fathers, and Wolfert Webber succeeded to the leathern bottomed arm chair in the inn parlour at Corlear's Hook; where he long reigned greatly honoured and respected, insomuch that he was never known to tell a story without its being believed, nor to utter a joke without its being laughed at.

THE ALHAMBRA

Contents

PREFACE TO THE REVISED EDITION.

Rough draughts of some of the following tales and essays, were actually written during a residence in the Alhambra; others were subsequently added, founded on notes and observations made there. Care was taken to maintain local coloring and verisimilitude; so that the whole might present a faithful and living picture of that microcosm, that singular little world into which I had been fortuitously thrown; and about which the external world had a very imperfect idea. It was my endeavor scrupulously to depict its half Spanish half Oriental character; its mixture of the heroic, the poetic, and the grotesque; to revive the traces of grace and beauty fast fading from its walls; to record the regal and chivalrous traditions concerning those who once trod its courts; and the whimsical and superstitious legends of the motley race now burrowing among its ruins.

The papers thus roughly sketched out lay for three or four years in my portfolio, until I found myself in London, in 1832, on the eve of returning to the United States. I then endeavored to arrange them for the press, but the preparations for departure did not allow sufficient leisure. Several were thrown aside as incomplete; the rest were put together somewhat hastily and in rather a crude and chaotic manner.

In the present edition I have revised and re-arranged the whole work, enlarged some parts, and added others, including the papers originally omitted; and have thus endeavored to render it more complete and more worthy of the indulgent reception with which it has been favored.

W. I.

Sunnyside, 1851.

The Journey

IN THE SPRING of 1829, the author of this work, whom curiosity had brought into Spain, made a rambling expedition from Seville to Granada in company with a friend, a member of the Russian Embassy at Madrid. Accident had thrown us together from distant regions of the globe, and a similarity of taste led us to wander together among the romantic mountains of Andalusia. Should these pages meet his eye, wherever thrown by the duties of his station, whether mingling in the pageantry of courts, or meditating on the truer glories of nature, may they recall the scenes of our adventurous companionship, and with them the recollection of one, in whom neither time nor distance will obliterate the remembrance of his gentleness and worth.*

And here, before setting forth, let me indulge in a few previous remarks on Spanish scenery and Spanish travelling. Many are apt to picture Spain to their imaginations as a soft southern region, decked out with the luxuriant charms of voluptuous Italy. On the contrary, though there are exceptions in some of the maritime provinces, yet, for the greater part, it is a stern, melancholy country, with rugged mountains, and long sweeping plains, destitute of trees, and indescribably silent and lonesome, partaking of the savage and solitary character of Africa. What adds to this silence and loneliness, is the absence of singing-birds, a natural consequence of the want of groves and hedges. The vulture and the eagle are seen wheeling about the mountain-cliffs, and soaring over the plains, and groups of shy bustards stalk about the heaths; but the myriads of smaller birds, which animate the whole face of other countries, are met with in but few provinces in Spain, and in those chiefly among the orchards and gardens which surround the habitations of man.

In the interior provinces the traveller occasionally traverses great tracts cultivated with grain as far as the eye can reach,

Note to the Revised Edition.—The Author feels at liberty to mention that his travelling companion was the Prince Dolgorouki, at present Russian minister at the Court of Persia.

waving at times with verdure, at other times naked and sun-burnt, but he looks round in vain for the hand that has tilled the soil. At length, he perceives some village on a steep hill, or rugged crag, with mouldering battlements and ruined watchtower; a strong-hold, in old times, against civil war, or Moorish inroad; for the custom among the peasantry of congregating together for mutual protection is still kept up in most parts of Spain, in consequence of the maraudings of roving freebooters.

But though a great part of Spain is deficient in the garni-ture of groves and forests, and the softer charms of ornamen-tal cultivation, yet its scenery is noble in its severity, and in unison with the attributes of its people; and I think that I better understand the proud, hardy, frugal and abstemious Spaniard, his manly defiance of hardships, and contempt of effeminate indulgences, since I have seen the country he in-habits.

There is something, too, in the sternly simple features of the Spanish landscape, that impresses on the soul a feeling of sublimity. The immense plains of the Castiles and of La Man-cha, extending as far as the eye can reach, derive an interest from their very nakedness and immensity, and possess, in some degree, the solemn grandeur of the ocean. In ranging over these boundless wastes, the eye catches sight here and there of a straggling herd of cattle attended by a lonely herds-man, motionless as a statue, with his long slender pike taper-ing up like a lance into the air; or, beholds a long train of mules slowly moving along the waste like a train of camels in the desert; or, a single horseman, armed with blunderbuss and stiletto, and prowling over the plain. Thus the country, the habits, the very looks of the people, have something of the Arabian character. The general insecurity of the country is evinced in the universal use of weapons. The herdsman in the field, the shepherd in the plain, has his musket and his knife. The wealthy villager rarely ventures to the market-town with-out his trabuco, and, perhaps, a servant on foot with a blun-derbuss on his shoulder; and the most petty journey is undertaken with the preparation of a warlike enterprise.

The dangers of the road produce also a mode of travelling, resembling, on a diminutive scale, the caravans of the east.

The arrieros, or carriers, congregate in convoys, and set off in large and well-armed trains on appointed days; while additional travellers swell their number, and contribute to their strength. In this primitive way is the commerce of the country carried on. The muleteer is the general medium of traffic, and the legitimate traverser of the land, crossing the peninsula from the Pyrenees and the Asturias to the Alpuxarras, the Serrania de Ronda, and even to the gates of Gibraltar. He lives frugally and hardily: his alforjas of coarse cloth hold his scanty stock of provisions; a leathern bottle, hanging at his saddle-bow, contains wine or water, for a supply across barren mountains and thirsty plains; a mule-cloth spread upon the ground is his bed at night, and his pack-saddle his pillow. His low, but clean-limbed and sinewy form betokens strength; his complexion is dark and sunburnt; his eye resolute, but quiet in its expression, except when kindled by sudden emotion; his demeanor is frank, manly, and courteous, and he never passes you without a grave salutation: "Dios guarde à usted!" "Va usted con Dios, Caballero!" "God Guard you!" "God be with you, Cavalier!"

As these men have often their whole fortune at stake upon the burden of their mules, they have their weapons at hand, slung to their saddles, and ready to be snatched out for desperate defence; but their united numbers render them secure against petty bands of marauders, and the solitary bandolero, armed to the teeth, and mounted on his Andalusian steed, hovers about them, like a pirate about a merchant convoy, without daring to assault.

The Spanish muleteer has an inexhaustible stock of songs and ballads, with which to beguile his incessant wayfaring. The airs are rude and simple, consisting of but few inflections. These he chants forth with a loud voice, and long, drawling cadence, seated sideways on his mule, who seems to listen with infinite gravity, and to keep time, with his paces, to the tune. The couplets thus chanted, are often old traditional romances about the Moors, or some legend of a saint, or some love-ditty; or, what is still more frequent, some ballad about a bold contrabandista, or hardy bandolero, for the smuggler and the robber are poetical heroes among the common people of Spain. Often, the song of the muleteer is composed at the instant, and relates to some local scene, or some incident of the journey. This talent of singing and improvising is frequent in Spain, and is said to have been inherited from the Moors. There is something wildly pleasing in listening to these ditties among the rude and lonely scenes they illustrate; accompanied, as they are, by the occasional jingle of the mule-bell.

It has a most picturesque effect also to meet a train of muleteers in some mountain-pass. First you hear the bells of the leading mules, breaking with their simple melody the stillness of the airy height; or, perhaps, the voice of the muleteer admonishing some tardy or wandering animal, or chanting, at the full stretch of his lungs, some traditionary ballad. At length you see the mules slowly winding along the cragged defile, sometimes descending precipitous cliffs, so as to present themselves in full relief against the sky, sometimes toiling up the deep arid chasms below you. As they approach, you descry their gay decorations of worsted tufts, tassels, and saddle-cloths, while, as they pass by, the ever-ready trabuco, slung behind the packs and saddles, gives a hint of the insecurity of the road.

The ancient kingdom of Granada, into which we were about to penetrate, is one of the most mountainous regions of Spain. Vast sierras, or chains of mountains, destitute of shrub or tree, and mottled with variegated marbles and granites, elevate their sunburst summits against a deep-blue sky; yet in their rugged bosoms lie ingulfed verdant and fertile valleys, where the desert and the garden strain for mastery, and the very rock is, as it were, compelled to yield the fig, the orange, and the citron, and to blossom with the myrtle and the rose.

In the wild passes of these mountains the sight of walled towns and villages, built like eagles' nests among the cliffs, and surrounded by Moorish battlements, or of ruined watch-towers perched on lofty peaks, carries the mind back to the chivalric days of Christian and Moslem warfare, and to the romantic struggle for the conquest of Granada. In traversing these lofty sierras the traveller is often obliged to alight, and lead his horse up and down the steep and jagged ascents and descents, resembling the broken steps of a staircase. Sometimes the road winds along dizzy precipices, without parapet to guard him from the gulfs below, and then will plunge down steep, and dark, and dangerous declivities. Sometimes it straggles through rugged barrancos, or ravines, worn by winter torrents, the obscure path of the contrabandista; while, ever and anon, the ominous cross, the monument of robbery and murder, erected on a mound of stones at some lonely part of the road, admonishes the traveller that he is among the haunts of banditti, perhaps at that very moment under the eye of some lurking bandolero. Sometimes, in winding through the narrow valleys, he is startled by a hoarse bellowing, and beholds above him on some green fold of the mountain a herd of fierce Andalusian bulls, destined for the combat of the arena. I have felt, if I may so express it, an agreeable horror in thus contemplating, near at hand, these terrific animals, clothed with tremendous strength, and ranging their native pastures in untamed wildness, strangers almost to the face of man: they know no one but the solitary herdsmen who attends upon them, and even he at times dares not venture to approach them. The low bellowing of these bulls, and their menacing aspect as they look down from their rocky height, give additional wildness to the savage scenery.

I have been betrayed unconsciously into a longer disquisition than I intended on the general features of Spanish travelling; but there is a romance about all the recollections of the Peninsula dear to the imagination.

As our proposed route to Granada lay through mountainous regions, where the roads are little better than mule paths, and said to be frequently beset by robbers, we took due travelling precautions. Forwarding the most valuable part of our luggage a day or two in advance by the arrieros, we retained merely clothing and necessaries for the journey and money for the expenses of the road; with a little surplus of hard dollars by way of *robber purse*, to satisfy the gentlemen of the road should we be assailed. Unlucky is the too wary traveller who, having grudged this precaution, falls into their clutches empty handed: they are apt to give him a sound ribroasting for cheating them out of their dues. "Caballeros like them cannot afford to scour the roads and risk the gallows for nothing."

A couple of stout steeds were provided for our own mounting, and a third of our scanty luggage and the conveyance of a sturdy Biscayan lad, about twenty years of age, who was to be our guide, our groom, our valet, and at all times our guard. For the latter office he was provided with a formidable trabuco or carbine, with which he promised to defend us against rateros or solitary footpads; but as to powerful bands, like that of the "sons of Ecija," he confessed they were quite beyond his prowess. He made much vainglorious boast about his weapon at the outset of the journey; though, to the discredit of his generalship, it was suffered to hang unloaded behind his saddle.

According to our stipulations, the man from whom we hired the horses was to be at the expense of their feed and stabling on the journey, as well as of the maintenance of our Biscayan squire, who of course was provided with funds for the purpose; we took care, however, to give the latter a private hint, that, though we made a close bargain with his master, it was all in his favor, as, if he proved a good man and true, both he and the horses should live at our cost, and the money provided for their maintenance remain in his pocket. This unexpected largess, with the occasional present of a cigar, won his heart completely. He was, in truth, a faithful, cheery, kind-hearted creature, as full of saws and proverbs as that miracle of squires, the renowned Sancho himself, whose name, by the by, we bestowed upon him, and like a true Spaniard, though treated by us with companionable familiarity, he never for a moment, in his utmost hilarity, overstepped the bounds of respectful decorum.

Such were our minor preparations for the journey, but above all we laid in an ample stock of good humor and a genuine disposition to be pleased; determining to travel in true contrabandista style; taking things as we found them, rough or smooth, and mingling with all classes and conditions in a kind of vagabond companionship. It is the true way to travel in Spain. With such disposition and determination, what a country is it for a traveller, where the most miserable inn is as full of adventure as an enchanted castle, and every meal is in itself an achievement! Let others repine at the lack of turnpike roads and sumptuous hotels, and all the elaborate comforts of a country cultivated and civilized into tameness and commonplace; but give me the rude mountain scramble;

the roving, haphazard, wayfaring; the half wild, yet frank and hospitable manners, which impart such a true game flavor to dear old romantic Spain!

Thus equipped and attended, we cantered out of "Fair Seville city" at half-past six in the morning of a bright May day, in company with a lady and gentleman of our acquaintance, who rode a few miles with us, in the Spanish mode of taking leave. Our route lay through old Alcala de Guadaira (Alcala on the river Aira), the benefactress of Seville, that supplies it with bread and water. Here live the bakers who furnish Seville with that delicious bread for which it is renowned; here are fabricated those roscas well known by the well-merited appellation of *pan de Dios* (bread of God); with which, by the way, we ordered our man, Sancho, to stock his alforjas for the journey. Well has this beneficent little city been denominated the "Oven of Seville;" well has it been called Alcala de los Panaderos (Alcala of the bakers), for a great part of its inhabitants are of that handicraft, and the highway hence to Seville is constantly traversed by lines of mules and donkeys laden with great panniers of loaves and roscas.

I have said Alcala supplies Seville with water. Here are great tanks or reservoirs, of Roman and Moorish construction, whence water is conveyed to Seville by noble aqueducts. The springs of Alcala are almost as much vaunted as its ovens; and to the lightness, sweetness, and purity of its water is attributed in some measure the delicacy of its bread.

Here we halted for a time, at the ruins of the old Moorish castle, a favorite resort for pic-nic parties from Seville, where we had passed many a pleasant hour. The walls are of great extent, pierced with loopholes; inclosing a huge square tower or keep, with the remains of masmoras, or subterranean granaries. The Guadaira winds its stream round the hill, at the foot of these ruins, whimpering among reeds, rushes, and pond-lilies, and overhung with rhododendron, eglantine, yellow myrtle, and a profusion of wild flowers and aromatic shrubs; while along its banks are groves of oranges, citrons, and pomegranates, among which we heard the early note of the nightingale.

A picturesque bridge was thrown across the little river, at one end of which was the ancient Moorish mill of the castle,

defended by a tower of yellow stone; a fisherman's net hung
against the wall to dry, and hard by in the river was his boat;
a group of peasant women in bright-colored dresses, crossing
the arched bridge, were reflected in the placid stream. Altogether it was an admirable scene for a landscape painter.

The old Moorish mills, so often found on secluded streams,
are characteristic objects in Spanish landscape, and suggestive
of the perilous times of old. They are of stone, and often in
the form of towers with loopholes and battlements, capable of
defence in those warlike days when the country on both sides
of the border was subject to sudden inroad and hasty ravage,
and when men had to labor with their weapons at hand, and
some place of temporary refuge.

Our next halting place was at Gandul, where were the
remains of another Moorish castle, with its ruined tower, a
nestling place for storks, and commanding a view over a vast
campiña or fertile plain, with the mountains of Ronda in the
distance. These castles were strong-holds to protect the plains
from the talas or forays to which they were subject, when the
fields of corn would be laid waste, the flocks and herds swept
from the vast pastures, and, together with captive peasantry,
hurried off in long cavalgadas across the borders.

At Gandul we found a tolerable posada; the good folks
could not tell us what time of day it was, the clock only struck
once in the day, two hours after noon; until that time it was
guess work. We guessed it was full time to eat; so, alighting,
we ordered a repast. While that was in preparation, we visited
the palace once the residence of the Marquis of Gandul. All
was gone to decay; there were but two or three rooms habit-
able, and very poorly furnished. Yet here were the remains of
grandeur; a terrace, where fair dames and gentle cavaliers may
once have walked; a fish-pond and ruined garden, with grape-
vines and date-bearing palm-trees. Here we were joined by a
fat curate, who gathered a bouquet of roses and presented it,
very gallantly, to the lady who accompanied us.

Below the palace was the mill, with orange-trees and aloes
in front, and a pretty stream of pure water. We took a seat in
the shade, and the millers, all leaving their work, sat down
and smoked with us; for the Andalusians are always ready for
a gossip. They were waiting for the regular visit of the barber,

who came once a week to put all their chins in order. He arrived shortly afterwards; a lad of seventeen, mounted on a donkey, eager to display his new alforjas or saddle-bags, just bought at a fair; price one dollar, to be paid on St. John's day (in June), by which time he trusted to have mown beards enough to put him in funds.

By the time the laconic clock of the castle had struck two we had finished our dinner. So, taking leave of our Seville friends, and leaving the millers still under the hands of the barber, we set off on our ride across the campiña. It was one of those vast plains, common in Spain, where for miles and miles there is neither house nor tree. Unlucky the traveller who has to traverse it, exposed as we were to heavy and re-peated showers of rain. There is no escape nor shelter. Our only protection was our Spanish cloaks, which nearly covered man and horse, but grew heavier every mile. By the time we had lived through one shower we would see another slowly but inevitably approaching; fortunately in the interval there would be an outbreak of bright, warm, Andalusian sunshine, which would make our cloaks send up wreaths of steam, but which partially dried them before the next drenching.

Shortly after sunset we arrived at Arahal, a little town among the hills. We found it in a bustle with a party of miquelets, who were patrolling the country to ferret out rob-bers. The appearance of foreigners like ourselves was an un-usual circumstance in an interior country town; and little Spanish towns of the kind are easily put in a state of gossip and wonderment by such an occurrence. Mine host, with two or three old wiseacre comrades in brown cloaks, studied our passports in a corner of the posada, while an Alguazil took notes by the dim light of a lamp. The passports were in for-eign languages and perplexed them, but our Squire Sancho assisted them in their studies, and magnified our importance with the grandiloquence of a Spaniard. In the mean time the magnificent distribution of a few cigars had won the hearts of all around us; in a little while the whole community seemed put in agitation to make us welcome. The corregidor himself waited upon us, and a great rush-bottomed arm-chair was ostentatiously bolstered into our room by our landlady, for the accommodation of that important personage. The commander of the patrol took supper with us; a lively, talk-ing, laughing Andaluz, who had made a campaign in South America, and recounted his exploits in love and war with much pomp of phrase, vehemence of gesticulation, and mys-terious rolling of the eye. He told us that he had a list of all the robbers in the country, and meant to ferret out every mother's son of them; he offered us at the same time some of his soldiers as an escort. "One is enough to protect you, se-ñors; the robbers know me, and know my men; the sight of one is enough to spread terror through a whole sierra." We thanked him for his offer, but assured him, in his own strain, that with the protection of our redoubtable squire, Sancho, we were not afraid of all the ladrones of Andalusia.

While we were supping with our drawcansir friend, we heard the notes of a guitar, and the click of castañets, and presently a chorus of voices singing a popular air. In fact mine host had gathered together the amateur singers and musi-cians, and the rustic belles of the neighborhood, and, on go-ing forth, the court-yard or patio of the inn presented a scene of true Spanish festivity. We took our seats with mine host and hostess and the commander of the patrol, under an arch-way opening into the court; the guitar passed from hand to hand, but a jovial shoemaker was the Orpheus of the place. He was a pleasant-looking fellow, with huge black whiskers; his sleeves were rolled up to his elbows. He touched the gui-tar with masterly skill, and sang a little amorous ditty with an expressive leer at the women, with whom he was evidently a favorite. He afterwards danced a fandango with a buxom An-dalusian damsel, to the great delight of the spectators. But none of the females present could compare with mine host's pretty daughter, Pepita, who had slipped away and made her toilette for the occasion, and had covered her head with roses; and who distinguished herself in a bolero with a handsome young dragoon. We ordered our host to let wine and refresh-ment circulate freely among the company, yet, though there was a motley assembly of soldiers, muleteers, and villagers, no one exceeded the bounds of sober enjoyment. The scene was a study for a painter: the picturesque group of dancers, the troopers in their half military dresses, the peasantry wrapped

in their brown cloaks; nor must I omit to mention the old
meagre Alguazil, in a short black cloak, who took no notice of
any thing going on, but sat in a corner diligently writing by
the dim light of a huge copper lamp, that might have figured
in the days of Don Quixote.

The following morning was bright and balmy, as a May
morning ought to be, according to the poets. Leaving Arahal
at seven o'clock, with all the posada at the door to cheer us
off, we pursued our way through a fertile country, covered
with grain and beautifully verdant; but which in summer,
when the harvest is over and the fields parched and brown,
must be monotonous and lonely; for, as in our ride of yesterday, there were neither houses nor people to be seen. The
latter all congregate in villages and strong-holds among the
hills, as if these fertile plains were still subject to the ravages
of the Moor.

At noon we came to where there was a group of trees,
beside a brook in a rich meadow. Here we alighted to make
our mid-day meal. It was really a luxurious spot, among wild
flowers and aromatic herbs, with birds singing around us.
Knowing the scanty larders of Spanish inns, and the houseless
tracts we might have to traverse, we had taken care to have
the alforjas of our squire well stocked with cold provisions,
and his bota, or leathern bottle, which might hold a gallon,
filled to the neck with choice Valdepeñas wine.* As we depended more upon these for our well-being than even his
trabuco, we exhorted him to be more attentive in keeping
them well charged; and I must do him the justice to say that
his namesake, the trencher-loving Sancho Panza, was never a
more provident purveyor. Though the alforjas and the bota
were frequently and vigorously assailed throughout the journey, they had a wonderful power of repletion, our vigilant

*It may be as well to note here, that the alforjas are square pockets at each
end of a long cloth about a foot and a half wide, formed by turning up its
extremities. The cloth is then thrown over the saddle, and the pockets hang
on each side like saddle-bags. It is an Arab invention. The bota is a leathern
bag or bottle, of portly dimensions, with a narrow neck. It is also oriental.
Hence the scriptural caution, which perplexed me in my boyhood, not to put
new wine into old bottles

squire sacking every thing that remained from our repasts at
the inns, to supply these junketings by the road-side, which
were his delight.

On the present occasion he spread quite a sumptuous variety of remnants on the green-sward before us, graced with an
excellent ham brought from Seville; then, taking his seat at a
little distance, he solaced himself with what remained in the
alforjas. A visit or two to the bota made him as merry and
chirruping as a grasshopper filled with dew. On my comparing his contents of the alforjas to Sancho's skimming of the
flesh-pots at the wedding of Cammacho, I found he was well
versed in the history of Don Quixote, but, like many of the
common people of Spain, firmly believed it to be a true
history.

"All that happened a long time ago, señor," said he, with
an inquiring look.

"A very long time," I replied.

"I dare say more than a thousand years"—still looking
dubiously.

"I dare say not less."

The squire was satisfied. Nothing pleased the simple-
hearted varlet more than my comparing him to the renowned
Sancho for devotion to the trencher; and he called himself by
no other name throughout the journey.

Our repast being finished, we spread our cloaks on the
green-sward under the tree, and took a luxurious siesta in the
Spanish fashion. The clouding up of the weather, however,
warned us to depart, and a harsh wind sprang up from the
southeast. Towards five o'clock we arrived at Osuna, a town
of fifteen thousand inhabitants, situated on the side of a hill,
with a church and a ruined castle. The posada was outside of
the walls; it had a cheerless look. The evening being cold, the
inhabitants were crowded round a brasero in a chimney corner; and the hostess was a dry old woman, who looked like a
mummy. Every one eyed us askance as we entered, as Spaniards are apt to regard strangers; a cheery, respectful salutation on our part, caballeroing them and touching our
sombreros, set Spanish pride at ease; and when we took our
seat among them, lit our cigars, and passed the cigar-box

round among them, our victory was complete. I have never known a Spaniard, whatever his rank or condition, who would suffer himself to be outdone in courtesy; and to the common Spaniard the present of a cigar (puro) is irresistible. Care, however, must be taken never to offer him a present with an air of superiority and condescension; he is too much of a caballero to receive favors at the cost of his dignity.

Leaving Osuna at an early hour the next morning, we entered the sierra or range of mountains. The road wound through picturesque scenery, but lonely; and a cross here and there by the road side, the sign of a murder, showed that we were now coming among the "robber haunts." This wild and intricate country, with its silent plains and valleys intersected by mountains, has ever been famous for banditti. It was here that Omar Ibn Hassan, a robber-chief among the Moslems, held ruthless sway in the ninth century, disputing dominion even with the caliphs of Cordova. This too was a part of the regions so often ravaged during the reign of Ferdinand and Isabella by Ali Atar, the old Moorish alcayde of Loxa, father-in-law of Boabdil, so that it was called Ali Atar's garden, and here "Jose Maria," famous in Spanish brigand story, had his favorite lurking places.

In the course of the day we passed through Fuente la Piedra near a little salt lake of the same name, a beautiful sheet of water, reflecting like a mirror the distant mountains. We now came in sight of Antiquera, that old city of warlike reputation, lying in the lap of the great sierra which runs through Andalusia. A noble vega spread out before it, a picture of mild fertility set in a frame of rocky mountains. Crossing a gentle river we approached the city between hedges and gardens, in which nightingales were pouring forth their evening song. About nightfall we arrived at the gates. Every thing in this venerable city has a decidedly Spanish stamp. It lies too much out of the frequented track of foreign travel to have its old usages trampled out. Here I observed old men still wearing the montero, or ancient hunting cap, once common throughout Spain; while the young men wore the little round-crowned hat, with brim turned up all round, like a cup turned down in its saucer; while the brim was set off with little black tufts like cockades. The women, too, were all in mantillas and basquinas. The fashions of Paris had not reached Antiquera.

Pursuing our course through a spacious street, we put up at the posada of San Fernando. As Antiquera, though a considerable city, is, as I observed, somewhat out of the track of travel, I had anticipated bad quarters and poor fare at the inn. I was agreeably disappointed, therefore, by a supper table amply supplied, and what were still more acceptable, good clean rooms and comfortable beds. Our man, Sancho, felt himself as well off as his namesake, when he had the run of the duke's kitchen, and let me know, as I retired for the night, that it had been a proud time for the alforjas.

Early in the morning (May 4th) I strolled to the ruins of the old Moorish castle, which itself had been reared on the ruins of a Roman fortress. Here, taking my seat on the remains of a crumbling tower, I enjoyed a grand and varied landscape, beautiful in itself, and full of storied and romantic associations; for I was now in the very heart of the country famous for the chivalrous contests between Moor and Christian. Below me, in its lap of hills, lay the old warrior city so often mentioned in chronicle and ballad. Out of yon gate and down yon hill paraded the band of Spanish cavaliers, of highest rank and bravest bearing, to make that foray during the war and conquest of Granada, which ended in the lamentable massacre among the mountains of Malaga, and laid all Andalusia in mourning. Beyond spread out the vega, covered with gardens and orchards and fields of grain and enamelled meadows, inferior only to the famous vega of Granada. To the right the Rock of the Lovers stretched like a cragged promontory into the plain, whence the daughter of the Moorish alcayde and her lover, when closely pursued, threw themselves in despair.

The matin peal from church and convent below me rang sweetly in the morning air, as I descended. The market place was beginning to throng with the populace, who traffic in the abundant produce of the vega; for this is the mart of an agricultural region. In the market-place were abundance of freshly plucked roses for sale; for not a dame or damsel of Andalusia thinks her gala dress complete without a rose shining like a gem among her raven tresses.

On returning to the inn I found our man Sancho, in high gossip with the landlord and two or three of his hangers-on. He had just been telling some marvellous story about Seville, which mine host seemed piqued to match with one equally marvellous about Antiquera. There was once a fountain, he said, in one of the public squares called *Il fuente del toro*, the fountain of the bull, because the water gushed from the mouth of a bull's head, carved of stone. Underneath the head was inscribed:

> En frente del toro
> Se hallen tesoro.

(In front of the bull there is treasure.) Many digged in front of the fountain, but lost their labor and found no money. At last one knowing fellow construed the motto a different way. It is in the forehead (frente) of the bull that the treasure is to be found, said he to himself, and I am the man to find it. Accordingly he came late at night, with a mallet, and knocked the head to pieces; and what do you think he found?

"Plenty of gold and diamonds!" cried Sancho eagerly.

"He found nothing," rejoined mine host dryly; "and he ruined the fountain."

Here a great laugh was set up by the landlord's hangers-on; who considered Sancho completely taken in by what I presume was one of mine host's standing jokes.

Leaving Antiquera at eight o'clock, we had a delightful ride along the little river, and by gardens and orchards, fragrant with the odors of spring and vocal with the nightingale. Our road passed round the Rock of the Lovers (el peñon de los enamorados), which rose in a precipice above us. In the course of the morning we passed through Archidona, situated in the breast of a high hill, with a three-pointed mountain towering above it, and the ruins of a Moorish fortress. It was a great toil to ascend a steep stony street leading up into the city, although it bore the encouraging name of Calle Real del Llano (the royal street of the plain), but it was still a greater toil to descend from this mountain city on the other side.

At noon we halted in sight of Archidona, in a pleasant little meadow among hills covered with olive-trees. Our cloaks were spread on the grass, under an elm by the side of a bubbling rivulet; our horses were tethered where they might crop the herbage, and Sancho was told to produce his alforjas. He had been unusually silent this morning ever since the laugh raised at his expense, but now his countenance brightened, and he produced his alforjas with an air of triumph. They contained the contributions of four days' journeying, but had been signally enriched by the foraging of the previous evening in the plenteous inn at Antiquera; and this seemed to furnish him with a set-off to the banter of mine host.

> En frente del toro
> Se hallen tesoro

would he exclaim, with a chuckling laugh, as he drew forth the heterogeneous contents one by one, in a series which seemed to have no end. First came forth a shoulder of roasted kid, very little the worse for wear; then an entire partridge; then a great morsel of salted codfish wrapped in paper; then the residue of a ham; then the half of a pullet, together with several rolls of bread, and a rabble rout of oranges, figs, raisins, and walnuts. His bota also had been recruited with some excellent wine of Malaga. At every fresh apparition from his larder, he would enjoy our ludicrous surprise, throwing himself back on the grass, shouting with laughter, and exclaiming "Frente del toro!—frente del toro! Ah, señors, they thought Sancho a simpleton at Antiquera; but Sancho knew where to find the *tesoro*."

While we were diverting ourselves with his simple drollery, a solitary beggar approached, who had almost the look of a pilgrim. He had a venerable gray beard, and was evidently very old, supporting himself on a staff, yet age had not bowed him down; he was tall and erect, and had the wreck of a fine form. He wore a round Andalusian hat, a sheep-skin jacket, and leathern breeches, gaiters, and sandals. His dress, though old and patched, was decent, his demeanor manly, and he addressed us with the grave courtesy that is to be remarked in the lowest Spaniard. We were in a favorable mood for such a visitor; and in a freak of capricious charity gave him some silver, a loaf of fine wheaten bread, and a goblet of our choice wine of Malaga. He received them thankfully, but without any grovelling tribute of gratitude. Tasting the wine, he held it up to the light, with a slight beam of surprise in his eye, then quaffing it off at a draught; "It is many years," said he, "since I have tasted such wine. It is a cordial to an old man's heart." Then, looking at the beautiful wheaten loaf, *"bendito sea tal pan!"* "blessed be such bread!" So saying, he put it in his wallet. We urged him to eat it on the spot. "No, señors," replied he, "the wine I had either to drink or leave; but the bread I may take home to share with my family."

Our man Sancho sought our eye, and reading permission there, gave the old man some of the ample fragments of our repast, on condition, however, that he should sit down and make a meal.

He accordingly took his seat at some little distance from us, and began to eat slowly, and with a sobriety and decorum that would have become a hidalgo. There was altogether a measured manner and a quiet self-possession about the old man, that made me think that he had seen better days: his language too, though simple, had occasionally something picturesque and almost poetical in the phraseology. I set him down for some broken-down cavalier. I was mistaken; it was nothing but the innate courtesy of a Spaniard, and the poetical turn of thought and language often to be found in the lowest classes of this clear-witted people. For fifty years, he told us, he had been a shepherd, but now he was out of employ and destitute. "When I was a young man," said he, "nothing could harm or trouble me; I was always well, always gay; but now I am seventy-nine years of age, and a beggar, and my heart begins to fail me."

Still he was not a regular mendicant: it was not until recently that want had driven him to this degradation; and he gave a touching picture of the struggle between hunger and pride, when abject destitution first came upon him. He was returning from Malaga without money; he had not tasted food for some time, and was crossing one of the great plains of Spain, where there were but few habitations. When almost dead with hunger, he applied at the door of a venta or country inn. *"Perdon usted por Dios hermano!"* (Excuse us, brother, for God's sake!) was the reply—the usual mode in Spain of refusing a beggar. "I turned away," said he, "with shame greater than my hunger, for my heart was yet too proud. I came to a river with high banks, and deep, rapid current, and felt tempted to throw myself in: 'What should such an old, worthless, wretched man as I live for?' But when I was on the brink of the current, I thought on the blessed Virgin, and turned away. I travelled on until I saw a country-seat at a little distance from the road, and entered the outer gate of the court-yard. The door was shut, but there were two young señoras at a window. I approached and begged:—'*Perdon usted por Dios hermano!*'—and the window closed. I crept out of the courtyard, but hunger overcame me, and my heart gave way: I thought my hour at hand, so I laid myself down at the gate, commended myself to the Holy Virgin, and covered my head to die. In a little while afterwards the master of the house came home: seeing me lying at his gate, he uncovered my head, had pity on my gray hairs, took me into his house, and gave me food. So, señors, you see that one should always put confidence in the protection of the Virgin."

The old man was on his way to his native place, Archidona, which was in full view on its steep and rugged mountain. He pointed to the ruins of its castle: "That castle," he said, "was inhabited by a Moorish king at the time of the wars of Granada. Queen Isabella invaded it with a great army; but the king looked down from his castle among the clouds, and laughed her to scorn! Upon this the Virgin appeared to the queen, and guided her and her army up a mysterious path in the mountains, which had never before been known. When the Moor saw her coming, he was astonished, and springing with his horse from a precipice, was dashed to pieces! The marks of his horse's hoofs," said the old man, "are to be seen in the margin of the rock to this day. And see, señors, yonder is the road by which the queen and her army mounted; you see it like a ribbon up the mountain's side; but the miracle is, that, though it can be seen at a distance, when you come near it disappears!"

The ideal road to which he pointed was undoubtedly a sandy ravine of the mountain, which looked narrow and defined at a distance, but became broad and indistinct on an approach.

As the old man's heart warmed with wine and wassail, he went on to tell us a story of the buried treasure left under the castle by the Moorish king. His own house was next to the foundations of the castle. The curate and notary dreamed three times of the treasure, and went to work at the place pointed out in their dreams. His own son-in-law heard the sound of their pickaxes and spades at night. What they found nobody knows; they became suddenly rich, but kept their own secret. Thus the old man had once been next door to fortune, but was doomed never to get under the same roof.

I have remarked that the stories of treasure buried by the Moors, so popular throughout Spain, are most current among the poorest people. Kind nature consoles with shadows for the lack of substantials. The thirsty man dreams of fountains and running streams; the hungry man of banquets; and the poor man of heaps of hidden gold: nothing certainly is more opulent than the imagination of a beggar.

Our afternoon's ride took us through a steep and rugged defile of the mountains, called Puerte del Rey, the Pass of the King; being one of the great passes into the territories of Granada, and the one by which king Ferdinand conducted his army. Towards sunset the road, winding round a hill, brought us in sight of the famous little frontier city of Loxa, which repulsed Ferdinand from its walls. Its Arabic name implies guardian, and such it was to the vega of Granada; being one of its advanced guards. It was the strong-hold of that fiery veteran, old Ali Atar, father-in-law of Boabdil; and here it was that the latter collected his troops, and sallied forth on that disastrous foray which ended in the death of the old alcayde and his own captivity. From its commanding position at the gate, as it were, of this mountain pass, Loxa has not unaptly been termed the key of Granada. It is wildly picturesque; built along the face of an arid mountain. The ruins of a Moorish alcazar or citadel crown a rocky mound which rises out of the centre of the town. The river Xenil washes its base, winding among rocks, and groves, and gardens, and meadows, and crossed by a Moorish bridge. Above the city all is savage and sterile, below is the richest vegetation and the freshest verdure. A similar contrast is presented by the river; above the bridge it is placid and grassy, reflecting groves and gardens; below it is rapid, noisy and tumultuous. The Sierra Nevada, the royal mountains of Granada, crowned with perpetual snow, form the distant boundary to this varied landscape; one of the most characteristic of romantic Spain.

Alighting at the entrance of the city, we gave our horses to Sancho to lead them to the inn, while we strolled about to enjoy the singular beauty of the environs. As we crossed the bridge to a fine alameda, or public walk, the bells tolled the hour of oration. At the sound the wayfarers, whether on business or pleasure, paused, took off their hats, crossed themselves, and repeated their evening prayer; a pious custom still rigidly observed in retired parts of Spain. Altogether it was a solemn and beautiful evening scene, and we wandered on as the evening gradually closed, and the new moon began to glitter between the high elms of the alameda. We were roused from this quiet state of enjoyment by the voice of our trusty squire hailing us from a distance. He came up to us, out of breath. "Ah, señores," cried he, "el pobre Sancho no es nada sin Don Quixote." (Ah, señors, poor Sancho is nothing without Don Quixote.) He had been alarmed at our not coming to the inn; Loxa was such a wild mountain place, full of contrabandistas, enchanters and infiernos; he did not well know what might have happened, and set out to seek us, inquiring after us of every person he met, until he traced us across the bridge, and, to his great joy, caught sight of us strolling in the alameda.

The inn to which he conducted us was called the Corona, or Crown, and we found it quite in keeping with the character of the place, the inhabitants of which seem still to retain the bold fiery spirit of the olden time. The hostess was a young and handsome Andalusian widow, whose trim basquiña of black silk, fringed with bugles, set off the play of a graceful form and round pliant limbs. Her step was firm and elastic; her dark eye was full of fire, and the coquetry of her air, and varied ornaments of her person, showed that she was accustomed to be admired.

She was well matched by a brother, nearly about her own

age; they were perfect models of the Andalusian Majo and Maja. He was tall, vigorous, and well-formed, with a clear olive complexion, a dark beaming eye, and curling chestnut whiskers that met under his chin. He was gallantly dressed in a short green velvet jacket, fitted to his shape, profusely decorated with silver buttons, with a white handkerchief in each pocket. He had breeches of the same, with rows of buttons from the hips to the knees; a pink silk handkerchief round his neck; gathered through a ring, on the bosom of a neatly-plaited shirt; a sash round the waist to match; bottinas, or spatterdashes, of the finest russet leather, elegantly worked, and open at the calf to show his stocking; and russet shoes, setting off a well-shaped foot.

As he was standing at the door, a horseman rode up and entered into low and earnest conversation with him. He was dressed in a similar style, and almost with equal finery; a man about thirty, square-built, with strong Roman features, handsome, though slightly pitted with the small-pox; with a free, bold, and somewhat daring air. His powerful black horse was decorated with tassels and fanciful trappings, and a couple of broad-mouthed blunderbusses hung behind the saddle. He had the air of one of those contrabandistas I have seen in the mountains of Ronda, and evidently had a good understanding with the brother of mine hostess; nay, if I mistake not, he was a favored admirer of the widow. In fact, the whole inn and its inmates had something of a contrabandista aspect, and a blunderbuss stood in a corner beside the guitar. The horseman I have mentioned passed his evening in the posada, and sang several bold mountain romances with great spirit. As we were at supper, two poor Asturians put in in distress, begging food and a night's lodging. They had been waylaid by robbers as they came from a fair among the mountains, robbed of a horse, which carried all their stock in trade, stripped of their money, and most of their apparel, beaten for having offered resistance, and left almost naked in the road. My companion, with a prompt generosity natural to him, ordered them a supper and a bed, and gave them a sum of money to help them forward towards their home.

As the evening advanced, the dramatis personæ thickened. A large man, about sixty years of age, of powerful frame, came strolling in, to gossip with mine hostess. He was dressed in the ordinary Andalusian costume, but had a huge sabre tucked under his arm; wore large moustaches, and had something of a lofty swaggering air. Every one seemed to regard him with great deference.

Our man Sancho whispered to us that he was Don Ventura Rodriguez, the hero and champion of Loxa, famous for his prowess and the strength of his arm. In the time of the French invasion he surprised six troopers who were asleep: he first secured their horses, then attacked them with his sabre, killed some, and took the rest prisoners. For this exploit the king allows him a peseta (the fifth of a duro, or dollar) per day, and has dignified him with the title of Don.

I was amused to behold his swelling language and demeanor. He was evidently a thorough Andalusian, boastful as brave. His sabre was always in his hand or under his arm. He carries it always about with him as a child does her doll, calls it his Santa Teresa, and says, "When I draw it, the earth trembles" (tiembla la tierra).

I sat until a late hour listening to the varied themes of this motley group, who mingled together with the unreserve of a Spanish posada. We had contrabandista songs, stories of robbers, guerrilla exploits, and Moorish legends. The last were from our handsome landlady, who gave a poetical account of the Infiernos, or infernal regions of Loxa, dark caverns, in which subterranean streams and waterfalls make a mysterious sound. The common people say that there are money-coiners shut up there from the time of the Moors; and that the Moorish kings kept their treasures in those caverns.

I retired to bed with my imagination excited by all that I had seen and heard in this old warrior city. Scarce had I fallen asleep when I was aroused by a horrid din and uproar, that might have confounded the hero of La Mancha himself whose experience of Spanish inns was a continual uproar. It seemed for a moment as if the Moors were once more breaking into the town; or the infiernos of which mine hostess talked had broken loose. I sallied forth half dressed to reconnoiter. It was nothing more nor less than a charivari to celebrate the nuptials of an old man with a buxom damsel. Wishing him joy of his bride and his serenade, I returned to my more quiet bed, and slept soundly until morning.

While dressing, I amused myself in reconnoitering the populace from my window. There were groups of fine-looking young men in the trim fanciful Andalusian costume, with brown cloaks, thrown about them in true Spanish style, which cannot be imitated, and little round majo hats stuck on with a peculiar knowing air. They had the same galliard look which I have remarked among the dandy mountaineers of Ronda. Indeed, all this part of Andalusia abounds with such game-looking characters. They loiter about the towns and villages; seem to have plenty of time and plenty of money; "horse to ride and weapon to wear." Great gossips; great smokers; apt at touching the guitar, singing couplets to their maja belles, and famous dancers of the bolero. Throughout all Spain the men, however poor, have a gentleman-like abundance of leisure; seeming to consider it the attribute of a true cavaliero never to be in a hurry; but the Andalusians are gay as well as leisurely, and have none of the squalid accompaniments of idleness. The adventurous contraband trade which prevails throughout these mountain regions, and along the maritime borders of Andalusia, is doubtless at the bottom of this galliard character.

In contrast to the costume of these groups was that of two long-legged Valencians conducting a donkey, laden with articles of merchandise; their musket slung crosswise over his back ready for action. They wore round jackets (jalecos), wide linen bragas or drawers scarce reaching to the knees and looking like kilts, red fajas or sashes swathed tightly round their waists, sandals of espartal or bass weed, colored kerchiefs round their heads somewhat in the style of turbans but leaving the top of the head uncovered; in short, their whole appearance having much of the traditional Moorish stamp.

On leaving Loxa we were joined by a cavalier, well mounted and well armed, and followed on foot by an escopetero or musketeer. He saluted us courteously, and soon let us into his quality. He was chief of the customs, or rather, I should suppose, chief of an armed company whose business it is to patrol the roads and look out for contrabandistas. The escopetero was one of his guards. In the course of our morning's ride I drew from him some particulars concerning the smugglers, who have risen to be a kind of mongrel chivalry in Spain. They come into Andalusia, he said, from various parts, but especially from La Mancha; sometimes to receive goods, to be smuggled on an appointed night across the line at the plaza or strand of Gibraltar; sometimes to meet a vessel, which is to hover on a given night off a certain part of the coast. They keep together and travel in the night. In the daytime they lie quiet in barrancos, gullies of the mountains or lonely farm-houses; where they are generally well received, as they make the family liberal presents of their smuggled wares. Indeed, much of the finery and trinkets worn by the wives and daughters of the mountain hamlets and farm-houses are presents from the gay and open-handed contrabandistas.

Arrived at the part of the coast where a vessel is to meet them, they look out at night from some rocky point or headland. If they descry a sail near the shore they make a concerted signal; sometimes it consists in suddenly displaying a lantern three times from beneath the folds of a cloak. If the signal is answered, they descend to the shore and prepare for quick work. The vessel runs close in; all her boats are busy landing the smuggled goods, made up into snug packages for transportation on horseback. These are hastily thrown on the beach, as hastily gathered up and packed on the horses, and then the contrabandistas clatter off to the mountains. They travel by the roughest, wildest, and most solitary roads, where it is almost fruitless to pursue them. The custom-house guards do not attempt it: they take a different course. When they hear of one of these bands returning full freighted through the mountains, they go out in force, sometimes twelve infantry and eight horsemen, and take their station where the mountain defile opens into the plain. The infantry, who lie in ambush some distance within the defile, suffer the band to pass, then rise and fire upon them. The contrabandistas dash forward, but are met in front by the horsemen. A wild skirmish ensues. The contrabandistas, if hard pressed, become desperate. Some dismount, use their horses as breastworks, and fire over their backs; others cut the cords, let the packs fall off to delay the enemy, and endeavor to escape with their steeds. Some get off in this way with the loss of their packages; some are taken, horses, packages, and all; others abandon every thing, and make their escape by scrambling up the mountains. "And then," cried Sancho, who had been listening with a greedy ear, *"se hacen ladrones legitimos,"*—and then they become legitimate robbers.

I could not help laughing at Sancho's idea of a legitimate calling of the kind; but the chief of customs told me it was really the case that the smugglers, when thus reduced to extremity, thought they had a kind of right to take the road, and lay travellers under contribution, until they had collected funds enough to mount and equip themselves in contrabandista style.

Towards noon our wayfaring companion took leave of us and turned up a steep defile, followed by his escopetero; and shortly afterwards we emerged from the mountains, and entered upon the far famed Vega of Granada.

Our last mid-day's repast was taken under a grove of olive-trees on the border of a rivulet. We were in a classical neighborhood; for not far off were the groves and orchards of the Soto de Roma. This, according to fabulous tradition, was a retreat founded by Count Julian to console his daughter Florinda. It was a rural resort of the Moorish kings of Granada, and has in modern times been granted to the Duke of Wellington.

Our worthy squire made a half melancholy face as he drew forth, for the last time, the contents of his alforjas, lamenting that our expedition was drawing to a close, for, with such cavaliers, he said, he could travel to the world's end. Our repast, however, was a gay one; made under such delightful auspices. The day was without a cloud. The heat of the sun was tempered by cool breezes from the mountains. Before us extended the glorious Vega. In the distance was romantic Granada surmounted by the ruddy towers of the Alhambra, while far above it the snowy summits of the Sierra Nevada shone like silver.

Our repast finished, we spread our cloaks and took our last siesta *al fresco*, lulled by the humming of bees among the flowers and the notes of doves among the olive-trees. When the sultry hours were passed we resumed our journey. After a time we overtook a pursy little man, shaped not unlike a toad and mounted on a mule. He fell into conversation with Sancho, and finding we were strangers, undertook to guide us to a good posada. He was an escribano (notary), he said, and knew the city as thoroughly as his own pocket. "Ah Dios Señores! what a city you are going to see. Such streets! such squares! such palaces! and then the women—ah Santa Maria purisima—what women!" "But the posada you talk of," said I, "are you sure it is a good one?"

"Good! Santa Maria! the best in Granada. Salones grandes —camas de luxo—colchones de pluma (grand saloons— luxurious sleeping rooms—beds of down). Ah, señores, you will fare like king Chico in the Alhambra."

"And how will my horses fare?" cried Sancho.

"Like king Chico's horses. *Chocolate con leche y bollos para almuerza*" (chocolate and milk with sugar cakes for breakfast), giving the squire a knowing wink and a leer.

After such satisfactory accounts nothing more was to be desired on that head. So we rode quietly on, the squab little notary taking the lead, and turning to us every moment with some fresh exclamation about the grandeurs of Granada and the famous times we were to have at the posada.

Thus escorted, we passed between hedges of aloes and Indian figs, and through that wilderness of gardens with which the vega is embroidered, and arrived about sunset at the gates of the city. Our officious little conductor conveyed us up one street and down another, until he rode into the court-yard of an inn where he appeared to be perfectly at home. Summoning the landlord by his Christian name, he committed us to his care as two cavaleros de mucho valor, worthy of his best apartments and most sumptuous fare. We were instantly reminded of the patronizing stranger who introduced Gil Blas with such a flourish of trumpets to the host and hostess of the inn at Pennaflor, ordering trouts for his supper, and eating voraciously at his expense. "You know not what you possess," cried he to the innkeeper and his wife. "You have a treasure in your house. Behold in this young gentleman the eighth wonder of the world—nothing in this house is too good for Señor Gil Blas of Santillane, who deserves to be entertained like a prince."

Determined that the little notary should not eat trouts at our expense, like his prototype of Pennaflor, we forbore to ask him to supper; nor had we reason to reproach ourselves with ingratitude; for we found before morning the little varlet, who was no doubt a good friend of the landlord, had decoyed us into one of the shabbiest posadas in Granada.

Palace of the Alhambra

To the traveller imbued with a feeling for the historical and poetical, so inseparably intertwined in the annals
of romantic Spain, the Alhambra is as much an object of devotion as is the Caaba to all true Moslems. How many legends and traditions, true and fabulous; how many songs and
ballads, Arabian and Spanish, of love and war and chivalry,
are associated with this oriental pile! It was the royal abode of
the Moorish kings, where, surrounded with the splendors and
refinements of Asiatic luxury, they held dominion over what
they vaunted as a terrestrial paradise, and made their last
stand for empire in Spain. The royal palace forms but a part
of a fortress, the walls of which, studded with towers, stretch
irregularly round the whole crest of a hill, a spur of the Sierra
Nevada or Snowy Mountains, and overlook the city; externally it is a rude congregation of towers and battlements, with
no regularity of plan nor grace of architecture, and giving
little promise of the grace and beauty which prevail within.

In the time of the Moors the fortress was capable of containing within in its outward precincts an army of forty thousand men, and served occasionally as a strong-hold of the
sovereigns against their rebellious subjects. After the kingdom
had passed into the hands of the Christians, the Alhambra
continued to be a royal demesne, and was occasionally inhabited by the Castilian monarchs. The emperor Charles V. commenced a sumptuous palace within its walls, but was deterred
from completing it by repeated shocks of earthquakes. The
last royal residents were Philip V. and his beautiful queen,
Elizabetta of Parma, early in the eighteenth century. Great
preparations were made for their reception. The palace and
gardens were placed in a state of repair, and a new suite of
apartments erected, and decorated by artists brought from
Italy. The sojourn of the sovereigns was transient, and
after their departure the palace once more became desolate.
Still the place was maintained with some military state. The
governor held it immediately from the crown, its jurisdiction extended down into the suburbs of the city, and was

independent of the captain-general of Granada. A considerable garrison was kept up, the governor had his apartments in the front of the old Moorish palace, and never descended into Granada without some military parade. The fortress, in fact, was a little town of itself, having several streets of houses within its walls, together with a Franciscan convent and a parochial church.

The desertion of the court, however, was a fatal blow to the Alhambra. Its beautiful halls became desolate, and some of them fell to ruin; the gardens were destroyed, and the fountains ceased to play. By degrees the dwellings became filled with a loose and lawless population; contrabandistas, who availed themselves of its independent jurisdiction to carry on a wide and daring course of smuggling, and thieves and rogues of all sorts, who made this their place of refuge whence they might depredate upon Granada and its vicinity. The strong arm of government at length interfered; the whole community was thoroughly sifted; none were suffered to remain but such as were of honest character, and had legitimate right to a residence; the greater part of the houses were demolished and a mere hamlet left, with the parochial church and the Franciscan convent. During the recent troubles in Spain, when Granada was in the hands of the French, the Alhambra was garrisoned by their troops, and the palace was occasionally inhabited by the French commander. With that enlightened taste which has ever distinguished the French nation in their conquests, this monument of Moorish elegance and grandeur was rescued from the absolute ruin and desolation that were overwhelming it. The roofs were repaired, the saloons and galleries protected from the weather, the gardens cultivated, the watercourses restored, the fountains once more made to throw up their sparkling showers; and Spain may thank her invaders for having preserved to her the most beautiful and interesting of her historical monuments.

On the departure of the French they blew up several towers of the outer wall, and left the fortifications scarcely tenable. Since that time the military importance of the post is at an end. The garrison is a handful of invalid soldiers, whose principal duty is to guard some of the outer towers, which serve occasionally as a prison of state; and the governor, abandoning the lofty hill of the Alhambra, resides in the centre of Granada, for the more convenient dispatch of his official duties. I cannot conclude this brief notice of the state of the fortress without bearing testimony to the honorable exertions of its present commander, Don Francisco de Serna, who is tasking all the limited resources at his command to put the palace in a state of repair, and by his judicious precautions, has for some time arrested its too certain decay. Had his predecessors discharged the duties of their station with equal fidelity, the Alhambra might yet have remained in almost its pristine beauty; were government to second him with means equal to his zeal, this relic of it might still be preserved for many generations to adorn the land, and attract the curious and enlightened of every clime.

Our first object of course, on the morning after our arrival, was a visit to this time-honored edifice; it has been so often, however, and so minutely described by travellers, that I shall not undertake to give a comprehensive and elaborate account of it, but merely occasional sketches of parts with the incidents and associations connected with them.

Leaving our posada, and traversing the renowned square of the Vivarrambla, once the scene of Moorish jousts and tournaments, now a crowded market-place, we proceeded along the Zacatin, the main street of what, in the time of the Moors, was the Great Bazaar, and where small shops and narrow alleys still retain the oriental character. Crossing an open place in front of the palace of the captain-general, we ascended a confined and winding street, the name of which reminded us of the chivalric days of Granada. It is called the Calle, or street of the Gomeres, from a Moorish family famous in chronicle and song. This street led up to the Puerta de las Granadas, a massive gateway of Grecian architecture, built by Charles V., forming the entrance to the domains of the Alhambra.

At the gate were two or three ragged superannuated soldiers, dozing on a stone bench, the successors of the Zegris and the Abencerrages; while a tall, meagre varlet, whose rusty-brown cloak was evidently intended to conceal the ragged state of his nether garments, was lounging in the sunshine and gossiping with an ancient sentinel on duty. He joined us as we entered the gate, and offered his services to show us the fortress.

I have a traveller's dislike to officious ciceroni, and did not altogether like the garb of the applicant.

"You are well acquainted with the place, I presume?"

"Ninguno mas; pues señor, soy hijo de la Alhambra."—(Nobody better; in fact, sir, I am a son of the Alhambra!)

The common Spaniards have certainly a most poetical way of expressing themselves. "A son of the Alhambra!" the appellation caught me at once; the very tattered garb of my new acquaintance assumed a dignity in my eyes. It was emblematic of the fortunes of the place, and befitted the progeny of a ruin.

I put some farther questions to him, and found that his title was legitimate. His family had lived in the fortress from generation to generation ever since the time of the conquest. His name was Mateo Ximenes. "Then, perhaps," said I, "you may be a descendant from the great Cardinal Ximenes"—"Dios Sabe! God knows, Señor! It may be so. We are the oldest family in the Alhambra,—*Christianos Viejos*, old Christians, without any taint of Moor or Jew. I know we belong to some great family or other, but I forgot whom. My father knows all about it: he has the coat-of-arms hanging up in his cottage, up in the fortress."—There is not any Spaniard, however poor, but has some claim to high pedigree. The first title of this ragged worthy, however, had completely captivated me, so I gladly accepted the services of the "son of the Alhambra."

We now found ourselves in a deep narrow ravine, filled with beautiful groves, with a steep avenue, and various footpaths winding through it, bordered with stone seats, and ornamented with fountains. To our left, we beheld the towers of the Alhambra beetling above us; to our right, on the opposite side of the ravine, we were equally dominated by rival towers on a rocky eminence. These, we were told, were the Torres Vermejos, or vermillion towers, so called from their ruddy hue. No one knows their origin. They are of a date much anterior to the Alhambra: some suppose them to have been built by the Romans; others, by some wandering colony of Phœnicians. Ascending the steep and shady avenue, we arrived at the foot of a huge square Moorish tower, forming a kind of barbican, through which passed the main entrance to the fortress. Within the barbican was another group of veteran invalids, one mounting guard at the portal, while the rest, wrapped in their tattered cloaks, slept on the stone benches. This portal is called the Gate of Justice, from the tribunal held within its porch during the Moslem domination, for the immediate trial of petty causes: a custom common to the oriental nations, and occasionally alluded to in the Sacred Scriptures. "Judges and officers shalt thou make thee *in all thy gates*, and they shall judge the people with just judgment."

The great vestibule, or porch of the gate, is formed by an immense Arabian arch, of the horseshoe form, which springs to half the height of the tower. On the keystone of this arch is engraven a gigantic hand. Within the vestibule, on the keystone of the portal, is sculptured, in like manner, a gigantic key. Those who pretend to some knowledge of Mohammedan symbols, affirm that the hand is the emblem of doctrine; the five fingers designating the five principal commandments of the creed of Islam, fasting, pilgrimage, alms-giving, ablution, and war against infidels. The key, say they, is the emblem of the faith or of power; the key of Daoud or David, transmitted to the prophet. "And the key of the house of David will I lay upon his shoulder; so he shall open and none shall shut, and he shall shut and none shall open." (Isaiah xxii. 22.) The key we are told was emblazoned on the standard of the Moslems in opposition to the Christian emblem of the cross, when they subdued Spain or Andalusia. It betokened the conquering power invested in the prophet. "He that hath the key of David, he that openeth and no man shutteth; and shutteth and no man openeth." (Rev. iii. 7.)

A different explanation of these emblems, however, was given by the legitimate son of the Alhambra, and one more in unison with the notions of the common people, who attach something of mystery and magic to every thing Moorish, and have all kind of superstitions connected with this old Moslem fortress. According to Mateo, it was a tradition handed down from the oldest inhabitants, and which he had from his father and grandfather, that the hand and key were magical devices on which the fate of the Alhambra depended. The Moorish king who built it was a great magician, or, as some believed, had sold himself to the devil, and had laid the whole fortress under a magic spell. By this means it had remained standing for several hundred years, in defiance of storms and earthquakes, while almost all other buildings of the Moors had fallen to ruin, and disappeared. This spell, the tradition went on to say, would last until the hand on the outer arch should reach down and grasp the key, when the whole pile would tumble to pieces, and all the treasures buried beneath it by the Moors would be revealed.

Notwithstanding this ominous prediction, we ventured to pass through the spell-bound gateway, feeling some little assurance against magic art in the protection of the Virgin, a statue of whom we observed above the portal.

After passing through the barbican, we ascended a narrow lane, winding between walls, and came on an open esplanade within the fortress, called the Plaza de los Algibes, or Place of the Cisterns, from great reservoirs which undermine it, cut in the living rock by the Moors to receive the water brought by conduits from the Darro, for the supply of the fortress. Here, also, is a well of immense depth, furnishing the purest and coldest of water; another monument of the delicate taste of the Moors, who were indefatigable in their exertions to obtain that element in its crystal purity.

In front of this esplanade is the splendid pile commenced by Charles V., and intended, it is said, to eclipse the residence of the Moorish kings. Much of the oriental edifice intended for the winter season was demolished to make way for this massive pile. The grand entrance was blocked up; so that the present entrance to the Moorish palace is through a simple and almost humble portal in a corner. With all the massive grandeur and architectural merit of the palace of Charles V., we regarded it as an arrogant intruder, and passing by it with a feeling almost of scorn, rang at the Moslem portal.

While waiting for admittance, our self-imposed cicerone, Mateo Ximenes, informed us that the royal palace was intrusted to the care of a worthy old maiden dame called Doña Antonia-Molina, but who, according to Spanish custom, went by the more neighborly appellation of Tia Antonia (Aunt Antonia), who maintained the Moorish halls and gardens in order and showed them to strangers. While we were talking, the door was opened by a plump little black-eyed Andalusian damsel, whom Mateo addressed as Dolores, but who from her bright looks and cheerful disposition evidently merited a merrier name. Mateo informed me in a whisper that she was the niece of Tia Antonia, and I found she was the good fairy who was to conduct us through the enchanted palace. Under her guidance we crossed the threshold, and were at once transported, as if by magic wand, into other times and an oriental realm, and were treading the scenes of Arabian story. Nothing could be in greater contrast than the unpromising exterior of the pile with the scene now before us. We found ourselves in a vast patio or court one hundred and fifty feet in length, and upwards of eighty feet in breadth, paved with white marble, and decorated at each end with light Moorish peristyles, one of which supported an elegant gallery of fretted architecture. Along the mouldings of the cornices and on various parts of the walls were escutcheons and ciphers, and cufic and Arabic characters in high relief, repeating the pious mottoes of the Moslem monarchs, the builders of the Alhambra, or extolling their grandeur and munificence. Along the centre of the court extended an immense basin or tank (estanque) a hundred and twenty-four feet in length, twenty-seven in breath, and five in depth, receiving its water from two marble vases. Hence it is called the Court of Alberca (from al Beerkah, the Arabic for a pond or tank). Great numbers of gold-fish were to be seen gleaming through the waters of the basin, and it was bordered by hedges of roses.

Passing from the court of the Alberca under a Moorish archway, we entered the renowned court of Lions. No part of the edifice gives a more complete idea of its original beauty than this, for none has suffered so little from the ravages of time. In the centre stands the fountain famous in song and story. The alabaster basins still shed their diamond drops; the twelve lions which support them, and give the court its name, still cast forth crystal streams as in the days of Boabdil. The lions, however are unworthy of their fame, being of miserable sculpture, the work probably of some Christian captive. The court is laid out in flower-beds, instead of its ancient and appropriate pavement of tiles or marble; the alteration, an instance of bad taste, was made by the French when in possession of Granada. Round the four sides of the court are light Arabian arcades of open filigree work supported by slender pillars of white marble, which it is supposed were originally gilded. The architecture, like that in most parts of the interior of the palace, is characterized by elegance, rather than grandeur; bespeaking a delicate and graceful taste, and a disposition to indolent enjoyment. When one looks upon the fairy tracery of the peristyles, and the apparently fragile fretwork of the walls, it is difficult to believe that so much has survived the wear and tear of centuries, the shocks of earthquakes, the violence of war, and the quiet, though no less baneful, pilferings of the tasteful traveller: it is almost sufficient to excuse the popular tradition, that the whole is protected by a magic charm.

On one side of the court a rich portal opens into the hall of the Abencerrages; so called from the gallant cavaliers of that illustrious line who were here perfidiously massacred. There are some who doubt the whole story, but our humble cicerone Mateo pointed out the very wicket of the portal through which they were introduced one by one into the court of Lions, and the white marble fountain in the centre of the hall beside which they were beheaded. He showed us also certain broad ruddy stains on the pavement, traces of their blood, which, according to popular belief, can never be effaced.

Finding we listened to him apparently with easy faith, he added, that there was often heard at night, in the court of Lions, a low confused sound, resembling the murmuring of a multitude; and now and then a faint tinkling, like the distant clank of chains. These sounds were made by the spirits of the murdered Abencerrages; who nightly haunt the scene of their suffering and invoke the vengeance of Heaven on their destroyer.

The sounds in questions had no doubt been produced, as I had afterwards an opportunity of ascertaining, by the bubbling currents and tinkling falls of water conducted under the pavement through pipes and channels to supply the fountains; but I was too considerate to intimate such an idea to the humble chronicler of the Alhambra.

Encouraged by my easy credulity, Mateo gave me the following as an undoubted fact, which he had from his grandfather:

There was once an invalid soldier, who had charge of the Alhambra to show it to strangers: as he was one evening, about twilight, passing through the court of Lions, he heard footsteps on the hall of the Abencerrages; supposing some strangers to be lingering there, he advanced to attend upon them, when to his astonishment he beheld four Moors richly dressed, with gilded cuirasses and cimeters, and poniards glittering with precious stones. They were walking to and fro, with solemn pace; but paused and beckoned to him. The old soldier, however, took to flight, and could never afterwards be prevailed upon to enter the Alhambra. Thus it is that men sometimes turn their backs upon fortune; for it is the firm opinion of Mateo, that the Moors intended to reveal the place where their treasures lay buried. A successor to the invalid soldier was more knowing; he came to the Alhambra poor; but at the end of a year went off to Malaga, bought houses, set up a carriage, and still lives there one of the richest as well as oldest men of the place; all which, Mateo sagely surmised, was in consequence of his finding out the golden secret of these phantom Moors.

I now perceived I had made an invaluable acquaintance in this son of the Alhambra, one who knew all the apocryphal history of the place, and firmly believed in it, and whose memory was stuffed with a kind of knowledge for which I have a lurking fancy, but which is too apt to be considered rubbish by less indulgent philosophers. I determined to cultivate the acquaintance of this learned Theban.

Immediately opposite the hall of the Abencerrages a portal, richly adorned, leads into a hall of less tragical associations. It is light and lofty, exquisitely graceful in its architecture, paved with white marble, and bears the suggestive name of the Hall of the Two Sisters. Some destroy the romance of the name by attributing it to two enormous slabs of alabaster which lie side by side, and form a great part of the pavement; an opinion strongly supported by Mateo Ximenes. Others are disposed to give the name a more poetical significance, as the vague memorial of Moorish beauties who once graced this hall, which was evidently a part of the royal harem. This opinion I was happy to find entertained by our little bright-eyed guide, Dolores, who pointed to a balcony over an inner porch; which gallery, she had been told, belonged to the women's apartment. "You see, señor," said she, "it is all grated and latticed, like the gallery in a convent chapel where the nuns hear mass; for the Moorish kings," added she, indignantly, "shut up their wives just like nuns."

The latticed "jalousies," in fact, still remain, whence the dark-eyed beauties of the harem might gaze unseen upon the zambras and other dances and entertainment of the hall below.

On each side of this hall are recesses or alcoves for ottomans and couches, on which the voluptuous lords of the Alhambra indulged in that dreamy repose so dear to the Orientalists. A cupola or lantern admits a tempered light from above and a free circulation of air; while on one side is heard the refreshing sound of waters from the fountain of the lions, and on the other side the soft plash from the basin in the garden of Lindaraxa.

It is impossible to contemplate this scene so perfectly Oriental without feeling the early associations of Arabian romance, and almost expecting to see the white arm of some mysterious princess beckoning from the gallery, or some dark eye sparkling through the lattice. The abode of beauty is here, as if it had been inhabited but yesterday; but where are the two sisters; where the Zoraydas and Lindaraxas!

An abundant supply of water, brought from the mountains by old Moorish aqueducts, circulates throughout the palace, supplying its baths and fishpools, sparkling in jets within its halls, or murmuring in channels along the marble pavements. When it has paid its tribute to the royal pile, and visited its gardens and parterres, it flows down the long avenue leading to the city, tinkling in rills, gushing in fountains, and maintaining a perpetual verdure in those groves that embower and beautify the whole hill of the Alhambra.

Those only who have sojourned in the ardent climates of the South, can appreciate the delights of an abode, combining the breezy coolness of the mountain with the freshness and verdure of the valley. While the city below pants with the noontide heat, and the parched Vega trembles to the eye, the delicate airs from the Sierra Nevada play through these lofty halls, bringing with them the sweetness of the surrounding gardens. Every thing invites to that indolent repose, the bliss of southern climes; and while the half-shut eye looks out from shaded balconies upon the glittering landscape, the ear is lulled by the rustling of groves, and the murmur of running streams.

I forbear for the present, however, to describe the other delightful apartments of the palace. My object is merely to give the reader a general introduction into an abode where, if so disposed, he may linger and loiter with me day by day until we gradually become familiar with all its localities.

NOTE ON MORISCO ARCHITECTURE

To an unpractised eye the light relievos and fanciful arabesques which cover the walls of the Alhambra appear to have been sculptured by the hand, with a minute and patient labor, an inexhaustible variety of detail, yet a general uniformity and harmony of design truly astonishing; and this may especially be said of the vaults and cupolas, which are wrought like honey-combs, or frostwork, with stalactites and pendants which confound the beholder with the seeming intricacy of their patterns. The astonishment ceases, however, when it is discovered that this is all stucco-work; plates of plaster of Paris, cast in moulds and skilfully joined so as to form patterns of every size and form. This mode of diapering walls with arabesques and stuccoing the vaults with grotto-work, was invented in Damascus; but highly improved by the Moors in Morocco, to whom Saracenic architecture owes its most graceful and fanciful details. The process by which all this fairy tracery was produced was ingeniously simple. The wall in its naked state was divided off by lines crossing at right angles, such as artists use in copying a picture; over these were drawn a succession of intersecting segments of circles. By the aid of these the artists could work with celerity and certainty, and from the mere intersection of the plain and curved lines arose the interminable variety of patterns and the general uniformity of their character.*

Much gilding was used in the stucco-work, especially of the cupolas; and the interstices were delicately pencilled with brilliant colors,

*See Urquhart's Pillars of Hercules, B. iii. C. 8.

such as vermilion and lapis lazuli, laid on with the whites of eggs. The primitive colors alone were used, says Ford, by the Egyptians, Greeks, and Arabs, in the early period of art; and they prevail in the Alhambra whenever the artist has been Arabic or Moorish. It is remarkable how much of their original brilliancy remains after the lapse of several centuries.

The lower part of the walls in the saloons, to the height of several feet, is incrusted with glazed tiles, joined like the plates of stucco-work, so as to form various patterns. On some of them are emblazoned the escutcheons of the Moslem kings, traversed with a band and motto. These glazed tiles (azulejos in Spanish, az-zulaj in Arabic) are of Oriental origin; their coolness, cleanliness, and freedom from vermin, render them admirably fitted in sultry climates for paving halls and fountains; incrusting bathing rooms and lining the walls of chambers. Ford is inclined to give them great antiquity. From their prevailing colors, sapphire and blue, he deduces that they may have formed the kind of pavements alluded to in the sacred Scriptures—"There was under his feet as it were a paved work of a sapphire stone" (Exod. xxiv. 10); and again, "Behold I will lay thy stones with fair colors, and lay thy foundations with sapphires" (Isaiah liv. 11).

These glazed or porcelain tiles were introduced into Spain at an early date by the Moslems. Some are to be seen among the Moorish ruins which have been there upwards of eight centuries. Manufacturers of them still exist in the peninsula, and they are much used in the best Spanish houses, especially in the southern provinces, for paving and lining the summer apartments.

The Spaniards introduced them into the Netherlands when they had possession of that country. The people of Holland adopted them with avidity, as wonderfully suited to their passion for household cleanliness; and thus these Oriental inventions, the azulejos of the Spanish, the az-zulaj of the Arabs, have come to be commonly known as Dutch tiles.

Important Negotiations—The Author
Succeeds to the Throne of Boabdil

THE DAY was nearly spent before we could tear ourself from this region of poetry and romance to descend to the city and return to the forlorn realities of a Spanish posada. In a visit of ceremony to the Governor of the Alhambra, to whom we had brought letters, we dwelt with enthusiasm on the scenes we had witnessed, and could not but express surprise that he should reside in the city when he had such a paradise at his command. He pleaded the inconvenience of a residence in the palace from its situation on the crest of a hill, distant from the seat of business and the resorts of social intercourse. It did very well for monarchs, who often had need of castle walls to defend them from their own subjects. "But señors," added he, smiling, "if you think a residence there so desirable, my apartments in the Alhambra are at your service."

It is a common and almost indispensable point of politeness in a Spaniard, to tell you his house is yours.—"Esta casa es siempre à la disposicion de Vm." "This house is always at the command of your Grace." In fact, any thing of his which you admire, is immediately offered to you. It is equally a mark of good breeding in you not to accept it; so we merely bowed our acknowledgments of the courtesy of the Governor in offering us a royal palace. We were mistaken, however. The Governor was in earnest. "You will find a rambling set of empty, unfurnished rooms," said he; "but Tia Antonia, who has charge of the palace, may be able to put them in some kind of order; and to take care of you while you are there. If you can make any arrangement with her for your accommodation, and are content with scanty fare in a royal abode, the palace of King Chico is at your service."

We took the Governor at his word, and hastened up the steep Calle de los Gomeres, and through the Great Gate of Justice, to negotiate with Dame Antonia; doubting at times if this were not a dream, and fearing at times that the sage Dueña of the fortress might be slow to capitulate. We knew we had one friend at least in the garrison, who would be in our favor, the bright-eyed little Dolores, whose good graces we had propitiated on our first visit; and who hailed our return to the palace with her brightest looks.

All, however, went smoothly. The good Tia Antonia had a little furniture to put in the rooms, but it was of the commonest kind. We assured her we could bivouac on the floor. She could supply our table; but only in her own simple way—we wanted nothing better. Her niece, Dolores, would wait upon us—and at the word we threw up our hats and the bargain was complete.

The very next day we took up our abode in the palace, and never did sovereigns share a divided throne with more perfect harmony. Several days passed by like a dream, when my worthy associate, being summoned to Madrid on diplomatic duties, was compelled to abdicate, leaving me sole monarch of this shadowy realm. For myself, being in a manner a hap-hazard loiterer about the world and prone to linger in its pleasant places, here have I been suffering day by day to steal away unheeded, spell-bound, for aught I know, in this old enchanted pile. Having always a companionable feeling for my reader, and being prone to live with him on confidential terms, I shall make it a point to communicate to him my reveries and researches during this state of delicious thraldom. If they have the power of imparting to his imagination any of the witching charms of the place, he will not repine at lingering with me for a season in the legendary halls of the Alhambra.

And first it is proper to give him some idea of my domestic arrangements; they are rather of a simple kind for the occupant of a regal palace; but I trust they will be less liable to disastrous reverses than those of my royal predecessors.

My quarters are at one end of the Governor's apartment, a suite of empty chambers, in front of the palace, looking out upon the great esplanade called *la plaza de los algibes* (the place of the cisterns); the apartment is modern, but the end opposite to my sleeping-room communicates with a cluster of little chambers, partly Moorish, partly Spanish, allotted to the *chatelaine* Doña Antonia and her family. In consideration of keeping the palace in order, the good dame is allowed all the perquisites received from visitors, and all the produce of the gardens; excepting that she is expected to pay an occasional tribute of fruits and flowers to the Governor. Her family consists of a nephew and niece, the children of two different brothers. The nephew, Manuel Molina, is a young man of sterling worth and Spanish gravity. He had served in the army, both in Spain and the West Indies; but is now studying medicine in the hope of one day or other becoming physician to the fortress, a post worth at least one hundred and forty dollars a year. The niece is the plump little black-eyed Dolores already mentioned; and who, it is said, will one day inherit all her aunt's possessions, consisting of certain petty tenements in the fortress, in a somewhat ruinous condition it is true, but which, I am privately assured by Mateo Ximenes, yield a revenue of nearly one hundred and fifty dollars; so that she is quite an heiress in the eyes of the ragged son of the Alhambra. I am also informed by the same observant and authentic personage, that a quiet courtship is going on between the discreet Manuel and his bright-eyed cousin, and that nothing is wanting to enable them to join their hands and expectations but his doctor's diploma, and a dispensation from the Pope on account of their consanguinity.

The good dame Antonia fulfills faithfully her contract in regard to my board and lodging; and as I am easily pleased, I find my fare excellent; while the merry-hearted little Dolores keeps my apartment in order, and officiates as handmaid at meal-times. I have also at my command a tall, stuttering, yellow-haired lad, named Pépe, who works in the gardens, and would fain have acted as valet; but, in this, he was forestalled by Mateo Ximenes, "the son of the Alhambra." This alert and officious wight has managed, somehow or other, to stick by me ever since I first encountered him at the outer gate of the fortress, and to weave himself into all my plans, until he has fairly appointed and installed himself my valet, cicerone, guide, guard, and historiographic squire; and I have been obliged to improve the state of his wardrobe, that he may not disgrace his various functions; so that he has cast his old brown mantle, as a snake does his skin, and now appears about the fortress with a smart Andalusian hat and jacket, to his infinite satisfaction, and the great astonishment of his comrades. The chief fault of honest Mateo is an over anxiety to be useful. Conscious of having foisted himself into my employ, and that my simple and quiet habits render his situation a sinecure, he is at his wit's end to devise modes of making himself important to my welfare. I am, in a manner, the victim of his officiousness; I cannot put my foot over the threshold of the palace, to stroll about the fortress, but he is at my elbow, to explain every thing I see; and if I venture to ramble among the surrounding hills, he insists upon attending me as a guard, though I vehemently suspect he would be more apt to trust to the length of his legs than the strength of his arms, in case of attack. After all, however, the poor fellow is at times an amusing companion; he is simple-minded, and of infinite good humor, with the loquacity and gossip of a village barber, and knows all the small-talk of the place and its environs; but what he chiefly values himself on, is his stock of local information, having the most marvellous stories to relate of every tower, and vault, and gateway of the fortress, in all of which he places the most implicit faith.

Most of these he has derived, according to his own account, from his grandfather, a little legendary tailor, who lived to the age of nearly a hundred years, during which he made but two migrations beyond the precincts of the fortress. His shop, for the greater part of a century, was the resort of a knot of venerable gossips, where they would pass half the night talking about old times, and the wonderful events and hidden secrets of the place. The whole living, moving, thinking, and acting, of this historical little tailor, had thus been bounded by the walls of the Alhambra; within them he had been born, within them he lived, breathed, and had his being; within them he died, and was buried. Fortunately for posterity, his traditionary lore died not with him. The authentic Mateo, when an urchin, used to be an attentive listener to the narratives of his grandfather, and of the gossip group assembled round the shopboard; and is thus possessed of a stock of valuable knowledge concerning the Alhambra, not to be found in books, and well worthy the attention of every curious traveller.

Such are the personages that constitute my regal household; and I question whether any of the potentates, Moslem or Christian, who have preceded me in the palace, have been waited upon with greater fidelity, or enjoyed a serener sway.

When I rise in the morning, Pépe, the stuttering lad from the gardens, brings me a tribute of fresh culled flowers, which are afterwards arranged in vases, by the skilful hand of Dolores, who takes a female pride in the decorations of my chamber. My meals are made wherever caprice dictates; sometimes in one of the Moorish halls, sometimes under the arcades of the court of Lions, surrounded by flowers and fountains: and when I walk out, I am conducted by the assiduous Mateo, to the most romantic retreats of the mountains, and delicious haunts of the adjacent valleys, not one of which but is the scene of some wonderful tale.

Though fond of passing the greater part of my day alone, yet I occasionally repair in the evenings to the little domestic circle of Doña Antonia. This is generally held in an old Moorish chamber, which serves the good dame for parlor, kitchen and hall of audience, and which must have boasted of some splendor in the time of the Moors, if we may judge from the traces yet remaining; but a rude fireplace has been made in modern times in one corner, the smoke from which has discolored the walls, and almost obliterated the ancient arabesques. A window, with a balcony overhanging the valley of the Darro, lets in the cool evening breeze; and here I take my frugal supper of fruit and milk, and mingle with the conversation of the family. There is a natural talent or mother wit, as it is called, about the Spaniards, which renders them intellectual and agreeable companions, whatever may be their condition in life, or however imperfect may have been their education: add to this, they are never vulgar; nature has endowed them with an inherent dignity of spirit. The good Tia Antonia is a woman of strong and intelligent, though uncultivated mind; and the bright-eyed Dolores, though she has read but three or four books in the whole course of her life, has an engaging mixture of naïveté and good sense, and often surprises me by the pungency of her artless sallies. Sometimes the nephew entertains us by reading some old comedy of Calderon or Lope de Vega, to which he is evidently prompted by a desire to improve, as well as amuse his cousin Dolores; though, to his great mortification, the little damsel generally falls asleep before the first act is completed. Sometimes Tia Antonia has a little levee of humble friends and dependents, the inhabitants of the adjacent hamlet, or the wives of the invalid soldiers. These look up to her with great deference, as the custodian of the palace, and pay their court to her by bringing the news of the place, or the rumors that may have straggled up from Granada. In listening to these evening gossipings I have picked up many curious facts, illustrative of the manners of the people and the peculiarities of the neighborhood.

These are simple details of simple pleasures; it is the nature of the place alone that gives them interest and importance. I tread haunted ground, and am surrounded by romantic associations. From earliest boyhood, when, on the banks of the Hudson, I first pored over the pages of old Gines Perez de Hytas's apocryphal but chivalresque history of the civil wars of Granada, and the feuds of its gallant cavaliers, the Zegries and Abencerrages, that city has ever been a subject of my waking dreams; and often have I trod in fancy the romantic halls of the Alhambra. Behold for once a day-dream realized; yet I can scarce credit my senses, or believe that I do indeed inhabit the palace of Boabdil, and look down from its balconies upon chivalric Granada. As I loiter through these Oriental chambers, and hear the murmur of fountains and the song of the nightingale; as I inhale the odor of the rose, and feel the influence of the balmy climate, I am almost tempted to fancy myself in the paradise of Mahomet, and that the plump little Dolores is one of the bright-eyed houris, destined to administer to the happiness of true believers.

Inhabitants of the Alhambra

I HAVE OFTEN observed that the more proudly a mansion has been tenanted in the day of its prosperity, the humbler are its inhabitants in the day of its decline, and that the palace of a king commonly ends in being the nestling-place of the beggar.

The Alhambra is in a rapid state of similar transition. Whenever a tower falls to decay, it is seized upon by some tatterdemalion family, who become joint-tenants, with the bats and owls, of its gilded halls; and hang their rags, those standards of poverty, out of its windows and loopholes.

I have amused myself with remarking some of the motley characters that have thus usurped the ancient abode of royalty, and who seem as if placed here to give a farcical termination to the drama of human pride. One of these even bears the mockery of a regal title. It is a little old woman named Maria Antonia Sabonea, but who goes by the appellation of la Reyna Coquina, or the Cockle-queen. She is small enough to be a fairy, and a fairy she may be for aught I can find out, for no one seems to know her origin. Her habitation is in a kind of closet under the outer staircase of the palace, and she sits in the cool stone corridor, plying her needle and singing from morning till night, with a ready joke for every one that passes; for though one of the poorest, she is one of the merriest little women breathing. Her great merit is a gift for story-telling, having, I verily believe, as many stories at her command, as the inexhaustible Scheherezade of the thousand and one nights. Some of these I have heard her relate in the evening tertulias of Dame Antonia, at which she is occasionally a humble attendant.

That there must be some fairy gift about this mysterious little old woman, would appear from her extraordinary luck, since, notwithstanding her being very little, very ugly, and very poor, she has had, according to her own account, five husbands and a half, reckoning as a half one a young dragoon, who died during courtship. A rival personage to this little fairy queen is a portly old fellow with a bottle-nose, who goes about in a rusty garb with a cocked hat of oil-skin and a red cockade. He is one of the legitimate sons of the Alhambra, and has lived here all his life, filling various offices, such as deputy alguazil, sexton of the parochial church, and marker of a fives-court established at the foot of one of the towers. He is as poor as a rat, but as proud as he is ragged, boasting of his descent from the illustrious house of Aguilar, from which sprang Gonzalvo of Cordova, the grand captain. Nay, he actually bears the name of Alonzo de Aguilar, so renowned in the history of the conquest; though the graceless wags of the fortress have given him the title of *el padre santo*, or the holy father, the usual appellation of the Pope, which I had thought too sacred in the eyes of true Catholics to be thus ludicrously applied. It is a whimsical caprice of fortune to present, in the grotesque person of this tatterdemalion, a namesake and descendant of the proud Alonzo de Aguilar, the mirror of Andalusian chivalry, leading an almost mendicant existence about this once haughty fortress, which his ancestor aided to reduce; yet, such might have been the lot of the descendants of Agamemnon and Achilles, had they lingered about the ruins of Troy!

Of this motley community, I find the family of my gossiping squire, Mateo Ximenes, to form, from their numbers at least, a very important part. His boast of being a son of the Alhambra, is not unfounded. His family has inhabited the fortress ever since the time of the conquest, handing down an hereditary poverty from father to son; not one of them having ever been known to be worth a maravedi. His father, by trade a ribbon-weaver, and who succeeded the historical tailor as the head of the family, is now near seventy years of age, and lives in a hovel of reeds and plaster, built by his own hands, just above the iron gate. The furniture consists of a crazy bed, a table, and two or three chairs; a wooden chest, containing, besides his scanty clothing, the "archives of the family." These are nothing more nor less than the papers of various lawsuits sustained by different generations; by which it would seem that, with all their apparent carelessness and good humor, they are a litigious brood. Most of the suits have been brought against gossiping neighbors for questioning the purity of their blood, and denying their being *Christianos viejos*,

i. e. old Christians, without Jewish or Moorish taint. In fact, I doubt whether this jealousy about their blood has not kept them so poor in purse: spending all their earnings on escribanos and alguazils. The pride of the hovel is an escutcheon suspended against the wall, in which are emblazoned quarterings of the arms of the Marquis of Caiesedo, and of various other noble houses, with which this poverty-stricken brood claim affinity.

As to Mateo himself, who is now about thirty-five years of age, he has done his utmost to perpetuate his line and continue the poverty of the family, having a wife and a numerous progeny, who inhabit an almost dismantled hovel in the hamlet. How they manage to subsist, he only who sees into all mysteries can tell; the subsistence of a Spanish family of the kind, is always a riddle to me; yet they do subsist, and what is more, appear to enjoy their existence. The wife takes her holiday stroll on the Paseo of Granada, with a child in her arms and half a dozen at her heels; and the eldest daughter, now verging into womanhood, dresses her hair with flowers, and dances gayly to the castañets.

There are two classes of people to whom life seems one long holiday, the very rich, and the very poor; one because they need do nothing, the other because they have nothing to do; but there are none who understand the art of doing nothing and living upon nothing, better than the poor classes of Spain. Climate does one half, and temperament the rest. Give a Spaniard the shade in summer, and the sun in winter; a little bread, garlic, oil, and garbances, an old brown cloak and a guitar, and let the world roll on as it pleases. Talk of poverty! with him it has no disgrace. It sits upon him with a grandiose style, like his ragged cloak. He is a hidalgo, even when in rags.

The "sons of the Alhambra" are an eminent illustration of this practical philosophy. As the Moors imagined that the celestial paradise hung over this favored spot, so I am inclined at times to fancy, that a gleam of the golden age still lingers about this ragged community. They possess nothing, they do nothing, they care for nothing. Yet, though apparently idle all the week, they are as observant of all holy days and saints' days as the most laborious artisan. They attend all fêtes and dancings in Granada and its vicinity, light bonfires on the hills on St. John's eve, and dance away the moonlight nights on the harvest-home of a small field within the precincts of the fortress, which yield a few bushels of wheat.

Before concluding these remarks, I must mention one of the amusements of the place which has particularly struck me. I had repeatedly observed a long lean fellow perched on the top of one of the towers, manœuvring two or three fishing-rods, as though he were angling for the stars. I was for some time perplexed by the evolutions of this aerial fisherman, and my perplexity increased on observing others employed in like manner on different parts of the battlements and bastions; it was not until I consulted Mateo Ximenes, that I solved the mystery.

It seems that the pure and airy situation of this fortress has rendered it, like the castle of Macbeth, a prolific breeding-place for swallows and martlets, who sport about its towers in myriads, with the holiday glee of urchins just let loose from school. To entrap these birds in their giddy circlings, with hooks baited with flies, is one of the favorite amusements of the ragged "sons of the Alhambra," who, with the good-for-nothing ingenuity of arrant idlers, have thus invented the art of angling in the sky.

The Hall of Ambassadors

IN ONE of my visits to the old Moorish chamber, where the good Tia Antonia cooks her dinner and receives her company, I observed a mysterious door in one corner, leading apparently into the ancient part of the edifice. My curiosity being aroused, I opened it, and found myself in a narrow, blind corridor, groping along which I came to the head of a dark winding staircase, leading down an angle of the tower of Comares. Down this staircase I descended darkling, guiding myself by the wall until I came to a small door at the bottom, throwing which open, I was suddenly dazzled by emerging into the brilliant antechamber of the Hall of Ambassadors; with the fountain of the court of the Alberca sparkling before me. The antechamber is separated from the court by an elegant gallery, supported by slender columns with spandrels of open work in the Morisco style. At each end of the antechamber are alcoves, and its ceiling is richly stuccoed and painted. Passing through a magnificent portal I found myself in the far-famed Hall of Ambassadors, the audience chamber of the Moslem monarchs. It is said to be thirty-seven feet square, and sixty feet high; occupies the whole interior of the Tower of Comares; and still bears the traces of past magnificence. The walls are beautifully stuccoed and decorated with Morisco fancifulness; the lofty ceiling was originally of the same favorite material, with the usual frostwork and pensile ornaments or stalactites; which, with the embellishments of vivid coloring and gilding, must have been gorgeous in the extreme. Unfortunately it gave way during an earthquake, and brought down with it an immense arch which traversed the hall. It was replaced by the present vault or dome of larch or cedar, with intersecting ribs, the whole curiously wrought and richly colored; still Oriental in its character, reminding one of "those ceilings of cedar and vermilion that we read of in the prophets and the Arabian Nights."*

*Urquhart's Pillars of Hercules.

From the great height of the vault above the windows the upper part of the hall is almost lost in obscurity; yet there is a magnificence as well as solemnity in the gloom, as through it we have gleams of rich gilding and the brilliant tints of the Moorish pencil.

The royal throne was placed opposite the entrance in a recess, which still bears an inscription intimating that Yusef I. (the monarch who completed the Alhambra) made this the throne of his empire. Every thing in this noble hall seems to have been calculated to surround the throne with impressive dignity and splendor; there was none of the elegant voluptuousness which reigns in other parts of the palace. The tower is of massive strength, domineering over the whole edifice and overhanging the steep hillside. On three sides of the Hall of Ambassadors are windows cut through the immense thickness of the walls, and commanding extensive prospects. The balcony of the central window especially looks down upon the verdant valley of the Darro, with its walks, its groves, and gardens. To the left it enjoys a distant prospect of the Vega, while directly in front rises the rival height of the Albaycin, with its medley of streets, and terraces, and gardens, and once crowned by a fortress that vied in power with the Alhambra. "Ill fated the man who lost all this!" exclaimed Charles V., as he looked forth from this window upon the enchanting scenery it commands.

The balcony of the window where this royal exclamation was made, has of late become one of my favorite resorts. I have just been seated there, enjoying the close of a long brilliant day. The sun, as he sank behind the purple mountains of Alhama, sent a stream of effulgence up the valley of the Darro, that spread a melancholy pomp over the ruddy towers of the Alhambra; while the Vega, covered with a slight sultry vapor that caught the setting ray, seemed spread out in the distance like a golden sea. Not a breath of air disturbed the stillness of the hour, and though the faint sound of music and merriment now and then rose from the gardens of the Darro, it but rendered more impressive the monumental silence of the pile which over-shadowed me. It was one of those hours and scenes in which memory asserts an almost magical power; and, like the evening sun beaming on these mouldering towers, sends back her retrospective rays to light up the glories of the past.

As I sat watching the effect of the declining daylight upon this Moorish pile, I was led into a consideration of the light, elegant, and voluptuous character, prevalent throughout its internal architecture; and to contrast it with the grand but gloomy solemnity of the Gothic edifices reared by the Spanish conquerors. The very architecture thus bespeaks the opposite and irreconcilable natures of the two warlike people who so long battled here for the mastery of the peninsula. By degrees, I fell into a course of musing upon the singular fortunes of the Arabian or Morisco-Spaniards, whose whole existence is as a tale that is told, and certainly forms one of the most anomalous yet splendid episodes in history. Potent and durable as was their dominion, we scarcely know how to call them. They were a nation without a legitimate country or name. A remote wave of the great Arabian inundation, cast upon the shores of Europe, they seem to have all the impetus of the first rush of the torrent. Their career of conquest, from the rock of Gibraltar to the cliffs of the Pyrenees, was as rapid and brilliant as the Moslem victories of Syria and Egypt. Nay, had they not been checked on the plains of Tours, all France, all Europe, might have been overrun with the same facility as the empires of the East, and the crescent at this day have glittered on the fanes of Paris and London.

Repelled within the limits of the Pyrenees, the mixed hordes of Asia and Africa, that formed this great irruption, gave up the Moslem principle of conquest, and sought to establish in Spain a peaceful and permanent dominion. As conquerors, their heroism was only equalled by their moderation; and in both, for a time, they excelled the nations with whom they contended. Severed from their native homes, they loved the land given them as they supposed by Allah, and strove to embellish it with every thing that could administer to the happiness of man. Laying the foundations of their power in a system of wise and equitable laws, diligently cultivating the arts and sciences, and promoting agriculture, manufactures, and commerce; they gradually formed an empire unrivalled for its prosperity by any of the empires of Christendom; and diligently drawing round them the graces and refinements which marked the Arabian empire in the East, at the time of its greatest civilization, they diffused the light of Oriental knowledge, through the Western regions of benighted Europe.

The cities of Arabian Spain became the resort of Christian artisans, to instruct themselves in the useful arts. The universities of Toledo, Cordova, Seville, and Granada, were sought by the pale student from other lands to acquaint himself with the sciences of the Arabs, and the treasured lore of antiquity; the lovers of the gay sciences resorted to Cordova and Granada, to imbibe the poetry and music of the East; and the steel-clad warriors of the North hastened thither to accomplish themselves in the graceful exercises and courteous usages of chivalry.

If the Moslem monuments in Spain, if the Mosque of Cordova, the Alcazar of Seville, and the Alhambra of Granada, still bear inscriptions fondly boasting of the power and permanency of their dominion; can the boast be derided as arrogant and vain? Generation after generation, century after century, passed away, and still they maintained possession of the land. A period elapsed longer than that which has passed since England was subjugated by the Norman Conqueror, and the descendants of Musa and Taric might as little anticipate being driven into exile across the same straits, traversed by their triumphant ancestors, as the descendants of Rollo and William, and their veteran peers, may dream of being driven back to the shores of Normandy.

With all this, however, the Moslem empire in Spain was but a brilliant exotic, that took no permanent root in the soil it embellished. Severed from all their neighbors in the West, by impassable barriers of faith and manners, and separated by seas and deserts from their kindred of the East, the Morisco-Spaniards were an isolated people. Their whole existence was a prolonged, though gallant and chivalric struggle, for a foothold in a usurped land.

They were the outposts and frontiers of Islamism. The peninsula was the great battle-ground where the Gothic conquerors of the North and the Moslem conquerors of the East, met and strove for mastery; and the fiery courage of the Arab was at length subdued by the obstinate and persevering valor of the Goth.

Never was the annihilation of a people more complete than that of the Morisco-Spaniards. Where are they? Ask the shores of Barbary and its desert places. The exiled remnant of their once powerful empire disappeared among the barbarians of Africa, and ceased to be a nation. They have not even left a distinct name behind them, though for nearly eight centuries they were a distinct people. The home of their adoption, and of their occupation for ages, refuses to acknowledge them, except as invaders and usurpers. A few broken monuments are all that remain to bear witness to their power and dominion, as solitary rocks, left far in the interior, bear testimony to the extent of some vast inundation. Such is the Alhambra. A Moslem pile in the midst of a Christian land; an Oriental palace amidst the Gothic edifices of the West; an elegant memento of a brave, intelligent, and graceful people, who conquered, ruled, flourished, and passed away.

The Jesuits' Library

S INCE INDULGING in the foregoing reverie, my curiosity
has been aroused to know something of the princes, who
left behind them this monument of Oriental taste and magnificence; and whose names still appear among the inscriptions
on its walls. To gratify this curiosity, I have descended from
this region of fancy and fable, where every thing is liable to
take an imaginary tint, and have carried my researches among
the dusty tomes of the old Jesuits' Library, in the University.
This once boasted repository of erudition is now a mere
shadow of its former self, having been stripped of its manuscripts and rarest works by the French, when masters of Granada; still it contains among many ponderous tomes of the
Jesuit fathers, which the French were careful to leave behind,
several curious tracts of Spanish literature; and above all, a
number of those antiquated parchment-bound chronicles for
which I have a particular veneration.

In this old library, I have passed many delightful hours of
quiet, undisturbed, literary foraging; for the keys of the doors
and bookcases were kindly intrusted to me, and I was left
alone, to rummage at my pleasure—a rare indulgence in these
sanctuaries of learning, which too often tantalize the thirsty
student with the sight of sealed fountains of knowledge.

In the course of these visits I gleaned a variety of facts concerning historical characters connected with the Alhambra,
some of which I here subjoin, trusting they may prove acceptable to the reader.

Alhamar, the Founder of the Alhambra

THE MOORS of Granada regarded the Alhambra as a miracle of art, and had a tradition that the king who founded it dealt in magic, or at least in alchemy, by means whereof he procured the immense sums of gold expended in its erection. A brief view of his reign will show the secret of his wealth. He is known in Arabian history as Muhamed Ibn-l-Ahmar; but his name in general is written simply Alhamar, and was given to him, we are told, on account of his ruddy complexion.*

He was of the noble and opulent line of the Beni Nasar, or tribe of Nasar, and was born in Arjona, in the year of Hegira 592 (A.D. 1195). At his birth the astrologers, we are told, cast his horoscope according to Oriental custom, and pronounced it highly auspicious; and a santon predicted for him a glorious career. No expense was spared in fitting him for the high destinies prognosticated. Before he attained the full years of manhood, the famous battle of the Navas (or plains) of Tolosa shattered the Moorish empire, and eventually severed the Moslems of Spain from the Moslems of Africa. Factions soon arose among the former, headed by warlike chiefs, ambitious of grasping the sovereignty of the Peninsula. Alhamar became engaged in these wars; he was the general and leader of the Beni Nasar, and, as such, he opposed and thwarted the ambition of Aben Hud, who had raised his standard among the warlike mountains of the Alpuxarras, and been proclaimed king of Murcia and Granada. Many conflicts took place between these warring chieftains; Alhamar dispossessed his rival of several important places, and was proclaimed king of Jaen by his soldiery; but he aspired to the sovereignty of the whole of Andalusia, for he was of a sanguine spirit and lofty ambition. His valor and generosity went hand in hand; what he gained by the one he secured by the other; and at the death of

*Et porque era muy rubio llamaban lo los Moros Abenalhamar, que quiere decir bermejo . . . . et porque los Moros lo llamaban Benalhamar que quiere decir bermejo tomo los señales bermejos, segun que los ovieron despues los Reyes de Granada.— BLEDA, *Cronica de Alfonso XI.*, P. i. C. 44.

Aben Hud (A.D. 1238), he became sovereign of all the territories which owned allegiance to that powerful chief. He made his formal entry into Granada in the same year, amid the enthusiastic shouts of the multitude, who hailed him as the only one capable of uniting the various factions which prevailed, and which threatened to lay the empire at the mercy of the Christian princes.

Alhamar established his court in Granada; he was the first of the illustrious line of Nasar that sat upon a throne. He took immediate measures to put his little kingdom in a posture of defence against the assault' to be expected from his Christian neighbors, repairing and strengthening the frontier posts and fortifying the capital. Not content with the provisions of the Moslem law, by which every man is made a soldier, he raised a regular army to garrison his strong-holds, allowing every soldier stationed on the frontier a portion of land for the support of himself, his horse, and his family; thus interesting him in the defence of the soil in which he had a property. These wise precautions were justified by events. The Christians, profiting by the dismemberment of the Moslem power, were rapidly regaining their ancient territories. James the Conqueror had subjected all Valencia, and Ferdinand the Saint sat down in person before Jaen, the bulwark of Granada. Alhamar ventured to oppose him in open field, but met with a signal defeat, and retired discomfited to his capital. Jaen still held out, and kept the enemy at bay during an entire winter, but Ferdinand swore not to raise his camp until he had gained possession of the place. Alhamar found it impossible to throw reinforcements into the besieged city; he saw that its fall must be followed by the investment of his capital, and was conscious of the insufficiency of his means to cope with the potent sovereign of Castile. Taking a sudden resolution, therefore, he repaired privately to the Christian camp, made his unexpected appearance in the presence of King Ferdinand, and frankly announced himself as the king of Granada. "I come," said he, "confiding in your good faith, to put myself under your protection. Take all I possess and receive me as your vassal;" so saying, he knelt and kissed the king's hand in token of allegiance.

Ferdinand was won by this instance of confiding faith, and

determined not to be outdone in generosity. He raised his late enemy from the earth, embraced him as a friend, and, refusing the wealth he offered, left him sovereign of his dominions, under the feudal tenure of a yearly tribute, attendance at the Cortes as one of the nobles of the empire, and service in war with a certain number of horsemen. He moreover conferred on him the honor of knighthood, and armed him with his own hands.

It was not long after this that Alhamar was called upon, for his military services, to aid King Ferdinand in his famous siege of Seville. The Moorish king sallied forth with five hundred chosen horsemen of Granada, than whom none in the world knew better how to manage the steed or wield the lance. It was a humiliating service, however, for they had to draw the sword against their brethren of the faith.

Alhamar gained a melancholy distinction by his prowess in this renowned conquest, but more true honor by the humanity which he prevailed upon Ferdinand to introduce into the usages of war. When in 1248 the famous city of Seville surrendered to the Castilian monarch, Alhamar returned sad and full of care to his dominions. He saw the gathering ills that menaced the Moslem cause; and uttered an ejaculation often used by him in moments of anxiety and trouble—"How straitened and wretched would be our life, if our hope were not so spacious and extensive." "Que angoste y miserabile seria nuestra vida, sino fuera tan dilatada y espaciosa nuestra esperanza!"

As he approached Granada on his return he beheld arches of triumph which had been erected in honor of his martial exploits. The people thronged forth to see him with impatient joy, for his benignant rule had won all hearts. Wherever he passed he was hailed with acclamations as "El Ghalib!" (the conqueror). Alhamar gave a melancholy shake of the head on hearing the appellation. "*Wa le ghalib ile Aláh!*" (there is no conqueror but God) exclaimed he. From that time forward this exclamation became his motto, and the motto of his descendants, and appears to this day emblazoned on his escutcheons in the halls of the Alhambra.

Alhamar had purchased peace by submission to the Christian yoke; but he was conscious that, with elements so discordant and motives for hostility so deep and ancient, it could not be permanent. Acting, therefore, upon the old maxim, "arm thyself in peace and clothe thyself in summer," he improved the present interval of tranquillity by fortifying his dominions, replenishing his arsenals, and promoting those useful arts which give wealth and real power. He confided the command of his various cities to such as had distinguished themselves by valor and prudence, and who seemed most acceptable to the people. He organized a vigilant police, and established rigid rules for the administration of justice. The poor and the distressed always found ready admission to his presence, and he attended personally to their assistance and redress. He erected hospitals for the blind, the aged, and infirm, and all those incapable of labor, and visited them frequently; not on set days with pomp and form, so as to give time for every thing to be put in order, and every abuse concealed; but suddenly, and unexpectedly, informing himself, by actual observation and close inquiry, of the treatment of the sick, and the conduct of those appointed to administer to their relief. He founded schools and colleges, which he visited in the same manner, inspecting personally the instruction of the youth. He established butcheries and public ovens, that the people might be furnished with wholesome provisions at just and regular prices. He introduced abundant streams of water into the city, erecting baths and fountains, and constructing aqueducts and canals to irrigate and fertilize the Vega. By these means prosperity and abundance prevailed in this beautiful city, its gates were thronged with commerce, and its warehouses filled with luxuries and merchandise of every clime and country.

He moreover gave premiums and privileges to the best artisans; improved the breed of horses and other domestic animals; encouraged husbandry; and increased the natural fertility of the soil twofold by his protection, making the lovely valleys of his kingdom to bloom like gardens. He fostered also the growth and fabrication of silk, until the looms of Granada surpassed even those of Syria in the fineness and beauty of their productions. He moreover caused the mines of gold and silver and other metals, found in the mountainous regions of his dominions, to be diligently worked, and was the first king of Granada who struck money of gold and silver with his name, taking great care that the coins should be skil-fully executed.

It was towards the middle of the thirteenth century, and just after his return from the siege of Seville, that he com-menced the splendid palace of the Alhambra; superintending the building of it in person; mingling frequently among the artists and workmen, and directing their labors.

Though thus magnificent in his works and great in his en-terprises, he was simple in his person and moderate in his enjoyments. His dress was not merely void of splendor, but so plain as not to distinguish him from his subjects. His harem boasted but few beauties, and these he visited but sel-dom, though they were entertained with great magnificence. His wives were daughters of the principal nobles, and were treated by him as friends and rational companions. What is more, he managed to make them live in friendship with one another. He passed much of his time in his gardens; especially in those of the Alhambra, which he had stored with the rarest plants and the most beautiful and aromatic flowers. Here he delighted himself in reading histories, or in causing them to be read and related to him, and sometimes, in intervals of leisure, employed himself in the instruction of his three sons, for whom he had provided the most learned and virtuous masters.

As he had frankly and voluntarily offered himself a tribu-tary vassal to Ferdinand, so he always remained loyal to his word, giving him repeated proofs of fidelity and attachment. When that renowned monarch died in Seville in 1254, Alha-mar sent ambassadors to condole with his successor, Alonzo X., and with them a gallant train of a hundred Moorish cava-liers of distinguished rank, who were to attend round the royal bier during the funeral ceremonies, each bearing a lighted taper. This grand testimonial of respect was repeated by the Moslem monarch during the remainder of his life on each anniversary of the death of King Ferdinand el Santo, when the hundred Moorish knights repaired from Granada to Seville, and took their stations with lighted tapers in the centre of the sumptuous cathedral round the cenotaph of the illustrious deceased.

Alhamar retained his faculties and vigor to an advanced

age. In his seventy-ninth year (A.D. 1272) he took the field on horseback, accompanied by the flower of his chivalry, to resist an invasion of his territories. As the army sallied forth from Granada, one of the principal adalides, or guides, who rode in the advance, accidentally broke his lance against the arch of the gate. The councillors of the king, alarmed by this circumstance, which was considered an evil omen, entreated him to return. Their supplications were in vain. The king persisted, and at noontide the omen, say the Moorish chroniclers, was fatally fulfilled. Alhamar was suddenly struck with illness, and had nearly fallen from his horse. He was placed on a litter, and borne back towards Granada, but his illness increased to such a degree that they were obliged to pitch his tent in the Vega. His physicians were filled with consternation, not knowing what remedy to prescribe. In a few hours he died, vomiting blood and in violent convulsions. The Castilian prince, Don Philip, brother of Alonzo X., was by his side when he expired. His body was embalmed, enclosed in a silver coffin, and buried in the Alhambra in a sepulchre of precious marble, amidst the unfeigned lamentations of his subjects, who bewailed him as a parent.

I have said that he was the first of the illustrious line of Nasar that sat upon a throne. I may add that he was the founder of a brilliant kingdom, which will ever be famous in history and romance, as the last rallying place of Moslem power and splendor in the peninsula. Though his undertakings were vast, and his expenditures immense, yet his treasury was always full; and this seeming contradiction gave rise to the story that he was versed in magic art, and possessed of the secret for transmuting baser metals into gold. Those who have attended to his domestic policy, as here set forth, will easily understand the natural magic and simple alchemy which made his ample treasury to overflow.

Yusef Abul Hagig,
the Finisher of the Alhambra

TO THE FOREGOING PARTICULARS, concerning the Moslem princes who once reigned in these halls, I shall add a brief notice of the monarch who completed and embellished the Alhambra. Yusef Abul Hagig (or as it is sometimes written, Haxis) was another prince of the noble line of Nasar. He ascended the throne of Granada in the year of grace 1333, and is described by Moslem writers as having a noble presence, great bodily strength, and a fair complexion, and the majesty of his countenance increased, say they, by suffering his beard to grow to a dignified length and dyeing it black. His manners were gentle, affable, and urbane; he carried the benignity of his nature into warfare, prohibiting all wanton cruelty, and enjoining mercy and protection towards women and children, the aged and infirm, and all friars and other persons of holy and recluse life. But though he possessed the courage common to generous spirits, the bent of his genius was more for peace than war, and though repeatedly obliged by circumstances to take up arms, he was generally unfortunate.

Among other ill-starred enterprises, he undertook a great campaign, in conjunction with the king of Morocco, against the kings of Castile and Portugal, but was defeated in the memorable battle of Salado, which had nearly proved a death-blow to the Moslem power in Spain.

Yusef obtained a long truce after this defeat, and now his character shone forth in its true lustre. He had an excellent memory, and had stored his mind with science and erudition; his taste was altogether elegant and refined, and he was accounted the best poet of his time. Devoting himself to the instruction of his people and the improvement of their morals and manners, he established schools in all the villages, with simple and uniform systems of education; he obliged every hamlet of more than twelve houses to have a mosque, and purified the ceremonies of religion, and the festivals and popular amusements, from various abuses and indecorums which had crept into them. He attended vigilantly to the police of

the city, establishing nocturnal guards and patrols, and superintending all municipal concerns. His attention was also
directed towards finishing the great architectural works
commenced by his predecessors, and erecting others on his
own plans. The Alhambra, which had been founded by the
good Alhamar, was now completed. Yusef constructed the
beautiful Gate of Justice, forming the grand entrance to
the fortress, which he finished in 1348. He likewise adorned
many of the courts and halls of the palace, as may be seen by
the inscriptions on the walls, in which his name repeatedly
occurs. He built also the noble Alcazar or citadel of Malaga,
now unfortunately a mere mass of crumbling ruins, but which
most probably exhibited in its interior, similar elegance and
magnificence with the Alhambra.

The genius of a sovereign stamps a character upon his time.
The nobles of Granada, imitating the elegant and graceful
taste of Yusef, soon filled the city of Granada with magnificent palaces; the halls of which were paved with Mosaic, the
walls and ceilings wrought in fretwork, and delicately gilded
and painted with azure, vermilion, and other brilliant colors,
or minutely inlaid with cedar and other precious woods; specimens of which have survived, in all their lustre, the lapse of
several centuries. Many of the houses had fountains, which
threw up jets of water to refresh and cool the air. They had
lofty towers also, of wood or stone, curiously carved and ornamented, and covered with plates of metal that glittered in
the sun. Such was the refined and delicate taste in architecture
that prevailed among this elegant people; insomuch that to
use the beautiful simile of an Arabian writer, "Granada, in the
days of Yusef, was as a silver vase filled with emeralds and
jacinths."

One anecdote will be sufficient to show the magnanimity of
this generous prince. The long truce which had succeeded the
battle of Salado was at an end, and every effort of Yusef to
renew it was in vain. His deadly foe, Alfonso XI. of Castile,
took the field with great force, and laid siege to Gibraltar.
Yusef reluctantly took up arms, and sent troops to the relief
of the place. In the midst of his anxiety, he received tidings
that his dreaded foe had suddenly fallen victim to the plague.
Instead of manifesting exultation on the occasion, Yusef

called to mind the great qualities of the deceased, and was touched with a noble sorrow. "Alas!" cried he, "the world has lost one of its most excellent princes; a sovereign who knew how to honor merit, whether in friend or foe!"

The Spanish chroniclers themselves bear witness to this magnanimity. According to their accounts, the Moorish cavaliers partook of the sentiment of their king, and put on mourning for the death of Alfonso. Even those of Gibraltar, who had been so closely invested, when they knew that the hostile monarch lay dead in his camp, determined among themselves that no hostile movement should be made against the Christians. The day on which the camp was broken up, and the army departed bearing the corpse of Alfonso, the Moors issued in multitudes from Gibraltar, and stood mute and melancholy, watching the mournful pageant. The same reverence for the deceased was observed by all the Moorish commanders on the frontiers, who suffered the funeral train to pass in safety, bearing the corpse of the Christian sovereign from Gibraltar to Seville.*

Yusef did not long survive the enemy he had so generously deplored. In the year 1354, as he was one day praying in the royal mosque of the Alhambra, a maniac rushed suddenly from behind and plunged a dagger in his side. The cries of the king brought his guards and courtiers to his assistance. They found him weltering in his blood. He made some signs as if to speak, but his words were unintelligible. They bore him senseless to the royal apartments, where he expired almost immediately. The murderer was cut to pieces, and his limbs burnt in public to gratify the fury of the populace.

The body of the king was interred in a superb sepulchre of white marble; a long epitaph, in letters of gold upon an azure ground, recorded his virtues. "Here lies a king and martyr, of an illustrious line, gentle, learned, and virtuous; renowned for the graces of his person and his manners; whose clemency, piety and benevolence, were extolled throughout the king-

---

*"Y los moros que estaban en la villa y Castillo de Gibraltar despues que sopieron que el Rey Don Alonzo era muerto, ordenaron entresi que ninguno non fuesse osado de fazer ningun movimiento contra los Christianos, ni mover pelear contra ellos, estovieron todos quedos y dezian entre ellos qui aquel dia muriera un noble rey y Gran principe del mundo."

dom of Granada. He was a great prince; an illustrious captain; a sharp sword of the Moslems; a valiant standard-bearer among the most potent monarchs," &c.

The mosque still exists which once resounded with the dying cries of Yusef, but the monument which recorded his virtues has long since disappeared. His name, however, remains inscribed among the delicate and graceful ornaments of the Alhambra, and will be perpetuated in connection with this renowned pile, which it was his pride and delight to beautify.

The Mysterious Chambers

As I was rambling one day about the Moorish halls, my attention was, for the first time, attracted to a door in a remote gallery, communicating apparently with some part of the Alhambra which I had not yet explored. I attempted to open it, but it was locked. I knocked, but no one answered, and the sound seemed to reverberate through empty chambers. Here then was a mystery. Here was the haunted wing of the castle. How was I to get at the dark secrets here shut up from the public eye? Should I come privately at night with lamp and sword, according to the prying custom of heroes of romance; or should I endeavor to draw the secret from Pépe the stuttering gardener; or the ingenuous Dolores, or the loquacious Mateo? Or should I go frankly and openly to Dame Antonia the chatelaine, and ask her all about it? I chose the latter course, as being the simplest though the least romantic; and found, somewhat to my disappointment, that there was no mystery in the case. I was welcome to explore the apartment, and there was the key.

Thus provided, I returned forthwith to the door. It opened, as I had surmised, to a range of vacant chambers; but they were quite different from the rest of the palace. The architecture, though rich and antiquated, was European. There was nothing Moorish about it. The first two rooms were lofty; the ceilings, broken in many places, were of cedar, deeply panelled and skilfully carved with fruits and flowers, intermingled with grotesque masks or faces.

The walls had evidently in ancient times been hung with damask; but now were naked, and scrawled over by that class of aspiring travellers who defile noble monuments with their worthless names. The windows, dismantled and open to wind and weather, looked out into a charming little secluded garden, where an alabaster fountain sparkled among roses and myrtles, and was surrounded by orange and citron trees, some of which flung their branches into the chambers. Beyond these rooms were two saloons, longer but less lofty, looking also in the garden. In the compartments of the panelled ceilings were baskets of fruit and garlands of flowers, painted by no mean hand, and in tolerable preservation. The walls also had been painted in fresco in the Italian style, but the paintings were nearly obliterated; the windows were in the same shattered state with those of the other chambers. This fanciful suite of rooms terminated in an open gallery with balustrades, running at right angles along another side of the garden. The whole apartment, so delicate and elegant in its decorations, so choice and sequestered in its situation along this retired little garden, and so different in architecture from the neighboring halls, awakened an interest in its history. I found on inquiry that it was an apartment fitted up by Italian artists in the early part of the last century, at the time when Philip V. and his second wife, the beautiful Elizabetta of Farnese, daughter of the Duke of Parma, were expected at the Alhambra. It was destined for the queen and the ladies of her train. One of the loftiest chambers had been her sleeping room. A narrow staircase, now walled up, led up to a delightful belvidere, originally a mirador of the Moorish sultanas, communicating with the harem; but which was fitted up as a boudoir for the fair Elizabetta, and still retains the name of *el tocador de la Reyna*, or the queen's toilette.

One window of the royal sleeping-room commanded a prospect of the Generalife and its embowered terraces, another looked out into the little secluded garden I have mentioned, which was decidedly Moorish in its character, and also had its history. It was in fact the garden of Lindaraxa, so often mentioned in descriptions of the Alhambra; but who this Lindaraxa was I had never heard explained. A little research gave me the few particulars known about her. She was a Moorish beauty who flourished in the court of Muhamed the Left-Handed, and was the daughter of his loyal adherent, the alcayde of Malaga, who sheltered him in his city when driven from the throne. On regaining his crown, the alcayde was rewarded for his fidelity. His daughter had her apartment in the Alhambra, and was given by the king in marriage to Nasar, a young Cetimerien prince descended from Aben Hud the Just. Their espousals were doubtless celebrated in the royal palace, and their honeymoon may have passed among these very bowers.*

Four centuries had elapsed since the fair Lindaraxa passed away, yet how much of the fragile beauty of the scenes she inhabited remained! The garden still bloomed in which she delighted; the fountain still presented the crystal mirror in which her charms may once have been reflected; the alabaster, it is true, had lost its whiteness; the basin beneath, overrun with weeds, had become the lurking-place of the lizard, but there was something in the very decay that enhanced the interest of the scene, speaking as it did of that mutability, the irrevocable lot of man and all his works.

The desolation too of these chambers, once the abode of the proud and elegant Elizabetta, had a more touching charm for me than if I had beheld them in their pristine splendor, glittering with the pageantry of a court.

When I returned to my quarters, in the governor's apartment, every thing seemed tame and common-place after the poetic region I had left. The thought suggested itself: Why could I not change my quarters to these vacant chambers? that would indeed be living in the Alhambra, surrounded by its gardens and fountains, as in the time of the Moorish sovereigns. I proposed the change to Dame Antonia and her family, and it occasioned vast surprise. They could not conceive any rational inducement for the choice of an apartment so forlorn, remote and solitary. Dolores exclaimed at its frightful loneliness; nothing but bats and owls flitting about—and then a fox and wild-cat kept in the vaults of the neighboring baths, and roamed about at night. The good Tia had more reasonable objections. The neighborhood was infested by vagrants; gipsies swarmed in the caverns of the adjacent hills; the palace was ruinous and easy to be entered in

---

*Una de las cosas en que tienen precisa intervencion los Reyes Moros es en el matrimonio de sus grandes: de aqui nace que todos los señores llegadas à la persona real si casan en palacio, y siempre huvo su quarto destinado para esta ceremonia.

One of the things in which the Moorish kings interfered was in the marriage of their nobles: hence it came that all the señors attached to the royal person were married in the palace; and there was always a chamber destined for the ceremony.—*Paseos por Granada*, Paseo XXI.

many places; the rumor of a stranger quartered alone in one of the remote and ruined apartments, out of the hearing of the rest of the inhabitants, might tempt unwelcome visitors in the night, especially as foreigners were always supposed to be well stocked with money. I was not to be diverted from my humor, however, and my will was law with these good people. So, calling in the assistance of a carpenter, and the ever officious Mateo Ximenes, the doors and windows were soon placed in a state of tolerable security, and the sleeping-room of the stately Elizabetta prepared for my reception. Mateo kindly volunteered as a body-guard to sleep in my antechamber; but I did not think it worth while to put his valor to the proof.

With all the hardihood I had assumed and all the precautions I had taken, I must confess the first night passed in these quarters was inexpressibly dreary. I do not think it was so much the apprehension of dangers from without that affected me, as the character of the place itself, with all its strange associations: the deeds of violence committed there; the tragical ends of many of those who had once reigned there in splendor. As I passed beneath the fated halls of the tower of Comares on the way to my chamber, I called to mind a quotation, that used to thrill me in the days of boyhood:

> Fate sits on these dark battlements and frowns;
> And, as the portal opens to receive me,
> A voice in sullen echoes through the courts
> Tells of a nameless deed!

The whole family escorted me to my chamber, and took leave of me as of one engaged on a perilous enterprise; and when I heard their retreating steps die away along the waste antechambers and echoing galleries, and turned the key of my door, I was reminded of those hobgoblin stories, where the hero is left to accomplish the adventure of an enchanted house.

Even the thoughts of the fair Elizabetta and the beauties of her court, who had once graced these chambers, now, by a perversion of fancy, added to the gloom. Here was the scene of their transient gayety and loveliness; here were the very traces of their elegance and enjoyment; but what and where

I now felt the poetic merit of the Arabic inscription on the walls: "How beauteous is this garden; where the flowers of the earth vie with the stars of heaven. What can compare with the vase of yon alabaster fountain filled with crystal water? nothing but the moon in her fulness, shining in the midst of an unclouded sky!"

On such heavenly nights I would sit for hours at my window inhaling the sweetness of the garden, and musing on the checkered fortunes of those whose history was dimly shadowed out in the elegant memorials around. Sometimes, when all was quiet, and the clock from the distant cathedral of Granada struck the midnight hour, I have sallied out on another tour and wandered over the whole building; but how different from my first tour! No longer dark and mysterious; no longer peopled with shadowy foes; no longer recalling scenes of violence and murder; all was open, spacious, beautiful; every thing called up pleasing and romantic fancies; Lindaraxa once more walked in her garden; the gay chivalry of Moslem Granada once more glittered about the Court of Lions! Who can do justice to a moonlight night in such a climate and such a place? The temperature of a summer night in Andalusia is perfectly ethereal. We seem lifted up into a purer atmosphere; we feel a serenity of soul, a buoyancy of spirits, an elasticity of frame, which render mere existence happiness. But when moonlight is added to all this, the effect is like enchantment. Under its plastic sway the Alhambra seems to regain its pristine glories. Every rent and chasm of time, every mouldering tint and weather-stain is gone; the marble resumes its original whiteness; the long colonnades brighten in the moonbeams; the halls are illuminated with a softened radiance—we tread the enchanted palace of an Arabian tale!

What a delight, at such a time, to ascend to the little airy pavilion of the queen's toilet (el tocador de la reyna), which, like a bird-cage, overhangs the valley of the Darro, and gaze from its light arcades upon the moonlight prospect! To the right, the swelling mountains of the Sierra Nevada, robbed of their ruggedness and softened into a fairy land, with their snowy summits gleaming like silver clouds against the deep blue sky. And then to lean over the parapet of the Tocador and gaze down upon Granada and the Albaycin spread out like a map below; all buried in deep repose; the white palaces and convents sleeping in the moonshine, and beyond all these the vapory Vega fading away like a dream-land in the distance.

Sometimes the faint click of castañets rise from the Alameda, where some gay Andalusians are dancing away the summer night. Sometimes the dubious tones of a guitar and the notes of an amorous voice, tell perchance the whereabouts of some moon-struck lover serenading his lady's window.

Such is a faint picture of the moonlight nights I have passed loitering about the courts and halls and balconies of this most suggestive pile; "feeding my fancy with sugared suppositions," and enjoying that mixture of reverie and sensation which steal away existence in a southern climate; so that it has been almost morning before I have retired to bed, and been lulled to sleep by the falling waters of the fountain of Lindaraxa.

Panorama from the Tower of Comares

IT IS A SERENE and beautiful morning: the sun has not gained sufficient power to destroy the freshness of the night. What a morning to mount to the summit of the Tower of Comares, and take a bird's-eye view of Granada and its environs!

Come then, worthy reader and comrade, follow my steps into this vestibule, ornamented with rich tracery, which opens into the Hall of Ambassadors. We will not enter the hall, however, but turn to this small door opening into the wall. Have a care! here are steep winding steps and but scanty light; yet up this narrow, obscure, and spiral staircase, the proud monarchs of Granada and their queens have often ascended to the battlements to watch the approach of invading armies, or gaze with anxious hearts on the battles in the Vega.

At length we have reached the terraced roof, and may take breath for a moment, while we cast a general eye over the splendid panorama of city and country; of rocky mountain, verdant valley, and fertile plain; of castle, cathedral, Moorish towers, and Gothic domes, crumbling ruins, and blooming groves. Let us approach the battlements, and cast our eyes immediately below. See, on this side we have the whole plain of the Alhambra laid open to us, and can look down into its courts and gardens. At the foot of the tower is the Court of Alberca, with its great tank or fishpool, bordered with flowers; and yonder is the Court of Lions, with its famous fountain, and its light Moorish arcades; and in the centre of the pile is the little garden of Lindaraxa, buried in the heart of the building, with its roses and citrons, and shrubbery of emerald green.

That belt of battlements, studded with square towers, straggling round the whole brow of the hill, is the outer boundary of the fortress. Some of the towers, you may perceive, are in ruins, and their massive fragments buried among vines, fig-trees and aloes.

Let us look on the northern side of the tower. It is a giddy height; the very foundations of the tower rise above the groves of the steep hill-side. And see! a long fissure in the massive walls, shows that the tower has been rent by some of the earthquakes, which from time to time have thrown Granada into consternation; and which, sooner or later, must reduce this crumbling pile to a mere mass of ruin. The deep narrow glen below us, which gradually widens as it opens from the mountains, is the valley of the Darro; you see the little river winding its way under imbowered terraces, and among orchards and flower-gardens. It is a stream famous in old times for yielding gold, and its sands are still sifted occasionally, in search of the precious ore. Some of those white pavilions, which here and there gleam from among groves and vineyards, were rustic retreats of the Moors, to enjoy the refreshment of their gardens. Well have they been compared by one of their poets to so many pearls set in a bed of emeralds.

The airy palace, with its tall white towers and long arcades, which breasts yon mountain, among pompous groves and hanging gardens, is the Generalife, a summer palace of the Moorish kings, to which they resorted during the sultry months to enjoy a still more breezy region than that of the Alhambra. The naked summit of the height above it, where you behold some shapeless ruins, is the Silla del Moro, or Seat of the Moor, so called from having been a retreat of the unfortunate Boabdil during the time of an insurrection, where he seated himself, and looked down mournfully upon his rebellious city.

A murmuring sound of water now and then rises from the valley. It is from the aqueduct of yon Moorish mill, nearly at the foot of the hill. The avenue of trees beyond is the Alameda, along the bank of the Darro, a favorite resort in evenings, and a rendezvous of lovers in the summer nights, when the guitar may be heard at a late hour from the benches along its walks. At present you see none but a few loitering monks there, and a group of water-carriers. The latter are burdened with water jars of ancient Oriental construction, such as were used by the Moors. They have been filled at the cold and limpid spring called the fountain of Avellanos. Yon mountain path leads to the fountain, a favorite resort of Moslems as well as Christians; for this is said to be the Adinamar

(Aynu-l-adamar), the "Fountain of Tears," mentioned by Ibn Batuta the traveller, and celebrated in the histories and romances of the Moors.

You start! 'tis nothing but a hawk that we have frightened from his nest. This old tower is a complete breeding-place for vagrant birds: the swallow and martlet abound in every chink and cranny, and circle about it the whole day long; while at night, when all other birds have gone to rest, the moping owl comes out of its lurking place, and utters its boding cry from the battlements. See how the hawk we have dislodged sweeps away below us, skimming over the tops of the trees, and sailing up to the ruins above the Generalife!

I see you raise your eyes to the snowy summit of yon pile of mountains, shining like a white summer cloud in the blue sky. It is the Sierra Nevada, the pride and delight of Granada; the source of her cooling breezes and perpetual verdure; of her gushing fountains and perennial streams. It is this glorious pile of mountains which gives to Granada that combination of delights so rare in a southern city; the fresh vegetation and temperate airs of a northern climate, with the vivifying ardor of a tropical sun, and the cloudless azure of a southern sky. It is this aerial treasury of snow, which, melting in proportion to the increase of the summer heat, sends down rivulets and streams through every glen and gorge of the Alpuxarras, diffusing emerald verdure and fertility throughout a chain of happy and sequestered valleys.

Those mountains may be well called the glory of Granada. They dominate the whole extent of Andalusia, and may be seen from its most distant parts. The muleteer hails them, as he views their frosty peaks from the sultry level of the plain; and the Spanish mariner on the deck of his bark, far, far off on the bosom of the blue Mediterranean, watches them with a pensive eye, thinks of delightful Granada, and chants, in low voice, some old romance about the Moors.

See to the south at the foot of those mountains a line of arid hills, down which a long train of mules is slowly moving. Here was the closing scene of Moslem domination. From the summit of one of those hills the unfortunate Boabdil cast back his last look upon Granada, and gave vent to the agony of his soul. It is the spot famous in song and story, "The last sigh of the Moor."

Further this way these arid hills slope down into the luxurious Vega, from which he had just emerged; a blooming wilderness of grove and garden, and teeming orchard, with the Xenil winding through it in silver links, and feeding innumerable rills; which, conducted through ancient Moorish channels, maintain the landscape in perpetual verdure. Here were the beloved bowers and gardens, and rural pavilions, for which the unfortunate Moors fought with such desperate valor. The very hovels and rude granges, now inhabited by boors, show, by the remains of arabesques and other tasteful decoration, that they were elegant residences in the days of the Moslems. Behold, in the very centre of this eventful plain, a place which in a manner links the history of the Old World with that of the New. Yon line of walls and towers gleaming in the morning sun, is the city of Santa Fe, built by the Catholic sovereigns during the siege of Granada, after a conflagration had destroyed their camp. It was to these walls Columbus was called back by the heroic queen, and within them the treaty was concluded which led to the discovery of the Western World. Behind yon promontory to the west is the bridge of Pinos, renowned for many a bloody fight between Moors and Christians. At this bridge the messenger overtook Columbus when, despairing of success with the Spanish sovereigns, he was departing to carry his project of discovery to the court of France.

Above the bridge a range of mountains bounds the Vega to the west; the ancient barrier between Granada and the Christian territories. Among their heights you may still discern warrior towns; their gray walls and battlements seeming of a piece with the rocks on which they are built. Here and there a solitary atalaya, or watchtower, perched on a mountain peak, looks down as it were from the sky into the valley on either side. How often have these atalayas given notice, by fire at night or smoke by day, of an approaching foe! It was down a cragged defile of these mountains, called the Pass of Lope, that the Christian armies descended into the Vega. Round the base of yon gray and naked mountain (the mountain of

Elvira), stretching its bold rocky promontory into the bosom of the plain, the invading squadrons would come bursting into view, with flaunting banners and clangor of drum and trumpet.

Five hundred years have elapsed since Ismael ben Ferrag, a Moorish king of Granada, beheld from this very tower an invasion of the kind, and an insulting ravage of the Vega; on which occasion he displayed an instance of chivalrous magnanimity, often witnessed in the Moslem princes; "whose history," says an Arabian writer, "abounds in generous actions and noble deeds that will last through all succeeding ages, and live for ever in the memory of man."—But let us sit down on this parapet and I will relate the anecdote.

It was in the year of Grace 1319, that Ismael ben Ferrag beheld from this tower a Christian camp whitening the skirts of yon mountain of Elvira. The royal princes, Don Juan and Don Pedro, regents of Castile during the minority of Alfonso XI., had already laid waste the country from Alcaudete to Alcalá la Real, capturing the castle of Illora and setting fire to its suburbs, and they now carried their insulting ravages to the very gates of Granada, defying the king to sally forth and give them battle.

Ismael, though a young and intrepid prince, hesitated to accept the challenge. He had not sufficient force at hand, and awaited the arrival of troops summoned from the neighboring towns. The Christian princes, mistaking his motives, gave up all hope of drawing him forth, and having glutted themselves with ravage, struck their tents and began their homeward march. Don Pedro led the van, and Don Juan brought up the rear, but their march was confused and irregular, the army being greatly encumbered by the spoils and captives they had taken.

By this time King Ismael had received his expected resources, and putting them under the command of Osmyn, one of the bravest of his generals, sent them forth in hot pursuit of the enemy. The Christians were overtaken in the defiles of the mountains. A panic seized them; they were completely routed, and driven with great slaughter across the borders. Both of the princes lost their lives. The body of Don Pedro was carried off by his soldiers, but that of Don Juan was lost in the darkness of the night. His son wrote to the Moorish king, entreating that the body of his father might be sought and honorably treated. Ismael forgot in a moment that Don Juan was an enemy, who had carried ravage and insult to the very gate of his capital; he only thought of him as a gallant cavalier and a royal prince. By his command diligent search was made for the body. It was found in a barranco and brought to Granada. There Ismael caused it to be laid out in state on a lofty bier, surrounded by torches and tapers, in one of these halls of the Alhambra. Osmyn and other of the noblest cavaliers were appointed as a guard of honor, and the Christian captives were assembled to pray around it.

In the mean time, Ismael wrote to the son of Prince Juan to send a convoy for the body, assuring him it should be faithfully delivered up. In due time, a band of Christian cavaliers arrived for the purpose. They were honorably received and entertained by Ismael, and, on their departure with the body, the guard of honor of Moslem cavaliers escorted the funeral train to the frontier.

But enough—the sun is high above the mountains, and pours his full fervor on our heads. Already the terraced roof is hot beneath our feet; let us abandon it, and refresh ourselves under the Arcades by the Fountain of the Lions.

The Truant

WE HAVE HAD a scene of a petty tribulation in the Alhambra, which has thrown a cloud over the sunny countenance of Dolores. This little damsel has a female passion for pets of all kinds, and from the superabundant kindness of her disposition one of the ruined courts of the Alhambra is thronged with her favorites. A stately peacock and his hen seem to hold regal sway here, over pompous turkeys, querulous guinea-fowls, and a rabble rout of common cocks and hens. The great delight of Dolores, however, has for some time past been centered in a youthful pair of pigeons, who have lately entered into the holy state of wedlock, and even supplanted a tortoise-shell cat and kittens in her affections.

As a tenement for them wherein to commence housekeeping, she had fitted up a small chamber adjacent to the kitchen, the window of which looked into one of the quiet Moorish courts. Here they lived in happy ignorance of any world beyond the court and its sunny roofs. Never had they aspired to soar above the battlements, or to mount to the summit of the towers. Their virtuous union was at length crowned by two spotless and milk-white eggs, to the great joy of their cherishing little mistress. Nothing could be more praiseworthy than the conduct of the young married folks on this interesting occasion. They took turns to sit upon the nest until the eggs were hatched, and while their callow progeny required warmth and shelter; while one thus stayed at home, the other foraged abroad for food, and brought home abundant supplies.

This scene of conjugal felicity has suddenly met with a reverse. Early this morning, as Dolores was feeding the male pigeon, she took a fancy to give him a peep at the great world. Opening a window, therefore, which looks down upon the valley of the Darro, she launched him at once beyond the walls of the Alhambra. For the first time in his life the astonished bird had to try the full vigor of his wings. He swept down into the valley, and then rising upwards with a surge, soared almost to the clouds. Never before had he risen to such a height, or experienced such delight in flying; and, like a young spendthrift just come to his estate, he seemed giddy with excess of liberty, and with the boundless field of action suddenly opened to him. For the whole day he has been circling about in capricious flights, from tower to tower, and tree to tree. Every attempt has been vain to lure him back by scattering grain upon the roofs; he seems to have lost all thought of home, of his tender helpmate, and his callow young. To add to the anxiety of Dolores, he has been joined by two *palomas ladrones*, or robber pigeons, whose instinct it is to entice wandering pigeons to their own dovecotes. The fugitive, like many other thoughtless youths on their first launching upon the world, seems quite fascinated with these knowing but graceless companions, who have undertaken to show him life, and introduce him to society. He has been soaring with them over all the roofs and steeples of Granada. A thunder-storm has passed over the city, but he has not sought his home; night has closed in, and still he comes not. To deepen the pathos of the affair, the female pigeon, after remaining several hours on the nest without being relieved, at length went forth to seek her recreant mate; but stayed away so long that the young ones perished for want of the warmth and shelter of the parent bosom. At a late hour in the evening, word was brought to Dolores, that the truant bird had been seen upon the towers of the Generalife. Now it happens that the *Administrador* of the ancient palace has likewise a dovecote, among the inmates of which are said to be two or three of these inveigling birds, the terror of all neighboring pigeon-fanciers. Dolores immediately concluded, that the two feathered sharpers who had been seen with her fugitive, were these bloods of the Generalife. A council of war was forthwith held in the chamber of Tia Antonia. The Generalife is a distinct jurisdiction from the Alhambra, and of course some punctilio, if not jealousy, exists between their custodians. It was determined, therefore, to send Pépe, the stuttering lad of the gardens, as ambassador to the Administrador, requesting that if such fugitive should be found in his dominions, he might be given up as a subject of the Alhambra. Pépe departed accordingly, on his diplomatic expedition, through the moonlit groves and avenues, but returned in an hour with the afflicting intelligence that no such bird was to be found in the dovecote of the Generalife. The Administrador, however, pledged his sovereign word that if such vagrant should appear there, even at midnight, he should instantly be arrested, and sent back prisoner to his little black-eyed mistress.

Thus stands the melancholy affair, which has occasioned much distress throughout the palace, and has sent the inconsolable Dolores to a sleepless pillow.

———"Sorrow endureth for a night," says the proverb, "but joy cometh in the morning." The first object that met my eyes, on leaving my room this morning, was Dolores, with the truant pigeon in her hands, and her eyes sparkling with joy. He had appeared at an early hour on the battlements, hovering shyly about from roof to roof, but at length entered the window, and surrendered himself prisoner. He gained little credit, however, by his return; for the ravenous manner in which he devoured the food set before him showed that, like the prodigal son, he had been driven home by sheer famine. Dolores upbraided him for his faithless conduct, calling him all manner of vagrant names, though, woman-like, she fondled him at the same time to her bosom, and covered him with kisses. I observed, however, that she had taken care to clip his wings to prevent all future soarings; a precaution which I mention for the benefit of all those who have truant lovers or wandering husbands. More than one valuable moral might be drawn from the story of Dolores and her pigeon.

The Balcony

I HAVE SPOKEN of a balcony of the central window of the Hall of Ambassadors. It served as a kind of observatory, where I used often to take my seat, and consider not merely the heaven above but the earth beneath. Besides the magnificent prospect which it commanded of mountain, valley, and vega, there was a little busy scene of human life laid open to inspection immediately below. At the foot of the hill was an alameda, or public walk, which, though not so fashionable as the more modern and splendid paseo of the Xenil, still boasted a varied and picturesque concourse. Hither resorted the small gentry of the suburbs, together with priests and friars, who walked for appetite and digestion; majos and majas, the beaux and belles of the lower classes, in their Andalusian dresses; swaggering contrabandistas, and sometimes half-muffled and mysterious loungers of the higher ranks, on some secret assignation.

It was a moving picture of Spanish life and character, which I delighted to study; and as the astronomer has his grand telescope with which to sweep the skies, and, as it were, bring the stars nearer for his inspection, so I had a smaller one, of pocket size, for the use of my observatory, with which I could sweep the regions below, and bring the countenances of the motley groups so close as almost, at times, to make me think I could divine their conversation by the play and expression of their features. I was thus, in a manner, an invisible observer, and, without quitting my solitude, could throw myself in an instant into the midst of society,—a rare advantage to one of somewhat shy and quiet habits, and fond, like myself, of observing the drama of life without becoming an actor in the scene.

There was a considerable suburb lying below the Alhambra, filling the narrow gorge of the valley, and extending up the opposite hill of the Albaycin. Many of the houses were built in the Moorish style, round patios, or courts, cooled by fountains and open to the sky; and as the inhabitants passed much of their time in these courts, and on the terraced roofs during the summer season, it follows that many a glance at their domestic life might be obtained by an aerial spectator like myself, who could look down on them from the clouds.

I enjoyed, in some degree, the advantages of the student in the famous old Spanish story, who beheld all Madrid un-roofed for his inspection; and my gossiping squire, Mateo Ximenes, officiated occasionally as my Asmodeus, to give me anecdotes of the different mansions and their inhabitants.

I preferred, however, to form conjectural histories for my-self, and thus would sit for hours, weaving, from casual inci-dents and indications passing under my eye, a whole tissue of schemes, intrigues, and occupations of the busy mortals be-low. There was scarce a pretty face or a striking figure that I daily saw, about which I had not thus gradually framed a dra-matic story, though some of my characters would occasionally act in direct opposition to the part assigned them, and discon-cert the whole drama. Reconnoitring one day with my glass the streets of the Albaycin, I beheld the procession of a novice about to take the veil; and remarked several circumstances which excited the strongest sympathy in the fate of the youth-ful being thus about to be consigned to a living tomb. I ascer-tained to my satisfaction that she was beautiful; and, from the paleness of her cheek, that she was a victim, rather than a votary. She was arrayed in bridal garments, and decked with a chaplet of white flowers, but her heart evidently revolted at this mockery of a spiritual union, and yearned after its earthly loves. A tall stern-looking man walked near her in the proces-sion; it was, of course, the tyrannical father, who, from some bigoted or sordid motive, had compelled this sacrifice. Amid the crowd was a dark handsome youth, in Andalusian garb, who seemed to fix on her an eye of agony. It was doubtless the secret lover from whom she was for ever to be separated. My indignation rose as I noted the malignant expression painted on the countenances of the attendant monks and friars. The procession arrived at the chapel of the convent; the sun gleamed for the last time upon the chaplet of the poor novice, as she crossed the fatal threshold, and disap-peared within the building. The throng poured in with cowl, and cross, and minstrelsy; the lover paused for a moment at the door. I could divine the tumult of his feelings; but he mastered them, and entered. There was a long interval—I pictured to myself the scene passing within; the poor novice despoiled of her transient finery, and clothed in the conventual garb; the bridal chaplet taken from her brow, and her beautiful head shorn of its long silken tresses. I heard her murmur the irrevocable vow. I saw her extended on a bier; the death-pall spread over her; the funeral service performed that proclaimed her dead to the world; her sighs were drowned in the deep tones of the organ, and the plaintive requiem of the nuns; the father looked on, unmoved, without a tear; the lover—no—my imagination refused to portray the anguish of the lover—there the picture remained a blank.

After a time the throng again poured forth, and dispersed various ways, to enjoy the light of the sun and mingle with the stirring scenes of life; but the victim, with her bridal chaplet, was no longer there. The door of the convent closed that severed her from the world for ever. I saw the father and the lover issue forth; they were in earnest conversation. The latter was vehement in his gesticulations; I expected some violent termination to my drama; but an angle of a building interfered and closed the scene. My eye afterwards was frequently turned to that convent with painful interest. I remarked late at night a solitary light twinkling from a remote lattice of one of its towers. "There," said I, "the unhappy nun sits weeping in her cell, while perhaps her lover paces the street below in unavailing anguish."

—The officious Mateo interrupted my meditations and destroyed in an instant the cobweb tissue of my fancy. With his usual zeal he had gathered facts concerning the scene, which put my fictions all to flight. The heroine of my romance was neither young nor handsome; she had no lover; she had entered the convent of her own free will, as a respectable asylum, and was one of the most cheerful residents within its walls.

It was some little while before I could forgive the wrong done me by the nun in being thus happy in her cell, in contradiction to all the rules of romance; I diverted my spleen, however, by watching, for a day or two, the pretty coquetries of a dark-eyed brunette, who, from the covert of a balcony shrouded with flowering shrubs and a silken awning, was carrying on a mysterious correspondence with a handsome, dark, well-whiskered cavalier, who lurked frequently in the street beneath her window. Sometimes I saw him at an early hour, stealing forth wrapped to the eyes in a mantle. Sometimes he loitered at a corner, in various disguises, apparently waiting for a private signal to slip into the house. Then there was the tinkling of a guitar at night, and a lantern shifted from place to place in the balcony. I imagined another intrigue like that of Almaviva; but was again disconcerted in all my suppositions.—The supposed lover turned out to be the husband of the lady, and a noted contrabandista; and all his mysterious signs and movements had doubtless some smuggling scheme in view.

—I occasionally amused myself with noting from this balcony the gradual changes of the scenes below, according to the different stages of the day.

Scarce has the gray dawn streaked the sky, and the earliest cock crowed from the cottages of the hill-side, when the suburbs give sign of reviving animation; for the fresh hours of dawning are precious in the summer season in a sultry climate. All are anxious to get the start of the sun, in the business of the day. The muleteer drives forth his loaded train for the journey; the traveller slings his carbine behind his saddle, and mounts his steed at the gate of the hostel; the brown peasant from the country urges forward his loitering beasts, laden with panniers of sunny fruit and fresh dewy vegetables: for already the thrifty housewives are hastening to the market.

The sun is up and sparkles along the valley, tipping the transparent foliage of the groves. The matin bells resound melodiously through the pure bright air, announcing the hour of devotion. The muleteer halts his burdened animals before the chapel, thrusts his staff through his belt behind, and enters with hat in hand, smoothing his coal-black hair, to hear a mass, and put up a prayer for a prosperous wayfaring across the sierra. And now steals forth on fairy foot the gentle Señora, in trim basquiña, with restless fan in hand, and dark eye flashing from beneath the gracefully folded mantilla; she seeks some well-frequented church to offer up her morning orisons; but the nicely-adjusted dress, the dainty shoe and cobweb stocking, the raven tresses exquisitely braided, the fresh plucked rose, gleaming among them like a gem, show that earth divides with Heaven the empire of her thoughts. Keep an eye upon her, careful mother, or virgin aunt, or vigilant duenna, whichever you be, that walk behind!

As the morning advances, the din of labor augments on every side; the streets are thronged with man, and steed, and beast of burden, and there is a hum and murmur, like the surges of the ocean. As the sun ascends to his meridian the hum and bustle gradually decline; at the height of noon there is a pause. The panting city sinks into lassitude, and for several hours there is a general repose. The windows are closed, the curtains drawn; the inhabitants retired into the coolest recesses of their mansions; the full-fed monk snores in his dormitory; the brawny porter lies stretched on the pavement beside his burden; the peasant and the laborer sleep beneath the trees of the Alameda, lulled by the sultry chirping of the locust. The streets are deserted, except by the water-carrier, who refreshes the ear by proclaiming the merits of his sparkling beverage, "colder than the mountain snow (*mas fria que la nieve*)."

As the sun declines, there is again a gradual reviving, and when the vesper bell rings out his sinking knell, all nature seems to rejoice that the tyrant of the day has fallen. Now begins the bustle of enjoyment, when the citizens pour forth to breathe the evening air, and revel away the brief twilight in the walks and gardens of the Darro and Xenil.

As night closes, the capricious scene assumes new features. Light after light gradually twinkles forth; here a taper from a balconied window; there a votive lamp before the image of a Saint. Thus, by degrees, the city emerges from the pervading gloom, and sparkles with scattered lights, like the starry firmament. Now break forth from court and garden, and street and lane, the tinkling of innumerable guitars, and the clicking of castañets; blending, at this lofty height, in a faint but general concert. "Enjoy the moment," is the creed of the gay and amorous Andalusian, and at no time does he practise it more zealously than in the balmy nights of summer, wooing his mistress with the dance, the love ditty, and the passionate serenade.

I was one evening seated in the balcony, enjoying the light

breeze that came rustling along the side of the hill, among the tree-tops, when my humble historiographer Mateo, who was at my elbow, pointed out a spacious house, in an obscure street of the Albaycin, about which he related, as nearly as I can recollect, the following anecdote.

The Adventure of the Mason

THERE WAS once upon a time a poor mason, or bricklayer, in Granada, who kept all the saints' days and holidays, and Saint Monday into the bargain, and yet, with all his devotion, he grew poorer and poorer, and could scarcely earn bread for his numerous family. One night he was roused from his first sleep by a knocking at his door. He opened it, and beheld before him a tall meagre, cadaverous-looking priest.

" 'Hark ye, honest friend!' said the stranger; 'I have observed that you are a good Christian, and one to be trusted; will you undertake a job this very night?'

" 'With all my heart, Señor Padre, on condition that I am paid accordingly.'

" 'That you shall be; but you must suffer yourself to be blindfolded.'

"To this the mason made no objection; so, being hoodwinked, he was led by the priest through various rough lanes and winding passages, until they stopped before the portal of a house. The priest then applied a key, turned a creaking lock, and opened what sounded like a ponderous door. They entered, the door was closed and bolted, and the mason was conducted through an echoing corridor, and a spacious hall, to an interior part of the building. Here the bandage was removed from his eyes, and he found himself in a patio, or court, dimly lighted by a single lamp. In the centre was the dry basin of an old Moorish fountain, under which the priest requested him to form a small vault, bricks and mortar being at hand for the purpose. He accordingly worked all night, but without finishing the job. Just before daybreak the priest put a piece of gold into his hand, and having again blindfolded him, conducted him back to his dwelling.

" 'Are you willing,' said he, 'to return and complete your work?'

" 'Gladly, Señor Padre, provided I am so well paid.'

" 'Well, then, to-morrow at midnight I will call again.'

"He did so, and the vault was completed.

813

" 'Now,' said the priest, 'you must help me to bring forth the bodies that are to be buried in this vault.'

"The poor mason's hair rose on his head at these words: he followed the priest with trembling steps, into a retired chamber of the mansion, expecting to behold some ghastly spectacle of death, but was relieved on perceiving three or four portly jars standing in one corner. They were evidently full of money, and it was with great labor that he and the priest carried them forth and consigned them to their tomb. The vault was then closed, the pavement replaced, and all traces of the work were obliterated. The mason was again hoodwinked and led forth by a route different from that by which he had come. After they had wandered for a long time through a perplexed maze of lanes and alleys, they halted. The priest then put two pieces of gold into his hand: 'Wait here,' said he, 'until you hear the cathedral bell toll for matins. If you presume to uncover your eyes before that time, evil will befall you:' so saying, he departed. The mason waited faithfully, amusing himself by weighing the gold pieces in his hand, and clinking them against each other. The moment the cathedral bell rang its matin peal, he uncovered his eyes, and found himself on the banks of the Xenil; whence he made the best of his way home, and revelled with his family for a whole fortnight on the profits of his two nights' work; after which, he was as poor as ever.

"He continued to work a little, and pray a good deal, and keep saints' days and holidays, from year to year, while his family grew up as gaunt and ragged as a crew of gipsies. As he was seated one evening at the door of his hovel, he was accosted by a rich old curmudgeon, who was noted for owning many houses, and being a griping landlord. The man of money eyed him for a moment from beneath a pair of anxious shagged eyebrows.

" 'I am told, friend, that you are very poor.'

" 'There is no denying the fact, señor—it speaks for itself.'

" 'I presume then, that you will be glad of a job, and will work cheap.'

" 'As cheap, my master, as any mason in Granada.'

" 'That's what I want. I have an old house fallen into decay, which costs me more money than it is worth to keep it in repair, for nobody will live in it; so I must contrive to patch it up and keep it together at as small expense as possible.'

"The mason was accordingly conducted to a large deserted house that seemed going to ruin. Passing through several empty halls and chambers he entered an inner court, where his eye was caught by an old Moorish fountain. He paused for a moment, for a dreaming recollection of the place came over him.

" 'Pray,' said he, 'who occupied this house formerly?'

" 'A pest upon him!' cried the landlord, 'it was an old miserly priest, who cared for nobody but himself. He was said to be immensely rich, and, having no relations, it was thought he would leave all his treasures to the church. He died suddenly, and the priests and friars thronged to take possession of his wealth; but nothing could they find but a few ducats in a leathern purse. The worst luck has fallen on me, for, since his death, the old fellow continues to occupy my house without paying rent, and there is no taking the law of a dead man. The people pretend to hear the clinking of gold all night in the chamber where the old priest slept, as if he were counting over his money, and sometimes a groaning and moaning about the court. Whether true or false, these stories have brought a bad name on my house, and not a tenant will remain in it.'

" 'Enough,' said the mason sturdily: 'let me live in your house rent-free until some better tenant present, and I will engage to put it in repair, and to quiet the troubled spirit that disturbs it. I am a good Christian and a poor man, and am not to be daunted by the Devil himself, even though he should come in the shape of a big bag of money!'

"The offer of the honest mason was gladly accepted; he moved with his family into the house, and fulfilled all his engagements. By little and little he restored it to its former state; the clinking of gold was no more heard at night in the chamber of the defunct priest, but began to be heard by day in the pocket of the living mason. In a word, he increased rapidly in wealth, to the admiration of all his neighbors, and became one of the richest men in Granada: he gave large sums to the church, by way, no doubt, of satisfying his conscience, and never revealed the secret of the vault until on his deathbed to his son and heir."

The Court of Lions

THE PECULIAR CHARM of this old dreamy palace, is its power of calling up vague reveries and picturings of the past, and thus clothing naked realities with the illusions of the memory and the imagination. As I delight to walk in these "vain shadows," I am prone to seek those parts of the Alhambra which are most favorable to this phantasmagoria of the mind; and none are more so than the Court of Lions, and its surrounding halls. Here the hand of time has fallen the lightest, and the traces of Moorish elegance and splendor exist in almost their original brilliancy. Earthquakes have shaken the foundations of this pile, and rent its rudest towers; yet see! not one of those slender columns has been displaced, not an arch of that light and fragile colonnade given way, and all the fairy fretwork of these domes, apparently as unsubstantial as the crystal fabrics of a morning's frost, exist after the lapse of centuries, almost as fresh as if from the hand of the Moslem artist. I write in the midst of these mementos of the past, in the fresh hour of early morning, in the fated Hall of the Abencerrages. The blood-stained fountain, the legendary monument of their massacre, is before me; the lofty jet almost casts its dew upon my paper. How difficult to reconcile the ancient tale of violence and blood with the gentle and peaceful scene around! Every thing here appears calculated to inspire kind and happy feelings, for every thing is delicate and beautiful. The very light falls tenderly from above, through the lantern of a dome tinted and wrought as if by fairy hands. Through the ample and fretted arch of the portal I behold the Court of Lions, with brilliant sunshine gleaming along its colonnades, and sparkling in its fountains. The lively swallow dives into the court, and, rising with a surge, darts away twittering over the roofs; the busy bee toils humming among the flower beds, and painted butterflies hover from plant to plant, and flutter up and sport with each other in the sunny air. It needs but a slight exertion of the fancy to picture some pensive beauty of the harem, loitering in these secluded haunts of Oriental luxury.

He, however, who would behold this scene under an aspect more in unison with its fortunes, let him come when the shadows of evening temper the brightness of the court, and throw a gloom into the surrounding halls. Then nothing can be more serenely melancholy, or more in harmony with the tale of departed grandeur.

At such times I am apt to seek the Hall of Justice, whose deep shadowy arcades extend across the upper end of the court. Here was performed, in presence of Ferdinand and Isabella, and their triumphant court, the pompous ceremonial of high mass, on taking possession of the Alhambra. The very cross is still to be seen upon the wall, where the altar was erected, and where officiated the Grand Cardinal of Spain, and others of the highest religious dignitaries of the land. I picture to myself the scene when this place was filled with the conquering host, that mixture of mitred prelate and shaven monk, and steel-clad knight and silken courtier; when crosses and crosiers and religious standards were mingled with proud armorial ensigns and the banners of the haughty chiefs of Spain, and flaunted in triumph through these Moslem halls. I picture to myself Columbus, the future discoverer of a world, taking his modest stand in a remote corner, the humble and neglected spectator of the pageant. I see in imagination the Catholic sovereigns prostrating themselves before the altar, and pouring forth thanks for their victory; while the vaults resound with sacred minstrelsy, and the deep-toned Te Deum.

The transient illusion is over—the pageant melts from the fancy—monarch, priest, and warrior, return into oblivion, with the poor Moslems over whom they exulted. The hall of their triumph is waste and desolate. The bat flits about its twilight vault, and the owl hoots from the neighboring tower of Comares.

Entering the Court of the Lions a few evenings since, I was almost startled at beholding a turbaned Moor quietly seated near the fountain. For a moment one of the fictions of the place seemed realized: an enchanted Moor had broken the spell of centuries, and become visible. He proved, however, to be a mere ordinary mortal; a native of Tetuan in Barbary, who had a shop in the Zacatin of Granada, where he sold rhubarb, trinkets, and perfumes. As he spoke Spanish fluently,

I was enabled to hold conversation with him, and found him shrewd and intelligent. He told me that he came up the hill occasionally in the summer, to pass a part of the day in the Alhambra, which reminded him of the old palaces in Barbary, being built and adorned in similar style, though with more magnificence.

As we walked about the palace, he pointed out several of the Arabic inscriptions as possessing much poetic beauty.

"Ah, señor," said he, "when the Moors held Granada, they were a gayer people than they are now-a-days. They thought only of love, music, and poetry. They made stanzas upon every occasion, and set them all to music. He who could make the best verses, and she who had the most tuneful voice, might be sure of favor and preferment. In those days, if any one asked for bread, the reply was, make me a couplet; and the poorest beggar, if he begged in rhyme, would often be rewarded with a piece of gold."

"And is the popular feeling for poetry," said I, "entirely lost among you?"

"By no means, señor; the people of Barbary, even those of the lower classes, still make couplets, and good ones too, as in old times; but talent is not rewarded as it was then; the rich prefer the jingle of their gold to the sound of poetry or music."

As he was talking, his eye caught one of the inscriptions which foretold perpetuity to the power and glory of the Moslem monarchs, the masters of this pile. He shook his head, and shrugged his shoulders, as he interpreted it. "Such might have been the case," said he; "the Moslems might still have been reigning in the Alhambra, had not Boabdil been a traitor, and given up his capital to the Christians. The Spanish monarchs would never have been able to conquer it by open force."

I endeavored to vindicate the memory of the unlucky Boabdil from this aspersion, and to show that the dissensions which led to the downfall of the Moorish throne, originated in the cruelty of his tiger-hearted father; but the Moor would admit of no palliation.

"Muley Abul Hassan," said he, "might have been cruel; but he was brave, vigilant, and patriotic. Had he been properly

seconded, Granada would still have been ours; but his son
Boabdil thwarted his plans, crippled his power, sowed treason
in his palace, and dissension in his camp. May the curse of
God light upon him for his treachery!" With these words the
Moor left the Alhambra.

The indignation of my turbaned companion agrees with an
anecdote related by a friend, who, in the course of a tour in
Barbary, had an interview with the Pacha of Tetuan. The
Moorish governor was particular in his inquiries about Spain,
and especially concerning the favored region of Andalusia, the
delights of Granada, and the remains of its royal palace. The
replies awakened all those fond recollections, so deeply cherished by the Moors, of the power and splendor of their ancient empire in Spain. Turning to his Moslem attendants, the
Pacha stroked his beard, and broke forth in passionate lamentations, that such a sceptre should have fallen from the sway
of true believers. He consoled himself, however, with the persuasion, that the power and prosperity of the Spanish nation
were on the decline; that a time would come when the Moors
would reconquer their rightful domains; and that the day was
perhaps not far distant, when Mohammedan worship would
again be offered up in the Mosque of Cordova, and a Mohammedan prince sit on his throne in the Alhambra.

Such is the general aspiration and belief among the Moors
of Barbary; who consider Spain, or Andaluz, as it was anciently called, their rightful heritage, of which they have been
despoiled by treachery and violence. These ideas are fostered
and perpetuated by the descendants of the exiled Moors of
Granada, scattered among the cities of Barbary. Several of
these reside in Tetuan, preserving their ancient names, such as
Paez and Medina, and refraining from intermarriage with any
families who cannot claim the same high origin. Their
vaunted lineage is regarded with a degree of popular deference, rarely shown in Mohammedan communities to any
hereditary distinction, except in the royal line.

These families, it is said, continue to sigh after the terrestrial paradise of their ancestors, and to put up prayers in their
mosques on Fridays, imploring Allah to hasten the time when
Granada shall be restored to the faithful: an event to which
they look forward as fondly and confidently as did the Chris-

tian crusaders to the recovery of the Holy Sepulchre. Nay, it is added, that some of them retain the ancient maps and deeds of the estates and gardens of their ancestors at Granada, and even the keys of the houses; holding them as evidences of their hereditary claims, to be produced at the anticipated day of restoration.

My conversation with the Moor set me to musing on the fate of Boabdil. Never was surname more applicable than that bestowed upon him by his subjects of el Zogoybi, or the Unlucky. His misfortunes began almost in his cradle, and ceased not even with his death. If ever he cherished the desire of leaving an honorable name on the historic page, how cruelly has he been defrauded of his hopes. Who is there that has turned the least attention to the romantic history of the Moorish domination in Spain, without kindling with indignation at the alleged atrocities of Boabdil? Who has not been touched with the woes of his lovely and gentle queen, subjected by him to a trial of life and death, on a false charge of infidelity? Who has not been shocked by his alleged murder of his sister and her two children, in a transport of passion? Who has not felt his blood boil, at the inhuman massacre of the gallant Abencerrages, thirty-six of whom, it is affirmed, he ordered to be beheaded in the Court of Lions? All these charges have been reiterated in various forms; they have passed into ballads, dramas, and romances, until they have taken too thorough possession of the public mind to be eradicated. There is not a foreigner of education that visits the Alhambra, but asks for the fountain where the Abencerrages were beheaded; and gazes with horror at the grated gallery where the queen is said to have been confined; not a peasant of the Vega or the Sierra, but sings the story in rude couplets, to the accompaniment of his guitar, while his hearers learn to execrate the very name of Boabdil.

Never, however, was name more foully and unjustly slandered. I have examined all the authentic chronicles and letters written by Spanish authors, contemporary with Boabdil; some of whom were in the confidence of the Catholic sovereigns, and actually present in the camp throughout the war. I have examined all the Arabian authorities I could get access to, through the medium of translation, and have found nothing to justify these dark and hateful accusations. The most of these tales may be traced to a work commonly called "The Civil Wars of Granada," containing a pretended history of the feuds of the Zegries and Abencerrages, during the last struggle of the Moorish empire. The work appeared originally in Spanish, and professed to be translated from the Arabic by one Gines Perez de Hita, an inhabitant of Murcia. It has since passed into various languages, and Florian has taken from it much of the fable of his Gonsalvo of Cordova; it has thus, in a great measure, usurped the authority of real history, and is currently believed by the people, and especially the peasantry of Granada. The whole of it, however, is a mass of fiction, mingled with a few disfigured truths, which give it an air of veracity. It bears internal evidence of its falsity; the manners and customs of the Moors being extravagantly misrepresented in it, and scenes depicted totally incompatible with their habits and their faith, and which never could have been recorded by a Mahometan writer.

I confess there seems to me something almost criminal, in the wilful perversions of this work: great latitude is undoubtedly to be allowed to romantic fiction, but there are limits which it must not pass; and the names of the distinguished dead, which belong to history, are no more to be calumniated than those of the illustrious living. One would have thought, too, that the unfortunate Boabdil had suffered enough for his justifiable hostility to the Spaniards by being stripped of his kingdom, without having his name thus wantonly traduced, and rendered a by-word and a theme of infamy in his native land, and in the very mansion of his fathers!

If the reader is sufficiently interested in these questions to tolerate a little historical detail, the following facts, gleaned from what appear to be authentic sources, and tracing the fortunes of the Abencerrages, may serve to exculpate the unfortunate Boabdil from the perfidious massacre of that illustrious line so shamelessly charged to him. It will also serve to throw a proper light upon the alleged accusation and imprisonment of his queen.

The Abencerrages

A GRAND LINE of distinction existed among the Moslems of Spain, between those of Oriental origin and those from Western Africa. Among the former the Arabs considered themselves the purest race, as being descended from the countrymen of the Prophet, who first raised the standard of Islam; among the latter, the most warlike and powerful were the Berber tribes from Mount Atlas and the deserts of Sahara, commonly known as Moors, who subdued the tribes of the sea-coast, founded the city of Morocco, and for a long time desputed with the oriental races the control of Moslem Spain.

Among the oriental races the Abencerrages held a distinguished rank, priding themselves on a pure Arab descent from the Beni Seraj, one of the tribes who were Ansares or Companions of the Prophet. The Abencerrages flourished for a time at Cordova; but probably repaired to Granada after the downfall of the Western Caliphat; it was there they attained their historical and romantic celebrity, being foremost among the splendid chivalry which graced the court of the Alhambra.

Their highest and most dangerous prosperity was during the precarious reign of Muhamed Nasar, surnamed El Hayzari, or the Left-handed. That ill-starred monarch, when he ascended the throne in 1423, lavished his favors upon this gallant line, making the head of the tribe, Jusef Aben Zeragh, his vizier, or prime minister, and advancing his relatives and friends to the most distinguished posts about the court. This gave great offence to other tribes, and caused intrigues among their chiefs. Muhamed lost popularity also by his manners. He was vain, inconsiderate and haughty; disdained to mingle among his subjects; forbade those jousts and tournaments, the delight of high and low, and passed his time in the luxurious retirement of the Alhambra. The consequence was a popular insurrection; the palace was stormed; the king escaped through the gardens; fled to the sea-coast, crossed in disguise to Africa, and took refuge with his kinsman, the sovereign of Tunis.

Muhamed el Zaguer, cousin of the fugitive monarch, took possession of the vacant throne. He pursued a different course from his predecessor. He not only gave fêtes and tourneys, but entered the lists himself, in grand and sumptuous array; he distinguished himself in managing his horse, in tilting, riding at the ring, and other chivalrous exercises; feasted with his cavaliers, and made them magnificent presents.

Those who had been in favor with his predecessor, now experienced a reverse; he manifested such hostility to them that more than five hundred of the principal cavaliers left the city. Jusef Aben Zeragh, with forty of the Abencerrages, abandoned Granada in the night, and sought the court of Juan the king of Castile. Moved by their representations, that young and generous monarch wrote letters to the sovereign of Tunis, inviting him to assist in punishing the usurper and restoring the exiled king to his throne. The faithful and indefatigable vizier accompanied the bearer of these letters to Tunis, where he rejoined his exiled sovereign. The letters were successful. Muhamed el Hayzari landed in Andalusia with five hundred African horse, and was joined by the Abencerrages and others of his adherents and by his Christian allies; wherever he appeared the people submitted to him; troops sent against him deserted to his standard; Granada was recovered without a blow; the usurper retreated to the Alhambra, but was beheaded by his own soldiers (1428), after reigning between two and three years.

El Hayzari, once more on the throne, heaped honors on the loyal vizier, through whose faithful services he had been restored, and once more the line of the Abencerrages basked in the sunshine of royal favor. El Hayzari sent ambassadors to King Juan, thanking him for his aid, and proposing a perpetual league of amity. The king of Castile required homage and yearly tribute. These the left-handed monarch refused, supposing the youthful king too much engaged in civil war to enforce his claims. Again the kingdom of Granada was harassed by invasions, and its Vega laid waste. Various battles took place with various success. But El Hayzari's greatest danger was near at home. There was at that time in Granada a cavalier, Don Pedro Venegas by name, a Moslem by faith, but Christian by descent, whose early history borders on romance. He was of the noble house of Luque, but captured when a child, eight years of age, by Cid Yahia Alnayar, prince of Almeria,* who adopted him as his son, educated him in the Moslem faith, and brought him up among his children, the Celtimerian princes, a proud family, descended in direct line from Aben Hud, one of the early Granadian kings. A mutual attachment sprang up between Don Pedro and the princess Cetimerien, a daughter of Cid Yahia, famous for her beauty, and whose name is perpetuated by the ruins of her palace in Granada; still bearing traces of Moorish elegance and luxury. In process of time they were married; and thus a scion of the Spanish house of Luque became engrafted on the royal stock of Aben Hud.

Such is the early story of Don Pedro Venegas, who at the time of which we treat was a man mature in years, and of an active, ambitious spirit. He appears to have been the soul of a conspiracy set on foot about this time, to topple Muhamed the Left-handed from his unsteady throne, and elevate in his place Yusef Aben Alhamar, the eldest of the Celtimerian princes. The aid of the king of Castile was to be secured, and Don Pedro proceeded on a secret embassy to Cordova for the purpose. He informed King Juan of the extent of the conspiracy; that Yusef Aben Alhamar could bring a large force to his standard as soon as he should appear in the Vega, and would acknowledge himself his vassal, if with his aid he should attain the crown. The aid was promised, and Don Pedro hastened back to Granada with the tidings. The conspirators now left the city, a few at a time, under various pretexts; and when King Juan passed the frontier, Yusef Aben Alhamar brought eight thousand men to his standard, and kissed his hand in token of allegiance.

It is needless to recount the various battles by which the kingdom was desolated, and the various intrigues by which one half of it was roused to rebellion. The Abencerrages stood by the failing fortunes of Muhamed throughout the struggle; their last stand was at Loxa, where their chief, the vizier Yusef Aben Zeragh, fell bravely fighting, and many of

*ALCANTARA, *Hist. Granad.*, O. 3, p. 226, note.

their noblest cavaliers were slain: in fact, in that disastrous war the fortunes of the family were nearly wrecked.

Again, the ill-starred Muhamed was driven from his throne, and took refuge in Malaga, the Alcayde of which still remained true to him.

Yusef Aben Alhamar, commonly known as Yusef II., entered Granada in triumph on the first of January, 1432, but he found it a melancholy city, where half of the inhabitants were in mourning. Not a noble family but had lost some member; and in the slaughter of the Abencerrages at Loxa, had fallen some of the brightest of the chivalry.

The royal pageant passed through silent streets, and the barren homage of a court in the halls of the Alhambra ill supplied the want of sincere and popular devotion. Yusef Aben Alhamar felt the insecurity of his position. The deposed monarch was at hand in Malaga; the sovereign of Tunis espoused his cause, and pleaded with the Christian monarchs in his favor; above all, Yusef felt his own unpopularity in Granada; previous fatigues had impaired his health, a profound melancholy settled upon him, and in the course of six months he sank into the grave.

At the news of his death, Muhamed the Left-handed hastened from Malaga, and again was placed on the throne. From the wrecks of the Abencerrages he chose as vizier Abdelbar, one of the worthiest of that magnanimous line. Through his advice he restrained his vindictive feelings and adopted a conciliatory policy. He pardoned most of his enemies. Yusef, the defunct usurper, had left three children. His estates were apportioned among them. Aben Celim, the oldest son, was confirmed in the title of Prince of Almeria and Lord of Marchena in the Alpuxarras. Ahmed, the youngest, was made Señor of Luchar; and Equivila, the daughter, received rich patrimonial lands in the fertile Vega, and various houses and shops in the Zacatin of Granada. The vizier Abdelbar counselled the king, moreover, to secure the adherence of the family by matrimonial connections. An aunt of Muhamed was accordingly given in marriage to Aben Celim, while the prince Nasar, younger brother of the deceased usurper, received the hand of the beautiful Lindaraxa, daughter of Muhamed's faithful adherent, the alcayde of Malaga. This was the Lindaraxa whose name still designates one of the gardens of the Alhambra.

Don Pedro de Venegas alone, the husband of the princess Cetimerien, received no favor. He was considered as having produced the late troubles by his intrigues. The Abencerrages charged him with the reverses of their family and the deaths of so many of their bravest cavaliers. The king never spoke of him but by the opprobrious appellation of the Tornadizo, or Renegade. Finding himself in danger of arrest and punishment, he took leave of his wife, the princess, his two sons, Abul Cacem and Reduan, and his daughter, Cetimerien, and fled to Jaen. There, like his brother-in-law, the usurper, he expiated his intrigues and irregular ambition by profound humiliation and melancholy, and died in 1434 a penitent, because a disappointed man.*

Muhamed el Hayzari was doomed to further reverses. He had two nephews, Aben Osmyn, surnamed el Anaf, or the Lame, and Aben Ismael. The former, who was of an ambitious spirit, resided in Almeria; the latter in Granada, where he had many friends. He was on the point of espousing a beautiful girl, when his royal uncle interfered and gave her to one of his favorites. Enraged at this despotic act, the prince Aben Ismael took horse and weapons and sallied from Granada for the frontier followed by numerous cavaliers. The affair gave general disgust, especially to the Abencerrages who were attached to the prince. No sooner did tidings reach Aben Osmyn of the public discontent than his ambition was aroused. Throwing himself suddenly into Granada, he raised a popular tumult, surprised his uncle in the Alhambra, compelled him to abdicate, and proclaimed himself king. This occurred in September, 1445. The Abencerrages now gave up the fortunes of the left-handed king as hopeless, and himself as incompetent to rule. Led by their kinsman, the vizier Abdelbar, and accompanied by many other cavaliers, they abandoned the court and took post in Montefrio. Thence Abdelbar wrote to Prince Aben Ismael, who had taken refuge

---

*SALAZAR Y CASTRO, *Hist. Genealog. de la Casa de Lara*, lib. v., c. 12, cited by Alcantara in his *Hist. Granad.*

in Castile, inviting him to the camp, offering to support his pretensions to the throne, and advising him to leave Castile secretly, lest his departure should be opposed by King Juan II. The prince, however, confiding in the generosity of the Castilian monarch, told him frankly the whole matter. He was not mistaken. King Juan not merely gave him permission to depart, but promised him aid, and gave him letters to that effect to his commanders on the frontiers. Aben Ismael departed with a brilliant escort, arrived in safety at Montefrio, and was proclaimed king of Granada by Abdelbar and his partisans, the most important of whom were the Abencerrages. A long course of civil wars ensued between the two cousins, rivals for the throne. Aben Osmyn was aided by the kings of Navarre and Aragon, while Juan II, at war with his rebellious subjects, could give little assistance to Aben Ismael.

Thus for several years the country was torn by internal strife and desolated by foreign inroads, so that scarce a field but was stained with blood. Aben Osmyn was brave, and often signalized himself in arms; but he was cruel and despotic, and ruled with an iron hand. He offended the nobles by his caprices, and the populace by his tyranny, while his rival cousin conciliated all hearts by his benignity. Hence there were continual desertions from Granada to the fortified camp at Montefrio, and the party of Aben Ismael was constantly gaining strength. At length the king of Castile, having made peace with the kings of Aragon and Navarre, was enabled to send a choice body of troops to the assistance of Aben Ismael. The latter now left his trenches in Montefrio, and took the field. The combined forces marched upon Granada. Aben Osmyn sallied forth to the encounter. A bloody battle ensued, in which both of the rival cousins fought with heroic valor. Aben Osmyn was defeated and driven back to his gates. He summoned the inhabitants to arms, but few answered to his call; his cruelty had alienated all hearts. Seeing his fortunes at an end, he determined to close his career by a signal act of vengeance. Shutting himself up in the Alhambra, he summoned thither a number of the principal cavaliers whom he suspected of disloyalty. As they entered, they were one by one put to death. This is supposed by some to be the massacre which gave its fatal name to the hall of the Abencerrages.

Having perpetrated this atrocious act of vengeance, and hearing by the shouts of the populace that Aben Ismael was already proclaimed king in the city, he escaped with his satellites by the Cerro del Sol and the valley of the Darro to the Alpuxarra mountains; where he and his followers led a kind of robber life, laying villages and roads under contribution.

Aben Ismael II, who thus attained the throne in 1454, secured the friendship of King Juan II by acts of homage and magnificent presents. He gave liberal rewards to those who had been faithful to him, and consoled the families of those who had fallen in his cause. During his reign, the Abencerrages were again among the most favored of the brilliant chivalry that graced his court. Aben Ismael, however, was not of a warlike spirit; his reign was distinguished rather by works of public utility, the ruins of some of which are still to be seen on the Cerro del Sol.

In the same year of 1454 Juan II died, and was succeeded by Henry IV of Castile, surnamed the Impotent. Aben Ismael neglected to renew the league of amity with him which had existed with his predecessor, as he found it to be unpopular with the people of Granada. King Henry resented the omission, and, under pretext of arrears of tribute, made repeated forays into the kingdom of Granada. He gave countenance also to Aben Osmyn and his robber hordes, and took some of them into pay; but his proud cavaliers refused to associate with infidel outlaws, and determined to seize Aben Osmyn; who, however, made his escape, first to Seville, and thence to Castile.

In the year 1456, on the occasion of a great foray into the Vega by the Christians, Aben Ismael, to secure a peace, agreed to pay the king of Castile a certain tribute annually, and at the same time to liberate six hundred Christian captives; or, should the number of captives fall short, to make it up in Moorish hostages. Aben Ismael fulfilled the rigorous terms of the treaty, and reigned for a number of years with more tranquillity than usually fell to the lot of the monarchs of that belligerent kingdom. Granada enjoyed a great state of prosperity during his reign, and was the seat of festivity and splendor. His sultana was a daughter of Cid Hiaya Abraham Alnayar, prince of Almeria; and he had by her two sons, Abul

Hassan, and Abi Abdallah, surnamed El Zagal, the father and uncle of Boabdil. We approach now the eventful period signalized by the conquest of Granada.

Muley Abul Hassan succeeded to the throne on the death of his father in 1465. One of his first acts was to refuse payment of the degrading tribute exacted by the Castilian monarch. His refusal was one of the causes of the subsequent disastrous war. I confine myself, however, to facts connected with the fortunes of the Abencerrages and the charges advanced against Boabdil.

The reader will recollect that Don Pedro Venegas, surnamed El Tornadizo, when he fled from Granada in 1433, left behind him two sons, Abul Cacim and Reduan, and a daughter, Cetimerien. They always enjoyed a distinguished rank in Granada, from their royal descent by the mother's side; and from being connected, through the princes of Almeria, with the last and the present king. The sons had distinguished themselves by their talents and bravery, and the daughter Cetimerien was married to Cid Hiaya, grandson of King Jusef and brother-in-law of El Zagal. Thus powerfully connected, it is not surprising to find Abul Cacim Venegas advanced to the post of vizier of Muley Abul Hassan, and Reduan Venegas one of his most favored generals. Their rise was regarded with an evil eye by the Abencerrages, who remembered the disasters brought upon their family, and the deaths of so many of their line, in the war fomented by the intrigues of Don Pedro, in the days of Jusef Aben Alhamar. A feud had existed ever since between the Abencerrages and the house of Venegas. It was soon to be aggravated by a formidable schism which took place in the royal harem.

Muley Abul Hassan, in his youthful days had married his cousin, the princess Ayxa la Horra, daughter of his uncle, the ill-starred sultan, Muhamed the Left-handed;* by her he had two sons, the eldest of whom was Boabdil, heir presumptive to the throne. Unfortunately at an advanced age he took another wife, Isabella de Solis, a young and beautiful Christian captive; better known by her Moorish appellation of Zoraya; by her he had also two sons. Two factions were produced in

*AL MAKKARI, B. viii. c. 7.

the palace by the rivalry of the sultanas, who were each anxious to secure for their children the succession to the throne. Zoraya was supported by the vizier Abul Cacim Venegas, his brother Reduan Venegas, and their numerous connections, partly through sympathy with her as being, like themselves, of Christian lineage, and partly because they saw she was the favorite of the doting monarch.

The Abencerrages, on the contrary, rallied round the sultana Ayxa; partly through hereditary opposition to the family of Venegas, but chiefly, no doubt, through a strong feeling of loyalty to her as daughter of Muhamed Alhayzari, the ancient benefactor of their line.

The dissensions of the palace went on increasing. Intrigues of all kinds took place, as is usual in royal palaces. Suspicions were artfully instilled in the mind of Muley Abul Hassan that Ayxa was engaged in a plot to depose him and put her son Boabdil on the throne. In his first transports of rage he confined them both in the tower of Comares, threatening the life of Boabdil. At dead of night the anxious mother lowered her son from a window of the tower by the scarfs of herself and her female attendants; and some of her adherents, who were in waiting with swift horses, bore him away to the Alpuxarras. It is this imprisonment of the sultana Ayxa which possibly gave rise to the fable of the queen of Boabdil being confined by him in a tower to be tried for her life. No other shadow of a ground exists for it, and here we find the tyrant jailer was his father, and the captive sultana, his mother.

The massacre of the Abencerrages in the halls of the Alhambra is placed by some about this time, and attributed also to Muley Abul Hassan, on suspicion of their being concerned in the conspiracy. The sacrifice of a number of the cavaliers of that line is said to have been suggested by the vizier Abul Cacim Venegas, as a means of striking terror into the rest.* If such were really the case, the barbarous measure proved abortive. The Abencerrages continued intrepid, as they were loyal, in their adherence to the cause of Ayxa and her son Boabdil, throughout the war which ensued, while the Venegas were

*ALCANTARA, *Hist. Granad.*, c. 17. See also AL MAKKARI, *Hist. Mohamd. Dynasties*, B. viii. c. 7, with the Commentaries of Don Pascual de Guyangos.

ever foremost in the ranks of Muley Abul Hassan and El Zagal. The ultimate fortunes of these rival families is worthy of note. The Venegas, in the last struggle of Granada, were among those who submitted to the conquerors, renounced the Moslem creed, returned to the faith from which their ancestors had apostatized, were rewarded with offices and estates, intermarried with Spanish families, and have left posterity among the nobles of the land. The Abencerrages remained true to their faith, true to their king, true to their desperate cause, and went down with the foundering wreck of Moslem domination, leaving nothing behind them but a gallant and romantic name in history.

In this historical outline, I trust I have shown enough to put the fable concerning Boabdil and the Abencerrages in a true light. The story of the accusation of his queen, and his cruelty to his sister, are equally void of foundation. In his domestic relations he appears to have been kind and affectionate. History gives him but one wife, Morayma, the daughter of the veteran alcayde of Loxa, old Aliatar, famous in song and story for his exploits in border warfare; and who fell in that disastrous foray into the Christian lands in which Boabdil was taken prisoner. Morayma was true to Boabdil throughout all his vicissitudes. When he was dethroned by the Castilian monarchs, she retired with him to the petty domain allotted him in the valleys of the Alpuxarras. It was only when (dispossessed of this by the jealous precautions and subtle chicanery of Ferdinand, and elbowed, as it were, out of his native land,) he was preparing to embark for Africa, that her health and spirits, exhausted by anxiety and long suffering, gave way, and she fell into a lingering illness, aggravated by corroding melancholy. Boabdil was constant and affectionate to her to the last; the sailing of the ships was delayed for several weeks, to the great annoyance of the suspicious Ferdinand. At length Morayma sank into the grave, evidently the victim of a broken heart, and the event was reported to Ferdinand by his agent, as one propitious to his purposes, removing the only obstacle to the embarkation of Boabdil.*

*For the authorities for these latter facts, see the Appendix to the author's revised edition of the Conquest of Granada.

Mementos of Boabdil

WHILE MY MIND was still warm with the subject of the unfortunate Boabdil, I set forth to trace the mementos of him still existing in this scene of his sovereignty and misfortunes. In the Tower of Comares, immediately under the Hall of Ambassadors, are two vaulted rooms, separated by a narrow passage; these are said to have been the prisons of himself and his mother, the virtuous Ayxa la Horra; indeed, no other part of the tower would have served for the purpose. The external walls of these chambers are of prodigious thickness, pierced with small windows secured by iron bars. A narrow stone gallery, with a low parapet, extends along three sides of the tower just below the windows, but at a considerable height from the ground. From this gallery, it is presumed, the queen lowered her son with the scarfs of herself and her female attendants during the darkness of the night to the hill-side, where some of his faithful adherents waited with fleet steeds to bear him to the mountains.

Between three and four hundred years have elapsed, yet this scene of the drama remains almost unchanged. As I paced the gallery, my imagination pictured the anxious queen leaning over the parapet; listening, with the throbbings of a mother's heart, to the last echoes of the horses' hoofs as her son scoured along the narrow valley of the Darro.

I next sought the gate by which Boabdil made his last exit from the Alhambra, when about to surrender his capital and kingdom. With the melancholy caprice of a broken spirit, or perhaps with some superstitious feeling, he requested of the Catholic monarchs that no one afterwards might be permitted to pass through it. His prayer, according to ancient chronicles, was complied with, through the sympathy of Isabella, and the gate was walled up.*

*Ay una puerta en la Alhambra por la qual salio Chica Rey de los Moros, quando si rindio prisionero al Rey de España D. Fernando, y le entregó la ciudad con el castillo. Pidio esta principe como por merced, y en memoria de tan importante conquista, al que quedasse siempre cerrada esta puerta. Consintio en allo el Rey Fernando, y des de aquel tiempo no solamente no se

I inquired for some time in vain for such a portal; at length my humble attendant, Mateo Ximenes, said it must be one closed up with stones, which, according to what he had heard from his father and grandfather, was the gateway by which King Chico had left the fortress. There was a mystery about it, and it had never been opened within the memory of the oldest inhabitant.

He conducted me to the spot. The gateway is in the centre of what was once an immense pile, called the Tower of the Seven Floors (*la Torre de los siete suelos*). It is famous in the neighborhood as the scene of strange apparitions and Moorish enchantments. According to Swinburne the traveller, it was originally the great gate of entrance. The antiquaries of Granada pronounce it the entrance to that quarter of the royal residence where the king's body-guards were stationed. It therefore might well form an immediate entrance and exit to the palace; while the grand Gate of Justice served as the entrance of state to the fortress. When Boabdil sallied by this gate to descend to the Vega, where he was to surrender the keys of the city to the Spanish sovereigns, he left his vizier Aben Comixa to receive, at the Gate of Justice, the detachment from the Christian army and the officers to whom the fortress was to be given up.*

The once redoubtable Tower of the Seven Floors is now a mere wreck, having been blown up with gunpowder by the French, when they abandoned the fortress. Great masses of the wall lie scattered about, buried in luxuriant herbage, or overshadowed by vines and fig-trees. The arch of the gateway, though rent by the shock, still remains; but the last wish of poor Boabdil has again, though unintentionally, been fulfilled, for the portal has been closed up by loose stones gathered from the ruins, and remains impassable.

Mounting my horse, I followed up the route of the

---

abrio la puerta sino tambien se construyo junto à ella fuerte bastion. — Mo-RERI's *Historical Dictionary*, Spanish Edition, Vol. i. p. 372.

*The minor details of the surrender of Granada have been stated in different ways even by eye-witnesses. The author, in his revised edition of the Conquest, has endeavored to adjust them according to the latest and apparently best authorities.

Moslem monarch from this place of his exit. Crossing the hill of Los Martyros, and keeping along the garden wall of a convent bearing the same name, I descended a rugged ravine beset by thickets of aloes and Indian figs, and lined with caves and hovels swarming with gipsies. The descent was so steep and broken that I was fain to alight and lead my horse. By this *via dolorosa* poor Boabdil took his sad departure to avoid passing through the city; partly, perhaps, through unwillingness that its inhabitants should behold his humiliation; but chiefly, in all probability, lest it might cause some popular agitation. For the last reason, undoubtedly, the detachment sent to take possession of the fortress ascended by the same route.

Emerging from this rough ravine, so full of melancholy associations, and passing by the *puerta de los molinos* (the gate of the mills), I issued forth upon the public promenade called the Prado; and pursuing the course of the Xenil, arrived at a small chapel, once a mosque, now the Hermitage of San Sebastian. Here, according to tradition, Boabdil surrendered the keys of Granada to King Ferdinand. I rode slowly thence across the Vega to a village where the family and household of the unhappy king awaited him, for he had sent them forward on the preceding night from the Alhambra, that his mother and wife might not participate in his personal humiliation, or be exposed to the gaze of the conquerors. Following on in the route of the melancholy band of royal exiles, I arrived at the foot of a chain of barren and dreary heights, forming the skirt of the Alpuxarra mountains. From the summit of one of these the unfortunate Boabdil took his last look at Granada; it bears a name expressive of his sorrows, *La Cuesta de las Lagrimas* (the hill of tears). Beyond it, a sandy road winds across a rugged cheerless waste, doubly dismal to the unhappy monarch, as it led to exile.

I spurred my horse to the summit of a rock, where Boabdil uttered his last sorrowful exclamation, as he turned his eyes from taking their farewell gaze: it is still denominated *el ultimo suspiro del Moro* (the last sigh of the Moor). Who can wonder at his anguish at being expelled from such a kingdom and such an abode? With the Alhambra he seemed to be yielding up all the honors of his line, and all the glories and delights of life.

It was here, too, that his affliction was embittered by the reproach of his mother, Ayxa, who had so often assisted him in times of peril, and had vainly sought to instil into him her own resolute spirit. "You do well," said she, "to weep as a woman over what you could not defend as a man;" a speech savoring more of the pride of the princess than the tenderness of the mother.

When this anecdote was related to Charles V. by bishop Guevara, the emperor joined in the expression of scorn at the weakness of the wavering Boabdil. "Had I been he, or he been I," said the haughty potentate, "I would rather have made this Alhambra my sepulchre than have lived without a kingdom in the Alpuxarra." How easy it is for those in power and prosperity to preach heroism to the vanquished! how little can they understand that life itself may rise in value with the unfortunate, when nought but life remains!

Slowly descending the "Hill of Tears," I let my horse take his own loitering gait back to Granada, while I turned the story of the unfortunate Boabdil over in my mind. In summing up the particulars I found the balance inclining in his favor. Throughout the whole of his brief, turbulent, and disastrous reign, he gives evidence of a mild and amiable character. He, in the first instance, won the hearts of his people by his affable and gracious manners; he was always placable, and never inflicted any severity of punishment upon those who occasionally rebelled against him. He was personally brave; but wanted moral courage; and, in times of difficulty and perplexity, was wavering and irresolute. This feebleness of spirit hastened his downfall, while it deprived him of that heroic grace which would have given grandeur and dignity to his fate, and rendered him worthy of closing the splendid drama of the Moslem domination in Spain.

Public Fêtes of Granada

M Y DEVOTED SQUIRE and whilom ragged cicerone Mateo Ximenes, had a poor-devil passion for fêtes and holidays, and was never so eloquent as when detailing the civil and religious festivals of Granada. During the preparations for the annual Catholic fête of Corpus Christi, he was in a state of incessant transition between the Alhambra and the subjacent city, bringing me daily accounts of the magnificent arrangements that were in progress, and endeavoring, but in vain, to lure me down from my cool and airy retreat to witness them. At length, on the eve of the eventful day I yielded to his solicitations and descended from the regal halls of the Alhambra under his escort, as did of yore the adventure-seeking Haroun Alraschid, under that of his Grand Vizier Giaffar. Though it was yet scarce sunset, the city gates were already thronged with the picturesque villagers of the mountains, and the brown peasantry of the Vega. Granada has ever been the rallying place of a great mountainous region, studded with towns and villages. Hither, during the Moorish domination, the chivalry of this region repaired, to join in the splendid and semi-warlike fêtes of the Vivarrambla, and hither the elite of its population still resort to join in the pompous ceremonies of the church. Indeed, many of the mountaineers from the Alpuxarras and the Sierra de Ronda, who now bow to the cross as zealous Catholics, bear the stamp of their Moorish origin, and are indubitable descendants of the fickle subjects of Boabdil.

Under the guidance of Mateo, I made my way through streets already teeming with a holiday population, to the square of the Vivarrambla, that great place for tilts and tourneys, so often sung in the Moorish ballads of love and chivalry. A gallery or arcade of wood had been erected along the sides of the square, for the grand religious procession of the following day. This was brilliantly illuminated for the evening as a promenade; and bands of music were stationed on balconies on each of the four façades of the square. All the fashion and beauty of Granada, all of its population of either sex that had good looks or fine clothes to display, thronged this arcade, promenading round and round the Vivarrambla. Here, too, were the *Majos* and *Majas*, the rural beaux and belles, with fine forms, flashing eyes, and gay Andalusian costumes; some of them from Ronda itself, that stronghold of the mountains, famous for contrabandistas, bull-fighters, and beautiful women.

While this gay but motley throng kept up a constant circulation in the gallery, the centre of the square was occupied by the peasantry from the surrounding country; who made no pretensions to display, but came for simple, hearty enjoyment. The whole square was covered with them; forming separate groups of families and neighborhoods, like gipsy encampments, some were listening to the traditional ballad drawled out to the tinkling of the guitar; some were engaged in gay conversation; some were dancing to the click of the castañet. As I threaded my way through this teeming region with Mateo at my heels, I passed occasionally some rustic party, seated on the ground, making a merry though frugal repast. If they caught my eyes as I loitered by, they almost invariably invited me to partake of their simple fare. This hospitable usage, inherited from their Moslem invaders, and originating in the tent of the Arab, is universal throughout the land, and observed by the poorest Spaniard.

As the night advanced the gayety gradually died away in the arcades; the bands of music ceased to play, and the brilliant crowd dispersed to their homes. The centre of the square still remained well peopled and Mateo assured me that the greater part of the peasantry, men, women, and children, would pass the night there, sleeping on the bare earth beneath the open canopy of heaven. Indeed a summer night requires no shelter in this favored climate; and a bed is a superfluity, which many of the hardy peasantry of Spain never enjoy, and which some of them affect to despise. The common Spaniard wraps himself in his brown cloak, stretches himself on his manta or mule-cloth, and sleeps soundly, luxuriously accommodated if he can have a saddle for a pillow. In a little while the words of Mateo were made good; the peasant multitude nestled down on the ground to their night's repose, and by

midnight, the scene on the Vivarrambla resembled the bivouac of an army.

The next morning, accompanied by Mateo, I revisited the
square at sunrise. It was still strewed with groups of sleepers;
some were reposing from the dance and revel of the evening;
others, who had left their villages after work on the preceding
day, having trudged on foot the greater part of the night,
were taking a sound sleep to freshen themselves for the festivities of the day. Numbers from the mountains, and the remote villages of the plain, who had set out in the night,
continued to arrive with their wives and children. All were in
high spirits; greeting each other and exchanging jokes and
pleasantries. The gay tumult thickened as the day advanced.
Now came pouring in at the city gates, and parading through
the streets, the deputations from the various villages, destined
to swell the grand procession. These village deputations were
headed by their priests, bearing their respective crosses and
banners, and images of the blessed Virgin and of patron
saints; all which were matters of great rivalship and jealousy
among the peasantry. It was like the chivalrous gatherings of
ancient days, when each town and village sent its chiefs, and
warriors, and standards to defend the capital or grace its
festivities.

At length all these various detachments congregated into
one grand pageant, which slowly paraded round the Vivarrambla, and through the principal streets, where every window and balcony was hung with tapestry. In this procession
were all the religious orders, the civil and military authorities,
and the chief people of the parishes and villages: every church
and convent had contributed its banners, its images, its relics,
and poured forth its wealth for the occasion. In the centre
of the procession walked the archbishop, under a damask
canopy, and surrounded by inferior dignitaries and their de-
pendants. The whole moved to the swell and cadence of
numerous bands of music, and, passing through the midst
of a countless yet silent multitude, proceeded onward to the
cathedral.

I could not but be struck with the changes of times and
customs, as I saw this monkish pageant passing through the
Vivarrambla, the ancient seat of Moslem pomp and chivalry.

The contrast was indeed forced upon the mind by the decorations of the square. The whole front of the wooden gallery erected for the procession, extending several hundred feet, was faced with canvas, on which some humble though patriotic artist had painted, by contract, a series of the principal scenes and exploits of the conquest, as recorded in chronicle and romance. It is thus the romantic legends of Granada mingle themselves with every thing, and are kept fresh in the public mind.

As we wended our way back to the Alhambra, Mateo was in high glee and garrulous vein. "Ah, Señor," exclaimed he, "there is no place in all the world like Granada for grand ceremonies, (*funciones grandes*), a man need spend nothing on pleasure here, it is all furnished him gratis. Pero, el dia de la Toma! Ah, Señor! el dia de la Toma! But the day of the Taking! ah, Señor, the day of the Taking;"—that was the great day which crowned Mateo's notions of perfect felicity. The Dia de la Toma, I found, was the anniversary of the capture or taking possession of Granada, by the army of Ferdinand and Isabella.

On that day, according to Mateo, the whole city is abandoned to revelry. The great alarm bell on the watchtower of the Alhambra (*la Torre de la vela*), sends forth its clanging peals from morn till night; the sound pervades the whole Vega, and echoes along the mountains, summoning the peasantry from far and near to the festivities of the metropolis. "Happy the damsel," says Mateo, "who can get a chance to ring that bell; it is a charm to insure a husband within the year."

Throughout the day the Alhambra is thrown open to the public. Its halls and courts, where the Moorish monarchs once held sway, resound with the guitar and castanet, and gay groups, in the fanciful dresses of Andalusia, perform their traditional dances inherited from the Moors.

A grand procession, emblematic of the taking possession of the city, moves through the principal streets. The banner of Ferdinand and Isabella, that precious relic of the Conquest, is brought forth from its depository, and borne in triumph by the Alferez mayor, or grand standard-bearer. The portable camp-altar, carried about with the sovereigns in all their campaigns, is transported into the chapel royal of the cathedral, and placed before their sepulchre, where their effigies lie in monumental marble. High mass is then performed in memory of the Conquest; and at a certain part of the ceremony the Alferez mayor puts on his hat, and waves the standard above the tomb of the conquerors.

A more whimsical memorial of the Conquest is exhibited in the evening at the theatre. A popular drama is performed, entitled AVE MARIA, turning on a famous achievement of Hernando del Pulgar, surnamed "el de las Hazañas" (he of the exploits), a madcap warrior, the favorite hero of the populace of Granada. During the time of the siege, the young Moorish and Spanish cavaliers vied with each other in extravagant bravadoes. On one occasion this Hernando del Pulgar, at the head of a handful of followers, made a dash into Granada in the dead of the night, nailed the inscription of AVE MARIA with his dagger to the gate of the principal mosque, a token of having consecrated it to the Virgin, and effected his retreat in safety.*

While the Moorish cavaliers admired this daring exploit, they felt bound to resent it. On the following day, therefore, Tarfe, one of the stoutest among them, paraded in front of the Christian army, dragging the tablet bearing the sacred inscription AVE MARIA, at his horse's tail. The cause of the Virgin was eagerly vindicated by Garcilaso de la Vega, who slew the Moor in single combat, and elevated the tablet in devotion and triumph at the end of his lance.

The drama founded on this exploit is prodigiously popular with the common people. Although it has been acted time out of mind, it never fails to draw crowds, who become completely lost in the delusions of the scene. When their favorite Pulgar strides about with many a mouthy speech, in the very midst of the Moorish capital, he is cheered with enthusiastic bravos; and when he nails the tablet to the door of the mosque, the theatre absolutely shakes with the thunders of applause. On the other hand, the unlucky actors who figure in the part of the Moors, have to bear the brunt of popular

---

*See a more detailed account of the exploit in the chronicle of the Conquest of Granada.

indignation; which at times equals that of the Hero of Lamanche, at the puppet-show of Gines de Passamonte; for, when the infidel Tarfé plucks down the tablet to tie it to his horse's tail, some of the audience rise in fury, and are ready to jump upon the stage to revenge this insult to the Virgin.

By the way, the actual lineal descendant of Hernando del Pulgar, was the Marquis de Salar. As the legitimate representative of that madcap hero, and in commemoration and reward of this hero's exploit, above mentioned, he inherited the right to enter the cathedral on certain occasions, on horseback; to sit within the choir, and to put on his hat at the elevation of the host, though these privileges were often and obstinately contested by the clergy. I met him occasionally in society; he was young, of agreeable appearance and manners, with bright black eyes, in which appeared to lurk some of the fire of his ancestors. Among the paintings in the Vivarrambla, on the fête of Corpus Christi, were some depicting, in vivid style, the exploits of the family hero. An old gray-headed servant of the Pulgars shed tears on beholding them, and hurried home to inform the marquis. The eager zeal and enthusiasm of the old domestic only provoked a light laugh from his young master; whereupon, turning to the brother of the marquis, with that freedom allowed in Spain to old family servants, "Come, Señor," cried he, "you are more considerate than your brother; come and see your ancestor in all his glory!"

In emulation of this great *Dia de la Toma* of Granada, almost every village and petty town of the mountains has its own anniversary, commemorating, with rustic pomp and uncouth ceremonial, its deliverance from the Moorish yoke. On these occasions, according to Mateo, a kind of resurrection takes place of ancient armor and weapons; great two-handed swords, ponderous arquebuses with matchlocks, and other warlike relics, treasured up from generation to generation, since the time of the Conquest; and happy the community that possesses some old piece of ordnance, peradventure one of the identical lombards used by the conquerors; it is kept thundering along the mountains all day long, provided the community can afford sufficient expenditure of powder.

In the course of the day, a kind of warlike drama is enacted.

Some of the populace parade the streets, fitted out with the old armor, as champions of the faith. Others appear dressed up as Moorish warriors. A tent is pitched in the public square, inclosing an altar with an image of the Virgin. The Christian warriors approach to perform their devotions; the infidels surround the tent to prevent their entrance; a mock fight ensues; the combatants sometimes forget that they are merely playing a part, and dry blows of grievous weight are apt to be exchanged. The contest, however, invariably terminates in favor of the good cause. The Moors are defeated and taken prisoners. The image of the Virgin, rescued from thraldom, is elevated in triumph; a grand procession succeeds, in which the conquerors figure with great applause and vainglory; while their captives are led in chains, to the evident delight and edification of the spectators.

These celebrations are heavy drains on the treasuries of these petty communities, and have sometimes to be suspended for want of funds; but, when times grows better, or sufficient money has been hoarded for the purpose, they are resumed with new zeal and prodigality.

Mateo informed me that he had occasionally assisted at these fêtes and taken a part in the combats; but always on the side of the true faith; *"porque Señor,"* added the ragged descendant of the cardinal Ximenes, tapping his breast with something of an air, *"porque Señor, soy Christiano viejo."*

Local Traditions

THE COMMON PEOPLE of Spain have an Oriental passion for story-telling, and are fond of the marvellous. They will gather round the doors of their cottages in summer evenings, or in the great cavernous chimney-corners of the ventas in the winter, and listen with insatiable delight to miraculous legends of saints, perilous adventures of travellers, and daring exploits of robbers and contrabandistas. The wild and solitary character of the country, the imperfect diffusion of knowledge, the scarceness of general topics of conversation, and the romantic adventurous life that every one leads in a land where travelling is yet in its primitive state, all contribute to cherish this love of oral narration, and to produce a strong infusion of the extravagant and incredible. There is no theme, however, more prevalent and popular than that of treasures buried by the Moors; it pervades the whole country. In traversing the wild sierras, the scenes of ancient foray and exploit, you cannot see a Moorish atalaya, or watchtower, perched among the cliffs, or beetling above its rock-built village, but your muleteer, on being closely questioned, will suspend the smoking of his cigarillo, to tell some tale of Moslem gold buried beneath its foundations; nor is there a ruined alcazar in a city but has its golden tradition, handed down from generation to generation among the poor people of the neighborhood.

These, like most popular fictions, have sprung from some scanty groundwork of fact. During the wars between Moor and Christian which distracted this country for centuries, towns and castles were liable frequently and suddenly to change owners, and the inhabitants, during sieges and assaults, were fain to bury their money and jewels in the earth, or hide them in vaults and wells, as is often done at the present day in the despotic and belligerent countries of the East. At the time of the expulsion of the Moors also, many of them concealed their most precious effects, hoping that their exile would be but temporary, and that they would be enabled to return and retrieve their treasures at some future day.

It is certain that from time to time hoards of gold and silver coin have been accidentally digged up, after a lapse of centuries, from among the ruins of Moorish fortresses and habitations; and it requires but a few facts of the kind to give birth to a thousand fictions.

The stories thus originating have generally something of an Oriental tinge, and are marked with that mixture of the Arabic and the Gothic which seems to me to characterize every thing in Spain, and especially in its southern provinces. The hidden wealth is always laid under magic spell, and secured by charm and talisman. Sometimes it is guarded by uncouth monsters or fiery dragons, sometimes by enchanted Moors, who sit by it in armor, with drawn swords, but motionless as statues, maintaining a sleepless watch for ages.

The Alhambra of course, from the peculiar circumstances of its history, is a strong-hold for popular fictions of the kind; and various relics, digged up from time to time, have contributed to strengthen them. At one time an earthen vessel was found containing Moorish coins and the skeleton of a cock, which, according to the opinion of certain shrewd inspectors, must have been buried alive. At another time a vessel was dug up containing a great scarabæus or beetle of baked clay, covered with Arabic inscriptions, which was pronounced a prodigious amulet of occult virtues. In this way the wits of the ragged brood who inhabit the Alhambra have been set woolgathering until there is not a hall, nor tower, nor vault, of the old fortress, that has not been made the scene of some marvellous tradition. Having, I trust, in the preceding papers made the reader in some degree familiar with the localities of the Alhambra, I shall now launch out more largely into the wonderful legends connected with it, and which I have diligently wrought into shape and form, from various legendary scraps and hints picked up in the course of my perambulations; in the same manner that an antiquary works out a regular historical document from a few scattered letters of an almost defaced inscription.

If any thing in these legends should shock the faith of the over-scrupulous reader, he must remember the nature of the place, and make due allowances. He must not expect here the same laws of probability that govern commonplace scenes and every-day life; he must remember that he treads the halls of an enchanted palace, and that all is "haunted ground."

The House of the Weathercock

ON THE BROW of the lofty hill of the Albaycin, the high-est part of Granada, and which rises from the narrow valley of the Darro, directly opposite to the Alhambra, stands all that is left of what was once a royal palace of the Moors. It has, in fact, fallen into such obscurity, that it cost me much trouble to find it; though aided in my researches, by the sagacious and all-knowing Mateo Ximenes. This edifice has borne for centuries the name of "The House of the Weathercock" (La casa del Gallo de Viento), from a bronze figure on one of its turrets, in ancient times, of a warrior on horseback, and turning with every breeze. This weathercock was considered by the Moslems of Granada a portentous tal-isman. According to some traditions, it bore the following Arabic inscription:

> Calet el Bedici Aben Habuz,
> Quidat ehahet Lindabuz.

Which has been rendered into Spanish:

> Dice el sabio Aben Habuz,
> Que asi se defiende el Anduluz.

And into English:

> In this way, says Aben Habus the wise,
> Andaluz guards against surprise.

This Aben Habuz, according to some of the old Moorish chronicles, was a captain in the invading army of Taric, one of the conquerors of Spain, who left him as Alcayde of Granada. He is supposed to have intended this effigy as a perpetual warning to the Moslems of Andaluz, that, surrounded by foes, their safety depended upon their being always on their guard and ready for the field.

Others, among whom is the Christian historian Marmol, affirms 'Badis Aben Habus' to have been a Moorish sultan of Granada, and that the weathercock was intended as a perpetual admonition of the instability of Moslem power, bearing the following words in Arabic:

"Thus Ibn Habus al badise predicts Andalus shall one day vanish and pass away."*

Another version of this portentous inscription is given by a Moslem historian, on the authority of Sidi Hasan, a faquir who flourished about the time of Ferdinand and Isabella, and who was present at the taking down of the weathercock, when the old Kassaba was undergoing repairs.

"I saw it," says the venerable faquir, "with my own eyes; it was of a heptagonal shape, and had the following inscription in verse:

"The palace at fair Granada presents a talisman."

"The horseman, though a solid body, turns with every wind."

"This to a wise man reveals a mystery. In a little while comes a calamity to ruin both the palace and its owner."

In effect it was not long after this meddling with the portentous weathercock that the following event occurred. As old Muley Abul Hassan, the king of Granada, was seated under a sumptuous pavilion, reviewing his troops who paraded before him in armor of polished steel, and gorgeous silken robes, mounted on fleet steeds, and equipped with swords, spears and shields, embossed with gold and silver; suddenly a tempest was seen hurrying from the south-west. In a little while, black clouds overshadowed the heavens and burst forth with a deluge of rain. Torrents came roaring down from the mountains, bringing with them rocks and trees; the Darro overflowed its banks; mills were swept away; bridges destroyed, gardens laid waste; the inundation rushed into the city, undermining houses, drowning their inhabitants, and overflowing even the square of the Great Mosque. The people rushed in affright to the mosques to implore the mercy of Allah, regarding this uproar of the elements as the harbinger of dreadful calamities; and, indeed, according to the Arabian historian, Al Makkari, it was but a type and prelude of the direful war which ended in the downfall of the Moslem kingdom of Granada.

*MARMOL, *Hist. Rebellion of the Moors.*

I have thus given historic authorities, sufficient to show the portentous mysteries connected with the House of the Weathercock, and its talismanic horseman.

I now proceed to relate still more surprising things about Aben Habuz and his palace; for the truth of which, should any doubt be entertained, I refer the dubious reader to Mateo Ximenes and his fellow-historiographers of the Alhambra.

Legend of the Arabian Astrologer

IN OLD TIMES, many hundred years ago, there was a Moorish king named Aben Habuz, who reigned over the kingdom of Granada. He was a retired conqueror, that is to say, one who having in his more youthful days led a life of constant foray and depredation, now that he was grown feeble and superannuated, "languished for repose," and desired nothing more than to live at peace with all the world, to husband his laurels, and to enjoy in quiet the possessions he had wrested from his neighbors.

It so happened, however, that this most reasonable and pacific old monarch had young rivals to deal with; princes full of his early passion for fame and fighting, and who were disposed to call him to account for the scores he had run up with their fathers. Certain distant districts of his own territories, also, which during the days of his vigor he had treated with a high hand, were prone, now that he languished for repose, to rise in rebellion and threaten to invest him in his capital. Thus he had foes on every side; and as Granada is surrounded by wild and craggy mountains, which hide the approach of an enemy, the unfortunate Aben Habuz was kept in a constant state of vigilance and alarm, not knowing in what quarter hostilities might break out.

It was in vain that he built watchtowers on the mountains, and stationed guards at every pass with orders to make fires by night and smoke by day, on the approach of an enemy. His alert foes, baffling every precaution, would break out of some unthought-of defile, ravage his lands beneath his very nose, and then make off with prisoners and booty to the mountains. Was ever peaceable and retired conqueror in a more uncomfortable predicament?

While Aben Habuz was harassed by these perplexities and molestations, an ancient Arabian physician arrived at his court. His gray beard descended to his girdle, and he had every mark of extreme age, yet he had travelled almost the whole way from Egypt on foot, with no other aid than a staff, marked with hieroglyphics. His fame had preceded him. His name was Ibrahim Ebn Abu Ayub; he was said to have lived ever since the days of Mahomet, and to be son of Abu Ayub, the last of the companions of the Prophet. He had, when a child, followed the conquering army of Amru into Egypt, where he had remained many years studying the dark sciences, and particularly magic, among the Egyptian priests.

It was, moreover, said that he had found out the secret of prolonging life, by means of which he had arrived to the great age of upwards of two centuries, though, as he did not discover the secret until well stricken in years, he could only perpetuate his gray hairs and wrinkles.

This wonderful old man was honorably entertained by the king; who, like most superannuated monarchs, began to take physicians into great favor. He would have assigned him an apartment in his palace, but the astrologer preferred a cave in the side of the hill which rises above the city of Granada, being the same on which the Alhambra has since been built. He caused the cave to be enlarged so as to form a spacious and lofty hall, with a circular hole at the top, through which, as through a well, he could see the heavens and behold the stars even at mid-day. The walls of this hall were covered with Egyptian hieroglyphics, with cabalistic symbols, and with the figures of the stars in their signs. This hall he furnished with many implements, fabricated under his directions by cunning artificers of Granada, but the occult properties of which were known only to himself.

In a little while the sage Ibrahim became the bosom counsellor of the king, who applied to him for advice in every emergency. Aben Habuz was once inveighing against the injustice of his neighbors, and bewailing the restless vigilance he had to observe to guard himself against their invasions; when he had finished, the astrologer remained silent for a moment, and then replied, "Know, O King, that when I was in Egypt I beheld a great marvel devised by a pagan priestess of old. On a mountain, above the city of Borsa, and overlooking the great valley of the Nile, was a figure of a ram, and above it a figure of a cock, both of molten brass, and turning upon a pivot. Whenever the country was threatened with invasion, the ram would turn in the direction of the enemy, and the cock would crow; upon this the inhabitants of the city knew of the danger, and of the quarter from which it was approaching, and could take timely means to guard against it."

"God is great!" exclaimed the pacific Aben Habuz, "what a treasure would be such a ram to keep an eye upon these mountains around me; and then such a cock to crow in time of danger! Allah Akbar! how securely I might sleep in my palace with such sentinels on the top!"

The astrologer waited until the ecstasies of the king had subsided, and then proceeded.

"After the victorious Amru (may he rest in peace!) had finished his conquest of Egypt, I remained among the priests of the land, studying the rites and ceremonies of their idolatrous faith, and seeking to make myself master of the hidden knowledge for which they are renowned. I was one day seated on the banks of the Nile, conversing with an ancient priest, when he pointed to the mighty pyramids which rose like mountains out of the neighboring desert. 'All that we can teach thee,' said he, 'is nothing to the knowledge locked up in those mighty piles. In the centre of the central pyramid is a sepulchral chamber, in which is inclosed the mummy of the high-priest, who aided in rearing that stupendous pile; and with him is buried a wondrous book of knowledge containing all the secrets of magic and art. This book was given to Adam after his fall, and was handed down from generation to generation to King Solomon the wise, and by its aid he built the temple of Jerusalem. How it came into the possession of the builder of the pyramids, is known to him alone who knows all things.'

"When I heard these words of the Egyptian priest, my heart burned to get possession of that book. I could command the services of many of the soldiers of our conquering army, and of a number of the native Egyptians: with these I set to work, and pierced the solid mass of the pyramid, until, after great toil, I came upon one of its interior and hidden passages. Following this up, and threading a fearful labyrinth, I penetrated into the very heart of the pyramid, even to the sepulchral chamber, where the mummy of the high-priest had lain for ages. I broke through the outer cases of the mummy, unfolded its many wrappers and bandages, and at length found the precious volume on its bosom. I seized it with a trembling hand, and groped my way out of the pyramid, leaving the mummy in its dark and silent sepulchre, there to await the final day of resurrection and judgment."

"Son of Abu Ayub," exclaimed Aben Habuz, "thou hast been a great traveller, and seen marvellous things; but of what avail to me is the secret of the pyramid, and the volume of knowledge of the wise Solomon?"

"This it is, O king! By the study of that book I am instructed in all magic arts, and can command the assistance of genii to accomplish my plans. The mystery of the Talisman of Borsa is therefore familiar to me, and such a talisman can I make; nay, one of greater virtues."

"O wise son of Abu Ayub," cried Aben Habuz, "better were such a talisman, than all the watchtowers on the hills, and sentinels upon the borders. Give me such a safeguard, and the riches of my treasury are at thy command."

The astrologer immediately set to work to gratify the wishes of the monarch. He caused a great tower to be erected upon the top of the royal palace, which stood on the brow of the hill of the Albaycin. The tower was built of stones brought from Egypt, and taken, it is said, from one of the pyramids. In the upper part of the tower was a circular hall, with windows looking towards every point of the compass, and before each window was a table, on which was arranged, as on a chess-board, a mimic army of horse and foot, with the effigy of the potentate that ruled in that direction, all carved of wood. To each of these tables there was a small lance, no bigger than a bodkin, on which were engraved certain Chaldaic characters. This hall was kept constantly closed, by a gate of brass, with a great lock of steel, the key of which was in possession of the king.

On the top of the tower was a bronze figure of a Moorish horseman, fixed on a pivot, with a shield on one arm, and his lance elevated perpendicularly. The face of this horseman was towards the city, as if keeping guard over it; but if any foe were at hand, the figure would turn in that direction, and would level the lance as if for action.

When this talisman was finished, Aben Habuz was all impatient to try its virtues; and longed as ardently for an invasion as he had ever sighed after repose. His desire was soon gratified. Tidings were brought, early one morning, by the sentinel appointed to watch the tower, that the face of the bronze horseman was turned towards the mountains of El-vira, and that his lance pointed directly against the Pass of Lope.

"Let the drums and trumpets sound to arms, and all Granada be put on the alert," said Aben Habuz.

"O king," said the astrologer, "let not your city be disquieted, nor your warriors called to arms; we need no aid of force to deliver you from your enemies. Dismiss your attendants, and let us proceed alone to the secret hall of the tower."

The ancient Aben Habuz mounted the staircase of the tower, leaning on the arm of the still more ancient Ibrahim Ebn Abu Ayub. They unlocked the brazen door and entered. The window that looked towards the Pass of Lope was open. "In this direction," said the astrologer, "lies the danger; approach, O king, and behold the mystery of the table."

King Aben Habuz approached the seeming chess-board, on which were arranged the small wooden effigies, when, to his surprise, he perceived that they were all in motion. The horses pranced and curveted, the warriors brandished their weapons, and there was a faint sound of drums and trumpets, and the clang of arms, and neighing of steeds; but all no louder, nor more distinct, than the hum of the bee, or the summer-fly, in the drowsy ear of him who lies at noontide in the shade.

"Behold, O king," said the astrologer, "a proof that thy enemies are even now in the field. They must be advancing through yonder mountains, by the Pass of Lope. Would you produce a panic and confusion amongst them, and cause them to retreat without loss of life, strike these effigies with the but-end of this magic lance; would you cause bloody feud and carnage, strike with the point."

A livid streak passed across the countenance of Aben Habuz; he seized the lance with trembling eagerness; his gray beard wagged with exultation as he tottered toward the table: "Son of Abu Ayub," exclaimed he, in chuckling tone, "I think we will have a little blood!"

So saying, he thrust the magic lance into some of the pigmy effigies, and belabored others with the but-end, upon which the former fell as dead upon the board, and the rest turning upon each other began, pell-mell, a chance-medley fight.

It was with difficulty the astrologer could stay the hand of the most pacific of monarchs, and prevent him from absolutely exterminating his foes; at length he prevailed upon him to leave the tower, and to send out scouts to the mountains by the Pass of Lope.

They returned with the intelligence, that a Christian army had advanced through the heart of the Sierra, almost within sight of Granada, where a dissension had broken out among them; they had turned their weapons against each other, and after much slaughter had retreated over the border.

Aben Hazuz was transported with joy on thus proving the efficacy of the talisman. "At length," said he, "I shall lead a life of tranquillity, and have all my enemies in my power. O wise son of Abu Ayub, what can I bestow on thee in reward for such a blessing?"

"The wants of an old man and a philosopher, O king, are few and simple; grant me but the means of fitting up my cave as a suitable hermitage, and I am content."

"How noble is the moderation of the truly wise!" exclaimed Aben Habuz, secretly pleased at the cheapness of the recompense. He summoned his treasurer, and bade him dispense whatever sums might be required by Ibrahim to complete and furnish his hermitage.

The astrologer now gave orders to have various chambers hewn out of the solid rock, so as to form ranges of apartments connected with his astrological hall; these he caused to be furnished with luxurious ottomans and divans, and the walls to be hung with the richest silks of Damascus. "I am an old man," said he, "and can no longer rest my bones on stone couches, and these damp walls require covering."

He had baths too constructed, and provided with all kinds of perfumes and aromatic oils: "For a bath," said he, "is necessary to counteract the rigidity of age, and to restore freshness and suppleness to the frame withered by study."

He caused the apartments to be hung with innumerable silver and crystal lamps, which he filled with a fragrant oil, prepared according to a receipt discovered by him in the tombs of Egypt. This oil was perpetual in its nature, and diffused a soft radiance like the tempered light of day. "The light of the sun," said he, "is too garish and violent for the eyes of an old man, and the light of the lamp is more congenial to the studies of a philosopher."

The treasurer of king Aben Habuz groaned at the sums daily demanded to fit up this hermitage, and he carried his complaints to the king. The royal word, however, had been given; Aben Habuz shrugged his shoulders: "We must have patience," said he, "this old man has taken his idea of a philosophic retreat from the interior of the pyramids, and of the vast ruins of Egypt; but all things have an end, and so will the furnishing of his cavern."

The king was in the right; the hermitage was at length complete, and formed a sumptuous subterranean palace. The astrologer expressed himself perfectly content, and, shutting himself up, remained for three whole days buried in study. At the end of that time he appeared again before the treasurer. "One thing more is necessary," said he, "one trifling solace for the intervals of mental labor."

"O wise Ibrahim, I am bound to furnish every thing necessary for thy solitude; what more dost thou require?"

"I would fain have a few dancing women."

"Dancing women!" echoed the treasurer, with surprise.

"Dancing women," replied the sage, gravely; "and let them be young and fair to look upon; for the sight of youth and beauty is refreshing. A few will suffice, for I am a philosopher of simple habits and easily satisfied."

While the philosophic Ibrahim Ebn Abu Ayub passed his time thus sagely in his hermitage, the pacific Aben Habuz carried on furious campaigns in effigy in his tower. It was a glorious thing for an old man, like himself, of quiet habits, to have war made easy, and to be enabled to amuse himself in his chamber by brushing away whole armies like so many swarms of flies.

For a time he rioted in the indulgence of his humors, and even taunted and insulted his neighbors, to induce them to make incursions; but by degrees they grew wary from repeated disasters, until no one ventured to invade his territories. For many months the bronze horseman remained on the peace establishment with his lance elevated in the air, and the worthy old monarch began to repine at the want of his accustomed sport, and to grow peevish at his monotonous tranquillity.

At length, one day, the talismanic horseman veered suddenly round, and lowering his lance, made a dead point towards the mountains of Guadix. Aben Habuz hastened to his tower, but the magic table in that direction remained quiet; not a single warrior was in motion. Perplexed at the circumstance, he sent forth a troop of horse to scour the mountains and reconnoitre. They returned after three days' absence.

"We have searched every mountain pass," they said, "but not a helm nor spear was stirring. All that we have found in the course of our foray, was a Christian damsel of surpassing beauty, sleeping at noontide beside a fountain, whom we have brought away captive."

"A damsel of surpassing beauty!" exclaimed Aben Habuz, his eyes gleaming with animation; "let her be conducted into my presence."

The beautiful damsel was accordingly conducted into his presence. She was arrayed with all the luxury of ornament that had prevailed among the Gothic Spaniards at the time of the Arabian conquest. Pearls of dazzling whiteness were entwined with her raven tresses; and jewels sparkled on her forehead, rivalling the lustre of her eyes. Around her neck was a golden chain, to which was suspended a silver lyre, which hung by her side.

The flashes of her dark refulgent eye were like sparks of fire on the withered, yet combustible, heart of Aben Habuz; the swimming voluptuousness of her gait made his senses reel. "Fairest of women," cried he, with rapture, "who and what art thou?"

"The daughter of one of the Gothic princes, who but lately ruled over this land. The armies of my father have been destroyed, as if by magic, among these mountains; he has been driven into exile, and his daughter is a captive."

"Beware, O king!" whispered Ibrahim Ebn Abu Ayub, "this may be one of these northern sorceresses of whom we have heard, who assume the most seductive forms to beguile the unwary. Methinks I read witchcraft in her eye, and sorcery in every movement. Doubtless this is the enemy pointed out by the talisman."

"Son of Abu Ayub," replied the king, "thou art a wise man, I grant, a conjuror for aught I know; but thou art little versed in the ways of woman. In that knowledge will I yield to no man; no, not to the wise Solomon himself, notwithstanding the number of his wives and concubines. As to this damsel, I see no harm in her; she is fair to look upon, and finds favor in my eyes."

"Hearken, O king!" replied the astrologer. "I have given thee many victories by means of my talisman, but have never shared any of the spoil. Give me then this stray captive, to solace me in my solitude with her silver lyre. If she be indeed a sorceress, I have counter spells that set her charms at defiance."

"What! more women!" cried Aben Habuz. "Hast thou not already dancing women enough to solace thee?"

"Dancing women have I, it is true, but no singing women. I would fain have a little minstrelsy to refresh my mind when weary with the toils of study."

"A truce with thy hermit cravings," said the king, impatiently. "This damsel have I marked for my own. I see much comfort in her; even such comfort as David, the father of Solomon the wise, found in the society of Abishag the Shunamite."

Further solicitations and remonstrances of the astrologer only provoked a more peremptory reply from the monarch, and they parted in high displeasure. The sage shut himself up in his hermitage to brood over his disappointment; ere he departed, however, he gave the king one more warning to beware of his dangerous captive. But where is the old man in love that will listen to council? Aben Habuz resigned himself to the full sway of his passion. His only study was how to render himself amiable in the eyes of the Gothic beauty. He had not youth to recommend him, it is true, but then he had riches; and when a lover is old, he is generally generous. The Zacatin of Granada was ransacked for the most precious merchandise of the East; silks, jewels, precious gems, exquisite perfumes, all that Asia and Africa yielded of rich and rare, were lavished upon the princess. All kinds of spectacles and festivities were devised for her entertainment; minstrelsy, dancing, tournaments, bull-fights:—Granada for a time was a scene of perpetual pageant. The Gothic princess regarded all this splendor with the air of one accustomed to magnificence. She received every thing as a homage due to her rank, or rather to her beauty; for beauty is more lofty in its exactions even than rank. Nay, she seemed to take a secret pleasure in exciting the monarch to expenses that made his treasury shrink; and then treating his extravagant generosity as a mere matter of course. With all his assiduity and munificence, also, the venerable lover could not flatter himself that he had made any impression on her heart. She never frowned on him, it is true, but then she never smiled. Whenever he began to plead his passion, she struck her silver lyre. There was a mystic charm in the sound. In an instant the monarch began to nod; a drowsiness stole over him, and he gradually sank into a sleep, from which he awoke wonderfully refreshed, but perfectly cooled for the time of his passion. This was very baffling to his suit; but then these slumbers were accompanied by agreeable dreams, which completely enthralled the senses of the drowsy lover; so he continued to dream on, while all Granada scoffed at his infatuation, and groaned at the treasures lavished for a song.

At length a danger burst on the head of Aben Habuz, against which his talisman yielded him no warning. An insurrection broke out in his very capital: his palace was surrounded by an armed rabble, who menaced his life and the life of his Christian paramour. A spark of his ancient warlike spirit was awakened in the breast of the monarch. At the head of a handful of his guards he sallied forth, put the rebels to flight, and crushed the insurrection in the bud.

When quiet was again restored, he sought the astrologer, who still remained shut up in his hermitage, chewing the bitter cud of resentment.

Aben Habuz approached him with a conciliatory tone. "O wise son of Abu Ayub," said he, "well didst thou predict dangers to me from this captive beauty: tell me then, thou who art so quick at foreseeing peril, what I should do to avert it."

"Put from thee the infidel damsel who is the cause."

"Sooner would I part with my kingdom," cried Aben Habuz.

"Thou art in danger of losing both," replied the astrologer.

"Be not harsh and angry, O most profound of philosophers; consider the double distress of a monarch and a lover, and devise some means of protecting me from the evils by which I am menaced. I care not for grandeur, I care not for power, I languish only for repose; would that I had some quiet retreat where I might take refuge from the world, and all its cares, and pomps, and troubles, and devote the remainder of my days to tranquillity and love."

The astrologer regarded him for a moment, from under his bushy eyebrows.

"And what wouldst thou give, if I could provide thee such a retreat?"

"Thou shouldst name thy own reward, and whatever it might be, if within the scope of my power, as my soul liveth, it should be thine."

"Thou hast heard, O king, of the garden of Irem, one of the prodigies of Arabia the happy?"

"I have heard of that garden; it is recorded in the Koran, even in the chapter entitled 'The Dawn of Day.' I have moreover, heard marvellous things related of it by pilgrims who had been to Mecca; but I considered them wild fables, such as travellers are wont to tell who have visited remote countries."

"Discredit not, O king, the tales of travellers," rejoined the astrologer, gravely, "for they contain precious rarities of knowledge brought from the ends of the earth. As to the palace and garden of Irem, what is generally told of them is true; I have seen them with mine own eyes—listen to my adventure; for it has a bearing upon the object of your request.

"In my younger days, when a mere Arab of the desert, I tended my father's camels. In traversing the desert of Aden, one of them strayed from the rest, and was lost. I searched after it for several days, but in vain, until, wearied and faint, I laid myself down at noontide, and slept under a palm-tree by the side of a scanty well. When I awoke, I found myself at the gate of a city. I entered, and beheld noble streets, and squares, and market-places; but all were silent and without an inhabitant. I wandered on until I came to a sumptuous palace with a garden adorned with fountains and fishponds, and groves and flowers, and orchards laden with delicious fruit; but still no one was to be seen. Upon which, appalled at this loneliness, I hastened to depart; and, after issuing forth at the gate of the city, I turned to look upon the place, but it was no longer to be seen; nothing but the silent desert extended before my eyes.

"In the neighborhood I met with an aged dervise, learned in the traditions and secrets of the land, and related to him what had befallen me. 'This,' said he, 'is the far-famed garden of Irem, one of the wonders of the desert. It only appears at times to some wanderer like thyself, gladdening him with the sight of towers and palaces and garden walls overhung with richly-laden fruit-trees, and then vanishes, leaving nothing but a lonely desert. And this is the story of it. In old times, when this country was inhabited by the Addites, King Sheddad, the son of Ad, the great grandson of Noah, founded here a splendid city. When it was finished, and he saw its grandeur, his heart was puffed up with pride and arrogance, and he determined to build a royal palace, with gardens which should rival all related in the Koran of the celestial paradise. But the curse of heaven fell upon him for his presumption. He and his subjects were swept from the earth, and his splendid city, and palace, and gardens, were laid under a perpetual spell, which hides them from human sight, excepting that they are seen at intervals, by way of keeping his sin in perpetual remembrance.'

"This story, O king, and the wonders I had seen, ever dwelt in my mind; and in after years, when I had been in Egypt, and was possessed of the book of knowledge of Solomon the wise, I determined to return and revisit the garden of Irem. I did so, and found it revealed to my instructed sight. I took possession of the palace of Sheddad, and passed several days in his mock paradise. The genii who watch over the place, were obedient to my magic power, and revealed to me the spells by which the whole garden had been, as it were, conjured into existence, and by which it was rendered invisible. Such a palace and garden, O king, can I make for thee, even here, on the mountain above thy city. Do I not know all the secret spells? and am I not in possession of the book of knowledge of Solomon the wise?"

"O wise son of Abu Ayub!" exclaimed Aben Habuz, trembling with eagerness, "thou art a traveller indeed, and hast seen and learned marvellous things! Contrive me such a paradise, and ask any reward, even to the half of my kingdom."

"Alas!" replied the other, "thou knowest I am an old man, and a philosopher, and easily satisfied; all the reward I ask is the first beast of burden, with its load, which shall enter the magic portal of the palace."

The monarch gladly agreed to so moderate a stipulation, and the astrologer began his work. On the summit of the hill, immediately above his subterranean hermitage, he caused a great gateway or barbican to be erected, opening through the centre of a strong tower.

There was an outer vestibule or porch, with a lofty arch, and within it a portal secured by massive gates. On the key-stone of the portal the astrologer, with his own hand, wrought the figure of a huge key; and on the key-stone of the outer arch of the vestibule, which was loftier than that of the portal, he carved a gigantic hand. These were potent talismans, over which he repeated many sentences in an unknown tongue.

When this gateway was finished he shut himself up for two days in his astrological hall, engaged in secret incantations; on the third he ascended the hill, and passed the whole day on its summit. At a late hour of the night he came down, and presented himself before Aben Habuz. "At length, O king," said he, "my labor is accomplished. On the summit of the hill stands one of the most delectable palaces that ever the head of man devised, or the heart of man desired. It contains sumptuous halls and galleries, delicious gardens, cool fountains, and fragrant baths; in a word, the whole mountain is converted into a paradise. Like the garden of Irem, it is protected by a mighty charm, which hides it from the view and search of mortals, excepting such as possess the secret of its talismans."

"Enough!" cried Aben Habuz, joyfully, "to-morrow morning with the first light we will ascend and take possession." The happy monarch slept but little that night. Scarcely had the rays of the sun begun to play about the snowy summit of the Sierra Nevada, when he mounted his steed, and, accompanied only by a few chosen attendants, ascended a steep and narrow road leading up the hill. Beside him, on a white palfrey, rode the Gothic princess, her whole dress sparkling with jewels, while round her neck was suspended her silver lyre. The astrologer walked on the other side of the king, assisting his steps with his hieroglyphic staff, for he never mounted steed of any kind.

Aben Habuz looked to see the towers of the palace brightening above him, and the imbowered terraces of its gardens stretching along the heights; but as yet nothing of the kind was to be descried. "That is the mystery and safeguard of the place," said the astrologer, "nothing can be discerned until you have passed the spell-bound gateway, and been put in possession of the place."

As they approached the gateway, the astrologer paused, and pointed out to the king the mystic hand and key carved upon the portal and the arch. "These," said he, "are the talismans which guard the entrance to this paradise. Until yonder hand shall reach down and seize that key, neither mortal power nor magic artifice can prevail against the lord of this mountain."

While Aben Habuz was gazing, with open mouth and silent wonder, at these mystic talismans, the palfrey of the princess proceeded, and bore her in at the portal, to the very centre of the barbican.

"Behold," cried the astrologer, "my promised reward; the first animal with its burden which should enter the magic gateway."

Aben Habuz smiled at what he considered a pleasantry of the ancient man; but when he found him to be in earnest, his grey beard trembled with indignation.

"Son of Abu Ayub," said he, sternly, "what equivocation is this? Thou knowest the meaning of my promise: the first beast of burden, with its load, that should enter this portal. Take the strongest mule in my stables, load it with the most precious things of my treasury, and it is thine; but dare not raise thy thoughts to her who is the delight of my heart."

"What need I of wealth," cried the astrologer, scornfully; "have I not the book of knowledge of Solomon the wise, and through it the command of the secret treasures of the earth? The princess is mine by right; thy royal word is pledged; I claim her as my own."

The princess looked down haughtily from her palfrey, and a light smile of scorn curled her rosy lip at this dispute between two gray-beards, for the possession of youth and beauty. The wrath of the monarch got the better of his discretion. "Base son of the desert," cried he, "thou may'st be master of many arts, but know me for thy master, and presume not to juggle with thy king."

"My master! my king!" echoed the astrologer—"The monarch of a mole-hill to claim sway over him who possesses the talismans of Solomon! Farewell, Aben Habuz; reign over thy petty kingdom, and revel in thy paradise of fools, for me, I will laugh at thee in my philosophic retirement."

So saying he seized the bridle of the palfrey, smote the earth with his staff, and sank with the Gothic princess through the centre of the barbican. The earth closed over them, and no trace remained of the opening by which they had descended.

Aben Habuz was struck dumb for a time with astonishment. Recovering himself, he ordered a thousand workmen to dig, with pickaxe and spade, into the ground where the astrologer had disappeared. They digged and digged, but in vain; the flinty bosom of the hill resisted their implements; or if they did penetrate a little way, the earth filled in again as fast as they threw it out. Aben Habuz sought the mouth of the cavern at the foot of the hill, leading to the subterranean palace of the astrologer; but it was nowhere to be found. Where once had been an entrance, was now a solid surface of primeval rock. With the disappearance of Ibrahim Ebn Abu Ayub ceased the benefit of his talismans. The bronze horseman remained fixed, with his face turned toward the hill, and his spear pointed to the spot where the astrologer had descended, as if there still lurked the deadliest foe of Aben Habuz.

From time to time the sound of music, and the tones of a female voice, could be faintly heard from the bosom of the hill; and a peasant one day brought word to the king that in the preceding night he had found a fissure in the rock, by which he had crept in, until he looked down into a subterranean hall, in which sat the astrologer, on a magnificent divan, slumbering and nodding to the silver lyre of the princess, which seemed to hold a magic sway over his senses.

Aben Habuz sought the fissure in the rock, but it was again closed. He renewed the attempt to unearth his rival, but all in vain. The spell of the hand and key was too potent to be counteracted by human power. As to the summit of the mountain, the site of the promised palace and garden, it remained a naked waste; either the boasted elysium was hidden from sight by enchantment, or was a mere fable of the astrologer. The world charitably supposed the latter, and some used to call the place "The King's Folly;" while others named it "The Fool's Paradise."

To add to the chagrin of Aben Habuz, the neighbors whom he had defied and taunted, and cut up at his leisure while master of the talismanic horseman, finding him no longer protected by magic spell, made inroads into his territories from all sides, and the remainder of the life of the most pacific of monarchs was a tissue of turmoils.

At length Aben Habuz died, and was buried. Ages have since rolled away. The Alhambra has been built on the eventful mountain, and in some measure realizes the fabled delights of the garden of Irem. The spell-bound gateway still exists entire, protected no doubt by the mystic hand and key, and now forms the Gate of Justice, the grand entrance to the fortress. Under that gateway, it is said, the old astrologer remains in his subterranean hall, nodding on his divan, lulled by the silver lyre of the princess.

The old invalid sentinels who mount guard at the gate hear the strains occasionally in the summer nights; and, yielding to their soporific power, doze quietly at their posts. Nay, so drowsy an influence pervades the place, that even those who watch by day may generally be seen nodding on the stone benches of the barbican, or sleeping under the neighboring trees; so that in fact it is the drowsiest military post in all Christendom. All this, say the ancient legends, will endure from age to age. The princess will remain captive to the astrologer; and the astrologer, bound up in magic slumber by the princess, until the last day, unless the mystic hand shall grasp the fated key, and dispel the whole charm of this enchanted mountain.

NOTE TO THE ARABIAN ASTROLOGER

Al Makkari, in his history of the Mahommedan Dynasties in Spain, cites from another Arabian writer an account of a talismanic effigy somewhat similar to the one in the foregoing legend.

In Cadiz, says he, there formerly stood a square tower upwards of one hundred cubits high, built of huge blocks of stone, fastened together with clamps of brass. On the top was the figure of a man, holding a staff in his right hand, his face turned to the Atlantic, and pointing with the forefinger of his left hand to the Straits of Gibraltar. It was said to have been set up in ancient times by the Gothic kings of Andalus, as a beacon or guide to navigators. The Moslems of Barbary and Andalus, considered it a talisman which exercised a spell over the seas. Under its guidance, swarms of piratical people of a nation called Majus, appeared on the coast in large vessels with a square sail in the bow, and another in the stern. They came every six or seven years; captured every thing they met with on the sea; guided by the statue, they passed through the Straits into the Mediterranean, landed on the coasts of Andalus, laid every thing waste with fire and sword; and sometimes carried their depredations on the opposite coasts even as far as Syria.

At length, it came to pass in the time of the civil wars, a Moslem Admiral who had taken possession of Cadiz, hearing that the statue on top of the tower was of pure gold, had it lowered to the ground and broken to pieces; when it proved to be of gilded brass. With the destruction of the idol, the spell over the sea was at an end. From that time forward, nothing more was seen of the piratical people of the ocean, excepting that two of their barks were wrecked on the coast, one at Marsu-l-Majus (the port of the Majus), the other close to the promontory of Al-Aghan.

The maritime invaders above mentioned by Al Makkari must have been the Northmen.

Visitors to the Alhambra

For nearly three months had I enjoyed undisturbed my dream of sovereignty in the Alhambra: a longer term of quiet than had been the lot of many of my predecessors. During this lapse of time the progress of the season had wrought the usual change. On my arrival I had found every thing in the freshness of May; the foliage of the trees was still tender and transparent; the pomegranate had not yet shed its brilliant crimson blossoms; the orchards of the Xenil and the Darro were in full bloom; the rocks were hung with wild flowers, and Granada seemed completely surrounded by a wilderness of roses; among which innumerable nightingales sang, not merely in the night, but all day long.

Now the advance of summer had withered the rose and silenced the nightingale, and the distant country began to look parched and sunburnt; though a perennial verdure reigned immediately round the city and in the deep narrow valleys at the foot of the snow-capped mountains.

The Alhambra possesses retreats graduated to the heat of the weather, among which the most peculiar is the almost subterranean apartment of the baths. This still retains its ancient Oriental character, though stamped with the touching traces of decline. At the entrance, opening into a small court formerly adorned with flowers, is a hall, moderate in size, but light and graceful in architecture. It is overlooked by a small gallery supported by marble pillars and moresco arches. An alabaster fountain in the centre of the pavement still throws up a jet of water to cool the place. On each side are deep alcoves with raised platforms, where the bathers, after their ablutions, reclined on cushions, soothed to voluptuous repose by the fragrance of the perfumed air and the notes of soft music from the gallery. Beyond this hall are the interior chambers, still more retired; the sanctum sanctorum of female privacy: for here the beauties of the Harem indulged in the luxury of the baths.

A soft mysterious light reigns through the place, admitted through small apertures (lumbreras) in the vaulted ceiling.

The traces of ancient elegance are still to be seen; and the alabaster baths in which the sultanas once reclined. The prevailing obscurity and silence have made these vaults a favorite resort of bats, who nestle during the day in the dark nooks and corners, and on being disturbed, flit mysteriously about the twilight chambers, heightening, in an indescribable degree, their air of desertion and decay.

In this cool and elegant, though dilapidated retreat, which had the freshness and seclusion of a grotto, I passed the sultry hours of the day as summer advanced, emerging towards sunset; and bathing, or rather swimming, at night in the great reservoir of the main court. In this way I was enabled in a measure to counteract the relaxing and enervating influence of the climate.

My dream of absolute sovereignty, however, came at length to an end. I was roused one morning by the report of firearms, which reverberated among the towers as if the castle had been taken by surprise. On sallying forth, I found an old cavalier with a number of domestics, in possession of the Hall of Ambassadors. He was an ancient count who had come up from his palace in Granada to pass a short time in the Alhambra for the benefit of purer air; and who, being a veteran and inveterate sportsman, was endeavoring to get an appetite for his breakfast by shooting at swallows from the balconies. It was a harmless amusement; for though, by the alertness of his attendants in loading his pieces, he was enabled to keep up a brisk fire, I could not accuse him of the death of a single swallow. Nay, the birds themselves seemed to enjoy the sport, and to deride his want of skill, skimming in circles close to the balconies, and twittering as they darted by.

The arrival of this old gentleman changed essentially the aspect of affairs, but caused no jealousy nor collision. We tacitly shared the empire between us, like the last kings of Granada, excepting that we maintained a most amicable alliance. He reigned absolute over the court of the Lions and its adjacent halls, while I maintained peaceful possession of the regions of the baths and the little garden of Lindaraxa. We took our meals together under the arcades of the court, where the fountains cooled the air, and bubbling rills ran along the channels of the marble pavement.

In the evenings a domestic circle would gather about the worthy old cavalier. The countess, his wife by a second marriage, would come up from the city accompanied by her stepdaughter Carmen, an only child, a charming little being, still in her girlish years. Then there were always some of his official dependents, his chaplain, his lawyer, his secretary, his steward, and other officers and agents of his extensive possessions, who brought him up the news or gossip of the city, and formed his evening party of tresillo or ombre. Thus he held a kind of domestic court, where each one paid him deference, and sought to contribute to his amusement, without, however, any appearance of servility, or any sacrifice of self-respect. In fact, nothing of the kind was exacted by the demeanor of the Count; for whatever may be said of Spanish pride, it rarely chills or constrains the intercourse of social or domestic life. Among no people are the relations between kindred more unreserved and cordial, or between superior and dependent more free from haughtiness on the one side, and obsequiousness on the other. In these respects there still remains in Spanish life, especially in the provinces, much of the vaunted simplicity of the olden time.

The most interesting member of this family group, in my eyes, was the daughter of the count, the lovely little Carmen; she was but about sixteen years of age, and appeared to be considered a mere child, though the idol of the family, going generally by the child-like, but endearing appellation of la Niña. Her form had not yet attained full maturity and development, but possessed already the exquisite symmetry and pliant grace so prevalent in this country. Her blue eyes, fair complexion, and light hair, were unusual in Andalusia, and gave a mildness and gentleness to her demeanor in contrast to the usual fire of Spanish beauty, but in unison with the guileless and confiding innocence of her manners. She had at the same time the innate aptness and versatility of her fascinating countrywomen. Whatever she undertook to do she did well and apparently without effort. She sang, played the guitar and other instruments, and danced the picturesque dances of her country to admiration, but never seemed to seek admiration. Every thing was spontaneous, prompted by her own gay spirits and happy temper.

The presence of this fascinating little being spread a new charm about the Alhambra, and seemed to be in unison with the place. While the count and countess, with the chaplain or secretary, were playing their game of tresillo under the vestibule of the court of Lions, she, attended by Dolores, who acted as her maid of honor, would sit by one of the fountains, and accompanying herself on the guitar, would sing some of those popular romances which abound in Spain, or, what was still more to my taste, some traditional ballad about the Moors.

Never shall I think of the Alhambra without remembering this lovely little being, sporting in happy and innocent girlhood in its marble halls, dancing to the sound of the Moorish castañets, or mingling the silver warbling of her voice with the music of its fountains.

Relics and Genealogies

IF I HAD BEEN pleased and interested by the count and his family, as furnishing a picture of a Spanish domestic life, I was still more so when apprised of historical circumstances which linked them with the heroic times of Granada. In fact, in this worthy old cavalier, so totally unwarlike, or whose deeds in arms extended, at most, to a war on swallows and martlets, I discovered a lineal descendant and actual representative of Gonsalvo of Cordova, "The Grand Captain," who won some of his brightest laurels before the walls of Granada, and was one of the cavaliers commissioned by Ferdinand and Isabella to negotiate the terms of surrender; nay, more, the count was entitled, did he choose it, to claim remote affinity with some of the ancient Moorish princes, through a scion of his house. Don Pedro Venegas, surnamed the Tornadizo; and by the same token, his daughter, the fascinating little Carmen, might claim to be rightful representative of the princess Cetimerien or the beautiful Lindaraxa.*

Understanding from the count that he had some curious relics of the Conquest, preserved in his family archives, I accompanied him early one morning down to his palace in Granada to examine them. The most important of these relics was the sword of the Grand Captain; a weapon destitute of all ostentatious ornament, as the weapons of great generals are apt to be, with a plain hilt of ivory and a broad thin blade. It

---

*Lest this should be deemed a mere stretch of fancy, the reader is referred to the following genealogy, derived by the historian Alcantara, from an Arabian manuscript, on parchment, in the archives of the marquis of Corvera. It is a specimen of the curious affinities between Christians and Moslems, produced by capture and intermarriages, during the Moorish wars. From Aben Hud, the Moorish king, the conqueror of Almohades, was descended in right line Cid Yahia Abraham Alnagar, prince of Almeria, who married a daughter of king Bermejo. They had three children, commonly called the Cetimerian Princes. 1st. *Jusef ben Alhamar*, who for a time usurped the throne of Granada. 2d. The *Prince Nasar*, who married the celebrated Lindaraxa. 3d. The *Princess Cetimerien*, who married Don Pedro Venegas, captured by the Moors in his boyhood, a younger son of the *House of Luque*, of which house the old count was the present head.

might furnish a comment on hereditary honors, to see the sword of the grand captain legitimately declined into such feeble hands.

The other relics of the Conquest were a number of espingardas or muskets of unwieldy size and ponderous weight, worthy to rank with those enormous two-edged swords preserved in old armories, which look like relics from the days of the giants.

Beside other hereditary honors, I found the old count was Alferez mayor, or grand standard-bearer, in which capacity he was entitled to bear the ancient standard of Ferdinand and Isabella, on certain high and solemn occasions, and to wave it over their tombs. I was shown also the caparisons of velvet, sumptuously embroidered with gold and silver, for six horses, with which he appeared in state when a new sovereign was to be proclaimed in Granada and Seville; the count mounting one of the horses, and the other five being led by lackeys in rich liveries.

I had hoped to find among the relics and antiquities of the count's palace, some specimens of the armor and weapons of the Moors of Granada, such as I had heard were preserved as trophies by the descendants of the Conquerors; but in this I was disappointed. I was the more curious in this particular, because an erroneous idea has been entertained by many, as to the costumes of the Moors of Spain; supposing them to be of the usual oriental type. On the contrary, we have it on the authority of their own writers, that they adopted in many respects the fashions of the Christians. The turban, especially, so identified in idea with the Moslem, was generally abandoned, except in the western provinces, where it continued in use among people of rank and wealth, and those holding places under government. A woollen cap, red or green, was commonly worn as a substitute; probably the same kind originating in Barbary, and known by the name of Tunis or Fez, which at the present day is worn throughout the east; though generally under the turban. The Jews were obliged to wear them of a yellow color.

In Murcia, Valencia, and other eastern provinces, men of the highest rank might be seen in public bareheaded. The warrior king, Aben Hud, never wore a turban, neither did his rival and competitor Al Hamar, the founder of the Alhambra. A short cloak called Taylasan, similar to that seen in Spain in the sixteenth and seventeenth centuries, was worn by all ranks. It had a hood or cape which people of condition sometimes drew over the head; but the lower class never.

A Moslem cavalier in the thirteenth century, as described by Ibnu Said, was equipped for war very much in the Christian style. Over a complete suit of mail he wore a short scarlet tunic. His helmet was of polished steel; a shield was slung at his back; he wielded a huge spear with a broad point, sometimes a double point. His saddle was cumbrous, projecting very much in front and in rear, and he rode with a banner fluttering behind him.

In the time of Al Khattib of Granada, who wrote in the fourteenth century, the Moslems of Andalus had resumed the oriental costumes, and were again clad and armed in Arabic fashion: with light helmet, thin but well tempered cuirass, long slender lance, commonly of reed, Arabian saddle and leathern buckler, made of double folds of the skin of the antelope. A wonderful luxury prevailed at that time in the arms and equipments of the Granadian cavaliers. Their armor was inlaid with gold and silver. Their cimeters were of the keenest Damascus blades, with sheaths richly wrought and enamelled, and belts of golden filagree studded with gems. Their daggers of Fez had jewelled hilts, and their lances were set off with gay banderoles. Their horses were caparisoned in correspondent style, with velvet and embroidery.

All this minute description, given by a contemporary, and an author of distinction, verifies those gallant pictures in the old Morisco-Spanish ballads which have sometimes been deemed apocryphal, and give a vivid idea of the brilliant appearance of the chivalry of Granada, when marshalled forth in warlike array, or when celebrating the chivalrous fêtes of the Vivarrambla.

The Generalife

HIGH ABOVE the Alhambra, on the breast of the mountain, amidst embowered gardens and stately terraces,
rise the lofty towers and white walls of the Generalife; a fairy
palace, full of storied recollections. Here is still to be seen the
famous cypresses of enormous size which flourished in the
time of the Moors, and which tradition has connected with
the fabulous story of Boabdil and his sultana.

Here are preserved the portraits of many who figured in the
romantic drama of the Conquest. Ferdinand and Isabella,
Ponce de Leon, the gallant marquis of Cadiz, and Garcilaso de
la Vega, who slew in desperate fight Tarfe the Moor, a champion of Herculean strength. Here too hangs a portrait which
has long passed for that of the unfortunate Boabdil, but
which is said to be that of Aben Hud, the Moorish king from
whom descended the princes of Almeria. From one of these
princes, who joined the standard of Ferdinand and Isabella
towards the close of the Conquest, and was Christianized by
the name of Don Pedro de Granada Venegas, was descended
the present proprietor of the palace, the marquis of Campote-
jar. The proprietor, however, dwells in a foreign land, and the
palace has no longer a princely inhabitant.

Yet here is every thing to delight a southern voluptuary;
fruits, flowers, fragrance, green arbors and myrtle hedges, delicate air and gushing waters. Here I had an opportunity of
witnessing those scenes which painters are fond of depicting
about southern palaces and gardens. It was the saint's day of
the count's daughter, and she had brought up several of her
youthful companions from Granada, to sport away a long
summer's day among the breezy halls and bowers of the
Moorish palaces. A visit to the Generalife was the morning's
entertainment. Here some of the gay company dispersed itself
in groups about the green walks, the bright fountains, the
flights of Italian steps, the noble terraces and marble balustrades. Others, among whom I was one, took their seats in an
open gallery or colonnade commanding a vast prospect; with
the Alhambra, the city, and the Vega, far below, and the dis-

tant horizon of mountains—a dreamy world, all glimmering to the eye in summer sunshine. While thus seated, the all-pervading tinkling of the guitar and click of the castañets came stealing up from the valley of the Darro, and half way down the mountain we descried a festive party under the trees enjoying themselves in true Andalusian style; some lying on the grass, others dancing to the music.

All these sights and sounds, together with the princely seclusion of the place, the sweet quiet which prevailed around, and the delicious serenity of the weather had a witching effect upon the mind, and drew from some of the company, versed in local story, several of the popular fancies and traditions connected with this old Moorish palace; they were "such stuff as dreams are made of," but out of them I have shaped the following legend; which I hope may have the good fortune to prove acceptable to the reader.

Legend of Prince Ahmed al Kamel; or, the Pilgrim of Love

THERE WAS ONCE a Moorish king of Granada, who had but one son, whom he named Ahmed, to which his courtiers added the surname of al Kamel, or the perfect, from the indubitable signs of superexcellence which they perceived in him in his very infancy. The astrologers countenanced them in their foresight, predicting every thing in his favor that could make a perfect prince and a prosperous sovereign. One cloud only rested upon his destiny, and even that was of a roseate hue; he would be of an amorous temperament, and run great perils from the tender passion. If, however, he could be kept from the allurements of love until of mature age, these dangers would be averted, and his life thereafter be one uninterrupted course of felicity.

To prevent all danger of the kind, the king wisely determined to rear the prince in a seclusion where he should never see a female face, nor hear even the name of love. For this purpose he built a beautiful palace on the brow of the hill above the Alhambra, in the midst of delightful gardens, but surrounded by lofty walls, being, in fact, the same palace known at the present day by the name of the Generalife. In this palace the youthful prince was shut up, and intrusted to the guardianship and instruction of Eben Bonabben, one of the wisest and dryest of Arabian sages, who had passed the greatest part of his life in Egypt, studying hieroglyphics, and making researches among the tombs and pyramids, and who saw more charms in an Egyptian mummy than in the most tempting of living beauties. The sage was ordered to instruct the prince in all kinds of knowledge but one—he was to be kept utterly ignorant of love. "Use every precaution for the purpose you may think proper," said the king, "but remember, O Eben Bonabben, if my son learns aught of that forbidden knowledge while under your care, your head shall answer for it." A withered smile came over the dry visage of the wise Bonabben at the menace. "Let your majesty's heart be as easy about your son, as mine is about my head: am I a man likely to give lessons in the idle passion?"

Under the vigilant care of the philosopher, the prince grew up, in the seclusion of the palace and its gardens. He had black slaves to attend upon him—hideous mutes who knew nothing of love, or if they did, had not words to communicate it. His mental endowments were the peculiar care of Eben Bonabben, who sought to initiate him into the abstruse lore of Egypt; but in this the prince made little progress, and it was soon evident that he had no turn for philosophy.

He was, however, amazingly ductile for a youthful prince, ready to follow any advice, and always guided by the last counsellor. He suppressed his yawns, and listened patiently to the long and learned discourses of Eben Bonabben, from which he imbibed a smattering of various kinds of knowledge, and thus happily attained his twentieth year, a miracle of princely wisdom—but totally ignorant of love.

About this time, however, a change came over the conduct of the prince. He completely abandoned his studies, and took to strolling about the gardens, and musing by the side of the fountains. He had been taught a little music among his various accomplishments; it now engrossed a great part of his time, and a turn for poetry became apparent. The sage Eben Bonabben took the alarm, and endeavored to work these idle humors out of him by a severe course of algebra; but the prince turned from it with distaste. "I cannot endure algebra," said he; "it is an abomination to me. I want something that speaks more to the heart."

The sage Eben Bonabben shook his dry head at the words. "Here is an end to philosophy," thought he. "The prince has discovered he has a heart!" He now kept anxious watch upon his pupil, and saw that the latent tenderness of his nature was in activity, and only wanted an object. He wandered about the gardens of the Generalife in an intoxication of feelings of which he knew not the cause. Sometimes he would sit plunged in a delicious reverie; then he would seize his lute, and draw from it the most touching notes, and then throw it aside, and break forth into sighs and ejaculations.

By degrees this loving disposition began to extend to inanimate objects; he had his favorite flowers, which he cherished with tender assiduity; then he became attached to various trees, and there was one in particular, of a graceful form and drooping foliage, on which he lavished his amorous devotion, carving his name on its bark, hanging garlands on its branches, and singing couplets in its praise, to the accompaniment of his lute.

Eben Bonabben was alarmed at this excited state of his pupil. He saw him on the very brink of forbidden knowledge — the least hint might reveal to him the fatal secret. Trembling for the safety of the prince and the security of his own head, he hastened to draw him from the seductions of the garden, and shut him up in the highest tower of the Generalife. It contained beautiful apartments, and commanded an almost boundless prospect, but was elevated far above that atmosphere of sweets and those witching bowers so dangerous to the feelings of the too susceptible Ahmed.

What was to be done, however, to reconcile him to this restraint and to beguile the tedious hours? He had exhausted almost all kinds of agreeable knowledge; and algebra was not to be mentioned. Fortunately Eben Bonabben had been instructed, when in Egypt, in the language of birds, by a Jewish Rabbin, who had received it in lineal transmission from Solomon the wise, who had been taught it by the queen of Sheba. At the very mention of such a study, the eyes of the prince sparkled with animation, and he applied himself to it with such avidity, that he soon became as great an adept as his master.

The tower of the Generalife was no longer a solitude; he had companions at hand with whom he could converse. The first acquaintance he formed was with a hawk, who built his nest in a crevice of the lofty battlements, whence he soared far and wide in quest of prey. The prince, however, found little to like or esteem in him. He was a mere pirate of the air, swaggering and boastful, whose talk was all about rapine and carnage, and desperate exploits.

His next acquaintance was an owl, a mighty wise looking bird, with a huge head and staring eyes, who sat blinking and goggling all day in a hole in the wall, but roamed forth at night. He had great pretensions to wisdom, talked something of astrology and the moon, and hinted at the dark sciences; he was grievously given to metaphysics, and the prince found his prosings even more ponderous than those of the sage Eben Bonabben.

Then there was a bat, that hung all day by his heels in the dark corner of a vault, but sallied out in slipshod style at twilight. He, however, had but twilight ideas on all subjects, derided things of which he had taken but an imperfect view, and seemed to take delight in nothing.

Besides these there was a swallow, with whom the prince was at first much taken. He was a smart talker, but restless, bustling, and for ever on the wing; seldom remaining long enough for any continued conversation. He turned out in the end to be a mere smatterer, who did but skim over the surface of things, pretending to know every thing, but knowing nothing thoroughly.

These were the only feathered associates with whom the prince had any opportunity of exercising his newly acquired language; the tower was too high for any other birds to frequent it. He soon grew weary of his new acquaintances, whose conversation spoke so little to the head, and nothing to the heart; and gradually relapsed into his loneliness. A winter passed away, spring opened with all its bloom and verdure and breathing sweetness, and the happy time arrived for birds to pair and build their nests. Suddenly, as it were, a universal burst of song and melody broke forth from the groves and gardens of the Generalife, and reached the prince in the solitude of his tower. From every side he heard the same universal theme—love—love—love—chanted forth, and responded to it in every variety of note and tone. The prince listened in silence and perplexity. "What can be this love," thought he, "of which the world seems so full, and of which I know nothing?" He applied for information to his friend the hawk. The ruffian bird answered in a tone of scorn: "You must apply," said he, "to the vulgar peaceable birds of earth, who are made for the prey of us princes of the air. My trade is war, and fighting my delight. I am a warrior, and know nothing of this thing called love."

The prince turned from him with disgust, and sought the

owl in his retreat. "This is a bird," said he, "of peaceful habits, and may be able to solve my question." So he asked the owl to tell him what was this love about which all the birds in the groves below were singing.

Upon this, the owl put on a look of offended dignity. "My nights," said he, "are taken up in study and research, and my days in ruminating in my cell upon all that I have learnt. As to these singing birds of whom you talk, I never listen to them—I despise them and their themes. Allah be praised, I cannot sing; I am a philosopher, and know nothing of this thing called love."

The prince now repaired to the vault, where his friend the bat was hanging by the heels, and propounded the same question. The bat wrinkled up his nose into a most snappish expression. "Why do you disturb me in my morning's nap with such an idle question?" said he, peevishly. "I only fly by twilight, when all birds are asleep, and never trouble myself with their concerns. I am neither bird nor beast, and I thank heaven for it. I have found out the villany of the whole of them, and hate them one and all. In a word, I am a misanthrope—and know nothing of this thing called love."

As a last resort, the prince now sought the swallow, and stopped him just as he was circling about the summit of the tower. The swallow, as usual, was in a prodigious hurry, and had scarce time to make a reply. "Upon my word," said he, "I have so much public business to attend to, and so many pursuits to follow, that I have had no time to think on the subject. I have every day a thousand visits to pay; a thousand affairs of importance to examine into, that leave me not a moment of leisure for these little sing-song matters. In a word, I am a citizen of the world—I know nothing of this thing called love." So saying, the swallow dived into the valley, and was out of sight in a moment.

The prince remained disappointed and perplexed, but with his curiosity still more piqued by the difficulty of gratifying it. While in this mood, his ancient guardian entered the tower. The prince advanced eagerly to meet him. "O, Eben Bonabben," cried he, "thou hast revealed to me much of the wisdom of the earth; but there is one thing of which I remain in utter ignorance, and would fain be informed."

"My prince has but to make the inquiry, and every thing within the limited range of his servant's intellect is at his command."

"Tell me then, O most profound of sages, what is the nature of this thing called love?"

Eben Bonabben was struck as with a thunderbolt. He trembled and turned pale, and felt as if his head sat but loosely on his shoulders.

"What could suggest such a question to my prince—where could he have learnt so idle a word?"

The prince led him to the window of the tower. "Listen, O Eben Bonabben," said he. The sage listened. The nightingale sat in a thicket below the tower, singing to his paramour the rose; from every blossomed spray and tufted grove arose a strain of melody; and love—love—love—was still the unvarying strain.

"Allah Akbar! God is great!" exclaimed the wise Bonabben. "Who shall pretend to keep this secret from the heart of man, when even the birds of the air conspire to betray it?"

Then turning to Ahmed—"Oh my prince," cried he, "shut thine ears to these seductive strains. Close thy mind against this dangerous knowledge. Know that this love is the cause of half the ills of wretched mortality. It is this which produces bitterness and strife between brethren and friends; which causes treacherous murder and desolating war. Care and sorrow, weary days and sleepless nights, are its attendants. It withers the bloom and blights the joys of youth, and brings on the ills and griefs of premature old age. Allah preserve thee, my prince, in total ignorance of this thing called love!"

The sage Eben Bonabben hastily retired, leaving the prince plunged in still deeper perplexity. It was in vain he attempted to dismiss the subject from his mind; it still continued uppermost in his thoughts, and teased and exhausted him with vain conjectures. Surely, said he to himself, as he listened to the tuneful strains of the birds, there is no sorrow in those notes; every thing seems tenderness and joy. If love be a cause of such wretchedness and strife, why are not these birds drooping in solitude, or tearing each other in pieces, instead of fluttering cheerfully about the groves, or sporting with each other among flowers?

He lay one morning on his couch meditating on this inexplicable matter. The window of his chamber was open to admit the soft morning breeze, which came laden with the perfume of orange blossoms from the valley of the Darro. The voice of the nightingale was faintly heard, still chanting the wonted theme. As the prince was listening and sighing, there was a sudden rushing noise in the air; a beautiful dove, pursued by a hawk, darted in at the window, and fell panting on the floor; while the pursuer, balked of his prey, soared off to the mountains.

The prince took up the gasping bird, smoothed its feathers, and nestled it in his bosom. When he had soothed it by his caresses, he put it in a golden cage, and offered it, with his own hands, the whitest and finest of wheat and the purest of water. The bird, however, refused food, and sat drooping and pining, and uttering piteous moans.

"What aileth thee?" said Ahmed. "Hast thou not every thing thy heart can wish?"

"Alas, no!" replied the dove; "am I not separated from the partner of my heart, and that too in the happy spring-time, the very season of love!"

"Of love!" echoed Ahmed; "I pray thee, my pretty bird, canst thou then tell me what is love?"

"Too well can I, my prince. It is the torment of one, the felicity of two, the strife and enmity of three. It is a charm which draws two beings together, and unites them by delicious sympathies, making it happiness to be with each other, but misery to be apart. Is there no being to whom you are drawn by these ties of tender affection?"

"I like my old teacher Eben Bonabben better than any other being; but he is often tedious, and I occasionally feel myself happier without his society."

"That is not the sympathy I mean. I speak of love, the great mystery and principle of life: the intoxicating revel of youth; the sober delight of age. Look forth, my prince, and behold how at this blest season all nature is full of love. Every created being has its mate; the most insignificant bird sings to its paramour; the very beetle woos its lady-beetle in the dust, and yon butterflies which you see fluttering high above the tower, and toying in the air, are happy in each other's loves.

Alas, my prince! hast thou spent so many of the precious days of youth without knowing any thing of love? Is there no gentle being of another sex—no beautiful princess nor lovely damsel who has ensnared your heart, and filled your bosom with a soft tumult of pleasing pains and tender wishes?"

"I begin to understand," said the prince, sighing; "such a tumult I have more than once experienced, without knowing the cause; and where should I seek for an object such as you describe, in this dismal solitude?"

A little further conversation ensued, and the first amatory lesson of the prince was complete.

"Alas!" said he, "if love be indeed such a delight, and its interruption such a misery, Allah forbid that I should mar the joy of any of its votaries." He opened the cage, took out the dove, and having fondly kissed it, carried it to the window. "Go, happy bird," said he, "rejoice with the partner of thy heart in the days of youth and springtime. Why should I make thee a fellow-prisoner in this dreary tower, where love can never enter?"

The dove flapped its wings in rapture, gave one vault into the air, and then swooped downward on whistling wings to the blooming bowers of the Darro.

The prince followed him with his eyes, and then gave way to bitter repining. The singing of the birds which once delighted him, now added to his bitterness. Love! love! love! Alas, poor youth! he now understood the strain.

His eyes flashed fire when next he beheld the sage Bonabben. "Why hast thou kept me in this abject ignorance?" cried he. "Why has the great mystery and principle of life been withheld from me, in which I find the meanest insect is so learned? Behold all nature is in a revel of delight. Every created being rejoices with its mate. This—this is the love about which I have sought instruction. Why am I alone debarred its enjoyment? Why has so much of my youth been wasted without a knowledge of its raptures?"

The sage Bonabben saw that all further reserve was useless; for the prince had acquired the dangerous and forbidden knowledge. He revealed to him, therefore, the predictions of the astrologers, and the precautions that had been taken in his education to avert the threatened evils. "And now, my prince," added he, "my life is in your hands. Let the king your father discover that you have learned the passion of love while under my guardianship, and my head must answer for it."

The prince was as reasonable as most young men of his age, and easily listened to the remonstrances of his tutor, since nothing pleaded against them. Besides, he really was attached to Eben Bonabben, and being as yet but theoretically acquainted with the passion of love, he consented to confine the knowledge of it to his own bosom, rather than endanger the head of the philosopher.

His discretion was doomed, however, to be put to still further proofs. A few mornings afterwards, as he was ruminating on the battlements of the tower, the dove which had been released by him came hovering in the air and alighted fearlessly upon his shoulder.

The prince fondled it to his heart. "Happy bird," said he, "who can fly, as it were, with the wings of the morning to the uttermost parts of the earth. Where has thou been since we parted?"

"In a far country, my prince, whence I bring you tidings in reward for my liberty. In the wild compass of my flight, which extends over plain and mountain, as I was soaring in the air, I beheld below me a delightful garden with all kinds of fruits and flowers. It was in a green meadow, on the banks of a wandering stream; and in the centre of the garden was a stately palace. I alighted in one of the bowers to repose after my weary flight. On the green bank below me was a youthful princess, in the very sweetness and bloom of her years. She was surrounded by female attendants, young like herself, who decked her with garlands and coronets of flowers; but no flower of field or garden could compare with her for loveliness. Here, however, she bloomed in secret, for the garden was surrounded by high walls, and no mortal man was permitted to enter. When I beheld this beauteous maid, thus young and innocent and unspotted by the world, I thought, here is the being formed by heaven to inspire my prince with love."

The description was a spark of fire to the combustible heart of Ahmed; all the latent amorousness of his temperament had at once found an object, and he conceived an immeasurable passion for the princess. He wrote a letter, couched in the most impassioned language, breathing his fervent devotion, but bewailing the unhappy thraldom of his person, which prevented him from seeking her out and throwing himself at her feet. He added couplets of the most tender and moving eloquence, for he was a poet by nature, and inspired by love. He addressed his letter—"To the unknown beauty, from the captive Prince Ahmed;" then perfuming it with musk and roses, he gave it to the dove.

"Away, trustiest of messengers!" said he. "Fly over mountain and valley and river and plain; rest not in bower, nor set foot on earth, until thou hast given this letter to the mistress of my heart."

The dove soared high in air, and taking his course darted away in one undeviating direction. The prince followed him with his eye until he was a mere speck on a cloud, and gradually disappeared behind a mountain.

Day after day he watched for the return of the messenger of love, but he watched in vain. He began to accuse him of forgetfulness, when towards sunset one evening the faithful bird fluttered into his apartment, and falling at his feet expired. The arrow of some wanton archer had pierced his breast, yet he had struggled with the lingerings of life to execute his mission. As the prince bent with grief over this gentle martyr to fidelity, he beheld a chain of pearls round his neck, attached to which, beneath his wing, was a small enamelled picture. It represented a lovely princess in the very flower of her years. It was doubtless the unknown beauty of the garden; but who and where was she—how had she received his letter, and was this picture sent as a token of her approval of his passion? Unfortunately the death of the faithful dove left every thing in mystery and doubt.

The prince gazed on the picture till his eyes swam with tears. He pressed it to his lips and to his heart; he sat for hours contemplating it almost in an agony of tenderness. "Beautiful image!" said he, "alas, thou art but an image! Yet thy dewy eyes beam tenderly upon me; those rosy lips look as though they would speak encouragement: vain fancies! Have they not looked the same on some more happy rival? But where in this wide world shall I hope to find the original? Who knows what mountains, what realms may separate us; what adverse chances may intervene? Perhaps now, even now, lovers may be crowding around her, while I sit here a prisoner in a tower, wasting my time in adoration of a painted shadow."

The resolution of Prince Ahmed was taken. "I will fly from this palace," said he, "which has become an odious prison; and, a pilgrim of love, will seek this unknown princess throughout the world." To escape from the tower in the day, when every one was awake, might be a difficult matter; but at night the palace was slightly guarded; for no one apprehended any attempt of the kind from the prince, who had always been so passive in his captivity. How was he to guide himself, however, in his darkling flight, being ignorant of the country? He bethought him of the owl, who was accustomed to roam at night, and must know every by-lane and secret pass. Seeking him in his hermitage, he questioned him touching his knowledge of the land. Upon this the owl put on a mighty self-important look. "You must know, O prince," said he, "that we owls are of a very ancient and extensive family, though rather fallen to decay, and possess ruinous castles and palaces in all parts of Spain. There is scarcely a tower of the mountains, or a fortress of the plains, or an old citadel of a city, but has some brother, or uncle, or cousin, quartered in it; and in going the rounds to visit this my numerous kindred, I have pryed into every nook and corner, and made myself acquainted with every secret of the land."

The prince was overjoyed to find the owl so deeply versed in topography, and now informed him, in confidence, of his tender passion and his intended elopement, urging him to be his companion and counsellor.

"Go to!" said the owl, with a look of displeasure; "am I a bird to engage in a love affair? I whose whole time is devoted to meditation and the moon?"

"Be not offended, most solemn owl," replied the prince; "abstract thyself for a time from meditation and the moon, and aid me in my flight, and thou shalt have whatever heart can wish."

"I have that already," said the owl: "a few mice are sufficient for my frugal table, and this hole in the wall is spacious
enough for my studies; and what more does a philosopher
like myself desire?"

"Bethink thee, most wise owl, that while moping in thy cell
and gazing at the moon, all thy talents are lost to the world. I
shall one day be a sovereign prince, and may advance thee to
some post of honor and dignity."

The owl, though a philosopher and above the ordinary
wants of life, was not above ambition; so he was finally prevailed on to elope with the prince, and be his guide and
mentor in his pilgrimage.

The plans of a lover are promptly executed. The prince collected all his jewels, and concealed them about his person as
travelling funds. That very night he lowered himself by his
scarf from a balcony of the tower, clambered over the outer
walls of the Generalife, and, guided by the owl, made good
his escape before morning to the mountains.

He now held a council with his mentor as to his future
course.

"Might I advise," said the owl, "I would recommend you
to repair to Seville. You must know that many years since I
was on a visit to an uncle, an owl of great dignity and power,
who lived in a ruined wing of the Alcazar of that place. In my
hoverings at night over the city I frequently remarked a light
burning in a lonely tower. At length I alighted on the battlements, and found it to proceed from the lamp of an Arabian
magician: he was surrounded by his magic books, and on his
shoulder was perched his familiar, an ancient raven who had
come with him from Egypt. I am acquainted with that raven,
and owe to him a great part of the knowledge I possess. The
magician is since dead, but the raven still inhabits the tower,
for these birds are of wonderful long life. I would advise you,
O prince, to seek that raven, for he is a soothsayer and a
conjurer, and deals in the black art, for which all ravens, and
especially those of Egypt, are renowned."

The prince was struck with the wisdom of this advice, and
accordingly bent his course towards Seville. He travelled only
in the night, to accommodate his companion, and lay by

during the day in some dark cavern or mouldering watch-tower, for the owl knew every hiding hole of the kind, and had a most antiquarian taste for ruins.

At length one morning at daybreak they reached the city of Seville, where the owl, who hated the glare and bustle of crowded streets, halted without the gate, and took up his quarters in a hollow tree.

The prince entered the gate, and readily found the magic tower, which rose above the houses of the city, as a palm-tree rises above the shrubs of the desert; it was in fact the same tower standing at the present day, and known as the Giralda, the famous Moorish tower of Seville.

The prince ascended by a great winding staircase to the summit of the tower, where he found the cabalistic raven, an old, mysterious, gray-headed bird, ragged in feather, with a film over one eye that gave him the glare of a spectre. He was perched on one leg, with his head turned on one side, poring with his remaining eye on a diagram described on the pavement.

The prince approached him with the awe and reverence naturally inspired by his venerable appearance and supernatural wisdom. "Pardon me, most ancient and darkly wise raven," exclaimed he, "if for a moment I interrupt those studies which are the wonder of the world. You behold before you a votary of love, who would fain seek your counsel how to obtain the object of his passion."

"In other words," said the raven, with a significant look, "you seek to try my skill in palmistry. Come, show me your hand, and let me decipher the mysterious lines of fortune."

"Excuse me," said the prince, "I come not to pry into the decrees of fate, which are hidden by Allah from the eyes of mortals; I am a pilgrim of love, and seek but to find a clue to the object of my pilgrimage."

"And can you be at any loss for an object in amorous Andalusia?" said the old raven, leering upon him with his single eye; "above all, can you be at a loss in wanton Seville, where black-eyed damsels dance the zambra under every orange grove?"

The prince blushed, and was somewhat shocked at hearing

an old bird with one foot in the grave talk thus loosely. "Believe me," said he, gravely, "I am on none such light and vagrant errand as thou dost insinuate. The black-eyed damsels of Andalusia who dance among the orange groves of the Guadalquivir are as naught to me. I seek one unknown but immaculate beauty, the original of this picture; and I beseech thee, most potent raven, if it be within the scope of thy knowledge or the reach of thy art, inform me where she may be found."

The gray-headed raven was rebuked by the gravity of the prince.

"What know I," replied he, dryly, "of youth and beauty? my visits are to the old and withered, not the fresh and fair; the harbinger of fate am I; who croak bodings of death from the chimney top, and flap my wings at the sick man's window. You must seek elsewhere for tidings of your unknown beauty."

"And where can I seek if not among the sons of wisdom, versed in the book of destiny? Know that I am a royal prince, fated by the stars, and sent on a mysterious enterprise on which may hang the destiny of empires."

When the raven heard that it was a matter of vast moment, in which the stars took interest, he changed his tone and manner, and listened with profound attention to the story of the prince. When it was concluded, he replied, "Touching this princess, I can give thee no information of myself, for my flight is not among gardens, or around ladies' bowers; but hie thee to Cordova, seek the palm tree of the great Abderahman, which stands in the court of the principal mosque: at the foot of it thou wilt find a great traveller who has visited all countries and courts, and been a favorite with queens and princesses. He will give thee tidings of the object of thy search."

"Many thanks for this precious information," said the prince. "Farewell, most venerable conjurer."

"Farewell, pilgrim of love," said the raven, dryly, and again fell to pondering on the diagram.

The prince sallied forth from Seville, sought his fellow-traveller the owl, who was still dozing in the hollow tree, and set off for Cordova.

He approached it along hanging gardens, and orange and citron groves, overlooking the fair valley of the Guadalquivir. When arrived at its gates the owl flew up to a dark hole in the wall, and the prince proceeded in quest of the palm-tree planted in days of yore by the great Abderahman. It stood in the midst of the great court of the mosque, towering from amidst orange and cypress trees. Dervises and Faquirs were seated in groups under the cloisters of the court, and many of the faithful were performing their ablutions at the fountains before entering the mosque.

At the foot of the palm-tree was a crowd listening to the words of one who appeared to be talking with great volubility. "This," said the prince to himself, "must be the great traveller who is to give me tidings of the unknown princess." He mingled in the crowd, but was astonished to perceive that they were all listening to a parrot, who with his bright green coat, pragmatical eye, and consequential top-knot, had the air of a bird on excellent terms with himself.

"How is this," said the prince to one of the bystanders, "that so many grave persons can be delighted with the garrulity of a chattering bird?"

"You know not whom you speak of," said the other; "this parrot is a descendant of the famous parrot of Persia, renowned for his story-telling talent. He has all the learning of the East at the tip of his tongue, and can quote poetry as fast as he can talk. He has visited various foreign courts, where he has been considered an oracle of erudition. He has been a universal favorite also with the fair sex, who have a vast admiration for erudite parrots that can quote poetry."

"Enough," said the prince, "I will have some private talk with this distinguished traveller."

He sought a private interview, and expounded the nature of his errand. He had scarcely mentioned it when the parrot burst into a fit of dry rickety laughter that absolutely brought tears in his eyes. "Excuse my merriment," said he, "but the mere mention of love always sets me laughing."

The prince was shocked at this ill-timed mirth. "Is not love," said he, "the great mystery of nature, the secret principle of life, the universal bond of sympathy?"

"A fig's end!" cried the parrot, interrupting him; "prithee

where hast thou learned this sentimental jargon? trust me, love is quite out of vogue; one never hears of it in the company of wits and people of refinement."

The prince sighed as he recalled the different language of his friend the dove. But this parrot, thought he, has lived about the court, he affects the wit and the fine gentleman, he knows nothing of the thing called love. Unwilling to provoke any more ridicule of the sentiment which filled his heart, he now directed his inquiries to the immediate purpose of his visit.

"Tell me," said he, "most accomplished parrot, thou who hast every where been admitted to the most secret bowers of beauty, hast thou in the course of thy travels met with the original of this portrait?"

The parrot took the picture in his claw, turned his head from side to side, and examined it curiously with either eye. "Upon my honor," said he, "a very pretty face; very pretty: but then one sees so many pretty women in one's travels that one can hardly—but hold—bless me! now I look at it again—sure enough this is the princess Aldegonda: how could I forget one that is so prodigious a favorite with me!"

"The princess Aldegonda!" echoed the prince; "and where is she to be found?"

"Softly, softly," said the parrot, "easier to be found than gained. She is the only daughter of the Christian king who reigns at Toledo, and is shut up from the world until her seventeenth birth-day, on account of some prediction of those meddlesome fellows the astrologers. You'll not get a sight of her; no mortal man can see her. I was admitted to her presence to entertain her, and I assure you, on the word of a parrot who has seen the world, I have conversed with much sillier princesses in my time."

"A word in confidence, my dear parrot," said the prince; "I am heir to a kingdom, and shall one day sit upon a throne. I see that you are a bird of parts, and understand the world. Help me to gain possession of this princess, and I will advance you to some distinguished place about court."

"With all my heart," said the parrot; "but let it be a sinecure if possible, for we wits have a great dislike to labor."

Arrangements were promptly made; the prince sallied forth

from Cordova through the same gate by which he had entered; called the owl down from the hole in the wall, introduced him to his new travelling companion as a brother savant, and away they set off on their journey.

They travelled much more slowly than accorded with the impatience of the prince, but the parrot was accustomed to high life, and did not like to be disturbed early in the morning. The owl on the other hand, was for sleeping at mid-day, and lost a great deal of time by his long siestas. His antiquarian taste also was in the way; for he insisted on pausing and inspecting every ruin, and had long legendary tales to tell about every old tower and castle in the country. The prince had supposed that he and the parrot, being both birds of learning, would delight in each other's society, but never had he been more mistaken. They were eternally bickering. The one was a wit, the other a philosopher. The parrot quoted poetry, was critical on new readings and eloquent on small points of erudition; the owl treated all such knowledge as trifling, and relished nothing but metaphysics. Then the parrot would sing songs and repeat bon mots and crack jokes upon his solemn neighbor, and laugh outrageously at his own wit; all which proceedings the owl considered as a grievous invasion of his dignity, and would scowl and sulk and swell, and be silent for a whole day together.

The prince heeded not the wranglings of his companions, being wrapped up in the dreams of his own fancy and the contemplation of the portrait of the beautiful princess. In this way they journeyed through the stern passes of the Sierra Morena, across the sunburnt plains of La Mancha and Castile, and along the banks of the "Golden Tagus," which winds its wizard mazes over one half of Spain and Portugal. At length they came in sight of a strong city with walls and towers built on a rocky promontory, round the foot of which the Tagus circled with brawling violence.

"Behold," exclaimed the owl, "the ancient and renowned city of Toledo; a city famous for its antiquities. Behold those venerable domes and towers, hoary with time and clothed with legendary grandeur, in which so many of my ancestors have meditated."

"Pish!" cried the parrot, interrupting his solemn antiquarian rapture, "what have we to do with antiquities, and legends, and your ancestry? Behold what is more to the purpose—behold the abode of youth and beauty—behold at length, O prince, the abode of your long-sought princess."

The prince looked in the direction indicated by the parrot, and beheld, in a delightful green meadow on the banks of the Tagus, a stately palace rising from amidst the bowers of a delicious garden. It was just such a place as had been described by the dove as the residence of the original of the picture. He gazed at it with a throbbing heart; "perhaps at this moment," thought he, "the beautiful princess is sporting beneath those shady bowers, or pacing with delicate step those stately terraces, or reposing beneath those lofty roofs!" As he looked more narrowly he perceived that the walls of the garden were of great height, so as to defy access, while numbers of armed guards patrolled around them.

The prince turned to the parrot. "O most accomplished of birds," said he, "thou hast the gift of human speech. Hie thee to yon garden; seek the idol of my soul, and tell her that prince Ahmed, a pilgrim of love, and guided by the stars, has arrived in quest of her on the flowery banks of the Tagus."

The parrot, proud of his embassy, flew away to the garden, mounted above its lofty walls, and after soaring for a time over the lawns and groves, alighted on the balcony of a pavilion that overhung the river. Here, looking in at the casement, he beheld the princess reclining on a couch, with her eyes fixed on a paper, while tears gently stole after each other down her pallid cheek.

Pluming his wings for a moment, adjusting his bright green coat, and elevating his top-knot, the parrot perched himself beside her with a gallant air: then assuming a tenderness of tone, "Dry thy tears, most beautiful of princesses," said he, "I come to bring solace to thy heart"

The princess was startled on hearing a voice, but turning and seeing nothing but a little green-coated bird bobbing and bowing before her; "Alas! what solace canst thou yield," said she, "seeing thou art but a parrot?"

The parrot was nettled at the question. "I have consoled many beautiful ladies in my time," said he; "but let that pass. At present I come ambassador from a royal prince. Know that

Ahmed, the prince of Granada, has arrived in quest of thee, and is encamped even now on the flowery banks of the Tagus."

The eyes of the beautiful princess sparkled at these words even brighter than the diamonds in her coronet. "O sweetest of parrots," cried she, "joyful indeed are thy tidings, for I was faint and weary, and sick almost unto death with doubt of the constancy of Ahmed. Hie thee back, and tell him that the words of his letter are engraven in my heart, and his poetry has been the food of my soul. Tell him, however, that he must prepare to prove his love by force of arms; to-morrow is my seventeenth birth-day, when the king my father holds a great tournament; several princes are to enter the lists and my hand is to be the prize of the victor."

The parrot again took wing, and rustling through the groves, flew back to where the prince awaited his return. The rapture of Ahmed on finding the original of his adored portrait, and finding her kind and true, can only be conceived by those favored mortals who have had the good fortune to realize day-dreams and turn a shadow into substance: still there was one thing that alloyed his transport—this impending tournament. In fact, the banks of the Tagus were already glittering with arms, and resounding with trumpets of the various knights, who, with proud retinues, were prancing on towards Toledo to attend the ceremonial. The same star that had controlled the destiny of the prince had governed that of the princess, and until her seventeenth birth-day she had been shut up from the world, to guard her from the tender passion. The fame of her charms, however, had been enhanced rather than obscured by this seclusion. Several powerful princes had contended for her hand; and her father, who was a king of wondrous shrewdness, to avoid making enemies by showing partiality, had referred them to the arbitrament of arms. Among the rival candidates were several renowned for strength and prowess. What a predicament for the unfortunate Ahmed, unprovided as he was with weapons, and unskilled in the exercises of chivalry! "Luckless prince that I am!" said he, "to have been brought up in seclusion under the eye of a philosopher! Of what avail are algebra and philosophy in affairs of love? Alas, Eben Bonabben! why hast thou neglected to instruct me in the management of arms?" Upon this the owl broke silence, preluding his harangue with a pious ejaculation, for he was a devout Mussulman.

"Allah Akbar! God is great!" exclaimed he; "in his hands are all secret things—he alone governs the destiny of princes! Know, O prince, that this land is full of mysteries, hidden from all but those who, like myself, can grope after knowledge in the dark. Know that in the neighboring mountains there is a cave, and in that cave there is an iron table, and on that table there lies a suit of magic armor, and beside that table there stands a spell-bound steed, which have been shut up there for many generations."

The prince stared with wonder, while the owl, blinking his huge round eyes, and erecting his horns, proceeded.

"Many years since, I accompanied my father to these parts on a tour of his estates, and we are sojourned in that cave; and thus became I acquainted with the mystery. It is a tradition in our family which I have heard from my grandfather, when I was yet but a very little owlet, that this armor belonged to a Moorish magician, who took refuge in this cavern when Toledo was captured by the Christians, and died here, leaving his steed and weapons under a mystic spell, never to be used but by a Moslem, and by him only from sunrise to mid-day. In that interval, whoever uses them will overthrow every opponent."

"Enough: let us seek this cave!" exclaimed Ahmed.

Guided by his legendary mentor, the prince found the cavern, which was in one of the wildest recesses of those rocky cliffs which rise around Toledo; none but the mousing eye of an owl or an antiquary could have discovered the entrance to it. A sepulchral lamp of everlasting oil shed a solemn light through the place. On an iron table in the centre of the cavern lay the magic armor, against it leaned the lance, and beside it stood an Arabian steed, caparisoned for the field, but motionless as a statue. The armor was bright and unsullied as it had gleamed in days of old; the steed in as good condition as if just from the pasture; and when Ahmed laid his hand upon his neck, he pawed the ground and gave a loud neigh of joy that shook the walls of the cavern. Thus amply provided with "horse to ride and weapon to wear," the prince determined to defy the field in the impending tourney.

The eventful morning arrived. The lists for the combat were prepared in the Vega, or plain, just below the cliff-built walls of Toledo, where stages and galleries were erected for the spectators, covered with rich tapestry, and sheltered from the sun by silken awnings. All the beauties of the land were assembled in those galleries, while below pranced plumed knights with their pages and esquires, among whom figured conspicuously the princes who were to contend in the tourney. All the beauties of the land, however, were eclipsed when the princess Aldegonda appeared in the royal pavilion, and for the first time broke forth upon the gaze of an admiring world. A murmur of wonder ran through the crowd at her transcendent loveliness; and the princes who were candidates for her hand, merely on the faith of her reported charms, now felt tenfold ardor for the conflict.

The princess, however, had a troubled look. The color came and went from her cheek, and her eye wandered with a restless and unsatisfied expression over the plumed throng of knights. The trumpets were about sounding for the encounter, when the herald announced the arrival of a strange knight; and Ahmed rode into the field. A steel helmet studded with gems rose above his turban; his cuirass was embossed with gold; his cimeter and dagger were of the workmanship of Fez, and flamed with precious stones. A round shield was at his shoulder, and in his hand he bore the lance of charmed virtue. The caparison of his Arabian steed was richly embroidered and swept the ground, and the proud animal pranced and snuffed the air, and neighed with joy at once more beholding the array of arms. The lofty and graceful demeanor of the prince struck every eye, and when his appellation was announced, "The Pilgrim of Love," a universal flutter and agitation prevailed among the fair dames in the galleries.

When Ahmed presented himself at the lists, however, they were closed against him: none but princes, he was told, were admitted to the contest. He declared his name and rank. Still worse!—he was a Moslem, and could not engage in a tourney where the hand of a Christian princess was the prize.

The rival princes surrounded him with haughty and menacing aspects; and one of insolent demeanor and herculean
frame sneered at his light and youthful form, and scoffed at
his amorous appellation. The ire of the prince was roused. He
defied his rival to the encounter. They took distance, wheeled,
and charged; and at the first touch of the magic lance, the
brawny scoffer was tilted from his saddle. Here the prince
would have paused, but alas! he had to deal with a demoniac
horse and armor; once in action nothing could control them.
The Arabian steed charged into the thickest of the throng; the
lance overturned every thing that presented; the gentle prince
was carried pell-mell about the field, strewing it with high and
low, gentle and simple, and grieving at his own involuntary
exploits. The king stormed and raged at this outrage on his
subjects and his guests. He ordered out all his guards—they
were unhorsed as fast as they came up. The king threw off his
robes, grasped buckler and lance, and rode forth to awe the
stranger with the presence of majesty itself. Alas! majesty
fared no better than the vulgar; the steed and lance were no
respectors of persons; to the dismay of Ahmed, he was borne
full tilt against the king, and in a moment the royal heels were
in the air, and the crown was rolling in the dust.

At this moment the sun reached the meridian; the magic
spell resumed its power; the Arabian steed scoured across the
plain, leaped the barrier, plunged into the Tagus, swam its
raging current, bore the prince breathless and amazed to the
cavern, and resumed his station, like a statue, beside the iron
table. The prince dismounted right gladly, and replaced the
armor, to abide the further decrees of fate. Then seating himself in the cavern, he ruminated on the desperate state to
which this demoniac steed and armor had reduced him. Never
should he dare to show his face at Toledo after inflicting such
disgrace upon its chivalry, and such an outrage on its king.
What too would the princess think of so rude and riotous an
achievement? Full of anxiety, he sent forth his winged messengers to gather tidings. The parrot resorted to all the public
places and crowded resorts of the city, and soon returned
with a world of gossip. All Toledo was in consternation. The
princess had been borne off senseless to the palace; the tournament had ended in confusion; every one was talking of

the sudden apparition, prodigious exploits, and strange disappearance of the Moslem knight. Some pronounced him a Moorish magician; others thought him a demon who had assumed a human shape, while others related traditions of enchanted warriors hidden in the caves of the mountains, and thought it might be one of these, who had made a sudden irruption from his den. All agreed that no mere ordinary mortal could have wrought such wonders, or unhorsed such accomplished and stalwart Christian warriors.

The owl flew forth at night and hovered about the dusky city, perching on the roofs and chimneys. He then wheeled his flight up to the royal palace, which stood on a rocky summit of Toledo, and went prowling about its terraces and battlements, eaves-dropping at every cranny, and glaring in with his big goggling eyes at every window where there was a light, so as to throw two or three maids of honor into fits. It was not until the gray dawn began to peer above the mountains that he returned from his mousing expedition, and related to the prince what he had seen.

"As I was prying about one of the loftiest towers of the palace," said he, "I beheld through a casement a beautiful princess. She was reclining on a couch with attendants and physicians around her, but she would none of their ministry and relief. When they retired I beheld her draw forth a letter from her bosom, and read and kiss it, and give way to loud lamentations; at which, philosopher as I am, I could but be greatly moved."

The tender heart of Ahmed was distressed at these tidings. "Too true were thy words, O sage Eben Bonabben," cried he; "care and sorrow and sleepless nights are the lot of lovers. Allah preserve the princess from the blighting influence of this thing called love!"

Further intelligence from Toledo corroborated the report of the owl. The city was a prey to uneasiness and alarm. The princess was conveyed to the highest tower of the palace, every avenue to which was strongly guarded. In the mean time a devouring melancholy had seized upon her, of which no one could divine the cause—she refused food and turned a deaf ear to every consolation. The most skilful physicians had essayed their art in vain; it was thought some magic spell had been practised upon her, and the king made proclamation, declaring that whoever should effect her cure should receive the richest jewel in the royal treasury.

When the owl, who was dozing in a corner, heard of this proclamation, he rolled his large eyes and looked more mysterious than ever.

"Allah Akbar!" exclaimed he, "happy the man that shall effect that cure, should he but know what to choose from the royal treasury."

"What mean you, most reverend owl?" said Ahmed.

"Hearken, O prince, to what I shall relate. We owls, you must know, are a learned body, and much given to dark and dusty research. During my late prowling at night about the domes and turrets of Toledo, I discovered a college of antiquarian owls, who hold their meetings in a great vaulted tower where the royal treasury is deposited. Here they were discussing the forms and inscriptions and designs of ancient gems and jewels, and of golden and silver vessels, heaped up in the treasury, the fashion of every country and age; but mostly they were interested about certain relics and talismans that have remained in the treasury since the time of Roderick the Goth. Among these was a box of sandal-wood secured by bands of steel of Oriental workmanship, and inscribed with mystic characters known only to the learned few. This box and its inscription had occupied the college for several sessions, and had caused much long and grave dispute. At the time of my visit a very ancient owl, who had recently arrived from Egypt, was seated on the lid of the box lecturing upon the inscription, and he proved from it that the coffer contained the silken carpet of the throne of Solomon the wise; which doubtless had been brought to Toledo by the Jews who took refuge there after the downfall of Jerusalem."

When the owl had concluded his antiquarian harangue the prince remained for a time absorbed in thought. "I have heard," said he, "from the sage Eben Bonabben, of the wonderful properties of that talisman, which disappeared at the fall of Jerusalem, and was supposed to be lost to mankind. Doubtless it remains a sealed mystery to the Christians of

Toledo. If I can get possession of that carpet, my fortune is secure."

The next day the prince laid aside his rich attire, and arrayed himself in the simple garb of an Arab of the desert. He dyed his complexion to a tawny hue, and no one could have recognized in him the splendid warrior who had caused such admiration and dismay at the tournament. With staff in hand, and scrip by his side, and a small pastoral reed, he repaired to Toledo, and presenting himself at the gate of the royal palace, announced himself as a candidate for the reward offered for the cure of the princess. The guards would have driven him away with blows. "What can a vagrant Arab like thyself pretend to do," said they, "in a case where the most learned of the land have failed?" The king, however, overheard the tumult, and ordered the Arab to be brought into his presence.

"Most potent king," said Ahmed, "you behold before you a Bedouin Arab, the greater part of whose life has been passed in the solitudes of the desert. These solitudes, it is well known, are the haunts of demons and evil spirits, who beset us poor shepherds in our lonely watchings, enter into and possess our flocks and herds, and sometimes render even the patient camel furious; against these our counter-charm is music; and we have legendary airs handed down from generation to generation, that we chant and pipe, to cast forth these evil spirits. I am of a gifted line, and possess this power in its fullest force. If it be any evil influence of the kind that holds a spell over thy daughter, I pledge my head to free her from its sway."

The king, who was a man of understanding and knew the wonderful secrets possessed by the Arabs, was inspired with hope by the confident language of the prince. He conducted him immediately to the lofty tower, secured by several doors, in the summit of which was the chamber of the princess. The windows opened upon a terrace with balustrades, commanding a view over Toledo and all the surrounding country. The windows were darkened, for the princess lay within, a prey to a devouring grief that refused all alleviation.

The prince seated himself on the terrace, and performed

several wild Arabian airs on his pastoral pipe, which he had learnt from his attendants in the Generalife at Granada. The princess continued insensible, and the doctors who were present shook their heads, and smiled with incredulity and contempt: at length the prince laid aside the reed, and, to a simple melody, chanted the amatory verses of the letter which had declared his passion.

The princess recognized the strain—a fluttering joy stole to her heart; she raised her head and listened; tears rushed to her eyes and streamed down her cheeks; her bosom rose and fell with a tumult of emotions. She would have asked for the minstrel to be brought into her presence, but maiden coyness held her silent. The king read her wishes, and at his command Ahmed was conducted into the chamber. The lovers were discreet: they but exchanged glances, yet those glances spoke volumes. Never was triumph of music more complete. The rose had returned to the soft cheek of the princess, the freshness to her lips, and the dewy light to her languishing eyes.

All the physicians present stared at each other with astonishment. The king regarded the Arab minstrel with admiration mixed with awe. "Wonderful youth!" exclaimed he, "thou shalt henceforth be the first physician of my court, and no other prescription will I take but thy melody. For the present receive thy reward, the most precious jewel in my treasury."

"O king," replied Ahmed, "I care not for silver or gold or precious stones. One relic hast thou in thy treasury, handed down from the Moslems who once owned Toledo—a box of sandal-wood containing a silken carpet: give me that box, and I am content."

All present were surprised at the moderation of the Arab; and still more when the box of sandal-wood was brought and the carpet drawn forth. It was of fine green silk, covered with Hebrew and Chaldaic characters. The court physicians looked at each other, shrugged their shoulders, and smiled at the simplicity of this new practitioner, who could be content with so paltry a fee.

"This carpet," said the prince, "once covered the throne of Solomon the wise; it is worthy of being placed beneath the feet of beauty."

So saying, he spread it on the terrace beneath an ottoman that had been brought forth for the princess; then seating himself at her feet—

"Who," said he, "shall counteract what is written in the book of fate? Behold the prediction of the astrologers verified. Know, O king, that your daughter and I have long loved each other in secret. Behold in me the Pilgrim of Love!"

These words were scarcely from his lips, when the carpet rose in the air, bearing off the prince and princess. The king and the physicians gazed after it with open mouths and straining eyes until it became a little speck on the white bosom of a cloud, and then disappeared in the blue vault of heaven.

The king in a rage summoned his treasurer. "How is this," said he, "that thou hast suffered an infidel to get possession of such a talisman?"

"Alas, sir, we knew not its nature, nor could we decipher the inscription of the box. If it be indeed the carpet of the throne of the wise Solomon, it is possessed of magic power, and can transport its owner from place to place through the air."

The king assembled a mighty army, and set off for Granada in pursuit of the fugitives. His march was long and toilsome. Encamping in the Vega, he sent a herald to demand restitution of his daughter. The king himself came forth with all his court to meet him. In the king he beheld the real minstrel, for Ahmed had succeeded to the throne on the death of his father, and the beautiful Aldegonda was his sultana.

The Christian king was easily pacified when he found that his daughter was suffered to continue in her faith; not that he was particularly pious; but religion is always a point of pride and etiquette with princes. Instead of bloody battles, there was a succession of feasts and rejoicings, after which the king returned well pleased to Toledo, and the youthful couple continued to reign as happily as wisely, in the Alhambra.

It is proper to add, that the owl and the parrot had severally followed the prince by easy stages to Granada; the former travelling by night, and stopping at the various hereditary possessions of his family; the latter figuring in gay circles of every town and city on his route.

Ahmed gratefully requited the services which they had

rendered on his pilgrimage. He appointed the owl his prime minister, the parrot his master of ceremonies. It is needless to say that never was a realm more sagely administered, nor a court conducted with more exact punctilio.

A Ramble Among the Hills

I USED FREQUENTLY to amuse myself towards the close of the day, when the heat had subsided, with taking long rambles about the neighboring hills and the deep umbrageous valleys, accompanied by my historiographic squire, Mateo, to whose passion for gossiping I on such occasions gave the most unbounded license; and there was scarce a rock, or ruin, or broken fountain, or lonely glen, about which he had not some marvellous story; or, above all, some golden legend; for never was poor devil so munificent in dispensing hidden treasures.

In the course of one of these strolls Mateo was more than usually communicative. It was toward sunset that we sallied forth from the great Gate of Justice, and ascended an alley of trees until we came to a clump of figs and pomegranates at the foot of the Tower of the Seven Floors (de los siete suelos), the identical tower whence Boabdil is said to have issued, when he surrendered his capital. Here, pointing to a low archway in the foundation, Mateo informed me of a monstrous sprite or hobgoblin, said to infest this tower, ever since the time of the Moors, and to guard the treasures of a Moslem king. Sometimes it issues forth in the dead of the night, and scours the avenues of the Alhambra, and the streets of Granada, in the shape of a headless horse, pursued by six dogs with terrible yells and howlings.

"But have you ever met with it yourself, Mateo, in any of your rambles?" demanded I.

"No, Señor, God be thanked! but my grandfather, the tailor, knew several persons that had seen it, for it went about much oftener in his time than at present; sometimes in one shape, sometimes in another. Every body in Granada has heard of the Belludo, for the old women and the nurses frighten the children with it when they cry. Some say it is the spirit of a cruel Moorish king, who killed his six sons and buried them in these vaults, and that they hunt him at nights in revenge."

I forbear to dwell upon the marvellous details given by the

simple-minded Mateo about this redoubtable phantom, which has, in fact, been time out of mind a favorite theme of nursery tales and popular tradition in Granada, and of which honorable mention is made by an ancient and learned historian and topographer of the place.

Leaving this eventful pile, we continued our course, skirting the fruitful orchards of the Generalife, in which two or three nightingales were pouring forth a rich strain of melody. Behind these orchards we passed a number of Moorish tanks, with a door cut into the rocky bosom of the hill, but closed up. These tanks, Mateo informed me, were favorite bathing-places of himself and his comrades in boyhood, until frightened away by a story of a hideous Moor, who used to issue forth from the door in the rock to entrap unwary bathers.

Leaving these haunted tanks behind us, we pursued our ramble up a solitary mule-path winding among the hills, and soon found ourselves amidst wild and melancholy mountains, destitute of trees, and here and there tinted with scanty verdure. Every thing within sight was severe and sterile, and it was scarcely possible to realize the idea that but a short distance behind us was the Generalife, with its blooming orchards and terraced gardens, and that we were in the vicinity of delicious Granada, that city of groves and fountains. But such is the nature of Spain; wild and stern the moment it escapes from cultivation; the desert and the garden are ever side by side.

The narrow defile up which we were passing is called, according to Mateo, *el Barranco de la tinaja*, or the ravine of the jar, because a jar full of Moorish gold was found here in old times. The brain of poor Mateo was continually running upon these golden legends.

"But what is the meaning of the cross I see yonder upon a heap of stones, in that narrow part of the ravine?"

"Oh, that's nothing—a muleteer was murdered there some years since."

"So then, Mateo, you have robbers and murderers even at the gates of the Alhambra?"

"Not at present, Señor; that was formerly, when there used to be many loose fellows about the fortress; but they've all been weeded out. Not but that the gipsies who live in caves

in the hill-sides, just out of the fortress, are many of them fit
for any thing; but we have had no murder about here for a
long time past. The man who murdered the muleteer was
hanged in the fortress."

Our path continued up the barranco, with a bold, rugged
height to our left, called the "Silla del Moro," or, Chair of the
Moor, from the tradition already alluded to, that the unfortunate Boabdil fled thither during a popular insurrection, and
remained all day seated on the rocky summit, looking mournfully down on his factious city.

We at length arrived on the highest part of the promontory
above Granada, called the mountain of the sun. The evening
was approaching; the setting sun just gilded the loftiest
heights. Here and there a solitary shepherd might be descried
driving his flock down the declivities, to be folded for the
night; or a muleteer and his lagging animals, threading some
mountain path, to arrive at the city gates before nightfall.

Presently the deep tones of the cathedral bell came swelling
up the defiles, proclaiming the hour of "oration" or prayer.
The note was responded to from the belfry of every church,
and from the sweet bells of the convents among the mountains. The shepherd paused on the fold of the hill, the muleteer in the midst of the road, each took off his hat and
remained motionless for a time, murmuring his evening
prayer. There is always something pleasingly solemn in this
custom, by which, at a melodious signal, every human being
throughout the land unites at the same moment in a tribute
of thanks to God for the mercies of the day. It spreads a transient sanctity over the land, and the sight of the sun sinking in
all his glory, adds not a little to the solemnity of the scene.

In the present instance the effect was heightened by the
wild and lonely nature of the place. We were on the naked
and broken summit of the haunted mountain of the sun,
where ruined tanks and cisterns, and the mouldering foundations of extensive buildings, spoke of former populousness,
but where all was now silent and desolate.

As we were wandering about among these traces of old
times, we came to a circular pit, penetrating deep into the
bosom of the mountain; which Mateo pointed out as one of
the wonders and mysteries of the place. I supposed it to be a

well dug by the indefatigable Moors, to obtain their favorite element in its greatest purity. Mateo, however, had a different story, and one much more to his humor. According to a tradition, in which his father and grandfather firmly believed, this was an entrance to the subterranean caverns of the mountain, in which Boabdil and his court lay bound in magic spell; and whence they sallied forth at night, at allotted times, to revisit their ancient abodes.

"Ah, Señor, this mountain is full of wonders of the kind. In another place there was a hole somewhat like this, and just within it hung an iron pot by a chain; nobody knew what was in that pot, for it was always covered up; but every body supposed it full of Moorish gold. Many tried to draw it forth, for it seemed just within reach; but the moment it was touched it would sink far, far down, and not come up again for some time. At last one who thought it must be enchanted touched it with the cross, by way of breaking the charm; and faith he did break it, for the pot sank out of sight and never was seen anymore."

"All this is fact, Señor; for my grandfather was an eye-witness."

"What! Mateo; did he see the pot?"

"No, Señor, but he saw the hole where the pot had hung."

"It's the same thing, Mateo."

The deepening twilight, which, in this climate, is of short duration, admonished us to leave this haunted ground. As we descended the mountain defile, there was no longer herdsman nor muleteer to be seen, nor any thing to be heard but our own footsteps and the lonely chirping of the cricket. The shadows of the valley grew deeper and deeper, until all was dark around us. The lofty summit of the Sierra Nevada alone retained a lingering gleam of daylight; its snowy peaks glaring against the dark blue firmament, and seeming close to us, from the extreme purity of the atmosphere.

"How near the Sierra looks this evening!" said Mateo; "it seems as if you could touch it with your hand; and yet it is many long leagues off." While he was speaking, a star appeared over the snowy summit of the mountain, the only one yet visible in the heavens, and so pure, so large, so bright and beautiful, as to call forth ejaculations of delight from honest Mateo.

"Que estrella hermosa! que clara y limpia es!—No pueda ser estrella mas brillante!"

(What a beautiful star! how clear and lucid—a star could not be more brilliant!)

I have often remarked this sensibility of the common people of Spain to the charms of natural objects. The lustre of a star, the beauty or fragrance of a flower, the crystal purity of a fountain, will inspire them with a kind of poetical delight; and then, what euphonious words their magnificent language affords, with which to give utterance to their transports!

"But what lights are those, Mateo, which I see twinkling along the Sierra Nevada, just below the snowy region, and which might be taken for stars, only that they are ruddy, and against the dark side of the mountain?"

"Those, Señor, are fires, made by the men who gather snow and ice for the supply of Granada. They go up every afternoon with mules and asses, and take turns, some to rest and warm themselves by the fires, while others fill the panniers with ice. They then set off down the mountains, so as to reach the gates of Granada before sunrise. That Sierra Nevada, Señor, is a lump of ice in the middle of Andalusia, to keep it all cool in summer."

It was now completely dark; we were passing through the barranco, where stood the cross of the murdered muleteer; when I beheld a number of lights moving at a distance, and apparently advancing up the ravine. On nearer approach, they proved to be torches borne by a train of uncouth figures arrayed in black: it would have been a procession dreary enough at any time, but was peculiarly so in this wild and solitary place.

Mateo drew near, and told me, in a low voice, that it was a funeral train bearing a corpse to the burying-ground among the hills.

As the procession passed by, the lugubrious light of the torches, falling on the rugged features and funeral-weeds of the attendants, had the most fantastic effect, but was perfectly ghastly, as it revealed the countenance of the corpse, which according to the Spanish custom, was borne uncovered on an open bier. I remained for some time gazing after the dreary train as it wound up the dark defile of the mountain. It put me in mind of the old story of a procession of demons bearing the body of a sinner up the crater of Stromboli.

"Ah! Señor," cried Mateo, "I could tell you a story of a procession once seen among these mountains, but then you'd laugh at me, and say it was one of the legacies of my grandfather the tailor."

"By no means, Mateo. There is nothing I relish more than a marvellous tale."

"Well, Señor, it is about one of those very men we have been talking of, who gather snow on the Sierra Nevada.

"You must know, that a great many years since, in my grandfather's time, there was an old fellow, Tio Nicolo (Uncle Nicholas) by name, who had filled the panniers of his mule with snow and ice, and was returning down the mountain. Being very drowsy, he mounted upon the mule, and soon falling asleep, went with his head nodding and bobbing about from side to side, while his surefooted old mule stepped along the edge of precipices, and down steep and broken barrancos, just as safe and steady as if it had been on plain ground. At length, Tio Nicolo awoke, and gazed about him, and rubbed his eyes—and, in good truth, he had reason. The moon shone almost as bright as day, and he saw the city below him, as plain as your hand, and shining with its white buildings, like a silver platter in the moonshine; but, Lord! Señor, it was nothing like the city he had left a few hours before! Instead of the cathedral, with its great dome and turrets, and the churches with their spires, and the convents with their pinnacles, all surmounted with the blessed cross, he saw nothing but Moorish mosques, and minarets, and cupolas, all topped off with glittering crescents, such as you see on the Barbary flags. Well, Señor, as you may suppose, Tio Nicolo was mightily puzzled at all this, but while he was gazing down upon the city, a great army came marching up the mountains, winding along the ravines, sometimes in the moonshine, sometimes in the shade. As it drew nigh, he saw that there were horse and foot all in Moorish armor. Tio Nicolo tried to scramble out of their way, but his old mule stood stock still, and refused to budge, trembling, at the same time, like a leaf—for dumb beasts, Señor, are just as much frightened at such things as human beings. Well, Señor, the hobgoblin army came marching by; there were men that seemed to blow trumpets, and others to beat drums and strike cymbals, yet never a sound did they make; they all moved on without the least noise, just as I have seen painted armies move across the stage in the theatre of Granada, and all looked as pale as death. At last, in the rear of the army, between two black Moorish horsemen, rode the Grand Inquisitor of Granada, on a mule as white as snow. Tio Nicolo wondered to see him in such company, for the Inquisitor was famous for his hatred of Moors, and indeed, of all kinds of Infidels, Jews, and Heretics, and used to hunt them out with fire and scourge. However, Tio Nicolo felt himself safe, now that there was a priest of such sanctity at hand. So making the sign of the cross, he called out for his benediction, when, hombre! he received a blow that sent him and his old mule over the edge of a steep bank, down which they rolled, head over heels, to the bottom! Tio Nicolo did not come to his senses until long after sunrise, when he found himself at the bottom of a deep ravine, his mule grazing beside him, and his panniers of snow completely melted. He crawled back to Granada sorely bruised and battered, but was glad to find the city looking as usual, with Christian churches and crosses. When he told the story of his night's adventure, every one laughed at him; some said he had dreamed it all, as he dozed on his mule; others thought it all a fabrication of his own—but what was strange, Señor, and made people afterwards think more seriously of the matter, was, that the Grand Inquisitor died within the year. I have often heard my grandfather, the tailor, say that there was more meant by that hobgoblin army bearing off the resemblance of the priest, than folks dared to surmise."

"Then you would insinuate, friend Mateo, that there is a kind of Moorish limbo, or purgatory, in the bowels of these mountains, to which the padre Inquisitor was borne off."

"God forbid, Señor! I know nothing of the matter. I only relate what I heard from my grandfather."

By the time Mateo had finished the tale which I have more succinctly related, and which was interlarded with many comments, and spun out with minute details, we reached the gate of the Alhambra.

The marvellous stories hinted at by Mateo, in the early part of our ramble about the Tower of the Seven Floors, set me as usual upon my goblin researches. I found that the redoubtable phantom, the Belludo, had been time out of mind a favorite theme of nursery tales and popular traditions in Granada, and that honorable mention had even been made of it by an ancient historian and topographer of the place. The scattered members of one of these popular traditions I have gathered together, collated them with infinite pains, and digested them into the following legend; which only wants a number of learned notes and references at bottom to take its rank among those concrete productions gravely passed upon the world for Historical Facts.

Legend of the Moor's Legacy

JUST WITHIN the fortress of the Alhambra, in front of the royal palace, is a broad open esplanade, called the Place or Square of the Cisterns, (la Plaza de los Algibes,) so called from being undermined by reservoirs of water, hidden from sight, and which have existed from the time of the Moors. At one corner of this esplanade is a Moorish well, cut through the living rock to a great depth, the water of which is cold as ice and clear as crystal. The wells made by the Moors are always in repute, for it is well known what pains they took to penetrate to the purest and sweetest springs and fountains. The one of which we now speak is famous throughout Granada, insomuch that water-carriers, some bearing great water-jars on their shoulders, others driving asses before them laden with earthen vessels, are ascending and descending the steep woody avenues of the Alhambra, from early dawn until a late hour of the night.

Fountains and wells, ever since the scriptural days, have been noted gossiping places in hot climates; and at the well in question there is a kind of perpetual club kept up during the livelong day, by the invalids, old women, and other curious donothing folk of the fortress, who sit here on the stone benches, under an awning spread over the well to shelter the toll-gatherer from the sun, and dawdle over the gossip of the fortress, and question every water-carrier that arrives about the news of the city, and make long comments on every thing they hear and see. Not an hour of the day but loitering house-wives and idle maid-servants may be seen, lingering with pitcher on head or in hand, to hear the last of the endless tattle of these worthies.

Among the water-carriers who once resorted to this well, there was a sturdy, strong-backed, bandy-legged little fellow, named Pedro Gil, but called Peregil for shortness. Being a water-carrier, he was a Gallego, or native of Gallicia, of course. Nature seems to have formed races of men, as she has of animals, for different kinds of drudgery. In France the shoeblacks are all Savoyards, the porters of hotels all Swiss, and in the days of hoops and hair-powder in England, no man could give the regular swing to a sedan-chair but a bog-trotting Irishman. So in Spain, the carriers of water and bearers of burdens are all sturdy little natives of Gallicia. No man says, "Get me a porter," but, "Call a Gallego."

To return from this digression, Peregil the Gallego had begun business with merely a great earthen jar which he carried upon his shoulder; by degrees he rose in the world, and was enabled to purchase an assistant of a correspondent class of animals, being a stout shaggy-haired donkey. On each side of this his long-eared aid-de-camp, in a kind of pannier, were slung his water-jars, covered with fig-leaves to protect them from the sun. There was not a more industrious water-carrier in all Granada, nor one more merry withal. The streets rang with his cheerful voice as he trudged after his donkey, singing forth the usual summer note that resounds through the Spanish towns: *"Quien quiere agua—agua mas fria que la nieve?"*—"Who wants water—water colder than snow? Who wants water from the well of the Alhambra, cold as ice and clear as crystal?" When he served a customer with a sparkling glass, it was always with a pleasant word that caused a smile; and if, perchance, it was a comely dame or dimpling damsel, it was always with a sly leer and a compliment to her beauty that was irresistible. Thus Peregil the Gallego was noted throughout all Granada for being one of the civilest, pleas-antest, and happiest of mortals. Yet it is not he who sings loudest and jokes most that has the lightest heart. Under all this air of merriment, honest Peregil had his cares and troubles. He had a large family of ragged children to support, who were hungry and clamorous as a nest of young swallows, and beset him with their outcries for food whenever he came home of an evening. He had a helpmate, too, who was any thing but a help to him. She had been a village beauty before marriage, noted for her skill at dancing the bolero and rattling the castañets; and she still retained her early propensities, spending the hard earnings of honest Peregil in frippery, and laying the very donkey under requisition for junketing parties into the country on Sundays, and saints' days, and those innu-merable holidays which are rather more numerous in Spain than the days of the week. With all this she was a little of a

slattern, something more of a lie-abed, and, above all, a gossip
of the first water; neglecting house, household, and every
thing else, to loiter slipshod in the houses of her gossip
neighbors.

He, however, who tempers the wind to the shorn lamb,
accommodates the yoke of matrimony to the submissive neck.
Peregil bore all the heavy dispensations of wife and children
with as meek a spirit as his donkey bore the water-jars; and,
however he might shake his ears in private, never ventured to
question the household virtues of his slattern spouse.

He loved his children too even as an owl loves its owlets,
seeing in them his own image multiplied and perpetuated; for
they were a sturdy, long-backed, bandy-legged little brood.
The great pleasure of honest Peregil was, whenever he could
afford himself a scanty holiday, and had a handful of mare-
vedis to spare, to take the whole litter forth with him, some in
his arms, some tugging at his skirts, and some trudging at his
heels, and to treat them to a gambol among the orchards of
the Vega, while his wife was dancing with her holiday friends
in the Angosturas of the Darro.

It was a late hour one summer night, and most of the
water-carriers had desisted from their toils. The day had been
uncommonly sultry; the night was one of those delicious
moonlights, which tempt the inhabitants of southern climes
to indemnify themselves for the heat and inaction of the day,
by lingering in the open air, and enjoying its tempered sweetness until after midnight. Customers for water were therefore
still abroad. Peregil, like a considerate, painstaking father,
thought of his hungry children. "One more journey to the
well," said he to himself, "to earn a Sunday's puchero for the
little ones." So saying, he trudged manfully up the steep avenue of the Alhambra, singing as he went, and now and then
bestowing a hearty thwack with a cudgel on the flanks of his
donkey, either by way of cadence to the song, or refreshment
to the animal; for dry blows serve in lieu of provender in
Spain for all beasts of burden.

When arrived at the well, he found it deserted by every one
except a solitary stranger in Moorish garb, seated on a stone
bench in the moonlight. Peregil paused at first and regarded
him with surprise, not unmixed with awe, but the Moor

feebly beckoned him to approach. "I am faint and ill," said he, "aid me to return to the city, and I will pay thee double what thou couldst gain by thy jars of water."

The honest heart of the little water-carrier was touched with compassion at the appeal of the stranger. "God forbid," said he, "that I should ask fee or reward for doing a common act of humanity." He accordingly helped the Moor on his donkey, and set off slowly for Granada, the poor Moslem being so weak that it was necessary to hold him on the animal to keep him from falling to the earth.

When they entered the city, the water-carrier demanded whither he should conduct him. "Alas!" said the Moor, faintly, "I have neither home nor habitation, I am a stranger in the land. Suffer me to lay my head this night beneath thy roof, and thou shalt be amply repaid."

Honest Peregil thus saw himself unexpectedly saddled with an infidel guest, but he was too humane to refuse a night's shelter to a fellow being in so forlorn a plight, so he conducted the Moor to his dwelling. The children, who had sallied forth open-mouthed as usual on hearing the tramp of the donkey, ran back with affright, when they beheld the turbaned stranger, and hid themselves behind their mother. The latter stepped forth intrepidly, like a ruffling hen before her brood when a vagrant dog approaches.

"What infidel companion," cried she, "is this you have brought home at this late hour, to draw upon us the eyes of the inquisition?"

"Be quiet, wife," replied the Gallego, "here is a poor sick stranger, without friend or home; wouldst thou turn him forth to perish in the streets?"

The wife would still have remonstrated, for although she lived in a hovel she was a furious stickler for the credit of her house; the little water-carrier, however, for once was stiff-necked, and refused to bend beneath the yoke. He assisted the poor Moslem to alight, and spread a mat and a sheep-skin for him, on the ground, in the coolest part of the house; being the only kind of bed that his poverty afforded.

In a little while the Moor was seized with violent convulsions, which defied all the ministering skill of the simple water-carrier. The eye of the poor patient acknowledged his kindness. During an interval of his fits he called him to his side, and addressing him in a low voice, "My end," said he, "I fear is at hand. If I die, I bequeath you this box as a reward for your charity:" so saying, he opened his albornoz, or cloak, and showed a small box of sandal-wood, strapped round his body. "God grant, my friend," replied the worthy little Gallego, "that you may live many years to enjoy your treasure, whatever it may be." The Moor shook his head; he laid his hand upon the box, and would have said something more concerning it, but his convulsions returned with increasing violence, and in a little while he expired.

The water-carrier's wife was now as one distracted. "This comes," said she, "of your foolish good nature, always running into scapes to oblige others. What will become of us when this corpse is found in our house? We shall be sent to prison as murderers; and if we escape with our lives, shall be ruined by notaries and alguazils."

Poor Peregil was in equal tribulation, and almost repented himself of having done a good deed. At length a thought struck him. "It is not yet day," said he, "I can convey the dead body out of the city, and bury it in the sands on the banks of the Xenil. No one saw the Moor enter our dwelling, and no one will know any thing of his death."

So said, so done. The wife aided him; they rolled the body of the unfortunate Moslem in the mat on which he had expired, laid it across the ass, and Peregil set out with it for the banks of the river.

As ill luck would have it, there lived opposite to the water-carrier a barber named Pedrillo Pedrugo, one of the most prying, tattling, and mischief-making of his gossip tribe. He was a weasel-faced, spider-legged varlet, supple and insinuating; the famous barber of Seville could not surpass him for his universal knowledge of the affairs of others, and he had no more power of retention than a sieve. It was said that he slept but with one eye at a time, and kept one ear uncovered, so that, even in his sleep, he might see and hear all that was going on. Certain it is, he was a sort of scandalous chronicle for the quid-nuncs of Granada, and had more customers than all the rest of his fraternity.

This meddlesome barber heard Peregil arrive at an unusual

hour at night, and the exclamations of his wife and children. His head was instantly popped out of a little window which served him as a look-out, and he saw his neighbor assist a man in Moorish garb into his dwelling. This was so strange an occurrence, that Pedrillo Pedrugo slept not a wink that night. Every five minutes he was at his loophole, watching the lights that gleamed through the chinks of his neighbor's door, and before daylight he beheld Peregil sally forth with his donkey unusually laden.

The inquisitive barber was in a fidget; he slipped on his clothes, and, stealing forth silently, followed the water-carrier at a distance, until he saw him dig a hole in the sandy bank of the Xenil, and bury something that had the appearance of a dead body.

The barber hied him home, and fidgeted about his shop, setting every thing upside down, until sunrise. He then took a basin under his arm, and sallied forth to the house of his daily customer the alcalde.

The alcalde was just risen. Pedrillo Pedrugo seated him in a chair, threw a napkin round his neck, put a basin of hot water under his chin, and began to mollify his beard with his fingers.

"Strange doings!" said Pedrugo, who played barber and newsmonger at the same time—"Strange doings! Robbery, and murder, and burial all in one night!"

"Hey!—how!—what is that you say?" cried the alcalde.

"I say," replied the barber, rubbing a piece of soap over the nose and mouth of the dignitary, for a Spanish barber disdains to employ a brush—"I say that Peregil the Gallego has robbed and murdered a Moorish Mussulman, and buried him, this blessed night. *Maldita sea la noche*—accursed be the night for the same!"

"But how do you know all this?" demanded the alcalde.

"Be patient, Señor, and you shall hear all about it," replied Pedrillo, taking him by the nose and sliding a razor over his cheek. He then recounted all that he had seen, going through both operations at the same time, shaving his beard, washing his chin, and wiping him dry with a dirty napkin, while he was robbing, murdering, and burying the Moslem.

Now it so happened that this alcalde was one of the most

overbearing, and at the same time most griping and corrupt curmudgeons in all Granada. It could not be denied, however, that he set a high value upon justice, for he sold it at its weight in gold. He presumed the case in point to be one of murder and robbery; doubtless there must be a rich spoil; how was it to be secured into the legitimate hands of the law? for as to merely entrapping the delinquent—that would be feeding the gallows; but entrapping the booty—that would be enriching the judge, and such, according to his creed, was the great end of justice. So thinking, he summoned to his presence his trustiest alguazil—a gaunt, hungry-looking varlet, clad, according to the custom of his order, in the ancient Spanish garb, a broad black beaver turned up at its sides; a quaint ruff; a small black cloak dangling from his shoulders; rusty black under-clothes that set off his spare wiry frame, while in his hand he bore a slender white wand, the dreaded insignia of his office. Such was the legal bloodhound of the ancient Spanish breed, that he put upon the traces of the unlucky water-carrier, and such was his speed and certainty, that he was upon the haunches of poor Peregil before he had returned to his dwelling, and brought both him and his donkey before the dispenser of justice.

The alcalde bent upon him one of the most terrific frowns. "Hark ye, culprit!" roared he, in a voice that made the knees of the little Gallego smite together—"hark ye, culprit! there is no need of denying thy guilt, every thing is known to me. A gallows is the proper reward for the crime thou hast committed, but I am merciful, and readily listen to reason. The man that has been murdered in thy house was a Moor, an infidel, the enemy of our faith. It was doubtless in a fit of religious zeal that thou hast slain him. I will be indulgent, therefore; render up the property of which thou hast robbed him, and we will hush the matter up."

The poor water-carrier called upon all the saints to witness his innocence; alas! not one of them appeared; and if they had, the alcalde would have disbelieved the whole calendar. The water-carrier related the whole story of the dying Moor with the straightforward simplicity of truth, but it was all in vain. "Wilt thou persist in saying," demanded the judge, "that this Moslem had neither gold nor jewels, which were the object of thy cupidity?"

"As I hope to be saved, your worship," replied the water-carrier, "he had nothing but a small box of sandal-wood which he bequeathed to me in reward for my services."

"A box of sandal-wood! a box of sandal-wood!" exclaimed the alcalde, his eyes sparkling at the idea of precious jewels. "And where is this box? where have you concealed it?"

"An' it please your grace," replied the water-carrier, "it is in one of the panniers of my mule, and heartily at the service of your worship."

He had hardly spoken the words, when the keen alguazil darted off, and reappeared in an instant with the mysterious box of sandal-wood. The alcalde opened it with an eager and trembling hand; all pressed forward to gaze upon the treasures it was expected to contain; when, to their disappointment, nothing appeared within, but a parchment scroll, covered with Arabic characters, and an end of a waxen taper.

When there is nothing to be gained by the conviction of a prisoner, justice, even in Spain, is apt to be impartial. The alcalde, having recovered from his disappointment, and found that there was really no booty in the case, now listened dispassionately to the explanation of the water-carrier, which was corroborated by the testimony of his wife. Being convinced, therefore, of his innocence, he discharged him from arrest; nay more, he permitted him to carry off the Moor's legacy, the box of sandal-wood and its contents, as the well-merited reward of his humanity; but he retained his donkey in payment of costs and charges.

Behold the unfortunate little Gallego reduced once more to the necessity of being his own water-carrier, and trudging up to the well of the Alhambra with a great earthen jar upon his shoulder.

As he toiled up the hill in the heat of a summer noon, his usual good humor forsook him. "Dog of an alcalde!" would he cry, "to rob a poor man of the means of his subsistence, of the best friend he had in the world!" And then at the remembrance of the beloved companion of his labors, all the kindness of his nature would break forth. "Ah, donkey of my heart!" would he exclaim, resting his burden on a stone, and wiping the sweat from his brow—"Ah, donkey of my heart! I warrant me thou thinkest of thy old master! I warrant me thou missest the water-jars—poor beast."

To add to his afflictions, his wife received him, on his return home, with whimperings and repinings; she had clearly the vantage-ground of him, having warned him not to commit the egregious act of hospitality which had brought on him all these misfortunes; and, like a knowing woman, she took every occasion to throw her superior sagacity in his teeth. If her children lacked food, or needed a new garment, she could answer with a sneer—"Go to your father—he is heir to king Chico of the Alhambra: ask him to help you out of the Moor's strong box."

Was ever poor mortal so soundly punished for having done a good action? The unlucky Peregil was grieved in flesh and spirit, but still he bore meekly with the railings of his spouse. At length, one evening, when, after a hot day's toil, she taunted him in the usual manner, he lost all patience. He did not venture to retort upon her, but his eye rested upon the box of sandal-wood, which lay on a shelf with lid half open, as if laughing in mockery at his vexation. Seizing it up, he dashed it with indignation to the floor: "Unlucky was the day that I ever set eyes on thee," he cried, "or sheltered thy master beneath my roof!"

As the box struck the floor, the lid flew wide open, and the parchment scroll rolled forth.

Peregil sat regarding the scroll for some time in moody silence. At length rallying his ideas: "Who knows," thought he, "but this writing may be of some importance, as the Moor seems to have guarded it with such care?" Picking it up therefore, he put it in his bosom, and the next morning, as he was crying water through the streets, he stopped at the shop of a Moor, a native of Tangiers, who sold trinkets and perfumery in the Zacatin, and asked him to explain the contents.

The Moor read the scroll attentively, then stroked his beard and smiled. "This manuscript," said he, "is a form of incantation for the recovery of hidden treasure, that is under the power of enchantment. It is said to have such virtue, that the strongest bolts and bars, nay the adamantine rock itself, will yield before it!"

"Bah!" cried the little Gallego, "what is all that to me? I am no enchanter, and know nothing of buried treasure." So saying, he shouldered his water-jar, left the scroll in the hands of the Moor, and trudged forward on his daily rounds.

That evening, however, as he rested himself about twilight at the well of the Alhambra, he found a number of gossips assembled at the place, and their conversation, as is not unusual at that shadowy hour, turned upon old tales and traditions of a supernatural nature. Being all poor as rats, they dwelt with peculiar fondness upon the popular theme of enchanted riches left by the Moors in various parts of the Alhambra. Above all, they concurred in the belief that there were great treasures buried deep in the earth under the tower of the seven floors.

These stories made an unusual impression on the mind of the honest Peregil, and they sank deeper and deeper into his thoughts as he returned alone down the darkling avenues. "If after all, there should be treasure hid beneath that tower: and if the scroll I left with the Moor should enable me to get at it!" In the sudden ecstasy of the thought he had well nigh let fall his water-jar.

That night he tumbled and tossed, and could scarcely get a wink of sleep for the thoughts that were bewildering his brain. Bright and early, he repaired to the shop of the Moor, and told him all that was passing in his mind. "You can read Arabic," said he, "suppose we go together to the tower, and try the effect of the charm; if it fails we are no worse off than before; but if it succeeds, we will share equally all the treasure we may discover.

"Hold," replied the Moslem; "this writing is not sufficient of itself; it must be read at midnight, by the light of a taper singularly compounded and prepared, the ingredients of which are not within my reach. Without such a taper the scroll is of no avail."

"Say no more!" cried the little Gallego; "I have such a taper at hand, and will bring it here in a moment." So saying he hastened home, and soon returned with the end of yellow wax taper that he had found in the box of sandal-wood.

The Moor felt it and smelt to it. "Here are rare and costly perfumes," said he, "combined with this yellow wax. This is the kind of taper specified in the scroll. While this burns, the strongest walls and most secret caverns will remain open. Woe to him, however, who lingers within until it be extinguished. He will remain enchanted with the treasure."

It was now agreed between them to try the charm that very night. At a late hour, therefore, when nothing was stirring but bats and owls, they ascended the woody hill of the Alhambra, and approached that awful tower, shrouded by trees and rendered formidable by so many traditionary tales. By the light of a lantern, they groped their way through bushes, and over fallen stones, to the door of a vault beneath the tower. With fear and trembling they descended a flight of steps cut into the rock. It led to an empty chamber damp and drear, from which another flight of steps led to a deeper vault. In this way they descended four several flights, leading into as many vaults one below the other, but the floor of the fourth was solid; and though, according to tradition, there remained three vaults still below, it was said to be impossible to penetrate further, the residue being shut up by strong enchantment. The air of this vault was damp and chilly, and had an earthy smell, and the light scarce cast forth any rays. They paused here for a time in breathless suspense, until they faintly heard the clock of the watchtower strike midnight; upon this they lit the waxen taper, which diffused an odor of myrrh and frankincense and storax.

The Moor began to read in a hurried voice. He had scarce finished when there was a noise as of subterraneous thunder. The earth shook, and the floor, yawning open, disclosed a flight of steps. Trembling with awe they descended, and by the light of the lantern found themselves in another vault, covered with Arabic inscriptions. In the centre stood a great chest, secured with seven bands of steel, at each end of which sat an enchanted Moor in armor, but motionless as a statue, being controlled by the power of the incantation. Before the chest were several jars filled with gold and silver and precious stones. In the largest of these they thrust their arms up to the elbow, and at every dip hauled forth handfuls of broad yellow pieces of Moorish gold, or bracelets and ornaments of the same precious metal, while occasionally a necklace of oriental pearl would stick to their fingers. Still they trembled and breathed short while cramming their pockets with the spoils; and cast many a fearful glance at the two enchanted Moors, who sat grim and motionless, glaring upon them with unwinking eyes. At length, struck with a sudden panic at some fancied noise, they both rushed up the staircase, tumbled over one another into the upper apartment, overturned and extinguished the waxen taper, and the pavement again closed with a thundering sound.

Filled with dismay, they did not pause until they had groped their way out of the tower, and beheld the stars shining through the trees. Then seating themselves upon the grass, they divided the spoil, determining to content themselves for the present with this mere skimming of the jars, but to return on some future night and drain them to the bottom. To make sure of each other's good faith, also, they divided the talismans between them, one retaining the scroll and the other the taper; this done, they set off with light hearts and well-lined pockets for Granada.

As they wended their way down the hill, the shrewd Moor whispered a word of counsel in the ear of the simple little water-carrier.

"Friend Peregil," said he, "all this affair must be kept a profound secret until we have secured the treasure, and conveyed it out of harm's way. If a whisper of it gets to the ear of the alcalde, we are undone!"

"Certainly," replied the Gallego, "nothing can be more true."

"Friend Peregil," said the Moor, "you are a discreet man, and I make no doubt can keep a secret: but you have a wife."

"She shall not know a word of it," replied the little water-carrier, sturdily.

"Enough," said the Moor, "I depend upon thy discretion and thy promise."

Never was promise more positive and sincere; but alas! what man can keep a secret from his wife? Certainly not such a one as Peregil the water-carrier, who was one of the most loving and tractable of husbands. On his return home, he found his wife moping in a corner. "Mighty well," cried she as he entered, "you've come at last; after rambling about until this hour of the night. I wonder you have not brought home another Moor as a house-mate." Then bursting into tears, she began to wring her hands and smite her breast: "Unhappy woman that I am!" exclaimed she, "what will become of me? My house stripped and plundered by lawyers and alguazils; my husband a do-no-good, that no longer brings home bread to his family, but goes rambling about day and night, with infidel Moors! O my children! my children! what will become of us? we shall all have to beg in the streets!"

Honest Peregil was so moved by the distress of his spouse, that he could not help whimpering also. His heart was as full as his pocket, and not to be restrained. Thrusting his hand into the latter he hauled forth three or four broad gold pieces, and slipped them into her bosom. The poor woman stared with astonishment, and could not understand the meaning of this golden shower. Before she could recover her surprise, the little Gallego drew forth a chain of gold and dangled it before her, capering with exultation, his mouth distended from ear to ear.

"Holy Virgin protect us!" exclaimed the wife. "What has thou been doing, Peregil? surely thou has not been committing murder and robbery!"

The idea scarce entered the brain of the poor woman, than it became a certainty with her. She saw a prison and a gallows in the distance, and a little bandy-legged Gallego hanging pendant from it; and, overcome by the horrors conjured up by her imagination, fell into violent hysterics.

What could the poor man do? He had no other means of pacifying his wife, and dispelling the phantoms of her fancy, than by relating the whole story of his good fortune. This, however, he did not do until he had exacted from her the most solemn promise to keep it a profound secret from every living being.

To describe her joy would be impossible. She flung her arms round the neck of her husband, and almost strangled him with her caresses. "Now, wife," exclaimed the little man with honest exultation, "what say you now to the Moor's legacy? Henceforth never abuse me for helping a fellow-creature in distress."

The honest Gallego retired to his sheep-skin mat, and slept as soundly as if on a bed of down. Not so his wife; she emptied the whole contents of his pockets upon the mat, and sat counting gold pieces of Arabic coin, trying on necklaces and earrings, and fancying the figure she should one day make when permitted to enjoy her riches.

On the following morning the honest Gallego took a broad golden coin, and repaired with it to a jeweller's shop in the Zacatin to offer it for sale, pretending to have found it among the ruins of the Alhambra. The jeweller saw that it had an Arabic inscription, and was of the purest gold; he offered, however, but a third of its value, with which the water-carrier was perfectly content. Peregil now bought new clothes for his little flock, and all kinds of toys, together with ample provisions for a hearty meal, and returning to his dwelling, sat all his children dancing around him, while he capered in the midst, the happiest of fathers.

The wife of the water-carrier kept her promise of secrecy with surprising strictness. For a whole day and a half she went about with a look of mystery and a heart swelling almost to bursting, yet she held her peace, though surrounded by her gossips. It is true, she could not help giving herself a few airs, apologized for her ragged dress, and talked of ordering a new basquina all trimmed with gold lace and bugles, and a new lace mantilla. She threw out hints of her husband's intention of leaving off his trade of water-carrying, as it did not altogether agree with his health. In fact she thought they should all retire to the country for the summer, that the children might have the benefit of the mountain air, for there was no living in the city in this sultry season.

The neighbors stared at each other, and thought the poor woman had lost her wits; and her airs and graces and elegant pretensions were the theme of universal scoffing and merriment among her friends, the moment her back was turned.

If she restrained herself abroad, however, she indemnified herself at home, and putting a string of rich oriental pearls round her neck, Moorish bracelets on her arms, and an aigrette of diamonds on her head, sailed backwards and forwards in her slattern rags about the room, now and then stopping to admire herself in a broken mirror. Nay, in the impulse of her simple vanity, she could not resist, on one occasion, showing herself at the window to enjoy the effect of her finery on the passers by.

As the fates would have it, Pedrillo Pedrugo, the meddlesome barber, was at this moment sitting idly in his shop on the opposite side of the street, when his ever-watchful eye caught the sparkle of a diamond. In an instant he was at his loophole reconnoitering the slattern spouse of the water-carrier, decorated with the splendor of an eastern bride. No sooner had he taken an accurate inventory of her ornaments, than he posted off with all speed to the alcalde. In a little while the hungry alguazil was again on the scent, and before the day was over the unfortunate Peregil was once more dragged into the presence of the judge.

"How is this, villain!" cried the alcalde, in a furious voice. "You told me that the infidel who died in your house left nothing behind but an empty coffer, and now I hear of your wife flaunting in her rags decked out with pearls and diamonds. Wretch that thou art! prepare to render up the spoils of thy miserable victim, and to swing on the gallows that is already tired of waiting for thee."

The terrified water-carrier fell on his knees, and made a full relation of the marvellous manner in which he had gained his wealth. The alcalde, the alguazil, and the inquisitive barber, listened with greedy ears to this Arabian tale of enchanted treasure. The alguazil was dispatched to bring the Moor who had assisted in the incantation. The Moslem entered half frightened out of his wits at finding himself in the hands of the harpies of the law. When he beheld the water-carrier standing with sheepish looks and downcast countenance, he comprehended the whole matter. "Miserable animal," said he, as he passed near him, "did I not warn thee against babbling to thy wife?"

The story of the Moor coincided exactly with that of his colleague; but the alcalde affected to be slow of belief, and threw out menaces of imprisonment and rigorous investigation.

"Softly, good Señor Alcalde," said the Mussulman, who by

this time had recovered his usual shrewdness and self-possession. "Let us not mar fortune's favors in the scramble for them. Nobody knows any thing of this matter but ourselves; let us keep the secret. There is wealth enough in the cave to enrich us all. Promise a fair division, and all shall be produced; refuse, and the cave shall remain for ever closed."

The alcalde consulted apart with the alguazil. The latter was an old fox in his profession. "Promise any thing," said he, "until you get possession of the treasure. You may then seize upon the whole, and if he and his accomplice dare to murmur, threaten them with the fagot and the stake as infidels and sorcerers."

The alcalde relished the advice. Smoothing his brow and turning to the Moor, "This is a strange story," said he, "and may be true, but I must have ocular proof of it. This very night you must repeat the incantation in my presence. If there be really such treasure, we will share it amicably between us, and say nothing further of the matter; if ye have deceived me, expect no mercy at my hands. In the mean time you must remain in custody."

The Moor and the water-carrier cheerfully agreed to these conditions, satisfied that the event would prove the truth of their words.

Towards midnight the alcalde sallied forth secretly, attended by the alguazil and the meddlesome barber, all strongly armed. They conducted the Moor and the water-carrier as prisoners, and were provided with the stout donkey of the latter to bear off the expected treasure. They arrived at the tower without being observed, and tying the donkey to a fig-tree, descended into the fourth vault of the tower.

The scroll was produced, the yellow waxen taper lighted, and the Moor read the form of incantation. The earth trembled as before, and the pavement opened with a thundering sound, disclosing the narrow flight of steps. The alcalde, the alguazil, and the barber were struck aghast, and could not summon courage to descend. The Moor and the water-carrier entered the lower vault, and found the two Moors seated as before, silent and motionless. They removed two of the great jars, filled with golden coin and precious stones. The water-carrier bore them up one by one upon his shoulders, but though a strong-backed little man, and accustomed to carry burdens, he staggered beneath their weight, and found, when slung on each side of his donkey, they were as much as the animal could bear.

"Let us be content for the present," said the Moor; "here is as much treasure as we can carry off without being perceived, and enough to make us all wealthy to our heart's desire."

"Is there more treasure remaining behind?" demanded the alcalde.

"The greatest prize of all," said the Moor, "a huge coffer bound with bands of steel, and filled with pearls and precious stones."

"Let us have up the coffer by all means," cried the grasping alcalde.

"I will descend for no more," said the Moor, doggedly; "enough is enough for a reasonable man—more is superfluous."

"And I," said the water-carrier, "will bring up no further burden to break the back of my poor donkey."

Finding commands, threats and entreaties equally vain, the alcalde turned to his two adherents. "Aid me," said he, "to bring up the coffer, and its contents shall be divided between us." So saying he descended the steps, followed with trembling reluctance by the alguazil and the barber.

No sooner did the Moor behold them fairly earthed than he extinguished the yellow taper; the pavement closed with its usual crash, and the three worthies remained buried in its womb.

He then hastened up the different flights of steps, nor stopped until in the open air. The little water-carrier followed him as fast as his short legs would permit.

"What hast thou done?" cried Peregil, as soon as he could recover breath. "The alcalde and the other two are shut up in the vault."

"It is the will of Allah!" said the Moor devoutly.

"And will you not release them?" demanded the Gallego.

"Allah forbid!" replied the Moor, smoothing his beard. "It is written in the book of fate that they shall remain enchanted until some future adventurer arrive to break the charm. The will of God be done!" so saying, he hurled the end of the waxen taper far among the gloomy thickets of the glen.

There was now no remedy, so the Moor and the water-carrier proceeded with the richly laden donkey toward the city, nor could honest Peregil refrain from hugging and kissing his long-eared fellow-laborer, thus restored to him from the clutches of the law; and in fact, it is doubtful which gave the simple hearted little man most joy at the moment, the gaining of the treasure, or the recovery of the donkey.

The two partners in good luck divided their spoil amicably and fairly, except that the Moor, who had a little taste for trinketry, made out to get into his heap the most of the pearls and precious stones and other baubles, but then he always gave the water-carrier in lieu magnificent jewels of massy gold, of five times the size, with which the latter was heartily content. They took care not to linger within reach of accidents, but made off to enjoy their wealth undisturbed in other countries. The Moor returned to Africa, to his native city of Tangiers, and the Gallego, with his wife, his children, and his donkey, made the best of his way to Portugal. Here, under the admonition and tuition of his wife, he became a personage of some consequence, for she made the worthy little man array his long body and short legs in doublet and hose, with a feather in his hat and a sword by his side, and laying aside his familiar appellation of Peregil, assume the more sonorous title of Don Pedro Gil: his progeny grew up a thriving and merry-hearted, though short and bandy-legged generation, while Señora Gil, befringed, belaced, and betasselled from her head to her heels, with glittering rings on every finger, became a model of slattern fashion and finery.

As to the alcalde and his adjuncts, they remained shut up under the great tower of the seven floors, and there they remain spell-bound at the present day. Whenever there shall be a lack in Spain of pimping barbers, sharking alguazils, and corrupt alcaldes, they may be sought after; but if they have to wait until such time for their deliverance, there is danger of their enchantment enduring until doomsday.

The Tower of Las Infantas

IN AN EVENING'S STROLL up a narrow glen, overshadowed by fig-trees, pomegranates, and myrtles, which divides the lands of the fortress from those of the Generalife, I was struck with the romantic appearance of a Moorish tower in the outer wall of the Alhambra, rising high above the tree-tops, and catching the ruddy rays of the setting sun. A solitary window at a great height commanded a view of the glen; and as I was regarding it, a young female looked out, with her head adorned with flowers. She was evidently superior to the usual class of people inhabiting the old towers of the fortress; and this sudden and picturesque glimpse of her reminded me of the descriptions of captive beauties in fairy tales. These fanciful associations were increased on being informed by my attendant Mateo, that this was the Tower of the Princesses (La Torre de las Infantas); so called, from having been, according to tradition, the residence of the daughters of the Moorish kings. I have since visited the tower. It is not generally shown to strangers, though well worthy attention, for the interior is equal, for beauty of architecture, and delicacy of ornament, to any part of the palace. The elegance of the central hall, with its marble fountain, its lofty arches, and richly fretted dome; the arabesques and stucco-work of the small but well-proportioned chambers, though injured by time and neglect, all accord with the story of its being anciently the abode of royal beauty.

The little old fairy queen who lives under the staircase of the Alhambra, and frequents the evening tertulias of Dame Antonia, tells some fanciful traditions about three Moorish princesses, who were once shut up in this tower by their father, a tyrant king of Granada, and were only permitted to ride out at night about the hills, when no one was permitted to come in their way under pain of death. They still, according to her account, may be seen occasionally, when the moon is in the full, riding in lonely places along the mountain side, on palfreys richly caparisoned and sparkling with jewels, but they vanish on being spoken to.

But before I relate any thing further respecting these princesses, the reader may be anxious to know something about the fair inhabitant of the tower with her head dressed with flowers, who looked out from the lofty window. She proved to be the newly-married spouse of the worthy adjutant of invalids; who, though well stricken in years, had had the courage to take to his bosom a young and buxom Andalusian damsel. May the good old cavalier be happy in his choice, and find the Tower of the Princesses a more secure residence for female beauty than it seems to have proved in the time of the Moslems, if we may believe the following legend!

Legend of the Three Beautiful Princesses

IN OLD TIMES there reigned a Moorish king in Granada, whose name was Mohamed, to which his subjects added the appellation of El Hayzari, or "The Left-handed." Some say he was so called on account of his being really more expert with his sinister than his dexter hand; others, because he was prone to take every thing by the wrong end; or in other words, to mar wherever he meddled. Certain it is, either through misfortune or mismanagement, he was continually in trouble; thrice was he driven from his throne, and, on one occasion, barely escaped to Africa with his life, in the disguise of a fisherman.* Still he was as brave as he was blundering; and though left-handed, wielded his cimeter to such purpose, that he each time re-established himself upon his throne by dint of hard fighting. Instead, however, of learning wisdom from adversity, he hardened his neck, and stiffened his left arm in wilfulness. The evils of a public nature which he thus brought upon himself and his kingdom may be learned by those who will delve into the Arabian annals of Granada; the present legend deals but with his domestic policy.

As this Mohamed was one day riding forth with a train of his courtiers, by the foot of the mountain of Elvira, he met a band of horsemen returning from a foray into the land of the Christians. They were conducting a long string of mules laden with spoil, and many captives of both sexes, among whom the monarch was struck with the appearance of a beautiful damsel, richly attired, who sat weeping on a low palfrey, and heeded not the consoling words of a duenna who rode beside her.

The monarch was struck with her beauty, and, on inquiring of the captain of the troop, found that she was the daughter of the alcayde of a frontier fortress, that had been surprised and sacked in the course of the foray. Mohamed claimed her as his royal share of the booty, and had her conveyed to his harem in the Alhambra. There every thing was devised to

---

*The reader will recognize the sovereign connected with the fortunes of the Abencerrages. His story appears to be a little fictionized in the legend.

soothe her melancholy; and the monarch, more and more enamored, sought to make her his queen. The Spanish maid at
first repulsed his addresses—he was an infidel—he was the
open foe of her country—what was worse, he was stricken in
years!

The monarch, finding his assiduities of no avail, determined
to enlist in his favor the duenna, who had been captured with
the lady. She was an Andalusian by birth, whose Christian
name is forgotten, being mentioned in Moorish legends by
no other appellation than that of the discreet Kadiga—and
discreet in truth she was, as her whole history makes evident.
No sooner had the Moorish king held a little private conversation with her, than she saw at once the cogency of his reasoning, and undertook his cause with her young mistress.

"Go to, now!" cried she; "what is there in all this to weep
and wail about? Is it not better to be mistress of this beautiful
palace, with all its gardens and fountains, than to be shut up
within your father's old frontier tower? As to this Mohamed
being an infidel, what is that to the purpose? You marry him,
not his religion: and if he is waxing a little old, the sooner
will you be a widow, and mistress of yourself; at any rate, you
are in his power, and must either be a queen or a slave. When
in the hands of a robber, it is better to sell one's merchandise
for a fair price, than to have it taken by main force."

The arguments of the discreet Kadiga prevailed. The Spanish lady dried her tears, and became the spouse of Mohamed
the Left-handed; she even conformed, in appearance, to the
faith of her royal husband; and her discreet duenna immediately became a zealous convert to the Moslem doctrines: it
was then the latter received the Arabian name of Kadiga, and
was permitted to remain in the confidential employ of her
mistress.

In due process of time the Moorish king was made the
proud and happy father of three lovely daughters, all born at
a birth: he could have wished they had been sons, but consoled himself with the idea that three daughters at a birth
were pretty well for a man somewhat stricken in years, and
left-handed!

As usual with all Moslem monarchs, he summoned his astrologers on this happy event. They cast the nativities of the

three princesses, and shook their heads. "Daughters, O king!" said they, "are always precarious property; but these will most need your watchfulness when they arrive at a marriageable age; at that time gather them under your wings, and trust them to no other guardianship."

Mohamed the Left-handed was acknowledged to be a wise king by his courtiers, and was certainly so considered by himself. The prediction of the astrologers caused him but little disquiet, trusting to his ingenuity to guard his daughters and outwit the Fates.

The three-fold birth was the last matrimonial trophy of the monarch; his queen bore him no more children, and died within a few years, bequeathing her infant daughters to his love, and to the fidelity of the discreet Kadiga.

Many years had yet to elapse before the princesses would arrive at that period of danger—the marriageable age: "It is good, however, to be cautious in time," said the shrewd monarch; so he determined to have them reared in the royal castle of Salobreña. This was a sumptuous palace, incrusted, as it were, in a powerful Moorish fortress on the summit of a hill overlooking the Mediterranean sea. It was a royal retreat, in which the Moslem monarchs shut up such of their relatives, as might endanger their safety; allowing them all kinds of luxuries and amusements, in the midst of which they passed their lives in voluptuous indolence.

Here the princesses remained, immured from the world, but surrounded by enjoyment, and attended by female slaves who anticipated their wishes. They had delightful gardens for their recreation, filled with the rarest fruits and flowers, with aromatic groves and perfumed baths. On three sides the castle looked down upon a rich valley, enamelled with all kinds of culture, and bounded by the lofty Alpuxarra mountains; on the other side it overlooked the broad sunny sea.

In this delicious abode, in a propitious climate, and under a cloudless sky, the three princesses grew up into wondrous beauty; but, though all reared alike, they gave early tokens of diversity of character. Their names were Zayda, Zorayda, and Zorahayda; and such was their order of seniority, for there had been precisely three minutes between their births.

Zayda, the eldest, was of an intrepid spirit, and took the

lead of her sisters in every thing, as she had done in entering into the world. She was curious and inquisitive, and fond of getting at the bottom of things.

Zorayda had a great feeling for beauty, which was the reason, no doubt, of her delighting to regard her own image in a mirror or a fountain, and of her fondness for flowers, and jewels, and other tasteful ornaments.

As to Zorahayda, the youngest, she was soft and timid, and extremely sensitive, with a vast deal of disposable tenderness, as was evident from her number of pet-flowers, and pet-birds, and pet-animals, all of which she cherished with the fondest care. Her amusements, too, were of a gentle nature, and mixed up with musing and reverie. She would sit for hours in a balcony, gazing on the sparkling stars of a summer's night; or on the sea when lit up by the moon; and at such times, the song of a fisherman, faintly heard from the beach, or the notes of a Moorish flute from some gliding bark, sufficed to elevate her feelings into ecstasy. The least uproar of the elements, however, filled her with dismay; and a clap of thunder was enough to throw her into a swoon.

Years rolled on smoothly and serenely; the discreet Kadiga, to whom the princesses were confided, was faithful to her trust, and attended them with unremitting care.

The castle of Salobreña, as has been said, was built upon a hill on the sea-coast. One of the exterior walls straggled down the profile of the hill, until it reached a jutting rock overhanging the sea, with a narrow sandy beach at its foot, laved by the rippling billows. A small watchtower on this rock had been fitted up as a pavilion, with latticed windows to admit the sea-breeze. Here the princesses used to pass the sultry hours of mid-day.

The curious Zayda was one day seated at a window of the pavilion, as her sisters, reclining on ottomans, were taking the siesta or noontide slumber. Her attention was attracted to a galley which came coasting along, with measured strokes of the oar. As it drew near, she observed that it was filled with armed men. The galley anchored at the foot of the tower: a number of Moorish soldiers landed on the narrow beach, conducting several Christian prisoners. The curious Zayda awakened her sisters, and all three peeped cautiously through the close jalousies of the lattice which screened them from sight. Among the prisoners were three Spanish cavaliers, richly dressed. They were in the flower of youth, and of noble presence; and the lofty manner in which they carried themselves, though loaded with chains and surrounded with enemies, bespoke the grandeur of their souls. The princesses gazed with intense and breathless interest. Cooped up as they had been in this castle among female attendants, seeing nothing of the male sex but black slaves, or the rude fishermen of the sea-coast, it is not to be wondered at that the appearance of three gallant cavaliers, in the pride of youth and manly beauty, should produce some commotion in their bosom.

"Did ever nobler being tread the earth than that cavalier in crimson?" cried Zayda, the eldest of the sisters. "See how proudly he bears himself, as though all around him were his slaves!"

"But notice that one in green!" exclaimed Zorayda. "What grace! what elegance! what spirit!"

The gentle Zorahayda said nothing, but she secretly gave preference to the cavalier in blue.

The princesses remained gazing until the prisoners were out of sight; then heaving long-drawn sighs, they turned round, looked at each other for a moment, and sat down, musing and pensive, on their ottomans.

The discreet Kadiga found them in this situation; they related what they had seen, and even the withered heart of the duenna was warmed. "Poor youths!" exclaimed she, "I'll warrant their captivity makes many a fair and high-born lady's heart ache in their native land! Ah! my children, you have little idea of the life these cavaliers lead in their own country. Such prankling at tournaments! such devotion to the ladies! such courting and serenading!"

The curiosity of Zayda was fully aroused; she was insatiable in her inquiries, and drew from the duenna the most animated pictures of the scenes of her youthful days and native land. The beautiful Zorayda bridled up, and slyly regarded herself in a mirror, when the theme turned upon the charms of the Spanish ladies; while Zorahayda suppressed a struggling sigh at the mention of moonlight serenades.

Every day the curious Zayda renewed her inquiries, and

every day the sage duenna repeated her stories, which were listened to with profound interest, though with frequent sighs, by her gentle auditors. The discreet old woman awoke at length to the mischief she might be doing. She had been accustomed to think of the princesses only as children; but they had imperceptibly ripened beneath her eye, and now bloomed before her three lovely damsels of the marriageable age. It is time, thought the duenna, to give notice to the king.

Mohamed the Left-handed was seated one morning on a divan in a cool hall of the Alhambra, when a slave arrived from the fortress of Salobreña, with a message from the sage Kadiga, congratulating him on the anniversary of his daughters' birth-day. The slave at the same time presented a delicate little basket decorated with flowers, within which, on a couch of vine and fig-leaves, lay a peach, an apricot, and a nectarine, with their bloom and down and dewy sweetness upon them, and all in the early stage of tempting ripeness. The monarch was versed in the Oriental language of fruits and flowers, and rapidly divined the meaning of this emblematical offering.

"So," said he, "the critical period pointed out by the astrologers is arrived: my daughters are at a marriageable age. What is to be done? They are shut up from the eyes of men; they are under the eyes of the discreet Kadiga—all very good,—but still they are not under my own eye, as was prescribed by the astrologers: I must gather them under my wing, and trust to no other guardianship."

So saying, he ordered that a tower of the Alhambra should be prepared for their reception, and departed at the head of his guards for the fortress of Salobreña, to conduct them home in person.

About three years had elapsed since Mohamed had beheld his daughters, and he could scarcely credit his eyes at the wonderful change which that small space of time had made in their appearance. During the interval, they had passed that wondrous boundary line in female life which separates the crude, unformed, and thoughtless girl from the blooming, blushing, meditative woman. It is like passing from the flat, bleak, uninteresting plains of La Mancha to the voluptuous valleys and swelling hills of Andalusia.

Zayda was tall and finely formed, with a lofty demeanor

and a penetrating eye. She entered with a stately and decided step, and made a profound reverence to Mohamed, treating him more as her sovereign than her father. Zorayda was of the middle height, with an alluring look and swimming gait, and a sparkling beauty, heightened by the assistance of the toilette. She approached her father with a smile, kissed his hand, and saluted him with several stanzas from a popular Arabian poet, with which the monarch was delighted. Zora-hayda was shy and timid, smaller than her sisters, and with a beauty of that tender beseeching kind which looks for fondness and protection. She was little fitted to command, like her elder sister, or to dazzle like the second, but was rather formed to creep to the bosom of manly affection, to nestle within it, and be content. She drew near to her father, with a timid and almost faltering step, and would have taken his hand to kiss, but on looking up into his face, and seeing it beaming with a paternal smile, the tenderness of her nature broke forth, and she threw herself upon his neck.

Mohamed the Left-handed surveyed his blooming daughters with mingled pride and perplexity; for while he exulted in their charms, he bethought himself of the prediction of the astrologers. "Three daughters! three daughters!" muttered he repeatedly to himself, "and all of a marriageable age! Here's tempting Hesperian fruit, that requires a dragon watch!"

He prepared for his return to Granada, by sending heralds before him, commanding every one to keep out of the road by which he was to pass, and that all doors and windows should be closed at the approach of the princesses. This done, he set forth, escorted by a troop of black horsemen of hideous aspect, and clad in shining armor.

The princesses rode beside the king, closely veiled, on beautiful white palfreys, with velvet caparisons, embroidered with gold, and sweeping the ground; the bits and stirrups were of gold, and the silken bridles adorned with pearls and precious stones. The palfreys were covered with little silver bells, which made the most musical tinkling as they ambled gently along. Wo to the unlucky wight, however, who lingered in the way when he heard the tinkling of these bells!—the guards were ordered to cut him down without mercy.

The cavalcade was drawing near to Granada, when it overtook on the banks of the river Xenil, a small body of Moorish soldiers with a convoy of prisoners. It was too late for the soldiers to get out of the way, so they threw themselves on their faces on the earth, ordering their captives to do the like. Among the prisoners were the three identical cavaliers whom the princesses had seen from the pavilion. They either did not understand, or were too haughty to obey the order, and remained standing and gazing upon the cavalcade as it approached.

The ire of the monarch was kindled at this flagrant defiance of his orders. Drawing his cimeter, and pressing forward, he was about to deal a left-handed blow that might have been fatal to at least one of the gazers, when the princesses crowded round him, and implored mercy for the prisoners; even the timid Zorahayda forgot her shyness, and became eloquent in their behalf. Mohamed paused, with uplifted cimeter, when the captain of the guard threw himself at his feet. "Let not your highness," said he, "do a deed that may cause great scandal throughout the kingdom. These are three brave and noble Spanish knights, who have been taken in battle, fighting like lions; they are of high birth, and may bring great ransoms."—"Enough!" said the king. "I will spare their lives, but punish their audacity—let them be taken to the Vermilion Towers, and put to hard labor."

Mohamed was making one of his usual left-handed blunders. In the tumult and agitation of this blustering scene, the veils of the three princesses had been thrown back, and the radiance of their beauty revealed; and in prolonging the parley, the king had given that beauty time to have its full effect. In those days people fell in love much more suddenly than at present, as all ancient stories make manifest: it is not a matter of wonder, therefore, that the hearts of the three cavaliers were completely captured; especially as gratitude was added to their admiration: it is a little singular, however, though no less certain, that each of them was enraptured with a several beauty. As to the princesses, they were more than ever struck with the noble demeanor of the captives, and cherished in their breasts all that they had heard of their valor and noble lineage.

The cavalcade resumed its march; the three princesses rode

pensively along on their tinkling palfreys, now and then stealing a glance behind in search of the Christian captives, and
the latter were conducted to their allotted prison in the Vermilion Towers.

The residence provided for the princesses was one of the
most dainty that fancy could devise. It was in a tower somewhat apart from the main palace of the Alhambra, though
connected with it by the wall which encircled the whole summit of the hill. On one side it looked into the interior of the
fortress, and had, at its foot, a small garden filled with the
rarest flowers. On the other side it overlooked a deep embowered ravine separating the grounds of the Alhambra from
those of the Generalife. The interior of the tower was divided
into small fairy apartments, beautifully ornamented in the
light Arabian style, surrounding a lofty hall, the vaulted roof
of which rose almost to the summit of the tower. The walls
and the ceiling of the hall were adorned with arabesque and
fretwork, sparkling with gold and with brilliant pencilling. In
the centre of the marble pavement was an alabaster fountain,
set round with aromatic shrubs and flowers, and throwing up
a jet of water that cooled the whole edifice and had a lulling
sound. Round the hall were suspended cages of gold and
silver wire, containing singing-birds of the finest plumage or
sweetest note.

The princesses had been represented as always cheerful
when in the castle of the Salobreña; the king had expected to
see them enraptured with the Alhambra. To his surprise, however, they began to pine, and grow melancholy, and dissatis-
fied with every thing around them. The flowers yielded them
no fragrance, the song of the nightingale disturbed their
night's rest, and they were out of all patience with the alabaster fountain with its eternal drop-drop and splash-splash from
morning till night, and from night till morning.

The king, who was somewhat of a testy, tyrannical disposition, took this at first in high dudgeon; but he reflected that
his daughters had arrived at an age when the female mind
expands and its desires augment. "They are no longer children," said he to himself, "they are women grown, and
require suitable objects to interest them." He put in requisition, therefore, all the dressmakers, and the jewellers, and the

artificers in gold and silver throughout the Zacatin of Granada, and the princesses were overwhelmed with robes of silk, and tissue, and brocade, and cashmere shawls, and necklaces of pearls and diamonds, and rings, and bracelets, and anklets, and all manner of precious things.

All, however, was of no avail; the princesses continued pale and languid in the midst of their finery, and looked like three blighted rose-buds, drooping from one stalk. The king was at his wits' end. He had in general a laudable confidence in his own judgment, and never took advice. "The whims and caprices of three marriageable damsels, however, are sufficient," said he, "to puzzle the shrewdest head." So for once in his life he called in the aid of counsel.

The person to whom he applied was the experienced duenna.

"Kadiga," said the king, "I know you to be one of the most discreet women in the whole world, as well as one of the most trustworthy; for these reasons I have always continued you about the persons of my daughters. Fathers cannot be too wary in whom they repose such confidence; I now wish you to find out the secret malady that is preying upon the princesses, and to devise some means of restoring them to health and cheerfulness."

Kadiga promised implicit obedience. In fact she knew more of the malady of the princesses than they did themselves. Shutting herself up with them, however, she endeavored to insinuate herself into their confidence.

"My dear children, what is the reason you are so dismal and downcast in so beautiful a place, where you have everything that heart can wish?"

The princesses looked vacantly round the apartment, and sighed.

"What more, then, would you have? Shall I get you the wonderful parrot that talks all languages, and is the delight of Granada?"

"Odious!" exclaimed the princess Zayda. "A horrid, screaming bird, that chatters words without ideas: one must be without brains to tolerate such a pest."

"Shall I send for a monkey from the rock of Gibraltar, to divert you with his antics?"

"A monkey! faugh!" cried Zorayda; "the destestable mimic of man. I hate the nauseous animal."

"What say you to the famous black singer Casem, from the royal harem, in Morocco? They say he has a voice as fine as a woman's."

"I am terrified at the sight of these black slaves," said the delicate Zorahayda; "besides, I have lost all relish for music."

"Ah! my child, you would not say so," replied the old woman, slyly, "had you heard the music I heard last evening, from the three Spanish cavaliers, whom we met on our journey. But, bless me, children! what is the matter that you blush so, and are in such a flutter?"

"Nothing, nothing, good mother; pray proceed."

"Well—as I was passing by the Vermilion Towers last evening, I saw the three cavaliers resting after their day's labor. One was playing on the guitar, so gracefully, and the others sang by turns; and they did it in such style, that the very guards seemed like statues, or men enchanted. Allah forgive me! I could not help being moved at hearing the songs of my native country. And then to see three such noble and handsome youths in chains and slavery!"

Here the kind-hearted old woman could not restrain her tears.

"Perhaps, mother, you could manage to procure us a sight of these cavaliers," said Zayda.

"I think," said Zorayda, "a little music would be quite reviving."

The timid Zorahayda said nothing, but threw her arms round the neck of Kadiga.

"Mercy on me!" exclaimed the discreet old woman; "what are you talking of, my children? Your father would be the death of us all if he heard of such a thing. To be sure, these cavaliers are evidently well-bred, and high-minded youths; but what of that? they are the enemies of our faith, and you must not even think of them but with abhorrence."

There is an admirable intrepidity in the female will, particularly when about the marriageable age, which is not to be deterred by dangers and prohibitions. The princesses hung round their old duenna, and coaxed, and entreated, and declared that a refusal would break their hearts.

What could she do? She was certainly the most discreet old woman in the whole world, and one of the most faithful servants to the king; but was she to see three beautiful princesses break their hearts for the mere tinkling of a guitar? Besides, though she had been so long among the Moors, and changed her faith in imitation of her mistress, like a trusty follower, yet she was a Spaniard born, and had the lingerings of Christianity in her heart. So she set about to contrive how the wish of the princesses might be gratified.

The Christian captives, confined in the Vermilion Towers, were under the charge of a big-whiskered, broad-shouldered renegado, called Hussein Baba, who was reputed to have a most itching palm. She went to him privately, and slipping a broad piece of gold into his hand, "Hussein Baba," said she; "my mistresses, the three princesses, who are shut up in the tower, and in sad want of amusement, have heard of the musical talents of the three Spanish cavaliers, and are desirous of hearing a specimen of their skill. I am sure you are too kind-hearted to refuse them so innocent a gratification."

"What! and to have my head set grinning over the gate of my own tower! for that would be the reward, if the king should discover it."

"No danger of any thing of the kind; the affair may be managed so that the whim of the princesses may be gratified, and their father be never the wiser. You know the deep ravine outside of the walls which passes immediately below the tower. Put the three Christians to work there, and at the intervals of their labor, let them play and sing, as if for their own recreation. In this way the princesses will be able to hear them from the windows of the tower, and you may be sure of their paying well for your compliance."

As the good old woman concluded her harangue, she kindly pressed the rough hand of the renegado, and left within it another piece of gold.

Her eloquence was irresistible. The very next day the three cavaliers were put to work in the ravine. During the noontide heat, when their fellow-laborers were sleeping in the shade, and the guard nodding drowsily at his post, they seated themselves among the herbage at the foot of the tower, and sang a Spanish roundelay to the accompaniment of the guitar.

The glen was deep, the tower was high, but their voices rose distinctly in the stillness of the summer noon. The princesses listened from their balcony, they had been taught the Spanish language by their duenna, and were moved by the tenderness of the song. The discreet Kadiga, on the contrary, was terribly shocked. "Allah preserve us!" cried she, "they are singing a love-ditty, addressed to yourselves. Did ever mortal hear of such audacity? I will run to the slave-master, and have them soundly bastinadoed."

"What! bastinado such gallant cavaliers, and for singing so charmingly!" The three beautiful princesses were filled with horror at the idea. With all her virtuous indignation, the good old woman was of a placable nature, and easily appeased. Besides, the music seemed to have a beneficial effect upon her young mistresses. A rosy bloom had already come to their cheeks, and their eyes began to sparkle. She made no further objection, therefore, to the amorous ditty of the cavaliers.

When it was finished, the princesses remained silent for a time; at length Zorayda took up a lute, and with a sweet, though faint and trembling voice, warbled a little Arabian air, the burden of which was, "The rose is concealed among her leaves, but she listens with delight to the song of the nightingale."

From this time forward the cavaliers worked almost daily in the ravine. The considerate Hussein Baba became more and more indulgent, and daily more prone to sleep at his post. For some time a vague intercourse was kept up by popular songs and romances, which, in some measure, responded to each other, and breathed the feelings of the parties. By degrees the princesses showed themselves at the balcony, when they could do so without being perceived by the guards. They conversed with the cavaliers also, by means of flowers, with the symbolical language of which they were mutually acquainted: the difficulties of their intercourse added to its charms, and strengthened the passion they had so singularly conceived, for love delights to struggle with difficulties, and thrives the most hardily on the scantiest soil.

The change effected in the looks and spirits of the princesses by this secret intercourse, surprised and gratified the Left-handed king; but no one was more elated than the discreet Kadiga, who considered it all owing to her able management.

At length there was an interruption in this telegraphic correspondence: for several days the cavaliers ceased to make their appearance in the glen. The princesses looked out from the tower in vain. In vain they stretched their swan-like necks from the balcony; in vain they sang like captive nightingales in their cage: nothing was to be seen of their Christian lovers; not a note responded from the groves. The discreet Kadiga sallied forth in quest of intelligence, and soon returned with a face full of trouble. "Ah, my children!" cried she, "I saw what all this would come to, but you would have your way; you may now hang up your lutes on the willows. The Spanish cavaliers are ransomed by their families; they are down in Granada, and preparing to return to their native country."

The three beautiful princesses were in despair at the tidings. Zayda was indignant at the slight put upon them, in thus being deserted without a parting word. Zorayda wrung her hands and cried, and looked in the glass, and wiped away her tears, and cried afresh. The gentle Zorahayda leaned over the balcony and wept in silence, and her tears fell drop by drop among the flowers of the bank where the faithless cavaliers had so often been seated.

The discreet Kadiga did all in her power to soothe their sorrow. "Take comfort, my children," said she, "this is nothing when you are used to it. This is the way of the world. Ah! when you are as old as I am, you will know how to value these men. I'll warrant these cavaliers have their loves among the Spanish beauties of Cordova and Seville, and will soon be serenading under their balconies, and thinking no more of the Moorish beauties in the Alhambra. Take comfort, therefore, my children, and drive them from your hearts."

The comforting words of the discreet Kadiga only redoubled the distress of the three princesses, and for two days they continued inconsolable. On the morning of the third, the good old woman entered their apartment, all ruffling with indignation.

"Who would have believed such insolence in mortal man!" exclaimed she, as soon as she could find words to express herself; "but I am rightly served for having connived at this deception of your worthy father. Never talk more to me of your Spanish cavaliers."

"Why, what has happened, good Kadiga?" exclaimed the princesses in breathless anxiety.

"What has happened?—treason has happened! or what is almost as bad, treason has been proposed; and to me, the most faithful of subjects, the trustiest of duennas! Yes, my children, the Spanish cavaliers have dared to tamper with me, that I should persuade you to fly with them to Cordova, and become their wives!"

Here the excellent old woman covered her face with her hands, and gave way to a violent burst of grief and indignation. The three beautiful princesses turned pale and red, pale and red, and trembled, and looked down, and cast shy looks at each other, but said nothing. Meantime, the old woman sat rocking backward and forward in violent agitation, and now and then breaking out into exclamations. "That ever I should live to be so insulted!—I, the most faithful of servants!"

At length, the eldest princess, who had most spirit and always took the lead, approached her, and laying her hand upon her shoulder, "Well, mother," said she, "supposing we were willing to fly with these Christian cavaliers—is such a thing possible?"

The good old woman paused suddenly in her grief, and looking up, "Possible," echoed she; "to be sure, it is possible. Have not the cavaliers already bribed Hussein Baba, the renegado captain of the guard, and arranged the whole plan? But, then, to think of deceiving your father! your father, who has placed such confidence in me!" Here the worthy woman gave way to a fresh burst of grief, and began again to rock backward and forward, and to wring her hands.

"But our father has never placed any confidence in us," said the eldest princess, "but has trusted to bolts and bars, and treated us as captives."

"Why, that is true enough," replied the old woman, again pausing in her grief; "he has indeed treated you most unreasonably, keeping you shut up here, to waste your bloom in a moping old tower, like roses left to wither in a flower-jar. But then, to fly from your native land!"

"And is not the land we fly to, the native land of our

mother, where we shall live in freedom? And shall we not each have a youthful husband in exchange for a severe old father?"

"Why, that again is all very true; and your father, I must confess, is rather tyrannical: but what then," relapsing into her grief, "would you leave me behind to bear the brunt of his vengeance?"

"By no means, my good Kadiga; cannot you fly with us?"

"Very true, my child; and, to tell the truth, when I talked the matter over with Hussein Baba, he promised to take care of me, if I would accompany you in your flight: but then, bethink you, my children, are you willing to renounce the faith of your father?"

"The Christian faith was the original faith of our mother," said the eldest princess; "I am ready to embrace it, and so, I am sure, are my sisters."

"Right again," exclaimed the old woman, brightening up; "it was the original faith of your mother, and bitterly did she lament, on her death-bed, that she had renounced it. I promised her then to take care of your souls, and I rejoice to see that they are now in a fair way to be saved. Yes, my children, I, too, was born a Christian, and have remained a Christian in my heart, and am resolved to return to the faith. I have talked on the subject with Hussein Baba, who is a Spaniard by birth, and comes from a place not far from my native town. He is equally anxious to see his own country, and to be reconciled to the church; and the cavaliers have promised, that, if we are disposed to become man and wife, on returning to our native land, they will provide for us handsomely."

In a word, it appeared that this extremely discreet and provident old woman had consulted with the cavaliers and the renegado, and had concerted the whole plan of escape. The eldest princess immediately assented to it; and her example, as usual, determined the conduct of her sisters. It is true, the youngest hesitated, for she was gentle and timid of soul, and there was a struggle in her bosom between filial feeling and youthful passion: the latter, however, as usual, gained the victory, and with silent tears, and stifled sighs, she prepared herself for flight.

The rugged hill, on which the Alhambra is built, was in old times, perforated with subterranean passages, cut through the rock, and leading from the fortress to various parts of the city, and to distant sally-ports on the banks of the Darro and the Xenil. They had been constructed at different times by the Moorish kings, as means of escape from sudden insurrections, or of secretly issuing forth on private enterprises. Many of them are now entirely lost, while others remain, partly choked with rubbish, and partly walled up; monuments of the jealous precautions and warlike stratagems of the Moorish government. By one of these passages, Hussein Baba had undertaken to conduct the princesses to a sally-port beyond the walls of the city, where the cavaliers were to be ready with fleet steeds, to bear the whole party over the borders.

The appointed night arrived: the tower of the princesses had been locked up as usual, and the Alhambra was buried in deep sleep. Towards midnight, the discreet Kadiga listened from the balcony of a window that looked into the garden. Hussein Baba, the renegado, was already below, and gave the appointed signal. The duenna fastened the end of a ladder of ropes to the balcony, lowered it into the garden and descended. The two eldest princesses followed her with beating hearts; but when it came to the turn of the youngest princess, Zorahayda, she hesitated, and trembled. Several times she ventured a delicate little foot upon the ladder, and as often drew it back, while her poor little heart fluttered more and more the longer she delayed. She cast a wistful look back into the silken chamber; she had lived in it, to be sure, like a bird in a cage; but within it she was secure; who could tell what dangers might beset her, should she flutter forth into the wide world! Now she bethought her of her gallant Christian lover, and her little foot was instantly upon the ladder; and anon she thought of her father, and shrank back. But fruitless is the attempt to describe the conflict in the bosom of one so young and tender and loving; but so timid, and so ignorant of the world.

In vain her sisters implored, the duenna scolded, and the renegado blasphemed beneath the balcony; the gentle little Moorish maid stood doubting and wavering on the verge of elopement; tempted by the sweetness of the sin, but terrified at its perils.

Every moment increased the danger of discovery. A distant tramp was heard. "The patrols are walking their rounds," cried the renegado; "if we linger, we perish. Princess, descend instantly, or we leave you."

Zorahayda was for a moment in fearful agitation; then loosening the ladder of ropes, with desperate resolution, she flung it from the balcony.

"It is decided!" cried she; "flight is now out of my power! Allah guide and bless ye, my dear sisters!"

The two eldest princesses were shocked at the thoughts of leaving her behind, and would fain have lingered, but the patrol was advancing; the renegado was furious, and they were hurried away to the subterraneous passage. They groped their way through a fearful labyrinth, cut through the heart of the mountain, and succeeded in reaching, undiscovered, an iron gate that opened outside of the walls. The Spanish cavaliers were waiting to receive them, disguised as Moorish soldiers of the guard, commanded by the renegado.

The lover of Zorahayda was frantic, when he learned that she had refused to leave the tower; but there was no time to waste in lamentations. The two princesses were placed behind their lovers, the discreet Kadiga mounted behind the renegado, and they all set off at a round pace in the direction of the Pass of Lope, which leads through the mountains towards Cordova.

They had not proceeded far when they heard the noise of drums and trumpets from the battlements of the Alhambra.

"Our flight is discovered!" said the renegado.

"We have fleet steeds, the night is dark, and we may distance all pursuit," replied the cavaliers.

They put spurs to their horses, and scoured across the Vega. They attained the foot of the mountain of Elvira, which stretches like a promontory into the plain. The renegado paused and listened. "As yet," said he, "there is no one on our traces, we shall make good our escape to the mountains." While he spoke, a light blaze sprang up on the top of the watchtower of the Alhambra.

"Confusion!" cried the renegado, "that bale fire will put all the guards of the passes on the alert. Away! away! Spur like mad,—there is no time to be lost."

Away they dashed—the clattering of their horses' hoofs echoed from rock to rock, as they swept along the road that skirts the rocky mountain of Elvira. As they galloped on, the bale fire of the Alhambra was answered in every direction; light after light blazed on the Atalayas, or watchtowers of the mountains.

"Forward! forward!" cried the renegado, with many an oath, "to the bridge,—to the bridge, before the alarm has reached there!"

They doubled the promontory of the mountains, and arrived in sight of the famous Bridge of Pinos, that crosses a rushing stream often dyed with Christian and Moslem blood. To their confusion, the tower on the bridge blazed with lights and glittered with armed men. The renegado pulled up his steed, rose in his stirrups and looked about him for a moment; then beckoning to the cavaliers, he struck off from the road, skirted the river for some distance, and dashed into its waters. The cavaliers called upon the princesses to cling to them, and did the same. They were borne for some distance down the rapid current, the surges roared round them, but the beautiful princesses clung to their Christian knights, and never uttered a complaint. The cavaliers attained the opposite bank in safety, and were conducted by the renegado, by rude and unfrequented paths, and wild barrancos, through the heart of the mountains, so as to avoid all the regular passes. In a word, they succeeded in reaching the ancient city of Cordova; where their restoration to their country and friends was celebrated with great rejoicings, for they were of the noblest families. The beautiful princesses were forthwith received into the bosom of the Church, and, after being in all due form made regular Christians, were rendered happy wives.

In our hurry to make good the escape of the princesses across the river, and up the mountains, we forgot to mention the fate of the discreet Kadiga. She had clung like a cat to Hussein Baba in the scamper across the Vega, screaming at every bound, and drawing many an oath from the whiskered renegado; but when he prepared to plunge his steed into the river, her terror knew no bounds. "Grasp me not so tightly,"

cried Hussein Baba; "hold on by my belt and fear nothing."
She held firmly with both hands by the leather belt that
girded the broad-backed renegado; but when he halted with
the cavaliers to take breath on the mountain summit, the
duenna was no longer to be seen.

"What has become of Kadiga?" cried the princesses in alarm.

"Allah alone knows!" replied the renegado; "my belt came
loose when in the midst of the river, and Kadiga was swept
with it down the stream. The will of Allah be done! but it was
an embroidered belt, and of great price."

There was no time to waste in idle regrets; yet bitterly did
the princesses bewail the loss of their discreet counsellor. That
excellent old woman, however, did not lose more than half of
her nine lives in the water: a fisherman who was drawing his
nets some distance down the stream, brought her to land, and
was not a little astonished at his miraculous draught. What
further became of the discreet Kadiga, the legend does not
mention; certain it is that she evinced her discretion in never
venturing within the reach of Mohamed the Left-handed.

Almost as little is known of the conduct of that sagacious
monarch when he discovered the escape of his daughters, and
the deceit practised upon him by the most faithful of servants.
It was the only instance in which he had called in the aid of
counsel, and he was never afterwards known to be guilty of a
similar weakness. He took good care, however, to guard his
remaining daughter, who had no disposition to elope: it is
thought, indeed, that she secretly repented having remained
behind: now and then she was seen leaning on the battlements of the tower, and looking mournfully towards the
mountains in the direction of Cordova, and sometimes the
notes of her lute were heard accompanying plaintive ditties, in
which she was said to lament the loss of her sisters and her
lover, and to bewail her solitary life. She died young, and,
according to popular rumor, was buried in a vault beneath
the tower, and her untimely fate has given rise to more than
one traditionary fable.

————

The following legend, which seems in some measure to
spring out of the foregoing story, is too closely connected

with high historic names to be entirely doubted. The Count's daughter, and some of her young companions, to whom it was read in one of the evening tertullias, thought certain parts of it had much appearance of reality; and Dolores, who was much more versed than they in the improbable truths of the Alhambra, believed every word of it.

Legend of the Rose of the Alhambra

FOR SOME TIME after the surrender of Granada by the Moors, that delightful city was a frequent and favorite residence of the Spanish sovereigns, until they were frightened away by successive shocks of earthquakes, which toppled down various houses, and made the old Moslem towers rock to their foundation.

Many, many years then rolled away, during which Granada was rarely honored by a royal guest. The palaces of the nobility remained silent and shut up; and the Alhambra, like a slighted beauty, sat in mournful desolation, among her neglected gardens. The tower of the Infantas, once the residence of the three beautiful Moorish princesses, partook of the general desolation; the spider spun her web athwart the gilded vault, and bats and owls nestled in those chambers that had been graced by the presence of Zayda, Zorayda, and Zorahayda. The neglect of this tower may partly have been owing to some superstitious notions of the neighbors. It was rumored that the spirit of the youthful Zorahayda, who had perished in that tower, was often seen by moonlight seated beside the fountain in the hall, or moaning about the battlements, and that the notes of her silver lute would be heard at midnight by wayfarers passing along the glen.

At length the city of Granada was once more welcomed by the royal presence. All the world knows that Philip V. was the first Bourbon that swayed the Spanish sceptre. All the world knows that he married, in second nuptials, Elizabetta or Isabella (for they are the same), the beautiful princess of Parma; and all the world knows that by this chain of contingencies a French prince and an Italian princess were seated together on the Spanish throne. For a visit of this illustrious pair, the Alhambra was repaired and fitted up with all possible expedition. The arrival of the court changed the whole aspect of the lately deserted place. The clangor of drum and trumpet, the tramp of steed about the avenues and outer court, the glitter of arms and display of banners about barbican and battlement, recalled the ancient and warlike glories of the fortress.

A softer spirit, however, reigned within the royal palace. There was the rustling of robes and the cautious tread and murmuring voice of reverential courtiers about the antechambers; a loitering of pages and maids of honor about the gardens, and the sound of music stealing from open casements.

Among those who attended in the train of the monarchs was a favorite page of the queen, named Ruyz de Alarcon. To say that he was a favorite page of the queen was at once to speak his eulogium, for every one in the suite of the stately Elizabetta was chosen for grace, and beauty, and accomplishments. He was just turned of eighteen, light and lithe of form, and graceful as a young Antinous. To the queen he was all deference and respect, yet he was at heart a roguish stripling, petted and spoiled by the ladies about the court, and experienced in the ways of women far beyond his years.

This loitering page was one morning rambling about the groves of the Generalife, which overlook the grounds of the Alhambra. He had taken with him for his amusement a favorite ger-falcon of the queen. In the course of his rambles, seeing a bird rising from a thicket, he unhooded the hawk and let him fly. The falcon towered high in the air, made a swoop at his quarry, but missing it, soared away, regardless of the calls of the page. The latter followed the truant bird with his eye, in its capricious flight, until he saw it alight upon the battlements of a remote and lonely tower, in the outer wall of the Alhambra, built on the edge of a ravine that separated the royal fortress from the grounds of the Generalife. It was in fact the "Tower of the Princesses."

The page descended into the ravine and approached the tower, but it had no entrance from the glen, and its lofty height rendered any attempt to scale it fruitless. Seeking one of the gates of the fortress, therefore, he made a wide circuit to that side of the tower facing within the walls.

A small garden, inclosed by a trellis-work of reeds overhung with myrtle, lay before the tower. Opening a wicket, the page passed between beds of flowers and thickets of roses to the door. It was closed and bolted. A crevice in the door gave him a peep into the interior. There was a small Moorish hall with fretted walls, light marble columns, and an alabaster fountain surrounded with flowers. In the centre hung a gilt cage containing a singing bird, beneath it, on a chair, lay a tortoise-shell cat among reels of silk and other articles of female labor, and a guitar decorated with ribbons leaned against the fountain.

Ruyz de Alarcon was struck with these traces of female taste and elegance in a lonely, and, as he had supposed, deserted tower. They reminded him of the tales of enchanted halls current in the Alhambra; and the tortoiseshell cat might be some spell-bound princess.

He knocked gently at the door. A beautiful face peeped out from a little window above, but was instantly withdrawn. He waited, expecting that the door would be opened, but he waited in vain; no footstep was to be heard within—all was silent. Had his senses deceived him, or was this beautiful apparition the fairy of the tower? He knocked again, and more loudly. After a little while the beaming face once more peeped forth; it was that of a blooming damsel of fifteen.

The page immediately doffed his plumed bonnet, and entreated in the most courteous accents to be permitted to ascend the tower in pursuit of his falcon.

"I dare not open the door, Señor," replied the little damsel, blushing, "my aunt has forbidden it."

"I do beseech you, fair maid—it is the favorite falcon of the queen: I dare not return to the palace without it."

"Are you then one of the cavaliers of the court?"

"I am, fair maid; but I shall lose the queen's favor and my place, if I lose this hawk."

"Santa Maria! It is against you cavaliers of the court my aunt has charged me especially to bar the door."

"Against wicked cavaliers doubtless, but I am none of these, but a simple harmless page, who will be ruined and undone if you deny me this small request."

The heart of the little damsel was touched by the distress of the page. It was a thousand pities he should be ruined for the want of so trifling a boon. Surely too he could not be one of those dangerous beings whom her aunt had described as a species of cannibal, ever on the prowl to make prey of thoughtless damsels; he was gentle and modest, and stood so entreatingly with cap in hand, and looked so charming.

The sly page saw that the garrison began to waver, and

redoubled his entreaties in such moving terms that it was not in the nature of mortal maiden to deny him; so the blushing little warden of the tower descended, and opened the door with a trembling hand, and if the page had been charmed by a mere glimpse of her countenance from the window, he was ravished by the full length portrait now revealed to him.

Her Andalusian bodice and trim basquiña set off the round but delicate symmetry of her form, which was as yet scarce verging into womanhood. Her glossy hair was parted on her forehead with scrupulous exactness, and decorated with a fresh plucked rose, according to the universal custom of the country. It is true her complexion was tinged by the ardor of a southern sun, but it served to give richness to the mantling bloom of her cheek, and to heighten the lustre of her melting eyes.

Ruyz de Alarcon beheld all this with a single glance, for it became him not to tarry; he merely murmured his acknowledgments, and then bounded lightly up the spiral staircase in quest of his falcon.

He soon returned with the truant bird upon his fist. The damsel, in the mean time, had seated herself by the fountain in the hall, and was winding silk; but in her agitation she let fall the reel upon the pavement. The page sprang and picked it up, then dropping gracefully on one knee, presented it to her; but seizing the hand extended to receive it, imprinted on it a kiss more fervent and devout than he had ever imprinted on the fair hand of his sovereign.

"Ave Maria, Señor!" exclaimed the damsel, blushing still deeper with confusion and surprise, for never before had she received such a salutation.

The modest page made a thousand apologies, assuring her it was the way, at the court, of expressing the most profound homage and respect.

Her anger, if anger she felt, was easily pacified, but her agitation and embarrassment continued, and she sat blushing deeper and deeper, with her eyes cast down upon her work, entangling the silk which she attempted to wind.

The cunning page saw the confusion in the opposite camp, and would fain have profited by it, but the fine speeches he would have uttered died upon his lips; his attempts at gallantry were awkward and ineffectual; and to his surprise, the adroit page, who had figured with such grace and effrontery among the most knowing and experienced ladies of the court, found himself awed and abashed in the presence of a simple damsel of fifteen.

In fact, the artless maiden, in her own modesty and innocence, had guardians more effectual than the bolts and bars prescribed by her vigilant aunt. Still, where is the female bosom proof against the first whisperings of love? The little damsel, with all her artlessness, instinctively comprehended all that the faltering tongue of the page failed to express, and her heart was fluttered at beholding, for the first time, a lover at her feet—and such a lover!

The diffidence of the page, though genuine, was short-lived, and he was recovering his usual ease and confidence, when a shrill voice was heard at a distance.

"My aunt is returning from mass!" cried the damsel in affright: "I pray you, Señor, depart."

"Not until you grant me that rose from your hair as a remembrance."

She hastily untwisted the rose from her raven locks. "Take it," cried she, agitated and blushing, "but pray begone."

The page took the rose, and at the same time covered with kisses the fair hand that gave it. Then, placing the flower in his bonnet, and taking the falcon upon his fist, he bounded off through the garden, bearing away with him the heart of the gentle Jacinta.

When the vigilant aunt arrived at the tower, she remarked the agitation of her niece, and an air of confusion in the hall; but a word of explanation sufficed. "A ger-falcon had pursued his prey into the hall!"

"Mercy on us! to think of a falcon flying into the tower. Did ever one hear of so saucy a hawk? Why, the very bird in the cage is not safe!"

The vigilant Fredegonda was one of the most wary of ancient spinsters. She had a becoming terror and distrust of what she denominated "the opposite sex," which had gradually increased through a long life of celibacy. Not that the good lady had ever suffered from their wiles, nature having set up a safeguard in her face that forbade all trespass upon her premises; but ladies who have least cause to fear for themselves are most ready to keep a watch over their more tempting neighbors.

The niece was the orphan of an officer who had fallen in the wars. She had been educated in a convent, and had recently been transferred from her sacred asylum to the immediate guardianship of her aunt, under whose overshadowing care she vegetated in obscurity, like an opening rose blooming beneath a brier. Nor indeed is this comparison entirely accidental; for, to tell the truth, her fresh and dawning beauty had caught the public eye, even in her seclusion, and, with that poetical turn common to the people of Andalusia, the peasantry of the neighborhood had given her the appellation of "the Rose of the Alhambra."

The wary aunt continued to keep a faithful watch over her tempting little niece as long as the court continued at Granada, and flattered herself that her vigilance had been successful. It is true, the good lady was now and then discomposed by the tinkling of guitars and chanting of love ditties from the moonlit groves beneath the tower; but she would exhort her niece to shut her ears against such idle minstrelsy, assuring her that it was one of the arts of the opposite sex, by which simple maids were often lured to their undoing. Alas! what chance with a simple maid has a dry lecture against a moonlight serenade?

At length king Philip cut short his sojourn at Granada, and suddenly departed with all his train. The vigilant Fredegonda watched the royal pageant as it issued forth from the Gate of Justice, and descended the great avenue leading to the city. When the last banner disappeared from her sight, she returned exulting to her tower, for all her cares were over. To her surprise, a light Arabian steed pawed the ground at the wicket-gate of the garden:—to her horror, she saw through the thickets of roses a youth, in gayly-embroidered dress, at the feet of her niece. At the sound of her footsteps he gave a tender adieu, bounded lightly over the barrier of reeds and myrtles, sprang upon his horse, and was out of sight in an instant.

The tender Jacinta, in the agony of her grief, lost all

thought of her aunt's displeasure. Throwing herself into her arms, she broke forth into sobs and tears.

"Ay de mi!" cried she, "he's gone!—he's gone!—he's gone! and I shall never see him more!"

"Gone!—who is gone?—what youth is that I saw at your feet?"

"A queen's page, aunt, who came to bid me farewell."

"A queen's page, child!" echoed the vigilant Fredegonda, faintly; "and when did you become acquainted with the queen's page?"

"The morning that the ger-falcon came into the tower. It was the queen's ger-falcon, and he came in pursuit of it."

"Ah silly, silly girl! know that there are no ger-falcons half so dangerous as these young prankling pages, and it is precisely such simple birds as thee that they pounce upon."

The aunt was at first indignant at learning that in despite of her boasted vigilance, a tender intercourse had been carried on by the youthful lovers, almost beneath her eye; but when she found that her simple-hearted niece, though thus exposed, without the protection of bolt or bar, to all the machinations of the opposite sex, had come forth unsinged from the fiery ordeal, she consoled herself with the persuasion that it was owing to the chaste and cautious maxims in which she had, as it were, steeped her to the very lips.

While the aunt laid this soothing unction to her pride, the niece treasured up the oft-repeated vows of fidelity of the page. But what is the love of restless, roving man? A vagrant stream that dallies for a time with each flower upon its bank, then passes on, and leaves them all in tears.

Days, weeks, months elapsed, and nothing more was heard of the page. The pomegranate ripened, the vine yielded up its fruit, the autumnal rains descended in torrents from the mountains; the Sierra Nevada became covered with a snowy mantle, and wintry blasts howled through the halls of the Alhambra—still he came not. The winter passed away. Again the genial spring burst forth with song and blossom and balmy zephyr; the snows melted from the mountains, until none remained but on the lofty summit of Nevada, glistening through the sultry summer air. Still nothing was heard of the forgetful page.

In the mean time, the poor little Jacinta grew pale and thoughtful. Her former occupations and amusements were abandoned, her silk lay entangled, her guitar unstrung, her flowers were neglected, the notes of her bird unheeded, and her eyes, once so bright, were dimmed with secret weeping. If any solitude could be devised to foster the passion of a love-lorn damsel, it would be such a place as the Alhambra, where every thing seems disposed to produce tender and romantic reveries. It is a very paradise for lovers: how hard then to be alone in such a paradise—and not merely alone, but for-saken!

"Alas, silly child!" would the staid and immaculate Frede-gonda say, when she found her niece in one of her despond-ing moods—"did I not warn thee against the wiles and deceptions of these men? What couldst thou expect, too, from one of a haughty and aspiring family—thou an orphan, the descendant of a fallen and impoverished line? Be assured, if the youth were true, his father, who is one of the proudest nobles about the court, would prohibit his union with one so humble and portionless as thou. Pluck up thy resolution, therefore, and drive these idle notions from thy mind."

The words of the immaculate Fredegonda only served to increase the melancholy of her niece, but she sought to in-dulge it in private. At a late hour one midsummer night, after her aunt had retired to rest, she remained alone in the hall of the tower, seated beside the alabaster fountain. It was here that the faithless page had first knelt and kissed her hand; it was here that he had often vowed eternal fidelity. The poor little damsel's heart was overladen with sad and tender recol-lections, her tears began to flow, and slowly fell drop by drop into the fountain. By degrees the crystal water became agi-tated, and—bubble—bubble—bubble—boiled up and was tossed about, until a female figure, richly clad in Moorish robes, slowly rose to view.

Jacinta was so frightened that she fled from the hall, and did not venture to return. The next morning she related what she had seen to her aunt, but the good lady treated it as a phantasy of her troubled mind, or supposed she had fallen asleep and dreamt beside the fountain. "Thou hast been thinking of the story of the three Moorish princesses that once inhabited this tower," continued she, "and it has entered into thy dreams."

"What story, aunt? I know nothing of it."

"Thou hast certainly heard of the three princesses, Zayda, Zorayda, and Zorahayda, who were confined in this tower by the king their father, and agreed to fly with three Christian cavaliers. The two first accomplished their escape, but the third failed in her resolution, and, it is said, died in this tower."

"I now recollect to have heard of it," said Jacinta, "and to have wept over the fate of the gentle Zorahayda."

"Thou mayest well weep over her fate," continued the aunt, "for the lover of Zorahayda was thy ancestor. He long bemoaned his Moorish love; but time cured him of his grief, and he married a Spanish lady, from whom thou art descended."

Jacinta ruminated upon these words. "That what I have seen is no phantasy of the brain," said she to herself, "I am confident. If indeed it be the spirit of the gentle Zorahayda, which I have heard lingers about this tower, of what should I be afraid? I'll watch by the fountain to-night—perhaps the visit will be repeated."

Towards midnight, when every thing was quiet, she again took her seat in the hall. As the bell in the distant watchtower of the Alhambra struck the midnight hour, the fountain was again agitated; and bubble—bubble—bubble—it tossed about the waters until the Moorish female again rose to view. She was young and beautiful; her dress was rich with jewels, and in her hand she held a silver lute. Jacinta trembled and was faint, but was reassured by the soft and plaintive voice of the apparition, and the sweet expression of her pale, melancholy countenance.

"Daughter of mortality," said she, "what aileth thee? Why do thy tears trouble my fountain, and thy sighs and plaints disturb the quiet watches of the night?"

"I weep because of the faithlessness of man, and I bemoan my solitary and forsaken state."

"Take comfort; thy sorrows may yet have an end. Thou beholdest a Moorish princess, who, like thee, was unhappy in her love. A Christian knight, thy ancestor, won my heart, and would have borne me to his native land and to the bosom of his church. I was a convert in my heart, but I lacked courage equal to my faith, and lingered till too late. For this the evil genii are permitted to have power over me, and I remain enchanted in this tower until some pure Christian will deign to break the magic spell. Wilt thou undertake the task?"

"I will," replied the damsel, trembling.

"Come hither then, and fear not; dip thy hand in the fountain, sprinkle the water over me, and baptize me after the manner of thy faith; so shall the enchantment be dispelled, and my troubled spirit have repose."

The damsel advanced with faltering steps, dipped her hand in the fountain, collected water in the palm, and sprinkled it over the pale face of the phantom.

The latter smiled with ineffable benignity. She dropped her silver lute at the feet of Jacinta, crossed her white arms upon her bosom, and melted from sight, so that it seemed merely as if a shower of dew-drops had fallen into the fountain.

Jacinta retired from the hall filled with awe and wonder. She scarcely closed her eyes that night; but when she awoke at daybreak out of a troubled slumber, the whole appeared to her like a distempered dream. On descending into the hall, however, the truth of the vision was established, for, beside the fountain, she beheld the silver lute glittering in the morning sunshine.

She hastened to her aunt, to relate all that had befallen her, and called her to behold the lute as a testimonial of the reality of her story. If the good lady had any lingering doubts, they were removed when Jacinta touched the instrument, for she drew forth such ravishing tones as to thaw even the frigid bosom of the immaculate Fredegonda, that region of eternal winter, into a genial flow. Nothing but supernatural melody could have produced such an effect.

The extraordinary power of the lute became every day more and more apparent. The wayfarer passing by the tower was detained, and, as it were, spell-bound, in breathless ecstasy. The very birds gathered in the neighboring trees, and hushing their own strains, listened in charmed silence.

Rumor soon spread the news abroad. The inhabitants of Granada thronged to the Alhambra to catch a few notes of the transcendent music that floated about the tower of Las Infantas.

The lovely little minstrel was at length drawn forth from her retreat. The rich and powerful of the land contended who should entertain and do honor to her; or rather, who should secure the charms of her lute to draw fashionable throngs to their saloons. Wherever she went her vigilant aunt kept a dragon watch at her elbow, awing the throngs of impassioned admirers, who hung in raptures on her strains. The report of her wonderful powers spread from city to city. Malaga, Seville, Cordova, all became successively mad on the theme; nothing was talked of throughout Andalusia but the beautiful minstrel of the Alhambra. How could it be otherwise among a people so musical and gallant as the Andalusians, when the lute was magical in its powers, and the minstrel inspired by love!

While all Andalusia was thus music mad, a different mood prevailed at the court of Spain. Philip V., as is well known, was a miserable hypochondriac, and subject to all kinds of fancies. Sometimes he would keep to his bed for weeks together, groaning under imaginary complaints. At other times he would insist upon abdicating his throne, to the great annoyance of his royal spouse, who had a strong relish for the splendors of a court and the glories of a crown, and guided the sceptre of her imbecile lord with an expert and steady hand.

Nothing was found to be so efficacious in dispelling the royal megrims as the power of music; the queen took care, therefore, to have the best performers, both vocal and instrumental, at hand, and retained the famous Italian singer Farinelli about the court as a kind of royal physician.

At the moment we treat of, however, a freak had come over the mind of this sapient and illustrious Bourbon that surpassed all former vagaries. After a long spell of imaginary illness, which set all the strains of Farinelli and the consultations of a whole orchestra of court fiddlers at defiance, the monarch fairly, in idea, gave up the ghost, and considered himself absolutely dead.

This would have been harmless enough, and even convenient both to his queen and courtiers, had he been content to remain in the quietude befitting a dead man; but to their annoyance he insisted upon having the funeral ceremonies performed over him, and to their inexpressible perplexity, began to grow impatient, and to revile bitterly at them for negligence and disrespect, in leaving him unburied. What was to be done? To disobey the king's positive commands was monstrous in the eyes of the obsequious courtiers of a punctilious court—but to obey him, and bury him alive, would be downright regicide!

In the midst of this fearful dilemma a rumor reached the court, of the female minstrel who was turning the brains of all Andalusia. The queen dispatched missions in all haste to summon her to St. Ildefonso, where the court at that time resided.

Within a few days, as the queen with her maids of honor was walking in those stately gardens, intended, with their avenues and terraces and fountains, to eclipse the glories of Versailles, the far-famed minstrel was conducted into her presence. The imperial Elizabetta gazed with surprise at the youthful and unpretending appearance of the little being that had set the world madding. She was in her picturesque Andalusian dress, her silver lute in hand, and stood with modest and downcast eyes, but with a simplicity and freshness of beauty that still bespoke her "the Rose of the Alhambra."

As usual she was accompanied by the ever-vigilant Fredegonda, who gave the whole history of her parentage and descent to the inquiring queen. If the stately Elizabetta had been interested by the appearance of Jacinta, she was still more pleased when she learnt that she was of a meritorious though impoverished line, and that her father had bravely fallen in the service of the crown. "If thy powers equal their renown," said she, "and thou canst cast forth this evil spirit that possesses thy sovereign, thy fortunes shall henceforth be my care, and honors and wealth attend thee."

Impatient to make trial of her skill, she led the way at once to the apartment of the moody monarch.

Jacinta followed with downcast eyes through files of guards and crowds of courtiers. They arrived at length at a great chamber hung with black. The windows were closed to exclude the light of day: a number of yellow wax tapers in silver sconces diffused a lugubrious light, and dimly revealed the figures of mutes in mourning dresses, and courtiers who glided about with noiseless step and woebegone visage. In the midst of a funeral bed or bier, his hands folded on his breast, and the tip of his nose just visible, lay extended this would-be-buried monarch.

The queen entered the chamber in silence, and pointing to a footstool in an obscure corner, beckoned to Jacinta to sit down and commence.

At first she touched her lute with a faltering hand, but gathering confidence and animation as she proceeded, drew forth such soft aerial harmony, that all present could scarce believe it mortal. As to the monarch, who had already considered himself in the world of spirits, he set it down for some angelic melody or the music of the spheres. By degrees the theme was varied, and the voice of the minstrel accompanied the instrument. She poured forth one of the legendary ballads treating of the ancient glories of the Alhambra and the achievements of the Moors. Her whole soul entered into the theme, for with the recollections of the Alhambra was associated the story of her love. The funeral chamber resounded with the animating strain. It entered into the gloomy heart of the monarch. He raised his head and gazed around: he sat up on his couch, his eye began to kindle—at length, leaping upon the floor, he called for sword and buckler.

The triumph of music, or rather of the enchanted lute, was complete; the demon of melancholy was cast forth; and, as it were, a dead man brought to life. The windows of the apartment were thrown open; the glorious effulgence of Spanish sunshine burst into the late lugubrious chamber; all eyes sought the lovely enchantress, but the lute had fallen from her hand, she had sunk upon the earth, and the next moment was clasped to the bosom of Ruyz de Alarcon.

The nuptials of the happy couple were celebrated soon afterwards with great splendor, and the Rose of the Alhambra became the ornament and delight of the court. "But hold— not so fast"—I hear the reader exclaim, "this is jumping to the end of a story at a furious rate! First let us know how Ruyz de Alarcon managed to account to Jacinta for his long neglect?" Nothing more easy; the venerable, time-honored excuse, the opposition to his wishes by a proud, pragmatical old father: besides, young people, who really like one another, soon come to an amicable understanding, and bury all past grievances when once they meet.

But how was the proud pragmatical old father reconciled to the match?

Oh! as to that, his scruples were easily overcome by a word or two from the queen; especially as dignities and rewards were showered upon the blooming favorite of royalty. Besides, the lute of Jacinta, you know, possessed a magic power, and could control the most stubborn head and hardest breast.

And what became of the enchanted lute?

O that is the most curious matter of all, and plainly proves the truth of the whole story. The lute remained for some time in the family, but was purloined and carried off, as was supposed, by the great singer Farinelli, in pure jealousy. At his death it passed into other hands in Italy, who were ignorant of its mystic powers, and melting down the silver, transferred the strings to an old Cremona fiddle. The strings still retain something of their magic virtues. A word in the reader's ear, but let it go no further—that fiddle is now bewitching the whole world—it is the fiddle of Paganini!

The Veteran

AMONG THE CURIOUS acquaintances I made in my rambles about the fortress, was a brave and battered old colonel of Invalids, who was nestled like a hawk in one of the Moorish towers. His history, which he was fond of telling, was a tissue of those adventures, mishaps, and vicissitudes that render the life of almost every Spaniard of note as varied and whimsical as the pages of Gil Blas.

He was in America at twelve years of age, and reckoned among the most signal and fortunate events of his life, his having seen General Washington. Since then he had taken a part in all the wars of his country; he could speak experimentally of most of the prisons and dungeons of the Peninsula; had been lamed of one leg, crippled in his hands, and so cut up and carbonadoed that he was a kind of walking monument of the troubles of Spain, on which there was a scar for every battle and broil, as every year of captivity was notched upon the tree of Robinson Crusoe. The greatest misfortune of the brave old cavalier, however, appeared to have been his having commanded at Malaga during a time of peril and confusion, and been made a general by the inhabitants, to protect them from the invasion of the French. This had entailed upon him a number of just claims upon government, that I feared would employ him until his dying day in writing and printing petitions and memorials, to the great disquiet of his mind, exhaustion of his purse, and penance of his friends; not one of whom could visit him without having to listen to a mortal document of half an hour in length, and to carry away half a dozen pamphlets in his pocket. This, however, is the case throughout Spain; every where you meet with some worthy wight brooding in a corner, and nursing up some pet grievance and cherished wrong. Besides, a Spaniard who has a lawsuit, or a claim upon government, may be considered as furnished with employment for the remainder of his life.

I visited the veteran in his quarters in the upper part of the Torre del Vino, or Wine Tower. His room was small but snug, and commanded a beautiful view of the Vega. It was arranged with a soldier's precision. Three muskets and a brace of pistols, all bright and shining, were suspended against the wall, with a sabre and a cane hanging side by side, and above them, two cocked hats, one for parade, and one for ordinary use. A small shelf, containing some half dozen books, formed his library, one of which, a little old mouldy volume of philosophical maxims, was his favorite reading. This he thumbed and pondered over day by day; applying every maxim to his own particular case, provided it had a little tinge of wholesome bitterness, and treated of the injustice of the world.

Yet he was social and kind-hearted, and provided he could be diverted from his wrongs and his philosophy, was an entertaining companion. I like these old weather-beaten sons of fortune, and enjoy their rough campaigning anecdotes. In the course of my visits to the one in question, I learnt some curious facts about an old military commander of the fortress, who seems to have resembled him in some respects, and to have had similar fortunes in the wars. These particulars have been augmented by inquiries among some of the old inhabitants of the place, particularly the father of Mateo Ximenes, of whose traditional stories the worthy I am about to introduce to the reader, was a favorite hero.

The Governor and the Notary

IN FORMER TIMES there ruled, as governor of the Alhambra, a doughty old cavalier, who, from having lost one arm in the wars, was commonly known by the name of el Gobernador Manco, or "the one-armed governor." He in fact prided himself upon being an old soldier, wore his mustaches curled up to his eyes, a pair of campaigning boots, and a toledo as long as a spit, with his pocket handkerchief in the basket-hilt.

He was, moreover, exceedingly proud and punctilious, and tenacious of all his privileges and dignities. Under his sway the immunities of the Alhambra, as a royal residence and domain, were rigidly exacted. No one was permitted to enter the fortress with firearms, or even with a sword or staff, unless he were of a certain rank; and every horseman was obliged to dismount at the gate, and lead his horse by the bridle. Now as the hill of the Alhambra rises from the very midst of the city of Granada, being, as it were, an excrescence of the capital, it must at all times be somewhat irksome to the captain-general, who commands the province, to have thus an *imperium in imperio*, a petty independent post in the very centre of his domains. It was rendered the more galling, in the present instance, from the irritable jealousy of the old governor, that took fire on the least question of authority and jurisdiction; and from the loose vagrant character of the people who had gradually nestled themselves within the fortress, as in a sanctuary, and thence carried on a system of roguery and depredation at the expense of the honest inhabitants of the city.

Thus there was a perpetual feud and heart-burning between the captain-general and the governor, the more virulent on the part of the latter, inasmuch as the smallest of two neighboring potentates is always the most captious about his dignity. The stately palace of the captain-general stood in the Plaza Nueva, immediately at the foot of the hill of the Alhambra, and here was always a bustle and parade of guards and domestics, and city functionaries. A beetling bastion of the fortress overlooked the palace and public square in front of it; and on this bastion the old governor would occasionally strut

968

backwards and forwards, with his toledo girded by his side, keeping a wary eye down upon his rival, like a hawk reconnoitering his quarry from his nest in a dry tree.

Whenever he descended into the city it was in grand parade, on horseback, surrounded by his guards, or in his state coach, an ancient and unwieldy Spanish edifice of carved timber and gilt leather, drawn by eight mules, with running footmen, outriders, and lackeys; on which occasions he flattered himself he impressed every beholder with awe and admiration as vicegerent of the king; though the wits of Granada, particularly those who loitered about the palace of the captain-general, were apt to sneer at his petty parade, and in allusion to the vagrant character of his subjects, to greet him with the appellation of "the king of the beggars." One of the most fruitful sources of dispute between these two doughty rivals was the right claimed by the governor to have all things passed free of duty through the city, that were intended for the use of himself or his garrison. By degrees this privilege had given rise to extensive smuggling. A nest of contrabandistas took up their abode in the hovels of the fortress, and the numerous caves in its vicinity, and drove a thriving business under the connivance of the soldiers of the garrison.

The vigilance of the captain-general was aroused. He consulted his legal adviser and factotum, a shrewd meddlesome escribano, or notary, who rejoiced in an opportunity of perplexing the old potentate of the Alhambra, and involving him in a maze of legal subtilties. He advised the captain-general to insist upon the right of examining every convoy passing through the gates of his city, and penned a long letter for him in vindication of the right. Governor Manco was a straightforward cut-and-thrust old soldier, who hated an escribano worse than the devil, and this one in particular worse than all other escribanos.

"What!" said he, curling up his mustaches fiercely, "does the captain-general set his man of the pen to practise confusions upon me? I'll let him see an old soldier is not to be baffled by schoolcraft."

He seized his pen and scrawled a short letter in a crabbed hand, in which, without deigning to enter into argument, he insisted on the right of transit free of search, and denounced vengeance on any custom house officer who should lay his unhallowed hand on any convoy protected by the flag of the Alhambra. While this question was agitated between the two pragmatical potentates, it so happened that a mule laden with supplies for the fortress arrived one day at the gate of Xenil, by which it was to traverse a suburb of the city on its way to the Alhambra. The convoy was headed by a testy old corporal, who had long served under the governor, and was a man after his own heart; as trusty and staunch as an old Toledo blade.

As they approached the gate of the city, the corporal placed the banner of the Alhambra on the pack-saddle of the mule, and drawing himself up to a perfect perpendicular, advanced with his head dressed to the front, but with the wary side-glance of a cur passing through hostile ground, and ready for a snap and a snarl.

"Who goes there?" said the sentinel at the gate.

"Soldier of the Alhambra!" said the corporal, without turning his head.

"What have you in charge?"

"Provisions for the garrison."

"Proceed."

The corporal marched straight forward, followed by the convoy, but had not advanced many paces before a posse of custom-house officers rushed out of a small toll-house.

"Hallo there!" cried the leader; "Muleteer, halt, and open those packages."

The corporal wheeled round, and drew himself up in battle array. "Respect the flag of the Alhambra," said he; "these things are for the governor."

"A figo for the governor, and a figo for his flag. Muleteer, halt, I say."

"Stop the convoy at your peril!" cried the corporal, cocking his musket; "Muleteer, proceed."

The muleteer gave his beast a hearty thwack; the custom-house officer sprang forward and seized the halter; whereupon the corporal levelled his piece, and shot him dead.

The street was immediately in an uproar.

The old corporal was seized, and after undergoing sundry kicks, and cuffs, and cudgellings, which are generally given impromptu by the mob in Spain, as a foretaste of the after penalties of the law, he was loaded with irons, and conducted to the city prison; while his comrades were permitted to proceed with the convoy, after it had been well rummaged, to the Alhambra.

The old governor was in a towering passion when he heard of this insult to his flag and capture of his corporal. For a time he stormed about the Moorish halls, and vapored about the bastions, and looked down fire and sword upon the palace of the captain-general. Having vented the first ebullition of his wrath, he dispatched a message demanding the surrender of the corporal, as to him alone belonged the right of sitting in judgment on the offences of those under his command. The captain-general, aided by the pen of the delighted escribano, replied at great length, arguing that as the offence had been committed within the walls of his city, and against one of his civil officers, it was clearly within his proper jurisdiction. The governor rejoined by a repetition of his demand; the captain-general gave a sur-rejoinder of still greater length and legal acumen; the governor became hotter and more peremptory in his demands, and the captain-general cooler and more copious in his replies; until the old lion-hearted soldier absolutely roared with fury at being thus entangled in the meshes of legal controversy.

While the subtle escribano was thus amusing himself at the expense of the governor, he was conducting the trial of the corporal, who, mewed up in a narrow dungeon of the prison, had merely a small grated window at which to show his iron-bound visage and receive the consolations of his friends.

A mountain of written testimony was diligently heaped up, according to Spanish form, by the indefatigable escribano; the corporal was completely overwhelmed by it. He was convicted of murder, and sentenced to be hanged.

It was in vain the governor sent down remonstrance and menace from the Alhambra. The fatal day was at hand, and the corporal was put *in capilla*, that is to say, in the chapel of the prison, as is always done with culprits the day before execution, that they may meditate on their approaching end and repent them of their sins.

Seeing things drawing to extremity, the old governor deter-

mined to attend to the affair in person. For this purpose he
ordered out his carriage of state, and, surrounded by his
guards, rumbled down the avenue of the Alhambra into the
city. Driving to the house of the escribano, he summoned
him to the portal.

The eye of the old governor gleamed like a coal at beholding the smirking man of the law advancing with an air of
exultation.

"What is this I hear," cried he, "that you are about to put
to death one of my soldiers?"

"All according to law—all in strict form of justice," said
the self-sufficient escribano, chuckling and rubbing his hands.
"I can show your excellency the written testimony in the
case."

"Fetch it hither," said the governor. The escribano bustled
into his office, delighted with having another opportunity of
displaying his ingenuity at the expense of the hard-headed
veteran.

He returned with a satchel full of papers, and began to read
a long deposition with professional volubility. By this time a
crowd had collected, listening with outstretched necks and
gaping mouths.

"Prithee, man, get into the carriage, out of this pestilent
throng, that I may the better hear thee," said the governor.

The escribano entered the carriage, when, in a twinkling,
the door was closed, the coachman smacked his whip—
mules, carriage, guards and all dashed off at a thundering rate,
leaving the crowd in gaping wonderment; nor did the governor pause until he had lodged his prey in one of the strongest
dungeons of the Alhambra.

He then sent down a flag of truce in military style, proposing a cartel or exchange of prisoners—the corporal for the
notary. The pride of the captain-general was piqued; he returned a contemptuous refusal, and forthwith caused a gallows, tall and strong, to be erected in the centre of the Plaza
Nueva for the execution of the corporal.

"Oho! is that the game?" said Governor Manco. He gave
orders, and immediately a gibbet was reared on the verge of
the great beetling bastion that overlooked the Plaza. "Now,"
said he in a message to the captain-general, "hang my soldier

when you please; but at the same time that he is swung off in the square, look up to see your escribano dangling against the sky."

The captain-general was inflexible; troops were paraded in the square; the drums beat, the bell tolled. An immense multitude of amateurs gathered together to behold the execution. On the other hand, the governor paraded his garrison on the bastion, and tolled the funeral dirge of the notary from the Torre de la Campana, or Tower of the Bell.

The notary's wife pressed through the crowd with a whole progeny of little embryo escribanos at her heels, and throwing herself at the feet of the captain-general, implored him not to sacrifice the life of her husband, and the welfare of herself and her numerous little ones, to a point of pride; "for you know the old governor too well," said she, "to doubt that he will put his threat in execution, if you hang the soldier."

The captain-general was overpowered by her tears and lamentations, and the clamors of her callow brood. The corporal was sent up to the Alhambra, under a guard, in his gallows garb, like a hooded friar, but with head erect and a face of iron. The escribano was demanded in exchange, according to the cartel. The once bustling and self-sufficient man of the law was drawn forth from his dungeon more dead than alive. All his flippancy and conceit had evaporated; his hair, it is said, had nearly turned gray with affright, and he had a downcast, dogged look, as if he still felt the halter round his neck.

The old governor stuck his one arm a-kimbo, and for a moment surveyed him with an iron smile. "Henceforth, my friend," said he, "moderate your zeal in hurrying others to the gallows; be not too certain of your safety, even though you should have the law on your side; and above all take care how you play off your schoolcraft another time upon an old soldier."

Governor Manco and the Soldier

WHILE GOVERNOR MANCO, or "the one-armed," kept up a show of military state in the Alhambra, he became nettled at the reproaches continually cast upon his fortress, of being a nestling place of rogues and contrabandistas. On a sudden, the old potentate determined on reform, and setting vigorously to work, ejected whole nests of vagabonds out of the fortress and the gipsy caves with which the surrounding hills are honeycombed. He sent out soldiers, also, to patrol the avenues and footpaths, with orders to take up all suspicious persons.

One bright summer morning, a patrol, consisting of the testy old corporal who had distinguished himself in the affair of the notary, a trumpeter and two privates, was seated under the garden wall of the Generalife, beside the road which leads down from the mountain of the sun, when they heard the tramp of a horse, and a male voice singing in rough, though not unmusical tones, an old Castilian campaigning song.

Presently they beheld a sturdy, sunburnt fellow, clad in the ragged garb of a foot-soldier, leading a powerful Arabian horse, caparisoned in the ancient Moresco fashion.

Astonished at the sight of a strange soldier descending, steed in hand, from that solitary mountain, the corporal stepped forth and challenged him.

"Who goes there?"

"A friend."

"Who and what are you?"

"A poor soldier just from the wars, with a cracked crown and empty purse for a reward."

By this time they were enabled to view him more narrowly. He had a black patch across his forehead, which, with a grizzled beard, added to a certain dare-devil cast of countenance, while a slight squint threw into the whole an occasional gleam of roguish good humor.

Having answered the questions of the patrol, the soldier seemed to consider himself entitled to make others in return.

"May I ask," said he, "what city is that which I see at the foot of the hill?"

"What city!" cried the trumpeter; "come, that's too bad. Here's a fellow lurking about the mountain of the sun, and demands the name of the great city of Granada!"

"Granada! Madre di Dios! can it be possible?"

"Perhaps not!" rejoined the trumpeter; "and perhaps you have no idea that yonder are the towers of the Alhambra."

"Son of a trumpet," replied the stranger, "do not trifle with me; if this be indeed the Alhambra, I have some strange matters to reveal to the governor."

"You will have an opportunity," said the corporal, "for we mean to take you before him." By this time the trumpeter had seized the bridle of the steed, the two privates had each secured an arm of the soldier, the corporal put himself in front, gave the word, "Forward—march!" and away they marched for the Alhambra.

The sight of a ragged foot-soldier and a fine Arabian horse, brought in captive by the patrol, attracted the attention of all the idlers of the fortress, and of those gossip groups that generally assemble about wells and fountains at early dawn. The wheel of the cistern paused in its rotations, and the slipshod servant-maid stood gaping, with pitcher in hand, as the corporal passed by with his prize. A motley train gradually gathered in the rear of the escort.

Knowing nods and winks and conjectures passed from one to another. "It is a deserter," said one; "A contrabandista," said another; "A bandalero," said a third;—until it was affirmed that a captain of a desperate band of robbers had been captured by the prowess of the corporal and his patrol. "Well, well," said the old crones, one to another, "captain or not, let him get out of the grasp of old Governor Manco if he can, though he is but one-handed."

Governor Manco was seated in one of the inner halls of the Alhambra, taking his morning's cup of chocolate in company with his confessor, a fat Franciscan friar, from the neighboring convent. A demure, dark-eyed damsel of Malaga, the daughter of his housekeeper, was attending upon him. The world hinted that the damsel, who, with all her demureness, was a sly buxom baggage, had found out a soft spot in the iron heart of the old governor, and held complete control over him. But let that pass—the domestic affairs of these mighty potentates of the earth should not be too narrowly scrutinized.

When word was brought that a suspicious stranger had been taken lurking about the fortress, and was actually in the outer court, in durance of the corporal, waiting the pleasure of his excellency, the pride and stateliness of office swelled the bosom of the governor. Giving back his chocolate cup into the hands of the demure damsel, he called for his basket-hilted sword, girded it to his side, twirled up his mustaches, took his seat in a large high-backed chair, assumed a bitter and forbidding aspect, and ordered the prisoner into his presence. The soldier was brought in, still closely pinioned by his captors, and guarded by the corporal. He maintained, however, a resolute self confident air, and returned the sharp, scrutinizing look of the governor with an easy squint, which by no means pleased the punctilious old potentate.

"Well, culprit," said the governor, after he had regarded him for a moment in silence, "what have you to say for yourself—who are you?"

"A soldier, just from the wars, who has brought away nothing but scars and bruises."

"A soldier—humph—a foot-soldier by your garb. I understand you have a fine Arabian horse. I presume you brought him too from the wars, besides your scars and bruises."

"May it please your excellency, I have something strange to tell about that horse. Indeed I have one of the most wonderful things to relate. Something too that concerns the security of this fortress, indeed of all Granada. But it is a matter to be imparted only to your private ear, or in presence of such only as are in your confidence."

The governor considered for a moment, and then directed the corporal and his men to withdraw, but to post themselves outside of the door, and be ready at a call. "This holy friar," said he, "is my confessor, you may say any thing in his presence—and this damsel," nodding towards the handmaid, who had loitered with an air of great curiosity, "this damsel is of great secrecy and discretion, and to be trusted with any thing."

The soldier gave a glance between a squint and a leer at the demure handmaid. "I am perfectly willing," said he, "that the damsel should remain."

When all the rest had withdrawn, the soldier commenced his story. He was a fluent, smooth-tongued varlet, and had a command of language above his apparent rank.

"May it please your excellency," said he, "I am, as I before observed, a soldier, and have seen some hard service, but my term of enlistment being expired, I was discharged, not long since, from the army at Valladolid, and set out on foot for my native village in Andalusia. Yesterday evening the sun went down as I was traversing a great dry plain of Old Castile."

"Hold," cried the governor, "what is this you say? Old Castile is some two or three hundred miles from this."

"Even so," replied the soldier, coolly; "I told your excellency I had strange things to relate; but not more strange than true; as your excellency will find, if you will deign me a patient hearing."

"Proceed, culprit," said the governor, twirling up his mustaches.

"As the sun went down," continued the soldier, "I cast my eyes about in search of quarters for the night, but as far as my sight could reach, there were no signs of habitation. I saw that I should have to make my bed on the naked plain, with my knapsack for a pillow; but your excellency is an old soldier, and knows that to one who has been in the wars, such a night's lodging is no great hardship."

The governor nodded assent, as he drew his pocket handkerchief out of the basket-hilt, to drive away a fly that buzzed about his nose.

"Well, to make a long story short," continued the soldier, "I trudged forward for several miles until I came to a bridge over a deep ravine, through which ran a little thread of water, almost dried up by the summer heat. At one end of the bridge was a Moorish tower, the upper end all in ruins, but a vault in the foundation quite entire. Here, thinks I, is a good place to make a halt; so I went down to the stream, took a hearty drink, for the water was pure and sweet, and I was parched with thirst; then, opening my wallet, I took out an onion and a few crusts, which were all my provisions, and seating myself on a stone on the margin of the stream, began to make my supper; intending afterwards to quarter myself for the night in the vault of the tower; and capital quarters they would have been for a campaigner just from the wars, as your excellency, who is an old soldier, may suppose."

"I have put up gladly with worse in my time," said the governor, returning his pocket-handkerchief into the hilt of his sword.

"While I was quietly crunching my crust," pursued the soldier, "I heard something stir within the vault; I listened—it was the tramp of a horse. By and by a man came forth from a door in the foundation of the tower, close by the water's edge, leading a powerful horse by the bridle. I could not well make out what he was by the starlight. It had a suspicious look to be lurking among the ruins of a tower, in that wild solitary place. He might be a mere wayfarer, like myself; he might be a contrabandista; he might be a bandalero! what of that? thank heaven and my poverty, I had nothing to lose; so I sat still and crunched my crusts.

"He led his horse to the water, close by where I was sitting, so that I had a fair opportunity of reconnoitering him. To my surprise he was dressed in a Moorish garb, with a cuirass of steel, and a polished skull-cap that I distinguished by the reflection of the stars upon it. His horse, too, was harnessed in the Moresco fashion, with great shovel stirrups. He led him, as I said, to the side of the stream, into which the animal plunged his head almost to the eyes, and drank until I thought he would have burst.

" 'Comrade,' said I, 'your steed drinks well; it's a good sign when a horse plunges his muzzle bravely into the water.'

" 'He may well drink,' said the stranger, speaking with a Moorish accent; 'it is a good year since he had his last draught.'

" 'By Santiago,' said I, 'that beats even the camels I have seen in Africa. But come, you seem to be something of a soldier, will you sit down and take part of a soldier's fare?' In fact, I felt the want of a companion in this lonely place, and was willing to put up with an infidel. Besides, as your excellency well knows, a soldier is never very particular about the faith of his company, and soldiers of all countries are comrades on peaceable ground."

The governor again nodded assent.

"Well, as I was saying, I invited him to share my supper, such as it was, for I could not do less in common hospitality. 'I have no time to pause for meat or drink,' said he, 'I have a long journey to make before morning.'

" 'In which direction?' said I.

" 'Andalusia,' said he.

" 'Exactly my route,' said I, 'so, as you won't stop and eat with me, perhaps you will let me mount and ride with you. I see your horse is of a powerful frame, I'll warrant he'll carry double.'

" 'Agreed,' said the trooper; and it would not have been civil and soldierlike to refuse, especially as I had offered to share my supper with him. So up he mounted, and up I mounted behind him.

" 'Hold fast,' said he, 'my steed goes like the wind.'

" 'Never fear me,' said I, and so off we set.

"From a walk the horse soon passed to a trot, from a trot to a gallop, and from a gallop to a harum-scarum scamper. It seemed as if rocks, trees, houses, every thing, flew hurry-scurry behind us.

" 'What town is this?' " said I.

" 'Segovia,' said he; and before the word was out of his mouth, the towers of Segovia were out of sight. We swept up the Guadarama mountains, and down by the Escurial; and we skirted the walls of Madrid, and we scoured away across the plains of La Mancha. In this way we went up hill and down dale, by towers and cities, all buried in deep sleep, and across mountains, and plains, and rivers, just glimmering in the starlight.

"To make a long story short, and not to fatigue your excellency, the trooper suddenly pulled up on the side of a mountain. 'Here we are,' said he, 'at the end of our journey.' I looked about, but could see no signs of habitation; nothing but the mouth of a cavern. While I looked I saw multitudes of people in Moorish dresses, some on horseback, some on foot, arriving as if borne by the wind from all points of the compass, and hurrying into the mouth of the cavern like bees into a hive. Before I could ask a question the trooper struck his long Moorish spurs into the horse's flanks, and dashed in with the throng. We passed along a steep winding way, that descended into the very bowels of the mountain. As we pushed on, a light began to glimmer up, by little and little, like the first glimmerings of day, but what caused it I could not discern. It grew stronger and stronger, and enabled me to see every thing around. I now noticed, as we passed along, great caverns, opening to the right and left, like halls in an arsenal. In some there were shields, and helmets, and cuirasses, and lances, and cimeters, hanging against the walls; in others there were great heaps of warlike munitions, and camp equipage lying upon the ground.

"It would have done your excellency's heart good, being an old soldier, to have seen such grand provision for war. Then, in other caverns, there were long rows of horsemen armed to the teeth, with lances raised and banners unfurled, all ready for the field; but they all sat motionless in their saddles like so many statues. In other halls were warriors sleeping on the ground beside their horses, and foot-soldiers in groups ready to fall into the ranks. All were in old-fashioned Moorish dresses and armor.

"Well, your excellency, to cut a long story short, we at length entered an immense cavern, or I may say palace, of grotto work, the walls of which seemed to be veined with gold and silver, and to sparkle with diamonds and sapphires and all kinds of precious stones. At the upper end sat a Moorish king on a golden throne, with his nobles on each side, and a guard of African blacks with drawn cimeters. All the crowd that continued to flock in, and amounted to thousands and thousands, passed one by one before his throne, each paying homage as he passed. Some of the multitude were dressed in magnificent robes, without stain or blemish and sparkling with jewels; others in burnished and enamelled armor; while others were in mouldered and mildewed garments, and in armor all battered and dented and covered with rust.

"I had hitherto held my tongue, for your excellency well knows it is not for a soldier to ask many questions when on duty, but I could keep silent no longer.

" 'Prithee, comrade,' said I, 'what is the meaning of all this?'

" 'This,' said the trooper, 'is a great and fearful mystery. Know, O Christian, that you see before you the court and army of Boabdil the last king of Granada.'

" 'What is this you tell me?' cried I. 'Boabdil and his court were exiled from the land hundreds of years agone, and all died in Africa.'

" 'So it is recorded in your lying chronicles,' replied the Moor, 'but know that Boabdil and the warriors who made the last struggle for Granada were all shut up in the mountain by powerful enchantment. As for the king and army that marched forth from Granada at the time of the surrender, they were a mere phantom train, or spirits and demons permitted to assume those shapes to deceive the Christian sovereigns. And furthermore let me tell you, friend, that all Spain is a country under the power of enchantment. There is not a mountain cave, not a lonely watchtower in the plains, nor ruined castle on the hills, but has some spell-bound warriors sleeping from age to age within its vaults, until the sins are expiated for which Allah permitted the dominion to pass for a time out of the hands of the faithful. Once every year, on the eve of St. John, they are released from enchantment, from sunset to sunrise, and permitted to repair here to pay homage to their sovereign; and the crowds which you beheld swarming into the cavern are Moslem warriors from their haunts in all parts of Spain. For my own part, you saw the ruined tower of the bridge in Old Castile, where I have now wintered and summered for many hundred years, and where I must be back again by daybreak. As to the battalions of horse and foot which you beheld drawn up in array in the neighboring caverns, they are the spell-bound warriors of Granada. It is written in the book of fate, that when the enchantment is broken, Boabdil will descend from the mountain at the head of this army, resume his throne in the Alhambra and his sway of Granada, and gathering together the enchanted warriors, from all parts of Spain, will reconquer the Peninsula and restore it to Moslem rule.'

" 'And when shall this happen?' said I.

" 'Allah alone knows: we had hoped the day of deliverance was at hand; but there reigns at present a vigilant governor in the Alhambra, a staunch old soldier, well known as Governor Manco. While such a warrior holds command of the very outpost, and stands ready to check the first irruption from the mountain, I fear Boabdil and his soldiery must be content to rest upon their arms.' "

Here the governor raised himself somewhat perpendicularly, adjusted his sword, and twirled up his mustaches.

"To make a long story short, and not to fatigue your excellency, the trooper, having given me this account, dismounted from his steed.

" 'Tarry here,' said he, 'and guard my steed while I go and bow the knee to Boabdil.' So saying, he strode away among the throng that pressed forward to the throne.

" 'What's to be done?' thought I, when thus left to myself, 'shall I wait here until this infidel returns to whisk me off on his goblin steed, the Lord knows where; or shall I make the most of my time and beat a retreat from this hobgoblin community?' A soldier's mind is soon made up, as your excellency well knows. As to the horse, he belonged to an avowed enemy of the faith and the realm, and was a fair prize according to the rules of war. So hoisting myself up from the crupper into the saddle, I turned the reins, struck the Moorish stirrups into the sides of the steed, and put him to make the best of his way out of the passage by which he had entered. As we scoured by the halls where the Moslem horsemen sat in motionless battalions, I thought I heard the clang of armor and a hollow murmur of voices. I gave the steed another taste of the stirrups and doubled my speed. There was now a sound behind me like a rushing blast; I heard the clatter of a thousand hoofs; a countless throng overtook me. I was borne along in the press, and hurled forth from the mouth of the cavern, while thousands of shadowy forms were swept off in every direction by the four winds of heaven.

"In the whirl and confusion of the scene I was thrown senseless to the earth. When I came to myself I was lying on the brow of a hill, with the Arabian steed standing beside me; for in falling, my arm had slipped within the bridle, which, I presume, prevented his whisking off to Old Castile.

"Your excellency may easily judge of my surprise, on looking round, to behold hedges of aloes and Indian figs and other proofs of a southern climate, and to see a great city below me, with towers, and palaces, and a grand cathedral.

"I descended the hill cautiously, leading my steed, for I was afraid to mount him again, lest he should play me some slippery trick. As I descended I met with your patrol, who let me into the secret that it was Granada that lay before me; and that I was actually under the walls of the Alhambra, the fortress of the redoubted Governor Manco, the terror of all enchanted Moslems. When I heard this, I determined at once to seek your excellency, to inform you of all that I had seen, and to warn you of the perils that surround and undermine you, that you may take measures in time to guard your fortress, and the kingdom itself, from this intestine army that lurks in the very bowels of the land."

"And prithee, friend, you who are a veteran campaigner, and have seen so much service," said the governor, "how would you advise me to proceed, in order to prevent this evil?"

"It is not for a humble private of the ranks," said the soldier, modestly, "to pretend to instruct a commander of your excellency's sagacity, but it appears to me that your excellency might cause all the caves and entrances into the mountain to be walled up with solid mason work, so that Boabdil and his army might be completely corked up in their subterranean habitation. If the good father, too," added the soldier, reverently bowing to the friar, and devoutly crossing himself, "would consecrate the barricadoes with his blessing, and put up a few crosses and relics and images of saints, I think they might withstand all the power of infidel enchantments."

"They doubtless would be of great avail," said the friar.

The governor now placed his arm a-kimbo, with his hand resting on the hilt of his Toledo, fixed his eye upon the soldier, and gently wagging his head from one side to the other,

"So, friend," said he, "then you really suppose I am to be gulled with this cock-and-bull story about enchanted mountains and enchanted Moors? Hark, ye, culprit!—not another word. An old soldier you may be, but you'll find you have an older soldier to deal with, and one not easily outgeneralled. Ho! guards there! put this fellow in irons."

The demure handmaid would have put in a word in favor of the prisoner, but the governor silenced her with a look.

As they were pinioning the soldier, one of the guards felt something of bulk in his pocket, and drawing it forth, found a long leathern purse that appeared to be well filled. Holding it by one corner, he turned out the contents upon the table before the governor, and never did freebooter's bag make more gorgeous delivery. Out tumbled rings, and jewels, and rosaries of pearls, and sparkling diamond crosses, and a profusion of ancient golden coin, some of which fell jingling to the floor, and rolled away to the uttermost parts of the chamber.

For a time the functions of justice were suspended; there was a universal scramble after the glittering fugitives. The governor alone, who was imbued with true Spanish pride, maintained his stately decorum, though his eye betrayed a little anxiety until the last coin and jewel was restored to the sack.

The friar was not so calm; his whole face glowed like a furnace, and his eyes twinkled and flashed at sight of the rosaries and crosses.

"Sacrilegious wretch that thou art!" exclaimed he; "what church or sanctuary hast thou been plundering of these sacred relics?"

"Neither one nor the other, holy father. If they be sacrilegious spoils, they must have been taken, in times long past, by the infidel trooper I have mentioned. I was just going to tell his excellency when he interrupted me, that on taking possession of the trooper's horse, I unhooked a leathern sack which hung at the saddle-bow, and which I presume contained the plunder of his campaigning in days of old, when the Moors overran the country."

"Mighty well; at present you will make up your mind to take up your quarters in a chamber of the vermilion tower, which, though not under a magic spell, will hold you as safe as any cave of your enchanted Moors."

"Your excellency will do as you think proper," said the prisoner, coolly. "I shall be thankful to your excellency for any accommodation in the fortress. A soldier who has been in the wars, as your excellency well knows, is not particular about his lodgings: provided I have a snug dungeon and regular rations, I shall manage to make myself comfortable. I would only entreat that while your excellency is so careful about me, you would have an eye to your fortress, and think on the hint I dropped about stopping up the entrances to the mountain."

Here ended the scene. The prisoner was conducted to a strong dungeon in the vermilion tower, the Arabian steed was led to his excellency's stable, and the trooper's sack was deposited in his excellency's strong box. To the latter, it is true, the friar made some demur, questioning whether the sacred relics, which were evidently sacrilegious spoils, should not be placed in custody of the church; but as the governor was peremptory on the subject, and was absolute lord in the Alhambra, the friar discreetly dropped the discussion, but determined to convey intelligence of the fact to the church dignitaries in Granada.

To explain these prompt and rigid measures on the part of old Governor Manco, it is proper to observe, that about this time the Alpuxarra mountains in the neighborhood of Granada were terribly infested by a gang of robbers, under the command of a daring chief named Manuel Borasco, who were accustomed to prowl about the country, and even to enter the city in various disguises, to gain intelligence of the departure of convoys of merchandise, or travellers with well-lined purses, whom they took care to waylay in distant and solitary passes of the road. These repeated and daring outrages had awakened the attention of government, and the commanders of the various posts had received instructions to be on the alert, and to take up all suspicious stragglers. Governor Manco was particularly zealous in consequence of the various stigmas that had been cast upon his fortress, and he now doubted not he had entrapped some formidable desperado of this gang.

In the mean time the story took wind, and became the talk, not merely of the fortress, but of the whole city of Granada. It was said that the noted robber Manuel Borasco, the terror of the Alpuxarras, had fallen into the clutches of old Governor Manco, and been cooped up by him in a dungeon of the

vermilion towers; and every one who had been robbed by
him flocked to recognize the marauder. The vermilion towers,
as is well known, stand apart from the Alhambra on a sister
hill, separated from the main fortress by the ravine down
which passes the main avenue. There were no outer walls, but
a sentinel patrolled before the tower. The window of the
chamber in which the soldier was confined was strongly
grated, and looked upon a small esplanade. Here the good
folks of Granada repaired to gaze at him, as they would at a
laughing hyena, grinning through the cage of a menagerie.
Nobody, however, recognized him for Manuel Borasco, for
that terrible robber was noted for a ferocious physiognomy,
and had by no means the good-humored squint of the prisoner. Visitors came not merely from the city, but from all
parts of the country; but nobody knew him, and there began
to be doubts in the minds of the common people whether
there might not be some truth in his story. That Boabdil and
his army were shut up in the mountain, was an old tradition
which many of the ancient inhabitants had heard from their
fathers. Numbers went up to the mountain of the sun, or
rather of St. Elena, in search of the cave mentioned by the
soldier; and saw and peeped into the deep dark pit, descending, no one knows how far, into the mountain, and which
remains there to this day—the fabled entrance to the subterranean abode of Boabdil.

By degrees the soldier became popular with the common
people. A freebooter of the mountains is by no means the
opprobrious character in Spain that a robber is in any other
country: on the contrary, he is a kind of chivalrous personage
in the eyes of the lower classes. There is always a disposition,
also, to cavil at the conduct of those in command, and many
began to murmur at the high-handed measures of old Governor Manco, and to look upon the prisoner in the light of a
martyr.

The soldier, moreover, was a merry, waggish fellow, that
had a joke for every one who came near his window, and a
soft speech for every female. He had procured an old guitar
also, and would sit by his window and sing ballads and love-
ditties to the delight of the women of the neighborhood, who
would assemble on the esplanade in the evenings and dance

boleros to his music. Having trimmed off his rough beard, his sunburnt face found favor in the eyes of the fair, and the demure handmaid of the governor declared that his squint was perfectly irresistible. This kind-hearted damsel had from the first evinced a deep sympathy in his fortunes, and having in vain tried to mollify the governor, had set to work privately to mitigate the rigor of his dispensations. Every day she brought the prisoner some crumbs of comfort which had fallen from the governor's table, or been abstracted from his larder, together with, now and then, a consoling bottle of choice Val de Peñas, or rich Malaga.

While this petty treason was going on, in the very centre of the old governor's citadel, a storm of open war was brewing up among his external foes. The circumstance of a bag of gold and jewels having been found upon the person of the supposed robber, had been reported, with many exaggerations, in Granada. A question of territorial jurisdiction was immediately started by the governor's inveterate rival, the captain-general. He insisted that the prisoner had been captured without the precincts of the Alhambra, and within the rules of his authority. He demanded his body therefore, and the *spolia opima* taken with him. Due information having been carried likewise by the friar to the grand inquisitor of the crosses, and rosaries, and other relics contained in the bag, he claimed the culprit as having been guilty of sacrilege, and insisted that his plunder was due to the church, and his body to the next auto da fe. The feuds ran high; the governor was furious, and swore, rather than surrender his captive, he would hang him up within the Alhambra, as a spy caught within the purlieus of the fortress.

The captain-general threatened to send a body of soldiers to transfer the prisoner from the vermilion tower to the city. The grand inquisitor was equally bent upon dispatching a number of the familiars of the Holy Office. Word was brought late at night to the governor of these machinations. "Let them come," said he, "they'll find me beforehand with them; he must rise bright and early who would take in an old soldier." He accordingly issued orders to have the prisoner removed, at daybreak, to the donjon keep within the walls of the Alhambra. "And d'ye hear, child," said he to his demure handmaid, "tap at my door, and wake me before cock-crowing, that I may see to the matter myself."

The day dawned, the cock crowed, but nobody tapped at the door of the governor. The sun rose high above the mountain-tops, and glittered in at his casement, ere the governor was awakened from his morning dreams by his veteran corporal, who stood before him with terror stamped upon his iron visage.

"He's off! he's gone!" cried the corporal, grasping for breath.

"Who's off—who's gone?"

"The soldier—the robber—the devil, for aught I know; his dungeon is empty, but the door locked: no one knows how he has escaped out of it."

"Who saw him last?"

"Your handmaid, she brought him his supper."

"Let her be called instantly."

Here was new matter of confusion. The chamber of the demure damsel was likewise empty, her bed had not been slept in: she had doubtless gone off with the culprit, as she had appeared, for some days past, to have frequent conversations with him.

This was wounding the old governor in a tender part, but he had scarce time to wince at it, when new misfortunes broke upon his view. On going into his cabinet he found his strong box open, the leather purse of the trooper abstracted, and with it, a couple of corpulent bags of doubloons.

But how, and which way had the fugitives escaped? An old peasant who lived in a cottage by the road-side, leading up into the Sierra, declared that he had heard the tramp of a powerful steed just before daybreak, passing up into the mountains. He had looked out at his casement, and could just distinguish a horseman, with a female seated before him.

"Search the stables!" cried Governor Manco. The stables were searched; all the horses were in their stalls, excepting the Arabian steed. In his place was a stout cudgel tied to the manger, and on it a label bearing these words, "A gift to Governor Manco, from an Old Soldier."

A Fête in the Alhambra

THE SAINT'S DAY of my neighbor and rival potentate, the count, took place during his sojourn in the Alhambra, on which occasion he gave a domestic fête; assembling round him the members of his family and household, while the stewards and old servants from his distant possessions came to pay him reverence and partake of the good cheer, which was sure to be provided. It presented a type, though doubtless a faint one, of the establishment of a Spanish noble in the olden time.

The Spaniards were always grandiose in their notions of style. Huge palaces; lumbering equipages, laden with footmen and lackeys; pompous retinues, and useless dependents of all kinds; the dignity of a noble seemed commensurate with the legions who loitered about his halls, fed at his expense, and seemed ready to devour him alive. This, doubtless, originated in the necessity of keeping up hosts of armed retainers during the wars with the Moors; wars of inroads and surprises; when a noble was liable to be suddenly assailed in his castle by a foray of the enemy, or summoned to the field by his sovereign.

The custom remained after the wars were at an end; and what originated in necessity was kept up through ostentation. The wealth which flowed into the country from conquests and discoveries fostered the passion for princely establishments. According to magnificent old Spanish usage, in which pride and generosity bore equal parts, a superannuated servant was never turned off, but became a charge for the rest of his days; nay, his children, and his children's children, and often their relatives, to the right and left, became gradually entailed upon the family. Hence the huge palaces of the Spanish nobility, which have such an air of empty ostentation from the greatness of their size compared with the mediocrity and scantiness of their furniture, were absolutely required in the golden days of Spain, by the patriarchal habits of their possessors. They were little better than vast barracks for the hereditary generations of hangers on, that battened at the expense of a Spanish noble.

These patriarchal habits of the Spanish nobility have declined with their revenues; though the spirit which prompted them remains, and wars sadly with their altered fortunes. The poorest among them have always some hereditary hangers on, who live at their expense, and make them poorer. Some who, like my neighbor the count, retain a modicum of their once princely possessions, keep up a shadow of the ancient system, and their estates are overrun and the produce consumed by generations of idle retainers.

The count held estates in various parts of the kingdom, some including whole villages; yet the revenues collected from them were comparatively small; some of them, he assured me, barely fed the hordes of dependents nestled upon them, who seemed to consider themselves entitled to live rent free and be maintained into the bargain, because their forefathers had been so since time immemorial.

The saint's day of the old count gave me a glimpse into a Spanish interior. For two or three days previous preparations were made for the fête. Viands of all kinds were brought up from town, greeting the olfactory nerves of the old invalid guards, as they were borne past them through the Gate of Justice. Servants hurried officiously about the courts; the ancient kitchen of the palace was again alive with the tread of cooks and scullions, and blazed with unwonted fires.

When the day arrived I beheld the old count in patriarchal state, his family and household around him, with functionaries who mismanaged his estates at a distance and consumed the proceeds; while numerous old worn-out servants and pensioners were loitering about the courts and keeping within smell of the kitchen.

It was a joyous day in the Alhambra. The guests dispersed themselves about the palace before the hour of dinner, enjoying the luxuries of its courts and fountains, and embosomed gardens, and music and laughter resounded through its late silent halls.

The feast, for a set dinner in Spain is literally a feast, was served in the beautiful Moresco Hall of "Las dos Hermanas." The table was loaded with all the luxuries of the season; there was an almost interminable succession of dishes; showing how truly the feast at the rich Camachos' wedding in Don Quixote was a picture of a Spanish banquet. A joyous conviviality prevailed around the board; for though Spaniards are generally abstemious, they are complete revellers on occasions like the present, and none more so than the Andalusians. For my part, there was something peculiarly exciting in thus sitting at a feast in the royal halls of the Alhambra, given by one who might claim remote affinity with its Moorish kings, and who was a lineal representative of Gonsalvo of Cordova, one of the most distinguished of the Christian conquerors.

The banquet ended, the company adjourned to the Hall of Ambassadors. Here every one endeavored to contribute to the general amusement, singing, improvising, telling wonderful tales, or dancing popular dances to that all pervading talisman of Spanish pleasure, the guitar.

The count's gifted little daughter was as usual the life and delight of the assemblage, and I was more than ever struck with her aptness and wonderful versatility. She took a part in two or three scenes of elegant comedy with some of her companions, and performed them with exquisite point and finished grace; she gave imitations of the popular Italian singers, some serious, some comic, with a rare quality of voice, and, I was assured, with singular fidelity; she imitated the dialects, dances, ballads, and movements and manners of the gipsies, and the peasants of the Vega, with equal felicity, but every thing was done with an all-pervading grace and a lady-like tact perfectly fascinating.

The great charm of every thing she did was its freedom from pretension or ambitious display, its happy spontaneity. Every thing sprang from the impulse of the moment; or was in prompt compliance with a request. She seemed unconscious of the rarity and extent of her own talent, and was like a child at home revelling in the buoyancy of its own gay and innocent spirits. Indeed I was told she had never exerted her talents in general society, but only, as at present, in the domestic circle.

Her faculty of observation and her perception of character must have been remarkably quick, for she could have had only casual and transient glances at the scenes, manners and customs, depicted with such truth and spirit. "Indeed it is a continual wonder to us," said the countess, "where the child (la Niña) has picked up these things; her life being passed almost entirely at home, in the bosom of the family."

Evening approached; twilight began to throw its shadows about the halls, and the bats to steal forth from their lurking-place and flit about. A notion seized the little damsel and some of her youthful companions, to set out, under the guidance of Dolores, and explore the less frequented parts of the palace in quest of mysteries and enchantments. Thus conducted, they peeped fearfully into the gloomy old mosque, but quick drew back on being told that a Moorish king had been murdered there; they ventured into the mysterious regions of the bath, frightening themselves with the sounds and murmurs of hidden aqueducts, and flying with mock panic at the alarm of phantom Moors. They then undertook the adventure of the Iron Gate, a place of baleful note in the Alhambra. It is a postern gate, opening into a dark ravine; a narrow covered way leads down to it, which used to be the terror of Dolores and her playmates in childhood, as it was said a hand without a body would sometimes be stretched out from the wall and seize hold of the passers by.

The little party of enchantment hunters ventured to the entrance of the covered way, but nothing would tempt them to enter, in this hour of gathering gloom; they dreaded the grasp of the phantom arm.

At length they came running back into the Hall of Ambassadors in a mock paroxysm of terror; they had positively seen two spectral figures all in white. They had not stopped to examine them; but could not be mistaken, for they glared distinctly through the surrounding gloom. Dolores soon arrived and explained the mystery. The spectres proved to be two statues of nymphs in white marble, placed at the entrance of a vaulted passage. Upon this a grave, but, as I thought, somewhat sly old gentleman present, who, I believe, was the count's advocate or legal adviser, assured them that these statues were connected with one of the greatest mysteries of the Alhambra; that there was a curious history concerning them, and moreover, that they stood a living monument in marble of female secrecy and discretion. All present entreated him to tell the history of the statues. He took a little time to recollect the details, and then gave them in substance the following legend.

Legend of the Two Discreet Statues

THERE LIVED ONCE in a waste apartment of the Alhambra, a merry little fellow named Lope Sanchez, who worked in the gardens, and was as brisk and blithe as a grasshopper, singing all day long. He was the life and soul of the fortress; when his work was over, he would sit on one of the stone benches of the esplanade, strum his guitar, and sing long ditties about the Cid, and Bernardo del Carpio, and Fernando del Pulgar, and other Spanish heroes, for the amusement of the old soldiers of the fortress, or would strike up a merrier tune, and set the girls dancing boleros and fandangos.

Like most little men, Lope Sanchez had a strapping buxom dame for a wife, who could almost have put him in her pocket; but he lacked the usual poor man's lot—instead of ten children he had but one. This was a little black-eyed girl about twelve years of age, named Sanchica, who was as merry as himself, and the delight of his heart. She played about him as he worked in the gardens, danced to his guitar as he sat in the shade, and ran as wild as a young fawn about the groves and alleys and ruined halls of the Alhambra.

It was now the eve of the blessed St. John, and the holiday-loving gossips of the Alhambra, men, women, and children, went up at night to the mountain of the sun, which rises above the Generalife, to keep their midsummer vigil on its level summit. It was a bright moonlight night, and all the mountains were gray and silvery, and the city, with its domes and spires, lay in shadows below, and the Vega was like a fairy land, with haunted streams gleaming among its dusky groves. On the highest part of the mountain they lit up a bale fire, according to an old custom of the country handed down from the Moors. The inhabitants of the surrounding country were keeping a similar vigil, and bale fires, here and there in the Vega, and along the folds of the mountain, blazed up palely in the moonlight.

The evening was gayly passed in dancing to the guitar of Lope Sanchez, who was never so joyous as when on a holiday revel of the kind. While the dance was going on, the little Sanchica with some of her playmates sported among the ruins of an old Moorish fort that crowns the mountain, when, in gathering pebbles in the fosse, she found a small hand curiously carved of jet, the fingers closed, and the thumb firmly clasped upon them. Overjoyed with her good fortune, she ran to her mother with her prize. It immediately became a subject of sage speculation, and was eyed by some with superstitious distrust. "Throw it away," said one; "it's Moorish—depend upon it there's mischief and witchcraft in it." "By no means," said another; "you may sell it for something to the jewelers of the Zacatin." In the midst of this discussion an old tawny soldier drew near, who had served in Africa, and was as swarthy as a Moor. He examined the hand with a knowing look. "I have seen things of this kind," said he, "among the Moors of Barbary. It is a great virtue to guard against the evil eye, and all kinds of spells and enchantments. I give you joy, friend Lope, this bodes good luck to your child."

Upon hearing this, the wife of Lope Sanchez tied the little hand of jet to a ribbon, and hung it round the neck of her daughter.

The sight of this talisman called up all the favorite superstitions about the Moors. The dance was neglected, and they sat in groups on the ground, telling old legendary tales handed down from their ancestors. Some of their stories turned upon the wonders of the very mountain upon which they were seated, which is a famous hobgoblin region. One ancient crone gave a long account of the subterranean palace in the bowels of that mountain where Boabdil and all his Moslem court are said to remain enchanted. "Among yonder ruins," said she, pointing to some crumbling walls and mounds of earth on a distant part of the mountain, "there is a deep black pit that goes down, down into the very heart of the mountain. For all the money in Granada I would not look down into it. Once upon a time a poor man of the Alhambra, who tended goats upon this mountain, scrambled down into that pit after a kid that had fallen in. He came out again all wild and staring, and told such things of what he had seen that every one thought his brain was turned. He raved for a day or two about the hobgoblin Moors that had pursued him in the cavern, and could hardly be persuaded to drive his goats up again to the mountain. He did so at last, but, poor man, he never came down again. The neighbors found his goats browsing about the Moorish ruins, and his hat and mantle lying near the mouth of the pit, but he was never more heard of."

The little Sanchica listened with breathless attention to this story. She was of a curious nature, and felt immediately a great hankering to peep into this dangerous pit. Stealing away from her companions she sought the distant ruins, and after groping for some time among them came to a small hollow, or basin, near the brow of the mountain, where it swept steeply down into the valley of the Darro. In the centre of this basin yawned the mouth of the pit. Sanchica ventured to the verge and peeped in. All was as black as pitch, and gave an idea of immeasurable depth. Her blood ran cold; she drew back, then peeped in again, then would have run away, then took another peep—the very horror of the thing was delightful to her. At length she rolled a large stone, and pushed it over the brink. For some time it fell in silence; then struck some rocky projection with a violent crash, then rebounded from side to side, rumbling and tumbling, with a noise like thunder, then made a final splash into water, far, far below— and all was again silent.

The silence, however, did not long continue. It seemed as if something had been awakened within this dreary abyss. A murmuring sound gradually rose out of the pit like the hum and buzz of a beehive. It grew louder and louder; there was the confusion of voices as if a distant multitude, together with the faint din of arms, clash of cymbals and clangor of trumpets, as if some army were marshalling for battle in the very bowels of the mountain.

The child drew off with silent awe, and hastened back to the place where she had left her parents and their companions. All were gone. The bale fire was expiring, and its last wreath of smoke curling up in the moonshine. The distant fires that had blazed along the mountains and in the Vega were all extinguished, and every thing seemed to have sunk to repose. Sanchica called her parents and some of her companions by name, but received no reply. She ran down the side of the mountain, and by the gardens of the Generalife, until she arrived in the alley of trees leading to the Alhambra, when she seated herself on a bench of a woody recess to recover breath. The bell from the watchtower of the Alhambra tolled midnight. There was a deep tranquillity as if all nature slept; excepting the low tinkling sound of an unseen stream that ran under the covert of the bushes. The breathing sweetness of the atmosphere was lulling her to sleep, when her eye was caught by something glittering at a distance, and to her surprise she beheld a long cavalcade of Moorish warriors pouring down the mountain side and along the leafy avenues. Some were armed with lances and shields; others with cimeters and battle-axes, and with polished cuirasses that flashed in the moonbeams. Their horses pranced proudly and champed upon their bits, but their tramp caused no more sound than if they had been shod with felt, and the riders were all as pale as death. Among them rode a beautiful lady, with a crowned head and long golden locks entwined with pearls. The housings of her palfrey were of crimson velvet embroidered with gold, and swept the earth; but she rode all disconsolate, with eyes ever fixed upon the ground.

Then succeeded a train of courtiers magnificently arrayed in robes and turbans of divers colors, and amidst them, on a cream-colored charger, rode king Boabdil el Chico, in a royal mantle covered with jewels, and a crown sparkling with diamonds. The little Sanchica knew him by his yellow beard, and his resemblance to his portrait, which she had often seen in the picture gallery of the Generalife. She gazed in wonder and admiration at this royal pageant, as it passed glistening among the trees; but though she knew these monarchs and courtiers and warriors, so pale and silent, were out of the common course of nature, and things of magic and enchantment, yet she looked on with a bold heart, such courage did she derive from the mystic talisman of the hand, which was suspended about her neck.

The cavalcade having passed by, she rose and followed. It continued on to the great Gate of Justice, which stood wide open; the old invalid sentinels on duty lay on the stone benches of the barbican, buried in profound and apparently charmed sleep, and the phantom pageant swept noiselessly by them with flaunting banner and triumphant state. Sanchica would have followed; but to her surprise she beheld an opening in the earth, within the barbican, leading down beneath the foundations of the tower. She entered for a little distance, and was encouraged to proceed by finding steps rudely hewn in the rock, and a vaulted passage here and there lit up by a silver lamp, which, while it gave light, diffused likewise a grateful fragrance. Venturing on, she came at last to a great hall, wrought out of the heart of the mountain, magnificently furnished in the Moorish style, and lighted up by silver and crystal lamps. Here, on an ottoman, sat an old man in Moorish dress, with a long white beard, nodding and dozing, with a staff in his hand, which seemed ever to be slipping from his grasp; while at a little distance sat a beautiful lady, in ancient Spanish dress, with a coronet all sparkling with diamonds, and her hair entwined with pearls, who was softly playing on a silver lyre. The little Sanchica now recollected a story she had heard among the old people of the Alhambra, concerning a Gothic princess confined in the centre of the mountain by an old Arabian magician, whom she kept bound up in magic sleep by the power of music.

The lady paused with surprise at seeing a mortal in that enchanted hall. "Is it the eve of the blessed St. John?" said she.

"It is," replied Sanchica.

"Then for one night the magic charm is suspended. Come hither, child, and fear not. I am a Christian like thyself, though bound here by enchantment. Touch my fetters with the talisman that hangs about thy neck, and for this night I shall be free."

So saying, she opened her robes and displayed a broad golden band round her waist, and a golden chain that fastened her to the ground. The child hesitated not to apply the little hand of jet to the golden band, and immediately the chain fell to the earth. At the sound the old man woke and began to rub his eyes; but the lady ran her fingers over the chords of the lyre, and again he fell into a slumber and began to nod, and his staff to falter in his hand. "Now," said the lady, "touch his staff with the talismanic hand of jet." The child did so, and it fell from his grasp, and he sank in a deep sleep on the ottoman. The lady gently laid the silver lyre on the ottoman, leaning it against the head of the sleeping magician; then touching the chords until they vibrated in his ear—"O potent spirit of harmony," said she, "continue thus to hold his senses in thraldom till the return of day. Now follow me, my child," continued she, "and thou shalt behold the Alhambra as it was in the days of its glory, for thou hast a magic talisman that reveals all enchantments." Sanchica followed the lady in silence. They passed up through the entrance of the cavern into the barbican of the Gate of Justice, and thence to the Plaza de los Algibes, or esplanade within the fortress.

This was all filled with Moorish soldiery, horse and foot, marshalled in squadrons, with banners displayed. There were royal guards also at the portal, and rows of African blacks with drawn cimeters. No one spoke a word, and Sanchica passed on fearlessly after her conductor. Her astonishment increased on entering the royal palace, in which she had been reared. The broad moonshine lit up all the halls and courts and gardens almost as brightly as if it were day, but revealed a far different scene from that to which she was accustomed. The walls of the apartments were no longer stained and rent by time. Instead of cobwebs, they were now hung with rich silks of Damascus, and the gildings and arabesque paintings were restored to their original brilliancy and freshness. The halls, no longer naked and unfurnished, were set out with divans and ottomans of the rarest stuffs, embroidered with pearls and studded with precious gems, and all the fountains in the courts and gardens were playing.

The kitchens were again in full operation; cooks were busy preparing shadowy dishes, and roasting and boiling the phantoms of pullets and partridges: servants were hurrying to and fro with silver dishes heaped up with dainties, and arranging a delicious banquet. The Court of Lions was thronged with guards, and courtiers, and alfaquis, as in the old times of the Moors; and at the upper end, in the saloon of judgment, sat Boabdil on his throne, surrounded by his court, and swaying a shadowy sceptre for the night. Notwithstanding all this throng and seeming bustle, not a voice nor a footstep was to be heard; nothing interrupted the midnight silence but the splashing of the fountains. The little Sanchica followed her conductress in mute amazement about the palace, until they came to a portal opening to the vaulted passages beneath the great tower of Comares. On each side of the portal sat the figure of a nymph, wrought out of alabaster. Their heads were turned aside, and their regards fixed upon the same spot within the vault. The enchanted lady paused, and beckoned the child to her. "Here," said she, "is a great secret, which I will reveal to thee in reward for thy faith and courage. These discreet statues watch over a treasure hidden in old times by a Moorish king. Tell thy father to search the spot on which their eyes are fixed, and he will find what will make him richer than any man in Granada. Thy innocent hands alone, however, gifted as thou art also with the talisman, can remove the treasure. Bid thy father use it discreetly, and devote a part of it to the performance of daily masses for my deliverance from this unholy enchantment."

When the lady had spoken these words, she led the child onward to the little garden of Lindaraxa, which is hard by the vault of the statues. The moon trembled upon the waters of the solitary fountain in the centre of the garden, and shed a tender light upon the orange and citron trees. The beautiful lady plucked a branch of myrtle and wreathed it round the head of the child. "Let this be a memento," said she, "of what I have revealed to thee, and a testimonial of its truth. My hour is come; I must return to the enchanted hall; follow me not, lest evil befall thee—farewell. Remember what I have said, and have masses performed for my deliverance." So saying, the lady entered a dark passage leading beneath the tower of Comares, and was no longer seen.

The faint crowing of a cock was now heard from the cottages below the Alhambra, in the valley of the Darro, and a pale streak of light began to appear above the eastern mountains. A slight wind arose, there was a sound like the rustling of dry leaves through the courts and corridors, and door after door shut to with a jarring sound.

Sanchica returned to the scenes she had so lately beheld thronged with the shadowy multitude, but Boabdil and his phantom court were gone. The moon shone into empty halls and galleries stripped of their transient splendor, stained and dilapidated by time, and hung with cobwebs. The bat flitted about in the uncertain light, and the frog croaked from the fish-pond.

Sanchica now made the best of her way to a remote staircase that led up to the humble apartment occupied by her family. The door as usual was open, for Lope Sanchez was too poor to need bolt or bar; she crept quietly to her pallet, and, putting the myrtle wreath beneath her pillow, soon fell asleep.

In the morning she related all that had befallen her to her father. Lope Sanchez, however, treated the whole as a mere dream, and laughed at the child for her credulity. He went forth to his customary labors in the garden, but had not been there long when his little daughter came running to him almost breathless. "Father! father!" cried she, "behold the myrtle wreath which the Moorish lady bound round my head."

Lope Sanchez gazed with astonishment, for the stalk of the myrtle was of pure gold, and every leaf was a sparkling emerald! Being not much accustomed to precious stones, he was ignorant of the real value of the wreath, but he saw enough to convince him that it was something more substantial than the stuff of which dreams are generally made, and that at any rate the child had dreamt to some purpose. His first care was to enjoin the most absolute secrecy upon his daughter; in this respect, however, he was secure, for she had discretion far beyond her years or sex. He then repaired to the vault, where stood the statues of the two alabaster nymphs. He remarked that their heads were turned from the portal, and that the regards of each were fixed upon the same point in the interior of the building. Lope Sanchez could not but admire this most discreet contrivance for guarding a secret. He drew a line from the eyes of the statues to the point of regard, made a private mark on the wall, and then retired.

All day, however, the mind of Lope Sanchez was distracted with a thousand cares. He could not help hovering within distant view of the two statues, and became nervous from the dread that the golden secret might be discovered. Every footstep that approached the place made him tremble. He would have given any thing could he but have turned the heads of

the statues, forgetting that they had looked precisely in the
same direction for some hundreds of years, without any person being the wiser.

"A plague upon them," he would say to himself, "they'll
betray all; did ever mortal hear of such a mode of guarding a
secret?" Then on hearing any one advance, he would steal off,
as though his very lurking near the place would awaken suspicions. Then he would return cautiously, and peep from a
distance to see if every thing was secure, but the sight of the
statues would again call forth his indignation. "Ay, there they
stand," would he say, "always looking, and looking, and looking, just where they should not. Confound them! they are just
like all their sex; if they have not tongues to tattle with,
they'll be sure to do it with their eyes."

At length, to his relief, the long anxious day drew to a
close. The sound of footsteps was no longer heard in the
echoing halls of the Alhambra; the last stranger passed the
threshold, the great portal was barred and bolted, and the bat
and the frog and the hooting owl gradually resumed their
nightly vocations in the deserted palace.

Lope Sanchez waited, however, until the night was far advanced before he ventured with his little daughter to the hall
of the two nymphs. He found them looking as knowingly and
mysteriously as ever at the secret place of deposit. "By your
leaves, gentle ladies," thought Lope Sanchez, as he passed between them, "I will relieve you from this charge that must
have set so heavy in your minds for the last two or three
centuries." He accordingly went to work at the part of the
wall which he had marked, and in a little while laid open a
concealed recess, in which stood two great jars of porcelain.
He attempted to draw them forth, but they were immovable,
until touched by the innocent hand of his little daughter.
With her aid he dislodged them from their niche, and found,
to his great joy, that they were filled with pieces of Moorish
gold, mingled with jewels and precious stones. Before daylight he managed to convey them to his chamber, and left the
two guardian statues with their eyes still fixed on the vacant
wall.

Lope Sanchez had thus on a sudden become a rich man;

but riches, as usual, brought a world of cares to which he had hitherto been a stranger. How was he to convey away his wealth with safety? How was he even to enter upon the enjoyment of it without awakening suspicion? Now, too, for the first time in his life the dread of robbers entered into his mind. He looked with terror at the insecurity of his habitation, and went to work to barricade the doors and windows; yet after all his precautions he could not sleep soundly. His usual gayety was at an end, he had no longer a joke or a song for his neighbors, and, in short, became the most miserable animal in the Alhambra. His old comrades remarked this alteration, pitied him heartily, and began to desert him; thinking he must be falling into want, and in danger of looking to them for assistance. Little did they suspect that his only calamity was riches.

The wife of Lope Sanchez shared his anxiety, but then she had ghostly comfort. We ought before this to have mentioned that Lope, being rather a light inconsiderate little man, his wife was accustomed, in all grave matters, to seek the counsel and ministry of her confessor Fray Simon, a sturdy, broad-shouldered, blue-bearded, bullet-headed friar of the neighboring convent of San Francisco, who was in fact the spiritual comforter of half the good wives of the neighborhood. He was moreover in great esteem among divers sisterhoods of nuns; who requited him for his ghostly services by frequent presents of those little dainties and knick-knacks manufactured in convents, such as delicate confections, sweet biscuits, and bottles of spiced cordials, found to be marvelous restoratives after fasts and vigils.

Fray Simon thrived in the exercise of his functions. His oily skin glistened in the sunshine as he toiled up the hill of the Alhambra on a sultry day. Yet notwithstanding his sleek condition, the knotted rope round his waist showed the austerity of his self-discipline; the multitude doffed their caps to him as a mirror of piety, and even the dogs scented the odor of sanctity that exhaled from his garments, and howled from their kennels as he passed.

Such was Fray Simon, the spiritual counsellor of the comely wife of Lope Sanchez; and as the father confessor is the domestic confidant of women in humble life in Spain, he was soon acquainted, in great secrecy, with the story of the hidden treasure.

The friar opened his eyes and mouth and crossed himself a dozen times at the news. After a moment's pause, "Daughter of my soul!" said he, "know that thy husband has committed a double sin—a sin against both state and church! The treasure he hath thus seized upon for himself, being found in the royal domains, belongs of course to the crown; but being infidel wealth, rescued as it were from the very fangs of Satan, should be devoted to the church. Still, however, the matter may be accommodated. Bring hither the myrtle wreath."

When the good father beheld it, his eyes twinkled more than ever with admiration of the size and beauty of the emeralds. "This," said he, "being the first-fruits of this discovery, should be dedicated to pious purposes. I will hang it up as a votive offering before the image of San Francisco in our chapel and will earnestly pray to him, this very night, that your husband be permitted to remain in quiet possession of your wealth."

The good dame was delighted to make her peace with heaven at so cheap a rate, and the friar putting the wreath under his mantle, departed with saintly steps toward his convent.

When Lope Sanchez came home, his wife told him what had passed. He was excessively provoked, for he lacked his wife's devotion, and had for some time groaned in secret at the domestic visitations of the friar. "Woman," said he, "what hast thou done? thou hast put every thing at hazard by thy tattling."

"What!" cried the good woman, "would you forbid my disburdening my conscience to my confessor?"

"No, wife! confess as many of your own sins as you please; but as to this money-digging, it is a sin of my own, and my conscience is very easy under the weight of it."

There was no use, however, in complaining; the secret was told, and, like water spilled on the sand, was not again to be gathered. Their only chance was, that the friar would be discreet.

The next day, while Lope Sanchez was abroad there was a

humble knocking at the door, and Fray Simon entered with meek and demure countenance.

"Daughter," said he, "I have earnestly prayed to San Francisco, and he has heard my prayer. In the dead of the night the saint appeared to me in a dream, but with a frowning aspect. 'Why,' said he, 'dost thou pray to me to dispense with this treasure of the Gentiles, when thou seest the poverty of my chapel? Go to the house of Lope Sanchez, crave in my name a portion of the Moorish gold, to furnish two candlesticks for the main altar, and let him possess the residue in peace.'"

When the good woman heard of this vision, she crossed herself with awe, and going to the secret place where Lope had hid the treasure, she filled a great leathern purse with pieces of Moorish gold, and gave it to the friar. The pious monk bestowed upon her, in return, benedictions enough, if paid by Heaven, to enrich her race to the latest posterity; then slipping the purse into the sleeve of his habit, he folded his hands upon his breast, and departed with an air of humble thankfulness.

When Lope Sanchez heard of this second donation to the church, he had well nigh lost his senses. "Unfortunate man," cried he, "what will become of me? I shall be robbed by piecemeal; I shall be ruined and brought to beggary!"

It was with the utmost difficulty that his wife could pacify him, by reminding him of the countless wealth that yet remained, and how considerate it was for San Francisco to rest contented with so small a portion.

Unluckily, Fray Simon had a number of poor relations to be provided for, not to mention some half-dozen sturdy bullet-headed orphan children, and destitute foundlings that he had taken under his care. He repeated his visits, therefore, from day to day, with solicitations on behalf of Saint Dominick, Saint Andrew, Saint James, until poor Lope was driven to despair, and found that unless he got out of the reach of this holy friar, he should have to make peace-offerings to every saint in the calendar. He determined, therefore, to pack up his remaining wealth, beat a secret retreat in the night, and make off to another part of the kingdom.

Full of his project, he bought a stout mule for the purpose, and tethered it in a gloomy vault underneath the tower of the seven floors; the very place whence the Belludo, or goblin horse, is said to issue forth at midnight, and scour the streets of Granada, pursued by a pack of hell-hounds. Lope Sanchez had little faith in the story, but availed himself of the dread occasioned by it, knowing that no one would be likely to pry into the subterranean stable of the phantom steed. He sent off his family in the course of the day with orders to wait for him at a distant village of the Vega. As the night advanced, he conveyed his treasure to the vault under the tower, and having loaded his mule, he led it forth, and cautiously descended the dusky avenue.

Honest Lope had taken his measures with the utmost secrecy, imparting them to no one but the faithful wife of his bosom. By some miraculous revelation, however, they became known to Fray Simon. The zealous friar beheld these infidel treasures on the point of slipping for ever out of his grasp, and determined to have one more dash at them for the benefit of the church and San Francisco. Accordingly, when the bells had rung for animas, and all the Alhambra was quiet, he stole out of his convent, and descending through the Gate of Justice, concealed himself among the thickets of roses and laurels that border the great avenue. Here he remained, counting the quarters of hours as they were sounded on the bell of the watchtower, and listening to the dreary hootings of owls, and the distant barking of dogs from the gipsy caverns.

At length he heard the tramp of hoofs, and, through the gloom of the overshadowing trees, imperfectly beheld a steed descending the avenue. The sturdy friar chuckled at the idea of the knowing turn he was about to serve honest Lope.

Tucking up the skirts of his habit, and wriggling like a cat watching a mouse, he waited until his prey was directly before him, when darting forth from his leafy covert, and putting one hand on the shoulder and the other on the crupper, he made a vault that would not have disgraced the most experienced master of equitation, and alighted well-forked astride the steed. "Ah ha!" said the sturdy friar, "we shall now see who best understands the game." He had scarce uttered the words when the mule began to kick, and rear, and plunge, and then set off full speed down the hill. The friar attempted to check him, but in vain. He bounded from rock to rock, and bush to bush; the friar's habit was torn to ribbons and fluttered in the wind, his shaven poll received many a hard knock from the branches of the trees, and many a scratch from the brambles. To add to his terror and distress, he found a pack of seven hounds in full cry at his heels, and perceived, too late, that he was actually mounted upon the terrible Belludo!

Away then they went, according to the ancient phrase, "pull devil, pull friar," down the great avenue, across the Plaza Nueva, along the Zacatin, around the Vivarrambla—never did huntsman and hound make a more furious run, or more infernal uproar. In vain did the friar invoke every saint in the calendar, and the holy Virgin into the bargain; every time he mentioned a name of the kind it was like a fresh application of the spur, and made the Belludo bound as high as a house. Through the remainder of the night was the unlucky Fray Simon carried hither and thither, and whither he would not, until every bone in his body ached, and he suffered a loss of leather too grievous to be mentioned. At length the crowing of a cock gave the signal of returning day. At the sound the goblin steed wheeled about, and galloped back for his tower. Again he scoured the Vivarrambla, the Zacatin, the Plaza Nueva, and the avenue of fountains, the seven dogs yelling and barking, and leaping up, and snapping at the heels of the terrified friar. The first streak of day had just appeared as they reached the tower; here the goblin steed kicked up his heels, sent the friar a somerset through the air, plunged into the dark vault, followed by the infernal pack, and a profound silence succeeded to the late deafening clamor.

Was ever so diabolical a trick played off upon a holy friar? A peasant going to his labors at early dawn found the unfortunate Fray Simon lying under a fig-tree at the foot of the tower, but so bruised and bedevilled that he could neither speak nor move. He was conveyed with all care and tenderness to his cell, and the story went that he had been waylaid and maltreated by robbers. A day or two elapsed before he recovered the use of his limbs; he consoled himself, in the meantime, with the thoughts that though the mule with the treasure had escaped him, he had previously had some rare pickings at the infidel spoils. His first care on being able to use his limbs, was to search beneath his pallet, where he had secreted the myrtle wreath and the leathern pouches of gold extracted from the piety of dame Sanchez. What was his dismay at finding the wreath, in effect, but a withered branch of myrtle, and the leathern pouches filled with sand and gravel!

Fray Simon, with all his chagrin, had the discretion to hold his tongue, for to betray the secret might draw on him the ridicule of the public, and the punishment of his superior: it was not until many years afterwards, on his death-bed, that he revealed to his confessor his nocturnal ride on the Belludo.

Nothing was heard of Lope Sanchez for a long time after his disappearance from the Alhambra. His memory was always cherished as that of a merry companion, though it was feared, from the care and melancholy observed in his conduct shortly before his mysterious departure, that poverty and distress had driven him to some extremity. Some years afterwards one of his old companions, an invalid soldier, being at Malaga, was knocked down and nearly run over by a coach and six. The carriage stopped; an old gentleman magnificently dressed, with a bag-wig and sword, stepped out to assist the poor invalid. What was the astonishment of the latter to behold in this grand cavalier his old friend Lope Sanchez, who was actually celebrating the marriage of his daughter Sanchica with one of the first grandees in the land.

The carriage contained the bridal party. There was dame Sanchez, now grown as round as a barrel, and dressed out with feathers and jewels, and necklaces of pearls, and necklaces of diamonds, and rings on every finger, altogether a finery of apparel that had not been seen since the days of Queen Sheba. The little Sanchica had now grown to be a woman, and for grace and beauty might have been mistaken for a duchess, if not a princess outright. The bridegroom sat beside her—rather a withered spindle-shanked little man, but this only proved him to be of the true-blue blood; a legitimate Spanish grandee being rarely above three cubits in stature. The match had been of the mother's making.

Riches had not spoiled the heart of honest Lope. He kept his old comrade with him for several days; feasted him like a king, took him to plays and bull-fights, and at length sent him away rejoicing, with a big bag of money for himself, and another to be distributed among his ancient messmates of the Alhambra.

Lope always gave out that a rich brother had died in America and left him heir to a copper mine; but the shrewd gossips of the Alhambra insist that his wealth was all derived from his having discovered the secret guarded by the two marble nymphs of the Alhambra. It is remarked that these very discreet statues continue, even unto the present day, with their eyes fixed most significantly on the same part of the wall; which leads many to suppose there is still some hidden treasure remaining there well worthy the attention of the enterprising traveller. Though others, and particularly all female visitors, regard them with great complacency as lasting monuments of the fact that women can keep a secret.

The Crusade of the Grand Master
of Alcántara

IN THE COURSE of a morning's research among the old chronicles in the Library of the University, I came upon a little episode in the history of Granada, so strongly character-istic of the bigot zeal, which sometimes inflamed the Chris-tian enterprises against this splendid but devoted city, that I was tempted to draw it forth from the parchment-bound vol-ume in which it lay entombed and submit it to the reader.

In the year of redemption, 1394, there was a valiant and devout grand master of Alcántara, named Martin Yañez de Barbudo, who was inflamed with a vehement desire to serve God and fight the Moors. Unfortunately for this brave and pious cavalier, a profound peace existed between the Christian and Moslem powers. Henry III. had just ascended the throne of Castile, and Yusef ben Mohammed had succeeded to the throne of Granada, and both were disposed to continue the peace which had prevailed between their fathers. The grand master looked with repining at Moorish banners and weap-ons, which decorated his castle hall, trophies of the exploits of his predecessors; and repined at his fate to exist in a period of such inglorious tranquillity.

At length his impatience broke through all bounds, and seeing that he could find no public war in which to engage, he resolved to carve out a little war for himself. Such at least is the account given by some ancient chronicles, though oth-ers give the following as the motive for this sudden resolution to go campaigning.

As the grand master was one day seated at table with several of his cavaliers, a man suddenly entered the hall; tall, meagre and bony, with haggard countenance and fiery eye. All recognized him for a hermit, who had been a soldier in his youth, but now led a life of penitence in a cave. He advanced to the table and struck upon it with a fist that seemed of iron. "Cavaliers," said he, "why sit ye here idly, with your weapons resting against the wall, while the enemies of the faith lord it over the fairest portion of the land?"

"Holy father, what wouldst thou have us do," asked the grand master, "seeing the wars are over and our swords bound up by treaties of peace?"

"Listen to my words," replied the hermit. "As I was seated late at night at the entrance of my cave, contemplating the heavens, I fell into a reverie, and a wonderful vision was presented to me. I beheld the moon, a mere crescent, yet luminous as the brightest silver, and it hung in the heavens over the kingdom of Granada. While I was looking at it, behold there shot forth from the firmament a blazing star, which, as it went, drew after it all the stars of heaven; and they assailed the moon and drove it from the skies; and the whole firmament was filled with the glory of that blazing star. While mine eyes were yet dazzled by this wondrous sight, some one stood by me with snowy wings and a shining countenance. 'Oh man of prayer,' said he, 'get thee to the grand master of Alcántara and tell him of the vision thou has beheld. He is the blazing star, destined to drive the crescent, the Moslem emblem, from the land. Let him boldly draw the sword and continue the good work begun by Pelazo of old, and victory will assuredly attend his banner.' "

The grand master listened to the hermit as to a messenger from heaven, and followed his counsel in all things. By his advice he dispatched two of his stoutest warriors, armed cap-a-pie, on an embassy to the Moorish king. They entered the gates of Granada without molestation, as the nations were at peace; and made their way to the Alhambra, where they were promptly admitted to the king, who received them in the Hall of the Ambassadors. They delivered their message roundly and hardily. "We come, oh king, from Don Martin Yañez de Barbudo, grand master of Alcántara; who affirms the faith of Jesus Christ to be true and holy, and that of Mahomet false and detestable, and he challenges thee to maintain the contrary, hand to hand, in single combat. Shouldst thou refuse, he offers to combat with one hundred cavaliers against two hundred; or, in like proportion, to the number of one thousand, always allowing thy faith a double number of champions. Remember, oh king, that thou canst not refuse this challenge; since thy prophet, knowing the impossibility of maintaining his doctrines by argument, has commanded his followers to enforce them with the sword."

The beard of king Jusef trembled with indignation. "The master of Alcántara," said he, "is a madman to send such a message, and ye are saucy knaves to bring it."

So saying, he ordered the ambassadors to be thrown into a dungeon, by way of giving them a lesson in diplomacy; and they were roughly treated on their way thither by the populace, who were exasperated at this insult to their sovereign and their faith.

The grand master of Alcántara could scarcely credit the tidings of the maltreatment of his messengers; but the hermit rejoiced when they were repeated to him. "God," said he, "has blinded this infidel king for his downfall. Since he has sent no reply to thy defiance, consider it accepted. Marshal thy forces, therefore; march forward to Granada; pause not until thou seest the gate of Elvira. A miracle will be wrought in thy favor. There will be a great battle; the enemy will be overthrown; but not one of thy soldiers will be slain."

The grand master called upon every warrior zealous in the Christian cause to aid him in this crusade. In a little while three hundred horsemen and a thousand foot-soldiers rallied under his standard. The horsemen were veterans; seasoned to battle and well armed; but the infantry were raw and undisciplined. The victory, however, was to be miraculous; the grand master was a man of surpassing faith, and knew that the weaker the means the greater the miracle. He sallied forth confidently, therefore, with his little army, and the hermit strode ahead bearing a cross on the end of a long pole, and beneath it the pennon of the order of Alcántara.

As they approached the city of Cordova they were overtaken by messengers, spurring in all haste, bearing missives from the Castilian monarch, forbidding the enterprise. The grand master was a man of a single mind and a single will; in other words, a man of one idea. "Were I on any other errand," said he, "I should obey these letters as coming from my lord the king; but I am sent by a higher power than the king. In compliance with its commands I have advanced the cross thus far against the infidels; and it would be treason to the standard of Christ to turn back without achieving my errand."

So the trumpets were sounded; the cross was again reared aloft, and the band of zealots resumed their march. As they passed through the streets of Cordova the people were amazed at beholding a hermit bearing a cross at the head of a warlike multitude; but when they learnt that a miraculous victory was to be effected and Granada destroyed, laborers and artisans threw by the implements of their handicrafts and joined in the crusade; while a mercenary rabble followed on with a view of plunder.

A number of cavaliers of rank who lacked faith in the promised miracle, and dreaded the consequences of this unprovoked irruption into the country of the Moor, assembled at the bridge of the Guadalquivir and endeavored to dissuade the grand master from crossing. He was deaf to prayers, expostulations or menaces; his followers were enraged at this opposition to the cause of the faith; they put an end to the parley by their clamors; the cross was again reared and borne triumphantly across the bridge.

The multitude increased as it proceeded; by the time the grand master had reached Alcala la Real, which stands on a mountain overlooking the Vega of Granada, upwards of five thousand men on foot had joined his standard.

At Alcala came forth Alonzo Fernandez de Cordova, Lord of Aguilar, his brother Diego Fernandez, Marshal of Castile, and other cavaliers of valor and experience. Placing themselves in the way of the grand master, "What madness is this, Don Martin?" said they; "the Moorish king has two hundred thousand foot-soldiers and five thousand horse within his walls; what can you and your handful of cavaliers and your noisy rabble do against such force? Bethink you of the disasters which have befallen other Christian commanders, who have crossed these rocky borders with ten times your force. Think, too, of the mischief that will be brought upon this kingdom by an outrage of the kind committed by a man of your rank and importance, a grand master of Alcántara. Pause, we entreat you, while the truce is yet unbroken. Await within the borders the reply of the king of Granada to your challenge. If he agree to meet you singly, or with champions two or three, it will be your individual contest, and fight it out in God's name; if he refuse, you may return home with great honor and the disgrace will fall upon the Moors."

Several cavaliers, who had hitherto followed the grand master with devoted zeal, were moved by these expostulations, and suggested to him the policy of listening to this advice.

"Cavaliers," said he, addressing himself to Alonzo Fernandez de Cordova and his companions; "I thank you for the counsel you have so kindly bestowed upon me, and if I were merely in pursuit of individual glory I might be swayed by it. But I am engaged to achieve a great triumph of the faith, which God is to effect by miracle through my means. As to you, cavaliers," turning to those of his followers who had wavered, "if your hearts fail you, or you repent of having put your hands to this good work, return in God's name, and my blessing go with you. For myself, though I have none to stand by me but this holy hermit, yet will I assuredly proceed; until I have planted this sacred standard on the walls of Granada, or perished in the attempt."

"Don Martin Yañez de Barbudo," replied the cavaliers, "we are not men to turn our backs upon our commander, however rash his enterprise. We spoke but in caution. Lead on, therefore, and if it be to the death, be assured to the death we will follow thee."

By this time the common soldiers became impatient. "Forward! forward!" shouted they. "Forward in the cause of faith." So the grand master gave the signal, the hermit again reared the cross aloft, and they poured down a defile of the mountain, with solemn chants of triumph.

That night they encamped at the river of Azores, and the next morning, which was Sunday, crossed the borders. Their first pause was at an atalaya or solitary tower, built upon a rock; a frontier post to keep a watch upon the border, and give notice of invasion. It was thence called el Torre del Exea (the tower of the spy). The grand master halted before it and summoned its petty garrison to surrender. He was answered by a shower of stones and arrows, which wounded him in the hand and killed three of his men.

"How is this, father?" said he to the hermit, "you assured me that not one of my followers would be slain!"

"True, my son; but I meant in the great battle of the infidel king; what need is there of miracle to aid in the capture of a petty tower?"

The grand master was satisfied. He ordered wood to be piled against the door of the tower to burn it down. In the mean time provisions were unloaded from the sumpter-mules, and the crusaders, withdrawing beyond bow-shot, sat down on the grass to a repast to strengthen them for the arduous day's work before them. While thus engaged, they were startled by the sudden appearance of a great Moorish host. The atalayas had given the alarm by fire and smoke from the mountain tops of "an enemy across the border," and the king of Granada had sallied forth with a great force to the encounter.

The crusaders, nearly taken by surprise, flew to arms and prepared for battle. The grand master ordered his three hundred horsemen to dismount and fight on foot in support of the infantry. The Moors, however, charged so suddenly that they separated the cavaliers from the foot-soldiers and prevented their uniting. The grand master gave the old war cry, "Santiago! Santiago! and close Spain!" He and his knights breasted the fury of the battle, but were surrounded by a countless host and assailed with arrows, stones, darts, and arquebuses. Still they fought fearlessly, and made prodigious slaughter. The hermit mingled in the hottest of the fight. In one hand he bore the cross, in the other he brandished a sword, with which he dealt about him like a maniac, slaying several of the enemy, until he sank to the ground covered with wounds. The grand master saw him fall, and saw too late the fallacy of his prophecies. Despair, however, only made him fight the more fiercely, until he also fell overpowered by numbers. His devoted cavaliers emulated his holy zeal. Not one turned his back nor asked for mercy; all fought until they fell. As to the foot-soldiers, many were killed, many taken prisoners; the residue escaped to Alcala la Real. When the Moors came to strip the slain, the wounds of the cavaliers were all found to be in front.

Such was the catastrophe of this fanatic enterprise. The

Moors vaunted it as a decisive proof of the superior sanctity of their faith, and extolled their king to the skies when he returned in triumph to Granada.

As it was satisfactorily shown that this crusade was the enterprise of an individual and contrary to the express orders of the king of Castile, the peace of the two kingdoms was not interrupted. Nay, the Moors evinced a feeling of respect for the valor of the unfortunate grand master, and readily gave up his body to Don Alonzo Fernandez de Cordova, who came from Alcala to seek it. The Christians of the frontier united in paying the last sad honors to his memory. His body was placed upon a bier, covered with the pennon of the order of Alcántara; and the broken cross, the emblem of his confident hopes and fatal disappointment, was borne before it. In this way his remains were carried back in funeral procession, through the mountain tract which he had traversed so resolutely. Wherever it passed, through a town or village, the populace followed, with tears and lamentations, bewailing him as a valiant knight and a martyr to the faith. His body was interred in the chapel of the convent of Santa Maria de Almocovara, and on his sepulchre may still be seen engraven in quaint and antique Spanish the following testimonial to his bravery:

"HERE LIES ONE WHOSE HEART NEVER KNEW FEAR."

(Aqui yaz aquel que par neua cosa nunca eve pavor en seu corazon.)*

*Torres. Hist. Ord. Alcántara. Cron. Enrique III., por Pedro Lopez de Ayala.

Spanish Romance

I<small>N THE LATTER PART</small> of my sojourn in the Alhambra, I made frequent descents into the Jesuit's Library of the University; and relished more and more the old Spanish chronicles, which I found there bound in parchment. I delight in those quaint histories which treat of the times when the Moslems maintained a foothold in the Peninsula. With all their bigotry and occasional intolerance, they are full of noble acts and generous sentiments, and have a high, spicy, oriental flavor, not to be found in other records of the times, which were merely European. In fact, Spain, even at the present day, is a country apart; severed in history, habits, manners, and modes of thinking, from all the rest of Europe. It is a romantic country; but its romance has none of the sentimentality of modern European romance; it is chiefly derived from the brilliant regions of the East, and from the high-minded school of Saracenic chivalry.

The Arab invasion and conquest brought a higher civilization, and a nobler style of thinking, into Gothic Spain. The Arabs were a quick-witted, sagacious, proud-spirited, and poetical people, and were imbued with oriental science and literature. Wherever they established a seat of power, it became a rallying place for the learned and ingenious; and they softened and refined the people whom they conquered. By degrees, occupancy seemed to give them an hereditary right to their foothold in the land; they ceased to be looked upon as invaders, and were regarded as rival neighbors. The peninsula, broken up into a variety of states, both Christian and Moslem, became, for centuries, a great campaigning ground, where the art of war seemed to be the principal business of man, and was carried to the highest pitch of romantic chivalry. The original ground of hostility, a difference of faith, gradually lost its rancor. Neighboring states, of opposite creeds, were occasionally linked together in alliances, offensive and defensive; so that the cross and crescent were to be seen side by side, fighting against some common enemy. In times of peace, too, the noble youth of either faith resorted to the same cities, Christian or Moslem, to school themselves in military science. Even in the temporary truces of sanguinary wars, the warriors who had recently striven together in the deadly conflicts of the field, laid aside their animosity, met at tournaments, jousts, and other military festivities, and exchanged the courtesies of gentle and generous spirits. Thus the opposite races became frequently mingled together in peaceful intercourse, or if any rivalry took place, it was in those high courtesies and nobler acts, which bespeak the accomplished cavalier. Warriors, of opposite creeds, became ambitious of transcending each other in magnanimity as well as valor. Indeed, the chivalric virtues were refined upon to a degree sometimes fastidious and constrained; but at other times, inexpressibly noble and affecting. The annals of the times teem with illustrious instances of high-wrought courtesy, romantic generosity, lofty disinterestedness, and punctilious honor, that warm the very soul to read them. These have furnished themes for national plays and poems, or have been celebrated in those all-pervading ballads, which are as the life-breath of the people, and thus have continued to exercise an influence on the national character, which centuries of vicissitude and decline have not been able to destroy; so that, with all their faults, and they are many, the Spaniards, even at the present day, are, on many points, the most high-minded and proud-spirited people of Europe. It is true, the romance of feeling derived from the sources I have mentioned, has, like all other romance, its affectations and extremes. It renders the Spaniard at times pompous and grandiloquent; prone to carry the 'pundonor,' or point of honor, beyond the bounds of sober sense and sound morality; disposed, in the midst of poverty, to affect the 'grande caballero,' and to look down with sovereign disdain upon 'arts mechanical,' and all the gainful pursuits of plebeian life; but this very inflation of spirit, while it fills his brain with vapors, lifts him above a thousand meannesses; and though it often keeps him in indigence, ever protects him from vulgarity.

In the present day, when popular literature is running into the low levels of life, and luxuriating on the vices and follies of mankind; and when the universal pursuit of gain is trampling down the early growth of poetic feeling, and wearing out the verdure of the soul, I question whether it would not be of service for the reader occasionally to turn to these records of prouder times and loftier modes of thinking; and to steep himself to the very lips in old Spanish romance.

With these preliminary suggestions, the fruit of a morning's reading and rumination, in the old Jesuit's Library of the University, I will give him a legend in point, drawn forth from one of the venerable chronicles alluded to.

Legend of Don Munio Sancho de Hinojosa

IN THE CLOISTERS of the ancient Benedictine convent of San Domingo, at Silos, in Castile, are the mouldering yet magnificent monuments of the once powerful and chivalrous family of Hinojosa. Among these reclines the marble figure of a knight, in complete armor, with the hands pressed together, as if in prayer. On one side of his tomb is sculptured in relief a band of Christian cavaliers, capturing a cavalcade of male and female Moors; on the other side, the same cavaliers are represented kneeling before an altar. The tomb, like most of the neighboring monuments, is almost in ruins, and the sculpture is nearly unintelligible, excepting to the keen eye of the antiquary. The story connected with the sepulchre, how-ever, is still preserved in the old Spanish chronicles, and is to the following purport.

———

In old times, several hundred years ago, there was a noble Castilian cavalier, named Don Munio Sancho de Hinojosa, lord of a border castle, which had stood the brunt of many a Moorish foray. He had seventy horsemen as his household troops, all of the ancient Castilian proof; stark warriors, hard riders, and men of iron; with these he scoured the Moorish lands, and made his name terrible throughout the borders. His castle hall was covered with banners, cimeters, and Mos-lem helms, the trophies of his prowess. Don Munio was, moreover, a keen huntsman; and rejoiced in hounds of all kinds, steeds for the chase, and hawks for the towering sport of falconry. When not engaged in warfare, his delight was to beat up the neighboring forests; and scarcely ever did he ride forth, without hound and horn, a boar-spear in his hand, or a hawk upon his fist, and an attendant train of huntsmen.

His wife, Doña Maria Palacin, was of a gentle and timid nature, little fitted to be the spouse of so hardy and adventur-ous a knight; and many a tear did the poor lady shed, when he sallied forth upon his daring enterprises, and many a prayer did she offer up for his safety.

As this doughty cavalier was one day hunting, he stationed himself in a thicket, on the borders of a green glade of the forest, and dispersed his followers to rouse the game, and drive it toward his stand. He had not been here long, when a cavalcade of Moors, of both sexes, came prankling over the forest lawn. They were unarmed, and magnificently dressed in robes of tissue and embroidery, rich shawls of India, bracelets and anklets of gold, and jewels that sparkled in the sun.

At the head of this gay cavalcade rode a youthful cavalier, superior to the rest in dignity and loftiness of demeanor, and in splendor of attire: beside him was a damsel, whose veil, blown aside by the breeze, displayed a face of surpassing beauty, and eyes cast down in maiden modesty, yet beaming with tenderness and joy.

Don Munio thanked his stars for sending him such a prize, and exulted at the thought of bearing home to his wife the glittering spoils of these infidels. Putting his hunting horn to his lips, he gave a blast that rung through the forest. His huntsmen came running from all quarters, and the astonished Moors were surrounded and made captives.

The beautiful Moor wrung her hands in despair, and her female attendants uttered the most piercing cries. The young Moorish cavalier alone retained self-possession. He inquired the name of the Christian knight, who commanded this troop of horsemen. When told that it was Don Munio Sancho de Hinojosa, his countenance lighted up. Approaching that cavalier, and kissing his hand, "Don Munio Sancho," said he, "I have heard of your fame as a true and valiant knight, terrible in arms, but schooled in the noble virtues of chivalry. Such do I trust to find you. In me you behold Abadil, son of a Moorish alcayde. I am on the way to celebrate my nuptials with this lady; chance has thrown us in your power, but I confide in your magnanimity. Take all our treasure and jewels; demand what ransom you think proper for our persons, but suffer us not to be insulted nor dishonored."

When the good knight heard this appeal, and beheld the beauty of the youthful pair, his heart was touched with tenderness and courtesy. "God forbid," said he, "that I should disturb such happy nuptials. My prisoners in troth shall ye be, for fifteen days, and immured within my castle, where I claim, as conqueror, the right of celebrating your espousals."

So saying, he dispatched one of his fleetest horsemen in advance, to notify Doña Maria Palacin of the coming of this bridal party; while he and his huntsmen escorted the cavalcade, not as captors, but as a guard of honor. As they drew near to the castle, the banners were hung out, and the trumpets sounded from the battlements; and on their nearer approach, the draw-bridge was lowered, and Doña Maria came forth to meet them, attended by her ladies and knights, her pages and her minstrels. She took the young bride, Allifra, in her arms, kissed her with the tenderness of a sister, and conducted her into the castle. In the mean time, Don Munio sent forth missives in every direction, and had viands and dainties of all kinds collected from the country round; and the wedding of the Moorish lovers was celebrated with all possible state and festivity. For fifteen days, the castle was given up to joy and revelry. There were tiltings and jousts at the ring, and bull-fights, and banquets, and dances to the sound of minstrelsy. When the fifteen days were at an end, he made the bride and bridegroom magnificent presents, and conducted them and their attendants safely beyond the borders. Such, in old times, were the courtesy and generosity of a Spanish cavalier.

Several years after this event, the king of Castile summoned his nobles to assist him in a campaign against the Moors. Don Munio Sancho was among the first to answer to the call, with seventy horsemen, all stanch and well-tried warriors. His wife, Doña Maria, hung about his neck. "Alas, my lord!" exclaimed she, "how often wilt thou tempt thy fate, and when will thy thirst for glory be appeased!"

"One battle more," replied Don Munio, "one battle more, for the honor of Castile, and I here make a vow, that when this is over, I will lay by my sword, and repair with my cavaliers in pilgrimage to the sepulchre of our Lord at Jerusalem." The cavaliers all joined with him in the vow, and Doña Maria felt in some degree soothed in spirit; still, she saw with a heavy heart the departure of her husband, and watched his banner with wistful eyes, until it disappeared among the trees of the forest.

The king of Castile led his army to the plains of Salmanara, where they encountered the Moorish host, near to Ucles. The battle was long and bloody; the Christians repeatedly wavered, and were as often rallied by the energy of their commanders. Don Munio was covered with wounds, but refused to leave the field. The Christians at length gave way, and the king was hardly pressed, and in danger of being captured.

Don Munio called upon his cavaliers to follow him to the rescue. "Now is the time," cried he, "to prove your loyalty. Fall to, like brave men! We fight for the true faith, and if we lose our lives here, we gain a better life hereafter."

Rushing with his men between the king and his pursuers, they checked the latter in their career, and gave time for their monarch to escape; but they fell victims to their loyalty. They all fought to the last gasp. Don Munio was singled out by a powerful Moorish knight, but having been wounded in the right arm, he fought to disadvantage, and was slain. The battle being over, the Moor paused to possess himself of the spoils of this redoubtable Christian warrior. When he unlaced the helmet, however, and beheld the countenance of Don Munio, he gave a great cry, and smote his breast. "Woe is me!" cried he, "I have slain my benefactor! The flower of knightly virtue! the most magnanimous of cavaliers!"

While the battle had been raging on the plain of Salmanara, Doña Maria Palacin remained in her castle, a prey to the keenest anxiety. Her eyes were ever fixed on the road that led from the country of the Moors, and often she asked the watchman of the tower, "What seest thou?"

One evening, at the shadowy hour of twilight, the warden sounded his horn. "I see," cried he, "a numerous train winding up the valley. There are mingled Moors and Christians. The banner of my lord is in the advance. Joyful tidings!" exclaimed the old seneschal: "my lord returns in triumph, and brings captives!" Then the castle courts rang with shouts of joy; and the standard was displayed and the trumpets were sounded, and the draw-bridge was lowered, and Doña Maria went forth with her ladies, and her knights, and her pages, and her minstrels, to welcome her lord from the wars. But as the train drew nigh, she beheld a sumptuous bier, covered with black velvet, and on it lay a warrior, as if taking his repose: he lay in his armor, with his helmet on his head, and his sword in his hand, as one who had never been conquered, and around the bier were the escutcheons of the house of Hinojosa.

A number of Moorish cavaliers attended the bier, with emblems of mourning, and with dejected countenances; and their leader cast himself at the feet of Doña Maria, and hid his face in his hands. She beheld in him the gallant Abadil, whom she had once welcomed with his bride to her castle; but who now came with the body of her lord, whom he had unknowingly slain in battle!

The sepulchre erected in the cloisters of the convent of San Domingo, was achieved at the expense of the Moor Abadil, as a feeble testimony of his grief for the death of the good knight Don Munio, and his reverence for his memory. The tender and faithful Doña Maria soon followed her lord to the tomb. On one of the stones of a small arch, beside his sepulchre, is the following simple inscription: *"Hic jacet Maria Palacin, uxor Munonis Sancij De Finojosa:"* Here lies Maria Palacin, wife of Munio Sancho de Hinojosa.

The legend of Don Munio Sancho does not conclude with his death. On the same day on which the battle took place on the plain of Salmanara, a chaplain of the Holy Temple at Jerusalem, while standing at the outer gate, beheld a train of Christian cavaliers advancing, as if in pilgrimage. The chaplain was a native of Spain, and as the pilgrims approached, he knew the foremost to be Don Munio Sancho de Hinojosa, with whom he had been well acquainted in former times. Hastening to the patriarch, he told him of the honorable rank of the pilgrims at the gate. The patriarch, therefore, went forth with a grand procession of priests and monks, and received the pilgrims with all due honor. There were seventy cavaliers, beside their leader, all stark and lofty warriors. They carried their helmets in their hands, and their faces were deadly pale. They greeted no one, nor looked either to the right or to the left, but entered the chapel, and kneeling before the sepulchre of our Saviour, performed their orisons in silence. When they had concluded, they rose as if to depart, and the patriarch and his attendants advanced to speak to them, but they were no more to be seen. Every one marvelled what could be the meaning of this prodigy. The patriarch carefully noted down the day, and sent to Castile to learn tidings of Don Munio Sancho de Hinojosa. He received for reply, that on the very day specified, that worthy knight, with seventy of his followers, had been slain in battle. These, therefore, must have been the blessed spirits of those Christian warriors, come to fulfil their vow of pilgrimage to the Holy Sepulchre at Jerusalem. Such was Castilian faith, in the olden time, which kept its word, even beyond the grave.

If any one should doubt of the miraculous apparition of these phantom knights, let him consult the History of the Kings of Castile and Leon, by the learned and pious Fray Prudencio de Sandoval, bishop of Pamplona, where he will find it recorded in the History of king Don Alonzo VI., on the hundred and second page. It is too precious a legend, to be lightly abandoned to the doubter.

Poets and Poetry of Moslem Andalus

URING THE LATTER PART of my sojourn in the Alhambra I was more than once visited by the Moor of Tetuan, with whom I took great pleasure in rambling through the halls and courts, and getting him to explain to me the Arabic inscriptions. He endeavored to do so faithfully; but, though he succeeded in giving me the thought, he despaired of imparting an idea of the grace and beauty of the language. The aroma of the poetry, said he, is all lost in translation. Enough was imparted, however, to increase the stock of my delightful associations with this extraordinary pile. Perhaps there never was a monument more characteristic of an age and people than the Alhambra; a rugged fortress without, a voluptuous palace within; war frowning from its battlements; poetry breathing throughout the fairy architecture of its halls. One is irresistibly transported in imagination to those times when Moslem Spain was a region of light amid Christian, yet benighted Europe; externally a warrior power fighting for existence; internally a realm devoted to literature, science, and the arts; where philosophy was cultivated with passion, though wrought up into subtleties and refinements; and where the luxuries of sense were transcended by those of thought and imagination.

Arab poetry, we are told, arrived at its highest splendor under the Ommiades of Spain, who for a long time centred the power and splendor of the western Caliphat at Cordova. Most of the sovereigns of that brilliant line were themselves poets. One of the last of them was Mahomed ben Abderahman. He led the life of a sybarite in the famous palace and gardens of Azahara, surrounding himself with all that could excite the imagination and delight the senses. His palace was the resort of poets. His vizier, Ibn Zeydun, was called the Horace of Moslem Spain, from his exquisite verses, which were recited with enthusiasm even in the saloons of the Eastern Caliphs. The vizier became passionately enamored of the princess Walada, daughter of Mahomed. She was the idol of her father's court, a poetess of the highest order, and renowned for beauty as well as talent. If Ibn Zeydun was the Horace of Moslem Spain, she was its Sappho. The princess became the subject of the vizier's most impassioned verses; especially of a famous risáleh or epistle addressed to her, which the historian Ash-Shakandi declares has never been equalled for tenderness and melancholy. Whether the poet was happy in his love, the authors I have consulted do not say; but one intimates that the princess was discreet as she was beautiful, and caused many a lover to sigh in vain. In fact, the reign of love and poetry in the delicious abode of Zahara, was soon brought to a close by a popular insurrection. Mahomed with his family took refuge in the fortress of Ucles, near Toledo, where he was treacherously poisoned by the Alcayde; and thus perished one of the last of the Ommiades.

The downfall of that brilliant dynasty, which had concentrated every thing at Cordova, was favorable to the general literature of Morisco Spain.

"After the breaking of the necklace and the scattering of its pearls," says Ash-Shakandi, "the kings of small states divided among themselves the patrimony of the Beni Ommiah."

They vied with each other in filling their capitals with poets and learned men, and rewarded them with boundless prodigality. Such were the Moorish kings of Seville of the illustrious line of the Beni Abbad, "with whom," says the same writer, "resided fruit and palm-trees and pomegranates; who became the centre of eloquence in prose and verse; every day of whose reign was a solemn festivity; whose history abounds in generous actions and heroic deeds, that will last through surrounding ages and live for ever in the memory of man!"

No place, however, profited more in point of civilization and refinement by the downfall of the Western Caliphat than Granada. It succeeded to Cordova in splendor, while it surpassed it in romantic beauty of situation. The amenity of its climate, where the ardent heats of a southern summer were tempered by breezes from snow-clad mountains; the voluptuous repose of its valleys and the bosky luxuriance of its groves and gardens all awakened sensations of delight, and disposed the mind to love and poetry. Hence the great number of amatory poets that flourished in Granada. Hence those amorous canticles breathing of love and war, and wreathing chivalrous grace round the stern exercise of arms. Those ballads which still form the pride and delight of Spanish literature are but the echoes of amatory and chivalric lays, which once delighted the Moslem courts of Andalus; and in which a modern historian of Granada pretends to find the origin of the *rima Castellana* and the type of the "gay science" of the troubadours.*

Poetry was cultivated in Granada by both sexes. "Had Allah," says Ash-Shakandi, "bestowed no other boon on Granada than that of making it the birth-place of so many poetesses; that alone would be sufficient for its glory."

Among the most famous of these was Hafsah; renowned, says the old chronicler, for beauty, talents, nobility, and wealth. We have a mere relic of her poetry in some verses, addressed to her lover, Ahmed, recalling an evening passed together in the garden of Maumal.

"Allah has given us a happy night, such as he never vouchsafes to the wicked and the ignoble. We have beheld the cypresses of Maumal gently bowing their heads before the mountain breeze,—the sweet perfumed breeze that smelt of gillyflowers: the dove murmured her love among the trees; the sweet basil inclined its boughs to the limpid brook."

The garden of Maumal was famous among the Moors for its rivulets, its fountains, its flowers, and above all, its cypresses. It had its name from a vizier of Abdallah, grandson of Aben Habuz, and Sultan of Granada. Under the administration of this vizier many of the noblest public works were executed. He constructed an aqueduct by which water was brought from the mountains of Alfacar to irrigate the hills and orchards north of the city. He planted a public walk with cypress-trees, and "made delicious gardens for the solace of the melancholy Moors." "The name of Maumal," says Alcántara, "ought to be preserved in Granada in letters of gold." Perhaps it is as well preserved by being associated with the garden he planted; and by being mentioned in the verses of Hafsah. How often does a casual word from a poet confer immortality!

Perhaps the reader may be curious to learn something of

---

*Miguel Lafuente Alcántara.

the story of Hafsah and her lover, thus connected with one of the beautiful localities of Granada. The following are all the particulars I have been able to rescue out of the darkness and oblivion which have settled upon the brightest names and geniuses of Moslem Spain.

Ahmed and Hafsah flourished in the sixth century of the Hegira; the twelfth of the Christian Era. Ahmed was the son of the Alcayde of Alcala la Real. His father designed him for public and military life and would have made him his lieutenant; but the youth was of a poetical temperament, and preferred a life of lettered ease in the delightful abodes of Granada. Here he surrounded himself by objects of taste in the arts, and by the works of the learned; he divided his time between study and social enjoyment. He was fond of the sports of the field, and kept horses, hawks, and hounds. He devoted himself to literature, became renowned for erudition, and his compositions in prose and verse were extolled for their beauty, and in the mouths of every one.

Of a tender, susceptible heart, and extremely sensible to female charms, he became the devoted lover of Hafsah. The passion was mutual, and for once the course of true love appeared to run smooth. The lovers were both young, equal in merit, fame, rank, and fortune, enamored of each other's genius as well as person, and inhabiting a region formed to be a realm of love and poetry. A poetical intercourse was carried on between them that formed the delight of Granada. They were continually interchanging verses and epistles; "the poetry of which," says the Arabian writer, Al Makkari, "was like the language of doves."

In the height of their happiness a change took place in the government of Granada. It was the time when the Almohades, a Berber tribe of Mount Atlas, had acquired the control of Moslem Spain, and removed the seat of government from Cordova to Morocco. The Sultan Abdelmuman governed Spain through his Walis and Alcaydes; and his son, Sidi Abu Said, was made Wali of Granada. He governed in his father's name with royal state and splendor, and with despotic sway. Being a stranger in the country, and a Moor by birth, he sought to strengthen himself by drawing round him popular persons of the Arab race; and to this effect made

Ahmed, who was then in the zenith of his fame and popularity, his vizier. Ahmed would have declined the post, but the Wali was peremptory. Its duties were irksome to him, and he spurned at its restraint. On a hawking party, with some of his gay companions, he gave way to his poetic vein, exulting in his breaking away from the thraldom of a despotic master like a hawk from the jesses of the falconer, to follow the soaring impulses of his soul.

His words were repeated to Sidi Abu Said. "Ahmed," said the informant, "spurns at restraint and scoffs at thy authority." The poet was instantly dismissed from office. The loss of an irksome post was no grievance to one of his joyous temperament; but he soon discovered the real cause of his removal. The Wali was his rival. He had seen and become enamored of Hafsah. What was worse, Hafsah was dazzled with the conquest she had made.

For a time Ahmed treated the matter with ridicule; and appealed to the prejudice existing between the Arab and Moorish races. Sidi Abu Said was of a dark olive complexion. "How canst thou endure that black man?" said he, scornfully. "By Allah, for twenty dinars I can buy thee a better than he in the slave market."

The scoff reached the ears of Sidi Abu Said and rankled in his heart.

At other times, Ahmed gave way to grief and tenderness, recalling past scenes of happiness, reproaching Hafsah with her inconstancy, and warning her in despairing accents that she would be the cause of his death. His words were unheeded. The idea of having the son of the Sultan for a lover had captivated the imagination of the poetess.

Maddened by jealousy and despair, Ahmed joined in a conspiracy against the ruling dynasty. It was discovered, and the conspirators fled from Granada. Some escaped to a castle on the mountains, Ahmed took refuge in Malaga, where he concealed himself, intending to embark for Valencia. He was discovered, loaded with chains and thrown into a dungeon to abide the decision of Sidi Abu Said.

He was visited in prison by a nephew, who has left on record an account of the interview. The youth was moved to tears at seeing his illustrious relative, late so prosperous and honored, fettered like a malefactor.

"Why dost thou weep?" said Ahmed. "Are these tears shed for me? For me, who have enjoyed all that the world could give? Weep not for me. I have had my share of happiness; banqueted on the daintiest fare; quaffed out of crystal cups; slept on beds of down; been arrayed in the richest silks and brocades; ridden the fleetest steeds; enjoyed the loves of the fairest maidens. Weep not for me. My present reverse is but the inevitable course of fate. I have committed acts which render pardon hopeless. I must await my punishment."

His presentiment was correct. The vengeance of Sidi Abu Said was only to be satisfied by the blood of his rival, and the unfortunate Ahmed was beheaded at Malaga, in the month Jumadi, in the year 559 of the Hegira (April, 1164). When the news was brought to the fickle-hearted Hafsah, she was struck with sorrow and remorse, and put on mourning; recalling his warning words, and reproaching herself with being the cause of his death.

Of the after fortunes of Hafsah I have no further trace than that she died in Morocco, in 1184, outliving both her lovers, for Sidi Abu Said died in Morocco of the plague in 1175. A memorial of his residence in Granada remained in a palace which he built on the banks of the Xenil. The garden of Maumal, the scene of the early lives of Ahmed and Hafsah, is no longer in existence. Its site may be found by the antiquary in poetical research.

The authorities for the foregoing, Alcantara, Hist. Granada. Al Makkari, Hist. Mohamed. Dynasties in Spain, B. ii., c. 3. Notes and illustrations of the same, by Gayangos, v. i., P. 440. Ibnu Al Kahttib, Biograph. Dic., cited by Gayangos. Conde Hist. Dom. Arab.

An Expedition in Quest of a Diploma

ONE OF the most important occurrences in the domestic life of the Alhambra, was the departure of Manuel, the nephew of Doña Antonia, for Malaga, to stand examination as a physician. I have already informed the reader that, on his success in obtaining a degree depended in a great measure the union and future fortunes of himself and his cousin Dolores; at least so I was privately informed by Mateo Ximenes, and various circumstances concurred to corroborate his information. Their courtship, however, was carried on very quietly and discreetly, and I scarce think I should have discovered it, if I had not been put on the alert by the all-observant Mateo.

In the present instance, Dolores was less on the reserve, and had busied herself for several days in fitting out honest Manuel for his expedition. All his clothes had been arranged and packed in the neatest order, and above all she had worked a smart Andalusian travelling jacket for him with her own hands. On the morning appointed for his departure, a stout mule on which he was to perform the journey was paraded at the portal of the Alhambra, and Tio Polo (Uncle Polo), an old invalid soldier, attended to caparison him. This veteran was one of the curiosities of the place. He had a leathern lantern visage, tanned in the tropics, a long Roman nose, and a black beetle eye. I had frequently observed him reading, apparently with intense interest, an old parchment-bound volume; sometimes he would be surrounded by a group of his brother invalids; some seated on the parapets, some lying on the grass, listening with fixed attention, while he read slowly and deliberately out of his favorite work, sometimes pausing to explain or expound for the benefit of his less enlightened auditors.

I took occasion one day to inform myself of this ancient book, which appeared to be his *vade mecum*, and found it to be an odd volume of the works of Padre Benito Geronymo Feyjoo; and that one which treats about the Magic of Spain, the mysterious caves of Salamanca and Toledo, the Purgatory of San Patricio (St. Patrick), and other mystic subjects of the kind. From that time I kept my eye upon the veteran.

On the present occasion, I amused myself with watching him fit out the steed of Manuel with all the forecast of an old campaigner. First, he took a considerable time in adjusting to the back of the mule a cumbrous saddle of antique fashion, high in front and behind, with Moorish stirrups like shovels; the whole looking like a relic of the old armory of the Alhambra; then a fleecy sheep-skin was accommodated to the deep seat of the saddle; then a maleta, neatly packed by the hand of Dolores, was buckled behind; then a manta was thrown over it to serve either as cloak or couch; then the all-important alforjas, carefully stocked with provant, were hung in front, together with the bota, or leathern bottle for either wine or water, and lastly the trabuco, which the old soldier slung behind, giving it his benediction. It was like the fitting out in old times of a Moorish cavalier for a foray or a joust in the Vivarrambla. A number of the lazzaroni of the fortress had gathered round, with some of the invalids, all looking on, all offering their aid, and all giving advice, to the great annoyance of Tio Polo.

When all was ready Manuel took leave of the household; Tio Polo held his stirrup while he mounted; adjusted the girths and saddle, and cheered him off in military style; then turning to Dolores, who stood admiring her cavalier as he trotted off; "Ah Dolorocita," exclaimed he, with a nod and a wink, *"es muy guapo Manuelito in su Xaqueta,"* (Ah Dolores, Manuel is mighty fine in his jacket.) The little damsel blushed and laughed, and ran into the house.

Days elapsed without tidings from Manuel, though he had promised to write. The heart of Dolores began to misgive her. Had any thing happened to him on the road? Had he failed in his examination? A circumstance occurred in her little household to add to her uneasiness and fill her mind with foreboding. It was almost equal to the escapado of her pigeon. Her tortoise-shell cat eloped at night and clambered to the tiled roof of the Alhambra. In the dead of the night there was a fearful caterwauling; some grimalkin was uncivil to her; then there was a scramble; then a clapper-clawing; then both parties rolled off the roof and tumbled from a great height among the trees on the hill side. Nothing more was seen or heard of the fugitive, and poor Dolores considered it but the prelude to greater calamities.

At the end of ten days, however, Manuel returned in triumph, duly authorized to kill or cure; and all Dolores' cares were over. There was a general gathering in the evening, of the humble friends and hangers-on of Dame Antonio to congratulate her, and to pay their respects to *el Señor Medico*, who, peradventure, at some future day, might have all their lives in his hands. One of the most important of these guests was old Tio Polo; and I gladly seized the occasion to prosecute my acquaintance with him. "Oh Señor," cried Dolores, "you who are so eager to learn all the old histories of the Alhambra. Tio Polo knows more about them than any one else about the place. More than Mateo Ximenes and his whole family put together. *Vaya—Vaya*—Tio Polo, tell the Señor all those stories you told us one evening, about enchanted Moors, and the haunted bridge over the Darro, and the old stone pomegranates, that have been there since the days of King Chico."

It was some time before the old invalid could be brought into a narrative vein. He shook his head—they were all idle tales! not worthy of being told to a cavallero like myself. It was only by telling some stories of the kind myself I at last got him to open his budget. It was a whimsical farrago, partly made up of what he had heard in the Alhambra, partly of what he had read in Padre Feyjoo. I will endeavor to give the reader the substance of it, but I will not promise to give it in the very words of Tio Polo.

The Legend of the Enchanted Soldier

E VERY BODY HAS HEARD of the Cave of St. Cyprian at Salamanca, where in old times judicial astronomy, necromancy, chiromancy, and other dark and damnable arts were secretly taught by an ancient sacristan; or, as some will have it, by the devil himself, in that disguise. The cave has long been shut up and the very site of it forgotten; though, according to tradition, the entrance was somewhere about where the stone cross stands in the small square of the seminary of Carvajal; and this tradition appears in some degree corroborated by the circumstances of the following story.

There was at one time a student of Salamanca, Don Vicente by name, of that merry but mendicant class, who set out on the road to learning without a penny in pouch for the journey, and who, during college vacations, beg from town to town and village to village to raise funds to enable them to pursue their studies through the ensuing term. He was now about to set forth on his wanderings; and being somewhat musical, slung on his back a guitar with which to amuse the villagers, and pay for a meal or a night's lodgings.

As he passed by the stone cross in the seminary square, he pulled off his hat and made a short invocation to St. Cyprian, for good luck; when casting his eyes upon the earth, he perceived something glitter at the foot of the cross. On picking it up, it proved to be a seal ring of mixed metal, in which gold and silver appeared to be blended. The seal bore as a device two triangles crossing each other, so as to form a star. This device is said to be a cabalistic sign, invented by king Solomon the wise, and of mighty power in all cases of enchantment; but the honest student, being neither sage nor conjurer, knew nothing of the matter. He took the ring as a present from St. Cyprian in reward of his prayer; slipped it on his finger, made a bow to the cross, and strumming his guitar, set off merrily on his wandering.

The life of a mendicant student in Spain is not the most miserable in the world; especially if he has any talent at making himself agreeable. He rambles at large from village to village, and city to city, wherever curiosity or caprice may conduct him. The country curates, who, for the most part, have been mendicant students in their time, give him shelter for the night, and a comfortable meal, and often enrich him with several quartos, or half-pence in the morning. As he presents himself from door to door in the streets of the cities, he meets with no harsh rebuff, no chilling contempt, for there is no disgrace attending his mendicity, many of the most learned men in Spain having commenced their career in this manner; but if, like the student in question, he is a good looking varlet and a merry companion; and, above all, if he can play the guitar, he is sure of a hearty welcome among the peasants, and smiles and favors from their wives and daughters.

In this way, then, did our ragged and musical son of learning make his way over half the kingdom; with the fixed determination to visit the famous city of Granada before his return. Sometimes he was gathered for the night into the fold of some village pastor; sometimes he was sheltered under the humble but hospitable roof of the peasant. Seated at the cottage door with his guitar, he delighted the simple folk with his ditties; or striking up a fandango or bolero, set the brown country lads and lasses dancing in the mellow twilight. In the morning he departed with kind words from host and hostess, and kind looks and peradventure a squeeze of the hand from the daughter.

At length he arrived at the great object of his musical vagabondizing, the far-famed city of Granada, and hailed with wonder and delight its Moorish towers, its lovely vega and its snowy mountains glistering through a summer atmosphere. It is needless to say with what eager curiosity he entered its gates and wandered through its streets, and gazed upon its oriental monuments. Every female face peering through a window or beaming from a balcony was to him a Zorayda or a Zelinda, nor could he meet a stately dame on the Alameda but he was ready to fancy her a Moorish princess, and to spread his student's robe beneath her feet.

His musical talent, his happy humor, his youth and his good looks, won him a universal welcome in spite of his ragged robes, and for several days he led a gay life in the old Moorish capital and its environs. One of his occasional haunts was the fountain of Avellanos, in the valley of the Darro. It is one of the popular resorts of Granada, and has been so since the days of the Moors; and here the student had an opportunity of pursuing his studies of female beauty; a branch of study to which he was a little prone.

Here he would take his seat with his guitar, improvise love-ditties to admiring groups of majos and majas, or prompt with his music the ever ready dance. He was thus engaged one evening, when he beheld a padre of the church advancing at whose approach every one touched the hat. He was evidently a man of consequence; he certainly was a mirror of good if not of holy living; robust and rosy-faced, and breathing at every pore, with the warmth of the weather and the exercise of the walk. As he passed along he would every now and then draw a maravedi out of his pocket and bestow it on a beggar, with an air of signal beneficence. "Ah, the blessed father!" would be the cry; "long life to him, and may he soon be a bishop!"

To aid his steps in ascending the hill he leaned gently now and then on the arm of a handmaid, evidently the pet-lamb of this kindest of pastors. Ah, such a damsel! Andalus from head to foot: from the rose in her hair, to the fairy shoe and lace-work stocking; Andalus in every movement; in every undulation of the body:—ripe, melting Andalus!—But then so modest!—so shy!—ever, with downcast eyes, listening to the words of the padre; or, if by chance she let flash a side glance, it was suddenly checked and her eyes once more cast to the ground.

The good padre looked benignantly on the company about the fountain, and took his seat with some emphasis on a stone bench, while the handmaid hastened to bring him a glass of sparkling water. He sipped it deliberately and with a relish, tempering it with one of those spongy pieces of frosted eggs and sugar so dear to Spanish epicures, and on returning the glass to the hand of the damsel pinched her cheek with infinite loving-kindness.

"Ah, the good pastor!" whispered the student to himself;

"what a happiness would it be to be gathered into his fold with such a pet-lamb for a companion!"

But no such good fare was likely to befall him. In vain he essayed those powers of pleasing which he had found so irresistible with country curates and country lasses. Never had he touched his guitar with such skill; never had he poured forth more soul-moving ditties, but he had no longer a country curate or country lass to deal with. The worthy priest evidently did not relish music, and the modest damsel never raised her eyes from the ground. They remained but a short time at the fountain; the good padre hastened their return to Granada. The damsel gave the student one shy glance in retiring; but it plucked the heart out of his bosom!

He inquired about them after they had gone. Padre Tomás was one of the saints of Granada, a model of regularity; punctual in his hour of rising; his hour of taking a paseo for an appetite; his hours of eating; his hour of taking his siesta; his hour of playing his game of tresillo, of an evening, with some of the dames of the Cathedral circle; his hour of supping, and his hour of retiring to rest, to gather fresh strength for another day's round of similar duties. He had an easy sleek mule for his riding; a matronly housekeeper skilled in preparing tid-bits for his table; and the pet lamb, to smooth his pillow at night and bring him his chocolate in the morning.

Adieu now to the gay, thoughtless life of the student; the side glance of a bright eye had been the undoing of him. Day and night he could not get the image of this most modest damsel out of his mind. He sought the mansion of the padre. Alas! it was above the class of houses accessible to a strolling student like himself. The worthy padre had no sympathy with him; he had never been *Estudiante sopista*, obliged to sing for his supper. He blockaded the house by day, catching a glance of the damsel now and then as she appeared at a casement; but these glances only fed his flame without encouraging his hope. He serenaded her balcony at night, and at one time was flattered by the appearance of something white at a window. Alas, it was only the nightcap of the padre.

Never was lover more devoted; never damsel more shy: the poor student was reduced to despair. At length arrived the eve of St. John, when the lower classes of Granada swarm into the country, dance away the afternoon, and pass midsummer's night on the banks of the Darro and the Xenil. Happy are they who on this eventful night can wash their faces in those waters just as the Cathedral bell tells midnight; for at that precise moment they have a beautifying power. The student, having nothing to do, suffered himself to be carried away by the holiday-seeking throng until he found himself in the narrow valley of the Darro, below the lofty hill and ruddy towers of the Alhambra. The dry bed of the river; the rocks which border it; the terraced gardens which overhang it were alive with variegated groups, dancing under the vines and fig-trees to the sound of the guitar and castañets.

The student remained for some time in doleful dumps, leaning against one of the huge misshapen stone pomegranates which adorn the ends of the little bridge over the Darro. He cast a wistful glance upon the merry scene, where every cavalier had his dame; or, to speak more appropriately, every Jack his Jill; sighed at his own solitary state, a victim to the black eye of the most unapproachable of damsels, and repined at his ragged garb, which seemed to shut the gate of hope against him.

By degrees his attention was attracted to a neighbor equally solitary with himself. This was a tall soldier, of a stern aspect and grizzled beard, who seemed posted as a sentry at the opposite pomegranate. His face was bronzed by time; he was arrayed in ancient Spanish armor, with buckler and lance, and stood immovable as a statue. What surprised the student was, that though thus strangely equipped, he was totally unnoticed by the passing throng, albeit that many almost brushed against him.

"This is a city of old-time peculiarities," thought the student, "and doubtless this is one of them with which the inhabitants are too familiar to be surprised." His own curiosity, however, was awakened, and being of a social disposition, he accosted the soldier.

"A rare old suit of armor that which you wear, comrade. May I ask what corps you belong to?"

The soldier gasped out a reply from a pair of jaws which seemed to have rusted on their hinges.

"The royal guard of Ferdinand and Isabella."

"Santa Maria! Why, it is three centuries since that corps was in service."

"And for three centuries have I been mounting guard. Now I trust my tour of duty draws to a close. Dost thou desire fortune?"

The student held up his tattered cloak in reply.

"I understand thee. If thou hast faith and courage, follow me, and thy fortune is made."

"Softly, comrade, to follow thee would require small courage in one who has nothing to lose but life and an old guitar, neither of much value; but my faith is of a different matter, and not to be put in temptation. If it be any criminal act by which I am to mend my fortune, think not my ragged cloak will make me undertake it."

The soldier turned on him a look of high displeasure. "My sword," said he, "has never been drawn but in the cause of the faith and the throne. I am a *Cristiano viejo*, trust in me and fear no evil."

The student followed him wondering. He observed that no one heeded their conversation, and that the soldier made his way through the various groups of idlers unnoticed, as if invisible.

Crossing the bridge, the soldier led the way by a narrow and steep path past a Moorish mill and aqueduct, and up the ravine which separates the domains of the Generalife from those of the Alhambra. The last ray of the sun shone upon the red battlements of the latter, which beetled far above; and the convent bells were proclaiming the festival of the ensuing day. The ravine was overshadowed by fig-trees, vines, and myrtles, and the outer towers and walls of the fortress. It was dark and lonely, and the twilight-loving bats began to flit about. At length the soldier halted at a remote and ruined tower, apparently intended to guard a Moorish aqueduct. He struck the foundation with the but-end of his spear. A rumbling sound was heard, and the solid stones yawned apart, leaving an opening as wide as a door.

"Enter in the name of the Holy Trinity," said the soldier, "and fear nothing." The student's heart quaked, but he made the sign of the cross, muttered his Ave Maria, and followed his mysterious guide into a deep vault cut out of the solid rock under the tower, and covered with Arabic inscriptions. The soldier pointed to a stone seat hewn along one side of the vault. "Behold," said he, "my couch for three hundred years." The bewildered student tried to force a joke. "By the blessed St. Anthony," said he, "but you must have slept soundly, considering the hardness of your couch."

"On the contrary, sleep has been a stranger to these eyes; incessant watchfulness has been my doom. Listen to my lot. I was one of the royal guards of Ferdinand and Isabella; but was taken prisoner by the Moors in one of their sorties, and confined a captive in this tower. When preparations were made to surrender the fortress to the Christian sovereigns, I was prevailed upon by an Alfaqui, a Moorish priest, to aid him in secreting some of the treasures of Boabdil in this vault. I was justly punished for my fault. The Alfaqui was an African necromancer, and by his infernal arts cast a spell upon me— to guard his treasures. Something must have happened to him, for he never returned, and here have I remained ever since, buried alive. Years and years have rolled away; earthquakes have shaken this hill; I have heard stone by stone of the tower above tumbling to the ground, in the natural operation of time; but the spell-bound walls of this vault set both time and earthquakes at defiance.

"Once every hundred years, on the festival of St. John, the enchantment ceases to have thorough sway; I am permitted to go forth and post myself upon the bridge of the Darro, where you met me, waiting until some one shall arrive who may have power to break this magic spell. I have hitherto mounted guard there in vain. I walk as in a cloud, concealed from mortal sight. You are the first to accost me for now three hundred years. I behold the reason. I see on your finger the seal-ring of Solomon the wise, which is proof against all enchantment. With you it remains to deliver me from this awful dungeon, or to leave me to keep guard here for another hundred years."

The student listened to this tale in mute wonderment. He had heard many tales of treasure shut up under strong enchantment in the vaults of the Alhambra, but had treated them as fables. He now felt the value of the seal-ring, which had, in a manner, been given to him by St. Cyprian. Still, though armed by so potent a talisman, it was an awful thing to find himself tête-a-tête in such a place with an enchanted soldier, who, according to the laws of nature, ought to have been quietly in his grave for nearly three centuries.

A personage of this kind, however, was quite out of the ordinary run, and not to be trifled with, and he assured him he might rely upon his friendship and good will to do every thing in his power for his deliverance.

"I trust to a motive more powerful than friendship," said the soldier.

He pointed to a ponderous iron coffer, secured by locks inscribed with Arabic characters. "That coffer," said he, "contains countless treasure in gold and jewels, and precious stones. Break the magic spell by which I am enthralled, and one-half of this treasure shall be thine."

"But how am I to do it?"

"The aid of a Christian priest, and a Christian maid is necessary. The priest to exorcise the powers of darkness; the damsel to touch this chest with the seal of Solomon. This must be done at night. But have a care. This is solemn work, and not to be effected by the carnal-minded. The priest must be a *Cristiano viejo*, a model of sanctity; and must mortify the flesh before he comes here, by a rigorous fast of four-and-twenty hours: and as to the maiden, she must be above reproach, and proof against temptation. Linger not in finding such aid. In three days my furlough is at an end; if not delivered before midnight of the third, I shall have to mount guard for another century."

"Fear not," said the student, "I have in my eye the very priest and damsel you describe; but how am I to regain admission to this tower?"

"The seal of Solomon will open the way for thee."

The student issued forth from the tower much more gayly than he had entered. The wall closed behind him, and remained solid as before.

The next morning he repaired boldly to the mansion of the priest, no longer a poor strolling student, thrumming his way with a guitar; but an ambassador from the shadowy world, with enchanted treasures to bestow. No particulars are told of his negotiation, excepting that the zeal of the worthy priest was easily kindled at the idea of rescuing an old soldier of the faith and a strong box of King Chico from the very clutches of Satan; and then what alms might be dispensed, what churches built, and how many poor relatives enriched with the Moorish treasure!

As to the immaculate handmaid, she was ready to lend her hand, which was all that was required, to the pious work; and if a shy glance now and then might be believed, the ambassador began to find favor in her modest eyes.

The greatest difficulty, however, was the fast to which the good Padre had to subject himself. Twice he attempted it, and twice the flesh was too strong for the spirit. It was only on the third day that he was enabled to withstand the temptations of the cupboard; but it was still a question whether he would hold out until the spell was broken.

At a late hour of the night the party groped their way up the ravine by the light of a lantern, and bearing a basket with provisions for exorcising the demon of hunger so soon as the other demons should be laid in the Red Sea.

The seal of Solomon opened their way into the tower. They found the soldier seated on the enchanted strong-box, awaiting their arrival. The exorcism was performed in due style. The damsel advanced and touched the locks of the coffer with the seal of Solomon. The lid flew open; and such treasures of gold and jewels and precious stones as flashed upon the eye!

"Here's cut and come again!" cried the student, exultingly, as he proceeded to cram his pockets.

"Fairly and softly," exclaimed the soldier. "Let us get the coffer out entire, and then divide."

They accordingly went to work with might and main; but it was a difficult task; the chest was enormously heavy, and had been imbedded there for centuries. While they were thus employed the good dominie drew on one side and made a vigorous onslaught on the basket, by way of exorcising the demon of hunger which was raging in his entrails. In a little while a fat capon was devoured, and washed down by a deep potation of Val de peñas; and, by way of grace after meat, he gave a kind-hearted kiss to the pet lamb who waited on him. It was quietly done in a corner, but the tell-tale walls babbled it forth as if in triumph. Never was chaste salute more awful in its effects. At the sound the soldier gave a great cry of despair; the coffer, which was half raised, fell back in its place and was locked once more. Priest, student, and damsel, found themselves outside of the tower, the wall of which closed with a thundering jar. Alas! the good Padre had broken his fast too soon!

When recovered from his surprise, the student would have re-entered the tower, but learnt to his dismay that the damsel, in her fright, had let fall the seal of Solomon; it remained within the vault.

In a word, the cathedral bell tolled midnight; the spell was renewed; the soldier was doomed to mount guard for another hundred years, and there he and the treasure remain to this day—and all because the kind-hearted Padre kissed his hand-maid. "Ah father! father!" said the student, shaking his head ruefully, as they returned down the ravine, "I fear there was less of the saint than the sinner in that kiss!"

Thus ends the legend as far as it has been authenticated. There is a tradition, however, that the student had brought off treasure enough in his pocket to set him up in the world; that he prospered in his affairs, that the worthy Padre gave him the pet lamb in marriage, by way of amends for the blunder in the vault; that the immaculate damsel proved a pattern for wives as she had been for handmaids, and bore her husband a numerous progeny; that the first was a wonder; it was born seven months after her marriage, and though a seven months boy, was the sturdiest of the flock. The rest were all born in ordinary course of time.

The story of the enchanted soldier remains one of the popular traditions of Granada, though told in a variety of ways; the common people affirm that he still mounts guard on midsummer eve, beside the gigantic stone pomegranate on the Bridge of the Darro; but remains invisible excepting to such lucky mortal as may possess the seal of Solomon.

NOTES TO THE ENCHANTED SOLDIER

Among the ancient superstitions of Spain, were those of the existence of profound caverns in which the magic arts were taught, either by the devil in person, or some sage devoted to his service. One of the most famous of these caves, was at Salamanca. Don Francisco de Torreblanca makes mention of it in the first book of his work on Magic, C. 2, No. 4. The devil was said to play the part of Oracle there; giving replies to those who repaired thither to propound fateful questions, as in the celebrated cave of Trophonius. Don Francisco, though he records this story, does not put faith in it: he gives it however as certain, that a Sacristan, named Clement Potosi, taught secretly the magic arts in that cave. Padre Feyjoo, who inquired into the matter, reports it as a vulgar belief, that the devil himself taught those arts there; admitting only seven disciples at a time, one of whom, to be determined by lot, was to be devoted to him body and soul for ever. Among one of these sets of students, was a young man, son of the Marquis de Villena, on whom, after having accomplished his studies, the lot fell. He succeeded, however, in cheating the devil; leaving him his shadow instead of his body.

Don Juan de Dios, Professor of Humanities in the University, in the early part of the last century, gives the following version of the story, extracted, as he says, from an ancient manuscript. It will be perceived he has marred the supernatural part of the tale, and ejected the devil from it altogether.

As to the fable of the Cave of San Cyprian, says he, all that we have been able to verify is, that where the stone cross stands, in the small square or place called by the name of the Seminary of Carvajal, there was the parochial church of San Cyprian. A descent of twenty steps led down to a subterranean Sacristy, spacious and vaulted like a cave. Here a Sacristan once taught magic, judicial astrology, geomancy, hydromancy, pyromancy, acromancy, chiromancy, necromancy, &c.

The extract goes on to state that seven students engaged at a time with the Sacristan, at a fixed stipend. Lots were cast among them which one of their number should pay for the whole, with the understanding that he on whom the lot fell, if he did not pay promptly, should be detained in a chamber of the Sacristy, until the funds were forthcoming. This became thenceforth the usual practice.

On one occasion the lot fell on Henry de Villena, son of the marquis of the same name. He having perceived that there had been trick and shuffling in the casting of the lot, and suspecting the Sacristan to be cognizant thereof, refused to pay. He was forthwith left in limbo. It so happened, that in a dark corner of the Sacristy was a huge jar or earthen reservoir for water, which was cracked and empty. In this the youth contrived to conceal himself. The Sacristan returned at night with a servant, bringing lights and a supper. Unlocking the door, they found no one in the vault, and a book of magic lying open on the table. They retreated in dismay, leaving the door open, by which Villena made his escape. The story went about that through magic he had made himself invisible.—The reader has now both versions of the story, and may make his choice. I will only observe that the sages of the Alhambra incline to the diabolical one.

This Henry de Villena flourished in the time of Juan II, King of Castile, of whom he was uncle. He became famous for his knowledge of the Natural Sciences; and hence, in that ignorant age was stigmatized as a necromancer. Fernan Perez de Guzman, in his account of distinguished men, gives him credit for great learning, but says he devoted himself to the arts of divination, the interpretation of dreams, of signs, and portents.

At the death of Villena, his library fell into the hands of the King, who was warned that it contained books treating of magic, and not proper to be read. King Juan ordered that they should be transported in carts to the residence of a reverend prelate to be examined. The prelate was less learned than devout. Some of the books treated of mathematics, others of astronomy, with figures and diagrams, and planetary signs; others of chemistry or alchemy, with foreign and mystic words. All these were necromancy in the eyes of the pious prelate, and the books were consigned to the flames, like the library of Don Quixote.

THE SEAL OF SOLOMON.—The device consists of two equilateral triangles, interlaced so as to form a star, and surrounded by a circle. According to Arab tradition, when the Most High gave Solomon the choice of blessings, and he chose wisdom, there came from heaven a ring, on which this device was engraven. This mystic talisman was the arcanum of his wisdom, felicity, and grandeur; by this he governed and prospered. In consequence of a temporary lapse from virtue, he lost the ring in the sea, and was at once reduced to the level of ordinary men. By penitence and prayer he made his peace with the Deity, was permitted to find his ring again in the belly of a fish, and thus recovered his celestial gifts. That he might not utterly lose them again, he communicated to others the secret of the marvellous ring.

This symbolical seal we are told was sacrilegiously used by the Mahometan infidels; and before them by the Arabian idolators, and before them by the Hebrews, for "diabolical enterprises and abominable superstitions." Those who wish to be more thoroughly informed on the subject, will do well to consult the learned Father Athanasius Kirker's treatise on the *Cabala Sarracenica*.

* * *

A word more to the curious reader. There are many persons in these skeptical times, who affect to deride every thing connected with the occult sciences, or black art; who have no faith in the efficacy of conjurations, incantations or divinations; and who stoutly contend that such things never had existence. To such determined unbelievers the testimony of past ages is as nothing; they require the evidence of their own senses, and deny that such arts and practices have prevailed in days of yore, simply because they meet with no instance of them in the present day. They cannot perceive that, as the world became versed in the natural sciences, the supernatural became superfluous and fell into disuse; and that the hardy inventions of art superseded the mysteries of magic. Still, say the enlightened few, those mystic powers exist, though in a latent state, and untasked by the ingenuity of man. A talisman is still a talisman, possessing all its indwelling and awful properties; though it may have lain dormant for ages at the bottom of the sea, or in the dusty cabinet of the antiquary.

The signet of Solomon the Wise, for instance, is well known to have held potent control over genii, demons, and enchantments; now who will positively assert that the same mystic signet, wherever it may exist, does not at the present moment possess the same marvellous virtues which distinguished it in the olden time? Let those who doubt repair to Salamanca, delve into the cave of San Cyprian, explore its hidden secrets, and decide. As to those who will not be at the pains of such investigation, let them substitute faith for incredulity, and receive with honest credence the foregoing legend.

The Author's Farewell to Granada

M Y SERENE and happy reign in the Alhambra, was suddenly brought to a close by letters which reached me, while indulging in oriental luxury in the cool hall of the baths, summoning me away from my Moslem elysium to mingle once more in the bustle and business of the dusty world. How was I to encounter its toils and turmoils, after such a life of repose and reverie! How was I to endure its common-place, after the poetry of the Alhambra!

But little preparation was necessary for my departure. A two-wheeled vehicle, called a tartana, very much resembling a covered cart, was to be the travelling equipage of a young Englishman and myself through Murcia, to Alicant and Valencia, on our way to France; and a long-limbed varlet, who had been a contrabandista, and, for aught I knew, a robber, was to be our guide and guard. The preparations were soon made, but the departure was the difficulty. Day after day was it postponed; day after day was spent in lingering about my favorite haunts, and day after day they appeared more delightful in my eyes.

The social and domestic little world also, in which I had been moving, had become singularly endeared to me; and the concern evinced by them at my intended departure, convinced me that my kind feelings were reciprocated. Indeed, when at length the day arrived, I did not dare venture upon a leave-taking at the good dame Antonia's; I saw the soft heart of little Dolores, at least, was brim full and ready for an overflow. So I bade a silent adieu to the palace and its inmates, and descended into the city, as if intending to return. There, however, the tartana and the guide were ready; so, after taking a noonday's repast with my fellow traveller at the Posada, I set out with him on our journey.

Humble was the cortege and melancholy the departure of El Rey Chico the second! Manuel, the nephew of Tia Antonia, Mateo, my officious but now disconsolate squire, and two or three old invalids of the Alhambra with whom I had grown into gossiping companionship, had come down to see me off; for it is one of the good old customs of Spain, to sally forth several miles to meet a coming friend, and to accompany him as far on his departure. Thus then we set out, our long-legged guard striding ahead, with his escopeta on his shoulder; Manuel and Mateo on each side of the tartana, and the old invalids behind.

At some little distance to the north of Granada, the road gradually ascends the hills; here I alighted and walked up slowly with Manuel, who took this occasion to confide to me the secret of his heart and of all those tender concerns between himself and Dolores, with which I had been already informed by the all knowing and all revealing Mateo Ximenes. His doctor's diploma had prepared the way for their union, and nothing more was wanting but the dispensation of the Pope, on account of their consanguinity. Then, if he could get the post of Medico of the fortress, his happiness would be complete! I congratulated him on the judgment and good taste he had shown in his choice of a helpmate; invoked all possible felicity on their union, and trusted that the abundant affections of the kind-hearted little Dolores would in time have more stable objects to occupy them than recreant cats and truant pigeons.

It was indeed a sorrowful parting when I took leave of these good people and saw them slowly descend the hills; now and then turning round to wave me a last adieu. Manuel, it is true, had cheerful prospects to console him, but poor Mateo seemed perfectly cast down. It was to him a grievous fall from the station of prime minister and historiographer, to his old brown cloak and his starveling mystery of ribbon-weaving; and the poor devil, notwithstanding his occasional officiousness, had, somehow or other, acquired a stronger hold on my sympathies than I was aware of. It would have really been a consolation in parting, could I have anticipated the good fortune in store for him, and to which I had contributed; for the importance I had appeared to give to his tales and gossip and local knowledge, and the frequent companionship in which I had indulged him in the course of my strolls, had elevated his idea of his own qualifications and opened a new career to him; and the son of the Alhambra has since become its regular and well-paid cicerone; insomuch that I am told he has never been obliged to resume the ragged old brown cloak in which I first found him.

Towards sunset I came to where the road wound into the mountains, and here I paused to take a last look at Granada. The hill on which I stood commanded a glorious view of the city, the Vega, and the surrounding mountains. It was at an opposite point of the compass from *La cuesta de las lagrimas* (the hill of tears) noted for the "last sigh of the Moor." I now could realize something of the feelings of poor Boabdil when he bade adieu to the paradise he was leaving behind, and beheld before him a rugged and sterile road conducting him to exile.

The setting sun as usual shed a melancholy effulgence on the ruddy towers of the Alhambra. I could faintly discern the balconied window of the tower of Comares, where I had indulged in so many delightful reveries. The bosky groves and gardens about the city were richly gilded with the sunshine, the purple haze of a summer evening was gathering over the Vega; every thing was lovely, but tenderly and sadly so, to my parting gaze.

"I will hasten from this prospect," thought I, "before the sun is set. I will carry away a recollection of it clothed in all its beauty."

With these thoughts I pursued my way among the mountains. A little further and Granada, the Vega, and the Alhambra, were shut from my view; and thus ended one of the pleasantest dreams of a life, which the reader perhaps may think has been too much made up of dreams.

THE END

Chronology

1783–86   Born April 3, 1783, at 131 William Street, New York City, youngest of eight surviving children of William Irving and Sarah Sanders Irving. (Father was born in 1731 on Shapinsay, in the Orkney Islands north of Scotland, the descendant of seamen, tradesmen, and shopkeepers. In 1761, while a petty officer in the Royal Navy, he married Sarah Sanders, born 1738, the granddaughter of an English curate, in Falmouth, England. They emigrated to New York in 1763, where father became successful merchant, with business at 75 William Street, and a Presbyterian deacon.) Mother names him Washington Irving in honor of George Washington. Within a few weeks after his birth, family moves across the street to 128 William Street. Baptized in 1784 in the Episcopal Church of St. Paul in a Presbyterian service. Father reads the Bible aloud to the family every evening, takes them to three sermons on Sundays, and makes the children study the catechism on Thursday afternoons. Irving feels close to his mother and is the favorite of his four brothers (William, Jr., b. 1766; Peter, b. 1772; Ebenezer, b. 1776; John Treat, b. 1778) and three sisters (Ann, b. 1770; Catharine, b. 1774; Sarah, b. 1780).

1787–89   Attends Mrs. Ann Kilmaster's kindergarten. Sister Ann marries Richard Dodge on February 14, 1788. On a walk in the summer of 1789, his Scottish nurse, Lizzie, sees President George Washington in a shop and asks him to bless his namesake, which he does.

1789–97   Attends school of Benjamin Romaine, a Revolutionary War veteran and strict disciplinarian. Reads romances and travel books, including *The World Displayed* (later writes that these volumes "were more delightful to me than a fairy tale and the plates by which they were illustrated are indelibly stamped on my reccollection"), John Bunyan's *Pilgrim's Progress*, Jonathan Swift's *Gulliver's Travels*, Daniel Defoe's *Robinson Crusoe*, and *Sinbad the Sailor*. Wanders among the wharves and watches ships sail out to sea. Begins attending theaters and pantomimes, sneaking out through the window and over the rooftop at night.

Visitors to the Irving home include Archibald and Alexander Robertson, artists whose drawing academy at 135 William Street Irving attends; the wood engraver Alexander Anderson, and his brother John, in whose drawings Irving takes an interest. Brother William marries Julia Paulding on November 7, 1793; sister Catharine marries John Daniel Paris on October 1, 1796.

1797–98 After Romaine retires from teaching to enter into business in the spring of 1797, Irving is sent by brothers to school of Josiah A. Henderson, author of *The Well-Bred Scholar* and an authority on theater; then, in December 1797, his brothers send him to Jonathan Fiske's school, where he studies Latin. Against his father's wishes, attends dancing school, takes long walks in the open country, and hunts squirrels along the Hudson River. Spends much time with his brothers and friends.

1799   Unlike his brothers Peter and John, does not attend Columbia College. Enters law offices of Henry Masterson, for whom John also clerked, in preference to the family import business. Shares literary interests with brothers Peter and William.

1800   Takes first extended trip up the Hudson River to visit sisters Ann and Catharine, now living with their families in Johnstown, near Albany (later writes, "of all the scenery of the Hudson, the Kaatskill Mountains had the most witching effect on my boyish imagination").

1801   Moves in summer to office of prominent attorney Brockholst Livingston, a Revolutionary War veteran and Jeffersonian Anti-Federalist.

1802   After Livingston is named to the state supreme court, Irving transfers to offices of Judge Josiah Hoffman, former attorney general of New York (1798–1801), a leading New York Federalist, and a wealthy landowner and real estate speculator. Becomes an intimate of Hoffman's family. Spends most of July visiting his sisters in Johnstown. In November, begins publishing letters under pseudonym "Jonathan Oldstyle, Gent." in the *Morning Chronicle*, edited by brother Peter; they attract generally favorable notice.

1803   Accompanies Hoffman, lawyer Ludlow Ogden, and members of their families on a trip through upstate New York in the summer. Visits Albany, Ballston, Johnstown, Utica, and Oswegatchie, where Ogden and Hoffman own land and plan to lay out a town (later Ogdensburg), before going on to Montreal. Travels through forests and across unbridged rivers and streams, participates in a deer hunt for the first time, and encounters Indians. Keeps journal for part of trip. In Montreal, meets Henry Brevoort of New York, who becomes a close friend.

1804   Writes in March and April for *The Corrector*, a newssheet supporting Aaron Burr's campaign for governor of New York, anonymously published by Peter, who is running for the assembly on Burr's ticket (neither Burr nor Peter is elected). Brothers William and Ebenezer, worried that Irving is becoming consumptive, finance trip to Europe, and he embarks for Bordeaux on May 19. Keeps journal of his travels through France and Italy. Successfully hides his money when his ship, bound for Sicily, is robbed by pirates.

1805   Watches the *Victory* and other ships of Admiral Nelson's fleet sail through the Strait of Messina in January. Participates in social life of Americans and English abroad. Explores Naples and surroundings (including Pompeii and Herculaneum) with Virginians Joseph Cabell and Colonel John Mercer. Departs on March 24 with Cabell for Rome, where he begins lifelong friendship with American artist Washington Allston and briefly considers becoming a painter; introduced to French writer Madame de Staël by Baron Wilhelm von Humboldt, the Prussian minister at Rome. Travels through Switzerland to Paris with Cabell, arriving May 24. Leaves on September 22 for London, via Belgium and Holland. Attends theaters throughout his travels, especially in England. Joins crowds in London mourning death of Admiral Nelson during the British victory at Trafalgar on October 21. Brother Ebenezer marries Elizabeth Kip on November 14.

1806   Sister Sarah marries Henry Van Wart on January 8. Irving sails for New York on January 17, arriving March 24. Brother

John marries Abigail Spicer Furman on April 27. Returns to Hoffman law offices. Becomes a member of "lads of Kilkenny" or "nine worthies," a social and literary club with brothers William, Peter, and Ebenezer, James Kirke Paulding (William's brother-in-law), Henry Brevoort, Henry Ogden, Peter and Gouverneur Kemble, David Porter, and Richard McCall. Assists brother Peter and George Caines in translating a French travel account by François Depons (published by I. Riley in New York as *A Voyage to the Eastern Part of Terra Firma, or the Spanish Main in South-America*). Continues to visit the Hoffman household and falls in love with 15-year-old Matilda Hoffman. Passes bar examination November 21; shares an office with brother John at 3 Wall Street.

1807　　Co-authors *Salmagundi* with William Irving and James Paulding (published serially by David Longworth in 20 numbers between January 24, 1807, and January 25, 1808); the pieces receive much praise. Among friends is Mary Fairlie ("Miss Sophy Sparkle" of *Salmagundi*). Attends the trial for treason of Aaron Burr in Richmond on an informal retainer from a friend of Burr's who hoped Irving might write in Burr's favor. (Irving privately writes to Mrs. Josiah Hoffman, "though opposed to him in political principles, yet I consider him as a man so fallen, so shorn of the power to do national injury, that I feel no sensation remaining but compassion for him," but is not known to have written publicly about the case.) Meets Congressman John Randolph, the foreman of the grand jury that indicted Burr; visits his Virginia friends from European travels, Colonel John Mercer and Joseph Cabell. Makes periodic visits to Philadelphia and becomes friends with merchant Michael Gratz and family, especially his children Rebecca, a close friend of Matilda Hoffman's, and Joseph. Father dies on October 25.

1808　　Begins work on a burlesque historical guidebook to New York, originally conceived in collaboration with brother Peter as a parody of Samuel L. Mitchill's *The Picture of New-York; or The Traveller's Guide through the Commercial Metropolis of the United States* (1807). Travels with Peter to Montreal in May; prevented by President Jefferson's embargo from taking the $9,000 in silver he is carrying into

Canada, Irving buys cashier's receipts in Burlington, Vermont, hoping to exchange them for cash in Montreal. Sister Ann Dodge dies May 10. Makes second trip to Montreal in December.

1809   Returns to New York in January. Develops friendship with 18-year-old John Howard Payne, actor and author. Matilda Hoffman dies of tuberculosis on April 26. Irving, who was present along with the Hoffmans and Rebecca Gratz throughout her final three-day agony, retires in mourning to Kinderhook, the country home of William P. Van Ness (Burr's second in his duel with Alexander Hamilton in July 1804). Works on *A History of New York*. Returns to New York in mid-June and spends late summer at Ravenswood, Judge Hoffman's farm in upper Manhattan. Travels to Philadelphia in October to put *A History* through the press. Perpetrates with Paulding and Brevoort a newspaper hoax in October and November concerning the disappearance of "Diedrich Knickerbocker," the fictitious author of the parody. *A History of New York* published on December 6 by Bradford and Inskeep in Philadelphia, where it had been printed to keep its contents a secret in New York until publication; it becomes an instant success.

1810   Travels to Albany in an unsuccessful attempt to obtain a clerkship in the state courts (Daniel Paris, Irving's brother-in-law, is on the council of appointments for New York). Visits the Hoffmans, travels in the Hudson Valley, keeps notebooks. After being approached by the brother of Scottish poet Thomas Campbell, arranges for a selection of Campbell's poems to be published in the United States by Charles I. Nicholas, and writes a brief biographical introduction. Brothers Peter and Ebenezer make him inactive partner in a new import business, P. & E. Irving, based in Liverpool and New York, giving him one-fifth interest. Enjoys being a literary celebrity in New York.

1811   Sent to Washington by brothers William and Ebenezer to lobby Congress for the interests of New York merchants. Stays with the family of John P. Van Ness, brother of William; attends, without invitation, a ball given by President Madison's wife, Dolly, but is well-received, meets the President, and becomes friends with Dolly Madison. Participates in Washington social life, meets naval officer Captain Stephen Decatur and Senator Henry Clay. Secretary of State Robert Smith suggests his name as secretary of legation to France, under Joel Barlow as minister; Irving correctly predicts that Barlow will not choose him. Returns to New York in May and moves from family home to share living quarters with Henry Brevoort at 16 Broadway. *Salmagundi* published in book form in London by J. M. Richardson, with introduction by John Lambert but otherwise unsigned.

1812   Corrects *A History of New York* for a new printing by Bradford and Inskeep. Congress declares war on Great Britain on June 18 and renews 1811 Nonimportation Act barring entry of British goods. Firm of P. & E. Irving, unaware of outbreak of war and believing that the 1811 act lapsed with the repeal on June 17 of British Orders in Council restricting American trade, brings ship laden with British imports to New York, where cargo is confiscated until firm posts bond. Irving returns to Washington in November as member of committee of merchants petitioning for remission of bonds (potential forfeitures by American importers total $18 million). Congressmen John C. Calhoun and Langdon Cheves lead successful opposition to Secretary of the Treasury Albert Gallatin's proposal for partial forfeiture (bonds are fully remitted). Meets Calhoun, Albert Gallatin, and the Gallatin family. Leaves Washington on December 14 for New York, stopping in Baltimore and Philadelphia. Moses Thomas, a Philadelphia bookseller, buys the magazine *Select Reviews*, and Irving accepts his offer to edit it, for which he is "handsomely paid" (salary $1,500 a year).

1813   Irving and Thomas change the name of *Select Reviews* to *Analectic Magazine*; Irving writes a regular column, biographical sketches of naval heroes, and literary criticism, but dislikes editing. Walter Scott praises *A History* in letter to Brevoort, who had presented him with a copy while visiting Britain. Brother William wins special election to the U.S. House of Representatives (serves in Congress from January 22, 1814, to March 3, 1819).

1814   Irving moves in the summer with Brevoort to new lodgings at the corner of Greenwich and Rector streets (Stephen

Decatur and his wife are among the other lodgers). His patriotism aroused by British burning of Washington in August 1814, Irving becomes aide-de-camp to Governor Daniel Tompkins of New York, with rank of colonel. Serves on the Canadian frontier but does not see action. Writes Moses Thomas in November that he intends to resign as editor of *Analectic Magazine* at the end of the year. David Longworth publishes revised edition of *Salmagundi* with woodcuts and plates by Irving's old friend Alexander Anderson.

1815   When Moses Thomas is financially hurt by the failure of Bradford and Inskeep, Irving assists with arrangements that permit *Analectic Magazine* to continue, but resigns as editor and swears never to edit again. Peace treaty with Great Britain is ratified February 16; Irving, feeling restless, resolves to travel abroad and leaves May 25. Arrives in Liverpool in late June on the *Mexico* after a rough passage ("mewed up together for thirty days in dirty cabins"). Sees brother Peter, now suffering from rheumatism and erysipelas, for the first time in seven years. Visits sister Sarah Van Wart and her family in Birmingham; travels to London in July to view the celebrations following the British victory at Waterloo on June 18. Travels through the English countryside and visits Wales with engineer James Renwick (who marries Brevoort's sister in 1816) for the first two weeks in August. Irving abandons further plans to travel to France, Italy, and possibly Greece when he discovers that Peter's health is worsening; goes to Liverpool in late August to take over the business while Peter convalesces in Birmingham. Forms friendship with English historian William Roscoe. Attends theaters during visits to London, and sees Edmund Kean, Charles Mayne Young, and Eliza O'Neill perform.

1816   Visits Van Warts in Birmingham from mid-January to early April. Firm of P. & E. Irving is increasingly troubled by lack of demand for British goods and by Peter's overpurchasing; Irving returns to Liverpool in effort to help redeem the firm's debts and the family's name ("anxious days and sleepless nights"); borrows from James Renwick to pay firm's debts. Tours Derbyshire with Peter in August for two weeks; Peter returns to Liverpool, while Irving travels along Welsh border before returning to stay with Van Warts in Birmingham.

1817   Returns to Liverpool February 23 to be with Peter to help "relieve the loneliness of his life." Resolves to return to New York to visit his mother, but then learns that she died April 9. In June, Virginian William Campbell Preston arrives in Liverpool and joins Irving and Peter on a walking tour in Wales. Irving takes lodgings in London in early August on Cockspur Lane, Westminster, and begins work on *The Sketch Book of Geoffrey Crayon, Gent.* ("to raise myself from the degradation into which I considered myself fallen," he later writes). Visits Thomas Campbell in Sydenham and tries through Brevoort to arrange an American lecture tour for the poet (Campbell later declines to go). Dines with publisher John Murray II, who introduces him to writer Isaac D'Israeli (father of Benjamin Disraeli) and publisher John Miller. Visits poet Samuel Taylor Coleridge. Renews friendships with James Oglivie (a teacher of oratory, whom Irving met at the Burr trial) and American artists Washington Allston and Charles Leslie, who are working on illustrations for *A History of New York* for Murray, and becomes friends with American artist Gilbert Stuart Newton. Interrupts work on *The Sketch Book* to travel to Scotland on August 25. Visits Francis Jeffrey, editor of the *Edinburgh Review*, and meets Walter Scott at Abbotsford, where he is invited to stay for a few days. Irving is amazed at "being under the roof of Scott . . . in the very centre of that region which had for some time past been the favorite scene of romantic fiction." Scott reads aloud from *Le Morte d'Arthur* and introduces him to German legend and literature. Tours Scottish Highlands with Preston. Returns to Liverpool in September but takes occasional trips to London. Learns of Brevoort's marriage to Laura Elizabeth Carson; in his congratulations Irving says the news makes him more "melancholy than glad" for "marriage is the grave of Bachelors intimacy." Brother William attempts unsuccessfully, through Henry Clay, to have Irving appointed as secretary to the American legation in London; Irving asks William to seek positions for Peter or Ebenezer instead.

1818   Irving and Peter appear before the Commissioners of Bankruptcy between January 27 and March 14, and their

ham in September, visiting Oxford, Stratford-on-Avon, Warwick, and Kenilworth en route. Suffers from severely inflamed ankles during his stay in Birmingham while preparing *Bracebridge Hall* for press. Two of sister Catharine's four daughters die; soon afterward, learns of death of brother William Irving of tuberculosis on November 9, and calls it "one of the dismallest events" of his life, saying William "was like a father to the family." Returns to London on December 26.

1822   Is enlisted by Charles Wiley, James Fenimore Cooper's American publisher, to help arrange publication by Murray of Cooper's *The Spy*, but Murray declines to publish it on the advice of William Gifford. Irving asks Murray for £1,575 for *Bracebridge Hall*, but accepts his counteroffer of £1,050. *Bracebridge Hall by Geoffrey Crayon, Gent.* published on May 21 by C. S. Van Winkle in New York and in London by Murray on May 23. Worried by the recurring inflammations on his legs, leaves England on July 6 and travels through Holland to the spas at Aachen, intending to make a short trip through Germany before going to Paris in the fall. Finds the treatments helpful, and takes baths for two weeks in Wiesbaden and three weeks in Mainz. Goes to Koblenz, visits the fair in Frankfurt, and spends two weeks taking baths at Heidelberg, before visiting Karlsruhe, Baden-Baden, Strasbourg, Ulm, Munich, Salzburg, and Vienna, where he spends four weeks exploring the city and surroundings. Travels through Moravia and Bohemia to Prague, then goes to Dresden. Finds that with parts of *The Sketch Book* already published in German and *Bracebridge Hall* being translated (published in Berlin in 1823), his presence is hailed as an event in Dresden when he arrives in late November.

1823   Becomes close friends with Mrs. Amelia Foster of England and her family, with whom he acts in amateur theatricals. Grows deeply attached to 18-year-old Emily Foster. Takes lessons in German (from two tutors), Italian (from Mrs. Foster), and French (from Emily Foster). Becomes a favorite of the court of Frederick Augustus I, King of Saxony. Meets the author and critic Ludwig Tieck. Attends theater often, seeing plays by Heinrich von

Kleist and Friedrich Schiller. Hears the music of Bee-
thoven and Mozart, and listens to Carl Maria von Weber
performing his own piano music in Dresden. Together
with Barham John Livius, translates and adapts Weber's
operas *Abu Hassan* and *Der Freischütz* (attends performances of the latter in four cities during his travels in Germany). Leaves on May 20 in the company of British
artillery officer Lieutenant John Cockburn for a tour of
Bohemia and Silesia, arriving in Prague on May 28; plans
to stay only a few days there, but Cockburn develops scarlet fever and they remain until June 24 before returning to
Dresden. Travels with the Fosters to Rotterdam in July on
their way back to England, then returns to Paris to write,
arriving August 3. Visits Peter in Le Havre for two weeks
in late September, where he again has problems with inflamed ankles. Moves into Payne's rooms at 89 Rue Rich-
elieu, a five-minute walk from the national library, on his
return to Paris on October 3. Begins collaboration on
plays with Payne, but insists on anonymity. Leads active
social life with Moore, Payne, the painter David Wilkie,
the American merchant Thomas Wentworth Storrow and
family, Pierre François Guestier (Reuben Beasley's
brother-in-law), Talma, Prince Frederick Augustus of
Saxony (later King Frederick Augustus II), and many
others. Takes care of two nephews (sons of the Van Warts)
who are going to school in Paris, and looks after Irving
Van Wart when he has smallpox. Peter moves in with
Irving in November.

1824   Writes Payne in January that he can no longer afford to
             collaborate on plays but must devote himself to his own
             writing, though he continues to offer help. Begins period
             of intense work that produces most of *Tales of a Traveller*.
             Tells Murray in March that he has abandoned plans for
             additional volumes of *The Sketch Book* in favor of *Tales*;
             rejects Murray's offer of £1,260 and asks for £1,575, which
             Murray later agrees to pay. Arrives in England on May 28,
             in time to see second night's performance of *Charles II*, a
             play written in collaboration with Payne. Introduced by
             Payne to Mary Wollstonecraft Shelley. Stays with the poet
             William Spencer at 4 Mount Street in London. Travels to
             Southampton and then meets Moore in Bath. Returns to
             London on June 30. Visits the Fosters in Bedford (soon

afterward Emily Foster marries Henry Fuller), then returns to London. Corrects proofs of *Tales*, writes additional material to fill two octavo volumes. Travels to
Auteuil, outside of Paris, to visit the Storrows for a month
before going to the city. *Tales of a Traveller by Geoffrey
Crayon, Gent.* published by Carey & Lea of Philadelphia
in four parts (appearing Aug. 24–Oct. 9); published in
London by Murray on August 25; receives mixed reviews
in both countries, with some calling it imitative, indecent,
and sycophantic. Depressed by criticism, visits friends in
Paris. Takes nine-day trip through the Loire Valley (Orléans, Tours) with Peter in October.

1825   Studies Spanish for distraction. Reads dramatist and poet
            Pedro Calderón de la Barca, dramatist Lope de Vega, and
            Spanish history. Invests £1,150 in Mexican and Peruvian
            copper mines (his hopes for an immediate return are dis-
            appointed and in 1829 he will ask that the stocks be for-
            feited to prevent further costs). Goes to Le Havre in mid-
            June to visit Peter, returning to Paris on July 9. Visits
            Compiègne with the Storrows in early September. Leaves
            Paris with Peter on September 21 to visit friends in and
            around Bordeaux; stays at the Hôtel de France, with the
            Guestiers at the Château Beychevelle, then takes lodgings
            at 24 Rue Rolland in late October to save money. Realizes
            he must write to earn money, as his investments are un-
            productive.

1826   Decides to go to Spain. Writes in January to Alexander H.
            Everett, American minister in Madrid, accepting Everett's
            previous offer of a diplomatic passport for protection
            amid civil unrest; becomes an attaché to the American le-
            gation in Madrid without official duties. Everett suggests
            that Irving translate Martín Fernández de Navarrete's two-
            volume work on Columbus' voyages. Arrives with Peter in
            Madrid on February 15, where he lives and works in the
            house of Obadiah Rich, acting secretary of the American
            legation, using Rich's extensive private library. Decides
            for artistic and financial reasons not to do a direct transla-
            tion of Navarrete's scholarly work, but to write instead a
            popular biography of Columbus. Presented to King
            Ferdinand VII of Spain by Everett on March 18.
            Visited for two weeks by nephew Pierre Munro Irving,

24-four-year-old son of William. Begins planning *Conquest of Granada* in August and works on it until mid-November, when he returns to *Columbus*. Meets American naval officer Alexander Slidell (later known as Alexander Slidell Mackenzie) in November. Regularly attends bull-fights in Madrid.

1827   Concentrates on his work, researching and writing *Colum-bus*, using Navarrete's books. Asks nephew Pierre Munro Irving to help see *Columbus* through the press in London (because of delays in preparing the manuscript, task is eventually done by Thomas Aspinwall, the American consul in London, who becomes Irving's English agent). Frequently visits the home of Pierre D'Oubril, Russian minister at Madrid, where he becomes friends with Prince Dmitri I. Dolgorouki, Russian diplomat and son of the poet Ivan M. Dolgorouki. Irving is visited in March by 20-year-old Henry Wadsworth Longfellow, who remains in Madrid until September. Sends first volume of *Colum-bus* to Murray on July 29, asking £3,150 for it; Murray is delighted with the book and accepts his terms. Works on stories with Spanish themes, and begins a life of the prophet Muhammad in November. David Wilkie arrives in Madrid on October 10.

1828   *Life and Voyages of Columbus*, which appears under Irving's own name, published by Murray in London on February 8 and by Carvill in New York on March 15. Ebenezer's son Theodore visits Madrid during February. Irving leaves Madrid on March 1 with two Russian diplomats for a tour of southern Spain; Peter, who is unable to accom-pany them due to poor health, returns to Paris with Theo-dore. Visits Cordova, Granada, Málaga, Gibraltar, Cádiz, and Seville, where he takes up residence in mid-April. Explores Seville and vicinity with Wilkie during the later half of April. Begins correcting first edition of *Columbus* in May. Carey & Lea buys the rights to *A History*, *The Sketch Book*, *Bracebridge Hall*, and *Tales* for seven years at $600 a year. In July, Irving moves to a cottage ("Casa de Cera") outside of Seville with John Nalder Hall, a con-sumptive young Englishman living in Spain for his health. Sends corrected copies of *Columbus* to England and Amer-ica on August 5. Goes with Hall to Puerto de Santa Maria, on the Bay of Cádiz, in late August. Visits with German scholar Johann Nikolaus Böhl von Faber, manager of a winery in Puerto de Santa Maria, whom Irving met in Seville (later meets his daughter Cecilia, the Marquise of Arco Hermosa, who will write novels and folklore under the name Fernán Cabellero). Sends final portion of *Granada* to Murray in London and Ebenezer in New York on October 19. Declines Murray's offers of £1,000 a year to edit a new periodical Murray is establishing, plus £105 for any articles for the *Quarterly Review* (writes to Everett that the *Review* "has been so hostile to our country, that I cannot think of writing a line for it"). Works on *Voyages and Discoveries of the Companions of Columbus*. Returns to Seville on November 3 to work in the cathedral, where the personal library of Fernando Columbus is kept. Completes abridged version of *Columbus* in 19 days after hearing from Peter on November 18 that a pirated abridgment was being planned in America (Carvill buys rights to both corrected edition and abridgment of *Columbus* for five years for $6,000; Murray receives abridgment "gratis"). Learns in late November of the death of John Nalder Hall at Puerto de Santa Maria. Elected to Spanish Royal Academy of History in December.

1829   Continues studying Spanish history and legend, working on *Companions of Columbus*, *Legends of the Conquest of Spain* (completed in June), *The Alhambra*, and *Mahomet. A Chronicle of the Conquest of Granada by Fray Antonio Agapida* published in Philadelphia on April 20 by Carey and Lea ($4,750 for five years) and in London on May 23 by Murray (Irving receives £2,100, but is annoyed that Murray placed Irving's name on the title page, and not only that of the fictional narrator, as he wished). Book is praised by Coleridge. In April, Prince Dolgorouki arrives from Madrid and Irving shows him Seville and vicinity. Their plan to visit North Africa ("to get a peep at the turbaned infidels in their own towns") is hindered by the Austrian bombardment of Tangiers, but in May they travel to the Alhambra palace in Granada, where they are met by Ebenezer's son Edgar. Remains in the Alhambra after Edgar and Dolgorouki leave in mid-May ("It absolutely appears to me like a dream; or as if I am spell bound in some fairy palace").

Feels more and more homesick and plans to return to America, but accepts instead appointment as first secretary at the American legation in London under Minister Louis McLane (salary $2,000) at the urging of his friends and brothers. Leaves Granada on July 28, traveling in the company of Ralph Sneyd, a young Englishman, through Alicante, Valencia, and Catalonia, leaving Spain "with feelings of great regret" on August 23. Meets Peter in Paris and visits Rouen with him. Arrives in London on September 19, taking lodgings on Chandos Street, Cavendish Square, across the street from McLane. Learns that Sneyd, who had fallen ill during their trip, died on his return to London. Nephew Theodore begins working at legation.

1830   Irving's wide friendships in English society are helpful to McLane, who is negotiating a new Anglo-American trade agreement covering the West Indies. Moves to 8 Argyll Street. Learns on his birthday that the Royal Society of Literature voted to present him with a gold medal. Sees Louis Philippe crowned king of France on a visit to Paris in August. Visits Van Warts in Birmingham in October and sees much of Prince Dolgorouki, who is now attached to the Russian embassy in London. Sees John Randolph, who has resigned his post as American minister to Russia, during Randolph's stay in London. Invests $5,000 in New York iron works and loans money to nephew Pierre P. Irving, son of Ebenezer, to establish a brewery. *Voyages and Discoveries of the Companions of Columbus* published on December 30 by Murray in London (published in Philadelphia by Carey & Lea on March 7, 1831).

1831   Goes to Birmingham for a month, hoping to write, but is unproductive. Arranges for Murray to publish Alexander Slidell's *A Year in Spain*, revises and edits it, and reviews it in the *Quarterly Review*. Receives honorary doctorate of civil law from Oxford. McLane sails in June for the United States, where he assumes duties as secretary of the treasury in August. Irving is acting chargé d'affaires until Martin Van Buren, the new minister, arrives on September 13. Attends coronation of William IV on September 8. Resigns his position at legation in late

September to devote himself to writing. Dines on September 27 with Sir Walter Scott, who is on his way to Italy (their last meeting before Scott's death in 1832). Irving visits the Van Warts in Birmingham, his nephew Irving Van Wart in Sheffield, and the Reverend C. R. Reaston Rodes at Barlborough Hall in Derbyshire, from where he makes an excursion to Newstead Abbey, ancestral home of Lord Byron. Returns to London on November 1. Sends first part of *Mahomet* to Murray in October with the understanding that he will receive £525 for it and £1,050 for *The Alhambra*; Murray balks at price, citing losses sustained on earlier books and the uncertain literary market. Irving takes Van Buren and his son on a three-week excursion, visiting Oxford, Stratford-on-Avon, Kenilworth, and the Van Warts in Birmingham, arriving on Christmas Eve at Barlborough Hall, where they spend two weeks before going on to Newstead Abbey.

1832   Irving remains after the Van Burens return to London, "visiting the haunts of Lord Byron and Robin Hood," sleeping in Byron's bed at Newstead Abbey, and dining with Duke of Sussex, brother to the king. Commiserates with Van Buren when his appointment as minister is not confirmed by the Senate. Unable to persuade Murray to publish William Cullen Bryant's poetry, Irving convinces John Andrews to bring out an English edition, sees it through the press, and writes preface in the form of a dedicatory letter to Samuel Rogers (is later criticized for having changed a line in "The Song of Marion's Men" that Andrews felt might injure British pride). Spends a week in Le Havre with Peter, who is too ill to travel. Leaves on the *Havre* for America, April 11. On board meets Englishman Charles Joseph Latrobe and Swiss count Albert-Alexandre de Pourtalès, as well as John Schell, an 11-year-old German boy whom Irving employs as a servant. (In 1835 Schell and his father move to Quincy, Illinois, and receive a $100 loan from Irving, which Schell eventually turns into an estate worth $70,000.) *The Alhambra* published in England by Colburn and Bentley on May 4 (Irving and Murray are unable to come to terms) and in America by Carey, Lea and Blanchard on June 11. Arrives in New York, May 21, after a 17-year absence, to an enthusiastic reception. Enjoys official dinner in his

honor on May 30, but declines invitations to ceremonies
in Philadelphia, Baltimore, and other cities. Dines in
Washington with President Andrew Jackson and Van Buren, now the vice-presidential nominee on Jackson's ticket.
Visits Clay, Jackson's National Republican opponent in
the 1832 election. Encounters his friend Thomas Cooper
(who is now married to Mary Fairlie) by chance in a Philadelphia hotel in June, then visits the Cooper family at
their home in Bristol, Pennsylvania. Takes steamboat trip
up the Hudson with Latrobe and Pourtalès to visit Gouverneur Kemble at West Point and the Catskill Mountains.
Sees Gilbert Stuart Newton and his fiancée in Boston,
continues on to the White Mountains in New Hampshire
with Latrobe and Pourtalès, then goes by himself to Tarrytown, where he considers buying the property and cottage
adjacent to his nephew Oscar's home. Rejoins Latrobe
and Pourtalès at Saratoga Springs in early August; in September they accompany Commissioner of Indian Affairs
Henry Ellsworth on his trip west to superintend removal
of Indians. Sees defeated Sauk chief Black Hawk at Jefferson Barracks outside St. Louis. Travels west by land into
Indian Territory (now Oklahoma), living "almost Indian
style"; hunts buffalo and wolf, fords rivers, eats skunk,
and is exhilarated by the adventure. Makes arrangements
in November for the financial support of niece Helen
Dodge, orphaned by the death of her father on September
2. Parts with Latrobe and Pourtalès at Fort Gibson, Indian
Territory, on November 11 and travels by steamboat down
the Arkansas and Mississippi rivers to New Orleans,
where he spends several days. Travels by mail coach
through Mississippi, Alabama, Georgia, South Carolina
(where he dines with William C. Preston, with whom he
toured Wales and Scotland), North Carolina, and Virginia, reaching Washington in mid-December. Stays with
McLane and sees Gouverneur Kemble.

1833   Attends congressional debates on the tariff bill, states'
rights, and nullification, in which Daniel Webster, Clay, and
Calhoun speak (writes to Peter, "I became so deeply interested in the debates of Congress, that I almost lived in the
capitol"). Leaves Washington in early March and spends
three weeks in Baltimore, where he visits writer John Pendleton Kennedy, who becomes a close friend. Arrives in
New York in late March. Lives with Ebenezer at 3 Bridge

Street. Receives diploma for honorary doctor of laws degree conferred on him by Harvard University while he was traveling in 1832. Takes trip up the Hudson to the Catskills with Van Buren in September. Travels at Van Buren's suggestion to Washington to persuade McLane not to resign as secretary of state in protest against President Jackson's removal of public deposits from the national bank (McLane remains in cabinet until June 1834). Begins writing *A Tour on the Prairies* in October.

1834   John Jacob Astor suggests that Irving write a history of Astor's fur trade in Oregon and the northwest; Irving agrees and enlists nephew Pierre Munro Irving to help organize the materials. (Astor pays Pierre $3,000 for his work, to which Irving later adds $1,000, but Irving receives no money from Astor for the book.) Completes *A Tour on the Prairies* in November.

1835   *The Crayon Miscellany* published in three volumes by Murray in London and by Carey, Lea and Blanchard in Philadelphia: *A Tour on the Prairies* appears in England in March and in America in April; *Abbotsford and Newstead Abbey* in May; and *Legends of the Conquest of Spain* in October (America) and December (England). Irving receives £900 and $4,500 for the three works. Carey, Lea buys the American rights to all of Irving's previous works (except the abridgment of *Columbus*) for seven years at $1,150 a year. Irving buys a "neglected cottage" and ten acres along the Hudson two miles south of Tarrytown (the property he had looked at in 1832), and begins renovating cottage. Begins writing *Astoria*, history of fur trade, in May. Helps nephew John Treat Irving publish *Indian Sketches*. Moves into Hell Gate, Astor estate on upper east side of Manhattan, to work on *Astoria*. Meets western explorer Captain Benjamin Bonneville at Hell Gate and purchases his papers.

1836   Completes *Astoria* in February. Peter arrives from France in June; stays with Ebenezer until cottage is ready. Irving moves into it with Peter in September (household later includes Ebenezer, five nieces, and visiting relatives) and calls his new home "Wolfert's Roost," after the original owner, Wolfert Acker. Grows especially fond of Sarah Paris, 23-year-old daughter of sister Catharine. Niece

Helen marries her cousin Pierre Munro Irving, whose first wife died in October 1832. *Astoria* published on October 28 by Carey, Lea & Blanchard in Philadelphia; Irving receives $4,000 for 5,000-copy printing, and £500 for later English edition. Engages in several western land speculations that fail to yield prompt returns he hopes for. Begins work on account of Bonneville's travels, based on his journals.

1837   Judge Hoffman dies January 24. Irving enjoys family life at Tarrytown cottage. Visited in the spring by Charles Louis Napoleon Bonaparte (later Napoleon III). *Adventures of Captain Bonneville, U.S.A.* published in London by Bentley in May and by Carey, Lea, and Blanchard in June as *The Rocky Mountains: Or, Scenes, Incidents and Adventures in the Far West; Digested from the Journal of Captain B.L.E. Bonneville, of the Army of the United States, and Illustrated from Various Other Sources*; Irving receives £900 and $3,000.

1838   Tells Kemble (now a congressman) in January that his growing political differences with Van Buren (now president) have not affected his personal regard for Van Buren. Declines Tammany Hall nomination for mayor of New York and Van Buren's offer to appoint him secretary of the navy. Judge John Treat Irving dies in March and Peter, Irving's closest brother, in June. Worries about lack of funds to support his household, because too much of his money is invested in unprofitable western lands. Begins work in the fall on a history of the conquest of Mexico, but abandons it with regret when he hears from scholar Joseph G. Cogswell that William Prescott is working on the same project.

1839   Writes letters that help get nephew Pierre Munro Irving job as notary at the New York Bank of Commerce. Becomes regular contributor to *Knickerbocker* at $2,000 a year (30 of his essays, tales, and sketches appear between March 1839 and October 1841). Attends wedding of nephew Irving Van Wart and Sarah Ames in New York. Praises Edgar Allan Poe's story "William Wilson" in a letter to Poe in November.

1840   Writes letter to editor of *Knickerbocker* in support of international copyright law. Concerned that Ebenezer's business is failing, writes to Van Buren, Kemble, and other politically influential people in attempt to have Ebenezer appointed to new subtreasury in New York. Angry over Van Buren's lack of response, Irving supports Whig slate of William Henry Harrison and John Tyler in the presidential election. Edits *Life and Works of Oliver Goldsmith* in two volumes for Harper & Brothers School District Library, reworking his three previous introductions to Goldsmith's works into a new biographical essay.

1841   Writes life of the young poet Margaret Miller Davidson (1823–38), using memoranda supplied by her mother. (*Biography and Poetical Remains of the Late Margaret Miller Davidson* published by Lea and Blanchard in June, with the profits going to the Davidson family.) Sarah, Irving's favorite niece, marries Thomas Storrow, Jr., (the son of his friend in Paris) on March 31 and leaves for Paris on May 1. Responds warmly to Charles Dickens after receiving an admiring letter from him. Takes trip through the Highlands of the Hudson in July and August to visit Brevoort and Gouverneur Kemble, whose sister Gertrude (James K. Paulding's wife) had recently died. Ebenezer, unemployed, lives at the Tarrytown cottage (which Irving now calls "Sunnyside"). Irving gathers materials and begins work on a life of George Washington.

1842   Appointed minister to Spain by President John Tyler, at the recommendation of Secretary of State Daniel Webster, with salary of $9,000. Spends time with Dickens when he visits America, but "breaks down" when he tries to give a speech at dinner in Dickens' honor on February 18. Arranges appointment of Joseph G. Cogswell, who has been advising John Jacob Astor on a proposed public library, as secretary of the legation. However, Cogswell remains in New York when Astor commits himself to the library project; Alexander Hamilton, Jr., a neighbor at Sunnyside and the grandson of Alexander Hamilton, replaces Cogswell. Irving offers Lea & Blanchard the rights to revised edition of his collected works, including works never before published, for $3,000 a year (they reject his offer, citing the depressed market for literature, as well as Irving's second offer to extend the present contract for two years). Submits petition to Congress in support of international copyright law. Travels to Washington in March to discuss position at legation. Dines with William Preston, now a U.S. senator from South Carolina. Makes provisions for Sunnyside and his nieces there and collects materials for his life of Washington before leaving on April 10 for England. Presented to Queen Victoria by American minister Edward Everett on May 4. Sees old friends Rogers, Leslie, Moore, and Murray, and attends dinner of the Literary Fund with Prince Albert presiding on May 11. Visits Beasley in Le Havre. Arrives in Paris on May 24, visits niece Sarah, and is presented by American minister Lewis Cass to King Louis Philippe at his palace at Neuilly, outside of Paris. Dines with Baron James de Rothschild. Visits Guestiers in Bordeaux before arriving in Madrid on July 25, accompanied by Hamilton and his assistants Hector Ames (brother-in-law of nephew Irving Van Wart) and Carson Brevoort (son of Henry Brevoort). Takes over his predecessor Aaron Vail's lodgings at 112 Calle de Alcalá, Plazuela de la Villa. Visited by the Duke de Gor, a friend from previous trip to Granada. Meets the Brazilian minister, José Francisco de Paula Cavalcanti de Albuquerque, and his wife (formerly Miss Oakey of New York), who become close friends. Finds himself well-known and well-received ("all welcome me as a 'friend of Spain' "). Spain is in political turmoil, with many factions seeking control of the regency of 12-year-old Isabella II, daughter of the exiled former consort María Christina; Irving maneuvers skillfully among the contenders. Writes dispatches to Webster (the first of five secretaries of state he will serve under in the next four years) describing the political situation in which ministers are "transient functionaries." Moves into Calle Victor Hugo in mid-September to be nearer the public promenades and theaters. Works on Spanish-American trade relations.

1843   Falls ill with herpetic inflammation in legs (similar to 1822 attack) that spreads over his entire body, accompanied by intermittent fever, and is forbidden to write by his physician. Carson Brevoort leaves legation in April to tour Europe before returning to America, and Hector Ames leaves for the United States in June. Several insurrections break out in June against the regency of General Baldomero Fernández Espartero and Madrid is briefly besieged by rebel forces in July. Irving hears sound of skirmishing outside city gates, and recommends that the diplomatic corps go to the palace to protect Isabella II in case Madrid is stormed (offer is rejected by the Spanish). Espartero is defeated by General Ramón María Narváez and goes into exile. Feeling sick and lonely, Irving places Hamilton in charge of the legation and leaves Madrid on September 7 to visit Sarah in France. Sees friends in Bordeaux en route, arriving in Versailles, where the Storrows are staying, on September 15. In Paris encounters Samuel Rogers by chance. Despite incomplete recovery, returns to Madrid to follow continuing political turmoil; arrives on November 30, shortly after Isabella II is declared of age and crowned. Becomes friend of Irish banker Henry O'Shea and his wife, Sabina.

1844   Feels somewhat better and takes greater part in social life. María Christina returns from exile in March. Marriage plans for Isabella II become main topic of debate among the various factions; Irving continues to closely follow fate of "the little Queen." Begins revising his works for new edition. Learns that nephew Pierre Munro Irving, who holds Irving's power of attorney in America, has received some money for him from his previously unproductive land investments in Green Bay, Wisconsin. Hamilton resigns post and leaves Spain on May 14; Jasper Livingston (son of Brockholst Livingston) replaces him as first secretary. Irving leaves Madrid on June 25 for Barcelona, where the court has gone for the summer, to deliver two official letters from President Tyler to Isabella II. Granted leave for reasons of health. Takes Spanish steamer to Marseilles on July 29, travels up the Rhone to Lyons, then continues by coach to Paris. Sees Sarah at Versailles for a week, then visits Beasley for a few days at Le Havre before leaving on August 21 for Birmingham. Spends three weeks with the Van Warts (sister Sarah is partially paralyzed from a stroke suffered the previous year) before returning to Paris to take baths. Visits King Louis Philippe at St. Cloud in October with William King, American minister at Paris. Returns to Madrid on November 17.

1845   Resumes writing. Reports to Secretary of State John C. Calhoun on debate in the Spanish parliament over new penal law against the slave trade (legislation is result of

British pressure; Calhoun suspects that Britain's anti-slavery efforts mask intention to seize Cuba). Irving tries to further American trade interests in Cuba. Remains in Madrid when the royal family travels in May to Barcelona for the summer. Begins discussions with publisher George Putnam about planned revised edition. Albuquerques return from Barcelona, and having no place to stay in Madrid, move in with him. Still troubled by herpetic malady, takes leave in September. Travels through Bordeaux, Nantes, and Orléans, on his way to visit Sarah in Paris. McLane, who is again serving as minister to Britain, requests Irving's help in November as Anglo-American dispute over the Oregon border intensifies. Irving writes letter of resignation as minister to Spain on December 12.

1846 Goes to London to help McLane with Oregon negotiations (treaty setting border along the 49th parallel is signed in May and ratified in June). Breakfasts with John Murray III (who inherited his father's firm in 1843) and Gansevoort Melville, secretary of the American legation in London; Melville reads from the manuscript of his brother Herman's forthcoming book *Typee*, which Irving praises. Visits Van Warts in Birmingham for ten days in late January. Goes to Paris in February to see Sarah, who is planning a trip to America, then returns to Madrid on March 6 to await the arrival of Romulus M. Saunders, his replacement. Has special audience with the queen and her mother on March 14. Explains American position in Mexican War to Spanish government. To the regret of Spanish court and government, leaves Spain permanently early in August. Visits Paris, Birmingham, and London, before sailing in early September on a steamer to Boston. Arrives on September 18 and goes the following day to Sunnyside. Begins work on repairs and improvements to his property, adding a tower to his "snuggery" to accommodate guests and family. Lives with nieces and brother Ebenezer.

1847 Inflammation of eyes and recurrence of inflammation in ankles slow work on revised edition. Revises several unpublished works on Spanish themes (published posthumously in *Spanish Papers* in 1866). Resumes work on life of Washington in September. Moves to New York in mid-December, staying with various relatives.

1848   Spends most of the year in New York, visiting Astor and
        other friends, attending opera and theater, and working
        on *Washington* and the revised edition of his works. Re-
        ceives $3,500 from company that plans to build railroad
        along Hudson River through his property (later com-
        plains of noise). Acts as pallbearer for John Jacob Astor,
        who died March 29, and is made one of six executors of
        his will (eventually receives $10,592 for this role) and pres-
        ident of the trustees of the Astor Library (which later be-
        comes part of the New York Public Library). Henry
        Brevoort dies May 17. Irving signs with Putnam on July 26
        for complete edition of his works (15 volumes appear over
        the next two years; Irving receives 12 1/2 percent of the
        retail price of all copies sold, and earns over $88,000 from
        Putnam by the time of his death).

1849   Visits former Irving family home at 128 William Street
        with nephew Pierre Munro Irving before it is torn down.
        *A Book of the Hudson. Collected from the Various Works of
        Diedrich Knickerbocker* published in April. Returns to Sun-
        nyside in summer, making regular trips to New York for
        meetings of the executors of Astor's estate and the trustees
        of the Astor Library, and to work on the revised edition.
        Visits niece Sarah Storrow and her family, who are living
        in New York (until summer 1850). First volume of *Maho-
        met and His Successors* published on December 15. Sister
        Catharine dies on December 23.

1850   Second volume of *Mahomet and His Successors* published
        on April 15. Supports John Murray III in struggle over the
        British copyrights for his writings. Meets Henry James,
        Sr., and his seven-year-old son Henry, Jr., on steamboat
        to Long Island in August and tells them that Margaret
        Fuller has drowned in a shipwreck off Fire Island. Visits
        Gouverneur Kemble at West Point and James K. Paulding
        in Cold Spring in September.

1851   Works on *Washington*, using 25 years of notes and Jared
        Sparks's earlier 12-volume edition of Washington's writ-
        ings. Writer Donald G. Mitchell (Ik Marvel) visits Sunny-
        side. Writes public letter in November correcting
        "erroneous statement" by explorer and historian of Amer-
        ican Indians Henry Schoolcraft that Irving had received
        $5,000 from Astor for writing *Astoria*.

1852   Writes to Nathaniel Hawthorne in January, praising his work. Continues to see returns from his western land investments. Irving is chairman of memorial committee formed in honor of James Fenimore Cooper (who died September 14, 1851) and makes short remarks at public meeting held in New York on February 25, with Daniel Webster presiding and William Cullen Bryant delivering the main eulogy. Thomas Storrow, Sr., Irving's friend from Paris and niece Sarah's father-in-law, visits Sunnyside in May. Travels to Saratoga Springs and Lake George in July and August; is surprised to meet Gouverneur Kemble, John Pendleton Kennedy, and other friends at Saratoga Springs. English writer William Makepeace Thackeray visits Sunnyside in November, accompanied by *Knickerbocker* contributor Frederick Cozzens.

1853   Irving is amazed by news of marriage of Eugenia de Montijo, whom he knew in Spain, and Napoleon III, who visited him at Tarrytown in 1837. Encounters Thackeray by chance at the ferry in New York and rides with him as far as Philadelphia, where Thackeray is delivering a series of lectures. Irving goes on to Baltimore, where he visits Edward Gray, John Pendleton Kennedy's father-in-law, with whom he becomes friends. Continues to Washington to stay with Kennedy, now secretary of the navy. Develops friendship with President and Mrs. Millard Fillmore. Does research on Washington in archives and visits Mount Vernon in January and February. Attends inauguration of President Franklin Pierce on March 4 and speaks with him afterwards; is favorably impressed when Pierce tells him that he is giving Hawthorne a consular post. Returns to Sunnyside in early March. Has Pierre Munro Irving read his *Washington* manuscript and is reassured when his nephew praises it. Visits the Kennedys and Edward Gray in Ellicotts Mills, Gray's home near Baltimore, in June. Travels with Kennedy through western Virginia, visiting Cassilis (estate near Harpers Ferry owned by Kennedy's brother Andrew), examining Washington manuscripts and sites, and taking the baths at Berkeley Springs. Returns to Sunnyside on July 12, then leaves on August 1 for Saratoga Springs, where he rejoins the Kennedys and Edward Gray. Goes with Kennedy by boat up Lake Champlain to Plattsburg and then by train to Ogdensburg, where he visits the old French fort he stayed at on his 1803 trip with the Hoffman and Ogden families. Continues by steamer to Lake Ontario and Lewiston, then by carriage to Niagara Falls. Visits niece Charlotte at Ingleside. After difficult trip in hot weather, returns to Sunnyside August 17, very ill with fever, chills, and delirium. Kennedys and Grays visit Sunnyside. Irving prepares family plot in cemetery of Sleepy Hollow Church and has his parents' remains moved there. Leaves on September 29 for another visit to the Kennedys at Ellicotts Mills and Andrew Kennedy at Cassilis. Travels with Andrew and John P. Kennedy to Greenway Court, the residence of Lord Fairfax, a colonial patron of Washington's. Goes to New York on October 26 for meeting of trustees of Astor Library, then returns to Sunnyside.

1854   Sick with fever in April; continued poor health often prevents him from writing. Dearman, the village and railroad station adjacent to Sunnyside, changes its name to Irvington in April. Visits Gouverneur Kemble in late May. Nephew William Irving, son of Ebenezer, dies of overdose of morphine on July 28. Writes reminiscence of Washington Allston for Evert Duyckinck's *Cyclopedia of American Literature* (published 1855). Visits the Kennedys in Virginia in August.

1855   Attends wedding of Mary Kennedy, daughter of Andrew, to Henry Pendleton Cooke, at Cassilis on January 1. Hears nephew Theodore Irving deliver sermon at nephew Pierre P. Irving's Episcopal church on Staten Island. Attends wedding on February 1 of grandniece Henrietta Eckford Irving, granddaughter of John Treat Irving, to Smith Thompson Van Buren, son of the former president. *Wolfert's Roost*, a miscellany from the *Knickerbocker* which Irving calls "garret trumpery," published in February by Putnam and is well-received by readers. Irving is badly bruised and in bed for a few days in April after being thrown from horse "Gentleman Dick." First volume of *Life of George Washington* published by Putnam in May. Visits Martin Van Buren in early September at his Kinderhook home (where Irving wrote part of *A History of New York*, when it belonged to the Van Ness family). Second volume of *Washington* published by Putnam in December. Hires Pierre Munro Irving as his literary assistant (formally authorizes salary of $135 a month in February 1856).

1856   With Pierre's help, continues work on *Washington*. Often ill, Irving seldom leaves Sunnyside, where he receives stream of admiring visitors. Exchanges letters with Emily Fuller (née Foster). Third volume of *Washington* published in July. Nephew Pierre Paris Irving visits the birthplace of Irving's father in the Orkneys and returns with a genealogical table of Irving family.

1857   Fourth volume of *Washington* published in May. Now comfortable financially, negotiates new contract and buys plates for entire edition from Putnam, who needs cash due to national economic depression.

1858   Health deteriorates. Works intermittently on last volume of *Washington*. Visits New York on September 1 to take part in celebrations of the laying of the Atlantic telegraph cable. Pierre Munro Irving and his wife, Helen, move to Sunnyside in December (will stay with Irving for the rest of his life). Writer Oliver Wendell Holmes, Sr., visits Sunnyside on December 20, accompanied by Frederick Cozzens.

1859   Pierre often reads aloud to him, to calm his nerves. Alexander Slidell's *A Year in Spain* is among his favorites. Finishes fifth and final volume of *Washington* March 15. Pierre does final revisions and sees it through the press, and it is published by Putnam in April. Visits New York with brother Ebenezer in May. Declines, for reasons of health, Kennedy's invitation to take a trip to St. Louis. Gouverneur Kemble visits Sunnyside on June 2 (their last meeting) and Evert Duyckinck visits on June 11. Offers to pay passage to America for niece Sarah and family (is disappointed that they will not come). Visits Barrett Ames (father of Hector Ames and Sarah Van Wart) in Orange, New Jersey, in early September, hoping that change will help his health. Visited by John P. Kennedy and writer Nathaniel P. Willis on October 30. Dies of heart attack at Sunnyside at 10:30 P.M. on November 28, surrounded by his family, and is buried at Sleepy Hollow Cemetery on December 1.

Note on the Texts

The texts of *Bracebridge Hall, Tales of a Traveller*, and *The Alhambra* presented in this volume are those established for the Twayne edition of *The Complete Works of Washington Irving* under the general editorship of Richard Dilworth Rust, and published in Boston by The Twayne Publishers: *Bracebridge Hall* in 1977, *Tales of a Traveller* in 1987, and *The Alhambra* in 1983. These texts were prepared according to the standards established by—and they have received the official approval of—the Center for Editions of American Authors of the Modern Language Association of America. (See its *Statement of Editorial Principles and Procedures*, revised edition, 1972.)

The three works included in this volume were written during the time Irving lived in Europe, and were published on both sides of the Atlantic. At that time, though the copyright laws were not clear and there was no agreement between the United States and Great Britain, it was possible for an American author living in Europe to secure copyright in both countries if the work was published and copyrighted in Great Britain before it was published in America and if the work was published in America almost simultaneously with the English edition. However, if the work was published in England, and the printed book was shipped to America before American copyright was obtained, any American publisher had the right to publish it without paying the author. The same understanding held for books published in America and then shipped to England before copyright had been secured there. Therefore, Irving had to send his manuscript to America for publication before he had finished making his final corrections in the work, and once he had sent his manuscript off, he had to make sure there was no delay in the publication date in England.

Partial manuscript exists for each of the works included here, and because Irving was a popular writer, all three works went through many printings and editions during his lifetime. Therefore, the amount of collation needed to establish Irving's texts was considerable.

Washington Irving began work on *Bracebridge Hall* during

his stay in Paris from August 1820 until July 1821. Apparently he began intensive work on it sometime in May, and on July 6, 1821, he wrote his publisher, John Murray II, that he had "a mass of writings" but that the constant interruptions caused by social engagements made concentrated writing difficult. He continued to work on the manuscript after his return to England in July 1821, but it was not until January 1822 that he prepared a fair copy to send to his brother Ebenezer for publication in America. The copy was sent in two installments: Volume I on January 29, and Volume II on February 25, 1822. (Although the installments were sent nearly a month apart, the second one arrived only eight days after the first, near the beginning of April 1822.) In his letter to his brother, sent with Volume I, giving him instructions about publishing the book, Irving told Ebenezer that it was very important to "put the first volume to press immediately," to give him "some chance of securing copyright." Irving went on to say that because time was so important, the first edition could be small in number and that another one could be based on the corrected proof sheets he was preparing for Murray. "There will doubtless be many alterations," Irving wrote, because he had not "had time to revise some parts of the work sufficiently" and was "apt to make alterations to the last moment." After sending the fair copy manuscripts to America, Irving continued to correct and revise his work, both in his working manuscript and on the proofs. Many sections were completely rewritten, four new sections were added, and the order of essays in the first volume was changed. *Bracebridge Hall* was published by Van Winkle in America on May 21, 1822, and by John Murray in England on May 23, 1822.

Herbert F. Smith, the editor for the Twayne edition of *Bracebridge Hall*, based his text on the first English edition of the work, because Irving made so many revisions in the proofs for that edition (these proofs are not known to be extant), and made no other revisions in the text until he prepared it for the Author's Revised Edition, published by George P. Putnam in 1849. In cases where Smith judged that Irving's intention was not carried out, he inserted emendations in the text, based on the English and American manuscripts and on the first American edition; one paragraph was added that appeared only in the later printings of the first English edition. Emendations were also made on the authority of the Author's Revised Edition in 1849, but not all of the revisions in that edition were accepted. According to Smith, these revisions can be divided into two categories: the first consists of corrections and includes the elimination not only of obvious typographical errors but also of unnecessary repetition; the second Smith defines as modernization, where changes are made in spelling and diction to accord better with later usage. Smith accepted only the first category and incorporated these revisions into the text. The Twayne edition text of *Bracebridge Hall* is printed in this volume.

Though Irving had written Murray from Paris just before Christmas 1823 that he would have two volumes ready for him by spring, he had not yet determined what they would include. By mid-February the book began to take shape, and on March 25, 1824, when he again wrote Murray, Irving had decided on the title *Tales of a Traveller*. He continued working in Paris until May 24, when he felt that the manuscript was almost ready for publication. He returned to England, made his arrangements with Murray (he was to be paid 1,500 guineas for the copyright), and gave his manuscript out to be copied. He made revisions and corrections in the copies, and by June 22, 1824, he had sent the last of four installments of copy to America. Concerned in early July that he had not yet received any proofs, he returned from the country, where he had been revising copy, and learned that Murray meant to delay the publication until November. Irving told him that copy had already been sent to America, and Murray agreed to publish the book in August instead. On July 5 Irving received his first proof sheets, and he mailed duplicate sheets to Ebenezer on July 8 to be used for a second American edition. Problems, however, developed. In late July, Murray told him there was not enough copy to make up the two volumes; Irving added a preface and four stories and revised and expanded others. A week before he was to leave England he received a letter from Murray telling him that William Gifford, Murray's friend and adviser, found some parts of Irving's treatment of Englishmen, college towns, and cathedral towns offensive. Irving reluctantly agreed to make changes in his text. The first

American edition was published by H. C. Carey & I. Lea of Philadelphia in four parts: on August 24, September 7, September 25, and October 9, 1824. The first English edition was published by Murray on August 25, 1824. Irving made a few revisions in the second English edition and many more in the Author's Revised Edition, published by George P. Putnam in 1849.

Judith Giblin Haig, the editor (with the cooperation of Brom Weber and David S. Wilson) of the Twayne edition of *Tales of a Traveller*, used the manuscript, of which about a third of the original is extant, as her basic text, and where the manuscript was missing she used the first American edition, since that version most closely reproduces the texture of Irving's manuscript; both of these were supplemented by the first English edition in those parts that were revised later. The last revisions made because of Gifford's censure were not considered authorial; the Twayne text of these sections is that of the manuscript and first American edition and retains Irving's original intentions. Emendations were made in the text only when they were clearly authorial; they were taken primarily from the first English edition when Irving made revisions in the proofs and from the Author's Revised Edition when the revisions were typical of the kind Irving made throughout his life. Every effort was made to retain Irving's own spelling, rhetorical punctuation, and diction. The text of the Twayne edition of *Tales of a Traveller* is printed here.

Irving had thought of a book called *The Alhambra* even before he had spent three months living in the Moorish palace. In a journal entry of January 10, 1829, he noted: "Write a little at tales of the Alhambra." During his stay in the palace he had taken down notes of the history, stories, and legends of the place from every source he encountered, written and oral. On October 18, 1830, during the time he spent in England as First Secretary of the American Legation, he wrote his brother Peter that he had finished three of the Alhambra tales. His official duties occupied much of his time, and he was also preparing *Voyages of the Companions of Columbus* for the press, which he finished in December 1830. It was not until he had resigned his diplomatic position in late September 1831 that he turned his full attention to writing *The*

Alhambra. On March 1, 1832, he sent the first volume to his brother Ebenezer for publication in America. Meanwhile the English publishing world was suffering a depression. When Murray, his English publisher, could not give him the price he asked, the work was sold to Colburn and Bentley for 1,000 guineas. Irving by now was eager to return to America after an absence of seventeen years and did not wait to read proofs. The first English edition was published on May 4, 1832, and the first American edition was published by Carey and Lea in Philadelphia on June 9, 1832. As usual, in the first American edition set from early manuscripts the contents were out of order and a few of the linking passages were misplaced. Irving revised the work for the second American edition, published by Carey, Lea and Blanchard in Philadelphia, in 1836. But it was not until he prepared the work for the Author's Revised Edition, published by George P. Putnam in 1851, that he actually changed its form. For this edition, Irving wrote new sections and rearranged and restructured old sections, creating a version that was more than a third larger than the original.

William T. Lenehan and Andrew B. Myers, the editors of the Twayne edition of *The Alhambra*, chose the Author's Revised Edition as their text. At points where they considered the Author's Revised Edition faulty, they emended it on the basis of the earlier versions. The text printed here is that of the Twayne edition.

This volume presents the texts of the original printings chosen for inclusion here but does not attempt to reproduce features of their typographic design, such as the display capitalization of chapter openings. The texts are printed without change, except for the correction of typographical errors. Spelling, punctuation, and capitalization are often expressive features, and they are not altered, even when inconsistent or irregular. The following is a list of typographical errors corrected, cited by page and line number: 15.6, Hall; 51.6, *Evan's*; 80.7, exquisiite; 81.18, Tibbetts; 155.5, feliciy; 160.19, inquistion; 252.31, enlivend; 265.30, transients; 272.14, longbodied; 275.12, predeliction; 280.2, supersitions; 289.32, housekeper; 299.13, afterthoughts; 310.31–32, houskeeper; 335.14, is; 343.19, point; 396.16, lanthern; 474.16, roar.; 513.2, scrape; 586.37, siezed; 734.18, bells; 742.15, by; 744.34, trip; 756.31, openeth.; 785.14, consernation; 786.1, *Hagig:*; 810.2, dark; 811.32, firmament,; 830.38, *Hist*; 839.14, gratis."; 839.15, "But; 853.26, moontide; 896.20, born; 938.38, thy; 960.15, are; 975.12, You; 988.37, manager; 1010.25, as; 1015.2, slain?" 1031.31, Condi; 1034.20, Chico.; 1039.12, castanets; 1048.35, Antonio.

Notes

In the notes that follow, the reference numbers denote page and line of this volume (the line count includes chapter headings). No note is made for material found in standard desk-reference books such as *Webster's Collegiate Dictionary* or *Webster's Biographical Dictionary*. Quotations from Shakespeare have been keyed to *The Riverside Shakespeare*, ed. G. Blakemore Evans (Boston: Houghton Mifflin, 1974). Notes at the foot of the page in the text are Irving's own. For more detailed notes, references to other studies, and further biographical background, see the following volumes in *The Complete Works of Washington Irving* (Boston: Twayne Publishers): *Bracebridge Hall*, ed. Herbert F. Smith (1977); *Tales of a Traveller*, ed. Judith Giblin Haig (1987); *The Alhambra*, ed. William T. Lenehan and Andrew B. Myers (1983); *Journals and Notebooks, 1803–1859*, 5 vols., ed. Nathalia Wright, Lillian Schlissel, Walter A. Reichart, Wayne R. Kime, Andrew B. Myers, Sue Fields Ross, et. al. (1969–84); *Letters, 1802–1859*, 4 vols., ed. Ralph M. Aderman, Herbert L. Kleinfield, Jenifer S. Banks, et. al. (1978–84). See also *Washington Irving and the House of Murray: Geoffrey Crayon Charms the British, 1817–1856*, ed. Ben Harris McClary (Knoxville: University of Tennessee Press, 1969); Pierre Munro Irving, *The Life and Letters of Washington Irving*, 4 vols. (New York: G. P. Putnam, 1862–64); Stanley T. Williams, *The Life of Washington Irving*, 2 vols. (New York: Oxford University Press, 1935).

BRACEBRIDGE HALL

1.6–10   Under . . . ORDINARY]   *The Christmas Ordinary*, A Private Show (1682), scene 7, by W. R., Master of Arts.

8.37–40   Tintern . . . Castle]   Tintern Abbey in southern Wales, near the English border, was founded in 1131 as a Cistertian abbey and then rebuilt in 1220–87. The fortress castle in Conway (now Conwy), northwest Wales, was built c. 1284 by Edward I.

10.7–8   St. John's . . . Magazine]   An engraving of the gate of St. John's Priory in the City of London served as the frontispiece of *The Gentleman's Magazine*, founded in 1731 by Edward Cave under the pseudonym Sylvanus Urban.

10.22   Monument . . . Magog]   The monument to the Great Fire of 1666, a 202-foot Doric column erected in 1671–77 in the City of London. Gogmagog was one of a tribe of giants who occupied Britain before the coming of Brut, great-grandson of Aeneas, according to Geoffrey of

Monmouth's 12th-century *Historia Regum Britanniae*. The name was divided in the 15th century between two figures carried in the Lord Mayor of London's procession. In 1708 14-foot wooden effigies of Gog and Magog were erected in the Guild Hall; they were destroyed in a German air raid in 1940.

10.27　　Mr. Newberry's shop] John Newbery (1713–67), the bookseller, writer, and publisher, especially of children's books, was the original proprietor of the shop in St Paul's Churchyard.

13.2–5　　The ancientest . . . *Beggars*] Richard Brome (c. 1590–1652), *A Joviall Crew or the Merry Beggars* (1641), a romantic comedy, act IV, scene i.

15.22　　*Mirror for Magistrates.*] An admonitory collection of verse accounts of the downfall of famous men and women. First issued in 1555 and immediately suppressed, it next appeared in 1559, and was published in at least seven variously enlarged editions by 1609.

16.2–6　　A decayed . . . *Crew*] See note 13.2–5.

17.1　　Newgate Calendar] The first *Newgate Calendar*, named for the famous London prison, is a record of notorious crimes from 1700, published in five volumes c. 1774. Similar compilations continued to appear through 1826.

18.20–21　　*casting . . . rangle*] Casting is anything given to a hawk to purge its gorge; imping is the repairing of its wing with supplemental feathers; gleaming is the cleansing of the gorge, i.e., vomiting of filth, after casting; enseaming is the process of causing it to lose excess fat; and rangle is gravel or small stones given to improve its digestion.

22.19　　Pamela] *Pamela, or Virtue Rewarded* (1740–41) by Samuel Richardson.

26.1–5　　"As . . . loyalty!"] By Shakespeare; II.iii.69–70.

27.2–9　　She . . . *Chaucer*] Cf. *Canterbury Tales* (c. 1400), General Prologue, lines 143–49, describing the Prioress.

28.32–33　　Sir Charles Grandison] Hero of the novel of the same name (1754) by Samuel Richardson.

29.22–23　　Castle of Otranto] A Gothic romance (1765) by Horace Walpole.

31.2–6　　Rise . . . *Solomon*] 2:10–12.

34.2–13　　My . . . *Dekker*] Thomas Dekker and Thomas Middleton, *The Honest Whore* (1604), Part I: V.i.34–37, 41–47.

35.2　　Nimrod] Genesis 10:9: "Nimrod, the mighty hunter before the Lord."

35.15　　Rippon spurs] Spurs made in Ripon, Yorkshire, which was famous at the time for their manufacture.

39.2–5　　I've worn . . . *Ordinary*] William Cartwright (1611–43), *The Ordinary* (1635?), I.iv.372–76.

39.37   Seringapatam]   The former capital of Mysore in southern India, captured by the British in 1799 during the Fourth Mysore War.

41.5–8   Why, . . . die!]   From a song that became known as "How Stands the Glass Around."

41.13   Tippoo Saib]   Tippu (1749?–99), Sultan of Mysore, was killed defending Seringapatam during the fourth Mysore War.

43.2–3   Little . . . Lear]   Shakespeare, *King Lear*, III.vi.62.

46.10   *Book of Hunting*]   The treatise on hunting attributed to Dam Julyans Barnes first appeared in the *Boke of St. Albans* (1486), along with treatises on "haulking" and "fyshing." The first two were reprinted in *The Gentleman's Academie* (1595) by Gervase Markham.

47.21   Pinner of Wakefield]   The pinner, i.e., pound-keeper, in *George-a-Greene, the Pinner of Wakefield* (c. 1595), a play attributed to Robert Greene.

50.16   Tusser's . . . Husbandrie,"]   *Hundreth good pointes of husbandrie* (augmented edition, 1573) by Thomas Tusser.

51.2–6   The Bachelor . . . *Ballads*]   Thomas Evans, *Old Ballads, Historical and Narrative, with Some of Modern Date*, (4 vols., 1784) Volume 3, ballad XXVIII, "The batchellor's plea against matrimony."

54.2–8   Believe . . . *Sidney*]   Sir Philip Sidney, *The Arcadia* (1593), third eclogue.

54.33–34   old play . . . Night-cap;"]   Robert Davenport, *The City-Night-Cap; or Crede quod habes, et habes* (1624).

54.37   Griselda]   The character in Boccaccio's *Decameron* (1349–51), "Day 10, Tale 10," later appeared in Latin, French, Italian, and English works including Chaucer's *Canterbury Tales* (1387?), "The Clerk's Tale," and *Patient Grissil* (1603) by Thomas Dekker, Henry Chettle, and William Haughton. The name came to refer to a patient sufferer.

58.31–37   "She . . . dies."]   Cf. Sermon XVIII, "The Marriage Ring; or the Mysteriousness and Duties of Marriage, Part II," in *XXV Sermons* (1653) by Jeremy Taylor.

59.6–14   "There . . . her."]   From Sermon XVII, "The Marriage Ring . . . , Part I."

60.17–19   Wandering . . . Lady]   In European tales dating from the 16th century, a Jew who taunted Jesus to carry the cross to Calvary faster is condemned to wander the world until the second coming of Christ. The Man in the Iron Mask, a prisoner in the reign of Louis XIV, whose face was concealed by an iron and velvet mask, was sometimes thought to be the twin brother of Louis XIV. The Pigfaced Lady, dating from about the 17th century, was often portrayed as a woman of rank with the face of a pig for whom a husband was being sought.

61.3–4   "I'll . . . *Hamlet*]   Shakespeare; I.i.127.

62.13   upper Benjamin]   An overcoat.

65.5   slammerkin]   Slattern.

65.20   Hunt]   Henry Hunt (1773–1835), a radical orator and campaigner for parliamentary reform and universal male suffrage.

67.6–7   Belcher handkerchiefs]   Multicolored neckerchiefs named for the boxer Jim Belcher.

67.8   sworn at Highgate]   A popular custom at pubs in Highgate, a village north of London, was to have travelers swear mock oaths on a ram's or stag's horn attached to a five-foot pole. These were oaths of self-indulgence such as "I shall not drink small beer while I can get strong."

71.2   "A living . . . trees."]   John Evelyn, *Silva: or, A Discourse of Forest-Trees* (1664), Book IV, fifth edition: "Dendrologia, An Historical Account of the Sacredness and Use of Standing Groves."

76.6   *Micro-Cosmographie*, 1628]   *Micro-cosmographie, or, a Peece of the World Discovered; in Essayes and Characters* by John Earle (c. 1601–65).

77.4   Perigord . . . *Strasbourg.*]   A truffled partridge pie and a goose-liver paté.

79.15–16   Captain . . . Moore's]   Probably the American captain Charles Morris (1739–1832), a favorite in fashionable society, writer of bacchanalian songs; George Alexander Stevens (1710–1784); and Thomas Moore (1779–1852). Moore, a close friend of Irving's, had translated *Odes of Anacreon* in 1800.

81.2–4   "Love . . . *Fletcher*]   *Monsieur Thomas* (1619), V.ii.54–55. The play is now thought to have been written solely by John Fletcher, who had collaborated with Francis Beaumont from about 1605 to 1613.

85.2–7   A coach . . . *Poet*]   *All the Works of John Taylor the Water Poet Being Sixty-and-Three in Number. Collected into One Volume by the Author; with Sundry New Additions, corrected, revised and newly imprinted* (1630), "The World runnes on Wheeles," by the Thames waterman John Taylor.

86.20   Nashe . . . Quaternio]   Thomas Nashe, *Quaternio; or a Fourefold Way to Happie Life, set forth in a Dialogue betweene a Countryman and a Citizen, a Divine and a Lawyer* (1663).

89.2–4   I will . . . *Marston*] John Marston, *The Parasitaster; or The Fawne* (1606), act IV.

90.39   *Morte d'Arthur.] Cycle of Arthurian legends (1483) by Sir Thomas Malory.

92.2–6   Ne . . . *Spenser*] Edmund Spenser, *The Fairie Queene*, Book VI, canto ii, 32.1–4.

92.30   Braithwate] Poet and satirist Richard Brathwait (1588–1673), author of *The English Gentleman* (1630) and *The English Gentlewoman* (1631), books concerned with teaching good manners and morals, and *Barnabae Itinerarium* (1636) translated (1638) as *Barnabee's Journall.*

92.36–37   tassel-gentel . . . jesses] A trained male hawk, held by short straps on the legs.

93.14–15   Juliana . . . Markham] See note 46.10.

96.2–10   The soaring . . . *Delites*] Cf. "The Lover compareth him self to the painful Falcon," in *A Handful of Pleasant Delights, containing sundry new Sonnets and delectable Histories in divers kinds of metre* (1584) by Clement Robinson et. al.

96.17–20   "In peascod . . . a-field,"] Cf. Thomas Churchyard's "A matter of fond Cupid, and vain Venus," first published in *A Pleasante Laberinthe called Churchyardes Chance* (1580): "In peascod time when hound to horne giv's eare til Buck be kilde / And little laddes with pipes of corne, sat keepyng beastes a filde."

98.23–30   Webster's . . . answers."] V.iii.3–5, 7–9.

98.38   *Bekker's Monde enchanté.] Balthasar Bekker, *Le Monde Enchanté*, I, 171, a French translation (1694) of the Dutch theologian's *De Betoverde Wereld* (1691–93).

102.2–9   O 'tis . . . *Dryden*] Cf. *Oedipus* (1679), III.i, by John Dryden and Nathaniel Lee.

105.7–8   Clemens Alexandrinus] Titus Flavius Clemens (c. 150–212), Saint Clement of Alexandria.

105.18   battle of Blenheim] During the War of the Spanish Succession, the English and Austrians under the Duke of Marlborough and Prince Eugene of Savoy defeated French and Bavarian forces at Blenheim, in Bavaria, on August 13, 1704.

105.34–35   "——walk . . . sleep."] John Milton, *Paradise Lost*, IV.677–78.

110.5   *Mirror for Magistrates*] See note 15.22.

III.23–27   his person . . . wit.] Cf. Henry Howard, Earl of Surrey (?1517–47), "Of the Death of the Same Sir T. W."

III.28–33   "They . . . style."] From George Puttenham's *The Arte of English Poesie* (1589).

112.37–113.11   Morte d'Arthur] See note 90.39.

114.2–8   Each . . . *Beggars*] Act I. See note 13.2–5.

119.2–5   Come, . . . *Suckling*] John Suckling, *The Goblins* (1646), Act IV.

122.3–5   "All . . . be."] In John Aubrey, *Miscellanies* (1696).

123.13   "Author of Waverley"] Sir Walter Scott (1771–1832) did not admit the authorship of his novels until 1827. *Waverly*, his first, appeared in 1814; fifteen were published by 1822, the year *Bracebridge Hall* went to press.

125.2–8   What . . . *Gallathea*] Cf. II.iii, by John Lyly.

139.20   Pietro d'Abano] D'Abano (1250?–1316?), also known as Petrus de Abano, a Padua physician and astrologer, author of treatises on medicine, philosophy, and astronomy, whose best-known work, *Conciliator differentiarum philosophorem*, was first published in Venice in 1476. He was denounced by the Inquisition after his death.

142.17–18   Sandivogius . . . Nuysment] Seventeenth-century alchemists Michael Sandivogius, Eirenaeus Pilalethes, and Dominus de Nuysement.

153.23   Henry Kuhnrade] Kunrath or Kunrade (1560–1605), author of theosophical and mystical books including of *Amphitheatrum Sapientiae Æternae Solius Verae* (c. 1609).

155.41   HOWELL'S LETTERS] James Howell, *Epistolae Ho-Elianae, Familiar Letters Domestic and Foreign*, 4 vols. (1645–55), written, largely in prison, mostly to imaginary correspondents.

167.32   Hermes Trismegestes] Hermes Trismegistros, a Greek name for the Egyptian god Thoth, reputedly the source of "Hermetic" writings, works of revelation on theology, medicine, astronomy, and magic.

181.32   *Rodd's . . . Grenada] A translation of *Historia de los bandos de Zegries y Abencerajes o Guerras Civiles de Granada* (1595–1604) by Ginés Pérez de Hita.

182.39   Gonsalvius] Reginald Gonsalvius Montanus, *Sanctae inquisitionis hispanicae* (1567).

191.3–10   His . . . *Fletcher*] Cf. Phineas Fletcher, *The Purple Island* (1633), canto XII, stanza 5.

198.2–3   "I'll . . . *Croydon*] William Haughton, *Grim the Collier of Croydon* (1622), Act IV, scene i.

198.11–12   "Go, . . . me;"] Edmund Waller, "Go, lovely rose" (1645), line 1.

203.37   campus phlegræ] A volcanic field, after the Campi Flegerei west of Naples, Italy.

205.10–13   Nashe . . . habiliments.' "] Thomas Nashe, *Christs Teares over Ierusalem* (1593), II.142.18–20.

207.2–6   What's . . . *Crew*] Act II. See note 13.2–5.

210.14–21   "Who . . . weather."] Shakespeare, *As You Like It*, II.v.38–45.

215.26–29   May-day . . . forgot."] From an old ballad lamenting the passing of May-Day games; it occurs, e.g., in Shakespeare's *Hamlet*, III.ii.135, and *Love's Labours Lost*, III.i. 29–30.

216.2–4   Nay, . . . *Croyden*] V.i. See note 198.2–3.

219.2–9   There . . . *Euphues*] John Lyly, *Euphues and his England* (1580).

224.26   Strutt] Joseph Strutt, *The Sports and Pastimes of the People of England* (1801).

227.2–6   *Goblins*] A play (1646) by John Suckling.

229.37   robber in Ariosto] Orillo, hewn by a thousand blows, puts himself back together in Ludovico Ariosto's *Orlando Furioso* (1532), canto XV, stanzas 82–84.

230.9–14   Tusser . . . claws.] See note 50.16.

231.2–6   But cawing rooks . . . *Cowper*] Lines 203–6 of "The Sofa," Book One in the six-book blank verse poem *The Task* (1785) by William Cowper.

238.2–8   It is the choice . . . *Actæon and Diana*] Robert Cox (d. 1655), *Actæon and Diana, with a pastoral Storæ of the Nimph Oenone, &c.*

269.2–8   A citizen . . . *Doctor Merrie-Man*, 1609] Samuel Rowlands, *Democritus, or Doctor Merryman his Medicines against Melancholy Humors* (1607); reprinted as *Doctor Merry-Man: or nothing but mirth* (1609), II.iii.1–6.

271.19–24   Tusser's . . . cost."] See note 50.16.

275.2–10   Farewell . . . *Bishop Corbet*] From "The Fairies' Farewell," poem by Richard Corbet (1582–1635), bishop first of Oxford, then Norwich.

277.30–39   "Tells . . . rings."] John Milton, "L'Allegro" (1645), lines 105–14.

278.23–39   "——Their dwellings . . . forsaken."] Thomas Heywood,

The Hierarchie of the Blessed Angells; their Names, Orders, and Offices: the Fall of Lucifer and his Angells (1635), Book IX, "The Angell."

280.35–281.5   Brown, . . . sat."]   William Browne, *Britannia's Pastoralls*, Book I (1613).

281.6–11   in a poem . . . minstrelsies."]   "Robin Good-fellow," often attributed to Ben Jonson.

283.2–4   From fire . . . *Widow*]   I.i.29–30, in the play (1652) by Thomas Middleton, perhaps with Ben Jonson and John Fletcher.

286.5   "dejected . . . side,"]   William Collins (1721–59), "The Passions: an Ode for Music," line 49.

289.2–4   "The night . . . *Macbeth*]   Shakespeare; cf. II.iii.60–61.

292.2–7   "The poor . . . *Song*]   This version of the song appears in Shakespeare's *Othello*, IV.iii.40–43, 51.

295.14–18   "My . . . singing it."]   *Othello*, IV.iii.26–30.

297.2–9   Hermione. . . . *Tale*]   Shakespeare; cf. II.i.22–26.

304.10   *Tale of a Tub*]   A comedy (1633) by Ben Jonson.

364.2–6   No more . . . *Braithwaite*]   Cf. *A Strappado for the Devell* (1615), epithalamium, by Richard Brathwait.

372.2–4   And so . . . *Hamlet*]   I.v.127–28.

TALES OF A TRAVELLER

379.4–7   *I am* . . . JONSON]   Ben Jonson, *Cynthia's Revels* (1600), I.iii. A babion is a baboon.

383.9   Mentz]   Mainz, also known by the French name Mayence. In 1815 the Congress of Vienna made it a federal fortress of the German Confederation.

383.20–21   studying . . . Katrine]   While staying at the Hotel de Darmstadt in Mainz in September 1822, Irving wrote his sister, Sarah Van Wart, that he had "daily lessons in French and German" from "la belle Katrina," the hotel manager Johann Adnot's convent-educated 16-year-old daughter.

383.23   *ich liebe*]   I love.

387.4–11   I'll . . . MONTH]   Act II, scene i, by John Fletcher (1579–1625). Letters of mart (marque) were a license to arm a vessel for capturing merchant ships of hostile nations. Their holder, called a privateer or corsair, was allowed by international law to commit acts which in other circumstances would be considered piracy.

389.10   author of Waverly]   Sir Walter Scott (1771–1832), whose novels were being published anonymously. He did not admit their authorship until 1827.

390.20   hunting . . . Nimrod]   Cf. Genesis 10:9: "Nimrod, the mighty hunter before the Lord."

393.7   Milesian]   According to legend, the Gaelic Milesians, sons of King Miledh or Milesius of Spain, conquered the kingdom of Ireland during the Bronze Age and became the ancestors of the present Irish.

396.3   wars of the League]   Civil wars (1588–94) in France primarily between Roman Catholics and the Protestant Huguenots. The League, led by Henry, third Duke de Guise (1550–88), and later by his brother the Duke de Mayenne, was formed in 1576 and revived in 1584 to prevent the accession of Henry of Navarre, later King Henry IV (1589–1610).

396.17   *ailes de pigeon*]   Pigeon wings.

397.1–3   sovereign . . . August]   On August 10, 1792, the Convention deprived the king of his powers, and the subsequent storming and seizure of the Tuileries palace by the people of Paris and the national guard marked the fall of the monarchy.

397.6   poissarde]   One of the Parisian marketwomen who led riots during the Revolution. The word connotes a woman of the lowest classes who is rough and foulmouthed.

399.5–6   Dolly's . . . London]   In Queen's Head Passage, Paternaster Row, built during the reign (1702–14) of Queen Anne and demolished in 1883.

401.25   civil . . . Fronde]   Two unsuccessful revolts against the absolutism of Cardinal Mazarin, chief minister to the young Louis XIV. The first, 1648–49, was led by the Paris bourgeoisie, the second, 1651–53, by nobles led by the Prince de Condé. The opponents of Mazarin became known as *frondeurs*, from *fronde*, "sling," i.e., those who "slung stones" at the chief minister.

401.28   affairs of the Barricadoes]   When two Parisian leaders were arrested by royal authorities on August 26, 1648, an insurrection began in the city that forced their release on August 28 and marked the beginning of the first Fronde.

401.29   Port Cocheres]   A cavalry force raised by requiring householders to furnish a man and a horse for each carriage gate (porte cochère).

409.3   Knight of the Post]   A malefactor; the post is a whipping post.

409.28   Botany Bay]   An English penal settlement on the southeast coast
of Australia, established in 1788. Although the colony was quickly moved to
nearby Port Jackson (the future site of Sydney), it was popularly called by its
original name into the early 19th century.

410.20–22   uncle Toby . . . Trim]   Laurence Sterne, *Tristram Shandy*
(1760–67), volume 3, chapter 11: " 'Our armies swore terribly in Flanders,'
cried my uncle Toby, 'but nothing to this.' " The account of Trim is in volume 5, chapters 35–40.

411.15–16   ya vrouws]   *Juffrouws*, maidens.

412.13   HEER . . . DRANK.]   Good drink sold here.

414.1–2   Ally Croaker]   Alley or Ally Croker, from a popular mid-18th
century Irish song.

420.15   ancient . . . Ville]   The original Hôtel de Ville (Town Hall), acquired in 1357. It was destroyed by the Commune in 1871.

421.28–29   statue . . . populace]   The statue of Henry IV, torn down by
the populace in 1792, was restored in 1818.

425.24   merry thought]   Wishbone.

429.15   humming ale]   Very strong ale, i.e., so strong it could make the
head "hum."

432.35   zendaletto]   Originally a cloth hanging over the hood of the gondola into the water; it later came to refer to the gondola itself.

468.26–27   'cut . . . again,']   There's plenty; have as many helpings as
you like. Cf. Jonathan Swift, *Polite Conversation* (1738), Dialogue II.

469.8–9   Booksellers . . . Abed-nego]   The London family publishing
firm established in 1724 by Thomas Longman (1699–1755) was known for its
many partners. Shadrach, Meshach, and Abednego appear in Daniel 3:12–30.

475.9   catch]   In singing, a kind of round for three or more unaccom-
panied voices where the effect becomes ludicrous when some words are sung
together.

476.30–34   circumstance . . . Tibbs']   Letter 55 in *Citizen of the World* by
Oliver Goldsmith, a series of imaginary letters first published from 1760 to
1761 in the *Public Ledger*.

479.34   Bernard Lintot]   Barnaby Bernard Lintot (1675–1736), a publisher
of Pope, Steel, Gay, and Farquhar. Alexander Pope compared his uncouth
appearance to that of a small water bird, the dabchick, in *The Dunciad*, Book
the Third (1728), line 63.

484.15   Crackscull Common]   "Crackscull Common" appears in Oliver

Goldsmith's comedy *She Stoops to Conquer, or The Mistakes of a Night* (1773), I.ii and V.ii.

485.15 Cockney pastorals] The poetry of Leigh Hunt and the "'Ampstead Circle," derided by John Lockhart as the "Cockney School of Poetry" in *Blackwood's Edinburgh Magazine*, October 1817, the first of a series of attacks on Hunt and other writers of "low birth," including John Keats and William Hazlitt.

486.2 Jack Straw's Castle] On Hampstead Heath, named for a leader of the Peasants' Revolt of 1381.

487.31 'under . . . tree.'] The phrase occurs in Shakespeare's *As You Like It*, II.i.1: "Under the greenwood tree / Who loves to lie with me, / And turn his merry note / Unto the sweet bird's throat, / Come hither . . . " In another meaning, the greenwood, a forest in leaf, came to refer to a scene of outlaw life; "to go to the greenwood" meaning "to become an outlaw."

488.15–16 Knights of the Post] See note 409.3.

489.5 yellow boys] Gold pieces.

489.24 Newgate Kalendar] The original *Newgate Calendar*, named for the famous London prison, is a record of notorious crimes from 1700 to 1774, published in five volumes c. 1774. Similar compilations continued to appear through 1826.

492.35 Lalla Rookh] Four Oriental tales in verse linked by a prose narrative (1817) by Thomas Moore.

493.31 "Shall . . . wind?"] Job 15:2.

494.22–23 Bow Street Office] Principal London police court and headquarters of the Bow Street Runners, a police force organized in 1753 by magistrates Henry Fielding, the novelist, and his half-brother John.

498.6 "sweet . . . adversity] Cf. *As You Like It*, II.i.12.

498.36–499.2 I care . . . eve——] James Thompson (1700–48), *The Castle of Indolence* (1748), Canto II.

502.2–4 volume . . . Sacharissa] The love poems to Sacharissa (Lady Dorothy Sidney) by Edmund Waller (1606–87).

505.2 Orson] In *Valentine and Orson*, an early French romance, Orson is kidnapped and raised by a bear.

506.7–10 Song . . . love.] Cf. Song of Solomon 2:5.

511.39–40 Simon . . . Lion] Cf. Shakespeare's *A Midsummer Night's Dream*, V.i.223–24.

512.34 Prince . . . associates] In Shakespeare's *1 Henry IV*.

516.11–12 "a little . . . kind"] Cf. Shakespeare's *Hamlet*, I.ii.65: "A little more than kin, and less than kind."

516.24–25 Belvidera . . . Jaffier] In the tragedy *Venice Preserv'd, or a Plot Discovered* (1682) by Thomas Otway.

516.30 melancholy . . . cat] Cf. *1 Henry IV*, I.ii.73–74: "I am as melancholy as a gib cat," i.e., a castrated cat.

520.26 Santissima Trinidada] One of the Spanish ships-of-the-line captured by the British fleet commanded by Viscount Nelson at the Battle of Trafalgar, October 21, 1805.

521.12 "preying . . . cheek."] Cf. Shakespeare, *Twelfth Night*, II.iv.112: "Feed on her damask cheek."

521.17–18 "had . . . choose."] Cf. Book XII, line 646, from the closing sentence of Milton's *Paradise Lost* (1667): "The world was all before them, where to choose."

522.6–7 Jack . . . Castle.] See note 486.2.

525.30 the Isis] A local name for the Thames at Oxford and upstream.

528.13 "come . . . might,"] Cf. Shakespeare, *Macbeth*, I.iii.146.

529.32–33 Peeping . . . Coventry] A wooden figure of Tom the Taylor, at the corner of Herford and Smithfield streets. According to one legend, Tom was struck blind for peeping at Lady Godiva.

531.18 "like . . . tears;"] *Hamlet*, I.ii.149.

535.6–7 Elegant Extracts] *Elegant Extracts: Or Useful and Entertaining Pieces of Poetry* (c. 1787), edited by Vicesimus Knox, frequently reprinted in the 19th century.

548.9 Caliban] The son of the witch Sycorax, in Shakespeare's *The Tempest*.

552.39–553.1 Lord Townly] A character in *The Provok'd Husband, or a Journey to London* (1728) by John Vanbrugh and Colly Cibber.

553.22 "Upon . . . spake"] Shakespeare, *Othello*, I.iii.166.

553.25–26 "The funeral . . . Hamlet says.] I.ii.180–81.

553.36 Bartlemy Fair] Bartholomew Fair, also called Bartlemy, held annually at West Smithfield from 1133–1855 around the feast of St. Bartholomew, August 24.

553.37 Astley's Troop] A circus company run by Philip Astley (1742–1814).

554.18 "to very . . . Hamlet says] III.ii.10.

555.6–7   "the high . . . joy,"]   Shakespeare, *Romeo and Juliet*, II.iv.190.

555.16   bloods]   Dandies.

556.13   breeches of Rosalind]   In *As You Like It*.

559.2–3   Mr. Walker's Eidouranion]   John Walker lectured on a clockwork model of the solar system called the Eidouranion, or orrery.

559.11   "a beggarly . . . boxes."]   *Romeo and Juliet*, V.i.45.

560.1–2   "one fell swoop,"]   *Macbeth*, IV.iii.219.

560.4   "be . . . all"]   *Macbeth*, I.vii.5.

560.9–10   "the bell . . . one,"]   *Hamlet*, I.i.39.

560.11   bumbailiffs]   A bailiff employed in arrests, especially of debtors.

560.12   "end . . . greatness."]   Cf. Shakespeare, *Henry VIII*, III.ii.351.

560.24   Richard . . . horse!"]   Shakespeare, *Richard III*, V.iv.7.

560.28–29   "Richard . . . arms,"]   Cf. Shakespeare, *2 Henry VI*, V.ii.7.

563.21   Banquo's shadowy line]   Cf. *Macbeth*, IV.i.111.

569.18   rosolio]   A sweet cordial.

569.21   San Gennaro!]   Saint Januarius (died c. 305), martyr whose blood relics are at Naples.

570.11   *Corpo di Bacco!*]   Body of Bacchus, a mild oath.

570.15   Pontine marshes]   Then a region of malarial swamps, separated from the sea by low sand hills, bounded on the north by the Lepini Mountains, and traversed by the Appian Way. The district is now called Pontino Agro.

572.12   *in cuerpo*]   Naked, stripped.

576.17   Harvey sauce]   Made from Harvey apples.

577.38   quanto . . . Inglesi.]   How peculiar these English are.

578.24   *O Sicuro*]   Oh, sure.

586.7   late . . . revolution]   The Neapolitan revolution of July 1820 forced the Bourbon King Ferdinand I to grant a liberal constitution before Austrian troops intervened in March 1821 and restored the monarchy to full power.

594.38–40   Loretto . . . shrine]   A place of pilgrimage, the Santa Casa was believed to be the house of Jesus' mother, Mary, which had been transported from Nazareth to Loretto by angels.

595.2   cockleshell]   A token of pilgrimage associated with the shrine of Saint James the Great at Compostella in Spain.

597.27   Cospetto!]   Usually translated "Good heavens!" From *al cospetto di Dio*, in the presence of God.

603.12–13   Throgmorton Street]   The address of the Stock Exchange in the City of London.

604.33–34   "Loves of the Angels;"]   Thomas Moore's poem (1823) about three fallen angels who fall in love with mortal women.

616.20   Sbirri]   A contemptuous term for police or police spies.

638.30   "Quanto . . . Inglesi!"]   See Irving's translation on page 637.31 in this volume.

640.34   "Scampa via!"]   Let's get away, now!

645.5–9   Now . . . MALTA]   Cf. act II, scene i. In Marlowe, the second line reads: "Who in my wealth would tell me winter's tales."

647.28–29   famous . . . Dreamer]   In Irving's *A History of New York*, Book II, chapter III, an "armament of canoes" on a voyage of discovery led by Oloffe and several other Dutchmen from the colony of Communipaw is tossed about in the channel and finally washes up "on the very point of the island where at present stands the delectable city of New York."

648.31   Pylorus]   Pelorus, now known as Cape Faro, where Sicily and Italy are divided by a channel two-and-a-half miles wide.

649.5–6   Devil's Stepping Stones]   At Throg's Neck.

649.18   Frogs Neck]   Throg's Neck.

649.26–29   just . . . Second]   In 1664 the Dutch colony (1613–64) of New Netherland was seized by England and granted by the king to his brother James, Duke of York.

649.34–35   valuable . . . jurist]   The memoir was read in 1816 by Egbert Benson and published the following year. It is reprinted in *Collections of the New-York Historical Society*, 2nd series (1848), vol. 2, pp. 28–148.

651.1   musquito built]   Built light for rapid maneuvering.

651.17   Quedah]   Kedah, a Malaysian state.

652.6   Execution . . . London]   At Wapping on the Thames.

668.3–4   John . . . Heyliger]   See *Bracebridge Hall*, p. 303 and pp. 304–38 in this volume.

668.21–22   Oloffe Van Kortlandt] See note 647.28–29.

676.38   Morgan] Henry Morgan (c. 1635–88) raided Dutch and Spanish colonies in the Caribbean as a privateer. Brought to England in 1672 to answer accusations of piracy, he gained favor with Charles II, was knighted, and in 1674 appointed lieutenant governor of Jamaica.

677.34   moidores . . . pistareens] Moidores were gold coins of Portugal, pistareens were silver Spanish coins. Ducats bore the likenesses of dukes and circulated in several European countries.

682.12   like . . . pot] Ecclesiastes 7:6: "For as the crackling of thorns under a pot, so is the laughter of the fool."

687.7   Devil's Dans Kammer] Devil's Dance Chamber, near Newburgh.

687.24–25   Bradish] Joseph Bradish (1672–1700), an American-born buccaneer.

689.14–16   Hen . . . Pan] The Pot is a whirlpool; the rest are rocks or reefs in the channel.

689.21   Blackwell's Island] In the East River; later called Welfare, now Roosevelt, Island.

697.16–17   dead lights] Porthole covers.

697.19   Dead Man's Isle] One of the Magdalene Islands in the Gulf of St. Lawrence.

698.21   greedy . . . Bagdad] "The Blind Baba-Abdalla" in *The Arabian Nights*.

699.31   Wallabout] Wallabout Bay, on the Brooklyn side of the East River, opposite Corlear's Point; later the site of the Brooklyn Navy Yard.

699.39–40   "most . . . smell"] Cf. *The Tempest*, II.ii.26.

700.26   Bloomen-dael] Valley of flowers, an early settlement near present-day 100th Street on the upper west side of Manhattan.

708.7–8   three . . . bowl] From the nursery rhyme. Gotham, a village in England, was proverbial for the foolishness and simplicity of its citizens. Irving appropriated the name for New York in *Salmagundi* (1807).

708.32   Turtle . . . Kip's Bay] Along the East River, respectively, north and south of 42d Street.

709.28   *Pots tausends*] Good God!

THE ALHAMBRA

723.1   *PREFACE*] The following dedication to the Scottish painter David Wilkie (1785–1841) appeared in the first English edition and continued, with minor changes, until the completely revised 1851 edition, from which Irving omitted the letter to his long deceased friend:

TO DAVID WILKIE, ESQ. R.A.

MY DEAR SIR,

You may remember, that in the rambles we once took together about some of the old cities of Spain, particularly Toledo and Seville, we remarked a strong mixture of the Saracenic with the Gothic, remaining from the time of the Moors; and were more than once struck with scenes and incidents in the streets, which reminded us of passages in the "Arabian Nights." You then urged me to write something that should illustrate those peculiarities, "something in the Haroun Alrasched style," that should have a dash of that Arabian spice which pervades everything in Spain. I call this to your mind to show you that you are, in some degree, responsible for the present work, in which I have given a few "Arabesque" sketches from the life, and tales founded on popular traditions, which were chiefly struck-off during a residence in one of the Morisco-Spanish places in the Peninsula.

I inscribe these pages to you as a memorial of the pleasant scenes we have witnessed together in that land of adventure, and as a testimonial of an esteem for your worth which is only exceeded by admiration of your talents.

Your friend and fellow-traveller,

May, 1832.   THE AUTHOR.

725.36   Prince Dolgorouki] Dmitri Ivanovitch Dolgorouki (1797–1867), Russian noble and son of the poet Ivan Mikhailovitch Dolgorouki.

730.6   sons of Ecija] In Cordova on March 4, 1828, on the way to Granada, Irving's party was assigned an additional escort, whom Irving described in his journal, March 9, as "our Robber guide Bautisto Serrano de Ecija." Pierre Munro Irving, in *Life and Letters of Washington Irving* (1862–64), Volume 2, says a landlord at Cordova described Serrano as a " . . . first-rate fellow—knows all the robbers—has been a robber himself." Ecija is an ancient town southeast of Seville.

731.12   roscas] Traditional twisted rolls.

733.4–5   St. . . . June] Two celebrations coincide on June 24: the Feast of the Nativity of St. John the Baptist (Fiesta de San Juan) and Midsummer Day.

733.30   Alguazil] A local constable or court bailiff.

733.37   corregidor] Magistrate.

734.14   drawcansir friend] A blustering braggart, from the character Drawcansir in *The Rehearsal* (1672) by George Villiers, second duke of Buckingham.

735.25   Valdepeñas] A large town in La Mancha long renowned for its red wine and cellars.

735.38–39   scriptural . . . bottles] Cf. Matthew 9:17, Mark 2:22, Luke 5:37.

736.10–11   Sancho's . . . Cammacho]   Cervantes' *Don Quixote de la Mancha* (1605–15), at the wedding feast of Camacho, Part II, xx and xxi.

738.2   basquinas]   Iberian outer petticoats or skirts.

738.11–12   namesake . . . kitchen]   *Don Quixote*, Part II, xxxi.

746.8–9   time . . . invasion]   France invaded Spain in 1808, beginning the Peninsular War, which ended in 1814 with the defeat of the French by Great Britain, Portugal, and Spanish guerillas.

749.22–23   Count Julian . . . Florinda]   According to legend, Florinda was raped by Roderick (d. 711?), the last Visigothic ruler of Spain. In revenge Julian, Byzantine governor of Ceuta in North Africa, called in North African Muslims to overthrow Roderick, and Tariq Ibn Ziyad began the conquest of the Iberian Peninsula (see note 777.22–25). The legend was popular in Spanish literature and versions of the story were used by Robert Southey in *Roderick, the Last of the Goths* (1814), Walter Landor in *Count Roderick* (1812), and by Irving in *Legends of the Conquest of Spain* (1835).

750.32   Gil Blas]   *Gil Blas de Santillane* (1715–35), set in Spain, by French novelist Alain Renée Le Sage.

752.5   Caaba]   The most sacred site in the Islamic world, the Caaba, or Kaaba, is the small, cube-shaped building of gray stone and marble in the courtyard of the Great Mosque of Mecca. Pilgrims to Mecca circle its interior seven times, and the faithful orient themselves toward it during the five daily prayers. It encloses the sacred Black Stone, believed to have been given to Adam on his fall from paradise.

752.25–26   Charles V. . . . palace]   Charles V (1500–58) destroyed part of the Alhambra to build a Renaissance-style palace. Begun in 1526 by Pedro Machuca, building continued through the 16th century but was never completed.

753.35   French . . . towers]   In 1812, under the French general Count Horace Sebastiani.

754.11–14   were government . . . zeal]   Restoration endowed by Ferdinand VII was begun by José Contreras in 1828, and continued after his death in 1847 by his son Rafael.

762.40   Urquhart's]   David Urquhart (1805–77), Scottish diplomat, member of Parliament, and author of *Pillars of Hercules; or, A Narrative of Travels in Spain and Morocco in 1848, 1850*.

763.2   Ford]   Richard Ford, author of *Handbook for Travellers in Spain* (1845) and *Gathering in Spain* (1846).

765.32   My quarters]   There is a plaque above the outer door indicating that Irving wrote his "cuentos" (tales) while residing in the palace, although the original 1832 edition was finished while he was living in London. The plaque reads:

WASHINGTON IRVING
Escribo En Estas Habitaciones Sus
CUENTOS DE LA ALHAMBRA
En El Año De 1829

769.15–17   Gines . . . Granada]   The soldier and writer Ginés Pérez de Hita (c. 1544–1619), who fought in the campaign against the Moriscos in the Alpujarros (1568–71). His historical novel *Historia de los bandos de Zegríes y Abencerajes o Guerras Civiles de Granada* (1595–1604) was translated by Thomas Rodd as *The Civil Wars of Granada* (1803). For Irving's opinion see page 821.3–18.

771.5   fives-court]   Three-sided court in which fives, a game similar to present-day handball, is played.

777.22–25   Musa . . . William]   Musa ibn Nusayr, the Arab ruler of Tunisia and Morocco, (c. 640–714) sent Tariq ibn Ziyad to lead the first Moorish invasion of Spain. Tariq began the conquest of the Iberian Peninsula in 711 and in 712 Musa led his own army to Spain, capturing Mérida, Toledo, and Saragossa. The Norseman Rollo or Hrolf (c. 860–932) became the first Duke of Normandy in 911 when the region was ceded to him by Charles III of France. His descendant William the Conqueror (1027?–87) invaded England in 1066 and ruled it until his death.

780.12   Hegira]   The Islamic era dates from July 16, 622, the first day in the lunar year in which the hegira, the prophet Muhammad's flight from Mecca to Yathrib (now Medina), occurred.

780.37   BLEDA]   Fray Jaime Bleda (1550–1622), a Dominican friar.

781.8–9   Alhamar . . . Nasar]   The Nasrid dynasty was founded and named for his grandfather Nasr by Abu Abdullah ibn Yusuf ibn Nasr al-Ahmar (1231–73), as sultan called Muhammad I al-Ghalib.

782.5   Cortes]   Parliament.

786.24   battle of Salado]   Alfonso XI of Castile defeated the Moroccan invaders on the Río Salado in 1340, but the Christian reconquest of Spain was then stemmed by internal strife among the Christian kingdoms.

792.40   *Paseos por Granada*]   *Walks through Granada* (1764; re-issued 1814), a guide book popular for its stories and anecdotes, by Padre Juan de Echeverría.

793.24–27   Fate . . . deed!]   Cf. Ann Radcliffe (1764–1823), *The Mysteries of Udolpho* (1794), motto. In Radcliffe, the third line reads: "A voice in hollow murmurs through the courts."

796.40   Albaycin]   The city of Granada is divided into three sections: Granada proper, Antequeruela (founded 1410), and Albaicín.

799.19   Generalife]   Jennat al Arif (Garden of the Builder), a palace-fortress built in the 13th century and restored several times.

806.9–10   "Sorrow . . . morning."]   Cf. Psalm 30:5: "Weeping may endure for a night, but joy cometh in the morning."

808.5   old Spanish story]   *El Diablo Cojuole* by Luis Vélez de Guevera, first translated into English (1741) as *The Devil on Two Sticks* and later as *Asmodeus — The Devil on Two Sticks.*

810.8–9   intrigue . . . Almaviva]   The action of Rossini's comic opera *Il Barbiere di Seviglia* (1816) centers on the devices Count Almaviva, with the barber's aid, uses to outwit Bartholo and win Rosaline, whom Bartholo has imprisoned and plans to force into marriage. Based on Beaumarchais' play *Le Barbier de Séville* (1775), Rossini's version became a constant in the repertoires of the Madrid opera, where Irving saw it often.

813.4   Saint Monday]   Another day off, to recover from the effects of Sunday's rest.

820.1   Holy Sepulchre]   The presumed site of Jesus' entombment on which Constantine I built the Church of the Holy Sepulchre (dedicated c. 336). The interruption of pilgrimages to the Holy Sepulchre by the advance of the Seljak Turks in the 11th century and by the taking of Jerusalem by the Muslims in the 12th was an immediate cause of the Crusades.

822.18   downfall . . . Caliphate]   In 1031.

830.38–39   AL MAKKARI . . . Guyangos]   Al Makkari (1591?–1632), born in Algeria, part of whose major work, "Breath of the Perfumes," was translated into English as *History of the Mohammedan Dynasties of Spain* (1840–43) by Don Pascual de Gayangos y Arce (1804–97).

840.38–39   *See . . . Granada.]   Chapter XCII, "Of the insolent Defiance of Tarfe the Moor, and the Daring Exploit of Hernando de Pulgar."

841.1–2   Hero . . . puppet-show]   *Don Quixote*, Part II, xxvi.

842.25   porque . . . Viejo]   Because, sir, I am an old Christian.

847.39   MARMOL]   Luis del Mármol y Carvajal, historian (fl. 1575) especially of 16th-century Spain.

857.23–24   such comfort . . . Abishag]   Cf. I Kings 1:1–4.

874.13–14   "such stuff . . . made of,"]   Cf. Shakespeare, *The Tempest*, IV.i.156–57: "We are such stuff / As dreams are made on."

887.37   zambra]   An ancient dance of Moorish origin.

895.1   "horse . . . wear,"]   Shakespeare, *King Lear*, III.iv.137.

913.20   Angosturas of the Darro]   In the narrows of the river Darro, in town below the Alhambra.

913.30   puchero]   Stew; everyday food.

929.28   tertulias]   Evening parties that meet for conversation.

935.31   prankling]   Prancing; capering.

958.3   "Ay de mi!"]   Alas for me!

965.19   Cremona]   The city in Lombardy, Italy, famous in the 17th and 18th centuries for violins made by the Amati, Guarneri, and Stradivari families.

990.39   "Las dos Hermanas."]   "The Two Sisters."

991.2–3   rich . . . Quixote]   See note 736.10–11.

1011.20   Pelazo]   Pelayo, the Gothic chieftain whose defeat of the Moors at Covadonga, c. 718, preserved Asturias as a Christian kingdom and marked the beginning of Christian resistance to the Moorish conquerors of Spain.

1032.35–36   Padre . . . Feyjoo]   Benito Jerónimo Feyóo (also, Feijóo) y Montenegro (1676–1764), Benedictine monk and professor of theology and philosophy at the University of Oviedo, and a writer on science, mathematics, medicine, law, political economy, education, literature, and popular superstitions; a leader in bringing the Enlightenment to Spain.

1035.9–10   Carvajal]   An old town on the main road from Málaga to Cádiz.

1045.6   cave of Trophonius]   According to legend, the architect Trophonius was swallowed into the earth after asking the gods to reward him for building Apollo's temple at Delphi, and thereafter gave oracles in a cave at Lebadea.

1046.41–42   the learned . . . Kirker's]   The German Jesuit scholar Athnasius Kircher (1601–80), whose subjects included hieroglyphics, archaeology, biology, physics, math, and Oriental languages.

1048.3   letters . . . me]   Informing Irving of his unexpected appointment as first secretary to the American legation in London.

Cataloging Information

Irving, Washington, 1783–1859.
    Bracebridge Hall, Tales of a Traveller, The Alhambra.
    Edited by Andrew B. Myers.

    (The Library of America ; 52)
    I. Title: Bracebridge Hall.   II. Title: Tales of a Traveller.
    III. Title: The Alhambra.   IV. Series.
PS2052   1991   813'.2—dc20   90–62267
ISBN 0–940450–59–3 (alk. paper)

For a list of titles in The Library of America, write to:
The Library of America
14 East 60th Street
New York, NY 10022

This book is set in 10 point Linotron Galliard,
a face designed for photocomposition by Matthew Carter
and based on the sixteenth-century face Granjon. The paper
is acid-free Ecusta Nyalite and meets the requirements for perma-
nence of the American National Standards Institute. The binding
material is Brillianta, a 100% woven rayon cloth made by
Van Heek-Scholco Textielfabrieken, Holland. The com-
position is by Haddon Craftsmen, Inc., and The
Clarinda Company. Printing and binding
by R. R. Donnelley & Sons Company.
Designed by Bruce Campbell.

THE LIBRARY OF AMERICA SERIES